ge mænne he þara mapa forð gen
gode onseah dagū spendel na
told buende no hie fæder cunnon
hwæþer him ænig wæs ær acenned
dyrnra gasta hie dygel lond
warigeað wulf hleoþu windige
næssas frecne fengelad ðær fyrgen
stream under næssa genipu niþer gewit
flod under foldan nis þæt feor heonon
mil gemearces þæt se mere standeð
ofer þæm hongiað hrinde bearwas
wudu wyrtum fæst wæter oferhelmað
þær mæg nihta gehwæm niðwundor
seon fyr on flode no þæs frod leofað
gumena bearna þone grund wite
ðeah þe hæðstapa hundum geswenced
heorot hornum trum holtwudu sece
feorran geflymed ær he feorh seleð
aldor on ofre ær he in wille hafelan
hydan nis þæt heoru stow þonon
yð ge blond up astigeð won to wolcnum
þon wind styreþ lað gewidru oð þæt
lyft drysmaþ roderas reotað nu is se ræd gelang

MS. COTT. VITELLIUS A. XV.
Fol. 184ᵃ (reduced). (ll. 2428–50.)

BEOWULF

AND

THE FIGHT AT FINNSBURG

EDITED, WITH INTRODUCTION, BIBLIOGRAPHY
NOTES, GLOSSARY, AND APPENDICES

BY

FR. KLAEBER

THIRD EDITION
WITH FIRST AND SECOND SUPPLEMENTS

D. C. HEATH AND COMPANY

BOSTON

COPYRIGHT, 1922, 1928, 1936, 1941, and 1950
BY D. C. HEATH AND COMPANY

No part of the material covered by this copyright may be reproduced in any form without written permission of the publisher.

6 B 7

CONTENTS

BEOWULF

INTRODUCTION	ix
1. Argument of the Poem	ix
2. The Fabulous or Supernatural Elements	xii
3. The Historical Elements	xxix
4. The Christian Coloring	xlviii
5. Structure of the Poem	li
6. Tone, Style, Meter	lviii
7. Language. Manuscript	lxxi
8. Genesis of the Poem	cii
BIBLIOGRAPHY	cxxv
TABLE OF ABBREVIATIONS	clxxxiv
TEXT	1
NOTES	121

THE FIGHT AT FINNSBURG

INTRODUCTION	231
BIBLIOGRAPHY	239
TEXT	245
NOTES	250

APPENDICES

I. PARALLELS	254
II. ANTIQUITIES	270

iv CONTENTS

III. TEXTUAL CRITICISM (GRAMMATICAL AND METRICAL NOTES) 274

IV. THE TEXT OF *Waldere, Deor*, SELECT PASSAGES OF *Widsið*, AND THE OHG. *Hildebrand* 283

GLOSSARIES

GLOSSARY OF *Beowulf* 293

PROPER NAMES. 433

GLOSSARY OF *The Fight at Finnsburg* 443

SUPPLEMENT 445

ADDITIONS TO THE SUPPLEMENT (1941) 460

SECOND SUPPLEMENT (1950) 463

FIG. 1.— THE GOKSTAD BOAT (*cir.* 900 A. D.; reconstructed).
Found in a grave mound near Gokstad, southern Norway, and preserved in Christiania (Oslo).
From O. Montelius, *Die Kultur Schwedens in vorchristlicher Zeit.* Berlin, G. Reimer. 2d ed., 1885, p. 174.

FIG. 2.— BRONZE PLATE FROM ÖLAND (Early Viking period?).
Preserved in the National Museum, Stockholm.
From Montelius, p. 151.

FIG. 3.—IRON HELMET WITH BRONZE PLATES.
From Vendel, Uppland (*cir.* close of 7th century).
From *Studier tillägnade Oscar Montelius af Lärjungar*. Stockholm, P. A. Norstedt & Söner, 1903, p. 104.

FIG. 4.—GOLD COLLAR FROM ÖLAND (5th to 8th century).
Preserved in the National Museum, Stockholm.
From Montelius, p. 124.

FIG. 5.—ENTRANCE TO A STONE GRAVE (*jættestue*), Zealand.
From M. Hoernes, *Die Urgeschichte des Menschen.*
Wien, A. Hartleben, 1892, p. 302.

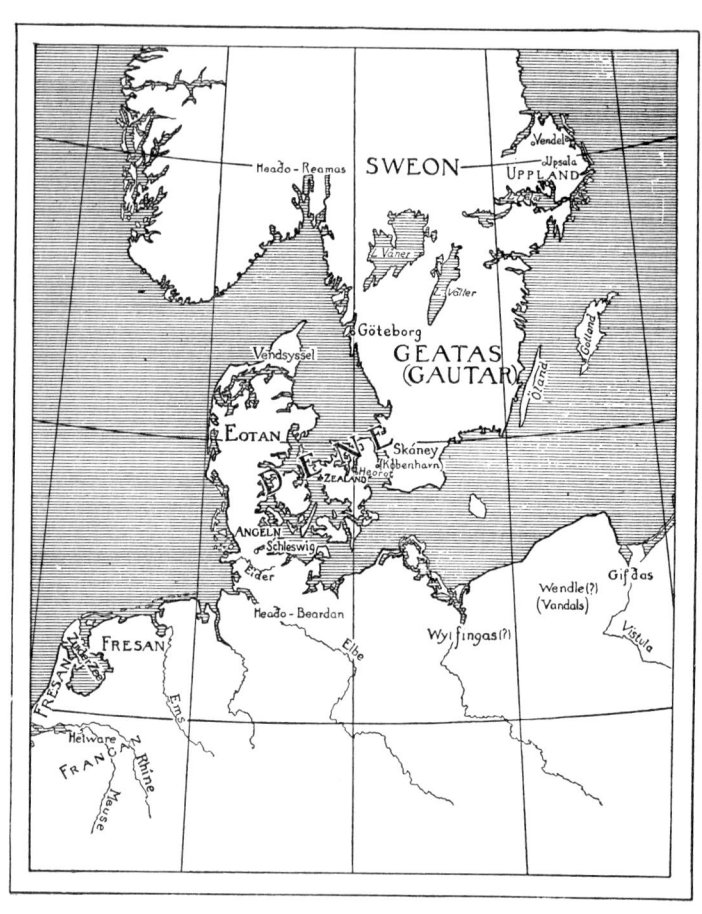

THE GEOGRAPHY OF BEOWULF.

INTRODUCTION

I. ARGUMENT OF THE POEM

Part I. Bēowulf the Young Hero
(His exploits in Denmark)

1. *The Fight with Grendel*

Bēowulfe wearð
gūðhrēð gyfeþe. (818 f.)

1-188. *Introductory. The building of Heorot by Hrōðgār; the ravages of Grendel.* The poem opens with the story of Scyld, the mythical founder of the Scylding dynasty, whose glorious reign and magnificent sea-burial are vividly set forth. — (53–85.) His line of descendants is carried down to king Hrōðgār, who builds the great hall Heorot for feasting and the dispensing of gifts. — (86–188.) Before long a fiendish monster, Grendel, angered by the daily sounds of rejoicing, comes to destroy the happiness of the Danes. One night he surprises them in their hall and kills thirty of the sleeping men. He repeats his murderous attack on the following night. For twelve years he continues his ravages. No one may with safety sleep in the hall. Hrōðgār, the good king, is bowed down by grief, his councilors can devise no help, his warriors are unable to check the visits of the demon.

189–661. *Bēowulf's voyage, reception in Denmark, and entertainment in the royal hall.* When Bēowulf, the nephew of Hygelāc, king of the Geats, hears of the doings of Grendel, he resolves to come to the assistance of Hrōðgār. An eminently fit man he is for that enterprise, since he has the strength of thirty men in his hand-grip. With fourteen chosen warriors he sails to the land of the Danes. On their arrival they are challenged by the coast-guard; but when the leader makes known their peaceful purpose, they are readily shown the way to Heorot. Bēowulf announces his name to the king's herald, Wulfgār, who in turn tells his lord. Hrōðgār bids that they be welcomed; Wulfgār bears the message. The Geats enter the royal hall. Bēowulf greets Hrōðgār and offers to cleanse Heorot. The king replies graciously and invites the Geats to the feast. — (499–661.) *Incidents at the banquet.* A dispute started by the Danish courtier, Unferð, gives Bēowulf an opportunity to narrate the true story of his daring swimming adventure with Breca and to predict his victory in the coming contest. In response to the courteous greeting of queen Wealhþēow he avows his determination to conquer or to die.

662-709. *The watch for Grendel.* At nightfall the Danes retire; Bēowulf with his men remains in charge of the hall. All the Geats fall asleep save Bēowulf. He watches for the demon. — **710-836.** *The fight.* Grendel sets out from the moor, approaches the hall, swings the door open, and quickly seizes and devours one of the Geats, Hondsciōh, but on seizing Bēowulf finds himself in the power of the hero's mighty grip. Long and bitter is the wrestling between the two; the hall rings with the sound of their fighting and seems on the point of tumbling down. Grendel gives forth a terrible howl of pain. Bēowulf by sheer strength tears off Grendel's arm. The demon escapes to his joyless abode, mortally wounded.

837-924. *Rejoicing of the retainers.* In the morning many of the warriors follow the tracks of Grendel and ride to see the blood-stained pool into which he had plunged. As they return, a court singer recites lays about Sigemund and Heremōd. — **925-990.** *The king's blessing.* Hrōðgār, who has proceeded to the hall, views the arm and claw of Grendel (hung up as a trophy) and utters a speech in praise of the hero's deed, to which Bēowulf makes appropriate reply. — **991-1250.** *Royal entertainment.* A feast is prepared in the hall. Rich presents are bestowed on Bēowulf and his band; the scop relates the Finnsburg tale; Wealhþēow, taking part in the entertainment, presents Bēowulf with costly gifts and bespeaks his kindness for her sons. After the banquet Hrōðgār as well as the Geats leave the hall, which is once more placed in guard of the Danish warriors.

2. *The Fight with Grendel's Mother*

Ofslōh ðā æt þǣre sæcce . . . hūses hyrdas. (1665 f.)

1251-1320. *Attack by Grendel's mother.* That night Grendel's mother makes her way into the hall to avenge her son; she carries off Æschere, a favorite thane of Hrōðgār, and, taking Grendel's arm with her, escapes to the fenland. In the morning Bēowulf is sent for by the king.

1321-1398. *Conversation between Hrōðgār and Bēowulf.* Hrōðgār bewails the loss of Æschere, describes graphically the weird haunt of the demons, and appeals to the Geat for help. Bēowulf, like a true hero, is ready to meet the monster at once.

1399-1491. *The expedition to Grendel's mere.* With a troop of Danes and Geats the king and the hero proceed to the lake. Bēowulf arms himself and addresses a few parting words to Hrōðgār. — **1492-1590.** *The fight.* He plunges into the water, at length reaches the bottom, and is carried by the troll-wife into her cavern. There they have a desperate struggle. The creature has him all but in her power, when he finds a curious giant-sword, with which he puts her to death. With it he also cuts off the head of the dead Grendel. — **1591-1650.** *The sequel of the fight and the triumphal return to Heorot.* In the meanwhile many of those on the shore having surmised Bēowulf's death from the discoloring of the

ARGUMENT OF THE POEM

water, the Danes depart to their hall. Bēowulf's faithful followers wait for him, until swimming upwards he comes to the surface, carrying with him Grendel's head and the golden hilt of the wondrous sword, whose blade has melted in the poisonous blood. They march with their trophies back to Heorot.

1651-1784. *Speeches by Bēowulf and Hrōðgār.* Bēowulf recounts his thrilling experience and assures the king of the completeness of the delivery. Hrōðgār replies by a lengthy moralizing discourse. — **1785-1887.** *The parting.* After the feast Bēowulf enjoys a much needed rest. In the morning friendly farewell speeches are exchanged, whereupon the Geats start for the shore.

3. *Bēowulf's Home-Coming and Report to Hygelāc*

Hū lomp ēow on lāde, lēofa Bīowulf . . . ? (1987.)

1888-1962. *Homeward voyage.* The fourteen warriors embark and in due time reach the land of the Geats. The mention of queen Hygd leads the poet to intersperse the legend of the haughty and cruel Þrȳð.

1963-2151. *Bēowulf's narrative.* Arrived at Hygelāc's court, Bēowulf relates his adventures and weaves in the account of events which are bound to happen in connection with the engagement of Frēawaru to Ingeld.

2152-2199. *Bēowulf and Hygelāc.* The presents he has brought from Denmark he shares with Hygelāc and Hygd and receives liberal gifts in return. He makes his home in Geatland, greatly honored and beloved by the king his uncle.

Part II. Bēowulf's Death

(The Fight with the Dragon)

Sceolde lǣndaga
æþeling ǣrgōd ende gebīdan,
worulde līfes, ond se wyrm somod. (2341 ff.)

2200-2323. *The robbing of the hoard and the ravages of the dragon.* After the death of Hygelāc and of his son Heardrēd, Bēowulf has ruled over the Geats for fifty years. Then it happens that the rich hoard (the early history of which is narrated in part) of a dragon is robbed by a fugitive slave, and the enraged monster in revenge lays waste the country by his fire.

2324-2537. *Preparation for the fight.* The veteran warrior-king, still young in spirit, resolves to meet the enemy single-handed. He has a strong iron shield made for this purpose and, accompanied by eleven men, sets out for the cave of the dragon. — (2417-2537.) Filled with forebodings of his end, he in a long speech reviews the days of his youth,

especially the events at the Geat court and the feud with the Swedes, and bids farewell to his comrades.
2538-2711. *The fight.* He calls the dragon out of the barrow and attacks him stoutly with his sword, but finds himself overwhelmed by deadly flames. His terrified companions flee to the wood, all save Wīglāf, who, mindful of the obligations of loyalty and gratitude, hastens to the assistance of his kinsman. Together they contend against the dreadful foe. Wīglāf deals him a decisive blow in the lower parts, and Bēowulf cuts him in two. But the king himself has received a fatal wound. — **2711-2820.** *Bēowulf's death.* Wīglāf tends his dying lord, and at his bidding brings part of the precious hoard out of the cave. Bēowulf gives thanks for having won the treasure for his people; he orders that a mound be built for him on the headland, and, after bequeathing his battle-gear to his faithful kinsman, he passes away.
2821-3030. *The spread of the tidings.* Wīglāf, full of sorrow and anger, rebukes the cowardly companions and sends a messenger to announce the king's death. The envoy foretells the disaster that will follow this catastrophe, recalling at length past wars with Franks and Swedes. — **3030-3136.** *Preliminaries of the closing scene.* The Geat warriors repair to the scene of the fight — the ancient curse laid on the gold having been grievously fulfilled — and at Wīglāf's command carry out the remaining treasure, push the dragon into the sea, and bear the king's body to the headland.
3137-3182. *The funeral of Bēowulf.* A funeral pyre is built. The hero is placed upon it and given over to the flames amid the lamentations of his people. Then they erect over the remains a royal mound in which they hide the dearly bought dragon's hoard. Twelve noble warriors ride round the barrow, lamenting their lord and praising his deeds and kingly virtues.

II. THE FABULOUS OR SUPERNATURAL ELEMENTS[1]

Hæfde þā gefǣlsod sē þe ǣr feorran cōm,
snotor ond swȳðferhð sele Hrōðgāres. (825 f.)
.   .   .   .   *oð ðone ānne dæg,*
þē hē wið þām wyrme gewegan sceolde. (2399 f.)

The subject-matter of *Beowulf* comprises in the first place, as the main plot, three fabulous exploits redolent of folk-tale fancy (the first two forming a closely connected series),[2] and secondly a number of ap-

---

[1] Cf. L 4.41 ff.; in particular Panzer, Boer (L 4.58 & 140); besides, Müllenhoff, Sarrazin St., Schück L 4.39, Symons L 4.29, Brandl, Chadwick H. A., Heusler L 4.37.2, Berendsohn L 4.141.1; Cha. Intr.; Lawrence L 4.22 c; Schneider L 4.13 a, 22 d. [*General note:* The necessarily summary treatment of some topics in chs. ii and iii of the Introduction may be supplemented by further utilizing the references, especially the more recent ones, in the corresponding sections of the Bibliography.]

[2] Outside the main action also, various supernatural elements are found, such as Sigemund's dragon fight (see note on 875-900), Scyld's mysterious arrival (see note on 4-52), the notion

parently historical elements which are introduced as a setting to the former and by way of more or less irrelevant digressions.

BĒOWULF'S FIGHT WITH GRENDEL AND HIS MOTHER[1]

Bēowulf's wonderful adventures with the Grendel race have called to mind folk-tales in various languages.[2] A systematic study of this aspect of the epic material was undertaken by Panzer, who recognized in the *Beowulf* story a version (raised to heroic proportions) of the time-honored, widespread ' Bear's Son Tale.'[3] The substance of this tale as extracted from over two hundred (European and other) variants is as follows.

(Introduction[4]) A demon appears at night in a house which has been built by an aged king. The elder sons of the king are unable to cope with the intruder, but the youngest one successfully gets hold of him. The demon is wounded but manages to get away. A bloody trail shows the way to his abode. — (Central part) The hero fights in a strange place, which in a great many instances is under the earth, against one or two demons (often a male and a female one). By this successful exploit he frees several maidens, who are then safely restored to the upper world. But he is himself betrayed by his faithless companions and must

---

of *eotenas, entas*, etc. (883, 2717, 2774, 112, etc., cf. *Angl.* xxxvi 169 f.). Special mention should be made of the motive of invulnerability (in encountering ordinary weapons, 804 f., 1522 ff.). Neither mythology nor history is to be appealed to in the case of the Breca episode (see note on 499 ff.).

[1] Additional special references: Gering L 4.48.1, Laistner L 4.50, Bugge 55 ff., 360 ff., Sarrazin L 4.32.4 & 5, Lawrence L 4.60, 62, Lehmann L 4.57, Mogk L 4.66 b2, von Sydow L 4.66 b, b3, Dehmer L 4.66 b5.

[2] Cf. W. Grimm L 4.41, Mone L 4.23.281 ff., Simrock L 3.21.177 ff., Laistner *l.c.* § 39, Cha. Intr. 62 ff., 365 ff. — Parallels from Irish legend were cited, e.g., by Cook (L 4.55 = P. Kennedy, *Legendary Fictions of the Irish Celts* [London, 1891], pp. 200 ff.; cf. Panzer 386 ff.), Brooke L 4.6.1.84 f., Deutschbein L 4.36. A Japanese version was pointed out by Powell L 4.56. A remarkable parallel was mentioned by Krappe, L 4.56a. Kittredge (in addition to Celtic variants) referred to a North American Indian tale (*Harvard Studies and Notes in Philology and Literature* viii 222 ff.). The stories cited by Laistner, Brooke, Cook, Krappe, and fully discussed by Kittredge and Dehmer, belong to the type known as ' The Hand and the Child.' (Its salient feature: a demonic arm stretches into the house to carry off human beings, especially children, but is finally seized and wrenched off by the hero.) Concerning it Kittredge remarked (*l.c.*, 229): "We must put behind us the temptation to genealogize. One fact is clear: the defence of a hall or a hut against the demon that haunts it is a simple theme, to which the theory of ' independent origins ' must apply if it ever applies to anything. That the defence should result in the demon's losing his arm seems a not unnatural development." Cf. Cha. Intr.[2] 478 ff. There is, of course, no reason why incidents representing different folkloristic types could not be found combined in a particular story.

[3] The name is derived from the hero who in some versions is the son of a bear. A more appropriate title would be ' Dat Erdmänneken,' ' the fairy of the mine ' (No. 91 of the Grimm collection of tales), denoting the strange demon whom the hero overcomes. (?)

[4] Of the Introductions to this tale which have been arranged by Panzer in three groups, the B-formula stands nearest to the *Beowulf*.

remain in the realm of monsters, until he finds means of escape. [The conclusion tells of the punishment of the traitors and the marriage of one of the maidens to her deliverer.]

Panzer thought he could show the ultimate derivation of numerous elements of the *Beowulf* narrative from the introductory and central parts of the Bear's Son Tale.[1] Thus, the building of the gold-decked royal hall, the nightly depredations of the giant demon; the watch against the monster; the character of the hero, who in his boyhood is looked down upon as sluggish and good for nothing, but gives an early proof of his extraordinary strength; the manner of the (first) fight, the enemy's loss of a limb, its exhibition and inspection; the mother of the monster, the fight in the cave under the water, the part played by the magic sword, the departure of the companions,[2] etc.

While these similarities are after all remote and generally vague, a genetic relation of some kind must clearly be admitted between the *Beowulf* and certain Scandinavian stories, in particular the one attached to Grettir the Strong.

The *Grettissaga* (dating from about 1300) is concerned with a historical personage, a headstrong, adventurous outlaw, who died in the year 1031, but it includes obvious fabulous elements derived, according to Panzer, from folk-tales of the ' Bear's Son ' and the ' Doughty Hans '[3] type. Chapters 64–66[4] relate two successive exploits of the Icelandic hero — ' the strongest man in the land of his age,' chapter 93 — which in several respects form the nearest parallel to the fight with Grendel and Grendel's mother.

At Yule-tide, so the story runs, the young wife Steinvǫr at Sandhills (*at Sandhaugum, í Bárðardal*) had gone to worship at *Eyjardalsá* and left her husband at home. In the night the men heard a huge crashing in the house; and in the morning it was found that the husband had disappeared, and no one knew what had become of him. The next year the same thing happened to a house-carle. Grettir the Strong heard the

---

[1] See his detailed comparison, pp. 254 ff. It should not fail to be noted that the parallels are gathered from widely scattered and varying versions (most of them modern), no single specimen or group answering precisely to the type represented by the *Beowulf*. And it may be remarked in general that the folk-tale element is not necessarily to be considered the germ pure and simple of the Beowulfian legend. Priority may be claimed for the heroic ' historical ' features.

[2] That is, the Danes only, 1600 ff. They are supposed to represent the faithless companions of the tale.

[3] Thus Grettir (and likewise Ormr) as a boy shows himself lazy and of a violent disposition and displays uncommon bodily strength. — It may be mentioned that Grettir gains fame by killing a mighty bear which no one else could overcome (ch. 21; also Biarco slays a big bear, Saxo ii 56, see Par. § 7). The bear's cave is described as being ' in a cliff by the sea where there was a cave under an overhanging rock, with a narrow path leading to the entrance.' (Hight's transl.)

[4] The version given here is in part a summary and in part follows the translation of Magnússon and Morris (L 10.6).

THE FABULOUS ELEMENTS

tale, and at Yule-eve he betook himself to the haunted place. He asked permission to stay there and called himself Gestr. The goodwife wished to go to church again, but thought it impossible to cross the river. It thawed fast abroad, and the river was in flood, and therein was the drift of ice great. But Grettir went with Steinvǫr and her little daughter and carried them both with one arm through the raging river, while with the other he pushed back the ice-floe.[1] He then returned to Sandhills and lay down at night, but did not take off his clothes.

Towards midnight Grettir heard great din without, and thereafter into the hall came a huge troll-wife, with a trough[2] in one hand and a chopper wondrous great in the other; she peered about when she came in, and saw where 'Gestr' lay, and ran at him; but he sprang up to meet her, and they fell a-wrestling terribly, and struggled together for long in the hall. She was the stronger, but he gave back with craft, and all that was before them was broken, yea, the cross-paneling withal of the chamber. She dragged him out through the door and labored away with him down towards the river, and right down to the deep gulfs. All night they wrestled furiously; never, he deemed, had he fought with such a monster; she held him to her so hard that he might turn his arms to no account save to keep fast hold on the middle of the witch. But now when they had come to the gulf of the river, he gives the hag a swing round, and therewith got his right hand free, and swiftly seized the short-sword (*sax*) that he was girt withal, and smote the troll therewith on the shoulder, and struck off her arm; and therewithal was he free, but she fell into the gulf and was carried down the 'force.'

After Yule-tide Grettir went with the *Eyjardalsá* priest (who doubted his tale and would not believe that the two men who had vanished had gone into the gulf) to the scene of his victory. When they came to the force-side, they saw a cave up under the cliff; a sheer rock that cliff was, so great that in no place might man come up thereby, and well-nigh fifty fathoms was it down to the water. Grettir bade the priest watch the upper end of a rope, which he let sink down into the water; then he leapt off the cliff into the gulf. He dived under the force, and hard work it was, because the whirlpool was strong, and he had to dive down to the bottom, before he might come up under the force. But thereby was a rock jutting out, and thereon he gat; a great cave was under the force, and the river fell over it from the sheer rocks. He went up into the cave, and there was a great fire flaming from amidst brands; and there he saw a giant (*jǫtunn*) sitting, marvelously great and dreadful to look on. But when Grettir came anigh, the giant leapt up and caught up a glaive and smote at the newcomer, for with that glaive might a man both cut and

---

[1] It is exceedingly doubtful whether this feat — a preliminary demonstration of strength, cf. the Bear's Son parallels, Panzer 34 ff. — can be regarded as an analogue of the Breca adventure (Brandl 994). Grettir's superiority as an endurance swimmer is mentioned in ch. 58.

[2] For holding her food — the human victim. Grendel brought a *glōf* for the same purpose with him (2085 ff.).

thrust; a wooden shaft it had, and that fashion of weapon men called then, heft-sax (*hepti-sax*). Grettir hewed back against him with his short-sword (*sax*), and smote the shaft so that he struck it asunder; then was the giant fain to stretch aback for a sword that hung up there in the cave; but therewithal Grettir smote him afore into the breast, and smote off well-nigh all the breast bone and the belly, so that the bowels tumbled out of him and fell into the river, and were driven down along the stream; and as the priest sat by the rope, he saw certain fibers all covered with blood swept down the swirls of the stream; then he grew unsteady in his place, and thought for sure that Grettir was dead, so he ran from the holding of the rope[1] (which had been fastened to a peg), and returned home. — In the meantime Grettir went up the cave; he kindled a light and examined the place. The story does not tell how much he got therein, but men deem that it must have been something great. He also found the bones of the two men and put them in a bag. Then he made off from the cave and swam to the rope and shook it, and thought that the priest would be there yet; but when he knew that the priest had gone home, then must he draw himself up by strength of hand, and thus he came up out on to the cliff. Then he fared back to *Eyjardalsá*, and brought into the church porch the bag with the bones, and therewith a rune-staff with verses cut on it. (The last verses: 'For from its mighty shaft of tree The heft-sax [*hepti-sax*] smote I speedily; And dulled the flashing war-flame [*gunn-logi*] fair In the black breast that met me there.')

(Chap. 67.) Grettir was thought to have done great deeds for the cleansing of the land (*mikla landhreinsun*).

Like Grettir, Ormr the Strong is known to have been a real person, but in the *Orms þáttr Stórólfssonar*[2] remarkable deeds of a fabulous character are ascribed to him.

Orm's sworn brother, Ásbjǫrn, we are told, sails to the Norwegian island Sandey (Saudey), where a man-eating giant Brúsi and his mother (in the shape of an enormous cat) dwell in a cave.[3] (He is slain by Brúsi after a severe struggle.[4] Twenty of his men are torn to pieces and devoured by the terrible fire-breathing cat.) When Ormr at his home in Iceland gets news of his friend's death, he determines to avenge him and

---
[1] This motive recurs in the story of Grettir's encounter with the ghost of Kárr, which in the manner of the fighting resembles also the Glámr incident (see below, p. xvii) and the first part of the *Sandhaugar* episode. — It may be mentioned that a submarine contest in the *Þorsteinssaga Víkingssonar* has been cited as a parallel to Bēowulf's fight with Grendel's mother (C. N. Gould, *MPh*. vii 214).

[2] See L 10.7. Ormr and Grettir are mentioned together as two of the strongest men ever known in Iceland, *Grettissaga*, ch. 58. See note on l. 901. It must be admitted that the *Orm* parallel is of less value than has often been assumed, especially as that text is largely dependent on the *Grettissaga* (and other sagas), cf. Boer L 4.140.177 ff.

[3] The cave is near the sea; in the Faroe versions it is reached by means of a small boat. See Bugge 361 ff.

[4] Bugge thought this Ásbjǫrn ultimately identical with Æschere, *Beow*. 1323 ff.

THE FABULOUS ELEMENTS xvii

sails to Brúsi's island. He enters the cave and fights first with the mother — the cat, who attacks him with her piercing claws.[1] He reels back, but when he calls on God and St. Peter for help,[2] he gets the better of the monster and breaks her back. Thereupon he struggles with Brúsi and overcomes him by sheer strength of arm. After cutting with his sword (*sax*) the ' blood-eagle ' into the dead giant's back, he leaves the cave with two chests of gold and silver.

The same story has been traced in the modern versions of two Faroe and two Swedish ballads.[3]

Another analogue (from the *Floressaga*) has been cited by M. Schlauch, L 4.62 e.

Of less significance, yet worthy of mention, as a parallel to the Grendel fight, is the *Glámr episode* of the *Grettissaga* (chaps. 32–35), which tells of how Glámr, a shepherd, who (had been killed by an evil spirit and who afterwards) haunted and made uninhabitable the house and farm of Þórhallr, was slain by Grettir in a mighty contest.

Grettir when told of the hauntings rode to the place (*Þórhallsstaðir*) and in the night awaited Glámr in the hall. When a third part of the night had passed, he heard a great noise without, then one went up upon the house, and afterwards came down and opened the door. Grettir lay quiet; Glámr went up to him and tried to pull him out of the house. They struggled wondrously hard, and seats and benches were broken before them. Glámr wanted to get out. Grettir resisted with all his might and finally succeeded in making his fiendish opponent reel back and fall open-armed out of the house. By drawing his short-sword (*sax*) and cutting off Glám's head he disposed of the hateful revenant. (But before he could do it, he beheld with terror in the moonlight Glám's horrible face and heard his dying curse, which was to be of disastrous consequences to him.)

A notable parallel of the second adventure has been detected (by Lawrence, L 4.62 c) in an episode of the (13th or 14th cent.) *Samsonssaga*. (A brief summary by Lawrence: " A she-troll dwelling under a waterfall has begotten a son, a supernatural being who haunts the forests. She is killed, like Grendel's dam, in a struggle under the waters. Afterwards the hero dives under the fall, and comes to a cave in which he finds precious objects. Gallyn the miller, seeing blood in the stream, immediately concludes, like the watchers in the tales of Bēowulf and Grettir, that the hero has been killed.") The characteristic ' waterfall-cave ' scenery is likewise found in the *Gullþórissaga* and the story of ' Gullbra and Skeggi.'[4]

---

[1] Cp. *Beow.* 1501 ff. [2] Cp. *Beow.* 1553 ff.

[3] An interesting detail of the Faroe ballads, viz. the exclamation in praise (blessing) of the hero's mother after the slaying of the giant, has been connected (by Bugge) with *Beow.* 942 ff., but the coincidence need not be considered of importance.

[4] Text and translation of the *Samsonssaga* episode by Lawrence, Cha. Intr.² 502 f., 456 f.; of the stories of Gullþórir and Gullbra by Cha. Intr.² 494 ff.

xviii   INTRODUCTION

The points of contact between the foregoing extracts and the *Beowulf* are unmistakable and need not be gone over in detail. The *Sandhaugar* episode in particular gives a strikingly similar description[1] of the monster's cave under a waterfall, and moreover seems to show a verbal agreement in the use of (the nonce word) *heptisax*, recalling the (equally unique) *hæftmēce*, *Beow.* 1457.[2] In some points, it should be noted, this important and highly instructive version presents an obscuration of the original folk-tale elements;[3] viz. in making not the male but the female monster (who, by the way, is not stated explicitly to be the giant's mother) provoke the first fight by attacking the house, the natural rôles of the two demons being thus reversed; in motivating the hero's visit to the cave by mere curiosity; in omitting all mention of the wounded she-demon in the second adventure; and in completely blurring the motive of the wonderful sword which is found hanging in the cave.

Some noteworthy innovations in the *Beowulf* account — apart from the general transformation incident to the epic setting and atmosphere — are the following. The mother of the slain Grendel leaves her cave, appears in the hall, and avenges her son in heroic fashion — an evident amplification (including a partial repetition) of the narrative. Again, Grendel, though (mortally wounded by Bēowulf and) found dead in the cave, is as it were slain again (1576 ff.) and definitely disposed of by beheading. In the original form of the story, it appears, the male demon had been merely wounded; when the hero had made his way to the dwelling place of the monsters, he put the wounded enemy to death (and afterwards killed the mother). A number of minor incongruities possibly arising from an imperfect remodeling of old folk-tale motives are pointed out in the Notes, see ll. 135, 703, 736 ff., 839 ff., cf. 1260. The theory that the Anglo-Saxon poet worked up different versions (relating to Grendel and to Grendel's mother respectively) has been repeatedly proposed as a means of accounting for disparities of the narrative; see especially Schneider (L 4.135) and Berendsohn (L 4.141.1.14 ff.).

Different and in a certain respect closer is the relation of *Beowulf* to the late *Hrólfssaga* (see Par. § 9, L 10.8). It is true, Bǫðvar's contest with a peculiar fanciful beast (chap. 23) has not nearly so much in common with the Grendel fight as Grettir's adventure in the cave has with Bēowulf's second encounter. Yet only in the *Hrólfssaga* do we find a story at all comparable to the Grendel part placed in a historical setting comparable to that in the Anglo-Saxon epic and attributed to a person

---

[1] It serves indeed to make clear the Beowulfian representation of the Grendel abode, see Lawrence L 4.62. Cf. also above, pp. xiv n. 3, xvi n. 3.

[2] The former is used by the giant, the latter by Bēowulf; a *seax* is used also by Grendel's mother (1545), as a *sax* is several times by Grettir. The kenning *gunnlogi* reminds us of *beadolēoma*, *Beow.* 1523. See further, notes on 1457, 1506 ff., 1555 f.

[3] Cf. Panzer 319.

THE FABULOUS ELEMENTS

who is possibly after all identical with Bēowulf himself.[1] Manifestly the relation of Bǫðvarr to Hrólfr is not unlike that of Bēowulf to Hrōðgār — both deliver the king from the ravages of a terrible monster, both are his honored champions and friends, Bǫðvarr the son-in-law, Bēowulf the 'adopted son' (946 ff., 1175 f.). Nor should the following parallels be denied consideration. Bǫðvarr goes from Gautland, whose king is his brother, to the Danish court at Hleiðra; Bēowulf goes from the land of the Geats, who are ruled by his uncle Hygelāc, to the court of the Danish king at Heorot. Bǫðvarr makes his entrance at the court in a brusque, self-confident manner and at the feast quarrels with the king's men; Bēowulf introduces himself with a great deal of self-reliance tempered, of course, by courtly decorum (407 ff.), and at the banquet has a dispute with an official of the king (499 ff.); also his scornful retort of ll. 590 ff. is matched by Bǫðvar's slighting remarks, 68. 17 ff. (Par. § 9.)

In addition, certain features in the Norse tradition of Bǫðvarr have been instanced as confirming the original identity of the two heroes.[2] The bear nature of Bǫðvarr which must be supposed to be his own by inheritance[3] and which is implied by his strange behavior in the great *Bjarkamál* battle (Saxo ii 59 ff., *Hrólfssaga*, chaps. 32 f.) has been compared to Bēowulf's bearlike wrestling propensities, dwelt upon in his

---

[1] Additional special references: ten Brink 185 ff., Olrik i 134 ff., Lawrence L 4.60, Olson L 4.65; von Sydow L 4.66 b3; Cha. Intr. 54 ff. (*ib.* 398, ²522: ref. to Brynjulfsson); Berendsohn L 4.40 a. — The value of the *Hrólfssaga* for purposes of comparison and the identity of Bǫðvarr and Bēowulf (insisted upon above all by Sarrazin) have been recognized by a number of scholars. It has been claimed that a comparison of Saxo (ii 56, Par. § 7; cf. above, p. xiv n. 3: *Grettissaga*, ch. 21), the *Hrólfssaga*, and the *Bjarkarímur* (Par. § 9.1) with each other, and with the *Beowulf* helps to throw light on certain elements of confusion in the Saga. The wings of the monster are thus considered to be a modern embellishment of the story. Besides, the real and the sham fight might seem to have arisen from a series of two real encounters, in the second of which the (previously wounded) troll was killed (in accordance with the supposedly older form of the Grendel part, see Panzer 371 f.). Furthermore, it has been supposed that in the original story the fighter's own sword actually failed him (cp. Par. § 9 with *Beow.* 1523 ff.), but a wonderful, gold-hilted sword brought him victory (cp. Par. § 9 with *Beow.* 1557 ff.). Sarrazin suggested that the two 'war-friends' (*Beow.* 1810), the unsuccessful *Hrunting* and the victorious *Gyldenhilt* (*Gullinhjalti*), were developed by a process of personification into the dual figure of *Hǫttr-Hjalti* (coward-champion), cf. *E St.* xxxv 19 ff. Olson endeavored to prove that the *Bjarkarímur* have no independent value in this connection, that the earliest type of Bjarki's fight is the one found in Saxo, and that the form of the monster overcome in the *Hrólfssaga* is derived from the Siward saga. See Cha. Intr.

[2] See Chadwick H. A. 120 f.; Clarke L 4.76.49 ff.

[3] On the use of this bear motive (which is not unknown in folk-tales, cf. above, p. xiii n. 3) in the *Gesta Herwardi*, in Saxo (x 345), and in the story of Siward, see Lawrence, pp. 234 ff.; Olrik i 215 ff., & *AfNF.* xix 199 ff.; Deutschbein, *Studien zur Sagengeschichte Englands,* pp. 249 ff.; and especially Olson, who, with Olrik, traces Bǫðvar's bear-ancestry to the Siward saga. — Did Bēowulf inherit his wrestling strength from his father (cp. *handbona* 460)? Incidentally, it may be noted that he became the forerunner of wrestling heroes celebrated in English literature (as in *The Tale of Gamelyn, Lorna Doone* ,etc.).

xx   INTRODUCTION

contest with Grendel and with the Frankish warrior Dæghrefn (2501 ff.). Also the fact that Bǫðvarr Bjarki (with other champions of Hrólfr) aids Aðils in his war (*Skáldskaparmál, Skjǫldungasaga, Bjarkarímur*, Par. §§ 5, 8.6, 9.1[1]) is paralleled, in a measure, by Bēowulf's 'befriending' the Swedish prince Ēadgils (2392 ff.).

The perplexing question of the precise relation between *Beowulf* and the various (late) Scandinavian stories briefly considered here has given rise to manifold earnest and ingenious discussions, and conflicting conclusions have been arrived at. On the whole, it seems safest to attribute the undeniable parallelisms to the use of the same or similar Scandinavian sources both in the Old English and the Old Norse accounts.[1a] There existed, we may assume, on the one hand a tale — made over into a local legend[2] — of the freeing of the Danish court from a strange monster through the prowess of a mighty warrior, and another one — like the former going back to a primitive folk-tale — about a similar adventure expanded to a fight with two monsters[3] and placed in picturesque Scandinavian surroundings. Both kinds of narrative circulated orally in the North. In course of time they were attached to various persons (two of whom are unquestionably historical characters),[3a] Bǫðvarr, Grettir, Ormr, Bēowulf respectively. A comparatively early combination of the two sets was perhaps effected in Scandinavia, though it is actually traceable in the Anglo-Saxon epic only. The artistic *Beowulf* version represents the final result of this formative process.

Attention, however, should be called also to the significant suggestion made from time to time, that the substance of the Grendel part goes back ultimately, if not directly, to Irish models.[4] Even a definite Irish analogue has been detected,[5] viz. Cuchulinn's adventures in the saga of

[1] The fame of Bjarki is attested also by the *Series Runica* and the *Annales Ryenses* (Par. § 8.4 & 5). That he came to be known in North England, is shown by the occurrence of the name *Boduwar Berki* in the *Liber Vitae Ecclesiae Dunelmensis* (in a 12th century entry); cf. also A. Bugge, *ZfdA*. li 35.

[1a] That the account of the *Sandhaugar* episode is not derived from the English version has been clearly demonstrated by Cha., Intr.[2] 461 ff., cf. L 4.62 d. By a comparison of the analogous versions (see pp. xv ff.) Cha. has managed to reconstruct what may be considered the outlines of the original form of the Grendel story, in particular of the second adventure. (See notes on 1506 ff., 1555 f.)

[2] For such a legend (showing at least a slight similarity) attached to the bay of Roskilde see Sarrazin St. 10 ff.

[3] The figures on a 6th century tablet found in Öland have been interpreted by Stjerna (31 f.) as representing a counterpart to Bēowulf's contest with the 'she-wolf,' Grendel's mother.

[3a] Also Gull-Þórir is historical.

[4] Cf. e.g., Brooke L 4.6.1.84 f., von Sydow, Dehmer, see above, p. xiii n. 1, 2; v. Sydow, *Anz. fdA*. xxxv 129 f. (Parallel British versions: Freymond, "Artus' Kampf mit dem Katzenungetüm," *Festgabe für Gröber* (1899), pp. 311 ff.) — See below, p. cxxiii.

[5] Deutschbein L 4.36, cf. *Anz.fdA*. xxxvi 224 f. A direct influence of the Irish saga (which has not been claimed) would be entirely out of the question on chronological grounds. Zimmer (*ZfdA*. xxxii 331 f.) had assumed, on the other hand, an (indirect) influence of the Bēowulf legend on that of Cuchulinn.

THE FABULOUS ELEMENTS   xxi

The Feast of Bricriu, though the parallelism noted is certainly not conspicuous.[1] Again, the motives and the general atmosphere of the second adventure have been alleged to point in the direction of Celtic sources. Indeed, the brilliant picture of the monsters' mysterious haunt (1357 ff.) might well remind us of Celtic fancy.[2] The notion of the female monster, Grendel's mother, foreshadowing ' the devil's dam,' has been cited in the same connection.[3]

Other analogies have been mentioned, such as the elegiac tone of certain passages (2247-66, 2435-71),[4] the mystic element of the Scyld legend (see note on 4-52), the position of the court *þyle*.[5] Moreover, in the selection of the peculiar kind of plot (supernatural adventures) and even in the general style and manner of the narrative the influence of Celtic types has been supposed to be visible.[6] Also the possibility of Celtic elements in the language of *Beowulf* has been discussed.[7]

While these observations and hypotheses are exceedingly interesting, it is only fair to say that so far no tangible proof has been produced.

BĒOWULF'S FIGHT WITH THE DRAGON[8]

Dragon fights are events of such ordinary occurrence in medieval literature that it may almost seem otiose to hunt for specific sources of the Beowulfian specimen. But mention has been very properly made of numerous modern parallels of folk legends[9] — the nearest of which is a Danish one, — and more especially of Frotho's dragon fight[10] in Saxo's History (ii 38 f., Par. § 7) as indicating a probable Danish origin of the story. It is true, one of the most sagacious students of Scandinavian legend[11] has pronounced the similarities between Saxo's account and the *Beowulf* version entirely irrelevant, imaginary, or common-

---

[1] See Olson L 4.63.
[2] The picturesque kennings for the sea have been instanced as suggesting the quality of Celtic imagination (Rankin, *JEGPh.* ix 75, 82).
[3] Ker L 4.120.1.198 f.; Lehmann L 4.57.428; von der Leyen L 4.67. n. 5.122; v. Sydow, *l.c.*
[4] Bugge 77 ff. (Some minor details are added.) But this is very questionable, see Sieper L 4.126.2.58 f.
[5] Deutschbein, *l.c.*   [6] Deutschbein, *l.c.*
[7] Sarrazin Käd. 69 ff. (Thus *Gārmund* 1962, in place of *Wǣrmund*, is explained as a Celticism, cf. also *E St.* xlii 17.) The MS. spellings *cames* 107, *camp* 1261 have been thought to evidence a Celtic source of information. (Bugge 82; cf. Emerson, *Publ. MLAss.* xxi 925, 885 n. 3; note on ll. 106 ff.)
[8] Additional special references: Sievers L 4.33, Olrik i 305 ff., Sarrazin L 4.32.1 & 5, Bugge and Olrik L 4.51, Bugge 45 ff., Berendsohn L 4.141.1.1 ff.; Lawrence L 4.62 a; Cha. Intr. 92 ff.; Schneider L 4.13 a.
[9] Panzer 294 ff. All of these parallels belong to the so-called Þórr type. Most of them are localized in Germany, a few in Denmark.
[10] Sievers, *l.c.* (Cf. Müllenhoff, *ZfdA*. vii 439; Müller L 10.4. ii. 74; Sarrazin St. 88.) A similar, briefer version is the dragon fight of Fridlevus, Saxo vi 180 f.
[11] Olrik, *l.c.*

place, emphasizing at the same time the fact that the stories taken as a whole are of a totally different order, — Frotho, who wages the fight for the sake of the dragon's treasure and who by this victory first establishes his fame, representing the Sigurðr type,[1] and, on the other hand, Bēowulf, who undertakes the venture primarily to save his people and, although victorious, loses his life, exemplifying in the main the Þórr type.[2] Yet it appears quite credible that some such lay as the one which Saxo deliberately turned into Latin verse was known to the Anglo-Saxon poet and perhaps even suggested to him Bēowulf's third great adventure. There is a notable agreement in a number of features which can hardly be accidental, — thus, in the description of the dragon (cp. *Beow.* 2561, 2569 ff., 2827, 2582 f.; 2304, 2524, 2580); the report of a countryman (cp. 2214 ff., 2280 ff., 2324 ff., 2404 ff.); the use of a specially prepared shield (cp. 2337 ff., 2522 ff.); the hero's desire to engage in the contest without help from others (cp. 2345 ff., 2529 ff.); the manner of the fight itself (cp. e.g., the details: 2699, 2705). It is also evident that far-reaching alterations would be deemed requisite by the poet who fitted this theme into the story of Bēowulf's life. Nothing could be more natural than that the high-minded slayer of the Grendel kin should appear again, above all else, in the rôle of a deliverer from distress, a benefactor of men. And when this great deed was added as the crowning event to the record of his long life, what better motivation of his death could have presented itself? The introduction of an associate in the person of Wīglāf served to provide not only a welcome helper in the fatal struggle, but an eyewitness and assistant at the king's pathetic death, besides an heir and executor who directs the impressive closing scene of the poem. Of course, if Sarrazin's thesis (see below, pp. xxiii, xliv) be adopted, Wīglāf (Viggo, Vǫggr) must be considered one of the original figures of the Scandinavian legend.[3]

It has been conjectured[4] that certain instances of an imperfect adaptation of the Danish original can be detected in our text of the *Beowulf*, viz. the reference to the *ēalond* 2334 (see note), answering to Saxo's island, and the puzzling line (*þone ðe ǣr gehēold* . . .) *æfter hæleða hryre hwate Scildingas* 3005 (see note), which was supposed to show that the dragon fight was originally attributed to the Danish king Bēowulf (I)[5] of ll. 18 ff., 53 ff., the predecessor of Healfdene, just as it was attached (Saxo ii 38) to Haldanus' predecessor Frotho. The latter assumption

---

[1] See *Reginsmál, Fáfnismál; Skáldskaparmál* (Prose Edda), ch. (37,) 38; *Vǫlsungasaga*, ch. (14,) 18.

[2] See *Vǫluspá* 55 (56) f.; *Gylfaginning* (Prose Edda), ch. 50.

[3] We may add that both the detailed story of how the hoard came into the possession of the dragon and the motive of the curse laid on the gold put us in mind of Scandinavian analogues, — even though the circumstances of the former are not at all identical. (See notes on 2231 ff., 3051 ff.) Cf. *Reginsmál, Fáfnismál, Skáldskaparmál*, chs. 37 ff.

[4] See Sievers, *l.c.;* Boer L 4.58.69 n., L 4.140.112.

[5] Or Bēowa (see below, pp. xxiii ff.), which Sievers (*l.c.*) also took for granted.

THE FABULOUS ELEMENTS xxiii

has been endorsed by Berendsohn, who — improving upon the formula 'combination of the Þórr and the Fáfnir (or Sigurðr) type' (Panzer) — suggests that two versions have been fused in the epic (itself), the hero of the first being originally Bēowulf I = Frotho, whilst the second was concerned with an aged king who fights a fiery dragon in order to save his people. It is one of a number of possibilities.

In some respects the other dragon fight told in the *Beowulf*, that of Sigemund (884 ff.), exhibits a closer affinity to Saxo's Frotho parallel. Both belong in the ' Sigurðr ' class, being the adventurous exploits of conquering heroes. Sigemund, like Frotho, is really alone in the fight (888 f.). He loads a boat with the dragon's treasures, just as Frotho is bidden to do by his informant (Par. § 7). (The scene of Bēowulf's fight is near the sea, but the boat is replaced by a wagon, 3134.)[1]

Several minor parallels between Bēowulf's and Sigemund's dragon fight should not be overlooked. Cp. *under hārne stān*[2] (. . . *āna genēðde* . . .) 887; 2553, 2744, 2213, 2540. — [*draca*] *morðre swealt* 892, 2782. — *wyrm hāt gemealt* 897 (see note), cf. 3040 f.: *wæs se lēgdraca . . . glēdum beswǣled*. (Similarly the victorious sword which avails against [Grendel and] Grendel's mother, is melted by the monster's hot blood, 1605 ff., 1666 ff.)[3] — . . . *selfes dōme, sǣbāt gehleōd* 895; *him on bearm hladon . . . sylfes dōme* 2775 f. — (*hordes hyrde* 887, cf. *beorges hyrde* 2304.) See further, *A.* l 238 ff.

That both ' Bēowulf's death ' and ' the fall of Boðvarr Bjarki '[4] (Saxo ii 59 ff., *Hrólfssaga*, chaps. 32 ff., Par. §§ 7, 9) go back ultimately to historical legend commemorating the fight between Hjǫrvarðr (= Heoroweard) and the Geat [king] Boðvarr (Bjarki) (= Bēowulf), that is, practically a war — the final, disastrous one — between Swedes and Geats,[5] has been argued with great keenness by Sarrazin (*E St.* xlii 24 ff.), who is supported by Berendsohn (*l.c.* 12 f.). Through subsequent intrusion of supernatural folk-tale elements, it is further assumed, the whole character of the legend underwent a radical metamorphosis, although the persistent allusions to the Swedish-Geatish affairs in the second part of the *Beowulf* serve as reminders of the actual historical background.

THE TWO BĒOWULFS. MYTHOLOGICAL INTERPRETATION[6]

The mention of Bēowulf the Dane (who may be designated as

[1] Sigurðr has his horse carry the treasures (*Fáfnismál, Skáldskaparmál*, ch. 38, *Vǫlsungasaga*, ch. 19).

[2] In the *Nibelungenlied* the hoard is carried *ūz eime holn berge*, 90.

[3] The light in the cave (2769 f.) recalls the second adventure (1570 ff.).

[4] That is, before the latter became connected with the story of Hrólfr Kraki.

[5] Cf. below, p. xl.

[6] Special references: Kemble L 4.43, Müllenhoff L 4.25.2, 3, 5 (besides L 4.19.1 ff.), Sarrazin L 4.32.3, Olrik i 223 ff., ii 250 ff., Binz, Lawrence L 4.60, Heusler L 4.37.2; Cha. Intr. 41 ff., 291 ff.

Bēowulf I in contradistinction to the hero Bēowulf [II] the Geat) has caused much perplexity to students of the poem. In the opening canto Scyld Scēfing and his son Bēowulf are given the place of honor in the genealogy of the Danish kings. Practically the same names, viz. Scēaf (Scēf), Scyld (Scyldwa, Sceldwea), Bēaw (Beo, Beowi(n)us, etc.[1]) occur among the ancestors of Wōden in a number of Anglo-Saxon and, similarly, Old Norse genealogies (Par. §§ 1, 5, 8.1). That those names in the Scandinavian pedigrees are derived from Anglo-Saxon sources, is clearly proved by their forms and by the explanatory translations which have been added. Again, a local appellation *Bēowan hamm*[2] is mentioned in the neighborhood of a *Grendles mere* in a Wiltshire charter issued by King Æðelstān in the year 931.[3] From these facts, aided by etymological interpretations of the name *Bēaw-Bēow*(a) (*Bēowulf*), it has been inferred that the hero of the poem was originally the same as Bēaw (Bēowa, Bēowulf I); i.e., a divine being worshiped by the Anglo-Saxons and credited with wondrous deeds of the mythological order, and who by contamination with a historical person of the name of Bēowulf, the nephew of king Hygelāc, was transformed into the mortal hero of the poem. Originated by Kemble and very generally accepted for generations (though varied in minor details), this hypothesis seemed to furnish the very key to a true understanding of the unique epic poem. It was enunciated by Müllenhoff, as a kind of dogma, in the following precise and supposedly authoritative formulation.

Bēow (whose name is derived from the root *bhū* [cp. OE. *būan*] 'grow,' 'dwell,' 'cultivate land'), in conjunction with Scēaf ('sheaf,' denoting husbandry) and Scyld ('shield,' i.e., protection against enemies), typifies the introduction of agriculture and civilization, the peaceful dwelling on the cultivated ground. He is virtually identical with Ing[4] and thus also with Frēa (ON. Freyr), the god of fruitfulness

---

[1] For the variant forms see Grimm D. M. iii 389 (1722); Kemble ii, p. xii. And see below, Par. §1.

[2] First pointed out by Kemble (L 9.1. i. 416) and turned to full account by Müllenhoff (*ZfdA*. xii 282 ff.). — *ham*(*m*) = 'dwelling,' 'fold,' perhaps 'piece of land surrounded with paling, wicker-work, etc., and so defended against the stream, which would otherwise wash it away' (see B.-T.); cf. H. Middendorff, *Ae. Flurnamenbuch* (1902), pp. 63 f. — Place-names like *Beas broc, Beodun* and, on the other hand, *Grindles bec, Grendeles pyt* and the like (Haack L 4.30.51 ff.; Binz 153 ff.; Napier and Stevenson, *Crawford Charters* (1895) 1.14, 3.5, and note on p. 50), occurring without any relation to each other, cannot be used as evidence.

[3] 'Ego Aeðelstanus rex Anglorum .... quandam telluris particulam meo fideli ministro Wulfgaro ... in loco quem solicolae æt Hamme vocitant tribuo .... Praedicta ... tellus his terminis circumcincta clarescit: *ærest on easteweardan on lin-leage geat ...... ðonon ondlong herpoðes on burghardes anstigo. ðonne forð to bares anstigon ... oð hit cimeð to ðære dic ... ðonne norð ofer dune ... ðonne á dune on ða yfre. on beowan hammes hecgan. on bremeles sceagan easteweardne ..... to ðære scortan dic. butan anan æcre. ðonne to fugel-mere to ðan wege; ondlong weges to ottes forda; ðonon to wudumere; ðonne io ðære ruwan hecgan; ðæt on langan hangran; ðonne on grendles mere; ðonon on dyrnan geat; ðonne eft on lin-leage geat.*' (*Cartularium Saxonicum* ed. by W. de Gray Birch ii 363 ff. [Kemble, *Cod. Dipl.* ii 171 ff.].)

[4] Cf. below, p. xxxvii.

THE FABULOUS ELEMENTS

and riches. In a similar mythological light are to be viewed the exploits of Bēowulf (that is, primarily, Bēow). Grendel is a personification of the (North) Sea, and so is Grendel's mother; and Bēowulf's fight against these demons symbolizes the successful checking of the inundations of the sea in the spring season. The contest with the dragon is its autumnal counterpart. In the death of the aged hero, which means the coming on of winter, an old seasons-myth is seen to lie back of the prevailing culture-myth conception.[1] Owing to the similarity of names, the ancient Anglo-Saxon myth of Bēowa was transferred to Bēowulf the Geat, a great warrior who distinguished himself in Hygelāc's ill-fated expedition against the Franks.

A number of other more or less ingenious mythological expositions have been put forward.[2] Bēowulf has been made out a superhuman being of the order of Þórr or Baldr, or a lunar deity,[3] a personification of wind, storm, or lightning, a patron of bee-keepers,[4] whilst his opponent Grendel has figured as the incarnation of the terrors of pestilential marshes, malaria or fog, or of the long winter nights, a storm being, a likeness of the ON. Loki or Ægir, even of the Lernaean hydra of old.[5] Also the dragon and Bēowulf's dragon fight have been subjected to various interpretations of a similar allegorizing character.

Grimm understood the name *Bēo-wulf* (of which *Bēow* was supposed to be a shortening) as ' bee-wolf ² (enemy of the bees), meaning ' woodpecker,'[6] which bird he conjectured to have been held sacred like the Picus of the Romans. Others have accepted this eminently plausible etymology of ' bee-wolf,' taking the word, however, in the sense of ' bear '[6a] (the ravager of bees, the hive plunderer). (Cosijn, *Aanteekeningen*, p. 42 [cf. *ZfdPh*. xxiv 17 n.] explained ' bee-wolf ' as *sigewulf* [with reference to the use of *sigewīf* for ' bees ' in the Ags. *Charms* 3.8, Grein-Wülcker i 320].)

Out of the bewildering mass of learned disquisitions along these lines a few facts emerge as fairly probable. Neither the Grendel nor the dragon fight is to be shifted back from Bēowulf (II) the Geat hero to Bēowulf (I) the Dane or the Anglo-Saxon progenitor. The evidence of the famous Wiltshire charter is far from conclusive as regards the attribution of the Grendel fight to Bēowa, especially as the latter name (in

---

[1] Even the swimming adventure with Breca has been explained mythologically, see note on 499 ff.

[2] See Wülker L 4.4.258 ff.; Panzer 250 ff.

[3] By reason of his dragon fight, cf. E. Siecke, *Drachenkämpfe, Untersuchungen zur indogermanischen Sagenkunde.* 1907.

[4] Hence, more generally, a representative of civilization (Müllenhoff, *ZfdA*. xii 283).

[5] Hagen, *MLN*. xix 71; cf. Kögel, *ZfdA*. xxxvii 270; see also Fog L 4.66 b1.

[6] Skeat at one time accepted this (*Academy* xi 163 c), but considered that the woodpecker on account of its fighting qualities was meant to typify a hero. Schröder L 4.66 b7 inclines to Grimm's view.

[6a] Presumably a taboo name. The conclusion reached by Krogmann (L 4.66 b8) leaves the troublesome questions unsettled.

xxvi INTRODUCTION

beowan hammes) could be explained as a shortened form (pet form) of Bēowulf.[1]

That Bēaw: Bēow was after all, originally, some kind of a divine being, has been shown to be probable by the investigations of folklorists,[2] who called attention to the corresponding figure of the Finnish Pekko, a god of grain, whom the Finns had taken over from Germanic tradition. In course of time it came to pass that the grain being Bēow (*bēow* = ' barley '), like the analogous personifications of ' sheaf ' and ' shield,'[3] was regarded as an epic personage, an early progenitor of royal races.

But outside of the introductory genealogy this shadowy divinity has no place in the Anglo-Saxon epic. Nothing but his name is recorded (ll. 18, 53). And that seems to have been introduced as a result of an accidental confusion. When detailing the ancestry of the Scyldingas (Skjǫldungar), the poet was reminded by the name Scyld (Skjǫldr) of the Anglo-Saxon Scyld(wa) and the beings associated with him,[4] and thus, mingling Danish and Anglo-Saxon tradition, he cited the series *Scyld Scēfing, Bēowulf* among the early kings of the Danes.[5] That the form *Bēowulf* of ll. 18, 53 in place of *Bēow*(*a*) or *Bēaw* is due to a mistake of the poet's or a scribe's, has been conjectured more than once.[6]

On the other hand, Bēowulf the Geat is entirely of Scandinavian origin. His name, if rightly interpreted as ' bear,'[7] agrees (though of course not etymologically) with that of *Bjarki*, which to begin with was apparently meant as a diminutive form of *bjǫrn* ' bear.'[8] His deeds are

---

[1] Thomas Miller (*Academy* xlv 396) thought that the *grendel* of *grendles mere* was meant as a common noun. (Cf. Lawrence *l.c.* 251 ff.; Panzer 395 ff.) But see Cha. Intr. 44.

[2] See Olrik ii 250 ff.; further, L 4.82 b. Cf. Cha. Intr. 84 ff., 296 ff.

[3] See note on 4-52.

[4] Cf. Heusler, *Anz.fdA*. xxx 32; *R.-L.* i 247.

[5] In the Anglo-Saxon genealogies the Danish Heremōd (Hermóðr) also appears, see note on Heremōd (901-15).

[6] Cf. Simrock L 3.21.176; Trautmann, *Bonn.B*. xvii 153; Child, *MLN*. xxi 198 f.; Lawrence 256; Binz, *Lit.bl*. xxxii 54; Heusler, *R.-L.* i 247; also Brandl 993.

[7] Cf. above, pp. xix, xxv. — A somewhat too realistic and simple explanation of his name and deeds was offered by Skeat, who conjectured (*Jour. of Philol*. xv 120 ff.) that a strong man once killed a bear or two, and was therefore given, as a mark of distinction, the name of ' bear ' himself. A similar suggestion as to the rise of the story was made by Bode (L 7.9.71 f.). Sidney Lanier asked curiously whether traditions of actual antediluvian monsters might not have been the starting point of legends of the Grendel kin (L 7.26). (Cf. Haigh's and Harrison's remarks on dragons, L 4.27.95 ff.; L 9.9.158.) Brooke (L 4.6.1.86, 4.6.2.66) reckoned with the cannibalism of primeval cave-dwellers as a possible germinal element of such folk-tales. Chadwick (H. A. 114) observed that the supernatural incidents in heroic stories " may often truly reflect the belief of an age which did not clearly distinguish between natural and supernatural." According to a novel theory of Hübener's (L 4.66 b4), the Grendel fight was fought out in the hero's soul.

[8] His first name, *Bǫðvarr*, is owing to a misunderstanding of an appellative *bǫðvar* (gen. sing. of *bǫð* ' fight '). Cp. Saxo ii 64: ' [ense,] a quo belligeri cepi cognomen.' (Sarrazin would take *Bǫðvarr* (from *Baðu-(h)arir*) as the real name, thus bringing it in line with the assumed form

THE FABULOUS ELEMENTS xxvii

plainly of the folk-tale order adjusted in the epic to the level of Germanic hero-life. The chief adversary of Bēowulf in the first part is naturally to be traced to the same source; but probably English traditions of a water-sprite have entered into the conceptions of the monster Grendel, whose very name seems to have been added on English soil. To inquire into the primitive mythological signification of those preternatural adventures is an utterly hopeless undertaking. Resting as they do on pure theory and diversified imagination, such romantic constructions merely obscure the student's vision of the real elements of the story.[1]

Are we now to believe that Bēowulf, the hero — like Grettir of the later Icelandic saga — belongs in part to history, or, in other words, that a Geat famed for strength and prowess attracted to himself wonderful tales of ultrahuman feats?[2] What the poem tells about his person, apart from his marvelous deeds, has not the appearance of history or of genuine historical legend.[3] He is out of place in the line of Geat kings, who bear names alliterating with *H*; and, still more strangely, his own *B* does not harmonize with the name of his father Ecgþēow and that of his family, the Wǣgmundingas.[4] He is a solitary figure in life, and he dies without leaving any children. Neither as Hygelāc's retainer nor as king of the Geats does he play any real part in the important events of the time.[5] He accompanies Hygelāc, indeed, on his historic continental expedition, but what is told of him in that connection is of a purely episodic nature, conventional, or fabulously exaggerated, in short, to all appearances, anything but authentic. There is hardly a trait assigned to him that is not more or less typical[6] or in some way associated with his extraordinary qualities or his definite rôle as a protecting and defending man of strength, in which the Anglo-Saxon poet rejoiced. That there is some substratum of truth in the extensive recital of his doings may well be admitted as a possibility; but that need not have been more than the merest framework of the narrative elements common to Bēowulf and Bǫðvarr Bjarki.[7] The elaboration of Bēowulf's character and actions plainly shows the hand of the author who made him the hero of a great epic poem.

Beaduwulf, see below, p. xxviii). No importance need be attached to the fact that the grandfather of Bǫðvarr Bjarki is called Bjór in the *Bjarkarímur*.

[1] Cf. Boer, *AfNF.* xix 43 f.; Lawrence 258 ff.; Panzer 252 ff. — That the ultimate relation between Bēow(a) and Bēowulf, after all, remains a problem is to be admitted.

[2] Grein (L 4.69.267, 278) ventured the guess that the deliverance of Denmark and Geatland from the attacks of pirates by a historical Bēowulf caused the Grendel and dragon combats to be attributed to him.

[3] The events of his life are briefly reviewed on p. xlv.

[4] See below, p. xxxii & n. 3.

[5] It is true, the assistance given to Ēadgils is alluded to in ll. 2392 ff., but even that did not amount to active participation.

[6] Thus the motive of the sluggish youth is, somewhat awkwardly, added to his person (2183 ff.) exactly as it was done in the case of Grettir and of Ormr (see above, p. xiv n. 3).

[7] A decidedly remote possibility of tracing a corresponding Scandinavian legendary prototype was reviewed, *A.* xlvi 193 ff. (L 4.92 b, c, d.)

INTRODUCTION

Note on the Etymology of Bēowulf, Bēow, and Grendel

The following etymologies of the names a) *Bēowulf*, b) *Bēow* have been proposed.[1]

a) 1) *Bēowulf* (= ON. *Bjólfr*), = 'bee-wolf.' So Grimm D. M. 306 (369); Simrock L 3.21.177; Müllenhoff, *ZfdA*. xii 283; Sweet, *Ags. Reader, & E St.* ii 312–4; Körner, *E St.* i 483 f.; Skeat, *Academy* xi 163 c, & *Jour. of Philol.* xv 120 ff.; Cosijn, *Aant*. 42; Sievers, *Beitr*. xviii 413; v. Grienberger 759; Panzer 392. This etymology is strongly supported by the form of the proper name *Biuulf* (i.e. *Biuuulf*) occurring in the *Liber Vitae Ecclesiae Dunelmensis* (Sweet, *Oldest English Texts*, p. 163, l. 342). Cf. Lang. § 17. Thus *Bēo-wulf*, Northumbr. *Bīu-wulf*, = ON. *Bjólfr*. Parallel OHG. form: *Biulfus*.

2) *Bēowulf* = ON. *Bjólfr* (as first seen by Grundtvig), i.e. Bœjólfr, Býjúlfr, from *bœr, býr* 'farm (yard).' So Bugge Tid. 287 ff., & *Beitr*. xii 56; Gering L 3.26.100 f.

3) *Bēowulf* a substitution for *Beadu-wulf*. So Thorpe (Gloss.); Grundtvig (Edit.), p. xxxiii; Morley L 4.2³.344; Sarrazin St. 47, *E St.* xvi 71 ff., xxiii 227 [ON. *Bǫðvarr* = **Badu-(h)arir;* cf. St. 151, *E St.* xlii 20: from **Bǫð-vargr*]; Ferguson L 4.52.4.

4) Laistner, L 4.47.264 f. connected the name with **bēawan*, Goth. (*us-)baugjan* ' sweep.' *Bēowulf* = ' sweeping wolf,' i.e. the cleansing wind that chases the mists away. Another, very far-fetched suggestion of Laistner's: L 4.50.24. And see Wadstein L 4.52.5.

b) *Bēow, Bēaw*, = ON. *Biár*,[2] belongs to OE. *bēow* ' grain,' ' barley? ' (*Epin. Gloss.* 645, *Leiden Gloss.* 184), OS. *beo(w), beuwod* ' harvest,' related to the root *bhū*. So Kemble ii, pp. xiii f.; Müllenhoff, *ZfdA*. vii 410 f., & L 4.19; Kögel, *ZfdA*. xxxvii 268 ff.; cf. Boer, *AfNF*. xix 20 ff. It corresponds to ON. *bygg* ' barley? ' (cp. *Byggvir*, note on 4–52, *fin*.). Cf. L 4.82 b.

Etymologies of Grendel[3]

1) *Grendel*, related to OE. *grindan* ' grind,' hence = ' destroyer? ' (Ettmüller, Transl., p. 20; Sweet, *Ags. Reader;* Laistner L 4.50.23; etc.; also Brandl [992], who at the same time suggests a possible allusion to the grinding of grain by slaves), and to OE. **grandor* (Sievers § 289) in *grandorlēas, Jul*. 271, ON. *grand* ' evil,' ' injury ' (Grein Spr.; Sarrazin, *Angl*. xix 374 n.; v. Grienberger 758). And see Pogatscher L 4.49.4.

2) *Grendel*, related to OE. (*Gen. B* 384) *grindel* ' bar,' ' bolt,' OHG. *grindel, krintil*.[4] Grimm D. M. 201 (243).

---

[1] Cf. Björkman L 4.66 a; Cha. Intr. 365 ff.; Schröder L 4.66 b7; Krogmann L 4.66 b8.

[2] Cf. Par. § 5, *Prologus*, also *Skáldskap*., ch. 55.

[3] Cf. Cha. Intr. 305 ff., 44; Philippson L 4.42. n. 10.84 f.; Zachrisson L 4.66 b6.

[4] Cf. *Schweizerisches Idiotikon* (ed. by Staub & Tobler) ii 757 ff., s.v. *grendel, grindel*, where reference is made to the names of numerous localities containing that stem; see also *Arch*. cxxx 154 f., cxxxi 427 n. 2; *E St.* i 485. — It has been pointed out, by the way, that a proper

3) *Grendel*, related to ON. *grindill*, one of the poetical terms for 'storm'; *grenja* 'to bellow.' See, e.g., Egilsson, *Lexicon poet. antiq. ling. septent.*; Sarrazin St. 65; Mogk, *P. Grdr.*² iii 301 f. (Cp. *Beow.* 1373 ff.?)

4) Formation by means of *-ila* (cp. *strengel*) from Lat. *grandis*. See Hagen, *MLN.* xix 70.[1]

5) *Grendel*, *grandil, from *grand, ' sand,' ' bottom (ground) of a body of water.' See Rooth L 4.49.3.

III. THE HISTORICAL ELEMENTS[2]

[*Ic wæs*] *mid Swēom ond mid Gēatum ond mid Sūþ-Denum.* (*Widsið* 58.)

How much of historical truth there is in the subjects considered under this heading cannot be made out with certainty.[3] The early Germanic poetry of heroic legend, though inspired by stirring events of the times, primarily those of the great period of tribal migrations, was anything but a record and mirror of historical happenings. What the singers and hearers delighted in was the warlike ideals of the race, the momentous situations that bring out a man's character; and the poet's imagination eagerly seized upon the facts of history to mold them in accordance with the current standards of the typical hero-life. The personality of the hero and the *comitatus* idea — mutual loyalty of chief and retainer — dominated the representation of events. The hostile encounters of Germanic tribes were depicted as feuds between families. (Cp. the Finn legend, the Heaðo-Bard story.) Moreover, all kinds of variation, shifting, and combination naturally attended the oral transmission of the ancient lays. Facts easily gave way to fiction. The figure of Eormenrīc, e.g., as known to the Anglo-Saxons (see note on 1197–1201), in all probability retained next to nothing of the actual traits, doings, and sufferings of the great king of the Goths. Yet with all due allowance for disintegrating influences, those elements of the *Beowulf* which we naturally class as 'historical,' i.e. based on history, in contradistinction to the frankly fabulous matter of a preternatural charac-

---

name *Aedric Grendel* occurs in the *Great Roll of the Pipe* for A.D. 1179–80 (Liebermann, *Arch.* cxxvi 180). — An adj. *grindel* ' angry,' ' impetuous ' is found in some ME. texts, see Stratmann-Bradley. [Cf. etymol. no. 3?]

[1] Imitation of an oriental name was vaguely suggested as a possibility by Bouterwek, *Germ.* i 401. — Also Hicketier's speculation (L 4.64) may be noted.

[2] See L 4.23 ff., L 4.67 ff. Comprehensive treatises and surveys: Müllenhoff, Grein L 4.69, Uhlenbeck L 4.72, Clarke L 4.76; cf. Heusler L 4.75, Chambers Wid.; Cha. Intr., Lawrence L 4.22 c; Schneider L 4.13 a. — It may be remarked that the map (' The Geography of Beowulf ') included in this edition is designed to show the main geographical and ethnological features as they seem to have been understood by the poet; it is not entirely consistent chronologically.

[3] On this general question, see Heusler L 4.37.1.

ter, have, in a large measure, an air of reality and historical truth about them which is quite remarkable and, in fact, out of the ordinary.

It is true, there is only one of the events mentioned in the poem, viz. the disastrous Frankish raid of Hygelāc, which we can positively claim as real history (see below, p. xxxix). But this very fact that the *Beowulf* narrative is fully confirmed by the unquestioned accounts of early chroniclers, coupled with the comparative nearness of the poem to the time of the events recounted, raises into probability the belief that we are dealing in the main with fairly authentic narrative.[1] It is certainly not too much to say that our Anglo-Saxon epos is to be considered the oldest literary source of Scandinavian history. This applies, of course, in the first place to the relation between the various tribes, and in a less degree to the record of individuals.

Much farther removed from history appear to us the Finn legend,[2] the allusion to Offa,[3] and the brief reference to Eormenrīc and Hāma.[4]

Of tribes outside of Scandinavia[5] we find mention of the Franks, Hætware, Frisians,[6] the Baltic group of the Gifðas, Wylfingas, Heaðo-Bards[7] and, perhaps, the Vandals.[8] With the possible exception of the family of Wealhþēow, England is not represented save for the ancient Angle legend of Offa.

THE DANES[9]

(Dene, Ingwine, Scyldingas, see Glossary of Proper Names.)

A genealogy of the royal line and a summary of the facts of Danish history extracted from the poem are presented below.

---

[1] That the references to Swedish kings have a definite foundation in fact is no longer open to doubt (see below, p. xlv).

[2] See Introd. to *The Fight at Finnsburg*.

[3] See note on 1931-62.

[4] See note on 1197-1201. A historical basis of the Sigemund legend cannot be reckoned with, see note on 875-900, nor could Wēland (l. 455) be considered in this class.

[5] In addition to Danes, 'Half-Danes,' Geats, and Swedes, the poem knows the Jutes (cf. Introd. to *The Fight at Finnsburg*, also below, p. xlvi), the (*Heaþo-*)*Rēamas* and the *Finna land* (see note on 499 ff.).

[6] See below, pp. xxxix f.

[7] See Gloss. of Proper Names; below, p. xxxvi.

[8] This is very doubtful. See Gloss. of Proper Names: *Wendlas*.

[9] Passages in the *Beowulf* serving as sources: 57 ff.; 467, 2158 (Heorogār), 2161 (Heoroweard); 612 ff., 1162 ff. (Wealhþēow); 1017, 1180 ff. (2166 ff.) (Hrōðulf); 1219 f., 1226 f., 1836 ff. (Hrēðrīc, Hrōðmund); 2020 ff., 81 ff. (Frēawaru, Ingeld). — Of especial value for the study of this Danish legendary history are the investigations of Grundtvig, Müllenhoff, Olrik, Heusler (L 4.35, L 4.73), Sarrazin (L 4.32.1 & 2), Malone, Herrmann L 4.35 a, (Schrøder L 4.69 a), Schneider ii 1 (L 4.13 a); for the Heaðo-Bard feud, see also L 4.83 ff. (chiefly 84: Bugge), Olrik (vol. ii), and Müllenhoff, *Deutsche Altertumskunde* v (1891), pp. 315 ff.

THE HISTORICAL ELEMENTS xxxi

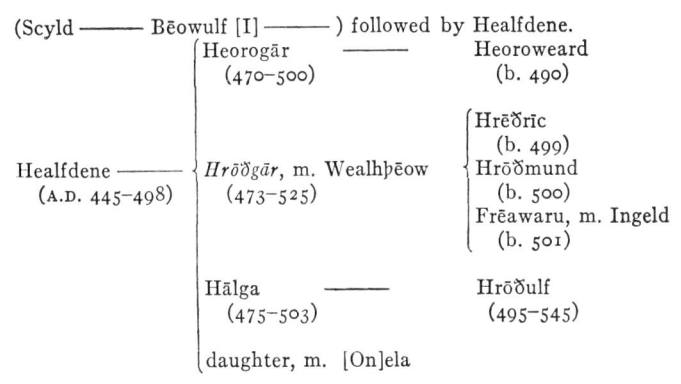

```
(Scyld ———— Bēowulf [I] ————) followed by Healfdene.
                ⎡ Heorogār              Heoroweard
                ⎢ (470–500)             (b. 490)
                ⎢
                ⎢                       ⎡ Hrēðrīc
                ⎢                       ⎢ (b. 499)
Healfdene  ———— ⎨ Hrōðgār, m. Wealhþēow ⎨ Hrōðmund
(A.D. 445–498)  ⎢ (473–525)             ⎢ (b. 500)
                ⎢                       ⎢ Frēawaru, m. Ingeld
                ⎢                       ⎣ (b. 501)
                ⎢
                ⎢ Hālga                 Hrōðulf
                ⎢ (475–503)             (495–545)
                ⎢
                ⎣ daughter, m. [On]ela
```

Note: For the sake of clearness the figures (which at best could represent approximate dates only) have been made quite definite. They are only designed to show the sequence of events in such an order as to satisfy the probabilities of the narrative.[1]

Healfdene (57 ff.), following the mythical founder Scyld and the equally fictitious Bēowulf (I), is the first one in the line of Danish kings belonging to semi-historical tradition. He was succeeded by his eldest son Heorogār, whose reign was apparently of short duration. After Heorogār's early death, the crown fell not to his son Heoroweard (who was perhaps considered too young or was held in disrespect[2]), but to his brother Hrōðgār, the central figure of Danish tradition in the *Beowulf*.

His is a reign of surpassing splendor. After gaining brilliant success in war (64 ff.),[3] he established his far-famed royal seat Heorot (68 ff.) and ruled for a long, long time (1769 ff.) in peace, honored by his people (863), a truly noble king. His queen Wealhþēow, of the race of the *Helmingas* (620), is a stately and gracious lady, remarkable for her tact and diplomacy.[4] Another person of great importance at the court is Hrōðulf. By the parallel Scandinavian versions it is definitely established that he was the son of Hālga, who in the *Beowulf* receives no further mention (i.e. after l. 61). Left fatherless at a tender age,[5] he was brought up kindly and honorably by Hrōðgār and Wealhþēow (1184 ff.), and when grown up, rose to a position of more than ordinary influence.

---

[1] They are in the main derived from Heusler (L 4.75). Somewhat different are the chronological tables of Gering (L 3.26) and Kier (L 4.78). See Par. §11, second note.

[2] In ll. 2155 ff. we hear of a valuable corslet which Heorogār did not care to bestow on his son.

[3] The definite reference to wars, 1828, possibly points to the Heaðo-Bards (see below, pp. xxxiv ff.) or to the Geats (see below, p. xliv).

[4] See 1169 ff., 1215 ff.

[5] At the age of eight according to the *Skjǫldungasaga*, ch. 12 (Par. § 8.6) and the *Ynglingasaga*, ch. 29 (33) (Par. § 6).

xxxii INTRODUCTION

Hrōðulf and Hrōðgār occupy seats of honor side by side in the hall Heorot (1163 f.), as befits near relatives of royal rank, who are called *suhtergefæderan* (1164; *suhtorfædran*, *Wids.* 46). In fact, it almost looks as if Hrōðulf were conceived of as a sort of joint-regent in Denmark.[1] With just a little imagination we may draw a fine picture of the two *Scyldingas* ruling in high state and glory over the Danes, Hrōðgār the old and wise, a peacemaker (470 ff., 1859 ff., 2026 ff.), a man of sentiment, and Hrōðulf, the young and daring, a great warrior, a man of energy and ambition. At a later time, however, as the poet intimates with admirable subtlety (1018 f., 1164 f., 1178 ff., 1228 ff.), the harmonious union was broken, and Hrōðulf, unmindful of the obligations of gratitude, behaved ill towards his cousins, Hrēðrīc and Hrōðmund (1180 ff.), that is to say — very likely — usurped the throne. One is tempted to regard Bēowulf's 'adoption' (946 ff., 1175 f.) as in some way connected with the anticipated treachery of Hrōðulf. In case of future difficulties among the *Scyldingas*, Bēowulf might come to the rescue of the Danish princes (in particular the elder one, cf. 1226 f., 1219 f.), or Hrēðrīc might find a place of refuge at the court of the Geats (*hē mæg þǣr fela / frēonda findan* 1837).

Regarding the chronology of Hrōðgār's life, the poet is clearly inconsistent in depicting him as a very old man, who looks back on a reign of sixty-two years (1769 ff., 147),[2] and, on the other hand, representing his sons as mere youngsters. Evidently neither the definite dates of the passages referred to nor the intimation of the helpless king's state of decrepitude could be taken literally.

Of these eight male names of the Danish dynasty, which are properly united by alliteration conformably to the Norse epic laws of name-giving in the period preceding the Viking age — the majority of them moreover containing one element recurring in one or more of the other names,[3] — all except Heorogār and Hrōðmund are well known in the analogous Scandinavian tradition.[4] It is true, the names do not always correspond precisely in form,[5] but this is only natural in different ver-

---

[1] In a somewhat similar manner uncle and nephew (in this case, the sister's son), namely Hygelāc and Bēowulf, are found living together in the land of the Geats: *him wæs bām samod/ on ðām lēodscipe lond gecynde,/eard ēðelriht, ōðrum swīðor/sīde rīce þām ðēr sēlra wæs* 2196 ff.

[2] And who may be expected to have to fight the Heaðo-Bards in years to come (2026 ff., cf. *Wids.* 45 ff.).

[3] See Olrik i 22 ff. The most frequent of the name elements, *hrōð* (*hrēð*), reflects the glory and splendor of the royal line. Also the genealogies of the Geats and the Swedes (likewise the Danish *Hōcingas* (1069, 1071, 1076), and the *Wǣgmundingas*) are marked by alliteration. Similarly, in the West Saxon line of kings — beginning with Ecgberht — vocalic alliteration is traceable for two centuries and a half. On (historical) exceptions to the rule of alliteration in name-giving among early Germanic tribes, see Gering (L 3.26, 2d ed.), p. vi, n. Cf. G. T. Flom, "Alliteration and Variation in Old Germanic Name-Giving," *MLN.* xxxii (1917), 7–17; also Holthausen, *Beibl.* xlii 201.

[4] See Par. §§ 4–9.

[5] Thus, *Hrōðgār* answers to an ON. *Hrōðgeirr*, whereas the names actually used, *Hróarr*,

THE HISTORICAL ELEMENTS xxxiii

sions separated by centuries and based on long continued oral transmission. We also find a good many variations in the treatment of the material due to shifting and confusion, but, thanks to the researches of farsighted scholars, the main outlines of the original tradition appear with gratifying clearness. On the whole, the *Beowulf* account is to be regarded as being not only in time but also in historical fidelity nearest to the events alluded to.

Heorogār, the eldest son of Healfdene, it is reasonable to believe, merely dropped out of the later versions of the Skjǫldung saga, whilst *Hrōðmund*, showing distinct English affiliations,[1] seems peculiar to the Anglo-Saxon account. The strange name of Hrōðgār's queen, *Wealhþēow* (i.e. ' Celtic servant ?'), indicates that she was considered of foreign descent.[2]

Heoroweard is the Norse Hjǫrvarðr (Hiarthwarus, Hyarwardus), whose fatal attack on his brother-in-law (not cousin) Hrólfr Kraki introduces the situation celebrated in the famous *Bjarkamál*.[3] The person of *Hrēðrīc* is curiously hidden in a few scanty references to Hrœrekr (hnǫggvanbaugi) and in a cursory but instructive allusion to King Rolvo's slaying of a Rǫricus (*Bjarkamál*, Saxo ii 62.4 ff.: ' [rex] qui natum Bǿki Rǿricum stravit avari, etc.').[4] That *Healfdene* (ON. Hálfdan(r), O.Dan. Haldan) figured also in Norse accounts as the father of Hrōðgār (Hróarr) and Hālga (Helgi), is abundantly proved, though his position became in time much confused. Even his designation as *hēah* and *gamol* (57 f.) is duplicated in Scandinavian sources (*Skáldskaparmál*, chap. 62: *Hálfdan gamli*; *Hyndluljóþ* 14: *Hálfdanr fyrri hæstr Skjǫldunga*).[5] An explanation of his peculiar name has been found in the fact that, according to the later *Skjǫldungasaga* (Par. § 8.6: chap. 9),

---

Roe would be *Hrōð-here in OE. Similar variations between different versions are OE. *Ēadgils*: ON. *Aðils*; OE. *Ēanmund*: ON. (Lat.) *Hömothus* (see below, p. xli); *Gārmund*: *Wērmund* (see note on 1931–62); *Ōslāf*: *Ordlāf* (see Introd. to *The Fight at Finnsburg*); and within the *Beowulf* itself, *Heorogār*: *Heregār* (61, 2158; 467); *Hrēðel*: *Hrǣdla*. Cf. Heusler, " Heldennamen in mehrfacher Lautgestalt," *ZfdA*. lii 97–107.

[1] Sarrazin, *E St.* xxiii 229.

[2] The non-Danish, i.e. English lineage of Hróar's wife in the *Hrólfssaga* (ch. 5, Par. § 9) and in Arngrím Jónsson's *Skjǫldungasaga* (ch. 11, Par. § 8.6) may or may not be connected with that fact; cf. Olson L 4.65.80, 97. — The name of Wealhþēow's family, *Helmingas*, possibly points to East Anglia (Binz 177 f.; Sarrazin, *l.c.*). The name Wealhþēow (whose second element need not be interpreted literally) may have been constructed as a characterizing one like Angelþēow in the Mercian genealogy (Par. § 2). Cp. also *Ecg-*, *Ongen-þēow*. A note by Deutschbein: *Anz.fdA*. xxxvi 225. See Malone, *Kl. Misc.* 156 f.

[3] Par. § 7 (ii 59 ff.), § 9 (chs. 32 ff.); § 8.2, 5, 6 (ch. 12). Edition of the ' Bjarkamál en fornu,' see L 10.1.4.

[4] As first seen by Grundtvig (Edition, p. 204). Cf. also Bugge, *Studien über die Entstehung der nordischen Götter- und Heldensagen* (1889), pp. 171 f.; Malone L 4.87 a. See Par. § 8.1.

[5] See Par. §§ 4, 7 (ii 51), 8, 9. Cf. *Angl.* xxix 378. — Kier (L 4.78.104 ff.) would identify Healfdene with Alewīh of *Wids.* 35 (see note on 1931–62).

his mother was the daughter of the Swedish king Jorundus.[1] Icelandic sources have it that he lost his life through his brother (Fróði).[2]

Two sons of Hálfdan(r), *Hróarr* (Roe) and *Helgi* (Helgo), are regularly known in the North, besides in a few versions a daughter Signý who married a jarl named Sævil,[3] — probably a mistake for Onela, the Swedish king. That her real name was Yrsa, was first argued by (Chadwick and) Clarke (L 4.76).[4] In contrast with the *Beowulf*, Helgi left a much stronger impression in Scandinavian legend than the quiet, inactive Hróarr; he even appears, under the guise of Helgi Hundingsbani, as the sole representative of the Skjǫldungar in the Eddic poems bearing his name.[5]

Still greater is the shifting in the relative importance of *Hrōðgār* (Hróarr) and his nephew *Hrōðulf* (Hrólfr [Kraki], Rolvo). All the glory of Hrōðgār seems to be transferred to Hrólfr, who became the most renowned and popular of the ancient Danish legendary kings, the most perfect of rulers, the center of a splendid court rivaling that of the Gothic Theodoric and the Celtic Arthur.[6] This development was perhaps first suggested by the significant contrast between the old, peace-loving Hrōðgār and his young, forceful, promising nephew; it was further aided by a change in the story of Helgi, who was made to survive his brother, whereby Hrólfr was dissociated from the traditions concerning his uncle.[7]

Another phase of Danish history is opened up in the allusions to the relation between the *Scyldingas* and the chiefs of the *Heaðo-Bards* (2024–2069), which are all the more welcome as they present one of the most truly typical motives of the old Germanic heroic life, viz. the sacred duty of revenge. To settle an old bloody feud Hrōðgār gave his daughter Frēawaru in marriage to Ingeld, the son of the Heaðo-Bard king Frōda, who in years gone by had been slain by the victorious Danes. But an old, grim warrior (*eald æscwiga*, 2042), chafing under the trying situation, which to his sense of honor is utterly humiliating, spurs a young comrade on to a realization of his duty, until hostility actually breaks out again. The outcome of the new war between the two tribes is related in *Widsið*, 45-49:

[1] On the name, see Schröder, L 4.78 g.
[2] According to Danish accounts Haldanus killed his brother (cf. Par. § 8.3).
[3] *Skjǫldungasaga*, ch. 10 (Par. § 8.6), *Hrólfssaga*, ch. 1 (Par. § 9).
[4] On Yrsa's relations with Helgi, (Áli, and) Aðils, see Clarke, pp. 64 ff., 82 ff. Chadwick and Clarke suggest that an (unknowingly) incestuous marriage between father and daughter (see *Grottasǫngr* 22, Par. § 5: ch. 40, *Hrólfssaga*, chs. 7, 9) may have been substituted in Norse tradition for that between brother and sister. See note on l. 62. — In the *Hrólfssaga* and (probably) the late *Skjǫldungasaga* Signý is the oldest of Halfdan's children, whereas in the *Beowulf* Healfdene's daughter is apparently younger than her brothers.
[5] Cf. Bugge L 4.84.
[6] See Par. § 5: ch. 41, § 7: ii 53, § 8.6: ch. 12, § 9: ch. 16.
[7] Heusler, *ZfdA*. xlviii 73 f. — That Hrōðulf was remembered in England at a comparatively late date, we see from the reference in a late *Brut* version to the ' gesta rodulphi et hunlapi, Unwini et Widie, horsi et hengisti, Waltef et hame ' (Imelmann, *D.Lit.z.* xxx 999).

THE HISTORICAL ELEMENTS

> Hrōþwulf ond Hrōðgār   hēoldon lengest[1]
> sibbe ætsomne   suhtorfædran,
> siþþan hȳ forwrǣcon   Wīcinga cynn
> ond Ingeldes   ord forbīgdan,
> forhēowan æt Heorote   Heaðo-Beardna þrym.

In other words, the Heaðo-Bards invade the land of the Danes and attack the royal stronghold, but are utterly defeated. On this occasion, as is to be inferred from ll. 82 ff., the famous hall Heorot was destroyed by fire.[2]

Curiously but not unnaturally (the memory of an independent Bard tribe having been lost in later times), Scandinavian sources regard the feud as arising from the enmity between two brothers of the Scylding family or — as in the case of Saxo — represent the former Bards as Danes, whilst their enemies, the Swerting family, are made over into Saxons.[3] Otherwise, Saxo's account is substantially a faithful counterpart of the *Beowulf* episode; in particular the fine, taunting speech of the old warrior, which sums up the ethical significance of the tragic conflict, is plainly echoed in the Latin verses — immoderately lengthened, diluted and in part vulgarized as they are — which are put in the mouth of the famous hero Starkaðr (' the Old '), the representative of the old, simple, honorable warlike life and of stern, unbending Viking[4] virtue.

A faint recollection of the Heaðo-Bard feud lingers in the tradition of Hothbrodus, king of Sweden (in Saxo and other Danish sources, Par. § 7: ii 52 f., § 8.4 & 5) and of Hǫðbroddr, the enemy of Helgi in the Eddic lays mentioned above. The very name Hǫðbroddr, as first pointed out by Sarrazin,[5] is the individualized form of the tribal name Heaðo-Beardan, though the phonetic agreement is not complete.[6]

In accordance with the spirit of the Germanic heroic legend, the personal element is strongly emphasized in viewing the events in the light

---

[1] According to Deutschbein's — rather doubtful — interpretation (L 4.97.296): ' had kept peace for the longest time . . . '; i.e., soon after the defeat of the Vikings they became estranged. Cp. *Wids.* 28: *lengest* ' for a very long time.'

[2] That the memory of this Ingeld (whom Müllenhoff [p. 22] thought identical with Ingjaldr illráði, *Ynglingasaga*, chs. 34 (38) ff.) was kept alive in songs, appears from a passage in Alcuin's letter (A.D. 797) to bishop Speratus of Lindisfarne: ' Verba Dei legantur in sacerdotali convivio. Ibi decet lectorem audiri, non citharistam; sermones patrum, non carmina gentilium. Quid enim Hinieldus cum Christo? Angusta est domus; utrosque tenere non poterit.' (O. Jänicke, *ZfdA*. xv 314; Haack L 4.30.49 f.)

[3] See note on 2024–69. In the later *Skjǫldungasaga*, chs. 9, 10, this Swerting figures as a Swedish ' baron ' (Par. § 8.6).

[4] Cf. *Wids.* 47: *Wīcinga cynn.*

[5] Sarr. St. 42. See also Bugge L 4.84.160; Sarrazin, *E St.* xxiii 233 ff.; Boer, *Beitr.* xxii 377 f. In like manner, the name of Starkaðr has been explained (Bugge, *l.c.* 166 f.) from *Stark-hǫðr, i.e., ' the strong Heaðo-Bard.' In the second *Helgi* lay he is called Hǫðbrodd's brother, and a king.

[6] Detter, who (like Müllenhoff) connected Ingeld (Ingellus) with Ingjaldr illráði, attempted to establish a mythological basis (a Freyr myth) for this episode (*Beitr.* xviii 90 ff.).

of a family feud of chiefs or petty kings; yet we have reason to believe that there existed a true historical background of considerable political significance.

But who are the Heaðo-Bards? Evidently, a seafaring people (*Wids.* 47: *wīcinga cynn*), who seem to have lived for some time on the southern coast of the Baltic (the home of the Hǫðbroddr of the Eddic *Helgi* lays). They have been identified with (1) the Langobards (Lombards), whose name is reasonably to be equated with that of the Heaðo-Bards, and some divisions of whom may have been left behind on the Baltic shore when the main body of the tribe migrated south,[1] and with (2) the Erulians (Heruli), who, according to Jordanes,[2] were driven from their dwellings (on the Danish islands, perhaps) by the powerful Danes and whose defeat has been supposed (by Müllenhoff) to have ushered in the consolidation of the Danish state. Besides, compromise theories have been proposed. Also the problematical *Myrgingas*[3] of *Widsið* have been connected with the Bards.[4] An authoritative decision is hardly possible.

Summing up, we may give the following brief, connected account of the outstanding events of Danish history as underlying the allusions of the poem.[5] Frōda, king of the Bards, slays Healfdene[6] (about A.D. 498); (Heorogār,) Hrōðgār, and Hālga make a war of revenge,[6] Frōda falls in battle (A.D. 499). After an interval of nearly twenty years, when Frōda's son, Ingeld (born A.D. 498) has grown up, Hrōðgār, the renowned and venerable king, desirous of forestalling a fresh outbreak of the feud, marries his daughter Frēawaru to the young Heaðo-Bard king (A.D. 518). Yet before long, the flame of revenge is kindled again, the Bards invade the Danish dominions and burn Heorot, but are completely routed, A.D. 520. The foreign enemy having been overcome, new trouble awaits the Danes at home. Upon Hrōðgār's death (A.D. 525), his nephew Hrōðulf forcibly seizes the kingship, pushing aside and slaying his cousin Hrēðrīc, the heir presumptive. [Of the subsequent attack of Heoroweard, who had a still older claim to the throne, and the fall of Hrōðulf (A.D. 545) no mention is made in the *Beowulf*.]

Thus the two tragic motives of this epic tradition are the implacable enmity between two tribes, dominated by the idea of revenge which no human bonds of affection can restrain, and the struggle for the crown among members of a royal family [which is to lead to the extinction of the dynasty].

---

[1] Attention has been called to the 'Bardengau,' the district of the modern Lüneburg (where the place-name Bardowieck persists).

[2] *De Origine Actibusque Getarum*, cap. iii. Cf. note on 82–85.

[3] Cf. Chambers Wid. 159 ff.; Much, *ZfdA*. lxii 122 ff.

[4] Möller 26 ff.; Sarrazin, *E St.* xxiii 234 ff., *Angl.* xix 388. [In a note, "Halfdan = Frode = Hadbardernes Konge, hvis Rige forenes med det danske," *Nordisk Tidsskrift for Filologi*, 4. Series, vi (1917), 78–80, J. Neuhaus assigns the Heaðo-Bards to North Schleswig. Cf. Cha. Intr.[2] 533.]

[5] Cf. Heusler, *ZfdA*. xlviii 72. On the meaning of the dates given, see above, p. xxxi.

[6] There is no mention of this in *Beowulf*. See Malone. *Kl. Misc.* 140 ff.

THE HISTORICAL ELEMENTS

The existence of a royal line preceding the *Scyldingas* is to be inferred from the allusions to Heremōd, see note on 901–15.[1]

The seat of the Danish power, the fair hall Heorot, corresponds to the ON. Hleiðr[2] (Hleiðargarðr, Lat. Lethra) of Scandinavian fame, which, although reduced to insignificance at an early date, and now a tiny, wretched village, Lejre (southwest of Roskilde on the island of Zealand), is habitually associated with the renown of the Skjǫldung kings.[3] It has been (doubtfully) regarded as the site of an ancient sanctuary devoted, perhaps, to the cult of Nerthus (Tacitus, *Germ.*, ch. 40, Par. § 10) and Ing (ON. Freyr, Yngvifreyr, Ingunafreyr).[4] Hleiðr was destroyed, we may imagine, on the occasion of Hrólf's fall, but in the memory of the people it lived on as the ideal center of the greatness of Denmark in the olden times.

Sarrazin claimed that the scenery of the first part of the *Beowulf* could be clearly recognized even in the present Lejre and its surroundings,[5] while others (including the present editor) have failed to see more than a very general topographical resemblance.

It should be noted that the name *Ingwine* twice applied to the Danes (1044, 1319) bears weighty testimony to the ancient worship of Ing.[6]

The designations *Scede-land* 19, *Sceden-īg* 1686 (used of the Danish dominion in general) point to the fact that the original home of the Danes was in *Skåne* (*Scania*, the southernmost district of the present kingdom of Sweden),[7] whence they migrated to the islands and later to Jutland.[8]

---

[1] On the name 'Half-Danes,' see note on 82–85.

[2] Note the regular alliteration in the names of the place and of the royal family (*Hrōðgār*, etc.); also *Hrēðel*, etc.: *Hrēosnabeorh* 2477; *Ongenþēow* etc.: *Uppsalir*; perhaps *Wīglāf: Wendel*.

[3] See Par. § 6: chs. 5, 29 (33); § 7: ii 52, § 8.2, § 8.3, § 8.6: ch. 1, § 9: chs. 16 ff. Only in late sources is Hrōðgār (Roe), the builder of Heorot (Hleiðr) in the *Beowulf*, credited with the founding of Roskilde; see Par. § 8.4. The identification of Heorot with present-day Lejre was called in question by S. J. Herben, see Lawrence L 4.22 c. 306.

[4] Cf. Sarrazin St. 5 f., *Angl.* xix 368 ff., *E St.* xlii 1 ff.; Much, *Beitr.* xvii 196 ff.; Mogk, P Grdr.³ iii 367. According to Sarrazin, the original meaning of *Hleiðr* is 'tent-like building,' 'temple' (cp. Go. *hleiþra*), and appears even in the OE. *æt hærgtrafum, Beow.* 175. That human and animal sacrifices were offered to the gods at the capital, 'Lederun,' is related by Thietmar of Merseburg (early in the 11th century); cf. Grimm D. M. 39 (48). But see Olrik i 192 ff., Olrik-Hollander 330 ff.

[5] See the detailed topographical descriptions, Sarr. St. 4 ff., *Beitr.* xi 167 ff.

[6] Cp. *Runic Poem* 67 ff. (See *Arch.* cxlii 250–53; Krappe, *Revue germanique* xxiv 23–25.) *Ingwine* has the appearance of being changed, by folk etymology, from (the equivalent of) **Ingvaeones* (the worshipers of Ing), the name by which Tacitus designates the Germanic North Sea tribes (Par. § 10: ch. 2). From Jutland and Zealand the cult of Ing spread to the other Danish islands, to Skåne, and thence to Sweden. (Cf. the name *Ynglingar*, below, p. xlii n. 1, etc.)

[7] It was not united politically with Sweden until 1658.

[8] In Wulfstān's account of his voyage (Ælfred's *Oros.* 19.35 f.) the form *Scōn-ēg* is used: *and on bæcbord him wæs Langaland, and Lǣland, and Falster, and Scōnēg; and þās land eall hȳrað*

xxxviii   INTRODUCTION

The Geats and Swedes[1]

(See Glossary of Proper Names: *Gēatas, Wederas, Hrēðlingas; Swēon, Scylfingas*.)

The Geatish *Royal Line*[2]

Hrēðel ──── { Herebeald (470–502)

Hæðcyn (472–510)

Hygelāc, m. Hygd (second wife)[3] (475–521) { daughter (from 1st marriage),[3] m. Eofor
Heardrēd (from 2d marriage) (511–533)

daughter, m. Ecgþēow }

(A.D. 445–503)

The Swedish *Royal Line*

Ongenþēow (450–510) { Ōhthere[4] (478–532) { Ēanmund[4] (505–533)

Ēadgils (b. 510, becomes king 535)

Onela [m. Healfdene's daughter] (480–535) }

Hrēðel, like his contemporary Healfdene the Dane, had three sons and one daughter. The eldest son Herebeald was accidentally killed by Hæðcyn, who, when shooting an arrow, missed his aim and struck his brother instead (2435 ff.).[5] The grief caused by this tragic fate ate away the king's life. Upon his death and the succession of Hæðcyn, war broke out between the Geats and Swedes (2472 ff., 2922 ff.). It is started by the Swedes, who attack their southern neighbors and after

tō Denemearcan. Cf. *Scani,* Par. § 1.3. See also Glossary: *Scedenīg;* Malone, *Studies in Philology* xxviii 574 ff.

[1] Ll. 1202–14, 2201–9, 2354–96, (2425–89:) 2425–43, 2462–89, 2501–8, 2611–19, 2910–98; also 1830 ff., 1923 ff., 2169 ff., 2190 ff. — For discussions, see especially L 4.28 (Bugge) and L 4.88–97 e, also references below, p. xlvi.

[2] As to the definite chronological figures used, see above, p. xxxi.

[3] So we may assume in the interest of chronological harmony.

[4] There is no direct proof that either Ōhthere or Ēanmund was the elder brother.

[5] At this point, chronology must not be insisted upon too rigidly. See note on 2432 ff.

THE HISTORICAL ELEMENTS xxxix

inflicting severe damage return home. An expedition of revenge into the land of the Swedes undertaken by Hæðcyn and Hygelāc, though at first successful (even Ongenþēow's queen is taken prisoner), seems destined to utter failure; the ' old, terrible ' king of the Swedes falls upon Hæðcyn's army, rescues the queen, kills the Geat king and forces his troops to seek refuge in the woods (*Hrefnesholt* 2935), threatening them all night long with death in the morning by the sword and the gallows. But at dawn the valorous Hygelāc appears with his division and inspires such a terror that the Swedes flee to their fastness, pursued by the Geats. Ongenþēow in a brave fight against two brothers, Eofor and Wulf, loses his life. Hygelāc, now king of the Geats, after his homecoming richly repaid the brothers and gave his only daughter as wife to Eofor.

This victory at the Ravenswood (A.D. 510) insured the Geats peace with the Swedes, who seem to have dreaded the power of the warlike Hygelāc. [The Geat king's arm was strengthened by his loyal nephew, the mighty Bēowulf, who, after his triumphant return from Denmark, where he had overcome the Grendel race (about A.D. 515), was the associate of Hygelāc.]

Not content with his success in the North, Hygelāc even undertook a ravaging expedition into the Frankish lands (' Gallias,' Par. § 11) about A.D. 521.[1] He arrived with a fleet in the land of the (West) Frisians (west of the Zuider Zee) (*syððan Higelāc cwōm / faran flotherge on Frēsna land* 2914 f., cp. 1206 f.), and sailed up the river Rhine as far as the district of the Frankish tribe Hætware (*Attoarii*, better known as *Chattuarii*).[2] [Supplementing the narrative by means of Gregory's version and the *Historia Francorum* (Par. § 11):] Having loaded their ships with prisoners and rich booty (*wælrēaf* 1205), the Geats return. The main force is sent out in advance, but the king with a smaller band remains on the shore (of either the Rhine or the North Sea). There (*Frēslondum on* 2357) he is overtaken by a strong army under the command of Theodebert, the son of the Frankish king Theoderic (the Merovingian 2921). King Hygelāc and his followers are slain, his fleet is pursued and utterly routed. The poem repeatedly dwells on the heroic deeds of prowess done by Bēowulf in the unequal encounter between the allied forces (*ofermægen* 2917) of the continental tribes and Hygelāc's guard: 2363 ff., 2501 ff.

The final battle is waged against the Franks (1210) or Hūgas (2914, 2502), Hetware (2363, 2916), and (no doubt) Frisians (2357, 2503). Of the four names mentioned, *Hūgas* is only an epic appellation of the

---

[1] See Par. § 11, second note. — The references in the poem occur in ll. 1202 ff., 2354 ff., 2501 ff., 2913 ff. (2201). The identity of the *Beowulf* allusions and the accounts of the Frankish histories was first recognized by Grundtvig (see his Transl., p. lxi).

[2] Between the rivers Rhine and Meuse (Maas), on the border of the present Rhenish Prussia and the Netherlands, in the neighborhood of the cities of Kleve (Cleves) and Geldern. Cf. Chambers Wid. 201 f.; Much, *R.-L.* i 371 f. The tribe is mentioned in *Wids.* 33: *Hūn [wēold] Hætwerum*.

Franks;[1] the *Hetware* seem to have belonged to the Frankish ' sphere of influence.' The two main tribes involved are thus the *Franks* and the *Frisians* (see 2912).[2] At the same time the rising power of the Franks is reflected in the allusion to the threatening unfriendliness of the Merovingian dynasty (2921). It is possible, however, that the poet did not consistently differentiate between the three or four terms (see especially 2502 f.). His use of the name *Dæghrefn*, by the way, shows that he followed a genuine tradition (see note on 2501).

The young Heardrēd now succeeded his father Hygelāc. Bēowulf [who by a marvelous swimming feat had escaped from the enemies] generously declined Hygd's offer of the throne, but acted as Heardrēd's guardian during the prince's minority (2367 ff.). When the latter had come into his rights, another series of warlike disputes with the Swedes arose (A.D. 532–535). After the fall of Ongenþēow in the battle of Ravenswood his son Ōhthere had become king,[3] but upon Ōhthere's death, Onela seized the throne, compelling his nephews Ēanmund and Ēadgils to flee the country. They find refuge at the court of Heardrēd. Soon after Onela enters Geatland with an army (A.D. 533), Heardrēd as well as Ēanmund is slain, whereupon the Swedish king returns, allowing Bēowulf to take over the government unmolested (2379 ff., 2611 ff., 2202 ff.). A few years later Ēadgils,[4] aided by a Geatish force,[5] reopens the war (2391 ff.), which results in his uncle Onela's death and Ēadgils's accession to the throne (A.D. 535).

However, trouble from their northern foes is likely to come upon the Geats again, in spite of their temporary alliance with a branch of the Scylfing dynasty; indeed it seems as if the downfall of their kingdom is virtually foreshadowed in the messenger's speech announcing the death of Bēowulf (2999 ff., 3018 ff.).

On the life of Bēowulf the Geat, see below, p. xlv.

Of the Geatish royal line, with the probable exception of Hygelāc,[6]

---

[1] Cf. Müllenhoff, *ZfdA.* vi 438; W. Grimm, L 4.67³.37. — *Annales Quedlinburgenses* (cir. A.D. 1000): ' Hugo Theodoricus ' (*Wids.* 24: *þēodrīc wēold Froncum*, =the Hug-Dietrich of the MHG. epic *Wolfdietrich* [13th century]) 'iste dicitur,id est Francus,quia olim omnes Franci Hugones vocabantur ' [with a spurious explanation added:] ' a suo quodam duce Hugone.' (According to E. Schröder (*ZfdA.* xli 26), that notice is derived from an OE. source, and the use of *Hūgas*=Franks really confined to the OE. [*Beowulf*].) — Regarding the question of the possible relation between the names *Hūgas* and *Chauci*, see the convenient references in Chambers Wid. 68 n. 2; Much, *R.-L.* ii 82.

[2] The prominence given to the Frisians and their seemingly unhistorical alliance with the Franks is attributed by Sarrazin (Käd. 90 f.) to the Frisian source of this story.

[3] This is nowhere stated, but the interpretation given above seems not unnatural.

[4] Had Ēadgils made his escape (when Onela attacked the Geats) and afterwards returned to Geatland, planning revenge and rehabilitation?

[5] Probably Bēowulf did not take part personally in this war; cf. note on 2395.

[6] Some of the other *names* also are found in Scandinavian sources, but in entirely different surroundings. Thus *Hrēðel* (*Hrōðil) is =ON. *Hrollr, Lat. *Rollerus* (' Regneri pugilis filius '), Saxo, Book v; *Heardrēd* =O. West Norse *Harðrāðr; Swerting* is mentioned as a Saxon and as a

THE HISTORICAL ELEMENTS xli

the Northern tradition is silent. But early Frankish chronicles, as noted above, have preserved a most valuable record of Hygelāc's daring expedition against the Franks, thereby confirming completely the account of the *Beowulf*.[1] The only discrepancy discoverable, viz. the designation of *Chogilaicus as ' Danorum rex ' is naturally accounted for by the assumption that the powerful Danes were taken as the representatives of the Scandinavian tribes, just as the later Anglo-Saxon annalists included under the name of ' Danes ' the Vikings of Norway. Moreover the *Liber Monstrorum* (Par. § 11.1) remembers the mighty warrior[2] as ' rex Getarum ' (suggesting an actual ' Gautarum ' or ' Got(h)orum ').

A faint reminiscence of *Hygelāc* seems to crop out in Saxo's brief notice (iv 117) of the Danish king Hugletus, ' who is said to have defeated in a naval battle the Swedish chiefs Hømothus and Høgrimus,' the former one (ON. *Eymóðr*) answering[3] to the Swedish prince *Ēanmund*, who falls in the land of the Geats (2612 ff.).[4] Some connection has also been traced between Bēowulf's uncle and the light-minded Hugleikr, king of Sweden (Saxo: Hugletus, king of Ireland), who is slain in an attack by the Danish king Haki (*Ynglingasaga*, chap. 22 (25); Saxo vi 185 f.).[4a]

The accidental killing of *Herebeald* by *Hæðcyn* has been repeatedly[5] compared with the unintentional slaying of Baldr by the blind Hǫðr, who is directed by Loki in shooting the mistletoe (Prose Edda, *Gylfaginning*, chap. 48). But it is difficult to believe that the story told in *Beowulf* has any mythological basis. It rather impresses us as a report of an ordinary incident that could easily happen in those Scandinavian communities and probably happened more than once. Maybe the motive was associated at an early date with names suggesting a warlike occupation, like Here-*beald*, *Hæð*-cyn (*Baldr*, *Hǫðr*).[6]

Swede (see above, p. xxxv). *Herebeald* is traceable only as a common noun *herbaldr*, ' warrior. The peculiar, abstract name of *Hygd* is entirely unknown outside of *Beowulf*.

[1] The names given in the MSS. (*Chlochilaichus*, etc., see Par. § 11) do not differ greatly from the true form which we should expect, viz. *Chogilaicus.

[2] That the giant Hugebold in the MHG. *Ecken Liet* (83) is to be ultimately identified with him (see Much, *Arch*. cviii 403), is a pure guess.

[3] Though we should expect *Eymundr*.

[4] A. Olrik, *Kilderne etc.*, L 4.100.2.190 f.

[4a] Cf. Herrmann L 4.35 a. ii 310 f., 433 ff.; also Malone, *Acta Philol. Scand.* ix 76 ff.

[5] Thus by Gísli Brynjúlfsson, *Antikv. Tidskrift* (1852/54), p. 132; Grundtvig (Ed.), pp. xliii, 175; Rydberg, *Undersökningar i germanisk mythologi* (1886), i 665 (who moreover called attention to Saxo's account (iii 69 ff.) of Hotherus' skill in archery [which was, however, only one of his numerous accomplishments]); Sarrazin St. 44; Bugge, *Studien über die Entstehung der nordischen Götter-und Heldensagen*, p. 262; Detter, *Beitr*. xviii 82 ff., xix 495 ff.; Much, *Arch*. cviii 413 f. See also Gering's note, L 3.26².104. Detter finds a direct parallel to the Herebeald-Hæðcyn version in the story of Alrekr and Eiríkr (*Ynglingasaga*, chap. 20 (23)), who are succeeded on the Swedish throne — though not immediately — by Hugleikr. — See further, note on 2435 ff.

[6] A slight similarity in the situation may be found in the story of Herthegn and his three sons, Herburt, Herthegn, and Tristram (Sintram), *Þiðrekssaga*, chs. 231 f. (Simrock L 3.21.191; Müllenhoff 17).

Turning to the Swedish affairs, we find the royal *Scylfingas*[1] well remembered in the North — *Óttarr* (Ōhthere) and his son *Aðils* (Ēadgils)[2] standing out prominently — but their true family relationships are somewhat obscured. Neither is Eymundr (Ēanmund) ever mentioned in conjunction with Aðils nor is Óttarr considered the brother of *Áli* (Onela), who in fact has been transformed into a Norwegian king. Besides, Ongenþēow's name has practically disappeared from the drama of exciting events in which he had taken a leading part.[3]

Also the two series of hostile complications between the Swedes and Geats reappear in Scandinavian allusions, though with considerable variations, since the Geats have been forgotten and replaced by the Jutes and Danes.

The conflict between *Ongenþēow* and the Geats recounted in *Beowulf* has undergone a change in the scene and the names of the actors, but the substance of the narrative and certain details of the great central scene can be readily identified in the story of the fall of King Óttarr Vendilkráka in the *Ynglingatal* and the *Ynglingasaga*, chap. 27 (31), see Par. § 6. The cruel nickname 'Vendel Crow' given the dead king, who was likened to a dead crow torn by eagles, recalls Ongenþēow's fierce threats of execution (2939 ff.), which by the irony of fate was visited upon his own person. Also the remarkable fact of the slaying of the Swedish king by two men is preserved; indeed, the names Vǫttr and Fasti[4] are evidently more authentic than the rather typical appellations Wulf and Eofor of the Anglo-Saxon epic. That the Old Norse account is at fault in associating the incident with Ōhthere (Óttarr) rather than with Ongenþēow is to be inferred from the testimony of Ari,[5] who in *Íslendingabók* (cir. A.D. 1135), chap. 12 calls Óttarr's father by the name of Egill Vendilkráka. The name Egill (in place of Angantýr = Ongenþēow)[6] is possibly, Bugge suggested, due to corruption, a pet form *Angila being changed to *AgilaR and Egill.[7] The scene

---

[1] In Old (West) Norse sources called *Ynglingar*.

[2] The phonetic correspondence is not complete, see above, pp. xxxii f.

[3] Kier (L 4.78.130 ff.) identifies *Ongenþēow* with *Angelþēow* of the Mercian genealogy (Par. § 2) and *Ongen* (Nennius § 60). The great fight at the Ravenswood he locates at Hedeby (at or near the present site of Schleswig). He further points out that *Ravnholt* is a very common place-name in Denmark.

[4] They are brothers in the *Historia Norvegiae* (cf. the following note) as in the *Beowulf*, whereas the *Ynglingatal* and the *Ynglingasaga* are silent on this point. — It may be noted that among the twelve champions of Hrólfr Kraki we find Vǫttr mentioned, *Skáldskaparmál*, ch. 41 (Par. § 5), and *Hrólfssaga*, ch. 32 (98.14, Par. § 9).

[5] Followed by the *Historia Norvegiae* (Bugge 15 n.).

[6] The names Angantýr and Óttarr are coupled in *Hyndl.* 9 (Par. § 4). Ongenþēow is remembered in *Wids.* 31: *Swēom [wēold] Ongendþēow*, see Chambers's note.

[7] Belden, L 4.96 (like Grundtvig, see Bugge 15) would equate Ongenþēow with Aun (or Áni), son of Jǫrundr and father of Egill (*Ynglingasaga*, ch. 25 [29]). On the relation between Egill and Ongenþēow, see Schück, *Studier i Ynglingatal* (*Uppsala Universitets Årsskrift*, 1907), 119 ff.; Björk. Eig. 91 ff.; Malone Haml. 117 ff.; Nerman L 4.97 c 4.100 f.; Cha. Intr.² 411 n. 2.

THE HISTORICAL ELEMENTS xliii

of the battle is according to the *Beowulf* in Ongenþēow's own land, i.e. Sweden, but in the *Ynglingatal* (*Ynglingasaga*) is shifted to Vendel in Jutland. Now it has been pointed out (by Stjerna, 52 f.) that the striking surname 'Vendel Crow'[1] cannot be a late literary invention, but must have originated immediately after the battle. As the king fell in his own land, the Vendel in question cannot be the large Jutish district of that name, but must be the place called Vendel in Swedish Uppland. Vendel is at present an insignificant church-village, some twenty English miles north of Upsala, but being favorably located for commercial traffic, it enjoyed a considerable importance in the Middle Ages. There are exceptionally numerous ancient cemeteries near Vendel, the principal one of which was evidently the burial place of a great chieftain's family. It may safely be concluded (with Stjerna) that about the year 500 there existed a royal fortress at Vendel, and that a noble family resided there.

On other possible recollections of this part of the Swedish-Geatish tradition, see note on 2922 ff.

The second series of encounters between the Geats and Swedes resolves itself in Scandinavian tradition into a contest between *Aðils* — a great saga hero — and *Áli*, who, through confusion of the Swedish Uppland with 'uplands' in Norway, was made into a Norwegian king. The battle in which Áli fell took place on the ice of Lake Väner. See *Skáldskaparmál*, chaps. 41, 55, *Ynglingasaga*, chap. 29 (33), *Ynglingatal*, Arngrím Jónsson's *Skjǫldungasaga*, chap. 12 (Par. §§ 5, 6, 8.6). A hint of Aðils's foreign (Geatish) support (2391 ff.) is found in the statement that Hrólfr Kraki sent his twelve champions (Bǫðvarr Bjarki among them) to assist him. Thus the Danes have stepped into the place originally occupied by the Geats. The memory of Ēadgils's brother, Ēanmund, is all but lost. He may be recognized, however, in the Eymundr of *Hyndluljóþ* 15 (Par. § 4) with whom Hálfdanr (the representative of the Danes) allies himself,[2] and in the above (p. xli) mentioned Hǿmothus of Saxo.

The dominating element in this second phase of the intertribal war, the dynastic struggle within the royal Swedish line, is perhaps to be explained (with Belden) by the existence of a foreign or pro-Danish party led by Onela (the son-in-law of Healfdene (l. 62), who was of Dano-Swedish extraction), and a native party led by Ēadgils and Ēanmund (who presumably followed their father's policy).[3] In this connection

---

[1] As to the name 'Vendel Crow,' cf. E. Linderholm, *Namn och Bygd* vii (1919), 37 f. (and references given there); Cha. Intr. 344, ²417 f.

[2] Áli, mentioned by the side of Hálfdanr (*Hyndl.* 14), was considered *Áli inn frǿkni* (i.e. the Bold), the Dane, but probably was at the outset no one but the Swedish Onela. See also Belden, L 4.96.152. — Ēanmund has also been equated with Aun of the *Ynglingasaga* (see Malone Haml. 67 ff.). A further allusion has been traced by Malone in an obscure passage of the (9th cent.) Swedish Rök inscription (L 4.97 b).

[3] No explanation is found (in the available sources) of the surprising fact that Heardrēd and Bēowulf side with the native and against the Danish faction.

it has been suggested by Belden that the ' Wendlas ' mentioned in l. 348 (Wulfgār, *Wendla lēod*) sided with the Danish faction. Accepting this view and assuming further (as was first conjectured by Stjerna[1]) that, like Wulfgār, the *Wǣgmundingas*, i.e. Wēohstān and his son Wīglāf,[2] belong to the Wendel family, i.e. a noble family of Vendel in Uppland, Sweden, we are able to understand not only that Wulfgār held an honored position at the Danish court, but also (what seems singular indeed) that Wēohstān,[3] the father of Bēowulf's most loyal kinsman Wīglāf, fought in the service of Onela, against the latter's nephews and the Geats who sheltered them.[4] After Ēadgils had been established on the throne, Wēohstān, who had slain Ēanmund (2612 ff.), was compelled to leave the country and settled in the land of the Geats. That Wīglāf[5] even in Bēowulf's last battle is still called *lēod Scylfinga* (2603),[6] is thus readily understood in the light of his father's antecedents. But what the relation is between the Geatish branch of the Wǣgmundingas (to which Bēowulf and his father Ecgþēow belong) and the Swedish branch (the only one which carries through the family alliteration), remains doubtful. The rich homestead of the Wǣgmundingas (2607) must clearly be sought in the land of the Geats.[7]

The (essentially hostile) relations between the Danes and Swedes have been traced in detail by Clarke, L 4.76.82 ff., 156, and Belden, *l.c.* The Geats, the hereditary enemies of the Swedes, are naturally on friendly terms with the Danes. It is true, we are told, in rather vague language (1857 f.), that in former times strife existed between the peoples of the Geats and Danes.[8] But, at any rate, since Bēowulf's deliverance of Heorot, peace and good will were loyally maintained (1829 ff., 1859 ff.).[9] (Possibly even before that event, friendly gifts were ex-

---

[1] Who called attention to the *w*-alliteration. That this is merely a conjecture is not denied. (Wulfgār may have come from Vendel in Jutland.)

[2] Belden conjectures also Wulf Wonrēding, who fights against Ongenþēow (2965 ff.), to be of the Wendel family.

[3] He is apparently the same as *Vésteinn* who is mentioned in conjunction with Áli riding to the battle (against Aðils), *Kálfsvísa* (Par. § 5).

[4] Another version has been proposed by Deutschbein (L 4.97). Setting aside as entirely unhistorical the rôle assigned to Bēowulf and regarding the Wǣgmundingas as the direct successors to the line of Hrēðel on the Geatish throne, he believes that Onela after the fall of Heardrēd appointed Wēohstān king of the Geats, whilst Ēadgils fled to the Danes and afterwards, gaining support from Hrōðulf (as told by Snorri and Arngrím Jónsson), returned to Sweden and defeated Onela.

[5] Wīglāf has been doubtfully identified with Saxo's Wiggo (ii 57, 67), the Vǫggr of the *Hrólfssaga* (chs. 28, 34; Arngrím Jónsson's *Skjǫldungasaga*, chs. 12 f., cp. *Skáldskaparmál*, ch. 41), the devoted retainer of Hrólfr and the avenger of his death (Bugge 50 f.; cf. Sarrazin, *E St.* xlii 28 ff.; Berendsohn, L 4.141.1.8 f.).

[6] Which does not necessarily mean that he is related to the royal line of Ongenþēow.

[7] See on these questions, Scherer L 5.5.475 f., Müllenhoff, *Anz.fdA.* iii 177 f. (Ecgþēow has been declared a Swede, L 4.97 d.)

[8] Can this be a reference to the period when the center of Danish power was still in Skåne?

[9] Deutschbein, *l.c.* would interpret the allusions of ll. 1832 ff., 1855 ff. as evidence of the

THE HISTORICAL ELEMENTS

changed [378 f.].) The excellent personal relations between Bēowulf's family and Hrōðgār date from the time when Ecgþēow, the hero's father, was befriended at the Danish court (459 ff.). They culminate in Bēowulf's adoption (946 ff., 1175 f.). On the strange allusion of l. 3005, see note on that passage.

The historical basis of the allusions to the Swedish kings has now been well established by the discoveries of Swedish archæologists relating to the Uppsala and Vendel grave-mounds. By a happy, almost exact agreement between the purely archæological datings and the dates previously arrived at on literary grounds, it has been proved beyond reasonable doubt that actually Aðils (Ēadgils), Egill (Ongenþēow), and Aun were laid in mound in Old Uppsala about 575, 510 (according to Nerman, 514 or 515), and 500 A.D. respectively, and that the Ottarshögen at Vendel, Uppland, rightly bears its ancient name as containing the ashes of Óttarr (Ōhthere) buried there about 525–530 A.D. This latter fact, by the way, clinches the arguments against the identification of the *Gēatas* and Jutes. See the very helpful survey, Cha. Intr.[2] 408 ff. (L 9.39, 4.97 c.)

Regarding Bēowulf the hero himself, the son of Ecgþēow[1] and grandson of Hrēðel (373 ff.), the facts of his life, *if fitted into the chronological scheme here adopted*, would show the following sequence. He was born about the year 495. At the age of seven he was brought to the court of his grandfather Hrēðel and nurtured there with loving care (2428 ff.). [He was, however, considered slack and of little promise (2183 ff.).] [He distinguishes himself in fighting giants and sea-monsters, 418 ff. and in a swimming adventure with Breca, 506 ff.] He takes no part in the engagements with the Swedes which culminate in the battle at Ravenswood. [In A.D. 515 he visits the Danes and delivers Hrōðgār from the plague of Grendel and his dam.] As a loyal thane he accompanies his uncle Hygelāc in his expedition against the Franks (A.D. 521), slays Dæghrefn (thus avenging Hygelāc's death, it seems), and escapes home by swimming (2356 ff., 2501 ff.). Refusing Hygd's offer of the throne, he acts as Heardrēd's guardian during the latter's minority (2369 ff.). After Heardrēd's death in the fight with the Swedes (A.D. 533), he becomes king and soon supports Ēadgils in his war on Onela, A.D. 535 (2389 ff.). [After a long reign he falls in a combat with a fire dragon. The date of his death must be left indefinite. At any rate, Bēowulf's fifty years' reign (2209) — which would leave him a nonagenarian at the time of the final battle — is meant only as a sort of poetic formula.][2]

---

fact that Heoroweard (Hjǫrvarðr) made his attack on Hrōðulf (Hrólfr) at Lejre with the assistance of the Geats, i.e., of Wīglāf. Further discussion by Berendsohn, *l.c.* 9 ff.

[1] The same *name*, i.e. Eggþér, occurs *Vǫluspá* 42.

[2] Cf. ll. 1769 ff., and above, p. xxxii.

The Nationality of the GEATS

This has been the subject of a prolonged controversy, which has brought out manifold aspects of the question, linguistic, geographical, historical, and literary. Grundtvig assigned the Geats to the island of Gotland (or, for a second choice, to Bornholm); Kemble to Angeln, Schleswig; Haigh (as a matter of course) to North England. But the only peoples that have been actually admitted as rival claimants to the title are the Jutes in the northern part of the Jutish peninsula, and the ON. *Gautar*, O.Swed. *Gǿtar*, i.e. the inhabitants of Väster- and Östergötland, south of the great Swedish lakes.[1]

Phonetically OE. *Gēatas*[2] answers precisely to ON. *Gautar*. The OE. name of the (West Germanic) Jutes[3] is Angl. *Ēote*, *Īote* (*Īotan*), LWS. *Ȳte*, *Ȳtan*,[4] as used in *Wids.* 26: *Ȳtum*, OE. *Bede* 308.11: *Ēota* (Var.: *Ȳtena*) *lond*, OE. *Chron.* A.D. 449: *Īotum*, *Īutna* (Baeda: *Iutarum*) *cyn.*[5] In linguistic respect, then, the identification of the Gēatas cannot be doubtful, and very weighty arguments indeed would be required to overthrow this fundamental evidence in favor of the Gǿtar.

Testimony of a geographical and historical character has been brought forward to support the Jutish claims, but it is somewhat impaired by the fact that the early history of Jutland as well as of Götland is enveloped in obscurity. It is clear from the poem that the Geats are a seafaring people.[6] Hygelāc's castle is situated near the sea (1924, 1963 ff.), the dragon is pushed over the sea-cliff (3131 ff.), and on the 'whale's headland' do the Geats erect the grave monument of their beloved king (2802 ff., 3136). The intercourse between the Swedes and Geats takes place *ofer sǣ* 2380, 2394, *ofer wīd wæter* 2473, *ofer heafo* 2477. Contrariwise, in historic times the Gǿtar are a typical inland people with their

---

[1] See Leo L 4.24, Schaldemose L 2.3, Fahlbeck L 4.71.1 & 2, Bugge 1 ff., Gering L 3.26, p. vii, Weyhe L 4.94, Schütte L 4.71.3, Kier L 4.78, Wadstein, Weibull L 4.74.6 [in favor of the Jutes]; — [and for the opposite view, especially:] Ettmüller Transl., Sarrazin St. 23 ff., ten Brink ch. 12; Schück, Björkman. Stjerna (L 4.74); Uhlenbeck L 4.72.187 ff.; Chambers Wid. 207; also Möller, *E St.* xiii 313 n.; Tupper, *MPh.* ix 266; Cha.Intr. 333 ff., ²401 ff. — Again, Schütte declared the Gēatas to be a Gautic colony in N. E. Jutland; see *Publ. of the Society for the Advancement of Scandinavian Study* i 185 f. (Summary of a paper read at Göteborg in August, 1912.) Cf. L 9.39; L 4.74.8. That a Geatish colony or state existed in Jutland (as a result of the overthrow of the Geatish kingdom), has been argued with especial force by Malone, L 4.74.5, 7, L 4.92 e; see note on l. 445ª. Cf. p. cxv n. 3; L 4.78 i.

[2] The solitary exception to the *Beowulf* practice in l. 443: *Gēotena* is of little consequence; cf. Lang. § 16.2.

[3] It is a plausible assumption that the (W. Germ.) name 'Jutes' was transferred to the Scandinavian settlers of Jutland, who became amalgamated with those of the original population that had remained in their old home. (Cf. Much, *R.-L.* ii 623.)

[4] See Introd. to *The Fight at Finnsburg*.

[5] The forms *Gēata*, *Gēatum* (for 'Jutes') found in one place only, OE. *Bede* 52.4, 9, have been explained in different ways; cf. *A.* xxvii 412; L 4.74.5.

[6] *Sǣ-Gēatas* 1850, 1986; *sǣmen* 2954, *brimwīsa* 2930.

capital Skara far away from the sea. It is possible, nevertheless, that formerly Halland and Bohuslän with an extensive coast line were included in the kingdom of Gautland,[1] and that it was only after their subjugation by the Swedes and the forfeiture of those domains that the Gautar — like the Anglo-Saxons after their settlement in Britain — lost their skill in matters nautical. Again, the water route by which the Swedes and Geats reached each other may very well have been by way of the great lakes, Väner and Vätter.[2] Even the passage by the Baltic Sea and Lake Mälar might have been less inconvenient than the impassable inland roads. Moreover, can we be sure that the Anglo-Saxon poet had a clear knowledge of Northern geography? Is it not rather likely that he would suppose all branches of the Scandinavians to be seafaring peoples? Certainly the topographical hints contained in the poem could not be used successfully for definite localization. The ' sea-cliffs ' (1911 f.), which would fit in better with the coast of Västergötland and Halland than with the shore of Jutland, seem to be part of a conventional description based on notions of English scenery. (They are attributed to Zealand also, 222 f.) ' Storms ' (implied by the terms *Weder-Gēatas, Wederas*) could visit the shores of Västergötland and Jutland alike, and nothing but poetic invention seems to be back of the place-names *Hronesnæs* 2805, *Earnanæs* 3031, cf. *Hrefnawudu* 2925, *Hrefnesholt* 2935 (see 2941, 3024 ff.).[2a]

As regards the hostile relations between the two tribes, we learn from the *Beowulf* that the wars extended over a considerable period and were plainly called forth by natural causes of a serious nature such as are easily to be found in the case of neighboring peoples. It would be difficult to understand, on the other hand, why the Jutes and Swedes should persist in warring upon each other in such inveterate fashion.

The military expedition of the Geats in another direction, viz. against the Franks and Frisians, it has been claimed, points to the Jutes rather than to the distant Gǿtar.[3] Especially the apprehension expressed, after Bēowulf's death, of future attacks from the Merovingians (2911 ff.) has been thought to be natural from the Jutland horizon only.[4] But just as the poet (through the mouth of the messenger) declared the Geats' fear of renewed wars with the Swedes (2922 f., 2999 ff., 3015 ff.), his thoughts would likewise turn to the continental enemies of Bēowulf's people, who might be expected to seize the opportunity of seeking re-

[1] See Schück's arguments, pp. 22 ff. According to Stjerna, p. 91 the Baltic Sea is meant.

[2] And, to some extent, by way of neighboring rivers. Cf. Schück, pp. 34 ff. If necessary, boats could be carried from one body of water to another. Cp. Ōhthere's Voyage (*Oros.* 19.6 f.): *and berað þā Cwēnas hyra scypu ofer land on ðā meras, and þanon hergiað on ðā Norðmen.*

[2a] But see Langenfelt L 4.92 h.

[3] Little light is obtained from the characterization of Hygelāc as king of the ' Danes ' (not ' Jutes,' by the way) by Gregory of Tours and as king of the ' Getae ' in the *Liber Monstrorum*, see above, p. xli.

[4] Sarrazin Käd. 90 f. ascribed this sentiment to the Frisians' point of view dating from an intermediate Frisian stage in the history of the poem. Cf. also Schück L 4.39.48.

venge. The death of the illustrious king, this is apparently the main idea he wishes to convey, will leave the country without protection against any of its foes.

It has been observed that in later literary sources the tradition became confused, and the place of the Geats was taken by Danes and Jutes. Thus, Hugletus (like Gregory's Ch(l)ochilaicus) figures as a Danish king (see above, p. xli), the scene of the first great encounter between Swedes and Geats is shifted (by an evident blunder) from Sweden to Jutland (Vendel),[1] and Aðils gains support from Hrólfr Kraki instead of from the Geat king. Yet the interesting fact remains that Boðvarr Bjarki, Hrólf's famous warrior, who assists Aðils in his fight against Áli, has come from Gautland to the Danish court. On the whole, the Danification of the legends seems to be naturally accounted for by the very early absorption of the Geats into the Swedish state. The loss of their independent existence caused the deeds of the Geatish kings to be attributed to members of other, prominent Scandinavian divisions.[2]

The probability is thus certainly on the side of the Gǿtar, and it requires no great stretch of the imagination to look upon this contest between the two Northern tribes as one of the most significant phases of early Scandinavian history.[3]

Of the territory occupied by the Gǿtar, Västergötland is commonly believed to correspond to Hygelāc's realm, and his royal town has been conjecturally located at Kungsbacka or at Kungälf (south and north of Göteborg respectively).[4]

IV. THE CHRISTIAN COLORING[5]

The presentation of the story-material in *Beowulf* has been influenced, to a considerable extent, by ideas derived from Christianity.

The poem abounds, to be sure, in supernatural elements of pre-Christian associations.[6] Heathen practices are mentioned in several places, such as the vowing of sacrifices at idol fanes (175 ff.), the observing of omens (204), the burning of the dead (3137 ff., 1107 ff., 2124 ff.), which was frowned upon by the Church. The frequent allusions to the power of fate (*wyrd*, cf. *Angl.* xxxvi 171 f.), the motive of blood revenge (1384 f., cp. 1669 f., 1256, 1278, 1546 f.), the praise of worldly glory (1387 ff., cp. 2804 ff., 884 f., 954 f.) bear testimony to

---

[1] On the archæological evidence, see p. xlv. See also the note on 2922 ff.

[2] Cf. Stjerna, ch. 4. — The shifting in the traditions of the Heaðo-Bards (see above, pp. xxxv f.) furnishes a kind of parallel.

[3] By archæological data Stjerna (*l.c.*) felt enabled to trace definitely the causes and the results of this struggle. Nerman L 4.97 c4.136 assigns the final defeat of the Geats to the third quarter of the sixth century.

[4] Stjerna, for archæological and geographical reasons, preferred the island of Öland.

[5] See especially L 4.147 ff.

[6] Cf. above, p. xii & notes.

THE CHRISTIAN COLORING xlix

an ancient background of pagan conceptions and ideals. On the other hand, we hear nothing of angels, saints, relics, of Christ and the cross, of divine worship, church observances, or any particular dogmatic points. Still, the general impression we obtain from the reading of the poem is certainly the opposite of pagan barbarism. We almost seem to move in normal Christian surroundings. God's governance of the world and of every human being, the evil of sin, the doings of the devil, the last judgment, heaven and hell are ever and anon referred to as familiar topics. (See the detailed discussion, *Angl.* xxxv 113 ff., 249 ff., 453 ff.) Though mostly short, these allusions show by their remarkable frequency how thoroughly the whole life was felt to be dominated by Christian ideas. The author is clearly familiar with the traditional Christian terminology in question and evinces some knowledge[1] of the Bible, liturgy, and ecclesiastical literature. Of specific motives derived from the Old Testament (and occurring in *Genesis A* also) we note the story of Cain, the giants, and the deluge (107 ff., 1261 ff., 1689 ff.), and the song of Creation (92 ff.).

Furthermore, the transformation of old heathen elements in accordance with Christian thought may be readily observed. The pagan and heroic cremation finds a counterpart in the peaceful burial of the dead, which the Church enforced (1007 f., 2457 f., cp. 445 f., 3107 ff.). The curse placed on the fateful treasure is clothed in a Christian formula (3071 ff.) and is declared to be void before the higher will of God (3054 ff.). By the side of the heathen fate is seen the almighty God. *Gǣð ā wyrd swā hīo scel*, exclaims Bēowulf in expectation of the Grendel fight, 455, but again, in the same speech, he avows: *ðǣr gelȳfan sceal/Dryhtnes dōme sē þe hine dēað nimeð* 440. The functions of fate[2] and God seem quite parallel: *wyrd oft nereð/unfǣgne eorl . . . 572; swā mæg unfǣge ēaðe gedīgan/wēan ond wrǣcsīð sē ðe Waldendes/hyldo gehealdeþ* 2291; cp. 2574 and 979, 2526 and 2527; 572 f. and 669 f. Yet God is said to control fate: *nefne him wītig God wyrd forstōde/ond ðæs mannes mōd* 1056.[3] Moreover, the fundamental contrast between the good God and the blind and hostile fate is shown by the fact that God invariably grants victory (even in the tragic dragon fight, 2874), whereas it is a mysterious, hidden spell that brings about Bēowulf's death, 3067 ff.

Predominantly Christian are the general tone of the poem and its ethical viewpoint. We are no longer in a genuine pagan atmosphere. The sentiment has been softened and purified. The virtues of moderation, unselfishness, consideration for others are practised and appreciated. The manifest readiness to express gratitude to God on all imaginable occasions (625 ff., 1397 f., 928 f., 1778 f., 1626 f., 1997 f., 2794 ff., 227 f.), and the poet's sympathy with weak and unfortunate

[1] Whether direct or secondary, cf. also *Angl.* xxxv 481 & n. 1 & 2.

[2] Still, *wyrd* is not felt to be a personal being; the term is often used in a colorless way cp., e.g., 1205 (*wyrd*) with 452 (*hild*), 1123 (*gūð*), 557 (*heaþorǣs*), 441 (*dēað*).

[3] However, the caution suggested in the preceding footnote certainly applies here.

INTRODUCTION

beings like Scyld the foundling (7, 46) and even Grendel (e.g. 105, 721, 973, 975, 1351) and his mother (1546 f.), are typical of the new note. Particularly striking is the moral refinement of the two principal characters, Bēowulf and Hrōðgār. Those readers who, impressed by Bēowulf's martial appearance at the beginning of the action, expect to find an aggressive warrior hero of the Achilles or Sigfrit type, will be disposed at times to think him somewhat tame, sentimental, and fond of talking. Indeed, the final estimate of the hero's character by his own faithful thanes lamenting his death is chiefly a praise of Bēowulf's gentleness and kindness: *cwǣdon þæt hē wǣre wyruldcyning[a]/manna mildust ond monðwǣrust,/lēodum līðost ond lofgeornost* 3180.

The Christian elements are almost without exception so deeply ingrained in the very fabric of the poem that they cannot be explained away as the work of a reviser or later interpolator.[1] In addition, it is instructive to note that whilst the episodes are all but free from those modern influences,[2] the main story has been thoroughly imbued with the spirit of Christianity. It is true, the action itself is not modified or visibly influenced by Christianization.[3] But the quality of the plot is changed. The author has fairly exalted the fights with fabled monsters into a conflict between the powers of good and of evil. The figure of Grendel, at any rate, while originally an ordinary Scandinavian troll,[4] and passing in the poem as a sort of man-monster,[5] is at the same time conceived of as an impersonation of evil and darkness, even an incarnation of the Christian devil. Many of his appellations are unquestionable epithets of Satan (e.g., *fēond mancynnes, Godes andsaca, fēond on helle, helle hæfta;* cf. *Angl.* xxxv 250 ff.), he belongs to the wicked progeny of Cain, the first murderer, his actions are represented in a manner suggesting the conduct of the evil one (cf. *ib.* 257), and he dwells with his demon mother[6] in a place which calls up visions of hell (see note on 1357 ff.). Even the antagonist of the third adventure, though less personally conceived than the Grendel pair, is not free from the suspicion of similar influences, especially as the dragon was in ecclesiastical tradition the recognized symbol of the archfiend. (*Angl.* xxxvi 188 f.)

That the victorious champion, who overcomes this group of monsters, is a decidedly unusual figure of very uncertain historical associations,

---

[1] See *Angl.* xxxvi 179 ff.; Cl. Hall, pp. xliv ff.; for interesting arguments to the contrary, see Chadwick H. A. 47 ff.; L 4.22.2.552 ff. (: the poem " has come down from heathen times and acquired its Christian character gradually and piecemeal from a succession of minstrels"). On possible interpolations, see below, Chapter viii: ' Genesis of the Poem.'

[2] The Christian turn given the Heremōd motive (901 ff., 1709 ff.) and some allusions in the Scyld prologue are the chief exceptions. (Cf. *Angl.* xxxv 472 f.)

[3] See note on 1555 f.; *Angl.* xxxv 482, xxxvi 178.

[4] In the poem called *eoten*, 761, cp. 668; *þyrs*, 426.

[5] See, e.g., 105, 1352, also 1379.

[6] Some of her epithets at least are redolent of devil nature, viz. *mānscaða, wælgǣst wǣfre*, perhaps *brimwylf* (?), *grundwyrgen* (?), cp. (*æfter*) *dēofla* (*hryre*) 1680. (*Angl.* xxxvi 188, cf. *ib.* xxxv 253, 256.)

has been pointed out before. The poet has raised him to the rank of a singularly spotless hero, a ' defending, protecting, redeeming being,'[1] a truly ideal character. We might even feel inclined to recognize features of the Christian Savior in the destroyer of hellish fiends, the warrior brave and gentle, blameless in thought and deed, the king that dies for his people.[2] Though delicately kept in the background, such a Christian interpretation of the main story on the part of the Anglo-Saxon author could not but give added strength and tone to the entire poem. It helps to explain one of the great puzzles of our epic. It would indeed be hard to understand why the poet contented himself with a plot of mere fabulous adventures so much inferior to the splendid heroic setting, unless the narrative derived a superior dignity from suggesting the most exalted hero-life known to Christians.

V. STRUCTURE OF THE POEM[3]

STRUCTURAL PLAN[4]

The poem of *Beowulf* consists of two distinct parts joined in a very loose manner and held together only by the person of the hero. The first of these does not in the least require or presuppose a continuation.[5] Nor is the second dependent for its interpretation on the events of the first plot, the two references to the ' Grendel part ' being quite cursory

[1] (See Kemble ii, p. x.) In his rôle as a deliverer from the ravages of monsters he might well be likened to ancient heroes like Hercules and Theseus. — With all the heroic attributes the poet has conferred on him, the dominant trait of the hero is his wonderful eagerness to help others. (Cf. note on 198 ff.)

[2] It is especially in the last adventure that we are strongly tempted to look for a deeper, spiritual interpretation. The duality of the motives which apparently prompt Bēowulf to the dragon fight may not be as unnatural as it has sometimes been considered. (See note on 2336.) Still, it is somewhat strange that the same gold which Bēowulf rejoices in having obtained for his people before the hour of his death (*þæs ðe ic mōste mīnum lēodum / ǣr swyltdæge swylc gestrȳnan* 2797) is placed by his mourning thanes into the burial mound; they give it back to the earth — *þǣr hit nū gēn lifað / eldum swā unnyt, swā hit ǣror wæs* 3167. (Cf. note on 3166 ff.) Nay, Wīglāf, in the depth of his sorrow which makes him oblivious of all else, expresses the wish that Bēowulf had left the dragon alone to hold his den until the end of the world (3079 ff.). The indubitably significant result of the adventure is the hero's death, and, in the structural plan of the poem, the aim and object of the dragon fight is to lead up to this event — a death, that is, which involves the destruction of the adversary, but is no less noteworthy in that it partakes of the nature of a self-sacrifice: *Nū ic on māðma hord mīne bebohte / frōde feorhlege* 2799. That also some incidents in the encounter with the dragon lend themselves to comparison with happenings in the garden of Gethsemane, is shown in the notes to ll. 2419 and 2596 ff. (See also notes on 942 ff., 1707 ff.)

[3] See in general: L 4.1 ff., L 4.120 ff.; L 7, *passim*.

[4] Cf. especially Ker L 4.120, Hart L 4.125, Smithson L 4.128, Heinzel L 7.2.1 & 2, Tolman L 7.11, ten Brink L 7.15, Haeuschkel L 7.20, Rönning L 4.15, Routh L 4.138. — On the division of the poem for purposes of reading, 1–1250, 1251–1887, 1888–3182, see *A*. lvi 429 f.

[5] Only a hint of Bēowulf's future kingship is vouchsafed after the second victory, 1850 ff.; a fainter echo of this note is heard after the first triumph, 861.

and irrelevant (2351 ff., 2521). The first part, again, contains two well-developed main incidents (which are closely enough bound together to constitute technically one story), while its third division, 'Bēowulf's Home-Coming,' serves as a supplement to the preceding major plot. As may be seen from the Argument of the Poem (above, pp. ix ff.), there is a decided structural parallelism in the unfolding of the three great adventures, the fights with the fabulous monsters, namely in setting forth the 'exciting cause,' the preliminaries of the main action, the fight itself, and the relaxation or pause following the climax.[1]

At the same time we note a remarkable gradation in the three great crises of the poem. The fight against Grendel is rather monotonous and seems altogether too short and easy to give much opportunity for excitement — in spite of the horrors of the darkness in which the scene is enacted. The second contest is vastly more interesting by reason of its elaborate, romantic scenery, the variety and definiteness of incidents, the dramatic quality of the battle. The hero is fully armed, uses weapons in addition to his 'hand-grip,' and yet is so hard pressed that only a kind of miracle saves him. There is, moreover, an element of justice in representing the combat with Grendel's mother as more formidable and pregnant with danger. Grendel, who has ravaged the hall because of the innate wickedness of his heart, deserves to be overcome without difficulty. His mother, on the contrary, is actuated by the laudable desire for revenge (1256 ff., 1278, 1305 f., 1546 f., cf. Antiq. § 5) and, besides, is sought out in her own home; hence a certain amount of sympathy is manifestly due her. Finally, the dragon (who likewise has a kind of excuse for his depredations) is entirely too much for his assailant. We tremble for the venerable king. He takes a special measure for protection (2337 ff.), and is strengthened by the help of a youthful comrade, but the final victory is won only at the cost of the hero's own life. The account of this fight, which, like that against Grendel's mother, falls into three clearly marked divisions, receives a new interest by the introduction of the companions, the glorification of one man's loyalty, and the added element of speech-making.

The plot of each part is surprisingly simple. In the use of genuine heroic motives the main story of *Beowulf* is indeed inferior to the Finnsburg legend. But the author has contrived to expand the narrative considerably in the leisurely epic fashion, which differentiates it completely from the type of the short lays. Subsidiary as well as important incidents are related in our epic. Extended speeches are freely introduced. There is not wanting picturesque description and elaborate setting. In the first part of the poem, the splendid life at the Danish court with its

---

[1] As regards individual motives, the function of the speeches (e.g. those uttered before the battles) may be compared. Parallels in minor details between the first and the second incident could be mentioned; cp. 129 ff., 473 ff. and 1321 ff.; 452 f. and 1482 f.; 625 f. and 1397 f.; 636 ff. and 1490 f.; likewise between the first and the second main part, cp. 1769 and 2209; 86 f. and 2302 f.; 1994 ff. and 3079 ff., and see above, p. xxiii.

STRUCTURE OF THE POEM

feastings and ceremonies is graphically portrayed in true epic style. The feelings of the persons are described, and general reflections on characters, events, and situations are thrown in. Last not least, matter more or less detached from the chief narrative is given a place in the poem by way of digressions and episodes.[1]

DIGRESSIONS AND EPISODES

About 450 verses in the first part and almost 250 in the second part are concerned with episodic matter, as the following list will show.

The origin of the Scylding line and Scyld's burial (1–52). The fate of Heorot (82^b–85). The song of Creation (90^b–98). Cain's punishment, and his offspring (107^b–114; 1261^b–1266^a). Youthful adventures of Bēowulf (419–424^a). Settling of Ecgþēow's feud (459–472). The Unferð intermezzo [Breca episode] (499–589). Stories of Sigemund and Heremōd (874^b–915). The Finnsburg Tale (1069–1159^b). Allusions to Eormenrīc and Hāma (1197–1201). The fall of Hygelāc (1202–1214^a). The destruction of the *gīgantas* (1689^b–1693). Heremōd's tragedy (1709^b–1722^a). Sermon against pride and avarice (1724^b–1757). Story of Þrȳð, the wife of Offa (1931^b–1962). The feud between Danes and Heaðo-Bards (2032–2066). Bēowulf's inglorious youth (2183^b–2189).

Elegy of the lone survivor of a noble race (2247–2266). Geatish history: Hygelāc's death in Friesland, Bēowulf's return by swimming, and his guardianship of Heardrēd; the second series of Swedish wars (2354^b–2396). Geatish history: King Hrēðel, the end of Herebeald [the Lament of the Father, 2444–2462^a], the earlier war with the Swedes, Bēowulf's slaying of Dæghrefn in Friesland (2428–2508^a). Wēohstān's slaying of Ēanmund in the later Swedish-Geatish war (2611–2625^a). Geatish history: Hygelāc's fall; the battle at Ravenswood in the earlier Swedish war (2910^b–2998).

It will be seen that several of these digressions contain welcome information about the hero's life; others tell of events relating to the Scylding dynasty and may be regarded as a legitimate sort of setting. The allusions to Cain and the giants are called forth by the references to Grendel's pedigree. The story of Creation is a concrete illustration of the entertainments in Heorot. Earlier Danish history is represented by Heremōd, and the relation between Danish and Frisian tribes is shown in the Finn story. Germanic are the legends of Sigemund and of Eormenrīc and Hāma. To the old continental home of the Angles belongs the allusion to Offa and his queen. The digressions of the second part are chiefly devoted to Geatish history, the exceptions being the 'Elegy of the Last Survivor' and the 'Lament of the Father,' which (like the central portion of Hrōðgār's harangue in the first part) are of a more

---

[1] A rigid distinction between 'digressions' and 'episodes' as attempted by Smithson (pp. 371, 379 ff.), who considers the accounts of Sigemund-Heremōd and the Finnsburg Tale the only episodes, need not be applied.

general character. The frequent mention of Hygelāc's Frankish raid is accounted for by the fact that it is closely bound up both with Geatish history in general and with Bēowulf's life in particular. Accordingly, sometimes the aggression and defeat of Hygelāc are dwelt upon (1202 ff., 2913 ff.), in other passages Bēowulf's bravery is made the salient point of the allusion (2354 ff., 2501 ff.).

Most of the episodes are introduced in a skilful manner and are properly subordinated to the main narrative. For example, the Breca story comes in naturally in a dispute occurring at the evening's entertainment.[1] The legends of Sigemund and of Finnsburg are recited by the scop. The glory of Scyld's life and departure forms a fitting prelude to the history of the Scyldings, who, next to the hero, claim our chief interest in the first part. In several instances the introduction is effected by means of comparison or contrast (in the form of a negative: 1197, 1709, 1931, 2354, [2922], cp. 901). Occasionally the episodic character is clearly pointed out: 2069 *ic sceal forð sprecan/gēn ymbe Grendel;* 1722 *ðū þē lǣr be þon . . . , ic þis gid be þē/āwræc.* The facts of Geatish history, it cannot be denied, are a little too much in evidence and retard the narrative of the second part rather seriously. Quite far-fetched may seem the digression on Þrȳð, which is brought in very abruptly and which, like the Heremōd tale, shows the poet's disposition to point a moral.

In extent the episodic topics range from cursory allusions of a few lines (82ᵇ-85, 1197-1201) to complete and complicated narratives (the adventure with Breca, the Finnsburg legend, the Heaðo-Bard feud, the battle at Ravenswood).

A few passages, like the old spearman's speech (2047-56) and the recital of the Ravenswood battle (2924 ff.), give the impression of being taken without much change (in substance) from older lays. The Elegy of the Last Survivor reminds us of similar elegiac passages in Old English poetry (see *Wanderer, passim,* and *Ruin*). The fine picture of Scyld's sea-burial, and the elaboration of detail in the Bēowulf-Breca adventure seem to be very largely, if not exclusively, the poet's own work. Most of the episodes, however, are merely summaries of events told in general terms and are far removed both from the style of independent lays (like the *Finnsburg* Fragment) and from the broad, expansive epic manner. The distinctly allusive character of a number of them shows that the poet assumed a familiarity with the full story on the part of his audience.

On the whole, we have every reason to be thankful for these episodes, which not only add fulness and variety to the central plot, but disclose a wealth of authentic heroic song and legend, a magnificent historic background. Still we may well regret that those subjects of intensely

---

[1] Inasmuch as the hero tells of his earlier life in the course of a festive entertainment, this episode may be compared to Æneas' narrative at Dido's court (*Æneid*, Books ii and iii) and its prototype, Odysseus' recital of his adventures before Alkinoos (*Odyssey*, Books ix-xii).

STRUCTURE OF THE POEM   lv

absorbing interest play only a minor part in our epic, having to serve as a foil to a story which in itself is of decidedly inferior weight.

SPEECHES[1]

Upwards of 1300 lines are taken up with speeches.[2] The major part of these contain digressions, episodes, descriptions, and reflections, and thus tend to delay the progress of the narrative. But even those which may be said to advance the action, are lacking in dramatic quality; they are characterized by eloquence and ceremonial dignity. The shortest speech consists of four lines (the coast-guard's words of God-speed, 316–19), the longest extends to 160 lines (Bēowulf's report to Hygelāc, 2000–2151, 2155–62); almost as long is the messenger's discourse (128 ll.: 2900–3027); next follow the Finn recital (90 ll.: 1069–1159[a]), Hrōðgār's harangue (85 ll.: 1700–1784), Bēowulf's reminiscences (84 ll.: 2426–2509), his answer to Unferð's version of the Breca story (77 ll.: 530–606).[3]

The formal character of the speeches is accentuated by the manner of their introduction. Most frequently the verb *maðelode* ' made a speech '[4] is employed, either in set expressions occurring with the formula-like regularity well known from the Homeric epic, as

Bēowulf maþelode, bearn Ecgþēowes
Hrōðgār maþelode, helm Scyldinga
Wīglāf maðelode, Wēohstānes sunu

(see Glossary of Proper Names), or in combination with descriptive, characterizing, explanatory matter intruded between the announcement and the actual beginning of the speech, e.g. *Bēowulf maðelode — on him byrne scān,/searonet seowed smiþes orþancum* 405 f.[5] Other terms of introduction like *meþelwordum frægn* 236, *andswarode . . . wordhord onlēac* 258 f., *lȳt swīgode . . . sægde ofer ealle* 2897 ff. (cp. 1215) likewise indicate the formality of the occasions.[6]

The prominent and rather independent position of the speeches is signalized by the fact that, in contrast with the usual practice of enjambment, nearly all the speeches begin and end with the full line. (The only exceptions are 287[b], 342[b], 350[b], 2511[b], 2518[b], 3114[b]; 389[a] (?) (1159[a]).)

About one tenth of the lines devoted to speech is in the form of indirect discourse, which is properly preferred for less important func-

[1] Cf. in particular: Heusler L 7.18.

[2] The proportion of (direct) speech to narrative is in the *Iliad* 7339 : 8635, in the *Odyssey* 8240 : 3879, in the *Æneid* 4632½ : 5263½.

[3] There are in the *Beowulf* some 40 instances of direct discourse averaging in the neighborhood of 30 lines (i.e., if the Finnsburg episode is included).

[4] ' Imperfective verb ' (never used with an object). See Glossary.

[5] Similarly 286 f., 348 ff., 499 ff., 925 ff., 1687 ff., 2510 f., 2631 f., 2724 ff. Cp. *Wids.* 1 ff., *Wald.* ii 11 ff., *Gen. B* 347 ff.; *Hel.* 139 ff., 914 f., 3137 ff., 3993 ff.

[6] Of the simpler expressions, *fēa worda cwæð* (2246, 2662, cp. *Hildebr.* 9), *ond þæt word ācwæð* (654, cp. 2046) may be noted as formulas (*ZfdA.* xlvi 267; *Arch.* cxxvi 357 n. 3).

tions (in 'general narrative') and in the case of utterances by a collection of people (175, 202, 227, 857, 987, 1595, 1626, 3172, 3180). The use of (*ge*)*cwæð* as immediate verb of introduction, following a preparatory statement of a more general character, should be mentioned here. E.g., *swā begnornodon Gēata lēode/hlāfordes* (*hry*)*re* . . . , *cwǣdon þæt* . . . 3180 (so 92, 1810, 2158, 2939; 857, 874).

By far the most felicitous use of the element of discourse is made in the first part, especially in the earlier division of it, from the opening of the action proper to the Grendel fight (189–709). The speeches occurring in it belong largely to the 'advancing' type, consist mainly of dialogue (including two instances of the type 'question: reply: reply,' 237–300, 333–355[1]), and are an essential factor in creating the impression of true epic movement. As the poem continues, the speeches increase in length and deliberation. The natural form of dialogue[2] is in the last part completely superseded by addresses without answer, some of them being virtually speeches in form only.[3]

The 'Grendel part' also shows the greatest variety, as regards the occasions for speech-making and the number of speakers participating (Bēowulf, the coast-guard, Wulfgār, Hrōðgār, Unferð, the scop, Wealhþēow). In its continuation (i 2) the use of discourse is practically limited to an interchange of addresses between Bēowulf and Hrōðgār.

In a class by itself stands the pathetic soliloquy, 2247 ff.

In spite of a certain sameness of treatment the poet has managed to introduce a respectable degree of variation in adapting the speeches to their particular occasions. Great indeed is the contrast between Bēowulf's straightforward, determined vow of bravery (632–638) and Hrōðgār's moralizing oration, which would do credit to any preacher (1700–1784). Admirable illustrations of varying moods and kinds of utterance are Bēowulf's salutation to Hrōðgār (407–455) and his brilliant reply to the envious trouble-maker Unferð (530–606). A masterpiece is the queen's exhibition of diplomatic language by means of veiled allusion (1169 ff.). A finely appropriate emotional quality characterizes Bēowulf's dying speeches (2729 ff., 2794 ff., 2813 ff.).

That some of the speeches follow conventional lines of heroic tradition need not be doubted. This applies to the type of the *gylpcwide* before the combat (675 ff., 1392 ff., 2510 ff.), the 'comitatus' speech or exhortation of the retainers (2633 ff., cp. *Bjarkamál* [Par. § 7: Saxo ii 59 ff.], *Mald*. 212 ff., 246 ff., *Finnsb*. 37 ff.), the inquiry after a stranger's name and home (237 ff.; cp. *Finnsb*. 22 f., *Hildebr*. 8 ff., also *Hel*. 554 ff.). The absence of battle challenge and defiance (see *Finnsb*. 24 ff.) is an obvious, inherent defect of our poem.

---

[1] Cp. 1318–1396 (indirect discourse: reply: reply).

[2] Cp. 1492: *æfter þǣm wordum Weder-Gēata lēod/efste mid elne, nalas andsware/bīdan wolde.*

[3] The length of several of these is somewhat disguised by the fact that they are broken up into two or three portions separated by a few lines of narrative or comment (2426–2537, 2633–2668, 2794–2816, 3077–3119; so in the preceding division: 2000–2162).

STRUCTURE OF THE POEM lvii

LACK OF STEADY ADVANCE

The reader of the poem very soon perceives that the progress of the narrative is frequently impeded. Looseness is, in fact, one of its marked peculiarities. Digressions and episodes, general reflections in the form of speeches, an abundance of moralizing passages (see below, pp. lx f.) interrupt the story. The author does not hesitate to wander from the subject. When he is reminded of a feature in some way related to the matter in hand, he thinks it perfectly proper to speak of it. Hence references to the past are intruded in unexpected places. The manner of Scyld's wonderful arrival as a child is brought out incidentally by way of comparison with the splendor of his obsequies (43 ff.). Bēowulf's renown at the height of his career calls to mind the days of his youth when he was held in disrespect (2183 ff.).[1] No less fond is the poet of looking forward to something that will happen in the near or distant future. The mention of the harmony apparently reigning at the court of Hrōðgār gives an opportunity to hint at subsequent treachery (1018 f., 1164 f., 1180 ff.). The building of the hall Heorot calls up the picture of its destruction by fire (82 ff.).[2] It is not a little remarkable that in the account of the three great fights of the hero, care has been taken to state the outcome of the struggle in advance (696 ff., 706 f., 734 ff., 805 ff.; 1553 ff.; 2341 ff., 2420 ff., 2573 ff., 2586 ff., cp. 2310 f.). Evidently disregard of the element of suspense was not considered a defect in story telling.[3]

Sometimes the result of a certain action is stated first, and the action itself mentioned afterwards (or entirely passed over). E.g., *þā wæs frōd cyning . . . on hrēon mōde,/syþðan hē aldorþegn unlyfigendne . . . wisse* 1306 f.[4] In this way a fine abruptness is attained: *hrā wīde sprong,/syþðan hē æfter dēaðe drepe þrōwade* 1588.[5] Thus it also happens that a fact of first importance is strangely subordinated (as in 1556).[6]

There occur obvious gaps in the narrative. That Wealhþēow left the hall in the course of the first day's festival, or that Bēowulf brought the sword Hrunting back with him from the Grendel cave, is nowhere mentioned, but both facts are taken for granted at a later point of the story (664 f., 1807 ff.).[7]

Furthermore, different parts of a story are sometimes told in different places, or substantially the same incident is related several times from different points of view. A complete, connected account of the history

[1] Similarly: 14 ff., 107 ff., 716 f., 1579 ff., 2771 f., 2777 ff. (In numerous episodes, of course.)
[2] Similarly, e.g., 1202 ff., 1845 ff., 3021 ff.; 2032 ff. (prediction of war with the Heaðo-Bards).
[3] The author of *Judith* uses the same method (ll. 16, 19, 59 f., 63 ff., 72 f.). On predictions of a tragic issue in the *Nibelungenlied*, see Radke L 7.37.47 f.
[4] Cf. notes on 208 ff., 2697 ff.
[5] Other cases of abrupt transition are enumerated by Schücking, Sa. 139 ff.
[6] Subordinate clauses introduced by *siððan* or by *oð þæt* (56, 100, 2210, 2280, 644) are used a number of times in place of a co-ordinate, independent statement.
[7] Cp. the omission of Heorogār's reign (64, 465 ff.).

lviii   INTRODUCTION

of the dragon's hoard is obtained only by a comparison of the passages, 3049 ff., 3069 ff., 2233 ff. The brief notice of Grendel's first visit in Heorot (122 f.) is supplemented by a later allusion containing additional detail (1580 ff.).[1] The repeated references to the various Swedish wars, the frequent allusions to Hygelāc's Frankish foray, the two versions of the Heremōd legend, the review of Bēowulf's great fights by means of his report to Hygelāc (and to Hrōðgār) and through Wīglāf's announcement to his companions (2874 ff.; cp. also 2904 ff.) are well-known cases in point.

Typical examples of the rambling, dilatory method — the forward, backward, and sideward movements — are afforded by the introduction of Grendel (see note on 86–114), by the Grendel fight (see note on 710 ff.), Grendel's going to Heorot (702 ff.),[2] and the odd sequel of the fight with Grendel's mother (1570–90). The remarkable insertion of a long speech by Wīglāf, together with comment on his family, right at a critical moment of the dragon fight (2602–60), can hardly be called felicitous. But still more trying is the circuitous route by which the events leading up to that combat are brought before the reader (see note on 2200 ff.: Second Part).

VI. TONE, STYLE, METER[3]

Although a poem of action, *Beowulf* is more than a narrative of notable events. Not that the author is lacking in the art of telling a story effectively. But a mere objective narration is not his chief aim. The poet is not satisfied with reciting facts, heroic and stirring though they be. Nor does he trouble to describe in a clear, concrete manner the outward appearance of the persons, even of the principal hero, though he sets forth, with eloquence, the striking impression he makes on others (247 ff., cp. 369 f.). But he takes the keenest interest in the inner significance of the happenings, the underlying motives, the manifestation of character. He loses no opportunity of disclosing what is going on in the minds of his actors. He is ever ready to analyze the thoughts and feelings of Bēowulf and Hrōðgār, the Danes and the Geats, Grendel and his kind, even down to the sea-monsters (549, 562, 1431) and the birds of prey (3024 ff.). Their intentions, resolutions, expectations, hopes, fears, longings, rejoicings, and mental sufferings engage his constant attention.[4] In a moment of intensest action, such as the combat with Grendel, the

---

[1] Cp. 83 ff. and 2029 ff. We might compare the account of Satan's rebellion in the first and the fifth and sixth books of *Paradise Lost*.

[2] The repetition of *cōm* 702, 710, 720 may be compared with *Dan.* 149 f., 158.

[3] Cf. L 7, L 8; also L 4, *passim*.

[4] See, e.g., 632 ff., 709, 758, 1272, 1442, 1536 f., 1539, 1565, 2419, 2572; 136, 154 ff., 599 f., 712, 723, 730 f., 739, 753 ff., 762, 769, 821; 1129, 1137 ff., 1150; 1719. See also Glossary: *myntan, wēn(an), þencan, gelȳfan, murnan, (ge)truwian, gefēa, gefēon, þancian, gebelgan, scamian, sorh, geōmor, fyrwyt(t), gemunan, sefa, mōd, ferhð*. (Cf. *Angl.* xxxv 470.)

state of mind of the characters is carefully taken note of (710 ff.). An elaborate psychological analysis runs through the central part of Hrōðgār's great moral discourse (1724 ff.).[1] Delicacy as well as strength of emotion are finely depicted (see 862 f., 1602 ff.,[2] 1853 ff., 1894, 1915 f., 2893 ff., 3031 f.), and numerous little touches indicate an appreciation of kind-heartedness (e.g., 46, 203^b, 469^b, 521^a, 1262^b, 1275, 1547^a, 2434^b, 3093^a).

With especial fondness does the author dwell on the feelings of grief and sadness. Hrōðgār's sorrow for his thanes (129 ff., 473 ff., 1322 ff.), his wonderfully sentimental farewell to his young friend (1870 ff.), Bēowulf's yielding to a morbid reverie when least expected (442 ff., cp. 562 f.), the gloomy forebodings of his men and their yearning love of home (691 ff.),[3] the ever recurring surgings of care,[4] the abundance of epithets denoting sadness of heart[5] give ample evidence of the pervading influence of this characteristic trait. It almost seems as if the victories of the hero and the revelries in the hall produce only a temporary state of happiness, since ' ever the latter end of joy is woe ' (119, 128, 1007 f., 1078 ff., 1774 f.).[6] Even Wīglāf's stern rebuke (*grim andswaru*) of his cowardly comrades is tinged with melancholy reflections (2862 ff.). Full of profound pathos are the elegies of the last survivor (2247 ff.) and the lonely father (2444 ff.). The regret for the passing of youth (2111 ff.), the lament for the dead (1117 f., 1323 ff., 2446 f., 3152 ff., 3171 ff.), the tragic conflict of duties (Hrēðel, 2462 ff.; Hengest, 1138 ff.; Ingeld, 2063 ff.),[7] the lingering fear of a catastrophe in the royal family of the Scyldings (cf. above, pp. xxxii, xxxvi), the anticipation of the downfall of the Geats' power (cf. above, p. xl) aptly typify the prevailing Teutonic mood of seriousness, solemnity, and sadness. But nowhere appears the tragic pathos more subtly worked into the story than in Bēowulf's own death. The venerable king succeeds in overcoming the deadly foe, but suffers death himself; he wins the coveted hoard, but it is of no use to him or his folk; he enters upon the task with the purest intention, even searching his heart for sins he may have unwittingly committed (2329 ff.), but he encounters a fatal curse of which he knew nothing (3067 f.).

The scenery of the poem — sea and seashore, lake and fen-district, the royal hall and its surroundings, the Grendel and the dragon cave — is in the main sketched briefly, yet withal impressively. The large part which the sea played in the life of the Beowulfian peoples, finds expres-

[1] A curious result of this mental attitude is a certain indirectness of expression which in numerous passages takes precedence over the natural, straightforward manner of statement, see, e.g., 715, 764, 1309, 1936, 1969; 814 f.; 866; 532, 677, 793 f., 1845; 1025 f., 2363, 2995.

[2] *Gistas sètan/mōdes sèoce ond on mere staredon* — words as moving in their simple dignity as any lines from Wordsworth's *Michael*.

[3] Cf. *Arch.* cxxvi 343.   [4] Cf. *Arch.* cxxvi 351.
[5] Cf. *Beitr.* xxx 392.   [6] Cf. *MPh.* iii 449, also *Angl.* xxxv 459 ff.

[7] A truly Germanic motive, perhaps best known from the stories of Rüedegēr, Kriemhilt, and Hildebrand.

sion in an astonishing wealth of terms applied to it[1] and in numerous allusions to its dominating geographical importance.[2] Clear visualization and detailed description of scenery should not be expected, as a rule.[3] Elements of nature are introduced as a background for human action or as symbols of sentiment. Nightfall, dawn, the advent of spring[4] signalize new stages in the narrative. The storm on the wintry ocean accompanies the struggle of the courageous swimmers.[5] The swirl of the blood-stained lake tells of deadly conflict (847 ff., 1422, 1593 f.). The funeral ship is covered with ice (33), and frost-bound trees hang over the forbidding water (1363). The moors of the dreary desert, steep stone-banks, windy headlands, mist and darkness are fit surroundings for the lonely, wretched stalkers of mystery. 'Joyless' (821) is their abode. Strikingly picturesque and emotional in quality is the one elaborate landscape picture representing the Grendel lake (1357 ff.), which conveys all the horror of the somber scenery and forcefully appeals to our imagination — a justly celebrated masterpiece of English nature poetry.

In such a gloomy atmosphere there is little room for levity, fun, or humor. Passages which to modern readers would seem to be humorous were possibly not so meant by the Anglo-Saxon author (e.g., 138 f., 560 f., 793 f., 841 f.).[5a] Apparently, he is always in earnest, notably intense, and bent on moralizing. Acting in a way like a Greek chorus, the poet takes pleasure in adding his philosophic comment or conclusion, or, it may be, his slightly emotional expression of approval or censure. Thus, individual occurrences are viewed as illustrations of a general rule, subject to the decrees of fate or of God.[6] The course of the world, the inevitableness of death are set forth.[7] The author bestows praise and blame upon persons and their actions, sometimes in brief quasi-exclamatory clauses like *þæt wæs gōd cyning* 11, 2390; *ne bið swylc earges sīð* 2541; *swā hyt nō sceolde/(īren ǣrgōd)* 2585;[8] sometimes, however, by turning aside and pointing a moral, with manifest relish, for its own sake. Thus, courage, loyalty, liberality, wisdom are held up

---

[1] See Schemann L 7.5.34 ff., 92 ff., Tolman L 7.11, Merbach L 7.27, Erlemann L 7.29.26 ff.

[2] Thus, *be sǣm twēonum* 858, 1297, 1685, 1956; *swā sīde swā sǣ bebūgeð/windgeard weallas* 1223; *ofer hronrāde* 10; 1826, 1861, 2473.

[3] On the somewhat vague use of color terms, see Mead L 7.29.

[4] See 649 ff., 1789 f.; 1801 ff.; 1136 f.

[5] Thus, *geofon ȳþum wēol,/wintrys wylm[um]* 515; *oþ þæt unc flōd tōdrāf,/wado weallende, wedera cealdost,/niþende niht, ond norþanwind/heaðogrim ondhwearf* 545.

[5a] A certain kind of grim humor or irony may have to be recognized. Cp. 157 f., 450 f. (?), 1228 ff.; note on 597.

[6] E.g., *oþ þæt hine yldo benam/mægenes wynnum, sē þe oft manegum scōd* 1886 f.; *oþ ðæt ōþer cōm/gēar in geardas,* — *swā nū gȳt dēð* etc. 1133 ff.; cp. 1058, 2859; 2470, 2590 f.

[7] E.g., *Oft sceall eorl monig ānes willan/wrǣc ādrēogan, swā ūs geworden is* 3077 f.; *gǣð ā wyrd swā hīo scel* 455; *nō þæt ȳðe byð/tō beflēonne* etc. 1002 ff.; 24 f.; 572 f., 2291 ff.; 2029 ff., 2764 ff., 3062 ff.

[8] Cp. 1250, 1812, 1885 f., 1372, 1691 f., 1940 ff. (amplified).

TONE, STYLE, METER

as qualities worthy of emulation. E.g., *swā sceal (geong g)uma gōde gewyrcean* etc. 20 ff.; *swā sceal mǣg dôn,/nealles inwitnet ōðrum bregdon* etc. 2166 ff.[1] The punishment of hell is commented upon by way of warning and of contrast with the joys of heaven: *wā bið þǣm ðe sceal . . . sāwle bescūfan/in fȳres fæþm.* . . . 183 ff.

As to form, the gnomic elements are clearly marked by the use of certain words or phrases, such as *swā sceal (man dōn)* (20);[2] *swylc sceolde (secg wesan)* (2708, 1328); *sēlre bið*[3] (1384, 2890, 1838 f.); *ā, ǣfre (ne)* (455, 930, 2600); *oft (oftost)* (572, 2029, 3077, 1663); *ēaðe mæg* (2291, 2764; cp. 1002); the *sceal* of necessity or certainty (24, 3077).

The abstracting, generalizing tendency often takes the form of recapitulating or explanatory remarks like *wæs se īrenþrēat/wǣpnum gewurþad* 330 f., *sume on wæle crungon* 1113, *wæs tō fæst on þām* 137, *swylc wæs þēaw hyra* 178;[4] of illustrative comparisons, e.g. *ne wæs his drohtoð þǣr,/swylce hē on ealderdagum ǣr gemētte* 756 f., *ne gefrægn ic frēondlīcor fēower mādmas . . . gummanna fela . . . ōðrum gesellan* 1027 ff.;[5] or of reviews of present conditions and comments on the results achieved, e.g. *hæfde Kyningwuldor/Grendle tōgēanes . . . seleweard āseted . . .* 665 ff.; *hæfde þā gefǣlsod . . . sele Hrōðgāres . . .* 825 ff.[6] The course of events is carefully analyzed, with cause and effect duly noted: *þā wæs gesȳne, þæt se sīð ne ðāh* etc. 3058 ff.

Although the moralizing turn and also some of the maxims may be regarded as a common Germanic inheritance,[7] the extent to which this feature as well as the fondness for introspection has been carried is distinctly Beowulfian and shows the didactic and emotional nature of the author himself.

The characters of the poem are in keeping with the nobility of its spirit and the dignity of its manner. Superior to, and different from, all the others, strides the mighty figure of Bēowulf through the epic. In his threefold rôle as adventurous man in arms (*wrecca*), loyal thane of his overlord, and generous, well-beloved king he shows himself a perfect hero, without fear and without reproach, — the strongest of his generation, valorous, resolute, great-hearted and noble of soul, wise and steadfast, kind, courteous, and unselfish, a truly 'happy warrior.'[8] Next to

---

[1] Similarly 1534 ff.; 287 ff., 3174 ff.

[2] The simpler form of this type (as in 1172) is well known in the *Heliand* and in Otfrid.

[3] Naturally the forms of *bēon* are used, see Glossary.

[4] Cp. 223 f., 359, 814 f., 1075, 1124, 1150 f., 133 f., 191 f., 1246 ff.

[5] Cp. 716 ff., 2014 ff., 1470 f.

[6] Cp. 1304 ff., 1620, 2823 ff.

[7] E.g., those expressing the power of fate or coupling fate and courage (cf. *Arch.* cxv 179 & n.). — See on the general subject of the moralizing element, the monograph by B. C. Williams, *Gnomic Poetry in Anglo-Saxon* (1914), Part i (Introduction).

[8] Passages of direct characterization: 196 ff., 858 ff., 913 ff., 1705 ff., 1844 ff., 2177 ff., (2736 ff.), 3180 ff. The poet very skilfully prepares the reader for a true appreciation of Bēowulf's greatness by dwelling on the impression which his first appearance makes on strangers, 247 ff., 369 f. Cf. above, p. lviii. — In a general way, Bēowulf reminds us of Vergil's *pius*

lxii INTRODUCTION

him rank Hrōðgār, the grand and kindly ruler, full of years, wisdom, and eloquence, and the young Wīglāf, who typifies the faithful retainer, risking his life to save his dear master. In a second group belong those lesser figures like Wealhþēow, the noble, gracious, farsighted queen, Unferð, that singular personality of the 'Thersites' order, Hygelāc, the admirable, if somewhat indefinitely sketched member of Geat royalty, and his still more shadowy queen Hygd. Thirdly we find that company of mostly nameless followers of the chiefs, Scyldings and Geats, among whom the coast-guard and the herald Wulfgār stand forth prominently. Finally the villains are represented by the three enemy monsters, partly humanized and one of them at least having a name of his own. Though the majority of the characters are still more or less types, they are, on the whole, clearly drawn and leave a distinct picture in our minds. Certainly the delineation of the chief actor surpasses by far anything we find in other Anglo-Saxon poems. Even some of the persons mentioned only episodically, like Ongenþēow, Hengest, and the old 'spear-warrior' of the Heaðo-Bards, seem to assume a lifelike reality. Of special psychological interest are Unferð, Heremōd, and Þrȳð. Characterization by contrast[1] is seen in the cases of Þrȳð-Hygd (1926 ff.) and Heremōd-Bēowulf (1709 ff., cp. 913 ff.).

The Beowulfian society is noble, aristocratic,[2] and, considering the age it represents, pre-eminently remarkable for its refinement and courtly demeanor. The old Germanic military ideals[3] are still clearly recognizable, notwithstanding the Christian retouching of the story — the prime requirement of valor, the striving for fame and the upholding of one's honor,[4] a stern sense of duty,[5] the obligation of blood revenge,[6] and above all the cardinal virtue of loyalty which ennobles the 'comitatus' relation[7] and manifests itself in unflinching devotion and self-sacrifice on the part of the retainer and in kindness, generosity, and protection on the part of the king. To have preserved for us a faithful

Æneas (cf. *Arch.* cxxvi 339). — The traits of the hero as a mighty 'champion' (*cempa*) have been elaborated by Keller L 4.92 g. — On the author's method of characterization by speeches, see Schücking L 7.25 i.

[1] The author also likes to contrast situations and events, see 128, 716 ff., 756 f., 1078 ff., 1774 f., 2594 f.; 183 ff.; 818 ff., 1470 ff.

[2] Outside of court circles (including retainers and attendants) we find mention of a fugitive slave only, 2223 ff., 2280 ff., 2406 ff. — Of course, the savage slaying of monsters and giants seems to us curiously out of keeping with the general refined atmosphere.

[3] Cf. the Introd. to *Finnsburg*. An interesting instance of the Germanization of the main story is the device of representing Grendel's relation to the Danes (and to God) in the light of a regular feud, see 154 ff., 811 (978, 1001).

[4] Cp. 2890 f.: *Dēað bið sēlla/eorla gehwylcum þonne edwītlīf*. See Grønbech L 9.24. i. 69 ff.

[5] "A profound and serious conception of what makes man great, if not happy, of what his duty exacts, testifies to the devout spirit of English paganism." (ten Brink, L 4.3.3.29.) For a classical illustration see 1384–89.

[6] Ll. 1384 f may be compared with *Odyssey* xxiv 432 ff.

[7] See Antiq. § 2; above, p. lvi.

picture of many phases of the ancient Germanic life in its material as well as its moral aspect, is indeed one of the chief glories of *Beowulf*, and one which, unlike its literary merit, has never been called in question. The poem is a veritable treasure-house of information on ' Germanic antiquities,' in which we seem at times to hear echoes of Tacitus' famous *Germania*, whilst the authenticity of its descriptions has been in various ways confirmed by rich archæological finds especially in the Scandinavian countries. A detailed consideration of this subject is of supreme interest, but cannot be attempted in this place. Its study will be facilitated, however, by the ' Index of Antiquities,' Appendix II, in addition to the general Bibliography, L 9.

In the matter of diction our poem is true to its elevated character and idealizing manner. The vocabulary of *Beowulf*, like that of most Old English poems, is very far removed from the language of prose. A large proportion of its words is virtually limited to poetic diction,[1] many of them being no doubt archaisms, while the abundance of compounds used testifies to the creative possibilities of the alliterative style. A good many terms are nowhere recorded outside of *Beowulf*, and not a few of these may be confidently set down as of the poet's own coinage. Indeed, by reason of its wealth, variety, and picturesqueness of expression the language of the poem is of more than ordinary interest. A host of synonyms enliven the narrative, notably in the vocabulary pertaining to kings and retainers,[2] war and weapons,[2] sea and seafaring.[3] Generously and withal judiciously the author employs those picturesque circumlocutory words and phrases known as ' kennings,'[4] which, emphasizing a certain quality of a person or thing, are used in place of the plain, abstract designation, e.g. *helmberend, wundenstefna, ȳðlida, lyftfloga, hǣðstapa, hronrād; bēaga brytta, goldwine gumena, homera lāf, ȳða gewealc*, or such as involve metaphorical language, like *rodores candel, heofenes gim, bānhūs, beadolēoma*.

Applying the term to verbal expressions also, we may mention, e.g., the concrete periphrases for ' going ' (*hwanon ferigeað gē fǣtte scyldas* etc. 333 ff., or 2539 f., 2661 f., 2754 f., 2850 f.), ' holding court ' (*hringas*

[1] At the same time the appearance of certain prose words which are not met with in any other poem, like *heor(r), sadol, web(b), yppe, dryncfæt, wīnærn, nōn, undernmǣl, uppriht, ūt(an)weard* (see Glossary), betokens a comparatively wide range of interests.

[2] See Antiq. §§ 1, 2, 8.

[3] See above, pp. lix f. Some 30 terms are used for ' hall,' ' house ' (those confined to poetry being marked here with†): *hūs, ærn, reced†, flet, heal(l), sǣld†, sǣlt†, sele(†), bold, burh, geard, hof, wīc*, besides compounds; some 20 for ' man,' ' men ': *mon(n), eorl, ceorl, wer, guma†, rinc†, beorn†, secg†, hæle(ð)†, fīras†, nīððas†, yldet; landbūend, grundbūend†, foldbūend(e)†; sāwlberend‡; ylda, nīðða, gumena bearn†;* 7 for ' son ': *sunu, maga†, mago†, byre, bearn, eafora†, yrfeweard;* 4 for ' heaven ': *heofon, rodor, swegl†, wolcnu;* 3 for ' hand ': *hand, mund(†), folm(†);* 4 for ' blood ': *blōd, drēor†, heolfor†, swāt(†)* (cp. l. 2692 f.); 3 for ' wound ': *wund, ben(n)†, (syn-)dolh(‡);* 6 (9) for ' mind ': *mōd, sefa, hyge†, myne†, ferhð†, brēosthord†, (mōdsefa†, -gehygd†, -geþonc(†));* 9 for ' time ': *tīd, hwīl, fyrst, fǣc, þrāg, sǣl, mǣl(†), stund, sīð;* 3 (6) for ' old ': *eald, frōd(†), gamol† (hār, gamolfeax†, blondenfeax†);* etc.

[4] ON. *kenning*, ' mark of recognition,' ' descriptive name,' ' poetical periphrasis.'

dǣlan 1970), 'conquering' (monegum mægþum meodosetla ofteah 5), 'dying' (ellor hwearf 55, cp. 264 f., 1550 f., 2254; gumdrēam ofgeaf, Godes lēoht gecēas 2469; etc.).

It is no matter for surprise that the kennings very often take the form of compounds. Obviously, composition is one of the most striking and inherently significant elements of the diction. Descriptive or intensive in character, — at times, it is true, merely cumbersome and otiose, the nominal (i.e. substantive and adjective) compounds make their weight strongly felt in the rhetoric of the poem. On an average there occurs a compound in every other line, and a different compound in every third line. Fully one third of the entire vocabulary, or some 1070 words, are compounds,[1] so that in point of numbers, the *Beowulf* stands practically in the front rank of Old English poems.

In comparison with the paramount importance of compounds or kennings, the use of characterizing adjectives is a good deal less prominent, at any rate less striking. These denote mostly general or permanent qualities and make a stronger appeal to sentiment and moral sense than to imagination. By means of the superlative[2] the rhetorical effect is occasionally heightened: *hūsa sēlest* 146, *hrægla sēlest* 454, *healsbēaga mǣst* 1195, etc. Stereotyped ornamental epithets of the familiar Homeric variety like πολύμητις Ὀδυσσεύς, γλαυκῶπις Ἀθήνη, *pius Æneas*, i.e. those appearing inseparably attached to certain persons and objects, are sought in vain in the *Beowulf*.[3]

On the whole, we note a scarcity of conscious poetic metaphors,[4] by the side of the more numerous ones of faded and only dimly felt metaphorical quality, and similes of the Homeric order are entirely lacking, only a few brief, formula-like comparisons being scattered through the first part of the poem.[5]

---

[1] *īsernscūr*‡, *ecgbana*‡, *gomenwudu*‡, *hāmweorðung*‡, *fāmigheals*‡, *stānfāh*‡; *þēodgestrēon*‡, *lēodcyning*‡, *ferhðgenīðla*‡, *brēostgehygd*‡, *bregorōf*‡; *ǣfengrom*‡, *bencswēg*‡ may be cited as typical samples. One of the two elements may be more or less devoid of distinct meaning; e.g., *ende*(*stæf*)(‡), *earfoð*(*þrāg*)‡, *orleg*(*hwīl*)‡, *geogoð*(*feorh*)‡, *ben*(*geat*)‡; (*ferhð*)*frec*‡, (*bealo*)-*cwealm*‡; several first elements like *sige-*, *frēa-*, *frēo-*, *dryht-*, *eorl-*, *eald-*, *þrȳð-*, may carry some general commendatory sense, 'noble,' 'splendid,' 'excellent.' Tautological compounds are not wanting; e.g., *dēaðcwealm*‡, *mægenstrengo*‡, *mægencræft*‡, *gryrebrōga*‡, *mōdsefa*‡, *wongstede*‡, *frēadrihten*‡, *dēaðfǣge*‡. There occur in *Beowulf* 28 alliterating compounds (cf. L 8.18) like *brȳdbūr*, *cwealmcuma*‡, *goldgyfa*‡, *heardhicgende*‡ and 2 (3) riming compounds: *foldbold*‡, *wordhord*‡, (*ðrȳðswȳð*‡). The resources of compound formation are illustrated by the observation that *gūð* is employed as the first element of (different) compounds 30 times, *wæl* 24, *hild*(*e*) 25, *heaðo* 20, *wīg* 16, *here* 14, *beadu* 12, *heoro* 7, *sǣ* 19, *medo* 11, *mægen* 9, *hyge* 8 times.

[2] It is akin to an exaggeration like *unrīm eorla* 1238.

[3] The set expression *mǣre þēoden* which occurs 15 times is applied to Hrōðgār, Bēowulf, Heremōd, Onela, and unnamed lords.

[4] Such as *wordhord onlēac* 259, *winter ȳþe belēac*/*īsgebinde* 1132 f., *mǣlceare* ... *sēað* 189 f., 1992 f., *wordes ord*/*brēosthord þurhbræc* 2791 f., *inwitnet bregdon* 2167, *hiorodryncum swealt* 2358.

[5] See 218: *fugle gelīcost*, 727: *ligge gelīcost*, 985: *stȳle gelīcost*, 1608: *þæt hit eal gemealt īse gelīcost* (amplified by a brief explanatory clause or two not unlike those used, e.g., in 1033 f.,

Highly characteristic and much fancied by the *Beowulf* poet is the familiar trope of litotes, which generally assumes the form of a negative expression, as in *nē mē swōr fela/āðа on unriht* 2738 f., *nō þæt ȳðe byð* (' impossible ') 1002; 793 f., 841 f., 1071 f., 1076 f., 1167 f., 1930; see also *lȳt, sum, dǣl, dēað-(fyl-, gūð-)wērig, forhealdan* in the Glossary. The negation sometimes appears in conjunction with a comparative as in 38, 1027 ff., 1842 f., 2432 f., and even with two comparatives: 1011 f.

As regards the handling of the sentence, by far the most important rhetorical figure, in fact the very soul of the Old English poetical style, is of course the device of ' variation,' which may be studied to perfection in the *Beowulf*.

The still more directly retarding element of parenthesis or parenthetic exclamation, though naturally far less essential and frequent, is likewise part and parcel of the stylistic apparatus. In contrast with variation, it is nearly always placed in (or begins with) the second half of the line.[1]

It should not fail to be observed that there is an organic relation between the rhetorical characteristics and certain narrower linguistic facts as well as the broader stylistic features and peculiarities of the narrative. Thus, tautological compounds like *dēaðcwealm*, redundant combinations like *bēga gehwæþres* 1043[2] and those of the type *wudu wælsceaftas*,[3] the ubiquitous element of variation, and the repetitions in the telling of the story are only different manifestations of the same general tendency. The freedom of word-order by which closely related words may become separated from each other (see e.g., 1 f., 270 f., 450 f., 473 f., 1285 ff., 1488 ff., 2098 f., 2448 f., 2886 ff.), and especially the retardation by means of variations and parenthetical utterances, find their counterpart in the disconnectedness of narration as shown in digressions, episodes, and irregular, circuitous movements. The following up of a pronoun by a complementary descriptive phrase — in the manner of variation —, as in *hī . . . swǣse gesīþas* 28 f., *þæt . . . . Grendles dǣda* 194 f. (cp. 1563, 1674 ff., 77 f., 350 ff.), is matched by the peculiar method of introducing the hero and his antagonist, who at their first mention are referred to as familiar persons and later on receive fuller attention by specifying the name and family history. (See 86 ff. [note the definite article], 194 ff., also 331 ff. [Wulfgār], cp. 12 ff.) Again, the very restatement of an idea in a set of different words (variation) may remind us of the noteworthy way of reporting a speech in studiously varied terms (361 ff.). The preponderance of the nominal over the verbal element,[4]

1327, 2544, 3117 ff., 1648). The pretty lines 1570 ff.: *Līxte se lēoma . . . efne swā of hefene hādre scīneð/rodores candel* can hardly be said to contain an imaginative comparison.

[1] The only exceptions are 2778, 3056, 3115.

[2] Or *uncer twēga* 2532, *worn fela*, see Glossary: *worn*.

[3] See note on 398.

[4] Typical instances are *ofost is sēlest/tō gecȳðanne, hwanan ēowre cyme syndon* (' whence you have come ') 256 f.; *hȳ bēnan synt* (' they ask ') 364, 352, 3140; *tō banan weorðan* (' kill ') 460, 587, 2203; *ic . . . wæs endesǣta* 240 f.; *wearð . . ingenga mīn* 1775 f.; *Ēadgilse wearð . . . frēond* 2392 f.; *æfter mundgripe* 1938, *æfter hēaðuswenge* 2581, *æfter billes bite* 2060; *wes þū ūs*

one of the outstanding features of the ancient diction, runs parallel to the favorite practice of stating merely the result of an action and of dwelling on a state or situation when a straightforward account of action would seem to be called for.[1] The choice of emotional epithets and the insertion of exclamatory clauses are typical of the noble pathos which inspires the entire manner of presentation, whilst the semantic indefiniteness of many words and expressions[2] recalls the lack of visualization, not to say of realism, in regard to persons and places. The indirectness of litotes is similar in kind to the author's veiled allusions to the conduct of Hrōðulf and to the remarkable reserve practised in the Christian interpretation of the story.

As a matter of course, the Beowulfian stylistic apparatus (taken in its widest sense) was to a great extent traditional, deeply rooted in timehonored Germanic, more particularly West Germanic, practice. Its conventional character can hardly be overestimated. Substantial evidence in detail is afforded by its large stock of formulas, set combinations of words, phrases of transition, and similar stereotyped elements.[3] One may mention, e.g., the *maðelode*-formulas (see above, p. lv); expressions marking transition like *næs ðā long tō ðon,/þæt* 2591, 2845 (83?, 134, 739); copulative alliterative phrases like *ord ond ecg, wǣpen ond gewǣdu, mēaras ond mādmas, wigum ond wǣpnum* (2395), *word ond weorc, synn ond sacu; nē lēof nē lāð* (511), *grim ond grǣdig, micel ond mǣre, habban ond healdan,* besides a few riming combinations: *hond ond rond, sǣl ond mǣl, gē wið fēond gē wið frēond* (1864), *frōd ond gōd;* prepositional phrases like *in (on) burgum, geardum, wīcum; under wolcnum, heofenum, roderum, swegle; mid yldum;* constructions of the type *brēac þonne mōste* 1487, 1177, *wyrce sē þe mōte* 1387, *hȳde sē ðe wylle* 2766, cp. 1003, 1379, 1394; first half-lines consisting of a noun or adjective (sometimes adverb) and prepositional phrase, like *geong in geardum* 13, *mǣrne be mǣste* 36, *aldor of earde* 56, *sinc æt symle* 81, *hlūdne in healle* 89, *heard under helme* (see Glossary: *under*), *hraþor on holme* 543, etc. Of especial interest are the *gefrægn*-formulas, which unmistakably point to the 'preliterary' stage of poetry, when the poems lived on the lips of singers, and oral transmission was the only possible source of information. Emphasizing, as they do, the importance of a fact — known by common report — or

---

lārena gōd 269; *þǣr him āglǣca ætgrǣpe wearð* 1269; *þǣr wæs Hondsciō hild onsǣge* 2076, 2482 f.; *þǣr wæs Æschere . . . feorh ūðgenge* 2122 f.; *Bēowulfe wearð/gūðhrēð gyfeþe* 818 f.; etc. Cp. periphrastic expressions for plain verbs, like *gewin drugon* 798, *sundnytte drēah* 2360, *sīð drugon* 1966, *līfgesceafta . . . brēac* 1953.

[1] See above, pp. lvii, lxi; also ten Brink L 4.7.527 f. Among the simpler illustrations may be mentioned ll. 328 f., 994 f., 1110 f., 1243 ff. (pictures rather than action).

[2] For the vague and elastic character of words, see e.g., *nīð, synn, torn, anda, sīð, heaðorēaf, āglǣca, fǣhðo, fāh, lāð, fǣge, mǣre, rōf, frōd.* Cf. Schücking Bd., *passim*. The vagueness of phrases like *cwealmbealu cȳðan* 1940 (cp. 276 f.), and the peculiar preference for passive constructions as in 1629 f.: *ðā wæs of þǣm hrōran helm ond byrne/lungre ālȳsed,* 642 f., 1103, 1399 f., 1787 f., 1896 f., 2284, 3021 f. (cf. *Arch.* cxxvi 355) should be noted.

[3] Cf. L 7.8, 12 f., 34 ff.

TONE, STYLE, METER

the truth of the story, they are naturally employed to introduce poems or sections of poems[1] (e.g., 1 f., 837, 2694, 2752), to point out some sort of progress in the narrative (74, 2480, 2484, 2773, 2172, 433, 776), to call attention to the greatness of a person, object, or action (38, 70, 1196, 1197, 1955, 2685, 2837, 575, 582, 1027). They add an element of variety to the plain statement of facts, and are so eminently useful and convenient that the poets may draw on this stock for almost any occasion.[2]

Owing to the accumulation of a vast store of ready forms and formulas, which could also be added to and varied at will, repetition of phrases (mostly half-lines, but also some full lines) is observable throughout the poem.[3] For example, to cite some recurrent phrases not found outside of *Beowulf*, — *hordweard hæleþa* occurs 1047, 1852; *æþeling ærgōd*, 130, 2342, [1329]; *wyrsan wīgfrecan*, 1212, 2496; *þrȳðlīc þegna hēap*, 400, 1627; *geongum gārwigan*, 2674, 2811; *eafoð ond ellen*, 602, 902, 2349; *feorhbealu frēcne*, 2250, 2537; *morþorbealo māga*, 1079, 2742; *sorhfullne sīð*, 512, 1278, 1429 (cp. 2119); *ealdsweord eotenisc*, 1558, 2616, 2979; *gomel on giohðe*, 2793, 3095; *heard hondlocen*, 322, 551; *ginfæstan gife þē him God sealde*, 1271, 2182; *æfter hæleþa hryre*, *hwate Scyldungas*, 2052, 3005 (MS.); *ǣr (þæt) hē þone grundwong ongytan mehte*, 1496, 2770; 1700, cp. 2864; 47ᵇ–48ᵃ, cp. 2767ᵇ–68ᵃ.

Apart from the matter of formulas, there are not wanting reminders of a primitive or, perhaps, 'natural' method of expression, suggesting the manner of conversational talk or of recitation before a crowd of listeners. E.g., the free and easy use of personal pronouns and the sudden change of subject which leave one in doubt as to the person meant,[4] the preference for paratactic construction,[5] the failure to express logical relations between facts,[6] the simple way of connecting sentences by the monotonous *þā* or of dispensing with connectives altogether, not to mention the exclamatory element, the fondness for repetition by the side of occasional omission, the jerky movement and lack of a steady flow in the narrative. On the other hand, no proof is needed to show that the style of our poem goes far beyond the limits of primitive art; the epic

---

[1] Translated into indirect discourse: *wēlhwylc gecwæð,/þæt hē fram Sigemunde[s] secgan hȳrde/ellendǣdum* 874.

[2] Cf. *MPh.* iii 243 f.

[3] A list of several hundred repeated half-lines is given by Kistenmacher, L 7.16.33 ff.; cf. Sarrazin St. 141 ff.; also *Arch.* cxxvi 357.

[4] See 902, 913, 915, 1305, 1900, 2490, 3074; 109, 115, 169, 748, 1809, 2618 f. (change of subject). The pronominal object (and, of course, subject) may be entirely omitted, see Lang. § 25.4.

[5] Sometimes it is hard to tell whether to consider a clause 'demonstrative' or 'relative'; see, e.g., *sē, sēo, þæt, þā* in the Glossary; *þǣr* 420, etc. — An unavoidable result of the paratactic tendency is the extreme frequency of the semicolon in editions.

[6] For a loose use of the conjunction *þæt* (and of *forðām, forðon*), see Glossary.

INTRODUCTION

manner of *Beowulf* is vastly different from that of the ballad or the short lay.[1]

The good judgment and taste of the author are shown in his finely discriminating way of handling the inherited devices of rhetoric. He increases the force of graphic description or pathetic utterance by bringing together groups of compounds, e.g. in 130 f., 320 ff., 475 ff., 1710 ff., 2900 ff., and achieves a wonderful impressiveness in a single line: *nȳdwracu nīþgrim, nihtbealwa mǣst* 193. A notably artistic effect is produced by the repetition of a couple of significant lines in prominent position, 196 f., 789 f.; cp. 133 f., 191 f. Accumulation of variations is indulged in for the sake of emphasis, as in characterizing a person, describing an object or a situation, and in address; e.g., 2602 ff., 1228 ff., 1557 ff., 3071 ff.; 50 ff., 1345 f., 1004 ff.; 426 ff., 1474 ff.; 1357 ff., 847 ff., 858 ff.; 512 ff., 910 ff. On the other hand, not a single variation interrupts Bēowulf's most manly and businesslike speech, 1384 ff., which thus contrasts strongly with the plaintive lingering on the depredations wrought by Grendel, 147 ff. Again, a succession of short, quick, asyndetic clauses is expressive of rapidity of action, 740 ff., 1566 ff., and appropriately applied to incisive exhortations, 658 ff., 2132 ff., whereas the long, elegant periods of Hrōðgār's farewell speech, 1841 ff., convey the sentimental eloquence of an aged ruler and fatherly friend. Clearly, the author has mastered the art of varying his style in response to the demands of the occasion.

Latin influence, it may be briefly mentioned, is perceptible in the figures of antithesis, 183 ff., anaphora, 864 ff., 2107 ff., polysyndeton, 1763 ff., 1392 ff. Also Latin models for certain kennings and metaphors (e.g., appellations of God and the devil [Grendel], and for terms denoting 'dying' and 'living') have been pointed out.[2]

Our final judgment of the style of *Beowulf* cannot be doubtful. Though lacking in lucidity, proportion, and finish of form as required by modern taste or by Homeric and Vergilian standards, the poem exhibits admirable technical skill in the adaptation of the available means to the desired ends. It contains passages which in their way are nearly perfect, and strong, noble lines which thrill the reader and linger in the memory. The patient, loving student of the original no longer feels called upon to apologize for *Beowulf* as a piece of literature.

---

[1] The vital difference between the style of the lay and of the epic has been clearly set forth by Ker L 4.120 and Heusler L 4.124.

[2] Cf. Rankin L 7.25, *passim; Angl.* xxxv 123 ff., 249 ff., 458 ff., 467 ff.; *Arch.* cxxvi 348 ff.; but also Lang. § 25.9 & n. Some examples are *liffrēa* ('auctor vitae'), *wuldres wealdend, wuldurcyning, kyningwuldor; fēond mancynnes, ealdgewinna, Godes andsaca, helle hæfta* ('captivus inferni'); *worolde brūcan; ylda bearn* ('filii hominum'). — Of Latin loan-words the following occur in *Beowulf: ancor, camp, (cempa), candel, cēap, ceaster(būend), dēofol, disc, draca, gīgant, gim, (ge-)lafian, mīl(gemearc), nōn, ōr, orc, orc(nēas), scrīfan (for-, ge-scrīfan), segn, strǣt, symbel(?), syrce(?), (hærg)træf, weal(l), wīc, wīn.*

TONE, STYLE, METER

METER

The impression thus gained is signally strengthened by a consideration of the metrical form, which is of course most vitally connected with the style of Old English poetry. It is easy to see, e.g., that there is a close relation between the principle of enjambment and the all-important use of variation, and that the requirement of alliteration was a powerful incentive to bringing into full play a host of synonyms, compounds,[1] and recurrent formulas. In the handling of the delicate instrument of verse the poet shows a strict adherence to regularity and a surprisingly keen appreciation of subtle distinctions which make *Beowulf* the standard of Anglo-Saxon metrical art. Suffice it to call attention to the judicious balancing of syntactical and metrical pause and the appropriate distribution of the chief metrical types (ascending, descending) and their subdivisions.

Naturally, our estimate of the intrinsic merit of various rhythmical forms does not rest on a basis of scientific exactitude. We can only guess the psychological values of the different types[2] and their combinations. One would like, indeed, to associate type A with steady progress or quiet strength, to call B the rousing, exclamatory type,[3] to consider type C the symbol of eagerness checked or excitement held in suspense; D 1-3, and D 4, though heavier and less nervous, would seem to have an effect similar to C and B respectively; E with its ponderous opening and short, emphatic close is likely to suggest solemnity and force.[4] However this may be, we can hardly fail to perceive the skill in the selection of successive types in syntactical units, like B+A/A: 80-81^a, C+A/A: 96-97^a, 99-100^a, B/A+E: 109^b-110, C+A/A+C/A: 2291-93^a, or in the case of longer periods, C+A/D4 +A/A//+C/A(//)+C/A//+B: 1368-72, and with totally different effect, A3+A/D4x+A/A3+A/C+A/A3+A/A//+B/C+A: 1728-34. A nice gradation is attained by the sequence of types, 49^b-50^a: *him wæs geōmor sefa,/murnende mōd.*[5]

Quite expressive appear the rhythmical variations of the elegy, 2247 ff. Again, the pleasing rhythm of the semi-lyrical passage, 92 ff. is in marked contrast with the vigor (aided by asyndeton and riming congruence) of 741^b-42: *slāt unwearnum,/bāt bānlocan, blōd ēdrum dranc.*

---

[1] The influence of alliteration on the choice of synonyms may be illustrated by a comparison of ll. 431, 633, 662, its influence on the use of varying compounds by a comparison of ll. 383, 392, 463, 616, 783; 479, 707, 712, 766; 2144, 2148. (For its influence on word-order compare, e.g., ll. 499, 529; 253, 1904; 2663, 2745.)

[2] According to Sievers's classification. (See, however, Appendix iii.)

[3] It is admirably adapted both to introducing a new element (see, e.g., 100^b, 2210^b, 2280^b, 2399^b) and to accentuating a conclusion, almost with the effect of a mark of exclamation (see, e.g., 52^b, 114^b, 455^b).

[4] It fittingly marks a close, as in 5^b, 8^b, 17^b, 19^b, 110^b, 193^b.

[5] Cf. also Heusler V. §§ 343, 346, 348.

INTRODUCTION

Repetition (as in the last instance) and parallelism of rhythmical forms are used to good purpose, e.g., in 2456–58^a; 183^b–187; 3181 f.; 1393–94^a, cp. 1763 ff. Nor does it seem altogether fanciful to recognize symbolic values in the slow, mournful movement (incident to the use of the smallest possible number of syllables) of l. 34: *ālēdon þā lēofne þēoden* compared with the brisk and withal steady progress of ll. 217: *gewāt þā ofer wǣgholm winde gefȳsed* and 234: *gewāt him þā tō waroðe wicge rīdan*.

Of the minor or secondary devices of versification a moderate, discriminating use has been made. Groups of emphatic hypermetrical types are introduced three times, 1163–68, 1705–7, 2995–96.[1] End rime occurs in the first and second half of the line in 726, 734, 1014, 2258, 3172, in a *b*-line and the following *a*-line: 1404^b-5^a, 1718^b–9^a, 2389^b–90^a, in two successive *a*- or *b*-lines: 465^a f., 1132^a f., 3070^a f., 890^b f., 1882^b f., 2590^b f., 2737^b f. (2377^b: 79^a), — aside from the rather frequent suffix rimes, which strike us as accidental. The so-called enjambment of alliteration,[2] i.e. the carrying over of a non-alliterating stressed letter of a *b*-line as the alliterating letter to the following line, is to be considered rather accidental; it occurs some two hundred times (sometimes in groups, as in 168 f., 169 f.; 178 f., 179 f.; 287 f., 288 f.; 3037 f., 3038 f.; etc.).[3] Regarding the much discussed phenomenon of transverse alliteration, of which over a hundred instances can be traced (mostly of the order *a b a b* as in *Hwæt, wē Gār-Dena in gēardagum* 1, 19, 32, 34, 39, 1131, etc., more rarely *a b b a* as in *þæt hit ā mid gemete* m*anna ǣnig* 779, 1728, 2615, etc.), no consensus of opinion has been reached, but it seems not unlikely that it was occasionally recognized as a special artistic form.[4]

The so-called stichic system of West Germanic verse, with its preference for the use of run-on lines and for the introduction of the new elements at the beginning of the *b*-line, appears in our poem in full bloom. At the same time, monotony is avoided by making the end of the sentence not infrequently coincide with the end of the line, especially in the case of major pauses, e.g. those marking the beginning and the end of a speech. In a large number of instances groups of 4 lines forming a syntactical unit could indeed be likened to stanzas.[5] But this does not

---

[1] Very doubtful is the hypermetrical character of the isolated *a*-lines, 2173^a (cf. T.C. § 19) and 2367^a (cf. T.C. § 24).

[2] Kaluza 93. Cf. Heusler V. § 340; also Oakden, *MLR*. xxviii 233.

[3] The use of the same alliterating letter in two successive lines (e.g. 63 f., 70 f., 111 f., 216 f.) was generally avoided; only 50 instances are found (counting all vocalic alliterations as identical ones); the repetition runs through three lines in 897–9. Cf. *MLR*. xxviii 233 f.

[4] Morgan (L 8.23.176) would recognize as many as 86 cases of intentional transverse alliteration. See Heusler V. § 132.

[5] To cite a few examples, 28–31, 43–46, 312–15, 316–19, 391–94, 395–98, 1035–38, 1039–42, 1046–49, 1110–13, 1184–87, 1188–91, 1288–91, 1386–89, 1836–39, 2107–10, 2111–14, 2397–2400, 2809–12, 2813–16, 2817–20 It has been claimed (cf. Kaluza L 8.9.3.18) that an effect of the old stanza division into 5 + 3 half-lines (e g. 2363–66) is traceable in the favorite practice of placing a syntactical unit of 1½ long lines at the end of a period, e.g. 24 f., 78 f., 162 f.,

LANGUAGE. MANUSCRIPT

imply that the normal stichic arrangement has replaced an older strophic form of the *Beowulf*.[1]

On certain metrical features bearing on textual criticism, Appendix III should be consulted.

If a practical word of advice may be added for the benefit of the student, it is the obvious one, that in order to appreciate the poem fully, we must by all means read it aloud with due regard for scansion and expression. Nor should we be afraid of shouting at the proper time.[2]

VII. LANGUAGE. MANUSCRIPT[3]

The transmitted text of *Beowulf*[4] shows on the whole West Saxon forms of language, the Late West Saxon ones predominating, with an admixture of non-West Saxon, notably Anglian, elements.[5]

VOWELS OF ACCENTED SYLLABLES[6]

§ *1. Distinctly Early West Saxon are*

a) *ie* in *hiera* 1164, (*gryre*)*gieste* 2560; *siex-*(*bennum*) 2904, this MS. spelling presupposing the form *sex* (= *seax* 1545, 2703, see § 8.3), which was mistaken for the numeral and altered to *siex*.[7]

b) *īe* in *nīehstan* 2511; *ī* in *nīdgripe* 976 (MS. *mid-*).

Late West Saxon Features

§ 2. *y*

1. = EWS. *i*. Cf. Siev. § 22, Bülb. §§ 306 n. 2, 283, 454.

scypon 1154 (*i* 6x); *swymman* 1624; *ācwyð* 2046 (*i* 2041), *-cwyde* 1841, 1979, 2753 (*i* 3x); (*fyr*)*wyt* 232; *wylle*, *wylt*, *wyllað* 7x (*i* 16x); (-)*hwylc*

---

256 f., 384 f., 756 f., 1435 f., 1527 f., 1598 f., 1616 f., 2890 f., 3108 f., etc. — Less frequently 2 lines could be arranged as stanzas, e.g. 126 f., 258 f., 489 f., 710 f., 1011 f., 1785 f., 1975 f., 2860 f., 2989 f., 3077 f. Also stanzas of 3 lines (and of 5 lines) could be made out.

[1] Cf. G. Neckel, *Beiträge zur Eddaforschung* (1908), pp. 1 ff., and *passim;* but also Sieper, L 4.126.2.40 ff. — Möller's violent reconstruction of the original (L 2.19), with its disregard of stylistic laws, proved a failure. — On the proper meaning of 'stichic' and 'strophic,' see Heusler V. §§ 349 ff.

[2] A notation of the 'speech melody' of the first 52 lines has been attempted by Morgan (L 8.23.101).

[3] See L 6; L 1.

[4] The same is true of the majority of the OE. poems. Cf. Jane Weightman, *The Language and Dialect of the later OE. Poetry*, University Press of Liverpool, 1907 [considers, besides others, the poems of the Vercelli and Exeter MSS.]; also, e.g., A. Kamp, *Die Sprache der altengl. Genesis*, Münster Diss., 1913.

[5] The following survey aims to bring out the characteristic features. A complete record of forms is contained in the Glossary.

[6] See L 6.4 (Davidson), L 6.5 (Thomas).

[7] This seems more natural than a direct transition of *ea* to *ie* (as explained by Cosijn, *Beitr.* viii 573 with reference to *Cur. Past.* [Hatton MS.] 111.23, *forsieh*).

lxxii INTRODUCTION

48x (*e* 148);[1] *swylc*(*e*) 37x (*i* 1152);[1] *swynsode* 611; *nymeð* 598, 1846 (*i* 8x); *sym*(*b*)*le* 2450, 2497, 2880; *lyfað* etc.[2] 5x (*i* 13x); *gyf* 6x (in A[3] only, *ī* 23x); *fyren* 15x (*i* 1932); *fyrst* 7x; *hylt* 1687 (*i* 8x); *ylca* 2239; *syn-* 743, 817, 1135 (*sin-* 6x); *gynne* 1551 (*i* 3x); *hyt*(*t*) 2649; *hwyder* 163 (*hwæder* 1331), *þyder* 3x; *nyðer* 3044 (*i* 1360); *syððan* 57x (*i* 17x; originally *ī*, cf. Bülb. § 336); *gerysne* 2653, *andrysno* 1796; *hrysedon* 226; *hyne* 30x (24x in B[3]) (*hine* 44x, mostly in A); *hyre* 7x (*hire* 8x, in A only); *hyt* 8x (in B only, *hit* 30x); *ys* 2093, 2910, 2999, 3084 (*is* 36x), *synt* 260, 342, 364, *syndon* 237, 257, 361, 393, 1230 (*sint* 388); *byð* 1002, 2277 (*bið* 22x).[4]

2. = EWS. *ie* from *e* after palatal *g*, *sc*. Cf. Wright § 91, Bülb. §§ 151, 306 & n. 3.

gyd(*d*) 7x (*i* 5x); *gyfan* etc. 13x (*i* 19x); *gyldan* 7x (no *i*); *gylþ*(-) 9x (*i* 4x in A); *gystran* 1334; *scyld*(-) 8x (*i* 3118), very often *Scyldingas* (*Scyld;* cf. *Scylfingas* 3x) (*scyldan* 1658).

3. = EWS. *ie*, *i*-umlaut of *ea* = Germanic *a* by breaking. See § 7: *æ*; § 8: *e*.

a) *ylde* 7x, *yldo* 4x, *yldan* 739, *yldra* 3x, *yldesta* 3x; *ylfe* 112; *byldan* 1094; (-)*fyl*(*l*) 5x, *gefyllan* 2x; (-)*wylm* 16x.

b) *yrfe*(-) 5x; *yrmþu* 2x; *byrgean* 448; (-)*dyrne* 10x; *fyrd-* 9x; *gyrwan* 9x (*gegiredan* 3137); (*ā*)*hyrdan* 1460; (*land*)*gemyrce* 209; *myrð*(*u*) 810 (see note); (-)*syrce* 6x; (-)*syrwan* 4x; (-)*wyrdan* 2x; (*grund*)*wyrgen* 1518; (*for*)*wyrnan* 2x;[5] *hwyrfan* 98.[5]

c) (*ge-*, *ond-*)*slyht* 3x; *lyhð* 1048 (*lŷhð*, see T. C. § 1).

4. = EWS. *ie*, *i*-umlaut of *ea* = Germanic *a* after palatal *g*. See § 1: *ie*, § 7: *æ*, § 8: *e*.

(-)*gyst* 2x (*gist* 4x in A).

5. EWS. *ie*, *i*-umlaut of *io* = Gmc. *i* by breaking. See § 13: *eo*.

yrre(-) 8x, *yrringa* 2x; (-)*hyrde* 17x; *hyrtan* 2593; *myrce* 1405; *gesyhð* 2x; *wyrsa* 5x;[6] *wyrðe* 5x;[6] *fyr* 2x.[6]

6. = EWS. *ie* before *ht*, from *eo* = Gmc. *e* by breaking. Cf. Siev. § 108.1.

cnyht 1219 (*cniht-* 372, 535).

7. = *eo*, *io*, = Gmc. *e*, *i* by *u*-umlaut. Cf. Siev. §§ 104.2, 105.2.

gyfen(*es*) 1394 (*i* 1690, *eo* 362, 515); *syfan*(-) 2428, 3122 (*eo* 517, 2195).

8. = *e* in the combination *sel-*,

---

[1] EWS. *hwelc*, *swelc*, cf. Siev. § 342 n. 2 & 3, Wright §§ 311 n. 2, 469 f.

[2] I.e., including various grammatical forms or derivatives from the same stem. This is to be understood also with regard to many of the following examples.

[3] A = the first part of the MS., B = the second part; see below, § 24.

[4] *þysses*, *þyssum*, *þysne* (7x) are already found in Ælfred's prose. It must be admitted that also some of the other *y* spellings quoted are not entirely unknown there; cf. Cosijn, *Altwestsächsische Grammatik* i, p. 65.

[5] Met with already in Ælfred's prose, cf. Cosijn, *op. cit.*, i, p. 34.

[6] Found already in Ælfred's prose, cf. Cosijn, i, p. 65. *byrnan* (2272, 2548, 2569) is likewise Alfredian; cf. Bülb. §§ 283 n. 2, 518, Wright § 98 n. 3, Cosijn, *l.c.*

LANGUAGE. MANUSCRIPT   lxxiii

a) from Gmc. *a* by *i*-umlaut. *syllan* 2160, 2729 (*e* 4x in A). Cf. Siev. § 407 n. 3.

b) Gmc. *e*. *syllīc* 2086, 2109, 3038 (*e* 1426); *sylf* 17x (16x in B, & 505; *e* 17x in A; *eo* 3067). Cf. Bülb. §§ 304, 306.

Note. On *swyrd, swurd, byrht, fyrian*, see § 8.6.

§ 3. *ȳ*

1. = Gmc. *ī*.

fȳf(-) 1582 (*ī* 6x); *fȳra* 2250 (*ī* 4x); *gȳtsað* 1749; *scȳran* 1939 (*scīr*(-) 5x in A); (-)*swȳð*(-) 8x (*ī* 20x); *swȳn* 1111 (*ī* 1286, 1453).

2. = EWS. *īe, i*-umlaut of *ēa* (mostly Gmc. *au*). See § 10: *ē*.

gecȳpan 2496; *geflȳmed* 846, 1370; (-)*gȳman* 4x; *hȳnan* 2319, *hȳnðo* 5x; *hȳran* uniformly, 19x; *gelȳfan* uniformly, 5x; *ālȳsan* 1630; *nȳd*(-) 10x (*ī* 976, *ē* 2223); *nȳhstan* 1203 (*īe* 2511); *scȳne* 3016; *bestȳmed* 486; *geþȳwe* 2332; *ȳðan* 421; *ȳðe*(-) 4x (see § 10.2: *ē*); (-)*ȳwan* 2149, 2834 (*ēo* [also used in WS.] 1738, *ēa* [practically non-WS.] 276, 1194, cf. Siev. § 408 n. 10, Cosijn i, p. 112). — (*ge*)*dȳgan* 2531, 2549. (*gedīgan* 7x — through palatal influence, cf. Bülb. § 306C; so *ācīgan* 3121, *līg* 83, 727, 781, 1122, 2305, 2341, etc.)

3. = *i*-umlaut of *īo* (older *iu*) and *īowj* (older *iuwj, ewwj*). Cf. Wright §§ 138, 90; Bülb. § 188. See § 16: *ēo, īo*.

dȳgel 1357 (*ēo* 275) [possibly *i*-umlaut of *ēa*, cf. Deutschbein, *Beitr.* xxvi 224 n. 2]; *dȳre* 2050, 2306, 3048, 3131 (*ēo* 7x, *īo* 1x); (*un-*) *hȳre* 2120 (*ēo* 2x, *īo* 1x); *gestrȳnan* 2798; (*an-*)*sȳn* 251, 928, 2772, 2834 (*īo* 995); (-)*trȳwe* 1165, 1228 (*ēo-* 1166); *þȳstru* 87 (cf. *ēo* 2332).

4. Varia. — *hȳ* (plur.) 10x (beside *hīe, hī*, see Gloss.; cf. Wright § 462); *sȳ* 3x (*sīe* 3x, *sī* 1x); (-)*gesȳne* 7x (umlaut of *ēa* or *īo*? Cf. Siev. § 222.2); *tȳn*(*e*) 5x (cf. Siev. § 113 n. 2.).

Interchange of *ē* and *ȳ* in *Frēsan, Frȳsan*.

§ 4. *i*

= *y, i*-umlaut of *u*. [Also occasionally in Angl.] Cf. Bülb. §§ 307 f., 161 n. 2, Siev. § 31 n.

bicgan 1305; *bisigu* 281, 1743 (*y* 2580; however, original vowel doubtful, cf. NED.: *busy;* Franck-vanWijk, *Etym. Woordenboek: bezig*); (-)*driht*(-) 10x (in A, *y* 11x); (-)*drihten* 17x (*y* 32x); *fliht* 1765; (-)*hicgan* 5x in A (*y* 3x in B); *hige*(-) 5x in A, 3x in B (*y* 2x in A, 3x in B, -*hȳdig* 723, 1749, 2667, 2810, cf. -*hēdig*, § 10.6), *Higelāc* 15x in A, 8x in B (*Hyge-* 8x in B, 1x in A, *Hȳ-* 1530, see Gloss.); *scildig* 3071 (*y* 3x); *scile* 3176 [found also in Ælfred and in Northumbr., cf. Bülb. § 308, Siev. § 423] (*scyle* 2657); *Wilfingum* 461 (*y* 471); *sinnig* 1379 (*synn*(-) 9x); *þincean* 4x (in A, *y* 2x in B).

§ 5. ī

= ȳ, i-umlaut of ū (un-). Cf. Bülb. §§ 163 n., 309.
-þīhtig 746 (ȳ 1558); wīston 1604 (n.).

Note 1. Predominantly LWS. is the spelling *ig* for *ī* (brought about after a change of forms like *fāmig* to *fāmī* 218). Cf. Siev. §§ 24 n., 214.5; Cosijn, i, pp. 91 f., 178. *hig* 1085, 1596; *sig* 1778; *big*(-) 2220?, 3047; *ligge* 727; *wigge* 1656, 1770; *wiglig* 1841; *-stigge* 924; *Scedan-igge* 1686; cp. *unigmetes* 1792.

Note 2. For some other LWS. features see § 7 n. 1 & 2; § 8.3 b, 4, 6 & n. 1; § 9.1; § 10.4, 5; § 15.2; § 18.5.

Non-West Saxon Elements

(This is a broad, general term. A number of forms included can be traced in the so-called Saxon patois also.)[1]

§ 6. a

1. Unbroken Gmc. *a* before *l+consonant*. [This is really a non-LWS. feature; besides being Angl., it is found not infrequently in EWS. and E. Kent.] Cf. Bülb. § 134, Cosijn i, pp. 8 ff.

alwalda 316, 955, 1314, *alwealda* 928 (always: *eal(l)*), *anwalda* 1272; *aldor* 29x (*ealdor* 20x; always: *eald*); *baldor* 2428 (*bealdor* 2567), -*balde* 1634; *balwon* (dp.) 977 (*ea* in inflected forms 6x); *galdre* 3052 (*gealdor* 2944); *galg(a)* 2446, 2940; *galgmōd* 1277; (-)*hals* 298, 1566 (*ea* 8x); *wald*- 1403; *waldend* 8x (*wealdend* 3x; always *wealdan*, 9x).

2. Original unbroken *a* before *r+consonant* is possibly hidden behind the MS. spelling *brand* in 1020, i.e. *barn. [This would savor of Angl., particularly Northumbr., influence.; cf. Bülb. § 132.]

Note 1. As to the interchange of *a* and *o* spellings before nasals, see below, § 24, p. lxxxix, n. 1. Parallel forms are, e.g., *gamen, gomen; gamol, gomol; gangan, gongan; hand, hond; hangian, hongian; sang, song*.

Note 2. It is very doubtful whether an original long *ā(ǣ)* could be claimed in the form *þara* of the MS., 1015, i.e., if thought an error for *wāran(=*wǣron*). (Cf. Bülb. § 129: *swāran*.)

§ 7. æ

1. WS. & Gmc. *e*. [Not infrequent in several Angl. texts, but sporadically found also elsewhere.] Cf. Bülb. § 92 n. 1; Deutschbein, *Beitr.* xxvi 195 f.; Gabrielson, *Beibl.* xxi 208 ff.

sprǣc 1171 (*sprecan* etc. 4x); *gebrǣc* 2259; *wǣs* 407 (*wes* 5x); *nǣfne* 250 (MS. *nǣfre*), 1353 (*e* 8x); the MS. spellings *hwǣðre* 2819 (i.e. *hrǣðre*), *fǣder*- 3119 (i.e. *fæðer*-); *þǣs* 411 (cf. Siev. § 338 n. 4).[2]

[1] Incidentally a few WS. forms are to be mentioned.
[2] Considered historically, *þæs* would belong under original Gmc. *a;* cf. Wright §§ 465 f.

2. =*i*-umlaut of Gmc. *a* (WS. broken *ea*) before *l*+*cons*. [Angl.] Cf. Wright § 65 n., Bülb. § 175. — See § 2.3: *y;* § 8.2: *e*.

bælde 2018 (n.; cp. *A,idr.* 1186: *bældest*); (-)*wælm* 2066, 2135, 2546.

3. = WS. broken *ea* before *rg, rh* and *h*+*cons*. (smoothing). [Angl.] Cf. Bülb. §§ 205 f. — See § 8.3: *e*.

hærg(*trafum*) 175; *geæhted* 1885 (*ea* 3x, *e* 1x), *geæhtle* 369.

4. = WS. *ea* after initial palatal *sc, g*. [Angl., but also met with in Sax. pat. and Kent.] Cf. Wright § 72 n. 1, Bülb. §§ 152 n., 155 f. — See § 8.4: *e*.

gescær 1526 (*e* 2973); *gescæp*- 26 (*ea* 650, 3084).

With conditions for *i*-umlaut: *gæst* 1800, 1893, 2312, 2670, 2699 (see also Gloss.: *gist* and *gāst, gæst*). Cf. Siev. § 75 n. 1.

5. = WS. *ryht, riht.* [Angl. smoothing of *eo* to *e* (*æ*); *ræht*- 2x in *Lindisf. Gosp.*] Cf. Siev. § 164 n. 1., Bülb. §§ 207, 211.

(*wiðer*)*ræhtes* 3039.

Note 1. Interchange of *æ* and *e* in cases of *i*-umlaut of a) *æ* and of b) *a, o* before nasals is seen in a) *æfnan, efnan; ræst, rest*(?)*; sæcc*(*e*), *secc*(*e*); *wræcca, wrecca; -mæcgas* 491, 2379, *-mecgas* 332, 363, 481, 799, 829; *æl*- 1500, 2371, *el*-, *ellor*, etc. (Cf. Bülb. §§ 168 f., Siev. § 89.) — b) -*hlæmm*, -*hlemm; læ*[*n*]*g, leng; mænigo, menigo*. [This *æ* is characteristic especially of South East Sax. pat., cf. Bülb. §§ 170 f.]

Note 2. *hwæder* 1331 (= *hwider*), occurs sporadically in OE.; it seems to suggest a LWS. scribe. Cf. Sievers, *Beitr.* ix 263; Deutschbein, *Beitr.* xxvi 201; Holt. Et.

Note 3. On the *æ* of *Ælfhere*, see Siev. § 80 n. 3, Cosijn i, p. 31.

§ 8. *e*

1. = WS. *æ.* [(Late) Kent., partly Merc.] Cf. Siev. § 151; Bülb. § 91; Wright § 54 n. 1.

drep 2880; *hreþe* 991, see 1914 Varr. (*æ* 1437, *a* 15x); *Hetware* 2363, 2916; *hrefn* 1801, 2448, 3024, *Hrefnes-holt* 2935, *Hrefna-wudu* 2925 (*e* owing to analogy of *hremn*, cf. Bülb. § 170 n.; not a dialect test); *meþel*(-) 236, 1082, 1876 (cf. Weyhe, *Beitr.* xxx 72 f.); *ren*- 770 ((-) *ærn* 7x, cf. below, § 19.7); *sel* 167 (*sæl* 3x; possibly compromise between *sæl* and *sele*); *þrec*- 1246 (*geþræc* 3102).

2. = EWS. *ie, i*-umlaut of *ea* (see § 2.3: *y*);

a) before *r*+*cons*. [Angl., Kent., also Sax. pat.] Cf. Bülb. § 179 n.; Wright § 181.

under[*ne*] 2911; *mercels* 2439; -*serce* 2539, 2755; *werhðo* 589; perhaps *wergan*, 133 (n.), 1747.

b) before *l*+*cons*. [Kent., also Sax. pat., partly Angl.] Cf. Bülb. §§ 175 & n., 179 n. 1, 180, Wright § 183. — See § 7.2: *æ*.

elde 2214, 2314, 2611, 3168, *eldo* 2111.

3. = WS. broken *ea* (see § 7.3: *æ*);

a) before *rg, rh*. [Angl.] Cf. Bülb. § 206.

hergum 3072.

lxxvi INTRODUCTION

b) before *h*, *h*+*cons.* [Partly Angl., Kent., (chiefly Late) WS.] Cf. Bülb. §§ 210, 313 & n.

ehtigað, 1222; *gefeh* 827, 1569, 2298 (*ea* 2x); *-fex* 2962, 2967 (*ea* 1647); *mehte* [frequent in Ælfred's *Orosius*] 1082, 1496, 1515, 1877 (often *meahte, mihte*); *genehost* 794 (*geneahhe* 783, 3152); *-seh* 3087 (*ea* 18x); *sex*-2904 (see § 1).

4. = WS. *ea* (Gmc. *a*) after initial palatal *g, sc.* [LWS., Kent., occasionally Merc.] Cf. Siev. §§ 109, 157, Bülb. § 314, Wright § 72 n. 1. — See § 7.4: *æ*.

(*be*)*get* 2872 (*be-, on-geat* 7x); *sceft* 3118 (*ea* 2x); *scel* 455, 2804, 3010 (very often *sceal*); *gescer* 2973.

With *i*-umlaut (of *ea* or *æ*), = EWS. *ie.* [Angl., Kent.] Cf. Bülb. § 182, Siev. § 75 n. 2, Wright § 181. — See § 2.4.

(-)*gest*(-) 994, 1976.

5. = WS. broken *eo* before *rg, rh.* [Angl. smoothing.] Cf. Bülb. § 203.

(*hlēor*)*ber*[*g*] 304 (*eo* 1030); *ferh*(-) 305, 2706 (*eo* very often); (-)*ferhð*(-) 19x.

6. The combination *weo-* (from *we-*) appears changed to *wu* [LWS.] in *wurðan* 282, 807, *swurd* 539, 890, 1901, to *wy-* [late WS. spelling, cf. Siev., *Beitr.* ix 202, Bülb. § 268 n. 1.] in *swyrd* 2610, 2987, 3048, *wyruld-*3180, to *wo-* [in general, L. Northumbr. and (partly) LWS., cf. Wright § 94, Bülb. §§ 265 ff., also Wood, *JEGPh.* xiv 505] in *hworfan* 1728 (*eo* 2888), (*for*)*sworceð* 1767 (*eo* 1737), *worc* 289, 1100 [Northumbr.: *werc, wærc*]; *worðmynd* 1186 (*eo* 4x); also in *worold*(-) 17x, *worðig* 1972 [both occurring also in EWS.].

In case the aforesaid spelling *wyr-* is considered to represent a real phonetic change, it might be likened to the change of *beorht* to *byrht*, 1199. Cp. the forms *-byrht* (*-bryht*) of proper names in *Bede* (cf. *Beitr.* xxvi 238), *Byrhte, Bede* 58.13, *-bryht* in the *OE. Chron.* (cf. Cosijn i § 22); *Byrht-nōð, -helm, -wold* in *Mald.; unbyrhtor, Boeth.* 82.1; *Sat.* 238; *Fat. Ap.* 21; etc. Another seemingly parallel case is *fyredon* 378 (*feredon* etc. 11 x).

Note 1. The form (*āð*)*sweord* 2064 perhaps represents an original *-swyrd*, which was erroneously 'corrected' to *-sweord* (because of association with *sweord* 'sword,' see Gloss.). — *hwyrfaþ* 98 (see § 2.3) admits, at any rate, of being identified with *hweorfaþ* (strong verb). — *swulces* (for *swylces*) 880 is a very late form, cf. Bülb. § 280.[1]

Note 2. It is doubtful whether *trem* 2525 contains Kent.[2] *e* = WS. *y* (Mald. 247: *trym*).

§ 9. *ǣ*

1. = WS. *ēa*, Gmc. (and specifically ON.) *au* in (*Heaþo-*) *Rǣmes* 519.

---

[1] See, e.g., *Andr.* 1713: *wunn, Fat. Ap.* 42: *wurd;* W. Schlemilch, *Beiträge zur Sprache und Orthographie spätaltengl. Sprachdenkmäler der Übergangszeit* (St. EPh. xxxiv), pp. 11 f., 14, 47.

[2] But cf. also Wright § 112 n. 1 ('Kentish' claimed to include dialects of East Anglia and Sussex).

[A change sometimes met with in LWS., L. Merc. and, at an earlier date, in Kentish documents.[1]] Cf. Schlemilch, *l.c.*, pp. 35 f.; Zupitza, *ZfdA*. xxxiii 55; Wolff, *Untersuchung der Laute in den kent. Urkunden* (Heidelberg Diss., 1893), pp. 54 f. — Is *lēanes* 1809 'inverted spelling' (for *lǣnes*)?

2. = WS. *ēa* before *g*. [Angl. smoothing.] Cf. Siev. § 163 n. 1, Bülb. § 200. *ǣg(weard)* 241 (see Gloss.).[2] — See § 10.5: *ē*.

3. = *ē*, *i*-umlaut of *ō*. Probably to be accounted for by alteration of original *ǣ* [i.e., archaic OE., and late Northumbr.; Bülb. §§ 165 f.]. Cf. Deutschbein, *Beitr*. xxvi 199 f.; but also Schlemilch, p. 21.

ǣht 2957 (n.); *(hige)mǣðum* 2909; *(on)sǣce*[3] 1942; *(ge-)sacan* 1004 (MS.) is perhaps miswritten for *sǣcan*, i.e. *sēcan*. *Hrǣdles*, *Hrǣdlan* have been similarly explained (L 4.22.2.503); see Glossary (and note on 2869 f.). (The MS. spelling *reote* 2457[3a] possibly points to original *roete*, i.e. *rēte*.)

Note. On the spelling *bęl*, 2126 (= *bǣl*), see note to l. 1981.

§ *10. ē*

1. = WS. & Gmc. *ǣ*. [Angl., Kent.]

ēdrum 742 (*ǣ* 2966); *gefēgon* 1627 (*ǣ* 1014); (-)*mēce* 12x[4]; *Ēomēr* (MS. *geomor*) 1960; *(folc)rēd* 3006, *Heardrēd* 2202, 2375, 2388, *Wonrēdes* 2971, *Wonrēding* 2965 (perhaps due to loss of chief stress, cf. Bülb. § 379); *sēle* 1135 (*ǣ* 8x); *gesēgan* 3038, 3128 (*ǣ* 1422); *sētan* 1602 (*ǣ* 564, 1164); *þēgon* 563, 2633 (*ǣ* 1014); *wēg*(-) 1907, 3132 (*ǣ* 1440).

1a. = WS. *ǣ*, *i*-umlaut of *ā*, Gmc. *ai*. [Kent.] Cf. Bülb. § 167 & n. *snēdeþ* 600 (MS. *sendeþ*).

2. = EWS. *īe*, *i*-umlaut of *ēa*. [Angl., Kent., Sax. pat.] Cf. Bülb. §§ 183 f. — See § 3.2 & 4: *ȳ*.

ēðe 2586, *ēþ-* 1110, 2861; *lēg*(-) 2549, 3040, 3115, *3145* (*ī* 10x); (*þrēa*)-*nēdla* 2223; (-)*rēc* 2661, 3144, 3155; (-)*gesēne* 1244; *(ge)hēgan* 425, 505; *gētan* 2940.

3. = (E)WS. *ēa* (from *ǣ*) after palatal *g*.[5] [Angl., Kent., LWS.]

(of)gēfan 2846 (*ēa* 1600); cf. *-begēte* 2861 (with conditions for *i*-umlaut).

4. = EWS. *ēa* (from Gmc. *au*) after palatal *sc*. [LWS.] Bülb. § 315. *ofscēt* 2439 (*ēa* 2319); *Scēfing* 4.

---

[1] Note also Baeda's spelling *Aeduini*, the *Ēd-* forms of the Northumbr. *Liber Vitae*, and a few *Ēd-* forms occurring in the *OE. Chronicle* (cf. Cosijn i § 93). But cf. Chadwick, *Studies in Old English* (1899), p. 4 (*ǣ*, *ē* due to umlaut).

[2] On the somewhat uncertain etymology, see *Beitr*. xxxi 88 n.; Holt. Et.

[3] Kock[5] 94 1. refers it to *onsacan*.

[3a] On similar *eo* spellings in late MSS., see Schlemilch, p. 22.

[4] This, the invariable form in OE., had become stereotyped through its use in Anglian poetry.

[5] The form *tōgēnes* 3114 (from *tōgēanes* (6x), *tōgeagnes*) occurs already in Alfredian prose; also *gēfe* (Cosijn i, p. 84, ii, p. 138) has been found there. Cf. Bülb. § 315. Note also *gēnunga*, 2871.

5. = WS. *ēa* before *c, g, h*. [Angl., partly LWS.] Cf. Bülb. §§ 316 f. — See § 9.2: *ǣ*.

bēcn 3160 (*ēa* 2x); *bēg* 3163 (*ēa* 30x); *ēg(strēamum)* 577 (*ēagor*-513); (*ā*)*lēh* 80 (*ēa* 3029); *nēh* [2215,] 2411 (*ēa* 12x); *þēh* 1613, 2967 (*ēa* 30x).[1]

6. = *ȳ* (from *yg*-, with *i*-umlaut of *u*). [Later Kent.] Cf. Wright § 132 n., but also § 3 n.

(*nīð*)*hēdige* 3165. (See § 4.)

7. = smoothing of primitive Angl. *ēu* (WS. *ēo*) from Gmc. *ī* in *fēl*(*a*) 1032 (n.). Cf. Bülb. §§ 147, 196, 199.

§ 11. *ī*

= WS. broken *īo, ēo* before *h*, from Gmc. *ī*. [Angl.] Cf. Wright § 127. — See § 10.7.

wīg(*weorþung*) 176 (WS. *wēoh*), *Wīhstān* 2752, 2907, 3076, 3110, 3120 (*ēo* 2602, 2613, 2862).

§ 12. *ea*

1. by *u*-, *o/a*-umlaut, = WS. *a*. [Merc., partly E. Kent.] Cf. Siev. § 103, Bülb. § 231.

beadu- 16x; *cearu* etc. 8x (*care* [3171]); *eafora* 14x; *eafoð* 7x (*eo*, see § 13.2); *eatol* 2074, 2478 (*a* 11x); *heafo* 1862, 2477; (-)*heafola* 2661, 2679, 2697 (*a* 11x); *heaþu*- 35x, *Heaðo*- 7x; -*heaðerod* 3072 (*a* 414?).

Note. *ealu*(-) (7x) has passed into WS. also. Cf. Wright § 78 n. 3.

2. = WS. *eo*, *u*-umlaut of *e*. [Paralleled in Northumbr. (especially *Durh. Rit.*) and E. Kent. (sporadically).] Cf. Bülb. §§ 236, 238.

eafor 2152 (*eo* 4x), *Eafores* 2964 (*eo* 1x, *io* 2x).

Note. *fealo* 2757 may stand for *feola* (*o/a*-umlaut of *e*, Angl., Kent., also Sax. pat., cf. Bülb. § 234) or be =*feala*, a form found in several (including WS.) texts, cf. Siev. § 107 n. 2 [influence of *fēawa* suggested]; Bülb. § 236, Tupper, *Publ. MLAss.* xxvi 246 f., Schlemilch, p. 34.[2] — Is *sealma* 2460 in the relation of ablaut to *selma*?

§ 13. *eo*

1. Non-WS. (though partly also Sax. pat.) cases of *u*-, *o/a*-umlaut (cf. Bülb. §§ 233–35).

a) of *e*.

eodor 428, 663, 1037, 1044; *eoton* etc. 112, 421, 668, 761, 883, 1558, 2979 (*e* 2616); *geofena* 1173 (*geofum* 1958), -*geofa* 2900 (see § 14.2: *io*, § 2.2: *i, y*); *meodu*- 5, 638, 1643, 1902, 1980 (*e* 13x); *meoto* 489 (n.); *meotod*- 1077 (*e* 14x); *weora* 2947 (9 corresponding instances of *e*).

b) of *i*.

---

[1] The forms *nēh* and *þēh* occur already in *Orosius*, see Bülb. § 317 n.

[2] The very form *fealo* is recorded in *Lind. Gosp., Luke* 12.48, *Durh. Rit.* 61.5.

(-)*freoðo*(-) 188, 522, 851, 1942, 2959[1] (see § 14.1: *io; i* 2017); *hleonian* 1415; *-hleoðu* 710, 820, 1358, 1427 (1 corresponding case of *i:* 1409); *leomum* 97; *leoðo*- 1505, 1890, 2769; *seonowe* 817; *seoððan* 1775, 1875, 1937; *weotena* 1098,[1] (-)*weotode* 1796, 1936, 2212 (*i* 9x); *wreoþen(hilt)* 1698 (*i* 3x); *heonan* 252, 1361. [On the occurrence of this umlaut before dentals and nasals in Sax. pat., see Bülb. § 235 n.]

2. *eo* for *ea*, a) *u*-umlaut of *a* (see § 12.1). [Found sporadically in Merc.] Cf. Bülb. § 231 n.

eofoðo 2534.

b) breaking of *a*. [So. Northumbr.] Cf. Bülb. § 144.

beorn 1880.

3. =EWS. *ie*, *i*-umlaut of *io*, Gmc. *i*; see § 2.5: *y*. [Merc., Kent., Sax. pat.] Cf. Bülb. §§ 141–43, 186 n., 187.

eormen- 859, 1201, 1957, 2234 (*Yrmen*- 1324); *eorres* 1447; *feorran* 156; *-heorde* 2930 (MS.), apparently presupposing a form *herde* (Sax. pat., cf. Bülb. § 186 n., — in place of original -*hredde*).

4. =breaking of *e* in *seolf(a)* 3067 (*e* 17x, *y* 17x). [Merc., No. Northumbr., Early Kent.] Cf. Bülb. § 138.[2]

5. *geong* 2743, for *gong*. [Northumbr.] Cf. Siev. § 396 n. 2, Bülb. § 492 n. 1.

For the combination *weo*- see § 8.6.

§ *14. io*

1. Non-WS. cases of *u*-umlaut of *i*.

frioðu- 1096, 2282 (see § 13.1: *eo*); *riodan* 3169; *scionon* 303 (*i* 994); *nioðor* 2699 (also Sax. pat., cf. Bülb. § 235 n.).

2. *io* for *eo*, *u*- or *o/a*-umlaut of *e*. [Kent. coloring.] Cf. Bülb. §§ 238, 141.

hioro- 2158, 2358, 2539, 2781 (*eo* 13x); *Hior(o)te* 1990, 2099 (*eo* 18x); *Iofore* 2993, 2997 (see § 12.2); *siomian* 2767 (*eo* 2x); *giofan* 2972 (might be Sax. pat., or EWS., cf. Bülb. § 253 & n. 2).[3]

3. *io* for *eo*, breaking of *e* before *r+cons*. [Kent., rarely WS.] Cf. Wright § 205, Bülb. §§ 141, 143, Cosijn i, p. 39.

biorg etc. 2272, 2807, 3066 (*eo* 18x); *biorn* 2404, 2559 (*eo* 11x).[4]

§ *15. ēa*

1. for *ēo* in *fēa* 156 (*fēo* 2x). [Might be Northumbr., or Merc., Kent.; cf. Siev. § 166 n. 2., Bülb. §§ 112 n. 1, 114.][5]

---

[1] For EWS. *Freoðo*-, *wiotan* etc., see Cosijn i, pp. 49 f., 52.

[2] According to W. F. Bryan, *Studies in the Dialects of the Kentish Charters of the OE. Period* (Chicago Diss., 1915), p. 20, *seolf(a)* is distinctively Anglian. Three instances from *Orosius* are noted by Cosijn, i, p. 36.

[3] Possibly *swioðol* 3145 is to be included.

[4] Possibly *giohðe* 2267, 2793 should be placed here (*e* broken before *h*); in that case *gehðo* 3095 would belong in § 8.5.

[5] For similar *ēa* forms in (very) late WS., see P. Perlitz, *Die Sprache der Interlin.-Version von Defensor's Liber Scintillarum* (Kiel Diss., 1904), § 17; also Schlemilch, p. 38.

2. *hrēa-* 1214 for *hrǣ(w)* (*ā* 277, 1588). [LWS.] Siev. § 118 n. 2.
3. On *ēaweð* etc., see § 3.2.
Note. Through shifting of stress *-glēaw* developed to (*-gleāw,*) *-glāw* 2564 MS. [but see Varr. and note on l.] (so *glāwne, Andr.* 143; *unglāunesse, Bede* 402.29 (Ca.); *glāunes, Blickl. Hom.* 99.31); cf. Bülb. § 333; Schlemilch, p. 36; Wood, *JEGPh.* xiv 506. — On *leanes* (MS.) 1809, see § 9.1.

§ 16. ēo

1. *ēo, īo* = WS. *īe, ȳ, i*-umlaut of *īo* (older *iu*) and *īowj* (older *iuwj, ewwj*). [Angl., Kent., Sax. pat., partly WS.] Cf. Wright § 138, Bülb. § 189 & n. 1, § 191. — See § 3.3: *ȳ*.

dēore 488, 561, 1309, 1528, 1879, 2236, 2254, *dīore* 1949[1]; (-)*hēoru* 987, 1372, *unhīore* 2413; *nēos(i)an* 115, 125, 1125, 1786, 1791, 1806, 2074, *nīos(i)an* 2366, 2388, 2486, 2671, 3045; *nīowan* 1789 (*ī* 9x); *-sīon* 995; *trēowde* 1166; *þēostrum* 2332.[2]

Note. For the forms *ēoweð* 1738, *dēogol* 275, see § 3.2, 3; cf. Cosijn i §§ 98, 100.

2. *ēo* = normal *ēa*.

a) = Gmc. *au*. [So. Northumbr. coloring.] Cf. Bülb. § 108.[3] (*ā*)*brēot*[4] 2930; *dēoð* 1278; *Gēotena* 443 (= *Gēata*).[5]

b) = WS. *ēa(h)* from *ǣ(h)* in *nēon* 3104. [Angl., Kent.] Cf. Bülb. § 146.

Note. *reote* 2457 may be Kentish spelling for *ǣ, i*-umlaut of *ō* (Wyld, *Short History of English* § 144). Cf. § 9.3.

§ 17. īo

1. = (L)WS. *ēo*. [Presumably Kent., though also EWS. and partly Merc.] Cf. Wright § 209, Siev. § 150 n. 2 & 3, Bülb. § 112.[6]

a) Gmc. *eu*.

bīodan 2892 (*ēo* 3x); *bīor* 2635 (*ēo* 9x); *cīosan* 2376 (*ēo* 2x); *dīop(e)* 3069 (*ēo* 3x); *dīor(-)* 2090, 3111 (*ēo* 11x); (-)*drīor(-)* 2693, 2789 (*ēo* 9x); *hīofende* 3142; *nīod(e)* 2116 (*ēo* 1320); *-sīoc* 2754, 2787 (*ēo* 4x); *þīod(-)* 2219, 2579 (*ēo* 21x), *þīoden* 2336, 2788, 2810 (*ēo* 37x).

b) Contractions [of *ī* + *ŏ, ī* + *ŭ, e* + *u,* cf. Bülb. §§ 118 f.; contraction to *īo* partly Northumbr. also, thus: *fīond, hīo, sīo, ðrīo, bīo* ' bee '].

---

[1] Cf. *Cur. Past.* 411.27, 439.32: *īo*.
[2] Cf. *Oros.* 256.16, 19: *ēo*.
[3] Also late Southern texts contain examples of this *ēo;* cf. Schlemilch, p. 36.
[4] Possibly influenced by redupl. preterites like *bēot*.
[5] Strong and weak declension of tribal names may be found side by side, cf. *Ēote, Ēotan,* Intr. xlvi (also note on 4–52, tenth footnote); Siev. § 264 n.
[6] Instances of *īo* by the side of *ēo* from EWS. (Cosijn i, pp. 37, 44, 66 f., 113 f.): a) *bīodan, bīor-, dīop, dīor, hīofan, sīoc, ðīod;* b) *bīon, fīond, hīo, hīold, sīo, ðīow, ðrīo.* On the use of *īo, ie* in EWS., see Sievers, *Zum ags. Vocalismus* (1900), pp. 39 ff.

LANGUAGE. MANUSCRIPT

bīo(ð) 2063, 2747 (ēo 5x); Bīowulf 15x (in B; ēo 40x [37x in A, see Gloss.]); (on)cnīow 2554; fīond(a) 2671 (ēo 26x); (ge)īode 2200 (ēo 20x); gīong 2214, 2409, 2715 (ēo 5x); hīo 11x (3x in A; hēo 18x in A); hīold 1954 (ēo 33x); sīo 16x (sēo 13x, see Gloss.); Swīo(rīce) 2383, 2495 (ēo 5x); Ongen-, Ecg-ðīo(w) 1999, 2387, 2398, 2924, 2951, 2961, 2986 (ēo 17x; Wealh-þēow 6x); þrīo 2174 (ēo 2278).

2. For īo, ēo = WS. i-umlaut of īo, see § 16.1.

3. iŏ, eŏ (rising diphthongs, unless the i, e were inserted merely to indicate the palatal nature of g) in (-)giōmor- 2267, 2408, 2894, 3150, (-)geōmor(-) 12x (from Gmc. ǣ before nasal).[1] Cf. Wright §§ 51 n., 121 n., Bülb. § 299.

Note. Compare the spelling io in Hondscio (Hondsciô) 2076, which may, however, be merely analogical for eo.[2]

UNACCENTED SYLLABLES

§ 18. Weakening (and interchange) of vowels (and inflexional syllables)

1. -um (dat. plur. ending) appears as -un, -on, -an. Cf. Siev. § 237 n. 6.

a) -un; herewǣsmun 677, wīcun 1304.
b) -on; hēafdon 1242, scypon 1154, grimmon 306 (n.).
c) -an; āþumswēoran (MS. swerian) 84, hlēorber[g]an 304, uncran eaferan 1185, feorhgenīðlan 2933, lǣssan 43, ǣrran 907, 2237, 3035, cp. 1064?

Note. On cases like heardan clammum (so 963; heardum clammum 1335), dēoran sweorde, see § 25.3. Note balwon (bendum) 977, hāton (heolfre) 849. — The erroneous spelling (ū, i.e.) -um for -an appears in 2860ᵃ.

2. -u appears as -o, -a. Cf. Siev. § 237 n. 5; H. C. A. Carpenter, Die Deklin. in d. nordhumbr. Evang. (1910), § 87.

a) -o; earfeþo 534, -gewǣdo 227, geþingo 1085, -hlīðo 1409, wado 546; fǣhðo 2489; -strengo 533, (sinc)þego 2884, etc.
b) -a; -gewǣda 2623 (n.), þūsenda 1829, 2994 (?) (cf. Bülb. § 364); -beala 136, geara 1914 (cf. Bu. Zs. 194, Angl. xxvii 419).

Note. Analogical use of -u for -a in the gen. & dat. sg. of sunu: 1278, 344, 1808(?), acc. pl.: 2013(?). (Cf. Siev. § 271 n. 2.) See also 1243.

3. -a (gen. plur.) appears as
a) -o. Cf. Sievers, Beitr. ix 230; MLN. xvi 17 f.; Sisam, MLR. xi 337. hȳnðo 475, 593, mēdo 1178, yldo 70 (n.).[3]
b) -e in myrðe 810, fyrene 811, sorge 2004, yrmðe 2005, [n]ǣnigre 949; also -hwīle 2710.

4. -an appears as -on
a) in infinitives (cf. Siev. § 363 n. 1), bregdon 2167, būon 2842, healdon

---

[1] Thus, e.g., Kent. Glosses, ZfdA. xxi 20.94: giōmras.
[2] It is possible that a falling diphthong had developed.
[3] The MS. form þrȳðo 1931 has sometimes been supposed to be an error for þrȳðe.

lxxxii   INTRODUCTION

(MS. *heoldon*) 3084 (but see note on l.), *hladon* (MS. *hlodon*) 2775, *ongyton* 308.

b) in *mannon* 577, *hæfton* 788.[1]

Note. The change of *-on* to *-an* in the ind. plur. pret. (cf. Siev. § 364 n. 4) is seen in 43, 650, 1945, 2116, 2475, 2479, 2852, etc.

5. -es (gen. sing.) appears as

a) *-as* (as found in various later texts, cf. Siev. § 237 n. 1; Carpenter, *op. cit.*, §§ 62 f.);[2] *Heaðo-Scilfingas* 63, *Merewīoingas* 2921, *yrfeweardas* 2453. — The spelling *-es* for *-as*, acc. pl., occurs only once, 519.

b) *-ys* (cf. Siev. § 44 n. 2, Bülb. § 360 n.: late, especially LWS.); *wintrys* 516.

A similar transition of *e* in inflexional syllables to *y* in: (*nīw*)*tyrwyd* 295, *feormynd* 2256 (cp. 2761).

6. Various changes of normal *-e-*.

(a) *-ende* (pres. ptc.) > *-inde; weallinde* 2464; > *-ande* (cf. Siev. § 363 n. 4); *-āgande* 1013.

(b) *-en* (pres. opt. plur.) > *-an* (cf. Siev. § 361); *fēran* 254, etc.; *-en* (pret. opt. plur.) > *-on* (cf. Siev. § 365); *feredon* 3113, etc.

(c) *-e* (before *n*) of middle syllables > *-on-*; in the pret. ptc. (cf. Siev. § 366.2): *gecorone* 206, (*þurh*)*etone* 3049 (cp. *Ruin* 6: *undereotone*); — gen. plur.: *sceaðona* 274 (cf. Siev. § 276 n. 2 & 3); — *ricone* 2983.

(d) > *æ* in infl. superl.: *gingæste* 2817.[3]

7. An *i* of the second element of a compound weakened to *e* (cf. Bülb. § 354); *fyrwet* 1985, 2784 (*fyrwyt* 232).[4]

8. Prefix *-ge-* > *-i-* in *unigmetes* 1792, which is reasonably to be considered = *unimetes*, showing a late transition of *ge-* to *i-* (Siev. § 212 n. 1, cp. *unilīc*, *uniwemmed*; *Met. Bt.* 7.33 & 10.9: *unigmet*), and analogical spelling *ig* (which is rather frequent in that portion of the MS.).[5]

9. The isolated *te* 2922 (see Gloss.: *tō*) shows an interesting weakening, cf. Wright § 656, Bülb. § 454, B.-T., s.v. *te*, Luick § 325.

10. The loss of the middle vowel of *Hygelāc* in *Hȳlāc*(*es*) 1530 (from *Hyglāc*) has been designated as largely Northumbrian, with reference to the analogous forms of the *Liber Vitae* (Siev. R. 463 f.).[6] The dropping of the posttonic vowel in *Heort* 78, 991, originally due to the

---

[1] On the spelling *frecnen* for *frēcnan* 1104, see T.C. § 16.

[2] Some examples from poetical texts: *Gen.* (*B*) 485, *Ex.* 248, *Dan.* 30, 115, *Wand.* 44. See Krapp's note on *Andr.* 523.

[3] Such weak *æ* may be found in some (late) texts, cf. Sweet, *Ags. Reader*, *Gra.* § 28 n.; *Angl.* xxv 307 (note on *Bede* 68.25). — The MS. spelling *onlīc næs* (for *onlīcnes* 1351) shows scribal misapprehension.

[4] *Hæðcen* 2925 may be a weakened form for *Hæðcyn* (2434, 2437, 2482) (or Kentish?).

[5] That this *ig* should stand, by mistake, for an old or dialectal *gi-* (cf. Bülb. § 455 n. 1) is a far less plausible hypothesis.

[6] Sievers posits the uniform use of the form *Hyglāc* (as well as *Wedra*) for the original text; similarly *Sigemund* 875, 884 might have been substituted for *Sigmund*. Also *Fitela* 879, 889 has been declared a Southern scribe's alteration of *Fitla* (Weyhe, *Beitr.* xxx 98). — On the forms *hilde-* and *hild-* in compounds, see T.C. § 14.

example of the inflected forms (see 2099; Bülb. §§ 405, 439), is demanded by the meter in l. 78 (cf. Siev. R. 248, T. C. § 5 n.).

Note. The weakening (leveling) of unstressed vowels, accompanied by orthographic confusion, has been dealt with by Malone, *A.* liv 97 f. and L 6.6 a. However, all of the cases cited are not equally clear. A typically ambiguous instance is *fyrene* corrected to *fyrena* 879.

CONSONANTS

§ 19.

1. g.

Loss of palatal *g*, transition of *-ig* to *-ī* (later *i*). Cf. Wright §§ 321, 324; Siev. § 214.5, Cosijn i, pp. 88, 178.

Wīlāf 2852 (*Wīg-* 6x); *Hȳlāc(es)* 1530 (see § 18.10); *-brǣd* 723, 1664, 2575, 2703, *frīn(an)* 351, 1322, *-hȳdig* etc. 434, 723, 1749, 1760, 2667, 2810, cf. 3165, *sǣde* etc. 1696, 1945, 3152; by analogy (cf. Siev. § 214 n. 8) also *gefrūnon* 2, 70, (*-)brōden* 552, 1443, 1548; — *fāmī-* 218, *-sǣlī* 105.

The disappearance of *g* in *gende* 1401 (*gengde* 1412) is perhaps merely an orthographic [L. Kent.] feature, cf. Siev. §§ 184, 215 n. 1, Bülb. § 533 d.

The prefixing of *g* in the spelling *geomor* 1960 (for *Ēomēr*) suggests a Kentish scribe, cf. Siev. § 212 n. 2.

Transition of final *ng* to *nc* in *ǣtspranc* 1121 (*-rinc* 1118 (n.) ?); cf. Siev. § 215, Bülb. § 504. *gecranc* 1209 is possibly to be referred to *-crincan*, a parallel form of *-cringan;* cf. *Beitr.* xxxvii 253 f.

Note. Interesting spellings. (a) *sorhge* 2468 (cp. an analogous spelling of *h* in *fǣghðe* 2465), *ābealch* 2280; cf. Siev. §§ 214 n. 5, 223. — (b) Spellings for *cg* (cf. Siev. § 216 n. 1, Cosijn i, p. 179): *secggende*[1] 3028, *fricgcean* 1985; *Ec-þēow, -lāf* 957, 980 (*Ec-* corrected to *Ecg-* 263), *sec* 2863.[2]

2. h.

Loss and addition of initial *h*. Cf. Siev. § 217 n. 1 & 2, Bülb. § 480 n.

The loss of initial *h* in the MS. spellings *of* 312, *-reade* 1194, *inne* 1868 may or may not be of phonetic significance.[3]

On the unwarranted spelling *h* in initial position in *hraþe* 1390, 1975, see T. C. § 15; on *-hnǣgdon* 2916 (cp. 1318), *hroden* 1151, see T. C. § 28; on *hun ferð* see note on 499 ff., tenth footnote. Obvious mistakes are *hand-, hond-* 1541, 2094, 2929, 2972, also *hattres* 2523.

3. n.

n before *f, þ*, changed to *m* (assimilation, cf. Siev. § 188. 1): *gimfæst* 1271, *hlimbed* 3034.

Loss of *n* in the form *cyniges* 3121, which arose perhaps as a cross

---

[1] Cp., e.g., *El.* 160, 387, 560.
[2] So *Wald.* i 5. — Whether *cg* is erroneously spelled for *g* in *ecgclif* 2893 is doubtful, see Gloss.
[3] The incorrect *beortre* [see however Siev. § 221 n. 2] 158 has been corrected by another hand to *beorhtre*.

between *cynig* and *cynges* (cf. Bülb. § 561) and may be found in several later texts.[1]

The absence of final *n* in *ræswa* (M 3.) 60 (=*ræswan*) has been explained as a Northumbrianism; cf. Siev. §§ 188.2, 276 n. 5, Bülb. § 557; Napier, *Furnivall Miscellany*, p. 379 n. The forms *lemede* 905, *oferēode* 1408, *weardode* 2164 possibly exhibit weakening from normal *-don*, but they (especially the first two instances) can be accounted for by lack of congruence, cf. § 25.6, note on 904 f.[2]

4. Doubling of consonants.

a) Normal doubling of *t* before *r* (cf. Wright § 260, Bülb. § 344) in *attres* 2523, *ættren* 1617, hence also *attor* 2715, 2839 (*āter* 1459).

b) Merely orthographic (or due to confusion) seems to be the doubling of intervocalic *t* after long vowel or diphthong (in open syllable) in *fǣttum* 716 (cf. Gloss.: *fǣted*), *gegrēttan* 1861, *gehēdde*[2a] 505 (cf. *hēdan*), *scēatta* 752 (cf. *sceat(t)*[3]).

c) Doubling of final *l* after short vowel: *sceall*[4] 2275, 2498, 2508, 2535, 3014, 3021, 3077; *till* 2721; *well* 1951, 2162, 2812. Cf. Bülb. §§ 547 f. (Doubled *l* in posttonic position: *æþellingum* 906.)

5. Simplification of double consonants.

a) *hh* between vowels simplified (in spelling) to *h* in *genehost* 794. Cf. Bülb. § 554 n. 2: quite frequent in Angl. texts, but found also in WS. MSS.[5]

b) *tt* spelt *t* in *hetende*[6] 1828; *nn* spelt *n* in *īrena* 673 (n.), 1697, 2259.

c) The simplification of *eorlīc* 637 (for *eorllīc*) is normal. Cf. Wright § 259.3.

6. Loss of the second of three successive consonants. Cf. Bülb. § 533; also *MLN.* xviii 243–45.

[1] See B.-T. Suppl.: *cyning; OE. Chron.* 409 (E), 755 (E); *Wonders of the East* ch. 19. Cf. also Luick § 344 n.

[2] Trautmann (Tr. 134) diagnosed *banu* 158 (MS., however, *banū*) as a Northumbr. form for *banan* (though it is more naturally explained as an error caused by the following *folmū*, cp. 2821, 2961), likewise *-sporu* 986, for *-sporan* (Tr. 177), and — vice versa — *walan* 1031, as an erroneously Westsaxonized form for *walu* (Bonn.B. xvii, p. 163); *lemede* 905 was suspected by him (Tr. 174) of standing for original Northumbr. *lemedu* (which is very questionable, cf. Siev. § 364 n. 4). Cosijn (Aant. 25) judged *-cempa* 1544 to be an Angl. form for *-cempan*.

[2a] The form *gehedde* has been defended as a legitimate pret. (Weyhe, *Sievers-Festschrift* (1925), 319; cf. Luick § 352 n. 4.)

[3] The same spelling, *Ex.* 429: *sceattas*. Such double spellings occur rather irregularly in Northumbr., see e.g., E. M. Lea, *The Lang. of the Northumbr. Gloss. to the Gospel of St. Mark, Angl.* xvi 131 ff.; Lindelöf, *Die Sprache des Rituals von Durham*, pp. 70 f. On such spellings in late Southern texts, see Schlemilch, pp. 64 ff. — The double *t* after shortened diphthong in *þreotteoða* 2406 is LWS., cf. Siev. §§ 328, 230 n. 1, Bülb. § 349.

[4] Frequent in LWS. (Siev. § 423). Cf. also Schlemilch, p. 63.

[5] Thus, e.g., *Gen.* 2843: *geneahe*, *Mald.* 269: *genehe*; *Gen.* 1582, 2066, *El.* 994: *hlihende*, *Blickl. Hom.* 25.23: *hlihaþ*; also *Kent. Gloss., ZfdA.* xxi 18.11: *hlihe; WS. Gosp., Luke* 6.21: *hlihaþ, Lind., ib.: hlæheð;* so 6.25.

[6] Perhaps influenced by *hete, hetelīc, hetol*. Thus *El.* 18, 119: *hetend(um)*. — The spelling *niða* 2215 (not uncommon in OE. MSS.) for *nīðða* seems to be due to analogy with the noun *nið*.

t. (*here*)*wæsmun* 677, and (in a case involving two words:) *siðas sige* 2710 MS. (see Varr.).

d. (*heaða*)*bearna* 2037 MS., (*heaðo*)*bearna* 2067 MS.[1] (Perhaps scribal confusion with the noun *bearn*.) The spelling *hearede* 2202 (= *Heardrēde*) is possibly a mere blunder.

Loss of *r* before one (or two) consonant(s): *sweodum* 567 MS. (see Varr.), *fyhtum* 457 MS. (for [*ge*]*wyrhtum*?).

Unfortunately, *-wæsmun* is the only fairly probable instance of intentional phonetic spelling.[2]

7. *Varia.* — Absence of metathesis of *r* (cf. *ærn*) is noted in (archaic) *ren*(*weard*) 770, cf. Siev. § 179. 1, Bülb. § 518.[3] — *bold* 773, 997, 1925, 2196, 2326, 3112 with *ld* from *þl* (WS. *tl*) is considered predominantly Angl. Cf. Siev. § 196.2, Bülb. § 522.

f. The solitary spelling *u* for intervocalic *f*, in *hlīuade* 1799 (*hlīfade* 1898) probably (though not necessarily) bespeaks the hand of a late scribe. Cf. Siev. § 194; Schlemilch, p. 49.[4]

INFLEXION

Only a few noteworthy forms in addition to those mentioned in §18 are to be pointed out here.

§ 20. Nouns

1. Of nouns used with more than one gender, *sǣ* once (2394) appears as fem. (later usage),[5] (*īsern*)*scūr* 3116 as fem. (archaism).[6] The (Angl.?) fem. gender of *bend* is seen in *wælbende* 1936. On (*hand*)*sporu*, see note on 984 ff.; on *wala*, *wrǣc*, Gloss.; on *frōfor*, note on 698; on *hlǣw*, note on 2297. See also notes on 48, 2338, and T. C. § 25. The apparent fem. use of *sār* 2468 (MS.) is to be charged against the scribe. For the neut. *hwealf* (Gloss.), cp. ON. *hválf*. On *hilt*, see § 21.

2. The fem. nouns of the *i*-declension regularly form the acc. sing. without *-e*, the only exception being *dǣde* 889.[7] The fem. *wynn* fluctuates between the *jō*- and the *i*- type, the acc. sing. (-)*wynne* occurring 8x, the acc. sing. *ēðelwyn* in 2493.[8] — The nom. plur. *lēoda* 3001 shows

---

[1] L. 2032: *-beardna*; Wids. 49: *-bearna* with *d* added above the line. — The spelling *-rædenne* 51 is interpreted by Malone, *A*. liii 335 f. as a legitimate form (so 1142). In view of the normal spelling *-rædende* 1346, the emended form has been preferred.

[2] Exceedingly doubtful are *hol* (*þegnas*) 1229, *-wyl* (*þa*) 1506, and *þeo* (*ge streona*) 1218.

[3] The same form is recorded in the early *Erfurt Glossary*, :137: *rendegn* = ' aedis minister'; besides, as the second element of compounds, in *hordren*, *ZfdA*. xxxiii 245.42, *gangren*, *ib*. 246.80.

[4] Thus, e.g., *El*. 834: *begrauene*, *Andr*. 142: *eaueðum*.

[5] Cf. Schröder, *ZfdA*. xliii 366; Hempl, *JGPh*. ii 100 f.

[6] So Gothic *skūra*; cf. *P.Grdr.*[2]i, p. 770.

[7] The forms *brȳde* 2956, *gumcyste* 1723, *sēle* 1135 must be understood as acc. plur.

[8] In l. 1782 Sievers would introduce the acc. sing. *-wynn*, in l. 2493, *-wynne*. Siev. § 269 ranges *wynn* with the *i*-stems, in *Beitr*. 1 494 f. he classes it, as, primarily, a *jō*-stem. OS. *wunnia* is *jō*-stem, OHG. *wunna jō*-stem, OHG. *wunnī i*-stem.

association of *lēod(e)* with *þēod* and the passing over to the *ō*-declension, cf. Siev. § 264; J. F. Royster, *MLN*. xxiii 121 f.; B.-T.

3. The form *nēodlaðu* 1320, though not impossible as a late, analogical dat. sing. (cf. Siev. § 253 n. 2), is probably meant for *-laðum* (*u* written for *ū*).

4. Of distinct interest is the archaic dat. (instr.) *dōgor* 1395 (cf. Varr.: 1797, 2573).[1] As to form, *-sigor* 1554 could also be an archaic dat. sing.,[1] though the perfective meaning of *gewealdan* harmonizes better with the acc.

§ 21. Adjectives

A remarkably late, analogical form of the acc. plur. neut. would be *fāge* 1615, if construed with a neut. *hilt*.[2] (Cf. Siev. § 293 n. 3.) However, *hilt* may be used here as a fem. (Cp. 1563?) Note also *wynsume* 612, *cwice* 98.

§ 22. Pronouns

On the apparent use of *sē=sēo*, *hē=hēo*, see notes to 1260, 1344, 1887.[3] — A single instance of *hīe*, nom. sg. fem., occurs 2019 (so regularly [twice] in the [Merc.] *Vesp. Psalter*, cf. Siev. § 334 n. 1 & 3). — The transmitted *sīe*, nom. sg. fem., 2219 (see Varr.) is well known [only once: *sēo*] in the *Vesp. Psalter* (cf. Siev. § 337 n. 4). — *þāra*, dat. sg. fem., 1625 suggests dialectal or late usage (cf. Siev. § 337 n. 2 & 4, and *Beitr.* ix 271). — The erroneous *here* 1199 could be interpreted as a blunder for *þĕre* (Kent., Merc., cf. Siev. § 337 n. 3 & 4), i.e. normal *þǣre*.[4] — The MS. form *si* 2237 is defended by Malone as an instance of the occasional raising of a close *ē*, cf. *Jesp. Misc.* 45 ff.

§ 23. Verbs

1. The uniform use of the full endings *-est, -eð* (2. & 3. sing. pres. ind.) of long-stemmed strong verbs and weak verbs of the 1. class, and of the unsyncopated forms (ending *-ed*) of the pret. ptc. of weak verbs of the 1. class terminating in a dental is in accord with the postulate of the Anglian origin of the poem.[5] Conclusive instances (guaranteed by

---

[1] See Weyhe, *Beitr.* xxxi 85 ff.

[2] See Glossary: *hilt*.

[3] Such a form *sē* is a dialectal possibility, cf. E. M. Brown, *The Lang. of the Rushworth Gloss to Matthew*, § 81; Bülb. § 454; Bu. Zs. 205; Hoops St. 7.

[4] The Merc. (*Vesp. Ps.*) form *ūr* has been conjecturally proposed for 2642[b], see Varr.

[5] See Siev. §§ 358.2, 402.2, 406, *Beitr.* ix 273; Siev. R. 464 ff., A. M. § 76.3. Those critics who have cast doubts on Sievers's formulation of this dialect test have intimated the value of these conjugational features as a criterion of early date, so far as Southern texts might be concerned. Cf. ten Brink 213; Trautmann Kyn. 71 n.; Tupper, *Publ. MLAss.* xxvi 255 ff., *JEGPh.* xi 84 f.

LANGUAGE. MANUSCRIPT   lxxxvii

the meter) are (a) *oferswȳðeþ* 279, 1768; *gedīgeð* (*-est*) 300, 661; *þenceð* 355, 448, 1535, 2601; *weorþeð* 414, 2913; *wēneþ* 600; *scīneð* 606, 1571; *brūceð* 1062; *healdest* 1705; *scēoteð* 1744; *gedrēoseð* 1754; etc. (For the absence of WS. umlaut, see Siev. § 371.) (b) *hyrsted* 672; *gecȳþed* 700; *āfēded* 693; *gelǣsted* 829; *forsended* 904; *scynded* 918; etc.[1] The dissyllabic value of the 2. & 3. sing. pres. ind. of short-stemmed verbs is likewise proved by the meter, e.g. *cymest* 1382, *nymeð* 1846, 2536, *gǣleð* 2460, *siteð* 2906.

2. An archaic, or Angl., feature is the ending -*u* in *fullēstu* 2668; cf. Siev. § 355. (See *hafu*, below, under 5.) Another archaism appears in the ending -*ǣ: fǣðmię* 2652 (see note on 1981); cf. Siev. § 361.

3. The pret. of (-)*findan* is both *funde* (6x, in accordance with the regular EWS. practice, cf. Cosijn ii, p. 132) and *fand* (11x), *fond* (2x). — The pret. of (-)*cuman* is both *cwōm*(-) (26x) and *cōm*(-) (24x). — The pret. sing. of (-)*niman* is *nōm* (2x, the normal Angl. form), *nam* (18x), pl. *nāmon* (2x). — The pret. (*ge*)*þah* 1024 looks like a WS. scribe's ineffectual respelling of Angl. *þæh*; cf. Siev. § 391 n. 8, *Beitr.* ix 283; Deutschbein, *Beitr.* xxvi 235 n. (Was there confusion with *þāh*?) Cf. *Beibl.* xxxvii 249 f., xxxviii 356 f. — Not strictly WS. are *sǣgon* 1422, *gesēgan* 3038, *gesēgon* 3128; cf. Siev. § 391 n. 7. — Late [Kent., LWS.] is *specan* 2864.[2] — Quite exceptional (found nowhere else, it seems,) is the pret. ptc. *dropen* 2981.

4. The unique pret. *gang* 1009, 1295, 1316 was referred by Grein Spr. to an inf. *gingan (by Krogmann, *A*. lvii 216 f. to an inf. *gungan). According to Horn (*Behaghel-Festschrift*, 1924, p. 72 f.), *gang* is shortened from *gegang. It has even been explained as an unreasonably mechanical transcription into WS. of a form *gēong* (which was taken for a Northumbr. imp. *geong* (So. Northumbr. *gong*), cf. § 13.5). The form (*ge*)-*gangeð* 1846 is perhaps Angl. (WS. *gǣð*).[3]

5. *hafu*, *hafo* 2150, 2523, 3000 (see § 23.2), *hafast* (uniformly, 5x), *hafað* (uniformly, 9x) are rather Angl. (or poetical); cf. Siev. § 416 n. 1.; (-)*lifi*(*g*)*ende* 468, etc. (10x) is not the standard WS. form, cf. Siev. § 416 n. 2.[4] — *telge* 2067 evidences a compromise between *telle* and *talige* (so 532, 677, 1845).[5] — The ending -*ade* as in *hlīfade* 81, *losade* 2096 (so -*ad* as in *geweorðad*, etc.) occurs sporadically in both parts of the MS., cf. Siev. § 413.[6]

---

[1] Metrically inconclusive cases are, e.g., 93, 1460, 1610, 2044, 2460ᵃ.

[2] Cf. Siev. § 180. The only other instance in OE. poetry: *spǣcon*, *Par. Ps.* 57.3. See also Holt. Et.: *specan*, *sprecan*.

[3] Cf. A. K. Hardy, *Die Sprache der Blickling Homilien* (Leipzig Diss., 1899), p. 75, n.

[4] K. Wildhagen, St. EPh. xiii 180 makes it out to be Angl. It is to be admitted, however, that *hafast*, *hafað*, and especially *lif*(*i*)*gende* are not unknown in WS.

[5] Cp. *Andr.* 1484: *tælige*.

[6] In *Rushw.*², e.g., the vowel *a* is used in such forms almost without exception, cf. Lindelöf, *Bonn.B.* x, §§ 228 f.

lxxxviii   INTRODUCTION

6. The archaic, poetical *dǣdon* (*dēdon*) [claimed as a Northumbrianism] has been demanded by metrical rigorists, 1828^b (cp. 44^b), see Varr. Cf. Siev. § 429 n. 1, Siev. R. 498; Tupper, *Publ. MLAss.* xxvi 264 n. 3.

7. The Angl. pres. ptc. formation in *-ende* of weak verbs of the 2. class (cf. Siev. § 412 n. 11, Siev. R. 482, A. M. § 76.7) is seen in *feormend-* 2761 (cf. Lang. § 18.5).

On the uninflected inf. after *tō*, see Siev. § 363 n. 3; T.C. § 12.

On important linguistic features bearing on scansion, see Appendix III (T.C.). See also below, Chapter viii: ' Genesis of the Poem ' (Date: Linguistic Tests).

§ 24. *Mixture of forms*

How can this mixture of forms, early[1] and late,[2] West Saxon, Northumbrian, Mercian, Kentish, Saxon patois be accounted for? The interesting supposition that an artificial, conventional standard, a sort of compromise dialect had come into use as the acknowledged medium for the composition of Anglo-Saxon poetry,[3] can be accepted only in regard to the continued employment of ancient forms (archaisms) and of certain Anglian elements firmly embedded in the vocabulary of early Anglian poetry. Witness, e.g., the use of *hēan*, *fēores*,[4] *heht* by the side of the later *hēan*, *feores*, *hēt*, or the forms *mēce* (never *mǣce*), *beadu*(-), *heaðu*- uniformly adhered to even in Southern texts. But the significant coexistence in the manuscript of different forms of one and the same word,[5] without any inherent principle of distribution being recognizable, points plainly to a checkered history of the written text as the chief factor in bringing about the unnatural medley of spellings. The only extant manuscript of *Beowulf* was written some two and a half centuries after the probable date of composition[6] and was, of course, copied from a previous copy. It is perfectly safe to assert that the text was copied a number of times, and that scribes of heterogeneous dialectal habits and

---

[1] Note, e.g., details like *ren-* § 19.7, *dōgor* § 20.4, *hafu*, *fullǣstu*, *fæðmię̄*, § 23.2 & 5; also T.C. § 1, etc.

[2] Note, e.g., *hlīuade* § 19.7, *specan* § 23.3, *fāge* § 21(?), *swyrd* § 8.6, *swulc* § 8 n. 1, *fāmī*, *unigmetes* §§ 18.8, 19.1.

[3] Cf. O. Jespersen, *Growth and Structure of the English Language*, 2d ed., 1912, § 53; see also H. Collitz, " The Home of the Heliand," *Publ. MLAss.* xvi 123 ff.

[4] Cf. T.C. §§ 1, 3.

[5] Thus, *gifan, gyfan, giofan; lifað, lyfað, leofað; giest, gist, gyst, gæst, gest; dēore, dīore, dȳre; sweord, swurd, swyrd; Eafores, Eofores, Iofore; ealdor, aldor; eahtian, æhtian, ehtian; dryhten, drihten;* etc.

[6] See below, ' Manuscript,' and Chapter viii (' Date ').

different individual peculiarities[1] had a share in that work.[2] Although the exact history of the various linguistic and orthographic strata cannot be recovered, the principal landmarks are still plainly discernible.

The origin of the poem on Anglian soil[3] to be postulated on general principles is confirmed by groups of Anglian forms and certain cases of faulty substitution (e.g., *næfre*, *hwæðre*, *fæder* § 7.1, *-beran* § 8.5, *þeod* (i.c. *deoð*) § 16.2),[4] to which some syntactical and lexical features are to be added (§§ 25.7, 26). See also below, pp. xc f. A decision in favor of either Northumbria or Mercia as the original home cannot be made on the basis of the language.[5]

Before receiving its broad, general LWS. complexion, the MS. — at any rate, part of it — passed through EWS. and Kentish hands.[5a] See especially §§ 1, 8 n. 2, 10.1 a & 6, 14.2 & 3, 17, 19.1. That these dialectal elements were superimposed on a stratum of a different type is suggested by a blunder like *siex-* 2904 (cf. §§ 1, 8.3) and a mechanical application of an *io* spelling in *Hondscio* 2076 (cf. § 17 n.). On the other hand, the scribal mistake *mid* of l. 976 (cf. § 1) would not be unnatural in a copyist unfamiliar with EWS. spelling traditions. It is worthy of note that these dialectal contributions have been almost completely obliterated in the first part of the MS.

The final copy which has been preserved is the work of two scribes, the second hand beginning at *mōste*, 1939. As the first of these scribes

---

[1] Striking illustrations of passing scribal moods are the occurrence of the spelling $ig = ī$ with any degree of frequency in a definitely limited portion only, see § 5 n. 1 (cp. the spasmodic appearance of *Hygelāc*, Gloss. of Proper Names); the solitary instances of *seoððan* in ll. 1775, 1875, 1937; the irregular use of the *a* and *o* spellings (exclusive of *þone*, etc.) before nasals which show the following ratios: ll. 1–927, 2: 1, ll. 928–1340, 8: 1, ll. 1341–1944, 7: 6, ll. 1945–2199, 31: 32, ll. 2200–3182, 4: 7 (Möller, *ESt*. xiii 258); the varying frequency of the preposition *in* (as over against *on*), which appears in ll. 1–185: 10x, in ll. 1300–2000: 5x, in ll. 2458–3182: 10x. — H. M. and N. K. Chadwick (L 4.22.2.503) recognize in the different linguistic strata " the different standard school languages which successively obtained currency."

[2] As contributing causes of the mixture of forms may be mentioned the occasional fluctuation between traditional and phonetic spelling, the pronounced Anglo-Saxon delight in variation (note, e.g., 2912: *Frȳsum*, 2915: *Frēsna*, 3032: *wundur*, 3037: *wundor*), and the mingling of dialects in monastic communities (cf. Stubbs, *Constitutional History of England*[6] i 243; W. F. Bryan, *Studies in the Dialects of the Kentish Charters* etc., pp. 34 f.).

[3] Cf. Siev. A. M. §§ 74 ff.

[4] It has been plausibly suggested that a form *gefǣgon* (so 1014) indicates a WS. remodeling of Angl. *gefēgon* (1627), since *gefǣgon* seems to be unknown in pure WS. texts; see Deutschbein, *Beitr*. xxvi 194. The same may be true of *sǣgon* 1422, cf. § 23.3.

[5] The strongest evidence supporting Mercia is the *u-*, *o/a-*umlaut of *a*, § 12.1. — It would be possible to argue for the existence of an original Northumbr. stretch from 986–1320; cf. *-sporu* 986, *gesacan* 1004 (orig. *ǣ*), *-āgande* 1013, *brand* 1020 MS., *walu* 1031, *fēla* 1032, *sēðan* 1106 (originally *sǣðan* — *seoð(ð)an* — *syððan* ?), *sprǣc* 1171, *sē* 1260 (?), *þēod* 1278 MS., *-laðu* 1320 (?). But most of the material is problematical.

[5a] Sievers L 8.13 e. 81 thought he could trace a Kentish recension of the Northumbrian text. On his modified views of ' Anglian,' cf. Förster, *Chapters on the Exeter Book*, 1933, p. 69.

(A, 1–1939) copied also the three preceding prose pieces, viz. a short *Christophorus* fragment,[1] *Wonders of the East*,[2] and *Letter of Alexander*,[3] and the second one (B, 1939–3182) copied the poem of *Judith* also, some inferences relating to their treatment of the *Beowulf* MS. and the condition in which they found it may be ventured. The most obvious difference between the language of A and of B is the multitude of *io*, *īo* spellings in the B part, a number of which, at least, may be assigned to the Kentish layer of the MS.,[4] in contrast with the almost total absence of such forms in the A part. As no *ĭo* forms at all are contained in the MS. of *Judith*, it has been reasonably argued (by ten Brink) that scribe B did not introduce those spellings into the *Beowulf*, but found them in his original, adhering to his text more faithfully than scribe A.[5] Some other features could likewise be interpreted as signs of conservatism on the part of the second copyist.

Thus we find, B: (-)*wælm*, (-)*wylm*, A: (-)*wylm*; B: *eldo*, *elde* (only 2117: *yldum*), A: *yldo*, *ylde*. (Cf. §§ 7.2, 8.2, 2.3.)

B: -*derne*, (-)*dyrne*, A: (-)*dyrne*; B: *mercels*, A: -*gemyrcu*; B: -*serce*, A: (-)*syrce*. (Cf. §§ 8.2, 2.3.)

B: *eatol*, *atol*, A: *atol* (*Jud.*: *atol*); B: (-)*heafola*, A: *hafela*. (Cf. § 12.1.)

B: *hafu*, *hafo*, A: *hæbbe* (§ 23.5); B: *gesēgon*, A: *sǣgon*, *gesāwon* (§§ 10.1, 23.3).

B: *lēg*(-), *līg*(-), A: *līg*. (Cf. § 10.2.)

B: *Wedra* (only (2186,) 2336: *Wedera*), A: *Wedera*. (Cf. § 18.10 n.)

B: *wundur*(-), *wundor*-, A: *wundor*(-), *wunder*(-); B: *wuldur*-, A: *wuldor*(-) (*Jud.*: *wuldor*); B: *sāwul*-, *sāwol*, A: *sāwol*-, *sāwl*-; B: *sundur*, A: *sundor*-. (Cf. Siev. §§ 139 f.; Bülb. § 364.)[6]

A preference for the spelling *y* in B, and for later *i* in A is shown in certain groups of words, thus B: *dryhten* (only 2186: *i*), A: *drihten*, *dryhten*; B: *dryht*, A: *driht*, *dryht*; B: *hycgan*, A: *hicgan*; B: *hyge*, *hige*, A: *hige*, rarely *hyge*; B: *Hygelāc*, *Higelāc*, A: *Higelāc* (nearly always); B: *þyncan*, A: *þincan*; see § 4. It is true that the spelling *y* is favored

[1] *Christophorus* fragment (ff. 94ᵃ–98ᵇ); ed. by G. Herzfeld, *ESt.* xiii 142–45.

[2] *De Rebus in Oriente Mirabilibus* (ff. 98ᵇ–106ᵇ); a modern edition by F. Knappe, Greifswald Diss., 1906.

[3] *Epistola Alexandri ad Aristotelem* (ff. 107ᵃ–131ᵇ); an easily accessible edition by W. M. Baskervill, *Angl.* iv 139–67. An edition of the three prose texts by Rypins, L 1.9.4. See also Förster L 1.8.76 ff. The identity of the handwriting of *Beowulf* A and the *Epistola Alexandri* was recognized by Sedgefield (Edition, 1910, p. 2, n.). That the same scribe wrote also the two other prose texts was pointed out by Sisam, *MLR.* xi 335 ff. Cf. Förster, *l.c.* 34 f.

[4] For details see §§ 14, 16.1, 17. In 'B' there occur 115 *io*, *ĭo*(*iŏ*) spellings, in 'A' only 11, viz. *scionon* 303, *hīo* 455, 623, 1929, *gewiofu* 697 (*u*-umlaut of *i* before labial), -*sīon* 995, *friođu*- 1096, *hiora* 1166, *giogođ* (*iogoþ*) 1190, 1674, *nīowan* 1789. All of these could be called WS. in the broader sense (including 'patois'); for *scionon*, *friođu*- (§ 14.1), see Bülb. § 235 n. — The frequent *ĭo* spellings in 'B') of the name *Bīowulf* are especially noteworthy.

[5] Cf. L 6.2 (ten Brink), L 6.3 (Davidson, Mc Clumpha). [Rypins L 1.9.2 combats ten Brink's view; he holds that scribe A was the more 'careful' copyist.]

[6] The same archaic *u* in posttonic syllable appears in A: *eodur* 663, *Heorute* 766; so 782, cf. 1075.

LANGUAGE. MANUSCRIPT

by B also in certain words in which *i* represents the earlier sound; thus B: *syðð an*, A: *syðð an*, *siðð an*, B: *hyt*, *hit*, A: *hit*, B: *hyne* (*hine*), A: *hine* (*hyne*), B: *is*, *ys*, A: *is*, B: *wylle*, A: *wille* (*y* 3x); cf. also B: *syllan*, A: *sellan*, B: *sylf*, A: *self* (only 505: *y*); see § 2.[1]

In A only do we find the remarkable gen. plur. forms in *-o* (§ 18.3), forms like *fāmī* (§ 19.1), *mænigo* (§ 7 n.1), *ēowan*, *ēawan* (cf. § 3.2), *hworfan*, *worc* (§ 8.6), *hreþe* (§ 8.1), *gefǣgon* (cf. p. lxxxix, n. 4).

That a number of these distinctive spellings of A were actually introduced by that particular scribe is made probable by a noteworthy agreement in various orthographic details between A and the three prose texts which precede the *Beowulf*. Thus we find *yldo*, *Ep.Al*. 419, 726; *līgit*, *ib*. 153, *līg*, *Christoph*. 14, 17; *self* 9x[2] in *Ep.Al*. (*y* 2x, *eo* 4x); *þurstī*, *ib*. 169, cf. 66, 102, 158, 246; *-wlitī*, *De Reb*. ch. 29, *nǣnīne*, *ib*. ch. 24; gen. plur. *-fato*, *Ep.Al*. 122, 295, *earfeðo* 332, *Mēdo* 400, *ondswaro* 423, etc.,[3] *hyro*, *De Reb*. ch. 3; *mænigo*, *Ep.Al*. 115, 195, 196, 204, 492, 516 (624), *De Reb*. chs. 1, 11, *Christoph*. 20, 29; *-ēawest*, *Ep.Al*. 51, *-ēowde*, etc. 28, 217, 363, 367, 451; *hworfeð*, *ib*. 164, 743, *geworc*, *Christoph*. 97; *hreðnisse*, *Ep.Al*. 70, *hredlīce*, *De Reb*. ch. 10; *fǣgon*, *Ep.Al*. 751.[4]

That also the second scribe of our *Beowulf* MS., in some respects, asserted his independence, we are fain to believe on account of some orthographic parallelisms between B and *Judith*, such as the uniform spellings *hyne*, *ys*, *sylf* in *Jud*.; *ȳwan*, *Jud*. 174 (*ēo* 240; see § 3.2); *dȳre*, *Jud*. 300, 319, and 4x in B (*ēo* 2x, *īo* 1x; A: *ēo* 5x; see §§ 16.1, 3.3); the regular use of *ymbe*, prepos., in *Jud*. (47, 268), B: *ymbe*(-) 7x (*ymb* 3x, A: *ymb;* cf. T.C. § 13); the form *swyrd*, preferred in *Jud*. (6x), and occurring 3x in the latter part of B's work (never *swurd* as 3x in A); the representation of *æ* by *e*, *Jud*. 150, and 4x in B (see note on 1981). Even the exclusive use of *ðām* (*þām*) in *Jud*. and the marked preference for *þǣm* (*ðǣm*) in *Ep.Al*. are plainly matched by the distribution of those forms in B and A respectively, see Glossary.

Syntax

§ 25.

Turning to the field of syntax,[5] we may briefly mention some features calling for the attention of students.

---

[1] By the side of *fyrwyt* A: 232 is found *fyrwet* B: 1985, 2784, cf. the analogous weakening to *e* in *Hæðcen* 2925, see § 18.7. It may be noted that A has *gedīgan*, B *gedīgan*, *gedȳgan* (§ 3.2).

[2] Cf. A. Braun, *Lautlehre der ags. Version der Epistola Alexandri ad Aristotelem*. Würzburg Diss., 1911.

[3] A strong preference for the vowel *o* in endings appears in this text.

[4] Of minor importance is the use in *Ep.Al*. of *gesāwon* 25, 229, etc.; *gemindig* 7; *gedīgde* 371; *wiscte and wolde* 40 (*wiston*, *Beow*. 1604); *hǣfdo* 315 (= *hēafdu*, cf. § 9.1), which may be a scribal blunder, being preceded and followed by *hæfdon;* *þēoh*, *ib*. 15 (cf. § 16.2); *eorre*, *ib*. 550 (cf. § 13.3); *fixas*, *ib*. 377 (though *-fiscas* 510), *Beow*. 540, 549 *-fixas* (LWS., cf. Siev. § 204.3, Bülb. § 520; Weyhe, *ESt*. xxxix 161 ff.).

[5] L 6.7 ff.

INTRODUCTION

1. The use of the singular of concrete nouns in a collective sense (see note on 794). The singular meaning of the plural of nouns such as *burh, geard, eard, wīc; rodor, heofon; bānhūs; folc; searo; list, lust, ēst, snyttru, geþyld* (semi-adverbial function of dat. plur., cp. *on sǣlum*); *cyme; oferhygd;* the use of the plural of abstract nouns with concomitant concretion of meaning, e.g. *hrōðor, liss, willa*.[1]

2. The absolute (substantival) use of adjectives in their strong inflexion, e.g. *gomele ymb gōdne ongeador sprǣcon* 1595.[2] The employment of the (more concrete) adjective in cases where our modern linguistic feeling inclines toward the (abstract) adverb, as *hādor* 497; 2553; 130, 3031; 626, 1290, 1566; 897; etc. The appearance of the comparative in a context where, according to our ideas, no real comparison takes place, e.g. *betera* 1703, *sēlran* 1839, *lēofre* 2651, *syllīcran* 3038.[3]

3. Of great interest, as a presumable archaism, is the frequency of the weak adjective when not preceded by the definite article, e.g. *gomela Scilding, hēapostēapa helm, widan rīces, ofer ealde riht*,[4] some 75 instances (apart from vocatives) being found, including however the doubtful instrumental (dative) forms like *dēoran (sweorde), heardan (clammum)*.[5] The comparative paucity of definite articles together with the more or less demonstrative force of (the attributive) *sē̆, sēo, þæt* recognizable in many places have likewise been considered a highly characteristic feature and have received much attention from investigators.[6] However, the value of the relative frequency of the article use (and the use of the weak adjective) in Old English poems as a criterion of chronology is greatly impaired by the fact that the scribes could easily tamper with their originals by inserting articles in conformity with later or prose use, not to mention the possibility of archaizing tendencies.[7]

4. Omission of the personal pronoun both as subject[8] and object[9] is

---

[1] *MPh.* iii 263 ff.; *Arch.* cxxvi 354.

[2] The substantival function cannot always be distinguished from the adjectival (appositive) one, e.g. *wīges heard* 886 is either 'he, being brave in battle' or 'the brave one.'

[3] Cf. *MPh.* iii 251 f. It may happen that the missing member of the comparison is easily supplied: *ðā wæs swigra secg* 980 ('more reticent,' sc. 'than before').

[4] The type of the order *hrefn blaca* is found in 1177, 1243, 1343, 1435, 1553, 1801, 1847, 1919, 2474; cp. 412. (The type *se maga geonga*: 2675, 3028.)

[5] *dēoran* might be a weakened form of the normal strong dat. sing. in *-um*, *heardan* might stand for the weak or strong dat. plur. Besides, the desire to avoid suffix rime may have to be taken into account, cf. Sarrazin, *ESt.* xxxviii 147.

[6] See L 6.7 (especially Lichtenheld, Barnouw).

[7] See L 5.48.2; Tupper's edition of the *Riddles*, p. lxxviii. Similarly inconclusive as chronological tests are the use of the preposition *mid* (in place of the instrumental case) and the construction of impersonal verbs with the formal subject *hit*. In both respects *Beowulf* would seem to occupy an intermediate position between the so-called Cædmonian and the Cynewulfian poetry. Cf. Sarrazin Käd. 5.

[8] Cf. A. Pogatscher, "Unausgedrücktes Subjekt im Altenglischen," *Angl.* xxiii 261-301. See 68, 286, 300, 470, 567, 1367, 1487, 1923, 1967, 2344, 2520, 3018.

[9] Cf. *MPh.* iii 253. See 24, 31, 48 f., 93, 387, 748, 1487, 1808, 2940.

LANGUAGE. MANUSCRIPT

abundantly exemplified in our poem; also the indefinite pronoun *man* is left unexpressed, 1365 (cp. 1290 f., 2547). That the possessive pronoun is dispensed with in many places where a modern English translation would use it, and that the personal pronoun in the dative may be found instead,[1] need hardly be mentioned.

5. The peculiar use of such adverbs of place as *hider, þonan, nēan, feor, ufan, sūþan*[2] and of certain prepositions, like *ofer, under*, and *on* with acc., *tō, of* furnishes numerous instructive instances of the characteristic fact that in the old Germanic languages the vivid idea of 'motion' (considered literally or figuratively) was predominant in many verbs[3] which are now more commonly felt to be verbs of 'rest.'[4] Sometimes, it should be added, motion was conceived in a different direction from the ordinary modern use,[5] and sometimes, contrary to our expectations, the idea of rest rather than motion determined the use (or regimen) of the preposition (see *æt, on* with dat.). The still fairly well preserved distinction of the 'durative' and 'perfective' (including 'ingressive' and 'resultative') function of verbs,[6] the concretion of meaning attending verbs denoting a state, or disposition, of mind,[7] and the unusual, apparently archaic regimen of some verbs[8] are further notable points which will come under the observation of students.

6. Lack of concord as shown in the interchange of cases,[9] the coupling of a singular verb with a plural subject,[10] the violation, or free handling, of the *consecutio temporum*[11] should cause no surprise or suspicion.

---

[1] E.g., in 40, 47, 49, 726, 755, 816, 1242, 1446. In the same way, of course, the dat. of a noun instead of a MnE. gen., as in 2044, 2122 f.

[2] Thus, in 394, 2408, 528, 1701, 1805, 330, 606.

[3] Including, e.g., such as *(ge)sēon, scēawian, (ge)hȳran, gefrignan, gefricgan, bīdan, sēcan, wilnian, wēnan, gelȳfan, gemunan, sprecan, scīnan, standan.*

[4] Cf. L 6.10 (Sievers, Dening); *MPh.* iii 255 ff. See those prepositions in the Glossary. Note the contrast between *æt-* and *tō-somne, -gæd(e)re.*

[5] See some examples under *tō.*

[6] E.g., *sittan, gesittan; standan, gestandan; feallan, gefeallan; gān, gegān; bīdan, gebīdan.* Cf. L 6.17; *MPh.* iii 262 f.

[7] E.g., *hatian* ('show one's hatred by deeds,' 'persecute'), *lufian, unnan, eahtian.* Cf. *MPh.* iii 260 f.

[8] Thus, the dative after *forniman, forgrindan, forswerian, forgrīpan* (so [*forgrīpan*] also Gen. 1275); cf. Grimm, *Deutsche Grammatik* iv², 812 ff. (684 ff.), 836 (700 f.); H. Winkler, *German. Casussyntax*, pp. 363 ff. The instrumental function of the genitive in connection with verbs: 845, 1439, 2206; 1825, 2035(??), 2791.

[9] Thus, *wið* with acc. and dat.: 424 ff., 1977 f.; an apposition in the acc. case following a noun in the dat., 1830 f.

[10] With the verb preceding, 1408; with the verb following, 904 f. (see note), and (in a dependent clause) 2163 f.

[11] Transition from preterite to present in dependent clauses: 1313 f., 1921 ff., 1925 ff., 2484 ff., 2493 ff., 2717 ff.

xciv   INTRODUCTION

7. The construction of *mid* with accus.[1] and the use of *in* (= WS. *on*)[2] are considered Anglianisms. — Both as a dialectal and a chronological test the mode of expressing negation has been carefully studied with the gratifying result of establishing *Beowulf* as an Anglian poem of about 725 A.D.[3]

8. In the matter of word-order the outstanding feature is the predominance, according to ancient Germanic rule, of the end-position of the verb both in dependent and, in a somewhat less degree, independent clauses, as exemplified in the very first lines of the poem. The opposite order: verb — subject is not infrequently found to mark a distinct advance in the narrative[4] (the more restful normal order being more properly adapted to description or presentation of situations and minor narrative links[5]) or to intimate in a vague, general way a connection of the sentence with the preceding one, such as might be expressed more definitely by ' and,' (negatively) ' nor,' ' so,' ' indeed,' ' for,' ' however.'[6] Besides, any part of the sentence may appear in the emphatic head-position, whereby the author is enabled to give effective syntactical prominence to the most important elements, as shown, e.g., in 1323: *dēad is Æschere*, 548: *hrēo wǣron ȳþa*, 769: *yrre wǣron bēgen*, 994 f.: *goldfāg scinon/web æfter wāgum*, 343: *Bēowulf is mīn nama*, 2583 f.: *hrēðsigora ne gealp/goldwine Gēata*, 1237 f.: *reced weardode/unrīm eorla*, 2582 f.: *wīde sprungon/hildelēoman*, 287 f.: *ǣghwæþres sceal/scearp scyldwiga gescād witan*. For a detailed study of this subject cf. Ries, L. 6.12.2. — See also notes on 122 f., 180 f., 575 f., 786 ff.

9. Traces of Latin influence are perhaps to be recognized in the use of certain appositive participles (thus in 815, 916, 1368, 1370, 1913, 2350) and, likewise, in the predilection for passive construction (in cases like 642 f., 1629 f., 1787 f., 1896 f., 3021 f., cf. above, p. lxvi, n. 2).[7] The use of the plur. form of the neuter, *ealra* 1727, is no doubt a Latinism, cf. *Angl.* xxxv 118. See also notes on 159, 991 f., 1838 f.; *Arch.* cxxvi 355 f.

VOCABULARY

§ 26.

The vocabulary of *Beowulf*, apart from the aspect of poetic diction,

[1] Cf. Napier, *Angl.* x 138 f.; Miller's edition of *Bede*, i, pp. xlv ff.

[2] Cf. Napier, *Angl.* x 139; Miller's edition of *Bede*, i, pp. xxxiii ff.; Gloss.: *in*. To state the case accurately, in the South *in* was early supplanted by *on*. (Erroneous substitution of *in* for *on:* 1029 (cp. 1052, etc.), 1952.)

[3] Cf. L 6.14.3.

[4] See, e.g., 217 f., 399, 620, 640 f., 675 f., 1125, 1397, 1506, 1518, 1870, 1903.

[5] Ll. 320 ff., 1898[b], 1906[b], 1992 ff., 2014 may serve as illustrations. Highly instructive is the interchange of the two orders, as in 399 ff., 688 ff., 702 ff., 1020 ff., 1600 ff., 1963 ff.

[6] Thus in 83[b], 109, 134, 191[b], 271[b] f., 411, 487[b] f., 609[b] f., 828[b] f., 969[b] f., 1010, 1620, 1791, 2461[b], 2555, 2975.

[7] H. M. and N. K. Chadwick (L 4.22.2.557 n.) issue a warning against such assumptions; they point to similar ON. usage.

LANGUAGE. MANUSCRIPT

invites attention as a possible means of determining the dialectal quality of the text. It must be confessed that extreme caution is necessary in speaking of Anglian elements in the vocabulary, since the testimony of prose texts of a *later* date is of only limited value. But the following words can with reasonable safety be claimed as belonging primarily to the Anglian area:[1] *gēn, gēna* (WS. *gīet(a)*), *nefne, nemne, nymþe*[2] (WS. *būtan*), *ac* used as interrogative particle,[3] the preposition *in* (see § 25.7), *bront, semninga*,[4] *worn, gnēaþ, rēc, bebycgan*,[5] *tēo(ga)n*,[6] and possibly *morðor* (WS. *morð*).[7] Typical examples of words which are absent, more or less, from the later WS., are *gefēon* (WS. *fægnian*), *tīd* ('time,' disappearing before *tīma*), *snyttru* (cp. *wīsdōm*), *bearn* (cp. *cild*).

MANUSCRIPT

The only existing manuscript of *Beowulf* is contained in a volume of the Cottonian collection in the British Museum which is known as Vitellius A. xv.[8] That volume consists of two originally separate codices[9] which were arbitrarily joined by the binder (early in the 17th century), and it holds nine different Old English texts, four of them belonging to the first part,[10] and five to the second. *Beowulf* (folios 129ᵃ–198ᵇ, or, according to the foliation of 1884, 132ᵃ–201ᵇ)[11] is the fourth number of the second codex, being preceded by three prose pieces and followed by the poem of *Judith.* (See above, p. xc.) We do not know where Sir Robert Bruce Cotton (1571–1631), to whose zealous efforts we are indebted for the precious collection of Cottonian manuscripts, obtained that codex.[12] But the name 'Laurence Nouell' (with date 1563) written

---

[1] See especially Jordan, L 6.20.

[2] Occurring, it is true, also *Ep.Al.* 566.

[3] Cf. Napier, *Angl.* x 138; also Sarrazin Käd. 69 f.

[4] Also, e.g., *Ep.Al.* 221, 347, 474, 489; *Wulfst.* 262.7.

[5] At least in the sense of 'sell,'— provided *unbeboht*, *Oros.* 18.10 is rightly rendered by unbought.'

[6] Also *Ep.Al.* 729.

[7] According to Wildhagen, St. EPh. xiii 184 ff., *-scua* (see l. 160), *winnan, gewin(n)* (?), and according to Scherer, *Zur Geographie und Chronologie des ags. Wortschatzes* (Berlin Diss., 1928), *līxan* and *unlīfigende* could be added.

[8] A dozen book-cases in the original library happened to be surmounted by busts of Roman emperors; hence the catalog designations of Vitellius, Tiberius, Nero, etc.

[9] Cf. K. Sisam's valuable observations, *MLR.* xi 335–37.

[10] The first codex contains the Alfredian version of St. Augustine's *Soliloquies*, the *Gospel of Nicodemus*, the prose *Dialogue of Solomon and Saturn*, and an extremely brief Fragment of a *Passio Quintini.* A short sixteenth century text (of one leaf) which had been stitched on to the codex, figures as no. 1 in Wanley's description.

[11] A former, temporary misplacing of some leaves is brought out by the fact that f. 131 (old style numbering) stands between 146 and 147, and f. 197 stands between 188 and 189. On different systems of numbering used and proposed, see esp. Hoops L 1.11.

[12] On the early history of the Cottonian collection and on Wanley's 'discovery' of the *Beowulf* MS., see Huyshe L 3.8, pp. lx ff.; Förster L 1.8.58 ff.

at the top of its first page justifies the belief[1] that Nowell, dean of Lichfield and one of the very earliest students of Anglo-Saxon (d. 1576), had something to do with its preservation in those years following the dissolution of monasteries which witnessed the wanton destruction of untold literary treasures. The date of the *Beowulf* codex is about the end of the tenth century, as is judged from the character of the handwriting exhibited by its two scribes. Thus it is not far removed in time from the three other great collections containing Old English poems, viz. the Exeter Book, the Vercelli Codex, and the so-called Cædmon Manuscript.

While the Cottonian library was lodged in Ashburnham House, in Little Deans Yard, Westminster, the manuscript, like numerous other volumes of the collection, was injured by a disastrous fire (in 1731) causing the scorching of margins and edges and their subsequent gradual crumbling away in many places. In Zupitza's words (1882), " the manuscript did not suffer so much from the fire of 1731 itself as from its consequences, which would, without doubt, have been avoided if the MS. had been at once rebound as carefully as it has been rebound in our days. . . . Further losses have been put a stop to by the new binding; but, admirably as this was done, the binder could not help covering some letters or portions of letters in every back page with the edge of the [transparent] paper which now surrounds every parchment leaf."[2] The great value of the two Thorkelin transcripts in supplying readings which in the meantime have been lost will become apparent to everyone that turns over the leaves of the excellent, annotated facsimile edition.

Of the one hundred and forty pages of the MS., seventy-nine (ff. 129^b–162^b, 171^a–174^a, 176^b–178^b) contain 20 lines each (including the line for the Roman numeral), forty-four (ff. 174^b–176^a, 179^a–198^b) 21 lines, sixteen (ff. 163^a–170^b) 22 lines, and the first page (f. 129^a) has 19 lines, the first of which is written in large capitals. In accordance with the regular practice of the period, the Old English text is written continuously like prose. There are on an average slightly less than 23 alliterative verses to the page; towards the end where the scribe endeavored to economize space, the percentage is highest.

Of the general mode of writing and of the difference between the two hands the facsimile pages included in this edition (f. 160^a = ll. 1352–77, f. 184^a = ll. 2428–50) will give a fairly good idea.[3] Attention is called to some details. Two forms of *y* (both punctuated) are used, as seen, e.g., in l. 7 of f. 184^a, — the second one being much rarer than the first,

---

[1] Cf. K. Sisam, *l.c.;* Förster, *l.c.* 56 f.; Flower, *Chapters on the Exeter Book* 91 f.

[2] *Autotypes* (L 1.5), p. vi.

[3] On Ags. paleography, see W. Keller, *Angelsächs. Palaeographie* (Palaestra xliii), 1906, and *R.-L.* i 98–103. On the preparation of parchment and ink, etc., see the quotations in Tupper's *Riddles*, pp. 126 ff.

LANGUAGE. MANUSCRIPT

and very seldom found in A. The three forms of *s* used in B appear, e.g., on f. 184ᵃ, l. 11, viz. the high *s* (long above the line), the low 'insular' *s* (long below the line), and the round, uncial *s*. In A the second of these varieties is completely lacking, and the third is rather sparingly used, — mostly in initial position, and (almost regularly) as a capital. A few times the high *s* is combined with a following *t* to a ligature, viz. in l. 168: *moste*, l. 646: *wiste*, l. 661: *gedigest* (?), l. 672: *hyrsted*, l. 673: *cyst*, l. 1096: *hengeste*, l. 1211: *breost*. The difference in the shape of *g* seen in the A and B specimens respectively applies, with absolute consistency, to the entire MS.

The letter *k* appears five times in *kyning*, ll. 619, 665, 2144, 2335, 3171. The runic character .ᛟ., for *ēþel*, is found three times, ll. 520, 913, 1702.[1]

Regarding the distribution of *þ* and *ð*,[2] B is decidedly averse to the use of *þ* in non-initial position, spelling a medial *þ* only in rare (about a dozen) instances, and a final *þ* only once (l. 2293), whereas initially both *þ* and *ð* are found. Scribe A makes a more liberal use of *þ* in initial and also — obviously — in medial position, avoiding it, however, generally at the end of words. (Two instances of final *þ* may be seen in the last but one line of folio 160ᵃ.) As a capital the more ornamental Ð is written. Only in ll. 642, 1896 there appears a somewhat larger *þ*, which may have been intended as a capital letter. A real large þ is used at the beginning of fit xlii.

That scribe B was, on the whole, following the traditions of a somewhat older school of penmanship is proved especially by his frequent use of the high *e*, e.g., before *n*, *m*, *r*, *t*, *o*, *a*, and by the shape of his *a*.

Small capital letters are found in a number of instances after periods,[3] and large ones appear regularly at the opening of the cantos. Twenty-one times the first letter only of the canto is capitalized, sixteen times[4] the first two letters (eight times: ÐA), once each the first syllable of *Hun-ferð* (viii) and *Beo-wulf* (xxiv),[5] twice the full name of *Beowulf* (xxi, xxii), once (xxvii) *cwom*, and the entire first line of the MS. is written in large capitals. But illuminated letters are completely lacking.

---

[1] Thus, *Wald.* i 31; *Oros.* 168. 11.

[2] The difference in this respect between the two parts of the MS. is paralleled, in a general way, by the distribution of *þ* and *ð* in *Epistola Alexandri* and *Judith* respectively. (In the MS. of *Judith* the *þ* is confined entirely to the initial position.) — In the Glossary to the present edition the variations in the employment of *þ* and *ð* could not be registered. The spelling used in the first form cited or the one used in the majority of forms has been selected for the headword.

[3] It is a question whether there is — or was — a period mark before the capital *O* in l. 1518 (*On-*) and before the capital *H* in l. 1550 (*Hæfde*).

[4] I.E., if the opening of canto xxxvi is included; however, the *g* of *Wiglaf*, though of the ordinary shape, is considerably enlarged.

[5] The large capital of *u* appears regularly in the *V*-shaped form; the small capital in l. 3101 (*Uton*) is somewhat different.

The commonest abbreviations of the MS. are 1) ⁊ = *ond*, uniformly used with the exception of ll. 600, 1148, 2040; also in ⁊ *sware* 354, 1493, 1840, 2860, ⁊ *swarode* 258, ⁊ *hwearf* 548, ⁊ *sacan* 786, 1682, ⁊ *langne* 2115 (see Gloss.: *and-*). 2) þ = *þæt*, exceedingly frequent, the full spellings *þæt*, *ðæt* forming a very small minority. 3) *þōn* (i.e., a stroke above the line, coming between *o* and *n*) = *þonne*, — frequent in both parts of the MS. (*ðōn* also in A).[1] 4) The sign for *m*, consisting of a line drawn over the preceding vowel. It is exceedingly common in the dat. ending *-um*, but is frequent also in *þā*, *ðā*, *hī*, i.e., *þām*, *ðām*, *him* (at least, in B). Other instances: *frā* 581, 2366, 2565, *frō* 2556, *hā* 374, 717, 2992, *gū* (*cystum*) 1486, 1723, 2469, 2543, 2765; *maðþū* 1023, 2055, 2193, 2405, 2750, 2757, 3016, *gegnū* 1404; *beaȓ* 896 (the only example of *m* abbreviated after a consonant); further (in B): *sū* 2279, 2301, 2401, 3123 f., *sū ne* 3061, *rū* 2461, *hī rū* 2690, *fultū* 2662, *frū gare* 2856, *glūpe* 2637, *grī* 2860, 3012, 3085, *brī* 2930, *for nā* 2772, *streā* 2545, *cwō* 2073, *dō* 2890, *wō mū* 3073, *-sōne* 3122, *ȳb*(*e*) 3169, 3172.

This abbreviation is never used for *n* in our MS.[2]

In B, which is much more partial to abbreviations than A, the following additional contractions occur.[3] *ḡ* = *ge*, as prefix: 2570, 2637, 2726, 3146, 3165, 3166, 3174, 3179, besides in *herge* 3175, *freoge* 3176;[4] — *m̄* = *men* in 3162: *men*, 3165: *men* and *genumen* (*ḡ num̄*); — *æft* = *æfter*, 2060, 2176, 2531, 2753; *of* = *ofer*, 3132, 3145; — *dryh* = *dryhten*, 3175.

The numerals are nearly always spelt out; only in ll. 147, 1867, 2401; 207; 379, 2361 the signs of the Roman numerals .XII., .XV., .XXX. respectively are substituted.

There are comparatively few instances of the mark of vowel length, the so-called apex of Latin inscriptions,[5] consisting of a "heavy dot, with a stroke sloping from it over the vowel."[6] Those who have examined the MS. itself are not agreed on the exact number, since the sloping line has frequently faded, but the following 126 cases, which are recognized both by Zupitza and Chambers, may be regarded as

[1] Strangely, the form *ðonne* (with initial *ð*) never occurs in B.

[2] It has been suggested, as a possibility, that in an earlier copy the same abbreviation for *n* occurred. This hypothesis would serve to explain the accidental omission of *n* in several places — thus in ll. 60, 255, 418, 591, 673 (see note), 1176, 1510, 1883, 2307, 2545, 2996, 3155, — and also the erroneous spelling *hrusam* 2279 (owing to a misinterpretation of the contraction). Cf. Schröer, *Angl.* xiii 344 n.; Sievers, *ib.* xiv 142 f. [strongly dissenting]; Chambers, p. xix; Hoops 16.

[3] On the last, very crowded leaf such economic devices are naturally much in evidence.

[4] On the facsimile page of *Judith* shown in Cook's edition (Belles-Lettres Series) no less than five examples of *ḡ* = *ge* may be seen.

[5] Cf. W. Keller, "Über die Akzente in den ags. Handschriften," *Prager Deutsche Studien* viii (1908), 97–120.

[6] Chambers, p. xxxviii. According to Sweet, *History of English Sounds* (1888), § 377, the accent was "generally finished off with a tag," and "there can be no doubt that it was written upwards" [from left to right].

LANGUAGE. MANUSCRIPT

practically certain.[1] It will be observed that only etymologically long vowels are marked, mostly in monosyllables, monosyllabic elements of full compounds, or monosyllabic verb forms compounded with prefixes. Twice the prefix ā- is provided with this 'accent' (*ábeag* 775, *áris* 1390), once the suffix *-líc* (*sarlíc* 2109), and twice the stem of an inflected adjectival form (*hárne* 2553, *fáne* 2655).

ád 3138, *ád fǽre* 3010; *án* 100, 2210 (see Varr.), 2280, *ángenga* 449; *ár* 336; *bád* 301, 1313, 2568, 2736, *gebád* 264, 2258, 3116, *ge bád* 1720, *onbád* 2302; *bán fag* 780, *bán cofan* 1445, *bán hus* 3147; *bát* 211; *fáh* 1038, *fáne* 2655; *gá* 1394, *gán* 386; *gád* 660; *gár*/[2] 1962, 2641, *hroðgár* 2155; *gársecg* 537; *hád* 1297; *hál* 300; *hám* 1407; *hár* 1307, *hárne* 2553, *un hár* 357; *hát* 386; *lác* 1863; *wig láf* 2631, 3076; *mán sceaða* 2514; *nát* 681; *here pád* 2258; *rád* 1883, *gerád* 2898; *sár* 975, 2468; *scán* 1965; *stán* 2553; *ge swác* 2584; *on swáf* 2559; *hilde swát* 2558; *ge wác* 2577; *wát* 1331; *gewát* 123, 210, *ge wát* 1274; *ábeag* 775, *áris* 1390.

ǽr 1187, 1388, 1587; *fǽr* 2230 (see Varr.); *rǽd* 1201; *sǽ*(-) 507, 544, 564, 579, 690, 895, 1149, 1223, 1882, 1896, 1924.

wælréc 2661, *wudu réc* 3144.

/*hwíl* 2002; *líc* 2080, *sarlíc* 2109; *líf* 2743, 2751; *scír hame* 1895; *síd* 2086; *wíc* 821, *wíc stede* 2607, *deaþ wíc* 1275; *wíd flogan* 2346; *wín* 1233; *wís hycgende* 2716.

cóm 2103, 2944, *becóm* 2992; *dóm* 1491, 1528, 2147, 2820, 2858, *cyne dóm* 2376; *dón* 1116, *gedón* 2090; *on fón* 911; *fór* 2308; *gód* 1562, 1870, *ǽr*(-)*gód* 2342, 2586; *mód* 1167; *mót* 442, 603; *róf* 2084, *ellen róf* 3063; *stód* 2679, 2769, *astód* 759; *brego stól* 2196; *onwóc* 2287; *wóp* 128.

brúc 1177; *brún ecg* 1546; *fús* 1966, 3025, 3119; *rún*/1325; *út fus* 33. *fýr* 2701, *fýr draca* 2689.

Full compounds are, as a general rule, written as two words; thus *þeod cyninga* 2, *meodo setla* 5, *fea sceaft* 7, *weorð myndum* 8; *ymb sittendra* 9; *healf dene* 57, *heoro gar* 61, etc. But also other words are freely divided; e.g., *ge frunon* 2, *of teah* 5, *ge scæp hwile* 26, *on woc* 56; *þæt te* 151, *wol de* 200, *wur don* 228, *fæt tum* 716, *alum þen* 733, *gefreme de* 811, *teoh hode* 951; *hea þo lafe* 460, *heoru grim me* 1847, etc. On the other hand, separate words are run together, as shown, e.g., on the specimen page of B, by *tolife, togebidanne, ongalgan, hissunu, tohroðre, nemæg;* or *swaða* 189, *þawæs* 223, *ærhe* 264, *þaselestan* 416, *awyrd* 455, *meto* 553, *forfleat* 1908–9, *arasða* 2538, *þenuða* 426, *þeheme* 2490, etc.[3] That these practices are liable to result in ambiguity and confusion, is illustrated by *nege leafnes word* 245, *mægen hreð manna* 445, *wist fylle wenne wæs* 734,

---

[1] Zupitza marks several more words with the accent; Chambers adds one case as certain, and several as probable; Sedgefield's list, differing in some points, is slightly shorter.

[2] I.e., *gar* stands at the end of the line and is thus separated from the second element of the compound.

[3] Cf. Keller, *För. Misc.* 89 ff.; M. Rademacher, *Die Worttrennung in ags. Handschriften*, Münster Diss., 1921; Förster, *Chapters on the Exeter Book* 64 f.

c   INTRODUCTION

*medo/stig ge **mæt** 924, onge byrd 1074, eallang twidig 1708, **wigge weorþad** 1783*,[1] *wind gereste 2456, mere wio ingasmilts 2921.*

Punctuation is rather sparingly used.[2] A period occurs on an average once in four or five lines, but with greatly varying degrees of frequency in different portions. It is usually placed at the end of the second half-line, occasionally at the end of the first half-line, and a few times — nearly always by sheer mistake — within the half-line (61ª, 273ª, 279ª, 423ª, 553ᵇ, 1039ª, 1159ª, 1585ᵇ, 2542ª, 2673ᵇ, 2832ᵇ, 2897ª). These marks may be said to correspond to major or minor syntactical pauses or, in a good many instances, merely to divisions of breath-groups. Twice a colon is found in the text, viz., after *hafelan* 1372ª, and after *gemunde* 2488ᵇ. After *reccan* 91ᵇ, at the end of the page, two raised periods followed by a comma occur. (Is this meant to stress a pause before a significant passage?) A colon followed by a curved dash is placed six times — in B only — at the end of a canto; once the same sign is found after the canto number (xl).

A pretty large number of corrections, mostly by the original hands, are scattered through the MS. Those which are of positive interest have been recorded among the Variants (or in Lang. § 19). On the freshening up of ff. 179 and 198ᵇ, and on the modern English gloss to l. 6ª and the Latin gloss to l. 3150ᵇ, see likewise the Variants.

Like all of the more extensive Old English poems, *Beowulf* is divided into ' cantos ' or ' chapters ' which were, in all likelihood, denoted by the term *fit(t)*.[3] They are marked by leaving space for one line vacant between sections,[4] by placing a colon with a short dash or curve at the close of a section,[5] by the use of capitals and the addition of Roman numerals at the head of a new division. Besides the unnumbered introductory canto,[6] they are forty-three in number. The numerals xxxviiii and xxviiii have been omitted, and there is no indication at all of division xxx.[7] Leaving out of account canto xxxv, which is exceptionally

---

[1] Possibly *wig ge* is to be read. " It is often very difficult, if not impossible, to decide whether the scribe intended one or more words " (Zupitza, p. vii).

[2] On metrical and syntactical pointing, see Luick, *Beibl.* xxiii 226 ff.; Förster L 1.8.83.

[3] This is to be deduced from the Latin ' Præfatio ' to the *Heliand* which states that the author — ' omne opus per vitteas distinxit, quas nos lectiones vel sententias possumus appellare ' and from the OE. *Erfurt Glossary* 1144: ... una lectio *fi*[*t*]*t*. — [Cf. *Boeth.* 68.6: *Ðā se Wīsdōm þā þās fitte āsungen hæfde.*] See Müllenhoff, *ZfdA*. xvi 141–43; Heusler, *R.-L.* i 444; Förster L 1.8.84 ff. The analogous use of *fit, fytte* in later English — e.g., in the ' Gest of Robyn Hode ' — is sufficiently known. Cf. *NED.*

[4] This is done almost always by scribe A, and once by scribe B.

[5] So six times in B.

[6] Cf. below, p. cvi, and note on 1 ff.

[7] The numeral xxx was no doubt already lacking in a previous copy; the canto probably opened at l. 2093. (Cp. ll. 2091 f. with 1554 ff.) The omission of numeral xxviiii seems to be due to scribe B. Presumably he had intended to insert it at the end of the first line of the fresh canto (as he did in the case of numeral xxxviii), but neglected to do so. The passing over of these two numbers may be connected with the confusion existing (and which seems to have

LANGUAGE. MANUSCRIPT

long,[1] the divisions vary from 112 lines (xli) to 43 lines (vii), the usual length being between 60 and 90.

Though sometimes appearing arbitrary and inappropriate, these divisions are not unnaturally to be attributed to the author himself, who may have considered his literary product incomplete without such formal marking of sections. Of course, it must be borne in mind that his conceptions of structure were different from our modern notions. He felt at liberty to pause at places where we would not, and to proceed without stop where we would think a pause indispensable. He cared more for a succession of separate pictures than for a steady progress of narration by orderly stages. Thus he interrupts, e.g., the three great combats by sectional divisions, but he plainly indicates by the character of the closing lines that he did so on purpose (ll. 788-90, 1555 f., 2600 f.). He even halts in the middle of a sentence, but the conjunction *oð þæt* which opens the ensuing sections, xxv, xxviiii, was not considered an inadequate means of introducing a new item of importance, cf. above, p. lvii. (See *Gen.* 1248.) On the other hand, the last great adventure is not separated by any pause from the events that happened fifty years before (see l. 2200). A closer inspection reveals certain general principles that guided the originator of those divisions. He likes to conclude a canto with a maxim, a general reflection, a summarizing statement, or an allusion to a turn in the events. He is apt to begin a canto with a formal speech, a resumptive paragraph,[2] or the announcement of an action, especially of the ' motion ' of individuals or groups of men.[3] Very clearly marked is the opening of cantos xxxvii and xxxviii (*Ðā ic snūde gefrægn* etc.)[4] and of xxxvi (*Wīglāf wæs hāten, Wēoxstānes sunu*).[5] Altogether there is too much method in the arrangement of ' fits ' to regard it as merely a matter of chance or caprice.[6]

It need hardly be mentioned that no title of the poem is found at the head of the MS. But since the days when Sharon Turner, J. J.

---

existed in an earlier copy) in the numbers from xxvi (perhaps from xxiiii) to xxviii which originally read xxvii (xxv) to xxviiii respectively, though they were subsequently corrected.

[1] A stop might be expected after l. 2537.

[2] Thus iii (*Swā ðā mælceare* etc.), ix, xxxi, xlii. In like manner, *Jud.* xi (l. 122), xii (l. 236); *El.* xiii, *Hel.* xxviii, xxviiii, xxxi, xlii.

[3] E.g., ii (*Gewāt ðā nēosian* etc.), x, xi, xiii, xvii, xxvii, xxviii, xxxv. On the use of *ðā* at the opening of ' fits,' see Glossary. Cf. *Hel.* x (*giwitun im thō*), xxiiii, xxv, xxvi, li, lvi.

[4] Cf. *Gen.* xxviii; *Hel.* xiii, xxxii, liiii.

[5] A typical mode of introducing a person at the beginning of a story or a section of it. It is exceedingly common in ON.; e.g. *Grettissaga*, ch. 1: *Onundr hét maðr, Hrólfssaga*, ch. 1: *Maðr hét Hálfdan*. OE. examples: *Psalm* 50 (C) 1: *Dāuid wæs hāten dīormōd hæleð, Gen.* 1082 f.; cf. *Angl.* xxv 288 f.; *För. Misc.* 19 n. (Also, e.g., Otfrid i 16.1.)

[6] H. Bradley suggested that the different sections of the *Beowulf* MS. represented the contents of the loose leaves or sheets of parchment on which the text was first written before it was transcribed into a regular codex. (L 4.21.) Cf. his supplementary investigation of other MSS., " The Numbered Sections in OE. Poetical MSS.," *Proceedings of the British Academy,* Vol. vii, 1915.

cii   INTRODUCTION

Conybeare, and N. F. S. Grundtvig first designated it as 'the Poem of Bēowulf,'[1] it has been regularly, and most appropriately, named after its great hero.

VIII. GENESIS OF THE POEM

Like nearly all of the Old English poems, like the epics of the *Chanson de Roland* and the *Nibelungenlied*, the *Beowulf* has come down to us anonymously. Nor do we find in Anglo-Saxon times any direct reference to it which would throw light on the vital questions of when, where, by whom, and under what circumstances the most important of the Anglo-Saxon literary monuments was composed. Hence, a bewildering number of hypotheses have been put forward with regard to its authorship and origin. A brief survey of the principal points at issue will be attempted in the following pages.

UNITY OF AUTHORSHIP[2]

It has been the fate of *Beowulf* to be subjected to the theory of multiple authorship, the number of its conjectural ' makers ' ranging up to six or more. At the outset, in this line of investigation, the wish was no doubt father to the thought.[3] Viewing the poem in the light of a ' folk epic ' based on long continued oral tradition, scholars labored hard to trace it back to its earliest and purest form or forms and to establish the various processes such as contamination, agglutination, interpolation, modernization by which it was gradually transformed into an epic of supposedly self-contradictory, heterogeneous elements. While Ettmüller, who first sounded this note, contented himself, at least in his translation (1840), with characterizing the *Beowulf* as a union of a number of originally separate lays and marking off in his text the lines added by clerical editors, daring dissectors like Müllenhoff, Möller, ten Brink, Boer undertook to unravel in detail the ' inner history ' of the poem, rigorously distinguishing successive stages, strata, or hands of authors and editors. With Möller this searching analysis was reinforced

---

[1] Turner in his *History of the Anglo-Saxons*, 2nd ed., 1807, Vol. ii, p. 294 speaks of ' the Ags. poem on Beowulf,' and on p. 316 of ' these poems, of Beowulf, Judith, and Cædmon.' [The 1st ed. has been out of reach.] For Conybeare's announcement of 1817, see Wülker's *Grundriss*, p. 44. ' Bjowulfs Drape,' i.e. ' Heroic, laudatory Poem of Beowulf ' — the title of Grundtvig's translation — seems to have been applied by him to the poem as early as 1808 in his *Nordens Mythologi*, cf. Wülker, pp. 251, 45. The (principal) title which Grundtvig gave to his edition, viz. ' Beowulfes Beorh,' is based on l. 2807.

[2] See L 4.130 ff.; besides, Ettmüller L 2.18, 3.19, Rönning L 4.15, ten Brink L 4.18, Heinzel's reviews: L 4.15, 4.134, 4.18; cf. Heinzel L 7.2, Schemann L 7.5, Banning L 7.10, Sonnefeld L 7.14, Haeuschkel L 7.20.

[3] Müllenhoff was decisively influenced by the criticism of the *Nibelungenlied* by K. Lachmann, who in his turn had followed in the footsteps of F. A. Wolf, the famous defender of the ' Liedertheorie ' (ballad theory) in relation to the Homeric poems.

GENESIS OF THE POEM

by the endeavor to reconstruct the primitive stanzaic form. Ten Brink emphasized the use of variants, that is, parallel versions of ancient lays which were eclectically combined for better or worse and became the basis of parts of the final epic poem. To instance some of the results arrived at, there existed, according to Müllenhoff, two short poems by different authors recounting the Grendel fight (I) and the Dragon fight (IV) respectively. To the first of these certain additions were made by two other men, namely a continuation (fight with Grendel's mother, II) and the Introduction. Then a fifth contributor (interpolator A) added the Home-Coming part (III) and interpolated parts I and II to make them harmonize with his continuation. A sixth man, the chief interpolator (B) and final editor, joined the Dragon fight (IV) to the Grendel part thus augmented (I, II, III) and also introduced numerous episodes from other legends and a great deal of moralizing and theological matter.[1] Schücking elaborated a special thesis concerning Bēowulf's Return. This middle portion, he endeavored to show, was composed and inserted as a connecting link between the expanded Grendel part (Bēowulf in Denmark) and the Dragon fight, by a man who likewise wrote the Introduction and interpolated various episodes of a historical character. Still more recently Boer thought he could recognize several authors by their peculiarity of manner,[2] e.g., the so-called ' episode poet ' who added most of the episodic material; a combiner of two versions of the Grendel part; another combiner who connected the combined Grendel part with the Dragon part, composed Bēowulf's Return and two or three episodes, remodeled the last part by substituting the Geats for the original Danes, and placed the introduction of the old Dragon poem at the head of the entire epic. Truly, an ingeniously complicated, perplexing procedure.

There is little trustworthy evidence to support positive claims of this sort.

It is true, the probability that much of his material had come to the author in metrical form, is to be conceded. But — quite apart from the question of the forms of language or dialect — we can never hope to get at the basic lays by mere excision, however ingeniously done. The Beowulfian epic style is incompatible with that of the short heroic lay, not to speak of the more primitive ballads which must be presumed to have existed in large numbers in early Anglo-Saxon times.

Contradictions, incongruities, and obscurities that have been detected in the story can, as a rule, be removed or plausibly accounted for by correct interpretation of the context[3] and proper appreciation of some

[1] Even the exact number of lines credited to each one of the six contributors was announced by Müllenhoff; thus A was held responsible for 226 lines of interpolation (32 in i, 194 in ii), B for 1169 lines (67 in the Introduction, 121 in ii, 265 in ii, 172 in iii, 544 in iv). Ettmüller in his edition (1875) pared the poem in its pre-Christian form down to 2896 lines, Möller condensed the text into 344 four-line stanzas.

[2] Similarly Berendsohn would discriminate three different strata of poetical transmission on the basis of broad, general stylistic criteria. [Note his important recent work, L 4.141.3.]

[3] See, e.g., 207 ff., 655 ff., 1355 ff., and notes.

civ INTRODUCTION

prevalent characteristics of the old style and narrative method. In stances of apparent incoherence, omissions, repetitions, digressions, or irrelevant passages can no longer be accepted as proof of the patchwork theory, since analogous cases have been traced in many Old English poems of undoubted single authorship, in addition to examples from other literatures.[1] A number of inconsistencies may also be naturally explained by the use of conventional elements, that is, current motives and formulas of style,[2] or by imperfect adaptation or elaborate refashioning of old saga material.[3] Chronological incompatibilities as observed in the case of Hrōðgār, Bēowulf, and (perhaps) Hygd are straightened out without difficulty.[4] Variations in detail between Bēowulf's report of his experiences in Denmark and the actual story of the first two divisions furnish no basis for the charge of separate workmanship (see note on 1994 ff.). Nor would it be at all reasonable to insist throughout on impeccable logic and lucidity of statement, which would indeed be strangely at variance with the general character of *Beowulf* and other Old English poems.

That the Christian elements have not been merely grafted on the text, but are most intimately connected with the very substance of the poem, has been remarked before.[5] A certain want of harmony that has resulted from the Christian presentation of heathen material is not such as to warrant the assumption that a professed redactor went over a previously existing version, revising it by interpolation or substitution of Christian touches. The mere technical difficulties of such a process would have been of the greatest,[6] and vestiges of imperfect suture would be expected to be visible in more than one passage of our text.

No serious differences of language, diction, or meter can be adduced in favor of multiple authorship.[7] A few seemingly unusual instances of the definite article,[8] some exceptional verse forms,[9] the occurrence of a

---

[1] See above, pp. lvii f.; notes on 86–114, 1202 ff., 1807 ff., etc. Cf. Routh L 4.138, Heinzel, *ll.cc.* For examples (culled from various literatures) of discrepancies and inconsistencies due to the authors' oversight, see Rönning 26 f.; Heinzel, *Anz. fdA.* x 235 f.; Brandl 1005 f.; cf. also *MLN.* xxvii 161 ff.

[2] See above, pp. li, n. 2, xxi f. (twofold purpose of dragon fight), xxvii (motive of the sluggish youth); notes on 660, 1175, 1331 f., 2147, 2683 ff.

[3] Cf. above, pp. xviii, xxii (?). Note the apparent incongruity involved in Bēowulf's refusal to use a sword against Grendel (note on 435 ff.).

[4] See above, pp. xxxii, xlv, xxxviii.

[5] See p. l.

[6] It has been observed, e.g., that most of the Christian allusions begin with the second half-line (or end with the first half-line); cf. *Angl.* xxxvi 180 ff.

[7] Some lexical and phraseological studies have led their authors to diametrically opposite conclusions. Thus Müllenhoff's views were thought to be both vindicated (Schönbach, and [with some reservation] Banning) and refuted (Schemann). On the strength of a similar investigation some confirmation of ten Brink's theory was alleged (Sonnefeld).

[8] Thus 92, 2255, 2264, 3024 (Lichtenheld L 6.7.1.342, Barnouw 48).

[9] Cf. Schubert L 8.1.7 (l.6ᵃ etc.), 52 (hypermetrical lines); Kaluza 50, 69.

GENESIS OF THE POEM

parenthetical exclamation in some first half-lines,[1] several minor syntactical and rhetorical features[2] have been suspected of indicating a later date than that attributed to the bulk of the poem. Words, formations, or combinations could be mentioned which occur only in definitely limited portions.[3] But it would be hazardous, in fact presumptuous to assign any decisive weight to such insecure and fragmentary criteria. Contrariwise, it is entirely pertinent to emphasize the general homogeneity of the poem in matters of form as well as substance and atmosphere.[4]

Not that style and tone are monotonously the same, as to kind and quality, in all parts of the poem. In particular, the second part (Dragon fight) differs in several respects appreciably from the first (Bēowulf in Denmark), though for very natural reasons. Its action is much simpler and briefer, not extending beyond one day;[5] there is less variety of incident and setting, a smaller number of persons, no dialogue. The disconnectedness caused by encumbering digressions is more conspicuous, episodic matter being thrown in here and there quite loosely, it seems, though according to a clearly conceived plan.[6] No allusions to non-Scandinavian heroes are inserted, but all the episodes[7] are drawn from Geatish tradition and show a curiously distinct historical air. A deeper

---

[1] Krapp L 7.21: ll. 2778ᵃ, 3056ᵃ, 3115ᵃ. (Cf. above, p. lxv.)

[2] Cf. Schücking L 4.139.53 ff., 63 f.

[3] Compound participles of the type *wiggeweorþad* 1783 are found only in two other places, 1913 *lyftgeswenced*, 1937 *handgewriþene*. (Cp. *sweglwered* 606, *hondlocen* 322, 551; *forðgerīmed* 59, *forðgewiten* 1479. Note Rieger's doubt about formations of the former type, *ZfdPh.* iii 405.) A number of remarkable nonce words are met with in ' Bēowulf's Return,' such as *āfengrom* 2074, *blōdigtōð* 2082, *mūðbona* 2079, *sinfrēa* 1934, *ligetorn* 1943, *friðusibb folca* 2017. — The postposition of the definite article is confined to the second main part: 2007 (*ūhthlem þone*), 2334, 2588, 2959, 2969, 3081, cp. 2734 (2722). In the second part only, occur words and phrases like *stearcheort, ondslyht, morgenlong, morgenceald, uferan dōgrum, sigora waldend*, etc. However, the repeated use, within a short compass, of one and the same word or expression (or rhythmical form or, indeed, spelling), especially a striking one, is rather to be considered a natural psychological fact (cf. Schröder L 8.18.367; Schücking L 4.139.7). Cf., e.g., *wlonc* 331, *wlenco* 338, *wlanc* 341; *mǣg Higelāces* 737, 758; *forgyteð ond forgȳmeð* 1751, *forsiteð ond forsworceð* 1767; *folces hyrde* 1832, 1849; *ǣghwæs untǣle* 1865, *ǣghwæs orleahtre* 1886; *syððan mergen cōm* 2103, 2124; *ungemete till* 2721, *ungemete nēah* 2728; *þæt se byrnwiga būgan sceolde,/ fēoll on fēðan* 2918 f., *þæt hē blōde fāh būgan sceolde,/fēoll on foldan* 2974 f.

[4] A number of words occurring in both of the main parts of *Beowulf* but not elsewhere in Anglo-Saxon poetry are cited by Clark Hall, pp. 236 f. Some examples of interesting phrasal agreement between the two parts: ll. 100 f., 2210 f., 2399; 561, 3174; 1327, 2544; 1700, 2864; 61, 2434; cf. above, pp. xxiii, lii, n. 1, lxvii.

[5] Excepting, of course, the vaguely sketched preliminaries and the ten days needed for the construction of the memorial mound. The action of the first part can be definitely followed up for a series of five (or six) days, see note on 219.

[6] The author's evident intention of detailing the fortunes of the Geat dynasty during three generations is completely carried out, though the events are not introduced one after another in their chronological sequence.

[7] The two elegies, 2247 ff., 2444 ff., are, of course, of a neutral character.

gloom pervades all of the second part, fitly foreshadowing the hero's death and foreboding, we may fancy, the downfall of Geat power. The moralizing tendency is allowed full sway and increases inordinately towards the end. Regarding the grave structural defects characteristic of the ' Dragon Fight,' it would not be unreasonable to charge them primarily to the nature of the material used by the poet. Unlike the Danish element of the first part, which was no doubt familiarly associated with the central contests, the heroic traditions of Geatish-Swedish history were entirely separate from the main story, and the author, desirous though he was of availing himself of that interesting subject-matter for the purpose of epic enlargement, failed to establish an organic relation between the two sets of sources. Hence what generally appears in ' Bēowulf's Adventures in Denmark ' as an integral part of the story, natural setting, or pertinent allusion, has been left outside the action proper in the Dragon part. No description of Geat court life has been introduced, no name of the royal seat (like the Danish *Heorot*)[1] is mentioned, the facts pertaining to Bēowulf's *hām* (in which he does not seem to live, 2324 ff.) remaining altogether obscure. Queen Hygd[2] is a mere shadow in comparison with Hrōðgār's brilliant consort, besides being suspicious because of her singular name. Whether King Bēowulf was married or not, we are unable to make out (see note on 3150 ff.).

In explanation of some discrepancies and blemishes of structure and execution it may also be urged that very possibly the author had no complete plan of the poem in his head when he embarked upon his work, and perhaps did not finish it until a considerably later date.[3] His original design — if we may indulge in an unexciting guess — seems to have included the main contents of i1, i2, i3,[4] or, to use a descriptive title: *Bēowulfes sīð*.[5] The Danish court being the geographical and historical center of the action, the poet not unnaturally started by detailing the Scylding pedigree[6] and singing the praise of Scyld, the mythical ancestor of the royal line. It is possible, of course, that some passages were inserted after the completion of the first draft; e.g., part of the thirteenth canto with its subtle allusion to Bēowulf's subsequent

[1] The lack of actual place-names (for which typical appellations like *Hrefnesholt, Earnanæs* (*Biowulfes biorh*) are used), even in the historical narratives, has been noted. [But cf. p. xlvii, n. 2ª.]

[2] Mentioned in 2369 (and in i3: 1926, 2172).

[3] May not signs of weariness be detected in a passage like 2697 ff.?

[4] See above, pp. ii f. The fact that some matters omitted in i1 were apparently reserved for use in i3 (see note on 1994 ff.) serves to indicate that ' Bēowulf's Home-Coming ' does not owe its existence to an afterthought of the poet's.

[5] L. 872: *sīð Bēowulfes*. Cf. Müllenhoff xiv 202; Möller 118.

[6] Pedigrees were a matter of the utmost importance to the Germanic peoples, as may be seen from the Anglo-Saxon and Scandinavian examples in Appendix i: Illustrative Parallels; cp. *ib.* § 10: Tacitus, *Germania*, c. ii; *Beow.* 1957 ff., 2602 ff., 897. (Of course, also the biblical genealogies became known to the Anglo-Saxons.) Even the pedigree of the monster Grendel is duly stated, 106 ff., 1261 ff.

GENESIS OF THE POEM

kingship (861), or the digression on (Hāma [?] and) Hygelāc the Geat (1202 [1197] — 1214), which can easily be detached from the text. The author may have proceeded slowly and may have considered the first adventure (up to 1250) substantial enough to be recited or read separately; hence, some lines of recapitulation were prefixed to the story of the second contest (1252 ff.); cf. p. li, n. 4. Gradually the idea of a continuation with Bēowulf's death as the central subject took shape in the author's mind; thus a hint of Bēowulf's expected elevation to the throne (1845 ff.) is met with in the farewell conversation. A superior unity of structure, however, was never achieved. The lines in praise of the Danish kings placed as motto at the head of the first division and those extolling the virtues of the great and good Bēowulf at the close of the poem typify, in a measure, the duality of subjects and compositions.

Whether the text after its completion has been altered by interpolations it is difficult to determine. The number of lines which could be eliminated straightway without detriment to the context or style is surprisingly small; see 51 (cp. 1355 f.), 73,[1] 141, 168 f., 181 f., 1410, 2087 f., 2329 ff., 2422–24, 2544 (?), 2857–59, 3056; of longer passages, 1197–1214 (Hāma, Hygelāc), 1925–62 (Þrȳð, Offa), 2177–89 (Bēowulf's conduct). A decided improvement would result from the removal of 1681[b]–84[a] (and perhaps of 3005).

It is possible, of course, that certain changes involving additions were made by the author himself or by a copyist who had some notions of his own. But the necessity of assuming any considerable interpolations cannot be conceded. Even the Þrȳð-Offa episode, far-fetched and out of place as it seems, can hardly have been inserted after the numbering of the sections was fixed by the author,[2] unless, indeed, it was substituted for a corresponding passage of the original. For the suspected Cynewulfian insertions, see the discussion of Hrōðgār's sermon, below ('Relation to other Poems').

DATE. RELATION TO OTHER POEMS

Obviously the latest possible date[3] is indicated by the time when the MS. was written, i.e. about 1000 A.D. It is furthermore to be taken for granted that a poem so thoroughly Scandinavian in subject-matter and evincing the most sympathetic interest in Danish affairs cannot well have been composed after the beginning of the Danish invasions toward the end of the 8th century.

---

[1] This line could be explained as a corrective addition. (Similarly perhaps 3054[b] ff.?) The legal allusion of 157 f. can also be spared.
[2] The 27th section minus that episode would be unaccountably short. Cf. above, pp. c f.
[3] Regarding the question of the date, see L 4.142–146 d, L 4.16, L 6.6, 6.7.1 & 3.

INTRODUCTION

Historical Allusions

The only direct historical data contained in the poem are the repeated allusions to the raid of Hygelāc (Chochilaicus), which took place about 521 A.D. (cf. above, p. xxxix), and the mention, at the close of one of those allusive passages, of the Merovingian line of kings (*Merewīoing* 2921). As the latter reference is primarily to a bygone period, and as, on the other hand, the use of that name could conceivably have been continued in tradition even after the fall of the Merovingian dynasty (in 751), no absolutely definite chronological information can be derived from its mention. The latest of the events classed as 'historical,' the death of Onela, has been conjecturally assigned to the year 535 (cf. above, p. xl).[1]

It should be added that the pervading Christian atmosphere points to a period not earlier than, say, the second half of the 7th century.

Linguistic Tests

Investigations have been carried on with a view to ascertaining the relative dates of Old English poems by means of syntactical and phonetic-metrical tests.

1. A study of the gradual increase in the use of the definite article (originally demonstrative pronoun), the decrease of the combination of weak adjective and noun (*wīsa fengel*), the increase of the combination of article and weak adjective and noun (*se grimma gǣst*).

2. Sound changes as inferred from the meter, viz.

a) earlier dissyllabic vs. later monosyllabic forms in the case of contraction, chiefly through loss of intervocalic *h*, e.g. *hēahan, hēan — hēan* (T.C. § 1).

b) earlier long vs. later (analogical) short diphthongs in the case of the loss of antevocalic *h* after *r* (or *l*), e.g. *mearhas, mēaras — mearas* (T.C. § 3).

c) forms with vocalic *r, l, m, n* to be counted as monosyllabic or dissyllabic, e.g. *wundr* (*wundor*) — *wundor* (T.C. § 6).

It must be admitted that these criteria are liable to lead to untrustworthy results when applied in a one-sided and mechanical manner and without careful consideration of all the factors involved.[2] Allowance

---

[1] The Þrȳð-Offa episode cannot be used for dating, since we have no right to connect it with Offa, king of Mercia (who died in 796).

[2] Surprisingly wide discrepancies between the computations made by different scholars who have applied the second set of tests (Sarrazin L 4.144, Richter L 6.6.1, Seiffert L 6.6.2) have resulted from (1) a failure to eliminate from the calculations of cases under 2 c) those words which always (or nearly always) are dissyllabic (e.g. *mōdor, ēðel*), (2) differences in the practice of scansion naturally arising from the fact of metrical latitude, and (3) unavoidable oversights in collecting the material. Contradictory conclusions are indicated by the fact that Barnouw, on the basis of his syntactical criteria, dated *Genesis* (*A*) at 740, *Daniel* between 800 and 830, *Beowulf* at 660, Cynewulf's poems between 850 and 880; whereas the dates arrived at by Richter (with the help of the more reliable phonetic-metrical tests) are 700, 700, 700–730, 750–800

GENESIS OF THE POEM

should be made for individual and dialectal[1] variations, archaizing tendencies, and (in the matter of the article and weak adjective tests)[2] scribal alterations. Above all, a good many instances of test 2 are to be judged non-conclusive, since it remains a matter of honest doubt what degree of rigidity should be demanded in the rules of scansion (cf. T.C. §§ 3 ff.). Yet it cannot be gainsaid that these tests, which are based on undoubted facts of linguistic development, hold good in a general way. They justify the conclusion, e.g., that the forms of the language used by Cynewulf are somewhat more modern than those obtaining in *Beowulf*. They tend to show that *Exodus* is not far removed in time from *Beowulf*.[3] The second set of tests makes it appear probable that *Genesis* (A) and *Daniel* are earlier than *Beowulf*.

A means of absolute chronological dating was proposed by Morsbach.[4] He collected, from early texts which can be definitely dated, evidence calculated to show that the loss of final -*u* after a long stressed syllable did not take place before 700 (slightly earlier than the loss of intervocalic and antevocalic *h*, see tests 2 a, b), and demonstrated that in a number of instances the use of the forms without -*u* (and of forms like *fēorum*) was positively established by the meter, thus arriving at the conclusion that *Beowulf* could not have been composed until after the year 700.[5] Though several examples cited by Morsbach and by Richter (pp. 8 f.) are doubtful on account of metrical uncertainty,[6] there occur indeed some lines in which the older forms with final -*u* would disturb the scansion, e.g. 104^b: *fīfelcynnes *eardu*, 2609^b: **hondu rond gefēng* (?).

There is a possibility that in our only extant MS. a few forms are preserved which would seem to indicate a date anterior to about 750 A.D.,[7] viz. *wundini* 1382 and *unigmetes* 1792. The latter, however, admits of a different interpretation (cf. Lang. § 18.8), and as to the former,

---

respectively. The corresponding dates set up by Sarrazin are 700, 700, 740, 760–80. For an earlier chronological list (1898) by Trautmann, see his *Kynewulf*, pp. 121–3.

[1] Cf. Seiffert L 6.6.2.

[2] Cf. Lang. § 25.3.

[3] Sarrazin and Richter date *Exodus* about the year 740.

[4] L 4.143.

[5] The linguistic evidence, chief of which is the form *flōdu* on the Franks Casket, is not entirely clear. It has been rejected as inconclusive by Chadwick, who would place the loss of the -*u* as much as seven decades earlier (H. A. 66 ff.) Cf. Bülb. § 358; Luick § 309; Cha. Intr. 110 f.; Imelmann L 4.129 a. 338.

[6] E.g., 1297^a *on gesīðes *hādu*, 1189^b *ond hæleþa *bearnu*. (Cf. T.C. § 23.) In *Genesis* (A) Sarrazin recognized several instances (e.g., 1217, 1308, 1417) in which defective half-lines would be set right by the insertion (restoration) of the -*u*, cf. *ESt*. xxxviii 178 f., Käd. 25 f. For the metrical use of the forms of the *fēorum* type see T.C. § 3.

[7] Cf. Holthausen, *Beibl*. xviii 77. The transition of unstressed *i* to *e* is assigned to the middle of the 8th century (cf. Sievers, *Angl*. xiii 13 ff.; Bülb. §§ 360 ff.). This *i* is still largely retained in the early Northumbrian text (written about 737 A.D.) of *Cædmon's Hymn* (composed about 670 A.D.), *Bede's Death Song*, *Proverb* in Gr.-W. ii 315, the *Leiden Riddle*. For critical doubts as to the value of this test, see Tupper, *Publ. MLAss*. xxvi 239 ff., and *Riddles*, p. lvi, n.

it is a question whether it is not more natural to assume a mere scribal blunder (for *wundnū*, i.e. *wundnum*) than a perpetuation — in thoroughly modern surroundings — of such an isolated form reflecting a much earlier state of language.

Relation to Other Old English Poems

Bearing in mind the conventional use of a remarkably large stock of stereotyped expressions and devices of alliterative poetry, and furthermore the fact that many Old English poems must have been lost chiefly as a result of the Danish and Norman invasions and of the dissolution of monasteries, it behooves us to exercise extreme caution in asserting a direct relation between different poems on the basis of so-called parallel passages.[1] Otherwise we are in grave danger of setting up an endless chain of interrelations or, it may be, of assigning to one man an unduly large number, if not the majority, of the more important poems. We must certainly reckon with the fact that Anglo-Saxon England was wonderfully productive of secular as well as of religious poetry, and that the number of individual authors must have been correspondingly large. It might well have been said of the pre-Norman period: *Vetus Anglia cantat*.

One of the reasonably certain relations brought to light by a close comparison of various Old English poems is the influence on *Beowulf* of the extensive poem of *Genesis* (*A*), which in its turn presupposes the poetical labors of Cædmon as described by the Venerable Bede. Not only do we discover numerous and noteworthy parallelisms of words and phrases, many of them being traceable nowhere else,[2] but the occurrence in both poems of the religious motives of the Creation, Cain's fratricide, the giants and deluge (not to mention what has been called the Old Testament atmosphere), tends to establish a clear connection between the two. More than that, certain minor traits and expressions are made use of in *Beowulf* in such a manner as to suggest a process of imitation, as may be seen, e.g., from the lines at the close of the poem referring to the praise of the hero, which vividly recall the opening of *Genesis* (1 ff., 15 ff.).[3]

Likewise the priority of *Daniel* has been fairly demonstrated.[4] It can hardly be doubted that the picture of a king (Nebuchadnezzar) living in splendor and opulence, who suffers punishment for his pride, is

[1] Cf. Kail, *Angl*. xii 21 ff.; Sarrazin, *Angl*. xiv 188; Brandl 1009; *ESt*. xlii 321 f.

[2] Thus, e.g., *G*. 230, *B*. 466; *G*. 1220 f., *B*. 2798; *G*. 1385, *B*. 2706; *G*. 1631 f., *B*. 196 f., 789 f.; *G*. 1742 f., *B*. 1179 f.; *G*. 1895 f., *B*. 138 f.; *G*. 1998, *B*. 1073; *G*. 2003 ff., *B*. 1554; *G*. 2008, *B*. 1665; *G*. 2155, *B*. 63; *G*. 2156 f., *B*. 595 ff.; *G*. 2430 f., *B*. 612 ff.; *G*. 2544, *B*. 114.

[3] The somewhat strange expression applied to Hrēðel's death, 2469 ff., seems reminiscent of the phraseology lavished on the dry genealogical lists, *Gen*. 1178 ff., 1192 ff., 1214 ff., etc. — See also Sarrazin, *Angl*. xiv 414, *ESt*. xxxviii 170 ff.; *ESt*. xlii 327 ff. (additional material); Sievers, *För. Misc*. 75 (serious objections).

[4] Cf. Thomas, *MLR*. viii 537–39.

GENESIS OF THE POEM cxi

reflected in Hrōðgār's edifying harangue, 1700 ff.[1] Also the 'devil' worship of the Danes, 175 ff., is curiously suggestive of the idolatry practised by the Babylonians.[2] In both instances the phraseological correspondence is sufficiently close.[3] That Hrōðgār should caution Bēowulf against the sin of pride, and that the poet should go out of his way to denounce the supposed heathen worship among the Danes, will not appear quite so far-fetched, if the author was guided by reminiscences of *Daniel* which he adapted — not entirely successfully — to the subject in hand.

Furthermore, the spirited poem of *Exodus* is marked by a large number of striking parallels, which, however, have been interpreted in different ways.[4]

On the other hand, the legend of *Andreas* exhibits abundant and unmistakable signs of having been written with *Beowulf* as a model. Wholesale borrowing of phrases, which more than once are forced into a strange context, and various parallelisms in situations and in the general heroic conception of the story leave no shadow of a doubt that the author of the religious poem was following in the footsteps of the great secular epic.[5]

That the famous Cynewulf was acquainted with *Beowulf* has been inferred from the character of certain parallel passages occurring especially in *Elene* and in the short *Fates of the Apostles*.[6] The case would be

[1] Note *D.* 107, 489–94, 589–92, 598; 604 *wearð ðā anhȳdig ofer ealle men,/swīðmōd in sefan for ðǣre sundorgife/þē him God sealde, gumena rīce,/world tō gewealde, in wera līfe* (cp. *B.* 1730 ff.); 614; 668 *swā him ofer eorðan andsaca ne wæs/gumena ǣnig, oð þæt him God wolde/þurh hryre hreddan hēa rīce./Siððan þēr his aferan ēad bryttedon,/welan, wunden gold*, also 563–66 (cp. *B.* 1772 f., 1754 ff.); 677, 751; also 113 *wearð him on slǣpe sōð gecȳðed,/þætte rīces gehwæs rēðe sceolde gelimpan,/eorðan drēamas ende wurðan* (cp. *B.* 1733 f.).

[2] Note *Dan.* 170 *ac hē wyrcan ongan wōh on felda;* 181 *onhnigon tō þām herige hǣðne þēode,/wurðedon wihgyld, ne wiston wrāstran rǣd,/efndon unrihtdōm;* 186 *him þæs æfter becwōm/yfel endelēan.* Besides, the punishment meted out to those who refuse to worship the idol: 212–5 *þæt hīe ... sceolde ... prōwigean ... frēcne fȳres wylm, nymðe hīe frīðes wolde/wilnian tō þām wyrrestan ...;* 222 *nē hīe tō fācne freoðo wilnedan;* 230 *hēt þā his scealcas scūfan þā hyssas/in bǣlblȳse ...;* 233 *in fǣðm fȳres*.

[3] Some further parallels: *D.* 73[b], *B.* 2886[a]; *D.* 229[a], *B.* 1277; *D.* 545[b], *B.* 398[b], 525[b], 709[b]; *D.* 616 f., *B.* 2129 f.; *D.* 274 f., *B.* 1570 f.; *D.* 417 f., 717 f., 730, *B.* 837 ff., 995 f., 1649 f. (cp. *Ex.* 278 f.); *D.* 84, 485, 535, *B.* 1726; *D.* 703, *B.* 1920, 2152; *D.* 524 f., *B.* 2227 (cp. *Ex.* 136 f., 201, 491).

[4] Note, e.g., *E.* 56 ff., *B.* 1408 ff.; *E.* 200 f., *B.* 128 f.; *E.* 214, *B.* 387, 729; *E.* 261, *B.* 1238; *E.* 293, *B.* 256, 3007; *E.* 456 f., *B.* 2365 f. See note on 1409 f.; p. cxxiv.

[5] Cf. especially Krapp's edition, pp. lv f.; Arnold, *Notes on Beowulf*, pp. 123 ff. Some examples: *A.* 303, *B.* 2995; *A.* 333, *B.* 1223; *A.* 360 ff., *B.* 38 ff.; *A.* 377 f., *B.* 691 f.; *A.* 429, *B.* 632, *A.* 454, *B.* 730; *A.* 459 f., *B.* 572 f.; *A.* 497, *B.* 218; *A.* 553 f., *B.* 1842 f.; *A.* 622, *B.* 3006; *A.* 668, *B.* 82; *A.* 985, *B.* 320; *A.* 999 f., *B.* 721 f.; *A.* 1011 ff., *B.* 1397, 1626 ff.; *A.* 1173 ff., *B.* 361 ff.; *A.* 1235 f., *B.* 1679, 2717, 2774, 320; *A.* 1240 f., *B.* 3147, 849, 1422 f.; *A.* 1492 ff., *B.* 2542 ff., 2716 ff.; *A.* 1526, *B.* 769.

[6] See, e.g., *El.* 148 f., *B.* 123 f.; *El.* 250 ff., *B.* 397 f.; *El.* 722 f., *B.* 2901 f.; *Fat. Ap.* 3, 8, *B.* 2 f., 2695; *Fat. Ap.* 6, *B.* 18; *Fat. Ap.* 59 f., *B.* 557 f. Cp. also, e.g., *Chr.* 616 f. with *B.* 459, 470.

INTRODUCTION

strengthened if we were to include in the list of his poems all of *Christ*[1] and *Guðlac B*, perhaps also *Guðlac A*. (The inclusion of *Phoenix* is rather doubtful, the exclusion of *Andreas* is practically certain.)

At the same time a peculiar and, in fact, puzzling relation is found to exist between *Christ* 681–85 (659 ff.), 756–78 and Hrōðgār's sermon, *Beow.* 1724 ff. We may note *Christ* 660: [*God*] *ūs giefe sealde, 662 ond ēac monigfealde mōdes snyttru/sēow ond sette geond sefan monna; 682. . . . his giefe bryttað;/nyle hē ǣngum ānum ealle gesyl:an/gǣstes snyttru, þȳ lǣs him gielp sceþþe/þurh his ānes cræft ofer ōþre forð; 756 forþon wē ā sculon īdle lustas,/synwunde forseōn, ond þæs sēllran gefēon* (cp. *Beow.* 1759). God, so we are told, sends his messengers to protect us from the arrows of the devil: 761 *þā ūs gescildaþ wið sceþþendra/eglum earhfarum, . . . þonne wrōhtbora . . . onsendeð/of his brægdbogan biterne strǣl./Forþon wē fæste sculon wið þām fǣrscyte/ . . . wearde healdan,/þȳ lǣs se attres ord in gebūge,/biter bordgelāc under bānlocan . . . þæt bið frēcne wund . . . Utan ūs beorgan þā.* (Cp. *Guðl.* 781 *beorgað him bealonīþ.*) The parallels, it will be seen, relate to 1. God's distribution of manifold gifts, 2. the danger of pride, 3. the guarding against the shafts of the devil.[2] In *Christ* the first two of those motives are based on the ascertained source (cf. Cook's edition, pp. 136, 141); the third[3] is consistently connected with one of Cynewulf's favorite motives, that of the baneful wound of sin.

Moreover, at the close of the runic passage which follows immediately, *Christ* 797 ff., we meet with the expression, 812 (*brond bið on tyhte,*) *ǣleð ealdgestrēon unmurnlīce* (*gǣsta gīfrast*),[4] which reminds us of *Beowulf* 1756 f. (*fēhð ōþer tō) sē þe unmurnlīce mādmas dǣleþ,/eorles ǣrgestrēon.* Again, in *Christ* iii 1550 we come across the phrase *sāwle weard*, which suggests the analogous expression, *Beow.* 1741 f. *se weard . . . sāwele hyrde.* Also *Christ* iii 1400 f. (*þā ic þē gōda swā fela forgiefen hæfde*) *ond þē on þām eallum ēades tō lȳt*[*el*]/*mōde þūhte* recalls *Beow.* 1748 *þinceð him tō lȳtel þæt hē lange hēold.* That the extended enumeration, *Beow.* 1763 ff., is entirely in the manner of Cynewulf (cp., e.g., *Christ* 591 ff., 664 ff.) should not be overlooked in this connection.

On the strength of these parallels it was suggested, in partial agreement with Sarrazin,[5] that the 'homiletic' part of Hrōðgār's address

---

[1] Cf. Gerould, *ESt.* xli 13 ff.; S. Moore, *JEGPh.* xiv 550–67. For a recent conservative, reasonable view of the Cynewulf canon, see K. Sisam, *Proceedings of the British Academy* xviii 308 ff.

[2] Cf. Sarrazin, *Angl.* xiv 409 ff., *ESt.* xxxviii 187, Käd. 155 f.

[3] It is found likewise in *Jul.* 382 ff., 402 ff., 651 f. Cf. also *Angl.* xxxv 128 ff. — We may also compare *gifstōl, Beow.* 168, *gǣsta giefstōl, Chr.* 572; *nē his myne wisse, Beow.* 169, *El.* 1301 f., *Chr.* 1536 f.; *Beow.* 588ᵇ–89ᵃ, *El.* 210 f., 950 f.; *Beow.* 3056, *El.* 790 f.

[4] *gǣsta gīfrast* (so *Beow.* 1123) may be described as a literary formula, cf. *Angl.* xxxv 468 [Lat. 'spiritus']; Gr. Spr.: *gīfre; Heliand: grādag.* (*Christ* (iii) 972, *se gīfra gǣst.*)

[5] Of course, we could never follow Sarrazin when he declares Cynewulf to be the redactor of *Beowulf* — there are, with all the similarities in stylistic respect, irreconcilable differences of viewpoint which preclude such an assumption. — Grau's sweeping assertion (L 4.150) of

GENESIS OF THE POEM

might have been interpolated by Cynewulf or, in fact, by somebody familiar with Cynewulf's poetry. The natural supposition had been that the author of a strictly religious poem (*Christ*) was more likely to have offered the results of a first-hand theological study than the author of our heroic epic, scholar though he was. Cook (L 4.146 c 3) strongly dissented, preferring to assume that the author of *Beowulf* went to Gregory directly (i.e., made use of several (unconnected) Gregorian passages). He also mentioned the interesting fact that in still another passage of Gregory's the danger of haughtiness in the case of a ruler is emphasized. No doubt such a view is on the whole much more satisfactory and, indeed, quite likely to gain approval. It only remains to ask whether the same (or nearly the same) sequence of motives in the two poems and the various verbal correspondences can thus be completely accounted for. (See also Chadwick L 4.22.2.559.) This criticism likewise applies to the discussion of the *Daniel* parallels.

Whether any Old English poems besides those mentioned have come under the influence of *Beowulf*, it is extremely difficult to say. It would be unsafe, e.g., to claim it in the case of *Judith* or *Maldon*.[1] Altogether, we should hesitate to attribute to *Beowulf* a commanding, central position in the development of Anglo-Saxon poetry.[2]

The chronological conclusion to be drawn from the ascertained relation to other poems agrees well enough with the linguistic evidence. Placing the poems of *Genesis, Daniel, Exodus* or the so-called Cædmon group in the neighborhood of 700 (to mention a definite date), and Cynewulf in the latter half of the eighth century (or, with Cook, in the period between 750 and 825),[3] we would naturally assign *Beowulf* to the first half of the eighth century.[4]

RISE OF THE POEM. AUTHORSHIP

In discussing this highly problematic subject[5] we confine ourselves in

---

Cynewulf's authorship on the basis of alleged borrowings and of the use of the same sources is not sufficiently fortified by proof.

[1] It seems not unlikely in the case of the *Metra of Boethius*, especially *Met.* i; cf. *ESt.* xlii 325 n. 1. On *Maldon*, see Phillpotts L 4.146 e.

[2] The specific Beowulfian reminiscences in Laȝamon hunted up by Wülcker (*Beitr.* iii 551 f.) may safely be laid on the table.

[3] On the dating of *Guðlac A*, see Gerould, *MLN.* xxxii 84–6. Of *Andreas* we can say only that it "belongs to the general school of Cynewulfian poetry" (Krapp's edition, p. xlix). — [See also Cook's edition of *Elene, etc.* (1919), p. xiii.] Sisam assigns Cynewulf to the ninth century (see p. cxii, n. 1).

[4] An earlier date is considered certain by Chadwick (H. A., ch. 4), who agrees in that respect with various older scholars.

[5] Cf. especially ten Brink, chs. 11, 13; Rönning L 4.15.88 ff.; Sarrazin L 4.16, 17, 144; Symons L 4.29; Brandl 952 ff., 999 ff.; Schück L 4.39, 137; Chadwick H. A. 51 ff.; also A. Erdmann, *Über die Heimat und den Namen der Angeln*, 1890, pp. 51 ff.; besides the editions of Thorpe, Arnold, Sedgefield, and the translations of Earle and Clark Hall; and, of course, Cha. Intr., also L 4.22 b; Lawrence L 4.22 c., ch. 8. [Further, Berendsohn L 4.141.3.]

cxiv   INTRODUCTION

the main to outlining what seems the most probable course in the development of the story-material into our epic poem.

1. That the themes of the main story, i.e. the contest with the Grendel race and the fight with the dragon, are of direct Scandinavian provenience, may be regarded as practically certain.[1] The same origin is to be assigned to the distinctly historical episodes of the Swedish-Geatish wars of which no other traces can be found in England.[2]

2. Of the episodic matter introduced into the first part, the allusions to the Germanic legends of *Eormenrīc* and *Hāma*[3] as well as of *Wēland*[4] are drawn from the ancient heroic lore brought over by the Anglo-Saxons from their continental home. The *Finn* legend of Ingvaeonic associations reached England through the same channels of popular transmission. Whether old Frisian lays were used as the immediate source of the Beowulfian episode is somewhat doubtful on account of the markedly Danish point of view which distinguishes the Episode even more than the Fragment.[5] That tales of *Breca*, chief of the *Brondingas*, were included in the repertory of the Anglo-Saxon *scop*, is possibly to be inferred from the allusion, *Wids*. 25 (cp. l. 63: *mid Heaþo-Rēamum*), but the brilliant elaboration of the story and its connection with the life of the great epic hero must be attributed to the author himself.[6] Ancient North German tradition was brought into relation with Danish matters in the story of *Scyld Scēfing*.[7] Danish legends form the direct basis of the *Heremōd* episodes[8] and possibly even of the *Sigemund* allusion.[9] That the tragedy of the Heaðo-Bard feud and the glory of Hrōðgār, Hrōðulf, and the fair hall Heorot were celebrated themes of Anglo-Saxon song, may be concluded from the references in *Widsið*, but the form in which the dynastic element is introduced so as to serve as historical setting, and the close agreement noted in the case of the old spearman's speech make it appear probable that ancient popular tradition was reinforced by versions emanating directly from Denmark.

A specific Frisian source has been urged for the story of Hygelāc's disastrous Viking expedition of which Scandinavian sources betray no definite knowledge.[10] A genuine Anglo-Saxon, or rather Angle, legend is contained in the episode of Offa and his strong-minded queen.[11]

[1] Cf. above, pp. xx, xxi f.
[2] The mere mention of the name *Ongen(d)þēow* in *Wids*. 31 (and of the tribal names of the *Swēon* and *Gēatas*, *Wids*. 58) and the occurrence in historical documents, notably the *Liber Vitae Ecclesiae Dunelmensis* [i.e., a list of benefactors to the Durham church] (cf. Binz, *passim*; Chadwick H. A. 64 ff.), of such names as *Ēanmund*, *Ēadgils*; *Hygelāc*, *Herebeald*, *Heardrēd*, have no probative value so far as the knowledge of the historical legends is concerned. — The name *Biu[u]ulf*, *Liber Vitae* 163.342, which according to Chadwick's calculation was borne by a person [a monk] of the seventh century, does not necessarily betoken an acquaintance with Bēowulf legend (or with the poem); it may have been a rarely used proper name.

[3] See notes on 1197–1201.
[4] See note on 455.
[5] Cf. Introd. to *The Fight at Finnsburg*.
[6] Cf. note on 499 ff.
[7] Cf. note on 4–52.
[8] Cf. note on 901–15.
[9] Cf. note on 875–900.
[10] See Sarrazin Käd. 90 f.; cf. Müllenhoff 107 f.
[11] Cf. note on 1931–62.

3. There is no evidence to show that ' a Bēowulf legend,' i.e., a legend centering in Bēowulf and embodying the substance of the epic account, had gradually grown up out of popular stories that had been brought over to England by the migrating Angles. Certainly, we cannot, as in the case of the *Nibelungenlied*, trace definite earlier stages and follow up step by step the unfolding of the literary product. The only possible indication of a basic story popularly current at some time in England is the often mentioned Wiltshire charter of 931 A.D. with its *Bēowan hamm* and *Grendles mere*. A theory which operates with a development of popular traditions extending over a considerable period fails to account for the uniform and almost exclusive interest shown in Scandinavian legends. It would be inexplicable why such a minute attention to Northern dynasties continued to be manifested in the epic.[1] It has been argued, indeed, that the well-known ' reciprocal trade of the Germanic nations in subjects for epic poems ' sufficiently explains the ubiquitous Scandinavian elements in the Old English poem. But it is not their mere presence but their curiously historical character that has to be accounted for. It is doubtless remarkable that we can trace the fortunes of the Danish, Swedish, and Geatish royal houses for three generations and all the time can feel sure that we are on fairly safe historical ground. *Beowulf* has rightly been recognized as a first-rate source of ancient Scandinavian history. On the other hand, how much history could be learned from the heroic poems of the *Edda*, from *Deor*, *Waldere-Waltharius*, from the *Chanson de Roland*, or the *Nibelungenlied?* That the historical quality characteristic of the *Beowulf* narrative should be due to the element of geographical and chronological proximity alone may well be doubted.

To account for this very peculiar state of affairs with any approach to probability is not quite easy. The most satisfactory explanation offered by way of a hypothesis[2] is that there may have existed close relations, perhaps through marriage, between an Anglian court and the kingdom of Denmark, whereby a special interest in Scandinavian traditions was fostered among the English nobility.[3] It is true, of direct intercourse between England and Denmark in those centuries preceding the Danish invasions we have no positive historical proof. But we have certainly no right to infer from the statement of the *OE. Chronicle* (A.D. 787) with regard to the earliest Danish attack: *on his [Beorhtrīces] dagum cuōmon ǣrest. iii. scipu . . . þæt wǣron þā ǣrestan scipu Deniscra monna þē Angelcynnes lond gesōhton*, that peaceful visits of Danes in England

---

[1] Cf. Sarrazin Käd. 89 f. — If the *Gēatas* were Jutes, i.e. a tribe with whom the Angles had formerly shared the Jutish peninsula (cf. Kier L 4.78.38 f.), the difficulty would be materially lessened. This must be conceded to the advocates of the Jutland theory.

[2] See Morsbach L 4.143.277. That this is a mere conjecture is to be admitted.

[3] Moorman (L 4.31.5) endeavored to show that there was a Geat colony in the North Riding of Yorkshire, and that the courtly epos of *Beowulf* was composed during the reign of Ēadwine. (Cf. above, p. xlvi, n. 1.) See also Strömholm L 4.78 i.

were unknown before, since the reference is clearly to hostile inroads which then occurred for the first time. Another conjecture that has proved attractive to several scholars tried to establish Friesland as a meeting-ground of Danes and Englishmen where a knowledge of Northern tales was acquired by the latter.[1]

4. Evidently, we cannot entertain the notion that there was in existence even an approximately complete Scandinavian original ready to be put into Anglo-Saxon verse. If nothing else, the style and tone of *Beowulf* would disprove it, since they are utterly unlike anything to be expected in early Scandinavian poetry. But a number of lays (possibly also some poems interspersed with prose narrative like many of the Eddic lays) dealing with a variety of subjects became known in England, and, with the comparatively slight differences between the two languages in those times,[2] could be easily mastered and turned to account by an Anglo-Saxon poet. We may well imagine, e.g., that the Englishman knew such a lay or two on the slaying of Grendel and his mother, another one on the dragon adventure, besides, at any rate, two Danish (originally Geatish) poems on the warlike encounters between Geats and Swedes leading up to the fall of Ongenþēow and Onela respectively.

Whether the picture of the life of the times discloses any traces of Scandinavian originals is a fascinating query that can be answered only in very general and tentative terms. An enthusiastic archæologist[3] set up the claim that a good deal of the original cultural background had been retained in the Old English poem, as shown, e.g., by the helmets and swords described in *Beowulf* which appear to match exactly those used in the Northern countries in the period between A.D. 550 and 650. Again, it would not be surprising if Norse accounts of heathen obsequies had inspired the brilliant funeral scene at the close of the poem, ll. 3137 ff. (see note, and 1108 ff., 2124 ff., also note on 4–52: Scyld's sea-burial). But, on the whole, it is well to bear in mind that Anglo-Saxon and Scandinavian conditions of life were too much alike to admit of drawing a clear line of division in our study of Beowulfian

[1] Thus, Arnold surmised that the author might have been a companion of St. Willibrord, the Anglo-Saxon missionary, who, with the permission of their king Ongendus, took thirty young Danes with him to Friesland to be brought up as Christians. (Arnold's edition, pp. xxx ff.; cf. his *Notes on Beowulf*, pp. 114 f.) [As early as 1816, Outzen expressed a similar view, see Wülker's *Grundriss*, p. 253.] Schück (L 4.39.40, 43 ff.) conceived of an Anglo-Saxon missionary who met Danish merchants in Friesland and eagerly listened to their stories. According to Sarrazin (Käd. 90 ff.) an intermediate Frisian version of a Danish original served as basis for the final literary redaction by the English poet [Cynewulf]; cf. above, p. xlvii, n. 4. That the Germanic heroic legends were quite generally brought to England by way of Friesland was also the opinion of Müllenhoff (pp. 104 ff.). Cf. also Wadstein, *On the Origin of the English*, 1927, p. 26; *id.*, L 4.74.6.

[2] The remark inserted in the *Gunnlaugssaga Ormstungu*, ch. 6: *ein var tunga í Englandi ok Noregi, áþr Vilhjálmr bastarþr vann England*, though exaggerated, contains an important element of truth.

[3] Stjerna, L 9.39.

GENESIS OF THE POEM   cxvii

antiquities. Certain features, however, can be mentioned that are plainly indicative of English civilization, such as the institution of the *witan*,[1] the use of the harp, the vaulted stone chamber (see note on 2717 ff.), the paved street (320, cp. 725), and, above all, of course, the high degree of gentleness, courtesy, and spiritual refinement.[2]

Some Norse parallels relating to minor motives of the narrative are pointed out in the notes on 20 ff., 244 ff., 499 ff., 804, 1459 f., 2157, 2683 ff., 3024 ff., 3167 f.[3]

It remains to ask whether it is possible to detect Norse influence in the language of *Beowulf*. Generally speaking, it must be confessed that so far the investigations along this line[4] have brought out interesting similarities rather than proofs of imitation. Assuredly, no such indisputable evidence has been gained as in the case of the *Later Genesis*, which is, indeed, on a different footing, being a real and even close translation of a foreign (Old Saxon) original. It is worth while, however, to advert to the agreement in the use of certain words and phrases, such as *atol, bront; eodor, lēod* (in their transferred, poetical meanings, cp. ON. *jaðarr, ljóði*);[5] *beadolēoma* (see Glossary), *bona Ongenþēoes* (see note on 1968), and other kennings; *gehēgan ðing* 425 f., cp. ON. *heyja þing; mǣl is mē tō fēran* 316, cp. ON. *mál er mér at ríþa* (*Helgakv. Hund.* ii 48, cf. Sarrazin St. 69), *ic þē . . . biddan wille . . . ānre bēne* 426 ff. (see note). On *hæftmēce*, see above, p. xviii; on the epithets *hēah* and *gamol* applied to Healfdene, p. xxxiii. The combination *beornas on blancum* 856 might be taken for a duplicate of a phrase like *Bjǫrn reið Blakki* (Par. § 5: *Kálfsvísa*). The employment of the 'historical present'[6] has been accounted for as a Norse syntactical feature (Sarrazin Käd. 87; see Lang. § 25.6, and especially l. 2486), but there is reason to suspect that it merely indicates the same sort of approximation to the brisk language of every-day life. That the much discussed *īsig*, 33 is a misunderstood form of a Scandinavian word has also been suggested.[7] Several others of the unexplained ἄπαξ λεγόμενα might be conjecturally placed in the same category.

5. The author's part in the production of the poem was vastly more than that of an adapter or editor. It was he who combined the Grendel

---

[1] Cf. Antiq. § 1.   [2] Cf. Müller L 9.28.

[3] Cf. also *Angl.* xxix 379 n. 4 (ll. 249 ff.); *Angl.* xxxvi 174 n. 2 (ll. 445 f.); *Arch.* cxv 179 n. (ll. 1002 f.); *JEGPh.* xiv 549 (ll. 1121 f.). Thanks to the abundance of original secular literature in ancient Scandinavia, illustrative parallels present themselves very readily.

[4] Sarrazin's exaggerated claims were vigorously combated by Sievers, see L 4.16, 17. Cf. also *ZfdPh.* xxix 224 ff.

[5] The general, non-technical meaning — normally expressed by *gifu* — which appears in (*feoh*)*gift* (21, 1025, 1089), is probably archaic rather than due to the influence of ON. *gipt*.

[6] Though not 'historical present' in the strict sense (never occurring in principal clauses). Cf. also J. M. Steadman, Jr., "The Origin of the Historical Present in English," *Studies in Philology* (Univ. of North Carolina), Vol. xiv, No. 1 (1917); further, L 4.85 b.

[7] L 5.26.15, 5.54; see note on 33.

stories with the dragon narrative and added, as a connecting link, the account of Bēowulf's return, in short, conceived the plan of an extensive epic poem with a great and noble hero as the central figure. Various modifications of the original legends were thus naturally introduced. (Cf., e.g., above, pp. xviii, xx, xxi f.)[1] Leisurely elaboration and expansion by means of miscellaneous episodic matter became important factors in the retelling of the original stories. Hand in hand with such fashioning of the legends into a poem of epic proportions went a spiritualizing and Christianizing process. A strong element of moralization was mingled with the narrative. The characters became more refined, the sentiment softened, the ethics ennobled. Bēowulf rose to the rank of a truly ideal hero, and his contests were viewed in the light of a struggle between the powers of good and of evil, thus assuming a new weight and dignity which made them appear a fit subject for the main narrative theme.

That the idea of creating an epic poem on a comparatively large scale was suggested to the author, directly or indirectly, by classic models is more than an idle guess, though incontrovertible proof is difficult to obtain.[2] In any event, it is clear that a biblical poem like the Old English *Genesis* paraphrase, consisting of a loose series of separate stories, could not possibly have served as a pattern. Whether there was any real epic among the lost poems of the Anglo-Saxon period we have no means of ascertaining.[2a]

The question of the influence of the *Æneid* has received a good deal of attention from scholars.[3] There is assuredly no lack of parallels calling for examination. (See, e.g., notes on 90–98, 707, 1085, 1322 ff., 1357 ff., 1368 ff., 1386 ff., 1409 f.) In fact, surprisingly large lists of analogies have been drawn up, and it is to be granted that certain verbal agreements look like instances of imitation on the part of the Anglo-Saxon poet. The great popularity of the *Æneid* in Ireland should be noted in this connection.[4] The even larger claim that the author derived some of his subject-matter from Vergil[5] is, of course, much more difficult to establish. The most important influence to be recognized is, after all, the new conception of a true epic poem which the Anglo-Saxon, very likely, learned from the Roman classic.

6. That the poem was composed in the Anglian parts of England is one of the few facts bearing on its genesis which can be regarded as

[1] The names of Hygd and Unferð were perhaps coined by the poet himself.

[2] Deutschbein would attribute this important advance in technique to Celtic influence, *GRM.* i 115 ff.

[2a] The *Waldere* fragments, of course, show epic proportions.

[3] Cf. especially Brandl 1008; *Arch.* cxxvi 40–48, 339–59; also L 4.129 a (Imelmann), L 4.129 g (Haber); L 4.66 b 9. For decided objections, see Chadwick H. A. 73–76; Girvan, *MLR.* xxvii 466 ff. — That the author was not ignorant of the language of Vergil may be taken for granted, cf. above, p. lxviii, Lang. § 25.9.

[4] Cf. Zimmer, *ZfdA.* xxxiii 326–28; L 4.66 b 3 (von Sydow).

[5] Brandl, L 4.129 e.

GENESIS OF THE POEM

fairly established. But whether it originated in Northumbria or Mercia is left to speculation.[1] The evidence of language, as seen above, is indecisive on that point. The strongest argument in favor of Mercia is, after all, the keen interest in the traditions of the Mercian dynasty, made apparent by the introduction of the Offa episode.

Needless to say, the list of Anglian kings has been diligently scanned by scholars with a view to finding the most suitable person to be credited with the rôle of a patron. Several of those presented for consideration, it is important to note, relinquished their royal station to take up life in the quiet of a monastery. Perhaps the most plausible case has been made out so far for King Aldfrið of Northumbria (who died in 705). That also some allusions to contemporary history are hidden in the lines of our poem is at least a possibility not to be ignored. Might not the spectacle of internal strife and treachery rampant in the Northern regions of England have prompted the apparently uncalled-for note of rebuke and warning, 2166 ff. (cp. 2741 f., 587 f., 1167 f.)?[2]

We may, then, picture to ourselves the author of *Beowulf* as a man connected in some way with an Anglian court, a royal chaplain or abbot of noble birth[3] or, it may be, a monk friend of his, who possessed an actual knowledge of court life and addressed himself to an aristocratic, in fact a royal audience.[4] A man well versed in Germanic and Scandinavian heroic lore, familiar with secular Anglo-Saxon poems of the type exemplified by *Widsið*, *Finnsburg*, *Deor*, and *Waldere*, and a student of biblical poems of the Cædmonian cycle, a man of notable taste and culture and informed with a spirit of broad-minded Christianity.

The work left behind by the anonymous author does not rank with the few great masterpieces of epic poetry. *Beowulf* is not an English *Iliad*, not a standard Germanic or national Anglo-Saxon epos. In respect to plot it is immeasurably inferior to the grand, heroic *Nibelungenlied*. Yet it deservedly holds the first place in our study of Old English literature. As an eloquent exponent of old Germanic life it

---

[1] Successive places were assigned to Northumbria and Mercia in ten Brink's complicated theory of the gradual building up of the poem from a number of original, as well as modified, lays.

[2] Earle, by bold and somewhat playful conjecture, fastened the authorship on Hygeberht whom the great Offa had chosen to be archbishop of Lichfield. He furthermore imagined that the poem was a sort of allegory written for the benefit of Offa's son Ecgferþ, being in fact ' the institution of a prince.' (Cf. note on 1931–62.) As to its genesis, he thought that the name and also part of the story of Hygelāc had been taken from the *Historia Francorum*, and that " the saga," though of Scandinavian origin, " came out of Frankland to the hand of the poet, and probably . . . was written in Latin." See the ingenious, if fanciful, arguments in *Deeds of Beowulf*, pp. lxxv ff.; they were first set forth in the London *Times*, September 30 and October 29, 1885.

[3] Cf. Plummer's *Baeda*, i, p. xxxv.

[4] He makes it plain that the king's authority must be scrupulously safeguarded; see especially 862 f., 2198 f.

stands wholly in a class by itself. As an exemplar of Anglo-Saxon poetic endeavor it reveals an ambitious purpose and a degree of success in its accomplishment which are worthy of unstinted praise. In noble and powerful language, and with a technical skill unequaled in the history of our ancient poetry, it portrays stirring heroic exploits and, through these, brings before us the manly ideals which appealed to the enlightened nobles of the age. It combines the best elements of the old culture with the aspirations of the new.

The poem has been edited many times. The main object which this edition aims to serve is to assist the student in the thorough interpretation of the text *by placing within his reach the requisite material for a serious study*. It is hoped that he will feel encouraged to form his own judgment as occasion arises — *nullius addictus iurare in verba magistri*.

A SUPPLEMENTARY NOTE CONCERNING THE GENESIS OF *BEOWULF*

After all that has been written on the subject, *Beowulf* remains to us a singular and, in a sense, problematic poem. It is not at all what could be termed an orthodox epic. That the author fully appreciated the heroic subjects he was dealing with is beyond dispute[1] — no argument is needed to prove the obvious. But to him they meant more than could be gathered from an ordinary outline of the narrative. When the entertaining story (which in the main he did not invent) had been refashioned by his hand, it had assumed a markedly edifying character which requires to be analyzed and explained.[2] In particular, the all-important person of the hero had been idealized and spiritualized in such a degree as to make him a truly unique figure in heroic poetry. In what light the author desired him to be viewed is well expressed in those decisively significant final words of praise[3] which almost sound as if spoken of some saintly person (*manna mildust ond mon(ðw)wǣrust*, cf. *Angl*. l 223 f.); even the epithet *lofgeornost*, of which so much has been made, does not necessarily point to warlike renown, cf. *Angl*. xlvi 237 f.

Now it would clearly be going too far to say that the author set out with the deliberate purpose of writing an allegorical poem with Christ himself as its true hero. But it is not deemed a reckless supposition

---

[1] Is it necessary to say that a modern reader who is not thrilled by the early heroic poetry of his race would be a poor judge of it?

[2] How urgently the necessity is felt of discovering an additional, ulterior motive of some kind, is illustrated by an attempt recently made to explain the dragon fight allegorically as symbolizing the historical downfall of the Geat kingdom (Strömholm, L 4.78 i). Cf. Intr. xxiii. Also Cook considered it possible that 'Grendel' was meant to denote the devastation wrought by the Picts and Scots (L 4.146 c 1.322) — even as Grein long ago thought of allusions to destructive raids by pirates. — A subtle philosophical scheme involving a large symbolic element has been detected by Du Bois (L 4.158).

[3] After the hero's soul had departed to seek 'the glory of the righteous,' 2819 f.; cp. 2741 ff.

GENESIS OF THE POEM   cxxi

that in recounting the life and portraying the character of the exemplary leader, whom he conceived as a fighter against the demons of darkness and a deliverer from evil, he was almost inevitably reminded of the person of the Savior, the self-sacrificing King, the prototype of supreme perfection. If the sensitive author of a frankly religious poem felt no incongruity in picturing Christ ' ascending ' the cross as a *geong hæleð . . . strang and stīðmōd* (*Dream of the Rood* 39 f.[1]), it is reasonable to hold that the *Beowulf* poet could easily have associated his idealized king and warrior with the highest type of Christian heroism he could imagine. Exactly how far he meant the parallelism to apply in matters of detail we have of course no means of determining beyond question.[2]

Such a reading of the epic is entirely compatible with the pleasing suggestion (Earle, Schücking L 4.146 a) that it was composed with a special didactic purpose for the benefit of a king's son, that it was, in fact, designed as the ' institution of a prince ' — a hypothesis which takes into full account the poet's eminently moral and moralizing disposition.[3] It is to be understood, by the way, that the works mentioned as illustrative parallels, the *Fürstenspiegel* of the Carolingian period,[4] are of a somewhat different order. They are undisguised treatises containing direct advice to rulers, whereas in our poem the educational motive is kept in the background — just as the Christian interpretation is delicately veiled. Special attention should be called to Schücking's admirable presentation of the ideal of royalty as conceived by the poet. (L 4.157.)

No serious difference of opinion is to be apprehended nowadays on the general proposition that the author was a man of respectable scholarly attainments. It seems to be widely recognized that he had studied his Vergil to good purpose, although individual views may naturally vary in regard to details. Even his acquaintance with the Homeric epics would not be entirely out of the question. It is possible, indeed, to adduce more or less striking parallels as shown above all in a number of articles by Cook,[5] who incidentally offers the ingenious suggestion that the learned Aldhelm may have had some share in directing the poet's attention to classic models. Yet we must certainly bear in mind that Homeric influence could never have gone very far. The whole manner

---

[1] The true reading of l. 39ᵃ may have been *gyrede hine geong hæleð* (cp. *Beow.* 1441); see also ll. 44, 56: (*rīcne*) *cyning*.

[2] The problem of finding a formula which satisfactorily explains the peculiar spiritual atmosphere of the poem is not met by maintaining a merely negative attitude.

[3] The didactic purpose of Cædmon's poetry is stressed in Bede's well-known words (iv 24): ' in quibus cunctis homines ab amore scelerum abstrahere, ad dilectionem vero et solertiam bonae actionis excitare curabat.'

[4] Cf. Albert Werminghoff, " Die Fürstenspiegel der Karolingerzeit," *Historische Zeitschrift* lxxxix 193–214; Roland M. Smith, " The Speculum Principum in Early Irish Literature," *Speculum* ii 411–45. — A monitory letter of St. Boniface to King Æðilbald of Mercia has been noted by Crawford, *RESt.* vii 448 f.

[5] L 4.129 b, 146 c. Cf. also, e.g., L 4.129 f.; Cha.'s notes on ll. 1808, 2675. (Chadwick H. A., chs. 15 ff.)

of our author, his artistic, rhetorical, subjective style would seem — in spite of obvious differences — to put him in a class with the writer of the Augustan epic rather than with Homer.[1]

In order to realize the possibility of such many-sided interests as are credited to the unknown author, we should turn to the only evidence to be had, concrete examples, that is, from Anglo-Saxon history.[2] To a man like Aldhelm, the bishop and scholar, who in Latin prose and verse discoursed on a series of saints and who wrote a dissertation on Latin prosody, but who was also known as the minstrel and poet of secular English verse; or, in fact, to King Alfred, the Christian soldier, the educator of his people, friend and patron of the clergy, and also the lover of well remembered ' Saxon poems ' an epic like *Beowulf* must have been thoroughly congenial. Altogether, there was no insuperable barrier between a churchman's and a layman's world. Some of the early kings could see with the eyes of both, could be preacher and fighter in one person. Thus, the pious, gentle, humble-minded Ōswald, the faithful interpreter of his bishop's sermons, proved a successful statesman and a soldier, a king who died in the defense of his people (*for his folces ware*, Ælfric, *Saints* xxvi 147; ' pro salute gentis,' Bede, *H.E.* iii 2). Nor should the mention of those happy times (*gesǣliglīca tīda* as praised by Alfred) be forgotten when, in Bede's words (iv 2), religion and learning flourished in the country, and the English had ' fortissimos Christianosque reges,' — a source of terror to all barbarous nations. That actually lays about the Beowulfian Ingeld were recited in the monastery of Lindisfarne is an often mentioned, highly valuable bit of historical information (cf. Intr. xxxv n. 2).

A courageous attempt to sketch the very conditions under which *Beowulf* was composed has been made by Cook (L 4.146 c 1). He fixes on the court of King Aldfrið of Northumbria as the most likely place where we may imagine the author to have lived.[2a] Many were indeed the qualifications of this ruler as a patron of various kinds of literature. The son of an Irish mother, he had, during a long residence in Ireland,

---

[1] The knowledge of Greek in Old England has been set forth by Cook, *Philol. Quarterly* ii 1 ff. For judicious remarks on the general question of classical influence, see Chambers Introd. 329 ff. For some critical comment on Cook's theory of Homeric traces in Bēowulf's funeral, see L 4.129 c. (The parallels that had been collected by Chadwick (cf. Antiq., n. 1) were meant to illustrate analogous social conditions.) — The " sophisticated " character of the style of *Beowulf*, as in fact of nearly all the OE. poetry, has been emphasized by Tatlock (L 7.38, *passim*), who notes the scarcity of recurrent " formulas " of the standard Homeric type. At the same time, we should not lose sight of the fact that along with the inherited alliterative verse-form there were necessarily transmitted numerous conventional modes of expression. The artistic use made of the time-honored formulas shows, indeed, the poet's individuality and training.

[2] This matter has been admirably elucidated by Chambers, Introd. 121 ff., 324 ff., & L 4.22 b; he has explained the case more convincingly than can be done in the present cursory statement.

[2a] The same suggestion had been briefly mentioned by Deutschbein, *GRM.* i 118.

GENESIS OF THE POEM   cxxiii

acquired religious and secular learning and withal a love of poetry; he was himself a poet (in the Irish tongue), a friend of the famous Aldhelm, " a man sympathetic with the adventurous spirit — eager for learning and wandering, and curious respecting foreign countries — of his Irish kin ";[1] a noble chief of his people, not lacking in valor, but preëminently known as ' the wise ' and ' the learned '; beyond question, one of " the most enlightened and justly popular princes of his time."[2] At such a court the author of *Beowulf* might well have found his inspiration. The singularly sweet, warm-hearted, and tolerant spirit of Irish Christianity, in particular, would no doubt have strongly appealed to him.[3] Of course, no one would say that this tempting possibility has been proved to be a positive fact; but, then, proof appears to be entirely out of our reach.[4]

The customary dating of *Beowulf* (early in the eighth century) has been assailed by Schücking (L 4.146 a), who would rather place it at the end of the ninth century. Although this thesis can hardly be said to commend itself[5] (cf. Chambers Introd. 322 ff.), the study is of distinct merit, especially as the critic invites close attention to the striking cultural advance represented by the poem and, furthermore, tries to find a substantial motive for the very remarkable interest taken in matters Scandinavian. This latter fact is, indeed, still calling for an adequate explanation. An entirely different line of argumentation would connect this particular question[6] with the problem of the *Gēatas*, see, e.g., L 4.78 i; p. cxv & n. 3.

That the linguistic tests should be used with great caution is, of course, to be conceded. (See also L 6.12.3.) Nor will it be denied that the

---

[1] Cook, *l.c.*, p. 305.

[2] Montalembert, as quoted by Cook, p. 310.

[3] The vexing question of Irish elements in *Beowulf* (cf. Intr. xx, xxi) has never yet been settled. It is much to be hoped that von Sydow (L 4.66 b, b 3) will find it possible soon to publish in full the material collected by him so as to enable us to form an accurate opinion concerning the justice of his contention.

[4] Allusions to English history would naturally be of great interest. Possibly ll. 1342 ff. permit the inference that the poet had in mind the legend of King Ōswald's blessed hand; cf. *Angl.* l 200 n. An interesting suggestion by Brandl, L 4.146 d. See also p. cxxi, n. 4. (It is, by the way, highly characteristic that he repeatedly adverts to the fact that the story he is telling pertains to an earlier age; see, e.g., ll. 178 ff. (1246); 1797 f. (197, 790, 806). The rather otiose *swā (hē) nū gīt (gēn) dēð* 1058, 1134, 2859, similarly 3167 recalls Ælfric's notable comment, *swā swā gȳt for-oft dēð* (*Homilies*, Vol. ii, p. 120), added to the story (by Bede) of an event which took place four hundred years before.) At the same time, our author shows his good sense in keeping his Northern story free from grotesque allusions to outward symbols and rites of the Christian faith. — That a definite English landscape can be recognized in the poem (as recently claimed by Cook) is extremely questionable.

[5] Malone shrewdly observes (*Speculum* vi 149) that in a poem of that late date " Hrōðulf, not Hrōðgār, would have been the Danish king served by the hero, and the historical allusions would have been more in keeping with Scandinavian tradition as we know it in Saxo and the Icelandic monuments."

[6] Which has ever haunted scholars since the days of Thorkelin and Thorpe; see also Wülker's *Grundriss*, p. 252.

INTRODUCTION

chronology of Old English poems is far from being settled. (Cf. Imelmann *L* 4.129 a.) — As regards the relation between *Beowulf* and *Exodus*, it has been plausibly assumed — in view of the Vergilian echo traced in ll. 1409 f. of the former — that the writer of the religious poem knew our *Beowulf*. (Cf. Imelmann, *l.c.* 419; also *Angl.* l 202 f.)[1] However, the general question of chronology is hardly affected by the case. On the other hand, an acquaintance with *Widsið* could, perhaps, be inferred from *Beowulf* 311 as compared with *Widsið* 99: *hyre lof lengde geond londa fela* (136ᵇ: *geond grunda fela*).

[1] See note on 1409 f.; also Gollancz, *The Cædmon Manuscript*, p. lxxxiv; *Angl.* l 221 n. 3.

BIBLIOGRAPHY

THIS Bibliography will be referred to by the letter L, as explained under ' Table of Abbreviations.'
Notices of reviews are preceded by ' R.: ' or ' r.: '.[1]

I. MANUSCRIPT

1. The only extant MS.: Cotton MSS. (British Museum, London), Vitellius A. xv, 129ª–198ᵇ (132ª–201ᵇ in the numbering of 1884).
2. First mention of it by H. Wanley in: *Antiquæ literaturæ septentrionalis liber alter, seu Humphredi Wanleii librorum vett. septentrionalium, qui in Angliæ bibliothecis extant,...... catalogus historico-criticus* (= Book ii, or Vol. iii, of George Hickes's *Thesaurus*), Oxoniæ, 1705, pp. 218 f. [Brief notice of the MS. and transcription of ll. 1–19, 53–73.]
3. The Thorkelin transcripts: A = *Poema anglosaxonicum de rebus gestis Danorum ex membrana bibliothecae cottonianae.... fecit exscribi* Londini A.D. 1787 Grimus Johannis Thorkelin, LL.D.; B = *Poema anglosaxonicum ...... exscripsit* Grimus Johannis Thorkelin, LL.D. Londini anno 1787.

These copies were made use of by Grundtvig in his translation (1820, cf. L 3.27), see his *Anmærkninger*, pp. 267–312. They are preserved in the Great Royal Library at Copenhagen.
4. Collations of the MS.: a) J. J. Conybeare, *Illustrations of Anglo-Saxon Poetry* (L 2.23), pp. 137–55. b) Early collations embodied in the editions of Kemble, Thorpe (collation of 1830), Grundtvig. c) E. Kölbing, " Zur Beowulfhandschrift, " *Arch.* lvi (1876), 91–118; *id., ESt.* v (1882), 241, & vii (1884), 482–86 (in reviews of Wülker's texts). d) Recent collations embodied in the editions of Sedgefield and Chambers.
5. Facsimile: *Beowulf. Autotypes of the unique Cotton MS. Vitellius A XV in the British Museum, with a Transliteration and Notes*, by Julius Zupitza. (E.E.T.S., No. 77.) London, 1882. [Almost of equal value with the MS. Zupitza's painstaking Notes include also a collation with the Thorkelin transcripts. Photographs by Mr. Praetorius.]
6. Diplomatic editions: a) Richard Paul Wülcker in the revision of Grein's *Bibliothek der angelsächsischen Poesie*, i, 18–148. Kassel, 1881. R.: E. Kölbing (L 1.4). b) Alfred Holder, *Beowulf. I: Abdruck der Handschrift.* Freiburg i. B., 1st ed., n. d. [1881]; 2d ed., 1882; 3d ed., 1895.
7. Kenneth Sisam, " The ' Beowulf ' Manuscript." *MLR.* xi (1916), 335–37. [A useful note on the different parts of the MS. volume.]

[1] It deserves to be noted that, in spite of its length, the Bibliography is a selected one.

8. Max Förster, " Die Beowulf-Handschrift." *Berichte über die Verhandlungen der Sächsischen Akademie der Wissenschaften*, Vol. lxxi, No. 4. Leipzig, 1919. 89 pp. [Highly important, comprehensive study.] R.: Wolfgang Keller, *Beibl*. xxxiv (1923), 1–5. [Keller mentions, as a plausible reason for the worn-off condition of the first and the last page (ff. 179ª, 198ᵇ) of Part II of the poem (' Dragon Fight '), that this division may have been especially popular with Ags. readers and therefore have been handled separately. He convincingly controverts Rypins's thesis (L 1.9.2) concerning the relative merits of scribes A and B.]

9. Stanley I. Rypins, (1) " The Beowulf Codex." *MPh*. xvii (1920), 541–47, and in a slightly modified version, *Colophon* X (1932), 9–12. (2) " A Contribution to the Study of the *Beowulf* Codex." *Publ. MLAss*. xxxvi (1921), 167–85. Cf. Intr. xc, n. 5. (3) " The OE. Epistola Alexandri ad Aristotelem." *MLN*. xxxviii (1923), 216–20. [*Alexander's Letter* and *Wonders of the East* were in Angl. dialect (*Life of St. Christopher* in WS.), when they came into the hands of the WS. scribe of our MS. A list of interesting lexical elements.] (4) *Three Old English Prose Texts* [i.e., those preceding the *Beowulf*] *in MS. Codex Vitellius A xv edited with an Introduction and Glossarial Index*. (E.E.T.S., No. 161.) London, 1924. [The Latin text of each is added. Introduction, pp. vii–xiv = L 1.9.1, pp. xiv–xxix = L 1.9.2, pp. xxxviii–xlii = L 1.9.3.] R.: F. P. Magoun, Jr., *MLN*. xlii (1927), 67–70; J. Hoops, *ESt*. lxi (1927), 435–40.

10. W. A. Craigie, " Interpolations and Omissions in Anglo-Saxon Poetic Texts." *Philologica* ii (1925), 5–19. [Pp. 16–19: Craigie, building on a theory propounded by Bradley (see Intr. ci, n. 6), argues that the text seems to have been originally written on sheets containing about 62 lines (the pages averaging 15 or 16 lines), and notes possible imperfections at the beginning and the end of some such pages. See the criticism, *Angl*. l 236 f. (L 5.35.19).]

11. Johannes Hoops, " Die Foliierung der *Beowulf*-Handschrift." *ESt*. lxiii (1928), 1–11. [Recommends retention of the old numbering of folios (*Beowulf* beginning on fol. 129), subject, however, to the correction of the errors that had arisen from a former misplacement of certain leaves.] Cf. Marjorie Daunt, *Year's Work* ix, 75. [The "official pagination " of 1884 recommended.]

12. James Root Hulbert, " The Accuracy of the B-scribe of *Beowulf*." *Publ. MLAss*. xliii (1928), 1196–99. [Refutes Rypins's view (L 1.9.2).]

13. Eduard Prokosch, " Two Types of Scribal Errors in the *Beowulf* MS." *Kl. Misc*. (1929), 196–207. [Phonetic errors by scribe A, who wrote from dictation (but cf. Förster, L 1.8.27 n. 2); mechanical errors by scribe B, who copied from a MS.]

See also L 5.22, 52, 53.

II. EDITIONS

a. Complete Editions

1. Grim. Johnson [Grímur Jónsson] Thorkelin, *De Danorum rebus gestis secul. III & IV. poëma danicum dialecto anglosaxonica.* Havniæ, 1815. [Of interest chiefly as the 'editio princeps.']
2. John M. Kemble, *The Anglo-Saxon Poems of Beowulf, The Traveller's Song, and the Battle of Finnesburh.* London (1st ed. [100 copies], 1833);[1] 2d ed., Vol. i, 1835, Vol. ii (Translation, Introduction, Notes, Glossary), 1837. [Scholarly; the first real edition.]
3. Frederik Schaldemose, *Beo-Wulf og Scopes Widsið.* Kjøbenhavn, 1847; 2d ed., 1851. [Dependent on Kemble.]
4. Benjamin Thorpe, *The Anglo-Saxon Poems of Beowulf, the Scop or Gleeman's Tale, and the Fight at Finnesburg.* Oxford, 1855; reprinted, 1875. [Meritorious, though not sufficiently careful in details.]
5. C. W. M. Grein in his *Bibliothek der angelsächsischen Poesie*, Vol. i, pp. 255–341. Göttingen, 1857. [Marked by sterling scholarship; text printed in long lines, not collated with the MS.]
6. Nik. Fred. Sev. Grundtvig, *Beowulfes Beorh eller Bjovulfs-Drapen.* Kiöbenhavn, 1861. [The two Thorkelin copies utilized; numerous conjectures indulged in.]
7. (1) Moritz Heyne, *Beowulf. Mit ausführlichem Glossar hrsg.* Paderborn, 1863; 1868; 1873; 1879. — (2) Revised by Adolf Socin: 5th ed., 1888 (r.: Sievers, L 5.16.2; Heinzel, L 5.20); 1898 (r.: Sarrazin, L 5.36); 1903 (r.: v. Grienberger, L 5.45.2; E. Kruisinga, *ESt.* xxxv (1905), 401 f.; F. Holthausen, *Beibl.* xviii (1907), 193 f.; Fr. Klaeber, *ib.* xviii, 289–91). — (3) Revised by Levin L. Schücking: 8th ed., 1908 [thoroughly improved, still conservative] (r.: Fr. Klaeber, *ESt.* xxxix (1908), 425–33; R. Imelmann, *D. Lit. z.* xxx (1909), 995–1000; v. Grienberger, *ZföG.* lx (1909), 1089 f.; W. W. Lawrence, *MLN.* xxv (1910), 155–57); 9th ed., 1910 (r.: W. J. Sedgefield, *ESt.* xliii (1911), 267–69); 10th ed., 1913 (r.: Fr. Klaeber, *Beibl.* xxiv (1913), 289–91); 11th and 12th ed., 1918 (r.: F. Holthausen, *ZfdPh.* xlviii (1919/20), 127–31); 13th ed., 1929, 14th ed., 1931 [reprint].
8. C. W. M. Grein, *Beovulf nebst den Fragmenten Finnsburg und Valdere.* Cassel & Göttingen, 1867. [Rather conservative.]
9. Thomas Arnold, *Beowulf. A Heroic Poem of the Eighth Century, with a Translation, Notes, and Appendix.* London, 1876. [Unsafe.] See reviews by H. Sweet, *Academy* x (1876), 588 c–89 a; R. Wülcker, *Angl.* i (1878), 177–86.
10. James A. Harrison and Robert Sharp, *Beowulf: An Anglo-Saxon Poem; The Fight at Finnsburh: A Fragment.* Boston, 1883. [Based on Heyne.] 4th ed., 1894 [with explanatory notes].
11. Richard Paul Wülcker in the revision of Grein's *Bibliothek der*

---

[1] The edition of 1833 has not been accessible.

angelsächsischen Poesie, Vol. i, pp. 149-277. Kassel, 1883. [Extensive critical apparatus.] (Cf. L 1.6.) Anastatic reprint, Hamburg, 1922.

12. Alfred Holder, *Beowulf. II^a: Berichtigter Text mit knappem Apparat und Wörterbuch.* Freiburg i. B., 1884; 2d ed., 1899. [Benefited by the advanced scholarship of Kluge and Cosijn.] *II^b: Wortschatz mit sämtlichen Stellennachweisen.* 1896. (Cf. L 1.6.)

13. (1) A. J. Wyatt, *Beowulf edited with Textual Foot-Notes, Index of Proper Names, and Alphabetical Glossary.* Cambridge, 1894; 2d ed., 1898, reprinted, 1901, 1908. [Judicious; conservative.] — (2) New edition, thoroughly revised by R. W. Chambers, 1914. [Excellent notes.] R.: W. W. Lawrence, *JEGPh.* xiv (1915), 611-13; J. W. Bright, *MLN.* xxxi (1916), 188 f.; J. D. Jones, *MLR.* xi (1916), 230 f.; L. L. Schücking, *ESt.* lv (1921), 88-100. Second ed., 1920 [with additional textual notes, pp. 255-57]. R.: O. L. Jiriczek, *Die Neueren Sprachen* xxix (1921), 67-9.

14. Moritz Trautmann, *Das Beowulflied. Als Anhang das Finn-Bruchstück und die Waldhere-Bruchstücke* (Bonn. B. xvi). Bonn, 1904. [Many tentative emendations introduced.] R.: Fr. Klaeber, *MLN.* xx (1905), 83-7; L. L. Schücking, *Arch.* cxv (1905), 417-21. (Cf. F. Tupper, *Publ. MLAss.* xxv (1910), 164-81.)

15. F. Holthausen, *Beowulf nebst dem Finnsburg-Bruchstück*. Part i.: *Texte und Namenverzeichnis*, Heidelberg, 1905; — 2d ed., 1908, and 3d ed., 1912 (including also *Waldere, Deor, Widsið*, and the OHG. *Hildebrandslied*). Part ii.: *Einleitung, Glossar und Anmerkungen.* 1906; 2d ed., 1909; 3d ed., 1913. [Up-to-date, rigorously conforming to Sievers's metrical types; a mine of information.] R.: L. L. Schücking, *ESt.* xxxix (1908), 94-111; W. W. Lawrence, *JEGPh.* vii (1908), 125-29; M. Deutschbein, *Arch.* cxxi (1908), 162-64; v. Grienberger, *ZföG.* lix (1908), 333-46 (chiefly etymological notes on the Glossary); Fr. Klaeber, *MLN.* xxiv (1909), 94 f.; A. Eichler, *Beibl.* xxi (1910), 129-33, xxii (1911), 161-65; L. L. Schücking, *ESt.* xlii (1910), 108-11; G. Binz, *Lit. bl.* xxxii (1911), 53-5. — 4th ed., Part i, 1914; Part ii, 1919. 5th ed., Part i, 1921; Part ii, 1929; 6th ed., Part i, 1929. R.: Fr. Klaeber, *Beibl.* xli (1930), 8-12; Kemp Malone, *Speculum* v (1930), 327 f., *JEGPh.* xxix (1930), 611-13.

16. W. J. Sedgefield, *Beowulf edited with Introduction, Bibliography, Notes,* [admirable, complete] *Glossary, and Appendices.* (Publ. of the University of Manchester, Engl. Series, No. ii.) Manchester, 1910. [Includes also the text of *The Fight at Finnsburg* and other OE. epic remains.] R.: P. G. Thomas, *MLR.* vi (1911), 266-68; W. W. Lawrence, *JEGPh.* x (1911), 633-40; *Nation* xcii (New York, 1911), 505 b-c (*anon.*); Fr. Klaeber, *ESt.* xliv (1911/12), 119-26; F. Wild, *Beibl.* xxiii (1912), 253-60. — 2d ed., 1913. R.: Fr. Klaeber, *Beibl.* xxv (1914), 166-68; W. W. Lawrence, *JEGPh.* xiv (1915), 609-11.

17. Hubert Pierquin, *Le Poème Anglo-Saxon de Beowulf*. Paris, 1912. 846 pp. [Kemble's text. With French prose translation, Ags. grammar, treatise on versification, chapters on Ags. institutions, etc. A hetero-

II. EDITIONS

geneous compilation.] R.: Fr. Klaeber, *Beibl.* xxiv (1913), 138 f.; W. J. Sedgefield, *MLR.* viii (1913), 550–52.

17 a. Fr. Klaeber, *Beowulf and The Fight at Finnsburg edited, with Introduction, Bibliography, Notes, Glossary, and Appendices.* Boston, 1922. R.: Ernst A. Kock, *AfNF.* xxxix (1923), 185–89; Henning Larsen, *Ph.Q.* ii (1923), 156–58; Robert J. Menner, *The Literary Review (New York Evening Post)*, Jan. 20, 1923, p. 394; F. Holthausen, *Beibl.* xxxiv (1923), 353–57; Hermann M. Flasdieck, *ESt.* lviii (1924), 119–24; Hans Hecht, *Anz.fdA.* xliii (1924), 46–51; William W. Lawrence, *JEGPh.* xxiii (1924), 294–300; E. E. Wardale, *Year's Work* iv, 39–43. Second ed., with Supplement, 1928. R.: Kemp Malone, *JEGPh.* xxviii (1929), 416 f.; [A. Brandl,] *Arch.* clvi (1929), 304 f.

17 b. Federico Olivero, *Beowulf.* Torino, 1934. [Contains an extensive introduction, the text (of Chambers), an Italian translation, and a select bibliography.]

An edition of the 'Beowulf Manuscript,' forming Vol. iv of *The Anglo-Saxon Poetic Records*, is in preparation.

b. Curtailed Editions

18. Ludwig Ettmüller, *Carmen de Beovulfi Gautarum regis rebus praeclare gestis atque interitu, quale fuerit ante quam in manus interpolatoris, monachi Vestsaxonici, inciderat.* Zürich, 1875. [2896 lines.] Cf. L 4.132.

19. Hermann Möller, *Das altenglische Volksepos*, Part ii. Kiel, 1883. [Reconstruction of the presumptive original text in 344 four-line stanzas.] See L 4.134.

c. Selected Portions

20. Ludwig Ettmüller, *Engla and Seaxna Scopas and Bōceras.* Quedlinburg and Leipzig, 1850. [ll. 210–498, 607–661, 710–836, 991–1650, 2516–2820, 3110–3182.]

21. Max Rieger, *Alt- und angelsächsisches Lesebuch.* Giessen, 1861. [ll. 867–915, 1008–1250, 2417–2541, 2724–2820, 2845–2891.]

22. Henry Sweet, *An Anglo-Saxon Reader.* Oxford, 1876; 8th ed., 1908. [ll. 1251–1650.] 9th ed., revised by C. T. Onions, 1922.

23. Further, e.g., Rasmus Kristian Rask, *Angelsaksisk Sproglære*, Stockhom, 1817 (English version by B. Thorpe, Copenhagen, 1830; revised, London, 1865); John Josias Conybeare, *Illustrations of Anglo-Saxon Poetry*, ed. by William Daniel Conybeare, London, 1826; Louis F. Klipstein, *Analecta Anglo-Saxonica*, Vol. ii, New York, 1849; Francis A. March, *An Anglo-Saxon Reader*, New York, 1870; C. Alphonso Smith, *An Old English Grammar and Exercise Book*, 2d ed., Boston, 1898 (6th reprint, 1913) [ll. 611–661, 739–836, 2711–2751, 2792–2820]; W. M. Baskervill, James A. Harrison, and J. Lesslie Hall, *Anglo-Saxon Reader*, 2d ed., New York, 1901 [ll. 499–594, 791–836]; Alfred J. Wyatt, *An Anglo-Saxon Reader*, Cambridge, 1919 [some 440 lines; with William Morris's summary of the parts omitted between selections]; *id., The*

Threshold of Anglo-Saxon, Cambridge, 1926 [some 600 lines (somewhat normalized) of selected extracts with William Morris's summary interspersed]; W. J. Sedgefield, *An Anglo-Saxon Verse-Book*, Manchester, 1922 [upwards of 1200 lines arranged according to their literary affinities]; Milton Haight Turk, *An Anglo-Saxon Reader*, New York, 1927 [some 320 lines]; George Philip Krapp and Arthur Garfield Kennedy, *An Anglo-Saxon Reader*, New York, 1929 [ll. 64–158, 710–836, 2550–2835]; W. A. Craigie, *Specimens of Anglo-Saxon Poetry* III, Edinburgh, 1931 [some 600 lines (of historical legend)]. For Schücking's *Kleines ags. Dichterbuch*, see L F. 2.13.

[24. A paraphrase of the first part in Old English prose composed by Henry Sweet is contained in his *First Steps in Anglo-Saxon*. Oxford, 1897.]

III. TRANSLATIONS

a. Complete Translations

I. English.

A. Prose versions, by:

1. John M. Kemble (in Vol. ii of the 2d ed. of his text, see L 2.2). London, 1837. [Literal.]

2. Benjamin Thorpe. (Opposite his text, see L 2.4.) Oxford, 1855, 1875. [Literal.]

3. Thomas Arnold. (At the foot of his text, see L 2.9.) London, 1876. [Literal.]

4. John Earle, *The Deeds of Beowulf*. Oxford, 1892. c+203 pp. [Literary, picturesque, with inconsistent use of archaisms. Introduction and notes are added.] See review (especially of the Introduction) by E. Koeppel, *ESt.* xviii (1893), 93–5. — Reprinted (translation only), Oxford, 1910.

5. John R. Clark Hall. London, 1901; 2d ed. (carefully revised), 1911. lxvi+287 pp. [Faithful rendering, with valuable illustrative matter and notes.]

6. Chauncey Brewster Tinker. New York, 1902; 2d ed., 1910. [Pleasing.]

7. Clarence Griffin Child. (The Riverside Literature Series, No. 159.) Boston, 1904. [Helpful.] R.: Fr. Klaeber, *Beibl.* xvi (1905), 225–27.

8. Wentworth Huyshe. London, 1907. [With notes and pictorial illustrations. Of no independent value.]

9. Ernest J. B. Kirtlan. London, 1913. [Not up-to-date.]

9 a. R. K. Gordon, *The Song of Beowulf rendered into English Prose*. (The King's Treasuries of Literature.) London and New York, n.d. [1923]. [Not entirely accurate.] It has been incorporated in Everyman's Library, No. 794: *Anglo-Saxon Poetry Selected and Translated* by R. K. Gordon. London and New York. [1927.] The volume also contains a translation of *The Fight at Finnsburg*.

III. TRANSLATIONS

9 b. Prose translations are included in George Wm. McClelland and Albert C. Baugh's *Century Types of English Literature*, New York, 1925 (Transl. by A. C. Baugh), and in Homer A. Watt and James B. Munn's *Ideas and Forms in English and American Literature*, Chicago, 1925 (Transl. by J. B. Munn).

9 c. Harry Morgan Ayres, *Beowulf, a Paraphrase*. Williamsport, Penna., 1933. [A *paraphrase* of distinct literary merit modeled somewhat after the manner of an Icelandic saga.]

B. Metrical versions, by:

10. A. Diedrich Wackerbarth. London, 1849. [Ballad measure; popular.]

11. H. W. Lumsden. London, 1881; 2d ed., 1883. [Ballad measure.]

12. James M. Garnett. Boston, 1882; 4th ed., 1900; reprinted, 1902. [Line-for-line rendering; imitative measure, with two accents to each half-line (cf. J. Schipper, L 8.11.1. § 65, L 8.11.2. § 73).]

13. John Lesslie Hall. Boston, 1892; reprinted, 1900. [Imitative, alliterative measure; archaic language; spirited.]

14. William Morris (and A. J. Wyatt). Hammersmith (Kelmscott Press) [308 copies], 1895; 2d ed. (cheaper), London and New York, 1898. [Fine imitative measure; extremely archaic, strange diction.]

15. Francis B. Gummere, in his *The Oldest English Epic. Beowulf, Finnsburg, Waldere, Deor, Widsith, and the German Hildebrand*. New York, 1909.[1] [Very successful version in ' the original meter '; with good notes and introduction.] Cf. L 3.44 (on verse form).

16. John R. Clark Hall. Cambridge, 1914. [Imitative measure.] R.: W. J. Sedgefield, *MLR*. x (1915), 387–89; Fr. Klaeber, *Beibl*. xxvi (1915), 170–72.

16 a. Charles Scott Moncrieff, *Beowulf translated*. London, 1921. [Alliterative; rather awkward. Also the minor heroic poems are included.] R.: Fr. Klaeber, *Beibl*. xxxiv (1923), 321–23.

16 b. William Ellery Leonard, *Beowulf, a new Verse Translation*. New York and London, 1923. Cf. L 3.44. [A brilliant poetic version in rhymed ' Nibelungen couplets.'] R.: Fr. Klaeber, *Beibl*. xxxiv (1923), 322 f. Leonard's Translation has been presented in an artistic setting: *The Random House Beowulf* (with six full-page lithographs, a title page and full colophon page in black and white by Rockwell Kent) [950 copies]. New York, 1932. Large 4to.

16 c. Archibald Strong, *Beowulf translated into Modern English Rhyming Verse; with a Foreword on ' Beowulf and the Heroic Age '* by R. W. Chambers. London, 1925. R.: Fr. Klaeber, *Beibl*. xxxvii (1926), 257–60; Elsie Blackman, *Review of English Studies* iii (1927), 115 f.; S. J. Crawford, *MLR*. xxii (1927), 325–27; Martin B. Ruud, *MLN*. xliii (1928), 54 f.

---

[1] Gummere's translation of *Beowulf* has been incorporated in *The Five-Foot Shelf of Books* (" The Harvard Classics ") ed. by Charles W. Eliot, Vol. xlix (1910), pp. 5–94.

16 d. D. H. Crawford, *Beowulf translated into English Verse, with an Introduction, Notes & Appendices.* (The Medieval Library, No. 27.) London, 1926. [" Four-stressed unrhymed " lines; a somewhat unfortunate medium.] R.: Kemp Malone, *MLN.* xlii (1927), 202 f.; Elsie Blackman, *Review of Engl. Studies* iii (1927), 237–39; S. J. Crawford, *MLR.* xxii (1927), 325–27; Malcolm S. MacLean, *Beibl.* xxxviii (1927), 312–14.

II. German.

A. Prose versions, by:

17. H. Steineck, in his *Altenglische Dichtungen*, pp. 1–102. Leipzig, 1898. [Literal; poor.]

18. Moritz Trautmann. (Opposite his text.) Bonn, 1904. [Literal.]

B. Metrical versions (with the exception of Nos. 22 and 24, in measures modeled more or less closely after the OE. meter), by:

19. Ludwig Ettmüller. Zürich, 1840. [Literal; obsolete, strange words (' Unwörter '). With introduction and notes.]

20. C. W. M. Grein, in his *Dichtungen der Angelsachsen stabreimend übersetzt.* Vol. i, pp. 222–308. Göttingen, 1857; reprinted, 1863; 2d ed. (*Beowulf* separately), Kassel, 1883. [Accurate; helpful.]

21. Karl Simrock. Stuttgart and Augsburg, 1859. [Faithful.]

22. Moritz Heyne. Paderborn, 1863; 2d ed., 1898; 3d ed., 1915. [Iambic pentameter; readable.]

23. Hans von Wolzogen. [Reclam's Universal-Bibliothek, No. 430.) Leipzig, n.d. [1872]. [Brisk; cursory.]

24. P. Hoffmann. Züllichau, [1893]; 2d ed., Hannover, 1900. [Nibelungen strophes; inaccurate.]

25. Paul Vogt. Halle a. S., 1905. [For the use of high school pupils; text partially rearranged and abridged.] R.: Fr. Klaeber, *Arch.* cxvii (1906), 408–10; G. Binz, *Beibl.* xxi (1910), 289–91.

26. Hugo Gering. Heidelberg, 1906. [Admirable in rhythm and diction; with valuable notes.] R.: W. W. Lawrence, *JEGPh.* vii (1908), 129–33; v. Grienberger, *ZföG.* lix (1908), 423–28; J. Ries, *Anz. fdA.* xxxiii (1909/10), 143–47; G. Binz, *Lit. bl.* xxxi (1910), 397 f. — 2d ed., 1913.

III. Danish.

27. Nik. Fred. Sev. Grundtvig, *Bjowulfs Drape.* Kjøbenhavn, 1820; 2d ed., 1865. [Ballad measure; highly paraphrastic. The 1st ed. contains critical notes and an extensive introduction.] R.: J. Grimm, *Göttingische gelehrte Anzeigen*, Jan. 2, 1823, pp. 1–12 (=J. Grimm's *Kleinere Schriften* iv (Berlin, 1869), 178–86).

28. Frederik Schaldemose. (Opposite his text, see L 2.3.) Kjøbenhavn, 1847; 2d ed., 1851. [Literal, with alliterative decoration.]

29. Adolf Hansen. København and Kristiania, 1910. (Completed, after H.'s death, and edited by Viggo J. von Holstein Rathlou.) [Imitative measure.]

III. TRANSLATIONS

IV. Norwegian Landsmaal.

29 a. Henrik Rytter, *Beowulf og Striden um Finnsborg frå Angelsaksisk.* Oslo, 1921. [Alliterative meter.]

V. Swedish.

30. Rudolf Wickberg. Westervik (Progr.), 1889. [Rhythmical without alliteration.] A new, handy ed., Uppsala, 1914.

VI. Dutch.

31. L. Simons. Gent, 1896. (Publ. by the K. Vlaamsche Academie voor Taal- & Letterkunde.) [Iambic pentameter, with alliteration; careful. Contains an introduction.]

VII. Latin.

32. Grim. Johnson Thorkelin. (Opposite his text, see L 2.1.) Havniæ, 1815. [Practically useless.]

VIII. French.

33. L. Botkine. Havre, 1877. [Prose; free.] R.: K. Körner, *ESt.* ii (1879), 248–51, cf. *ib.* i (1877), 495–96.

34. H. Pierquin. (Opposite his text, see L 2.17.) Paris, 1912. [Prose; unsafe.]

35. W. Thomas, Paris, 1919. [Literal; line-for-line; with an introduction of 32 pages.] Also *Deor, Finnsburg,* and *Waldere* are included. (The translation was originally published in *Revue de l'Enseignement des Langues Vivantes* xxx (1913) ff.)

IX. Italian.

36. C. Giusto Grion, in *Atti della Reale Accademia Lucchese,* Vol. xxii. Lucca, 1883. [Loosely imitative measure; faithful; with introduction.] R.: Th. Krüger, *ESt.* ix (1886), 64–77.

36 a. Numerous passages (some 1100 lines) translated into Italian by Federico Olivero in his *Traduzioni dalla Poesia Anglo-Sassone.* Bari, 1915. [With some notes and a brief general introduction. Contains also *The Fight at Finnsburg* and many other specimens of OE. poetry.] A complete translation in his edition, L 2.17 b.

A. Benedetti's translation, Palermo, 1916 has been out of reach.

b. Partial Translations

37. Sharon Turner, *History of the Anglo-Saxons,* Vol. iv, London, 1805; 6th ed., 1836; 7th ed., 1852. (Reprinted, Philadelphia, 1841.) [Select passages; faulty.]

38. John Josias Conybeare, *Illustrations of Anglo-Saxon Poetry.* London, 1826. (See L 2.23.) [Paraphrastic extracts in blank verse (inserted in a prose analysis), and literal Latin rendering.]

39. The Grendel part (ll. 1–836) in German by G. Zinsser, Forbach Progr. Saarbrücken, 1881. [Iambic pentameter; free, readable.]

40. Selections from Chauncey B. Tinker's translation in *Translations*

from Old English Poetry ed. by Albert S. Cook and Chauncey B. Tinker, Boston, 1902. Revised ed., 1926.

41. The Dragon part (ll. 2207–3182) in Swedish by Erik Björkman in *Världslitteraturen i urval och öfversättning* redigerad af Henrik Schück. Andra Serien: Medeltiden. Stockholm, 1902. [Rhythmical prose.]

41 a. Henry Cecil Wyld, "Experiments in Translating *Beowulf.*" *Kl. Misc.* (1929), 217–31. [Specimens of passages translated in a variety of meters. "A modern version of a work so essentially poetical in form and diction ought certainly to be in verse, and . . . the meter should be one of those . . . familiar in modern English poetry."]

42. Selections included in anthologies of English literature. 1) Kate M. Warren, *A Treasury of English Literature.* London, 1906. (Contains also part of *The Fight at Finnsburg.*) 2) Walter C. Bronson, *English Poems: Old English and Middle English Periods.* Chicago, 1910. (E. S. Bronson's translation.) 3) A. G. Newcomer and A. E. Andrews, *Twelve Centuries of English Poetry and Prose.* Chicago, 1910. (An improved version of Thorpe's rendering.) 4) Henry S. Pancoast and John Duncan Spaeth, *Early English Poems.* New York, 1911. (Spaeth's translation, pp. 5–29; notes, pp. 389–403.) J. Duncan Spaeth, *Old English Poetry: Translations into Alliterative Verse, with Introductions and Notes.* Princeton, 1921, 1922. [Contains two thirds of *Beowulf.*] 5) J. W. Cunliffe, J. F. A. Pyre, Karl Young, *Century Readings for a Course in English Literature.* New York, 1915. (Contains the greater part of Earle's translation.) 6) *English Literature, The Beginnings to 1500*, ed. by James Dow McCallum. New York, 1929. (Several passages, chiefly episodes, are omitted.) 7) *Old English and Medieval Literature* ed. by G. H. Gerould. New York, 1929. (Gerould's metrical version (imitative measure) includes about one half of *Beowulf.*[1]

c. Criticism of Translations

43. A useful review of the translations published up to 1902 is found in Chauncey B. Tinker's *The Translations of Beowulf: a critical Bibliography.* (Yale Studies in English xvi.) New York, 1903. The earlier translations are surveyed by R. P. Wülcker in *Angl.* iv, *Anz.* (1881), 69–

---

[1] Paraphrases for the general public or for children: 1) Ferdinand Bässler, *Beowulf, Wieland der Schmied, und die Ravennaschlacht. Für die Jugend und das Volk bearbeitet*, 2d ed., Berlin, 1875. 16mo. 2) Clara L. Thomson, *The Adventures of Beowulf.* London, 1899; 2d ed., 1904. (A good paraphrase for school children.) 3) A popular summary in *A Book of Famous Myths and Legends*, with an Introduction by Thomas J. Shahan, Boston, 1901; included in Hamilton W. Mabie's *Legends that Every Child Should Know*, New York, 1906. 4) *Stories of Beowulf Told to the Children* by H. E. Marshall. (With pictures.) London and New York, 1908. 16mo. 5) *Brave Beowulf* (in *Every Child's Library*) by Thos. Cartwright. (With pictures.) London, 1908. 16mo. 6) A paraphrase of the first division (ll. 1–1250) for school children: R. A. Spencer, *The Story of Beowulf and Grendel retold in Modern English Prose.* London and Edinburgh, n.d. [1923]. 7) Other selections as well as digests and paraphrases are mentioned in Tinker's monograph (L 3.43), pp. 121 ff.

IV. LITERARY CRITICISM

78; some later ones by James M. Garnett, *Publ. MLAss.* xviii (1903), 445–51.

44. For a discussion of the verse-form most suitable for a translation, see J. Schipper, *Angl.* vi, *Anz.* (1883), 120–24; Francis B. Gummere, *Am. Jour. Phil.* vii (1886), 46–78; James M. Garnett, *ib.* ii (1881), 356 f., *Publ. MLAss.* vi (1891), 95–105, *ib.* xviii (1903), 446 f., 455–58; Prosser Hall Frye, *MLN.* xii (1897), 79–82; Edward Fulton, *Publ. MLAss.* xiii (1898), 286–96; M. Trautmann, *Bonn. B.* v (1900), 189–91; John Ries, L 3.26. Cf. also F. B. Gummere, *MLN.* xxv (1910), 61–3 (in a reply to C. G. Child's criticism of the use of verse, *ib.* xxiv (1909), 253 f.), and C. G. Child's rejoinder, *ib.* xxv (1910), 157 f.; further W. J. Sedgefield, *ESt.* xli (1910), 402 f., and M. Trautmann, *Beibl.* xxi (1910), 353–60 (in reviews of Gummere's translation); J. D. Spaeth in *Early English Poems* (L 3.42.4), pp. 376–80; A. Blyth Webster, *Essays and Studies by Members of the English Association* v (1914), 153–71; William Ellery Leonard, " Beowulf and the Niebelungen Couplet," *Univ. of Wisconsin Studies in Language and Literature*, No. 2 (1918), pp. 99–152 [a spirited exposition of the merits of the ' Nibelungen couplet ' as verse-medium; the added specimens convincingly support the arguments]. Review of W. E. Leonard's monograph by Fr. Klaeber, *Beibl.* xxxii (1921), 145–48. Cf. Leonard's supplementary study, " The Scansion of Middle English Alliterative Verse," *Univ. of Wisconsin Studies in Language and Literature*, No. 11 (1920), 57–103. And see L 3.41 a (H. C. Wyld).

[45. A drama on the subject of Beowulf (written in 1899–1900), entitled *Beowulf: An Epical Drama* by Percy MacKaye is in preparation for the press.][1]

IV. LITERARY CRITICISM. FABULOUS AND HISTORICAL ELEMENTS

A. GENERAL REFERENCES

a. *Handbooks of Literature*

1. Thomas Warton, *History of English Poetry*. Ed. by W. Carew Hazlitt. Vol. ii, pp. 3–19: Henry Sweet, *Sketch of the History of Anglo-Saxon Poetry*. London, 1871.

2. Henry Morley, *English Writers*. Vol. i, ch. vi (1st ed., 1864), 2d ed. (completely revised), London, 1887; 3d ed., 1891.

3. Bernhard ten Brink, (1) *Geschichte der englischen Litteratur*. Vol. i, Berlin, 1877; (2) 2d ed. revised by Alois Brandl, 1899. [Admirable.] (3) English translation of the first edition by Horace M. Kennedy. London and New York, 1884.

4. Richard Wülker, *Grundriss zur Geschichte der angelsächsischen Lit-*

---

[1] It may be mentioned that Howard Hanson has composed a choral work, " The Lament for Beowulf " (for mixed chorus and orchestra). (Boston, 1925.)

teratur. Leipzig, 1885. [Of great value on account of its bibliographies and critical summaries of books and papers.]

5. Adolf Ebert, *Allgemeine Geschichte der Literatur des Mittelalters im Abendlande.* Vol. iii, pp. 27 ff. Leipzig, 1887.

6. Stopford A. Brooke, (1) *The History of Early English Literature.* London and New York, 1892. [Interesting.] (2) *English Literature from the Beginning to the Norman Conquest.* London and New York, 1898. [A shorter version.]

7. Bernhard ten Brink, *Altenglische Literatur* in *P. Grdr.*[1], ii[a]. Strassburg, 1893. [Unfinished.] Reprinted in L 4.3.2, pp. 431–78.

8. Rudolf Koegel, *Geschichte der deutschen Litteratur bis zum Ausgange des Mittelalters.* Vol. i[a], *passim.* Strassburg, 1894.

9. W. J. Courthope, *A History of English Poetry.* Vol. i, ch. iii. London and New York, 1895.

10. *The Cambridge History of English Literature.* Ed. by A. W. Ward and A. R. Waller. Vol. i, ch. iii: H. Munro Chadwick, *Early National Poetry.* London and New York, 1907.[1] [Admirable, succinct account.]

11. Alois Brandl, *Englische Literatur: A. Angelsächsische Periode* in *P. Grdr.*[2], ii[a], pp. 980–1024. Strassburg, 1908. [The most successful scholarly treatment.]

12. Illustrated works of a somewhat popular character: (1) Richard Wülker, *Geschichte der englischen Litteratur.* Leipzig, 1896; 2d ed., 1907. (2) Richard Garnett and Edmund Gosse, *English Literature: An Illustrated Record.* Vol. i, by Richard Garnett. London and New York, 1903, 1923.

13. Shorter Handbooks: (1) John Earle, *Anglo-Saxon Literature.* London, 1884. 16mo, 262 pp. (2) F. J. Snell, *The Age of Alfred.* London, 1912. 12mo, 257 pp. (3) M. M. A. Schröer, *Grundzüge und Haupttypen der englischen Literaturgeschichte.* Part i. (Sammlung Göschen, No. 286.) 3. ed., 1927. [A stimulating primer.]

13 a. Andreas Heusler, *Die altgermanische Dichtung.* (*Handbuch der Literaturwissenschaft* hrsg. von Oskar Walzel, Vol. xi.) Berlin-Neubabelsberg, 1923. 4to, 200 pp. *Passim.* [A brilliant work covering the entire field; the ripe fruit of scholarship and literary insight. For *Beowulf,* see esp. §§ 148 ff.; for *Widsið,* §§ 77 f.]

Cf. also Levin L. Schücking, *Die angelsächsische und frühmittelenglische Dichtung* (Walzel's *Handbuch* etc.), *passim.* Pp. 1–35: the OE. period. (1927.) — Hermann Schneider, *Germanische Heldensage,* Vol. i. (*P. Grdr.* 10.1.) Berlin, 1928. 442 pp. [Contains a general informative introduction and a study of " Deutsche Heldensage."] R.: A. Heusler, *Anz. fdA.* xlviii (1929), 160–70. Vol. ii. 1 (*P. Grdr.* 10.2): " Nordger-

---

[1] George Sampson's *The Cambridge Book of Prose and Verse* (Cambridge, 1924; xxxviii+438 pp.) " offers to general readers a selection of passages to illustrate the first volume of *The Cambridge History of English Literature.*" [It contains a few short passages of *Beowulf* taken from various earlier translations.]

IV. LITERARY CRITICISM cxxxvii

manische Heldensage," 1933. Vol. ii. 2 (*P. Grdr.* 10.3): " Englische Heldensage, etc.," 1934. [Masterly studies.]

13 b. Emile Legouis, *A History of English Literature* 650–1660 (Vol. i of *A History of English Literature* by Emile Legouis and Louis Cazamian). Translated from the French by Helen Douglas Irvine. London and Toronto, 1926. Ch. i: 'Anglo-Saxon Literature' (pp. 1–34). [Remarkable for a certain unwillingness to appreciate Old English poetry. *Beowulf* is called " a poem which has come out of a cold cell in a Northumbrian cloister; it breathes the air of the tomb."] R.: Kemp Malone, *JEGPh.* xxvi (1927), 413–19. (" The mature philologist will read Mr. Legouis's work with interest and, now and again, with profit. The beginner (for whom the book was written) is likely to be led into false paths.")

b. Comprehensive Treatises (touching on various lines of inquiry)[1]

14. K. W. Bouterwek, " Das Beowulflied. Eine Vorlesung." *Germ.* i (1856), 385–418. [Analysis of the poem, with a general introduction.][2]

15. F. Rönning, *Beovulfs-Quadet: en literær-historisk undersøgelse.* København Diss. 1883. 175 pp. [Arguments against Müllenhoff's *Liedertheorie;* authorship, date, genesis, literary character of the *Beowulf.*] R.: R. Heinzel, *Anz. fdA.* x (1884), 233–39.

16. Gregor Sarrazin, (1) *Beowulf-Studien: ein Beitrag zur Geschichte altgermanischer Sage und Dichtung.* Berlin, 1888. 220 pp. (A summary in English by Phoebe M. Luehrs in *The Western Reserve University Bulletin*, Vol. vii, No. 5 (Nov., 1904), pp. 146–65.) [Scandinavian origin of the legends and the poem; Cynewulf's authorship.] R.: R. Heinzel, *Anz.fdA.* xv (1889), 182–89; E. Koeppel, *ESt.* xiii (1889), 472–80, cf. Sarrazin, *ib.* xiv (1890), 421–27; Koeppel, *ib.* xiv, 427–32. — Further: G. Sarrazin, (2) " Die Abfassungszeit des Beowulfliedes," *Angl.* xiv (1892), 399–415. (Cf. L 4.142.) (3) *Von Kädmon bis Kynewulf. Eine litterar-historische Studie.* Berlin, 1913. 173 pp. [Genesis of *Beowulf*, its relation to other OE. poems, date, authorship (Cynewulf).] R.: L. Dudley, *JEGPh.* xv (1916), 313–17; O. Funke, *Beibl.* xxxi (1920), 121–34.

17. Studies preparatory to his *Beowulf-Studien* are found in the following papers by G. Sarrazin: (1) " Der Schauplatz des ersten Beowulfliedes und die Heimat des Dichters," *Beitr.* xi (1886), 159–83; (2) " Altnordisches im Beowulfliede," *ib.* xi, 528–41; (3) " Die Beowulfsage in Dänemark," *Angl.* ix (1886), 195–99; (4) " Beowa und Böthvar," *ib.* ix,

---

[1] Here would belong also the introductions to certain editions and translations of *Beowulf*, especially those of Grundtvig (translation and edition), Kemble, Ettmüller (translation), Thorpe, Simrock, Arnold, Garnett, Grion, Earle, Simons, Clark Hall, Gering, Huyshe, Gummere, Sedgefield, *et al.*

[2] A very brief survey of the poem and its salient features is contained in Frederico Garlanda's *Beowulf: origini, bibliografia, metrica, contenuto, saggio di versione letterale, significato storico, etico, sociologico.* Roma, 1906. 15 pp.

200-4; (5) " Beowulf und Kynewulf," *ib.* ix, 515-50. — Cf. E. Sievers, " Die Heimat des Beowulfdichters," *Beitr.* xi (1886), 354-62; " Altnordisches im Beowulf?", *ib.* xii (1887), 168-200; J. H. Gallée, " *haf, gamel, bano*," *ib.* xii, 561-63; J. Kail, " Über die Parallelstellen in der angelsächsischen Poesie," *Angl.* xii (1889), 21-40; G. Sarrazin, " Parallelstellen in altenglischer Dichtung," *Angl.* xiv (1892), 186-92. Other papers of importance by Sarrazin are mentioned under L 4.32, 144.

18. Bernhard ten Brink, *Beowulf: Untersuchungen* (Quellen und Forschungen etc. lxii.). Strassburg, 1888. 248 pp. [Component elements ('variations'); nationality (English) and origin of the *Beowulf;* language, MS.] R.: R. Heinzel, *Anz.fdA.* xv (1889), 153-82; H. Möller, *ESt.* xiii (1889), 247-315.

19. Karl Müllenhoff, *Beowulf: Untersuchungen über das angelsächsische Epos und die älteste Geschichte der germanischen Seevölker.* Berlin, 1889. 165 pp. [a. Myths; historical elements (most valuable); b. " The inner history of *Beowulf*." See L 4.130.] R.: R. Heinzel, *Anz.fdA.* xvi (1890), 264-75; G. Sarrazin, *ESt.* xvi (1892), 71-85. — Cf. K. Müllenhoff in *Nordalbingische Studien* i (Kiel, 1844), 166-73. [A first, brief study of some of the historical elements.]

20. Thomas Arnold, *Notes on Beowulf.* London and New York, 1898. 12mo, 140 pp. [Helpful as an introduction.] R.: G. Sarrazin, *ESt.* xxviii (1900), 410-18.

21. Henry Bradley, " Beowulf." *Encyclopædia Britannica*, 11th ed., Vol. iii (1910), 758-61. [Brief, conservative survey.]

22. H. Munro Chadwick, (1) *The Heroic Age.* Cambridge, 1912. 474 pp. [An important work of wide scope. It includes an illuminating comparison of the Germanic with the Greek heroic poetry.] R.: A. Mawer, *MLR.* viii (1913), 207-9; R. W. Chambers, *ESt.* xlviii (1914/15), 162-66. (2) H. Munro Chadwick and N. Kershaw Chadwick, *The Growth of Literature.* Vol. i: *The Ancient Literatures of Europe.* Cambridge (Engl.) and New York, 1932. 672 pp. [The opening volume of a monumental undertaking. The comparative treatment has been extended to the old Norse, Welsh, and Irish literatures.] R.: A. H. Krappe, *Speculum* viii (1933), 270-78; H. V. Routh, *RESt.* ix (1933), 209-13. — [Cf. also I. S. Peter, *Beowulf and the Rāmāyaṇa: A Study in Epic Poetry.* London, 1934. 139 pp.]

22 a. R. W. Chambers, *Beowulf: An Introduction to the Study of the Poem with a Discussion of the Stories of Offa and Finn.* Cambridge, 1921. 417 pp. [Historical elements, non-historical elements, origin of the poem; illustrative documents, special appendices, full bibliography, etc. A very important, scholarly work, indispensable to advanced students. Thorough discussion of problems.] R.: Frederick Tupper, *JEGPh.* xxi (1922), 680-84; Bernhard Fehr, *Beibl.* xxxiii (1922), 121-26; Eilert Ekwall, *ib.*, 177-85; Howard R. Patch, *MLN.* xxxvii (1922), 418-27; Robert J. Menner, *The Literary Review (New York Evening Post)*, Jan. 20, 1923, p. 394; Allen Mawer, *MLR.* xviii (1923), 96-98;

IV. LITERARY CRITICISM

J. R. H[ulbert], *MPh.* xx (1923), 436 f.; O. L. Jiriczek, *Die Neueren Sprachen* xxxi (1923), 412–16; R. C. Boer, *Eng. Studies* v (Amsterdam, 1923), 105–18; E. E. Wardale, *Year's Work* ii, 33–35. Second ed., 1932. 565 pp. R.: Fr. Klaeber, *MLR.* xxvii (1932), 462–66; Kemp Malone, *Eng. Studies* xiv (1932), 190–93; *Medium Ævum* i (1932), 229–31 (*anon.*); F. Mossé, *Revue germanique* xxiv (1933), 49–52; Howard R. Patch, *Speculum* viii (1933), 278 f.; C. L. Wrenn, *RESt.* ix (1933), 204–09; W. Fischer, *Beibl.* xliv (1933), 332–35.

22 b. R. W. Chambers's delightful essay, "Beowulf and the Heroic Age" (L 3.16 c) deserves special mention; likewise, his paper, "The Lost Literature of Medieval England," *Transactions of the Bibliographical Society* (*The Library*), London, March, 1925, pp. 293–321.

22 c. William Witherle Lawrence, *Beowulf and Epic Tradition.* Cambridge (Harvard Univ. Press), 1928, 1930. 349 pp. [A very helpful book, similar in its scope to Chambers's *Introduction*, but not exclusively addressed to scholars. The author's aim has been "to review the subject-matter of the poem, both the main plot and the chief subsidiary material, and to show how this appears to have been gradually combined into an epic, giving due attention to the social and political background."] R.: Kemp Malone, *Speculum* iii (1928), 612–15; R. W. Chambers, *MLR.* xxiv (1929), 334–37; Elsie Blackman, *RESt.* v (1929), 333–35; Henning Larsen, *MLN.* xliv (1929), 189 f.; O. L. Jiriczek, *Beibl.* xl (1929), 193–202; Marjorie Daunt, *Year's Work* ix, 66 f.

22 d. Hermann Schneider, *Englische und nordgermanische Heldensage.* (Sammlung Göschen, No. 1064.) 1933. [A primer containing very brief but independent comments on *Finnsburg*, *Beowulf*, etc.] For a fuller account, see L 4.13 a.

B. THE LEGENDS. (*Component Elements of the Story*)

a. Fabulous (or Supernatural) and Historical Elements[1]

23. Franz Joseph Mone, *Untersuchungen zur Geschichte der teutschen Heldensage.* Quedlinburg and Leipzig, 1836. 292 pp.

24. H. Leo, *Ueber Beowulf: Beowulf, das älteste deutsche, in angelsächsischer Mundart erhaltene Heldengedicht nach seinem Inhalte, und nach seinen historischen und mythologischen Beziehungen betrachtet.* Halle, 1839. 120 pp.

25. Karl Müllenhoff, (1) "Die austrasische Dietrichssage," *ZfdA.* vi (1848), 435 ff. [Hygelāc's expedition against the Franks, etc.]; (2) "Scēaf und seine Nachkommen," *ib.* vii (1849), 410–19; (3) "Der Mythus von Bēowulf," *ib.* vii, 419–41; (4) "Zur Kritik des angelsäch-

---

[1] The various subdivisions do not necessarily exclude each other; a certain amount of overlapping is in fact unavoidable in this Bibliography. Occasional deviations from the chronological order are intentional.

sischen Volksepos," *ib.* xi (1859), 272–94; (5) " Zeugnisse und Excurse zur deutschen Heldensage," *ib.* xii (1865, paper dated: 1860), 253 ff. [Important testimonies.]

26. Ludwig Uhland, " Zur deutschen Heldensage. I. Sigemund und Sigeferd." *Germ.* ii (1857), 344–63. (=L. Uhland's *Schriften zur Geschichte der Dichtung und Sage* viii (Stuttgart, 1873), 479–504.)

27. Daniel H. Haigh, *The Anglo-Saxon Sagas.* London, 1861. 178 pp. [English history discovered in the poem; fanciful, superficial.]

28. Sophus Bugge, " Studien über das Beowulfepos." *Beitr.* xii (1887), 1–79; 360–65. [Sterling contribution.]

29. B. Symons, *Heldensage* in *P. Grdr.*, ii^a (1893), §§ 17–18; 2d ed. (1900), iii, §§ 23–25: " Beowulfsage." [Careful, conservative summary.]

30. Otto Haack, *Zeugnisse zur altenglischen Heldensage.* Kiel Diss., 1892. 56 pp.

31. (1) G. Binz, " Zeugnisse zur germanischen Sage in England." *Beitr.* xx (1895), 141–223. [Valuable collection of material based on an examination of proper names recorded in England.] (2) A few supplementary references by F. Kluge, *ESt.* xxi (1895), 446–48. — (3) Further: F. Kluge, " Der Beowulf und die Hrolfs Saga Kraka." *ESt.* xxii (1896), 144 f. — (4) Erik Björkman, *Nordische Personennamen in England in alt- u. frühmittelenglischer Zeit.* (St.EPh. xxxvii.) Halle a. S., 1910. *Passim.* (5) F. W. Moorman, " English Place-Names and Teutonic Sagas." *Essays and Studies by Members of the English Association* v (Oxford, 1914), 75–103. (6) A. Brandl, " Siegmund, Siegfried und Brünhilde in Ortsnamen des nordwestlichen Englands." *Arch.* cxxxiii (1915), 408 f. (7) Hans Naumann, *Altnordische Namenstudien,* pp. 179–82. Berlin, 1912. (8) Erik Björkman, *Studien über die Eigennamen im Beowulf.* (St.EPh. lviii.) Halle a. S., 1920. 122 pp. [A complete survey, of great value for the criticism of the legends.] (9) Elias Wessén, " Nordiska namnstudier." *Uppsala Universitets Årsskrift,* 1927. (Filos., Språkvet. och histor. Vetensk. 3.) 118 pp. [Pp. 5 ff.: ' Forngermanska kunganamn ' (cf. Intr. xxxii & n. 3); pp. 110 ff.: ' Nordiska personnamn på -*þióƒr* '; pp. 53 ff.: names in *Beowulf.*]

32. Gregor Sarrazin, (1) " Neue Beowulf-Studien. I. König Hrodhgeirr und seine Familie. II. Das Skjöldungen-Epos. III. Das Drachenlied. IV. Das Beowulflied und Kynewulfs Andreas." *ESt.* xxiii (1897), 221–67; (2) " Hrolf Krake und sein Vetter im Beowulfliede." *ESt.* xxiv (1898), 144 f.; (3) " Die Hirsch-Halle "; " Der Balder-Kultus in Lethra." *Angl.* xix (1897), 368–92; 392–97; (4) " Neue Beowulf-Studien. V. Beowulfs Kampfgenossen." *ESt.* xxxv (1905), 19–27; (5) " Neue Beowulf-Studien. VI. *Æt hærgtrafum.* VII. *Fyrgenstrēam.* VIII. Der Grendelsee. IX. Personennamen; Herkunft der Sage. X. Beowulfs Ende und Bödhvar Bjarkis Fall." *ESt.* xlii (1910), 1–37. [A series of highly ingenious but somewhat inconclusive studies.] See also L 4.20.

33. E. Sievers, " Beowulf und Saxo." *Berichte der Königl. Säch-*

IV. LITERARY CRITICISM

sischen Gesellschaft der Wissenschaften, July 6, 1895, pp. 175–92. [1. Heremōd. 2. Bēowulf's Dragon Fight. 3. Scyld.]

34. Max Förster, *Beowulf-Materialien zum Gebrauch bei Vorlesungen.* Braunschweig, 1900, 1908, 1912. 5th ed., Heidelberg, 1928. 28 pp. [Convenient collection of illustrative parallels.]

35. Axel Olrik, *Danmarks Heltedigtning.* Part i. *Rolf Krake og den ældre Skjoldungrække.* København, 1903. 352 pp. R.: A. Heusler, *Anz.fdA.* xxx (1906), 26–36. Part ii. *Starkad den gamle og den yngre Skjoldungrække.* 1910. 322 pp. R.: A. Heusler, *Anz.fdA.* xxxv (1912), 169–83. [A brilliant scholarly work.] — An English version of Vol. i: Axel Olrik, *The Heroic Legends of Denmark.* Translated from the Danish and revised in collaboration with the author by Lee M. Hollander. New York, The American-Scandinavian Foundation, 1919. [Considerably revised, rearranged, and thus made still more helpful.] R.: G. T. Flom, *JEGPh.* xix (1920), 284–90.

35 a. Paul Herrmann, *Die Heldensagen des Saxo Grammaticus.* (Continuation of the volume containing his translation, L 10.4. General title of the work: *Erläuterungen zu den ersten neun Büchern der dänischen Geschichte des Saxo Grammaticus.* Part i: Translation. Leipzig, 1901.) Part ii: Commentary. Leipzig, 1922. 668 pp. [A careful, detailed commentary; in fact, an extremely useful handbook.]

35 b. (1) R. C. Boer, "Studier over Skjoldungedigtningen." *Aarbøger for Nordisk Oldkyndighed og Historie*, 1922, pp. 133–266. [An elaborate survey differing considerably from Olrik's interpretation.] (Cf. Cha. Intr.² 424 ff.) — (2) Vilh. la Cour, "Skjoldungefejden." *Danske Studier*, 1926, pp. 147–56. [Refutes Boer's view of the Skjoldung family feud.]

36. Max Deutschbein, "Die sagenhistorischen und literarischen Grundlagen des Beowulfepos." *GRM.* i (1909), 103–19. [Notices Celtic influences.]

37. Andreas Heusler, (1) "Geschichtliches und Mythisches in der germanischen Heldensage." *Sitzungsberichte der Königl. Preussischen Akademie der Wissenschaften*, 1909, No. xxxvii, pp. 920–45. [Of fundamental importance.] (2) "Beowulf," *R.-L.* i, 245–48. (1912.)

38. H. Munro Chadwick, *The Origin of the English Nation.* Cambridge, 1907. 351 pp. *Passim.* [Distinguished by learning and acumen.]

39. Henrik Schück, *Studier i Beowulfsagan.* (Upsala Universitets Årsskrift. 1909. Program 1.) Upsala, 1909. 50 pp. [Analyzes the component saga elements; presents a clear-cut theory of the genesis of *Beowulf.*] R.: V. O. Freeburg, *JEGPh.* xi (1912), 488–97.

40. See W. A. Berendsohn, L 4.141. Cf. Berendsohn, "Altgermanische Heldendichtung." *Neue Jahrbücher für das klassische Altertum etc.* xxxv (1915), 633–48.

40 a. W. A. Berendsohn, "Hrolfssaga kraka und Beowulf-Epos." *Niederdeutsche Studien, Festschrift für Conrad Borchling*, pp. 328–37. Neumünster, 1932. (Cf. L 4.141.)

40 b. Gustav Hübener, " Beowulf und die Psychologie der Standesentwicklung." *GRM.* xiv (1926), 352–71. [Comments, in sociological terms, on the presence of folk-tale elements and of elements belonging to heroic legend.]

b. Studies devoted mainly to the Supernatural (and Mythical) Elements

41. Wilhelm Grimm in *Irische Elfenmärchen. Übersetzt von den Brüdern Grimm*, pp. cxix ff. Leipzig, 1826. (= W. Grimm's *Kleinere Schriften* i (Berlin, 1881), 467 ff.) [Refers to folk-tale motives.]

42. Jacob Grimm, *Deutsche Mythologie.* 1835; 4th ed., Berlin, 1875–78. 3 vols. Vol. iii, pp. 377 ff. (Anglo-Saxon genealogies); and *passim*.[1] English translation: *Teutonic Mythology*, by J. S. Stallybrass. London, 1880–88. 4 vols.

43. John M. Kemble, *Über die Stammtafel der Westsachsen.* München, 1836. (Preparatory to part of his ' Postscript to the Preface ' in his edition,[2] Vol. ii, pp. i-lv.) R.: J. Grimm, *Göttingische gelehrte Anzeigen*, April 28, 1836, pp. 649–57 (= J. Grimm's *Kleinere Schriften* v (Berlin, 1871), 240–45).

44. John M. Kemble, *The Saxons in England.* London, 1849; 2d ed. by Walter de Gray Birch, 1876. Vol. i, pp. 413 ff.

45. K. W. Bouterwek, *Cædmon's des Angelsachsen biblische Dichtungen* hrsg. Gütersloh, 1854. Vol. i, pp. c–cxiv.

46. Nathanael Müller, *Die Mythen im Beowulf in ihrem Verhältnis zur germanischen Mythologie betrachtet.* Heidelberg Diss. Leipzig, 1878. [Unprofitable compilation.]

---

[1] Handbooks of mythology, besides J. Grimm's monumental work, to be consulted with advantage are: (1) Elard Hugo Meyer, (a) *Germanische Mythologie*, Berlin, 1891; (b) *Mythologie der Germanen*, Strassburg, 1903; cf. (c) *Indogermanische Mythen* ii, 634 f. [on Beowulf], Berlin, 1887. (2) E. Mogk, (a) *Mythologie* in *P. Grdr.*, (1891), i, pp. 982–1138; 2d ed. (1900), iii, pp. 230–406; (b) *Germanische Mythologie* (Sammlung Göschen, No. 15), Leipzig, 1906. [Primer.] A revised ed., *Germanische Religionsgeschichte und Mythologie*, 1921. (3) Wolfgang Golther, (a) *Handbuch der germanischen Mythologie*, Leipzig, 1895; (b) *Götterglaube und Göttersagen der Germanen*, 1894; 2d ed., 1910. 12mo. [Handy school book.] (4) P. D. Chantepie de la Saussaye, *The Religion of the Teutons*, translated from the Dutch by Bert J. Vos. Boston and London, 1902. [Commendable.] (5) Friedrich von der Leyen, *Die Götter und Göttersagen der Germanen.* (Part i of *Deutsches Sagenbuch*, see L 4.67. n.) München, 1909, 3d ed., 1924. [Semi-popular.] (6) Richard M. Meyer, *Altgermanische Religionsgeschichte.* Leipzig, 1910. R.: W. Golther, *Lit. bl.* xxxii (1911), 265–72. (7) Karl Helm, *Altgermanische Religionsgeschichte. I.* Heidelberg, 1913. (8) Cf. *Die Kultur der Gegenwart* hrsg. von P. Hinneberg, i. 3, 1, 2d ed., pp. 258–72; Andreas Heusler, *Die altgermanische Religion.* Leipzig, 1913. [Stimulating sketch.] (9) Gudmund Schütte, *Dänisches Heidentum.* Heidelberg, 1923. 154 pp. (A revised and abridged version of his *Hjemligt Hedenskab*, Copenhagen, 1919.) R.: C. C. Uhlenbeck, *Acta Philologica Scandinavica* i (1926), 293–300; H. de Boor, *Lit. bl.* xlviii (1927), 416–18. (10) Cf. Ernst A. Philippson, *Germanisches Heidentum bei den Angelsachsen.* (Kölner Angl. Arbeiten iv.) Leipzig, 1929. 239 pp. R.: Kemp Malone, *MLN.* xlv (1930), 259 f.; G. Hübener, *Lit. bl.* lii (1931), 37–41; O. Ritter, *Zs. f. Ortsnamenforschung* viii (1932), 78–91 (critical remarks on place-names).

IV. LITERARY CRITICISM

47. Ludwig Laistner, *Nebelsagen*, pp. 88 ff., 264 ff. Stuttgart, 1879.
48. (1) Hugo Gering, " Der Beowulf und die isländische Grettissaga." *Angl.* iii (1880), 74–87. [Translation and discussion of chs. 64–67 of the *Grettissaga*.] (2) This parallel was first pointed out by Gudbrand Vigfusson in his edition of the *Sturlunga Saga*, Vol. i, p. xlix. Oxford, 1878.
49. Walter W. Skeat, (1) " On the signification of the monster Grendel in the poem of Beowulf; with a discussion of lines 2076–2100." *Journal of Philology* xv (1886), 120–31. (2) Cf. *id.*, " The name ' Beowulf,' " *Academy* xi (Febr. 24, 1877), 163 c. (3) Erik G. T. Rooth, " Der Name Grendel in der Beowulfsage." *Beibl.* xxviii (1917), 335–40. (4) A. Pogatscher, " Altenglisch *Grendel*." *Neusprachliche Studien, Festgabe für Karl Luick* (*Die Neueren Sprachen*, 6. Beiheft, 1925), p. 151. [Etymology: **grandilaz*, ' hostile pursuer,' cp. Gmc. *gram*.] — It may be added that H. Kern in his notes (§ 264) on J. H. Hessels's ed. of the *Lex Salica* (1880) referred to the word *granderba* (i.e., **grand-derba*, ' nequitiae audax (mulier) ') as related to OE. *grandor-*, *Grendel*.
50. Ludwig Laistner, *Das Rätsel der Sphinx. Grundzüge einer Mythengeschichte.* Berlin, 1889. Vol. ii, pp. 15–34. [Traces folk-tale motives in the Grendel story.]
51. Sophus Bugge and Axel Olrik, " Røveren ved Gråsten og Beowulf." *Dania* (*Tidsskrift for Folkemål og Folkeminder*) i (1891), 233–45. [On ll. 2231–71.] — Cf. Knut Stjerna (L 9.39), pp. 37 ff., 136 ff.
52. (1) Rudolf Kögel, " Beowulf." *ZfdA.* xxxvii (1893), 268–76. [Etymology of " Beowulf."] (2) Cf. *id.*, *Anz.fdA.* xviii (1892), 56; (3) E. Sievers, *Beitr.* xviii (1894), 413. (4) R. Ferguson, " The Anglo-Saxon name Beowulf." *Athenæum*, No. 3372 (June 11, 1892), p. 763 a-b. [=Beadowulf.] (5) Elis Wadstein, " Beowulf. Etymologie und Sinn des Namens." *Germanica, Sievers-Festschrift zum 75. Geburtstage.* Halle a. S., 1925, pp. 323–26. [Cp. Dutch *bui(e)*, ' strong gust of wind.' (?)]
53. Felix Niedner, " Die Dioskuren im Beowulf." *ZfdA.* xlii (1898), 229–58. [Mythological speculations.]
54. R. C. Boer, " Zur Grettissaga." *ZfdPh.* xxx (1898), 53–71.
55. Albert S. Cook, " An Irish Parallel to the Beowulf Story." *Arch.* ciii (1899), 154–56.
56. F. York Powell, " Beowulf and Watanabe-No-Tsuna " in *An English Miscellany presented to Dr. Furnivall*, pp. 395 f. Oxford, 1901.
56 a. Alexander Haggerty Krappe, " Eine mittelalterlich-indische Parallele zum Beowulf," *GRM.* xv (1927), 54–58.
57. Edv. Lehmann, " Fandens Oldemor." *Dania* viii (1901), 179–94; in a German version: " Teufels Grossmutter." *Archiv für Religionswissenschaft* viii (1905), 411–30. [On folk-lore affinities of Grendel and his dam.]
58. R. C. Boer, " Die Beowulfsage." *AfNF.* xix (1902), 19–88. [Highly interesting.] Cf. L 4.140.

59. Sivert N. Hagen, " Classical Names and Stories in the Beowulf."
MLN. xix (1904), 65–74; 156–65. [Problematic suggestions.]

60. William W. Lawrence, " Some Disputed Questions in Beowulf-Criticism." *Publ. MLAss.* xxiv (1909), 220–73. [On the *Hrólfssaga* analogue; Bēowa and Bēowulf; criticism of mythological interpretation.] Cf. A. Brandl, *Arch.* cxxiii (1910), 473.

61. Friedrich Panzer, *Studien zur germanischen Sagengeschichte. I. Beowulf.* München, 1910. 409 pp. [Noteworthy investigation of the original folk-tale elements of the Grendel and Dragon stories, together with a study of the relations between the *Beowulf* version and the Norse parallels.] R.: A. Heusler, *ESt.* xlii (1910), 289–98; B. Kahle, *ZfdPh.* xliii (1911), 383–94; A. Brandl, *Arch.* cxxvi (1911), 231–35; C. W. v. Sydow, *Anz.fdA.* xxxv (1911), 123–31 [opposes Panzer]; W. W. Lawrence, *MLN.* xxvii (1912), 57–60; G. Binz, *Beibl.* xxiv (1913), 321–37.

61 a. *Anmerkungen zu den Kinder- und Hausmärchen der Brüder Grimm.* Neu bearbeitet von Johannes Bolte und Georg Polívka. 5 vols., Leipzig, 1913–32. Vol. ii (1915), pp. 297 ff.: Notes on No. 91, ' Dat Erdmänneken.' [Connection of Grendel story with that tale doubted.]

62. William W. Lawrence, " The Haunted Mere in *Beowulf*." *Publ. MLAss.* xxvii (1912), 208–45. [Includes a comparison with the *Grettissaga* parallel.] — 62a. *id.*, " The Dragon and his Lair in *Beowulf*," *ib.* xxxiii (1918), 547–83. [Interpretation of the story.]

62 b. Frank Gaylord Hubbard, " The Plundering of the Hoard in Beowulf." *Univ. of Wisconsin Studies in Language and Literature*, No. 11 (1920), pp. 5–20. [Opposes Lawrence's interpretation of the story.]

62 c. William Witherle Lawrence, " *Beowulf* and the *Saga of Samson the Fair*." *Kl. Misc.* (1929), 172–81; cf. *id., Beowulf and Epic Tradition*, pp. 188 ff. [On an episode in the *Saga* telling of a fight with a female troll who dwells in a cave under a waterfall.]

62 d. R. W. Chambers, " Beowulf's Fight with Grendel, and its Scandinavian Parallels." *Eng. Studies* xi (1929), 81–100. [Lucid comment on the relation between the Beowulfian and Scandinavian accounts, by way of a reply to R. C. Boer's criticism, L 4.22 a.] Cf. Chambers, " Beowulf and Waterfall-Trolls," *The Times Literary Supplement*, London, May 9, 1929, p. 383. (Katherine M. Buck, " Water-Trolls," *ib.*, May 16, p. 403.)

62 e. Margaret Schlauch, " Another Analogue of *Beowulf*." *MLN.* xlv (1930), 20 f.

63. Oscar L. Olson, " ' Beowulf ' and ' The Feast of Bricriu.' " *MPh.* xi (1914), 407–27. [Opposes Deutschbein (L 4.36).]

64. Fritz Hicketier, *Grendel*. Berlin, 1914. 39 pp. [Far-fetched Iranian (mythological) parallel.]

65. Oscar L. Olson, *The Relation of the Hrólfs Saga Kraka and the Bjarkarímur to Beowulf*. (Publ. of the Society for the Advancement of Scandinavian Study, Vol. iii, No. 1; also Univ. of Chicago Diss.) Urbana, Ill., 1916. 104 pp. R.: L. M. Hollander, *JEGPh.* xvi (1917), 147–49.

IV. LITERARY CRITICISM cxlv

66. Cf. A. Heusler, " Beowulf " (L. 4.37.2); R. C. Boer, *Beowulf* (L 4.140).

66 a. Erik Björkman " Bēow, Bēaw und Bēowulf." *ESt.* lii (1918), 145–93. [On the etymology of the names Bēow and Bēowulf and the provenience of the respective legends. Cf. L 4.82 a.]

66 a 1. Erik Björkman, " Beowulfforskning och mytologi." *Finsk Tidskrift för Vitterhet, Vetenskap, Konst och Politik* lxxxiv (Helsingfors, 1918), 250–71.

66 b. C. W. v. Sydow, " Grendel i anglosaxiska ortnamn." *Namn och Bygd, Tidskrifṭ för Nordisk Ortnamnsforskning* ii (1914), 160–64. [Grendel, an Ags. water-sprite, was identified by the poet with a similar figure in Irish tradition. ' Bēowulf's fight with Grendel and his mother ' based on an Irish prose tale.] Cf. *id.*, " Irisches im Beowulf." *Verhandlungen der 52. Versammlung deutscher Philologen und Schulmänner (Marburg, 1913)*, pp. 177–80. Leipzig, 1914. (See Intr. xx n. 4.)

66 b 1. Reginald Fog, " Trolden Grendel i Bjovulf. En Hypothese." *Danske Studier* xiv (1917), 134–40. [Considers Grendel a disease-spreading demon; Bēowulf disinfects Heorot.]

66 b 2. Eugen Mogk, " Altgermanische Spukgeschichten. Zugleich ein Beitrag zur Erklärung der Grendelepisode im Beowulf." *Neue Jahrbücher für das klassische Altertum etc.* xliii (1919), 103–17. [Recognizes in the Grendel tale the type of a ghost-story (cf. *Grettissaga*); rejects Panzer's theory.]

66 b 3. C. W. von Sydow, " Beowulf och Bjarke." *Studier i Nordisk Filologi* ed. by H. Pipping, Vol. xiv, No. 3. Helsingfors, 1923. 46 pp. [The ' Grendel ' fights and Bjarki's fight with a monster are unrelated. Irish origin of Grendel. The author of *Beowulf* substituted the Irish story for a Scandinavian tradition which was the prototype of the Bjarki adventure. The ' bear's son ' theory rejected. The *Grettissaga* episode derived indirectly from Beowulfian version. Importance of oral tradition emphasized.] R.: A. Heusler, *Anz.fdA.* xliii (1924), 52–54; Kemp Malone, *JEGPh.* xxiii (1924), 458–60. — Further, C. W. von Sydow, " Beowulfskalden och nordisk tradition." *Yearbook of the New Society of Letters at Lund, Årsbok* 1923, pp. 77–91. [Declares, *inter alia*, that the author studied at an Irish ' university,' where he became acquainted with Irish legends and with the *Æneid*. Several traditions are combined in the Beowulfian version of the dragon fight.]

66 b 4. Gustav Hübener, " Beowulf und nordische Dämonenaustreibung. (Grettir, Herakles, Theseus usw.)" *ESt.* lxii (1927–28), 293–327. [The rôle of the " heroic exorcist " the original root of the ' Grendel ' and ' dragon ' exploits. — The question of the genesis of *Beowulf* is not discussed.] Cf. *id.*, *England und die Gesittungsgrundlage der europäischen Frühgeschichte*, Frankfurt a. M., 1930, pp. 67–104. Further *id.*, " *Beowulf* and Germanic Exorcism." *RESt.* xi (1935), 163–81. [An exorcistic custom is considered " the foundation of the most important Indo-Germanic saga traditions."]

66 b 5. Heinz Dehmer, (1) " Die Grendelkämpfe Beowulfs im Lichte moderner Märchenforschung." *GRM*. xvi (1928), 202–18. [The specific form of the ' Grendel fights ' represents an Irish type.] Cf. *id*., (2) *Primitives Erzählungsgut in den Íslendinga-Sögur*, Leipzig, 1927, pp. 51 ff. R.: Wolfgang Krause, *Anz.fdA*. xlviii (1929), 157–60.

66 b 6. R. E. Zachrisson, " Grendel in *Beowulf* and in Local Names.": *Jesp. Misc*. (1930), 39–44.

66 b 7. Edward Schröder, " Beowulf." *Angl*. lvi (1932), 316 f., lvii (1933), 400. [Comments, rather approvingly, on J. Grimm's explanation of the name.]

66 b 8. Willy Krogmann, " Bēowulf." *ESt*. lxvii (1932), 161–64. [In the light of numerous similar old Gmc. names compounded with *-wulf*, the name ' Bee-wolf ' cannot be held to possess a specific significance.]

66 b 9. Roberta D. Cornelius, " Palus inamabilis." *Speculum* ii (1927), 321–25.

c. Studies devoted mainly to the Historical Legends

67. Wilhelm Grimm, *Die deutsche Heldensage* (No. 6, and *passim*). Göttingen, 1829; 3d ed., Gütersloh, 1889. 536 pp.[1]

68. M. Rieger, " Ingävonen, Istävonen, Herminonen." *ZfdA*. xi (1859), 177–205.

69. C. W. M. Grein, " Die historischen Verhältnisse des Beowulfliedes " (Habilitationsvorlesung). *Eberts Jahrbuch für romanische und englische Literatur* iv (1862), 260–85. [Helpful, clear survey.]

69 a. Ludvig Schrøder, *Om Bjovulfs-drapen*. Kjøbenhavn, 1875. See Cha. Intr. 30.

70. Hermann Dederich, *Historische und geographische Studien zum angelsächsischen Beowulfliede*. Köln, 1877. 233 pp. See reviews by K. Müllenhoff, *Anz.fdA*. iii (1877), 172–82; K. Körner, *ESt*. i (1877), 481–95.

71. Pontus Fahlbeck, (1) " Beovulfskvädet såsom källa för nordisk fornhistoria." *Antikvarisk Tidskrift för Sverige* viii, No. 2 (1884), 1–88; (2) " Beowulfskvädet som källa för nordisk fornhistoria." *N.F.K. Vitterhets Historie och Antikvitets Akademiens Handlingar* xiii, No. 3 (1913) = xxxiii, No. 2 (1924), 17 pp. [Identification of *Gēatas* and

---

[1] On Germanic heroic legends in general, see further (1) L. Uhland, *Schriften zur Geschichte der Dichtung und Sage*, Vols. i. vii. Stuttgart, 1865; 1868. [Stimulating.] (2) B. Symons, *Heldensage* (L 4.29). (3) An excellent primer: Otto L. Jiriczek, *Die deutsche Heldensage* (Sammlung Göschen, No. 32), 1894; 4th ed., 1913; English translation of it (in The Temple Primers), entitled *Northern Hero Legends*, by M. Bentinck Smith, London and New York, 1902; 16mo., 146 pp. (4) Max Koch und Andreas Heusler, *Urväterhort. Die Heldensagen der Germanen*. Berlin, n.d. [1904]. Fol., 64 pp. [Fine popular summaries; artistic illustrations by M. K.] (5) Friedrich von der Leyen, *Die deutschen Heldensagen*. (Part ii of *Deutsches Sagenbuch*, see L. 4.42. n.) München. 1912, 1923. 352 pp. [Semi-popular.] (6) Cf. R. Koegel (L 4.8); L. F. Anderson (L 9.18); H. M. Chadwick (L 4.22); L 4.13 a (Heusler, Schneider); L 4.129 e (Brandl).

IV. LITERARY CRITICISM cxlvii

'Jutes,' etc.] (3) Gudmund Schütte, " The Geats of Beowulf." *JEGPh.* xi (1912), 574–602. [Supports the Jutland theory.]

72. C. C. Uhlenbeck, " Het Beowulf-epos als geschiedbron." *Tijdschrift voor Nederlandsche Taal- en Letterkunde* xx (1901), 169–96. [Useful survey.]

73. Andreas Heusler, " Zur Skiöldungendichtung." *ZfdA.* xlviii (1906), 57–87; *R.-L.* iv, 187 ff.

74. (1) Henrik Schück, *Folknamnet Geatas i den fornengelska dikten Beowulf* (Upsala Universitets Årsskrift 1907, Program 2). Upsala, 1907. [Identification of *Gēatas* and ON. *Gautar.*] R.: V. O. Freeburg, *JEGPh.* xi (1912), 279–83. (2) Cf. Erik Björkman, " Über den Namen der Jüten." *ESt.* xxxix (1908), 356–61; *id.*, " Zu ae. *Eote*, *Yte*, usw., dän. *Jyder* ' Jüten.' " *Beibl.* xxviii (1917), 275–80. (3) Cf. Knut Stjerna, L 9.39.4.

74.4. Erik Björkman, " Beowulf och Sveriges historia.", *Nordisk Tidskrift för Vetenskap, Konst och Industri*, 1917, 161–79. [*Gēatas* = *Gautar;* Bēowulf a historical person.]

74.5. Kemp Malone, " King Alfred's ' Geats.' " *MLR.* xx (1925), 1–11. [On allusions to the existence of a Geatish state in Jutland (as a result of extensive immigration, after the overthrow of the Geatish kingdom by the Swedes). Discussion of the ' Alfredian ' rendering of Bede i 15; ON. *Hreiðgotar*, etc.] See Intr. xlvi (esp. n. 1).

74.6. Elis Wadstein, " Norden och Västeuropa i gammal tid." *Populärt vetenskapliga föreläsningar vid Göteborgs Högskola*, Ny följd xxii, Stockholm, 1925. 192 pp. Pp. 10–32, 159–67. [*Gēatas* = Jutes; the form of the name due to Frisian sources. The poem is assigned to the ninth century, though no tangible evidence is presented.] *Id.*, " The Beowulf Poem as an English National Epos." *Acta Philologica Scandinavica* viii (1933–34), 273–91. — Curt Weibull's paper (in which the *Gēatas* are identified with the Jutes), " Om det svenska och det danska rikets uppkomst," *Historisk Tidskrift för Skåneland* vii, 300–60 has been out of reach.

74.7. Kemp Malone, " The Identity of the *Geatas*.", *Acta Philologica Scandinavica* iv (1929), 84–90. [Refutes Wadstein's identification of the *Gēatas* with the Jutes.] Cf. *id.*, " King Alfred's ' Gōtland.' ", *MLR.* xxiii (1928), 336–39.

74.8. Gudmund Schütte, " Geaterspørgsmaalet." *Danske Studier*, 1930, pp. 70–81. [Geography and historical legend point to Jutland; Geatish colonization in Jutland suggested.]

75. Andreas Heusler, " Zeitrechnung im Beowulfepos." *Arch.* cxxiv (1910), 9–14.

76. M. G. Clarke, *Sidelights on Teutonic History during the Migration Period.* Cambridge, 1911. 283 pp. [A handy survey; not sufficiently critical. Supports Chadwick's views.]

77. R. W. Chambers, *Widsith. A Study in Old English Heroic Legend.* Cambridge, 1912. 263 pp. [Extremely valuable discussions, text of

Widsith, and notes.] R.: W. W. Lawrence, *MLN.* xxviii (1913), 53–5.

78. Chr. Kier, *Beowulf: et Bidrag til Nordens Oldhistorie*. København, 1915. 195 pp. [Argues strongly for identity of ' Jutes ' and *Gēatas*.] R.: E. Björkman, *Beibl.* xxvii (1916), 244–46.

78 a. H. V. Clausen, " Kong Hugleik." *Danske Studier* xv (1918), 137–49. [Identifies Geats and Jutes; recognizes Hygelāc's name in the place-name Hollingsted.]

78 b. Vilh. la Cour, " Lejrestudier." *Danske Studier* xvii (1920), 49–67 [Lejre the ancient seat of Danish royalty; objections answered]; *ib.* xviii (1921), 147–66, xxi (1924), 13–22.

78 c. Erik Björkman, " Zu einigen Namen im Beowulf. 3. Wealhþēow." *Beibl.* xxx (1919), 177–80.

78 d. Willy Meyer, " Wealhþēo(w)." *Beibl.* xxxiii (1922), 94–101. [Fanciful.]

78 e. Kemp Malone, *The Literary History of Hamlet. I. The Early Tradition*. (Ang. F. lix.) Heidelberg, 1923. 268 pp. [Contains very ingenious (and, in part, boldly speculative) interpretations of the historical (Scandinavian) elements; e.g., Onela, Hrōðulf, Yrsa.] R.: A. Le Roy Andrews, *Philol. Quarterly* iii (1924), 318–20 (cf. Malone, *ib.* iv, 158–60); William D. Briggs, *JEGPh.* xxiv (1925), 413–24.

78 f. Kemp Malone, " Danes and Half-Danes." *AfNF.* xlii (1926), 234–40. [*Healf-Dene*, old name for ' Scylding ' family.] *Id., ESt.* lxx 74–6.

78 g. Edward Schröder, " Der Name Healfdene." *A.* lviii (1934), 345–50. [King Healfdene historical; his mother was of foreign extraction or of lower rank than the father.]

78 h. Kemp Malone, " The Daughter of Healfdene." *Kl. Misc.* (1929), 135–58. [Ȳrse of l. 62 was really Healfdene's daughter-in-law (wife of Hālga); Wealhþēow originally nickname of Ȳrsa. — The true name of Hrōðgār's daughter was Hrūt.]

78 i. D. Strömholm, " Försök över Beowulfdikten och Ynglingasagan." *Edda* xxv (1926), 233–49. [The continued treatment in verse of the elements relating to Geatish-Swedish history was primarily due to poets attached to a settlement of Geatish nobles in England (perhaps members of the royal family) who had emigrated after the fall of the Geat power. (A similar suggestion by Björkman, L 4.66 a 1.) Bēowulf's dragon fight was intended as an allegorical representation of the fall of (Heardrēd and of) the Geat kingdom; an echo of it is to be noticed in the story of the Brávalla battle. — Tradition of Ingeld. Ynglingatal.]

78 k. Elias Wessén, " De nordiska folkstammarna i Beowulf." *Kungl. Vitterhets Historie och Antikvitets Akademiens Handlingar*, Del 36: 2. Stockholm, 1927. 86 pp. [' Heruler och Daner '; ' Skjoldungar och Hadbarder '; ' Frode och Halvdan '; ' Geatas ' (= Gautar): etc.] R.: Kemp Malone, *Speculum* v (1930), 134 f.

78 l. Gudmund Schütte, " Daner og Eruler." *Danske Studier*, 1927, pp. 65–74. [Opposes Wessén; cf. also note on ll. 82 ff.]

79. For the study of Germanic tribes see (1) Kaspar Zeuss, *Die*

IV. LITERARY CRITICISM cxlix

Deutschen und die Nachbarstämme. München, 1837. 780 pp. Reprinted, Heidelberg, 1925. (2) Otto Bremer, *Ethnographie der germanischen Stämme* in *P. Grdr.*² iii (1900), 735-950. (3) Rudolf Much, *Deutsche Stammeskunde* (Sammlung Göschen, No. 126). Leipzig, 1900; 2d ed., 1905; 3d ed., 1920. (4) M. Schönfeld, *Wörterbuch der altgermanischen Personen- und Völkernamen etc.* Heidelberg, 1911. 309 pp. (5) Also R. W. Chambers (L 4.77).

d. Individual Legends

(*Additional* references.)

aa. Scēaf, Scyld, (Bēow):

80. E. Sievers, " Sceaf in den nordischen Genealogien." *Beitr.* xvi (1892), 361-63.

81. R. Henning, " Sceaf und die westsächsische Stammtafel." *ZfdA.* xli (1897), 156-69.

82. Knut Stjerna, " Skölds hädanfärd " in *Studier tillägnade Henrik Schück*, pp. 110-34. Stockholm, 1905. (See L 9.39.5.)

82 a. Erik Björkman, " Sköldungaättens mytiska stamfäder." *Nordisk Tidskrift för Vetenskap, Konst och Industri*, 1918, 163-82.

82 a 1. Erik Björkman, " Bedwig in den westsächsischen Genealogien." *Beibl.* xxx (1919), 23-5.

82 b (1). Kaarle Krohn, " Sampsa Pellervoinen<Njordr Freyr?" *Finnisch-Ugrische Forschungen* iv (1904), 231-48. [The Finnish Sampsa compared with the Norse Njǫrðr-Freyr.] — (2) M. J. Eisen, " Über den Pekokultus bei den Setukesen," *ib.* vi (1906), 104-11. [On the Finnish Pekko.] (It was Olrik (ii 250 ff.) that proposed the conclusion: Scyld-Scēaf=Sampsa, Bēow=Pekko. Cf. Intr. xxvi.) — (3) Wolf von Unwerth, " Fiolnir." *AfNF.* xxxiii (1917), 320-35. [Connects Fiolnir with Pellon-Pecko, Byggvir, Bēow.]

82 c. A. Brandl, " Die Urstammtafel der Westsachsen und das Beowulf-Epos." *Arch.* cxxxvii (1918), 6-24. [Assumes influence of *Beowulf* on Ethelwerd; rejects the mythological (ritual) origin of Scēaf and Scyld in the sense proposed by Chadwick; explains Sce(a)fing from Lat. scapha ' boat.']

82 d. Alois Brandl, " Einige Tatsachen betreffend Scyld Scefing." *Jesp. Misc.* (1930), 31-37. [*scefing* from Lat. scapha, ' boat.']

82 e. C. W. v. Sydow, ' Scyld Scefing.' *Namn och Bygd* xii (1924), 63-95. [v. S., approaching the subject from the folklorist's point of view, recognizes in the account of Scyld primarily a foundling story. The ship which carries Scyld back to the mysterious land of his origin, should not be thought of as a funeral ship. Scēaf is named from the sheaf on which he was found lying. There is no connection between this story and those ritual practices which have been cited as explanatory analogues.]

82 f. Walter A. Berendsohn, " Healfdenes Vater." *AfNF.* l (1934), 148-56.

bb. The Heaðo-Bard Feud:

83. Ferd. Detter, (1) " Über die Heaðobarden im Beowulf." *Verhandlungen der Wiener Philologenversammlung* (May, 1893), pp. 404 ff. Leipzig, 1894. (Cf. the brief summary, *ESt.* xix (1894), 167 f.) (2) " Zur Ynglingasaga. 4. Ingeld und die Svertinge." *Beitr.* xviii (1894), 90–6

84. Sophus Bugge, *The Home of the Eddic Poems with especial reference to the Helgi-Lays* translated from the Norwegian by W. H. Schofield. London, 1899. (The original was published in Copenhagen, 1896.) Chap. xiii: " The account of Helgi Hundingsbani in its relation to Anglo-Saxon Epics."

85. Gustav Neckel, in " Studien über Fróði," *ZfdA.* xlviii (1906), 181–86.

85 a. Kemp Malone, " Ingeld." *MPh.* xxvii (1930), 257–76. [Interpretation of the Heaðo-Bard episode and comparison with Scandinavian tradition.]

85 b. J. M. Steadman, Jr., " The Ingeld Episode in *Beowulf:* History or Prophecy?" *MLN.* xlv (1930), 522–25. [No historical present tense.]

cc. Hróðulf, Hrēðrīc:

86. Wilbur C. Abbott, " Hrothulf.'' *MLN.* xix (1904), 122–25.

87. Fr. Klaeber, " Hrothulf." *MLN.* xx (1905), 9–11.

87 a. Kemp Malone, " Hrethric." *Publ. MLAss.* xlii (1927), 268–313. [A remarkably elaborate discussion of the varying rôle of Hrēðrīc in Scandinavian tradition. The historical sequence of events is supposed to have been as follows. Hrōðgār was slain by Hrōðulf; Hrēðrīc, with Geatish aid, put Hrōðulf to flight and mounted his father's throne; Hrōðulf, having gathered a fleet, attacked Hrēðrīc at his hall, Hrēðrīc fell and Hrōðulf became once more king of the Danes. — The two epithets of Hrēðrīc, ' ring-stingy ' and ' ring-lavish ' (cf. Par. § 8.1) are incidentally explained.] Cf. Par. § 8.1, 3, 6, Intr. xxxiii; P. Herrmann, *Saxo* ii, 243–45.

dd. Herebeald, Hæðcyn; Hygelāc; (Bēowulf;) Breca:

88. Ferd. Detter, (1) " Zur Ynglingasaga. 2. Der Baldrmythus; König Hygelāc." *Beitr.* xviii (1894), 82–8. (2) " Der Baldrmythus." *Beitr.* xix (1894), 495–516.

88 a. Erik Björkman, " Hæðcyn und Hákon.'' *ESt.* liv (1920), 24–34.

88 b. Gustav Neckel, *Die Überlieferungen vom Gotte Balder dargestellt und vergleichend untersucht.* Dortmund, 1920. 265 pp. [See pp. 141 ff.: Herebeald, Hæðcyn; also pp. 55 ff.: Heremōd, and *passim.*] Cf. a brief critical note (relating to various Balder theories) by A. H. Krappe, *Litteris* ii (1925), 170–73.

89. M. Haupt, " Zum Beowulf." *ZfdA.* v (1845), 10. (See Par. § 11.1.)

90. Karl Müllenhoff, *ZfdA.* vi (1848), 437 f. (See L 4.25.1.)

91. William W. Lawrence. " The Breca Episode in ' Beowulf .' "

IV. LITERARY CRITICISM

Anniversary Papers by Colleagues and Pupils of George L. Kittredge, pp. 359–66. Boston, 1913.

92. See also M. Deutschbein, L 4.97.

92 a. Erik Björkman, " Zu einigen Namen im Beowulf. 1. Breca. 2. Brondingas." *Beibl.* xxx (1919), 170–77.

92 b. Alfred Anscombe, " Beowulf in High-Dutch Saga." *Notes and Queries*, August 21, 1915, pp. 133 f. [Ventures to identify Boppe ūz Tenelant in the MHG. *Biterolf* with Bēowulf.]

92 c. Wolf von Unwerth, " Eine schwedische Heldensage als deutsches Volksepos." *AfNF.* xxxv (1919), 113–37. [Finds traces of the stories of Hæðcyn (Herebeald) and Hygelāc in the MHG. *Biterolf*, the ON. *þiðrekssaga*, etc.] Cf. Intr. xli and n. 6.

92 d. Fr. Klaeber, " Der Held Bēowulf in deutscher Sagenüberlieferung?" *Angl.* xlvi (1922), 193–201.

92 e. Kemp Malone, " *Widsith* and the *Hervararsaga*." *Publ. MLAss.* xl (1925), 769–813. *Passim.* [Allusions to Geatish and Swedish history, etc.; e.g., Hæðcyn (Herebeald), pp. 783 f., 799; Hrēðel, 800 f.; Ongenþēow, 780 f.; Gautish colonization of Jutland, 785 f., 802 f.; also, (Saxo's) Lotherus, Humblus, 804 ff.]

92 f. (1) Emil Äng. Fredborg, *Det första årtalet i Sveriges historia.* Umeå Progr., 1917. 4to, 29 pp. — (2) Albert S. Cook, " Theodebert of Austrasia." *JEGPh.* xxii (1923), 424–27.

92 g. Cf. Wolfgang Keller, " Beowulf der riesige Vorkämpfer." *ESt.* lxviii (1934), 321–38. (Cf. *ib.* lxix, 154–58.)

92 h. Cf. Gösta Langenfelt, " Beowulf Problems." *ESt.* lxvi (1932), 236–44. [Beowulfian place-names in Vestergötland.]

ee. The Swedish Kings:

93. Knut Stjerna, " Vendel och Vendelkråka." *AfNF.* xxi (1904), 71–80. (See L 9.39.3.) [Vendel in Uppland, Sweden is shown to be the place of Ongenþēow's last battle.]

94. Hans Weyhe, " König Ongentheows Fall." *ESt.* xxxix (1908), 14–39. [Study of a parallel Danish version.]

94 a. Gudmund Schütte, " Vidsid og Slægtssagnene om Hengest og Angantyr." *AfNF.* xxxvi (1919/20), 1–32.

95. Lars Levander, " Sagotraditioner om Sveakonungen Adils." *Antikvarisk Tidskrift för Sverige* xviii, No. 3. (1908.) 55 pp. [Traces the tradition about Aðils (Ēadgils) as found in the *Beowulf*, and its development in Denmark, Sweden, and Norway.]

96. H. M. Belden, " Onela the Scylfing and Ali the Bold." *MLN.* xxviii (1913), 149–53.

97. Max Deutschbein, " Beowulf der Gautenkönig." *Festschrift für L. Morsbach* (=St.EPh. l), pp. 291–97. Halle a. S., 1913.

97 a. Oscar Montelius, " Ynglingaätten." *Nordisk Tidskrift för Vetenskap, Konst och Industri*, 1918, 213–38.

97 b. Kemp Malone, " King Aun in the Rök Inscription." *MLN.* xxxix (1924), 223–26. [Aun II=Ēanmund.]

97 c. Birger Nerman, (1) *Vilka konungar ligga i Uppsala högar?* Uppsala, 1913. 15 pp. [The three Kings' Mounds at Gamla Uppsala contain the remains of Aun, Egill, and Aðils.] Cf. *id.*, (2) *Studier över Svärges hedna litteratur* (Akademisk Avhandling), Uppsala, 1913. 212 pp. — (3) On a similar identification of Óttar's Mound at Vendel, see references in Björkman, L 4.31.8.84 ff., Chambers Introd. 356. — (4) Birger Nerman, *Det svenska rikets uppkomst*, Stockholm, 1925. 280 pp. [Chs. v (' Beowulf ') and vi (Geatish and Swedish affairs).]

97 d. Edith Wardale, " Beowulf: the nationality of Ecgðēow." *MLR.* xxiv (1929), 322. [Swedish.]

ff. Offa (Ēomǣr, Hemming); þrȳð:

98. Joseph Bachlechner, " Eomær und Heming (Hamlac)." *Germ.* i (1856), 297–303 (I. Eomær); 455–61 (II. Heming).

99. Hermann Suchier, " Ueber die Sage von Offa und þrȳðo." *Beitr.* iv (1877), 500–21.

100. Axel Olrik, (1) " Er Uffesagnet indvandret fra England?" *AfNF.* viii (1892), 368–75. (2) *Kilderne til Sakses Oldhistorie. II. Norröne sagaer og danske sagn*, pp. 177 f., 182 ff. København, 1894.

101. A. B. Gough, *The Constance Saga.* (Palaestra xxiii.) Berlin, 1902. 84 pp.

102. Gordon H. Gerould, " Offa and Labhraidh Maen." *MLN.* xvii (1902), 201–3.

103. R. C. Boer, " Eene episode uit den Beowulf." *Handelingen van het 3de Nederlandsche Philologen-Congres* (1903), pp. 84–94.

104. Edith Rickert, " The Old English Offa Saga." *MPh.* ii (1904/5), 29–76; 321–76.

105. Fr. Klaeber, " Zur þryðo-Episode." *Angl.* xxviii (1905), 448–52.

106. Svet. Stefanović, " Ein Beitrag zur angelsächsischen Offa-Sage." *Angl.* xxxv (1911), 483–525; *id.*, " Zur Offa-Thryðo-Episode im *Beowulf.*" *ESt.* lxix (1934), 15–31.

106 a. Rudolf Imelmann, *Forschungen zur altenglischen Poesie*, pp. 456–63. Berlin, 1920. [l. 1931 (perh.): Mōd þrȳð ō wæg.]

106 b. H. Patzig, " Zur Episode von þrȳð im Beowulf." *Angl.* xlvi (1922), 282–85.

106 c. J. Schick," Die Urquelle der Offa-Konstanze-Sage." *För. Misc.* (1929), 31–56.

106 d. And see Cha. Intr. 31–40; Craigie L 1.10; L 5.35.19; Hoops St. 64–71.

gg. Sigemund, Fitela:

107. Jacob Grimm, " Sintarfizilo." *ZfdA.* i (1841), 2–6.

108. Karl Müllenhoff, " Die alte Dichtung von den Nibelungen. I. Von Sigfrids Ahnen." *ZfdA.* xxiii (1879), 131 f., 147 f., 161–63. —Cf. also L 4.26 (Uhland).

109. Julius Goebel, (1) " On the Original Form of the Legend of Sig-

IV. LITERARY CRITICISM

frid." *Publ. MLAss.* xii (1897), 461–74. (2) "The Evolution of the Nibelungensaga." *JEGPh.* xvii (1918), 1–20.

110. Eugen Mogk, " Die germanische Heldendichtung mit besonderer Rücksicht auf die Sage von Siegfried und Brunhild." *Neue Jahrbücher für das klassische Altertum etc.* i (1898), 68–80.

111. William Henry Schofield, " Signy's Lament." *Publ. MLAss.* xvii (1902), 262–95.

112. Sophus Bugge, " Mundo und Sigmund." *Beitr.* xxxv (1909), 262–67. [Suggests a possible historical basis.] *Ib.*, 490–93.

113. R. C. Boer, *Untersuchungen über den Ursprung und die Entwicklung der Nibelungensage.* Vol. iii, ch. iv. Halle a. S., 1909.

114. Hermann Schneider, " Zur Sigmundsage." *ZfdA.* liv (1913), 339–43.

115. See F. W. Moorman (L 4.31.5), pp. 89–103.

115 a. Gustav Neckel, " Sigmunds Drachenkampf." *Edda* xiii (1920), 122–40, 204–29.

hh. Eormenrīc (Hāma; Brīsinga mene):

116. Otto L. Jiriczek, *Deutsche Heldensagen.* I. Strassburg, 1898. 331 pp. [Weland; Ermanaric; Theodoric.]

117. Friedrich Panzer, *Deutsche Heldensage im Breisgau.* Heidelberg, 1904. 90 pp.

118. A. Brandl, " Zur Gotensage bei den Angelsachsen." *Arch.* cxx (1908), 1–8.

119. R. C. Boer, *Die Sagen von Ermanarich und Dietrich von Bern,* espec. pp. 181 ff. Halle a. S., 1910.

119 a. Henning Larsen, " Wudga: A Study in the Theodoric Legends." *Ph.Q.* i (1922), 128–36. Cf. notes on ll. 1197 ff.

119 b. Alexander Haggerty Krappe, *La Légende des Harlungen,* in *Études de Mythologie et de Folklore germaniques,* pp. 137–74. Paris, 1928.

119 c. Howard W. Hintz, " The ' Hama ' Reference in Beowulf: 1197–1201." *JEGPh.* xxxiii (1934), 98–102.

C. LITERARY CRITICISM

a. General and Historical[1]

120. W. P. Ker, (1) *Epic and Romance. Essays on Medieval Literature.* London and New York, 1897, 451 pp.; 2d ed. (' Eversley Series,' cheaper), 1908. [A most stimulating study throwing into relief the nature of the narrative art of *Beowulf.*] R.: A. Brandl, *Arch.* c (1898),

---

[1] Entirely popular are (1) J. Wight Duff's *Homer and Beowulf: a Literary Parallel.* (Saga-Book of the Viking Club, Vol. iv, Part ii, pp. 382–406.) London, 1906; (2) Sarah J. McNary's " Beowulf and Arthur as English Ideals." *Poet-Lore* vi (1894), 529–36. — A stimulating lecture on " Beowulf " is contained in William W. Lawrence's *Medieval Story* (Columbia University Lectures), pp. 27–53. New York, 1911; 2. ed., 1931. See also W. Macneile Dixon, *English Epic and Heroic Poetry* (The Channels of English Literature Series), ch. 3. London, 1912.

198–200; (2) *The Dark Ages*, espec. pp. 249–54. Edinburgh and London, 1904.

121. Francis B. Gummere, (1) *The Beginnings of Poetry*, espec. pp. 192 f., 222 ff., 331, 434 ff. New York and London, 1901; (2) *The Popular Ballad*, espec. ch. i, § 3. Boston and New York, 1907.

122. Irene T. Myers, *A Study in Epic Development* (Yale Studies in English xi). New York, 1901. 159 pp.

123. Friedr. Panzer, *Das altdeutsche Volksepos*. Halle a. S., 1903. 34 pp.

124. Andreas Heusler, (1) *Lied und Epos in germanischer Sagendichtung*. Dortmund, 1905. 52 pp. [Supplements Ker's study (L 4.120.1).] (2) " Dichtung," *R.-L.* i, 439 ff. (1912/13.) (3) " Heliand, Liedstil und Epenstil." *ZfdA*. lvii (1919/20), 1–48. [Contains a lucid comment on style and meter of Germanic poems.]

125. Walter Morris Hart, *Ballad and Epic. A Study in the Development of the Narrative Art*. (Harvard Studies and Notes in Philology and Literature xi.) Boston, 1907. 315 pp. [Traces the development of narrative method, through the different classes of the Ballad (simple ballads, border and outlaw ballads, Gest of Robin Hood, heroic ballads), to the Epic (Beowulf, Roland).]

126. (1) Levin Ludwig Schücking, " Das angelsächsische Totenklagelied." *ESt.* xxxix (1908), 1–13. — (2) Ernst Sieper, *Die altenglische Elegie*. Strassburg, 1915. 294 pp. Introduction, *passim*. R.: L. L. Schücking, *ESt.* li (1917), 97–115. — Sister Mary Angelica O'Neill's *Elegiac Elements in Beowulf* (Cath. Univ. of Amer. Diss., 1932) has not been accessible.

127. Axel Olrik, " Epische Gesetze der Volksdichtung." *ZfdA*. li (1909/10), 1–12. A (somewhat different) Danish version: " Episke love i folkedigtningen." *Danske Studier*, 1908, 69–89.

128. George Arnold Smithson, *The Old English Christian Epic. A Study in the Plot Technique of the Juliana, the Elene, the Andreas, and the Christ, in comparison with the Beowulf and with the Latin Literature of the Middle Ages*. (University of California Publications in Modern Philology, Vol. i, No. 4.) Berkeley, 1910. [A useful study; the Latin sources are not considered.]

129. Fr. Klaeber, " Aeneis und Beowulf." *Arch.* cxxvi (1911), 40–8, 339–59. [On the possible influence of the *Æneid*.]

129 a. Cf. R. Imelmann's *Forschungen zur altenglischen Poesie* (L 4.106 a), *passim*, and review by A. Heusler, *Anz.fdA*. xli (1922), 27–35.

129 b. Albert S. Cook, (1) " Greek Parallels to Certain Features of the *Beowulf*." *Ph. Q.* v (1926), 226–34. (2) " Beowulfian and Odyssean Voyages." *Transactions of the Connecticut Academy of Arts and Sciences* xxviii (1926), 1–20. (3) " The Beowulfian *maðelode*." *JEGPh.* xxv (1926), 1–6. (4) " Hellenic and Beowulfian Shields and Spears." *MLN*. xli (1926), 360–63. [Traces of Homeric influence. See L 4.146 c. Cf. M. Daunt, *Year's Work* vii, 54–57.] (5) " *Beowulf* 1039 and the Greek ἀρχι-." *Speculum* iii (1928), 75–81.

IV. LITERARY CRITICISM

129 c. Fr. Klaeber, " Attila's and Beowulf's Funeral." *Publ. MLAss.* xlii (1927), 255–67. [Discussion of the Jordanes parallel and the classical parallels of Bēowulf's obsequies.]

129 d. Richard Leicher, *Die Totenklage in der deutschen Epik von der ältesten Zeit bis zur Nibelungen- Klage.* (German. Abhandl. lviii.) Breslau, 1927. 172 pp. (§ 5: Jordanes, ch. 49; § 10: *Beowulf.*) [Largely a collection of material.]

129 e. A. Brandl, " Hercules und Beowulf." *Sitzungsberichte der Preussischen Akademie der Wissenschaften, Phil.-hist. Klasse,* 1928, No. xiv, pp. 161–67. [Vergil (*Æn.* viii, 193 ff., vi, 131 ff.) a direct source of prime importance. (Cf. Imelmann L 4.129 a. 464 ff.) The semi-learned character of *Beowulf* is emphasized.] Cf. *id.*, " Zur Entstehung der germanischen Heldensage, gesehen vom angelsächsischen Standpunkt." *Arch.* clxii (1933), 191–202. [Classical origins (for legends of Eormenric, Theodoric, Niblungs) suggested.]

129 f. James A. Work, " Odyssean Influence on the *Beowulf.*" *Ph. Q.* ix (1930), 399–402. [Odyssean parallel (Book viii) of the Bēowulf-Unferð incident.]

129 g. Tom Burns Haber, " A Comparative Study of the *Beowulf* and the *Æneid.* Princeton, 1931. 145 pp. [A copious collection of parallels.] R.: P. F. Jones, *MLN.* xlvii (1932), 264–66; Fr. Klaeber, *Beibl.* xliii (1932), 229–32; R. Girvan, *MLR.* xxvii (1932), 466–70; M. Ashdown, *RESt.* viii (1932), 462 f.; F. M., *Revue germanique* xxiv (1933), 52.

129 h. Coolidge Otis Chapman, " *Beowulf* and *Apollonius of Tyre.*" *MLN.* xlvi (1931), 439–43. [Some parallels touching upon Bēowulf's reception at Heorot.]

b. Composition; Date

130. K. Müllenhoff, " Die innere Geschichte des Beovulfs." *ZfdA.* xiv (1869), 193–244. (Reprinted in Müllenhoff's *Beovulf* (L 4.19), pp. 110–60.) [Famous application of the *Liedertheorie.*]

131. Artur Köhler, (1) " Die Einleitung des Beovulfliedes. Ein Beitrag zur Frage über die Liedertheorie." *ZfdPh.* ii (1870), 305–14; (2) " Die beiden Episoden von Heremod im Beovulfliede," *ib.* ii, 314–20. [Favors multiple authorship.]

132. Anton Schönbach, in a review of Ettmüller's edition (L 2.18), *Anz.fdA.* iii (1877), 36–46. [Endorses Müllenhoff.]

133. Dr. Hornburg, *Die Composition des Beowulf.* Metz Progr., 1877 (=*Arch.* lxxii (1884), 333–404). [Opposes Müllenhoff.]

134. Hermann Möller, *Das altenglische Volksepos in der ursprünglichen strophischen Form. I. Teil: Abhandlungen.* Kiel, 1883. (Cf. L 2.19.) [Multiple authorship; the original parts composed in four-line stanzas.] R.: R. Heinzel, *Anz.fdA.* x (1884), 215–33.

135. Friedrich Schneider, *Der Kampf mit Grendels Mutter. Ein Beitrag zur Kenntnis der Komposition des Beowulf.* Berlin Progr., 1887. [Supports without much skill the patch-work theory.]

136. Max Hermann Jellinek & Carl Kraus, " Die Widersprüche im Beowulf." *ZfdA*. xxxv (1891), 265–81. [Apparent contradictions cleared up by proper interpretation.]

137. Henrik Schück in the Introduction to E. Björkman's translation (L 3.41), *Världslitteraturen* ii, 463–74. Stockholm, 1902. [The poem based on Geatish and Danish originals.]

138. James Edward Routh, Jr., *Two Studies on the Ballad Theory of the Beowulf*. Johns Hopkins Diss. Baltimore, 1905. [1. The legend of Grendel. 2. Irrelevant episodes and parentheses.] R.: L. L. Schücking, *D.Lit.z.* xxvi (1905), 1908–10; A. Heusler, *Anz.fdA*. xxxi (1908), 115 f.

139. Levin Ludwig Schücking, *Beowulfs Rückkehr*. (St.EPh. xxi.) Halle a. S., 1905. 74 pp. R.: A. Brandl, *Arch*. cxv (1905), 421–23.

140. R. C. Boer, *Die altenglische Heldendichtung. I. Beowulf*. Halle a. S., 1912. 200 pp. [Composite formation of the poem (cf. L 4.130, 18); comparison with Scandinavian analogues, cf. L 4.58.] R.: R. Imelmann, *D.Lit.z.* xxxiv (1913), 1064–66; W. E. Berendsohn, *Lit.bl*. xxxv (1914), 152–54.

141. Walter A. Berendsohn, (1) " Drei Schichten dichterischer Gestaltung im Beowulf-Epos." *Münchener Museum für Philologie des Mittelalters und der Renaissance* ii (1913), 1–32. [Definitely marked strata of tradition and formation confidently distinguished.] — (2) " Die Gelage am Dänenhof zu Ehren Beowulfs," *ib*. iii, 31–55. [Similar analysis.] Cf. L 4.40 a, 82 f. — (3) *Zur Vorgeschichte des "Beowulf."* Kopenhagen, 1935. 302 pp. [Could not yet be utilized.]

On *dating:*

142. G. Sarrazin, " Die Abfassungszeit des Beowulfliedes." *Angl*. xiv (1892), 399–415. (L 4.16.2.) [Cynewulf's redaction dated after *Christ* (A+B), and before *Elene* and *Andreas*.]

143. Lorenz Morsbach, " Zur Datierung des Beowulfepos." *Nachrichten der K. Gesellschaft der Wissenschaften zu Göttingen, Philologisch-historische Klasse*, 1906, pp. 251–77. [Linguistic criteria.] Cf. F. Holthausen, *Beibl*. xviii (1907), 77; H. M. Chadwick, L 4.22.66–72; C. Richter, L 6.6.1.

144. G. Sarrazin, " Zur Chronologie und Verfasserfrage angelsächsischer Dichtungen." *ESt*. xxxviii (1907), 145–95 (espec. 170 ff.).

145. Fr. Klaeber, (1) " Die Ältere Genesis und der Beowulf." *ESt*. xlii (1910), 321–38. [On the influence of *Genesis* on *Beowulf*.] (2) *id*., " Concerning the Relation between ' Exodus ' and ' Beowulf.' " *MLN*. xxxiii (1918), 218–24.

145 a. Levin L. Schücking, " Noch einmal: enge ānpaðas, uncūð gelād." *Kl. Misc.* (1929), 213–16. [Even if the *Beowulf* poet should have recalled a Vergilian passage, he adopted the phrasing of *Exodus*.] Cf. L 6.22.12 ff., 37 ff.

146. P. G. Thomas, " ' Beowulf ' and ' Daniel A.' " *MLR*. viii (1913), 537–39. [Priority of *Daniel A* and its influence on *Beowulf*.]

IV. LITERARY CRITICISM

146 a. Levin L. Schücking, (1) " Wann entstand der Beowulf? Glossen, Zweifel und Fragen." *Beitr.* xlii (1917), 347–410. [An important study including a criticism of the current chronological criteria and an examination of the literary and cultural background of the poem. It is suggested that *Beowulf* may have been composed about the end of the ninth century, at the request of a Scandinavian prince reigning in the Danelaw territory.] (2) " Die Beowulfdatierung. Eine Replik." *Beitr.* xlvii (1923), 293–311. [Includes a defense of his noteworthy theory against the criticism of Liebermann (L 4.146 b) and of Chambers (Introd. 322 ff.).]

146 b. F. Liebermann, " Ort und Zeit der Beowulfdichtung." *Nachrichten von der K. Gesellschaft der Wissenschaften zu Göttingen, Philol.-hist. Klasse*, 1920, pp. 255–76. [The epic may have been composed at the court of Cūþburg, sister of King Ine of Wessex, who became queen of Northumbria and later presided over the monastery at Wimborne.]

146 c. Albert S. Cook, (1) " The Possible Begetter of the Old English *Beowulf* and *Widsith*". *Transactions of the Connecticut Academy of Arts and Sciences* xxv (1922), 281–346. [King Aldfrið of Northumbria (685–705) the author's royal patron; influence exerted by Aldhelm; Homeric parallels of Bēowulf's funeral.] R.: F. Liebermann, *Arch.* cxliii (1922), 281 f.; E. Ekwall, *Beibl.* xxxiv (1923), 37–39; H. M. Flasdieck, *ESt.* lviii (1924), 124–26. — (2) " The Old English *Andreas* and Bishop Acca of Hexham," *ib.* xxvi (1924), 245–332. [Pp. 270 ff.: the chronological position of *Andreas* and *Beowulf;* pp. 324 ff.: classical parallels.] — (3) " Cynewulf's Part in our Beowulf," *ib.* xxvii (1925), 385–406. [Cynewulfian influence on Hrōðgār's ' sermon,' ll. 1724–52 denied. The author of *Beowulf* drew his inspiration and knowledge from Gregory directly. Homeric parallels.] R.: S. J. Crawford, *MLR.* xxii (1927), 94–96. — (4) " ' Beowulf ' 1422," *MLN.* xxxix (1924), 77–82; " Aldhelm and the Source of ' Beowulf ' 2523," *ib.* xl (1925), 137–42. [Influence of Aldhelm.]

146 d. Alois Brandl, " Beowulf und die Merowinger." *Sitzungsberichte der Preussischen Akademie der Wissenschaften, Phil.-hist. Klasse*, 1929, No. xi, pp. 207–11; *Kl. Misc.* (1929), 182–88. [The true significance of the allusion of ll. 2920 f. is explained from Ags. history: bitter feeling of Mercians against Merovingian princesses.]

146 e. B. S. Phillpotts, " ' The Battle of Maldon ': Some Danish Affinities." *MLR.* xxiv (1929), 172–90. [Pp. 183 ff.: relation between *Beowulf, Maldon*, and Danish verse.]

c. Christian Coloring; Spirit of the Poem

147. George Lyman Kittredge, " Zu Beowulf 107 ff." *Beitr.* xiii (1888), 210.

148. F. A. Blackburn, " The Christian Coloring in the Beowulf." *Publ. MLAss.* xii (1897), 205–25. [The various Christian passages examined.]

149. Oliver F. Emerson, " Legends of Cain, especially in Old and Middle English." *Publ. MLAss.* xxi (1906), 831–929 (*passim*). [Important investigation.]

149 a. S. J. Crawford, " Grendel's Descent from Cain." *MLR.* xxiii (1928), 207 f.; xxiv (1929), 63.

150. Gustav Grau, *Quellen und Verwandtschaften der älteren germanischen Darstellungen des Jüngsten Gerichtes.* (St.EPh. xxxi.) Halle a. S., 1908. Pp. 145–56. [Concludes that Cynewulf is the author of *Beowulf.*] R.: H. Hecht, *Arch.* cxxx (1913), 424–30.

151. G. Ehrismann, " Religionsgeschichtliche Beiträge zum germanischen Frühchristentum." *Beitr.* xxxv (1909), 209–39.

152. Fr. Klaeber, " Die christlichen Elemente im Beowulf." *Angl.* xxxv (1911), 111–36, 249–70, 453–82; xxxvi (1912), 169–99. (Further references: *Angl.* xxxv, 111 f., etc. Cf. also L 4.45 (Bouterwek, pp. cvii–cxiv), L 4.14 (Bouterwek, pp. 396, 401); L 7.25 (Rankin).)

153. Enrico Pizzo, " Zur Frage der ästhetischen Einheit des Beowulf." *Angl.* xxxix (1915), 1–15. [Recognizes a consistent representation of the early Ags.-Christian ideal.]

154. Oliver F. Emerson, " Grendel's Motive in Attacking Heorot." *MLR.* xvi (1921), 113–19. [The motive of envy according to Christian conceptions.]

155. H. V. Routh, *God, Man, and Epic Poetry. A Study in Comparative Literature.* Vol. ii: *Medieval.* Cambridge, 1927. 283 pp. *Passim;* esp. pp. 1 ff., 64 ff., 78 ff. [P. 79: " it seems . . . incontestable that the man who put his soul into *Beowulf* was not . . . a Christian in thought and spirit."] A [destructive] review by F. P. Magoun, Jr., *Speculum* iii (1928), 124–27.

156. Bertha S. Phillpotts, " Wyrd and Providence in Anglo-Saxon Thought." *Essays and Studies by Members of the English Association* (1927) xiii (1928), 7–27. [P. 21: " *Beowulf* may . . . be considered the first English compromise."] R.: S. B. Liljegren, *Beibl.* xl (1929), 12 f.; M. Daunt, *Year's Work* ix, 64–66. (Cf. also L 6.23.)

157. Levin L. Schücking, " Das Königsideal im Beowulf." *Bulletin of the Modern Humanities Research Association* iii (1929), 143–54, = *ESt.* lxvii (1932), 1–14. [While both Germanic-heroic and Christian elements are to be recognized, the ideal of royalty represented by Bēowulf and Hrōðgār recalls St. Augustine's *imperator felix* or *rex justus.* Considered broadly, the ethical standard is characterized by the basic virtue of ' mensura ' or ' sobrietas,' poise and self-restraint. An admirable exposition of the general spirit of the poem.]

158. Arthur E. Du Bois, " The Unity of *Beowulf.*" *PMLA.* xlix (1934), 374–405. [Theme and structure; historical element; fabulous elements; the poet's philosophy of history.]

For special studies of the ' Style ' see Bibliography VII.

V. TEXTUAL CRITICISM AND INTERPRETATION

1. Joseph Bachlechner, "Die Merovinge im Beowulf," *ZfdA.* vii (1849), 524–26 [l. 2921].[1]
2. K. W. Bouterwek, "Zur Kritik des Beowulfliedes," *ZfdA.* xi (1859), 59–113. [Some useful comments by the side of unprofitable guesses.]
3. Franz Dietrich, "Rettungen," *ZfdA.* xi (1859), 409–48 (*passim*).
4. Adolf Holtzmann, *Germ.* viii (1863), 489–97.
5. Wilhelm Scherer, in a review of L 2.7.1, 2d ed., *ZföG.* xx (1869), 89–112 (= W. Scherer's *Kleine Schriften* i (1893), 471–96).
6. Sophus Bugge, (1) *Tidskrift for Philologi og Pædagogik* viii (1868/69), 40–78; 287–305; (2) *ZfdPh.* iv (1873), 192–224; (3) in his "Studien über das Beowulfepos" (cf. L 4.28), *Beitr.* xii (1887), 79–112; 366–75. [Masterly.]
7. Max Rieger, *ZfdPh.* iii (1871), 381–416. [Penetrating.]
8. Karl Körner, (1) in a review of L 4.70, *ESt.* i (1877), 481–95; (2) in a review of H. Sweet, *An Anglo-Saxon Reader, ib.* i, 500; (3) in a review of L 3.33, *ib.* ii (1879), 248–51 [ll. 168 ff., 287, 489 f.].
9. H. Kern, *Taalkundige Bijdragen* i (1877), 193 ff. (*passim*). [l. 2766; *ofsittan.*]
10. P. J. Cosijn, (1) *Taalkundige Bijdragen* i (1877), 286 [l. 1694]; (2) *Beitr.* viii (1882), 568–74; (3) *Aanteekeningen op den Beowulf.* Leiden, 1892. [Concise, acute, illuminating.]
11. Richard Wülcker, in a review of L 2.9, *Angl.* i (1878), 177–86.
12. Eugen Kölbing, (1) *ESt.* iii (1880), 92 f. [ll. 168 f.]; (2) *ib.* xxii (1896), 325 [ll. 1027 ff.]; (3) in a review of L 4.12.1, *ib.* xxiii (1897), 306 [l. 748].
13. Hugo Gering, in a review of L 2.7.1, 4th ed., *ZfdPh.* xii (1881), 122–25 [ll. 303, 208 f., 643].
14. Oscar Brenner, in a review of L 2.7.1, 4th ed., *ESt.* iv (1881), 135–39 [*eolot*, l. 224: cp. Gr. ἐλαύνω].
15. F. Kluge, (1) *Beitr.* viii (1882), 532–34 [ll. 63, 1026, 1234 & 1266]; (2) *ib.* ix (1884), 187–92; (3) *ESt.* xxii (1896), 144 f. (cf. L 4.31.3) [ll. 62, 752, 924, 1677 (*Gyldenhilt*)].
16. E. Sievers, (1) *Beitr.* ix (1884), 135–44; 370 [acute observations]; (2) in a review of L 2.7.2, 5th ed., *ZfdPh.* xxi (1889), 354–65 [helpful corrections]; (3) *Angl.* xiv (1892), 133–46 [in opposition to Schröer L 5.24]; (4) *Beitr.* xviii (1894), 406 f. [on *earfoðþrāg*]; (5) *Beitr.* xxvii (1902), 572 [l. 33]; (6) *ib.* xxviii (1903), 271 f. [ll. 48 f.]; (7) *ib.* xxix (1904), 305–31 [against Trautmann, L 5.34.1]; (8) *ib.* xxix, 560–76 [concerning Kock's note on l. 6, L 5.44.1]; (9) *ib.* xxxvi (1910), 397–434 [against von Grienberger, L 5.45.3]; (10) *ESt.* xliv (1912), 295–97 [on L 5.48.4]; (11) "Beowulf 3066 ff.," *Beitr.* lv (1931), 376. [ll. 3069–73 a "Chris-

[1] Only in the case of certain shorter papers can the lines discussed be added.

tian-Kentish interpolation" inserted in a Northumbrian text; etc.]
17. Th. Krüger, *Beitr.* ix (1884), 571–78.
18. H. Corson, *MLN.* iii (1888), 97 [l. 2724].
19. Thomas Miller, "The position of Grendel's arm in Heorot." *Angl.* xii (1889), 396–400. [ll. 834 ff., 925 ff., 982 ff.]
20. R. Heinzel, in a review of L 2.7.2, 5th ed., *Anz.fdA.* xv (1889), 189–94.
21. J. Zupitza, *Arch.* lxxxiv (1890), 124 f. [l. 850].
22. Eugen Joseph, "Zwei Versversetzungen im Beowulf." *ZfdPh.* xxii (1890), 385–97.
23. Max Hermann Jellinek and Carl Kraus, "Die Widersprüche im Beowulf," *ZfdA.* xxxv (1891), 265–81. (Cf. L 4.136.)
24. A. Schröer, *Angl.* xiii (1891), 333–48.
25. (1) J. W. Pearce, "Ags. *scúrheard.*" *MLN.* vii (1892), 193 f., 253 f. Cf. (2) Albert S. Cook, *ib.* vii, 253; (3) Arthur H. Palmer, *ib.* viii (1893), 61; (4) James M. Hart, *ib.* viii, 61; (5) George Philip Krapp, *ib.* xix (1904), 234.
26. Ferd. Holthausen, (1) *Beitr.* xvi (1892), 549 f. [l. 1117: *ēame*]; (2) in a review of L 3.13, *Beibl.* iv (1894), 33–6; (3) *IF.* iv (1894), 384 f. [l. 2706]; (4) in a review of L 5.10.3, *Lit. bl.* xvi (1895), 82 [l. 600]; (5) *Angl.* xxi (1899), 366 [ll. 2298 f., 2488]; (6) in a review of L 3.22, 2d ed., *Arch.* ciii (1899), 373–76; (7) *Arch.* cv (1900), 366 f. [ll. 497 f., 568]; (8) in a review of L 2.7.2, 6th ed., *Beibl.* x (1900), 265–74 [extensive list of scholarly corrections]; (9) in a review of L 2.12, 2d ed., *Lit. bl.* xxi (1900), 60–62; (10) in a review of Trautmann (L 5.34.1), *ib.* xxi, 64; (11) *Angl.* xxiv (1901), 267 f. [l. 719]; (12) *Beibl.* xii (1901), 146 [l. 3157]; (13) *ib.* xiii (1902), 78 f. [l. 2577], 204 f. [l. 665], 363 f. [ll. 1107 f., 1745 ff.]; (14) in a review of L 3.5, *ib.* xiii, 227; (15) *ib.* xiv, 49 [*wægbora*, l. 1440], 82 f. [*īsig*, l. 33]; (16) *IF.* xiv (1903), 339 [*hrinde*, l. 1363]; (17) "Beiträge zur Erklärung des altenglischen Epos," *ZfdPh.* xxxvii (1905), 113–25 [notes on numerous passages]; (18) *Beibl.* xviii (1907), 77 [l. 719]; (19) *Vietor-Festschrift (Die Neueren Sprachen* (1910)), 127 [ll. 224, 2251]; (20) *Beibl.* xxi (1910), 300 f. [l. 1440]; (21) *ESt.* li (1917), 180 [l. 1141]; (22) *Beibl.* xl (1929), 90 f. [ll. 489 f., 3114 f.]; " onsǣl meoto," *ib.* xlii (1931), 249 f.; (23) " Zu Beowulf 3074 f.," *ib.* xliii (1932), 157 [*goldhwæt*, and *næfde*]; (24) *ESt.* lxix (1935), 433 [l. 224: *eoleces,*=*ēa-lāces*].
27. H. Lübke, in a review of L 5.10.3, *Anz.fdA.* xix (1893), 341 f. [l. 305, etc.].
28. Clarence G. Child, (1) "stapol=patronus," *MLN.* viii (1893), 252 f. [l. 926]; (2) "*Beowulf* 30, 53, 1323, 2957," *ib.* xxi (1906), 175–77; 198–200.
29. Albert S. Cook, (1) *MLN.* viii (1893), 59 [ll. 572 f.]; (2) "Beowulf 1009," *ib.* ix (1894), 237 f.; (3) "Beowulf 1408 ff.," *ib.* xvii (1902), 209 f.; *ib.* xxii (1907), 146 f. [Classical and English parallels]; (4) "Bitter Beer-Drinking," *ib.* xl (1925), 285–88 [*Andr.* 1526, cf. *Beow.* 769]; *ib.*, 352–54 [ll. 159–63]. And see L 5.25.2.

V. TEXTUAL CRITICISM clxi

30. A. Pogatscher, *Beitr.* xix (1894), 544 f. [ll. 168 f.]
31. James W. Bright, (1) *MLN*. x (1895), 43 f. [ll. 30, 306, 386 f., 622, 736]; (2) " An Idiom of the Comparative in Anglo-Saxon," *MLN*. xxvii (1912), 181–83 [l. 69]; (3) " Anglo-Saxon *umbor* and *seld-guma*," *MLN*. xxxi (1916), 82–4; (4) " Beowulf, 489–490," *ib*. xxxi, 217–23.
32. E. Martin, in a review of L 8.9.1 & 2, *ESt.* xx (1895), 295 [ll. 1514, 3027].
33. W. Konrath, *Arch.* xcix (1897), 417 f. [ll. 445 f.].
34. Moritz Trautmann, (1) *Berichtigungen, Vermutungen und Erklärungen zum Beowulf. Erste Hälfte* (Bonn. B. ii, pp. 121–92), Bonn, 1899 [numerous conjectures]. R.: Holthausen (L 5.26.10), Binz (L. 5.39), Sievers (L 5.16.7); (2) in a review of Heyne-Socin's ed.⁶, Wyatt's ed.², Holder's ed.², *Beibl.* x (1900), 257–62; (3) *Finn und Hildebrand*, see Bibliography of *The Fight at Finnsburg;* (4) *Auch zum Beowulf* (Bonn. B. xvii, pp. 143–74), Bonn, 1905 [reply to Sievers's criticisms].
35. Fr. Klaeber, (1) " Aus Anlass von Beowulf 2724 f.," *Arch.* civ (1900), 287–92; (2) *MLN*. xvi (1901), 15–8 [ll. 459, 423 and 1206, 847 f., 3170, 3024 ff., 70; on normalizations]; (3) *Arch.* cviii (1902), 368–70 [ll. 1745 ff., 497 f.]; (4) *ib.* cxv (1905), 178–82; (5) " Hrothulf," *MLN.* xx (1905), 9–11 (L 4.87); (6) " *Beowulf*, 62," *ib.* xxi (1906), 255 f., xxii (1907), 160 (cf. L 5.42 & 43); (7) in a review of L 2.14, *ib.* xx, 83–7; (8) " Studies in the Textual Interpretation of ' Beowulf,' " *MPh.* iii (1905/6), 235–65; 445–65 [I. Rhetorical notes. II. Syntactical notes. III. Semasiological notes. IV. Notes on various passages]; (9) *Angl.* xxviii (1905), 439–47 (cf. *ib.* xxix, 272); (10) *ib.* xxviii (1905), 448–56 [1. " Zur Þryðo-Episode " (L 4.105). 2. " Textkritische Rettungen "]; (11) *ib.* xxix (1906), 378–82; (12) *JEGPh.* vi (1907), 190–96; (13) *ESt.* xxxix (1908), 463–67; (14) in a review of L 2.7.3, *ib.* xxxix, 425–33; (15) *JEGPh.* viii (1909), 254–59; (16) in a review of L 2.16, *ESt.* xliv (1911/12), 119–26; (17) *Beibl.* xxii (1911), 372–74 [ll. 769 (*ealuscerwen*), 1129 f.]; (18) *MLN.* xxxiv (1919), 129–34; (19) " Beowulfiana." *Angl.* l (1926), 107–22, 195–244. [1. Textual Notes. 2. Finnsburg. 3. The Þryð-Offa Episode. 4. A Note on the two Dragon Fights. 5. The Date of Hygelāc's Death.]; (20) *Angl.* lvi (1932), 421–31 [ll. 850, 1140 ff., 1724 ff., 3074 f.; etc.]; (21) in reviews, L 5.60.5, 6; also L 5.60.3.
36. G. Sarrazin, in a review of L 2.7.2, 6th ed., *ESt.* xxviii (1900), 408–10. [ll. 2561, 3084].
37. A. J. Barnouw, *Textkritische Untersuchungen etc.* (L 6.7.3), p. 232 (' Stellingen '). Leiden, 1902. [ll. 987 ff., 1151 f., 2524 ff.]
38. Elizabeth M. Wright, *ESt.* xxx (1902), 341–43 [*hrinde*, l. 1363].
39. Gustav Binz, in a review of L 5.34.1, *Beibl.* xiv (1903), 358–60.
40. Otto Krackow, *Arch.* cxi (1903), 171 f. [ll. 1224, 2220].
41. James M. Hart, (1) *MLN.* xviii (1903), 117 f. [Þryð; Bēanstān]; (2) *ib.* xxvii (1912), 198 [ll. 168 f.].
42. Wilbur C. Abbott, " Hrothulf," *MLN.* xix (1904), 122–25 (cf. L 4.86).

BIBLIOGRAPHY

43. Frank E. Bryant, "*Beowulf* 62," *MLN*. xix (1904), 121 f.; *ib.* xxi (1906), 143–45, *ib.* xxii (1907), 96; cf. replies by Fr. Klaeber (L 5.35.5 and 6).

44. Ernst A. Kock, (1) " Interpretations and Emendations of Early English Texts. III," *Angl.* xxvii (1904), 218–37; (2) *ib.* xxviii (1905), 140–42 [reply to Sievers's criticism, cf. L 5.16.8]; (3) " Interpretations and Emendations etc. IV," *ib.* xlii (1918), 99–124 (cf. L 5.35.18); (4) " Jubilee Jaunts and Jottings: 250 Contributions to the Interpretation and Prosody of Old West Teutonic Alliterative Poetry." *Lunds Universitets Årsskrift*, N. F. Avd. 1, Bd. 14, No. 26 (1918), pp. 7–9, and *passim;* (5) *Angl.* xliii (1919), 303–5 [ll. 2030, 2423]; (6) *ib.* xliv (1920), 98–104 [ll. 24, 154 ff., 189 f., 489 f., 583, 1747, 1820 f., 1931 f., 2164]; *ib.*, 246–48 [l. 1231, 1404, 1555 f.]; (7) *ib.* xlv (1921), 105–22 [notes on numerous passages]; (8) *ib.* xlvi (1922), 63–96 (esp. 75–96), 173–90. See also, *passim*, his papers in *Lunds Universitets Årsskrift*, N.F. Avd. 1, Vol. 17, No. 7 (1922) (" Plain Points and Puzzles, 60 Notes on Old English Poetry "); Vol. 18, No. 1 (1922) (" Fornjermansk Forskning"); cf. " Notationes Norrœnæ," *ib.*, Vols. 19 ff. (1923 ff.). [By his consistent use of the comparative method, with especial reference to the important stylistic figure of variation, Kock has been enabled to throw much valuable light on textual interpretation.]

45. von Grienberger, (1) *Angl.* xxvii (1904), 331 f. [l. 1107: *ondicge*]; (2) in a review of L 2.7.2, 7th ed., *ZföG*. lvi (1905), 744–61 [suggestive]; (3) *Beitr.* xxxvi (1910), 77–101 [notes on certain words and passages]. (Cf. L 5.16.9.)

46. George Philip Krapp, (1) "*Scūrheard, Beowulf* 1033, *Andreas* 1133," *MLN*. xix (1904), 234 (cf. L 5.25); (2) *MPh*. ii (1905), 405–7 [*waroð, faroð*].

47. Grace F. Swearingen, " Old Norse *bauni*," *MLN*. xx (1905), 64.

48. L. L. Schücking, (1) in a review of L 2.14, *Arch*. cxv (1905), 417–21; (2) in a review of Barnouw L 6.7.3, *Göttingische gelehrte Anzeigen*, 167. Jahrgang (1905), Vol. ii, pp. 730–40 [instructive]; (3) in reviews of L 2.15, *ESt*. xxxix (1908), 94–111, xlii (1910), 108–11 [scholarly comments]; (4) *ESt*. xliv (1911/12), 155–57 [ll. 106, 1174]; (5) " Wiðergyld (Beowulf 2051)," *ESt*. liii (1919/20), 468–70; (6) in a review, L 2.13.2. And see L 6.15; L 4.139; L 4.126.1.

49. Chauncey B. Tinker, *MLN*. xxiii (1908), 239 f. [ll. 166 ff., 311, 760, 783 ff.].

50. John R. Clark Hall, *MLN*. xxv (1910), 113 f. [ll. 1142–5].

51. W. J. Sedgefield, *MLR*. v (1910), 286–88; *ib.* xviii (1923), 471 f. [ll. 223 f.]; *ib.* xxvii (1932), 448–51 [emendations: 33 (*ūrig*), 367, 489 f., 617, 936, 1107, 1375, 2577, 2766, 2989, 3074 f.]; *ib.* xxviii (1933), 226–30 [further emendations]; in a review, L 5.60.6. And see LF. 4.41.

52. F. A. Blackburn, " Note on *Beowulf* 1591–1617," *MPh*. ix (1912), 555–66. [Assumes a misplacement of some lines in the MS.]

53. R. W. Chambers, " The ' Shifted Leaf ' in ' Beowulf,' " *MLR*. x (1915), 37–41. [Refutes Blackburn.]

V. TEXTUAL CRITICISM

54. L. M. Hollander, " Beowulf 33," *MLN.* xxxii (1917), 246 f.
55. Alexander Green, " An Episode in Ongenþeow's Fall, ll. 2957–60," *MLR.* xii (1917), 340–43.
56. Frank G. Hubbard, " Beowulf 1598, 1996, 2026; uses of the impersonal verb *geweorþan*," *JEGPh.* xvii (1918), 119–24. Cf. Fr. Klaeber, *ib.* xviii (1919), 250 ff.
57. Cyril Brett, *MLR.* xiv (1919), 1–17. [ll. 2385, 2771 ff., 2792 ff., 2999 ff., 3066 ff., etc.]
58. Samuel Moore, (1) " Beowulf Notes," *JEGPh.* xviii (1919), 205–16. [ll. 489 f., 599, 1082 ff., 3005 f., 3074 f., 3123 f., etc.]; (2) " Notes on *Beowulf*," *Kl. Misc.* (1929), 208–12. [ll. 1106, 2032 ff., 2037 f., 3119.]
59. W. F. Bryan, " Beowulf Notes," *JEGPh.* xix (1920), 84 f. [ll. 306, 534, 868.] And see L 6.29, 7.25 g.
60. Johannes Hoops, (1) " Das Verhüllen des Haupts bei Toten, ein angelsächsisch-nordischer Brauch," *ESt.* liv (1920), 19–23 [l. 446]; (2) " War Beowulf König von Dänemark? " *För. Misc.* (1929), 26–30, and Hoops St. 78 ff. [l. 3005: *hwate scildwigan*]; (3) (a) " Altenglisch *ealuscerwen, meoduscerwen*," *ESt.* lxv (1931), 177–80. Cf.: (b) Fr. Klaeber, *ESt.* lxvi (1931), 1–3, J. Hoops, *ib.*, 3–5; (c) R. Imelmann, L 5.76; (d) W. Krogmann, *ESt.* lxvi (1932), 346, lxvii (1932), 15–23; (e) Fr. Klaeber, *ib.*, 24–26; (f) Hoops St. 41 ff.; (4) " Das Preislied auf Beowulf und die Sigemund-Heremod-Episode." *Beiträge zur neueren Literaturgeschichte* xvi (*Deutschkundliches, Fr. Panzer überreicht*), Heidelberg, 1930, pp. 34–36, =Hoops St. 52–55. [A single lyrical-narrative lay of praise.] (5) *Beowulfstudien.* (Ang. F. lxxiv.) Heidelberg, 1932. 140 pp. [A large number of difficult passages (and words) judiciously discussed; distinctly conservative attitude.] R.: F. Holthausen, *Beibl.* xliii (1932), 357 f.; Fr. Klaeber, *ESt.* lxvii (1932/33), 399–402; R. Girvan, *MLR.* xxviii (1933), 244–46; Kemp Malone, *Eng. Studies* xv (1933), 94–96; C. L. W., *RESt.* x (1934), 94 f. (review of (5) and (6)). (6) *Kommentar zum Beowulf.* Heidelberg, 1932, 333 pp. [An extremely helpful, up-to-date commentary on the entire text.] R.: W. J. Sedgefield, *MLR.* xxviii (1933), 373–75; Fr. Klaeber, *ESt.* lxviii (1933), 112–15; F. Holthausen, *Beibl.* xliv (1933), 225–27; Kemp Malone, *Eng. Studies* xv (1933), 149–51. (7) *ESt.* lxx (1935), 77–80. [l. 457: *werefyhtum.*]
61. J. D. Bush, *MLN.* xxxvi (1921), 251. [l. 1604.]
62. P. G. Thomas, *MLR.* xvii (1922), 63 f. [ll. 1604 f., 2085–91]; *ib.* xxii (1927), 70–73.
63. E. D. Laborde, " Grendel's Glove and his Immunity from Weapons." *MLR.* xviii (1923), 202–04.
64. H. Patzig, " Zum Beowulf-Text." *Angl.* xlvii (1923), 97–104.
65. William A. P. Sewell, " A Reading in Beowulf." *The Times Literary Supplement.* London, Sept. 11, 1924. [l. 6: *egsode Eorlas.*]
66. A. C. Dunstan, *MLR.* xx (1925), 317 f. [ll. 223 f.]
67. W. S. Mackie, " *Beowulf*, ll. 223–24." *MLR.* xxi (1926), 301. [*þā wæs sundlidan/eoletes æt ende.*]

68. S. J. Crawford, (1) " Ealu-scerwen," *MLR.* xxi (1926), 302 f.; (2) " Beowulf, ll. 168-9," *ib.* xxiii (1928), 336; (3) " Beowulfiana," *RESt.* vii (1931), 448-50 [1. ll. 1724-68, cp. letter of St. Boniface to Æðilbald of Mercia; 2. *sendeþ* 600; 3. a dragon in 15th century England.]

69. Oliver Farrar Emerson, " The Punctuation of *Beowulf* and Literary Interpretation." *MPh.* xxiii (1926), 393-405. [The logical basis of the sentence structure is emphasized.] (It should be borne in mind, however, that our modern stylistic feeling is not necessarily a safe guide for properly judging of OE. sentences, periods, and paragraphs.)

Note. It will often be found difficult to agree on the best mode of punctuation. The ubiquitous figure of variation, e.g., would seem to call for an abundance of commas; but, in practice, awkward cases of overpunctuation are liable to result from a rigorous regard for logical distinctions of this nature. Cf. *MPh.* iii, 241 f.; Ed., notes on 36 f., 55 f., also on 398 (asyndetic parataxis like *wudu wælsceaftas;* cp., e.g., 3049ª, 2378ª). If the student thoroughly understands the principle of variation, the constant insertion of commas may be dispensed with. On the other hand, it should be noted that a rather frequent use of semicolons and of dashes is necessitated by the quality of the old style.

70. F. P. Magoun, Jr., " The Burning of Heorot: an Illustrative Note." *MLN.* xlii (1927), 173 f. [ll. 82 f.; cf. Bede, *Eccl. Hist.* iii 16 & 10.]

71. Kemp Malone, (1) " A Note on *Beowulf* 1231," *MLN.* xli (1926), 466 f. [in defense of *dōð*]; (2) " The Kenning in ' Beowulf ' 2220," *JEGPh.* xxvii (1928), 318-24 [*bū folcbeorna*]; *ib.* xxix (1930), 233-36 [ll. 303 ff., 646 f., (708 f.), 1056]; (3) " A Note on *Beowulf* 2928 and 2932," *Ph. Q.* viii (1928), 406 f. [Ōhthere the elder brother; cf. Intr., pp. xl, xxxviii]; (4) " A Note on ' Beowulf,' l. 2034," *MLR.* xxiv (1929), 322 f. [*mid = tō* (?)]; *ib.* xxv (1930), 191 [in defense of *felasinnigne secg* 1379; cf. 445, 2220]; (5) " Notes on Beowulf," *Angl.* liii (1929), 335 f. [l. 51: *selerǣdenne*]; *ib.* liv (1930), 1-7, 97 f. [ll. 3005, 3059, 3074 f., 2003 ff.]; *ib.* lvi (1932), 436 f. [Ecg-wēla, ' sword-vexer,' i.e., = Scyld]; *ib.* lvii (1933), 218-20 [l. 2061], 313-16 [' dative of accompaniment,' l. 1068, etc. (?)]; (6) " Beowulfiana," *Medium Ævum* ii (1933), 58-64 [ll. 304, 3005, 646 f., 3074 f.] And see L 4.85 a, LF. 4.36, 37; L 5.60.5, 6; L 6.6 a.

72. E. E. Wardale, " ' Beowulf,' ll. 848 ff." *MLR.* xxiv (1929), 62 f. [*dēog*, pret. of **dēagan*, ' to conceal.']

73. Margaret Ashdown, " ' Beowulf,' ll. 1543 ff." *MLR.* xxv (1930), 78.

74. Putnam Fennell Jones, " *Beowulf* 2596-99." *MLN.* xlv (1930), 300 f.

75. Henry G. Lotspeich, " *Beowulf* 1363, *hrinde bearwas.*" *JEGPh.* xxix (1930), 367-69.

76. Rudolf Imelmann, " Beowulf 489 f." *ESt.* lxv (1931), 190-96

VI. LANGUAGE

[*onsǣl mē tō*]; *ib.* lxvi (1932), 321–45 [ll. 489 f., 600, 769]; *ib.* lxvii (1932/33), 325–39 [ll. 303 ff., 3074 f.], *ib.* lxviii (1933), 1–5 [3074 f.]. And see L 4.106 a.

77. Åke Furuhjelm, (1) " Note on a Passage in Beowulf," *Neuphilol. Mitteilungen* xxxii (1931), 107–09 [ll. 3066–75]; (2) " Beowulfiana," *Angl.* lvii (1933), 317–20 [ll. 224 (*ēfenes æt ende*), 303 ff., 3074 f.].

78. Heinrich Henel, *Angl.* lv (1931), 273–81. [*stānboga*, like *hringboga*, = the dragon. (?)]

79. Edmund Weber, " Seelenmörder oder Unholdtöter? " *Neuphilol. Monatsschrift* ii (1931), 293–95. [On ll. 171–79.]

80. Clifford P. Lyons, " A Note on *Beowulf* 760." *MLN.* xlvi (1931), 443 f.

81. Willy Krogmann, " Bemerkungen zum Beowulf." *ESt.* lxviii (1933), 317–19; " Ae. *ēolet*." *A.* lviii (1934), 351–57 [etymol. attempt]. And see L 5.60.3, 6.30.

82. D. E. Martin Clarke, " Beowulfiana." *MLR.* xxix (1934), 320 f. [On ll. 984 ff., 760, etc.]

83. Hope Traver, *Arch.* clxvii (1935), 253-56. [ll. 646 ff.]

VI. LANGUAGE

a. Studies of Phonology and Inflexion

1. James A. Harrison, " List of irregular (strong) verbs in Beowulf." *Am. Jour. Phil.* iv (1883), 462–77.

2. Bernhard ten Brink, *Beowulf* (L 4.18), 1888. Ch. xiv: *Die Beowulfhandschrift und ihre Vorstufen*. Cf. H. Möller, *ESt.* xiii (1889) (L 4.18), 258–62, 314 f., and *passim*.

3. Charles Davidson, " Differences between the scribes of ' Beowulf.' " *MLN.* v (1890), 43–5. Cf. Charles F. McClumpha, *ib.* v, 123; Chas. Davidson, *ib.* v, 189 f.

4. Charles Davidson, " The Phonology of the stressed vowels of Beowulf." *Publ. MLAss.* vi (1891), 106–33. R.: G. E. Karsten, *ESt.* xvii (1892), 417–20.

5. P. G. Thomas, " Notes on the Language of Beowulf." *MLR.* i (1906), 202–7. [Convenient summary of dialectal forms.]

5 a. Gerhard Heidemann, " Die Flexion des Verb. subst. im Ags." *Arch.* cxlvii (1924), 30–46. [Includes a study of dialectal differences.]

6. (1) Carl Richter, *Chronologische Studien zur angelsächsischen Literatur auf Grund sprachlich-metrischer Kriterien*. (St.EPh. xxxiii.) Halle a. S., 1910. (2) Friedrich Seiffert, *Die Behandlung der Wörter mit auslautenden ursprünglich silbischen Liquiden oder Nasalen und mit Kontraktionsvokalen in der Genesis A und im Beowulf*. Halle Diss., 1913. — See also Morsbach, L 4.143; Sarrazin, L 4.144.

6 a. Kemp Malone, " When did Middle English Begin? " *Curme Volume of Linguistic Studies*, 1930, pp. 110–17. [On the leveling of vowels of final unstressed syllables.]

Syntactical and Lexical Studies

7. (1) A. Lichtenheld, "Das schwache Adjectiv im Angelsächsischen." *ZfdA*. xvi (1873), 325–93. [Careful investigation.] (2) Hermann Osthoff, *Zur Geschichte des schwachen deutschen Adjectivums*. Jena, 1876. 183 pp. (*Passim.*) (3) A. J. Barnouw, *Textkritische Untersuchungen nach dem Gebrauch des bestimmten Artikels und des schwachen Adjectivs in der altenglischen Poesie*. Leiden, 1902. 236 pp. [Serviceable, but not always reliable.] R.: E. A. Kock, *ESt*. xxxii (1903), 228 f.; L. L. Schücking, see L 5.48.2. (4) B. Delbrück, *IF*. xxvi (1909), 187–99. (5) George O. Curme, *JEGPh*. ix (1910), 439–82.

8. E. Nader, (1) *Zur Syntax des Beowulf* (*Accusativ*). I. II. Brünn Progr., 1879, 1880; (2) *Der Genetiv im Beowulf*, Brünn Progr., 1882; (3) *Dativ und Instrumental im Beowulf*, Wien Progr., 1883. R.: E. Klinghardt, *ESt*. vii (1884), 368–70. (4) George Shipley, *The Genitive Case in Anglo-Saxon Poetry*. Johns Hopkins Diss., Baltimore, 1903. (5) Alexander Green, *The Dative of Agency. A Chapter of Indo-European Case-Syntax*. (Columbia Univ. Germanic Studies.) Pp. 95–102. New York, 1913.

9. Karl Köhler, *Der syntaktische Gebrauch des Infinitivs und Particips im " Beowulf."* Münster Diss., 1886.

10. (1) E. Sievers, *Beitr*. xii (1887), 188–200 (cf. L 4.17). [On verbs of motion and of rest.] (2) Wilhelm Dening, *Zur Lehre von den Ruhe- und Richtungskonstruktionen*. Leipzig Diss., 1912.

11. (1) E. Nader, " Tempus und Modus im Beowulf." *Angl*. x (1888), 542–63; xi (1889), 444–99. (2) Cf. Berthold Delbrück, " Der germanische Optativ im Satzgefüge." *Beitr*. xxix (1904), 201–304. (3) V. E. Mourek, " Zur Syntax des Konjunktivs im Beowulf." *Prager Deutsche Studien* viii (1908), 121–37. (4) Hans Glunz, *Die Verwendung des Konjunktivs im Altenglischen* (Beitr. z. engl. Phil. hrsg. von M. Förster. xi.). Leipzig, 1930. 144 pp. (5) Morgan Callaway, Jr., *The Temporal Subjunctive in Old English*. University of Texas, 1931. 222 pp. (6) Frank Behre, *The Subjunctive in Old English Poetry*. Göteborg, 1934. 320 pp.

12. (1) August Todt, " Die Wortstellung im Beowulf." *Angl*. xvi (1894), 226–60. (2) John Ries, *Die Wortstellung im Beowulf*. Hallea. S., 1907. 416 pp. [Elaborate investigation with a view to finding the laws of the Old Germanic word order.] R.: B. Delbrück, *Anz.fdA*. xxxi (1907/8), 65–76; G. Binz, *Beibl*. xxii (1911), 65–78. Cf. G. Hübener, *Angl*. xxxix (1915), 277 ff. [Psychological interpretation.] (3) Martin Cohn, " Ist die Wortstellung ein brauchbares Kriterium für die Chronologie angelsächsischer Denkmäler? " *ESt*. lvii (1923), 321–29. (Cf. G. Hübener, *Beitr*. xlv, 85 ff., whose view is combated.) [The late *Metra of Boethius* show about the same trend toward end-position of the verb as *Beowulf* and *Genesis A*. The word-order remained conventional in poetry.]

13. (1) Ernst A. Kock, *The English Relative Pronouns*. Lund, 1897, 4to. 94 pp. (2) Berthold Delbrück, *Abhandl. der philol.-hist. Klasse der Königl. Sächsischen Gesellschaft der Wissenschaften*, Vol. xxvii, No. 19.

VI. LANGUAGE clxvii

Leipzig, 1909; (3) George O. Curme, *JEGPh.* x (1911), 335–59, xi (1912), 10–29, 180–204, 355–80.

14. (1) V. E. Mourek, *Zur Negation im Altgermanischen* [i.e., Otfrid, *Heliand, Beowulf*]. Prag, 1903. 67 pp. (2) Richard Schuchardt, *Die Negation im Beowulf.* Berlin, 1910. 149 pp. (3) Eugen Einenkel, " Die englische Verbalnegation." *Angl.* xxxv (1911), 187–248; 401–24.

15. Levin Ludwig Schücking, *Die Grundzüge der Satzverknüpfung im Beowulf. I. Teil.* (St.EPh. xv.) Halle a. S., 1904. 149 pp. [Thorough study.] R.: H. Grossmann, *Arch.* cxviii (1907), 176–79.

15 a. Ernst Glogauer, *Die Bedeutungsübergänge der Konjunktionen in der angelsächsischen Dichtersprache.* (Neue angl. Arbeiten hrsg. von L. L. Schücking u. M. Deutschbein, No. 6.) Leipzig, 1922. 48 pp. (Cf. L 6.22.)

15 b. L. L. Schücking, " *Sōna* im Beowulf." *För. Misc.* (1929), 85–88. [*sōna* = *sōna swā?*]

16. Fr. Klaeber, " Syntactical Notes," " Semasiological Notes." *MPh.* iii (1905/6), 249–65. (Cf. L 5.35.8.)

17. Anton Lorz, *Aktionsarten des Verbums im Beowulf.* Würzburg Diss., 1908.

17 a. George F. Lussky, " The Verb Forms Circumscribed with the Perfect Participle in the Beowulf." *JEGPh.* xxi (1922), 32–69.

18. Reinhard Wagner, *Die Syntax des Superlativs im Gotischen, Altniederdeutschen, Althochdeutschen, Frühmittelhochdeutschen, im Beowulf und in der älteren Edda.* (Palaestra xci.) Berlin, 1910.

19. Paul Grimm, *Beiträge zum Pluralgebrauch in der altenglischen Poesie.* Halle Diss., 1912.

19 a. Walter Phoenix, *Die Substantivierung des Adjektivs, Partizips und Zahlwortes im Angelsächsischen.* Berlin Diss., 1918.

---

20. Richard Jordan, *Eigentümlichkeiten des anglischen Wortschatzes.* (Ang. F. xvii.) Heidelberg, 1906.

21. Albert S. Cook, *A Concordance to Beowulf.* Halle a. S., 1911. 436 pp. R.: Fr. Klaeber, *JEGPh.* xi (1912), 277–79. Cf. Holder's *Wortschatz,* L 2.12.

22. Levin L. Schücking, *Untersuchungen zur Bedeutungslehre der angelsächsischen Dichtersprache.* Heidelberg, 1915. 109 pp. [Searching analysis of a number of words.]

23. Alfred Wolf, *Die Bezeichnungen für Schicksal in der angelsächsischen Dichtersprache.* Breslau Diss., 1919. — Cf. also Alois Brandl, " Zur Vorgeschichte der *weird sisters* im ' Macbeth.' " *Texte und Untersuchungen zur englischen Kulturgeschichte, Festgabe für Felix Liebermann,* Halle, 1921, pp. 252–70.

24. Richard Jente, *Die mythologischen Ausdrücke im altenglischen Wortschatz.* (Ang. F. lvi.) Heidelberg, 1921. 344 pp. *Passim.* [Helpful lexical collections, including etymologies.]

25. Fr. Klaeber, " Zum Bedeutungsinhalt gewisser altenglischer

Wörter und ihrer Verwendung." *Angl.* xlvi (1922), 232–38. [*bēorscealc, weorod, cyst, lof.*]

26. Walther Heinrich Vogt, *Stilgeschichte der eddischen Wissendichtung*. Vol. i: *Der Kultredner (þulr)*. Kiel, 1927. R.: E. Mogk, *Beibl.* xxxix (1928), 254–56; Kemp Malone, *MLN.* xliv (1929), 129 f.; H. de Boor, *Anz.fdA.* xlviii (1929), 9–14; L. M. Hollander, *JEGPh.* xxviii (1929), 414 f.

27. Johannes Hoops, (1) " Altenglisch *gēaþ, horngēaþ, sǣgēaþ*," *ESt.* lxiv (1929), 201–11; (2) " Das Meer als Schwanenstrasse." *Wörter und Sachen* xii (1929), 251 f. [cygnus musicus.]

28. Ernst A. Kock, " Old West Germanic and Old Norse." *Kl. Misc.* (1929), 14–20. [On *heaðu-, hilde-, gryre-, wæl-, heoru-* and similar compounds showing a generalized meaning of the first element; etc.]

29. W. F. Bryan, " *Ǣrgōd* in *Beowulf*, and Other Old English Compounds of *ǣr*." *MPh.* xxviii (1930), 157–61.

30. Willy Krogmann, " Altengl. *īsig*." *Angl.* lvi (1932), 438 f. [Cf. L 5.26.15.] *Angl.* lviii 351 ff. [*ēolet*]; *ESt.* lxx 40 ff. [*āntīd*].

See also under " Style ": Krapp (L 7.21); Merbach (L 7.27); Mead (L 7.29); Schemann (L 7.5); Banning (L 7.10); Sonnefeld (L 7.14); Scheinert (L 7.22); Wyld (L 7.25 f); Bryan (L 7.25 g); Magoun (L 7.25 h); Buckhurst (L 7.33 d); under " Old Germanic Life ": Keller (L 9.42); Stroebe (L 9.45.2); Padelford (L 9.15).

VII. STYLE

1. Jacob Grimm, in his edition of *Andreas und Elene*, pp. xxiv–xliv. Cassel, 1840.

2. Richard Heinzel, (1) *Über den Stil der altgermanischen Poesie* (Quellen und Forschungen x). Strassburg, 1875. 54 pp. [Very suggestive essay]; (2) in a review of Möller (L 4.134) and of Rönning (L 4.15), *Anz.fdA.* x (1884), 215–39; (3) in a review of ten Brink (L 4.18), *Anz.fdA.* xv (1889), 153–82.

3. Francis B. Gummere, *The Anglo-Saxon Metaphor*. Freiburg Diss. Halle a. S., 1881. [Scholarly, interesting.]

4. Francis A. March, " The World of Beowulf." *Transactions of the Am. Philol. Assoc.* xiii (1882). Proceedings, pp. xxi–xxiii.

5. Karl Schemann, *Die Synonyma im Beowulfsliede mit Rücksicht auf Composition und Poetik des Gedichtes*. Münster Diss. Hagen, 1882.

6. A. Hoffmann, " Der bildliche Ausdruck im Beowulf und in der Edda." *ESt.* vi (1883), 163–216. (Part I also published as Breslau Diss., 1882.) [Useful observations.]

7. Reinhold Merbot, *Ästhetische Studien zur angelsächsischen (altenglischen) Poesie*. Breslau Diss., 1883. [Meagre.]

8. Otto Hoffmann, *Reimformeln im Westgermanischen*. Freiburg Diss. Darmstadt, 1885. [Copulative formulas like *ord* and *ecg*.]

9. Wilhelm Bode, *Die Kenningar in der angelsächsischen Dichtung*. Strassburg Diss. Darmstadt and Leipzig, 1886.

VII. STYLE

10. Adolf Banning, *Die epischen Formeln im Beowulf. I. Teil: Die verbalen Synonyma.* Marburg Diss., 1886.
11. Albert H. Tolman, " The Style of Anglo-Saxon Poetry." *MLAss. Transactions and Proceedings* iii (1887), 17–47. (Reprinted in Tolman's *The Views about Hamlet and other Essays*, pp. 337–82. Boston and New York, 1904.)
12. Richard M. Meyer, *Die altgermanische Poesie nach ihren formelhaften Elementen beschrieben.* Berlin, 1889. 549 pp. [Abundance of material and ideas.]
13. J. Kail, " Über die Parallelstellen in der angelsächsischen Poesie." *Angl.* xii (1889), 21–40. (See L 4.17.)
14. Gottfried Sonnefeld, *Stilistisches und Wortschatz im Beowulf.* Strassburg Diss. Würzburg, 1892.
15. Bernhard ten Brink, *Altenglische Literatur* in *P. Grdr.*[1], ii[a], pp. 522–32. 1893. (L 4.7.) [Excellent sketch.]
16. Richard Kistenmacher, *Die wörtlichen Wiederholungen im Beowulf.* Greifswald Diss., 1898. [Cursory.]
17. Ernst Otto, *Typische Motive in dem weltlichen Epos der Angelsachsen.* Berlin, 1901. 99 pp.
18. Andreas Heusler, " Der Dialog in der altgermanischen erzählenden Dichtung." *ZfdA.* xlvi (1902), 189–284. [A luminous paper.] (Cf. also Werner Schwartzkopff, *Rede und Redeszene in der deutschen Erzählung bis Wolfram von Eschenbach.* (Palaestra lxxiv.) Berlin, 1909. 148 pp.)
19. Otto Krackow, *Die Nominalcomposita als Kunstmittel im altenglischen Epos.* Berlin, 1903. 86 pp.
20. Bruno Haeuschkel, *Die Technik der Erzählung im Beowulfliede.* Breslau Diss., 1904. [Serviceable survey.]
21. George Philip Krapp, " The parenthetic exclamation in Old English Poetry." *MLN.* xx (1905), 33–7.
22. Moritz Scheinert, " Die Adjectiva im Beowulfepos als Darstellungsmittel." *Beitr.* xxx (1905), 345–430.
23. Fr. Klaeber, " Rhetorical Notes." *MPh.* iii (1905/6), 237–49. (L 5.35.8.)
24. Walther Paetzel, *Die Variationen in der altgermanischen Alliterationspoesie.* (Palaestra xlviii.) Berlin, 1913. 216 pp. (The first part issued as Berlin Diss., 1905.) [Attempts a more precise definition and grouping of variations.] R.: J. Franck, *Anz.fdA.* xxxvii (1914), 6–14. (Cf. Krauel, L 8.25.)
25. James Walter Rankin, " A Study of the Kennings in Anglo-Saxon Poetry." *JEGPh.* viii (1909), 357–422, ix (1910), 49–84. [Traces the kennings back to their (Christian) Latin sources.]
25 a. Alberta J. Portengen, *De Oudgermaansche dichtertaal in haar ethnologisch verband.* Leiden Diss., 1915. 208 pp. [Speculations on the origin of kennings.]

BIBLIOGRAPHY

25 b. Cf. Rudolf Meissner, *Die Kenningar der Skalden. Ein Beitrag zur skaldischen Poetik.* Bonn u. Leipzig, 1921. 437 pp.

25 c. Hendrik van der Merwe Scholtz, *The Kenning in Anglo-Saxon and Old Norse Poetry.* Utrecht Diss., 1927. 180 pp.

25 d. Wolfgang Krause, *Die Kenning als typische Stilfigur der germanischen und keltischen Dichtersprache.* Halle, 1930. 4to. 26 pp. R.: S. Singer, *IF.* li (1933), 164–67. — Wolfgang Mohr, *Kenningstudien.* Stuttgart, 1933. Cf. *Arch.* clxv, 290.

25 e. Ludwig Wolff, " Über den Stil der altgermanischen Poesie." *Deutsche Vierteljahrsschrift für Literaturwissenschaft und Geistesgeschichte* i (1923), 214–29. [Brief survey of salient features.]

25 f. Henry Cecil Wyld, " Diction and Imagery in Anglo-Saxon Poetry." *Essays and Studies by Members of the English Association* xi (1925), 49–91. [1. ' Poetical ' words and phrases. 2. Figurative or metaphorical use of words (ref. to sea, ships, sun, body, death, etc.) and typical epithets used in connection with these. 3. Individual use of words and phrases with striking poetic effect.]

25 g. William Frank Bryan, " Epithetic Compound Folk-Names in *Beowulf.*" *Kl. Misc.* (1929), 120–34. [The characterizing folk-name compounds were, in most instances, chosen by the poet with particular reference to the specific situation in which they are used.]

25 h. Francis P. Magoun, Jr., " Recurring First Elements in Different Nominal Compounds in *Beowulf* and in the *Elder Edda.*" *Kl. Misc.* (1929), 73–78. Cf. J. R. Hulbert, " A Note on Compounds in *Beowulf.*" *JEGPh.* xxxi (1932), 504–08.

And see L 6.28.

25 i. Levin L. Schücking, " Heldenstolz und Würde im Angelsächsischen. Mit einem Anhang: Zur Charakterisierungstechnik im Beowulfepos." *Abhandlungen der Sächsischen Akademie der Wissenschaften, Philol.-histor. Klasse,* Vol. xlii, No. 5. 1933. 4to, 46 pp. [Illuminating exposition.] Cf. L 4.157.

25 k. John O. Beaty, " The Echo-Word in *Beowulf* with a Note on the *Finnsburg* Fragment." *PMLA.* xlix (1934), 365–73. [Cf. *A.* xxviii, 453 f.]

---

26. Sidney Lanier, *Shakespere and his Forerunners.* Vol. i, ch. iii: " Nature in Early English and in Shakspere: ' Beowulf ' and ' Midsummer Night's Dream.' " New York, [printed:] 1902. (S. Lanier died in 1881.)

27. Hans Merbach, *Das Meer in der Dichtung der Angelsachsen.* Breslau Diss., 1884.

28. Otto Lüning, *Die Natur in der altgermanischen und mittelhochdeutschen Epik.* Zürich, 1889. 314 pp.

29. William E. Mead, " Color in Old English Poetry." *Publ. MLAss.* xiv (1899), 169–206.

30. J. E. Willms, *Untersuchung über den Gebrauch der Farbenbezeich-*

nungen in der Poesie Altenglands. Münster Diss., 1902. [Covers the OE. and ME. periods.]

31. Edmund Erlemann, *Das landschaftliche Auge der angelsächsischen Dichter.* Berlin Diss., 1902. [Incomplete.]

32. Frederic W. Moorman, *The Interpretation of Nature in English Poetry from Beowulf to Shakespeare*, ch. i. (Quellen und Forschungen xcv.) Strassburg, 1905.

33. Elizabeth Deering Hanscom, "The Feeling for Nature in Old English Poetry." *JEGPh.* v (1905), 439–63.

33 a. Emile Pons, "Le thème et le sentiment de la nature dans la poésie anglo-saxonne." *Publications de la Faculté des Lettres de l'Université de Strasbourg*, Fasc. 25. 1925. 162 pp. R.: C[arleton] B[rown], *MLR.* xxi (1926), 343 f.; E. C. B[atho], *Review of English Studies* ii (1926), 496 f.; Fr. Klaeber, *Beibl.* xxxviii (1927), 129–32; Kemp Malone, *MLN.* xliii (1928), 406–08.

33 b. Robert Ashton Kissack, Jr., "The Sea in Anglo-Saxon and Middle English Poetry." *Washington University Studies*, Humanistic Series, Vol. xiii, No. 2 (1926), 371–89. [A suggestive little sketch.]

33 c. Anne Treneer, *The Sea in English Literature from Beowulf to Donne.* Liverpool and London, 1926. 299 pp. (Ch. i: 'The Sea in Old English Literature.') [A pleasing general survey.]

33 d. Helen Thérèse McMillan Buckhurst, "Terms and Phrases for the Sea in Old English Poetry." *Kl. Misc.* (1929), 103–19. [Study of single terms, epithets, compounds, and phrases. Old Norse poetry is referred to for comparison.]

33 e. James R. Hulbert, "A Note on the Psychology of the *Beowulf* Poet." *Kl. Misc.* (1929), 189–95. [The poet was not accustomed to visualizing anything (hence, e.g., inconsistencies in the description of the haunted mere), but was interested in moods and states of mind.]

Supplementary:

34. Eduard Sievers, Edition of the *Heliand*, pp. 389–495: *Formelverzeichnis.* Halle, 1878. [Valuable collection including numerous OE. parallels.]

35. F. Schulz, *Die Sprachformen des Hildebrands-Liedes im Beowulf.* Königsberg Progr., 1882. [Lexical and phraseological parallels.]

36. R. Heinzel, "Beschreibung der isländ. Saga." *Sitzungsberichte der philos.-histor. Classe der Kaiserl. Akademie der Wissenschaften*, xcvii, 107–308. Wien, 1881.

37. Georg Radke, *Die epische Formel im Nibelungenliede.* Kiel Diss., 1890.

38. John S. P. Tatlock, (1) "Epic Formulas, especially in Laȝamon," *Publ. MLAss.* xxxviii (1923), 494–529; (2) "Laȝamon's Poetic Style and its Relations." *The Manly Anniversary Studies in Language and Literature*, Chicago, 1923, pp. 3–11.

And see R. Koegel (L 4.8), Vol. i[a], pp. 333–40 [excellent sketch], Vol. i[b], pp. 27 ff., 88 ff., 335 ff.; Heusler (L 4.124.3).

VIII. VERSIFICATION

1. Hermann Schubert, *De Anglo-Saxonum arte metrica*. Berlin Diss., 1870.
2. Max Rieger, " Die alt- und angelsächsische Verskunst." *ZfdPh.* vii (1876), 1–64. (Also printed separately.) [Still of considerable value.]
3. Eduard Sievers, " Zur Rhythmik des germanischen Alliterationsverses." *Beitr.* x (1885), 209–314 (220–314: " Die Metrik des Beowulf "); 451–545. Anastatic reprint, New York, 1909. [Masterly presentation of Sievers's system of types; of fundamental importance.] Also *Beitr.* xii (1887), 454–82: " Der angelsächsische Schwellvers."
4. Eduard Sievers, *Altgermanische Metrik*. Halle, 1893. 252 pp. [Has been largely regarded as standard.] (An abridged version in *P. Grdr.*, ii^a (1893), pp. 861–97; 2d ed., ii^b (1905), pp. 1–38 (under the supervision of F. Kauffmann and H. Gering).
5. James W. Bright, *An Anglo-Saxon Reader*. Appendix II (pp. 229–40): " Anglo-Saxon Versification." New York, 1891; 4th ed., 1917. [Admirable, condensed account of Sievers's system.]
6. Karl Fuhr, *Die Metrik des westgermanischen Alliterationsverses. Sein Verhältnis zu Otfried, den Nibelungen, der Gudrun etc.* Marburg, 1892. 147 pp.
7. Bernhard ten Brink, *Altenglische Literatur* (L 4.7) in *P. Grdr.*[1] ii^a (1893), pp. 515–22.
8. H. Frank Heath, " The Old English Alliterative Line." *Transactions of the Philological Society*, 1891–1894, pp. 375–95. London, 1894. [Presentation of ten Brink's views; on the construction of the expanded line.]
9. Max Kaluza, *Der altenglische Vers: eine metrische Untersuchung.* (1) *I. Teil: Kritik der bisherigen Theorien.* [Attempts to reconcile the four-accent theory with Sievers's types.] (2) *II. Teil: Die Metrik des Beowulfliedes.* [Including a scansion of the first 1000 lines.] Berlin, 1894. 96+102 pp. Cf. R. Fischer (in a review of F. Graz, *Die Metrik der sog. Cædmonschen Dichtungen*), *Anz.fdA.* xxiii (1897), 40–54. [Criticism of Kaluza's system, and suggestions as to the psychological function of the OE. rhythm.] (3) Max Kaluza, *Englische Metrik in historischer Entwicklung dargestellt*. Berlin, 1909. 384 pp. [A practical handbook; contains a clear, concise survey of existing theories.] English translation by A. C. Dunstan: *A Short History of English Versification*. New York, 1911.
10. Edwin B. Setzler, *On Anglo-Saxon Versification from the standpoint of Modern-English Versification*. (University of Virginia Studies in Teutonic Languages, No. v.) Baltimore, 1904. [Exposition of Sievers's system, for students.]
11. J. Schipper, (1) *Grundriss der englischen Metrik*. Wien and Leipzig, 1895. (2) English translation: *A History of English Versification*. Oxford, 1910. 390 pp. (An older handbook by J. Schipper: *Altenglische Metrik*. Bonn, 1881. [OE. and ME. versification.]

12. Moritz Trautmann, (1) "Zur Kenntnis des altgermanischen Verses. vornehmlich des altenglischen." *Beibl.* v (1894/5), 87–96; (2) *Die neuste Beowulfausgabe und die altenglische Verslehre* (Bonn. B. xvii, pp. 175–91). Bonn, 1905; (3) *Verhandlungen der 50. Versammlung deutscher Philologen und Schulmänner* (Graz, 1909), pp. 15–19. Leipzig, 1910; (4) *ESt.* xliv (1912), 303–42; cf. also L 3.44. (5) Cf. Theodor Schmitz, "Die Sechstakter in der altenglischen Dichtung," *Angl.* xxxiii (1910), 1–76, 172–218. [Study of the expanded lines on the basis of Trautmann's theory.]

13. For certain other treatises setting forth views dissenting from Sievers (such as those of Möller, Hirt, Heusler, Franck), see references in Sievers (L 8.4), Schipper (L 8.11), Kaluza (L 8.9.3), Brandl's bibliography (L 4.11); R. C. Boer, *Studiën over de Metriek van het Alliteratievers*, 1916, cf. Frantzen, *Neophilologus* iii (1917), 30–35; also W. E. Leonard (L 3.44); a paper by John Morris, "Sidney Lanier and Anglo-Saxon Verse-Technic," *Am. Jour. Phil.* xx (1899), 435–38 [opposing the fundamentals of Sievers's system]. — See further P. Fijn van Draat, "The Cursus in Old English Poetry." *Angl.* xxxviii (1914), 377–404; *id., ESt.* xlviii (1915), 394–428.

Cf. also Franz Saran's summary in *Ergebnisse und Fortschritte der germanistischen Wissenschaft im letzten Vierteljahrhundert* ed. by R. Bethge (1902), pp. 158–70. — Ernst Martin, *Der Versbau des Heliand und der altsächsischen Genesis.* (Quellen und Forschungen c.) Strassburg, 1907.

13 a. Wilhelm Heims, *Der germanische Allitterationsvers und seine Vorgeschichte. Mit einem Exkurs über den Saturnier.* Münster Diss., 1914.

13 b. James Routh, "Anglo-Saxon Meter." *MPh.* xxi (1923–24), 429–34. [Explains Sievers's five types from a common basis, unstressed syllables being allowed to interchange with pauses.]

13 c. W. W. Greg, "The 'Five Types' in Anglo-Saxon Verse." *MLR.* xx (1925), 12–17. [Sievers's types " represent the abstractly possible mutations of a two-stressed group, with the exclusion of such forms as we may reasonably suppose were unsuited to OE. Verse." D and E are declared non-fundamental types.] (Kaluza (L 8.9) had classed D1 (Da) with C, D2 (Db) with B.)

13 d. Eduard Sievers, "Metrische Studien IV. Die altschwedischen Upplandslagh nebst Proben formverwandter germanischer Sagdichtung." *Abhandlungen der K. Sächsischen Gesellschaft der Wissenschaften, Philol.-hist. Klasse*, Vol. xxxv. Leipzig, 1918. 1919. 4to. 620 pp. §§ 163 ff., and *passim*. [Sievers's later views on certain aspects of metrics, speech-melody, etc.] For a practical application of his system to textual criticism, see E. Sievers, "Zum Widsith." *Texte und Forschungen zur englischen Kulturgeschichte, Festgabe für Felix Liebermann*, pp. 1–19. Halle a. S., 1921.

13 e. Eduard Sievers, "Zu Cynewulf." *Neusprachliche Studien, Festgabe für Karl Luick (Die Neueren Sprachen*, 6. Beiheft, 1925), pp. 60–81.

BIBLIOGRAPHY

[Showing Sievers's radically changed metrical views, together with certain new linguistic observations. S. recognizes the musical element of regularly recurring measures, rejects the dynamic basis of alliteration, admits deviations from the normal (prose) accentuation, relies on his feeling for speech melody. The thesis that alliteration is not confined to rhythmically accented syllables, raises serious doubts.]

13 f. Andreas Heusler, *Deutsche Versgeschichte mit Einschluss des altenglischen und altnordischen Stabreimverses*. Vol. i: 1. Einführendes; Grundbegriffe. 2. Der altgermanische Vers. (*P. Grdr.* 8.1.) Berlin u. Leipzig, 1925. 314 pp. (See also *Die altgermanische Dichtung* (L 4.13 a), ch. 6: ' Verskunst; Vortrag '; *R.-L.* iv, 231–40: ' Stabreim.' Cf. L 4.124.3; also L 8.13.) [An inspiring book. The different forms of verse (half-line) are viewed as variations of the general *rhythmical* type of two bars[1] (' 2 Langtakte '), . . | x́xx̀x | x́xx̀x, freely admitting, however, pauses in place of speech-material. The ' swelling ' lines are not ' hypermetrical.' The valuable statistical material embodied in Sievers's researches (L 8.3 & 4) now appears capable of being fitted into a new interpretative scheme.]

13 g. William Ellery Leonard, " Four Footnotes to Papers on Germanic Metrics." *Kl. Misc.* (1929), 1–13. (See L 3.44.) [The basic eight-beat long-line; the rest-beat; the " expanded " lines are expanded in speech-material only. L. remarks on Heusler's *Deutsche Versgeschichte* (L 8.13 f): " In spite of great differences in terminology and manner of approach, and above all in the detail and comprehensiveness of his overwhelming scholarship, I feel I have at last found a friend and helper."] Cf. *id.*, " The Recovery of the Metre of the *Cid*," *Publ. MLAss.* xlvi (1931), 289–306. (An extensive version in Spanish: *Revista de Archivos*, 1928 ff.) But note also: *PMLA*. xlviii, 965 ff.

13 h. E. W. Scripture, " Die Grundgesetze des altenglischen Stabreimverses," *Angl.* lii (1928), 69–75; *id.*, " Experimentelle Untersuchungen über die Metrik in *Beowulf*," *Archiv für die gesamte Psychologie* lxvi (1928), 203–15; cf. *id.*, *Grundzüge der englischen Verswissenschaft*, Marburg, 1929. 98 pp. [Experimental (kymographic) researches on the physical nature of verse.] R.: R. A. Williams, *Beibl.* xli (1930), 357–62.

13 i. Paull F. Baum, " The Character of Anglo-Saxon Verse." *MPh.* xxviii (1930–31), 143–56. [A suggestive, slight sketch.]

13 k. S. O. Andrew, *The Old English Alliterative Measure*. Croydon, 1931. 82 pp. [A refreshingly subjective, rather amateurish criticism of Sievers's views of 1885 A.D.] R.: A. Brandl, *Arch.* clxi (1932), 145 f.; S. Potter, *RESt.* ix (1933), 85–87; K. Brunner, *Beibl.* xliv (1933), 71–73.

Studies of special features:

14. F. Kluge, " Zur Geschichte des Reimes im Altgermanischen." *Beitr.* ix (1884), 422–50.

---

[1] " Each line consists of four bars " — this was the formula laid down by Sidney Lanier, poet and musician (*The Science of English Verse*, 1880, p. 150).

VIII. VERSIFICATION

14 a. Cf. also J. W. Rankin, " Rhythm and rime before the Norman Conquest." *Publ. MLAss.* xxxvi (1921), 401–28. [On traces of popular, non-literary songs.]

14 b. (Cf. L 4.146 c 4) Albert S. Cook, "' Beowulf ' 1422." *MLN.* xxxix (1924), 77–82. [The employment of 'internal rime,' like *flōd blōde*, is attributed to the example of Aldhelm (thus, *fluenta cruenta*).]

15. John Lawrence, *Chapters on Alliterative Verse.* London Diss., 1893. [E.g., crossed alliteration, vowel alliteration.]

16. O. Brenner, " Zur Verteilung der Reimstäbe in der alliterierenden Langzeile." *Beitr.* xix (1894), 462–66.

17. James W. Bright, " Proper Names in Old English Verse." *Publ. MLAss.* xiv (1899), 347–68.

18. Edward Schröder, " Steigerung und Häufung der Allitteration in der westgermanischen Dichtung. I. Die Anwendung allitterierender Nominalcomposita." *ZfdA.* xliii (1899), 361–85.

19. Oliver F. Emerson, " Transverse Alliteration in Teutonic Poetry." *JGPh.* iii (1900), 127–37.

20. Julian Huguenin, *Secondary Stress in Anglo-Saxon (determined by metrical criteria).* Johns Hopkins Diss., Baltimore, 1901.

21. Eduard Sokoll, " Zur Technik des altgermanischen Alliterationsverses," in *Beiträge zur neueren Philologie, Jakob Schipper dargebracht,* pp. 351–65. Wien and Leipzig, 1902. [Inquiry as to laws governing the union of rhythmical types in the full line.]

22. M. Deutschbein, *Zur Entwicklung des englischen Alliterationsverses.* Leipzig Habilitationsschrift. Halle a. S., 1902. 69 pp. [Enjambment; statistics of the frequency of the different types. Follows the Sievers school.]

23. B. Q. Morgan, " Zur Lehre von der Alliteration in der westgermanischen Dichtung." *Beitr.* xxxiii (1908), 95–181 (also Leipzig Diss., 1907). [Application of the theory of speech-melody[1] to the problems of alliteration; discussion of crossed alliteration; criteria for punctuation.]

24. Adolf Bohlen, *Zusammengehörige Wortgruppen, getrennt durch Cäsur oder Versschluss, in der angelsächsischen Epik.* Berlin Diss., 1908.

25. Hans Krauel, *Der Haken- und Langzeilenstil im Beowulf.* Göttingen Diss., 1908. [' Mid-stopped ' and ' end-stopped ' lines; variation. Opposes Sievers and Deutschbein.]

26. E. Classen, *On Vowel Alliteration in the Old Germanic Languages.* (University of Manchester Publ., Germanic Series, No. i.) Manchester, 1913. 91 pp. R.: E. Noreen, *IF.Anz.* xxxiii (1914), 62–5; E. Brate, *AfNF.* xxxii (1915), 125–28. Cf. F. N. Scott, " Vowel Alliteration in MnE.," *MLN.* xxx (1915), 233–37.

26 a. Erich Neuner, *Über ein- und dreihebige Halbverse in der altenglischen alliterierenden Poesie.* Berlin Diss., 1920. R.: J. W. Bright, *MLN.* xxxvi (1921), 59–63.

[1] See E. Sievers, *Rhythmisch-melodische Studien.* Heidelberg, 1912. 141 pp. [Collection of five papers.]

26 b. Alfred Bognitz, *Doppelt-steigende Alliterationsverse (Sievers'. Typus B) im Angelsächsischen.* Berlin Diss., 1920.

27. See also H. Möller, *Das altenglische Volksepos in der ursprünglichen strophischen Form* (L 4.134, 2.19).

IX. OLD GERMANIC LIFE

1. John M. Kemble, *The Saxons in England*, 1849; 2d ed., 1876. 2 vols. (Cf. L 4.44.)
2. Jacob Grimm, " Über das Verbrennen der Leichen " (paper read in the Berlin Academy of Sciences, Nov. 29, 1849). *Kleinere Schriften* ii (Berlin, 1865), 211–313. [Famous essay.]
3. Thomas Wright, *The Celt, the Roman and the Saxon.* London, 1852; 4th ed., 1885. (Cf. xv: ' Anglo-Saxon Antiquities.')
4. (1) Moritz Heyne, *Ueber die Lage und Construction der Halle Heorot.* Paderborn, 1864. 60 pp. — (2) K. G. Stephani, *Der älteste deutsche Wohnbau und seine Einrichtung.* i, 388 ff. Leipzig, 1902–3.
5. Artur Köhler, " Germanische Alterthümer im Beowulf." *Germ.* xiii (1868), 129–58.
6. W. Scherer, *ZföG.* xx (1869), 89 ff. (L 5.5), *passim.* [Legal antiquities, etc.]
7. Artur Köhler, " Über den Stand berufsmässiger Sänger im nationalen Epos germanischer Völker." *Germ.* xv (1870), 27–50.
8. Martin Schultze, *Altheidnisches in der ags. Poesie, speciell im Beowulfsliede.* Berlin, 1877. 31 pp. — On Germanic heathendom, see also Kemble (L 9.1), Vol. i, ch. xii; Bouterwek (L 4.45), Introd., ch. iv; handbooks of mythology (L 4.42, note), also Philippson (*ib.*, 10).
9. James A. Harrison, " Old Teutonic Life in Beowulf." *The Overland Monthly* iv [Second Series] (San Francisco, 1884), 14–24, 152–61. See also F. A. March, L 7.4.
10. (1) Karl von Amira, *Recht*, in *P. Grdr.* ii[b] (1889), pp. 35–200; 2d ed., iii (1900), pp. 51–222; 3d ed. (separate, 1913), 302 pp. — (2) Cf. F. Liebermann, *Die Gesetze der Angelsachsen.* ii. 2 (pp. 255–758): *Rechts- und Sachglossar.* Halle a. S., 1912.
11. Francis B. Gummere, *Germanic Origins. A Study in Primitive Culture.* New York, 1892. 490 pp. [Excellent.] Re-issued under the title *Founders of England*, by Francis P. Magoun, Jr. New York, 1930. [With supplementary notes (pp. 485–99) containing up-to-date bibliographies.]
12. J. R. Green, *A Short History of the English People. Illustrated Edition.* Ed. by Mrs. J. R. Green and Miss Kate Norgate. London and New York, 1893.
13. *Social England.* Ed. by H. D. Traill. Vol. i, ch. ii; 2d ed., London and New York, 1894. Illustrated ed. by H. D. Traill and J. S. Mann, 1909.
14. (1) Karl Müllenhoff, *Deutsche Altertumskunde*, Vol. iv. Berlin,

IX. OLD GERMANIC LIFE

1900. 751 pp. 2d ed., 1920. [Elaborate commentary on Tacitus' *Germania*.] — (2) Theodor Schauffler, *Zeugnisse zur Germania des Tacitus aus der altnord. und ags. Dichtung*. Ulm Progr. I. II. Ulm, 1898. 1900.

15. Frederick Morgan Padelford, *Old English Musical Terms*. (Bonn. B. iv.) Bonn, 1899.

16. Moriz Heyne, *Fünf Bücher deutscher Hausaltertümer*. 3 vols. Leipzig, 1899–1903. 406+408+373 pp.

17. Frederic Seebohm, *Tribal Custom in Anglo-Saxon Law*. Ch. iii. London and New York, 1902.

18. L. F. Anderson, *The Anglo-Saxon Scop*. (University of Toronto Studies, Philological Series, No. i.) 1903. 45 pp. Cf. R. Merbot (L 7.7).

19. Laurence Marcellus Larson, *The King's Household in England before the Norman Conquest*. University of Wisconsin Diss., 1904. (Bulletin of the University of Wisconin, No. 100.)

20. Wilhelm Pfändler, " Die Vergnügungen der Angelsachsen." *Angl.* xxix (1906), 417–526.

21. Erich Budde, *Die Bedeutung der Trinksitten in der Kultur der Angelsachsen*. Jena Diss., 1906.

22. H. Munro Chadwick, *The Origin of the English Nation*, 1907 (L 4.38), and *The Heroic Age*, 1912 (L 4.22).

23. Edmund Dale, *National Life and Character in the Mirror of Early English Literature*. Cambridge, 1907. [Collection of illustrative material.]

24. Vilhelm Grønbech, *Vor Folkeæt i Oldtiden: I. Lykkemand og Niding*. København, 1909. 220 pp. [A psychological study of Old Germanic ideals; clanship, honor, duty of revenge. Decidedly original.] R.: L. M. Hollander, *JEGPh.* ix (1910), 269–78. — *II. Midgård og Menneskelivet. III. Hellighed og Helligdom. IV. Menneskelivet og Guderne.* 1912. 269+208+133 pp. R.: G. Neckel, *ESt.* xlvii (1913/14), 108–16; L. M. Hollander, *JEGPh.* xiv (1915), 124–35. — An English translation, entitled *The Culture of the Teutons*, appeared 1932, Copenhagen and London. 2 vols.

25. Klara Stroebe, " Altgermanische Grussformen." *Beitr.* xxxvii (1911/12), 173–212.

26. Friedrich Kauffmann, *Deutsche Altertumskunde*. *I.* München, 1913. 4to. 508 pp.

27. Arthur Bartels, *Rechtsaltertümer in der ags. Dichtung*. Kiel Diss., 1913.

28. Johannes Müller, *Das Kulturbild des Beowulfepos*. (St.EPh. liii.) Halle a. S., 1914. 88 pp. [Claims Beowulfian conditions of life as Ags.]

28 a. Gustav Neckel, " Adel und Gefolgschaft. Ein Beitrag zur germanischen Altertumskunde." *Beitr.* xli (1916), 385–436.

28 b. Gustav Neckel, *Altgermanische Kultur* (' Wissenschaft und Bildung,' No. 208), Leipzig, 1925. 131 pp.

28 c. Andreas Heusler, " Altgermanische Sittenlehre und Lebens-

BIBLIOGRAPHY

weisheit," in *Germanische Wiedererstehung* ed. by Hermann Nollau, Heidelberg, 1926, pp. 156–204. Cf. *id.*, *Germanentum: Vom Lebens- und Formgefühl der alten Germanen*. Heidelberg, 1934. 143 pp.

28 d. G. Baldwin Brown, *The Arts and Crafts of our Teutonic Forefathers*. Edinburgh and Chicago, 1911. 250 pp. [General survey.]

28 e. G. Baldwin Brown, *Saxon Art and Industry in the Pagan Period* (=Vols. 3 and 4 of *The Arts in Early England*). London, 1915. 825 pp.

28 f. Edmund Weber, " Die Halle Heorot als Schlafsaal." *Arch.* clxii (1932), 114–16. [Historical evidence of a large hall being used for sleeping purposes.]

---

29. Fritz Roeder, *Die Familie bei den Angelsachsen. I: Mann und Frau.* (St.EPh. iv.) Halle a. S., 1899.

30. Francis B. Gummere, *The Sister's Son*, in *An English Miscellany presented to Dr. Furnivall*, pp. 133–49. Oxford, 1901.

30 a. Cf. Albert William Aron, " Traces of Matriarchy in Germanic Hero-Lore." *Univ. of Wisconsin Studies in Language and Literature*, No. 9 (1920). 77 pp.

31. Ada Broch, *Die Stellung der Frau in der ags. Poesie*. Zürich Diss., 1902.

---

32. Karl Weinhold, *Altnordisches Leben*. Berlin, 1856. 512 pp. [Comprehensive account.]

33. Oscar Montelius, (1) *The Civilisation of Sweden in Heathen Times*. Translated, from the 2d Swedish edition, by F. H. Woods. London and New York, 1888. 214 pp. German translation, *Die Kultur Schwedens in vorchristlicher Zeit*, by C. Appel. Berlin, 1885. [With numerous illustrations; famous sketch.] (2) *Kulturgeschichte Schwedens von den ältesten Zeiten bis zum elften Jahrhundert nach Christus*. Leipzig, 1906. [With 540 illustrations.]

34. Kristian Kålund, *Sitte: Skandinavische Verhältnisse*, in *P. Grdr.* ii^b (1889), pp. 208–52; 2nd ed., iii (1900), pp. 407–79 (by Valtýr Guðmundsson & Kristian Kålund).

35. Paul B. du Chaillu, *The Viking Age*. London, 1889. 2 vols. 591+562 pp. [With numerous illustrations; popular.]

36. Oliver Elton, *The first nine Books of the Danish History of Saxo Grammaticus translated.* Introduction, § 7: ' Folk-lore Index ' (by F. York Powell). London, 1894. Cf. *Corpus Poeticum Boreale* (L 10.1), Vol. ii, pp. 685–708, Index III: ' Subjects.' Oxford, 1883.

37. Sophus Müller, *Nordische Altertumskunde nach Funden und Denkmälern aus Dänemark und Schleswig gemeinfasslich dargestellt*. Translated (from the Danish) by O. L. Jiriczek. 2 vols. Strassburg, 1897, 1898. 472+324 pp. The Danish version: *Vor Oldtid, Danmarks Forhistoriske Archæologi*, Kjøbenhavn, 1897. [With numerous illustrations; admirable.]

38. Axel Olrik, *Nordisches Geistesleben in heidnischer und frühchrist-*

IX. OLD GERMANIC LIFE

licher Zeit. Translated (from the Danish) by Wilhelm Ranisch. Heidelberg, 1908. 230 pp. The Danish version in the Encyclopedia *Verdenskulturen*, Vol. iii, pp. 253-352, København and Kristiania. [A lucid, popular account.] Translated into English (by Jacob W. Hartmann and Hanna A. Larsen): *Viking Civilization*, revised by Hans Ellekilde. New York, The American-Scandinavian Foundation, 1930.

39. Knut Stjerna, *Essays on Questions connected with the Old English Poem of Beowulf*. Translated and edited by John R. Clark Hall. Viking Club Publications, Extra Series, Vol. iii. Coventry, 1912. 4to, xxxv +284 pp. [Archæological papers issued between 1903 and 1908 in various Swedish journals and special publications. 1. Helmets and Swords in Beowulf. 2. Archæological Notes on Beowulf. 3. Vendel and the Vendel Crow (L 4.93). 4. Swedes and Geats during the Migration Period. 5. Scyld's Funeral Obsequies (L 4.82). 6. The Dragon's Hoard in Beowulf. 7. The Double Burial in Beowulf. 8. Beowulf's Funeral Obsequies.] — R.: *Nation* xcv (New York, 1912), 386[b]-87[a] *(anon.)*; A. Mawer, *MLR.* viii (1913), 242 f.; Fr. Klaeber, *JEGPh.* xiii (1914), 167-73; Gudmund Schütte, *AfNF.* xxxiii (1917), 64-96 [discusses, e.g., (pp. 86 f.) the theory that the Geats may have been a Gautic colony in N.E. Jutland].

---

40. Hans Lehmann, (1) *Brünne und Helm im ags. Beowulfliede*. Göttingen Diss., Leipzig, 1885; (2) " Über die Waffen im ags. Beowulfliede." *Germ.* xxxi (1886), 486-97.

41. Richard Wegner, *Die Angriffswaffen der Angelsachsen*. Königsberg Diss., 1899. [Spear only.]

42. May Lansfield Keller, *The Anglo-Saxon Weapon Names treated archæologically and etymologically*. (Ang.F. xv.) Heidelberg, 1906. 275 pp.

43. Karl Pfannkuche, *Der Schild bei den Angelsachsen*. Halle Diss., 1908.

44. Hjalmar Falk, " Altnordische Waffenkunde." *Videnskapsselskapets Skrifter. II. Hist.-Filos. Klasse*, 1914, No. 6, Kristiania. 4to. 211 pp. [Comprehensive study.]

45. Cf. (1) S. A. Brooke (L 4.6.1), ch. viii: ' Armor and War in Poetry.' — (2) Lilly L. Stroebe, *Die altenglischen Kleidernamen*. Heidelberg Diss., Leipzig, 1904. — (3) Knut Stjerna (L 9.39), ch. 1. — (4) The old work by L. Lindenschmit, *Handbuch der deutschen Alterthumskunde*, Part I: *Die Alterthümer der merovingischen Zeit*, Braunschweig, 1880-89 (514 pp.) may still be mentioned.

---

46. George H. Boehmer, " Prehistoric Naval Architecture of the North of Europe." *Report of the U. S. National Museum, under the direction of the Smithsonian Institution*, pp. 527-647. 1891. [With numerous illustrations.]

47. Heinrich Schnepper, *Die Namen der Schiffe und Schiffsteile im Altenglischen*. Kiel Diss., 1908. Cf. Merbach, L 7.27.

BIBLIOGRAPHY

48. Hjalmar Falk, " Altnordisches Seewesen." *Wörter und Sachen* iv (1912), 1–122. 4to.

48 a. W. Vogel, " Schiff (und seine Teile)." *R.-L.* iv, 94–114.

49. (1) *Reallexikon der germanischen Altertumskunde. Unter Mitwirkung zahlreicher Fachgelehrten* hrsg. von Johannes Hoops. Strassburg-Berlin, 1911–19. 4 vols. [Standard.] (2) O. Schrader's excellent *Reallexikon der indogermanischen Altertumskunde*, Strassburg, 1901 may serve as a supplement. Revised edition by A. Nehring, 1917–29. 2 vols. (3) A new encyclopedic reference work: *Reallexikon der Vorgeschichte* ed. by Max Ebert. Berlin, 1924–32. 15 vols.

50. Valuable material is found also in the translations of *Beowulf* by L. Simons (L 3.31), Clark Hall (L 3.5) [useful Index], and W. Huyshe (L 3.8). — Besides, studies of ' Teutonic Antiquities ' in other poems deserve notice: A. F. C. Vilmar (*Heliand*) [full of enthusiasm], C. W. Kent (*Andreas and Elene*), M. Rau (*Exodus*), C. Ferrell (*Genesis*), M. B. Price (' *Cynewulf* '), F. Brincker (*Judith*); F. Tupper (Edition of *Riddles, passim*); E. Lagenpusch, *Das germanische Recht im Heliand*, Breslau, 1894; O. Hartung, *Die deutschen Altertümer des Nibelungenliedes und der Kudrun*, Cöthen, 1894; H. Althof, *Waltharii Poesis, Das Waltharilied Ekkehards I.* hrsg. und erläutert, Part II: Commentary, Leipzig, 1905 (*passim*, and pp. 372–416: ' Kriegsaltertümer ').

X. OLD NORSE PARALLELS

1. *The Elder Edda* [*Eddic Poems*]. (9th to 13th century.) (1) Ed. by Sophus Bugge (Christiania, 1867); K. Hildebrand (Paderborn, 1904; re-edited by H. Gering, 1904, 1912, 1922); B. Sijmons (Halle, 1888–1906); F. Detter and R. Heinzel (Leipzig, 1903; with copious annotations); G. Vigfusson and F. York Powell, *Corpus Poeticum Boreale*, Vol. i (Oxford, 1883; with introduction, notes, and English translation; Vol. ii: Court Poetry); G. Neckel (Heidelberg, 1914, 2. ed., 1927; Vol. ii: ' Kommentierendes Glossar,' 1927); R. C. Boer, 's-Gravenhage, 1922 (Vol. i: Introduction and Text, Vol. ii: Commentary). — A commentary by H. Gering (ed. by B. Sijmons), 2 vols., Halle, 1927, 1931. — (2) English translations by Vigfusson and Powell, see (1); O. Bray, London, 1908: I. The mythological poems (includes ON. text); Henry A. Bellows (' Scandinavian Classics,' Vols. xxi & xxii), New York, The American-Scandinavian Foundation, 1923 (with introduction and notes); Lee M. Hollander, Univ. of Texas, 1928 (with introduction and explanatory notes). — German translations by H. Gering (Leipzig, 1892; with notes); F. Genzmer (' Thule,' Nos. 1 and 2, Jena, 1912, 1920, I. Heldendichtung, II. Götterdichtung und Spruchdichtung; with notes by A. Heusler). K. Simrock's German translation was re-edited (with introductions) by G. Neckel, Berlin, 1926. — (3) Glossaries by H. Gering:

X. OLD NORSE PARALLELS   clxxxi

Glossar etc. (Paderborn, 4th ed., 1915), and *Vollständiges Wörterbuch* (Halle a. S., 1903; 1404 cols.). — (4) *Eddica Minora* ed. by A. Heusler and W. Ranisch. Dortmund, 1903. [Pp. xxi–xxvi, 21–32: *Biarkamál*, i.e., the fragments of the Icelandic poem and Saxo's Latin version.]

2. Snorri Sturluson (A.D. 1178–1241), [*Prose*] *Edda*. Ed. by Þorleifr Jónsson (Kaupmannahöfn, 1875), E. Wilken (Paderborn, 1877, incomplete; 2d ed., 1912–13), Finnur Jónsson (København, 1900 [used for quotations in this edition]). — Important selections translated into English by I. A. Blackwell (London, 1847; reprinted, with B. Thorpe's transl. of the Elder Edda (1866), in the Norrœna Series, 1906); by A. G. Brodeur (American-Scandinavian Foundation, New York, 1916; more complete); into German, by H. Gering (in the Appendix to his translation of the Elder Edda). A complete German translation by G. Neckel and F. Niedner ('Thule,' No. 20, 1925; with introduction by G. Neckel).

Other 'Thule' volumes (see L 10.3, 5, 6, 8):
Heimskringla translated by F. Niedner (Nos. 14–16, 1922–23); *Vǫlsungasaga*, and *Hrólfssaga*, by P. Herrmann (No. 21, 1923, pp. 39–136; 221–306, a revision of his earlier translation); *Grettissaga*, by P. Herrmann (No. 5, 1913).

Peter Andreas Munch's *Norse Mythology, Legends of Gods and Heroes* ('Norrøne Gude- og Heltesagn, ordnet og fremstillet,' Kristiania, 1840, as revised by Magnus Olsen (1922)), translated by Sigurd B. Hustvedt. New York, The American-Scandinavian Foundation, 1926. 392 pp. [Intended as a companion volume to Bellows's *Poetic Edda* and Brodeur's *Prose Edda*. A pleasing, helpful handbook.]

3. Snorri Sturluson, *Heimskringla: Nóregs Konunga Sǫgur*. Ed. by Finnur Jónsson. 4 vols. København, 1893–1901. Vol. i, pp. 9–85: *Ynglingasaga*. — English translation by William Morris and Eiríkr Magnússon in The Saga Library, Vols. iii–vi. London, 1893–1905. Vol. iii, pp. 11–73: *Ynglingasaga*. Translation by Erling Monsen (and A. H. Smith), Cambridge, 1932.

4. Saxo Grammaticus (born cir. A.D. 1150), *Gesta Danorum*. Ed. by P. E. Müller and J. M. Velschow (Vol. i. Havniæ, 1839. Vol. ii [*Prolegomena et notae uberiores*]. Havniæ, 1858); by Alfred Holder (Strassburg, 1886; used for quotations); *Saxonis Gesta Danorum primum a C. Knabe et P. Herrmann recensita recognoverunt et ediderunt J. Olrik et H. Ræder. Vol. i: Text. Copenhagen, 1931. fol., li+609 pp. — Translation of the first nine books into English by Oliver Elton (London, 1894) (L 9.36); into German by Hermann Jantzen (Berlin, 1900; with notes and index of subjects); Paul Herrmann (Leipzig, 1901). (Cf. L 4.35 a, 35, 100).

For minor Latin chronicles see Appendix I: Par. § 8.

5. *Vǫlsungasaga* (cir. A.D. 1250). Ed. by S. Bugge (Christiania, 1865); E. Wilken (Paderborn, 1877, see L 10.2); W. Ranisch (Berlin, 1891). English translation by E. Magnússon and W. Morris (London, 1870;

reprinted and supplemented with Legends of the Wagner Trilogy, in the Norrœna Series, 1906). German translation by A. Edzardi (Stuttgart, 1880, and 1881).

6. *Grettis Saga Ásmundarsonar* (cir. A.D. 1300). Ed. by R. C. Boer (Altnordische Saga-Bibliothek, No. viii). Halle a. S., 1900. Chs. 64–66 also in F. Holthausen's *Altisländisches Lesebuch*, pp. 79 ff. Weimar, 1896; ch. 35 also in Vigfusson and Powell's *Icelandic Prose Reader*, pp. 209 ff. Oxford, 1879; chs. 32–35 and 64–66 (with translation) in Cha. Intr. 146 ff.; ch. 35 in E. V. Gordon's *Introduction to Old Norse*, Oxford, 1927 (No. 8). — English translations by Eiríkr Magnússon and William Morris (London and New York, 1900), and by George A. Hight (Everyman's Library, 1914). (Cf. L 4.48, 54.)

7. *Orms þáttr Stórólfssonar* (early 14th century). Ed. by G. Vigfússon and C. R. Unger in *Flateyjarbók* i, 521–33. Christiania, 1860. Extract with translation in Cha. Intr. 186 ff.

8. *Hrólfs Saga Kraka* (14th century). Ed. by Finnur Jónsson. København, 1904. (On pp. 109–63 the *Bjarkarímur* (15th century).) Part of ch. 23 in Cha. Intr. 138 ff. (with translation) and in Gordon's *Introduction* (No. 3). Complete translation by Stella M. Mills (with an introduction by E. V. Gordon), Oxford, 1933. Extracts from *Bjarkarímur* with translation in Cha. Intr. 182 ff. — German translation (with useful notes) by Paul Herrmann. Torgau Progr., 1905. (Cf. L 4.65.)

9. Finnur Jónsson, *Den Oldnorske og Oldislandske Litteraturs Historie*. København, 1894–1901; 2. ed., 1920–24. — Eugen Mogk, *Norwegisch-Isländische Literatur* in *P. Grdr.*², ii[a], pp. 555–923. 1902. — Primers: W. Golther, *Nordische Literaturgeschichte. I.* (Sammlung Göschen, No. 254.) 1905; 2. ed., 1921. G. Neckel, *Die altnordische Literatur* ('Aus Natur und Geisteswelt,' No. 782.) 1923. Bertha S. Phillpotts, *Edda and Saga*. (Home University Library, No. 155.) 1931.

NOTE 1. — A list of the best books in English suitable for an introduction to the subject and its wider relations should, by all means, include
Chadwick's *Heroic Age* (L 4.22)
Ker's *Epic and Romance* (L 4.120)
Chambers's *Widsith* (L 4.77) and *Introduction* (L 4.22 a)
Lawrence's *Beowulf and Epic Tradition* (L 4.22 c)
Gummere's *Germanic Origins* (L 9.11).
To these we may add the two most helpful translations, viz. those of Gummere and Clark Hall (Hall's prose translation).
Of books in other languages, Brandl's *Angelsächsische Literatur* (L 4.11) and Olrik's *Danmarks Heltedigtning* (L 4.35) — each in its own way — invite particular attention on the part of students. (The latter now also available in English.) Bugge's *Studien über das Beowulfepos* (L 4.28, L 5.6.3) may serve as a model of philological method. Hoops's *Kommentar* (L 5.60.6) is a most useful guide.

NOTE 2. — Reports of the progress of *Beowulf* studies have appeared

X. OLD NORSE PARALLELS

at various times. See Wülker's *Grundriss* (L 4.4); J. Earle, L 3.4, pp. ix–liii; F. Dieter in *Ergebnisse und Fortschritte der germanistischen Wissenschaft im letzten Vierteljahrhundert* ed. by R. Bethge (1902), pp. 348–56; cf. A. Brandl, "Über den gegenwärtigen Stand der Beowulf-Forschung," *Arch.* cviii (1902), 152–55; R. C. Boer, L 4.140, pp. 1–24. (Th. Krüger, *Zum Beowulfliede*, Bromberg Progr. (1884), and *Arch.* lxxi (1884), 129–52; C. B. Tinker, L 3.43, *passim*.) Bohumil Trnka, "Dnešní stav badání o Beowulfovi," *Časopis pro moderní filologii* xii (1925–26), 35–48, 124–36, 247–54. (Has not been read by the editor.) Walther Fischer, "Von neuerer deutscher Beowulf-Forschung," *Germanische Philologie, Festschrift für O. Behaghel* (1934), pp. 419–31.

NOTE 3. — For biographical accounts of some prominent *Beowulf* scholars, see Salmonsen's *Konversationsleksikon:* G. J. Thorkelin (1752–1829), N. F. S. Grundtvig (1783–1872); — *JEGPh.* vii, No. 2, pp. 105–114 (E. Mogk): S. Bugge (1833–1907); — *The Dictionary of National Biography:* J. M. Kemble (1807–1857), B. Thorpe (1782–1870); — *Allgemeine Deutsche Biographie:* C. W. M. Grein (1825–1877) (a fuller statement in Grein-Wülker's *Bibliothek der ags. Poesie* iii. 2, pp. vii–xii), K. Müllenhoff (1818–1884), J. Zupitza (1844–1895), B. ten Brink (1841–1892); — Heyne's *Das altdeutsche Handwerk*, pp. vii–xiv (E. Schröder): M. Heyne (1837–1906); — *ESt.* l, 192–97 (L. L. Schücking): Gregor Sarrazin (1857–1915); *Arch.* cxxxvi, 1–15 (A. Heusler), *Danske Studier* 1917, 1–12 (Marius Kristensen): Axel Olrik (1864–1917); *GRM.* ii, 577–92 (W. Streitberg), *Beitr.* lvii, pp. i–xviii (Th. Frings), *PMLA.* xlvii, 607 f. (F. H. Wilkens): Eduard Sievers (1850–1932).

TABLE OF ABBREVIATIONS

NOTE. *L* (Bibliographical List) signifies the Bibliography of this edition, pp. cxxv ff. In referring to it, the ten main divisions are denoted by Arabic numerals separated by a period from the given number of the respective title; thus L 2.16 means W. J. Sedgefield, *Beowulf*. Figures referring to subdivisions of the numbered items and to pages of books and articles are preceded by additional periods; thus L 6.12.2.379 means John Ries, *Die Wortstellung im Beowulf*, p. 379.

Aant. Cosijn's Aanteekeningen op den Beowulf. (L 5.10.3.)
AfNF. Arkiv för Nordisk Filologi.
Ang.F. Anglistische Forschungen hrsg. von J. Hoops.
Angl. or *A.* Anglia.
Anz.fdA. Anzeiger für deutsches Altertum.
Arch. Archiv für das Studium der neueren Sprachen und Literaturen.
Arn(old). Arnold's edition. (L 2.9.)
Barnouw. Barnouw's Textkritische Untersuchungen etc. (L 6.7.3.)
Beibl. Beiblatt zur Anglia.
Beitr. Beiträge zur Geschichte der deutschen Sprache und Literatur.
Binz. Binz's Zeugnisse zur germanischen Sage in England. (L 4.31.1.)
Björk. Eig. Björkman's Eigennamen im Beowulf. (L 4.31.8.)
Boer. Boer, Die altenglische Heldendichtung. (L 4.140.)
Bonn. B. Bonner Beiträge zur Anglistik hrsg. von M. Trautmann.
Bout. Bouterwek's paper in ZfdA. xi. (L 5.2.)
Brandl. Brandl's Angelsächsische Literatur. (L 4.11.)
B.-T. Bosworth and Toller, Anglo-Saxon Dictionary; *B.-T. Suppl.* Supplements thereto (1908, 1916, 1921).
Bu(gge). Bugge's Studien über das Beowulfepos, Beitr. xii (L 4.28, 5.6.3); *Bu.Tid.* Bugge's paper in Tidskrift for Philologi etc. viii. (L 5.6.1); *Bu.Zs.* Bugge's paper in ZfdPh. iv. (L 5.6.2.)
Bülb. Bülbring's Altenglisches Elementarbuch. I. 1902.
Cha(mbers). Chambers's edition of Beowulf (L 2.13.2); *Cha. Intr.* Chambers's Introduction (L 4.22 a); *Cha.Wid.* Chambers's edition of Widsið (L 4.77).
Chadwick H. A. Chadwick's Heroic Age (L 4.22); *Chadwick Or.* Chadwick's Origin of the English Nation (L 4.38).
Cl. Hall. Clark Hall's prose translation. (L 3.5.)
Cos. VIII. Cosijn's paper in Beitr. viii. (L 5.10.2.)
Dial.D. English Dialect Dictionary.
D. Lit. z. Deutsche Literaturzeitung.
E. Ettmüller's edition (L 2.18); *E.Sc.* his Engla and Seaxna Scopas etc. (L 2.20); *E.tr.* his translation (L 3.19).

TABLE OF ABBREVIATIONS   clxxxv

Earle. Earle's translation: Deeds of Beowulf. (L 3.4.)
ESt. Englische Studien.
För. Misc. Britannica, Festschrift für Max Förster, 1929.
Germ. Germania, Vierteljahrsschrift für deutsche Alterthumskunde, 1856–92.
Gr. (*Gr.*[1], *Gr.*[2]). Grein's editions (L 2.5, L 2.8); *Gr.Spr.* Grein's Sprachschatz der angelsächsischen Dichter, 1861–64. (Re-issued by Köhler & Holthausen, 1912.)
Grienb. von Grienberger's paper in ZföG. lvi. (L 5.45.2.)
Grimm D. M. Jacob Grimm's Deutsche Mythologie. (L 4.42.) References are to the 4th edition, with the page numbers in Stallybrass' translation added in parentheses. *Grimm R. A.* Jacob Grimm's Deutsche Rechtsalterthümer. References are in accordance with the pagination of the 1st ed. (1828), which is indicated also in the margin of the 4th ed. (1899).
GRM. Germanisch-Romanische Monatsschrift.
Gru. Grundtvig's edition (L 2.6); *Gru.tr.* his translation, 1st ed. (L 3.27.)
Gummere. Gummere's translation (L 3.15); *Gummere G. O.* his Germanic Origins (L 9.11).
Heusler V. Heusler's Deutsche Versgeschichte. (L 8.13 f.)
He(yne) (also: *He.-Soc.*, *He.-Schü.*). Heyne's editions. (L 2.7.)
Hold. Holder's editions. (L 2.12.)
Holt. Holthausen's editions. (L 2.15.) (References are primarily to the 6th ed.) *Holt.Zs.* his paper in ZfdPh. xxxvii. (L 5.26.17.)
Holt.Et. his Altenglisches etymologisches Wörterbuch, 1934.
Holtzm. Holtzmann's paper in Germ. viii. (L 5.4.)
Hoops. Hoops's Kommentar (L 5.60.6); *Hoops St.* his Beowulfstudien (L 5.60.5.)
IF. Indogermanische Forschungen.
J(E)GPh. The Journal of (English and) Germanic Philology.
Jesp. Misc. A Grammatical Miscellany offered to Otto Jespersen, 1930.
Kal(uza). Kaluza's Metrik des Beowulfliedes. (L 8.9.2.)
Ke(mble). Kemble's edition (of 1835); *Ke. II* the second volume (of 1837). (L 2.2.)
Keller. Keller's Anglo-Saxon Weapon Names. (L 9.42.)
Ker. Ker's Epic and Romance, 1897. (L 4.120.)
Kl. Misc. Studies in English Philology, a Miscellany in Honor of Frederick Klaeber, 1929.
Klu. IX. Kluge's paper in Beitr. ix. (5.15.2.)
Kock. Kock's paper in Angl. xxvii (L 5.44.1); *Kock*[2] his paper in Angl. xlii (L 5.44.3); so *Kock*[3], Angl. xliv; *Kock*[4], Angl. xlv; *Kock*[5], Angl. xlvi.
Lit.bl. Literaturblatt für germanische and romanische Philologie.
Lorz. Lorz's Aktionsarten des Verbums im Beowulf. (L 6.17.)

Luick. Luick's Historische Grammatik der englischen Sprache, 1914 ff.
Malone Haml. Malone's Literary History of Hamlet. I. (L 4.78 e.)
MLN. Modern Language Notes.
MLR. Modern Language Review.
Mö(ller). Möller, Das altenglische Volksepos. (L 4.134, 2.19.)
Montelius. Montelius, The Civilisation of Sweden in Heathen Times. (L 9.33.1.)
MPh. Modern Philology.
Müll(enhoff). Müllenhoff's Beovulf (L 4.19); *Müll. XIV* his paper in ZfdA. xiv (see L 4.130).
NED. New English Dictionary.
Notat. Norr. Kock's Notationes Norrœnæ (Lunds Universitets Årsskrift), 1923 ff.
Olrik. Olrik's Danmarks Heltedigtning. (Also *Olrik-Hollander.*) (L 4.35.)
Pal. Palaestra, Untersuchungen und Texte aus der deutschen und englischen Philologie.
Panzer. Panzer's Studien etc. I. Beowulf. (L 4.61.)
P. Grdr. Grundriss der germanischen Philologie hrsg. von H. Paul.
Ph. Q. Philological Quarterly. (University of Iowa.)
Publ. MLAss. or *PMLA.* Publications of the Modern Language Association of America.
RESt. Review of English Studies.
Rie. L. Rieger's Lesebuch (L 2.21); *Rie. V.* his Alt- & angelsächsische Verskunst (L 8.2); *Rie. Zs.* his paper in ZfdPh. iii. (L 5.7.)
Ritter. O. Ritter's Vermischte Beiträge zur englischen Sprachgeschichte, 1922.
R.-L. Reallexikon der germanischen Altertumskunde. (L 9.49.)
Sarr(azin) St. Sarrazin's Beowulf-Studien (L 4.16.1); *Sarr. Käd.* Sarrazin, Von Kädmon bis Kynewulf (L 4.16.3).
Schü. Schücking's editions (L 2.7.3). (References are primarily to the 14th ed.) *Schü. Bd.* his Untersuchungen zur Bedeutungslehre (L 6.22); *Schü. Sa.* his Grundzüge der Satzverknüpfung (L 6.15); *Schü. XXXIX* his paper in ESt. xxxix (L 5.48.3).
Sed. Sedgefield's editions (L 2.16) (References are primarily to the 2d ed.)
Siev. (§). Sievers's Angelsächsische Grammatik, 3d ed., 1898; also Cook's translation of it, 1903; *Siev. A. M.* Sievers's Altgermanische Metrik (L 8.4); *Siev. R.* his paper, Zur Rhythmik des germanischen Alliterationsverses (L 8.3); *Siev. IX, XXIX, XXXVI* his papers in Beitr. (L 5.16.1, 7, 9.)
S. Müller. Sophus Müller's Nordische Altertumskunde. (L 9.37.)
St.EPh. Studien zur englischen Philologie hrsg. von L. Morsbach.
Stjer. Stjerna's Essays etc. (L 9.39.)
t.Br. or *ten Brink.* ten Brink's Beowulf. (L 4.18.)

TABLE OF ABBREVIATIONS clxxxvii

Thk. Thorkelin's edition. (L 2.1.)
Tho. Thorpe's edition. (L 2.4.)
Tr(autmann). Trautmann's edition (L 2.14); *Tr.*[1] his paper in Bonn. B. ii (L 5.34.1); *Tr. F.* his Finn & Hildebrand (LF. 2.10); *Tr. Kyn.* his Kynewulf, Bonn. B. i, 1898.
Wright (§). Wright (J. & E. M.), Old English Grammar. 2d ed., 1914.
Wy. Wyatt's edition. (L 2.13.1.)
Year's Work. The Year's Work in English Studies.
Z. or *Zupitza.* Zupitza's facsimile edition. (L 1.5.)
ZfdA. Zeitschrift für deutsches Altertum.
ZfdPh. Zeitschrift für deutsche Philologie.
ZföG. Zeitschrift für die österreichischen Gymnasien.
Zfvgl. Spr. Zeitschrift für vergleichende Sprachforschung.

The poems of *Brun(anburh)*, *Dan(iel)*, *Ex(odus)*, *Jud(ith)*, *Mald(on)* have been quoted from the editions in the Belles-Lettres Series; *Andr(eas)*, *Chr(ist)*, *Fat(a)* *Ap(ostolorum)*, *Rid(dles)*, from the editions in the Albion Series; other OE. poems, from the Grein-Wülker *Bibliothek der angelsächsischen Poesie.* (For Tupper's *Riddles,* see also L 9.50.) — *Hel(iand)* has been quoted from Heyne's (4th) edition; *Hildebr(andslied)*, from Braune's *Althochd. Lesebuch;* *Nibel(ungenlied)*, from Lachmann's edition.

The following abbreviations of references to this edition need to be mentioned. *Intr.* = Introduction; *Lang.* (§) = Introduction, VII: Language; — *LF.* = Bibliography of the Fight at Finnsburg; — *Par.* = Appendix I: Parallels; *Antiq.* = Appendix II: Index of Antiquities; *T.C.* = Appendix III: Note on Textual Criticism; — (*n.*) refers to the Notes on the Text; thus (n.), placed after 2195, means: see note on l. 2915; — *Varr.* = Variant Readings.

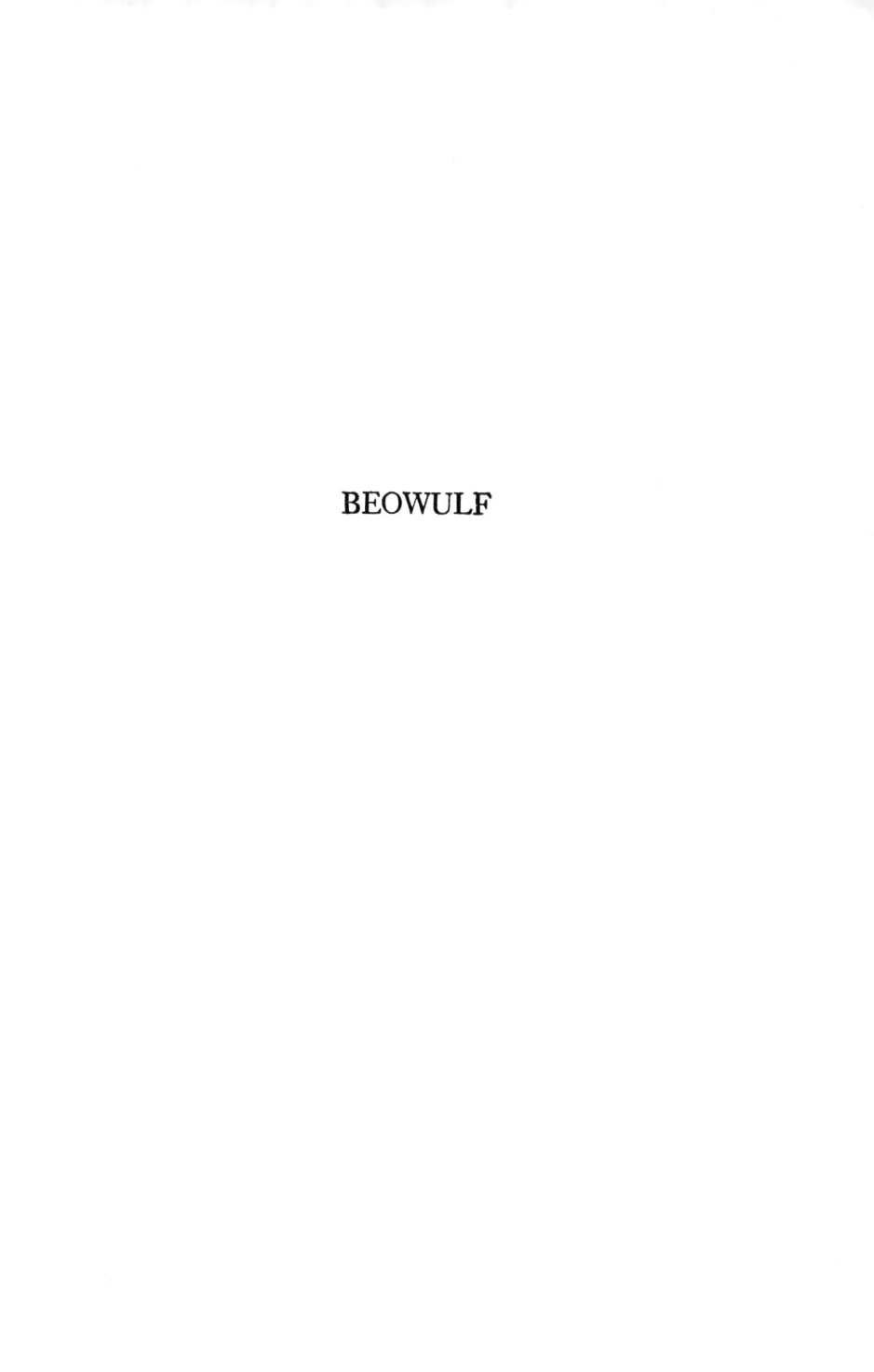

BEOWULF

THE TEXT

ITALICS indicate alteration of words by emendation. Letters or words added by emendation are placed within square brackets. Parentheses are used when the conjecturally inserted letters correspond to letters of the MS. which on account of its damaged condition are missing or illegible and were so when the Thorkelin transcripts were made. Expansion of the usual scribal contractions for *þæt*, *-um*, etc., is not marked.

The apparatus of variant readings, it is believed, has been made sufficiently full, although a system of careful selection had, necessarily, to be applied. Indeed, the inclusion of many useless guesses would have served no legitimate purpose. The emendations adopted are regularly credited to their authors. Of other conjectures, a number of the more suggestive and historically interesting ones have been added. Scholars who have given their support to certain readings have been frequently mentioned; also the expedient of the impersonal *et al.* has been freely — no doubt somewhat arbitrarily — employed. (?) after a name or a citation indicates that an emendation has been regarded as more or less doubtful by its author. In many cases it has seemed helpful to record the views of the four most recent editors. *4 Edd.* = Holt.[6], Schü.[14], Sed.[2], Cha.; *3 Edd.* = the same editions except the one specified. — *Edd.* = (all, or most) editions, or the subsequent editions, with the exception of those specified. (Readings of the previous issues (1922, 1928) of the present edition which have been abandoned are not mentioned.) In quoting the readings of various scholars normalization has been practised to the extent of providing the proper marks of quantity, etc., in every instance.

A and *B* denote the two Thorkelin transcripts, see L 1.3; whenever they are referred to, it is understood that the MS. in its present condition is defective. *MS. Ke.*, etc., means Kemble's (etc.) reading of the MS. The number of colons used in citing MS. readings (see, e.g., 159[a]) marks the presumable number of lost letters; in case their approximate number cannot be made out, dots are used. In quoting the readings of *A* and *B* — from Zupitza's notes — the plain dots have been kept. The beginning of a new line in the MS. is sometimes indicated by a bar; thus, 47[b] *MS.* g . . / denne. *Fol.* (*130*[a], etc.) followed by a word (or part of it) signifies that a page of the MS. begins with that word, which, however, is very often no longer fully visible in the MS. itself.

For other abbreviations see the Table of Abbreviations.

Regarding the somewhat uncertain matter of punctuating, it has been held desirable that the punctuation, while facilitating the student's understanding of the text, should also, in a measure, do justice to the old style and sentence structure. Cf. L 5.69.

The student is advised to go carefully through the Note on Textual Criticism (T.C.) in Appendix III, and to study the explanatory Notes constantly in connection with the variant readings.

BEOWULF

HWÆT, WĒ GĀR-DEna   in gēardagum,
þēodcyninga   þrym gefrūnon,
hū ðā æþelingas   ellen fremedon!
Oft Scyld Scēfing   sceaþena þrēatum,
5 monegum mǣgþum   meodosetla oftēah,
egsode eorl[as],   syððan ǣrest wearð
fēasceaft funden;   hē þæs frōfre gebād,
wēox under wolcnum   weorðmyndum þāh,
oð þæt him ǣghwylc   ymbsittendra
10 ofer hronrāde   hȳran scolde,
gomban gyldan;   þæt wæs gōd cyning!
Ðǣm eafera wæs   æfter cenned
geong in geardum,   þone God sende
folce tō frōfre;   fyrenðearfe ongeat,
15 þē hīe ǣr drugon   aldor(lē)ase
lange hwīle;   him þæs Līffrēa,
wuldres Wealdend   woroldāre forgeaf,
Bēowulf wæs brēme   — blǣd wīde sprang —
Scyldes eafera   Scedelandum in.
20 Swā sceal (geong g)uma   gōde gewyrcean,
fromum feohgiftum   on fæder (bea)rme,

1ᵃ *Fol. 129ᵃ begins.* — 4ᵇ *MS. (now)*, *AB* sceaþen, *Wanley L 1.2* sceaþena. — 6ᵃ *MS.* feared *over* egsode ' *in a 16th century hand* ' (*Z.*). — *Schubert L 8.1.7 inserts* [hīe]. — *Ke., Siev. L 4.33.188 f., xxix 560 ff., 4 Edd.* eorl[as]. — 9ᵇ *MS.* þara y.; *Siev. R. 256, L 4.33.190 cancels* þara; *so 4 Edd. Cf. T.C.* § 24 — 14ᵇ *Schü.*⁸⁻¹⁴ (*Krauel*) fyrn-. — 15ᵃ *MS.* þ; *Holt., Cha.* þæt; *Bouterwek L 4.45, Tr., Schü., Sed., (cf. Z.,)* þā; *Thk., Ke.* þē. — 15ᵇ *MS.* aldor (:): : ase; *Rask* (*in Gru. tr.* 267), *Edd.* -lēase; *Holt.*²⁻⁴ -lēaste. — 18ᵃ Bēowulf, *see* 53ᵇ *Varr.* — 19ᵃ *Ke.* eafera[n]; *so Schü. See note.* — 20ᵃ *MS.* : : : : : : (:)uma; *Ke.* gūðfruma; *Gr.*¹ glēaw guma; *Gr.*² geong guma, *so 4 Edd.* — 21ᵇ *Fol. 129ᵇ MS. Z.* (:): : rme; *Ke.* feorme; *Bouterwek L 4.45, Holt., Cha.* bearme; *Gr.*¹, *Schü., Sed.* ærne.

þæt hine on ylde   eft gewunigen
wilgesīþas,   þonne wīg cume,
lēode gelǣsten;   lofdǣdum sceal
25 in mǣgþa gehwǣre   man geþēon.

Him ðā Scyld gewāt   tō gescæphwīle
felahrōr fēran   on Frēan wǣre;
hī hyne þā ætbǣron   tō brimes faroðe,
swǣse gesīþas,   swā hē selfa bæd,
30 þenden wordum wēold   wine Scyldinga —
lēof landfruma   lange āhte.
þǣr æt hȳðe stōd   hringedstefna
īsig ond ūtfūs,   æþelinges fær;
ālēdon þā   lēofne þēoden,
35 bēaga bryttan   on bearm scipes,
mǣrne be mǣste.   þǣr wæs mādma fela
of feorwegum   frætwa gelǣded;
ne hȳrde ic cȳmlīcor   cēol gegyrwan
hildewǣpnum   ond heaðowǣdum,
40 billum ond byrnum;   him on bearme læg
mādma mænigo,   þā him mid scoldon
on flōdes ǣht   feor gewītan.
Nalǣs hī hine lǣssan   lācum tēodan,
þēodgestrēonum,   þon þā dydon,
45 þē hine æt frumsceafte   forð onsendon
ǣnne ofer ȳðe   umborwesende.

25[a] *Siev. R. 485, Holt., Schü., Sed.* gehwām. *Cf. T.C.* § *11*. — 28[b] *Krapp MPh. ii 407* waroðe (*so Thk.*). See *Angl. xxviii 455 f*. — 30[a] *Bright MLN. x 43* wordum geweald; *so Child ib. xxi 175 f*. — 31[b] *Rie. Zs. 381 f.* līf (*for* lēof). — 31[b] *Gr.*[1] (*?*), (*Siev. ix 136 ?*), *Aant. 1 f.* þrāge (*for* āhte); *Klu. ix 188* lǣndagas (*for* lange); *Holt.*[2-5] [hī] āhte.—*Cf. Bu. 80; Kock 221 ff*.— 33[a] īsig; *Tr.*[1] *127* īcig *or* ītig (*cp.* icge *1107 ?*) 'resplendent' (?); *Holt. Beibl. xiv 82 f.* īsig, *cp. ON.* eisa 'rush on,' *si. Krogmann A. lvi 438 f.; Tr. Bonn. B. xvii 151 f.* isig 'ready' (*cp.* eoset *224*[a] *Varr.*); *Hollander MLN. xxxii 246 f.* ītig 'splendid' (*cp. ON.* ítr); *cf. Grienb. Beitr. xxxvi 95*. — 44[b] *MS., Arn., Tr.* þon; *Thk., Edd.* þon[ne]. — *Tr., Holt.*[1] dǣdon. *Cf. Lang.* § *23.6*. — 46[b] *Fol. 130*[a] sende.

þā gȳt hīe him āsetton   segen g(yl)denne
hēah ofer hēafod,   lēton holm beran,
gēafon on gārsecg;   him wæs geōmor sefa,
50 murnende mōd.   Men ne cunnon
secgan tō sōðe,   selerædende,
hæleð under heofenum,   hwā þǣm hlæste onfēng.

1   Ðā wæs on burgum   Bēowulf Scyldinga,
lēof lēodcyning   longe þrāge
55 folcum gefrǣge   — fæder ellor hwearf,
aldor of earde —,   oþ þæt him eft onwōc
hēah Healfdene;   hēold þenden lifde
gamol ond gūðrēouw   glæde Scyldingas.
Ðǣm fēower bearn   forðgerīmed
60 in worold wōcun,   weoroda rǣswa[n],
Heorogār ond Hrōðgār   ond Hālga til,
hȳrde ic þæt [. . . . . .   wæs On]elan cwēn,
Heaðo-Scilfingas   healsgebedda.

þā wæs Hrōðgāre   herespēd gyfen,
65 wīges weorðmynd,   þæt him his winemāgas
georne hȳrdon,   oðð þæt sēo geogoð gewēox,
magodriht micel.   Him on mōd bearn,
þæt healreced   hātan wolde,
medoærn micel   men gewyrcean

47[b] MS. g . ./ denne; Ke. gyldenne. — 51[b] MS. rædenne; Ke. ii -rǣdende (cp. 1346).
— 53[b] Intr. xxvi n. 6: Bēow or Bēaw; cp. 18[a]. — Fuhr L 8.6.49, Kal. 56, Tr.[1] 128, Tr.
Bēowulf Scylding; but see Siev. xxix 309 ff.; T.C. § 20. — 58[a] Gr.[1], et al. -rēow (so Conybeare
L 1.4 misread MS.); Bu.Zs. 193 -rōf; E., Grienb. 746 -hrēow 'weary' [?]; Tr. -rōuw
'weary.' See T.C. § 2. — 60[b] MS. ræswa (and period after heoro gar); Ke., et al., Holt.,
Cha. rǣswa[n]. Cf. Lang. § 19.3. — 62 MS. no gap; He.[1] (cf. E. tr.), Gr.[2] Elan cwēn [Ongen-
þēowes wæs]; Gru. ix: Brage og Idun iv (1841) 500 [On]elan cwēn, cf. Gru.; Bu. Tid. 42 f.,
Holt., Cha., Schü. [. . . . . . wæs On]elan cwēn; Klu. ESt. xxii 144 f., et al., Sed. [Sigenēow
wæs Sǣw]elan cwēn, see Intr. xxxiv. Cf. E., Tr. Beibl. x 261, Tr., Holt. ii 105; Belden
MLN. xxviii 149, xxxiii 123 f. (Yrse, cf. Intr. xxxiv n. 4.) See note. — 68[a] Rask L 2.23,
et al. þæt [hē]. See Lang. § 25.4. — 69 Fol. 130[b] medo. Schönbach Anz. fdA. iii 42 māre
for micel (cf. E.); Harrison-Sharp[4] L 2.10 micle mā, Tr. micel, mā, Bright L 5.31.2 micle
māre (Holt.[4,5] mērre) gewyrcean.

<pre>
 70 þon[n]e yldo bearn   ǣfre gefrūnon,
     ond þǣr on innan   eall gedǣlan
     geongum ond ealdum,   swylc him God sealde
     būton folcscare   ond feorum gumena.
     Ðā ic wīde gefrægn   weorc gebannan
 75 manigre mǣgþe   geond þisne middangeard,
     folcstede frætwan.   Him on fyrste gelomp,
     ǣdre mid yldum,   þæt hit wearð ealgearo,
     healærna mǣst;   scōp him Heort naman
     sē þe his wordes geweald   wīde hæfde.
 80 Hē bēot ne ālēh,   bēagas dǣlde,
     sinc æt symle.   Sele hlīfade
     hēah ond horngēap;   heaðowylma bād,
     lāðan līges;   ne wæs hit lenge þā gēn,
     þæt se ecghete   āþumswēoran
 85 æfter wælnīðe   wæcnan scolde.

     Ðā se ellengǣst   earfoðlīce
     þrāge geþolode,   sē þe in þȳstrum bād,
     þæt hē dōgora gehwām   drēam gehȳrde
     hlūdne in healle;   þǣr wæs hearpan swēg,
 90 swutol sang scopes.   Sægde sē þe cūþe
     frumsceaft fīra   feorran reccan,
     cwæð þæt se Ælmihtiga eorðan worh(te),
     wlitebeorhtne wang,   swā wæter bebūgeð,
     gesette sigehrēþig   sunnan ond mōnan
 95 lēoman tō lēohte   landbūendum,
     ond gefrætwade   foldan scēatas
     leomum ond lēafum,   līf ēac gesceōp
</pre>

70ᵃ *MS.* þone; *Gr.*¹, *4 Edd.* þon[n]e; *Tr.* þon (*cp. 44*). — 77ᵇ *Ke., et al., Cha.* eal gearo. *So 1230ᵇ* (*2241ᵇ*). — 84ᵃ *MS.* secg; *Gr.*¹ ecg-. — 84ᵇ *MS.* aþum swerian; *Bu. Tid. 45 f.* āþumswerian; *Tr.*¹ *130* -swēorum, *Binz Beibl. xiv 359* -swēoran. — 86ᵃ *Gr.*¹ (?), *Rie.Zs. 383* ellorgǣst, *Tr.*¹ *130*, *Tr.* ellorgǣst. *See 1617ᵃ Varr.* — 92ᵃ *Fol. 132ᵃ* cwæð. — 92ᵇ *Ke.* worh(te).

cynna gehwylcum þāra ðe cwice hwyrfaþ. —
Swā ðā drihtguman drēamum lifdon,
100 ēadiglīce, oð ðæt ān ongan
fyrene fre(m)man fēond on helle;
wæs se grimma gǣst Grendel hāten,
mǣre mearcstapa, sē þe mōras hēold,
fen ond fæsten; fīfęlcynnes eard
105 wonsǣlī wer weardode hwīle,
siþðan him Scyppend forscrifen hæfde
in Cāines cynne — þone cwealm gewræc
ēce Drihten, þæs þe hē Ābel slōg;
ne gefeah hē þǣre fǣhðe, ac hē hine feor forwræc,
110 Metod for þȳ māne mancynne fram.
Þanon untȳdras ealle onwōcon,
eotenas ond ylfe ond orcnēas,
swylce gīgantas, þā wið Gode wunnon
lange þrāge; hē him ðæs lēan forgeald.

II 115 Gewāt ðā nēosian, syþðan niht becōm,
hēan hūses, hū hit Hring-Dene
æfter bēorþege gebūn hæfdon.
Fand þā ðǣr inne æþelinga gedriht
swefan æfter symble; sorge ne cūðon,
120 wonsceaft wera. Wiht unhǣlo,
grim ond grǣdig, gearo sōna wæs,
rēoc ond rēþe, ond on ræste genam
þrītig þegna; þanon eft gewāt
hūðe hrēmig tō hām faran,
125 mid þǣre wælfylle wīca nēosan.

101ª *Ke.* fre(m)man. — 101ᵇ *Bu. 80* healle *for* helle. — 106ª *MS.* scyppen **with d added above the line.** — 107ª *MS.* caines *altered from* cames. (*Confusion of Cain and Cham. Cf. Intr. xxi n. 7.*) *Siev. Zum ags. Vocalismus (1900) p. 7* Caines (*perh.* diphthong ai?). — 113ª *Fol. 132ᵇ* gantas. — 115ª *Siev. R. 298* nēosan. *Cf. T.C.* § 9. — 120ª *Siev. ix 137, Holt.* weras. — 120ᵇ *Rie. Zs. 383* unfǣlo.

6 BEOWULF

Đā wæs on ūhtan   mid ærdæge
Grendles gūðcræft   gumum undyrne;
þā wæs æfter wiste   wōp up āhafen,
micel morgenswēg.   Mǣre þēoden,
130 æþeling ǣrgōd,   unblīðe sæt,
þolode ðrȳðswȳð   þegnsorge drēah,
syðþan hīe þæs lāðan   lāst scēawedon,
wergan gāstes;   wæs þæt gewin tō strang,
lāð ond longsum!   Næs hit lengra fyrst,
135 ac ymb āne niht   eft gefremede
morðbeala māre,   ond nō mearn fore,
fæhðe ond fyrene;   wæs tō fæst on þām.
Þā wæs ēaðfynde   þē him elles hwǣr
gerūmlīcor   ræste [sōhte],
140 bed æfter būrum,   ðā him gebēacnod wæs,
gesægd sōðlīce   sweotolan tācne
healðegnes hete;   hēold hyne syðþan
fyr ond fæstor   sē þǣm fēonde ætwand.
Swā rīxode   ond wið rihte wan,
145 āna wið eallum,   oð þæt īdel stōd
hūsa sēlest.   Wæs sēo hwīl micel;
twelf wintra tīd   torn geþolode
wine Scyldinga,   wēana gehwelcne,
sīdra sorga;   forðām [secgum] wearð,
150 ylda bearnum   undyrne cūð
gyddum geōmore,   þætte Grendel wan
hwīle wið Hrōþgār,   hetenīðas wæg,
fyrene ond fæhðe   fela missēra,

134[b] *Fol. 133[a]* fyrst. — 139[b] *Gr.*[1] ge rūmlīcor. — 139[b] *Gr.*[1] [sōhte]. — 142[a] *E. tr.* (?) *Bu. 80, Sed.* helðegnes. — 148[a] *MS.* scyldenda; *Gru.tr. 269* Scyldinga. — 149[b] *Tho.* (*in Ke.*) [syððan], *so Sed., Cha.; Gr.*[2] [sorgcearu]; *E.* [sōcen]; *Bu. 367* [sārcwidum]; *Tr.*[1] *132 f.* sārlēoðum, *Tr.* sārspellum (*for* forðām); *Siev. xxix 313* for ðām [sōcnum]; *JEGPh. vi 191, Schü. xxxix 101 f., Schü., Holt.*[6] [secgum]; *Holt.*[2-5] [sōna].

singāle sæce;   sibbe ne wolde
155 wið manna hwone   mægenes Deniga,
feorhbealo feorran,   fēa þingian,
nē þǣr nǣnig witena   wēnan þorfte
beorhtre bōte   tō ban*an* folmum;
(ac se) ǣglǣca   ēhtende wæs,
160 deorc dēaþscua,   duguþe ond geogoþe,
seomade ond syrede;   sinnihte hēold
mistige mōras;   men ne cunnon,
hwyder helrūnan   hwyrftum scrīþað.
Swā fela fyrena   fēond mancynnes,
165 atol āngengea   oft gefremede,
heardra hȳnða;   Heorot eardode,
sincfāge sel   sweartum nihtum; —
nō hē þone gifstōl   grētan mōste,
māþðum for Metode,   nē his myne wisse. —
170 Þæt wæs wrǣc micel   wine Scyldinga,
mōdes brecða.   Monig oft gesæt
rīce tō rūne;   rǣd eahtedon,
hwæt swīðferhðum   sēlest wǣre
wið fǣrgryrum   tō gefremmanne.
175 Hwīlum hīe gehēton   æt *hæ*rgtrafum
wīgweorþunga,   wordum bǣdon,
þæt him gāstbona   gēoce gefremede
wið þēodþrēaum.   Swylc wæs þēaw hyra,
hǣþenra hyht;   helle gemundon
180 in mōdsefan,   Metod hīe ne cūþon,
dǣda Dēmend,   ne wiston hīe Drihten God,

156[b] *Ke.* fēo, *so Holt., Schü., Sed. See Lang.* § *15.1.* — 157[a] *Holt., Sed.* witena nǣnig (*cf. Siev. R. 286*). — 158[b] *MS.* banū; *Ke.* banan. *Cp. 2821*[b]*, 2961*[b]. — 159[a] *Fol. 133*[b] : : : : ; *Tho. (in Ke.)* atol, *so Sed., Cha.; Rie.Zs. 384* ac se, *so Holt., Schü.* — 175[b] *MS.* hrærg; *Ke.* hearg-; *Gru., Edd.* hærg-.

nē hīe hūru heofena Helm   herian ne cūþon,
wuldres Waldend.   Wā bið þǣm ðe sceal
þurh slīðne nīð   sāwle bescūfan
185 in fȳres fæþm,   frōfre ne wēnan,
wihte gewendan!   Wēl bið þǣm þe mōt
æfter dēaðdæge   Drihten sēcean
ond tō Fæder fæþmum   freoðo wilnian!

III   Swā ðā mǣlceare   maga Healfdenes
190 singāla sēað;   ne mihte snotor hæleð
wēan onwendan;   wæs þæt gewin tō swȳð,
lāþ ond longsum,   þē on ðā lēode becōm,
nȳdwracu nīþgrim,   nihtbealwa mǣst.

Þæt fram hām gefrægn   Higelāces þegn
195 gōd mid Gēatum,   Grendles dǣda;
sē wæs moncynnes   mægenes strengest
on þǣm dæge   þysses līfes,
æþele ond ēacen.   Hēt him ȳðlidan
gōdne gegyrwan;   cwæð, hē gūðcyning
200 ofer swanrāde   sēcean wolde,
mǣrne þēoden,   þā him wæs manna þearf.
Ðone sīðfæt him   snotere ceorlas
lȳthwōn lōgon,   þēah hē him lēof wǣre;
hwetton hige(r)ōfne,   hǣl scēawedon.
205 Hæfde se gōda   Gēata lēoda
cempan gecorone   þāra þe hē cēnoste
findan mihte;   fīftȳna sum
sundwudu sōhte,   secg wīsade,
lagucræftig mon   landgemyrcu.
210 Fyrst forð gewāt;   flota wæs on ȳðum,
bāt under beorge.   Beornas gearwe

<sub>182^a *Fol. 134^a* ne. — 186^a *Rie. Zs. 385* wīte. (*Cf. Bout. 74; Gr.¹note.*) — 203^b *Fol. 134^b*
þeah. — 204^a *A* þofne, *B* forne; *Rask* (*in Gru.tr. 270*) -rōfne. — 207^b *MS.* .x̄v̄. — 210^a
Gru. (?) fyrd.</sub>

on stefn stigon, — strēamas wundon,
sund wið sande; secgas bǣron
on bearm nacan beorhte frætwe,
215 gūðsearo geatolīc; guman ūt scufon,
weras on wilsīð wudu bundenne.
Gewāt þā ofer wǣgholm winde gefȳsed
flota fāmīheals fugle gelīcost,
oð þæt ymb āntīd ōþres dōgores
220 wundenstefna gewaden hæfde,
þæt ðā līðende land gesāwon,
brimclifu blīcan, beorgas stēape,
sīde sǣnæssas; þā wæs sund liden,
eoletes æt ende. Þanon up hraðe
225 Wedera lēode on wang stigon,
sǣwudu sǣldon, — syrcan hrysedon,
gūðgewǣdo; Gode þancedon
þæs þe him ȳþlāde ēaðe wurdon.

Þā of wealle geseah weard Scildinga,
230 sē þe holmclifu healdan scolde,
beran ofer bolcan beorhte randas,
fyrdsearu fūslicu; hine fyrwyt bræc
mōdgehygdum, hwæt þā men wǣron.
Gewāt him þā tō waroðe wicge rīdan
235 þegn Hrōðgāres, þrymmum cwehte
mægenwudu mundum, meþelwordum frægn:
' Hwæt syndon gē searohæbbendra,
byrnum werede, þē þus brontne cēol
ofer lagustrǣte lǣdan cwōmon,

223[b] *Tho.* sundlida, so *Holt.*[2-5], *Sed.* — 224[a] *Tho.* ēalāde (ȳðlāde?); *Gru.* ēalondes (?); ten Brink L 4.7.527 n. eodores; *Tr.* eosetes; *Holt. L 5.26.19* ēares; *Holt.*[3-5] ēoledes. See L 5.14. — 226[b] *Schlutter ESt. xxxviii 301 n. 2* (?) hryscedon (*cf. ib. xxxix 344 f.*). — 229[a] *Fol. 135[a]* þa. — 232[a] *Siev. R. 280* (?), *Holt.* fūslīc; *cf. Siev. xxix 566, 568; T.C. § 19.*

240 hider ofer holmas? [Hwæt, ic hwī]le wæs
endesǣta, ǣgwearde hēold,
þē on land Dena lāðra nǣnig
mid scipherge sceðþan ne meahte.
Nō hēr cūðlīcor cuman ongunnon
245 lindhæbbende, nē gē lēafnesword
gūðfremmendra gearwe ne wisson,
māga gemēdu. Nǣfre ic māran geseah
eorla ofer eorþan, ðonne is ēower sum,
secg on searwum; nis þæt seldguma,
250 wǣpnum geweorðad, næfne him his wlite lēoge,
ǣnlīc ansȳn. Nū ic ēower sceal
frumcyn witan, ǣr gē fyr heonan
lēassceaweras on land Dena
furþur fēran. Nū gē feorbūend,
255 merelīðende, mīn[n]e gehȳrað
ānfealdne geþōht: ofost is sēlest
tō gecȳðanne, hwanan ēowre cyme syndon.'

IIII   Him se yldesta andswarode,
werodes wīsa, wordhord onlēac:
260 ' Wē synt gumcynnes Gēata lēode
ond Higelāces heorðgenēatas.
Wæs mīn fæder folcum gecȳþed,
æþele ordfruma, Ecgþēow hāten;
gebād wintra worn, ǣr hē on weg hwurfe,

240[b] *Bu. 83* [hwīle ic on weal]le]; *Siev. Angl. xiv 146* [hwæt, ic hwī]le, so *Holt., Sed., Cha.;
Kal. 47, Schü.* [ic hwī]le; *Tr.[1] 140* [ic on hyl]le, *cf. Siev. xxix 327 f.* — 242[a] *MS.* þe; *Thk.,
Tho.* þæt; *Gru.* [þæt] þe. See *Gloss.: þē.* — 243[b] *Cos. viii 572* sceaðana (=lāðra). — 245[b]
Ke., E.Sc., Tho., Gru., E., Z., Holt. nē gelēafnesword. — 249[b] *Cl. Hal.* (?), *Bright MLN.
xxxi 84* is *for* nis. — *Thk., Ke., E.Sc., Tho., He.[1], E.* seld (*cp.* 'seldom') guma; *Gr.[1]*
seldguma. — 250[b] *MS.* næfre; *Ke.* næfne. — 252[b] *Fol. 135[b]* heonan. — 253[a] *E.Sc., E.,
Tho., et al.* lēase; *Holt.Zs. 113* [swā] l. *Cf. Earle 117.* — 255[b] *MS.* mine; *Ke.* mīn[n]e. —
262 *Tr.[1] 141 f.* fæder [monegum]; *Tr.* f. [foldan], *Holt.Zs. 113* f. [on foldan]; *Holt.[2], Sed.
]frōd] f.: Holt.[3-6]* f. folcum]feor]. See *T.C.* § *17*.

265 gamol of geardum;   hine gearwe geman
   witena wēlhwylc   wīde geond eorþan.
   Wē þurh holdne hige   hlāford þīnne,
   sunu Healfdenes   sēcean cwōmon,
   lēodgebyrgean;   wes þū ūs lārena gōd!
270 Habbað wē tō þǣm mǣran   micel ǣrende
   Deniga frēan;   ne sceal þǣr dyrne sum
   wesan, þæs ic wēne.   þū wāst, gif hit is
   swā wē sōþlīce   secgan hȳrdon,
   þæt mid Scyldingum   sceaðona ic nāt hwylc,
275 dēogol dǣdhata   deorcum nihtum
   ēaweð þurh egsan   uncūðne nīð,
   hȳnðu ond hrāfyl.   Ic þæs Hrōðgār mæg
   þurh rūmne sefan   rǣd gelǣran,
   hū hē frōd ond gōd   fēond oferswȳðeþ —
280 gyf him edwenden   ǣfre scolde
   bealuwa bisigu   bōt eft cuman — ,
   ond þā cearwylmas   cōlran wurðaþ;
   oððe ā syþðan   earfoðþrāge,
   þrēanȳd þolað,   þenden þǣr wunað
285 on hēahstede   hūsa sēlest.'
   Weard maþelode,   ðǣr on wicge sæt,
   ombeht unforht: 'Ǣghwæþres sceal
   scearp scyldwiga   gescād witan,
   worda ond worca,   sē þe wēl þenceð.
290 Ic þæt gehȳre,   þæt þis is hold weorod
   frēan Scyldinga.   Gewītaþ forð beran
   wǣpen ond gewǣdu,   ic ēow wīsige;
   swylce ic maguþegnas   mīne hāte
   wið fēonda gehwone   flotan ēowerne,

273[b] *Fol. 136[a]* secgan.— 275[a] *Klu. ix 188* dǣdhwata. — 280[a] *A B* edwendan, **Bu. Tid.** 281 (cf. *Gru. p. 117*) edwendan=edwenden; *Hold.*[1], *Holt.*, *Sed.* edwenden. — 282[b] *Gr.*[1] (?), *t. Br. 49* wurðan; *E.* weorðan.

BEOWULF

295 nīwtyrwydne   nacan on sande
ārum healdan,   oþ ðæt eft byreð
ofer lagustrēamas   lēofne mannan
wudu wundenhals   tō Wedermearce,
gōdfremmendra   swylcum gifeþe bið,
300 þæt þone hilderǣs   hāl gedīgeð.'
    Gewiton him þā fēran, — flota stille bād,
seomode on *sāle*   sīdfæþmed scip,
on ancre fæst.   Eoforlīc scionon
ofer hlēorber[g]an   gehroden golde,
305 fāh ond fȳrheard, —   ferhwearde hēold
gūþmōd *grimmon.*   Guman ōnetton,
sigon ætsomne,   oþ þæt hȳ [s]æl timbred
geatolīc ond goldfāh   ongyton mihton;
þæt wæs foremǣrost   foldbūendum
310 receda under roderum,   on þǣm se rīca bād;
līxte se lēoma   ofer landa fela.
Him þā hildedëor   [h]of mōdigra
torht getǣhte,   þæt hīe him tō mihton
gegnum gangan;   gūðbeorna sum
315 wicg gewende,   word æfter cwæð:
'Mǣl is mē tō fēran;   Fæder alwalda
mid ārstafum   ēowic gehealde
sīða gesunde!   Ic tō sǣ wille,
wið wrāð werod   wearde healdan.'

297[a] *Fol. 136[b]* mas. — 299[a] *Gru., et al.* gūðfremmendra. — 302[a] *MS.* sole; *E.Sc.* sāle. — 303[b] *E.Sc.* scīone (*or* scīonum); *Bu.Zs. 196* līcscīonon; *Sed.* scīonon (*wk. apn.*). — 304[a] *MS.* beran; *E.Sc.* ofer hlēor bǣron; *Sed.* ofer hleoþu bēran; *E., Gering ZfdPh. xii 123* hlēorber[g]an. — 305[b] *Gr., et al.* ferh (=fearh) w. h.; *Aant. 7* (?), *Lübke Anz.fdA. xix 342, Tr.* (*cf. Tr.*[1] *145*) færwearde h. — 306[a] *MS.* guþmod grummon; *Ke., et al.* gūðmōd[e] grummon (*from* grimman 'rage'); — construed w. 305[b]: *Bu. 83 f.* gūþmōdgum men; *Lübke l.c.* gūþmōdegra sum; *Bright MLN. x 43* gūþmōd grimmon (*adv.*), *so Sed.* (grimmon, *dp.*); *Tr.*[1] *145, Tr.* g. grīmmon; *Holt.*[1,3] g. gummon. — 307[b] *MS.* æltimbred; *Ke. ii* [s]æl timbred. — 312[b] *MS.* of; *Ke.* [h]of. — 319[a] *Fol. 137[a]* wrað.

V 320 Strǣt wæs stānfāh, stīg wīsode
gumum ætgædere. Gūðbyrne scān
heard hondlocen, hringīren scīr
song in searwum, þā hīe tō sele furðum
in hyra gryregeatwum gangan cwōmon.
325 Setton sǣmēþe sīde scyldas,
rondas regnhearde wið þæs recedes weal;
bugon þā tō bence, — byrnan hringdon,
gūðsearo gumena; gāras stōdon,
sǣmanna searo samod ætgædere,
330 æscholt ufan grǣg; wæs se īrenþrēat
wǣpnum gewurþad.
                   þā ðǣr wlonc hæleð
ōretmecgas æfter *æþel*um frægn:
' Hwanon ferigeað gē fǣtte scyldas,
grǣge syrcan, ond grīmhelmas,
335 heresceafta hēap? Ic eom Hrōðgāres
ār ond ombiht. Ne seah ic elþēodi̯ge
þus manige men mōdiglīcran.
Wēn' ic þæt gē for wlenco, nalles for wræcsīðum,
ac for higeþrymmum Hrōðgār sōhton.'
340 Him þā ellenrōf andswarode,
wlanc Wedera lēod, word æfter sprǣc
heard under helme: ' Wē synt Higelāces
bēodgenēatas; Bēowulf is mīn nama.
Wille ic āsecgan sunu Healfdenes,
345 mǣrum þēodne mīn ǣrende,
aldre þīnum, gif hē ūs geunnan wile,
þæt wē hine swā gōdne grētan mōton.'
Wulfgār maþelode — þæt wæs Wendla lēod,

323ᵇ *Tr.* furður. — 332ᵇ *MS.* hæleþum; *Gr.* æþelum (*cp. 392*). — 339ᵃ *Fol. 137ᵇ* þrymmum. — 344ᵇ *Ke., et al., Sed.* suna. *See Lang.* § 18.2.

BEOWULF

wæs his mōdsefa   manegum gecȳðed,
350 wīg ond wīsdōm — :   ' Ic þæs wine Deniga,
frēan Scildinga   frīnan wille,
bēaga bryttan,   swā þū bēna eart,
þēoden mǣrne   ymb þīnne sīð,
ond þē þā andsware   ǣdre gecȳðan,
355 ðē mē se gōda   āgifan þenceð.'

    Hwearf þā hrædlīce   þǣr Hrōðgār sæt
eald ond *a*nhār   mid his eorla gedriht;
ēode ellenrōf,   þæt hē for eaxlum gestōd
Deniga frēan;   cūþe hē duguðe þēaw.
360 Wulfgār maðelode   tō his winedrihtne:
' Hēr syndon geferede,   feorran cumene
ofer geofenes begang   Gēata lēode;
þone yldestan   ōretmecgas
Bēowulf nemnað.   Hȳ bēnan synt,
365 þæt hīe, þēoden mīn,   wið þē mōton
wordum wrixlan;   nō ðū him wearne getēoh
ðīnra gegncwida,   glædman Hrōðgār!
Hȳ on wīggetāwum   wyrðe þinceað
eorla geæhtlan;   hūru se aldor dēah,
370 sē þǣm heaðorincum   hider wīsade.'

VI   Hrōðgār maþelode,   helm Scyldinga:
' Ic hine cūðe   cnihtwesende;
wæs his ealdfæder   Ecgþēo hāten,
ðǣm tō hām forgeaf   Hrēþel Gēata
375 āngan dohtor;   is his eafor*a* nū
heard hēr cumen,   sōhte holdne wine.

357[a] *MS.* un hár; *Tr.*[1] *147* (?), *Tr., Holt., Cha.* anhār. — 360[b] *Fol. 138*[a] to. — 361[b] *Klu. ix 188, Holt.*[1–5] feorrancumene. — 367[b] *E.Sc., Gr.*[2], *E.* glæd man; *Gru., Sed.* glædmōd. — 368[a] *He.*[2–4], *Siev. R. 273 f.* (?), *Kal. 75, Holt., Schü., Sed.* wīggeatwum. See *T.C.* § 23. — 373[a] *Gr.*[1], *Gru., Tr., Cha.* eald fæder. — 375[b] *MS.* eaforan; *Gru.tr. 272, Ke.* eafora.

Ðonne sægdon þæt   sælīþende,
þā ðe gifsceattas   Gēata fyredon
þyder tō þance,   þæt hē þrītiges
380 manna mægencræft   on his mundgripe
heaþorōf hæbbe.   Hine hālig God
for ārstafum   ūs onsende,
tō West-Denum,   þæs ic wēn hæbbe,
wið Grendles gryre.   Ic þǣm gōdan sceal
385 for his mōdþræce   mādmas bēodan.
Bēo ðū on ofeste,   hāt in gân
sēon sibbegedriht   samod ætgædere;
gesaga him ēac wordum,   þæt hīe sint wilcuman
Deniga lēodum.'   [Þā tō dura ēode
390 wīdcūð hæleð,]   word inne ābēad:
'Ēow hēt secgan   sigedrihten mīn,
aldor Ēast-Dena,   þæt hē ēower æþelu can,
ond gē him syndon   ofer sǣwylmas
heardhicgende   hider wilcuman.
395 Nū gē mōton gangan   in ēowrum gūðgetāwum,
under heregrīman   Hrōðgār gesēon;
lǣtað hildebord   hēr onbīdan,
wudu wælsceaftas   worda geþinges.'
Ārās þā se rīca,   ymb hine rinc manig,
400 þrȳðlīc þegna hēap;   sume þǣr bidon,
heaðorēaf hēoldon,   swā him se hearda bebēad.
Snyredon ætsomne,   þā secg wīsode,

378[b] *Tho., Bu. 85 f., Tr.* Gēatum. — 379[a] *Aant. 7* hyder. — 379[b] *MS.* .xxxtiges. *Fol. 138[b]* tiges. — 386[b] *Rie.V. 47* gan[gan], *Siev. R. 268 f., 477* gā[a]n. *See T.C. § 1.* — *Bright MLN x 44* hāt [þæt] in gǣe. — 387[a] *t.Br. 53 n.* on sǣl*for* sēon; *Bright l.c.* sēo. — *t.Br. l.c., Holt. (cf. Beibl. x 267)* sib(b)gedriht, *see Gloss.* — 389[b]-90[a] [þā wið duru healle/Wulfgār ēode] *supplied by Gr.[1], 4 Edd. (4 half-lines inserted by E.Sc.); A. l 120: as in text above.* — 395[b] *MS.* geata/wum; *E.Sc., et al.* -getāwum; *Siev. R. 246* -geatwum; *Holt.* -searwum. *Cf. T.C. § 28, also § 23.* — 397[b] *MS. Z.* on bidman *w. incomplete erasure of* m; *Thk. on* bidian, *Gru., et al., Holt., Schü.* onbidian. — 401[b] *Fol. 139[a]* hearda. — 402[b] *AB* þa (*before* secg), *canceled by Siev. R. 256, Holt., Sed. Cf. T.C. § 24.*

BEOWULF

under Heorotes hrōf;   [heaþorinc ēode,]
heard under helme,   þæt hē on heo[r]ðe gestōd.
405 Bēowulf maðelode   — on him byrne scān,
searonet seowed   smiþes orþancum — :
' Wæs þū, Hrōðgār, hāl!   Ic eom Higelāces
mǣg ond magoðegn;   hæbbe ic mǣrða fela
ongunnen on geogoþe.   Mē wearð Grendles þing
410 on mīnre ēþeltyrf   undyrne cūð;
secgað sǣlīðend,   þæt þæs sele stande,
reced sēlesta   rinca gehwylcum
īdel ond unnyt,   siððan ǣfenlēoht
under heofenes hādor   beholen weorþeð.
415 Þā mē þæt gelǣrdon   lēode mīne,
þā sēlestan,   snotere ceorlas,
þēoden Hrōðgār,   þæt ic þē sōhte,
forþan hīe mægenes cræft   mīn[n]e cūþon;
selfe ofersāwon,   ðā ic of searwum cwōm,
420 fāh from fēondum,   þǣr ic fīfe geband,
ȳðde eotena cyn,   ond on ȳðum slōg
niceras nihtes,   nearoþearfe drēah,
wræc Wedera nīð   — wēan āhsodon — ,
forgrand gramum;   ond nū wið Grendel sceal,
425 wið þām āglǣcan   āna gehēgan
ðing wið þyrse.   Ic þē nū ðā,

403ᵇ *Gr.*¹, *Edd.* [hygerōf ēode]; *E.Sc.*, *E.* [(þā) mid (his) hæleðum gē(o)ng]. — 404ᵇ *Tho.* (*in Ke.*), *Holtzm. 490*, *Holt.*, *Sed.* heo[r]ðe; *but cf. Hoops 64; Bu. 86* hlēoðe ('hearing distance'?). — 407ᵃ *MS.*, *Hold.*², *Tr.*, *4 Edd.* wæs; *Ke., et al.* wes. *Cf. Lang.* § *7.1.* — 411ᵇ *MS.* þæs, *so Cha.; Thk., Ke., 3 Edd.* þes. *Cf. Lang.* § *7.1.* — 414ᵃ *MS.* hador; *Gr.*¹, *Holt.*¹⁻⁵, *Schü.* haðor. *Cf. also Sed. MLR. v 286 & Ed., note.* — 418ᵇ *MS.* mine; *Gr.*¹ mīn[n]e. *Cp. 255ᵇ; note on 2181.* — 419ᵇ *Gr.*¹ (?), *Bu. 368* on (*for* of). — 420ᵇ *Gr.*¹ fīfel *or* fīfle (?); *Bu. 367* [on] fīfelgeban (=-geofon), *t.Br. 50* fīfelgeban (*and* 421ᵃ hām *for* cyn); *L. Hall L 3.13* fīfelgeband, *Tr.*¹ *150*, *T.* fīfla gebann ('levy'?). — 423ᵃ *Fol. 139*ᵇ wedra *A*, .edera (*altered to* wedera *w. another ink*) *B. Cf. Lang.* § *18.10 n.; Intr. xc.* — 424ᵇ *Ke. ii*, *E.Sc.*, *E. Krüger Beitr. ix 571* Grendle. *See Lang.* § *25.6.*

brego Beorht-Dena, biddan wille,
eodor Scyldinga, ānre bēne,
þæt ðū mē ne forwyrne, wīgendra hlēo,
430 frēowine folca, nū ic þus feorran cōm,
þæt ic mōte āna [ond] mīnra eorla gedryht,
þes hearda hēap, Heorot fælsian.
Hæbbe ic ēac geāhsod, þæt se æglǣca
for his wonhȳdum wǣpna ne recceð;
435 ic þæt þonne forhicge, swā mē Higelāc sīe,
mīn mondrihten mōdes blīðe,
þæt ic sweord bere oþðe sīdne scyld,
geolorand tō gūþe, ac ic mid grāpe sceal
fōn wið fēonde ond ymb feorh sacan,
440 lāð wið lāþum; ðǣr gelȳfan sceal
Dryhtnes dōme sē þe hine dēað nimeð.
Wēn' ic þæt hē wille, gif hē wealdan mōt,
in þǣm gūðsele Gēotena lēode
etan unforhte, swā hē oft dyde,
445 mægen Hrēðmanna. Nā þū mīnne þearft
hafalan hȳdan, ac hē mē habban wile
d[r]ēore fāhne, gif mec dēað nimeð;
byreð blōdig wæl, byrgean þenceð,
eteð āngenga unmurnlīce,
450 mearcað mōrhopu; nō ðū ymb mīnes ne þearft
līces feorme leng sorgian.
Onsend Higelāce, gif mec hild nime,
beaduscrūda betst, þæt mīne brēost wereð,

430ᵃ *E.Sc., Tho., E., Arn.* frēawine. — 431ᵇ-32ᵃ *Ke. ii, Gr.¹, 4 Edd.* [ond] *(transposing it from before* þes); *MS.* ⁊ þes; *Tho.* [mid] m. e. g. — 435ᵇ *Siev. R. 237* sī. *Cf. T.C.* § *1.*
— 443ᵇ *MS.* geo/tena; *Holt.* Gēotna; *Cha.* Gēotena; *Gr.¹, Sed.* Gēatena; *Rie.Zs. 400 f.*,
Schü. Gēata. *Cf. Lang.* § *16.2.* — 444ᵇ *Fol. 140ᵃ* oft. — 445ᵃ *MS.* mægen hrēð manna;
Edd. mægen Hrēðmanna; *Tr.* mægenþrȳð manna; *Schü. xxxix 102, Schü., Holt.* mægenhrēð manna. — 447ᵃ *MS.* deore; *Gru. tr. 273, Ke. ii* d[r]ēore.

hrægla sēlest;   þæt is Hrǣdlan lāf,
455 Wēlandes geweorc.   Gǣð ā wyrd swā hīo scel!'

VII   Hrōðgār maþelode,   helm Scyldinga:
'For [g]ewy[r]htum þū,   wine mīn Bēowulf,
ond for ārstafum   ūsic sōhtest.
Geslōh þīn fæder   fǣhðe mǣste;
460 wearþ hē Heaþolāfe   tō handbonan
mid Wilfingum;   ðā hine *Wede*ra cyn
for herebrōgan   habban ne mihte.
Þanon hē gesōhte   Sūð-Dena folc
ofer ȳða gewealc,   Ār-Scyldinga;
465 ðā ic furþum wēold   folce Den*i*ga
ond on geogoðe hēold   gi*nn*e rīce,
hordburh hæleþa;   ðā wæs Heregār dēad,
mīn yldra mǣg   unlifigende,
bearn Healfdenes;   sē wæs betera ðonne ic!
470 Siððan þā fǣhðe   fēo þingode;
sende ic Wylfingum   ofer wæteres hrycg
ealde mādmas;   hē mē āþas swōr.
Sorh is mē tō secganne   on sefan mīnum
gumena ǣngum,   hwæt mē Grendel hafað
475 hȳnðo on Heorote   mid his heteþancum,
fǣrnīða gefremed;   is mīn fletwerod,
wīghēap gewanod;   hīe wyrd forswēop
on Grendles gryre.   God ēaþe mæg

454[b] *E.Sc.* (?), *Müll. ZfdA. xii 260, Holt., Sed.* Hrēðlan. See *Gloss. of Proper Names.*
— 457[a] *MS.* fere fyhtum; *Ke.* Fore fylstum (þū, frēond); *E.Sc., Tho., Schü.* Fore fyhtum (þū, frēond); *Gr.*[1] Fore wyhtum; *Gru.* For werefyhtum; *Tr., Cha.* For gewyrhtum; *Sed.* fore wyrhtum; *Holt.* Fer wīgum. — 459[a] *Holt., Schü., Sed.* þīn fæder geslōh. See *T.C.* § 17. *Cf. also Tr.*[1] *153 f.* — 461[b] *MS.* gara; *Gru.*, 4 *Edd.* Wedera. — 464[b] *Fol. 140[b]* scyldinga *A(B).* — 465[b] *MS.* de/ninga (*standing under* scyldinga), *Schü.* Deninga; *Tho.*, 3 *Edd.* Deniga. *Cp. 1686[a] Varr.* — 466[b] *MS.* gim merice; *Schü.* gimme rīce; *Cha.* gimmerīce; *Sed.* gumena rīce; *E.Sc., (Tho.), Holt.* ginne rīce (*so Gen. 230*). — 473[a] *MS.* secganne; *Siev. R. 312, Holt., Schü., Sed.* secgan. *Cf. T.C.* § 12.

BEOWULF 19

þone dolsceaðan dǣda getwǣfan!
480 Ful oft gebēotedon bēore druncne
ofer ealowǣge ōretmecgas,
þæt hīe in bēorsele bīdan woldon
Grendles gūþe mid gryrum ecga.
Ðonne wæs þēos medoheal on morgentīd,
485 drihtsele drēorfāh, þonne dæg līxte,
eal bencþelu blōde bestȳmed,
heall heorudrēore; āhte ic holdra þȳ lǣs,
dēorre duguðe, þē þā dēað fornam.
Site nū tō symle ond onsǣl meoto,
490 sigehrēð secgum, swā þīn sefa hwette.'
Þā wæs Gēatmæcgum geador ætsomne
on bēorsele benc gerȳmed;
þǣr swīðferhþe sittan ēodon,
þrȳðum dealle. Þegn nytte behēold,
495 sē þe on handa bær hroden ealowǣge,
scencte scīr wered. Scop hwīlum sang
hādor on Heorote. Þǣr wæs hæleða drēam,
duguð unlȳtel Dena ond Wedera.

VIII *Un*ferð maþelode, Ecglāfes bearn,
500 þē æt fōtum sæt frēan Scyldinga,
onband beadurūne — wæs him Bēowulfes sīð,
mōdges merefaran, micel æfþunca,
forþon þe hē ne ūþe, þæt ǣnig ōðer man
ǣfre mǣrða þon mā middangeardes

486ᵃ *Fol. 141ᵃ* benc. — 489ᵇ–90ᵃ *MS.* on sæl meoto; *Ke. ii* on sǣlum ete; *Tho.* onsǣl meodo sigehreðer; *Dietrich ZfdA. xi 411* onsǣl meoto, sigehrēð secgum; *Gr.³*, (*cf. Aant. 10*), sigehrēðsecgum; *Klu. ix 188* sigehrēðegum; *Holt.Zs. 114* on sǣlum weota sigehrēðgum secgum; *Schü. xxxix 103, Schü.* on sǣl weota sigehrēð secgum; *JEGPh. vi 192, Holt.²⁻ᵇ* on sǣl meota (*imp. of* metian) (*Holt.:* sighrēð secgum), *cf. Kock² 105, MLN. xxxiv 132; Sed.²* on sǣlum tēo ('award') s. s.; *Bright MLN. xxxi 217 ff.* onsǣl mētto s. s. *See note.* — 499ᵃ *MS.* HVN ferð; *Rie.Zs. 414* Unferð (*allit.; confusion w. Hūn-, see note on 499 ff.*). — 501ᵇ *Tr.¹ 155 cancels* sīð (*or:* Bēowan sīð [?]). — 504ᵃ *Fol. 141ᵇ* mærða *A.*

505 gehē*de* under heofenum   þonne hē sylfa — :
' Eart þū sē Bēowulf,   sē þe wið Brecan wunne,
on sīdne sǣ   ymb sund flite,
ðǣr git for wlence   wada cunnedon
ond for dolgilpe   on dēop wæter
510 aldrum nēþdon?   Nē inc ǣnig mon,
nē lēof nē lāð,   belēan mihte
sorhfullne sīð,   þā git on sund rēon;
þǣr git ēagorstrēam   earmum þehton,
mǣton merestrǣta,   mundum brugdon,
515 glidon ofer gārsecg;   geofon ȳþum wēol,
wintrys wylm[um].   Git on wæteres ǣht
seofon niht swuncon;   hē þē æt sunde oferflāt,
hæfde māre mægen.   Þā hine on morgentīd
on Heaþo-Rǣmes   holm up ætbær;
520 ðonon hē gesōhte   swǣsne ēþel,
lēof his lēodum,   lond Brondinga,
freoðoburh fægere,   þǣr hē folc āhte,
burh ond bēagas.   Bēot eal wið þē
sunu Bēanstānes   sōðe gelǣste.
525 Đonne wēne ic tō þē   wyrsan geþingea,
ðēah þū heaðorǣsa   gehwǣr dohte,
grimre gūðe,   gif þū Grendles dearst
nihtlongne fyrst   nēan bīdan.'

Bēowulf maþelode,   bearn Ecgþēowes:
530 ' Hwæt, þū worn fela,   wine mīn *U*nferð,

505ᵃ *MS.* ge/hedde; *Holt.*¹ gehēde; *Holt.*²⁻⁶ gehēgde. *Cf. Siev. ZfdPh. xxi 357; T.C. § 16; Lang.* § *19.4.* — 516ᵃ *MS.* wylm; *Tho.*, (*Rie.Zs. 387, 404,*) *Siev. R. 271, Schü., Cha.* wylm[e]; *Mö. 131, Holt.*¹⁻⁵, *Sed.* [þurh] w. w.; *Klu.* (*in Hold.*¹) wylm[um]; *cp. Andr. 451 f.* — 519ᵃ *MS.* heaþoræmes; *Munch Samlede Afhandlinger ii* (*1849–51*) *371,* (*cf. E.tr.*), *Müll. ZfdA. xi 287, Holt., Schü., Sed.* -Rēamas; *Gr.*¹, *Cha.* -Rǣmas. *See Lang.* §§ *9.1, 18.5.* — 520ᵇ *MS.* ♃. (=ēþel). *So 913ᵃ, 1702ᵃ.* — 523ᵇ *Fol. 142ᵃ* beot. — 524ᵃ *Bu.Zs. 198* (?), *Krüger Beitr. ix 573* Bānstānes; *Bu.Zs. 198* Bēahstānes (?). — 525ᵇ *Ke. ii* þinges (?); *Rie. Germ. ix 303, Rie.Zs. 389, Sed.* geþinges. — 530ᵇ *MS.* hun ferð. *See 499ᵃ.*

BEOWULF

bēore druncen   ymb Brecan sprǣce,
sægdest from his sīðe!   Sōð ic talige,
þæt ic merestrengo   māran āhte,
earfeþo on ȳþum,   ðonne ǣnig ōþer man.
535 Wit þæt gecwǣdon   cnihtwesende
ond gebēotedon   — wǣron bēgen þā gīt
on geogoðfēore —   þæt wit on gārsecg ūt
aldrum nēðdon,   ond þæt geæfndon swā.
Hæfdon swurd nacod,   þā wit on sund reon,
540 heard on handa;   wit unc wið hronfixas
werian þōhton.   Nō hē wiht fram mē
flōdȳþum feor   flēotan meahte,
hraþor on holme,   nō ic fram him wolde.
Ðā wit ætsomne   on sǣ wǣron
545 fīf nihta fyrst,   oþ þæt unc flōd tōdrāf,
wado weallende,   wedera cealdost,
nīpende niht,   ond norþanwind
heaðogrim ondhwearf;   hrēo wǣron ȳþa.
Wæs merefixa   mōd onhrēred;
550 þǣr mē wið lāðum   līcsyrce mīn
heard hondlocen   helpe gefremede,
beadohrægl brōden,   on brēostum læg
golde gegyrwed.   Mē tō grunde tēah
fāh fēondscaða,   fæste hæfde
555 grim on grāpe;   hwæþre mē gyfeþe wearð,
þæt ic āglǣcan   orde gerǣhte,
hildebille;   heaþorǣs fornam
mihtig meredēor   þurh mīne hand.

534ᵃ *He.¹ Gloss. (?), Bu.Zs. 198, Tr.¹ 156* eafeþo. See 577. — 540ᵇ *Schü. Bd. 55 f.* hornfiscas, *cp. Andr. 370. But Epist. Alex. 510* hronfiscas. — 544ᵃ *Fol. 142ᵇ* somne *A B*. — 548ᵃ *MS.* ⁊ hwearf; *Gr.* and hwearf (*adj., cp. Finnsb. 34*); *Tr.¹ 156, Tr. Holt.* onhwearf. — 552ᵇ *Siev. ix 138, Holt.* [þæt mē] on.

BEOWULF

VIIII   Swā mec gelōme   lāðgetēonan
560   þrēatedon þearle.   Ic him þēnode
dēoran sweorde,   swā hit gedēfe wæs.
Næs hīe ðǣre fylle   gefēan hæfdon,
mānfordǣdlan,   þæt hīe mē þēgon,
symbel ymbsǣton   sǣgrunde nēah;
565 ac on mergenne   mēcum wunde
be ȳðlāfe   uppe lǣgon,
sweo[r]dum āswefede,   þæt syðþan nā
ymb brontne ford   brimlīðende
lāde ne letton.   Lēoht ēastan cōm,
570 beorht bēacęn Godes,   brimu swaþredon,
þæt ic sǣnæssas   gesēon mihte,
windige weallas.   Wyrd oft nereð
unfǣgne eorl,   þonne his ellen dēah!
Hwæþere mē gesǣlde,   þæt ic mid sweorde ofslōh
575 niceras nigene.   Nō ic on niht gefrægn
under heofones hwealf   heardran feohtan,
nē on ēgstrēamum   earmran mannon;
hwæþere ic fāra feng   fēore gedīgde
sīþes wērig.   Ðā mec sǣ oþbær,
580 flōd æfter faroðe   on Finna land,
wadu weallendu.   Nō ic wiht fram þē
swylcra searonīða   secgan hȳrde,
billa brōgan.   Breca nǣfre gīt
æt heaðolāce,   nē gehwæþer incer,
585 swā dēorlīce   dǣd gefremede
fāgum sweordum   — nō ic þæs [fela] gylpe —,

565[b] *Fol. 143[a]* wunde. — 567[a] *A* sweodum; *Ke.* sweo[r]dum. — 574[b] *Rie.V. 9* mēce (*for* sweorde); *Holt.Zs. 114* ābrēat (*for* ofslōh). *Cf. T.C.* § *28.* — 578[a] *MS.* hwaþere; *Gru.* (*cf. Tho., Gr.*[1]) hwæþere. — 581[a] *MS.* wudu; *Gru.tr. 275, Ke. ii* wadu. — 586[b] *Gr.*[1]*, Sed.* [fela]; *Klu. ix 188, Holt., Schü., Cha.* [geflites].

þēah ðū þīnum brōðrum   tō banan wurde,
hēafodmǣgum;   þæs þū in helle scealt
werhðo drēogan,   þēah þīn wit duge.
590 Secge ic þē tō sōðe,   sunu Ecglāfes,
þæt nǣfre Gre[n]del swā fela   gryra gefremede,
atol ǣglǣca   ealdre þīnum,
hȳnðo on Heorote,   gif þīn hige wǣre,
sefa swā searogrim,   swā þū self talast;
595 ac hē hafað onfunden,   þæt hē þā fǣhðe ne þearf,
atole ecgþrǣce   ēower lēode
swīðe onsittan,   Sige-Scyldinga;
nymeð nȳdbāde,   nǣnegum āfað
lēode Deniga,   ac hē lust wigeð,
600 swefeð ond snēdeþ,   secce ne wēneþ
tō Gār-Denum.   Ac ic him Gēata sceal
eafoð ond ellen   ungeāra nū,
gūþe gebēodan.   Gǣþ eft sē þe mōt
tō medo mōdig,   siþþan morgenlēoht
605 ofer ylda bearn   ōþres dōgores,
sunne sweglwered   sūþan scīneð!'
þā wæs on sālum   sinces brytta
gamolfeax ond gūðrōf;   gēoce gelȳfde
brego Beorht-Dena;   gehȳrde on Bēowulfe
610 folces hyrde   fæstrǣdne geþōht.

Ðǣr wæs hæleþa hleahtor,   hlyn swynsode,
word wǣron wynsume.   Ēode Wealhþēow forð,

588[b] *Fol. 143[b]* helle *AB*. — 591[a] *MS.* gre del; *Thk.* Gre[n]del. — 596[b] *E.* ēowerra lēoda; *Klu.* (*in Hold.*[2]) ēowra lēoda; *Tr.*[1] *157 f., Tr., Sed.* ēowre lēode. *See 599*[a]*, 1124*[a]*.* — 599[b] *Ke. ii* [on] lust wīgeð (?); *Bu.Tid. 48 f.* [on] lust þigeð. — 600[a] *MS.* sendeþ; *Tho., Arn., B.-T.* s. o. scendeð; *Gru.* (*cf. Gru.tr., Ke.*) swefen onsendeð (*see Gr. Bibl. ii p. 414, Aant. 13*); *E., Holt. L 5.26.4* swendeþ (*for* sendeþ), *Holt. L 5.26.6 & 8* swenceþ, *Tr.*[1] *158, Tr.* swelgeþ, *Sed.* serweþ (*cp. 161*); *He.-Soc.*[6] swēfeð o. s.; *Imelmann ESt. lxvi 324 ff.* snēdeþ. — 601[b] *Tho., Gr. Bibl. ii p. 414 (?), Holtzm. 491 cancel* ic. — 609[a] *Fol. 144*[a] brego *AB*. — 612[a] *Kal. 56* wynsum (?); *Tr. cancels* wǣron.

cwēn Hrōðgāres　　cynna gemyndig,
grētte goldhroden　　guman on healle,
615 ond þā frēolīc wīf　　ful gesealde
ǣrest Ēast-Dena　　ēþelwearde,
bæd hine blīðne　　æt þǣre bēorþege,
lēodum lēofne;　　hē on lust geþeah
symbel ond seleful,　　sigerōf kyning.
620 Ymbēode þā　　ides Helminga
duguþe ond geogoþe　　dǣl ǣghwylcne,
sincfato sealde,　　oþ þæt sǣl ālamp,
þæt hīo Bēowulfe,　　bēaghroden cwēn
mōde geþungen　　medoful ætbǣr;
625 grētte Gēata lēod,　　Gode þancode
wīsfæst wordum　　þæs ðe hire se willa gelamp,
þæt hēo on ǣnigne　　eorl gelȳfde
fyrena frōfre.　　Hē þæt ful geþeah,
wælrēow wiga　　æt Wealhþēon,
630 ond þā gyddode　　gūþe gefȳsed,
Bēowulf maþelode,　　bearn Ecgþēowes:
'Ic þæt hogode,　　þā ic on holm gestāh,
sǣbāt gesæt　　mid mīnra secga gedriht,
þæt ic ānunga　　ēowra lēoda
635 willan geworhte,　　oþðe on wæl crunge
fēondgrāpum fæst.　　Ic gefremman sceal
eorlīc ellen,　　oþðe endedæg
on þisse meoduhealle　　mīnne gebīdan!'
Ðām wīfe þā word　　wēl līcodon,
640 gilpcwide Gēates;　　ēode goldhroden
frēolicu folccwēn　　tō hire frēan sittan.

Þā wæs eft swā ǣr　　inne on healle
þrȳðword sprecen,　　ðēod on sǣlum,

629ᵇ *Fol. 144ᵇ æt AB.* — 643 *Sed. transposes order of half-lines. But see MPh. iii 240.*

BEOWULF

sigefolca swēg, oþ þæt semninga
645 sunu Healfdenes sēcean wolde
ǣfenræste; wiste þǣm āhlǣcan
tō þǣm hēahsele hilde geþinged,
siððan hīe sunnan lēoht gesēon meahton,
oþ ðe nīpende niht ofer ealle,
650 scaduhelma gesceapu scrīðan cwōman
wan under wolcnum. Werod eall ārās.
[Ge]grētte þā guma ōþerne,
Hrōðgār Bēowulf, ond him hǣl ābēad,
wīnærnes geweald, ond þæt word ācwæð:
655 ' Nǣfre ic ǣnegum men ǣr ālȳfde,
siþðan ic hond ond rond hebban mihte,
ðrȳþærn Dena būton þē nū ðā.
Hafa nū ond geheald hūsa sēlest,
gemyne mǣrþo, mægenellen cȳð,
660 waca wið wrāþum! Ne bið þē wilna gād,
gif þū þæt ellenweorc aldre gedīgest.'
Ðā him Hrōþgār gewāt mid his hæleþa gedryht,
eodur Scyldinga ūt of healle;
wolde wīgfruma Wealhþēo sēcan,
665 cwēn tō gebeddan. Hæfde Kyningwuldor
Grendle tōgēanes, swā guman gefrungon,
seleweard āseted; sundornytte behēold
ymb aldor Dena, eotonweard' ābēad.
Hūru Gēata lēod georne truwode

648[b] *E.Sc., Tho.,* 4 *Edd.* insert [ne] (*cf. Ke. ii 27, E.tr.*). — 649[a] *Ke., et al.,* 4 *Edd.* oþðe; *Gru.tr. 276, Gru.* oð þæt. — 652[a] *MS.* grette; *Gru.tr. 276* [Ge]grētte; *cp. 2516[a], 1870[a], 34[a], etc.* — 653[b] *Gr.*[1] heal (?); *Cos. (in Hold.*[2]) healle. *But see MPh. iii 240 (bēod..n used w. two widely different objects).* — 654[a] *Fol. 145[a]* geweald. — 665[b] *Ke. ii (?), Tho., Sed.* kyning[a]w. *See also MPh. iii 454.* — 668[b] *Ke. ii* ēotnes weard ābād; *Tho.* eoten weard ābēad; *Tr.*[1] *161, Tr.* e. w. ābād; *Sed.* eotonweard ābād; *Binz Beibl. xiv 360 (Lit.bl. xxxii 55)* eotenwearde bēad. — 669[b] *Siev. R., Holt.*[1-3]*, Schü.* trēowde. *So 1095[a]* (-trēowdon), *1533[b], 1993[b], 2322[b], 2370[b], 2540[b], 2953[b]. See T.C. § 10.*

26 BEOWULF

670 mōdgan mægnes,   Metodes hyldo. —
Đā hē him of dyde   īsernbyrnan,
helm of hafelan,   sealde his hyrsted sweord,
īrena cyst   ombihtþegne,
ond gehealdan hēt   hildegeatwe.
675 Gespræc þā se gōda   gylpworda sum,
Bēowulf Gēata,   ǣr hē on bed stige:
'Nō ic mē an herewæsmun   hnāgran talige
gūþgeweorca,   þonne Grendel hine;
forþan ic hine sweorde   swebban nelle,
680 aldre benēotan,   þēah ic eal mæge;
nāt hē þāra gōda,   þæt hē mē ongēan slēa,
rand gehēawe,   þēah ðe hē rōf sīe
nīþgeweorca;   ac wit on niht sculon
secge ofersittan,   gif hē gesēcean dear
685 wīg ofer wǣpen,   ond siþðan wītig God
on swā hwæþere hond   hālig Dryhten
mǣrðo dēme,   swā him gemet þince.'
Hylde hine þā heaþodēor,   hlēorbolster onfēng
eorles andwlitan,   ond hine ymb monig
690 snellīc sǣrinc   selereste gebēah.
Nǣnig heora þōhte,   þæt hē þanon scolde
eft eardlufan   ǣfre gesēcean,
folc oþðe frēoburh,   þǣr hē āfēded wæs;
ac hīe hæfdon gefrūnen,   þæt hīe ǣr tō fela micles
695 in þǣm wīnsele   wældēað fornam,
Denigea lēode.   Ac him Dryhten forgeaf
wīgspēda gewiofu,   Wedera lēodum,

672[b] *Schü. ESt. lv 92* hyrsted-sweord. — 673[a] *Siev. R. 308, Tr., Holt., Schü., Sed.* īren[n]a. *See note.* So 1697[a] (2259[b]). — 676[a] *Fol. 145[b]* geata. — 677[a] *Gru.tr. 277* -wæs[t]-mum; *Aant. 13* -rǣsum (?); *Tr.[1] 162, Tr.* -wǣpnum. — 681[a] *Tho.* þære gūðe. — 684[b] *MS.* het; *Ke.* hē. — 688[b] *Ke., Tho., et al.* hlēor bolster; *He.[1], 4 Edd.* hlēorbolster. — 694[b] *Tho.* hyra (*for* hīe) (?); *Gr.[1], Gru.* þætte ǣr; *Bu. 89* þæt ǣr; *Klu. ix 189, Sed.* hiera (*for* hīe ǣr). *Cf. MPh. iii 455.* — 697[b] *Fol. 146[a]* wedera.

frōfor ond fultum, þæt hīe fēond heora
ðurh ānes cræft ealle ofercōmon,
700 selfes mihtum. Sōð is gecȳþed,
þæt mihtig God manna cynnes
wēold wīdeferhð.
　　　　　　　　Cōm on wanre niht
scrīðan sceadugenga. Scēotend swǣfon,
þā þæt hornreced healdan scoldon,
705 ealle būton ānum. Þæt wæs yldum cūþ,
þæt hīe ne mōste, þā Metod nolde,
se s[c]ynscaþa under sceadu bregdan; —
ac hē wæccende wrāþum on andan
bād bolgenmōd beadwa geþinges.
XI 710 Ðā cōm of mōre under misthleoþum
Grendel gongan, Godes yrre bær;
mynte se mānscaða manna cynnes
sumne besyrwan in sele þām hēan.
Wōd under wolcnum tō þæs þe hē wīnreced,
715 goldsele gumena gearwost wisse
fǣttum fāhne. Ne wæs þæt forma sīð,
þæt hē Hrōþgāres hām gesōhte;
nǣfre hē on aldordagum ǣr nē siþðan
heardran hǣle, healðegnas fand!
720 Cōm þā tō recede rinc sīðian
drēamum bedǣled. Duru sōna onarn
fȳrbendum fæst, syþðan hē hire folmum (æthr)ān;

702ᵃ *A B* ride; *Gru.tr. 277* wīde-. — 707ᵃ *MS.* syn; *Gr.*¹ s[c]in- (?), *Gr.*² s[c]yn-; *so H.lt.,
Schü., Cha.* See *T.C.* § 28 *n.* 2. — 709ᵇ Ke. ii, *Holt.* beadwe. — 718ᵇ *Fol. 146ᵇ* ne *A*. —
719ᵃ *Siev. R. 275* (?), *Holt. Angl. xxiv 267, Tr., Sed., Cha.* hǣle; *Holt. Beibl. xviii 77* hilde;
Schü. hǣle[ðas]; *Holt.*² *ii 170, Holt.*³⁻⁶ hǣle[scipes]; *Tr.*¹ *165* hwīle *or* mǣle. — 719ᵇ *E.Sc.*
(?), *Gr. Bibl. ii p. 414* (?), *E.* healþegen; *Bu. 368* helðegn onfand. — 722ᵇ *MS.* ∷ (hr)an
(*see Z., Cha.*); *Gru.tr. 277* (?), *Rask* (*see Ke., Gru.*), *Cha.* æthrān; *cp. 2270ᵃ; Z., Holt.*
gehrān; *Schü., Sed.* hrān. (*Perh.* onhrān?)

onbræd þā bealohȳdig,   ðā (hē ge)bolgen wæs,
recedes mūþan.   Raþe æfter þon
725 on fāgne flōr   fēond treddode,
ēode yrremōd;   him of ēagum stōd
ligge gelīcost   lēoht unfæger.
Geseah hē in recede   rinca manige,
swefan sibbegedriht   samod ætgædere,
730 magorinca hēap.   þā his mōd āhlōg;
mynte þæt hē gedælde,   ær þon dæg cwōme,
atol āglæca   ānra gehwylces
līf wið līce,   þā him ālumpen wæs
wistfylle wēn.   Ne wæs þæt wyrd þā gēn,
735 þæt hē mā mōste   manna cynnes
ðicgean ofer þā niht.   Þrȳðswȳð behēold
mæg Higelāces,   hū se mānscaða
under færgripum   gefaran wolde.
Nē þæt se āglæca   yldan þōhte,
740 ac hē gefēng hraðe   forman sīðe
slæpendne rinc,   slāt unwearnum,
bāt bānlocan,   blōd ēdrum dranc,
synsnædum swealh;   sōna hæfde
unlyfigendes   eal gefeormod,
745 fēt ond folma.   Forð nēar ætstōp,
nam þā mid handa   higeþīhtigne
rinc on ræste,   ræhte ongēan
fēond mid folme;   hē onfēng hraþe
inwitþancum   ond wið earm gesæt.
750 Sōna þæt onfunde   fyrena hyrde,

723[b] *MS.* : : : : : : bolgen; *Gru.tr. 277, Z., 4 Edd.* hē gebolgen; *Ke., et al.* hē ābolgen. — 729[a] *t.Br., Holt.* sibb-. See *387[a]*. — 739[a] *Gru.* Nō þær; *Holt.Zs. 115* Nō þæt. *But see ESt. xxxix 430* — 740[a] *Fol. 131[a]* feng *A B.* — 747[b] *MS.* on gean; *Siev. R. 265, 4 Edd.* tōgēanes; *Tr.[1] 107, Tr.* [him]r. o.; *Sed. MLR xxviii 227* [ond]r. o. *Cf. T.C.* § 22. — 749[a] *Aant. 14, Hoops* inwitþanc(u)lum. (*Gr.[1] ncte:* inwitþanc *used as adj., so Kock[4] 115.*)

þæt hē ne mētte   middangeardes,
eorþan scēata   on elran men
mundgripe māran;   hē on mōde wearð
forht on ferhðe;   nō þȳ ǣr fram meahte.
755 Hyge wæs him hinfūs,   wolde on heolster flēon,
sēcan dēofla gedræg;   ne wæs his drohtoð þǣr
swylce hē on ealderdagum   ǣr gemētte.
Gemunde þā se gōda,   mǣg Higelāces,
ǣfensprǣce,   uplang āstōd
760 ond him fæste wiðfēng;   fingras burston;
eoten wæs ūtweard,   eorl furþur stōp.
Mynte se mǣra,   (þ)ǣr hē meahte swā,
wīdre gewindan   ond on weg þanon
flēon on fenhopu;   wiste his fingra geweald
765 on grames grāpum.   Þæt wæs gēocor sīð,
þæt se hearmscaþa   tō Heorute ātēah!
Dryhtsele dynede;   Denum eallum wearð,
ceasterbūendum,   cēnra gehwylcum,
eorlum ealuscerwen.   Yrre wǣron bēgen,
770 rēþe renweardas.   Reced hlynsode.
Þā wæs wundor micel,   þæt se wīnsele
wiðhæfde heaþodēorum,   þæt hē on hrūsan ne fēol,
fǣger foldbold;   ac hē þæs fæste wæs
innan ond ūtan   īrenbendum
775 searoþoncum besmiþod.   Þǣr fram sylle ābēag

752ᵃ MS. sceat/ta; E.Sc., et al. scēata. Cf. Lang. § 19.4. — 758ᵃ MS. goda; Rie.V. 24, 43, 4 Edd. mōdga. See T.C. § 26. — 762ᵇ Fol. 131ᵇ . . . ær A, hwær (hw w. another ink & crossed out in pencil) B; Schü. hwǣr; E.Sc., 3 Edd. þǣr. See 797ᵇ; Gloss.: þǣr . — 763ᵃ Tr.¹ 169, Tr. wīdor; Tr.¹ (?), Sed. wīde. See MPh. iii 263. — 765ᵇ MS. he wæs; Gr.¹ wæs. — 766ᵃ Siev. ix 138 þone (?) (for þ); Cos. (in Hold.²), Tr. þē. — 769ᵃ Ke., et al. ealu scerwen; He.¹⁻³ e. scerpen (suggested by a misreading of Andr. 1526); Bu.Tid. 292 ff. ealuscerwen; Grienb. Beitr. xxxvi 85, Sed. ealuscerpen. — 770ᵃ Earlier Edd. took ren- as rēn-, regn-, cp. 326ᵃ; t.Br. 39 n. 2 rēnhearde (?). See Weyhe Beitr. xxx 59 n., JEGPh. vi 193; Lang. § 10.7.

medubenc monig　　mīne gefrǣge
golde geregnad,　　þǣr þā graman wunnon.
Þæs ne wēndon ǣr　　witan Scyldinga,
þæt hit ā mid gemete　　manna ǣnig
780 betlīc ond bānfāg　　tōbrecan meahte,
listum tōlūcan,　　nymþe līges fæþm
swulge on swaþule.　　Swēg up āstāg
nīwe geneahhe:　　Norð-Denum stōd
atelīc egesa,　　ānra gehwylcum
785 þāra þe of wealle　　wōp gehȳrdon,
gryrelēoð galan　　Godes andsacan,
sigelēasne sang,　　sār wānigean
helle hæfton.　　Hēold hine fæste
sē þe manna wæs　　mægene strengest
790 on þǣm dæge　　þysses līfes.

XII　　Nolde eorla hlēo　　ǣnige þinga
þone cwealmcuman　　cwicne forlǣtan,
nē his līfdagas　　lēoda ǣnigum
nytte tealde.　　Þǣr genehost brægd
795 eorl Bēowulfes　　ealde lāfe,
wolde frēadrihtnes　　feorh ealgian,
mǣres þēodnes,　　ðǣr hīe meahton swā.
Hīe þæt ne wiston,　　þā hīe gewin drugon,
heardhicgende　　hildemecgas,
800 ond on healfa gehwone　　hēawan þōhton,
sāwle sēcan:　　þone synscaðan
ǣnig ofer eorþan　　īrenna cyst,
gūðbilla nān　　grētan nolde;

779ᵇ *Holt.* ǣnig manna. *Cf. T.C.* § *18*. — 780ᵃ *MS.* hetlic; *Gru.tr. 278* bethc. — *Holt. Beibl. xliv 226* bōnfāg (bōn, ' ornament '). — 782ᵃ *E.Sc.* swolaðe (?); *Tho.* swaloðe; *Gru.* staðule. — 782ᵇ *Fol. 147ᵃ* up. — 788ᵃ *Tho., et al.* helle-hæftan(-on); *Holt.Zs. 124, Holt.*¹⁻⁴ helle hæftling (*so Andr. 1342, Jul. 246*). — 788ᵇ *Conybeare L 1.4, et al.* [tō] fæste. — 793ᵇ *MS.* ænigum. — 801ᵇ *E.Sc., et al., Sed.* [þæt] þ. *Cp. 199ᵇ*.

BEOWULF

    ac hē sigewǣpnum   forsworen hæfde,
805 ecga gehwylcre.   Scolde his aldorgedāl
    on ðǣm dæge   þysses līfes
    earmlīc wurðan,   ond se ellorgāst
    on fēonda geweald   feor sīðian. —
    Ðā þæt onfunde   sē þe fela ǣror
810 mōdes myrðe   manna cynne,
    fyrene gefremede   — hē [wæs] fāg wið God —,
    þæt him se līchoma   lǣstan nolde,
    ac hine se mōdęga   mǣg Hygelāces
    hæfde be honda;   wæs gehwæþer ōðrum
815 lifigende lāð.   Līcsār gebād
    atol ǣglǣca;   him on eaxle wearð
    syndolh sweotol,   seonowe onsprungon,
    burston bānlocan.   Bēowulfe wearð
    gūðhrēð gyfeþe;   scolde Grendel þonan
820 feorhsēoc flēon   under fenhleoðu,
    sēcean wynlēas wīc;   wiste þē geornor,
    þæt his aldres wæs   ende gegongen,
    dōgera dægrīm.   Denum eallum wearð
    æfter þām wælrǣse   willa gelumpen.
825 Hæfde þā gefǣlsod   sē þe ǣr feorran cōm,
    snotor ond swȳðferhð,   sele Hrōðgāres,
    genered wið nīðe.   Nihtweorce gefeh,
    ellenmǣrþum.   Hæfde Ēast-Denum
    Gēatmecga lēod   gilp gelǣsted,
830 swylce oncȳþðe   ealle gebētte,
    inwidsorge,   þē hīe ǣr drugon
    ond for þrēanȳdum   þolian scoldon,
    torn unlȳtel.   Þæt wæs tācen sweotol,

804[b] *Fol. 147[b] for A B.* — 8·0[a] *Gering L 3.26* mo[r]ð[r]es m. — 811[b] *Kö., Holt., Schü., Sed.* hē [wæs]. — 827[a] *Fol. 148[a]* nīðe.

syþðan hildedēor hond ālegde,
835 earm ond eaxle — þǣr wæs eal geador
Grendles grāpe — under gēapne hr(ōf).
XIII Ðā wæs on morgen mīne gefrǣge
ymb þā gifhealle gūðrinc monig;
fērdon folctogan feorran ond nēan
840 geond wīdwegas wundor scēawian,
lāþes lāstas. Nō his līfgedāl
sārlīc þūhte secga ǣnęgum
þāra þe tīrlēases trode scēawode,
hū hē wērigmōd on weg þanon,
845 nīða ofercumen, on nicera mere
fǣge ond geflȳmed feorhlāstas bær.
Ðǣr wæs on blōde brim weallende,
atol ȳða geswing eal gemenged,
hāton heolfre, heorodrēore wēol;
850 dēaðfǣge dēog, siððan drēama lēas
in fenfreoðo feorh ālegde,
hǣþene sāwle; þǣr him hel onfēng.
Þanon eft gewiton ealdgesīðas
swylce geong manig of gomenwāþe,
855 fram mere mōdge mēarum rīdan,
beornas on blancum. Ðǣr wæs Bēowulfes
mǣrðo mǣned; monig oft gecwæð,
þætte sūð nē norð be sǣm twēonum
ofer eormengrund ōþer nǣnig

835ᵇ-36ᵃ *Punctuat. in text w.* Gru., Bu. Tid. 49, Cos. Beitr. xxi 20, Holt., Cha., et al. *Several Edd. take* 835ᵇ *as a complete clause.* — 836ᵇ MS. B hr. .; Rask (in Gru.tr. 279, cf. Gru. ed. note), Edd. hrōf; Miller Angl. xii 398 horn. — 845ᵃ Kal. 82 n. oferwunnen (?); Holt. n. genǣged. Cf. T.C. § 17. — 846ᵇ Gr.¹, Tr.¹ 171, Tr. feorlāstas. — 849ᵇ Fol. 148ᵇ heoro A B. — 850ᵃ MS. deog; Ke. dēag ('the dye'), Tho. dēog ('dyed'), Leo (in He.) dēog ('concealed himself'); Siev. ix 138 d. dēop (no punct. after wēol), cf. Ke. ii, E.tr.; Bu. 89 f. dēaðfǣges dēop; Aant. 15 dēaðfāge dēop; Z. Arch. lxxxiv 124 f. dēaf; so Schü., Sed.; Tr.¹ 172, Holt. dēof = dēaf.

860 under swegles begong   sēlra nǣre
rondhæbbendra,   rīces wyrðra. —
Nē hīe hūru winedrihten   wiht ne lōgon,
glædne Hrōðgār,   ac þæt wæs gōd cyning. —
Hwīlum heaþorōfe   hlēapan lēton,
865 on geflit faran   fealwe mēaras,
ðǣr him foldwegas   fægere þūhton,
cystum cūðe.   Hwīlum cyninges þegn,
guma gilphlæden,   gidda gemyndig,
sē ðe ealfela   ealdgesegena
870 worn gemunde,   word ōþer fand
sōðe gebunden;   secg eft ongan
sīð Bēowulfes   snyttrum styrian,
ond on spēd wrecan   spel gerāde,
wordum wrixlan; ⁄ wēlhwylc gecwæð,
875 þæt hē fram Sigemunde[s]   secgan hȳrde
ellendǣdum,   uncūþes fela,
Wælsinges gewin,   wīde sīðas,
þāra þe gumena bearn   gearwe ne wiston,
fǣhðe ond fyrena,   būton Fitela mid hine,
880 þonne hē swulces hwæt   secgan wolde,
ēam his nefan,   swā hīe ā wǣron
æt nīða gehwām   nȳdgesteallan;
hæfdon ealfela   eotena cynnes
sweordum gesǣged.   Sigemunde gesprong
885 æfter dēaðdæge   dōm unlȳtel,
syþðan wīges heard   wyrm ācwealde,
hordes hyrde;   hē under hārne stān,
æþelinges bearn   āna geneōðde
frēcne dǣde,   ne wæs him Fitela mid;

871ᵇ *Rie.Zs. 390* secg[an]. — 872ᵇ *Fol. 149ᵃ* styrian. — 875ᵃ *MS.* sige **munde**; *Gr.¹, Schü., Sed.* Sigemunde[s]; *Holt.* (*cf. Siev. R. 463 f.*) Sigmunde[s], *so 884ᵇ*: **Sigmunde** *Cf. Lang.* § *18.10 n.* — 879ᵃ *MS.* fyrenē.

BEOWULF

890 hwæþre him gesælde, ðæt þæt swurd þurhwōd
wrætlīcne wyrm, þæt hit on wealle ætstōd,
dryhtlīc īren; draca morðre swealt.
Hæfde āglǣca elne gegongen,
þæt hē bēahhordes brūcan mōste
895 selfes dōme; sǣbāt gehlēod,
bær on bearm scipes beorhte frætwa,
Wælses eafera; wyrm hāt gemealt.
Sē wæs wreccena wīde mǣrost
ofer werþēode, wīgendra hlēo,
900 ellendǣdum — hē þæs ǣr onðāh —,
siððan Heremōdes hild sweðrode,
eafoð ond ellen. Hē mid Ēotenum wearð
on fēonda geweald forð forlācen,
snūde forsended. Hine sorhwylmas
905 lemede tō lange; hē his lēodum wearð,
eallum æþellingum tō aldorceare;
swylce oft bemearn ǣrran mǣlum
swīðferhþes sīð snotor ceorl monig,
sē þe him bealwa tō bōte gelȳfde,
910 þæt þæt ðēodnes bearn geþēon scolde,
fæderæþelum onfōn, folc gehealdan,
hord ond hlēoburh, hæleþa rīce,
ēþel Scyldinga. Hē þǣr eallum wearð
mǣg Higelāces manna cynne,
915 frēondum gefǣgra; hine fyren onwōd.
Hwīlum flītende fealwe strǣte

895[b] *Fol. 149[b]* sǣ. — *Tho., most Edd.* gehlōd. — 897[b] *Scherer L 5.5.494, Tr.*[1] *174* hāte. *Cf. MPh. iii 251.* — 900[b] *Cos. viii 568, Holt.*[1–5] āron ðāh; *Boer 26* ār onþāh ('received honor'). — 902[a] *MS.* earfoð; *Grimm Andr. & Elene p. 101* (?), *Gr.*[1], *most Edd.* eafoð. — 902[b] *Ke., et al., Cha.* eotenum; *Ke. ii, et al.* Ēotenum. — 904[b] *Bu. 41* sorhwylma hrine. — 905[a] *Gru.tr. 280, Ke., Holt.* lemedon. — 911[a] *Tho., et al.* fæder æþelum. — 913[a] *MS.* ℟. — 915[a] *Ke. ii* gef[r]ǣgra; *Gru.* gefægenra (?). — 916[b] *Aant. 16* fealwum.

mearum mæton.   Ðā wæs morgenlēoht
scofen ond scynded.   Ēode scealc monig
swīðhicgende   tō sele þām hēan
920 searowundor sēon;   swylce self cyning
of brȳdbūre,   bēahhorda weard,
tryddode tīrfæst   getrume micle,
cystum gecȳþed,   ond his cwēn mid him
medostigge mæt   mægþa hōse.
XIIII 925 Hrōðgār maþelode   — hē tō healle gēong,
stōd on stapole,   geseah stēapne hrōf
golde fāhne   ond Grendles hond — :
'Ðisse ansȳne   Alwealdan þanc
lungre gelimpe!   Fela ic lāþes gebād,
930 grynna æt Grendle;   ā mæg God wyrcan
wunder æfter wundre,   wuldres Hyrde.
Ðæt wæs ungeāra,   þæt ic ǣnigra mē
wēana ne wēnde   tō wīdan feore
bōte gebīdan,   þonne blōde fāh
935 hūsa sēlest   heorodrēorig stōd, —
wēa wīdscofen   witena gehwylc*um*
ðāra þe ne wēndon,   þæt hīe wīdeferhð
lēoda landgeweorc   lāþum beweredon
scuccum ond scinnum.   Nū scealc hafað
940 þurh Drihtnes miht   dǣd gefremede,
ðē wē ealle   ǣr ne meahton
snyttrum besyrwan.   Hwæt, þæt secgan mæg
efne swā hwylc mægþa   swā ðone magan cende
æfter gumcynnum,   gyf hēo gȳt lyfað,
945 þæt hyre Ealdmetod   ēste wǣre

918[b] *Fol. 150[a]* eode. — 926[a] *Rask (in Gru.), Gr.[1] p. 369 (?), Bu. 90, Tr.* staþole. — 936[a] *Gru.tr. 281* wēan wīdscufon; *Gru.* wēan wiðscufon (?); *Tr.* [hæfde] (*cf. Bu. 90*) wēa wiðscofen (*cf. Gr.[2]*); *Holt.[2] ii (?), Sed.* wēan wīde scufon. — 936[b] *MS.* ge hwylcne; *Ke. ii, Holt., Schü., Cha.* gehwylcum; *cf. ESt. xlii 326.* — 939[a] *Fol. 150[b]* scuccum *A B.* — 945[a] *Tho., Gr., Gru., et al.* eald Metod.

BEOWULF

bearngebyrdo. Nū ic, Bēowulf, þec,
secg betsta, mē for sunu wylle
frēogan on ferhþe; heald forð tela
nīwe sibbe. Ne bið þē [n]ænigre gād
950 worolde wilna, þē ic geweald hæbbe.
Ful oft ic for læssan lēan teohhode,
hordweorþunge hnāhran rince,
sæmran æt sæcce. Þū þē self hafast
dædum gefremed, þæt þīn [dōm] lyfað
955 āwa tō aldre. Alwalda þec
gōde forgylde, swā hē nū gȳt dyde!'
Bēowulf maþelode, bearn Ec[g]þēowes:
'Wē þæt ellenweorc ēstum miclum,
feohtan fremedon, frēcne genēðdon
960 eafoð uncūþes. Ūþe ic swīþor,
þæt ðū hine selfne gesēon mōste,
fēond on frætewum fylwērigne!
Ic hine hrædlīce heardan clammum
on wælbedde wrīþan þōhte,
965 þæt hē for mundgripe mīnum scolde
licgean līfbysig, būtan his līc swice;
ic hine ne mihte, þā Metod nolde,
ganges getwǣman, nō ic him þæs georne ætfealh,
feorhgenīðlan; wæs tō foremihtig
970 fēond on fēþe. Hwæþere hē his folme forlēt
tō līfwraþe lāst weardian,
earm ond eaxle; nō þær ǣnige swā þēah
fēasceaft guma frōfre gebohte;

₉₄₇^a *Siev. R. 312, Tr., 4 Edd.* secg[a]; *Tr.*¹ *175* secg [se] (?). *See T.C.* § 22. — 949^b *MS.*
ænigre; *Gr.*¹ (*see Bu.Zs. 203 f.*), *Schü., Cha.* [n]ænigra; *Tr.*¹ *175* (?), *Sed., Holt.* [n]ænges.
Cf. Lang. § *18.3.* — 954^a *Holt. Lit.bl. xxi 64, Holt.*², *Cha.* [mid] d.; *Holt.*^{3–6} d. gefremed[ne].
Cf. T.C. § *17.* — 954^b *Ke., Edd.* [dōm]. — 957^b *MS.* ec; *Tho., many Edd.* Ec[g]-. *So 980*^b.
— 962^a *Gru.tr. 281* fæterum. — 963^a *MS.* him; *Tho.* hine. — 963^b *Fol. 151*^{c.} heardan. —
965^a *MS.* hand; *Ke.* mund-

nō þȳ leng leofað lāðgetēona
975 synnum geswenced, ac hyne sār hafað
in nīdgripe nearwe befongen,
balwon bendum; ðǣr ābīdan sceal
maga māne fāh miclan dōmes,
hū him scīr Metod scrīfan wille.'
980 Ðā wæs swīgra secg, sunu Ec[g]lāfes,
on gylpsprǣce gūðgeweorca,
siþðan æþelingas eorles cræfte
ofer hēanne hrōf hand scēawedon,
fēondes fingras; foran ǣghwylc wæs,
985 stīð[r]a nægla gehwylc stȳle gelīcost,
hǣþenes handsporu hilderinces
egl[u] unhēoru; ǣghwylc gecwæð,
þæt him heardra nān hrīnan wolde
īren ǣrgōd, þæt ðæs āhlǣcan
990 blōdge beadufolme onberan wolde.
XV Ðā wæs hāten hreþe Heort innanweard
folmum gefrætwod; fela þǣra wæs,
wera ond wīfa, þē þæt wīnreced,
gestsele gyredon. Goldfāg scinon
995 web æfter wāgum, wundorsīona fela
secga gehwylcum þāra þe on swylc starað.
Wæs þæt beorhte bold tōbrocen swīðe

976ᵃ *MS.* mid; *Tho., Sed.* nīð-; *Gru. p. 209, Bu.Tid. 49, Cha.* nȳd-; *Schü.* (*see ESt. xxxix 105 f.*), *Holt.* mid nȳd-. — 980ᵇ. *See 957ᵇ.* — 984ᵇ *Miller Angl. xii 397* ǣghwylcne. — 985ᵃ *MS.* steda; *Gru.* stedig; *E., Siev. ix 138, Holt.* stīð[r]a; *Sed.* (*cf. MLR. v 287*) stīðnægla; *see 1533ᵃ.* — *MS.* nægla ge hwylc; *Tho., E., Siev.l.c., Holt. cancel* gehwylc. — 986ᵃ *Rie.Zs. 390* -speru, *Holt.* -speoru. — 986ᵇ hilde *last word of Fol. 151ᵃ erroneously repeated on Fol. 151ᵇ.* — 987ᵃ *MS.* egl; *Ke. ii* egl[e] (*noun*); *Rie.Zs. 391, Holt., Schü.* egl' (*adj.*); *Tr.* egl[u] (*adj.*). *Cf. T.C. § 25.* — 989ᵇ, 990ᵇ *Gru. p. 131, Siev. ix 139, Holt.*¹⁻⁵, *Sed.* þē *for* þæt (*ref. to* him *988, i.e. Bēowulf*). — *Siev. l.c., Holt.*¹⁻⁵ āberan mihte. — 991ᵃ *Gru.tr. 282, Gru.* hēa(h)timbrede (?) (*for* hāten hreþe), *Bu.Tid. 50* hēatimbred; *Tr.* handum *for* hāten. *Cf. also Klu. ix 189; Bu. 91; Tr.*¹ *178; Sed.* (& *MLR. v 287*).

eal inneweard īrenbendum fæst,
heorras tōhlidene; hrōf āna genæs
1000 ealles ansund, þē se āglǣca
fyrendǣdum fāg on flēam gewand,
aldres orwēna. Nō þæt ȳðe byð
tō beflēonne — fremme sē þe wille —,
ac gesēcan sceal sāwlberendra
1005 nȳde genȳdde, niþða bearna,
grundbūendra gearwe stōwe,
þǣr his līchoma legerbedde fæst
swefeþ æfter symle.
þā wæs sǣl ond mǣl,
þæt tō healle gang Healfdenes sunu;
1010 wolde self cyning symbel þicgan,
Ne gefrægen ic þā mǣgþe māran weorode
ymb hyra sincgyfan sēl gebǣran.
Bugon þā tō bence blǣdāgande,
fylle gefǣgon; fǣgere geþǣgon
1015 medoful manig māgas þāra
swīðhicgende on sele þām hēan,
Hrōðgār ond Hrōþulf. Heorot innan wæs
frēondum āfylled; nalles fācenstafas
Þēod-Scyldingas þenden fremedon. —
1020 Forgeaf þā Bēowulfe bearn Healfdenes
segen gyldenne sigores tō lēane,
hroden hildecumbor, helm ond byrnan;
mǣre māðþumsweord manige gesāwon

---

998 *Holt.*²⁻⁵ eal inneweard fæst/īrenbendum. — 1000ᵇ *E.Sc., Tho., Holt., Sed.* þā (*for* þē). *See Gloss.*: þē. — 1004ᵃ *MS.* ge sacan; *Ke.* ii, 4 *Edd.* gesēc(e)an, *cf. Siev. R. 291, Lang.* § 9.3. — 1009ᵃ *Fol. 152ᵃ* gang. — 1015ᵇ *MS.* þara; *t.Br. 73, Angl. xxviii 442, Holt.*²⁻⁵ wǣron(-an); *Schü., Sed.* wāron, *Cha.* wāran (*cf. Lang.* § 6 n. 2); *Hornburg L 4.133-23, Tr.*¹ *180, Tr.* þwǣre. *Cf. Bu. 91.* — 1020ᵇ *MS.* brand; *Gru.tr. 282* bearn. — 1022ᵃ *MS.* hilte cumbor; *E.Sc., Gr.*¹, *Rie.Zs. 392, Holt., Schü., Hoops* hilde-; *Cos.* (*in Hold.*²) bilt-; *Tr.*¹ *180* hilted. (*Ke., Tho.* hrodenhilte.)

BEOWULF 39

    beforan beorn beran.   Bēowulf geþah
1025 ful on flette;   nō hē þǣre feohgyfte
    for sc[ē]oten[d]um   scamigan ðorfte, —
    ne gefrægn ic frēondlīcor   fēower mādmas
    golde gegyrede   gummanna fela
    in ealobence   ōðrum gesellan.
1030 Ymb þæs helmes hrōf   hēafodbeorge
    wīrum bewunden   wal*a* ūtan hēold,
    þæt him fēla lāf   frēcne ne meaht*e*
    scūrheard sceþðan,   þonne scyldfreca
    ongēan gramum   gangan scolde.
1035 Heht ðā eorla hlēo   eahta mēaras
    fǣtedhlēore   on flet tēon,
    in under eoderas;   þāra ānum stōd
    sadol searwum fāh,   since gewurþad;
    þæt wæs hildesetl   hēahcyninges,
1040 ðonne sweorda gelāc   sunu Healfdenes
    efnan wolde, —   nǣfre on ōre læg
    wīdcūþes wīg,   ðonne walu fēollon.
    Ond ðā Bēowulfe   bēga gehwæþres
    eodor Ingwina   onweald getēah,
1045 wicga ond wǣpna;   hēt hine wēl brūcan.
    Swā manlīce   mǣre þēoden,
    hordweard hæleþa   heaþorǣsas geald
    mēarum ond mādmum,   swā hȳ nǣfre man lȳhð,
    sē þe secgan wile   sōð æfter rihte.
XVI 1050   Ðā gȳt ǣghwylcum   eorla drihten
    þāra þe mid Bēowulfe   brimlāde tēah,

1024[b] *Holt.*[1–5], *Hoops* geþeah; *Holt.*[6] geþāh. See *Lang.* § 23.3. — 1026[a] *MS.* scotenum; *Ke. ii, 4 Edd.* sc[ē]oten[d]um. — 1031[b] *MS.* walan; *E.Sc., Holt., Schü., Cha.* wala; *Siev. R. 257, Bu. 369, Sed.* walu. — 1032[a] *Tho.* fealo; *Rie.L., Sed.* fēola. — *Fol. 152*[b] laf *A B; Gr.*[1], *et al.* lāf[e]. — 1032[b] *MS.* meahton; *Ke. ii, Schü., Sed.* meahte. — 1037[b] *Aant. 18, Holt.*[2–5] [on] ānum. — 1048[b] *Siev. R. 269* [ne] lyhð, *or* leïð. *Cf. T.C.* § 1. — 1051[b] *MS.* leade; *Ke.* -lāde.

40 BEOWULF

on þǣre medubence   māþðum gesealde,
yrfelāfe,   ond þone ǣnne heht
golde forgyldan,   þone ðe Grendel ǣr
1055 māne ācwealde, —   swā hē hyra mā wolde,
nefne him wītig God   wyrd forstōde
ond ðæs mannes mōd.   Metod eallum wēold
gumena cynnes,   swā hē nū gīt dêð.
Forþan bið andgit   ǣghwǣr sēlest,
1060 ferhðes foreþanc.   Fela sceal gebīdan
lēofes ond lāþes   sē þe longe hēr
on ðyssum windagum   worolde brūceð!
Þǣr wæs sang ond swēg   samod ætgædere
fore Healfdenes   hildewīsan,
1065 gomenwudu grēted,   gid oft wrecen,
ðonne healgamen   Hrōþgāres scop
æfter medobence   mǣnan scolde,
[be] Finnes eaferum,   ðā hīe se fǣr begeat,
hæleð Healf-Dena,   Hnæf Scyldinga
1070 in Frēswæle   feallan scolde.
Nē hūru Hildeburh   herian þorfte
Ēotena trēowe;   unsynnum wearð
beloren lēofum   æt þām *lin*dplegan
bearnum ond brōðrum;   hīe on gebyrd hruron
1075 gāre wunde;   þæt wæs geōmuru ides!
Nalles hōlinga   Hōces dohtor
meotodsceaft bemearn,   syþðan morgen cōm,
ðā hēo under swegle   gesēon meahte

1053ᵃ *Fol. 153ᵃ* fe lafe. — 1064ʰ *Mö. ESt. xiii 180* ofer ('concerning,' *for* fore); *Holt.*
for. — *Lübke Anz.fdA. xix 342* H. [suna]; *Tr.- 183* Hrōðgāres, *Tr. F. 11, Tr., Malone
JEGPh. xxv 116* Healfdena. — 1065ᵇ *Lübke l.c., Tr.* eft. — 1068ᵃ *Tho.* (*in Ke.*) [be];
*Tr.*¹ *183, Holt.*²⁻⁴, *Schü.* eaferan; *Tr. F. 11 f., Tr.* gefēran; *Rie.L., Holt.*¹, *Imelmann LF.
4.24, Sed. assume lacuna before* 1068. — 1069ᵃ *Gru.tr. 283, Ke., et al.* Healfdenes. — 1072ᵇ
Gru. unsynnig *or* unsynnigum; *Holt.*¹⁻⁵ (*cf. Beibl. x 273*), *Tr. F. 13, Tr.* unsyn(n)gum.
See 2089ᵇ. Cf. Krapp MPh. ii 404 & note on Andr. 109. — 1073ᵇ *MS.* hild; *Ke.* lind-. —
1075ᵃ *Fol. 153ᵇ* wunde *AB*.

BEOWULF

<blockquote>

morþorbealo māga, þǣr hē[o] ǣr mǣste hēold
1080 worolde wynne. Wīg ealle fornam
Finnes þegnas nemne fēaum ānum,
þæt hē ne mehte on þǣm meðelstede
wīg Hengeste wiht gefeohtan,
nē þā wēalāfe wīge forþringan
1085 þēodnes ðegne; ac hig him geþingo budon,
þæt hīe him ōðer flet eal gerȳmdon,
healle ond hēahsetl, þæt hīe healfre geweald
wið Ēotena bearn āgan mōston,
ond æt feohgyftum Folcwaldan sunu
1090 dōgra gehwylce Dene weorþode,
Hengestes hēap hringum wenede
efne swā swīðe sincgestrēonum
fǣttan goldes, swā hē Frēsena cyn
on bēorsele byldan wolde.
1095 Ðā hīe getruwedon on twā healfa
fæste frioðuwǣre. Fin Hengeste
elne unflitme āðum benemde,
þæt hē þā wēalāfe weotena dōme
ārum hēolde, þæt ðǣr ǣnig mon
1100 wordum nē worcum wǣre ne brǣce,
nē þurh inwitsearo ǣfre gemǣnden,
ðēah hīe hira bēaggyfan banan folgedon
ðēodenlēase, þā him swā geþearfod wæs;
gyf þonne Frȳsna hwylc frēcnan sprǣce

</blockquote>

<small>1079^b MS. he; E.Sc., Tho., Edd. hē[o]; Cha. hē (begins sentence w. þǣr hē). — 1081^b MS. feaᵘ — 1083 Gr.¹ Wīg-Hengeste (?) [cp. e.g. 63, 1108; Bǫðvarr Bjarki, Intr. xxvi n. 8]; Rie.L. & Zs. 394 wiht H. wið g.; Holt.³⁻⁵ wiþ for wiht. Cf. also Tr. F. 15f., Tr., Angl. xxviii 444; Binz ZfdPh. xxxvii 530. — 1085ᵃ Brown ðegna (see note). — 1087ᵇ ESc. (?), Tho., Tr. F. 17, Tr., Holt.¹⁻⁵, Sed. healfne. — 1095ᵃ See 669ᵇ Varr. — 1097ᵃ Gru. unhlytme (?), see 1129; Tr.¹ 185 unslāwe (cp. Guðl. 923); Tr. F. 24, Tr. unblinne; Holt. Lit. bl. xxi 64 unslitne. — 1097ᵇ Fol. 154ᵃ be. — 1104ᵇ MS. frecnen; Tho. frecnan, Gr.¹ frēcnan. Cf. T.C. § 16.</small>

1105 ðæs morþorhetes myndgiend wære,
þonne hit sweordes ecg sēðan scolde. —
Ād wæs geæfned, ond icge gold
āhæfen of horde. Here-Scyldinga
betst beadorinca wæs on bǣl gearu.
1110 Æt þǣm āde wæs ēþgesȳne
swātfāh syrce, swȳn ealgylden,
eofer īrenheard, æþeling manig
wundum āwyrded; sume on wæle crungon!
Hēt ðā Hildeburh æt Hnæfes āde
1115 hire selfre sunu sweoloðe befæstan,
bānfatu bærnan, ond on bǣl dōn
ēame on eaxle. Ides gnornode,
geōmrode giddum. Gūðrinc āstāh.
Wand tō wolcnum wælfȳra mǣst,
1120 hlynode for hlāwe; hafelan multon,
bengeato burston, ðonne blōd ætspranc,
lāðbite līces. Līg ealle forswealg,
gǣsta gīfrost, þāra ðe þǣr gūð fornam
bēga folces; wæs hira blǣd scacen.
XVII 1125 Gewiton him ðā wīgend wīca nēosian

1105b *Tr. F. 32, Tr., Holt.* myndgend. — 1106b *MS.* syððan; *Tr. F. 19 (?), Tr., Sed.* sehtan; *JEGPh. viii 255* sēðan (*or* sēman (?), *so Tr. F. 19 (?)); Holt.*³⁻⁵ swȳðan (*or* snyð-ðan); *Imelmann D. Lit.z. xxx 998* scȳran; *Siev. ix 130: gap after* scolde; *Schü. (ESt. xlii 109 f.) thinks* myndgiend wesan *understood. So Hoops.* — 1107ª *MS.* að, *Edd.* Āð; *Gru.tr. 283, Gru.* Ād. — 1107b *MS.* ⁊ icge; *Ke. ii* īcge ('vegetus'?); *E.Sc. (?), Rie.L. (?), Singer Beitr. xii 213* incge (*cp. 2577*); *Bu. 30* ondīege ('openly,' *cp. 1935ª Varr.); Holt. Beibl. xiii 364*=īdge (Īdig 'resplendent'), *Holt.*² ītge (*cp. ON.* ītr, *see 33ª Varr.); Holt.*³ īcge ('eagerly,'=īdge, *Phoen. 407). Cf. also Tr.*¹ *185, Tr. F. 20, Tr.; Grienb. Angl. xxvii 331 f., Beitr. xxxvi 95, Siev. ib. 421.* — 1115ª *Tho., Gr.*¹ suna, *cf. Cos. viii 569.* — 1117ª *MS.* earme; *Holt. Beitr. xvi 549 f., Sed.* ēame; *Tho.* axe ('ashes') *for* eaxle; *Boer ZfdA. xlvii 135* earm ond eaxle (?). — 1118b *Gru.tr. 284, Gru., Rie.Zs. 395* gūðrēc (*cp. 3144); Gr.*¹ (?) gūðhring (='clamor'?), *so Sed.* (='spirals of smoke'); *Scherer L 5.5.494, Boer l.c.* gūðrincas tāh. — 1119ª *Fol. 154*b *to AB.* — 1120ª *Gru., Tr. F. 21, Tr.* from *for* for. — *Holt. Zs. 116* hrāwe. *Cf. also ESt. xxxix 463.* — 1121b *Many Edd. connect* ætspranc *w.* lāðbite, *omitting comma. But see Schü. ESt. xlii 110.* — 1125b *Holt., Schü.* nēosan. *See T.C. § 9.*

freōndum befeallen,   Frȳsland gesēon,
hāmas ond hēaburh.   Hengest ðā gȳt
wælfāgne wintẹr   wunode mid Finne
[ea]l unhlitme;   eard gemunde,
1130 þēah þe *ne* meahte   on mere drīfan
hringedstefnan, —   holm storme wēol,
won wið winde,   wintẹr ȳþe belēac
īsgebinde,   oþ ðæt ōþer cōm
gēar in geardas, —   swā nū gȳt dêð,
1135 þā ðe syngāles   sēle bewitiað,
wuldọrtorhtan weder.   Ðā wæs winter scacen,
fæger foldan bearm;   fundode wrecca,
gist of geardum;   hē tō gyrnwræce
swīðor þōhte   þonne tō sælāde,
1140 gif hē torngemōt   þurhtēon mihte,
þæt hē Ēotena bearn   īrne gemunde.
Swā hē ne forwyrnde   w[e]oro*d*ræden*d*e,
þonne him Hūnlāfing   hildelēoman,
billa sēlest   on bearm dyde;
1145 þæs wæron mid Ēotenum   ecge cūðe.
Swylce ferhðfrecan   Fin eft begeat
sweordbealo slīðen   æt his selfes hām,
siþðan grimne gripe   Gūðlāf ond Ōslāf
æfter sæsīðe   sorge mændon,

1128ᵇ⁻²⁹ᵃ *MS.* finnel unhlitme; *Ke.* Finne/elne (*cp. 1097ᵃ*) unhlitme; *so Holt.*¹⁻⁸, *Schü., Cha.; He.*¹⁻⁵ Finne/ealles unhlitme; *Tho.* Finne/unflitme (*cp. 1097ᵃ*); *Rie.L. & Zs. 397, Sed.* F./elne unflitme; *Gr.*¹ F./ēðles unhlitme; *Kock*² *110* F./unhlīte ('misfortune,' 'exile') in. *Cf. Tr.*¹ *187 f., Tr. F. 23 f.* — 1130ᵃ *MS.* þeah þe he; *Gru.tr. 284, many Edd., Sed., Cha.* [ne] meahte; *Holt.*⁵,⁶ þēah þe ne. — 1134ᵇ–35ᵃ *Tho.* dōð; *Aant. 20, Holt., Schü.* dōað. — *Gr.*¹, *Sed.* (*cf. MLR. v 287*) dēð/þām ðe. *Cf. also Siev. ix 139; Bu. 30 f.* — 1139ᵃ *Fol. 155ᵃ* þohte *AB.* — 1140ᵃ *Gru.* torngemōd. — 1141ᵃ⁻ᵇ *Tho.* þæs *for* þæt; *Gru.* þæt hyt *for* þæt hē; *Siev. Beitr. xii 193, Holt.*³ þǣr hē; *Cos. Beitr. xxi 26, Sed., Holt.*⁴⁻⁶ þæt hē [wið]. — *Rie.L.* bearnum *and* gemynte. — *MS.* inne; *Tr. F. 25, Tr.* īrne *for* inne. — *Cf. Rie.Zs. 397; Bu. 31; ESt. xxxix 430.* — 1142ᵇ *MS.* worold rædenne; *Mö. 68, Bu. 32, Sed.* worodrædenne; *Malone JEGPh. xxv 159* (*cf. Haml. 22*) woroldrædende; *A. lvi 421* worodrædende. *Schü.* makes 1142 *subordinate clause, close of period.* — 1143ᵃ *Bu. 32, Tr. F. 26, Tr.* Hūn Lāfing. — 1143ᵇ *Holt.* Hildelēoman.

1150 ætwiton wēana dǣl;   ne meahte wǣfre mōd
forhabban in hreþre.   Ðā wæs heal *r*oden
fēonda fēorum,   swilce Fin slægen,
cyning on corþre,   ond sēo cwēn numen.
Scēotend Scyldinga   tō scypon feredon
1155 eal ingesteald   eorðcyninges,
swylce hīe æt Finnes hām   findan meahton
sigla searogimma.   Hīe on sǣlāde
drihtlīce wīf   tō Denum feredon,
lǣddon tō lēodum.
                   Lēoð wæs āsungen,
1160 glēomannes gyd.   Gamen eft āstāh,
beorhtode bencswēg,   byrelas sealdon
wīn of wundẹrfatum.   Þā cwōm Wealhþēo forð
gān under gyldnum bēage   þǣr þā gōdan twēgen
sǣton suhtergefæderan;   þā gȳt wæs hiera sib ætgædere,
ǣghwylc ōðrum trȳwe.   Swylce þǣr *U*nferþ þyle
æt fōtum sæt frēan Scyldinga;   gehwylc hiora his ferhþe
                                    trēowde,
þæt hē hæfde mōd micel,   þēah þe hē his māgum nǣre
ārfæst æt ecga gelācum.   Spræc ðā ides Scyldinga:
'Onfōh þissum fulle,   frēodrihten mīn,
1170 sinces brytta!   Þū on sǣlum wes,
goldwine gumena,   ond tō Gēatum spræc
mildum wordum,   swā sceal man dôn!
Bēo wið Gēatas glæd,   geofena gemyndig,
nēan ond feorran   þū nū hafast.

1151ᵇ *MS*. hroden; *Bu.Tid. 64, 295* roden. *See T.C.* § *28*. — 1156ᵃ *Tr., Holt*. swylc.
— 1159ᵃ *Fol*. 155ᵇ *to AB*. — 1161ᵃ *Sed*. (*cf. MLR. v 287*) beorhtmode (*cþ*. bearhtm). —
1165ᵇ *MS*. hun ferþ; *Rie.Zs. 414* Unferð. *See 499ᵃ*. — 1174ᵇ *E.Sc., et al*. þ. n. [friðu] h.
[*metr. objectionable: Rie.V. 29, T.C.* § *5 n*.]; *Rie. l.c.* þ. nȳd h. (*and punct. after* feorran,
like Ke., Tho., Gru.); *Bu. 92 inserts after* 1174ᵇ [secgas ætsomne in sele þām hēan]; *Tr.*¹
191 [þā] *or* [þē] þ., *Sed*. [þē] þ.; *Siev. ESt. xliv 297* [þē] þ., *and lacuna before* 1174. *Cf.
JEGPh. viii 256 f.; Schü. ESt. xliv 157*.

1175 Mē man sægde, þæt þū ðē for sunu wolde
hereri[n]c habban.   Heorot is gefælsod,
bēahsele beorhta;   brūc þenden þū mōte
manigra mēdo,   ond þīnum māgum læf
folc ond rīce,   þonne ðū forð scyle,
1180 metodsceaft sēon.   Ic mīnne can
glædne Hrōþulf,   þæt hē þā geogoðe wile
ārum healdan,   gyf þū ǣr þonne hē,
wine Scildinga,   worold oflǣtest;
wēne ic þæt hē mid gōde   gyldan wille
1185 uncran eaferan,   gif hē þæt eal gemon,
hwæt wit tō willan   ond tō worðmyndum
umborwesendum ǣr   ārna gefremedon.'
Hwearf þā bī bence,   þǣr hyre byre wǣron,
Hrēðrīc ond Hrōðmund,   ond hæleþa bearn,
1190 giogoð ætgædere;   þǣr se gōda sæt,
Bēowulf Gēata   be þǣm gebrōðrum twǣm.

XVIII   .Him wæs ful boren,   ond frēondlaþu
wordum bewægned,   ond wunden gold
ēstum geēawed,   earm[h]rēade twā,
1195 hrægl ond hringas,   healsbēaga mǣst
þāra þe ic on foldan   gefrægen hæbbe.
Nǣnigne ic under swegle   sēlran hȳrde
hordmāðum hæleþa,   syþðan Hāma ætwæg
tō þǣre byrhtan byrig   Brōsinga mene,
1200 sigle ond sincfæt, —   searonīðas flēah
Eormenrīces,   gecēas ēcne rǣd. —

1175ª *Gru.* [swā] mē. — 1175ᵇ *Fol. 156ª* þu *AB.* — 1176ª *MS.* here ric; *Ke.* hereri[n]c. *Cp. 2466ª MS.* heaðo riⁿc. — 1178ª *MS. AB* medo; *Ke., et al.* mēda; *Gr.*¹ māðma (?); *Tr.*¹ *191* mērða (?); *Tr.* mēða. *Cf. Lang.* § *18.3.* — 1194ᵇ *MS.* reade; *Gr.*¹ -[h]rēade. — 1195ª *Fol. 156ᵇ* gas *AB.* — 1198ª *MS.* mad mum; *E.Sc.* -māðum (?); *Gr.* -māððum; *Gru.* -māðm; *Cha.* -mādm. *See Siev. A. M.* § *85 n. 2. Cp. 2193ª.* — 1199ª *MS.* here; *E.Sc.* þǣre. — 1199ᵇ *Grimm D. M. 255 (307), Bu. 75* Brīsinga. — 1200ᵇ *MS.* fealh; *Leo L 4.24.44, Gru.* flēah.

Þone hring hæfde   Higelāc Gēata,
nefa Swertinges   nȳhstan sīðe,
siðþan hē under segne   sinc ealgode,
1205 wælrēaf werede;   hyne wyrd fornam,
syþðan hē for wlenco   wēan āhsode,
fæhðe tō Frȳsum.   Hē þā frætwe wæg,
eorclanstānas   ofer ȳða ful,
rīce þēoden;   hē under rande gecranc.
1210 Gehwearf þā in Francna fæþm   feorh cyninges,
brēostgewǣdu,   ond se bēah somod;
wyrsan wīgfrecan   wæl rēafedon
æfter gūðsceare,   Gēata lēode
hrēawīc hēoldon. —   Heal swēge onfēng.
1215 Wealhðēo maþelode,   hēo fore þǣm werede sprǣc:
' Brūc ðisses bēages,   Bēowulf lēofa,
hyse, mid hǣle,   ond þisses hrægles nēot,
þēo[d]gestrēona,   ond geþēoh tela,
cen þec mid cræfte,   ond þyssum cnyhtum wes
1220 lāra līðe!   Ic þē þæs lēan geman.
Hafast þū gefēred,   þæt ðē feor ond nēah
ealne wīdeferhþ   weras ehtigað,
efne swā sīde   swā sǣ bebūgeð,
windgeard, weallas.   Wes þenden þū lifige,
1225 æþeling, ēadig!   Ic þē an tela
sincgestrēona.   Bēo þū suna mīnum
dǣdum gedēfe,   drēamhealdende!

1208ᵃ *Gru.tr. 285, et al.* eorcnan-. — 1210ᵇ *Siev. ix 139* ieoh. — 1212ᵇ *MS.* **reafeden;** *E.Sc.* rēafedon. *Cf. T.C.* § *16.* — 1213ᵃ *Holtzm. 494* gūðceare. — 1213ᵇ *E.Sc., Gru., E., Schü., Sed. place comma after* lēode. — 1214ᵇ *Cos. viii 570, Aant. 21* healsbēge (=-bēage). — 1217ᵇ *Fol. 157ᵃ* ⁊ *A.* — 1218ᵃ *MS.* þeo; *Gru.tr. 285, Ke.* þēo[d]-. — 1224ᵃ *MS.* **wind geard weallas;** *Ke., et al.* windge eardweallas; *E.Sc.* windige weallas; *Krackow Arch. cxi 171, cf. L 7.19.44* windgeard weallas. *See T.C.* § *28 n. 2.* — 1225ᵃ *Several Edd. omit comma after* æþeling. *See MPh. iii 457.*

Hēr is ǣghwylc eorl   ōþrum getrȳwe,
mōdes milde,   mandrihtne hol[d],
1230 þegnas syndon geþwǣre,   þēod ealgearo,
druncne dryhtguman   dōð swā ic bidde.'
Ēode þā tō setle.   Þǣr wæs symbla cyst,
druncon wīn weras.   Wyrd ne cūþon,
geōsceaft grim*m*e,   swā hit āgangen wearð
1235 eorla manegum,   syþðan ǣfen cwōm,
ond him Hrōþgār gewāt   tō hofe sīnum,
rīce tō ræste.   Reced weardode
unrīm eorla,   swā hīe oft ǣr dydon.
Bencþelu beredon;   hit geondbrǣded wearð
1240 beddum ond bolstrum.   Bēorscealca sum
fūs ond fǣge   fletræste gebēag.
Setton him tō hēafdon   hilderandas,
bordwudu beorhtan;   þǣr on bence wæs
ofer æþelinge   ȳþgesēne
1245 heaþostēapa helm,   hringed byrne,
þrecwudu þrymlīc.   Wæs þēaw hyra,
þæt hīe oft wǣron   an wīg gearwe,
gē æt hām gē on herge,   gē gehwæþer þāra
efne swylce mǣla,   swylce hira mandryhtne
1250 þearf gesǣlde;   wæs sēo þēod tilu.

XVIIII Sigon þā tō slǣpe.   Sum sāre angeald
ǣfenræste,   swā him ful oft gelamp,
siþðan goldsele   Grendel warode,

1229ᵇ *MS.* hol (*changed from* heol); *Thk., Ke.* hol[d]. — 1230ᵇ. *See* 77ᵇ. — 1231ᵇ *MS.* dōð; *Siev. ix 140, Holt., Sed.* dō. — 1234ᵃ *Klu. Beitr. viii 533 f., Holt.*¹⁻⁵ geasceaft (*supposed ancient form of* gesceaft *w. stressed prefix*). *So* 1266ᵃ. — *MS.* grim*m*ne; *E.Sc.* grimme. — 1235 *Several Edd.* (*thus Schü., Sed., cf. Schü. Sa. pp. xxiv, 119*) *begin a fresh sentence at* syþðan *and make it end w.* ræste 1237ᵃ; *Cha. includes in that sentence* 1235ᵇ-38ᵇ. *But see* 2103ᵇ-4, 1784ᵇ, 2124ᵇ, 2303ᵇ. — 1241ᵇ *Fol.* 157ᵇ beag *AB.* — 1247ᵇ *E.Sc., Cha., Prokosch Kl. Misc. 201* ānwīggearwe; *Cos. viii 570* an(d)wīg-, *Holt., Sed.* anwīg-. *See Rie.Zs. 405; MPh. iii 458; Gloss.: on.* — 1248ᵇ *E.Sc., et al. cancel* gē.

unriht æfnde,　oþ þæt ende becwōm,
1255 swylt æfter synnum.　Þæt gesȳne wearþ,
wīdcūþ werum,　þætte wrecend þā gȳt
lifde æfter lāþum,　lange þrāge,
æfter gūðceare;　Grendles mōdor,
ides āglǣcwīf　yrmþe gemunde,
1260 sē þe wæteregesan　wunian scolde,
cealde strēamas,　siþðan Cā*in* wearð
tō ecgbanan　āngan brēþer,
fæderenmǣge;　hē þā fāg gewāt,
morþre gemearcod　mandrēam fleōn,
1265 wēsten warode.　Þanon wōc fela
geōsceaftgāsta;　wæs þǣra Grendel sum,
heorowearh hetelīc,　sē æt Heorote fand
wæccendne wer　wīges bīdan;
þǣr him āglǣca　ætgrǣpe wearð;
1270 hwæþre hē gemunde　mægenes strenge,
gimfæste gife,　ðē him God sealde,
ond him tō Anwaldan　āre gelȳfde,
frōfre ond fultum;　ðȳ hē þone fēond ofercwōm,
gehnǣgde helle gāst.　Þā hē hēan gewāt,
1275 drēame bedǣled　dēaþwīc seōn,
mancynnes fēond.　Ond his mōdor þā gȳt
gīfre ond galgmōd　gegān wolde
sorhfulne sīð,　sunu *d*ēoð wrecan.
　　Cōm þā tō Heorote,　ðǣr Hring-Dene
1280 geond þæt sæld swǣfun.　Þā ðǣr sōna wearð
edhwyrft eorlum,　siþðan inne fealh

1258ᵃ *Tr.* gūðsceare. — 1260ᵃ *E.Sc., et al.* sē[o]. — 1261ᵇ *MS.* camp; *Gru.tr.* 286, *Ke.* Cāin. *See 107ᵃ Varr.* — 1264ᵇ *Fol. 158ᵃ* man *AB*. — 1266ᵃ *See 1234ᵃ.* — 1278ᵇ *MS.* sunu þeod; *E.Sc.* (?), *Gr.²* (?), *Scherer L 5.5.495, Rie.Zs. 401* suna (*or* sunu) dēað. (*deoð - ðeodþeod. Cf. Lang. § 16.2.*) — 1280ᵇ *Holt.* (*cf. Zs. 117*) sō[c]na.

Grendles mōdor. Wæs se gryre læssa
efne swā micle,   swā biðˇ mægþa cræft,
wīggryre wīfes   be wæpnedmen,
1285 þonne heoru bunden,   hamere geþrūen,
sweord swāte fāh   swīn ofer helme
ecgum dyhtig   andweard scireðˇ.
Ðā wæs on healle   heardecg togen
sweord ofer setlum,   sīdrand manig
1290 hafen handa fæst;   helm ne gemunde,
byrnan sīde,   þā hine se brōga angeat.
Hēo wæs on ofste,   wolde ūt þanon,
fēore beorgan,   þā hēo onfunden wæs;
hraðˇe hēo æþelinga   ānne hæfde
1295 fæste befangen,   þā hēo tō fenne gang.
Sē wæs Hrōþgāre   hæleþa lēofost
on gesīðˇes hād   be sǣm twēonum,
rīce randwiga,   þone ðˇe hēo on ræste ābrēat,
blǣdfæstne beorn.   Næs Bēowulf ðˇǣr,
1300 ac wæs ōþer in   ǣr geteohhod
æfter māþðˇumgife   mǣrum Gēate.
Hrēam wearðˇ in Heorote;   hēo under heolfre genam
cūþe folme;   cearu wæs genīwod,
geworden in wīcun.   Ne wæs þæt gewrixle til,
1305 þæt hīe on bā healfa   bicgan scoldon
frēonda fēorum!
                  Þā wæs frōd cyning,
hār hilderinc   on hrēon mōde,
syðˇþan hē aldorþegn   unlyfigendne,
þone dēorestan   dēadne wisse.

1285[b] *MS.* geþuren; *Gr.*[1] (?), *Siev. Beitr. ix 282, 294, cf. Siev. R. 265, 458* geþrūen. —
1287[a] *Fol. 158[b]* dyhttig *A*, dyttig *B; Gr.*[1] dyhtig. — 1291[b] *Gr.*[1] (?), *Bu. Tid. 296, Rie. Zs. 401*
þe *for* þā. — 1302[a] *MS.* o¦n. — 1307[b] *Fol. 159[a]* mode *A B*.

50   BEOWULF

1310 Hraþe wæs tō būre   Bēowulf fetod,
sigorēadig secg.   Samod ǣrdæge
ēode eorla sum,   æþele cempa
self mid gesīðum   þǣr se snotera bād,
hwæþer him Alwalda   ǣfre wille
1315 æfter wēaspelle   wyrpe gefremman.
Gang ðā æfter flōre   fyrdwyrðe man
mid his handscale   — healwudu dynede —,
þæt hē þone wīsan   wordum nǣgde
frēan Ingwina,   frægn gif him wǣre
1320 æfter nēodlaðu[m]   niht getǣse.
XX   Hrōðgār maþelode,   helm Scyldinga:
'Ne frīn þū æfter sǣlum!   Sorh is genīwod
Denigea lēodum.   Dēad is Æschere,
Yrmenlāfes   yldra brōþor,
1325 mīn rūnwita   ond mīn rǣdbora,
eaxlgestealla,   ðonne wē on orlege
hafelan weredon,   þonne hniton fēþan,
eoferas cnysedan.   Swy(lc) scolde eorl wesan,
[æþeling] ǣrgōd,   swylc Æschere wæs!
1330 Wearð him on Heorote   tō handbanan
wælgǣst wǣfre;   ic ne wāt hwæðer
atol ǣse wlanc   eftsīðas tēah,
fylle gefægnod.   Hēo þā fǣhðe wræc,
þē þū gystran niht   Grendel cwealdest

1314ᵃ *MS.* hwæþre; *Siev. ZfdPh. xxi 357, Holt., Sed.* hwæþer. *See 2844ᵃ.* — *MS.* alf walda; *Thk.* alwealda, *Tho.* Alwalda. — 1317ᵃ *Tho., Sweet L 2.22, Wy., Holt., Hoops* -scole. *See Gloss.* — 1318ᵇ *MS.* (*AB*) hnægde; *E.Sc.* nēgde, *Gr.*¹ nǣgde. — 1320ᵃ *MS.* neod laðu; *E.Sc.* -lāde; *E., Holt., Sed.* -laðu[m]; *Sweet L 2.22* -laðe; *Cos. viii 570* nēadlāðum. *See Lang.* § 20.3. — 1328ᵇ *Fol. 159ᵇ* swy .. scolde *B*(*A*); *Thk.* swylc. — 1329ᵃ *Gru.* [ædeling], *Gr.*² [æðeling]. *See 130ᵃ.* — 1331ᵇ *MS.* hwæþer; *Gr.*¹ (?), *Rie.V. 45, Sweet*¹ *L 2.22, Bu. 93* hwider; *Gr.*², *Schü., Sed., Cha.* hwæder. (*He.*¹, *Holt.* hwæþer=hwider.) — 1333ᵃ *MS.* ge frægnod; *Ke. ii, et al., Holt., Sed.* gefægnod; *cp. 562, 1014; see Gloss.; Tho., Tr.* gefrēfrod; *Gru.* gefrecnod.

BEOWULF

¹³³⁵ þurh hæstne hād   heardum clammum,
forþan hē tō lange   lēode mīne
wanode ond wyrde.   Hē æt wīge gecrang
ealdres scyldig,   ond nū ōþer cwōm
mihtig mānscaða,   wolde hyre mæg wrecan,
¹³⁴⁰ gē feor hafað   fæhðe gestæled,
þæs þe þincean mæg   þegne monegum,
sē þe æfter sincgyfan   on sefan grēoteþ, —
hreþerbealo hearde;   nū sēo hand ligeð,
sē þe ēow wēlhwylcra   wilna dohte.
¹³⁴⁵   Ic þæt londbūend,   lēode mīne,
selerædende   secgan hȳrde,
þæt hīe gesāwon   swylce twēgen
micle mearcstapan   mōras healdan,
ellorgæstas.   Ðæra ōðer wæs,
¹³⁵⁰ þæs þe hīe gewislīcost   gewitan meahton,
idese onlīcnes;   ōðer earmsceapen
on weres wæstmum   wræclāstas træd,
næfne hē wæs māra   þonne ænig man ōðer;
þone on gēardagum   Grendel nemdon
¹³⁵⁵ foldbūende;   nō hīe fæder cunnon,
hwæþer him ænig wæs   ær ācenned
dyrnra gāsta.   Hīe dȳgel lond
warigeað wulfhleoþu,   windige næssas,
frēcne fengelād,   ðær fyrgenstrēam
¹³⁶⁰ under næssa genipu   niþer gewīteð,
flōd under foldan.   Nis þæt feor heonon
mīlgemearces,   þæt se mere standeð;
ofer þæm hongiað   hrinde bearwas,

---

^{1344a} *E.Sc., et al.* sē[o]. — ^{1351a} *MS.* onlic næs; *Ke., et al., Schü., Sed., Cha.* onlīcnes; *Gru.tr. 287, Sweet L 2.22, Holt.* onlīc. (*Sweet adds* wæs *before* ōðer 1351^b.) — 1352^b *Fol. 160^a* træd. — 1354^b *MS. (AB)* nemdod; *Ke.* nemdon. — 1362^b *MS.* stanðeð; *Thk.* standeþ. — 1363^b *Morris in Preface (p. vi f.) to Blickl. Hom., Sweet L 2.22, Wülcker.* He.-Soc.^b

wudu wyrtum fæst   wæter oferhelmað.
1365 Þær mæg nihta gehwæm   nīðwundor sēon,
fȳr on flōde.   Nō þæs frōd leofað
gumena bearna,   þæt þone grund wite.
Ðēah þe hæðstapa   hundum geswenced,
heorot hornum trum   holtwudu sēce,
1370 feorran geflȳmed,   ǣr hē feorh seleð,
aldor on ōfre,   ǣr hē in wille,
hafelan [beorgan];   nis þæt hēoru stōw!
þonon ȳðgeblond   up āstīgeð
won tō wolcnum,   þonne wind styreþ
1375 lāð gewidru,   oð þæt lyft drysmaþ,
roderas rēotað.   Nū is se rǣd gelang
eft æt þē ānum.   Eard gīt ne const,
frēcne stōwe,   ðǣr þū findan miht
sinnigne secg;   sēc gif þū dyrre!
1380 Ic þē þā fæhðe   fēo lēanige,
ealdgestrēonum,   swā ic ǣr dyde,
wund*num* golde,   gyf þū on weg cymest.'
XXI   Bēowulf maþelode,   bearn Ecgþēowes:
' Ne sorga, snotor guma!   Sēlre bið ǣghwǣm,
1385 þæt hē his frēond wrece,   þonne hē fela murne.
Ūre ǣghwylc sceal   ende gebīdan
worolde līfes;   wyrce sē þe mōte
dōmes ǣr dēaþe;   þæt bið drihtguman
unlifgendum   æfter sēlest.

---

hrīmge (*see note to 1357 ff.*); *Cos. viii 571* hrīmde (=hrīmge); *B.-T. s.v.* hrind, *Sarrazin Beitr. xi 163 n., Sed.* hringde (*cp.* hring ' circle '); *Wright ESt. xxx 342 f.* hrinde, *see Gloss.* 1372ᵃ *MS.* hafelan : ; *Ke. ii, Edd.* [hȳdan]; *Holt. note* [beorgan] (?). *See 1293ᵃ.* — 1377ᵃ *Fol. 160ᵇ* þe *AB.* — 1379ᵃ *MS.* fela sinnigne; *He.², most Edd. cancel* fela; *Holt.* (*cf. Zs. 117*): *lacuna before* fela, *which he makes the last word of the preceding line; Malone MLR. xxv 191, Hoops* felasinnigne. — 1382ᵃ *MS. Z.* wun/dini *or* /dmi; *Gru.tr. 287* wunden-; *E.Sc., et al., Bu. 93, Schü., Sed.* wundnum; *Thk., Hold.², Holt., Cha., Hoops* wundini. *See Intr. cix f.*

1390 Ārīs, rīces weard, uton hraþe fēran,
Grendles māgan gang scēawigan.
Ic hit þē gehāte: nō hē on helm losaþ,
nē on foldan fæþm, nē on fyrgenholt,
nē on gyfenes grund, gā þǣr hē wille!
1395 Ðȳs dōgor þū geþyld hafa
wēana gehwylces, swā ic þē wēne tō.'
Āhlēop ðā se gomela, Gode þancode,
mihtigan Drihtne, þæs se man gespræc.
Þā wæs Hrōðgāre hors gebǣted,
1400 wicg wundenfeax. Wīsa fengel
geatolīc gende; gumfēþa stōp
lindhæbbendra. Lāstas wǣron
æfter waldswaþum wīde gesȳne,
gang ofer grundas, [swā] gegnum fōr
1405 ofer myrcan mōr, magoþegna bær
þone sēlestan sāwollēasne
þāra þe mid Hrōðgāre hām eahtode.
Oferēode þā æþelinga bearn
stēap stānhliðo, stīge nearwe,
1410 enge ānpaðas, uncūð gelād,
neowle næssas, nicorhūsa fela;
hē fēara sum beforan gengde
wīsra monna wong scēawian,
oþ þæt hē fǣringa fyrgenbēamas
1415 ofer hārne stān hleonian funde,
wynlēasne wudu; wæter under stōd
drēorig ond gedrēfed. Denum eallum wæs,

1392ᵇ *Tho., et al.* hē[o]; so 1394ᵇ. — *Tho. (in Ke.), et al., Aant.* 23 holm. — 1393ᵇ *Z. translit.* no (*misprint*). — 1398ᵇ *Fol. 161ᵃ* spræc *A*, spręc *B*. — 1401ᵃ *E.Sc., et al., Holt., Schü., Sed.* gen[g]de; see *1412. Cf. Lang.* § *19.1*. — 1404ᵇ *MS.* gegnū for; *Siev. ix 140, Holt., Sed., Cha.* [þǣr hēo] g. f.; *Bu. 94* [hwǣr hēo] g. f.; *Aant. 24* gegnunga (?); *JEGPh. vi 195* [swā] (or fērde *for* fōr, so *Schü.*). — 1407ᵇ *Tho.* (?), *Tr.* ealgode.

winum Scyldinga   weorce on mōde
tō geþolianne,   ðegne monegum,
1420 oncȳð eorla gehwǣm,   syðþan Æscheres
on þām holmclife   hafelan métton.
Flōd blōde wēol   — folc tō sǣgon —,
hātan heolfre.   Horn stundum song
fūslīc f(yrd)lēoð.   Fēþa eal gesæt.
1425 Gesāwon ðā æfter wætere   wyrmcynnes fela,
sellice sǣdracan   sund cunnian,
swylce on næshleoðum   nicras licgean,
ðā on undernmǣl   oft bewitigað
sorhfulne sīð   on seglrāde,
1430 wyrmas ond wildēor.   Hīe on weg hruron
bitere ond gebolgne;   bearhtm ongēaton,
gūðhorn galan.   Sumne Gēata lēod
of flānbogan   fēores getwǣfde,
ȳðgewinnes,   þæt him on aldre stōd
1435 herestrǣl hearda;   hē on holme wæs
sundes þē sǣnra,   ðē hyne swylt fornam.
Hræþe wearð on ȳðum   mid eofersprēotum
heorohōcyhtum   hearde genearwod,
nīða genǣged,   ond on næs togen,
1440 wundọrlīc wǣgbora;   weras scēawedon
gryrelīcne gist.
                   Gyrede hine Bēowulf
eorlgewǣdum,   nalles for ealdre mearn;
scolde herebyrne   hondum gebrōden,
sīd ond searofāh   sund cunnian,
1445 sēo ðe bāncofan   beorgan cūþe,

1418ª *Tr.* wigum. — 1423ª *Fol. 161ᵇ* hatan *AB.* — 1424ª *B(A)* f . . . ; *Bout. 92* fyrd-.
— 1430ª *Holt.* (*cf. Beibl. xiii 205*) wildor. — 1440ª *Tr.* wǣgfara; *ESt. xxxix 463* -dēor (?),
cp. Chr. 987; Holt. Beibl. xxi 300 -þora, *cp.* þweran. *See Gloss.*

þæt him hildegrāp hreþre ne mihte,
eorres inwitfeng aldre gesceþðan;
ac se hwīta helm hafelan werede,
sē þe meregrundas mengan scolde,
1450 sēcan sundgebland since geweorðad,
befongen frēawrāsnum, swā hine fyrndagum
worhte wǣpna smið, wundrum tēode,
besette swīnlīcum, þæt hine syðþan nō
brond nē beadomēcas bītan ne meahton.
1455 Næs þæt þonne mǣtost mægenfultuma,
þæt him on ðearfe lāh ðyle Hrōðgāres;
wæs þǣm hæftmēce Hrunting nama;
þæt wæs ān foran ealdgestrēona;
ecg wæs īren, ātertānum fāh,
1460 āhyrded heaþoswāte; nǣfre hit æt hilde ne swāc
manna ǣngum þāra þe hit mid mundum bewand,
sē ðe gryresīðas gegān dorste,
folcstede fāra; næs þæt forma sīð,
þæt hit ellenweorc æfnan scolde.
1465 Hūru ne gemunde mago Ecglāfes
eafoþes cræftig, þæt hē ǣr gespræc
wīne druncen, þā hē þæs wǣpnes onlāh
sēlran sweordfrecan; selfa ne dorste
under ȳða gewin aldre genēþan,
1470 drihtscype drēogan; þǣr hē dōme forlēas,
ellenmǣrðum. Ne wæs þǣm ōðrum swā,
syðþan hē hine tō gūðe gegyred hæfde.
XXII Bēowulf maþelode, bearn Ecgþēowes:
' Geþenc nū, se mǣra maga Healfdenes,
1475 snottra fengel, nū ic eom sīðes fūs,

<small>1448ᵇ Fol. 162ᵃ hafelan A B. — 1454ᵃ Aant. 24 (?), Tr., Holt.¹⁻⁵, Sed. brogdne. — 1459ᵇ Cos. viii 571, Aant. 24 ātertǣrum (= -tēarum, ' poison drops '); Tr. -tācnum. — 1471ᵃ Fol. 162ᵇ mærdam A B, : : rðum Z. (?).</small>

BEOWULF

goldwine gumena, hwæt wit geō sprǣcon,
gif ic æt þearfe þīnre scolde
aldre linnan, þæt ðū mē ā wǣre
forðgewitenum on fæder stǣle.
1480 Wes þū mundbora mīnum magoþegnum,
hondgesellum, gif mec hild nime;
swylce þū ðā mādmas, þē þū mē sealdest,
Hrōðgār lēofa, Higelāce onsend.
Mæg þonne on þǣm golde ongitan Gēata dryhten,
1485 gesēon sunu Hrǣdles, þonne hē on þæt sinc staraðˊ,
þæt ic gumcystum gōdne funde
bēaga bryttan, brēac þonne mōste.
Ond þū Unferð lǣt ealde lāfe,
wrǣtlīc wǣgsweord wīdcūðne man
1490 heardecg habban; ic mē mid Hruntinge
dōm gewyrce, oþðe mec dēað nimeð!'
Æfter þǣm wordum Weder-Gēata lēod
efste mid elne, — nalas andsware
bīdan wolde; brimwylm onfēng
1495 hilderince. Ðā wæs hwīl dæges,
ǣr hē þone grundwong ongytan mehte.
Sōna þæt onfunde sē ðe flōda begong
heorogīfre behēold hund missēra,
grim ond grǣdig, þæt þǣr gumena sum
1500 ælwihta eard ufan cunnode.
Grāp þā tōgēanes, gūðrinc gefēng
atolan clommum; nō þȳ ǣr in gescōd
hālan līce; hring ūtan ymbbearh,
þæt hēo þone fyrdhom ðurhfōn ne mihte,
1505 locene leoðosyrcan lāþan fingrum.

_{1481^a *Gru., Holt.*^{1–4} hondgesteallum. (*Holt. ii* -geseldum?) — 1485^a *Tho., et al.* Hrēðles. See *454^b*. — 1488^a *MS.* hunferð; *Rie.Zs. 414* Unferð. See *499^a*. — 1489^a *Tho.* wīg- (*for* wǣg-); *Klu.* (*in Hold.*¹) wæl·. — 1491^b *Fol. 163^a* oþðe.}

Bær þā sēo brimwyl[f], þā hēo tō botme cōm,
hringa þengel tō hofe sīnum,
swā hē ne mihte — nō hē þæs mōdig wæs —
wǣpna gewealdan, ac hine wundra þæs fela
1510 swe[n]cte on sunde, sǣdēor monig
hildetūxum heresyrcan bræc,
ēhton āglǣcan. Ðā se eorl ongeat,
þæt hē [in] nīðsele nāthwylcum wæs,
þǣr him nænig wæter wihte ne sceþede,
1515 nē him for hrōfsele hrīnan ne mehte
fǣrgripe flōdes; fȳrlēoht geseah,
blācne lēoman beorhte scīnan.
    Ongeat þā se gōda grundwyrgenne,
merewīf mihtig; mægenrǣs forgeaf
1520 hildebille, hond sweng ne oftēah,
þæt hire on hafelan hringmǣl āgōl
grǣdig gūðlēoð. Ðā se gist onfand,
þæt se beadolēoma bītan nolde,
aldre sceþðan, ac sēo ecg geswāc
1525 ðēodne æt þearfe; ðolode ǣr fela
hondgemōta, helm oft gescær,
fǣges fyrdhrægl; ðā wæs forma sīð
dēorum māðme, þæt his dōm ālæg.
    Eft wæs ānrǣd, nalas elnes læt,
1530 mǣrða gemyndig mǣg Hȳlāces:
wearp ðā wundenmǣl wrǣttum gebunden

1506ª *MS.* wyl; *Ke.* -wyl[f]. — 1508ª⁻ᵇ *Thk., Ke., Gru., Siev. ix 140, Hold., Aant. 24, Holt.*¹⁻⁵, *Schü. place* nō *in b-line, Wy., et al., in a-line.* — *MS.* þæm; *Gru., Holt.*¹⁻⁵ þæs; *Gr.*¹, *Cha.* þēah; *Aant. 24* (?), *Schü., Sed.* þǣr. — 1510ª *MS.* swecte; *Ke. ii* swe[n]cte. — 1513ª *Tho.* [in]. — 1514ª *Martin ESt. xx 295* wæter[a]; *Holt.* (*cf. Lit.bl. xxi 61*), *Morgan Beitr. xxxiii 126* wæter nænig. *See T.C.* § *17 f.* — 1516ᵇ *Fol. 163*ᵇ fyr *AB.* — 1520ᵇ *MS.* hord swenge; *Bout. 92* hondsweng; *Gr.*¹, *Edd.* hond swenge; *Tr., Schü., Sed., Holt.* sweng. — 1530ᵇ *MS.* hylaces; *most Edd.* Hygelāces; *MPh. iii 458, Schü., Cha.* Hȳlāces; *Holt.* Hyglāces. *See Lang.* §§ *18.10, 19.1.* — 1531ª *MS.* wundel; *Ke.* wunden-.

yrre ōretta, þæt hit on eorðan læg,
stīð ond stȳlecg; strenge getruwode,
mundgripe mægenes.   Swā sceal man dôn,
1535 þonne hē æt gūðe gegān þenceð
longsumne lof;   nā ymb his līf cearað.
Gefēng þā be eaxle   — nalas for fæhðe mearn —
Gūð-Gēata lēod   Grendles mōdor;
brægd þā beadwe heard,   þā hē gebolgen wæs,
1540 feorhgenīðlan,   þæt hēo on flet gebēah.
Hēo him eft hraþe *a*ndlēan forgeald
grimman grāpum   ond him tōgēanes fēng;
oferwearp þā wērigmōd   wigena strengest,
fēþecempa,   þæt hē on fylle wearð.
1545 Ofsæt þā þone selegyst,   ond hyre sea*x* getēah
brād [ond] brūnecg;   wolde hire bearn wrecan,
āngan eaferan.   Him on eaxle læg
brēostnet brōden;   þæt gebearh fēore,
wið ord ond wið ecge   ingang forstōd.
1550 Hæfde ðā forsīðod   sunu Ecgþēowes
under gynne grund,   Gēata cempa,
nemne him heaðobyrne   helpe gefremede,
herenet hearde, —   ond hālig God
gewēold wīgsigor;   wītig Drihten,
1555 rodera Rǣdend   hit on ryht gescēd
ȳðelīce,   syþðan hē eft āstōd.

XXIII   Geseah ðā on searwum   sigeēadig bil,
ealdsweord eotenisc   ecgum þȳhtig,
wigena weorðmynd;   þæt [wæs] wǣpna cyst, —

1533ᵇ *See 669ᵇ Varr.* — 1537ᵃ *Rie.V. 24, Sweet L 2.22, 4 Edd., Morgan Beitr. xxxiii 117*
feaxe. *Cf. T.C. § 26.* — 1541ᵇ *MS.* handlean; *Rie.Zs. 414, Holt., Schü., Cha.* andlēan.
See 2094 (2929, 2972). — 1542ᵃ *Fol. 164ᵃ* man. — 1543ᵃ *E.Sc. (?), Sed.* oferwearp [hine].
— 1543ᵇ-44ᵃ *E.Sc.* strengestan, *A ant. 24* strengel; *E.Sc., A ant. 25* -cempan. — 1545ᵇ *MS.*
seaxe; *E.Sc., most Edd.* seax. — 1546ᵃ *Gru. þ. 150, He.², 4 Edd.* [ond]. *Cp. Mald. 163.* —
1558ᵃ *Ke., Tho., Gr., et al.* eald sweord. *So 1663ᵃ, 2616ᵃ, 2979ᵃ.* — 1559ᵇ *Gru.tr. 190 (?),*
Ke. [wæs].

1560 būton hit wæs māre   ðonne ænig mon ōðer
tō beadulāce   ætberan meahte,
gōd ond geatolīc,   gīganta geweorc.
Hē gefēng þā fetelhilt,   freca Scyldinga
hrēoh ond heorogrim,   hringmǣl gebrægd
1565 aldres orwēna,   yrringa slōh,
þæt hire wið halse   heard grāpode,
bānhringas bræc;   bil eal ðurhwōd
fǣgne flǣschoman;   hēo on flet gecrong,
sweord wæs swātig,   secg weorce gefeh.
1570   Līxte se lēoma,   lēoht inne stōd,
efne swā of hefene   hādre scīneð
rodores candel.   Hē æfter recede wlāt;
hwearf þā be wealle,   wǣpen hafenade
heard be hiltum   Higelāces ðegn
1575 yrre ond anrǣd, —   næs sēo ecg fracod
hilderince,   ac hē hraþe wolde
Grendle forgyldan   gūðræsa fela
ðāra þe hē geworhte   tō West-Denum
oftor micle   ðonne on ænne sīð,
1580 þonne hē Hrōðgāres   heorðgenēatas
slōh on sweofote,   slǣpende frǣt
folces Denigea   fȳftȳne men,
ond ōðer swylc   ūt offerede,
lāðlicu lāc.   Hē him þæs lēan forgeald,
1585 rēþe cempa,   tō ðæs þe hē on ræste geseah
gūðwērigne   Grendel licgan,
aldorlēasne,   swā him ǣr gescōd
hild æt Heorote.   Hrā wīde sprong,
syþðan hē æfter dēaðe   drepe þrōwade,
1590 heorosweng heardne,   ond hine þā hēafde becearf

1565^b *Fol. 164^b* sloh *AB*.

60 BEOWULF

    Sōna þæt gesāwon   snottre ceorlas,
þā ðe mid Hrōðgāre   on holm wliton,
þæt wæs ȳðgeblond   eal gemenged,
brim blōde fāh.   Blondenfeaxe,
1595 gomele ymb gōdne   ongeador sprǣcon,
þæt hig þæs æðelinges   eft ne wēndon,
þæt hē sigehrēðig   sēcean cōme
mǣrne þēoden;   þā ðæs monige gewearð,
þæt hine sēo brimwylf   ābroten hæfde.
1600 Ðā cōm nōn dæges.   Næs ofgēafon
hwate Scyldingas;   gewāt him hām þonon
goldwine gumena.   Gistas sētan
mōdes sēoce   ond on mere staredon;
wīston ond ne wēndon,   þæt hīe heora winedrihten
1605 selfne gesāwon. —   Þā þæt sweord ongan
æfter heaþoswāte   hildegicelum,
wīgbil wanian;   þæt wæs wundra sum,
þæt hit eal gemealt   īse gelīcost,
ðonne forstes bend   Fæder onlǣteð,
1610 onwindeð wælrāpas,   sē geweald hafað
sǣla ond mǣla;   þæt is sōð Metod.
Ne nōm hē in þǣm wīcum,   Weder-Gēata lēod,
māðmǣhta mā,   þēh hē þǣr monige geseah,
būton þone hafelan   ond þā hilt somod
1615 since fāge;   sweord ǣr gemealt,
forbarn brōdenmǣl;   wæs þæt blōd tō þæs hāt,
ǣttren ellorgǣst,   sē þǣr inne swealt.
Sōna wæs on sunde   sē þe ǣr æt sæcce gebād
wīghryre wrāðra,   wæter up þurhdēaf;

1591[b] *Fol. 165[a]* ceorlas. — 1599[b] *MS.* abreoten; *Ke. ii* ābroten. — 1602[b] *MS.* secan; *Gru.tr. 290* sǣton, *Gr.*[2] sētan. — 1604[a] *Ke. ii* wȳs[c]ton, *Tho., Gru.* wīs[c]ton. — 1610[a] *Gru.tr. 291* (?), *Ke., et al.* wǣgrāpas. — 1616[b] *Fol. 165[b]* to *AB*. — 1617[a] *MS.* ellor *altered from* ellen. — 1619[a] *Gr.Spr.* (?), *Aant. 25* wīggryre.

BEOWULF

<pre>
1620 wǣron ȳðgebland   eal gefælsod,
     ēacne eardas,   þā se ellorgāst
     oflēt līfdagas   ond þās lǣnan gesceaft.
       Cōm þā tō lande   lidmanna helm
     swīðmōd swymman;   sǣlāce gefeah,
1625 mægenbyrþenne   þāra þe hē him mid hæfde.
     Ēodon him þā tōgēanes,   Gode þancodon,
     ðrȳðlīc þegna hēap,   þēodnes gefēgon,
     þæs þe hī hyne gesundne   gesēon mōston.
     Đā wæs of þǣm hrōran   helm ond byrne
1630 lungre ālȳsed.   Lagu drūsade,
     wæter under wolcnum,   wældrēore fāg.
       Fērdon forð þonon   fēþelāstum
     ferhþum fægne,   foldweg mǣton,
     cūþe strǣte;   cyningbalde men
1635 from þǣm holmclife   hafelan bǣron
     earfoðlīce   heora ǣghwæþrum
     felamōdigra;   fēower scoldon
     on þǣm wælstenge   weorcum geferian
     tō þǣm goldsele   Grendles hēafod, —
1640 oþ ðæt semninga   tō sele cōmon
     frome fyrdhwate   fēowertȳne
     Gēata gongan;   gumdryhten mid
     mōdig on gemonge   meodowongas trǣd.
       Đā cōm in gān   ealdor ðegna,
1645 dǣdcēne mon   dōme gewurþad,
     hæle hildedēor,   Hrōðgār grētan.
     Þā wæs be feaxe   on flet boren
     Grendles hēafod,   þǣr guman druncon,
</pre>

1624ᴸ *Tr.* (?), *Holt.* (*cf. Zs. 117*), *Delbrück L 6.13.2.682* -lāca. — 1625ᵇ *E. omits* þāra; *He.-Soc.*⁵⁻⁷ þǣre. — 1634ᵇ *Gr., E., Aant. 25, Sed.* cynebalde; *Bu. 369* cyningholde. *Cf. MPh. iii 459.* — 1640ᵃ *Fol. 166ᵃ* semninga. — 1644ᵃ gân. *See 386ᵇ.*

egeslīc for eorlum ond þǣre idese mid,
1650 wlitesēon wrǣtlīc; weras on sāwon.

XXIIII Bēowulf maþelode, bearn Ecgþēowes:
'Hwæt, wē þē þās sǣlāc, sunu Healfdenes,
lēod Scyldinga, lustum brōhton
tīres tō tācne, þē þū hēr tō lōcast.
1655 Ic þæt unsōfte ealdre gedīgde,
wigge under wætere, weorc genēþde
earfoðlīce; ǣtrihte wæs
gūð getwǣfed, nymðe mec God scylde.
Ne meahte ic æt hilde mid Hruntinge
1660 wiht gewyrcan, þēah þæt wǣpen duge;
ac mē geūðe ylda Waldend,
þæt ic on wāge geseah wlitig hangian
ealdsweord ēacen —oftost wīsode
winigea lēasum—; þæt ic ðȳ wǣpne gebrǣd.
1665 Ofslōh ðā æt þǣre sæcce, þā mē sǣl āgeald,
hūses hyrdas. Þā þæt hildebil
forbarn brogdenmǣl, swā þæt blōd gesprang,
hātost heaþoswāta. Ic þæt hilt þanan
fēondum ætferede; fyrendǣda wræc,
1670 dēaðcwealm Denigea, swā hit gedēfe wæs.
Ic hit þē þonne gehāte, þæt þū on Heorote mōst
sorhlēas swefan mid þīnra secga gedryht,
ond þegna gehwylc þīnra lēoda,
duguðe ond iogoþe, þæt þū him ondrǣdan ne þearft,
1675 þēoden Scyldinga, on þā healfe,
aldorbealu eorlum, swā þū ǣr dydest.'

1650 *Punct. in text w.* Siev. *ZfdPh. xxi 360; cp. 1422ᵇ.* Earlier Edd., *Schü.* (*cf. Bd. 81*) onsāwon, *most of them taking* wlitesēon *as its object.*—1656 *Tho.* weorce; *Aant.* 25 **wīg and** weorce. (*Cf. ESt. xxxix 463f.*) *Many Edd. make* 1656–57ᵃ *one clause.*—1658ᵃ *Gru.,* **Bu.**Tid. 52, Tr., *Sed.* gūðe (1657 wæs *1 sg.*). *Cf. Aant. 25.*—1662ᵇ *Fol. 166ᵇ* hangian *A.* —1663ᵃ *See 1558ᵃ.*—1663ᵇ *Siev. R. 256* (?), *Holt., Sed.* oft. *See T.C.* § 20.

Ðā wæs gylden hilt   gamelum rince,
hārum hildfruman   on hand gyfen,
enta ærgeweorc;   hit on ǣht gehwearf
1680 æfter dēofla hryre   Denigea frēan,
wundorsmiþa geweorc;   ond þā þās worold ofgeaf
gromheort guma,   Godes andsaca,
morðres scyldig,   ond his mōdor ēac;
on geweald gehwearf   woroldcyninga
1685 ðǣm sēlestan   be sǣm twēonum
ðāra þe on Scedenigge   sceattas dǣlde.
   Hrōðgār maðelode —   hylt scēawode,
ealde lāfe,   on ðǣm wæs ōr writen
fyrngewinnes,   syðþan flōd ofslōh,
1690 gifen gēotende   gīganta cyn,
frēcne gefērdon;   þæt wæs fremde þēod
ēcean Dryhtne;   him þæs endelēan
þurh wæteres wylm   Waldend sealde.
Swā wæs on ðǣm scennum   scīran goldes
1695 þurh rūnstafas   rihte gemearcod,
geseted ond gesǣd,   hwām þæt sweord geworht,
īrena cyst   ǣrest wǣre,
wreoþenhilt ond wyrmfāh.   Ðā se wīsa sprǣc
sunu Healfdenes   — swīgedon ealle — :
1700 ' Þæt, lā, mæg secgan   sē þe sōð ond riht
fremeð on folce,   feor eal gemon,
eald ēþelweard,   þæt ðes eorl wǣre
geboren betera!   Blǣd is ārǣred
1704 geond wīdwegas,   wine mīn Bēowulf,

1677ª *Kluge ESt. xxii 145, Holt.* Gyldenhilt. *See Intr. xix n. 1.*—1681ᵇ *Müll.* (*xiv 213*), *Holt., Sed. drop* ond. — 1685ᵇ *Fol. 167ª* sæm. — 1686ª *MS.* scedenigge (*the first* g *altered from* n). — 1697ª *See 673ª Varr.* — 1702ª *MS.* .ẋ. — 1702ᵇ *Bu.Tid. 52 f., Tr.* þæt ðē eorl nǣre. *See Lang.* § *25.2, Gloss.:* betera; *note on 1850.*

ðīn ofer þēoda gehwylce.   Eal þū hit geþyldum healdest,
mægen mid mōdes snyttrum.   Ic þē sceal mīne gelæstan
frēode, swā wit furðum spræcon.   Đū scealt tō frōfre weorþan
   eal langtwīdig   lēodum þīnum,
   hæleðum tō helpe.
                     Ne wearð Heremōd swā
1710 eaforum Ecgwelan,   Ār-Scyldingum;
   ne gewēox hē him tō willan,   ac tō wælfealle
   ond tō dēaðcwalum   Deniga lēodum;
   brēat bolgenmōd   bēodgenēatas,
   eaxlgesteallan,   oþ þæt hē āna hwearf,
1715 mære þēoden   mondrēamum from,
   ðēah þe hine mihtig God   mægenes wynnum,
   eafeþum stēpte,   ofer ealle men
   forð gefremede.   Hwæþere him on ferhþe grēow
   brēosthord blōdrēow;   nallas bēagas geaf
1720 Denum æfter dōme;   drēamlēas gebād,
   þæt hē þæs gewinnes   weorc þrōwade,
   lēodbealo longsum.   Đū þē lær be þon,
   gumcyste ongit!   Ic þis gid be þē
   āwræc wintrum frōd.
                     Wundor is tō secganne,
1725 hū mihtig God   manna cynne
   þurh sīdne sefan   snyttru bryttað,
   eard ond eorlscipe;   hē āh ealra geweald.
   Hwīlum hē on lufan   læteð hworfan
   monnes mōdgeþonc   mæran cynnes,
1730 seleð him on ēþle   eorþan wynne

1707ᵃ *MS. (Thk., Tho., Cha.)* freode *(cf. Gru.tr. 292), MS. (Ke., Gru., Z.)* freoðe. —
1709ᵃ *Fol. 167ᵇ* hæleðum *B(A)*. — 1710ᵃ *Schaldemose L 2.3, Holtzm. 495, Müll. 50* eafora.
— 1724ᵇ *MS.* secganne; *see T.C. § 12.* — 1728ᵃ *Gru.* on luste (?); *Holt.* on lustan; *Sed.*²
 r hlīsan.

BEOWULF

tō healdanne   hlēoburh wera,
gedēð him swā gewealdene   worolde dǣlas,
sīde rīce,   þæt hē his selfa ne mæg
his unsnyttrum   ende geþencean.
1735 Wunað hē on wiste;   nō hine wiht dweleð
ādl nē yldo,   nē him inwitsorh
on sefa(n) sweorceð,   nē gesacu ōhwǣr
ecghete ēoweð,   ac him eal worold
wendeð on willan;   hē þæt wyrse ne con — ,
XXV 1740 oð þæt him on innan   oferhygda dǣl
weaxeð ond wrīdað;   þonne se weard swefeð,
sāwele hyrde;   bið se slǣp tō fæst,
bisgum gebunden,   bona swīðe nēah,
sē þe of flānbogan   fyrenum scēoteð.
1745 Þonne bið on hreþre   under helm drepen
biteran strǣle   — him bebeorgan ne con — ,
wōm wundorbebodum   wergan gāstes;
þinceð him tō lȳtel,   þæt hē lange hēold,
gȳtsað gromhȳdig,   nallas on gylp seleð
1750 fætte bēagas,   ond hē þā forðgesceaft
forgyteð ond forgȳmeð,   þæs þe him ǣr God sealde,
wuldres Waldend,   weorðmynda dǣl.
Hit on endestæf   eft gelimpeð,
þæt se līchoma   lǣne gedrēoseð,
1755 fǣge gefealleð;   fēhð ōþer tō,
sē þe unmurnlīce   māðmas dǣleþ,
eorles ǣrgestrēon,   egesan ne gȳmeð.
Bebeorh þē ðone bealonīð,   Bēowulf lēofa,

1732ᵃ *Fol. 168ᵃ* ge deð. — 1733ᵇ *Tr.* sēlþa. — 1734ᵃ *MS. (AB, Ke., Z.), Wy., Sed., Cha.*
his; *Thk., Tho., Edd.* [for] his. — 1737ᵃ *MS. Z.* sefa :, *AB* sefad; *Gru.tr. 292, Ke.* sefan.
— 1737ᵇ *Gr.², Holt., Sed.* gesaca. — 1748ᵇ *MS.* to lange *w.* to '*imperfectly erased*' (Z.).
— 1750ᵃ *MS.* fædde; *Tho.* fætte. — 1752ᵃ *Fol. 168ᵇ* waldend *AB.*

secg betsta,   ond þē þæt sēlre gecēos,
1760 ēce rǣdas;   oferhȳda ne gȳm,
mǣre cempa!   Nū is þīnes mægnes blǣd
āne hwīle;   eft sōna biðˇ,
þæt þec ādl oððe ecg   eafoþes getwǣfeð,
oððe fȳres feng,   oððe flōdes wylm,
1765 oððe gripe mēces,   oððe gāres fliht,
oððe atol yldo;   oððe ēagena bearhtm
forsiteð ond forsworceð;   semninga bið,
þæt ðec, dryhtguma,   dēað oferswȳðeð.
Swā ic Hring-Dena   hund missēra
1770 wēold under wolcnum   ond hig wigge belēac
manigum mǣgþa   geond þysne middangeard,
æscum ond ecgum,   þæt ic mē ǣnigne
under swegles begong   gesacan ne tealde.
Hwæt, mē þæs on ēþle   edwenden cwōm,
1775 gyrn æfter gomene,   seoþðan Grendel wearð,
ealdgewinna,   ingenga mīn;
ic þǣre sōcne   singāles wæg
mōdceare micle.   Þæs sig Metode þanc,
ēcean Dryhtne,   þæs ðe ic on aldre gebād,
1780 þæt ic on þone hafelan   heorodrēorigne
ofer eald gewin   ēagum starige!
Gā nū tō setle,   symbȩlwynne drēoh
wīggeweorþad;   unc sceal worn fela
māþma gemǣnra,   siþðan morgen bið.'
1785 Gēat wæs glædmōd,   gēong sōna tō,

1759ᵃ *Tho. (in Ke.), Siev. R. 312, 4 Edd.* secg[a]; *Gru. p. 153, He.*²⁻⁵ secg [se]. *See 947ᵃ.*
— 1774ᵇ *MS.* ed wendan; *Gr.*¹ (?), *Spr., Gr.*², *most Edd.* edwenden. *See 280ᵃ.* — 1776ᵃ *Tho., Gr.*¹, *Gru., et al.* eald gewinna. — 1777ᵃ *Fol. 169ᵃ* Ic. — 1781ᵃ *Holt.*²·³ ealdgewinnan.
— 1782ᵇ *Siev. R. 266, Holt.* symbelwynn. *See Lang.* § 20.2. — 1783ᵃ *MS.* wigge weorþad, *so Gr.*¹, *Wy., Schü., Cha., Hoops; Cos. viii 571, Holt.*¹⁻⁵, *Sed.* wigge (*Holt.* wīge) geweorþad; *Ke., Holt.*⁶ wīggeweorþad. *See Intr. cv n. 3.* — 1784ᵃ *Kock*² *115* gemǣne. *Cf. MLN. xxxiv 132 f.*

BEOWULF

setles nēosan,   swā se snottra heht.
Þā wæs eft swā ǣr   ellenrōfum,
fletsittendum   fægere gereorded
nīowan stefne. —   Nihthelm geswearc
1790 deorc ofer dryhtgumum.   Duguð eal ārās;
wolde blondenfeax   beddes nēosan,
gamela Scylding.   Gēat unigmetes wēl,
rōfne randwigan   restan lyste;
sōna him seleþegn   sīðes wērgum,
1795 feorrancundum   forð wīsade,
sē for andrysnum   ealle beweotede
þegnes þearfe,   swylce þȳ dōgǫre
heaþolīðende   habban scoldon.

Reste hine þā rūmheort;   reced hlīuade
1800 gēap ond goldfāh;   gæst inne swæf,
oþ þæt hrefn blaca   heofones wynne
blīðheort bodode.   Ðā cōm beorht scacan
[scīma ofer sceadwa];   scaþan ōnetton,
wǣron æþelingas   eft tō lēodum
1805 fūse tō farenne;   wolde feor þanon
cuma collenferhð   cēoles nēosan.

Heht þā se hearda   Hrunting beran
sunu Ecglāfes,   heht his sweord niman,
lēoflīc īren;   sægde him þæs lēanes þanc,
1810 cwæð, hē þone gūðwine   gōdne tealde,

1792[b] *MS.* unig/metes; (*Gru. tr. 293*), *Tho., et al.* ungemetes; *E.* ungimetes. *See Lang.*
§ *18.8.* — 1796[b] *MS.* be weotene; *Gru. tr. 293, Ke. ii* beweotede. — 1797[b] *MS.* e *of* dogore
'*added in another hand*' (*Z.*) [*doubtful*]; *Siev. R. 233, 245, Holt., Weyhe Beitr. xxxi 85*
dōgor. *So 2573[b]. See 1395; Lang.* § *20.4.* — 1802[b] *Fol. 169[b]* ða com *B.* — 1802[b]-3[b] *MS.*
ða com beorht scacan scaþan onetton; *Gr.*[1] cōman beorhte [lēoman/ofer scadu] s. S. o.;
Gr.[2] ð. c. b. [lēoma]/s. [ofer scadu]. S. o.; *He.*[2] Ð. c. b. [sunne/scacan [ofer grundas]; s. o.;
Siev. Angl. xiv 137 f., 3 Edd. Ð. c. b. scacan/[scīma æfter sceadwe] etc.; *Sed.* Ð. c. b.
scacan/[scīma scyndend] etc. — 1805[a] *MS.* farene ne; *Ke.* farenne. — 1808[a] *Gru.* suna. —
1809[b] *Müll. (xiv 175)* lǣnes.

68 BEOWULF

wīgcræftigne, nales wordum lōg
mēces ecge; þæt wæs mōdig secg. —
Ond þā sīðfrome, searwum gearwe
wīgend wǣron; ēode weorð Denum
1815 æþeling tō yppan, þǣr se ōþer wæs,
hæle hildedēor Hrōðgār grētte.

XXVI Bēowulf maþelode, bearn Ecgþēowes:
'Nū wē sǣlīðend secgan wyllað
feorran cumene, þæt wē fundiaþ
1820 Higelāc sēcan. Wǣron hēr tela,
willum bewenede; þū ūs wēl dohtest.
Gif ic þonne on eorþan ōwihte mæg
þīnre mōdlufan māran tilian,
gumena dryhten, ðonne ic gȳt dyde,
1825 gūðgeweorca, ic bēo gearo sōna.
Gif ic þæt gefricge ofer flōda begang,
þæt þec ymbsittend egesan þȳwað,
swā þec hetende hwīlum dydon,
ic ðē þūsenda þegna bringe,
1830 hæleþa tō helpe. Ic on Higelāce wāt,
Gēata dryhten, þēah ðe hē geong sȳ,
folces hyrde, þæt hē mec fremman wile
wordum ond weorcum, þæt ic þē wēl herige
ond þē tō gēoce gārholt bere,
1835 mægenes fultum, þǣr ðē bið manna þearf.

1813[a] *Sed. omits* ond. — 1814 *Most Edd. place comma after* wǣron (*subordinate clause*): *so Schü. Sa. 110, Ries L 6.12.2.379.* — *MS.: point after* wǣron; *MS. (A)* Eode (*capital E*) *See 1681[b].* — 1815[b]–16. *On the punctuation see Ries L 6.12.2.379 f.* — *MS.* helle; *Ke. is* hæle. — 1826[a] *Fol. 170[a]* fricge. — 1828[a] *Gr.[1], Siev. R. 296, Holt., Schü., Sed.* hettende. *See Lang. § 19.5.* — 1828[b] *Siev. R. 498, Tr., Schü.* dædon, *Holt.* dēdon; *Sed.* ðȳdon. *Cf. T.C. § 17; Lang. § 23.6.* — 1830[b]–31[a] *Tr., Holt.* -lāc. *Sed.* Ic wāt on Higelāce. — *MS. Z.* wāt *altered from* wāc *w. another ink.* — *Klu. (in Hold.), Sed.* dryhtne. *See note.* — 1833[a] *MS.* weordum ⁊ worcum; *Tho., Schü., Cha.* wordum ond weorcum; *He.[1–4], Holt., Sed.* wordum ond worcum. *See 1902[b].*

Gif him þonne Hrēþrīc   tō hofum Gēata
geþingeð þēodnes bearn,   hē mæg þǣr fela
frēonda findan;   feorcȳþðe bēoð
sēlran gesōhte   þǣm þe him selfa dēah.'
1840 Hrōðgār maþelode   him on andsware:
' Þē þā wordcwydas   wigtig Drihten
on sefan sende;   ne hȳrde ic snotorlīcor
on swā geongum feore   guman þingian.
Þū eart mægenes strang,   ond on mōde frōd,
1845 wīs wordcwida!   Wēn ic talige,
gif þæt gegangeð,   þæt ðe gār nymeð,
hild heorugrimme   Hrēþles eaferan,
ādl oþðe īren   ealdor ðīnne,
folces hyrde,   ond þū þīn feorh hafast,
1850 þæt þe Sǣ-Gēatas   sēlran næbben
tō gecēosenne   cyning ǣnigne,
hordweard hæleþa,   gyf þū healdan wylt
māga rīce.   Mē þīn mōdsefa
līcað leng swā wēl,   lēofa Bēowulf.
1855 Hafast þū gefēred,   þæt þām folcum sceal,
Gēata lēodum   ond Gār-Denum
sib gemǣne,   ond sacu restan,
inwitnīþas,   þē hīe ǣr drugon,
wesan, þenden ic wealde   wīdan rīces,
1860 māþmas gemǣne,   manig ōþerne
gōdum gegrēttan   ofer ganotes bæð;
sceal hringnaca   ofer heafu bringan
lāc ond luftācen.   Ic þā lēode wāt

1836ᵃ *MS.* hreþrinc; *Gru. tr. 294* Hrēþrīc. — 1837ᵃ *MS.* geþinged; *Ke.* geþingað, *Gr. Spr., Gr.*² geþingeð. — 1840 *Holt. (cf. Zs. 125)* inserts *after* maþelode, [helm Scyldinga,/eorl æðelum gōu]. — 1850ᵃ *Fol. 170*ᵇ sǣ *A (B).* — 1854ᵃ *Gr. Spr. ii 498, Holt., Schü., Sed.* sēl *for* wēl; *E.* bet; *Bu. 96* bet *or* sēl. — 1857ᵃ *MS.* ge mænum; *Siev. ix 140* gemǣne. — 1862ᵃ l *after* sceal *erased.* — 1862ᵇ *MS.* hea þu; *Klu. ix 190, Siev. R. 235, 4 Edd.* heafu.

gē wið fēond gē wið frēond   fæste geworhte,
1865 æghwæs untǣle   ealde wīsan.'
Ðā gīt him eorla hlēo   inne gesealde,
mago Healfdenes   māþmas twelfe;
hēt [h]ine mid þǣm lācum   lēode swǣse
sēcean on gesyntum,   snūde eft cuman.
1870 Gecyste þā   cyning æþelum gōd,
þēoden Scyldinga   ðegn betstan
ond be healse genam;   hruron him tēaras
blondenfeaxum.   Him wæs bēga wēn
ealdum infrōdum,   ōþres swīðor,
1875 þæt h[ī]e seoððа(n) [nō]   gesēon mōston,
mōdige on meþle.   Wæs him se man tō þon lēof,
þæt hē þone brēostwylm   forberan ne mehte;
ac him on hreþre   hygebendum fæst
æfter dēorum men   dyrne langað
1880 beorn wið blōde.   Him Bēowulf þanan,
gūðrinc goldwlanc   græsmoldan træd
since hrēmig;   sǣgenga bād
āge[n]dfrēan,   sē þe on ancre rād.
Þā wæs on gange   gifu Hrōðgāres
1885 oft geæhted;   þæt wæs ān cyning
æghwæs orleahtre,   oþ þæt hine yldo benam
mægenes wynnum,   sē þe oft manegum scōd.

XXVII   Cwōm þā tō flōde   felamōdigra,
hægstealdra [hēap];   hringnet bǣron,

1867ᵇ *MS.* .xii. — 1868ᵃ *MS.* inne; *Tho.* hine. — 1871ᵇ *MS.* ðegn; *Ke., Schubert* ᴌ
8.1.41, Siev. R. 232, 4 Edd. ðegn[a]. *See 947ᵃ, 1759ᵃ.* — 1874ᵃ *Fol. 171ᵃ* frodum. — 1875̊-
MS. he; *Gru. tr. 294* h[ī]e. — *Thk.* seoþþa(n); *Bu. 96, Siev. Angl. xiv 141 (cf. E., Siev. ix
141), Holt., Sed., Cha.* [nā]. — 1880ᵃ *MS.* beorn; *Tho., Siev. ZfdPh. xxi 363, 3 Edd.* born:
Gr., Wy., Cha. bearn; *Thomas MLR. xxii 72, Hoops* beorn. *Cf. Lang. § 13.* — 1883ᵃ *MS.*
agedfrean; *Ke.* āge[n]d-. — 1887ᵇ *Gr.¹(?), et al.* sēo. — 1889ᵃ *Gr.¹* [hēap]. *Cf. T.C. §§ 22,
17 n.* — 1889ᵇ *Siev. R. 224 (?), Tr.* beran, *Holt.* beron *(infin. w.* cwōm). (*MS.* bæron,
cf. Siev.)

1890 locene leoðosyrcan.   Landweard onfand
eftsīð eorla,   swā hē ǣr dyde;
nō hē mid hearme   of hlīðes nosan
gæs(tas) grētte,   ac him tōgēanes rād,
cwæð þæt wilcuman   Wedera lēodum
1895 scaþan scīrhame   tō scipe fōron.
þā wæs on sande   sǣgēap naca
hladen herewǣdum   hringedstefna,
mēarum ond māðmum;   mǣst hlīfade
ofer Hrōðgāres   hordgestrēonum.
1900 Hē þǣm bātwearde   bunden golde
swurd gesealde,   þæt hē syðþan wæs
on meodubence   māþme þȳ weorþra,
yrfelāfe.   Gewāt him on naca
drēfan dēop wæter,   Dena land ofgeaf.
1905 Þā wæs be mǣste   merehrægla sum,
segl sāle fæst;   sundwudu þunede;
nō þǣr wēgflotan   wind ofer ȳðum
sīðes getwǣfde;   sǣgenga fōr,
flēat fāmigheals   forð ofer ȳðe,
1910 bundenstefna   ofer brimstrēamas,
þæt hīe Gēata clifu   ongitan meahton,
cūþe næssas;   cēol up geþrang
lyftgeswenced,   on lande stōd.
Hraþe wæs æt holme   hȳðweard geara,
1915 sē þe ǣr lange tīd   lēofra manna
fūs æt faroðe   feor wlātode;

1892ᵃ *Tr.* hrēame. (*Cf. Ags. Laws, Eadw.-Guðr. 6.6.*) — 1892ᵇ *Siev R. 248, 4 Edd.* nōsan, *Hoops* nosan. *So* 2803ᵇ. — 1893ᵃ *Fol. 171ᵇ* gæs . . . *A; Gru. tr. 294* gæstas. — 1894ᵇ *Gr.* lēode. — 1895ᵃ *MS.* sca/: : : , *A* scawan, *B* scaþan; *Gr.* scaþan. — 1902ᵇ *MS.* maþma, weorþre; *Tho.* -me, -ra. — 1903ᵇ *MS.* nacan; *Gr.* [ȳð]nacan; *Rie. Zs. 402, MPh. iii 461, 3 Edd.* naca; *Sed.* [eft] on nacan. [*Bu. 97 assumed loss of 2 half-lines before* gewāt.] — 1913ᵃ *Tr.* (*cf. Rie. Zs. 405*) lyfte (?). *See* 1783ᵃ. — 1913ᵇ *Siev. ix 141, Holt., Sed.* [þæt hē] o. l. s. — 1914ᵃ *MS.* hreþe *corrected to* hraþe. *Fol. 172ᵃ* holme. — 1916ᵃ *Krapp MPh. ii 407* waroðe. *See 28ᵇ Varr*

sælde tō sande sīdfæþme scip
oncẹrbendum fæst, þȳ læs hym ȳþa ðrym
wudu wynsuman forwrecan meahte.
1920 Hēt þā up beran æþelinga gestrēon,
frætwe ond fǣtgold; næs him feor þanon
tō gesēcanne sinces bryttan,
Higelāc Hrēþling, þǣr æt hām wunað
selfa mid gesīðum sǣwealle nēah.
1925 Bold wæs betlīc, bregorōf cyning,
hēa[h on] healle, Hygd swīðe geong,
wīs wēlþungen, þēah ðe wintra lȳt
under burhlocan gebiden hæbbe,
Hærehes dohtor; næs hīo hnāh swā þēah,
1930 nē tō gnēað gifa Gēata lēodum,
māþmgestrēona. Mōdþrȳðo wæg,
fremu folces cwēn, firen' ondrysne;
nǣnig þæt dorste dēor genēþan
swǣsra gesīða, nefne sinfrēa,
1935 þæt hire an dæges ēagum starede;
ac him wælbende weotode tealde
handgewriþene; hraþe seoþðan wæs
æfter mundgripe mēce geþinged,

1918ª *MS.* oncear; *Gru. tr. 295* oncer-. — 1923ᵇ *Tho., et al.* wunode. See *Intr. cxvii;
Lang.* § *25.6.* [*Cf. Siev. ix 141.*] — 1925ᵇ *Ke., Gru., Holt.* bregorōf (*cp. 1634ᵇ*); *Tho., Gr.,
Schü., Sed., Cha.* brego rōf; *Tr., Scheinert Beitr. xxx 386* (?) beadorōf. — 1926ª *Klu.* (*in
Hold.*) on hēan healle; *Sed.* on hēahealle (*cf. Grienb. 750, Schü.*); *Kock² 116* hēah on healle.
— 1928ᵇ *Tho., Tr.* (?) hæfde. See *1923ᵇ*. — 1931ᵇ *MS.* mod þryðo wæg; *Ke., Tho.* mōdþrȳðo; *Holt. Zs. 118, Sed.* mōdþrȳðe (*cp. Gen. 2238, etc.*); *Gr.* Mōdþrȳðo (*proper name*);
E. Mōdþrȳð onwæg; *Gru., et al.* mōd þrȳðo; *Schü.* (*cf. ESt. xxxix 108 f.*), *3 Edd.* mōd
þrȳðe [ne] wæg; *Imelmann L 4.106a.456 ff., Holt.*⁶ Mōd þrȳð ō wæg; *Hoops St. 64 ff.*
Mōdþrȳð ō wæg (or Mōdþrȳðo wæg). — 1932ª *Tho.* frome (?); *Rie. Zs. 403* fremu =
frempu, *Tr.* frempu; *Bu. Zs. 206, Sed.* fre(o)mu; *Cos. viii 572* frēcnu. — 1932ᵇ *Gr.*¹ firen-
ondrysne; *E.* firena o., *Rie. Zs. 402* firenum o., *Cos. viii 572* firenon o.; *Cha. suggests a
masc. use of* firen (*cp. 698ᵃ*). See *T.C.* § *25.* (*Type D1.*) — 1934ᵇ *Gru., et al., Holt., Cha.*
sīn f. See *Rie. V. 31.* — 1935ª *Holt.²* hīe *for* hire; *cf. Holt. Zs. 119.* — *Ke., Tho.* āndæges
(' daily '); (*Munch, in*) *Bu. Tid. 296* and-ēges (' openly ', *cp. Go.* andaugjō). — 1936ᵇ *Fol.
172ᵇ* weotode *AB*.

þæt hit sceādenmǣl scȳran mōste,
1940 cwealmbealu cȳðan. Ne bið swylc cwēnlīc þēaw
idese tō efnanne, þēah ðe hīo ǣnlicu sȳ,
þætte freoðuwebbe fēores onsǣce
æfter ligetorne lēofne mannan.
Hūru þæt onhōhsnod[e] Hemminges mǣg:
1945 ealodrincende ōðer sǣdan,
þæt hīo lēodbealewa lǣs gefremede,
inwitnīða, syððan ǣrest wearð
gyfen goldhroden geongum cempan,
æðelum dīore, syððan hīo Offan flet
1950 ofer fealone flōd be fæder lāre
sīðe gesōhte; ðǣr hīo syððan well
in gumstōle, gōde mǣre,
līfgesceafta lifigende brēac,
hīold hēahlufan wið hæleþa brego,
1955 ealles moncynnes mīne gefrǣge
þone sēlestan bī sǣm twēonum,
eormencynnes; forðām Offa wæs
geofum ond gūðum, gārcēne man,
wīde geweorðod, wīsdōme hēold
1960 ēðel sīnne;— þonon Ēomēr wōc
hæleðum tō helpe, Hem[m]inges mǣg,
nefa Gārmundes, nīða cræftig.

XXVIII Gewāt him ðā se hearda mid his hondscole
sylf æfter sande sǣwong tredan,
1965 wīde waroðas. Woruldcandel scān,

1939[b] *With* moste *the work of the second scribe begins.* — 1941[a] *Siev. R. 312, Holt., Schü., Sed.* efnan. *See T.C.* § *12.*—1942[b] *MS.* on sæce; *Ke. ii, Rie. Zs. 403, Holt., Schü., Sed.* onsēce. *See Lang.* § *9.3.* — 1944[a] *MS.* on hohsnod; *Tho.* onhōhsnod[e]. — 1944[b] *MS.* hem ninges; *Ke., Müll. (xiv 243), Siev. R. 501* Hemminges. (*Gr.*[1], *Siev. R. 264* Hēminges.) — 1956[a] *MS.* þæs; *Tho.* þone. — 1957[b] *Fol. 173*[a] wæs. — 1960[b] *MS.* geomor; *Tho.* Ēomēr, *Bachlechner Germ. i 298* Ēomǣr. — 1961[b] *MS.* hem inges. *See 1944*[b]. (*Ke. ii p. 80:* mm).

sigel sūðan fūs.   Hī sīð drugon,
elne geēodon,   tō ðæs ðe eorla hlēo,
bonan Ongenþēoęs   burgum in innan,
geongne gūðcyning   gōdne gefrūnon
1970 hringas dǣlan.   Higelāce wæs
sīð Bēowulfes   snūde gecȳðed,
þæt ðǣr on worðig   wīgendra hlēo,
lindgestealla   lifigende cwōm,
heaðolāces hāl   tō hofe gongan.
1975 Hraðe wæs gerȳmed,   swā se rīca bebēad,
fēðegestum   flet innanweard.
   Gesæt þā wið sylfne   sē ðā sæcce genæs,
mǣg wið mǣge,   syððan mandryhten
þurh hlēoðorcwyde   holdne gegrētte,
1980 mēaglum wordum.   Meoduscencum hwearf
geond þæt *heal*ręced   Hæreðes dohtor,
lufode ðā lēode,   līðwǣge bær
hæ*le*ðum tō handa.   Higelāc ongan
sīnne geseldan   in sele þām hēan
1985 fægre fricgcean,   hyne fyrwet bræc,
hwylce Sǣ-Gēata   sīðas wǣron:
'Hū lomp ēow on lāde,   lēofa Bīowulf,
þā ðū fǣringa   feorr gehogodest
sæcce sēcean   ofer sealt wæter,
1990 hilde tō Hiorote?   Ac ðū Hrōðgāre
wī*d*cūðne wēan   wihte gebēttest,
mǣrum ðēodne?   Ic ðæs mōdceare
sorhwylmum sēað,   sīðe ne truwode

1978[b] *Fol. 173[b]* syððan *B.* — 1981[a] *MS.* side ręced (side *added over the line*); *Ke.* (?), *Tho., 4 Edd.* healreced; *Gr.*[2] hēa reced; *Holt.*[1–4] (*cf. Zs. 119*): 2 *half-lines dropped out after* s. r. — 1983[a] *MS.* hæ nū (ð *erased after* æ); *Gr.*[1], *Sed.* hǣlum; *Bu. 9 f., Schü., Cha.* Hǣnum =Hǣðnum; *Tr., Holt.* (*cf. Zs. 125*) hæleðum. — 1989[a] *MS.* sęcce. — 1991[a] *MS.* wið; *Thk., Tho.* wīd-. — 1993[b] *See 669[b] Varr.*

lēofes mannes; ic ðē lange bæd,
1995 þæt ðū þone wælgǣst wihte ne grētte,
lēte Sūð-Dene sylfe geweorðan
gūðe wið Grendel. Gode ic þanc secge,
þæs ðe ic ðē gesundne gesēon mōste.'
Bīowulf maðelode, bearn Ecgðīoes:
2000 ' þæt is undyrne, dryhten Higelāc,
(micel) gemēting, monegum fīra,
hwylc (orleg)hwīl uncer Grendles
wearð on ðām wange, þǣr hē worna fela
Sige-Scyldingum sorge gefremede,
2005 yrmðe tō aldre; ic ðæt eall gewræc,
swā begylpan [ne] þearf Grendeles māga
(ǣnig) ofer eorðan ūhthlem þone,
sē ðe lengest leofað lāðan cynnes,
f(ācne) bifongen. — Ic ðǣr furðum cwōm
2010 tō ðām hringsele Hrōðgār grētan;
sōna mē se mǣra mago Healfdenes,
syððan hē mōdsefan mīnne cūðe,
wið his sylfes sunu setl getǣhte.
Weorod wæs on wynne; ne seah ic wīdan feorh
2015 under heofones hwealf healsittendra
medudrēam māran. Hwīlum mǣru cwēn,
friðusibb folca flet eall geondhwearf,
bǣdde byre geonge; oft hīo bēahwriðan

2000ᵃ *Fol. 174ᵃ* þ. — 2001ᵃ *MS. defective, see* 2002ᵃ, 2003ᵃ (Z.), 2006ᵃ, 2007ᵃ, 2009ᵃ, *etc.* — *Gr.* (mǣre); *Moore JEGPh. xviii 210* (mǣru). *Perh.* (micel), *cp.* 2354ᵇ–55ᵃ. — 2002ᵃ *Tho.* (orleg-). — 2004ᵃ *MS.* dingū *altered from* dungū. *See* 2052ᵇ, 2101ᵇ, 2159ᵃ. — 2006ᵃ *MS. A* swabe, *B* swal . . ; *Gru. tr. 296, Ke., et al., Sed.* swā ne gylpan; *Gr.*², *3 Edd.* swā begylpan [ne]; *cf. ESt. xxxix 431.* — 2007ᵃ *B* en . . ; *Ke.* ǣnig. — 2009ᵃ *MS. A* fæ . . , *B* fer . . ; *Ke., et al.* fǣr-; *Ke. ii* fen- (?), *Gru., et al.* fenne; *Bu. 97, Schü., Sed., Cha.* fācne (*so Jul. 350*) (*cf. Schröder ZfdA. xliii 365; Angl. xxxv 135*); *Tr., Holt.* flǣsce (*cp.* 2424). — 2018ᵃ *MS.* bædde; *MPh. iii 461, Holt., Schü.* bǣlde.

secge (sealde),   ǣr hīe tō setle gēong.
2020 Hwīlum for (d)uguðe   dohtor Hrōðgāres
eorlum on ende   ealuwǣge bær,
þā ic Frēaware   fletsittende
nemnan hȳrde,   þǣr hīo (næ)gled sinc
hæleðum sealde.   Sīo gehāten (is),
2025 geong goldhroden,   gladum suna Frōdan;
(h)afað þæs geworden   wine Scyldinga,
rīces hyrde,   ond þæt rǣd talað,
þæt hē mid ðȳ wīfe   wælfǣhða dǣl,
sæcca gesette.   Oft seldan hwǣr
2030 æfter lēodhryre   lȳtle hwīle
bongār būgeð,   þēah sēo brȳd duge!

Mæg þæs þonne ofþyncan   ðeod*ne* Heaðo-Beardna
ond þegna gehwām   þāra lēoda,
þonne hē mid fǣmnan   on flett gǣð:
2035 dryhtbearn Dena,   duguða biwenede;
on him gladiað   gomelra lāfe,
heard ond hringmǣl   Heaða-Bear[d]na gestrēon,
þenden hīe ðām wǣpnum   wealdan mōston, —
[XXVIIII–XXX] oð ðæt hīe forlǣddan   tō ðām lindplegan
2040 swǣse gesīðas   ond hyra sylfra feorh.

Þonne cwið æt bēore   sē ðe bēah gesyhð,
eald æscwiga,   sē ðe eall gem(an),

2019[a] *Fol. 174*[b] . . . . . . ǣr B; *Tho.* (sealde). — 2019[b] *MS., Ke., Tho., Holt., Schü., Cha.* hīe; *Gr., Edd.* hīo. *See Lang.* § 22. — 2020[a] *Gru. tr. 296* (d)uguðe. — 2021[a] *Aant. 29* on handa (?). — 2023[b] *Gr.*[1] (næ)gledsinc, *Gr.*[2] nægled sinc. — 2024[b] *Ke., et al.* (wæs), *Klu.* (*in Hold.*), *4 Edd.* (is). — 2026[a] *Ke.* (h)afað. — 2029[b] *Ke. ii, E.* Seldan ōhwǣr; *He.*[1–7]*, et al.* Oft [nō] seldan; *Klu.* (*in Hold.*) oft seldan (=sealdon) wǣre; *Holt.*[3] oft [bið] sēl and wǣr; *Sed.* (*cf. MLR. v 287*) oft sēlð onhwearf. [*Cf. Rie. Zs. 404; Bu. 369.*] — 2032[b] *MS.* ðeoden; *Ke., et al., Holt., Sed.* ðēodne. — 2035[a] *Klu. ix 191* (?), *Hold.*[1]*, Holt.*[1] dryhtbeorn. — 2035[b] *Tho.* duguðe beþēnede; *Gr., et al., Holt.*[1–3]*, Cha.* duguða (*Holt.:* duguðe) bī werede. — 2037[b] *MS.* heaða bearna; *Tho.* Heaðo-beardna. *See Lang.* § 19.6. — 2039[a] *The canto division is indicated by a large capital* O. *Cf. Intr. cf.* — 2041[b] *Gr.*[1] bill (?) (*for* bēah); *Bu. 98* bā; *Holt. Zs. 119, Sed.* beorn. — *Fol. 175*[a] gesyhð. — 2042[b] *Gru. tr. 296* gem(on), *Tho.* gem(an).

gārcwealm gumena — him biðgrim sefa —,
onginneð geōmormōd geong(um) cempan
2045 þurh hreðra gehygd higes cunnian,
wīgbealu weccean, ond þæt word ācwyð:
" Meaht ðū, mīn wine, mēce gecnāwan,
þone þīn fæder tō gefeohte bær
under heregrīman hindeman sīðe,
2050 dȳre īren, þǣr hyne Dene slōgon,
wēoldon wælstōwe, syððan Wiðergyld læg,
æfter hæleþa hryre, hwate Scyldungas?
Nū hēr þāra banena byre nāthwylces
frætwum hrēmig on flet gǣð,
2055 morðres gylpeð, ond þone māðþum byreð,
þone þe ðū mid rihte rǣdan sceoldest."
Manað swā ond myndgað mǣla gehwylce
sārum wordum, oð ðæt sǣl cymeð,
þæt se fǣmnan þegn fore fæder dǣdum
2060 æfter billes bite blōdfāg swefeð,
ealdres scyldig; him se ōðer þonan
losað (li)figende, con him land geare.
Þonne bīoð (āb)rocene on bā healfe
āðsweord eorla; (syð)ðan Ingelde
2065 weallað wælnīðas, ond him wīflufan
æfter cearwælmum cōlran weorðað.
Þȳ ic Heaðo-Bear[d]na hyldo ne telge,
dryhtsibbe dǣl Denum unfǣcne,
frēondscipe fæstne.

Ic sceal forð sprecan

2044[b] *Gru. tr. 296, Schü.* geong(ne); *Ke.* (*1st ed., 1833, see Cha.*), *Gr.*, *3 Edd.* geong(um). — 2048[a] *Holt.*[2], *Sed.* [frōd] fæder; *Holt.*[3-6] fæder [fǣge]. *Cf. T.C.* § 17. — 2051[b] *Gru. tr. 296, Gr.*[1], *et al.* wiðergyld. — 2055[a] *MS. B* gylped; *Ke.* gylpeð. — 2059[a] *Barnouw 23* fǣmnan-þegn. *See note on 910 f.* — 2059[b] *He.*[1-3], *Holt.* for. — 2062[a] *Fol. 175*[b] figende *A*, eigende *B; He.*[2] (li)figende. — 2063[a] *MS. A* orocene, *B* .orocene; *Ke., Z., 3 Edd.* ābrocene; *Tho., Schü.* brocene. — 2064[a] *MS.* sweorð (?); *Thk.* -sweord. — 2064[b] *Ke.* (syþ)ðan. — 2067[a] *MS.* bearna; *Tho.* -beardna.

2070 gēn ymbe Grendel,   þæt ðū geare cunne,
sinces brytta,   tō hwan syððan wearð
hondrǣs hæleða.   Syððan heofones gim
glād ofer grundas,   gǣst yrre cwōm,
eatol ǣfengrom   ūser nēosan,
2075 ðǣr wē gesunde   sæl weardodon.
þǣr wæs Hondsciô   hild onsǣge,
feorhbealu fǣgum;   hē fyrmest læg,
gyrded cempa;   him Grendel wearð,
mǣrum magu̇þegne   tō mūðbonan,
2080 lēofes mannes   līc eall forswealg.
Nō ðȳ ǣr ūt ðā gēn   īdelhende
bona blōdigtōð,   bealewa gemyndig,
of ðām goldsele   gongan wolde;
ac hē mægnes rōf   mīn costode,
2085 grāpode gearọfolm.   Glōf hangode
sīd ond syllīc,   searobendum fæst;
sīo wæs orðoncum   eall gegyrwed
dēofles cræftum   ond dracan fellum.
Hē mec þǣr on innan   unsynnigne,
2090 dīor dǣdfruma   gedōn wolde
manigra sumne;   hyt ne mihte swā,
syððan ic on yrre   uppriht āstōd.
Tō lang ys tō reccenne,   hū i(c ð)ām lēodsceaðan
yfla gehwylces   ọndlēan forgeald;
2095 þǣr ic, þēoden mīn,   þīne lēode
weorðode weorcum.   Hē on weg losade,

2070[a] *Gr., Holt.* ymb. *See T.C.* § *13.* — 2076[b] *MS.* hilde; *Holtzm. 496, Rie. Zs. 405* hild
See 2483. — 2079[a] *MS.* magū; *Ke.* magu-. — 2085[a] *Fol. 176[a]* grapode *AB.* — *MS. A*
geareo; *Thk.* gearo, *Ke.* geara-, *Ke. ii* gearo-. — 2088[b] *Tr.* of (*for* ond). *Cf. MPh. iii 240.*
— 2093[a] *Siev. R. 312, Holt., Schü., Sed.* reccan. *See T.C.* § *12.* — 2093[b] *MS. A* huiedā;
Gru. tr. 297, Ke. hū ic ðām. — 2094[b] *MS.* hond; *Gr.*[1] (?), *Ric. Zs. 415, Holt., Schü., Cha.*
ond-. *See 1541[b].*

lȳtle hwīle   līfwynna br(ēa)c;
hwæþre him sīo swīðre   swaðe weardade
hand on Hiorte,   ond hē hēan ðonan,
2100 mōdes geōmor   meregrund gefēoll.
Mē þone wælrǣs   wine Scildunga
fættan golde   fela lēanode,
manegum māðmum,   syððan mergen cōm,
ond wē tō symble   geseten hæfdon.
2105 Þǣr wæs gidd ond glēo;   gomela Scilding,
felafricgende   feorran rehte;
hwīlum hildedēor   hearpan wynne,
gome*n*wudu grētte,   hwīlum gyd āwræc
sōð ond sārlīc,   hwīlum syllīc spell
2110 rehte æfter rihte   rūmheort cyning;
hwīlum eft ongan   eldo gebunden,
gomel gūðwiga   gioguðe cwīðan,
hildestrengo;   hreðer inne wēoll,
þonne hē wintrum frōd   worn gemunde.
2115 Swā wē þǣr inne   andlangne dæg
nīode nāman,   oð ðæt niht becwōm
ōðer tō yldum.   Þā wæs eft hraðe
gearo gyrnwræce   Grendeles mōdor,
sīðode sorhfull;   sunu dēað fornam,
2120 wīghete Wedra.   Wīf unhȳre
hyre bearn gewræc,   beorn ācwealde
ellenlīce;   þǣr wæs Æschere,
frōdan fyrnwitan   feorh ūðgenge.
Nōðer hȳ hine ne mōston,   syððan mergen cwōm,
2125 dēaðwērigne   Denia lēode

2097ᵇ *MS. A* brǣc, *B* brene *altered to* brec; *Ke.* brēac. — 2105ᵇ *Fol. 176ᵇ* scilding *AB*. — 2106ᵃ *Most Edd.* fela fricgende. *See MPh. iii 262.* — 2108ᵃ *MS.* go/mel (*AB*); *Gru. tr. 297* gomen-. — 2109ᵃ *Gr.¹* (?), *Scheinert Beitr. xxx 366* (?), *Holt.* searolīc.

BEOWULF

bronde forbærnan, nē on bēl hladan,
lēofne mannan; hīo þæt līc ætbær
fēondes fæð(mum un)der firgenstrēam.
þæt wæs Hrōðgāre hrēowa tornost
2130 þāra þe lēodfruman lange begēate.
þā se ðēoden mec ðīne līfe
healsode hrēohmōd, þæt ic on holma geþring
eorlscipe efnde, ealdre genēðde,
mærðo fremede; hē mē mēde gehēt.
2135 Ic ðā ðæs wælmes, þē is wīde cūð,
grim*n*e gryrelīcne grundhyrde fond.
þær unc hwīle wæs hand gemǣne;
holm heolfre wēoll, ond ic hēafde becearf
in ðām [gūð]sele Grendeles mōdor
2140 ēacnum ecgum; unsōfte þonan
feorh oðferede; næs ic fǣge þā gȳt;
ac mē eorla hlēo eft gesealde
māðma menigeo, maga Healfdenes.

XXXI   Swā ʒe ðēodkyning   þēawum lyfde;
2145 nealles ic ðām lēanum forloren hæfde,
mægnes mēde, ac hē mē (māðma)s geaf,
sunu Healfdenes on (mīn)ne sylfes dōm;
ðā ic ðē, beorncyning, bringan wylle,
ēstum geȳwan. Gēn is eall æt ðē
2150 lissa gelong; ic lȳt hafo
hēafodmāga nefne, Hygelāc, ðec.'

2126[b] *MS.* bęl; *see note on 1981; Edd. exc. Holt. & Cha. normalize to* bǣl. — 2127[b] *Fol.* 177[a] hio *AB.* — 2128[a–b] *MS.* fæð. . . . . . . ; *Ke.* fæðrunga, under; *Gr.*[2] fæðmum under. — 2136[a] *MS.* grimme; *Tho.* grimne. — 2137[b] *Gru. tr. 297, Ke., et al., Cha.* hand-gemǣne. — 2139[a] *Tho., Holt., Sed., Panzer 281, Lawrence Publ. MLAss. xxvii 237 n. 2* [gūð-], *cp. 1513; Gru. tr. 297, E. tr., et al., Schü., Cha.* [grund-]. — 2146[b] *Fol.* 177[b]. . . . is *B(A); Gru. tr. 297, Ke.* māðmas. — 2147[b] *Ke., most Edd.* (mīn)ne; *Gru.* (sīn)ne. — 2150[a] *Holt. Beibl. x 269 (cf. Siev. R. 312), Tr., Sed.* gelenge; *Holt. Lit. bl. xxi 61* gelong lissa; *JEGPh. viii 257, Cha.* [mīnra]; *Siev.* (*in Schü.*) gelong[ra], (*cp. 1784*[a]).

Hēt ðā in beran   eafor hēafodsegn,
heaðostēapne helm,   hāre byrnan,
gūðsweord geatolīc,   gyd æfter wræc:
2155 'Mē ðis hildesceorp   Hrōðgār sealde,
snotra fengel;   sume worde hēt,
þæt ic his ǣrest ðē   ēst gesægde;
cwæð þæt hyt hæfde   Hiorogār cyning,
lēod Scyldunga   lange hwīle;
2160 nō ðȳ ǣr suna sīnum   syllan wolde,
hwatum Heorowearde,   þēah hē him hold wǣre,
brēostgewǣdu.   Brūc ealles well!'
Hȳrde ic þæt þām frætwum   fēower mēaras
lungre, gelīce   lāst weardode,
2165 æppelfealuwe;   hē him ēst getēah
mēara ond māðma. —   Swā sceal mǣg dôn,
nealles inwitnet   ōðrum bregdon
dyrnum cræfte,   dēað rēn(ian)
hondgesteallan.   Hygelāce wæs
2170 nīða heardum   nefa swȳðe hold,
ond gehwæðer ōðrum   hrōþra gemyndig. —
Hȳrde ic þæt hē ðone healsbēah   Hygde gesealde,
wrǣtlicne wundurmāððum,   ðone þe him Wealhðēo geaf,
ðēod(nes) dohtor,   þrīo wicg somod
2175 swancor ond sadolbeorht;   hyre syððan wæs
æfter bēahðege   br[ē]ost geweorðod.
   Swā bealdode   bearn Ecgðēowes,
guma gūðum cūð,   gōdum dǣdum,
drēah æfter dōme;   nealles druncne slōg
2180 heorðgenēatas;   næs him hrēoh sefa,

2152ᵇ *Most Edd., Holt., Sed.* eaforhēafodsegn. *Cf. MPh. iii 462.* — 2154ᵇ *Z. translit* sprǣc (*misprint*). — 2157ᵃ *Conybeare L 1.4 (?), Tho.* ǣrend; *Gr.*¹ (?), *Rie. Zs. 405 f.* ǣrist ('origo'?). — 2164ᵇ *Ke., et al., Holt.* weardodon. *See note on 904 f.* — 2166ᵇ *Fol. 178ᵃ* mǣg. — 2168ᵇ *Ke. ii* rēn(ian). — 2174ᵃ *Ke.* ðēod(nes). — 2176ᵇ *MS.* brost; *Tho.* br[ē]ost.

BEOWULF

ac hē mancynnes mæste cræfte
ginfæstan gife, þē him God sealde,
hēold hildedēor. Hēan wæs lange,
swā hyne Gēata bearn gōdne ne tealdon,
2185 nē hyne on medobence micles wyrðne
drihten We*dera* gedōn wolde;
swȳðe (wēn)don, þæt hē slēac wǣre,
æðeling unfrom. Edwenden cwōm
tīrēadįgum menn torna gehwylces. —
2190 Hēt ðā eorla hlēo in gefetian,
heaðorōf cyning Hrēðles lāfe
golde gegyrede; næs mid Gēatum ðā
sincmāðþųm sēlra on sweordes hād;
þæt hē on Bīowulfes bearm ālegde,
2195 ond him gesealde seofan þūsendo,
bold ond bregostōl. Him wæs bām samod
on ðām lēodscipe lond gecynde,
eard ēðelriht, ōðrum swīðor
sīde rīce þām ðǣr sēlra wæs.

2200   Eft þæt geīode ufaran dōgrum
hildehlæmmum, syððan Hygelāc læg,
ond Hear[dr]ēde hildemēceas
under bordhrēoðan tō bonan wurdon,
ðā hyne gesōhtan on sigeþēode
2205 hearde hil*d*frecan, Heaðo-Scilfingas,
nīða genǣgdan nefan Hererīces — :
syððan Bēowulfe brāde rīce

<small>2186ⁿ *Fol. 178ᵇ* drihten *B*. — *MS.* wereda; *Aant. 31, Holt., Sed., Cha.* Wedera. — 2187ⁿ *Gr.* (wēn)don. — 2202ⁿ *MS.* hearede; *Gru. tr. 298* Hear[dr]ēde. — 2205ⁿ *MS.* hilde; *Gru., Siev. R. 305 (?), Holt., Schü.* hild-. *See T.C. § 14*. — 2207ⁿ *Fol. 179ᵃ* beowulfe. *Folio 179, with the last page (Fol. 198ᵇ), is the worst part of the entire MS. It has been freshened up by a later hand, but not always correctly. Information on doubtful readings is in the notes of Zupitza and Chambers.*</small>

on hand gehwearf;   hē gehēold tela
fīftig wintra   — wæs ðā frōd cyning,
2210 eald ēþelweard —,   oð ðæt ān ongan
deorcum nihtum   draca rīcs[i]an,
sē ðe on hēa(ụm) h(æþ)e   hord beweotode,
stānbeorh stēapne;   stīg under læg
eldum uncūð.   Þǣr on innan gīong
2215 nið[ð]a nāthwylc,   (sē þe nē)h gefe(al)g
hǣðnum horde,   hond (wǣge nam),
(sīd,) since fāh;   nē hē þæt syððan (bemāð),
þ(ēah) ð(e hē) slǣpende   besyre(d wur)de
þēofes cræfte;   þæt sīe ðīod (onfand),
2220 b(ig)folc beorna,   þæt hē gebolge(n) wæs.

XXXII   Nealles mid gewealdum   wyrmhord ābræc,
sylfes willum,   sē ðe him sāre gescēod,
ac for þrēanēdlan   þ(ēow) nāthwylces
hæleða bearna   heteswengeas flēah,
2225 (ærnes) þearfa,   ond ðǣr inne fealh,

2209ᵃ *MS. later hand* wintru. — 2209ᵇ *Tho., Rie. Zs. 406, Sed.* þæt *for* ðā. — 2210ᵇ *MS. later hand* ón. — 2211ᵇ *A B* ricsan; *Ke.* rīcs[i]an. — 2212ᵃ *MS. letters between* hea *and* hord *very indistinct; Z. translit.* heaðo hlæwe (*so Holt.*¹⁻⁵, *Schü.*), *but* ðo *seems too short and* hlæwe *too long for the space in the MS.; Cha. seems to recognize* um *and afte- it either* hæþe (*so Siev. xxxvi 418*) *or* hope; *Sed., Holt.*⁶ hēaum hæþe, *Cha.* hēaum hope, *Kock*ᵇ *176* h. hofe. — 2215ᵃ *Klu.* (*in Hold.*²) nið[ð]a. — 2215ᵇ *MS.* : : : : : : : h gefe :(:)g; *Sed.* sē (þe) n(ē)h (*so Tr.*) geþ(ra)ng. *Restoration of* 2215ᵇ-17ᵇ *by Bu. 99 f.:* nēode tō gefēng/hǣðnum horde; hond ætgenam/seleful since fāh; nē hē þæt syððan āgeaf. *Cf. also Holt.* — 2216ᵇ-17ᵃ *Tr.* hond (wǣge nam),/(sigle) since fāch. 2217ᵃ *MS. originally* fac, *but* h *written over* c. 2217ᵇ *Angl. xxviii 446* (bemāð). *Sed.* since fāhne; hē þæt syððan (wræc). — 2218ᵃ *MS. Z.* þ(eah) ð(e he). — 2218ᵇ *Klu.* (*in Hold.*²) besyre(d wur)de. — 2219ᵇ *A B* sie, *Klu.* (*in Hold.*¹) sīo (*which may very well have been the original reading before the freshening up of the page* [*Cha.*]). — *Gr.*² (onfand). — 2220ᵃ *MS. apparently* bu (?) *or by* (?); *Bu. 100* (bȳ)folc; *Tr., Sed., Cha.* (bū)folc; *Klu.* (*in Hold.*²), *Holt.* (burh)folc [*too long*]. *Thk., et al.* . . . . . folcbiorn. *Malone JEGPh. xxvii 320 ff.* bū folcbeorna. *See T.C.* § 28 n. 2. *Cf. Krackow L 7.19.44.* — 2220ᵇ *Gr.*¹ gebolge(n). — 2221ᵃ *MS.* ge wealdū *w. a changed to* o *by later hand.* — 2221ᵇ *MS.* horda/cræft; *Tr.* -hord āstrēad; *Kaluza* (*in Holt.*), *4 Edd.* -hord ābræc. — 2223ᵇ *Ke., Z., Holt., Schü., Lawrence L 4.62a.554 f.* þ(egn); *Gru., Bu. Zs. 210, Sed., Cha.* þ(ēow); *Lawrence l.c.* prece *or* þrym(?). — 2224ᵇ *MS.* fleah *w. a changed to* o *by later hand.* — 2225ᵃ *MS. Z.* (ærnes) ('æ *and* n *are almost certain*' *Z.*). — 2225ᵇ *MS.* weal:, *A B* weall. w w *apparently standing on an orig.* f (*Z.*); *Gr.*¹ fealh.

secg synbysig.   Sōna †mwatide
þæt : : : : : ðām gyst(e   gryre)brōga stōd;
hwæðre (earm)sceapen   ....
.... sceapen
2230 ....   (þā hyne) se fǣr begeat.
Sincfæt .....
                    þǣr wæs swylcra fela
in ðām eorð(hū)se   ǣrgestrēona,
swā hȳ on gēardagum   gumena nāthwylc,
eormenlāfe   æðelan cynnes,
2235 þanchycgende   þǣr gehȳdde,
dēore māðmas.   Ealle hīe dēað fornam
ǣrran mǣlum,   ond sē ān ðā gēn
lēoda duguðe,   sē ðǣr lengest hwearf,
weard winegeōmor,   wēnde þæs ylcan,
2240 þæt hē lȳtel fæc   longgestrēona
brūcan mōste.   Beorh eallgearo
wunode on wonge   wæterȳðum nēah,
nīwe be næsse,   nearocræftum fæst;
þǣr on innan bær   eorlgestrēona
2245 hringa hyrde   hordwyrðne dǣl,
fǣttan goldes,   fēa worda cwæð:

2226[b] *MS.* mwatide [*the sign* † *in this ed. indicates that the reading is hopelessly corrupt*]; *Tho.,* (*cf. Bu. 101,*) *Schü., Cha.* inwlātode; *Holt.* hē wagode; *Sed.*[2] þæt geīode. — 2227 *MS. Z.: apparently* gyst(e gryre)brōga; *Gr.*[1] *had conjectured* gryre. *Cp. Dan. 524 f.* — 2228[a] *MS. Z.* (?), *MS. Ke.* (earm). — 2229[a] *Fol. 179*[b]. — 2230[b] *MS. Z.* (?), *MS. Cha.* (þā hyne). — *MS. Z., MS. Cha. orig.* fǣr *w.* r *altered to* s. — 2231[a] *Gr.*[1] (sōhte) (?); *He.*[2], *Tr., Cha.* (geseah); *Holt.* (genōm). — 2232[a] *Ke.* (scræfe); *Z.* (hū)se; *Klu.* (*in Hold.*[2]) (sel)e. — 2234[b] *A* æþelan, *B* æðelan. — 2237[b] *MS.* si; *Ke. ii* se. — 2239[a] *MS. B* weard (*A* feard), *MS. Z.: orig.* wearð (ð *doubted by Cha.*); *Gru., Tr., Schü., Cha., Holt.* weard; *Tho., Sed.* wearð. — 2239[b] *MS. Z.:* 'rihde *the later hand, but* wende *the first.*' — *MS.* yldan, *but Sed. established the fact that* d *had been clumsily altered from* c. — 2241[b] *Tho., et al., Cha.* eall gearo. *See* 77[b]. — 2244[a] *MS. Z.* innon *w.* o *altered fr.* a (*alteration doubted by Cha.*). — 2245[b] *MS. Z.* hard wyrðne (*or* f *instead of* w?); *Gr.* hardfyrdne; *Bout. 98* hord byrhtne; *Bu. 102* hordwynne; *Schü.* hord, wyrðne; *ESt. xxxix 431, Sed., Cha., Holt.* hordwyrðne. — 2246[b] *MS.* fea *w.* a *altered to* c (*Z.*).

' Heald þū nū, hrūse,   nū hæleð ne mōstan,
eorla æhte!   Hwæt, hyt ǣr on ðē
gōde begēaton;   gūðdēað fornam,
2250 feorhbealo frēcne   fȳra gehwylcne
lēoda mīnra   þāra ðe þis [līf] ofgeaf,
gesāwon seledrēam.   Nāh, hwā sweord wege
oððe fe(o)r(mie)   fǣted wǣge,
dryncfæt dēore;   dug(uð) ellor s[c]eōc.
2255 Sceal se hearda helm   (hyr)stedgolde,
fǣtum befeallen;   feormynd swefað,
þā ðe beadogrīman   bȳwan sceoldon;
gē swylce sēo herepād,   sīo æt hilde gebād
ofer borda gebræc   bite īrena,
2260 brosnað æfter beorne.   Ne mæg byrnan hring
æfter wīgfruman   wīde fēran,
hæleðum be healfe.   Næs hearpan wyn,
gomen glēobēames,   nē gōd hafoc
geond sæl swingeð,   nē se swifta mearh
2265 burhstede bēateð.   Bealocwealm hafað
fela feorhcynna   forð onsended! '
Swā giōmormōd   giohðo mǣnde
ān æfter eallum,   unblīðe hwe(arf)
dæges ond nihtes,   oð ðæt dēaðes wylm
2270 hrān æt heortan.   Hordwynne fond
eald ūhtsceaða   opene standan,

2247[b] *MS.* mæstan; *Z.: perh. orig.* mostun (*or* -on); *Cha.:* ' all very obscure.' — 2250[b] *MS.* fyrena; *Ke. ii* fira, *Tho.* fȳra. — 2251[b] *MS.* þana; *Ke. ii* þāra. — *Ke. ii, 3 Edd.* [līf]; *Holt.* (*cf. L 5.26.19*) [lēoht]. — 2252 *MS.* gesawon; *Rie. Zs. 408*, *Holt.*[1–2] gesība; *Tr., JEGPh. vi 193* secga; *Bu. 102* geswǣfon seledrēamas. *MS.* dream *or* dream : : (*erasure?*); *Holt., Sed., Cha.* (Ic) nāh. *Fol. 180*[a] nah. — 2253[a] *MS. Z.* fe : r : : : ; *Gr.*[1] feormie. — 2254[b] *Ke.* (*ii*) dug(uð). — *MS.* seoc; *Gr.*[1] scōc. — 2255[b] *Gru. tr. 299*, *Edd.* (hyr)sted golde; *Kock*[2] *118*, *Kock*[5] *177* (hyr)stedgolde. (*Cp. Gen. 2155.*) — 2256[b] (*Ke.,*) *Gr.*[2], *et al.* feormend, *Ke. ii, et al.* feormiend. — 2259[b] *Siev. R. 253*, *Tr., Holt., Schü., Sed.* īren[n]a. *See 673*[a] *Varr.* — 2262[b] *Tho., Bu. Zs. 212, 4 Edd.* nis. — 2266[b] *MS. Z.* feorð (*i.e.* forð). — 2268[b] *MS. Ke.* hweop, *MS. Tho.* hwæ . . ; *A* hweir *w. another ink*; *Gr. Spr.* (*s.v. hvōpan*), *Schü.*[9,10] wēop; *Gr.*[2], *4 Edd.* hwearf.

sē ðe byrnende   biorgas sēceð,
nacod nīðdraca,   nihtes flēogeð
fȳre befangen;   hyne foldbūend
2275 (swīðe ondræ)da(ð).   Hē gesēcean sceall
(ho)r(d on) hrūsan,   þær hē hæðen gold
warað wintrum frōd;   ne byð him wihte ðȳ sēl.
    Swā se ðēodsceaða   þrēo hund wintra
hēold on hrūsan   hordærna sum
2280 ēacencræftig,   oð ðæt hyne ān ābealch
mon on mōde;   mandryhtne bær
fæted wæge,   frioðowære bæd
hlāford sīnne.   Ðā wæs hord rāsod,
onboren bēaga hord,   bēne getīðad
2285 fēasceaftum men;   frēa scēawode
fīra fyrngeweorc   forman sīðe. —
    Þā se wyrm onwōc,   wrōht wæs genīwad;
stonc ðā æfter stāne,   stearcheort onfand
fēondes fōtlāst;   hē tō forð gestōp
2290 dyrnan cræfte   dracan hēafde nēah.
Swā mæg unfæge   ēaðe gedīgan
wēan ond wræcsīð   sē ðe Waldendes
hyldo gehealdeþ!   Hordweard sōhte
georne æfter grunde,   wolde guman findan,
2295 þone þe him on sweofote   sāre getēode;
hāt ond hrēohmōd   hlǣw oft ymbehwearf
ealne ūtanweardne;   nē ðær ænig mon

2275ᵃ *Fol. 180ᵇ Z.* (swiðe ondræ)da(ð). — 2276ᵃ *Gr.*² (hea)r(h on); *Z.* (ho)r(d on). — 2279ᵃ *MS.* hrusam; *Thk.* hrūsan. — 2280ᵇ *Gru. tr. 300, Tho., et al.* ābealh. — 2283ᵇ *Bu. Zs. 212* hearh (?), *Holt. Zs. 120, Sed.* hlǣw (*for* hord). — 2284ᵃ *Bu. Zs. 212* dǣl (?), *Cos. viii 572* sum (?) (*for* hord). — 2295ᵇ *Aant. 33, Holt., Schü., Sed.* sār. — 2296ᵇ *Fol. 181ᵃ* hlǣwū; *Ke., 4 Edd.* hlǣw; *Gru., et al.* hlǣw nū. — *Siev. R. 258, Holt., Schü.* ymb-. *See T.C.* § *13.* — 2297ᵃ *MS.* ealne utanweardne; *Siev. R. 306, Holt.*¹⁻⁵ eal ūtanweard; *Siev. A. M.* § *85 n. 8* (?), *Wroblewski Über d. ae. Gesetze d. Königs Knut (Berlin Diss. 1901) p. 61, Schü.* ealne ūtweardne; *Tr., Holt.*⁶ ealne ūtanweard; *Sed.* ealne ūtan. — 2297ᵇ *MS.* ne; *Gr.*¹ ne [wæs]; *Gr.*¹ (?), *Aant. 34, Holt., Schü., Cha.* næs; *Sed.* ne [wearð].

on þære wēstenne, — hwæðre *wīges* gefeh,
bea(du)[we] weorces;   hwīlum on beorh æthwearf,
2300 sincfæt sōhte;   hē þæt sōna onfand,
ðæt hæfde gumena sum   goldes gefandod,
hēahgestrēona.   Hordweard onbād
earfoðlīce,   oð ðæt æfen cwōm;
wæs ðā gebolgen   beorges hyrde,
2305 wolde *se* lāða   līge forgyldan
drincfæt dȳre.   Þā wæs dæg sceacen
wyrme on willan;   nō on wealle læ[n]g
bīdan wolde,   ac mid bæle fōr,
fȳre gefȳsed.   Wæs se fruma egeslīc
2310 lēodum on lande,   swā hyt lungre wearð
on hyra sincgifan   sāre geendod.

XXXIII Ðā se gæst ongan   glēdum spīwan,
beorht hofu bærnan, —   brynelēoma stōd
eldum on andan;   nō ðær āht cwices
2315 lāð lyftfloga   læfan wolde.
Wæs þæs wyrmes wīg   wīde gesȳne,
nearofāges nīð   nēan ond feorran,
hū se gūðsceaða   Gēata lēode
hatode ond hȳnde;   hord eft gescēat,
2320 dryhtsele dyrnne   ǣr dæges hwīle.
Hæfde landwara   līge befangen,
bæle ond bronde;   beorges getruwode,
wīges ond wealles;   him sēo wēn gelēah.
Þā wæs Bīowulfe   brōga gecȳðed
2325 snūde tō sōðe,   þæt his sylfes hām,

<small>2298 *Rie. Zs. 408* assumes lacuna after wēstenne, *Sed.* after gefeh; *Koeppel ZfdPh. xxiii 121* would strike out 2296ᵇ–98ᵃ. — MS. hilde; *Tr., Schü., Holt., Cha.* wīges. [*Cf. Bu. 103; t. Br. 132.*] — 2299ᵃ *Ke.* bea(du)-; *JEGPh. viii 257 f., 3 Edd.* bea(du)[we]; *Holt. Angl. xxi 366, Sed.* bea(du)weorces [georn]. — 2305ᵃ MS. fela ða; *Bu. Zs. 212* se lāða. — 2307ᵇ MS. læg; *Gru. tr. 300* leng; *Aant. 34* læng. — 2315ᵇ *Fol. 181ᵇ* wolde *AB*. — 2322ᵇ See 669ᵇ *Varr.* — 2325ᵇ MS. him; *Gru. tr. 301* hām.</small>

bolda sēlest   brynewylmum mealt,
gifstōl Gēata.   þæt ðām gōdan wæs
hrēow on hreðre,   hygesorga mæst;
wēnde se wīsa,   þæt hē Wealdende
2330 ofer ealde riht   ēcean Dryhtne
bitre gebulge;   brēost innan wēoll
þēostrum geþoncum,   swā him geþȳwe ne wæs.
Hæfde līgdraca   lēoda fæsten,
ēalond ūtan,   eorðweard ðone
2335 glēdum forgrunden;   him ðæs gūðkyning,
Wedera þīoden   wræce leornode.
Heht him þā gewyrcean   wīgendra hlēo
eallīrenne,   eorla dryhten,
wīgbord wrætlīc;   wisse hē gearwe,
2340 þæt him holtwudu   he(lpan) ne meahte,
lind wið līge.   Sceolde *lǣn*daga
æþeling ǣrgōd   ende gebīdan,
worulde līfes,   ond se wyrm somod,
þēah ðe hordwelan   hēolde lange.
2345 Oferhogode ðā   hringa fengel,
þæt hē þone wīdflogan   weorode gesōhte,
sīdan herge;   nō hē him *þā* sæcce ondrēd,
nē him þæs wyrmes wīg   for wiht dyde,
eafoð ond ellen,   forðon hē ǣr fela
2350 nearo nēðende   nīða gedīgde,
hildehlemma,   syððan hē Hrōðgāres,
sigorēadig secg,   sele fælsode,
ond æt gūðe forgrāp   Grendeles mǣgum

2334ᵇ *Sweet Ags. Dict.* eorðgeard (?). — *Gr.*¹, *Gru.*, *Sed.* ðonne. — 2338ᵃ *Bu. Tid. 56* eallīrenne [scyld]; *Holt. Lit. bl. xxi 61 & Zs. 120* īrenne [scyld] (*Holt.*³·⁴: 2337ᵇ wīgena hlēo [scyld]); *Kock*² *119 f.* eallīren ner ('protection'). — 2339ᵇ *Fol. 182ᵃ* wisse. — 2340ᵇ *Thk.* he(lpan). — 2341ᵇ *MS.* þend; *Gru. tr. 301* (?), *Ke. ii* lǣn-. — 2347ᵇ *MS.* hī þā (*i.e.* him þām); *Ke. ii* him þā.

lāðan cynnes.
      Nō þæt lǣsest wæs
2355 hondgemōt[a], þǣr mon Hygelāc slōh,
syððan Gēata cyning gūðe rǣsum,
frēawine folca Frēslondum on,
Hrēðles eafora hiorodryncum swealt,
bille gebēaten. Þonan Bīowulf cōm
2360 sylfes cræfte, sundnytte drēah;
hæfde him on earme (āna) þrītig
hildegeatwa, þā hē tō holme (st)āg.
Nealles Hetware hrēmge þorf(t)on
fēðewīges, þē him foran ongēan
2365 linde bǣron; lȳt eft becwōm
fram þām hildfrecan hāmes nīosan!
Oferswam ðā sioleða bigong sunu Ecgðēowes,
earm ānhaga eft tō lēodum;
þǣr him Hygd gebēad hord ond rīce,
2370 bēagas ond bregostōl; bearne ne truwode,
þæt hē wið ælfylcum ēþelstōlas
healdan cūðe, ðā wæs Hygelāc dēad.
Nō ðȳ ǣr fēasceafte findan meahton
æt ðām æðelinge ǣnige ðinga,
2375 þæt hē Heardrēde hlāford wǣre,
oððe þone cynedōm cīosan wolde;
hwæðre hē hine on folce frēondlārum hēold,
ēstum mid āre, oð ðæt hē yldra wearð,
Weder-Gēatum wēold.
       Hyne wræcmæcgas
2380 ofer sǣ sōhtan, suna Ōhteres;

2354[a] t. Br. 151 (?), Tr., Holt.[1,6], Kock[5] 178 cynne. — 2355[a] MS. AB gemot; Ke. -gemōt[a]. — 2356[b] Hoops gūðerǣsum; si. 2626[b]. — 2361[b] Fol. 182[b] Z. . . . . xxx.; Gr.[1] (āna). — 2362[b] Ke. (st)āg. — 2363[b] Ke. þorf(t)on. — 2367[a] Tho. siol-ēðel (drops bigong); Bout. 100 seolhbaða; Gr.[1] siolēða (=-ȳða). — 2370[b] See 669[b] Varr. — 2377[a] MS. hī; Tho. hine.

BEOWULF

hæfdon hȳ forhealden   helm Scylfinga,
þone sēlestan   sǣcyninga
þāra ðe in Swīorīce   sinc brytnade,
mǣrne þēoden. Him þæt tō mearce wearð;
2385 hē þǣr [f]or feorme   feorhwunde hlēat,
sweordes swengum,   sunu Hygelāces;
ond him eft gewāt   Ongenðīoes bearn
hāmes nīosan,   syððan Heardrēd læg,
lēt ðone bregostōl   Bīowulf healdan,
2390 Gēatum wealdan;   þæt wæs gōd cyning.

XXXIIII Sē ðæs lēodhryres   lēan gemunde
uferan dōgrum,   Ēadgilse wearð
fēasceaftum frēond;   folce gestēpte
ofer sǣ sīde   sunu Ōhteres,
2395 wigum ond wǣpnum;   hē gewræc syððan
cealdum cearsīðum,   cyning ealdre binēat.

Swā hē nīða gehwane   genesen hæfde,
slīðra geslyhta,   sunu Ecgðīowes,
ellenweorca,   oð ðone ānne dæg,
2400 þē hē wið þām wyrme   gewegan sceolde.
Gewāt þā twelfa sum   torne gebolgen
dryhten Gēata   dracan scēawian;
hæfde þā gefrūnen,   hwanan sīo fǣhð ārās,
bealonīð biorna;   him tō bearme cwōm
2405 māðþumfæt mǣre   þurh ðæs meldan hond.
Sē wæs on ðām ðrēate   þreottēoða secg,
sē ðæs orleges   ōr onstealde,
hæft hygegiōmor,   sceolde hēan ðonon

2383ª *MS*.ðe/ðe; *Ke.* ðe. — 2384ª *Fol. 183*ª þeoden *AB.* — 2385ª *MS.* orfeorme; *Gr.* on feorme; *Mö. 111, 4 Edd.* [f]or feorme. — 2387ᵇ *Siev. R. 266, Holt* Ongenðīoes. *Cf T.C.* §§ 7, 2. — 2394ª *Schröder ZfdA. xliii 366 f., Schü.*⁸⁻¹⁰ sǣsīðe. *But see ESt. xxxix 432.* — 2396ª *Aant. 35* cealde cearsīðas; *Tr.* cwealm cearsīðum. — 2401ª *MS.* .xīī. — 2404ᵇ *Fol. 183ᵇ* cwom *AB.*

wong wīsian. Hē ofer willan gīong
2410 tō ðæs ðe hē eorðsele ānne wisse,
hlǣw under hrūsan holmwylme nēh,
ȳðgewinne; sē wæs innan full
wrǣtta ond wīra. Weard unhīore,
gearo gūðfreca goldmāðmas hēold
2415 eald under eorðan; næs þæt ȳðe cēap
tō gegangenne gumena ǣnigum.
Gesæt ðā on næsse nīðheard cyning;
þenden hǣlo ābēad heorðgenēatum,
goldwine Gēata. Him wæs geōmor sefa,
2420 wǣfre ond wælfūs, wyrd ungemete nēah,
sē ðone gomelan grētan sceolde,
sēcean sāwle hord, sundur gedǣlan
līf wið līce; nō þon lange wæs
feorh æþelinges flǣsce bewunden.
2425 Bīowulf maþelade, bearn Ecgðēowes:
' Fela ic on giogoðe gūðrǣsa genæs,
orleghwīla; ic þæt eall gemon.
Ic wæs syfanwintre, þā mec sinca baldor,
frēawine folca æt mīnum fæder genam;
2430 hēold mec ond hæfde Hrēðel cyning,
geaf mē sinc ond symbel, sibbe gemunde;
næs ic him tō līfe lāðra ōwihte,
beorn in burgum, þonne his bearna hwylc,
Herebeald ond Hæðcyn oððe Hygelāc mīn.
2435 Wæs þām yldestan ungedēfelīce
mǣges dǣdum morþorbed strêd,

2421ª *Gr., et al.* sēo. See *1887*ᵇ. — 2423ᵇ *Gru., Sed.* (?) þonne. — *Gr.*¹ leng ne (?); *Aant.*
35 længe. — 2428ª *Fol. 184*ª ic. — 2430ᵇ *Holt.*¹ (*cf. Zs. 120*), *Sed.* geaf mē H. c.; *Holt.*²⁻⁴
Hrēðel cyning geaf. See *T.C.* § *17*. — 2432ᵇ *Siev. R. 256* (?), *Holt.*¹⁻⁵, *Schü.* wihte, *Tr.*
ōwiht, *Holt.*⁶ ōhte. See *T.C.* § *20*. — 2435ᵇ *MS.* ungedefelice; *Siev. R. 234, A. M.* § *85*
n. 8 ungedēfe; *Hoops St. 10* ungedēfelīce.

BEOWULF

syððan hyne Hæðcyn   of hornbogan,
his frēawine   flāne geswencte,
miste mercelses   ond his mǣg ofscēt,
2440 brōðor ōðerne   blōdigan gāre.
   Þæt wæs feohlēas gefeoht,   fyrenum gesyngad,
hreðre hygemēðe;   sceolde hwæðre swā þēah
æðeling unwrecen   ealdres linnan.
   Swā bið geōmorlīc   gomelum ceorle
2445 tō gebīdanne,   þæt his byre rīde
giong on galgan;   þonne hē gyd wrece,
sārigne sang,   þonne his sunu hangað
hrefne tō hrōðre,   ond hē him helpe ne mæg
eald ond infrōd   ǣnige gefremman.
2450 Symble bið gemyndgad   morna gehwylce
eaforan ellorsīð;   ōðres ne gȳmeð
tō gebīdanne   burgum in innan
yrfeweardas,   þonne se ān hafað
þurh dēaðes nȳd   dǣda gefondad.
2455 Gesyhð sorhcearig   on his suna būre
wīnsele wēstne,   windge reste
reōte berofene, —   rīdend swefað,
hæleð in hoðman;   nis þǣr hearpan swēg,
gomen in geardum,   swylce ðǣr iū wǣron.
XXXV 2460 Gewīteð þonne on sealman,   sorhlēoð gæleð
ān æfter ānum;   þūhte him eall tō rūm,
wongas ond wīcstede.

                Swā Wedra helm

2438[a] *Bu. 103, Tr.* frēowine. — 2442[a] *Ke.* Hrēðel; *Gr.*[1], *Tr., Holt.*[1–5], *Sed.* Hreðle. — *Tr., Scheinert Beitr. xxx 387* (?), *Holt.* -mēðo. — 2446[b] *Gr., Holt., Sed.* wreceð. — 2448[b] *MS.* helpan; *Ke.* helpe, *cf. Siev. ZfdPh. xxi 357.* — 2451[a] *Fol. 184*[b] eaforan *A B.* — 2454 *Gru., Müll.* (*xiv 232*) þurh dǣda nȳd (*or Gru. p. 176, Bu. Zs. 215:* nīð) dēaðes gefondad. — 2457[a] *MS.* reote; *Tho.* rōte (' rote '); *Gr.*[1], *Rie. L.* rēoce; *Bu. Zs. 215* r(e)ōte (' rest '); *Hold.* rōte (' joy '); *Holt.*[2–6] rēte (*orig.* rǣte); *Sed. MLR. xxviii 229* reorde. — 2457[b] *Gr.*[1] (?),[2], *Rie. L.* swefeð.

æfter Herebealde   heortan sorge
weallinde wæg;   wihte ne meahte
1465 on ðām feorhbonan   fǣghðe gebētan;
nō ðȳ ǣr hē þone heaðorinc   hatian ne meahte
lāðum dǣdum,   þēah him lēof ne wæs.
Hē ðā mid þǣre sorhge,   þē him *tō* sār belamp,
gumdrēam ofgeaf,   Godes lēoht gecēas;
2470 eaferum lǣfde,   swā dēð ēadig mon,
lond ond lēodbyrig,   þā hē of līfe gewāt.

Þā wæs synn ond sacu   Swēona ond Gēata
ofer *w*īd wæter   wrōht gemǣne,
herenīð hearda,   syððan Hrēðel swealt,
2475 oððe him Ongenðeowes   eaferan wǣran
frome fyrdhwate,   frēode ne woldon
ofer heafo healdan,   ac ymb Hrēosnabeorh
eatolne inwitscear   oft gefremedon.
Þæt mǣgwine   mīne gewrǣcan,
2480 fǣhðe ond fyrene,   swā hyt gefrǣge wæs,
þēah ðe ōðer his   ealdre gebohte,
heardan cēape;   Hæðcynne wearð,
Gēata dryhtne   gūð onsǣge.
Þā ic on morgne gefrægn   mǣg ōðerne
2485 billes ecgum   on bonan stǣlan,
þǣr Ongenþēow   Eofores nīosað;
gūðhelm tōglād,   gomela Scylfing
hrēas [heoro]blāc;   hond gemunde
fǣhðo genōge,   feorhsweng ne oftēah.

2468[b] *MS.* sio; *Rie. L., Gr.*[2], *E., Holt.*[1,2], *Sed.* swā; *Holt.*[3–5] giō; *dropped by Schü. Cf Lang.* § *20.1; note on 2295; Sed. MLR. xxviii 229* sīo þe him. — 2472[a] *Fol. 185*[a] wæs *AB.* — 2473[a] *MS.* A rid; *Gru. tr. 303* wīd. — 2477[a] *Sarr. St. 27 f.* heaþo. — 2477[b] *Bu. Zt 216*(?), *Sed* Hrefna beorh; *but see Bu. 11.* — 2478[b] *MS.* ge gefremedon; *Thk. drops first* ge. — 2481 *Gr.*[1] þ. ð. ō. [hit]/h. e. g.; *He.*[2], *Schü., Sed.* þ. ð. ō. hit/e.g.; *Hold.*[2], *Holt.*, *Cha* þ. ð. ō. his/e.g. — 2486[b] *Gr., et al.* nīosade. *See 1923*[b]. — 2488[a] *Gr., et al., Hoops* [heoro-]blāc; *Bu. Tid. 297* [hrēa-]blāc; *Holt. Angl. xxi 366, 4 Edd.* [hilde-]blāc (*metri causa*). — 2489[b] *Holt.*[1–5] (*cf. Zs. 121*) -swenge, *Cp. 1520*[b].

2490 Ic him þā māðmas, þē hē mē sealde,
geald æt gūðe, swā mē gifeðe wæs,
lēohtan sweorde; hē mē lond forgeaf,
eard ēðelwyn. Næs him ǣnig þearf,
þæt hē tō Gifðum oððe tō Gār-Denum
2495 oððe in Swīorīce sēcean þurfe
wyrsan wīgfrecan, weorðe gecȳpan;
symle ic him on fēðan beforan wolde,
āna on orde, ond swā tō aldre sceall
sæcce fremman, þenden þis sweord þolað,
2500 þæt mec ǣr ond sīð oft gelǣste,
syððan ic for dugeðum Dæghrefne wearð
tō handbonan, Hūga cempan; —
nalles hē ðā frætwe Frēscyning[e],
brēostweorðunge bringan mōste,
2505 ac in campe gecrong cumbles hyrde,
æþeling on elne; ne wæs ecg bona,
ac him hildegrāp heortan wylmas,
bānhūs gebræc. Nū sceall billes ecg,
hond ond heard sweord ymb hord wīgan.'
2510 Bēowulf maðelode, bēotwordum spræc
nīehstan sīðe: ' Ic genēðde fela
gūða on geogoðe; gȳt ic wylle,
frōd folces weard fǣhðe sēcan,
mǣrðu fremman, gif mec se mānsceaða
2515 of eorðsele ūt gesēceð.'
Gegrētte ðā gumena gehwylcne,
hwate helmberend hindeman sīðe,

2493[a] *Siev. ix 141* -wynne. *See Lang.* § 20.2. — 2495[b] *Bu. Zs. 216* þorfte. *See 1928[b].*
— 2496[a] *Fol. 185[b]* wyrsan *A*. — 2500[b] *Gr., Schü., Sed.: period after* gelǣste. — 2503[b]
MS. cyning; *Gru. tr. 304* -cyning[e]. — 2505[a] *MS.* cempan; *Ke., Tho , 4 Edd.* campe
(compe). — 2509[a] *Morgan Beitr. xxxiii 105 f., Holt., Sed.* heardsweord. *So 2987[a].* (*Cp.
2638[a]*.) — 2514[a] *MS.* mærðū (i.e. mærðum, *so Cha.*); *Ke. ii* mǣrðo, *Bu. 104, 3 Edd.*
mǣrðu. *Cp. 2079[a], 2347[b].*

BEOWULF

swǽse gesīðas: ' Nolde ic sweord beran,
wǽpen tō wyrme,   gif ic wiste hū
2520 wið ðām āglǽcean   elles meahte
gylpe wiðgrīpan,   swā ic giō wið Grendle dyde;
ac ic ðǽr heaðufȳres   hātes wēne,
[o]reðes ond *attres*;   forðon ic mē on hafu
bord ond byrnan.   Nelle ic beorges weard
2525 oferflēon fōtes trem,   ac unc [furður] sceal
weorðan æt wealle,   swā unc wyrd getēoð,
Metod manna gehwæs.   Ic eom on mōde from,
þæt ic wið þone gūðflogan   gylp ofersitte.
Gebīde gē on beorge   byrnum werede,
2530 secgas on searwum,   hwæðer sēl mǽge
æfter wælrǽse   wunde gedȳgan
uncer twēga.   Nis þæt ēower sīð,
nē gemet mannes,   nefn(e) mīn ānes,
þæt hē wið āglǽcean   eofoðo dǽle,
2535 eorlscype efne.   Ic mid elne sceall
gold gegangan,   oððe gūð nimeð,
feorhbealu frēcne   frēan ēowerne! '

Ārās ðā bī ronde   rōf ōretta,
heard under helme,   hiorosercean bær
2540 under stāncleofu,   strengo getruwode
ānes mannes;   ne bið swylc earges sīð!
Geseah ðā be wealle   sē ðe worna fela
gumcystum gōd   gūða gedīgde,
hildehlemma,   þonne hnitan fēðan,

2519[b] Fol. 186[a] gif AB. — 2520[a] MS. ðam; Siev. ix 141, Holt. ðæs. — 2521[a] Schröer Angl. xiii 345 gūþe (for gylpe). — 2523[a] MS. reðes ⁊ hattres; Gru. tr. 304, Ke. ii attres: Gr. [o]reðes. See 2557, 2715, 2839. — 2525[a] MS. ofer fleon; Bu. 104, Barnouw 232, Sed. flēo(ha)n (flēon); Tr. forflēon, Holt. ferflēon. — 2525[b] Schubert L 8.1.46, Barnouw 232, Tr. [fæhðo]; Bu. 104, Schü.8-10 [feohte]; Arch. cxv 181 [furðor], Cha. [furður]. — 2528[a] Siev. ix 141 þæs (for þæt). See Gloss.: þæt. — 2533[b] Gru. tr. 304 nefn(e). — 2534[a] MS. wat; Gru. tr. 304 þæt. — 2540[b] See 609[b] Varr. — 2542[b] Fol. 186[b] seðe A(B).

96   BEOWULF

2545 sto[n]dan stānbogan,   strēam ūt þonan
brecan of beorge;   wæs þǣre burnan wælm
heaðofȳrum hāt,   ne meahte horde nēah
unbyrnende   ǣnige hwīle
dēop gedȳgan   for dracan lēge.
2550 Lēt ðā of brēostum,   ðā hē gebolgen wæs,
Weder-Gēata lēod   word ūt faran,
stearcheort styrmde;   stefn in becōm
heaðotorht hlynnan   under hārne stān.
Hete wæs onhrēred,   hordweard oncnīow
2555 mannes reorde;   næs ðǣr māra fyrst
frēode tō friclan.   From ǣrest cwōm
oruð āglǣcean   ūt of stāne,
hāt hildeswāt;   hrūse dynede.
Biorn under beorge   bordrand onswāf
2560 wið ðām gryregieste,   Gēata dryhten;
ðā wæs hringbogan   heorte gefȳsed
sæcce tō sēceanne.   Sweord ǣr gebrǣd
gōd gūðcyning,   gomele lāfe,
ecgum unslāw;   ǣghwæðrum wæs
2565 bealohycgendra   brōga fram ōðrum.
Stīðmōd gestōd   wið stēapne rond
winia bealdor,   ðā se wyrm gebēah
snūde tōsomne;   hē on searwum bād.
Gewāt ðā byrnende   gebogen scrīðan,
2570 tō gescipe scyndan.   Scyld wēl gebearg

2545ᵃ *MS.* stodan; *Tho.* sto[n]dan. — 2549ᵃ *Gru. tr. 305, Gru.* dēor ('animal'), *Bu. Tid. 297, Sed.* dēor (*adj.*). — 2550ᵃ *Sed.* (*cf. MLR. v 288*) born (*comma after* dynede, *semicolon after* beorge). — 2561ᵃ *Sarr. ESt. xxviii 409 f.* hringboran (*i.e. Bēowulf*). — 2562ᵃ *Siev. R. 312, Holt., Schü., Sed.* sēc(e)an. *See T.C.* § *12*. — 2564ᵃ *MS.* un/glaw (*letter erased after* l), *B* gleap; *Tho.* unslēaw; *Bu. 104, 4 Edd.* unslāw. — 2565ᵇ *Fol. 187ᵃ* broga *A B.* — 2567ᵃ *Gu. tr. 305, Gru., Tr.* wigena. *See 1418ᵃ.* — 2570ᵃ *Tho.* gesceape; *E.* gescepe; *He.*⁴⁻⁷ gescīfe ('headlong,' *placed in 2569ᵇ*); *Holt.* gescīfe (gescife), *Sed.* gescife ('precipitation,' *see B.-T.:* (*niþer*)*scyfe, cp. scūfan*).

BEOWULF

life ond līce   lǣssan hwīle
mǣrum þēodne,   þonne his myne sōhte,
ðǣr hē þȳ fyrste   forman dōgọre
wealdan mōste,   swā him wyrd ne gescrāf
2575 hrēð æt hilde.   Hond up ābrǣd
Gēata dryhten,   gryrefāhne slōh
incge-lāfe,   þæt sīo ecg gewāc
brūn on bāne,   bāt unswīðor,
þonne his ðīodcyning   þearfe hæfde
2580 bysigum gebǣded.   Þā wæs beorges weard
æfter heaðuswenge   on hrēoụm mōde,
wearp wælfȳre;   wīde sprungon
hildelēoman.   Hrēðsigora ne gealp
goldwine Gēata;   gūðbill geswāc
2585 nacod æt nīðe,   swā hyt nō sceolde,
īren ǣrgōd. —   Ne wæs þæt ēðe sīð,
þæt se mǣra   maga Ecgðēowes
grundwong þone   ofgyfan wolde;
sceolde [ofer] willan   wīc eardian
2590 elles hwergen,   swā sceal ǣghwylc mon
ālǣtan lǣndagas.
                Næs ðā long tō ðon,
þæt ðā āglǣcean   hȳ eft gemētton.
Hyrte hyne hordweard,   hreðer ǣðme wēoll,
nīwan stefne;   nearo ðrōwode
2595 fȳre befongen   sē ðe ǣr folce wēold.
Nealles him on hēape   handgesteallan,
æðelinga bearn   ymbe gestōdon

2573ᵇ See 1797ᵇ. — 2577ᵃ Ke. ii Gloss. s.v. lāf īcge-; Tho., E., Sed. Incges, Gru. (?) Ingwina, Holt.³ Ingwines (cf. Grienb. 757); Tr. isigre; Tr. Beibl. xxiv 42 irfe-. [Cf. Holt. Beibl. xiii 78 f.: yrrincga or æðelincges.] — 2577ᵇ Hoops St. 129 þ=þā. Cf. note on 15. — 2589ᵃ Gr.² [wyrmes]; Aant. 35 [wyrme tō]; Rie. Zs. 410, 4 Edd. [ofer]. — 2590ᵇ Fol. 187ᵇ sceal AB. — 2596ᵇ MS. heand; Ke. hand-.

hildecystum, ac hȳ on holt bugon,
ealdre burgan. Hiora in ānum wēoll
2600 sefa wið sorgum; sibb' ǣfre ne mæg
wiht onwendan þām ðe wēl þenceð.

XXXVI Wīglāf wæs hāten, Wēoxstānes sunu,
lēoflīc lindwiga, lēod Scylfinga,
mǣg Ælfheres; geseah his mondryhten
2605 under heregrīman hāt þrōwian.
Gemunde ðā ðā āre, þē hē him ǣr forgeaf,
wīcstede weligne Wǣgmundinga,
folcrihta gehwylc, swā his fæder āhte;
ne mihte ðā forhabban, hond rond gefēng,
2610 geolwe linde, gomel swyrd getēah;
þæt wæs mid eldum Ēanmundes lāf,
suna Ōhtere[s]; þām æt sæcce wearð,
wræcca(n) winelēasum Wēohstā*n* bana
mēces ecgum, ond his māgum ætbær
2615 brūnfāgne helm, hringde byrnan,
ealdsweord etonisc; þæt him Onela forgeaf,
his gǣdelinges gūðgewǣdu,
fyrdsearo fūslīc, — nō ymbe ðā fǣhðe sprǣc,
þēah ðe hē his brōðor bearn ābredwade.
2620 Hē [ðā] frætwe gehēold fela missēra,
bill ond byrnan, oð ðæt his byre mihte
eorlscipe efnan swā his ǣrfæder;
geaf him ðā mid Gēatum gūðgewǣda,
ǣghwæs unrīm, þā hē of ealdre gewāt
2625 frōd on forðweg. — Þā wæs forma sīð
geongan cempan, þæt hē gūðe rǣs

<small>2612ᵃ *Fol. 188ᵃ* suna *AB.* — *MS.* ohtere; *Gru. tr. 305* Ōhtere[s] (*Thk.* Oþeres). — 2613ᵃ *E.Sc.* wrecca(n). — 2613ᵇ *MS.* weohstanes; *Gru. tr. 306* Wēohstā*n*. — 2615ᵃ *Tr.* hasufāgne. — 2615ᵇ *Rie. V. 21, Holt.* byrnan hringde. See *T.C.* § 27. — 2616ᵃ See *1558ᵃ.* — 2620ᵃ *Gru., E., Siev. ix 141, Holt.* [þā]. — 2623ᵇ *E.Sc.* -gewǣdu. — 2626ᵇ *Hoops* gūðerǣs.</small>

BEOWULF

mid his frēodryhtne fremman sceolde.
Ne gemealt him se mōdsefa, nē his mǣges lāf
gewāc æt wīge; þæt se wyrm onfand,
2630 syððan hīe tōgædre gegān hæfdon.
Wīglāf maðelode, wordrihta fela
sægde gesīðum — him wæs sefa geōmor — :
'Ic ðæt mǣl geman, þǣr wē medu þēgun,
þonne wē gehēton ūssum hlāforde
2635 in bīorsele, ðē ūs ðās bēagas geaf,
þæt wē him ðā gūðgetāwa gyldan woldon,
gif him þyslicu þearf gelumpe,
helmas ond heard sweord. Ðē hē ūsic on herge gecēas
tō ðyssum sīðfate sylfes willum,
2640 onmunde ūsic mǣrða, ond mē þās māðmas geaf,
þē hē ūsic gārwīgend gōde tealde,
hwate helmberend, — þēah ðe hlāford ūs
þis ellenweorc āna āðōhte
tō gefremmanne, folces hyrde,
2645 forðām hē manna mǣst mǣrða gefremede,
dǣda dollīcra. Nū is sē dæg cumen,
þæt ūre mandryhten mægenes behōfað,
gōdra gūðrinca; wutun gongan tō,
helpan hildfruman, þenden hyt sŷ,
2650 glēdegesa grim! God wāt on mec,
þæt mē is micle lēofre, þæt mīnne līchaman
mid mīnne goldgyfan glēd fæðmię.
Ne þynceð mē gerysne, þæt wē rondas beren

2628[b] *MS.* mægenes; *E.Sc.* mæges. — 2629[b] *MS.* þa; *Tho.* þæt. — 2633[a] *Fol. 188[b]* mæl *A.* — 2636[a] *MS.* getawa; *He.*[2], *Siev. R. 273 f., Holt., Schü., Sed.* -geatwa. *See Gloss.; T.C.* § *23.* — 2638[a] *Holt.* heardsweord. *See 2509[a].* — 2640[b] *Bu. 49* ond mēda gehēt. — 2642[b] *Gru. tr. 306* ūre (*for* ūs); *E.Sc., Tho., Bu. Zs. 216* ūser; *Aant. 36* ūr (?). — 2649[b] *Ke. ii, Bu. 105* hit [hāt]; *Ke. ii, Tho., Sed.* hāt (*for* hyt); *Gr.* hit (='heat'); *Gr. Spr.* (?) hitsie (*from* *hitsian). — 2650[a] *Siev. R. 463, Holt.* -egsa. *So 2780[b]. See T.C.* § *5.*

eft tō earde, nemne we ǣror mægen
2655 fāne gefyllan, feorh ealgian
Wedra ðēodnes.   Ic wāt geare,
þæt nǣron ealdgewyrht, þæt hē āna scyle
Gēata duguðe gnorn þrōwian,
gesīgan æt sæcce; ūrum sceal sweord ond helm,
2660 byrne ond beaduscrūd bām gemǣne.'
Wōd þā þurh þone wælrēc, wīgheafolan bær
frēan on fultum, fēa worda cwæð:
'Lēofa Bīowulf, lǣst eall tela,
swā ðū on geoguðfēore gēara gecwǣde,
2665 þæt ðū ne ālǣte be ðē lifigendum
dōm gedrēosan; scealt nū dǣdum rōf,
æðeling anhȳdig, ealle mægene
feorh ealgian; ic ðē fullǣstu.'
Æfter ðām wordum wyrm yrre cwōm,
2670 atol inwitgæst ōðre sīðe
fȳrwylmum fāh fīonda nīos(i)an,
lāðra manna. Līgȳðum forborn
bord wið rond, byrne ne meahte
geongum gārwigan gēoce gefremman,
2675 ac se maga geonga under his mǣges scyld
elne geēode, þā his āgen w(æs)
glēdum forgrunden.   þā gēn gūðcyning
m(ǣrða) gemunde, mægenstrengo slōh
hildebille, þæt hyt on heafolan stōd

2655ᵇ *Fol. 197ᵃ* feorh *AB*. — 2659ᵇ *MS.* urū; *and* ð (=deest) *above the line, ref. to*
ð˙sceal· *which has been inserted in the margin; Tho., Gr.*¹ unc (*for* ūrum), *Gr.*² unc nū, *Sed.*
(*cf. MLR. v 288*) hūru. — 2660ᵃ *MS.* byrdu scrud; *E. Sc., Tho., 4 Edd.* beaduscrūd (*cf.
JEGPh. viii 258*). — *Aant. 36, Holt.*¹⁻⁵ bord (*for* byrne). — [*Bu. Tid. 58 f. & Zs. 216 f.,
Rie. Zs. 411; Grienb. Beitr. xxxvi 83.*] — 2665ᵃ *Perh.* ālēte (?). — 2671ᵇ *MS.* B niosnan,
A mosum; *Ke., Holt., Schü.* nīosan, *Gr.*² nīosian. *See T.C.* § 9. — 2673ᵃ *MS.* rond; *Ke., 4
Edd.* rond[e] (*cf. Martin ESt. xx 295*); *Hoops St. 12* rond. — 2676ᵇ *Gru.tr. 306* w(æs). —
2678ᵃ *Gru.tr. 306* m(ǣrða). — 2678ᵇ *Rie. V. 34 n., Holt.: comma after* slōh. *But cp. 235 f.,
1519 f.*

2680 nīþe genȳded;   Nægling forbærst,
geswāc æt sæcce   sweord Bīowulfes
gomol ond grǣgmǣl.   Him þæt gifeðe ne wæs,
þæt him īrenna   ecge mihton
helpan æt hilde;   wæs sīo hond tō strong,
2685 sē ðe mēca gehwane   mīne gefrǣge
swenge ofersōhte,   þonne hē tō sæcce bær
wǣpen wund[r]um heard;   næs him wihte ðē sēl.
   Þā wæs þēodsceaða   þriddan sīðe,
frēcne fȳrdraca   fǣhða gemyndig,
2690 rǣsde on ðone rōfan,   þā him rūm āgeald,
hāt ond heaðogrim,   heals ealne ymbefēng
biteran bānum;   hē geblōdegod wearð
sāwuldrīore,   swāt ȳðum wēoll.

XXXVII   Ðā ic æt þearfe [gefrægn]   þēodcyninges
2695 andlongne eorl   ellen cȳðan,
cræft ond cēnðu,   swā him gecynde wæs.
Ne hēdde hē þæs heafolan,   ac sīo hand gebarn
mōdiges mannes,   þǣr hē his mǣges healp,
þæt hē þone nīðgæst   nioðor hwēne slōh,
2700 secg on searwum,   þæt ðæt sweord gedēaf
fāh ond fǣted,   þæt ðæt fȳr ongon
sweðrian syððan.   Þā gēn sylf cyning
gewēold his gewitte,   wæll-seaxe gebrǣd
biter ond beaduscearp,   þæt hē on byrnan wæg;
2705 forwrāt Wedra helm   wyrm on middan.

2682ª *Fol. 197ᵇ* gomol *A B.* — 2684ᵇ *considered parenthetical by Schü.* (*cf. Sa. 139*), *Holt., Cha.* — 2685ª *Tho., et al.* sēo. *See 1344.* — 2686ᵇ *Bu. 105, Holt.* þone. — 2687ª *MS.* wundū (*cp. 1460ª?*); *Tho.* wund[r]um. — 2691ᵇ *Tho., Tr., Holt.* ymb-. *See T.C.* § *13.* — 2694ª *Ke.* [gefrægn]. — 2698ᵇ *MS.* mægenes; *Ke.* mæges. *See 2879ᵇ.* — 2699ª *Ke., Tho., Rie. Zs. 407* þā (*for* þæt). — 2700ᵇ *Siev. ix 141* (*cf. E.*), *Holt. cancel* ðæt; *Hoops* þā ðæt. — 2701ᵇ *Gru., Siev. ix 141, Sed.* þā ðæt. *See MPh. iii 463 f.* — 2703ᵇ *E.Sc., Holt., Sed.* -seax. *See 1830 f.; 1545 f.* — 2705ª *Fol. 189ª* helm *A B.*

Fēond gefyldan — ferh ellen wræc —,
ond hī hyne þā bēgen ābroten hæfdon,
sibæðelingas; swylc sceolde secg wesan,
þegn æt ðearfe! Þæt ðām þēodne wæs
2710 sīðas[t] sigehwīle sylfes dædum,
worlde geweorces.
 Ðā sīo wund ongon,
þē him se eorðdraca ǣr geworhte,
swelan ond swellan; hē þæt sōna onfand,
þæt him on brēostum bealonīð(e) wēoll
2715 attor on innan. Ðā se æðeling gīong,
þæt hē bī wealle wīshycgende
gesæt on sesse; seah on enta geweorc,
hū ðā stānbogan stapulum fæste
ēce eorðreced innan healde.
2720 Hyne þā mid handa heorodrēorigne,
þēoden mǣrne þegn ungemete till,
winedryhten his wætere gelafede
hilde sædne ond his hel(m) onspēon.
 Bīowulf maþelode — hē ofer benne spræc,
2725 wunde wælblēate; wisse hē gearwe,
þæt hē dæghwīla gedrogen hæfde,
eorðan wynn(e); ðā wæs eall sceacen
dōgorgerīmes, dēað ungemete nēah - - :
' Nū ic suna mīnum syllan wolde

2706ᵃ *E.Sc., Tho., Siev. ix 141 f., Sed.* gefylde. — 2706ᵇ *Ke.* ferh-ellen; *Klu. ix 192* ealne (*for* ellen), *Aant. 37, Hoops* ellor. — 2710ᵃ *MS.* siðas sige hwile; *Ke.* sīðes sigehwīl; *Gru. tr. 307* sīþest; *Gr., Schü., Holt.* sīðast sigehwīla (*cp. 2427*); *Gru., Bu. Zs. 217* sīðast sigehwīle; *Tr., Sed., Cha.* sīðast sigehwīl. *Cf. Lang.* § *19.6.* — 2714ᵇ *MS. A* mð, *B* niði; *Schubert L 8.1.35, Siev. R. 269, 4 Edd.* -nīðe. -·- 2719ᵃ *Holt.*²⁻⁴ ēcne (=ēacne). — 2719ᵇ *E.Sc., Rie. Zs. 411* hēoldon. — 2721ᵇ *Z.*: ' *there is a sort of angle above the* t *of* till, *the meaning of which I do not know.*' *The same sign above the* n *of* unriht *2739ᵃ, and above the* u *of* up *2893ʰ.* — 2723ᵇ *MS. A* helo, *B* heb; *E.Sc.* (*after Grimm*) helm. — 2725ᵃ *Gr. Spr. i 128* (?), *Scheinert Beitr. xxx 375, Holt.* -blāte. (*Cp. Chr. 771.*) — 2727ᵃ *Thk., Gru.tr. 307* wynn(e).

2730 gūðgewǣdu,   þǣr mē gifeðe swā
ǣnig yrfeweard   æfter wurde
līce gelenge.   Ic ðās lēode hēold
fīftig wintra;   næs sē folccyning,
ymbesittendra   ǣnig ðāra,
2735 þē mec gūðwinum   grētan dorste,
egesan ðēon.   Ic on earde bād
mǣlgesceafta,   hēold mīn tela,
ne sōhte searonīðas,   nē mē swōr fela
āða on unriht.   Ic ðæs ealles mæg
2740 feorhbennum sēoc   gefēan habban;
forðām mē wītan ne ðearf   Waldend fīra
morðorbealo māga,   þonne mīn sceaceð
līf of līce.   Nū ðū lungre geong
hord scēawian   under hārne stān,
2745 Wīglāf lēofa,   nū se wyrm ligeð,
swefeð sāre wund,   since berēafod.
Bīo nū on ofoste,   þæt ic ǣrwelan,
goldǣht ongite,   gearo scēawige
swegle searogimmas,   þæt ic ðȳ sēft mæge
2750 æfter māððumwelan   mīn ālǣtan
līf ond lēodscipe,   þone ic longe hēold.'
XXXVIII Ðā ic snūde gefrægn   sunu Wīhstānes
æfter wordcwydum   wundum dryhtne
hȳran heaðosīocum,   hringnet beran,
2755 brogdne beadusercean   under beorges hrōf.
Geseah ðā sigehrēðig,   þā hē bī sesse gēong,
magoþegn mōdig   māððumsigla fealo,

2731ᵃ Fol. 189ᵇ weard AB. — 2734ᵃ Tho., Tr., Holt. ymb-. See T.C. § 13. — 2743ᵇ Ke. gang; Tho., Holt. gong. See Lang. § 13.5. — 2748ᵇ E., Aant. 41 gearwe. — 2749ᵃ Tho. sigel (for swegle), Rie. L. (?), Holt. siglu, Rie. Zs. 411 f. sigle (see 1157, MPh. iii 250). — 2755ᵇ MS. urder; Thk. under. — 2757ᵃ Fol. 190ᵃ modig. — 2757ᵇ Ke., et al. fela; Rie. L., et al., Sed. feola. See Lang. § 12.2 n.

BEOWULF

gold glitinian   grunde getenge,
wundur on wealle,   ond þæs wyrmes denn,
2760 ealdes ūhtflogan,   orcas stondan,
fyrnmanna fatu,   feormendlēase,
hyrstum behrorene;   þǣr wæs helm monig
eald ond ōmig,   earmbēaga fela
searwum gesǣled. — Sinc ēaðe mæg,
2765 gold on grund(e)   gumcynnes gehwone
oferhīgian,   hȳde sē ðe wylle! —
Swylce hē siomian geseah   segn eallgylden
hēah ofer horde,   hondwundra mǣst,
gelocen leoðocræftum;   of ðām lēoma stōd,
2770 þæt hē þone grundwong   ongitan meahte,
wrǣte giondwlītan.   Næs ðæs wyrmes þǣr
onsȳn ǣnig,   ac hyne ecg fornam.
Ðā ic on hlǣwe gefrægn   hord rēafian,
eald enta geweorc   ānne mannan,
2775 him on bearm hladon   bunan ond discas
sylfes dōme;   segn ēac genōm,
bēacna beorhtost.   Bill ǣr gescōd
— ecg wæs īren —   ealdhlāfordes
þām ðāra māðma   mundbora wæs
2780 longe hwīle,   līgegesan wæg
hātne for horde,   hioroweallende
middelnihtum,   oð þæt hē morðre swealt.
Ār wæs on ofoste,   eftsīðes georn,

2759[b] *Tr., Holt., Sed.* geond (*for* ond). — 2760[b] *E., Mö. ii, Aant. 37* (?), *Holt.*[1-5] stōdan.
— 2765[a] *Gru. tr. 307* grund(e). — 2766[a] *Klu. ix 192* -hȳdgian, *Schü.* -hīdgian; *Gru.* (?),
Sed.[1] (*cf. MLR. v 288*) -hīwian; *Sed.*[2] ofer hige hēan. — 2769[b] *MS.* leoman; *Ke.* lēoma. —
2771[a] *MS.* wrǣce; *Tho.* wrǣte. — 2775[a] *MS.* hlodon; *Gru. tr. 308, et al., Sed.* hladan;
Hold., 3 Edd. hladon. — 2777[b] *Ke., et al.*, [*cf. Brett MLR. xiv 4 f.*] ǣrgescōd ('brass-shod');
Bu. Tid. 299 (*cf. Gru. note*) ǣr gescōd. (*Cp. 1587*[b], *1615*[b], *etc.*) — 2778[b] *Rie. Zs. 412, Aant.
37, Sed.* -hlāforde (*i.e., the dragon*). — 2780[b] See *2650*[a]. — 2782[b] *Fol. 190*[b] oð.

frætwum gefyrðred;   hyne fyrwet bræc,
2785 hwæðer collenferð   cwicne gemētte
in ðām wongstede   Wedra þēoden
ellensīocne,   þǣr hē hine ǣr forlēt.
Hē ðā mid þām māðmum   mǣrne þīoden,
dryhten sīnne   drīorigne fand
2790 ealdres æt ende;   hē hine eft ongon
wæteres weorpan,   oð þæt wordes ord
brēosthord þurhbræc.
                                [Biorncyning spræc]
gomel on gio*h*ðe   — gold scēawode — :
' Ic ðāra frætwa   Frēan ealles ðanc,
2795 Wuldurcyninge   wordum secge,
ēcum Dryhtne,   þē ic hēr on starie,
þæs ðe ic mōste   mīnum lēodum
ǣr swyltdæge   swylc gestrȳnan.
Nū ic on māðma hord   mī*n*e bebohte
2800 frōde feorhlege,   fremmað gēna
lēoda þearfe;   ne mæg ic hēr leng wesan.
Hātað heaðomǣre   hlǣw gewyrcean
beorhtne æfter bǣle   æt brimes nosan;
sē scel tō gemyndum   mīnum lēodum
2805 hēah hlīfian   on Hronesnæsse,
þæt hit sǣlīðend   syððan hātan
Bīowulfes biorh,   ðā ðe brentingas
ofer flōda genipu   feorran drīfað.'

2785ᵃ *E.* (*cf. E.Sc.*) -ferhðne. — 2791ᵃ *Ke. ii* (?), *E.Sc.*, *Tho.*, *Bu. Zs. 218* (?) wætere;
Rie. Zs. 412, *Tr.* wætere sweorfan. *See Gloss.: weorpan.* [*Holt. note:* 2790ᵇ [on] hine (?).]
— 2792ᵇ *Gru.tr. 308, et al., Sed.* [Bēowulf maþelode]; *Schü.* (*cf. ESt. xxxix 110*) [þā se beorn
gespræc]; *Holt., Cha.* [Bīowulf reordode]. — 2793ᵃ *MS.* giogoðe; *Ke. ii* gehðo (?), *Grimm*
(*note on Andr. 66*), *E. Sc.* giohðe. — 2799ᵇ *MS.* minne; *E.Sc.* mīne. — 2800ᵇ *Tho., Bu. 96,
most Edd.* gē nū. — 2803ᵃ *Siev. R. 306, Holt.*¹,² beorht. — 2803ᵇ *See 1892ᵇ. Cf. T.C.* § *5 n. 2*,
— 2804ᵃ *Siev. i.c., Holt.*¹,² þæt (*for* sē). — 2808ᵃ *Fol. 191ᵃ* floda *B*.

106　BEOWULF

　　　Dyde him of healse　　hring gyldenne
2810　þīoden þrīsthȳdig,　　þegne gesealde,
　　　geongum gārwigan,　　goldfāhne helm,
　　　bēah ond byrnan,　　hēt hyne brūcan well — ;
　　　' þū eart endelāf　　ūsses cynnes,
　　　Wǣgmundinga;　　ealle wyrd forswēop
2815　mīne māgas　　tō metodsceafte,
　　　eorlas on elne;　　ic him æfter sceal.'
　　　Þæt wæs þām gomelan　　gingæste word
　　　brēostgehygdum,　　ǣr hē bǣl cure,
　　　hāte heaðowylmas;　　him of hræðre gewāt
2820　sāwol sēcean　　sōðfæstra dōm.

[XXXVIIII]　Ðā wæs gegongen　　guman unfrōdum
　　　earfoðlīce,　　þæt hē on eorðan geseah
　　　þone lēofestan　　līfes æt ende
　　　blēate gebǣran.　　Bona swylce læg,
2825　egeslīc eorðdraca　　ealdre berēafod,
　　　bealwe gebǣded.　　Bēahhordum leng
　　　wyrm wōhbogen　　wealdan ne mōste,
　　　ac him īrenna　　ecga fornāmon,
　　　hearde heaðoscearþe　　homera lāfe,
2830　þæt se wīdfloga　　wundum stille
　　　hrēas on hrūsan　　hordærne nēah.
　　　Nalles æfter lyfte　　lācende hwearf
　　　middelnihtum,　　māðmǣhta wlonc
　　　ansȳn ȳwde,　　ac hē eorðan gefēoll
2835　for ðæs hildfruman　　hondgeweorce.
　　　Hūru þæt on lande　　lȳt manna ðāh

2814[b] *MS.* speof; *Ke. ii* (*cf. Grimm D. M. 336*) -swēop. — 2819[b] *MS.* hwæðre; *Ke., et al.* hreðre; *Gr. Spr.* hræðre. — 2821[a] *No canto number in MS., but* Ða (*capital* Ð) *begins new line.* — 2821[b] *MS.* gumū; *He.*[1] guman. — 2828[a] *Gr.*[1] (?), *Rie. Zs. 412, et al.* hine. *See Lang.* § 25.5. — 2829[a] *MS.* scear/de; *cf. Schü. xxxix 110; Tho., et al., Scheinert Beitr. xxx 378, Hoops* -scearpe. — 2832[a] *Fol. 191*[b] *æfter.*

mægenāgendra mīne gefrǣge,
þēah ðe hē dǣda gehwæs dyrstig wǣre,
þæt hē wið attorsceaðan oreðe gerǣsde,
2840 oððe hringsele hondum styrede,
gif hē wæccende weard onfunde
būon on beorge. Bīowulfe wearð
dryhtmāðma dǣl dēaðe forgolden;
hæfde ǣghwæðer ende gefēred
2845 lǣnan līfes.
          Næs ðā lang tō ðon,
þæt ðā hildlatan holt ofgēfan,
tȳdre trēowlogan tȳne ætsomne,
ðā ne dorston ǣr dareðum lācan
on hyra mandryhtnes miclan þearfe;
2850 ac hȳ scamiende scyldas bǣran,
gūðgewǣdu þǣr se gomela læg;
wlitan on Wīlāf. Hē gewērgad sæt,
fēðecempa frēan eaxlum nēah,
wehte hyne wætre; him wiht ne spēow.
2855 Ne meahte hē on eorðan, ðēah hē ūðe wēl,
on ðām frumgāre feorh gehealdan,
nē ðæs Wealdendes wiht oncirran;
wolde dōm Godes dǣdum rǣdan
gumena gehwylcum, swā hē nū gēn dêð.
2860 Þā wæs æt ðām geongan grim andswaru
ēðbegēte þām ðe ǣr his elne forlēas.
Wīglāf maðelode, Wēohstānes sunu,
sec[g] sārigferð — seah on unlēofe — :

2844ᵃ *MS.* æghwæðre; *Ke. ii* æghwæðer; *cf. Rie. Zs. 412.* — 2852ᵃ *Ke., Siev. R. 272, Holt., Sed.* wlītan. — 2854ᵇ *MS.* speop; *Thk.* spēow. — 2857ᵃ *JEGPh. viii 258* weorldendes (?). — 2857ᵇ *Tho., Schü.* willan (*for* wiht). — 2858ᵃ *Fol. 192ᵃ* godes *AB.* — 2858ᵇ *Bu. 106* dēað ārǣdan. — 2860ᵃ *MS.* geongū; *Barnouw 36, Holt., Schü.* geongan. [geongum *doubtfully defended by Lichtenheld ZfdA. xvi 353, 355.*] — 2863ᵃ *MS.* sec; *Thk.* sec[g.]

' þæt, lā, mæg secgan   sē ðe wyle sōð specan,
2865 þæt se mondryhten,   sē ēow ðā māðmas geaf,
ēoredgeatwe,   þē gē þǣr on standað, —
þonne hē on ealubence   oft gesealde
healsittendum   helm ond byrnan,
þēoden his þegnum,   swylce hē þrȳdlīcost
2870 ōwer feor oððe nēah   findan meahte — ,
þæt hē gēnunga   gūðgewǣdu
wrāðe forwurpe,   ðā hyne wīg beget.
Nealles folccyning   fyrdgesteallum
gylpan þorfte;   hwæðre him God ūðe,
2875 sigora Waldend,   þæt hē hyne sylfne gewræc
āna mid ecge,   þā him wæs elnes þearf.
Ic him līfwraðe   lȳtle meahte
ætgifan æt gūðe,   ond ongan swā þēah
ofer mīn gemet   mǣges helpan;
2880 symle wæs þȳ sǣmra,   þonne ic sweorde drep
ferhðgenīðlan,   fȳr unswīðor
wēoll of gewitte.   Wergendra tō lȳt
þrong ymbe þēoden,   þā hyne sīo þrāg becwōm.
Nū sceal sincþego   ond swyrdgifu,
2885 eall ēðelwyn   ēowrum cynne,
lufen ālicgean;   londrihtes mōt
þǣre mǣgburge   monna ǣghwylc
īdel hweorfan,   syððan æðelingas
feorran gefricgean   flēam ēowerne,
2890 dōmlēasan dǣd.   Dēað bið sēlla
eorla gehwylcum   þonne edwītlīf! '

2867ᵇ *Tr.* ēow (*for* oft). — 2869ᵇ *MS.* þryd-; *Thk., Edd.* (*exc. Arn., Cha.*) þrȳð-; *Hoops St. 136* þrȳd-. — 2878ⁿ *Perh.* gifan. — 2880ᵇ *Siev. ix 142* þone *and* 2881ⁿ -genīðla. — 2881ᵇ *MS.* fyrun (u *altered from* a) swiðor; *Tho.* fȳr ran swīðor; *Rie. L.* (*cf. Zs. 413*), *4 Edd.* fȳr unswīðor. — 2882ᵇ *MS.* fergendra; *Gru.tr. 309* wergendra. — 2883ᵇ *Fol. 192ᵇ* þrag *A B.* — 2884ⁿ *MS.* hu, so (*i.e.* Hū) *Gru., Cha.* (*exclamatory, cf. Holt. ii note*); *Ke., 3 Edd.* Nū. — 2886ⁿ *Grimm R. A. 731, Ke., Tr.* leofen (' sustenance '); *Tho.* lēofum; *Sed. note* lungre (?).

BEOWULF

XL   Heht ðā þæt heaðoweorc   tō hagan bīodan
         up ofer ecgclif,   þǣr þæt eorlweorod
         morgenlongne dæg   mōdgiōmor sæt,
2895   bordhæbbende,   bēga on wēnum,
         endedōgores   ond eftcymes
         lēofes monnes.   Lȳt swīgode
         nīwra spella   sē ðe næs gerād,
         ac hē sōðlīce   sægde ofer ealle:
2900 ' Nū is wilgeofa   Wedra lēoda,
         dryhten Gēata   dēaðbedde fæst,
         wunað wælreste   wyrmes dǣdum;
         him on efn ligeð   ealdorgewinna
         sexbennum sēoc;   sweorde ne meahte
2905   on ðām āglǣcean   ǣnige þinga
         wunde gewyrcean.   Wīglāf siteð
         ofer Bīowulfe,   byre Wīhstānes,
         eorl ofer ōðrum   unlifigendum,
         healdeð higemǣðum   hēafodwearde
2910   lēofes ond lāðes.
                           Nū ys lēodum wēn
         orleghwīle,   syððan under[ne]
         Froncum ond Frȳsum   fyll cyninges
         wīde weorðeð.   Wæs sīo wrōht scepen
         heard wið Hūgas,   syððan Higelāc cwōm
2915   faran flotherge   on Frēsna land,
         þǣr hyne Hetware   hilde genǣgdon,
         elne geēodon   mid ofermægene,

2893ᵃ Ke. ii, 4 Edd. ēg-. — 2904ᵃ MS. siex; Ke. ii, et al. seax-; Holt., Sed. sex-. See Lang. § 1. — 2909ᵃ MS. hige mæðum; Gr., et al., Schü.: dþ. of hygemǣð 'reverence '[?] (Sed.: 'measure of ability '); Ke., et al. -mēðum (Rie. Zs. 413: dþ. of -mēðe, Ke., Bu. 106, Holt.¹: dþ. of -mēðu); Siev. ix 142 -mēðe (but cf. Siev. xxxvi 419). See Lang. § 9.3. — 2909ᵇ Fol. 193ᵃ heafod A B. — 2911ᵇ MS. under; Gr. under[ne]. — 2916ᵇ MS. ge hnægdon; Gr.¹ (?), Bu. Tid. 64, Holt., Sed., Cha. genǣgdon. See T.C. § 28.

þæt se byrnwiga   būgan sceolde,
fēoll on fēðan;   nalles frætwe geaf
2920 ealdor dugoðe.   Ūs wæs ā syððan
Merewīoingas   milts ungyfeðe. —
Nē ic te Swēoðēode   sibbe oððe trēowe
wihte ne wēne,   ac wæs wīde cūð,
þætte Ongenðīo   ealdre besnyðede
2925 Hæðcen Hrēþling   wið Hrefnawudu,
þā for onmēdlan   ǣrest gesōhton
Gēata lēode   Gūð-Scilfingas.
Sōna him se frōda   fæder Ōhtheres,
eald ond egesfull   *o*ndslyht āgeaf,
2930 ābrēot brimwīsan,   brȳd āh*redd*e,
gomela iōmēowlan   golde berofene,
Onelan mōdor   ond Ōhtheres;
ond ðā folgode   feorhgenīðlan,
oð ðæt hī oðēodon   earfoðlīce
2935 in Hrefnesholt   hlāfordlēase.
Besæt ðā sinherge   sweorda lāfe
wundum wērge;   wēan oft gehēt
earmre teohhe   ondlonge niht,
cwæð, hē on mergenne   mēces ecgum
2940 gētan wolde,   sum[e] on galgtrēowu[m]
[fuglum] tō gamene.   Frōfọr eft gelamp
sārigmōdum   somod ǣrdæge,

2921ᵃ *MS.* mere wio ingas; *Gru.tr. 309, Ke.* Merewīcinga; *Schü. ESt. lv 95 f., Holt.¹* merewīcingas; *Tho., Gr.* Merewīoinga; *Bu. Tid. 300, 3 Edd.* Merewīoingas. — 2921ᵇ *Luick Beitr. xi 475* ungyfðe (?) (*metri causa*). — 2922ᵃ *MS.* te; *Tho., most Edd.* tō. *See Lang.* § *18.9.* — 2929ᵇ *MS.* hond; *Gr.¹* (?), *Rie. Zs. 414, Holt., Schü., Cha.* ond-. *So 2972ᵇ. See 1541ᵇ.* — 2930ᵃ *Ke., Gr., Sed.* ābrēat. *See Lang.* § *16.2.* — 2930ᵇ *MS.* bryda heorde; *Gr., Schü., Cha.* brȳd āheorde ('liberated') [?]; *Bu. 107* (?), *Holt.³⁻⁶* brȳd āhredde, *cf. ESt. xlii 329* (*Gen. 2032, 2085*); *Lang.* § *13.3*; *Holt.¹·²* (*cf Zs. 122*), *Sed.* brȳd āfeorde ('removed'). — 2931ᵃ *Ke. ii* gomele; *Gr.¹* (?), *Lichtenheld ZfdA. xvi 330* gomelan; *Barnouw 40* gomel *or* gomelan. — 2937ᵇ *Fol. 193ᵇ* wean *A B.* — 2940ᵃ⁻41ᵃ *Tho., Sed.* g[r]ētan. — *MS.* sum on galg treowu: *Tho.* sum[e] *and* [fuglum]; *Ke.* -trēowu[m]. *Cf. Siev. ix 143; Bu. Tid. 60, Bu. 107, 372.*

syððan hīe Hygelāces   horn ond bȳman,
gealdor ongēaton,   þā se gōda cōm
2945 lēoda dugoðe   on lāst faran.
XLI Wæs sīo swātswaðu   Sw[ē]ona ond Gēata,
wælrǣs weora   wīde gesȳne,
hū ðā folc mid him   fǣhðe tōwehton.
Gewāt him ðā se gōda   mid his gædelingum,
2950 frōd felageōmor   fæsten sēcean,
eorl Ongenþīo   ufor oncirde;
hæfde Higelāces   hilde gefrūnen,
wlonces wīgcræft;   wiðres ne truwode,
þæt hē sǣmannum   onsacan mihte,
2955 heaðolīðendum   hord forstandan,
bearn ond brȳde;   bēah eft þonan
eald under eorðweall.   Þā wæs ǣht boden
Swēona lēodum,   segn Higelāce[s]
freoðowong þone   forð oferēodon,
2960 syððan Hrēðlingas   tō hagan þrungon.
Þǣr wearð Ongenðīow   ecgum sweorda,
blondenfexa   on bid wrecen,
þæt se þēodcyning   ðafian sceolde
Eafores ānne dōm.   Hyne yrringa
2965 Wulf Wonrēding   wǣpne geræhte,
þæt him for swenge   swāt ǣdrum sprong
forð under fexe.   Næs hē forht swā ðēh,
gomela Scilfing,   ac forgeald hraðe
wyrsan wrixle   wælhlem þone,
2970 syððan ðēodcyning   þyder oncirde.

2946[b] *MS.* swona; *Thk.* Sw[ē]ona. — 2948[b] *Tr.* f. geworhton. — 2953[b] *See 669[b] Varr.*
— 2957[b]–58[b] *Holt.* ōht. — *Siev. ix 143* sæcc (*for* segn). — *Ke., Bu. Tid. 61, Bu. 108, Holt.*
Higelāce[s]. — *Cl. Hall, Holt., Child MLN. xxi 200 punctuate as in text, other Edd. after*
Higelāce(s). — 2959[b] *MS.* ford; *Thk.* forþ. — 2961[b] *MS.* sweordū; *Ke.* sweorda. — 2964[a]
Fol. 194[a] anne.

BEOWULF

Ne meahte se snella sunu Wonrēdes
ealdum ceorle ondslyht giofan,
ac hē him on hēafde helm ǣr gescer,
þæt hē blōde fāh būgan sceolde,
2975 fēoll on foldan; næs hē fǣge þā gīt,
ac hē hyne gewyrpte, þēah ðe him wund hrine.
Lēt se hearda Higelāces þegn
brād[n]e mēce, þā his brōðor læg,
ealdsweord eotonisc entiscne helm
2980 brecan ofer bordweal; ðā gebēah cyning,
folces hyrde, wæs in feorh dropen.
Ðā wǣron monige, þē his mǣg wriðon,
ricone ārǣrdon, ðā him gerȳmed wearð,
þæt hīe wælstōwe wealdan mōston.
2985 Þenden rēafode rinc ōðerne,
nam on Ongenðīo īrenbyrnan,
heard swyrd hilted, ond his helm somod;
hāres hyrste Higelāce bær.
Hē ð(ām) frætwum fēng ond him fægre gehēt
2990 lēana (mid) lēodum, ond gelǣste swā;
geald þone gūðrǣs Gēata dryhten,
Hrēðles eafora, þā hē tō hām becōm,
Iofore ond Wulfe mid ofermāðmum,
sealde hiora gehwæðrum hund þūsenda
2995 landes ond locenra bēaga, — ne ðorfte him ðā lēan
oðwītan
mon on middangearde, syððа[n] hīe ðā mǣrða geslōgon;

2972[b] *See 2929[b].* — 2977[a] *Siev. ix 143, Holt., Sed.* Lēt [þā]. — 2978[a] *MS.* brade; *Tho.* brād[n]e. — 2979[a] *See 1558[a].* — 2987[a] *See 2509[a].* — 2989[a] *Gru. tr. 310* ð(ām). — 2990[a] *MS.* leana . . . ; *Ke.* (on); *Gr.* (his); *Gru., 4 Edd.* (mid) (*Bu. 108*: *cp. 2623, 2611*); *He.*[4] (fore), *Hold.*[1], *Wy., Tr.* (for). *Cf. Kock*[4] *121 f.; A. l 220 f.* — *Fol. 194[b]* leodū. — 2990[b] *MS.* gelæsta; *Ke.* gelǣste. — 2995[b]–96[a] *placed in parenthesis by Bu. 108.* — 2996[b] *Gru. tr. 310* syððа[n].

ond ðā Iofore forgeaf   āngan dohtor,
hāmweorðunge,   hyldo tō wedde.
  þæt ys sīo fæhðo   ond se fēondscipe,
3000 wælnīð wera,   ðæs ðe ic [wēn] hafo,
þē ūs sēceað tō   Swēona lēoda,
syððan hīe gefricgeað   frēan ūserne
ealdorlēasne,   þone ðe ǣr gehēold
wið hettendum   hord ond rīce,
3005 æfter hæleða hryre,   hwate scild*wiga*n,
folcrēd fremede,   oððe furður gēn
eorlscipe efnde. — Nū is ofǫst betost,
þæt wē þēodcyning   þǣr scēawian,
ond þone gebringan,   þē ūs bēagas geaf,
3010 on ādfære.   Ne scel ānes hwæt
meltan mid þām mōdigan,   ac þǣr is māðma hord,
gold unrīme   grimme gecēa(po)d,
ond nū æt sīðestan   sylfes fēore
bēagas (geboh)te;   þā sceall brond fretan,
3015 ǣled þeccean, —   nalles eorl wegan
māððum tō gemyndum,   nē mægð scȳne
habban on healse   hringweorðunge,
ac sceal geōmormōd,   golde berēafod
oft nalles ǣne   elland tredan,
3020 nū se herewīsa   hleahtor ālegde,
gamen ond glēodrēam.   Forðon sceall gār wesan
monig morgenceald   mundum bewunden,
hæfen on handa,   nalles hearpan swēg
wīgend weccean,   ac se wonna hrefn

3000ᵇ *Ke.* [wēn]. — 3001ᵇ *Ke., et al.* lēode. — 3005 *E.* hæleðes. — *MS.* scildingas; *JEGPh. viii 259* Sǣ-Gēatas; *He.*¹ Scilfingas; *so E., Holt.*²⁻⁵, *Sed. (inserting the line after 3001); Hoops St. 78 ff.* scildwigan. — 3007ᵇ *MS.* me; *Ke.* Nū. — 3012ᵇ *Ke.* gecēa(po)d. — 3014ᵃ *Gru.tr. 311* (beboh)te, *Gru.* (geboh)te. — 3015ᵃ *Holt. Beibl. x 273, Tr.* þicgean. *See JEGPh. vi 196; Sed. MLR. xxviii 230* þecgean. — 3015ᵇ *Fol. 195ᵃ* nalles.

3025 fūs ofer fǣgum   fela reordian,
earne secgan,   hū him æt ǣte spēow,
þenden hē wið wulf   wæl rēafode.'
   Swā se secg hwata   secggende wæs
lāðra spella;   hē ne lēag fela
3030 wyrda nē worda.   Weorod eall ārās;
ēodon unblīðe   under Earnanæs,
wollentēare   wundur scēawian.
Fundon ðā on sande   sāwullēasne
hlimbed healdan   þone þe him hringas geaf
3035 ǣrran mǣlum;   þā wæs endedæg
gōdum gegongen,   þæt se gūðcyning,
Wedra þēoden   wundọrdēaðe swealt.
Ǣr hī þǣr gesēgan   syllīcran wiht,
wyrm on wonge   wiðerræhtes þǣr
3040 lāðne licgean;   wæs se lēgdraca
grimlīc gry(refāh)   glēdum beswǣled;
sē wæs fīftiges   fōtgemearces
lang on legere;   lyftwynne hēold
nihtes hwīlum,   nyðer eft gewāt
3045 dennes nīosian;   wæs ðā dēaðe fæst,
hæfde eorðscrafa   ende genyttod.
Him big stōdan   bunan ond orcas,
discas lāgon   ond dȳre swyrd,
ōmige þurhetone,   swā hīe wið eorðan fæðm
3050 þūsend wintra   þǣr eardodon;
þonne wæs þæt yrfe   ēacencræftig,

3027ᵃ *MS.* wulf; *Gru. tr. 311, et al., Siev. R. 289* wulf[e]; *Hoops St 12* wulf. See *2673ᵃ*. — 3028ᵃ *Gr. Spr., Gr.², Z.* secghwata. See *Lang.* § 25.3. — 3035ᵃ *MS. Z.:* ærrun w. u *altered from a* by *erasure; MS. Sed. & Cha.:* ærran w. a *partially obliterated.* — 3038ᵃ *Tho. ac, Gru.* ǣc (= ēac) (*for* ǣr); *Bu. Zs. 219 drops* þǣr; *Siev. ix 143, Holt.*¹⁻⁵, *Sed.* þǣr hī þā. [*Cf. Bu. 372 f.; Aant. 39.*] — 3041ᵃ *MS. defective* (*end of last line of page*); *after* gry *there was perh. room for five letters* (*Cha.*); *Thk.* gryre; *He.*⁴ gryregæst; *Bu. Tid. 62, Sed., Cha.* gryrefāh. — 3041ᵇ *Fol. 195ᵇ* gledū. — 3045ᵃ *Holt., Schü.* nīosan. See *T.C.* § 9. — 3049ᵃ *Scheinert Beitr. xxx 377* ōme(?).

BEOWULF

iūmonna gold galdre bewunden,
þæt ðām hringsele hrīnan ne mōste
gumena ǣnig, nefne God sylfa,
3055 sigora Sōðcyning sealde þām ðe hē wolde
— hē is manna gehyld — hord openian,
efne swā hwylcum manna, swā him gemet ðūhte.

XLII Þā wæs gesȳne, þæt se sīð ne ðāh
þām ðe unrihte inne gehȳdde
3060 wrǣ*te* under wealle. Weard ǣr ofslōh
fēara sumne; þā sīo fǣhð gewearð
gewrecen wrāðlīce. Wundur hwār þonne
eorl ellenrōf ende gefēre
līfgesceafta, þonne leng ne mæg
3065 mon mid his (mā)gum meduseld būan.
Swā wæs Bīowulfe, þā hē biorges weard
sōhte searonīðas; seolfa ne cūðe,
þurh hwæt his worulde gedāl weorðan sceolde.
Swā hit oð dōmes dæg dīope benemdon
3070 þēodnas mǣre, þā ðæt þǣr dydon,
þæt se secg wǣre synnum scildig,
hergum geheaðerod, hellbendum fæst,
wommum gewītnad, sē ðone wong str*u*de,
næ*fn*e goldhwǣte gearwor hæfde
3075 Āgendes ēst ǣr gescēawod.

Wīglāf maðelode, Wīhstānes sunu:
' Oft sceall eorl monig ānes willan
wræc ādrēog*an*, swā ūs geworden is.

<small>3056ᵃ *Gru. (?), Bu. 109* gehyht.— *Bu 109, Morgan Beitr. xxxiii 110, Holt., Schü.* hæleða (*for* manna); *Holt. note, Sed.* gehyld manna. *Cf. T.C.* § *18.* [*Gr.*¹ (?),²: 3056ᵃ hēlsmanna g. (*parallel w.* hord); *Holt. Zs. 122.*]— 3059ᵇ *Bu. 109, Holt.* gehȳðde (*ref. to the thief*).— 3060ᵃ *MS.* wræce; *Tho.* wrǣte.— 3065ᵃ *Ke.* (mā)gum.— 3066ᵇ *Fol. 196ᵃ* þa. — 3069ᵇ *Holt. Zs. 122* (?), *Sed.* dīore.— 3073ᵇ *MS.* strade; *Gru.tr. 311* strude.— 3074ᵃ *MS.* næshe; *Holt.*⁴ᐟ⁶ (*cf. Siev. ix 144*), *Lawrence L 4.62 a. 562* næfne *for* Næs, *and comma after* strude.— *Siev. ix 143* goldhwǣte[s]; *He.*⁴ -hwǣt; *Holt. Zs. 122, Schü.* -ǣhte; *Holt.*¹ *note* (?), *Sed.* -frǣtwe.— 3078ᵃ *MS.* wræc a dreogeð; *Ke.* wræca drēogan; *Gr.* wræc ādrēogan.</small>

Ne meahton wē gelǣran   lēofne þēoden,
3080 rīces hyrde   rǣd ǣnigne,
þæt hē ne grētte   goldweard þone,
lēte hyne licgean,   þǣr hē longe wæs,
wīcum wunian   oð woruldende.
Hēold on hēahgesceap;   hord ys gescēawod,
3085 grimme gegongen;   wæs þæt gifeðe tō swīð,
þē ðone [þēodcyning]   þyder ontyhte.
Ic wæs þǣr inne   ond þæt eall geondseh,
recedes geatwa,   þā mē gerȳmed wæs,
nealles swǣslīce   sīð ālȳfed
3090 inn under eorðweall.   Ic on ofoste gefēng
micle mid mundum   mægenbyrðenne
hordgestrēona,   hider ūt ætbær
cyninge mīnum.   Cwico wæs þā gēna,
wīs ond gewittig;   worn eall gespræc
3095 gomol on gehðo,   ond ēowic grētan hēt,
bæd þæt gē geworhton   æfter wines dǣdum
in bǣlstede   beorh þone hēan,
micelne ond mǣrne,   swā hē manna wæs
wīgend weorðfullost   wīde geond eorðan,
3100 þenden hē burhwelan   brūcan mōste.
Uton nū efstan   ōðre [sīðe],
sēon ond sēcean   searo[gimma] geþræc,
wundur under wealle,   ic ēow wīsige,
þæt gē genōge   nēon scēawiað
3105 bēagas ond brād gold.   Sīe sīo bǣr gearo,

3084ª *MS.* heoldon; *Ke.* healdan, *Bu. Zs. 221* healdon (=-an); *Gr.*[1], *Schü.* hēoldon (*1 pl., period after* -ende); *Wy., Cha.* hēold on ('he held (on) to his high fate'). — 3084ᵇ *Gru., Sarr. ESt. xxviii 410* gecēapod. — 3086ª *Gru.tr. 311* [þēoden]; *Gr.*[2], *4 Edd.* [þēodcyning]. — 3092ᵇ *Fol. 196ᵇ* ut. — 3096ᵇ *Bu. Tid. 300, Siev. ix 144, Holt.*[1-5] wine dēadum. — 3101ᵇ *Gru. tr. 312* [sīðe]. — 3102ᵇ *Bu. 109 (cf. Siev. R. 269), 4 Edd.* [-gimma]. — 3104ª *Siev. ix 144, Holt.*[1-5] þǣr (*for* þæt) (*and* 3103ᵇ *in parenthesis*).

ǣdre geæfned, þonne wē ūt cymen,
ond þonne geferian frēan ūserne,
lēofne mannan þǣr hē longe sceal
on ðæs Waldendes wǣre geþolian.'
3110 Hēt ðā gebēodan byre Wīhstānes,
hæle hildedīor hæleða monegum,
boldāgendra, þæt hīe bælwudu
feorran feredon, folcāgende,
gōdum tōgēnes: 'Nū sceal glēd fretan
3115 (weaxan wonna lēg) wigena strengel,
þone ðe oft gebād īsernscūre,
þonne strǣla storm strengum gebǣded
scōc ofer scildweall, sceft nytte hēold,
fæðergearwum fūs flāne fullēode.'
3120 Hūru se snotra sunu Wīhstānes
ācīgde of corðre cyniges þegnas
syfone (tō)somne, þā sēlestan,
ēode eahta sum under inwithrōf
hilderinc[a]; sum on handa bær
3125 ǣledlēoman, sē ðe on orde gēong.
Næs ðā on hlytme, hwā þæt hord strude,
syððan orwearde ǣnigne dǣl
secgas gesēgon on sele wunian,
lǣne licgan; lȳt ǣnig mearn,
3130 þæt hī ofostlīc(e) ūt geferedon
dȳre māðmas; dracan ēc scufun,
wyrm ofer weallclif, lēton wēg niman,
flōd fæðmian frætwa hyrde.

3115ᵃ *Tr.* wēstan; *Holt.*⁶ weasan. — 3119ᵃ *MS.* fæder; *Thk.* fæþer, *Ke., Edd.* feðer-. — 3121ᵇ *Fol. 198ᵃ* cyniges; *Thk., most Edd.* cyni[n]ges. — 3122ᵃ *Ke., Edd.* (tō)somne; *Gr.*¹, *E., Wy., Cha.* (æt)somne. — 3124ᵃ *MS.* rinc; *E. Sc., Siev. ix 144, R. 314, 4 Edd.* -rinc[a] (*cp. 1412 f.*). *Punctuat. in text agrees w. Siev.; earlier Edd., Aant. 41, Moore JEGPh. xviii 215 f.:* 3124ᵃ -rinc sum (*E.Sc.* -rinca sum). — 3130ᵃ *E.Sc.* ofostlīc(e).

118   BEOWULF

þā wæs wunden gold   on wǣn hladen,
3135 ǣghwæs unrīm,   æþeling boren,
  hār hilde[rinc]   tō Hronesnæsse.

XLIII   Him ðā gegiredan   Gēata lēode
  ād on eorðan   unwāclīcne,
  helm[um] behongen,   hildebordum,
3140 beorhtum byrnum,   swā hē bēna wæs;
  ālegdon ðā tōmiddes   mǣrne þēoden
  hæleð hīofende,   hlāford lēofne.
  Ongunnon þā on beorge   bǣlfȳra mǣst
  wīgend weccan;   wud(u)rēc āstāh
3145 sweart ofer swioðole,   swōgende lēg
  wōpe bewunden   — windblond gelæg —,
  oð þæt hē ðā bānhūs   gebrocen hæfde
  hāt on hreðre.   Higum unrōte
  mōdceare mǣndon,   mondryhtnes cw(e)alm;
3150 swylce giōmorgyd   (s)īo g(eō)mēowle
  (æfter Bīowulfe   b)undenheorde
  (song) sorgcearig,   sǣde geneahhe,
  þæt hīo hyre (hearmda)gas   hearde (ondrē)de,
  wælfylla worn,   (wīgen)des egesan,
3155 hȳ[n]ðo (ond) h(æftnȳ)d.   Heofon rēce swe(a)lg.

_{3134^a MS. þ; Thk., Ke., E.Sc., Sed., Cha. þā; Ke. ii, Edd. þǣr; Tr. þon. — 3135^b MS. æþelinge; Ke. æþeling (geboren); Bu. 110 æþelingc; Barnouw 9 [ond se]æ., Tr. [ond] æ. — 3136^a MS. blank between hilde and to and possibly erasure of one letter; Gru.tr. 312 hilde[dēor]; E.Sc. hilde[rinc]. — 3139^a MS. helm; Gr. helm[um]. — Tr., Holt.¹, Sed. behēngon. — 3144^b Ke. wud(u)-. — 3145^a MS. swicðole; Tho. Swīo-ðole ('Swedish pine'); Bout. 82 ff., Gr. swioðole; Tr. swioloðe. — 3145^b MS. let; Tho. lēg. — 3146^b Grimm L 9.2.263 windblond [ne] gelæg; cf. JEGPh. vi 196. But see Aant. 41 f., Lüning L 7.28.75. [Cf. Bu. 110.] — 3149^b Ke. cw(e)alm. — 3150^a Wy., Cha. giōmor gyd. — 3150^b Fol. 198^b. 'Almost all that is legible in this page freshened up in a late hand' Z.; 'Versus ... miserrime lacerati sunt' E.Sc. — MS. Z. (s)ia (a perh. orig. o, erroneously freshened up) g(eo)meowle (w. Lat. anus written over it); geo first conjectured by E.Sc. — 3151^a-55^a Bugge's restoration (Bu. 110 f.) has been adopted in this edition, cf. his detailed comment. [Earlier conjectures by E.Sc., Gr.^{1,2}, Bu. Zs. 223 f., E.] — 3151^b Bu. Bēowulfe. — 3151^b Gr.² first conjectured (b)unden- (i.e., bundenheorte). — 3152^b MS. sælðe. — 3154^a MS. wonn. — 3154^b Zu pitza on one day 'thought (he) was able to read (w)igendes.' — 3155^a MS. hyðo. — 3155^b E.Sc. swe(a)lg.}

BEOWULF

Geworhton ðā Wedra lēode
hl(ǣw) on [h]līðe, sē wæs hēah ond brād,
(wǣ)glīðendum wīde g(e)sȳne,
ond betimbredon on tȳn dagum
3160 beadurōfes bēcn, bronda lāfe
wealle beworhton, swā hyt weorðlīcost
foresnotre men findan mihton.
Hī on beorg dydon bēg ond siglu,
eall swylce hyrsta, swylce on horde ǣr
3165 nīðhēdige men genumen hæfdon;
forlēton eorla gestrēon eorðan healdan,
gold on grēote, þǣr hit nū gēn lifað
eldum swā unnyt, swā hi(t ǣro)r wæs.
Þā ymbe hlǣw riodan hildedēore,
3170 æþelinga bearn, ealra twelfe,
woldon (care) cwīðan, [ond] kyning mǣnan,
wordgyd wrecan, ond ymb w(er) sprecan;
eahtodan eorlscipe ond his ellenweorc
duguðum dēmdon, — swā hit gedē(fe) bið,
3175 þæt mon his winedryhten wordum herge,
ferhðum frēoge, þonne hē forð scile
of līchaman (lǣded) weorðan.
Swā begnornodon Gēata lēode
hlāfordes (hry)re, heorðgenēatas;

3157ª *Ke.* hl(ǣw). — *MS.* liðe, *but freshened up* lide; *Tho.* [h]liðe; *Holt.*²⁻⁴, *Schü.* [h]liðeis nōsan]. *Cf. T.C.* § *17.* — 3158ª *Ke.* (wǣ)g-. — 3158ᵇ *Thk., et al.* to syne; *MS. Kölbing L 1.4* gēsyne, *Z.* g(e)syne, *He.*⁴, *Edd.* gesȳne. — 3163ᵇ *Tho.* bēag[as], *Tr., Holt.* bēg[as]. *Cf. MPh. iii 250.* — 3168ᵇ *Ke.* hi(t ǣro)r. — 3170ᵇ *MS.* twelfa; *E.Sc.* twelfe. — 3171ª *MS. Z.* : : : : ; *Gr., Edd.* ceare (*cp. Wand. 9*); *Sed.* hīe. — 3171ᵇ *Siev. R. 232, Hold.², Tr., Holt.* [ond]. — 3172ᵇ *Gr.* w(er). — 3174ᵇ *Ke.* gedē(fe). — 3177ª *MS. Z.* lachaman, *but 'there can be little doubt that* lac *instead of* lic *is owing only to the late hand'* Z. — 3177ᵇ *MS. Z.* : : : : ; *Ke., et al.* lǣne; *Bu. Tid. 65* ǣnum; *Klu.* (*in Hold.²*), *Sed.* lȳsed; *Kock*⁴ *118* lēored; *Tr.* (?), *Jacobsen D. synt. Gebrauch d. Präpos. for etc.* (*Kiel Diss. 1908*) *p. 57*, *Holt., Cha.* lǣded (*cp. Discourse of Soul 21, etc.*). *See Angl. xxxv 463.* — 3179ª *Tho.* (hry)re.

3180 cwǣdon þæt hē wǣre   wyruldcyning[a]
　　manna mildust   ond mon(ðw)ǣrust,
　　lēodum līðost   ond lofgeornost.

3180[b] *MS.* wyruldcyning; *Ke., Schubert L 8.1.35, Siev. R. 232, Holt., Scht., Sed.* -cyning[a]. — 3181[b] *Gru.tr. 312* -(ðw)ǣrust.

NOTES

Omnia autem probate:
quod bonum est, tenete.

1-188. Introductory. (See Argument, Intr. ix ff.)

1-52. Founding of the glorious Danish dynasty. Being considered a sort of prelude, this canto (' fit ') was left outside the series of numbered sections. Bradley (L 4.21) thought this opening section had originally belonged to a different poem, viz. one concerning Bēowulf, Scyld's son. According to Boer (110 ff.), it was at the outset the opening of the dragon lay (Intr. ciii). But see Intr. cvi.

1-3. Hwæt, see Gloss. — **wē ... gefrūnon.** The only instance in *Beowulf* of *wē* — the more inclusive, emphatic plural — in the list of the *gefrægn-* formulas (Intr. lxvi f.). Cp. the opening of *Exodus, Juliana, Andreas; Nibelungenlied, Annolied* (early MHG.). — **in gēardagum** is to be understood with reference to *þrym;* see note on 575.

4-52. The Story of Scyld. ' Scyld,' the poet tells us, ' arrived as a little boy, alone and destitute, on the shores of the Danes; he became their king, a great and glorious chief, beloved by his loyal people; he conquered many tribes beyond the sea; he was blessed with a son; and when at the fated hour he had passed away, he was sent out into the sea with all the pomp of military splendor.' Thus his illustrious career fittingly foreshadows the greatness of his royal line.

Scyld[1] is well known in Scandinavian tradition as Skjǫldr, the eponymous ancestor of the Skjǫldungar.[2] Especially, the account of Saxo, who pays high tribute to his warlike and royal qualities, resembles the *Beowulf* version so closely as to suggest the use of the same kind of original Danish source. (See quotations in notes on 4 f., 6ᵇ, 12 ff., 18 f., 20 ff.) But nowhere outside of *Beowulf* do we find Scyld's strange arrival and his wonderful passing narrated.

Mystery surrounds him, signalizing a being of supernatural, divine origin. He is sent by unknown powers on his high mission, and when his life work is done, he withdraws to the strange world whence he had

---

[1] On Scyld and Scēaf, see Ke. ii, pp. iii ff.; Leo L 4.24.19 ff.; Müll. L 4.25.2, L 4.19.6–12; Köhler *ZfdPh.* ii 305–14; Mö. 40–45; Binz 147 ff.; Siev. L 4.33; Olrik i 223 ff., ii 250 ff., Olrik-Hollander 381 ff.; Chadwick Or. 274 ff.; Neckel, *GRM.* ii 4 f., 678 f.; Cha. Wid. 117 ff., 201, Intr. 68 ff.; L 4.80–82 f (espec. Stjerna, Björkman, v. Sydow, Berendsohn); also G. Schütte, *Oldsagn om Godtjod: bidrag til etnisk kildeforsknings metode med særligt henblik på folke-stamsagn* (Kjøbenhavn, 1907), pp. 137–39.

[2] See Par. §§ 4, 5, 6; 8.1, 3, & 6. It has been suggested that the existence of Scyld was inferred from the name *Scyldingas* (' shield men,' see Olrik i 274 f., Chadwick Or. 284). For Scyld(wa) etc. in Ags. genealogies, see Par. § 1.

come.¹ Whether he is conceived of as arriving in royal splendor (which is rather likely) or — making allowance for the wide range of litotes (*MPh.* iii 249) — merely as a helpless foundling,² has been questioned (ll. 43 ff.). But we feel that our poet's heart goes out in sympathy for the poor, lonely boy (*fēasceaft* 7, ... *ǣnne ofer ȳðe umbọrwesende* 46).

Scyld's famous sea-burial — one of the gems of the poem — is not to be interpreted, however, merely as a symbolical act, but reflects the actual practice of a previous age. Based on the belief that the soul after death had to take a long journey (*feor* 42; cp. 808) to the realm of spirits, the custom of sea-burial arose among various peoples living near the sea or great lakes³ and was prevalent (according to Stjerna) in Scandinavia from the end of the fourth to the middle of the sixth century A.D. Sometimes the dead were burned on ship-board.⁴ This custom was subsequently replaced by the ship-burial on land, both with and without the burning of the body, as shown unmistakably by the numerous finds of boat-graves belonging to the period beginning about 600 A.D.,⁵ until finally, through a still further development of the spiritual element, the outlines of corpse-ships were merely suggested by stones suitably piled about the graves.⁶

[1] Like Arthur (Tennyson, *The Coming of Arthur* 410, *The Passing of Arthur* 445), 'from the great deep to the great deep he goes.' The similarity of the Scyld legend to the famous (originally, perhaps, Netherlandish) story of the 'swan knight' was first recognized by J. Grimm (L 3.27, D. M. 306 (370), iii 108 (1391)). Cf. O. Rank, *Der Mythus von der Geburt des Helden* (1909), pp. 55 ff.

[2] On the motive of exposure, which occurs in various forms and is especially frequent in Irish legend, see Earle-Plummer, *Two of the Saxon Chronicles* ii 103–105; Schofield, *Publ. MLAss.* xviii 42 n.; Deutschbein, *Studien zur Sagengeschichte Englands* (1906), pp. 68–75; also Grimm R. A. 701 (punishment by exposure as in the story of Drida, see note on Þrȳð, ll. 1931–62).

[3] Thus, among the Celts of Ireland and Britain and the natives of North and South America. Hence its appearance in literature: Arthur departing for Avalon; the Lady of Shalott (in a modern version in Tennyson's poem, Part iv); 'The corpse-freighted Barque' (P. Kennedy, *Legendary Fictions of the Irish Celts* (1891), pp. 294–6; Sinfjǫtli's disappearance in a boat in *Frá dauþa Sinfjǫtla* (Elder Edda); Longfellow's *Hiawatha*, last canto. [Such a departure in the family canoe was reported from Alaska in 1909.]

[4] Illustrations in literature: Baldr (*Gylfaginning* [Prose Edda], ch. 48); King Haki (*Ynglingasaga*, ch. 23 (27), see Par. § 6), Sigvard Ring (see Par. § 8.7).

[5] Grave finds in Öland, Skåne, Vendel (Uppland), etc.; also the famous Gokstad and Oseberg (Norway) boats. Cf. Cha. Intr. 362 ff. Literary parallels are found, e g., in *Atlamál* 97 and in various sagas. (Frotho's law, Saxo v 156.)

[6] See especially Boehmer L 9.46.558 ff. This stage finds its analogue in the conception of a supernatural boat appearing in poetry and legend (cp. the Flying Dutchman, also Sinfjǫtli). — On ship-burials in general, see besides: Grimm D. M. 692 ff. (830 ff.); iii 248 (1549 ff.); Weinhold L 9.32.479 ff.; Montelius, S. Müller, *passim;* du Chaillu L 9.35. ch. 19; Gummere G. O. 322–8; H. Schurtz, *Urgeschichte der Kultur*, pp. 197 f., 574 ff.; H. Schetelig, *Ship-Burials* (Saga-Book of the Viking Club, Vol. iv, Part ii, pp. 326–63); Schnepper L 9.47.17; B. Schnittger, *R.-L.* iv 116 f.; G. Neckel, *Balder* (L 4.88 b) 163 ff.; also F. W. Hodge, *Handbook of American Indians* i (1906), 946 f. — On other modes of burial, see note on Bēowulf's Funeral Obsequies, ll. 3137 ff.

A counterpart of the story of Scyld's wonderful arrival appears in the chronicles of Ethelwerd and William of Malmesbury, but is told of Scēaf, the father of Scyld and progenitor of the West Saxon kings. (Par. § 1.3 & 4.) Notable variations in the later one of these two versions are the mention of Schleswig in the old Anglian homeland of the English as Scēaf's royal town, and the explanation of his name from the sheaf of grain lying at his head, which has taken the place of the weapons in Ethelwerd's tale. How to account for the attributing of the motive on the one hand to Scyld and on the other to Scēaf (who has no place in authentic Norse tradition[1]), is an interesting problem. It has been argued that Scyld Scēfing of the *Beowulf* meant originally *Scyld scēfing*, 'Scyld child of the sheaf' (?) or 'Scyld with the sheaf,' but by folk etymology was understood in the sense of 'Scyld son of Scēaf,' and that in course of time the story was transferred from Scyld to his putative father Scēaf. Taking, however, the patronymic designation as the (naturally) original one, we might think that Scēaf, who can hardly be separated from *Scēafa*, the legendary ruler of the Langobards,[2] owes his introduction into the Danish pedigree in the *Beowulf* to the Anglo-Saxon predilection for extensive genealogizing. (Olrik.) According to (Kemble and) Müllenhoff, Scēaf was in ancient tradition a God-sent mythical being to whom Northern German tribes attributed the introduction of agriculture and kingly rule. That the sheaf as a religious symbol among the heathen English was, indeed, an original element of the conceptions underlying the foundling ancestor story, and that a sheaf (and a shield) played a part in some ritual practice, has been suggested by Chadwick, — an idea elaborated and studied from a broad comparative point of view by Olrik (ii 250 ff.).[3] (Cf. Intr. xxvi.) So far as the *Beowulf* is concerned, the linking of Scēaf (Scyld, Bēow) with the undoubtedly Danish (ancestor) Scyld may be regarded as a characteristic instance of the blending of English and Scandinavian tradition (cf. Cha. Wid. 120). [Björkman (L 4.82 a) is convinced that Scēaf, Scyld, Bēow were originally divine beings of fruitfulness known to the (continental) Anglo-Saxons, and that the ancestor story was shifted by the poet from Scēaf to Scyld, whom he spontaneously identified with the eponymous ancestor of the Skjǫldungar. The poet's inconsistency in retaining the epithet Scēfing for the founder of the race is thus naturally explained. Björkman compares Bēow to Byggvir mentioned in *Lokasenna* (Elder Edda). Cf. Cha. Intr. 291 ff. — On corn-spirits, see also Mogk, *R.-L.* iii 91–3.]

That Scyld as the progenitor of the Danish *Scyldingas* had stepped

[1] Sievers, *Beitr.* xvi 361–63.

[2] *Wids.* 32: *Scēafa [wēold] Longbeardum.* For the coexistence of the strong and weak forms cp. *Hrēðel, Hrǣdla; Bēaw, Bēo(w), Bēowa.*

[3] Cf. Cha. Intr. 303 f. A note on a certain modern analogue, by H. M. Belden, *MLN.* xxxiii 315. See also Brandl (L 4.82 c, d: Lat. *scapha*); cf. W. Jaeger, *Arch.* clix 274 f. (instances of the occurrence of *scapha*).

into the place formerly occupied by Ing, the ancestor of the *Ingwine* (cp. *Runic Poem* 67 ff.; Intr. xxxvii), is an ingenious and pleasing hypothesis (Olrik, Chadwick).

4 f. sceaþena þrēatum .... meodosetla oftēah. Saxo's report (i 12) of Scioldus: 'cum Scato Allemannie satrapa ..... dimicavit, interfectoque eo omnem Allemannorum gentem .... tributaria pensione perdomuit' sounds like an echo of the same poetic tradition. — 5ᵇ. *meodosetla oftēah*, i.e. 'subjugated.' (Cf. Intr. lxiii f.) Exactly the same metrical variety of type E occurs in 14ᵇ, 17ᵇ. *meodosell* is hardly to be identified with *meduseld* 3065; 'mead(hall)-seats'? (cp. *medostīg* 924), by synecdoche, = 'hall.'

6ᵃ. egsode eorl[as]. The emendation *eorlas*, strongly advocated by Sievers, has been adopted as, after all, a desirable improvement. The metrical form of *egsode eorl*, though rare, need not be rejected (T.C. § 21), but stylistically, the sing. *eorl* would be suspiciously harsh. It is true that the sing. in a collective sense is well substantiated (see note on 794 f.), but this use of *eorl* (in the acc. sing.) as variation of the preceding collective noun plurals (*þrēatum*, *mǣgþum*) would not be satisfactory. A still less acceptable type of variation would result from the interpretation of *eorl* as nom. sing., 'the hero terrified [them]'? (von Grienberger, *Beitr.* xxxvi 94 f.; B.-T. Suppl., s.v. *egesian*), the ponderous (plural) object requiring a variation in preference to the subject. [See L 5.65: *Eorlas*, i.e., Erulians (cf. p. xxxvi, note on 82 ff.). The mention of an individual tribe would be extremely doubtful in this place.]

6ᵇ. syððan ǣrest; *ǣrest* (somewhat redundantly) accentuates the meaning of the conjunction *syððan* (cp. MnE. 'when ... first'). No doubt Scyld was believed to have distinguished himself in his early youth. Cp. Saxo i 11: 'while but fifteen years of age he was of unusual bodily size, and displayed mortal strength in its perfection ..... ; the ripeness of Skiold's spirit outstripped the fulness of his strength, and he fought battles at which one of his tender years could scarcely look on.' (Elton's transl.) [Only one night old, Váli avenged the slaying of Baldr, see (Elder Edda:) *Vǫluspá* 33, *Baldrs Draumar* 11.]

7ᵇ. þæs, 'for that'? (see Gloss.: *sē*), refers to 6ᵇ–7ᵃ, i.e. his destitute condition. Similarly the OHG. *Ludwigslied* (3 ff.) says of King Louis: *kind uuarth her faterlōs; thes uuarth imo sār buoz,/holōda inan truhtīn, magaczogo uuarth her sīn;/gab er imo dugidi*, etc. (Cp. *Jud.* 157 f., *Hel.* 3363 f.)

8. wēox, perhaps 'prospered,' practically synonymous with *þāh* (so that no comma is needed before *weorðmyndum*, cp. 131 and note on 36 f.). **under wolcnum,** see Intr. lxvi; Gloss.: *under, wolcen*.

9ᵃ. oð is stressed in this line, though it is doubtful whether it was felt to alliterate (Siev. R. 282, A. M. § 28); so 219ᵃ, 1740ᵃ, 2934ᵃ, further 2039ᵃ, 3147ᵃ (clearly type A3); but more frequently it remains unstressed, as in 56ᵇ, 66ᵇ, 100ᵇ, 145ᵇ, 296ᵇ, etc. In similar manner particles and formulas like *þā, þǣr, þā gēn, þā gȳt, þonan, hwīlum, hȳrde* (*ic*), *gefrægn, cwæð* show variable accentuation.

10. ofer hronrāde. *ofer* with acc., see Lang. § 25.5. *hronrād*, a typical kenning, see Intr. lxiii. Whales were well known to the Anglo-Saxons, see R. Jordan, *Die ae. Säugetiernamen* (Ang. F. xii, 1903), pp. 209 f., 212; Tupper's *Riddles*, p. 169. An instance of the same kenning in Old Irish poetry: Knowlton, *PMLA*. xliv 102.

11. gomban gyldan. See quotation from Saxo in the note on 4 f. — **þæt wæs gōd cyning!** The omission of the mark of exclamation would be tantamount to the suppression of a significant stylistic feature; to leave it out in a MnE. translation is a different matter.

12 ff. Scyld has a son, Bēowulf, who gives promise of a continuation of dynastic splendor. So the Danes need not fear a recurrence of the terrible 'lordless' time they had experienced before Scyld came, i.e., after the fall of Heremōd (see note on 901–915). [Also Saxo's Scioldus had a son, named 'Gram, whose wondrous parts savored so strongly of his father's virtues, that he was deemed to tread in their very footsteps' (i 12). However, this parallelism may be purely accidental.]

12. æfter is not exactly 'afterwards,' but denotes rather 'coming after him,' as in 2731.

14. The subject of **ongeat** is 'God.'

15. þ (=*þæt*) seems to have been introduced for *þē* or *þā* by the late scribe. On *þæt* standing for the relat. pron. with a sing. masc. or fem. or a plur. antecedent, see Kock L 6.13.1.30 f.; on a few cases of þ used for *þā*, see Zupitza's note; also l. 3134 (?). Cf. J. M. Hart, *MLN*. i, col. 175–7; Napier, *Philol. Soc. Transact.*, 1907–10, p. 188 (þ used as contraction for *þē*); F. Wende, *Über die nachgestellten Präpositionen im Ags.* (Palaestra lxx, 1915), p. 37 (interchange of *þē* and *þæt*). See also 649 (*oþ ðe = oþ þæt*) and note on 1141. [Cha. would retain *þæt* (conj.) and take *lange hwīle* as the object of *drugon*, 'a long time of sorrow' (?); Kock² 100 takes *drugon* intransitively, 'they lived without a lord.' The rendering 'that they had lived without a lord' has been repeatedly urged by him (cf. *Angl.* xlv 123, *AfNF.* xxxix 187). But it seems on the whole more likely that the passage contains a direct reference to the distress *which* the Danes had suffered; cp. ll. 422, 831, 1858, *Jud.* 158, *Christ* 615, etc. (*Angl.* l 108).]

16. him, probably dat. sing. — **þæs,** see 7. Earle: "in consideration thereof."

18 f. On **Bēowulf (I)** the Dane, see Intr. xxiii ff., espec. xxv f. That this form of the name is an error for *Bēow*, is likely enough. — The emendation *blǣd wīde sprang/Scyldes eafera[n] Scedelandum in*, supported by Siev. (ix 135) in view of the apparently imitated passage, *Fat. Ap.* 6 ff., is unnecessary and even unsafe, since *springan* should be followed by *geond* or *ofer* with acc., not by *in* with dat. (*ESt.* xxxix 428). — 18ᵇ. **blǣd wīde sprang.** Type D4. — According to Saxo (i 12), 'the days of Gram's youth were enriched with surpassing gifts of mind and body, and he raised them to the crest of renown ('ad summum glorie cumulum perduxit'). Posterity did such homage to his greatness that in the most ancient poems of the Danes royal dignity is implied in his very name.' (ON. *gramr* ' chief.')

20 ff. Swā, ' in such a way [as he (Bēowulf or, possibly, Scyld [?]) did].' The missing reference to Scyld's liberality might be implied in the previous statements concerning him. For how could the king have been so successful in war, had he not been conspicuous for generosity, which gained for him the loyalty of his followers? These two ideas were inseparably connected in the minds of the ancient Teutons. Saxo says in his praise of Scioldus' liberality (i 12): ' Proceres non solum domesticis stipendiis colebat, sed eciam spoliis ex hoste quesitis, affirmare solitus, pecuniam ad milites, gloriam ad ducem redundare debere.' Cp. *Hrólfssaga* 43.3 ff., 45.28 ff. (Par. § 9), 62.4 ff. (Hrólfr Kraki); Baeda, *H.E.* iii, c. 14 (Ōswini). However, it must be admitted that the author, very likely, alludes to Scyld's son. — **gewyrcean** (perfective), ' bring about.' The reading *wine* (thus Grundtvig, Heyne), in place of (**bea**)**rme**, has been recommended by Kock (*Angl.* xlv 108), but it appears to conflict with the evidence of the MS. Also the meaning ' act on,' ' influence,' assigned by him to *gewyrcean on*, is doubtful. On the other hand, it is to be granted that the sense of ' possession ' assumed for *bearm* (cf. *JEGPh.* vi 190, *Beibl.* xl 30) is in fact based on its use in connection with verbs like *dōn, ālecgan, cuman.* [Earle translates: ' in his father's nurture.'] A dogmatic assertion in this case (*as in various other cases*) is inadvisable. (*Angl.* l 108 f.) — Those who believe that the poem was intended for the instruction of a prince will certainly reject the idea that these lines could refer to anyone but Bēowulf (I).

24. lēode gelǣsten. The object, i.e. probably *hine* (see 2500), is understood, cf. Lang. § 25.4. (In *Andr.* 411 f., *Mald.* 11 f. the dat. is used with *gelǣstan.*) There is no need to take *lēode* as dat. sing. (Kock, *Angl.* xlii 100, xliv 98: *lēode gelǣsten*=' follow their prince '). See *MLN.* xxxiv 129 f., *Angl.* l 109 f. — **sceal**, ' will,' ' is sure to ' (in 20: ' should,' ' ought to ').

29–31. Scyld's men prepare the funeral of their beloved king, as he bade them while he still ' wielded his words.' (Cf. Siev. xxix 308, Kock[2] 101. See ll. 2802 ff., 3140.) L. 31, **lēof landfruma lange āhte**, added paratactically, conveys the very appropriate idea: ' his had been a long reign.' (Cp. *Helgakv. Hund.* i 10; for the paratactic clause, cp. *OE. Chron.* A.D. 871: *Ond þæs ofer Ēastron gefōr Æþerēd cyning, ond hē rīcsode fīf gēar.*) The implied object of *āhte* (it need not be expressed, see 2208[b]) is *hī*, cp. 522, 2732, 911, 2751; *folcāgend(e)*. Practically the same interpretation would result from construing 31[a] as a variation of 30[b] (as to the brief clause *lange āhte*, cp. 1913[b]). [It would not seem impossible to regard 31 as parallel to 30, i.e. dependent on *þenden;* in that case the somewhat peculiar *lange* might be compared to *oft*, 2867.] Cf. *MPh.* iii 446. Hoops's explanation (St. 13 ff.): *lange*=acc. pl. of *lang*, to which he assigns the meaning of ' related,' ' relative ' (OHG. *gilang-(ēr)* ' relative ') is stylistically satisfactory, but this use of *lang* appears somewhat uncertain. Prokosch (Kl. Misc. 201) would place a period after *wēold*, thus making an independent sentence of 30ᵇ and 31.

33. īsig, not ' shining like ice ' (Kemble, Heyne⁵-Schücking), but ' covered with ice ' (see Bu. Tid. 69 f.; Siev. *Beitr.* xxvii 572, xxxvi 422 ff.; Intr. lx). Readings like *ītig* (see Varr.) provide very acceptable sense, but involve the introduction of otherwise unrecorded words. [Sedgefield, *MLR.* xxvii 448: *ūrig.*] **ūtfūs,** ' ready (i.e. eager) to set out ' (personification), cp. the use of *fundian* 1137.

36 f. mǣrne be mǣste etc. Scyld's body was placed amidships with his back against the mast. The remains of the Vendel ship-graves indicate a similar position for the dead. (Stjer. 127 f.) Also swords, corslets, splendid shield bosses, and other costly objects, including glass beakers of foreign origin, have been found in these graves. (Stjer. 128 ff.) — **of feorwegum** occupying a medial position between two terms of variation (**mādma, frǣtwa**), belongs with both. Similar ἀπὸ κοινοῦ function at the beginning of the line: 754, 935, 3067 (probably 281, 1109); at the beginning of the second half-line: 131 (8).

40. him, ref. to Scyld.

44. þon ' than ' (sometimes ' then ') is comparatively rare. It is best known from *Bede's Death Song* 2: *than.* Cf. Tr. Kyn. 86 f., & *Angl.* xxxvii 363 f.; Deutschbein, *Beitr.* xxvi 172; *Angl.* xxvii 248; O. Johnsen, *ib.* xxxix 103 f.

47. segen g(yl)denne (cp. 1021, 2767; Antiq. § 8). An emblem of royalty; cp. Baeda, *H.E.* ii, c. 16. The banner was flying on a long pole (see 1022?), which was fastened to the mast (Stjer. 130). On the meaning of *gylden*, see Gloss.: *eal(l)gylden*.

48. hēah is apparently left uninflected, perhaps on account of its semi-adverbial function. Or is there a shifting from the masc. to the neut. gender (see Gloss.: *segn*)? Cp. 2767 f. For the absence of inflexional endings of adjectives and participles qualifying a preceding noun (or pronoun), see 46ᵇ, 372ᵇ, 1126ᵃ, 2704ᵃ; H. Bauch, *Die Kongruenz in der ags. Poesie,* Kiel Diss., 1912, *passim;* Kock L 5.44.4.19 f. (numerous examples from OE. poetry); cf. also Lang. § 25.6. — **lēton holm beran.** The object *hine* is understood (so in 49ᵃ). — See 3132ᵇ: *lēton wēg niman.*

49 f. The predicate is: **wæs geōmor ..., murnende.** Cf. Lang. § 25.4.

51. Malone, *A.* liii 335 f. defends **selerǣdenne** (MS.), from **-rǣden*, earlier *-rǣdend;* he cites similar forms in 106, 1026 (?), 1142. The poet no doubt used the proper form *-rǣdende* (as in 1346).

53–85. The Danish line of kings. The building of Heorot.

53. Bēowulf Scyldinga. See, e.g., 1069, 676, 620, 2603. Grimm, *Deutsche Grammatik* iv 303 ff. (261).

55 f. folcum gefrǣge, ' famous among peoples.' The same use of the dative after *foremǣrost,* 309. — **fæder ellor hwearf** (type D4). Note the periphrasis for ' dying ' (Intr. lxiii f.). The pret. *hwearf* carries pluperf.

sense. **aldor of earde;** *of earde* is variation of *ellor*. The insertion of a comma (*aldor, of earde*) has not been deemed advisable in cases of this kind; cp., e.g., 36ª: *mærne be mæste*, 140ª, 213ª, 265ª, 420ª, etc.

57. Healfdene. On the Danish genealogy, see Intr. xxx ff.

58. glæde seems to be acc. plur. (*Angl.* xxix 379); it is usually explained as adv. (cp. 1173).

59. forðgerīmed. A variant of a conventional phrase, *geteled rīme(s)*, see Grein Spr.: *rīm*.

61. Heorogār ond Hrōðgār ond Hālga til. In accordance with an ancient idiom (Hirt, *Indogerm. Gra.* i, § 118), well known from Homer (e.g., Δουλίχιόν τε Σάμη τε καὶ ὑλήεσσα Ζάκυνθος, *Odyss.* ix 24), the last of three coordinate nouns, in particular proper names, is marked by the addition of an epithet or some other qualifying element; thus, ll. 2434, 112, cp. 1189. Similar examples from OE. and other Old Germanic languages are readily found. (Cf. *A.* lvi 425 ff.) Numerous instances in ME. alliterative poems have been collected by J. P. Oakden, *RESt.* ix 50–53. In a broader sense, this type illustrates the general principle of ' emphasis by increase of weight ' (Behaghel, *IF.* xxv 110 ff.).

62 f. hȳrde ic practically serves as poetic formula of transition, cf. Intr. lxvi f., *MPh.* iii 243 f.; see ll. 2163, 2172. — The name of the **daughter** (which need not alliterate with the names of her brothers and father, cp. Frēawaru) apparently began with a vowel. Cf. Intr. xxxiv; *MPh.* iii 447. — A supposed erasure under *heaðo* which was taken as evidence of scribal confusion after the word *cwēn*, and which gave rise to the unfortunate conjecture *hȳrde ic þæt Elan cwēn Hrōðulfes wæs* (see L 5.42 f.), has now been definitely pronounced non-existent in the MS. (Chambers). A Germanic name for a woman, *Elan*, would, indeed, be more than doubtful. The name **Yrse** (cf. Intr. xxxiv and n. 4, Varr.) has been confidently put in the text by Malone: *hȳrde ic þæt Yrse wæs Onelan cwēn* (see his *Hamlet* 101 ff., 230 ff., L 4.78 h). But he thinks Yrse was in reality Healfdene's daughter-in-law. — See also Herrmann's *Saxo* (L 4.35 a) ii 152–55. For the name Yrsa (*Annales Lundenses:* Yrsa, Ursula), see Olrik-Hollander 269 ff. (A Latin loan-word; not an old, inherited word as was urged, *AfNF.* xxxi 155, *Anz.fdA.* xxxvii 68.) — On the gen. sing. in *-as* (*Scilfingas*), see Lang. § 18.5.

64. Heorogār's reign, being irrelevant, is not mentioned here. See 465 ff., 2158 ff.; Intr. xxxi, lvii.

66ᵇ–67ª. magodriht micel represents the variation, as it were, of the preceding clause (*MPh.* iii 247). — Cf. Par. § 10: Tacitus' *Germania*, c. xiii.

67ᵇ. bearn, see Gloss.: *be-irnan*.

69 f. It has been plausibly assumed that the positive **micel** is used here for the comparative, or that the comparative idea is left unexpressed, cf. Gr. Spr.: *þanne, ii;* Bu. Zs. 193; Aant. 1; Koeppel, *ESt.* xxx 376 f.; Horn, *Arch.* cxiv 362 f., *Angl.* xxix 130 f. (blending of two constructions); so Hoops St. 92 f. [Bright (L 5.31.2) threw strong doubts on the idiomatic status of that construction by showing that, apart from *Epistola Alexandri* (*Angl.* iv 154) 405 f., the examples available for support (*Par. Ps.* 117.8 f., etc.) are due to imitation of the original (i.e., the Latin form of a Hebraism of the *Septuagint*). His emendation would remove the syntactical difficulty. Again, the possibility remains that after l. 69 a line containing a compar. has dropped out (so, e.g., Holt.[2,3]). It would be tempting to supply a line containing a superl., 'the most magnificent hall (*sele*),' and thus to account for *þone;* but in that case *þāra þe* would probably have been used.] — **yldo bearn.** See Gloss.: *bearn.* The ending *-o* (cf. Lang. § 18.3; § 24, p. xci) possibly suggests association, by folk etymology, with *yldo* 'age'; see *Angl.* xxxv 467 f. (*yldo bearn* also *Ex.* 28, *Gen.* [B] 464.)

73. būton folcscare ond feorum gumena. See Antiq. § 1; Intr. cvii n. 1.

74. Ðā ic wīde gefrægn ... As to the position of *wīde*, see note on 575.

76ª. frætwan, unless it be considered to depend directly on *gefrægn*, is to be connected with *weorc gebannan*, which was probably felt to be of the same import as *hātan.* — *folcstede frætwan*, ' to make a beautiful hall '; *frætwan* = ' to make in beautiful fashion.' Similarly OHG. *giziaren* Otfrid i 1.54. Cp. OE. *trymman*, ' to establish firmly,' *Gen.* (B) 248, 276.

76ᵇ–77ª. Him on fyrste gelomp,/ǣdre mid yldum. The work was done quickly (*ǣdre*), considering the magnitude of the undertaking; *on fyrste* 'in due time' (cf. B.-T. Suppl.: *first;* not to be rendered, with Schü. Bd. 26 ff., by ' speedily '). The rapid construction of the hall seems to be one of the folk-tale elements of the story, cf. Panzer 257 n. 1. — *mid yldum*, a formula-like expletive, see Intr. lxvi.

78. The hall has been supposed to be named **Heor(o)t** from horns (antlers) fastened to the gables, although the appellation *horn* = ' gable ' (*horn-gēap* 82, *-reced* 704, *hornas*, *Finnsb.* 4, *horn-sǣl*, *-sele* in other poems) seems to be derived merely from ' horn-shaped projections on the gable-ends ' (B.-T., cf. Miller, *Angl.* xii 396 f.). But the name may have been primarily symbolical, the hart signifying royalty (A. Bugge, *ZfdPh.* xli 375 n.). On the Danish royal hall, see Intr. xxxvii. — The name Heorot was explained by Sarrazin from an ancient worship of a ' hart deity ' (*Angl.* xix 372 f.) — a claim that has more recently been reinforced by Schütte, L 4.42 n. 9.88. — A popular, illustrated sketch of present-day Leire by Maurice P. Dunlap may be found in the *American-Scandinavian Review* xi (1923), 147–53.

79. sē þe his wordes geweald wīde hæfde. The relative clause (' he who ... '), containing the subject of the sentence, follows the predicate. So in 90, 138, 143, 809, 825, 1497, 1618, etc.

82–85. Allusion to the destruction of the hall by fire in the course of the **Heaðo-Bard** conflict. See Intr. xxxiv f., lvii and n. 2. (The allusion of 83ᵇ–85ᵇ cannot be separated from that of 82ᵇ–83ª.) Heorot was to be burned (cf. L 5.70) in the progress of the Heaðo-Bard feud. Evidently, the destruction of Hleiðr by fire in consequence of hostile engagements was part of the regular tradition connected with the ancient royal seat, although Scandinavian versions differ as to the occasion when the conflagration occurred. (Cf. *Angl.* l 111 f.) — As regards the references to the conflict between the Danes and Bards, Wessén (L 4.78 k) endeavors to show that they are connected with the defeat of the Erulians (Heruli) by the Danes as mentioned by Jordanes, ch. 3.; cf. Intr. xxxvi. However, the Erulians, it is argued, really correspond to the *Scyldingas* of the poem, whereas the Danes are disguised as Bards. The latter shifting is accounted for by the crushing defeat of (a division of) the Erulians under their king Rodulfus ('Ροδοῦλφος) by the Lombards in Hungary about 500 A.D. (Procopius, *Bell. Goth.* ii 14). Hrólf's (Hrōðulf's) fall (in Scandinavian tradition) is thus considered a significant counterpart of that historic fact. The Danish conquest of the land of the Erulians, we are to assume, resulted in an early amalgamation of the two tribes, a fact testified to by the name — originally a surname — *Healfdene*, denoting the ancestor king in *Beowulf*. Thus it happened that the traditions of the *Scyldingas* came to be regarded as Danish. (For a refutation of this theory, see Cha. Intr.[2] 434 ff.) [That '**Half-Danes**' as a tribal, or dynastic, name, occurring once in *Beowulf* (l. 1069), can be traced in Scandinavian sources also, is argued by Malone, L 4.78 f. (A new rendering of the much discussed passage, *Grottasǫngr* 22 (see Par. § 5, footnote 4) is proposed; regarding the form *Halfdana*, cf. also Kock, *AfNF.* xxxvii 134 f.) The old dynastic name *Healf-Dene*, it is held, was supplanted by the name *Scyldingas* when a mythical ancestor, Scyld, had been introduced.] — 82. **bād.** Similar light personifications: 1882, 397; 320, 688, 33 (*ūtfūs*), 1464 (in contrast with the more vigorous instance: 1521 f.), etc. — 83. **ne wæs hit lenge þā gēn** admits of being explained as a variety of a formula (see 134, 739, 2591, 2845), 'it was by no means (cp. 734) longer' (i.e. long, cf. Lang. § 25.2); see *MPh.* iii 245 f. (The analogical *lenge: Chr.* 1684, *Guðl.* 109, *Jul.* 375; also Varr.: 2423[b].) But as the reference is not to something to happen immediately (as in the other cases), *lenge* is with a little more probability taken as an adj. (cp. *gelenge* 2732), recorded in one other place, *Gnom. Ex.* 121, 'belonging to,' hence perhaps 'at hand'; 'the time was not yet (cp. 2081) come.' (Rie. Zs. 382.)

84. **āþumswēoran**, MS. *aþum swerian*. A copulative (or 'dvandva') compound, like *suhtergefæderan* (see Gloss.), *gisunfader* (*Hel.*), *sunufatarungo* (*Hildebr.*), first recognized by Bugge (Tid. 45 f.). Though the existence of a form *sweri(g)a* showing a suffixal extension like that seen in *suhtriga*, *suhterga* is within the bounds of possibility (so Bugge, *l.c.*), it appears more likely that a scribe blundered, having in mind *āþ* and *swerian*. For the dat. plur. in -*an*, see Lang. § 18.1.

85. **æfter wælnīðe.** See 2065.

86-114. The introduction of Grendel. The thought of this passage, though proceeding by a circuitous route, is not obscure. An evil spirit is angered by the rejoicing in Heorot (86–90ᵃ). One of the songs recited in the hall is mentioned (90ᵇ–98). After looking back for a moment the poet returns to the demon, Grendel, who is now spoken of as dwelling in the moors (100ᵇ–104ᵃ). This leads the author to relate how Grendel came to live there, viz. by being descended from Cain, whom God had exiled for the murder of Abel (104ᵇ–114). (Whereupon Grendel's first attack on Heorot is narrated.)

86. se ellengǣst (or, quite possibly, *ellorgǣst*, see Gloss.); the name is stated in 102. Cf. Intr. lxv. — Kock[2] 102 would connect *earfoðlīce* (acc. sing. fem.) with *þrāge*, 87 (cp. 283 f.). See Gloss.: *þrāg;* cp. 2302 f.

88 ff. Grendel, in accordance with the nature of such demons (Panzer 264; Grimm D. M. 380 [459]), is angered by the noisy merriment in the hall. This motive is given a peculiar Christian turn. (*Angl.* xxxv 257.)

90–98. The Song of Creation bears no special resemblance to Cædmon's famous Hymn, but follows pretty closely upon the lines suggested by the biblical account. Cp. 94 f. and Gen. i 16 f., 97ᵇ–98 and Gen. i 21, 24, 26, 28. For some slight similarities to *Ex.* 24 ff., see *MLN.* xxxiii 221. The theme is often touched upon in Ags. poetry. See *Angl.* xxxv 113 ff. [Also Vergil has a court minstrel recite the creation of the world, *Æn.* i 742 ff.] — The rare note of joy in the beauty of nature contrasts impressively with the melancholy inspired by the dreary, somber abode of Grendel. (God's bright sun: 570, cp. 606, 1571 f., 1801 ff., 1965, 2072.)

90ᵃ. swutol sang scopes. Type D2. **90ᵇ. Sǣgde,** used absolutely like *sang* 496, *rehte* 2106. Cf. *MPh.* iii 245.

93. swā wǣter bebūgeð, lit. ' as (far as) the water surrounds (it) '; cp. 1223 f., *Andr.* 333 f., etc.; also *Beow.* 2608. (*ESt.* xxxix 429.)

94. sigehrēþig. See 2875, 3055; *Angl.* xxxv 115, 120 f. [Cp. *Ex* 27.] — 94ᵃ: Type Dx, see T.C. § 24.

95. lēoman, in apposition to *sunnan ond mōnan,* recalls Gen. i 16: ' duo luminaria '; **tō lēohte landbūendum,** Gen. i 17: ' ut lucerent super terram.'

97ᵇ. līf ēac gesceōp. Type E1. — **98. cynna gehwylcum þāra ðe cwice hwyrfaþ.** Cp. Gen. i 21: ' creavitque ... omnem animam viventem atque motabilem,' i 26, 28.

99. drēamum lifdon. Cp. 2144, *Wīds.* 11, *Chr.* 621, etc.

100ᵇ. oð ðæt ān ongan ... So 2210ᵇ; cp. 2280ᵇ, 2399ᵇ. *ān,* ' one,' ' a certain,' is used to introduce a person, object, or situation even if mentioned before (thus, also in 2280, 2410); it looks as if the poet, after a digression, were starting afresh. A really demonstrative function of *ān* in these cases cannot be admitted. [Discussion by He.-Schü. (Gloss.), Scherer L 5.5.472; Lichtenheld, *ZfdA.* xvi 381 ff.; Heinzel, *Anz.fdA.* x 221; Braune, *Beitr.* xi 518 ff., xii 393 ff., xiii 586 f.; Bugge, *ib.* xii 371; Luick, *Angl.* xxix 339 ff., 527 f.; Grienb., *Beitr.* xxxvi 79 f., Siev., *ib.* 400; von Kraus, *ZfdA.* lxvii 1 ff.]

101. fēond on helle. See Gloss.: *on.*

103 f. Grendel's dwelling in the fen-districts reflects popular belief, cp. *Gnom. Cott.* 42 f.: *þyrs sceal on fenne gewunian,/āna innan lande*. There existed also, in popular imagination, a connection between hell and morasses. See Bugge L 4.84, p. lxxiv; *Angl.* xxxvi 185 ff.; *ib.* l 113; L 4.66 b 9.; ll. 845 ff., 1357 ff.

106 ff. Grendel's descent from Cain. The conception of the descent of monsters (evil spirits) and giants from Cain (cp. also 1261 ff.), and of the destruction of the giants by the deluge (so also 1688 ff.) is based ultimately on the biblical narrative, a causal relation being established between Gen. iv, vi 2, 4 (*gigantes*) and vi 5–7, vii. The direct source has not been discovered in this case, though Hebrew tradition (like that contained in the apocalyptic *Book of Enoch*) and Christian interpretation of Scripture have been adduced. See Emerson L 4.149. 865 ff., 878 ff.; *Angl.* xxxv 259 ff.; also notes on 1555 f., 1688 ff. Crawford, *MLR.* xxiii 207 refers to Job xxvi 5: 'gigantes gemunt sub aquis, et qui habitant cum eis' (cp. Apoc. xiii 1); *MLR.* xxiv 63: according to Irish belief, Cham (see 107 Varr.) inherited the curse of Cain and became the progenitor of monsters. — On Grendel, see Intr. l.

106–8. siþðan him Scyppend forscrifen hæfde/in Cāines cynne. This looks strongly theological. Originally, of course, it was Cain who was proscribed and exiled, but, being one of Cain's offspring, Grendel is included in the condemnation. Note the close correspondence of 104 ff. and 1260 ff. — **108. þæs þe hē Ābel slōg** is explanatory (or variation) of *þone cwealm;* cp. 2794 ff., 1627 f. (See *Beibl.* xl 25 f.) Cain's fratricide is mentioned again in 1261 ff. (cp. 2741 f., 587 f., 1167 f.). [Cf. Siev. ix 136 f.; Bu. 80; *MPh.* iii 255, 448. Nearly all edd. begin a fresh sentence with 107[a].]

109[a]. ne gefeah hē . . . , 'he [Cain] had no joy . . .' (cp. 827, 1569, also 2277); **109[b]. hē,** i.e. God.

111 f. The general term **untȳdras** is specified by the following nouns.

114[b]. hē him ðæs lēan forgeald. Allusion to the deluge. See 1689 ff.

115–188. Grendel's reign of terror.

115. nēosian. The 'visit' implies 'search' (cp. 118: *Fand*); this accounts for *hū*.

120. Wiht unhǣlo (type D1), 'creature of evil' (*Angl.* xxxv 252), has been taken by several scholars as 'anything of evil' and made the close of the preceding clause (a second variation). However, 121[a] would be unusually heavy as the opening of a sentence.

121[b]. gearo sōna wæs. Type D4.

122 f. on ræste genam/þrītig þegna. *On* (see Gloss.; Lang. § 25.5) may be translated by 'from,' but the underlying syntactical conception is not that of motion, *on ræste* belonging in fact with the object of the verb (cp. 747, 1298, 1302); see note on 575. — Of the disposal of the thirty men we are told in 1580 ff.

123[b]. þanon eft gewāt. Probably type E1.

126. Ðā . . . . , 128 þā . . . . A characteristic case of parataxis (cf.

Intr. lxvii). For a genuine correlative use of 'demonstrative' and 'relative' particles, see Gloss.: *þonne, swā, ǣr*, also *þā, þǣr*.

128. *þā wæs æfter wiste wōp up ahafen*; i.e., there was weeping where there was formerly feasting. Cp. 1007 f., 1774 f., 1078 ff., 119 f. — 128ᵇ. Type D4.

131. *þegnsorge* belongs both with *þolode* and *drēah*. Or is *þolode* to be taken intransitively?

133. *wergan gāstes*. Sievers, guided by linguistic and metrical considerations, strongly contended for *wĕrgan*, gen. sing. of *wĕrig* 'weary,' then 'wretched,' 'evil' (see *IF*. xxvi 225–35). Yet it seems unnatural to separate *wergan* in this well-known combination from *wearg* (see Gloss.: *heorowearh, werhðo*), (*ā*)*wergan*, (*ā*)*wyrgan*, '(ac)curse' (*se āwyrg(e)da gāst*, etc.). Thus, an adj. *wer(i)g* (from **wargi*), or (better) *werge* (from **wargja*) has been postulated (Hart, *MLN*. xxii 220 ff.; Trautmann, *Bonn. B.* xxiii 155 f.) in substantial agreement with the older explanation (Ke., Tho., Gr. Spr., et al.: *wērig*). The line of division between the two sets is often difficult to determine.

134ᵇ. *Næs hit lengra fyrst*. Formula of transition, cf. note on 83.

135 f. We are told here that Grendel made an attack on two successive nights (as the troll does on two successive Yule-eves, before the final defeat, in the *Grettissaga* [Intr. xiv] and the *Hrólfssaga* [Par. § 9], cp. analogous folk-tales, Panzer 96 ff., 266). But in fact, he wrought destruction 'much oftener' (1579), see 147 ff., 473 ff., 646 ff. — On *māre* 136, 'additional,' see *MPh*. iii 450.

137. *wæs tō fæst on þām*. An allusion to the fetters of sin. See 2009; *El*. 908: *on firenum fæstne;* etc.; *Angl*. xxxv 135 f.

140. *æfter* is to be construed with [*sōhte*], 139.

141. *gesægd*, i.e. made known (by deeds), manifested; cp. *cȳðan, ȳwan*.

142. The compound *healðegn* is coined for the occasion, like *renweard* 770, *cwealmcuma* 792, *mūðbona* 2079, etc.

145. *īdel*, i.e. at night. See 411 ff.

147. *twelf wintra tīd*. Other conventional uses of typical figures: *50* years, ll. 1498, 1769, 2209; *300*, l. 2278; *1000*, l. 3050; — *5* days, l. 545, *Finnsb*. 41; 7, l. 517; — *15* comrades, l. 207; *12*, ll. 2401, 3170; *8*(7), l. 3122 f.; *1000* warriors, l. 1829; *15+15* victims, l. 1582 f. (123); strength of *30* men, l. 379, cp. 2361; — *12* gifts, l. 1867; ll. 1027, 1035 (*4+8*); — *7000* hides of land (?), l. 2195; *100,000* (*sceattas*): l. 2994 (n.). *Three* sons: Heorogār, Hrōðgār, Hālga; Herebeald, Hæðcyn, Hygelāc. (Cf. Müllenhoff L 9.14. 1.115: trilogy of names in genealogies.) *Two* sons: Hrēðrīc, Hrōðmund; Ōhthere, Onela; Ēanmund, Ēadgils; Wulf, Eofor. The use of *5* in l. 420 seems rather accidental. On the use of *9* in l. 575, see Müllenhoff, *op. cit.*, 642 f; Gering's commentary (L 10.1) i 148.

151 ff. *þætte Grendel wan* etc. The profusion of parallel expressions is apt to suggest an actual paraphrase of 'plaints' concerning the distress of the Danes (which certainly became widely known, 1991).

154 ff. feorhbealo feorran is best taken as variation of the term **sibbe** (Bu. 82, *MPh*. iii 238). By construing *sibbe* as dat. (instr.) and removing the comma after *Deniga* the meaning would be slightly modified; cf. Siev. xxix 316 f. — 157 f. **nē þǣr nǣnig wítenà** (Heusler) etc. An indirect form of statement expressing the same idea as the preceding phrase, ... **fēa þingian**. From the legal point of view Grendel, being guilty of murder, was under obligation to compound for it by payment; see Antiq. § 5: Feud; Intr. lxii n. 3.

159. ēhtende wæs. The periphrastic form (so 3028: *secggende wæs*, 1105: *myndgiend wǣre*) in this instance seems to signify continuation. Cf. C. Pessels, *The Present and Past Periphrastic Tenses in Ags.*, Johns Hopkins Diss. (1896), pp. 49 f., 81 f. [possibility of Lat. influence?]; Sweet, *New English Grammar* ii §§ 2203 ff.; Curme, *Publ.MLAss.* xxviii 181; C. R. Goedsche, *JEGPh*. xxxi 473 [Lat. influence]. — It is of interest to note that the devil was often represented as 'persecuting' men, cf. *Angl.* xxxv 257 f.

160. deorc dēaþscua — used as epithet of Satan in *Chr.* (i) 257 (MS.: *deor dædscua;* see Cook's note) — is generally understood as 'deadly sprite.' But it was perhaps meant principally as a symbol of 'darkness,' cf. *Angl.* xxxv 255.

161. seomade (*ond syrede*), perhaps 'lay in wait' (and ambushed), or 'lingered' (and ...), i.e. kept on ambushing. *syrwan* calls to mind Lat. 'insidiari,' which is frequently applied to the devil; *Angl.* xxxv 257 f.

163. hwyder helrūnan (type C1) **hwyrftum scrīþað**. In this context *helrūnan* implies 'such demons.' The nom. sing. of this form has been posited as *helrūne*, which is recorded in Glosses (denoting 'witch,' 'sorceress'), cp. (Lat.) Go. *haljarunae* (emend.), = 'magae mulieres,' Jordanes, c. 24; OHG. *hellirūna* 'necromancia.' Cf. Grimm D. M. 1025 (1225); Bu.Zs. 194 f.; Kauffmann, *Beitr.* xviii 156; Förster, *Arch.* cviii 23 f. The use of this noun denoting primarily female evil beings is paralleled by Go. *unhulþō* serving as translation of δαιμόνιον, cf. Grimm D. M. 827 (990). — *hwyrftum* merely amplifies *scrīþað*, 'go' (moving).

164 f. fela ... oft. A similar redundant combination is that of *monig* and *oft*, 4 f., 171, 857, 907 f.

168 f. nō hē þone gifstōl etc. The difficulties experienced in the interpretation of this passage arise chiefly from (1) the ambiguity of *gifstōl*, which could denote either God's or Hrōðgār's throne, (2) the possibility of rendering *grētan* either by 'approach' or 'attack,' (3) the uncertainty as to the real force of *myne*. (The possibility of identifying *hē* with the king is too remote to be seriously considered.) If **gifstōl** is understood as Hrōðgār's throne, the lines might be thought to mean that Grendel was not allowed, because he was 'prevented by the Lord' (cp. 706, *Gen. B* 359), to approach the royal throne; i.e., though making his home in the hall at night, he was unlike a dutiful retainer, who receives gifts from his lord. See espec. Kock 225 f. & L 5.44.4.7 f. This explanation is sufficiently strange, but, perhaps, less far-fetched than the one resting on the interpretation of this noun as the throne of God; *māþðum* could thus be the ordinary 'treasured object,' 'precious thing,' used as a somewhat loose variation of *gifstōl* (cp. *Gnom. Ex.* 69). *witan* is to be understood in the well-established sense of 'be conscious of,' 'feel,' 'show,' cp. *Wand.* 27: [*mīn*] *mine wisse* (*JEGPh.* viii 254 f.). **mȳne** 'gratitude' (Kock)? *nē his myne wisse* 'nor did he have joy of it' (Sievers, Crawford)? (*myne* = 'desire' seems rather out of place.) — Still, the strange *for Metode* sets one speculating whether there may not be hidden, after all, behind the plain meaning 'royal throne' a veiled allusion to the throne of God from which the evildoer was barred. There remains the possibility that in either case 'God' was felt to be the subject of **myne wisse:** 'nor did he take (kind) thought of him'; the import of the clause would be similar to *Godes yrre bær* 711. For the change of subject, cp. 109. — When all is said, the passage appears singularly awkward. One might suspect an inept interpolation here; see Intr. cvii, cxii n. 3. [Cf. also Holtzm. 489 f.; Aant. 5; Pogatscher, *Beitr.* xix 544 f.; Tr.[1] 135, *Bonn. B.* xvii 160 f.; Siev. xxix 319; Emerson L 4.149.863, 870; Tinker, *MLN.* xxiii 239; Hart, *MLN.* xxvii 198; *Angl.* xxxv 254; *ib.* l 113 f.; Crawford, *MLR.* xxiii 336; Hoops 38 f.]

171[b]. **Monig oft gesæt.** Type E1.

175-88. **Hwīlum hīe gehēton æt hærgtrafum** etc. A passage remarkable both for the reference to the heathen practice of the Danes and the author's pointed Christian comment. Since Hrōðgār is throughout depicted as a good Christian, the Danes' supplication to a heathen deity (termed **gāstbona,** 'devil,' cf. *Angl.* xxxv 137) might conceivably indicate that in time of distress they returned to their former ways — as was done repeatedly in England, see Baeda, *H.E.* iii, c. 30; iv, c. 27, cp. ii, c. 15. (Routh L 4.138.54 n.; *Angl.* xxxv 134 f., xxxvi 184.) But it is at least equally possible that the author, having in mind the conditions existing among the Danes of the sixth century (on the pagan sanctuary at Hleiðr, see Intr. xxxvii), at this point, failed to live up to his own modernized representation of them. Besides, he seems to have been influenced by reminiscences of the idol worship of the Babylonians described in *Daniel*, see Intr. cx f. Cf. also Hoops 39. — On sacrifices offered for relief from affliction, see *P. Grdr.*[2] iii 389. The killing of oxen by the Anglo-Saxons 'in sacrificio daemonum' is mentioned in Baeda's *H.E.* i, c. 30. — [Imelmann L 4.129 a. 464 ff.: a Vergilian (*Æn.* viii 102 ff.) reminiscence. (?) Cf. *Angl.* l 114. — *gāstbona* = ' slayer of demons (trolls),' cp. ON. Þórr(Weber L 5.79)?; = 'destroyer of life' (murderer, cp. *feorhbana*, etc.)(Hoops St. 24 ff.)?]

178. **Swylc wæs þēaw hyra.** A conventional phrase of explanation, cp. 1246; Grein Spr.: *þēaw;* Sievers (*Heliand*), L 7.34.446.

180[b], 81[b]. **Metod hīe ne cūþon** etc. A similar inverted arrangement of words in two successive clauses (chiasmus) occurs in 301^b–2, 817^b–18^a, 1160^b–61^a, 1615^b–16^a, 2680^b–81, 3047 f.

183^b. Wā biðþǣm ðe sceal. Type E. So 186^b.

184–86. þurh sliðne nið, hardly ' through fierce hostility '; rather ' in dire distressful wise ' (Cl. Hall), see *Arch.* cxv 178. — **sāwle bescūfan** (cp. Lat. ' trudere ')/**in fȳres fæþm;** cf. *Angl.* xxxv 265 f. — Both **wihte gewendan** and **frōfre** depend on **wēnan** (*M Ph.* iii 238: variation).

189–498. Bēowulf's voyage. His reception in Denmark. (A translation of ll. 189–257 by Longfellow may be found in his *Poets and Poetry of Europe* [and among his *Poems*].)

189 f. ðā mǣlceare ... sēað; similarly 1922 f. The unique phrase, lit. ' he caused the care to well up,' i.e. ' he was agitated by cares,' shows an individualized application of the favorite metaphor of the surgings of care (*Arch.* cxxvi 351, *MLN.* xxxiv 131 f.). In its accentuation of personal action it may be compared to *sāwle bescūfan* etc., 184 f. [The general sense of the expression is not obscure, but the grammatical construction has been debated. For a final comment on the explanation offered (which had been called in question by Kock, *Angl.* xlii 104, xliv 100, *AfNF.* xxxix 187), see *Angl.* l 115 f. (The Greek κήδεα πέσσειν may be noted.) (Kock, like Heyne (1863), would take *-ceare* as instrumental and *sēoðan* as an intransitive verb (not recorded elsewhere).)]

194 f. þæt .... Grendles dǣda; see Intr. lxv. — **fram hām gefrægn**, practically ' heard at home ' (cp. 410), see Lang. § 25.5; Sievers, *Beitr.* xi 361 f., xii 188 ff. The addition of the phrase *fram hām* bespeaks the shifting of the scene from Denmark to Geatland. — **Higelāces þegn.** His name is not mentioned before l. 343.

197. on þǣm dæge þysses līfes. See Gloss.: *dæg, sē* (note); *Angl.* xxxv 461.

198 ff. Why does Bēowulf resolve to visit Hygelāc? The terse answer: *þā him wæs manna þearf* characterizes the hero, whose unselfishly helpful spirit manifests itself even on somewhat unexpected occasions, cp. 567–69, 1427–35.

200. swanrād. Cp. *hronrād* 10, *ganotes bæð* 1861. According to the *Encyclopædia Britannica*[11], xxvi 179 f., the (mute or tame) swan (cygnus olor) " is known to breed as a wild bird not farther from the British shores than the extreme south of Sweden." The whooper, whistling or wild swan (cygnus musicus) " was doubtless always a winter-visitant to Britain, ... it is a native of Iceland, eastern Lapland, and northern Russia, whence it wanders southward in autumn." Cf. Hoops 44, L 6.27.2. — See the 8th *Riddle*.

202 f. Ðone sīðfæt him snotere ceorlas/lȳthwōn lōgon. See 415 ff.; Antiq. § 1. The meaning of *lȳthwōn lōgon* is, of course, ' they urged him on '[2] (litotes); but, as shown by *þēah*, the clause is to be rendered literally. Cp. 2618 f.

204. hǣl scēawedon. Cp. Tacitus, *Germania*, c. x: ' auspicia ...

observant ' (Par. § 10). See Grimm D. M. 944 ff. (1128 ff.), 77 ff. (94 ff.), iii 324 ff. (1639 ff.); Müllenhoff L 9.14.1.222 ff.; Gummere G. O. 467; Liebermann L 9.10.2.574. That the omens which are watched by the men are favorable is understood. Cf. *ESt.* xliv 123. [Tr.[1] 137, & Ed.; Siev. xxix 322; Sed., *MLR.* v 286, & Ed.]

205 f. Gēata lēoda belongs with **cempan.** The peculiar enclosing of the superl. in the relat. clause is found in OE. (see 2869 f., 3161 f.) as well as in ON. and Lat.; cf. Wagner L 6.18.98.

208 ff. There is no reason for assuming an unskilful blending of two versions, or suspecting any other kind of disorder (ten Brink 32; Tr.[1] 137 f.); **sundwudu sōhte** means ' went to the ship ' (not ' on board '); the **lagucræftig mon,** i.e. Bēowulf, who like Sigfrit, *Nibel.* 367, is an experienced seaman, ' led the way to the shore.' The characteristic paratactic expression **Fyrst forð gewāt** would be, in modern usage, ' in course of time '; **flota wæs on ȳðum** states the ' result of an action ' (Intr. lvii, lxvi); i.e., the ship, which had been ashore, was now launched (cf. Falk L 9.48.28; Cleasby-Vigfússon, *Icel.-Eng. Dict.*: *hlunnr*). An interesting parallel to this scene: *Odyssey* iv 778 ff.

216. wudu bundenne. (Gummere: " the well-braced craft.") Cp. [*s*]*æl timbred* 307, (*næ*)*gled sinc* 2023; 2764, 406 (and note on 455), 322, 551 f., 1548, 2755; 1679, 2717, 2774; *nægledcnear, Brun.* 53; perhaps *bundenstefna* (see Gloss.), — epithets exhibiting the ancient pride in skill of workmanship.

217. winde gefȳsed. It is important to observe that a sailboat is used; see 1905 f. (one sail). Cf. Antiq. § 11; Schnepper L 9.47.25 ff.; Falk L 9.48.56. Its size may be judged from 1896 ff.

218. flota fāmīheals fugle gelīcost. The top part of the prow of smaller vessels in ancient Scandinavian times frequently had the shape of a goose's neck. See Falk, p. 38; Gloss.: *wunden-hals, -stefna, hringedstefna.*

219. ymb āntīd, ' after the lapse of a normal space of time '; **ōþres dōgores,** ' on the following day.' Cf. Siev. xxix 326 f., Gloss.: *āntīd.* It seems possible, however, to construe *ōþres dōgores* as depending on *āntīd;* the voyage takes one day and a reasonable space of time (as much as is to be expected) of another day. [Leonard, L 3.16a, returning to Grein's suggestion ' *āntīd* = hora prima,' translates " after the risen sun Of the next day "; cf. 569 ff.] Whether the distance from Bēowulf's home to the coast near Hleiðr (see Intr. xxxvii, xlviii) could really have been covered in so short a time, is to be doubted. (In the brief account of the return voyage, 1903 ff., no mention is made of the passing of a day.) The measuring of distance by the days required for the voyage (ON. *dǿgr,* i.e. 12 hours) was customary among the Scandinavians (see Falk, p. 17; Ōhthere's voyage in Ælfred's *Orosius* [ed. Sweet] 17.9 ff. and *passim*). — The different **days** are clearly marked off in the first main part: 3rd day, l. 837; 4th day, l. 1311 (*nōn* 1600); 5th day, l. 1802; (arrival on the 6th day? l. 1912, *sigel sūðan fūs* 1966).

223ᵇ-24ᵃ. **þā wæs sund liden,/eoletes æt ende.** One of the frequent summing-up remarks, Intr. lxi. *eoletes*, possibly representing an otherwise unrecorded OE. word, is still unexplained. We expect the gen. sing. of a noun meaning ' voyage,' ' sea,' or (perhaps) ' land.' Several conjectures are mentioned under Varr. But the list of possible guesses is not yet exhausted. Holthausen's (ed.³⁻⁵) *ēoledes*, i.e. *ēa-lādes*, fits the context well enough, but the form is questionable (*lād* is fem., see 228; *gelād* is neut., see 1410). [Cf. also Bu. Tid. 46 f.; Brenner, *ESt.* iv 139; Tr.¹ 139; Sed., *MLR.* v 286; xviii 471 f.; L 5.66, 67, 77.2, 81, 26.24; *A.* l 117 f.]

229. weard Scildinga. A man of importance (see 293). It is not unlikely that the office of coast-guard was established in early times in the Scandinavian countries as well as in Britain.

230. scolde. See Gloss.: *sculan*.

232. hine fyrwyt bræc; so 1985, 2784. One would like to know the origin of this quaint expression. For analogous phrases, see *A.* l 118; Notat. Norr. §§ 254, 331.

235. þrymmum. The plur. of abstract nouns is often used with sing. meaning, in many instances semi-adverbially. So, e.g., *ārum*, *duguðum*, *ēstum*, *fyrenum*, *geþyldum*, *listum*, *lustum*, *searwum*, *orþancum*, *weorcum*, *wundrum*; *on sǣlum*, *tō gemyndum*; (gp.:) *oferhygda*, *nīða*. See Lang. § 25.1.

237 ff. Hwæt syndon gē etc. On the typical motive of such ' question and answer,' see Ehrismann, *Beitr.* xxxii 275 f.; Intr. lvi. (*Odyssey* iii 71 ff., xv 263 ff., *Iliad* vi 123 ff.) — For the meaning of *hwæt*, see Gloss.

243. sceðþan. See Gloss.: *Epinal Gloss.* 736: *wīcing-sceaða*, ' pirate.'

244-47. Nō hēr cūðlīcor cuman ongunnon... Cp. *Hel.* 558 f.: *nio hēr ēr sulīka kumana ni wurðun/ēri fon ōðrun thiodun.* — An alternative interpretation takes *cuman* as a noun and assigns to *onginnan* the (recorded) meaning of ' behave,' ' act '; ' visitors never behaved less as strangers.' (Bu. Tid. 290; *Angl.* xxviii 439; cf. B.-T. Suppl.: *angin*.) However, the chief emphasis seems to be placed on their entering the country without permission. (Cp. *Vǫlsungasaga*, ch. 26; *Hrólfssaga* 36.23 ff.) — **246.** Probably **gearwe** is an error for *gearo* (predicative adj.); ' you were not sure that permission would be readily granted.' — **247. māga gemēdu.** (Cp. *māga rīce* 1853.) *māgas* refers to those in authority at the court, see Antiq. § 2. Kock⁵ 75 ff. renders *māgas* by ' compatriots.'

249. nis þæt seldguma. Bugge's explanation (Tid. 290 f.) of *seldguma* as ' hall-man,' ' retainer '? (cp. ON. *húskarl*) is the most convincing one; ' that is not a [mere] retainer [but a chief himself].' Two of the other meanings attributed to it, viz. ' stay-at-home '? (Grein), ' a man who possesses only a small homestead ' (Heyne², et al., similarly Förster [*Beibl.* xiii 168 n. 2], who thought of equating it with *cotsetla* ' cottager '), are rendered improbable by the fact that OE. *seld* (*sæld*) denotes a (royal) hall, palace. Bright's emendation *is þæt* [or: *þæt is* (?)] *seldguma*

NOTES

(cp. *seldan*, 'seldom,' see Varr.), 'that is a rare, or superior, man,' makes admirable sense, but the formation proposed is open to doubt, since the other *seld-* compounds cited in support (*seldcūð, -sīene, -cyme, -hwanne*) are of a different order, showing a more or less adverbial function of the first element.

252 f. ǣr, 'rather than,' see Gloss. Only in case they should attempt to proceed without an explanation are they liable to be taken for spies. lēassceāweras, type D2.

254 f. feor-būend, mere-līðende. On the inflexion and stylistic function of nouns of agency in *-end*, see K. Kärre, *Nomina agentis in Old English*. Part I, Upsala Diss., 1915. 243 pp.

256 f. ofost is sēlest etc. Cp. 3007 f., *Ex.* 293 f. (*MLN.* xxxiii 223.)

259. wordhord onlēac; so *Wids.* 1, *Andr.* 316, 601, *Met. Bt.* 6.1. Cp. ll. 489, 501, (2791 f.); *Andr.* 470: *wordlocan onspēonn*, 671; *Jul.* 79: *ferðlocan onspēon; Wand.* 13: *þæt hē his ferðlocan fæste binde.*

260. gumcynnes, probably gen. of specification, 'as to race'; cp. *Hel.* 557 f., 2986 f. (A variant rendering: 'people of the Geatish nation.')

262. 265 f. Wæs mīn fæder etc. Similarly Hadubrand says of his father: *chūd was her* [*allēm*, Holt.] *chōnnēm mannum, Hildebr.* 28.

272ᵃ. þæs ic wēne, 'as I think' (cp. colloq. 'I guess'). See 383, 3000. — **272ᵇ-73. gif,** 'if (in case)' it is . . . A peculiarly guarded, polite remark.

274ᵇ. sceaðona ic nāt hwylc. Type A1. See 2233ᵇ.

278ᵃ. (þurh) rūmne sefan, like (*þurh*) *sīdne sefan* 1726ᵃ, 'wisdom'; or 'magnanimity.'

280 f. Though **edwendan** (MS.) might be considered a verb (*edwendende* = 'rediens' occurs *Regius Psalter* 77.39), it seems more likely that the noun **edwenden** was intended, see 1774, 2188 (predic. *cwōm*). The genitive phrase **bealuwa bisigu** belongs both with *edwenden* and bōt (see 909, 933 f.).

283ᵃ. oððe ('else') **ā syþðan.** Type C1.

284. Note the alliteration of **þǣr.**

286. ðǣr ('where') **on wicge sæt.** Cp. *Mald.* 28: *þǣr hē on ōfre stōd; El.* 70, *Hel.* 716. (*Par. Lost* vi 671, viii 41, etc.) See 356, *þǣr* 'to where . . . ,' etc.

287ᵇ-89. Ǣghwæþres sceal etc. The purport of this general remark applied to the particular situation is: 'it was my duty to scrutinize your words and your conduct.' The coast-guard apologizes, as it were, for his previous official attitude. **sē þe wēl þenceð,** 'who has a clear mind'; cp. 2601: (*þām*) *ðe wēl þenceð*, 'who is right-minded.' Schücking (following a suggestion of Krauel's) and Holthausen[3-5] place these lines in parenthesis, making the speech begin at 290. However, although the insertion of some descriptive and explanatory matter between the announcement and the beginning of a speech is quite customary (Intr. lv), the intercalated statement never takes the form of an abstract maxim, but relates directly to the person or event in question. On the other hand, a maxim is placed at the beginning of a speech, 3077 f.

297. lēofne mannan; 299 f. gōdfremmendra swylcum gifeþe bið etc. Probably the whole band is referred to ('to whomsoever of the brave ones it will be granted'), the sing. of the noun and pronoun being used in a collective sense. (Cf. Rie. Zs. 385; *MPh*. iii 250.) The def. article: *þone* (*hilderǣs*) perhaps signifies 'such (a battle).' It is very unlikely that Bēowulf alone should have been meant (*swylcum*='to such a one').

302 f. On the *anchor*, see Falk, L 9.48.23; Vogel, *R.-L.* i 105–7. See note on 1918. — As to the MS. spelling *sole*, cp. Varr. 2210ᵇ (2221ᵃ, 2224ᵇ); T.C. § 16.

303ᵇ–6ᵃ. A much discussed passage, see Varr.; Bryan L 5.59; Malone L 5.71.2, 6; Imelmann L 5.76; Furuhjelm L 5.77; Hoops St. 27 ff. No doubt, *-beran* is a blunder for **(hlēor-)bergan** (which, however, should not be referred to a weak fem. *hlēorberge*); and *grummon*, most likely, is in need of emendation. Bugge's reading (which was formerly adopted): **eoforlīc scionon . . . , ferhwearde hēold**/*gūþmōdgum men* involves not only a transition from the plur. to the sing., which, although somewhat harsh, is not without parallel (*MPh*. iii 250, 451), but a decided alteration of the text. Bright's suggestion, improved upon by Sedgefield: **ferh** *wearde hēold*/*gūþmōd grimmon*, the 'warlike boar kept guard over the fierce ones' offers a simpler solution. (Cf. also Kock, *Angl*. xlvi 77 ff.) It is true, doubts concerning the *fe(a)rh*, 'porcellus,' are not without foundation, although there is no decisive proof that *fearh* was a hopelessly plebeian word, absolutely barred from poetical usage. (The regular terms applied to the boar-helmets are *swīn* and *eofor;* the common noun *swīn* figures in OE. poetry both in the heroic and the every-day domestic sense.) On the other hand, we do not like to sacrifice the eminently satisfactory compound **ferhweard,** and — putting up with the change of number — we may translate: 'the warlike one kept life-watch over the fierce ones.' Similar is the rendering of Imelmann, who refers, however, *gūþmōd* to the coast-guard. (Did the doughty warriors really need protection on their way?) [Malone would derive *grummon* from an unrecorded adj. *grum* 'fierce,' 'cruel'; it has also been taken as pret. plur. of *grimman* 'rage,' 'hasten' (?), cf. Bryan; B.-T. Suppl.; Holt. ii.⁵] — On helmets, see Antiq. § 8; Figure 2 showing helmets surmounted by a boar; Par. § 5, ch. 41 (*Hildisvín*). One such helmet has been found in England, viz. at Benty Grange, Derbyshire. As the boar was sacred to (ON.) Freyr (OE. Frēa, cf. Intr. xxiv, xxxvii), this decoration of helmets no doubt had originally a religious significance. Cf. Grimm D. M. 176 ff. (213 ff.); Gummere G. O. 433 f.; Par. § 10, c. xlv.

308. goldfāh. The lavish use of gold, even on the roof of the hall (see 927, 311; cp. 777, 994), recalls analogous folk-tales, see Panzer 96 ff., 257. Scandinavian imagination delighted in such pictures (e.g., *Vǫluspá* 37, 64; *Grímnismál* 8, 12, 15; Prose Edda, *Gylfaginning* 2).

NOTES

The immense gold hoards of Germanic chiefs of the migration period (see note on Eormenrīc, 1197 ff.), the precious ornaments found in the Scandinavian countries, and the splendor of Anglo-Saxon court life indicate the historical background of this poetic fancy. Cf. Montelius 164 ff.; Chadwick Or. 185 ff.; *R.-L.* ii 264 ff.; W. H. Stevenson's ed. of Asser's *De Rebus Gestis Ælfredi*, pp. 329 f.; Ang. F. lxi, p. 5, n. 2. See Gloss.: *gold*, and cpds. (Silver is never mentioned in *Beowulf*.)

311. līxte se lēoma ofer landa fela. Cp. *Wīds.* 99.

313. him tō, i.e. *tō hofe*, cp. 1974.

314. gūðbeorna sum. This use of *sum* (so 1312) may be compared to that of *ān*, 100.

320. Strǣt wæs stānfāh. So *Andr.* 1236: *strǣte stānfāge*. The street was "paved in the Roman fashion" (Gummere G. O. 98). Or was it, by poetic extravagance, thought to be paved with stones of various colors?

322 f. hringīren scīr/song. See 1521 f., *Finnsb.* 6 f.

325. sǣmēþe. Similarly *sīþes wērig* 579, 1794; *sīðwōrig*, *Hel.* 660, 670, 678, 698, 2238; *Kudrun* 1348; *Nibel.* 682. (Cf. *Arch.* cxxvi 45.)

328. gāras stōdon; i.e., the spears were placed (stacked together). Cf. Intr. lxvi & n. 1.

330. (æscholt) ufan grǣg, lit. ' grey (looked at from) above '; ref. to the iron point. Cf. Lang. § 25.5.

331. wlonc hæleð, named Wulfgār, 348.

333 ff. The normal equipment of warriors; cf. Antiq. § 8.

348. Wendla lēod. See Gloss.: *Wendlas;* Intr. xxx, xliv, xlviii. Two possible reasons for a foreigner's staying at Hrōðgār's court are suggested by ll. 461 ff., 2493 ff.

349 f. The general term **mōdsefa**, ' mind,' ' character,' is followed by the more specific, explanatory words *wīg ond wīsdom*.

350. þæs is preliminary to the exegetical phrase *ymb þīnne sīð*, 353.

356. Hwearf þā hrædlīce þǣr Hrōðgār sæt. Similarly 1163, etc., see Gloss.: *þǣr*. Cp. *Nibel.* 1348: *si īlten harte balde dā der künic saz*, 442, etc. On this idiom (and that of l. 286) see För. Misc. 1 ff.

357. anhār. MS. *un hár. un-* has sometimes been looked upon as a variant of *an-*, or an intensive prefix (Heyne, Bu. Tid. 71, 303, Bu. Zs. 197, Aant. 18; B.-T.; *Angl.* xxix 381), but the evidence is, indeed, insufficient. Sed., *MLR.* xxviii 226 suggests *inhār* (cp. *infrōd*), so his ed.[2], p. 254.

358. for eaxlum might be rendered by ' before the face,' 'in front.' Cf. *MLR.* xxii 70; *Ph. Q.* v 229 f.; *Beibl.* xl 29 f.

361 ff. By no means a verbatim report of the speech. The same is true of the report, 391 ff. Cf. Intr. lxv.

374. tō hām forgeaf, ' gave in marriage.' *A.* l 120.

377. Ðonne, ' further,' ' moreover '; **sægdon þæt sǣlīþende**, see 411, *Hildebr.* 42.

378. Gēata, objective gen.; 'gifts for the Geats' (*MPh.* iii 452). See 1860 ff.

383. West-Denum, simply 'Danes.' See 392, 463, 783; Intr. lxix n. 1; Hoops 62. (In a case like 463, 1996 a clear geographical designation was perhaps intended, see Bryan, Malone, Kl. Misc. 124 f.)

386 f. hāt in gân/sēon sibbegedriht samod ætgædere. *sibbegedriht* probably refers to Bēowulf and his men, as in 729; the object of *sēon* is understood, viz. *mē*, see 396. (*MPh.* iii 253.) In case the company of Danes were meant by *sibbegedriht*, the object of *hāt* would have to be supplied: 'command them to go in.'

390. inne, i.e., being still inside the hall.

397 f. The weapons are to remain outside. So *Nibel.* 1583, 1683 f.

398. wudu wælsceaftas. An interesting type of asyndetic parataxis. So *sigla searogimma* 1157, *windgeard weallas* (?) 1224, *ides āglǣcwīf* 1259, *eafor hēafodsegn* 2152, *eard ēðelriht* 2198, *eard ēðelwyn* 2493. (Siev. ix 137; *MPh.* iii 250.) Similar collocations of adjectives, e.g., *ealdum infrōdum* 1874, *frome fyrdhwate* 1641, 2476; probably *undyrne cūð* 150, 410 (*Angl.* xxviii 440).

404. heoðe (MS.) ('interior'?) is to all appearances spurious; the form *hel-heoðo* which has been quoted from *Sat.* 700 is extremely doubtful.

407. Wæs ... hāl! A common Germanic form of salutation. So *Andr.* 914; *OE. Gosp., Mat.* 28.9, *Luke* 1.28 (cp. *Par. Lost* v 385 ff.), Laȝamon's *Brut* 14309: *Lauerd king, wæs hæil.* Cf. Grimm, *Deutsche Grammatik* iv 356 (298 f.); Stroebe, *Beitr.* xxxvii 190, 197. On *wæs* (=*wes*), see Lang. § 7.1.

408ᵇ-9ᵃ. hæbbe ic mærða fela/ongunnen on geogoþe. This proud self-introduction is in line with the best epic usage: *Æneid* i 378 f.; *Odyssey* ix 19 f.; *Finnsb.* 25.

409ᵇ. Grendles þing, 'the affair of Grendel,' with the subaudition of 'case,' 'dispute' (see 425 f.).

413ᵃ. (stande ...) īdel ond unnyt. So *Gen.* 106 (*stōd ...*) *īdel ond unnyt.* A familiar phrase of somewhat didactic (and religious) flavor, occurring both in prose and poetry. (Also *Ormulum*, Dedic., 41.) Cf. *Angl.* xxxv 468.

413ᵇ-14. siððan ǣfenlēoht/under heofenes hādor beholen weorþeð. The plain meaning is: 'after the sun disappears from the firmament.' The conjectured *heofenes hador* (misspelling *d* for *ð* occurs in 1837, 2959, 3119; cp. *headerian; Rid.* 21.13: (ds.) *heaþore,* 66.3: *headre*) would be a periphrasis like *swegles begong, heofones hwealf, foldan fæþm* (see Gloss.). (Generally in OE. poetry the setting sun or stars are said to pass under the earth or the sea.) The reading of *hador* as *hādor* ('brightness,' so Ke., Tho., et al.) has been urged by Kock⁴ 110 f. (*heofenes hādor* = 'the clear sky'), though *hādor* is nowhere else found as a noun. — Other poetical expressions for the coming of night, 649 ff., 1789 f.

NOTES

420–24. It is not clear whether these feats were performed in the course of a single adventure or on several occasions. In the latter case, the slaying of the **niceras** could refer to the Breca episode, 549 ff. (cp. 567 ff. (1428 f.) with 423ª). By the term *niceras* (cp. *sǣdracan* 1426, *wyrmas ond wildēor* 1430, *wundra .. fela* 1509; 1510, 558, 549) were understood strange sea-beasts of some kind; the definite sense of ' walrus,' ' hippopotamus ' (Rie Zs. 388 f., Bu.Zs. 197) need not be looked for in the *Beowulf*. The fight against giants, five of whom were bound, seems reminiscent of folk-tales. Did Bēowulf bring those five with him as prisoners? (Cf. Panzer 44 ff., 58 ff.) — 423. The subject of **āhsodon** is *niceras*.

425 f. gehēgan/ðing, ' hold a meeting,' ' settle the dispute,' ' fight the case out.' A legal term applied to battle. See Antiq. § 6.

426ᵇ. Ic þē nū ðā. Type C1. See 657ᵇ, (*El.* 539, 661). *nū ðā* became ME. *nouthe*.

427 f. (Ic þē . . .) biddan wille . . . ānre bēne. *bēn* is here ' favor ' rather than ' petition,' cp. MnE. *boon*. The same expression occurs *Sigurþarkv. en skamma* 64: *biþja munk þik bǫnar einnar*.

430ᵇ. nū ic þus feorran cōm; cp. 825ᵇ, 361, 1819ª. An appeal to Hrōðgār's sense of fairness. Very similar sentiments: *OE. Bede* 60.5 ff. (i, c. 25), *Mald.* 55 ff.

432. fǣlsian. The notion of the ' cleansing ' of infested places was in accord with popular tradition (see Intr. xvi: *Grettissaga*, ch. 67; Ker L 4.120.1.196; Panzer 100 f., 266). It also admitted of a Christian interpretation (*Fat. Ap.* 66, *El.* 678; cf. *Angl.* xxxvi 191 n. 1).

433ª. Hæbbe ic ēac geāhsod. Type A3.

434. wǣpna ne recceð, ' does not care to use weapons.'

435 ff. Bēowulf wishes to meet Grendel on equal terms (so 679 ff.); that the monster cannot be wounded by ordinary weapons, he does not yet know (791 ff.). No doubt, the story called for a wrestling contest, which is also Bēowulf's favorite method of fighting (2506 ff., 2518 ff.; Intr. xix & n. 3), — though he sometimes does use weapons (note 2684 ff.). The introduction of the motive of Bēowulf's chivalry, or self-confidence, makes a modern impression. [Yet there is no need to operate with different structural layers in this connection, as Boer (59 f.) does.]

435ᵇ–6. swā mē Higelāc sīe . . . A form of asseveration; ' as [I wish that] H. may be . . . ' (or: ' so may H. be . . . '). In the same measure as Bēowulf will acquit himself heroically, Higelāc will feel kindly disposed towards him. Cp. Ælfric's *Gen.* 42.15: *swā ic āge Pharaones helde*.

440ª. lāð wið lāþum. ' Grammatical rime ' within the half-line; so 931ª, 1978ª, 2461ª.

444ᵇ. swā hē oft dyde. Some edd. have omitted the comma after *dyde*, construing *dyde* as ' verbum vicarium ' with the object *mægen* (cp. 1828; Grein Spr.: *dōn, 9*); but 444ᵇ has all the appearance of a complete formula, see 1238ᵇ, 1381ᵇ, 1676ᵇ, 1891ᵇ. The literalness of the statement must not be pressed any more than in 1891ᵇ.

445ª. The reading *mægenhrēð manna*, 'the pride (or flower) of men,' in place of **mægen Hrēðmanna** has been strongly objected to by Malone (see *Hamlet* 150 ff., 48 ff.; L 4.92 e. 785 ff., 812 f.; cf. L 4.74.5). By a noteworthy chain of arguments he arrives at the conclusion that *Hrēðmen(n)* was meant as a name for the Geats. Referring to the old Scandinavian use of *Reiðgotaland*, i.e., the land of the *Hreiðgotar*, which is found to denote both Jutland and the region on the south Baltic coast which for a considerable time was inhabited by Goths[1] (see *Wids.* 120: *Hrǣda here*), he holds that this tribal name was originally likewise applied to the Gauts[2] in their old home before it came to be used with regard to a Gautish state established in Jutland (after the Swedish conquest of the Gauts), and hence, by extension, was understood to signify Jutland generally. That the translator of Bede's *H.E.* (i 15) used *Gēatas* with reference to Jutland, is cited as an important piece of evidence in this connection. As to the OE. *Hrēð*-forms with *ē* instead of *ǣ* (ON. *Hreið*-) — thus, *Hrēðgotan*, *Hrēðcyning*, *Hrēðas* applied to the Goths in *Widsið* and *Elene* — , they have been plausibly explained by association with *hrōð*-, *hrēð*, 'glory'; cf. Cha. Wid. 252 f. — It must be admitted that the metrical argument formerly adduced in favor of *mægenhrēð manna* (cf. T.C. § 28 n. 2) is not so strong as in the case of *s[c]ynscaþa* 707.

445 ff. Nā þū mīnne þearft/hafalan hȳdan etc. The general sense of this passage is clear: there will be no need of funeral rites (cp. 2124 ff.). *hafalan hȳdan* refers either to interment (*Wand.* 83 f., cf. Notat. Norr. § 1147) or, more likely, to the custom of covering the head of the dead with a cloth (Konrath, *Arch.* xcix 417; *Angl.* xxxvi 174 n. 2). [Heyne thought of a guard of honor (see He.-Schü.), Simrock L 3.21.199, Schücking L 4.126.1.5, of a 'lichwake.'] Hoops (*ESt.* liv 19 ff.) infers from an incident related in Bede's *H.E.* iv 19 (17) that the custom of covering the head of the dead with a cloth obtained among the Anglo-Saxons as well as among the Scandinavians. It seems a natural enough usage. An explanation from folklore: Dehmer L 4.66 b5.2.28, n. 140. — 448. The meaning '(single) corpse' (*wæl*) inferred from this line is doubtful (the plur. *walu* 1042, *Ruin* 26 is non-conclusive); **byreð blōdig wæl** may have been a formula-like expression (so Neckel, *Walhall* (1913), pp. 6 f.); perhaps it was understood in the general sense of 'booty,' 'spoil.' — 450ª. **mearcað**, probably 'marks with blood,' 'stains.' [Bu. Tid. 70: 'marks with his footprints,' 'traverses'; Gr. Spr.: 'inhabits' (?).] — 450ᵇ–51. **nō ðū ymb mīnes ne þearft/līces feorme leng sorgian.** The rendering 'sustenance of my body,' although trivial and rather odd in view of Bēowulf's very brief visit, is not altogether out of

---

[1] According to von Friesen's brilliant etymology (*Rökstenen* (1920), p. 134), *Hreiðgotar* is literally 'nest-Goths,' i.e., 'home-Goths,' meaning those who had not emigrated. — [See further, Johannson, *Acta Philol. Scand.* vii 97 ff., Schütte, *ib.* viii 247 ff.]

[2] Cf. Bugge, *Antiqvarisk Tidskrift för Sverige* v, 35–37.

the question; an alternative sense of *feorm* is 'taking care of,' 'disposal,' being another allusion to the funeral. *nō . . . leng* 'no longer,' i.e. 'not a moment,' 'not at all' (Aant. 9).

452ᵃ. Onsend Higelāce. Type C1. Cp. 460ᵃ.

455. Wēlandes geweorc. If a weapon or armor in Old Germanic literature was attributed to Wēland, this was conclusive proof of its superior workmanship and venerable associations.[1] The figure of this wondrous smith — the Germanic Vulcanus (Hephaistos) — symbolizing at first the marvels of metal working as they impressed the people of the stone age, was made the subject of a heroic legend, which spread from North Germany to Scandinavia and England. Evidence that the striking story of Wēland's captivity and revenge told in the Eddic *Vǫlundarkviþa* (in a later, expanded, and somewhat diluted form, in the *þiðrekssaga*, chs. 57–79) was known to the Anglo-Saxons, is furnished by the allusions in the first two[2] ' stanzas ' of *Deor* and the carving on the front of the Franks Casket (dating from the beginning of the eighth century).[3] The tradition of Wēland was continued until modern times in connection with the motive of the 'silent trade.' It became attached to a cromlech in the White Horse valley in Berkshire called ' Wayland Smith's Cave,' or ' Forge '[4] and was used also, in a rather peculiar way, by Walter Scott in his *Kenilworth* (chs. 9 ff.).[5]

457. For [g]ewy[r]htum is parallel to *for ārstafum* (*for* denoting cause, not purpose); ' because of deeds done ' (ref. to the good services rendered to Bēowulf's father, 463 ff.) — and ' the resultant obligations you are under.' Accordingly, the meaning of 457 f. is: 'from a sense of duty and kindness you have come to us.' (*JEGPh.* vi 191 f.) [Cf. also Siev. ix 138, xxxvi 401 f.; Bu. 87 f.; Aant. 9 f.; Tr.[1] 152 f.; Holt. Zs. 114; *MPh.* iii 452 f.; Grienb., *Beitr.* xxxvi 80 f.; Boer 44 n.; Holt., *Beibl.* xlv 19: *wyhtum*, ' fights.' Hoops L 5.60.7 (cf. Gru.): *werefyhtum* (*for:* purpose).]

459. Geslōh þīn fæder fæhðe mæste. *geslēan* is understood in the perfective (resultative) sense: ' thy father brought about by fight the greatest feud ' (or, ' of feuds,' since *fǣhðe* perhaps stands for *fǣhða*, cp. *Chr.* 617, *Beow.* 78, 193, 1119, 2328, etc.). See Müllenhoff, *Anz.fdA.* iii 179; *MLN.* xvi 15, *MPh.* iii 262. The feud was probably considered

---

[1] Such references occur in the OE. *Waldere*, *Boethius* (prose and verse), in Middle English, Old French, and Latin texts (Binz 186 ff.). — The admiration for the works of (unnamed) smiths (cp. Longfellow's *Evangeline*, 117 f.) crops out in passages like *Beow.* 406, 1451 f., 1681. On *gīganta geweorc* 1562 and similar expressions, see note in *Angl.* xxxv 260 f.

[2] Or three? See Tupper, *MPh.* ix (1911), 265–67.

[3] See Napier, *Furnivall Miscellany* (1901), pp. 362 ff.

[4] Formerly ' Wayland-Smith ' = OE. *Wēlandes smiðöe* (in a charter of 955 A.D.). — Cp. also Kipling's *Puck of Pook's Hill* (' Weland's Sword ').

[5] On Wēland see especially: Grimm D. M. 312 ff. (376 ff.), Jiriczek L 4.116.1 ff.; P. Maurus, *Die Wielandsage in der Literatur* (Münch. Beitr. z. rom. u. engl. Phil. xxv), 1902; M. Förster, " Stummer Handel und Wielandsage," *Arch.* cxix (1907), 303–8; A. H. Krappe, *Arch.* clviii (9 ff.) ff.; Schneider (L 4.13 a) ii 2. 72 ff.

memorable on account of the persons or circumstances connected with it. — The chief alternative renderings advocated are: 'fought the greatest fight' (see Kock 226 f.), and 'fought out the greatest feud' (see Lorz 64; Chambers). The former, while not entirely impossible (cp. 1083), ignores the customary perfective function of *geslēan*. The latter is unconvincing, since the slaying of Heaþolāf by no means finishes the feud. Moreover, Hrōðgār is not interested primarily in relating a great exploit of Ecgþēow's, but means to emphasize the friendly relations existing between the Danes and Geats, his main point being the subsequent settlement of that feud (*þā* [demonstr.] *fǣhðe* 470).

461 f. for herebrōgan, 'on account of [anticipated] war-terror.' (*Angl.* xxviii 440.) Ecgþēow was compelled to leave the country after the manslaughter. Interesting parallels: *Odyssey* xv 271 ff.; *Grettissaga*, chs. 16, 24, 27; *Vǫlsungasaga*, ch. 1 (Sigi kills a man — *ok má hann nú eigi heima vera með feðr sínum*); Æþelberht's *Laws* 23 (*gif bana of lande gewīteþ* . . .).

463. Þanon. Evidently Ecgþēow had returned home from the land of the *Wylfingas*.

465. Is Deningas a by-form (of emotional connotation) of *Dene* (cp. *þyringas: (Ermun-)Duri*)? Cf. *ZfdA.* lxx 42.

466. ginne, Ms. *gimme*. The scribal blunder is not unnatural in the case of the rare, poetical adj. *gin(n)*; cf. *MPh.* ii 141.

472. hē mē āþas swōr. Ecgþēow promised Hrōðgār (who assumed responsibility for his good behavior) that he would keep the peace. Oaths of reconciliation between two warring parties are mentioned 1095 ff. — Or did he vow allegiance to the Danish king?

478. God ēaþe mæg . . . A conventional combination; *Angl.* xxxv 119 f.

480 f. Ful oft gebēotedon (type C2) **bēore druncne** . . . A kind of *gylpcwide* (Intr. lvi); cp. 2633 ff.; *Iliad* xx 83 ff. [Schücking L 7.25 i. 5 ff.: *bēot: gylp*.] — Different beverages are spoken of quite indiscriminately, *ealowǣge* 481, *bēorsele* 482, *medoheal* 484, *wered* 496, *wīn* 1162, etc. Cf. Gummere G. O. 71 ff.

487 f. þē þā dēað fornam, 'since death had taken those away.' Cp. 1435 f.; *Rid.* 10.11 f.

489 f. onsǣl meoto,/sigehrēð secgum. See Varr. The apparent metrical objection to an imper. *onsǣl*, which prompted the reading *on sǣl(um)*, has been shown by Bright to be largely imaginary, the occurrence of imperatives under the first metrical stress of the second half-line being not infrequent. For such imperatives taking precedence, in alliteration, of a following noun, see *Finnsb.* 11[b], 12[b], *Gen.* 1513[b], (*Andr.* 914[a]), *Gr.-Wü.* ii 219.38[b]; similarly, *Wald.* i 22[k], *Gen.* 1916[b], *Andr.* 1212[b] (cf. Siev. A. M. § 24.3; T.C. § 26). On the other hand, no really appropriate function of *on sǣl* can be presented. Bright's rendering, " do thou, victory-famous one, disclose to these men what thou hast in mind" (emend. *mētto*, found in no other place, but cp. *ofermētto*), makes very satisfactory sense; for the figurative meaning of *onsǣlan*, see *onlūcan* 259, *onbindan* 501; for the use of the dative, cp. *Andr.* 171 f., 315 f. In fact, the king's exhortation, 'enjoy yourself and speak your mind freely,' leaves nothing to be desired. But the assumption of an adj. *sigehrēð* (a ' possessive compound,' so He.[1-3], Tr.[1] 154 & ed.) is open to doubt. May not the noun *sigehrēð* refer to the hero's glorious deeds which he is expected to relate? Dietrich and Grein Spr. took **meoto** for a fem. noun, ' meditation,' ' thoughts,' so Hoops, who presents an admirable survey, St. 33 ff. (cp. Go. *mitōn*, wk. v. 2); Grein[2], Bu. Tid. 292, Tr.[1] 154, for the plur. of a neut. noun *met* (cp. *gemet*), ' measure,' ' etiquette' (Bu.: ' courtly words,' cf. He.[1-3] [Leo]). [Moore, *JEGPh.* xviii 206 (like Körner, *ESt.* ii 251, and Kock[2] 105,[3] 100, *AfNF.* xxxix 187): " think of good fortune (or joy) (*on sǣl meoto*), victory-renown to men"; si. *JEGPh.* vi 192, cf. *A.* l 121 f. — Further suggestions: *Holt., Beibl.* xl 90, xlii 249 f.; Imelmann, *ESt.* lxv 190 ff., lxvi 321 ff.]

494 ff. Cupbearers are mentioned again, 1161. Cf. Budde L 9.21.31 f.

497[a]. hādor; i.e., ' with a clear voice '; Lang. § 25.2. Cp. *Wids.* 103: *scīran reorde.*

497[b]**-98.** *þār wæs hæleða drēam,/duguð unlȳtel Dena ond Wedera.* A somewhat loose variation. Emerson's suggestion (*MPh.* xxiii 397) that **duguð** is used as a synonym for **drēam**, ' happiness,' ' rejoicing,' fails to carry conviction, especially in view of the parallel of *Andr.* 1269 f. (which looks like an imitation): *ðā cōm hæleða þrēat,/ . . . duguð unlȳtel.* Cf. *Arch.* cviii 370; *MPh.* iii 240.

499–661. The Unferð Intermezzo: Account of Bēowulf's swimming adventure with Breca. Entertainment in the hall.

Bēowulf, taunted by Unferð with having been beaten in a swimming match with **Breca**,[1] corrects him by telling the true story of the incident; whereupon he makes a spirited attack upon his critic's character and record, winding up with a confident prediction of his own success against Grendel.

Unferð represents the swimming tour as a contest (506 f., 517). Bēowulf, on the other hand, explains that the adventure was entered upon solely to fulfill a boastful pledge (*bēot*, 536) without any idea of rivalry (543), although he does consider himself superior to any contestant whatever. In fact, he makes much more of his struggles with the sea-monsters.

This swimming exploit, which has frequently been assumed to rest on a mythological basis,[2] looks rather like an exaggerated account of

[1] On the Breca episode, see especially Bu. 51–55; Cha. Wid. 110 f.; Lawrence L 4.91; Björkman, *Beibl.* xxx 170 ff.

[2] Thus, to Müllenhoff (1 f.) Breca meant the stormy sea, to Möller (22), the gulf stream, to Laistner (L 4.47.265), the sun; Sarrazin (St. 65 f.) considered the story a specialized form of a Baldr myth; Niedner (L 4.53) recognized in Bēowulf-Breca the Dioscurian twins.

one of those sporting feats common among the sea-loving Northern people (and which naturally often took the form of contests).[1] In particular, a somewhat similar tale of a swimming match in the *Egils Saga ok Ásmundar* (of the 14th century) has been cited,[2] but the parallelism noted is far from exact. That Breca was known to Ags. heroic legend,[3] is proved by the allusion in *Wids.* 25: *Breoca [wēold] Brondingum.* But nothing points to an old tradition in which the Breca incident was connected with the person of Bēowulf. It should be added that the story of the swimming could not well have formed the subject of a separate lay.

The narrative of this youthful trial of strength, inspiring, as it does, confidence in Bēowulf's ability to cope with the fearful monster, is eminently appropriate at this point. It may also be abundantly illustrated by analogies from folk-tales.[4]

The distance covered by the two endurance swimmers is very considerable. The *Finna land* 580 (land of the Finns or rather Lapps?) where Beowulf comes ashore is usually identified with *Finmarken* in the north of Norway. By the land of the *Heaþo-Rǣmas*[5] 519 is probably meant the region of the modern *Romerike* (to the north of Christiania), called in ON.: *Raumaríki*, and cited as a tribal name *Raumaricii* by Jordanes, c. 3. In prehistoric times it may very well have included a strip of seashore.[6] However, we are by no means compelled to believe that the poet had very clear notions of the geography of the scene.

Unferð, a most interesting personage of our poem, has been declared[7] an impersonation of the type of 'the wicked counselor' — like Bikki, e.g., at Jǫrmunrek's court —, well known in Germanic legend, although there is only a vague hint of a suspicion (see 1164 ff.) that he is fomenting dissensions within the Scylding dynasty. The name *Unferð*, i.e., more properly, *Unfrið*, 'mar-peace,'[8] it should be noted, appears

[1] See Weinhold L 9.32.311 f.; Panzer 270 f.; cf. Müllenhoff L 9.14.1.334 f. — Bēowulf himself on a later occasion swims from Friesland to his own home in southern Sweden, with thirty armors on his arm (2359 ff.).

[2] Bugge, *l.c.*

[3] Perhaps in connection with the sea; see also Glossary of Proper Names.

[4] See Panzer 272. That the name of *Breca*, *Bēanstān's* son, is derived from a **Stānbreca* (cf. *Steinhauer*, etc.) of some such folk-tales, is a rather far-fetched hypothesis of Panzer's.

[5] *Heaþo-* serves as epitheton ornans, cp. *Heaðo-Beardan*, *Heaðo-Scilfing*(as).

[6] The enormous distance separating the landing places of Bēowulf and Breca would be lessened if we assume either that the 'land of the Finns' is the district of *Finnheden* (*Finnved*) in Småland, Sweden (see Schück L 4.74.1.28), or that the term *Heaþo-Rǣmas* refers to *Romsdalen* (ON. *Raumsdalr*) on the west coast of Norway (Boer L 4.58.46; cf. Ettmüller's ed. of *Widsið* [1839], p. 22). The mention of the probably fictitious *Brondingas* 521 does not add to our knowledge. Unfortunately we do not even know from what place the swimmers started. On the Finns, see also R. Much, *R.-L.* ii 51 ff.

[7] Olrik i 25 ff. Cf. Malone, *PMLA*. xlii 302 ff.

[8] Hardly *Unfer(h)ð*, 'nonsense.' (For the interchange of -*ferð* and -*frið* see Bülb. § 572.) — The erroneous MS. spelling *Hunferð* was apparently suggested by the *Hūn*- compounds, e.g. *Hūnlāf* (see 1143); *Hunferþ*, *OE. Chron.* A.D. 744 (MS. E: *Unferð*), A.D. 754, MS. B: *Húnferþ* — [Etymological speculation: *PMLA*. xlii 302 f. (*Ivarr — Unferþ*), xlv 335 f., 626–28.]

to have been coined on English soil, such descriptive abstract appellations pointing to West Germanic rather than Scandinavian origin.[1] On the other hand, it has been suggested[2] that his peculiar position would seem to reflect conditions at the Irish courts where the *fili* (member of the learned poets' guild) enjoyed a remarkable influence and surprising freedom of speech.[3]

What the title þyle applied to Unferð (1165, 1456) meant, cannot be determined with certainty. The *þyle* (ON. *þulr*)[4] has been variously described as a sage, orator, poet of note, historiologer, major domus, or the king's right-hand man. The OE. noun occurs several times as the rendering of ' orator,' besides the compound *þelcræft* = ' rethorica ' (see B.-T.); hence the meanings of ' orator,' ' spokesman,' ' official entertainer ' suggest themselves as applicable to the situation in the *Beowulf*. As to the *þulr*, the characteristics of his office seem to have been " age, wisdom, extended knowledge, and a seat of honor " (Larson). Also Unferð has a seat of distinction: *æt fōtum sæt frēan Scyldinga* (500, 1166) — like the *scop* of *The Fates of Men*, 80 ff.[5] And by his reference to the Breca incident he shows that he is the best informed man at the court.

He is depicted by our poet as a sharp-witted (589) court official of undoubted influence and a reputation for valor (1166 f.), which he is jealously (501 ff.) anxious to guard. He has laid himself open to the terrible charge of fratricide (587 ff., 1167 f.), which, strange to say, does not seem to have imperiled his prominent position at the court,[6] although he is certain — so the Christian author informs us through the

[1] Cp. *Unwēn* (*Wids.* 114); *Wonrēd* (*Beow.* 2971); *Oftfōr; Wīdsīð;* OHG. *Unfrid*.

[2] By Deutschbein, *GRM.* i 114. It is strongly opposed by Olson, *MPh.* xi 419 ff.

[3] In his behavior to Bēowulf, Unferð shows a noteworthy similarity to Drances, *Æneid* xi 336 ff.; also Bēowulf's reply may be compared to that of Turnus, *ib.* xi 376 ff. (Earle 126, *Arch.* cxxvi 340 f.). Attention has also been called to the (decidedly less civilized) word-combat between Guþmundr and Sinfjǫtli in the Eddic lays of *Helgi Hundingsbani* i 33 ff., ii 22 ff. (Bugge L 4.84.163). — The taunting and trying of strangers at entertainments is not unknown in ON. sagas; see, e.g., *Gunnlaugssaga*, ch. 5, cp. *Hrólfssaga*, ch. 23. (Also *Odyssey* viii 158 ff.) But Unferð's disrespectful treatment of Bēowulf contrasts strangely with the dignified courtesy reigning at Hrōðgār's court.

[4] See the discussions of Müllenhoff, *Deutsche Altertumskunde* v 289 ff., Fr. Kauffmann in *Philologische Studien: Festgabe für E. Sievers*, pp. 159 ff., Koegel in *P. Grdr.*[2] ii[a], p. 33; Mogk, *ib.*, p. 575; Heusler, *R.-L.* i 443 f.; Larson L 9.19.120 f. (convenient summary); B. C. Williams, *Gnomic Poetry in Anglo-Saxon*, pp. 72 ff.; Phillpotts, *The Elder Edda and ancient Scandinavian Drama* (1920), 180 ff.; Heusler, *Altgerm. Dichtung* § 95; Vogt L 6.26; Chadwick L 4.22.2.619. — As a proper name, *þyle* occurs *Wids.* 24.

[5] W. H. Stevenson in his edition of Asser's *Life of King Alfred* (Oxford, 1904), p. 165 connects the office of Unferð with that of a *pedisequus, pedisecus*, — a term " appearing occasionally in the earlier charters as the name of an important official . . . " B. C. Williams (*l.c.*) compares Unferð to the later court fools.

[6] That Unferð remained unmolested in spite of the murder, because there can be no ' feud ' within one and the same family (cp. 2441 ff.), is scarcely believable.

mouth of Bēowulf (588 f.) — to receive his punishment in hell (cf. *Angl.* xxxv 133, 265).

In noteworthy contrast with the original conception of his character as expressed by his name, Unferð evinces a spirit of generosity, courtesy, and sportsmanlike fairness toward Bēowulf when the latter has demonstrated his superiority (1455 ff., 1807 ff.), — a feature obviously added by the poet himself. — [Cp. the Homeric parallel (from *Odyss.*, b. viii), p. 149, n. 3; Cha.'s note on l. 1808; Work, *Ph. Q.* ix 399 ff.]

The speeches of Unferð (506–528) and Bēowulf (530–606), if rather ornate considering the occasion, show the style of the poem at its best. The admirable use of variation, the abundance of sea terms (508 ff.), the strong description of the scene (545 ff., cp. *Wand.* 101 ff.) chiming in with the hardy spirit of the Northern heroes are conspicuous features of this famous passage.

501ª. onband beadurūne, 'unbound a battle-rune,' i.e. 'disclosed a hidden quarrel' (see note on *eardlufan* 692), 'began a bellicose speech.' It is probable that only the vaguest suggestion of ancient heathen belief (Müllenhoff in R. v. Liliencron & K. Müllenhoff, *Zur Runenlehre* [1852], p. 44) was lingering in *beadurūn*. Cp. *El.* 28: *wælrūne ne māð*, 1098: *hygerūne ne māð*. The use of *onbindan* is illustrated by *Beow.* 259, 489.

501ᵇ. Bēowulfes sīð. *sīð* should be understood in a rather general sense, 'undertaking'; cp. *Grendles þing* 409. (*Discourse of Soul* 20, Ex. MS.: *sāwle sīð*, Verc. MS.: *sāwle þing*.)

502. æfþunca, which has been found in one other passage only, viz. *Lib. Scint.* 176.12, need not be changed to *æfþanca* (Tr.¹ 155) or considered a weakened variant of it (Bülb. § 408, cf. B.-T. & Suppl.). Its genuineness is vouched for by the well-known verb *ofþyncan*.

503. forþon þe hē ne ūþe, þæt ǣnig ōðer man. Types A3: ×‖⌣́×××|⌣́× and B1: ×××⌣́|×⌣́.

504. middangeardes. Adverbial gen. of place (in quasi-negative clause). So 751 f.

506. sē Bēowulf, sē þe . . . , 'that Bēowulf who . . . ' (Cf. *Arch.* cxxvi 48 n. 3.)

525. wyrsan geþingea. Partitive gen. after a compar. (as in 247 f.), unless *wyrsan* be considered a rare, analogical by-form of the gen. plur. (Siev. § 304 n. 2). So *Gr.-Wü.* i 353.7: *wyrsan gewyrhta*.

526. The gen. **heaðoræsa** is construed with *dohte* (cp. 1344) rather than with *gehwǣr*.

543ᵇ. nō ic fram him wolde. Type C1.

545. fīf nihta fyrst. See 517: *seofon niht*. They kept on swimming for two days after their separation. That Bēowulf meant to correct Unferð's statement is not very likely. It is true, from a literal interpretation of the following passage one might conclude that Bēowulf landed on the sixth day; but it is more reasonable to believe that the poet omitted further details of the time element (which he neglected

NOTES 151

altogether in the account of Bēowulf's return voyage, 1903 ff.).

548. ondhwearf. The usual form of this (unstressed) verbal prefix is *on;* see Gloss.: *on-, and-*.

553 f. Mē tō grunde tēah/fāh fēondscaða. This incident foreshadows the hero's experience in his second great adventure, 1501 ff., 1509 ff.

557 f. heaþorǣs fornam/mihtig meredēor þurh mīne hand. Back of this remarkably impersonal manner of viewing the action lies the idea of fate. Cf. Intr. xlix & n. 2.

561. dēoran sweorde, 'with my good sword.' See 1528, 2050. (Laȝamon's *Brut* 28051: *mid deore mine sweorede*.)

565. mēcum. 567. sweo[r]dum. A 'generic plural,' used for the logically correct sing., perhaps even hardened into a kind of epic formula, cp. e.g. 583, 2140, 2485, 3147; *Andr.* 512. See Aant. 11; note on 1074ª. [Cf. also Heinzel, *Anz.fdA.* x 220 f.; ten Brink 37 n.; Möller, *ESt.* xiii 272, 278: old instrum. form.]

569 ff. Both the approach of morning and the subsiding of the storm enable Bēowulf to see the shore. Another description of the coming of morning, 1801 ff. (917 ff.).

572 f. Wyrd oft nereð/unfǣgne eorl, þonne his ellen dēah. Fate does not render manly courage unnecessary. A proverbial saying. ('Fortune favors the brave.') Frequently God is substituted for fate: 669 f., 1056 f., 1270 ff., 1552 ff., *Andr.* 459 f. Cf. Grimm D. M. iii 5 (1281 f.); Gummere G. O. 236 f.; Cook, *MLN.* viii 59 (classical and ME. parallels); *Arch.* cxv 179.

575 f. Nō ic on niht gefrǣgn etc. Prepositional phrases or adverbs of time and place modifying the object of the verb *gefrignan* or the infinitive phrase dependent on it, are placed before *gefrignan;* so 74, 2484, 2694, 2752, 2773. (Cf. Sievers, *Beitr.* xii 191.) See also 1197 (*hȳran*). The case is modified and complicated by the addition of the element of variation: 1 f.

581ᵇ–83ª. Nō . . wiht . . . swylcra searonīða . . . , billa brōgan. Terms of variation expressed by different grammatical forms; see 2067 ff. (2028 f.?), *MPh.* iii 238. Kock³ 101 takes *brōgan* as gen. plur.

588 f. þæs þū in helle scealt/werhðo drēogan. Cp. *El.* 210 f.

597. Sige-Scyldinga. A mechanical use of *sige-* as a general commendatory word (Intr. lxiv n. 1) without regard to the specific situation (cp. 663 f.). Or was irony intended? (Bryan, Kl. Misc. 128.)

599. ac hē lust wigeð,/swefeð ond sendeþ (MS.). *lust wigeð,* 'feels joy,' 'enjoys himself' (or, according to Moore, *JEGPh.* xviii 208, " has his own way "), placed paratactically by the side of the two following verbs. The force of this **sendan** is left to conjecture. The meaning of 'feasting' formerly (orig. by Leo in Heyne¹) attributed to it — on the basis of the noun *sand* ' dish of food,' ' repast ' ('that which is sent to the table ') has been generally given up. It has been credited with the sense of 'send to death,' like *forsendan* 904, *forð onsendan* 2266 (see Schü. xxxix 103 f.); cp. Lat. ' mittere Orco, umbris,' etc.

(e.g. *Æn.* ix 785, xi 81). Again, it has been suspected of being a relic of old heathen sacrificial terminology. Cp. *Hávamál* 145.3 f.: *veiztu hvé blóta skal?/veiztu hvé senda skal, veiztu hvé sóa skal?* (*blóta* and *sóa* = ' sacrifice '; the semantic development of *senda* (' send ') as used in this passage is not quite certain.) Possibly *sendan* was taken to convey a vague idea of ' sacrifice.' But the case is happily simplified by adopting Imelmann's emendation **snēdeþ.** (Holt., ed. ii⁵: *snǣdeþ?*)

603ᵇ. (Gǣþ eft) sē þe mōt. A mere formula; so 1387ᵇ (cp. 1177ᵇ, 1487ᵇ); *Hildebr.* 60; Rieger, *Germ.* ix 310; Sievers's note on *Hel.* 224. — 603ᵇ, either type D4 or E1.

605. ōþres dōgores; adv. gen., ' on the next day.'

606. sūþan scīneð; i.e., in full daylight. Is this meant as a literal reference to 917 ff., 1008 ff.?

610. folces hyrde. On possible affinities, see Glossary, also *A.* xxvii 256; *Speculum* viii 273 f.

612 ff. Appearance of nobie ladies at the banquet; see 1162 ff., 1980 ff., 2020 ff. Cf. Budde L 9.21.39 ff.; Tupper's *Riddles*, p. 218. A parallel to Wealhþēow's part in this passage: *Gnom. Ex.* 85–93.

617. bæd hine bliðne. Omission of *wesan*, see Gloss.: *eom*.

620ᵃ. Ymbēode þā. Type B1.

622. sincfato sealde; i.e., she passed the cups. On Ags. cups, see Tupper's *Riddles*, p. 204. No drinking horns are mentioned in *Beowulf*.

627 f. þæt hēo on ǣnigne eorl gelȳfde/fyrena frōfre; i.e., she counted on help *from* a hero. An instance of a peculiar mode of viewing direction (Lang. § 25.5). Quite parallel to this use of *on* with acc. is *tō*: 909, 1272 f.

628. Hē þæt ful geþeah etc. Evidently a definite drinking ceremony. Cp. the salutation, 617, 625. See 1024 f.

635. on wæl crunge. Note the use of *on* with acc. (cp. 772, 1540, 1568, etc.). On the other hand, 1113: *sume on wæle crungon*.

644. oþ þæt semninga; so 1640. It looks as if the adverb were added merely to accentuate the meaning of the conjunction. Cp. *oþ þæt fǣringa* 1414. See also Kock⁴ 113 f.; *A.* l 111 n. 2.

646 ff. The emendation adopted by nearly all recent edd.: **siððan hīe sunnan lēoht gesēon [ne] meahton** has a false ring; one would expect, at least, something like *leng gesēon ne meahton*. (Cf. also Schuchardt L 6.14.2.25.) Ll. 648 ff. plainly mean: ' from the time that they could see the light of the sun, until (oþ ðe) night came '; exactly as *Brun.* 13 ff. (*siþþan . . . oð . . .*). Thus, the meaning (of *oþ ðe*, or *oþðe*) ' until ' (so some earlier edd., like Grein, Arnold, cf. Heyne¹⁻³) need not be given up for Bugge's *oþðe* = ' and ' (i.e., a variant of the regular ' or,' see Bu. Tid. 57, cf. E. tr.). Nor do we need to assume a lacuna (Grein, cf. Gru.). In other words, the king knew that fight had been in Grendel's mind all day long; Grendel had been waiting from morning till night to renew his attacks in the hall, just as the dragon — *hordweard onbād/earfoðlīce, oð ðæt ǣfen cwōm* 2302 f. — Close parallels to the use of tō (þǣm hēahsele) are found in 1990, 1207. Whether we consider *āhlǣcan* as ' dat. used as instr.' (Sedgefield), as ' dat. of personal agency ' (Green L 6.8.5.98: " a fight was contemplated by the monster "), or a variety of the dat. of interest (cp. Lat. ' mihi consilium captum est,' see also Heusler, *Altisl. Elementarbuch* § 383), is immaterial to the general interpretation of the context. [Cf. also Bu. 89; ten Brink 52; Tr.¹ 160; Malone, *J EGPh*. xxix 234 f., *Medium Ævum* ii 61 f.; Hoops St. 100 f.; Traver L 5.83.] No general agreement as yet.

652. The type **guma ōþerne** (similarly 2484, 2908, 2985) is a counterpart of the repetition of the noun (' grammatical rime '), see note on 440ª. (Kluge, *Beitr.* ix 427.) Cp. *Gnom. Cott.* 52: *fyrd wið fyrde, fēond wið ōðrum*.

655. ǣnegum men, ' any man,' i.e. excepting, of course, Hrōðgār's own men. (Cf. Jellinek & Kraus, *ZfdA*. xxxv 272.)

660 f. It may jar on our feelings that Hrōðgār should offer a material reward to the high-minded hero, but he did just what was expected of him. Cp. 384 f., 1380 ff., 2134, also 1484 ff.

662-709. The watch for Grendel. 710-836. The fight with Grendel.

664. That Wealhþēow left the hall, the poet has omitted to mention. Cf. Intr. lvii.

666. swā guman gefrungon. A species of the *gefrægn-* formula.

667 f. Change of subject; Bēowulf **(seleweard)** is the subject of *behēold* and *ābēad*.

670. mōdgan probably qualifies *mægnes;* i.e., attrib. adj.

671. Ðā hē him of dyde. Type C2.

673ª. īrena cyst. *īrena* (so 1697ª, 2259ᵇ) stands for older *īrenna* (so 802ᵇ, 2683ª, 2828ª). Cf. Lang. § 19.5. Even if the *n* was really meant to be single, this would not necessarily involve a gross violation of meter. (T.C. § 21.)

675 ff. Bēowulf is made to utter his ' boast,' **gylpworda sum**, in deference to general epic practice. (Intr. lvi.) The occasion is singular enough, but the circumstances of the fight allowed no chance for oratory immediately before the action. — How are the beds procured? See 1239 f. — 677 f. **an herewæsmun hnāgran ... gūþgeweorca.** Cp. 980 f.: *swīgra ... on gylpsprǣce gūðgeweorca*.

681. nāt hē þāra gōda. Semi-partitive gen. in connection with the negation. The following *þæt-* clause explains *gōda*. Cp. Ælfric, *Hom.* i 190.31: *þæt folc ne cūðe ðǣra gōda, þæt hī cwǣdon þæt hē God wǣre;* also *Mald.* 176 f. (*MPh.* iii 455.)

691. Nǣnig heora þōhte, þæt hē þanon scolde. Types A3, C1.

692. eardlufu, ' dear home '; see *ēðel-, hord-, lyft-wyn(n), wæteregesa, mid gryrum ecga* 483. ' Concretion ' of meaning. (Aant. 13; *MPh.* iii 263 f.)

694ᵇ. The co-ordination of **hīe** and **(tō) fela** seems quite permissible, at least if we may trust the analogy of *fēa(we)* and *sume* (*hīe sume*, etc., cf. *MLN*. xvii 29).

697. wīgspēda gewiofu. As the context shows, the conception of the 'weaving' of destiny (by the Parcae, Norns, Valkyrias, cf. Grimm D. M. 343 ff. (414 ff.), W. Grimm L 4.67³.435, Kemble L 9.1. i 401, Mogk, *P. Grdr.*² iii 271) has become a mere figure of speech. See *Rim. Poem* 70: *mē þæt wyrd gewæf, Guðl.* 1325: *wefen wyrdstafum.* [Njálssaga, ch. 157.29: poem on 'the woof of war.']

698ª. frōfor ond fultum, acc. sing.; 1273: *frōfre ond fultum.* Occasionally, in later texts, *frōfor* is treated as a masc. (also neut.?); cf. Sievers, *Beitr.* i 493. Has, in this case, a spelling *frōfr* (=*frōfr*', see 668) been erroneously changed to *frōfor?*

698ᵇ–99. fēond is acc. sing. (not plur.), **ealle,** nom. plur. (not acc. plur.). See 939 ff., 705; *Angl.* xxxv 470.

700ᵇ–2ª. 'It is well known that God has always (in every instance up to this time) ruled over the race of men.' Cp. 1663 f.

703. How is it possible for the Geats to fall asleep in this situation? Obviously, their failing enhances the achievement of Bēowulf. Or does this feature reflect ancient tales in which preliminary unsuccessful attempts to cope with the intruder are incident to the defenders' failure to keep awake? Cf. Panzer 96 f., 99, 267.

707. under sceadu bregdan; *under* 'down to,' or 'to the inside of,' see Gloss. The 'shades' might well be of classical origin; cp., e.g., *Æneid* xi 831, xii 952: 'vitaque cum gemitu fugit indignata sub umbras.' Cf. *MPh.* iii 257; *Arch.* cxxvi 349. *Hel.* 1113 ff.: *giwēt im the mēnskaðo ... undar ferndalu; Par. Lost* vi 141 f.: 'and whelm'd Thy legions under darkness.'

710 ff. The presentation of the Grendel fight, the first climax of the poem, shows the author's characteristic manner. (Cf. Intr. lii, lviii.) Partly excellent, vigorous narrative — yet the story is very much interrupted by interspersed general reflections on the situation and by remarks on the persons' thoughts and emotions, which greatly lengthen it and detract from its effectiveness. The corresponding combat of Grettir (Intr. xiv f.) is a good deal shorter, and also more direct and realistic.

710. Ðā cōm. After a digression, the poet returns to the subject, see *Cōm* 702; likewise *Cōm þā* 720 is an entirely natural expression. No appeal to a patchwork theory is necessary to explain this repetition. Some enthusiasts have found the threefold bell-like announcement of Grendel's approach a highly dramatic device. (Cf. also Intr. lviii & n. 2.)

719. heardran hǣle, healðegnas fand. *hǣle, hilde, hǣlescipes,* and the like are metrically, at any rate, safer than *hǣle* (T.C. § 17). Holthausen's former interpretation (*Angl.* xxiv 267) of *heardran hǣle* (from *hǣl* 'omen') as 'in a worse plight' (or with A. J. Daniels's modification [*Kasussyntax zu den Predigten Wulfstans,* Leiden Diss., 1904, p. 162]: 'tot een rampzaliger omen,' i.e. in effect, ' with a more disastrous result ') was a happy suggestion — cp. ME. expressions like *to wroþer hele, till illerhayle, with il a hail* (see, e.g., Mätzner, *AE. Sprachproben, Wbch.* ii 391 a), ON. *illu heilli* — , but this use of the dat. appears rather

NOTES

doubtful. The same is true of Sedgefield's rendering 'with sterner greeting' (from *hǣlo*). We may venture to take *heardran hǣle* as acc. sing., 'worse luck' — cp. the meaning of *heardsǣlþ, heardsǣlig* —, *heardran* referring at the same time to the second object, *healðegnas*. That seemingly incongruous objects may be governed by one and the same verb, is seen from 653 f.

721. drēamum bedǣled. A permanent characteristic (epitheton perpetuum) of Grendel, like *wonsǣlī* 105, *fēasceaft* 973, *earmsceapen* 1351, *synnum geswenced* 975.

723. onbrǣd þā; i.e., then he swung the door wide open; not a mere repetition of *Duru onarn*, 721.

724ᵇ. Raþe æfter þon. Type D4. As to the accent on the preposition, cf. Rie. V. 31 f., also 61.

725. fāgne (flōr), perhaps 'fair-paved' (Gummere); see 320.

736. ðicgean ofer þā niht.   þrȳðswȳð behēold. Types A 1 (´×××|´×), E 1.

736ᵇ–38. Why does Bēowulf in the meantime remain lying on his bed? Presumably this is a feature of the original story (see Intr. xv, xvii; *Grettissaga*, chs. 65, 35) retained by the poet, though he had added the incident of a previous attack on one of the comrades (named *Hondsciōh*, 2076). — **under (fǣrgripum)** denotes attending circumstances ('with') rather than time ('during,' Aant. 14); "set to work with his sudden snatchings" (Cl. Hall). Cp. the use of *mid*, 2468, and *OE. Chron.* A.D. 1132 (MS. E): *hē fēorde mid suīcdōm*.

744 f. eal . . . fēt ond folma, 'all, (even) feet and hands,' or 'feet, hands, and all' (Aant. 14).

748 f. fēond, i.e. Grendel; **hē onfēng . . . inwitþancum,** 'he (Bēowulf) received him (pron. object understood, cf. Lang. § 25.4) with hostile intent'; see *A*. l 122. [Cf. also Schü. xxxix 105; Hoops St. 102 f.: *inwitþanclum* (adj.).] — **wið earm gesæt** (ingressive function), 'sat up supporting himself on his arm.' Thus *Sat.* 432: *ārās þā ānra gehwylc and wið earm gesæt,/hleonade wið handa.* (Cf. *Arch.* cix 312, *MPh.* iii 263.) Note the progress in 759: *uplang āstōd*.

756. sēcan dēofla gedræg. This cannot be literally true, as Grendel is supposed to live alone with his mother.

758. Gemunde þā se gōda, mæg Higelāces. The exceptional alliteration (see Varr., T.C. § 26) seems permissible, especially in view of the syntactical pause assumed here (comma after *gōda*). The usual type of alliteration in such lines may be seen in 1474, 2971, 2977.

760. (fingras) burston; perh. 'broke' (cracked, snapped), as in *burston bānlocan* 818, when a more serious stage of the fight has been reached. Tinker, *MLN.* xxiii 240 suggested: 'bled' (cp. 1121), — a result brought about by gripping, *Nibel.* 623; cp. *Salman und Morolf* 1609. See likewise *Ragnars saga Loðbrókar*, ch. 16. Lyons, *MLN.* xlvi 443 f.: an instance from *Gesta Herwardi;* Clarke, *MLR.* xxix 320: a MHG. parallel.

764f. wiste his fingra geweald/on grames grāpum, 'he realized etc.' Cp. 821; ON. *vita* (e.g., *Vǫlundarkv.* 14.3).

766. þæt se hearmscaþa tō Heorute ātēah. Kock[2] 106 ff. argues for the relative character of this clause, *þæt* (instead of *þone*) being justified by *þæt* 765; *sīð ātēon*, 'take a journey.' Cp. 1455 f. This is indeed more satisfactory than to take *þæt* as conjunct. and *ātēon* as intrans. verb (as suggested, *MPh.* iii 455).

769. ealuscerwen. *-scerwen*, related to **scerwan* 'grant,' 'allot' (*bescerwan* = 'deprive'). 'Dispensing of ale,' or, in a pregnant sense, of 'bitter or fateful drink' might have come to be used as a figurative expression for 'distress' (Bu. Tid. 292 ff.; *Beibl.* xxii 372 f.). It is to be noted that the author of *Andreas* (a better judge than modern scholars) understood the corresponding formation *meoduscerwen* (1526) in a sense which precludes the rendering 'taking away of (strong) drink'; to him it was 'plenty of (fateful) drink.' The alternative interpretation 'taking away of ale,' 'terror' (at the loss of ale) (Heyne[4]) has found much favor; a particularly tempting argument has been adduced (by Hoops) from ll. 5 f. (Spaeth L 3.42.4 describes the term as "reminiscent of the wild oversetting of tankards and spilling of ale when the hall was suddenly attacked.") Of course, the original form as well as meaning may have been obscured. [Cf. Cosijn, *Beitr.* xxi 19; Krapp's note on *Andr.* 1526; Grienb., *Beitr.* xxxvi 84 f., Siev., *ib.* 410; Sedgefield's note; Kock[4] 105 f.; Liebermann, *Arch.* cxliii 247 f.; (L 5.29;) *A.* l 122, *Beibl.* xl 28; Crawford, *MLR.* xxi 302 f.; L 5.60.3 a-f; also Hoops 97 f. (a clear summing-up).]

770 ff. The havoc made of the building and the furniture is naturally emphasized in encounters of this sort; cp. 997 ff.; *Grettissaga*, chs. 65, 35 (Intr. xv, xvii); *Bjarkarímur* iv 12.

777. golde geregnad. Does this imply gold-embroidered covers on the benches? (Falk, *R.-L.* i 166.)

779. The neuter **hit** seems to refer to the hall in a general way, without grammatical regard to the gender of any of the nouns that might have been used; see 770–73.

781 f. nymþe līges fæþm/swulge. See 82 f.

783[a]. nīwe geneahhe. See Gloss.; *nīwe* is naturally taken as adj. [Kock L 5.44.4.8: *nīwe, geneahhe*, "(the din arose) in manner strange and strong."]

785. þāra þe of wealle wōp gehȳrdon. As *of wealle*, in all probability, denotes the standpoint of the subject of *gehȳrdon* (Sievers, *Beitr.* xii 192; see l. 229), the meaning appears to be that the Danes heard the wailing from the wall(s) of their sleeping apartments. (We might translate: 'through the walls.') Sievers supposed that they had fled in terror to the shore, but this would seem a little far-fetched. Lawrence (*JEGPh.* xxiii 297) suggests that the frightened Danes " may have taken refuge on the wall surrounding the *tūn*." This is less forced than Sievers's explanation of *weall* as 'shore.' [Tinker (*MLN.* xxiii 240), who connects *of wealle* with the object, is enabled to render: " who heard the howling in the house (Heorot)."]

786 ff. gryre!ēoð galan Godes andsacan etc. Cries of pain and lamentation denoted by the use of *galan* and similar terms: 2460 (?); *Andr.* 1127, 1342, *Guðl.* 587, etc. Cf. Siev. A. M. § 5.3, *Beitr.* xxix 314 ff. (Numerous examples are found in Chaucer.) — The infin. phrases are variations of the preceding noun (*wōp*). Cp. 221 f., 1431 f., 1516 f.; 728 f., 2756 ff. (*MPh.* iii 237 f.) — In acc. with infin. constructions after *gehȳran, gefrignan* we note the tendency to give the acc. of the *object* the first place; so also 1027 ff., 2022 f., 2773 f. (but see 2484 f., 2694 f.); so after *hātan*, 68 f. [according to the MS. reading] (but see 2802); after *forlǣtan*, 3166.

793 f. nē his līfdagas lēoda ǣnigum/nytte tealde. Litotes, cf. Intr. lxv. *his* refers, of course, to Grendel.

794ᵇ-5. Þǣr genehost brægd/eorl Bēowulfes ealde lāfe; virtually, ' many a man brandished his sword.' The sing. of concrete nouns is often used in a collective sense; thus in connection with *manig, oft, genehost, ȳþgesēne*, 794 ff., 1065, 1110 ff., 1243 ff., 1288 ff., 2018 f.; also without any such auxiliary word suggesting the collective function, 296 ff., 492 (?), 1067, 1284 ff. Cf. Kock 219, Siev. xxix 569 ff., *MPh.* iii 249 f.

800. on healfa gehwone hēawan, lit. ' strike on (towards) all sides.'

804. ac hē sigewǣpnum forsworen hæfde. Grendel had laid a spell on swords. Cp. Saxo vii 219, where a certain Haquinus is called ' hebetandi carminibus ferri peritus '; *Sal.* 161 ff. (Cf. Falk L 9.44.44.) See note on 1523. [Laborde, *MLR.* xviii 202 ff.; *Angl.* l 195.]

805 ff. Scolde his aldorgedāl .... earmlīc wurðan. Is this an allusion to the fact that Grendel is not slain by swords, but suffers death in an ignominious manner? See also *ESt.* lvii 191 n. 3.

810. mōdes myrðe, in accordance with Holthausen's explanation of *myrð(u)* as ' trouble,' ' affliction ' (cp. OHG. *merrida*), is stylistically preferable to *mōdes myr(h)ðe*, ' joy of heart,' whether *myr(h)ðe* be taken as dat. or as gen. (parallel with *fyrene;* Cl. Hall, Lawrence, *MLN.* xxv 156: " had accomplished much of the joy of his heart "). Cp. *mōdes brecða* 171; 164 ff., 474 ff., 591 ff., 2003 ff. See *Angl.* l 195.

811. hē [wæs] fāg wið God. See 154 ff.; Intr. lxii n. 3; *Angl.* xxxvi 178 f. For the scribal omission of *wæs*, cp. 1559, and see Glossary: *eom*.

814ᵇ-15ᵃ. wæs gehwæþer ōðrum/lifigende lāð, ' each one was hateful to the other while living.' A pointed phrase (involving litotes) of an almost classic ring; cf. *Arch.* cxxvi 357 & n. 1. See 2564 f., *Mald.* 133.

816 f. wearð .. sweotol, ' became visible.'

833. Þæt wæs tācen sweotol, ' that was clearly proved.' (*MPh.* iii 456; *Angl.* xxv 280.)

834. hond ālegde. Much has been made of the tearing off of Grendel's arm and of the fact that such a feature can be traced in various Irish stories (cf. Dehmer L 4.66 b5). See Intr. xiii n. 2.

836. under gēapne hr(ōf). The victor places Grendel's right (2098) arm above the door outside the hall (on some projection perhaps) **as high as he can reach**. See 926 f., 982 ff. [Cf. also note in Krapp and Kennedy's *Reader*, L 2.23.]

837–924. Rejoicing of the retainers. Stories of Sigemund and Heremōd.

839 ff. This excursion to Grendel's *mere* has been declared an unwarranted duplication of the trip preceding Bēowulf's second adventure, 1399 ff.; see Panzer 276 ff. It might as well be called a legitimate expansion of the story. **folctogan** a high-sounding term like *selerǣdende* 51, 1346.

850–52. dēog is pluperf.; **siððan**, conj. Leo's explanation of *dēog* (see Varr.) was defended by E. E. Wardale, *MLR*. xxiv 62 f. [Krogmann, *ESt*. lxviii 317 conjectures for *dēog* the sense of ' raged.'] — Grendel's abode is vaguely identified with hell, cp. 756; he is even said to pass into the power of devils, *on fēonda geweald* 808 (in contrast with *on Frēan wǣre*, 27). No conscious personification is contained in the expression **þǣr him hel onfēng**. Cf. *Angl*. xxxv 267 f.

862 f. Nē hīe hūru winedrihten etc. Note the delicacy of feeling and the author's unshakable respect for kingship.

867[b]–915. Summary of songs recited (while the thanes ride slowly), the subjects being **Bēowulf, Sigemund, Heremōd**. Starting with a lay of praise concerning Bēowulf's exploit, which has just been extolled by the warriors in informal, yet highly eloquent language (856–61), the court poet, well versed in ancient heroic lore, proceeds to recite the adventures of Sigemund, thus raising Bēowulf, as it were, to the rank of pre-eminent Germanic heroes. From indirect discourse the account passes almost imperceptibly to direct statement, and when the Heremōd theme is taken up, we feel like questioning whether Hrōðgār's thane has not been altogether forgotten by the Ags. poet. — We have here a valuable testimony both of the improvisation of lays in connection with great, stirring events and of the circulation of famous short epic poems comparable in scale to *The Fight at Finnsburg*. — We might guess at the opening of the Sigemund and the Heremōd lay; thus: *ic Sigemundes secgan hȳrde/ellendǣda*, and *hwæt, wē Heremōdes hilde gefrūnon*. It should be added that Hoops (L 5.60.4) regards the entire passage as a summary of a single lay in praise of Bēowulf, of which the Sigemund and Heremōd verses are integral parts.

870 f. According to the punctuation introduced by Rieger (Rie. L., see Zs. 390) and approved by Bugge (Bu. Zs. 203), **word ōþer fand/sōðe gebunden** was understood as a parenthetical clause, ' one word found another rightly bound.' (See also Earle's note; *MPh*. iii 456, Ed.[1]) But it is certainly simpler to place a semicolon after *gebunden*, and to interpret *word ōþer* (and similarly *eft*) as expressing a contrast to *ealdgesegena*. For the use of *fand*, cp. *Fat. Ap*. 1: *ic þysne sang sīðgeōmor fand*, also Otfrid I 1.8; for the true alliteration ' binding,' *sōðe gebunden*, cp. *Gawain and the Green Knight* 35: *with lel letteres loken*. See Hoops St. 49 ff.

871[b]. secg eft ongan. Type E1.

NOTES 159

874. wordum wrixlan, here (unlike its use in 366, cp. *Runic Poem* 57) = ' vary words ' (cp. *Phoen.* 127, *Rid.* 9.2 f.) in the customary manner of Germanic poetry.

875–900. Sigemund.[1] The cursory, epitomizing report embodies two separate stories, going back, perhaps, to two originally separate lays, viz. 1) Sigemund's *wīde sīðas* of fierce fighting, especially those undertaken in company with Fitela, 2) his dragon fight.

1) The vague abstract of the former receives full light from the *Vǫlsungasaga*, chs. 3–8.[2] Sigmundr, we are told, is the eldest son of King Vǫlsungr, a descendant of Óþinn. His twin sister Signý is married against her will to Siggeirr, king of Gautland. While on a visit at Siggeir's court, Vǫlsungr and his men are treacherously slain (cp. the Finnsburg legend); his sons are taken prisoners and meet death one after another except Sigmundr, who escapes into the forest. Sigmundr and Signý brood revenge. Seeing that her sons by Siggeirr are lacking in valor and that only a true Vǫlsung son will be able to help in the work of revenge, Signý, impelled by a desperate resolve, disguises herself as a witch and visits her brother in the forest, and when her time comes, she gives birth to a son, who is named Sinfjǫtli. Ten years old, the boy at his mother's bidding joins Sigmundr (who does not know until the final catastrophe that Sinfjǫtli is his son) and is trained by him in deeds of strength and hardship. ' In summer they fare far through the woods and kill men to gain booty ' (ch. 8); living for a time as werewolves ' they performed many famous deeds in the realm of King Siggeirr.' (Cp. *Beow.* 883 f., *fǣhðe ond fyrena* 879 [*Helgakv. Hund.* i 43: *firinverkum* (?)].) Finally Sigmundr and Sinfjǫtli accomplish the revenge by setting fire to Siggeir's hall.

How far the version known to the author of *Beowulf* agreed with this part of the *Vǫlsungasaga*, it is impossible to determine. The fact that **Fitela** is referred to as Sigemund's *nefa* only (881), might perhaps be held to betoken Sigemund's own ignorance of their true relation, or it may be attributed to the Christian author's desire to suppress that morally revolting motive. But we do not know, indeed, whether the Anglo-Saxons of that time were at all acquainted with a story answering to the Sigmundr-Signý motive. The form *Fitela* differs from the established Norse compound name *Sinfjǫtli* (whose bearer figures in the *Eddas* and in *Eiríksmál*[3]) and from the High German *Sintarfizzilo* (merely

---

[1] References: L 4.107–115; besides: W. Grimm L 4.67.³17 f.; Jiriczek L 4.67. n. 55 ff., 89 ff.; Koegel L 4.8. iᵃ 172 ff., iᵇ 198 ff.; Binz 190 ff.; Symons L 4.29 § 27; Chadwick Or. 148 f.; Neckel L 4.115 a; Schneider L 4.13 a. i 157 ff.; Krappe, *Arch.* clxvii 161 ff. (on brother-sister marriage).

[2] For a modern version in poetical form, see William Morris's *The Story of Sigurd the Volsung and the Fall of the Niblungs*, the first part of Book i. Cf. H. Bartels, *William Morris, The Story of Sigurd the Volsung etc.: Studie über das Verhältnis des Epos zu den Quellen.* Münster (Diss.), 1906.

[3] Sigmundr and Sinfjǫtli are bidden by Óðinn to welcome King Eiríkr on entering Valhǫll (Valhalla). (*Corp. Poet. Bor.* [L 10.1] i 261.)

recorded, by the side of *Fezzilo, Fizzilo*, as a man's name). Also the designation of Sigemund's father as *Wæls* (897; Sigemund = *Wælsing* 877) differs from his Norse name *Vǫlsungr*, which latter is presumably the result of confusion, the patronymic form being taken for a proper name. It is possible, though, that *Wæls* itself (used in *Wælses eafera* 897 = *Wælsing*) is a (secondary) ' back formation ' inferred from *Wælsing* (Sievers, *Zum ags. Vocalismus* [1900], p. 22; Boer L 4.113.93). — It should be mentioned that a perplexing OE. poem in the Exeter MS., the so-called First Riddle, has been interpreted by Schofield as a lyric, ' Signý's Lament,' referring to the Sigmund-Signý-Fitela incident, but the evidence is by no means conclusive.[1]

2) Sigemund's **dragon fight** is peculiar to the *Beowulf*. It naturally suggests the far-famed dragon fight of his still greater son, (ON.) Sigurðr, (MHG.) Sigfrit, which kindled the imagination of the Scandinavians[2] and was not forgotten by the Germans,[3] and which in fact — especially as part of the great Nibelungen cycle — has been celebrated in modern Germanic epic, drama, and music. As Sigemund is called *wreccena wide mǣrost/ofer werþēode* 898, Sigurðr, in the seer's words, is to be ' the greatest man under the sun, and the highest-born of all kings ' (*Grípispá* 7); and the slaying of the dragon brings no little renown to Sigemund (*æfter dēaðdæge dōm unlȳtel* 885) just as to his illustrious son ('this great deed will be remembered as long as the world stands,' *Vǫlsungasaga*, ch. 19). But there are differences between the two stories, quite apart from the greater fulness of detail found in the narrative of Sigurð's exploit. The manner of the fight itself is not the same, Sigemund's deed appearing the more genuinely heroic one. Noteworthy incidents of the *Beowulf* version are the dissolving of the dragon in its own heat (897) and the carrying away of the hoard in a boat (895).[4] For points of contact with Bēowulf's and Frotho's dragon fights, see Intr. xxiii.

It is widely held that the dragon fight belongs properly to Sigfrit and not to Sigemund, his father;[5] yet there is no positive evidence to prove that the Ags. poet was in error when he attributed that exploit to the latter. Sigurðr-Sigfrit may, in fact, have been unknown to him. It is, on the whole, probable that in his allusions to Sigemund as well as to Here-

[1] An excellent historical sketch of scholarly opinion on this poem is found in Wyatt's edition of the *Old English Riddles* (Belles-Lettres Series, 1912), pp. xx–xxviii. Cf. also Imelmann L 4.129 a. 73 ff., 180 ff.

[2] Witness the *Eddas, Vǫlsungasaga*, and notable representations in Northern art, see Olrik L 9.38.111 f.

[3] *Nibel.* 101, 842 (cp. 88 ff.), *Seyfridslied*, cf. *Þiðrekssaga*.

[4] In *Guþrúnarkv.* ii 16 Sigmundr is represented as a maritime king.

[5] Thus, according to Goebel, " there seems little doubt that Siegfried's famous deed was transferred to Sigmund when through the latter the legend began to connect Siegfried with the chosen clan of the Volsungs and their special protector, Oðinn." (*JEGPh.* xvii 2 f.) Excepting this variation in respect to the name, the Beowulfian account has been thought to contain the oldest form of the legend of Siegfried. (Cf. Goebel, *l.c.*)

mōd he followed good old Danish tradition,[1] and that at that time no connection had yet been established between the Sigemund (Wælsing) legends and those of Sigfrit and of the Burgundians. Grundtvig's ingenious attempt to read Sigfrið into the *Beowulf* episode (Gru., pp. xxxviii f.) rests on violent emendation and interpretation; and the more recent claim of [Söderberg and] Wadstein (*The Clermont Runic Casket*, 1900) that the figures and runic inscription on the right side of the Franks Casket refer to scenes from the Sigurðr saga has not been substantiated, see Napier, *Furnivall Miscellany* (1901), pp. 371 ff.; Schück, *Studier i nordisk litteratur- och religionshistoria*, i (1904), pp. 176 f.[2] The antiquity of the heroic lore embedded in *Beowulf* need not be insisted upon anew. — It may be added that Neckel fully vindicates Sigemund's dragon fight as in fact based on genuine old tradition, considering it even the prototype of various later dragon fights in old Germanic literature. Cf. *Angl.* l 238 f. See also von Sydow's folkloristic study, "Sigurds Strid med Fåvne," *Lunds Universitets Årsskrift*, N.F. Avd. 1, Bd. 14, No. 16 (1918). The Beowulfian version, Neckel thinks, goes back to an originally Frankish lay — historically connected with the Burgundian king Sigimund (cf. Heusler, *R.-L.* iv 443) — which had been carried over to Gautland and which inevitably suffered certain changes incident to the new localization.

878. **þāra þe gumena bearn gearwe ne wiston.** Though *ne wiston* admits of being construed with the genitive (see 681), it is probable that its use here is due mainly to the partitive idea suggested by *uncūþes fela*, 876. The *þāra þe* combination regularly agrees with the syntactical requirements of the governing clause, cf. Delbrück L 6.13.2.682 f.

879. **Fitela** is merely the follower of Sigemund. So the Norse Sinfjǫtli appears in the rôle of a subordinate, not an independent saga figure (Bugge L 4.84.200).

880. **þonne hē swulces hwæt secgan wolde.** The reference is to deeds done by Sigemund before Fitela joined him. For *swulces*, see Lang. § 8 n. 1.

885. **æfter dēaðdæge dōm unlȳtel.** ' Renown after death ? was the ideal hero's chief aim in life. See 1387 ff.; Intr. xlviii, lxii; *Angl.* xxxvi 173.

887. **hordes hyrde.** The hoard motive appears here properly connected with the dragon fight. In the *Nibelungenlied* the winning of the hoard is separated from Sigfrit's slaying of the dragon.

---

[1] *Perhaps* of a semi-historical nature, see Chadwick Or. 148 f. The tradition of Sigemund has commonly been held to be of Frankish provenience, though Bugge (L 4.112) argued for an East Gothic origin. Moorman (L 4.115) conjectures that Sigemund was the leader of a band of Burgundian (Wælsing) exiles that settled in Norfolk. Boer (*ZfdA.* xlvii 130 n.), like Chadwick, believes in Scandinavian sources.

[2] Certain interesting motives have been pointed out as being common to the ' Beowulf ' and the ' Nibelungen ' narrative, see note on 3051 ff. For some parallels between the ' Finnsburg ' and the ' Nibelungen ' story, see Introd. to *The Fight at Finnsburg*.

888. āna genēðde ... A single-handed fight is, of course, especially glorious. Cp. 431, 2541, 2345 ff. (Bēowulf); Saxo ii 39 (Frotho: ' solitarius,' see Par. § 7); *Nibel.* 89 (Sigfrit: ' aleine ān alle helfe '); Nennius, *Historia Britonum* § 56 (Arthur: ' ipse solus '); Plutarch, *Theseus* § 29 (μηδενὸς συμμάχου δεηθέντα).

890-92. According to Norse legend, Sigmundr — an ' Óðinn hero,' like Hermóðr — received a wondrous sword from the great god. See *Hyndl.* 2 (Par. § 4), *Vǫlsungasaga*, ch. 3 (a detailed account of Sigmund's obtaining the sword). — The dragon is, as it were, nailed on the wall, [*swurd*] *on wealle ætstōd;* a variation of a typical feature, see *A.* l 239 n. 1. — Note the end rime of 890[b]: 891[b].

895. selfes dōme; i.e., such treasures — and as many — as he desired. Cp. 2775 f.; 2147. — **gehlēod.** The spelling *eo* for *o* (i.e. *ō*) after *l* is occasionally met with (*Angl.* xxv 272; cf. *ZfdPh.* iv 215). Was it caused in this case by analogy with (Mercian) *hleadan?* Or was the scribe thinking of *gehēold?*

896[a]. bær on bearm scipes. Type D. See Deutschbein L 8.22. 32 ff.

897. wyrm hāt (' being hot,' i.e. ' by its own heat ') **gemealt.** (Cp. 3040 f.; 1605 ff., 1666 ff.; Intr. xxiii.) This motive — cp. *Seyfridslied* 10, 147 — has been enlarged upon (and modified) in the accounts of the dragon fight of Sigurðr-Sigfrit. Cf. L. Polak, *Untersuchungen über die Sigfridsagen* (Berlin Diss., 1910), pp. 47 f. — Note the *w*-alliteration in three successive lines. (Intr. lxx n. 3.)

898[a]. Sē wæs wreccena. Type C2, see *ESt.* xxxix 427. Holt.: wreccena (type A3).

901-915. This digression on **Heremōd**[1] is to be interpreted in conjunction with a similar one (occurring in Hrōðgār's famous harangue after the second combat), 1709-1722.[2] The main point of the story referred to in these two allusive passages is that Heremōd was a strong, valiant hero, pre-eminent among his fellows, giving promise of a brilliant career, but subsequently proved a bad ruler, cruel and stingy, and having become a burden to his people, ended miserably. A minor feature, which in the *Beowulf* itself remains obscure, is connected with certain events preceding his accession (907-13).

Müllenhoff looked upon Heremōd as a mere allegorical personification setting forth the dangers of *here-mōd*, i.e. ' warlike disposition.'[3] But later studies have shown him to be a definite figure in Danish

---

[1] Chief references: Müll. 50 f.; Bu. 37-45; Sievers L 4.33. Further: ten Brink L 4.7.536, Koegel L 4.8.167 f., Binz 168, Sarrazin, *Angl.* xix 392-7, Otto L 7.17.30 f., Chadwick Or. 149 f., Heusler, *R.-L.* ii 574-76, Herrmann, *Saxo* ii 65-67, Malone, Haml. 160 ff., 74 f., and L 4.92 e. 804 ff., Hoops 113 ff., Schneider L 4.13 a. ii 2.145 ff. For a list of earlier studies, see Joseph, *ZfdPh.* xxii 386 (L. 5.22).

[2] An indirect reference to the character of Heremōd has been detected in the praise of Bēowulf, 2177-83.

[3] Similarly ten Brink.

historical-legendary tradition.[1] Thus Saxo tells of Olo who was a wonderfully strong and gifted youth, but later showed himself a cruel and unrighteous king, so that twelve generals (' duces '), moved by the distress of their country, plotted against his life and induced Starcatherus to kill the king while alone at the bath (viii 265). This Olo as well as the figure of Olavus, on whom the three goddesses of fate bestowed ' beauty and favor in the eyes of men,' ' the virtue of generosity,' but also ' the vice of niggardliness ' (Saxo vi 181), is identical with the Danish king Áli inn frøkni,[2] who after a long, vigorous reign was killed by Starkaðr (*Ynglingasaga*, ch. 25 (29); *Skjǫldungasaga*, ch. 9). In view of the fact, however, that according to the *Nornagestsþáttr* (cir. 1300 A.D.) and the *Egils Saga ok Ásmundar* (14th century) it is King Armóðr that was slain by Starkaðr while bathing, there is good reason to believe (with Bugge) that the name Heremōd applied to this saga figure in *Beowulf* goes back to true old Danish legend, the names Heremōd (ON. Hermóðr) and Armóðr (Ár-?) being insignificant variations.

Another version of the story (transferred to **Lotherus**), which is apt to throw light on the hidden meaning of ll. 907–13, occurs in Saxo i 11. (A brief mention in the *Annales Ryenses*, Par. §8.5.) Of the two sons of Dan — the fabulous eponymous ancestor of the Danish kings — ' Humblus[3] was elected king at his father's death; but [later on] by the malice of ensuing fate . . . . he was taken by Lotherus in war, and bought his life by yielding up his crown . . . . . But Lotherus played the king as insupportably as he had played the soldier, inaugurating his reign straightway with arrogance and crime; for he counted it uprightness to strip all the most eminent of life or goods, and to clear his country of its loyal citizens, thinking all his equals in birth his rivals for the crown. He was soon chastised for his wickedness; for he met his end in an insurrection of his country; which had once bestowed on him his kingdom, and now bereft him of his life.' Putting together the veiled allusion of the last clause (' which had once bestowed on him his kingdom ') and *Beow.* 907 ff., Sievers concluded that Lotherus gained the throne through the support of an active minority of the people which had been from the beginning in favor of his succession and regretted (*ǣrran mǣlum* 907) the turn Danish affairs had taken under the rule of his [weaker] brother.

A faint and confused echo of this narrative has been discovered by Sarrazin (*Angl.* xix 392 ff.) in the *Scondia illustrata* of the Swedish chronicler Johannes Messenius (beginning of the 17th century). ' Lo-

---

[1] A slight similarity is found in the case of the Danish king Harald Hildetan, who became ' ob senectam severitatemque civibus . . onustus ' and devised means for an honorable death (Saxo vii 255). A Vergilian parallel is the cruel tyrant Mezentius, who was driven out of the land by the ' fessi cives,' *Æn.* viii 481 ff.

[2] Cp. *Hyndl.* 14 (Par. § 4).

[3] Translation by Elton.

therus igitur Danorum rex ' — we are informed — ' ope suorum propter nimiam destitutus tyrannidem, superatusque in Jutiam profugit . . . . .' He returns from this exile, slays the rival king Balderus[1] and temporarily regains possession of his kingdom, but loses his life in a war of revenge instigated by Othinus.

Sievers's subtle interpretation of Saxo's wording (i 11: Lotherus, Humblus) has the merit of clearing up the otherwise dark allusion of ll. 907 ff. It has naturally been called in question; indeed, the connection between the Beowulfian account and Saxo's story has been altogether denied. It has been pointed out that the names Lotherus and Humblus have a counterpart in Hlǫðr and Humli of the *Hervararsaga*. But what is told of these and of Angantýr (*Wids*. 116: Hlīþe, Incgenþēow) does not add much light to our understanding of Saxo's all too cursory statement. (Cf. Malone, *ll. cc*.)

That the Ags. poet recognized Heremōd as a Danish king, is seen from *ēþel Scyldinga* 913 and *Ār-Scyldingum* 1710 (*Scyldingas* being used in the wider sense of ' Danes,' without regard to the Scyld dynasty). Moreover, both in Ags. and Norse genealogies (Par. §§ 1.1 & 2, 5, 8.1, cp. 1.4), Heremōd figures as the father, i.e. predecessor of Scyld(wa) (Skjǫldr), just as Saxo (i 11) represents Scioldus as Lotherus' son and follower on the Danish throne. More precisely, he belonged to an earlier line of kings,[2] and it was after his fall that the Danes endured distress — *aldorlēase* 15, until the God-sent Scyld inaugurated a new dynasty.

The coupling of Heremōd and Sigemund as heroes of greatest renown springs from a Scandinavian tradition (which may have arisen even before Heremōd was given a place among the Danish kings). This is proved by *Hyndluljóð* 2 (Par. § 4) and, indirectly, by a comparison of *Hákonarmál*, l. 38[3] with *Eiríksmál*, l. 16[4] (Chadwick, *The Cult of Othin* (1899), p. 51).

In contrast with the Sigemund episode, which is introduced as a pure heroic tale, our author has infused into the Heremōd story a strong spirit of Christian moralization (cf. *Angl*. xxxv 475, 479 f.), adding besides a touch of sentimental softness (904 f., 907, 909). In both of the passages Heremōd is made to serve as a foil to the exemplary Bēowulf.

901. siððan Heremōdes hild sweðrode. For the punctuation, see *MPh*. iii 457. Sigemund's glory survived that of Heremōd (who in

---

[1] The fact that in *Gylfaginning* (Prose Edda), ch. 48, Hermóðr — the same one as the 'Óðinn hero' of *Hyndluljóð* — appears as (Óðin's son and) Baldr's brother, furnishes additional proof of the identity of Lother and Heremōd.

[2] Was *Ecgwela* (1710) supposed to be the founder of this line? Sarrazin (*Angl.* xix 396) conjectured Heremōd to be the leader of the Heruli who were expelled by the Danes. Möller (100 ff.) thought him identical with Finn. Koegel and Binz regarded him as an Anglian hero.

[3] See *Corp. Poet. Bor.* i 264. (Hermóðr and Bragi are bidden by Óðinn to welcome King Hákon.)

[4] See above, p. 159, n. 3.

Hyndluljóð is mentioned before Sigmund). It was unrivaled after Heremōd's decline, — *sweðrode* refers either to his advancing years or (probably) to his lamentable death. (Cp. *Grettissaga*, ch. 58: ' Grettir was the strongest man ever known in the land, since Ormr Stórólfsson and Þórálfr Skólmsson left off their trials of strength.' Similarly two heroes, Offa and Alewīh, are set against one another in *Wids.* 35 ff., see the quotation in note on 1931–62.)

A gratuitous transposition of ll. 901–915 (861, 901–915, 862–900, 916 ff.) was proposed by Joseph (L 5.22). (Cf. ten Brink 60.)

902ᵇ–4ᵃ. Hē mid Ēotenum wearð etc. Heremōd, forced to flee the country (cp. 1714), sought refuge in the land of the *Ēotan* (' Jutes,' see the quotation from Messenius, p. 163 f.), the enemies of the Danes (cf. Introd. to *The Fight at Finnsburg*), exactly as the rebellious Swedish princes Ēanmund and Ēadgils were sheltered by the hereditary foes of their country, the Geats (Intr. xl). There he was slain (as Ēanmund was in Geatland). His death was brought about by treachery (*forlācen* 903), but the circumstances are unknown. (Bugge, who reads *mid eotenum*, points to the murder of Áli (Olo, Armóðr) by Starkaðr, who was sometimes regarded as a *jǫtunn*.) — **on fēonda geweald . . . . forsended** possibly means: ' he was sent to hell,' cp. 808; 1721 f. — Kock (*Angl.* xlv 117) takes ll. 902–04 to mean that Heremōd was treacherously ' sent to the Jutes '; he would place a comma after *wearð*, regarding *mid Ēotenum* and *on fēonda geweald* as parallel terms. This stylistic explanation will be approved by those who are willing to accept Neckel's interpretation (L 4.88 b.55 ff.) of the Heremōd allusion in regard to *mid eotenum* (*sic*) and *sīð* 908, cp. 1714 f. The *Beowulf* passages, according to Neckel, seem to reflect the story of Heremōd's riding to hell (in order to rescue his brother Balder). However, such vague hints leave the subject very much in the air. — In any case, we realize that the author of the OE. epic has very successfully obscured his allusions.

904ᵇ–5ᵃ. Hine sorhwylmas/lemede tō lange. Heremōd was unhappy during the greater part of his life (*tō lange*); first because excluded from the throne and exiled, later because hated by his own people and put to death. The singular of the verb may be explained syntactically, *sorhwylmas* being felt to be equal to *sorh*. Cf. Lang. §§ 25.6, 19.3; also Dietrich, *ZfdA.* x 332 f., xi 444 ff. Only sporadically do we find the ending *-on* of the pret. ind. plur. of wk. verbs weakened to *-e;* cf. E. M. Brown, *The Lang. of the Rushw. Gloss to Matthew*, ii (1892), § 38; O. Eger, *Dialekt. in den Flexionsverhältnissen der ags. Bedaübersetzung* (Leipzig Diss., 1910), § 13.

908. sīð, either ' lot,' ' fate ' or ' journey,' referring to Heremōd's going into exile when his brother (Humblus in Saxo) was elected king. Hoops 117 considers it an allusion to Heremōd's (Lotherus') war against his brother by which he gained the throne.

909. sē þe him bealwa tō bōte gelȳfde. Connect *tō* with *him*. Similarly 1272. Cp. 627 f. (608).

910 f. þæt þæt ðēodnes bearn geþēon scolde etc. In accordance with the rule: 'no article before qualifying nounal genitive and noun,' Barnouw (p. 22) would strike out the second *þæt*, which may very well be a late scribe's addition (cf. Schücking L 5.48.2). But *ðēodnes bearn* (cp. 888) was perhaps felt to be a compound, see 2059[a] and Varr. (Of course, Heremōd is meant, not his son.) — With *geþēon scolde* cp. *geþēoh tela* 1218. — **fæderæþelu,** 'ancestral (nobility, or) rank.' Cp. *Ex.* 338 f.: *frumbearnes riht . . . ēad and æðelo.*

913-15. Hē, i.e. Bēowulf; **915 hine,** i.e. Heremōd. — **eallum . . . manna cynne** (1057 f.: *eallum . . . gumena cynnes*) recalls the *al irmindeot* of *Hildebr.* 13 (see Braune, *Beitr.* xxi 1 ff.; French *tout le monde* 'everybody'). — **frēondum gefægra.** Bēowulf was universallly liked (cp. the ON. adj. *vinsæll*). *gefægra* is best explained as the compar. of **gefæg* (cp. OHG. *gifag(o)* 'content,' MHG. *gevage* 'satisfied,' 'acceptable'; so Grein[2], *Corrigendum;* Siev., *ZfdPh.* xxi 356; *Angl.* xxviii 440 f.), — though it would not be impossible to derive a compar. *gefāgra* from **gefāge* (see *gefēon*), 'causing joy' (Bu. 42), or 'cheerful,' 'genial' (B.-T. Suppl.), 'gracious' (cp. meanings of *glæd*). — **hine fyren onwōd.** Sin entered Heremōd's heart (*Angl.* xxxv 128).

917 f. Ðā wæs morgenlēoht/scofen ond scynded; i.e., morning wore on (see 837). A similar use of *scūfan* is found *Gen.* 136: *Metod æfter scēaf/scīrum scīman . . . æfen ærest.* (*ESt.* xlii 326.)

922. getrume micle. 924. mægþa hōse. King and queen appear with a train of attendants. A common epic trait. Cf. Cook, *JEGPh.* v 155; *Arch.* cxxvi 45.

925-990. Speech-making by Hrōðgār and Bēowulf.

926. stōd on stapole. The interpretation, 'stood by the (central) pillar' (Heyne[1], see L 9.4.1.48), has been largely discarded, since Hrōðgār is supposed to stand outside the hall, and such a use of *on* would be, at least, out of the ordinary. *stapol* more likely denotes "the steps leading up to the hall, or the landing at the top of the flight" (Miller, *Angl.* xii 398 f.) or, possibly, "an erection in the open air, standing in the area in front of the hall" (Earle, *Hand-Book to Land-Charters* [1888], p. 467, see also his note on *Beow.* 926; Middendorff, *AE. Flurnamenbuch* [1902], pp. 123 f.). Cf. NED.: *staple,* sb.[1] [Child *MLN.* viii 252 f., referring to Weinhold (L 9.32.239): 'pillar,' i.e. "the largest of the double row of pillars (in the Scandinavian hall) which came out above the house"; cf. Falk, *R.-L.* i 382. S. O. Addy, *Notes and Queries,* May 21, 1927, pp. 363-65: "There was an upper chamber annexed to Hrothgar's hall, that chamber having a separate entrance from without. The entrance was approached by a *stapol,* or flight of steps."]

932 f. mē goes with **wēnde.**

936. wēa wīdscofen. A loosely joined elliptic clause; see 1343, 2035. For the general thought of the passage, cp. 170 f.

942 ff. The praise of the hero's mother is possibly a biblical reminis-

NOTES

cence (Luke xi 27, etc.), cf. *Angl.* xxviii 441 f., xxxv 468; see also Intr. xvii n. 3. — 943. **ðone magan**, ' such a son '; cp. 1758. — 944. **æfter gumcynnum** serves the same purpose as *mid yldum*, 77.

946 ff. Nū ic, Bēowulf, þec etc. See 1175 f., 1479. The relationship entered into by Hrōðgār and Bēowulf does not signify adoption in the strict legal sense, but implies fatherly friendship and devoted helpfulness respectively, suggesting at any rate the bonds of loyal retainership (see Antiq. § 2). Cf. Chadwick H. A. 374; v. Amira L 9.10.1 § 60. [Scherer L 5.5.480 ff.; Müller L 9.28.19 f.; Rietschel, *R.-L.* i 38 f.]

947ᵃ. The original reading, most likely, was **secga betsta**. See 1759ᵃ, 1871ᵇ. T.C. § 22. (Cp. *Hel.* 3102, 5047.)

958. Wē. Bēowulf generously includes his men. See 431, 1652, 1987.

962. (fēond) on frætewum, ' in his trappings,' or ' in full gear '; a rather forced expression as applied to a fighter who uses only his own physical equipment. Cf. Aant. 17. [Tr.¹ 176.]

964. on wælbedde wrīþan. An allusion to the fetters of death, cp. 3045, 2901, 1007. (*Angl.* xxxv 465.) Bēowulf did not intend to catch Grendel alive.

966. būtan his līc swice seems to refer to the possibility of Grendel's escaping (see 967 ff.). Or does it involve a recollection of the curious ' disappearing trick ' of certain folk-tales pointed out by Panzer (L 4.61.89, 274 ff.)? Cf. P. G. Thomas, *MLR.* xxii 70.

968. nō ic him þæs georne ætfealh. 1508. *nō hē þæs* (MS. *þæm*) *mōdig wæs.* **2423 f.** *nō þon lange wæs/feorh æþelinges flæsce bewunden.* In these three clauses Kock (*Angl.* xliii 304, xlvi 83 f.) would recognize a Germanic idiom as shown in his translation: ' however eagerly I clung to him '; ' no matter how brave he was '; ' however long his life had been bound in flesh.' This is an interesting observation requiring, however, some qualification as to details. See *Angl.* l 197, also xlix 368 (on *Gen.* (*B*) 832). The first instance is perfectly clear and shows how such an idiom could arise: ' [I pressed him hard, but] I did not press him so hard [that he had to stay in my power].' And see note on 2423ᵇ.

983. ofer hēanne hrōf hand scēawedon. They looked over the high roof, i.e. they ' looked up to ' or ' in the direction of the high roof, and beheld the hand.' (*MPh.* iii 256.)

984ᵇ–87ᵃ. The treatment of this passage has not yet reached the stage of finality. Even the commonly accepted form of 984ᵇ, **foran ǣghwylc wæs** (advocated by Sievers, ix 138, R. 232, in place of *foran ǣghwylc* [with *wæs* added to the following l.] as printed by Grein, Heyne, et al.), has been assailed on syntactical grounds by Ries (L 6.12.2.378 f.), who suggests, as alternatives, *wæs foran ǣghwylc* or *foran wæs ǣghwylc.* The retention of the MS. reading *steda nægla gehwylc* 985ᵃ, ' each of the places of the nails ' (Schücking, Chambers), has recently been urged again (Clarke, *MLR.* xxix 320: ' the finger-tips '). On the other hand, *gehwylc* might be a thoughtless repetition like *hilde* of 986. Regarding **handsporu** 986, it seems that *spora*, elsewhere a wk. masc., has passed over into the fem. class (cf. Siev. § 278 n. 1). The form **egl** of the MS. has been taken by many scholars (e.g., Kemble, Grein, Heyne, Sedgefield, Chambers) as a noun, 'spike,' 'talon' (Kemble: 'molestia'), but the only substantiated meanings of *egl*, *egle* (the latter being the usual form) are 'awn' ('ail'), 'beard of barley' (B.-T. Suppl.), 'mote' (*Luke* 6.41 f.). As to *eglu*, see T.C. § 25. [Cf. also Aant. 17; Tr.[1] 176–8; *Arch.* cxv 179.]

988. him refers to Grendel. **heardra**; the adj. (gen. plur.) used absolutely, cf. Lang. § 25.2.

989[b]. þæt, conjunction, '(in such a way) that.'

991–1250. Royal entertainment in Heorot.

991 f. Ðā wæs hāten ... Heort ... gefrætwod. The inf. *wesan* is to be understood in connection with *gefrætwod*, cf. Aant. 18. The construction of the passive of *hātan* with a passive inf. looks like a Latinism, see *Arch.* cxxvi 355. [Chambers places a comma after *hreþe*. He is followed by J. F. Royster, who cites the sentence as an example of 'mixed construction,'— the idea of the 'ordering' or 'causing' giving way to that of the 'completion' of action, see *JEGPh.* xvii 89 n. 28.] — 992[b]. **fela þǣra wæs.** Type D4.

994 f. The hanging of the walls with tapestries is in conformity with Scand. and Ags. (also German) custom. See Montelius 150; Kålund and Guðmundsson, *P. Grdr.*[2] iii 432, 477; *Guþrúnarkv.* ii 15; Tupper's *Riddles*, p. 194; *Hel.* 4544 f.; Müller L 9.28.65; Falk, *Altwestnord. Kleiderkunde*, p. 201; Ang. F. lxi 52 ff. A close parallel to this particular instance is found *Æneid* i 637 ff. (*Arch.* cxxvi 342.)

996[b]. þāra þe on swylc starað. See 1485[b], 2796[b], 1654[b].

1002[b]–3[a]. Nō þæt ȳðe byð/tō beflēonne. The import of the vague *þæt* is fully cleared up by the context: it is impossible to escape death (fate). A proverbial saying well known in ON. literature; e.g., Saxo viii 295: 'fatis arduum obstare.' Cp. *Iliad* vi 488: μοῖραν δ' οὔτινά φημι πεφυγμένον ἔμμεναι ἀνδρῶν. (*Arch.* cxv 179 n.)

1003[b]. fremme sē þe wille, 'do (or, try) it who will.' (Imperfective function of *fremman*.) A kind of formula; see 2766[b], 1394[b]; note on 603[b].

1004–6. The parallel genitives **sāwlberendra, niþða bearna, grundbūendra** depend on **gearwe stōwe** (cp. *Hel.* 4453); **nȳde genȳdde ... stōwe** 'the place forced (upon him) by necessity' (cp. *Chr.* [i] 68 f.). No *gehwylc* or *ǣghwylc* need be inserted, since a pronominal subject is easily supplied from the preceding lines (cp. 1290 f.). Cf. Bu. 368 f.; *MPh.* iii 241, 457; *Angl.* xxxv 466. [Rie. Zs. 391; Tr.[1] 179; Sed., note.] — The MS. reading *gesacan* is strange as to meter and sense. Brett's rendering (*MLR.* xiv 7): "gain in spite of his striving" is a desperate guess; cf. also B.-T.

1008. swefeþ æfter symle; i.e., sleeps after the feast of life. See 128, 119; Earle's note; Cook, *MLN.* ix 237 f. (classical and modern parallels). — The dat. of *symbel* and the adv. *sym(b)le* have sometimes been confused.

1011 f. **Ne gefrægen ic þā mǣgþe māran weorode ... sēl gebǣran.**
A combination of two types, viz. a) *ne hȳrde ic cȳmlīcor cēol gegyrwan* 38 (1027, 1197, 1842); b) *ðā ic wīde gefrægn weorc gebannan* 74 (2484, 2694, 2752, 2773). Accordingly, *þā* is adverb. — *sēl gebǣran;* i.e., they behaved properly, as the occasion required, cp. *Finnsb.* 38. The reference here is to the etiquette (cp. *fægere* 1014) or to the splendid appearance of the retainers on the festive occasion (cp. *Nibel.* 593: *swie wol man dā gebārte*).

1013 ff. A much discussed passage. Cf. Varr.; Kock[5] 75 ff.; Hoops 127 f. The **þāra** of 1015[b] is held to refer to 1013–14[a]. According to an alternative interpretation, a comma would be placed after *gefǣgon* 1014, a semicolon after *manig* 1015, and *þāra* would be changed to *wǣran.* Cf. *A.* xxviii 442, l 198. Of course, it is an advantage to be able to dispense with an emendation.

1018 f. nalles fācenstafas / Þēod-Scyldingas þenden fremedon. Unquestionably an allusion to Hrōðulf's treachery in later times. Intr. xxxii.

1022. hildecumbor. As *hilt* is normally a st. neut. i. (occasionally a fem. or masc.), a compound *hiltecumbor* (MS.) cannot well be admitted. (Siev. xxxvi 420.) Hence, *hiltcumbor*, meaning perhaps a banner fastened to a staff with a sort of handle at its lower end (cp. the designation *hæftmēce*, 1457), was tentatively put in its place (Ed.[1]). The change to *hilde-* provides a more plausible meaning, although it is strange that the very common *hilde-* should have been thus misspelt.

1023 f. manige gesāwon practically serves the same purpose as a *gefrægn-* formula of transition (*MPh.* iii 244), enlivening the plain enumeration and signalizing the value of the fourth present. This consideration precludes the punctuation mark (colon, semicolon, comma) placed after *sweord* by several edd. (thus Holthausen, Schücking, Sedgefield). Cf. Aant. 18.

1024[b]–25[a]. Bēowulf geþah / ful on flette. Bēowulf empties the cup and expresses his thanks, no doubt in obedience to well-regulated courtly custom. See 628.

1025[b]–26. See 1048, 1901 f., 2995 f. A form *scotenum*, though not impossible in the later language (Siev. § 277 n. 1), would be objectionable on metrical grounds. Besides, no instance of *scota* seems to be recorded. (*gescota*, Wr.-Wü., *Ags. & OE. Vocab.* i 15.1, 207.7.)

1028. gummanna fela. Litotes; cf. *MPh.* iii 248.

1031. The exact nature of a **wala**, which seems to be an ornamental as well as useful part of the helmet, is not known. Stjerna (2 f.) guessed that " there was an inner head-covering of cloth, leather or the like ... and that this was fastened to an outer convex plate " (*wala*). Cf. Rie. Zs. 392–4; Bu. 369; Falk L 9.44.158.

1032. fēla lāf, ' that which is left after the files have done their work.' A notable kenning for ' sword,' see Gloss.: *lāf.* A form *fēl* (by the side of *fēol, fīl*) may well have existed (Bülb. § 199; see Lang. § 10.7). But it is equally possible that an earlier MS. had *feola* (=*fēola*), which by a thoughtless scribe was taken for *feola* 'much' and normalized to *fela*. This might also account for the plur. *meahton*. — With 1032 ff. cp. 1453 f.

1036. on flet teon. The horses are led directly into the hall. A custom frequently mentioned in ballads and romances; see Gummere G. O. 105, Earle's note.

1045. hēt hine wēl brūcan. A formula; see 1216, 2162, 2812. Cf. Meyer L 7.12.389.

1053 ff. Hrōðgār, who feels responsible for the safety of his guests, compounds for the loss of a man by the payment of *wergild*.

1056–62. God and mōd, 1056 f. constitute the dual subject; see note on 572 f. The apparent subordination of fate to God (Intr. xlix) does not justify us in recognizing in this passage the influence of Boethius' *Consolation of Philosophy* (as Earle did, see his note; H. F. Stewart, *Boethius, an Essay* [1891], pp. 163 ff.). Nor do we need to follow the earlier dissecting critics who condemned this passage as an interpolation. It is merely one of those interspersed reflections in which the author of the poem delighted. It enjoins rational trust in the governance of the Almighty and readiness to accept whatever may be in store for us, be it good or evil. (Cf. *Angl.* xxxv 118.) With 1060–62 cp. *Gnom. Cott.* 11 f.: *gomol [bið] snoterost,/fyrngēarum frōd, sē þe ǣr feala gebīdeð.* [The adversative meaning 'yet' proposed, though "very tentatively," for *Forþan* 1059 (M. Daunt, *MLR.* xiii 478) does not improve the context.]

1064. fore Healfdenes hildewīsan, 'in the presence of Healfdene's battle-leader,' i.e. of Hrōðgār. We may assume that the title appertaining to Hrōðgār during his father's reign is here retained, in violation of chronology. For the use of *fore*, see 1215, *Wids.* 55, 104. Cf. *Angl.* xxviii 449 n. 3. [Cf. Aant. 18 ("louter onzin"); ten Brink 68; Tr.[1] 183: *hildewīsan* = -*wīsum*, dat. plur. (quite possible). Cp. *Atlakv.* 14: *Buðla greppar* (Bugge).]

1069–1159. The Finn Episode. See **Introduction to The Fight at Finnsburg** and **Finnsburg Bibliography** (LF.).

1066–70. Scholars are not at all agreed on the punctuation and construction of these lines. A detailed survey of the various modes of interpretation has been offered by Green (LF. 4.27). See also Varr.; Williams LF. 4.36.1.10 ff.; Malone, *JEGPh.* xxv 157 f.; Hoops 134; Sedgefield LF. 4.33.

The present edition adopts the reading of Schücking (cf. *ESt.* xxxix 106, lv 92 ff.) and Holthausen, who make the Episode (direct statement) begin at 1071, and who — virtually returning to the practice of the earliest edd. — place a comma after *begeat*, thus considering 1069–70 the continuation of the subordinate clause introduced by *ðā* 1068. It presupposes the rendering of *fǣr* by 'disaster,' 'calamity' rather than 'sudden attack.' 1068 [be] **Finnes eaferum, ðā hīe se fǣr begeat** refers, by a characteristic anticipation, to the final triumph of the Danes over their enemies (see 1146 f.: *Swylce . . . Finn eft begeat/sweordbealo*, 1151 ff.), 1069 f. **hæleð Healf-Dena, Hnæf . . . feallan scolde**, to an earlier phase of the conflict. — **healgamen** 1066, ' entertainment,' hence ' entertaining tale '; with **ðonne** 1066 cp. 880. **gid oft wrecen** 1065[b], ' many a song was recited ' (cf. Siev. xxix 571; note on 794[b]–5); whereupon a definite specimen of the scop's repertory is exhibited in summary and paraphrase. It may seem that the author passes very abruptly to the new theme, leaving unexpressed the thought: ' and thus he sang.' However, this difficulty vanishes, if the phrase of 1065[b] is understood in a more general sense: ' there was plenty of entertainment by the minstrel ' (or if *gid* is interpreted as part or ' fit ' of a lay). The insertion of *be* in 1068: [*be*] *Finnes eaferum*, ' about Finn's men ' or ' about Finn and his men ' (cp. *Hrēðlingas* 2960, *eaforum Ecgwelan* 1710; *Sat.* 63 (?); Aant. 26) is on the whole more natural than the change to *eaferan* (a second object of *mǣnan*), though the latter would be quite possible stylistically (*Angl.* xxviii 443).

Dispensing with an emendation in 1068, Ettmüller, Grein, and others mark the beginning of the Episode at *Finnes eaferum*. Moreover, Grein, Bugge (29), Green construe *hæleð* as acc. plur. (parallel with *hīe*), thus arriving at the rendering: ' By Finn's men — when onset befell them, the heroes of the Half-Danes — Hnæf was fated to fall.' See Green, *l.c.*, also L 6.8.5; cf. Kock[2] 109, Notat. Norr. § 1113. This must be admitted to be an acceptable interpretation, provided it can be justified on syntactical and stylistic grounds. However, it is still a question whether *feallan* could be construed with a dative of personal agency, especially as this intrans. verb is elsewhere used absolutely (or with an expression denoting instrumentality in a more indirect way, see 2834 f., cp. 2902, *Mald.* 71). Besides, the opening of the sentence by such heavy, complex phraseology (1068–69[a]) is decidedly harsh, and the use of the so-called proleptic pronoun *hīe* (cf. *MPh.* iii 255; Intr. lxv) in this context is felt to be unnatural. [A ' comitative dative,' *Finnes eaferum*, ' with Finn's sons(s),' is assumed by Williams 19 ff., Malone, *A.* lvii 313 ff.]

1071 f. Nē hūru Hildeburh etc. Litotes. 1071[a]: Type B1, ××× ́ | × ́.

1074[a]. **bearnum ond brōðrum.** Generic plural: ' son and brother '; see 565. Möller (59) thought the combination an archaic idiom derived from the (elliptic) ' dvandva dual ' (cf. note on 2002); but see Osthoff, *IF.* xx 204 f.

1074[b]. **hīe on gebyrd hruron.** Cp. 2570. A variant, but hardly convincing rendering of *on gebyrd* is ' in succession,' ' one after another ' (Aant. 18; cf. B.-T. Suppl.).

1077. syþðan morgen cōm. This may or may not mean the first morning after the night attack; see *Finnsb.* 41.

1082–85[a]. The purport of these lines as commonly understood is: ' he could be successful neither in the offensive nor in the defensive.'

gefeohtan does not mean here (as might be expected): 'obtain by fighting'; wīg serves as 'cognate accus.' (Cf. Lorz 50; *JEGPh*. xiv 548.) As to forþringan, the meaning 'rescue' generally assigned to it has been questioned — it would certainly fit *oðþringan* — ; the only prose instance of the verb, *Ben. R.* (ed. Schröer, in Gr.-Wü., *Bibl. d. ags. Prosa* iii) 115.7 (cp. *Ormulum* 6169), would favor the sense 'displace.' Carleton Brown (*MLN*. xxxiv 181 ff.) suggests the change of ðegne to *ðegna;* thus the object of *forþringan* ('crush') would be 'the remnant of the thanes of the prince,' *wēalāfe* referring in 1084 as well as in 1098 to the Danish party. — The stress laid by the poet on the weakening of the Frisians (cp. 1080 f.) attests his desire to exalt the valor and success of the Danes. (Cf. Lawrence, *Publ. MLAss*. xxx 403.) [Moore, *JEGPh*. xviii 208 f., like Brown, understands *forþringan* as 'put down,' but takes *þēodnes ðegne* as variation of *Hengeste* and considers 1084 semi-parenthetic.] Williams 41 ff., 166 ff. concludes that *forþringan* is synonymous with *opþringan* 'force away (from one)'; Malone, *JEGPh*. xxv 115: 'expel' (i.e., from the hall). Hoops St. 57 f.: 'expel by fight [from the hall] the poor remnant [of the Danes],' *ðegne* to be taken as 'dat. of interest.' [Malone, *Eng. Studies* xv 150: 'dat. of accompaniment.'] Still, it seems strange that the Frisians should not have resorted to the customary device of firing the hall. — After all, it is not an extravagant assumption that *forþringan* — like *forstandan* — , construed with accus. and dat. (instr.), carries the sense of 'rescue,' 'defend,' 'protect.' Cp. 2954 f. (*Met. Bt.* 1.22: *ne meahte þā sēo wēalāf wīge forstandan/Gotan mid gūðe . . . gestrīon.*)

1085[b]. hig, i.e. the Frisians; so hīe, 1086[a]. — A Vergilian parallel of the peace treaty (*Æn*. xii 190 ff.): Imelmann LF. 4.30.376 f.; *Beibl.* xliii 230.

1086-88. þæt hīe him ōðer flet eal gerȳmdon,/healle ond hēahsetl. If we insist at all on the force of *eal* (taken as adverb), we might argue that this clause of the treaty, 'that the Frisians should make room for the Danes "completely" in another hall,' qualified by the provision granting equal rights to Danes and 'Jutes,' *þæt hīe* [the Danes] *healfre geweald/wið Ēotena bearn āgan mōston*, practically implies: 'making room for all the Danes'; 'another hall' would be a different one from that wrecked in the fight. A rationalizing commentator could add that, owing to the equally great loss of 'man power' on both sides, there was sufficient room for the two parties (both of which were reduced to a *wēalāf*). — Another exegetical possibility has been opened up by Heusler, *Anz.fdA*. xli 32. (Cf. Malone, *JEGPh*. xxv 116; Hoops St. 59 f.) He takes *ōðer* in the sense of 'one of two' (and *eal* as acc. sing. neut.), and *healle* as gen. sing.: 'that they should yield (clear) to them one of the 'bench-floors' of the hall together with the high-seat (belonging thereto).' However, *healle ond hēahsetl* has all the appearance of being parallel to *flet*. (Cf. also Williams, *MLR*. xxii 310 ff.) Also the sense attributed to OE. *flet* is not certain, although its possibility should be granted. In case (ōðer) flet was really meant to refer to one of the long bench-rows (cp. bencþelu) — it being understood that there are two — , the following nouns might have been employed rather loosely by way of variation (healle implying 'hall space'). At any rate, whether another hall was meant or not, it is shared by the two parties. (Cp., e.g., Vǫlsungasaga, ch. 11: skipa báþir konungar eina hǫll.)

1097. unflitme is unexplained. It may be connected with flītan 'contend,' cp. unbefliten 'uncontested'; elne unflitme: 'with undisputed zeal.' It has been held that the instr. elne has the force of an intensive adverb, 'much,' 'very,' (and that unflitme is an adv. form), which is but adding another guess. Kock[2] 109 proposes elne, unflitme: "strongly and indisputably." No light is obtained from the equally obscure unhlitme 1129. [Grienb. 748 would translate 'firmly' or 'inviolably,' deriving unflitme from flēotan 'float.']

1098. weotena dōme. A noteworthy allusion to the authority of the king's advisory council. Cp. Jul. 98: ofer witena dōm. King Ælfred undertook the codification of the laws ' mid mīnra witena geðeahte,' Ælfr. Laws, Introd. 49.9. Cf. F. Purlitz, König u. Witenagemot bei den Angelsachsen, Leipzig Diss., 1892; F. Liebermann, The National Assembly in the Anglo-Saxon Period, Halle a.S., 1913.

1099ᵇ-1101. Which of the two parties is meant? According to Williams 65 f., Malone, JEGPh. xxv 158, 163, Hoops St. 60, the reference is to the Frisians. If the Danes are meant, þæt 1099 denotes 'upon condition that,' and þonne 1104, ' on the other hand ' (A. xxviii 444). The use of gemǣnden seems to point to the Danes; the meaning ' complain ' is supported by mǣndon 1149, ǣtwiton 1150.

1102. ðēah hīe hira bēaggyfan banan folgedon. Whether Finn himself slew Hnæf we do not know; see note on 1968. — Making peace with the slayers of one's lord was entirely contrary to the Germanic code of honor. Cp. OE. Chron. A.D. 755 (' Cynewulf and Cyneheard '): Ond þā cuǣdon hīe þæt him nǣnig mǣg lēofra nǣre þonne hiera hlāford, ond hīe nǣfre his banan folgian noldon.

1106ᵇ remains problematical. The reading sēðan (JEGPh. viii 255, cf. Lang. § 24, p. lxxxix, n. 5) would mean 'declare the truth,' 'settle'; cp. scȳran 1939; Antiq. § 6. Kock[2] 109 argues for the existence of a wk. verb syððan (rel. to sēoðan), 'atone,' 'clear.' See also Varr.; Moore, Kl. Misc. 208 ff.; ESt. lxvii 402.

1107-8ᵃ. Ād (MS. að) **wæs geæfned, ond icge gold/āhæfen of horde.** Why is gold fetched from the hoard? Presumably the reference is to precious objects to be placed on the funeral pile — cp. 1111 f., 3138 ff., perhaps 3134 f.; 3163 ff.; 36 ff.; Par. § 7: Saxo viii 264 — , which points to ād as the proper reading; see also 1110: Æt þǣm āde. (If āð were meant, we should expect the plural, cp. 1097.) For (wæs) geæfned, see 3105 f. Cf. A. l 230 f. [Lawrence, Publ. MLAss. xxx 406 suggests that Finn intended to reward his warriors with presents of gold. — The payment of wergild seems out of the question.] — **icge** is entirely obscure;

see Varr., B.-T; Brett, *MLR.* xiv 2; Zachrisson, *Studia Neophilologica* i 75. One of many possibilities is to explain it as a corruption of the adj. *ǣce* found once in the runic inscription of the Isle of Wight sword, which perhaps means 'one's own' (Hempl, *Publ. MLAss.* xviii 95 ff.); *ǣce gold* = 'aurum domesticum'; *JEGPh.* viii 256. [Du Bois, *ESt.* lxix 321 ff.: a curiously daring speculation on *icge* and *incge* 2577.]

1109ᵃ. betst beadorinca, i.e. Hnæf. — **1109ᵇ. wæs on bǣl gearu,** 'was ready to be placed on the funeral pile.'

1116. bānfatu bærnan, ond on bǣl dôn. The same hysteron proteron in 2126. Evidently the purpose, or the result, of the action was uppermost in the author's mind.

1117ᵇ-18. Ides gnornode,/geōmrode giddum. The song of lament by Hildeburh is in keeping with primitive custom. See 3150 ff., 2446 f. Cf. Gummere L 4.121.1.222; Schücking L 4.126.1.7 ff. (The reading *gūðhring* or the interpretation of *-rinc* as *-hring* (so Holthausen (?); cp. *ǣtspranc* 1121), 'loud lamentation,' would add the wailing of a chorus as a kind of refrain; cp. *Iliad* xxiv 719 ff.) **Gūðrinc āstāh;** i.e., the warrior was placed on the funeral pile. Cf. Bu. Tid. 50 f.; Sarrazin, *Beitr.* xi 530. [Grimm L 9.2.262: 'the warrior's spirit rose into the air.'] The expression has been well compared to the Eddic *áþr á bál stigi, Vafþrúþ. 54*; similarly *ādfaru* 3010 (cp. 1109ᵇ) is matched by *bálfǫr, Gylfag.,* ch. 48.

1120. hlynode for hlāwe. Does *hlāw* denote the place where the mound is to be built, or an old mound which is to be used again? See 2241 ff., 2802 ff., 3156 ff.

1121 f. bengeato burston, ðonne blōd ǣtspranc,/lāðbite līces. This seems to be an accurate description of what might easily happen during the initial stage of the heating of the bodies by the funeral fire; cf. *JEGPh.* xiv 549. *lāðbite* is parallel with *bengeato*.

1125 ff. The Frisian warriors — presumably men who had been summoned by Finn in preparation for his encounter with the Danes — return to their homes in the country (*hēaburh* is a high-sounding epic term that should not be pressed), whilst Hengest stays with Finn in *Finnes burh* (where the latter is afterwards slain: *æt his selfes hām* 1147). There is no basis for the inference that *Finnes burh* (see *Finnsb.* 36) lies outside of Friesland proper. Cf. *JEGPh.* vi 193; *A.* l 229 (in reply to Cha. Intr. 258). — *Frȳsland . . . , hāmas ond hēaburh* is one of the favorite paratactic constructions (Lawrence, *PMLA.* xxx 402 n. 17).

1128. wælfāgne wintęr. The unique epithet of winter has been surmised to mean 'slaughter-stained' or 'deadly hostile,' 'forbidding,' or (reading *wǣlfāgne*) 'hostile to moving waters' (cp. 1610, 1132 f.). Could *wǣlfāg* mean 'marked by troubled (orig. 'battling') waters' (see 1131ᵇ-32ᵃ)? Note *scūrfāh winter,* 'stormy winter' (M. Förster, St. EPh. l 172). Quite possibly *wælfāg* is nothing but a back-formation from *wælfǣhð*.

1129ᵃ. [ea]l unhlitme. The puzzling *unhlitme* may be an adverb re-

lated to *hlytm* 'lot' (3126): 'very unhappily' (?), 'involuntarily (?).
B.-T., Grienb. 749: *unhlytm* 'ill-sharing,' 'misfortune'; B.-T.: 'and his lot was not a happy one.'

1129ᵇ-30. eard gemunde,/þēah þe hē (MS.) **meahte** etc.; i.e., he thought longingly of his home, if ... [speculating whether ..., wishing for a chance to sail]. See the parallel lines, 1138ᵇ-40. Cf. *Beibl.* xxii 373 f. Of course, a smoother text is obtained by substituting *ne* for *hē*.

1134-36ª. swā nū gȳt dêð. A trivial statement of a matter-of-course fact (cp. 1058). *dêð* refers to *ōþer gēar*, i.e. spring; *weder*, with its preceding relative clause (1135), is amplifying variation of the implied subject of *dêð*. The bright spring 'weathers' always observe (hold to) the proper time; cp. 1610 f. [Boer, *ZfdA.* xlvii 138, Schücking xxxix 106 understand 1134ᵇ with reference to 1129 ff.: 'as those people do (or, as is the case with those) who watch for the coming of spring.' Similarly Thorpe, Grein, Arnold, Sedgefield.]

1137 ff. fundode, 'he was anxious to go.' [Lawrence, *l.c.* 421 n. 2: "he hastened."] That Hengest actually sailed is extremely doubtful. [In case he did, it would have been primarily for the sake of furthering his plans for revenge.]

1141. þæt hē Ēotena bearn īrne gemunde. The adv. *inne* (MS.), 'inside,' 'within' (cp. *hreðer inne wēoll* 2113), in combination with *gemunde* would signify 'in the bottom of his heart'; *gemunan*, by concretion, means 'show one's remembrance by deeds.' Kock L 6.13.1.35 would connect *inne* with *þæt* (=*þe*), 'in which.' However, Trautmann's emendation *īrne*, for *inne*, greatly improves the sense; it also fits in admirably with the immediately following mention of the bestowal of the sword.

1142-44. A passage that has received most divergent comments. **him .... on bearm dyde,** which has been sometimes rendered by 'plunged into his bosom' (killing him) (so Kemble, Ettmüller, Grein, cf. Heinzel, *Anz.fdA.* x 227), very likely means 'placed on his lap,' i.e., gave to him as a present; cp. 2194, 2404; also *Gnom. Cott.* 25: *sweord sceal on bearme.* — The reading *Hūn* (nom.) *Lāfing* (acc., name of sword) is less acceptable than **Hūnlāfing**, meaning 'son of *Hūnlāf*,' i.e. quite possibly, nephew of *Gūðlāf* and *Ōslāf*, see Introd. to *The Fight at Finnsburg.* — The conjectural *worodrǣdenne* (an unknown word; according to Bugge's interpretation: 'he did not refuse retainership,' i.e. he agreed to become Finn's liegeman [by accepting from Hūn, one of Finn's followers, the sword Lāfing]) has been very generally rejected. **woroldrǣden** has been variously explained as law, way, rule, or custom, of the world, implying such diverse ideas as 'death,' 'fate,' 'revenge,' 'duty,' 'sanctity of oath,' 'universal obligation.' Another conjectural sense was proposed, *JEGPh.* xiv 547, viz. 'condition,' 'stipulation,' the rather redundant *worold*- vaguely referring to something which is in accordance with the ordinary course of life (cp., e.g., *woruldmāgas, Gen.* 2178), and the following rendering was offered: 'Under these circumstances (or, in this frame of mind) he did not refuse [him, i.e. Hūnlāfing] the condition, when Hūnlāfing placed the battle-flame (or: Battle-Flame), the best of swords, on his lap.' In other words, Hengest is presented with a famous sword (which has wrought havoc in the fight against the Frisians, 1145) with the stipulation [we now supply by conjecture:] that the vengeance he is brooding over is to be carried into execution. Hengest accepts and keeps his word. — Malone (*JEGPh.* xxv 158 f., cf. *Hamlet* 22) emends the problematic compound of 1142[b] to *woroldrǣdende* [though he would admit *-rǣdenne* as a phonetic variant, *A.* liii 335 f.], ' earthly ruler ' [?], places a comma after *gemunde*, and translates: ' since he did not prevent his lord when he [Hnæf] laid in his [Hengest's] lap Hūnlāfing, the battle-gleamer, the best of bills.' (That is to say, the dying Hnæf had given his sword to Hengest; for *Hūnlāfing* = ' the sword owned by Hūnlāf,' see Olrik-Hollander 145 f.; cp. Bugge's *Lāfing*.) The idea is so brilliant that one might wish it could be forthwith assented to.

The emendation **weorodrǣdende** (cp. *weoroda rǣswa* 60) enables us to translate: ' So, then, he did not refuse [it, i.e. *torngemōtes*] to the ruler of the host (i.e., Finn), when Hūnlāfing placed a famous, well-tried sword on his lap.' (Hūnlāf's sword? Hnæf's sword?) [On Malone's plea for *Hūnlāfing* = sword-name (as first suggested by Arnold and Olrik), see *MLN.* xliii 300 ff.; on objections to *Swā ne* introducing a main clause, see Malone, *JEGPh.* xxv 158 n. 7, Ericson, *Collitz Miscellany* (1930) 159 ff. But cf. *A.* lvi 422 f.] — [Cf. Rie Zs. 396 ff.; Heinzel, *Anz.fdA.* x 226 f.; Bu. 32 ff.; Aant. 20 f.; Shipley L 6.8.4.32; Tr. F. 25 f., Bonn. B. xvii 122; Boer, *ZfdA.* xlvii 139; Schü. Sa. 11; R. Huchon, *Revue germanique* iii 626 n.; Imelmann, *D. Lit. z.* xxx 997; Cl. Hall, *MLN.* xxv 113 f.; Lawrence, *Publ. MLAss.* xxx 417 ff.; Williams, LF. 4.36.1.93 ff.]

1145. þæs wǣron mid Ēotenum ēcgē cūðe. (Heusler.) The same idea is brought out more definitely in the Prose Edda, *Gylfag.*, ch. 20 (21): " ... [Thor's] hammer Mjölnir, which the Rime-Giants and the Hill-Giants know, when it is raised on high; and that is no wonder, — it has bruised many a skull among their fathers or their kinsmen." (Brodeur's transl.)

1146 f. Swylce ferhðfrecan Fin eft begeat/sweordbealo sliðen. *Swylce*, "likewise," seems to be used with reference to the former destructive work of the sword presented to Hengest (according to Bugge, with reference to the slaying of Hnæf); *eft*, ' in his turn.'

1148 ff. siþðan grimne gripe etc. We may imagine that an attack on the Frisians was being planned by Hengest. But the fight broke out prematurely when Gūðlāf and Ōslāf, losing their temper (1150[b]–51[a]), upbraided the Frisians for the treacherous onset (*grimne gripe* 1148, i.e. the Finnsburg Fight) and their resultant humiliation. (Cf. Bu. 36.) Both *sorge* and *grimne gripe* are the objects of *mǣndon;* with *æfter sæsīðe sorge* we may compare *æfter dēaðdæge dōm* 885.

1159-1250. Further entertainment, Wealhþēow taking a leading part.

1162. wīn. On the culture of the vine by the Anglo-Saxons, see Hoops, *Waldbäume und Kulturpflanzen im german. Altertum* (1905), p. 610; Plummer's note on Baeda, *H. E.* i, c. 1.

1163 ff. The first set of hypermetrical lines; cf. Intr. lxx.

1163ª. gān under gyldnum bēage. Does the queen wear a golden diadem? Or is a *healsbēag* (1195) meant? The prepos. *under* would not be incompatible with the latter sense. Cf. also Stjer. 35 f.

1164 f. þā gȳt wæs hiera sib ætgædere etc. Hint at Hrōðulf's disloyalty. See 1018 f., 1180 ff., 1228 ff.

1165 ff. Is Unferð's presence mentioned here because he was regarded as Wealhþēow's antagonist who incited Hrōðulf to treachery (Olrik i 25 ff., cf. Scherer L 5.5.482)? Or did the poet merely wish to complete the picture of the scene in the hall?

1167 f. þēah þe hē his māgum nǣre/ārfæst etc. Litotes; see 587 f. [Cf. also Lawrence, *MLN*. xxv 157.]

1171. sprǣc. Cf. Lang. § 7.1.

1174. nēan ond feorran þū nū hafast. 'You have them (i.e. gifts) now from near and far' (cp. 2869 f.) is not a very satisfactory version. If we supply mentally, as the object, 'people' (Kock, *Angl*. xlvi 80), the text is equally inadequate. (Trautmann's violent alteration *þū genōg hafast* (cp. *Husband's Message* 34 f.?) reappears, slightly modified, in Wyatt's *Threshold of Anglo-Saxon* (L 2.23): *þū nū genōg hafast.*) Probably at least one line has dropped out either before or after 1174. Cf. Varr.

1175. Mē man sægde. The remark may seem surprising, since the queen did not need to be told about the 'adoption' of Bēowulf (946 ff.), having been present at the king's speech. But it is entirely natural to suppose that the author, perhaps a little thoughtlessly, employed a variety of the *gefrægn-* formula, thereby securing a slight stylistic advantage. (*MPh.* iii 244.)

1177 f. brūc ... manigra mēdo, 'make use of many rewards,' i.e. 'dispense many gifts.' Cp. *mēdgebo, Hel.* (MS. M) 1200.

1193 ff. wunden gold (distinguished from *brād gold* 3105, *fǣted gold, fǣtgold*) probably refers to earm[h]rēade twā, the term hringas 1195ª being another variation of it. (Cf. *MPh.* iii 242 f.) The hrægl is called *brēostgewǣdu*, 1211. The great collar, healsbēaga mǣst, is called *hring*, 1202, *bēag*, 1211.

1197-1201. The allusion to Hāma and Eormenrīc, though very much discussed, is only imperfectly understood.[1]

Ermanaric, the great and powerful king of the East Goths, who, on the disastrous inroad of the Huns, died by his own hands (cir. 375 A.D.),

[1] See L 4.116-19 c; besides, Müllenhoff, *ZfdA*. xii 302 ff., xxx 217 ff.; Bu. 69 ff.; Cha. Wid. 15 ff., 48 ff.; Mogk, *R.-L.* i 314; Heusler, *ib.* i 627-9. Brandl (L 4.129 e) would attribute the strangely un-Germanic features in the representation of Ermanaric to classical influence ('Hercules furens'). But see also Schneider, *Deutsche Vierteljahrsschrift f. Literaturwiss. etc.* xii 13 f.

became in heroic poetry the type of a ferocious, covetous, and treacherous tyrant. (Thus *Deor* 23: *grim cyning*, 22: *wylfenne geþōht*, *Wids.* 9: *wrāþes wǣrlogan*.) He causes the fair Swanhild to be trodden to death by horses, and his son (cp. *Wids.* 124: Freoþerīc?) to be hanged at the instigation of his evil counselor, (ON.) Bikki (*Wids.* 115: Becca?); he slays his nephews, the (Ger.) Harlunge (*Wids.* 112: Herelingas); and — in the singularly unhistorical fashion of the later tradition — wars upon and oppresses Theodoric, king of the East Goths, the celebrated Dietrich von Bern of German legend. Great is the fame of his immense treasure (see, e.g., Saxo viii 278), which in a MHG. epic[1] is stated to include the Harlungs' gold.

Hāma (MHG. Heime), usually met with in the company of Widia (or Wudga, MHG. Witege), plays a somewhat dubious part in the MHG. epics of the Theodoric cycle as a follower now of Theodoric (Dietrich) and then again of the latter's enemy Ermanaric (Ermenrich). Whether his character was originally conceived as that of a traitor or rather that of an exile, adventurer, and outlaw,[2] is a mooted question.

A more or less complete knowledge of these legends among the Anglo-Saxons is to be inferred from allusions and mention of names (*Deor* 21 ff., *Wids.* 7 ff., 18, 88 ff., 111 ff.).[3]

As to the wonderfully precious **Brōsinga mene**,[4] we should naturally believe it to be the same as the ON. *Brísinga men*, which figures as the necklace of Freyja in the Elder Edda (*þrymskviþa*) and elsewhere. Reading between the lines of the *Beowulf* passage, we judge that Hāma had robbed Eormenrīc of the famous collar. As Ermenrich had come into possession of the Harlungs' gold (see above), it has been concluded that the *Brīsinga mene* originally belonged to the Harlung brothers, whom (late) tradition localized in Breisach on the Rhine ('castellum vocabulo Brisahc,'[5] not far from Freiburg). (In other words, the Harlungs, OE. *Herelingas* = *Brīsingas*.) Upon this unsafe basis Müllenhoff reared an elaborate structure of a primitive sun myth about Frīja's necklace and the heavenly twins (Harlungs), which, however, compels admiration rather than acceptance.[6]

The nearest parallel to the *Beowulf* allusion has been found in the *Þiðrekssaga*,[7] which relates that Heimir was forced to flee from the

---

[1] *Dietrichs Flucht* (cir. 1300 A.D.), l. 7857.

[2] *Wids.* 129: *wrǣccan þǣr wēoldan wundnan golde. ... Wudga ond Hāma.* See Cha. Wid. 52 ff. Boer (L 4.119.195 f.) surmised that Hāma joined Theodoric in his exile

[3] A reference to Hāma (Widia, Hrōðulf, etc.) dating from the ME. period was brought to light by Imelmann, *D. Lit.z.* xxx 999, cf. Intr. xxxiv n. 7. — See also E. Schröder, *ZfdA.* xli 24–32.

[4] For an archæological illustration, see Figure 4 included in this edition.

[5] See the quotation from *Ekkehardi Chronicon universale* (cir. 1100 A.D.), Grimm L 4.67.42, Panzer L 4.117.86.

[6] *ZfdA.* xxx 217 ff. Cf. also Krappe, L 4.119 b. 137–74. — Bugge (72 f.) found a reminiscence of Hāma in the god Heimdallr, who recovers the *Brísinga men*.

[7] Compiled from Low German sources in Norway about 1250 A.D. (Ed. by H. Bertelsen, København, 1905–11.)

enmity of Erminrı́kr (ch. 288), and that later he entered a monastery, bringing with him his armor and weapons as well as ten pounds in gold, silver, and costly things (ch. 429). The latter feature looks like a further step in the Christianization of the legend which is seen in its initial stage in *Beowulf*, l. 1201. Probably the expression **gecēas ēcne rǣd** implies that Hāma became a good Christian and that he died as such.[1] The 'bright city' to which he carried the treasure (= the monastery of the *þidrekssaga*), is possibly hinted at in *Wids.*, l. 129 (see above),[2] but the details of the original story are lost beyond recovery.

1200ᵃ. Neither 'jewel' nor 'ornamental casket' seems to be the proper rendering of **sincfæt**. It is more likely to signify 'precious setting,' cp. *Phoen.* 303; *sigle ond sincfæt* (sing. understood in a collective sense), 'precious gems in fine settings.' (*JEGPh.* vi 194.) [Cf. also Schü. Bd. 88.]

1200ᵇ-1ᵃ. **searonīðas flēah/Eormenrīces**. In *Hildebr.* 18 we are told (in accordance with earlier tradition) that Hiltibrant (with Dietrich) —*flōh . . Ōtachres nīd*, 'fled from the enmity of Odoacer.' That is to say, Odoacer's place as the adversary of Theodoric was afterwards taken by Ermanaric. [A hazardous interpretation of *fealh* (MS.): L 4.119 c.]

1202-14ᵃ. The first of the allusions to Hygelāc's fateful expedition. See Intr. xxxix f., liv.

1202. **þone hring hæfde Higelāc** etc. The apparent discrepancy between this statement and a later passage, 2172 ff., where Bēowulf presents to Hygd the necklace bestowed upon him by Wealhþēow, may be explained in two ways. Either Hygd gave the necklace to her husband before he set out on his raid, or the poet entirely forgot his earlier account (1202 ff.), when he came to tell of the presentation to Hygd (2172 ff.). The second alternative is the more probable one, especially if we suppose that at an earlier stage of his work the author had not yet thought at all of queen Hygd; cf. Intr. cvi. (*JEGPh.* vi 194.)

1213ᵇ-14ᵃ. **Gēata lēode/hrēawīc hēoldon**. Their bodies covered the battlefield. Cp. *Jud.* 322: *hīe on swaðe reston*, *Ex.* 590 f.: *werigend lāgon/on dēaðstede*; also *hlimbed healdan*, *Beow.* 3034. (*Æneid* x 741: 'eadem mox arva tenebis.') Cf. *A.* l 198 f.

1214ᵇ. Cosijn's brilliant emendation *healsbēge* (= -*bēage*) *onfēng* (or Sedgefield's tentatively mentioned improvement, *heals bēge onfēng*) is not needed. Why not assume that **swēg** signifies the applause that accompanies the bestowal of the wonderful gifts?

1219ᵇ-20 and 1226ᵇ-27. The queen, anticipating trouble after Hrōðgār's death, entreats Bēowulf to act as protector of her sons, especially of Hrēðrīc, the elder one and heir presumptive. Cf. Intr. xxxii.

1220ᵇ. **geman**, 'I will remember.'

1223ᵃ. **efne swā sīde**. Type A3; see 1249ᵃ, 1283ᵃ.

---

[1] Bu. 70; *Angl.* xxxv 456. Cp. also l. 2469.
[2] Cf. Cha. Wid. 223. According to Boer (*l.c.* 196) it is = Verona ('Bern').

1223 f. ... swā sǣ bebūgeð,/windgeard, weallas. Is *windgeard* subject or object? We recall at once *windige weallas* 572, *windige nǣssas* 1358. Yet, in a case of asyndetic parataxis like *wudu wælsceaftas* (see note on 398), the compound member normally occupies the second place (*Andr.* 494, *þrȳðbearn hæleð[a]*, does not belong in the list); hence, *windgeard* was probably meant as variation of *sǣ*. A somewhat similar use in Old Norse (kennings) is mentioned by Kock, *Angl.* xlii 110.

1225ᵇ-26ᵃ. In the light of the preceding imper. clause, the general sense of **Ic þē an tela/sincgestrēona** seems to be: 'I shall rejoice in your prosperity.' (Gummere: "I pray for thee rich possessions.") Others have interpreted the clause as an allusion to the gifts just bestowed on Bēowulf or to future rewards (cp. 1220).

1231ᵃ. druncne is used attributively.

1231ᵇ. dōð swā ic bidde. Kock (*Angl.* xliv 246 f.) and Malone (*MLN.* xli 466 f.) have urged the translation: 'the retainers do (*dōð*) my bidding (or, as I ask),' the latter scholar viewing the remark as an ironical climax. Cf. Intr. xxxi f., *Angl.* l 199. [The conjectural *dō*, imp. sing. (addressed to Bēowulf), seemed a tempting reading. The queen's abrupt return to her favorite topic would, indeed, cause no surprise. *dō swā ic bidde* is a formula; see *Gen.* 2225ᵇ, 2323ᵇ, 2465ᵇ, *Hel.* 1399ᵇ. But the emendation has been given up in this revised edition.]

1238. unrīm eorla; i.e., Danes. The Geat guests are assigned other quarters, see 1300 f.

1240. Bēorscealca sum. 'Many a one of the beer-drinkers.' See Gloss.: *sum*. It is true, only one man is actually killed, but the fate was, so to speak, hanging over them all; cp. 1235: *eorla manegum;* 713. (Cf. *MPh.* iii 457.) The meaning 'a certain one' could be vindicated only if *fūs ond fǣge* be declared the 'psychological predicate,' which is rather unlikely.

1248ᵇ. (gē æt hām gē on herge,) gē gehwæþer þāra, 'and each of them,' i.e. 'in either case.' The third *gē* ('and that') is no more objectionable than the third *nē* in *Institutes of Polity* § 9: *nē æt hām nē on sīðe nē on ǣnigre stōwe.* (*JEGPh.* vi 194 f.) See also *Beow.* 584.

1251-1320. Attack by Grendel's mother.

1257. lange þrāge. An exaggeration which is not borne out by the story. [Malone, *Eng. Studies* xv 151 would connect *lange þrāge* with *wīdcūþ* 1256.]

1260. sē þe, instead of *sēo þe*, applied to Grendel's mother just as in 1497, or *hē*, instead of *hēo*, in 1392, 1394. (See also 1344, 1887, 2421, 2685.) That it was the author, not a scribe, who at times lost sight of her sex, may be concluded from the equally inaccurate appellation *sinnigne secg* 1379 (*mihtig mānscaða* 1339, *gryrelīcne grundhyrde* 2136). We are reminded of *Par. Lost* i 423 f.: 'For spirits when they please Can either sex assume, or both.' (On the use of *helrūne*, see note on 163. Cp. the Go. transl., *Mat.* 9.33: *usdribans warþ unhulþō.*) Certainly, we cannot regard such masc. designations as evidence of an earlier version in which the hero killed Grendel himself in the cave, or of an old variant of the contest with Grendel which was subsequently worked into a story of the encounter with the mother. [Cf. Schneider L 4.135; ten Brink 92 ff., 110; Boer 66 ff.; Berendsohn L 4.141.1.14 ff.]

1261ᵇ–76ᵃ. Recapitulation; see Intr. cvii. On the descent of the Grendel race from Cain, see note on 106 ff.

1282 ff. The inserted remark that Grendel's mother is less dangerous than Grendel in as much as she is a woman, seems at variance with the facts, for the second fight is far more difficult for Bēowulf than the first, although he is well armed. It is evidently to be explained as an endeavor to discredit the unbiblical notion of a woman's superiority.

1287. andweard goes with *swīn*.

1290 f. helm ne gemunde etc. An indefinite subject, 'any one,' 'the one in question' is understood. Cf. Lang. § 25.4.

1295. A gratuitous transposition of lines involving the transference of ll. 1404–7 so as to follow 1295ᵇ *þā hēo tō fenne* [*eft*], and the elimination of the supposedly interpolated ll. 1296–98 was proposed by Joseph, *ZfdPh.* xxii 393 ff.

1302ᵇ–3ᵃ. under heolfre ... folme, 'the hand covered with blood' (*blōdge beadufolme* 990). Cf. note on 122 f.

1303ᵇ–4ᵃ. The addition of **geworden** emphasizes the fact that a change has taken place (**cearu wæs genīwod**).

1304ᵇ–6ᵃ. frēonda fēorum refers primarily to Grendel and Æschere; the two parties involved (cp. **on bā healfa**) are the Grendel race and the Danes with their guests.

1306ᵇ–9. þā wæs .. cyning ... on hrēon mōde,/syðþan etc. On the stylistic features of this passage, see Intr. lvii, lix n. 1. Cp. *OS. Gen.* 84 f.: *thes warð Ādamas hugi ... an sorogun, thuo hē wissa is sunu dōðan.*

1312. As to (**eorla**) **sum**, see 314.

1314. wille. For the change of tense, see Lang. § 25.6.

1317. handscale. The unique *scalu*, quite possibly, owes its existence to a scribal blunder, cp. *hondscole* 1963.

1321–1398. Conversation between Hrōðgār and Bēowulf.

1322 ff. These lines may be compared with *Æn.* vi 867 ff., see *A.* l 200.

1323ᵇ. Dēad is Æschere. Type Dx, see T.C. § 20. (Cp. *Mald.* 69.) Child, *MLN.* xxi 199 suggested the possibility of an original Scand. half-line: *dauþr es Askar*[*r*]. (?) A notable stylistic parallel is *Hildebr.* 44ᵃ: *tōt ist Hiltibrant.*

1331. ic ne wāt hwæder (*atol æse wlanc eftsīðas tēah*). It might be urged, in defense of a literal interpretation, that Hrōðgār, as a matter of fact, did not know the abode of Grendel's mother quite accurately. But it is more important to observe that the phrase is suggestive of formula-like expressions and that, in addition, a general statement of this kind is not altogether unsuited, since the allusion is to the ' uncanny ' dwelling-place of the mysterious *ellorgǣstas;* cp. 162 f. (*MPh.* iii 246.) [Möller 136, ten Brink 96, Heinzel, *Anz.fdA.* xv 173, 190: *hwæþer* ' which one of the two '; on the other hand, see, e.g., Bu. 93, Aant. 22: ' whither.']

1336 f. forþan hē tō lange etc. A recapitulation and an explanation which sounds almost apologetic.

1340–43ᵃ. feor, i.e. (going) far (in accomplishing her purpose). The phrase **fǣhðe stǣlan** (cp. *Gen.* 1351 f.), in all probability, denotes ' avenge hostility,' ' retaliate ' (in the prosecution of a feud), cf. Kock 229 ff. There appears to be no warrant for the meaning ' institute,' ' carry on ' attributed to *stǣlan* (thus, e.g., Aant. 23). **hreþerbealo hearde** could be regarded as acc., parallel with *fǣhðe*, but this would result in a rather unnatural breaking up of the context (1340–44). Also the construction of *grēoteþ* with *hreþerbealo hearde* as object (parallel with *æfter sincgyfan*) is questionable. [It is claimed to be the correct one by Kock⁵ 82, cf. Notat. Norr. § 1099.] We may venture to take the combination as a loosely connected, semi-exclamatory noun phrase, cp. 936, 2035. — 1342. **æfter sincgyfan.** Æschere, who occupied an exalted position, receives a title fit for a king.

1343 f. nū sēo hand ligeð,/sē þe ēow wēlhwylcra wilna dohte, ' which was good (liberal) to you as regards all good things.' *sē þe*, instead of *sēo þe*, could be justified as referring to the man; cp. 2685. (See also 1260, 1887, 2421.) — Did the author have in mind the legend of King Ōswald's generous hand? (*A.* l 200 n.)

1351ᵇ. ōðer earmsceapen. Type C2: ××⌣́|⌣̀×.

1355ᵇ–57ᵃ. nō hīe fæder cunnon, ' they have no knowledge of a father.' The meaning of **hwæþer him ǣnig wæs ǣr ācenned/dyrnra gāsta** is brought out in Earle's rendering, " whether they [i.e., the two demons] had any in pedigree before them of mysterious goblins"; with *ǣr*, ' previously ' (prior to them), cp. *æfter* 12, 2731. It is of interest to note that the Danes know less than the poet (see 106 ff., 1261 ff.).

1357 ff. Description of Grendel's abode. Read in the light of the corresponding version of the *Grettissaga* (Intr. xv, cf. xiv n. 3), the outlines of the scenery are fairly well understood — a pool surrounded by cliffs and overhung with trees, a stream descending into it, and a large cave behind the fall. The pool is situated in a dreary fen-district, *mōras*, *fen ond fæsten* (103 f., etc.) — a feature not improbably introduced in England. (See also note on 103 f. It has been suggested by Lawrence [see *infra*] 229 f. that the localization in the desolate moors was added in connection with Grendel's descent from the exiled tribe of Cain; cp. 1265.) That Grendel lives in the sea, or in a pool connected with the sea, or in an " almost land-locked arm of the sea " (Cl. Hall, p. 5; cf. Sarrazin, *ESt.* xlii 7 f., who recognized this very feature in the Roskilde bay), cannot be conceded. It certainly seems that the *nicras* and similar creatures (1425 ff., *nicorhūsa fela* 1411) have been brought in chiefly for epic elaboration without regard for absolute consistency. (See

NOTES

also note on 1428 f.) — It should be added that manifestly conceptions of the **Christian hell** have entered into the picture as drawn by the poet. The moors and wastes, mists and darkness, the cliffs, the bottomless deep (cp. 1366 f.), the loathsome *wyrmas* (1430) can all be traced in early accounts of hell, including Ags. religious literature. (See also notes on 1365 f., 850–52.) Especially close is the relation between this Beowulfian scenery and that described in the last portion of the 17th *Blickling Homily* which is based on a *Visio Pauli*. Cp. *Blickl. Hom.* 209. 29 ff.: *Sanctus Paulus wæs geseonde on norðanweardne þisne middangeard, þær ealle wætero niðer gewītað, and hē þær geseah ofer ðǣm wætere sumne hārne stān; and wǣron norð of ðǣm stāne āwexene swīðe hrīmige bearwas, and ðǣr wǣron þȳstro genipu, and under þǣm stāne wæs nicera eardung and wearga, ... on ðǣm īsgean bearwum.* . . . It is hardly going too far to attribute the remarkable agreement to the use of the same or a very similar source. — That the different features of the 'Grendel landscape' as a whole cannot easily be harmonized has to be admitted. (Hulbert L 7.33 e.) There occur, moreover, apparent echoes of the Æneid, vi 131 ff., 237 ff., besides xi 524 f. (see B. 1410, Hrōðgār passing the *enge ānpaðas* on horseback); cf. note on 1368 ff. In fact, those passages which we are tempted to regard as 'Vergilian' are especially striking in this section. — (See Lawrence, *Publ. MLAss.* xxvii 208–45; Sarrazin, *ESt.* xlii 4 ff.; *Angl.* xxxvi 185–87; Schü. Bd. 60 ff.; Earle's note [parallels]; Brooke L 4.6.1.45 [cave under the sea]; Cook L 5.29.3; Lawrence L 4.62 c; Chambers L 4.62 d, Intr.² 451 ff.) [A picture of the waterfall 'Godafoss,' in the Skjalfandafljot river, Iceland, which has been traditionally associated with Grettir's exploit, *Grettissaga*, ch. 66, may be found in P. Herrmann's translation of the *Grettissaga* (Thule, No. 5, Jena, 1913), opposite p. 174. A description of it: *MLR.* xxix 321.]

1359–61. ðǣr fyrgenstrēam/under nǣssa genipu niþer gewīteð,/flōd under foldan. Lawrence, *l.c.* 212, thinks that *fyrgenstrēam* signifies a waterfall, and that *nǣssa genipu* may be "the fine spray thrown out by the fall in its descent, and blown about over the windy nesses." But *nǣssa genipu* might as well denote the cliffs with the overhanging trees darkening the water, and *foldan*, which is naturally to be regarded as parallel with it, might also refer to the rocky ground, or cliffs. See Gloss.: *under, i 2*. (Cf. Lawrence 213.) Malone, *Eng. Studies* xiv 191 f. argues for *fyrgenstrēam* = 'ocean' ? ("an underground arm of the sea penetrating to the mere").

1363. hrinde (bearwas). The epithet is eminently suitable symbolically; cp. *hrīmige bearwas* (of the Northern region), *Blickl. Hom.* 209.32, *on ðǣm īsgean bearwum, ib.* 35. (See Intr. lx.) It is not to be imagined that Bēowulf found the trees covered with hoar-frost. He would not have sailed for Denmark in winter (see 1130 ff.).

1365–66ᵃ. Þǣr mæg nihta gehwǣm nīðwundor sēon,/fȳr on flōde. Although the mysterious fire may be nothing but the will-o'-the-wisp, it is worth noting that "the burning lake or river ... is one of the commonest features of all, Oriental as well as Christian, accounts of hell" (E. Becker, *The Medieval Visions of Heaven and Hell* [Johns Hopkins Diss., 1899], p. 37); cf. *Angl.* xxxvi 186. — The subject (indef. pronoun *man*) is left unexpressed, just as 'he?' in 1367[b]. Cf. Lang. § 25.4.

1366[b]. Nō þæs frōd leofað ... (þæt ... wite). A formula. Cp. *Wonders of Creation* (Gr.-Wü. iii 154) 76 f., *Ex.* 439 f., *Chr.* (i) 219 ff., *Rid.* 2.1 f., *Andr.* 544 ff., *Hel.* 4245 ff., etc.

1368 ff. Ðēah þe hǣðstapa hundum geswenced etc. The elegant period might put us in mind of Vergil. Cf. *Arch.* cxxvi 341 f.; besides *Æn.* vi 239 ff.; also Tupper's *Riddles*, p. 236 (on stag hunting among the Anglo-Saxons).

1374 f. þonne wind styreþ/lāð gewidru. Kock[4] 118 takes *lāð gewidru* as variation of *wind*, placing a comma after *styreþ* (intrans.). Cf. *A.* 1 201 f.; Hoops 165.

1379. felasinnigne secg is incompatible with the regular alliterative practice. See Siev. A. M. § 23.2.

1386 ff. A striking Vergilian parallel, *Æn.* x 467 ff. (cp. also vi 95), has been cited (*Arch.* cxxvi 43; Chambers Introd. 330). Is it more than a parallel? Of course, a hero's striving for fame would seem to be in no need of explanation or comment.

1392 ff. nō hē on helm losaþ etc. Biblical and Vergilian parallels have been pointed out, viz. *Ps.* lxvii 23 (68.22), cxxxviii (139) 7 ff., *Amos* ix 2 f.; *Æneid* xii 889 ff., x 675 ff. (Earle's and Holthausen's notes; *Arch.* cxxvi 344 f.) Cp. Otfrid i 5.53 ff. — The figure of polysyndeton has suggested Latin influence; cf. *Arch.* cxxvi 358.

1399-1491. Preparations for the second combat. 1492-1590. The fight with Grendel's mother. 1591-1650. Triumphal return to Heorot.

1404[b]. [swā] gegnum fōr. The subject has to be supplied indirectly from *Lāstas* 1402, *gang* 1404[a] (nouns used with reference to Grendel's mother). The insertion of *swā* is justified on stylistic grounds.

1408. æþelinga bearn is probably to be taken as plur., as in 3170. See Lang. § 25.6. [*JEGPh.* xxiii 298; *A.* 1 202; Hoops 169.] (1412 *hē*, i.e. Hrōðgār.)

1409 f. stīge nearwe,/enge ānpaðas, uncūð gelād. *Exod.* 58: *enge ānpaðas, uncūð gelād*. The correspondence between the Beowulfian passage and *Æn.* xi 524 f.: 'tenuis quo semita ducit,/angustaeque ferunt fauces aditusque maligni?' was pointed out by Imelmann, L 4.129 a. 419. Cf. Schü. Bd. 38 ff., L 4.145 a; *MLN.* xxxiii 219, *A.* l 202 f. (Intr. cxi, cxxiv.)

1418. winum Scyldinga. *wine*, a frequent term for 'lord,' is applied to retainers here and in 2567. Similarly in MHG., *goltwine* is sometimes used of vassals, and in O. French the retainer is often called the *amis* of his lord. Cf. *JEGPh.* vi 195; Stowell, *Publ. MLAss.* xxviii 390 ff.; Kock[2] 111 f. (See also Saxo ii 59, Par. § 7.)

1422ᵃ. **Flōd blōde wēol** (cp. *Exod.* 463ᵇ), see L 8.14 b.
1422ᵇ. **folc tō sǣgon.** Type D1. See 1650ᵇ; cp. 1654ᵇ, 2796ᵇ.
1423 f. **Horn stundum song/fūslīc** (Earle: 'spirited') **f(yrd)lēoð.** Apparently a signal for the company to gather or to stop. [Stern, *ESt.* lxviii 172 f. thinks of a 'death-song' (or 'terrifying notes of the war horn').]
1428 f. **ðā on undernmǣl oft bewitigað** . . . ; i.e., water-monsters 'such as' (of the same kind as those which) . . . These *nicras* do not ply in the sea (*seglrād*). Cf. Lawrence, *Publ. MLAss.* xxvii 219; Schü. Bd. 66. In any case, consistency is not to be postulated in the descriptions of the scenery.
1446 f. **him . . hreþre . . . . aldre gesceþðan,** 'injure . . . . his breast, his life'; cp. 2570 ff.; Lang. § 25.4.
1453. **besette swīnlīcum.** This helmet differs from the ordinary 'boar helmets' in that several boar-figures (or figures of helmeted warriors?) are engraved on the lower part of the helmet proper. See Keller 87; Stjer. 10 f.; Figure 3 inserted in this edition.
1454ᵃ. **brond nē beadomēcas.** Practically a tautological combination, see 2660ᵃ, note on 398.
1455. **Nǣs þæt þonne mǣtost** . . . . Transition by means of negation, see e.g., 2354. *þonne*, 'further.'
1457. **hæftmēce;** *Grettissaga:* **heptisax** (Intr. xv f.). It appears that in the original story much was made of a sword with a wonderful 'haft' (or 'hilt'), which latter, as a result of the fight, was detached from the blade. Bēowulf brings back from the cave a curious hilt with a runic inscription on it; cp. the runic verses of the *Grettissaga* relating to the *heptisax*. The unique sword-names, *Hornhjalti* (*Gullþórissaga*), *Gullinhjalti* (*Hrólfssaga,* Par. § 9, p. 265), together with the Beowulfian *gylden hilt* 1677 (*Gyldenhilt?*) should also be noted. It was a part of such a marvelous sword, we imagine, to bring about the hero's victory. This feature is obliterated in the *Grettissaga;* in the *Beowulf*, the term *hæftmēce* has been transferred to an entirely different sword. See the thorough discussion, Cha. Intr.² 468 ff.
1459ᵇ-60ᵃ. **ātertānum fāh.** *āter* is perhaps used figuratively with regard to the acid employed in the process of (false) damascening. Another possibility is that the serpentine ornamentation (cp. *wyrmfāh* 1698, also *wǣgsweord* 1489) was supposed to have a miraculous poisoning effect (Stjerna), the figures of serpents suggesting their well-known attribute (cp. *attorsceaða* 2839, also 2523). It is less likely that the edge was really meant to be poisoned. Several ON. passages have been cited as parallels; thus *Brot af Sigurþarkv.* 20 (interpreted in different ways), *Helgakv. Hjǫrv.* 9, *Helgakv. Hund.* i 8. Cf. Bu. Tid. 65 f.; Grienb. 754; Gering's note; Stjer. 20 ff.; Ebert, *R.-L.* i 386; Falk L 9.44.3 f. (Cook's note on *Chr.* 768.) — **āhyrded heaþoswāte.** The sword was believed to be hardened by the blood of battle; cp. *Njálssaga*, ch. 130.13; *scūrheard*, *Beow.* 1033 (?). Or is the reference to some kind of a fluid employed for

the hardening (cf. Scheinert [Sievers], *Beitr.* xxx 378)? In that case, 1460ᵃ could be regarded as, practically, a variation of 1459ᵇ. [Swords hardened by poison (*eitr*): *Hjálmar's Death Song* 2 (*Eddica Minora*, p. 52); *Vǫlsungasaga*, ch. 31; etc. According to Neckel (L 4.115 a. 208 ff.), the ultimate source of the motive of ' poisoned ' weapons in Germanic heroic legend is the notion of the dragon fight in which the hero's sword received its poisonous quality by the act of piercing the dragon. Thus swords and coats of mail are called ' hardened in dragon's blood.']

1461. mid mundum. Presumably generic plural. However, it has been observed that in the ON. sagas frequently both hands were used, either simultaneously or alternately, in handling the sword. (Falk L 9.44.44 f.) Similarly in MHG. epics, cf. *A.* l 203 (e.g., *Nibel.* 1899).

1474. se mǣra. The def. article retained in the vocative; similarly *Chr.* 441, *El.* 511, *Rood* 78, 95, *Guðl.* 1049, *Gen.* (*B*) 578; cp. Varr.: 947, 1759.

1476. hwæt wit geō sprǣcon. Cp. 1707; note on 946 ff.

1484 ff. Mæg þonne on þǣm golde ongitan etc. An interesting parallel: *Hildebr.* 46 f.

1488. ealde lāfe. Bēowulf's own sword (cp. 1023?).

1495. hwīl dæges, ' a good part of the day,' not ' the space of a day ' (see 1600). A long time is required for the same purpose in several corresponding folk-tales, see Panzer 119.

1506 ff. þā hēo tō botme cōm. Grendel's dam, aroused by a stranger's appearance in the water, goes to the bottom of the lake (to which Bēowulf had plunged, like Grettir, " in order to avoid the whirlpool and thus get up underneath the waterfall," Lawrence, *l.c.* 237) and drags him to her cave. **1508. swā hē ne mihte — nō hē þæs** (MS. *þæm*) **mōdig wæs.** Metrically, *nō* might be included either in the first or in the second half-line. But the sense (' no matter how brave he was,' see note on 968) is decisive for the latter. [In the 1st ed. *hē þǣm mōdig wæs* was explained as ' he was angry at them,' *þǣm* referring both to the she-demon and, by anticipation, to the *wundra fela*.] — In the *Grettissaga* the hero straightway enters the cave to fight the monster; in the *Samsonssaga* the hero is seized by the troll-woman in the water and dragged by her to the bottom. This dual conception, possibly, is responsible for the lack of clearness in *Beowulf*. See Cha. Intr.² 470 ff.

1511. bræc is used imperfectively, ' was in the act of breaking,' ' tried to pierce.' Cp. 2854.

1512. āglǣcan is more plausibly to be construed as nom. plur. than as gen. sing.; see 556. The object (*his*) is to be mentally supplied.

1516. fȳrlēoht geseah. The light in the ' hall ' (which enables Bēowulf to see his adversary, 1518) is met with in analogous folk-tales and in the *Grettissaga* (see Panzer 286, Intr. xv), likewise in hell (see *Sat.* 128 f.). Cp. *Beow.* 2767 ff.

1518. Beginning of the real combat. There are three distinct phases of it; the second begins at 1529, the third at 1557.

1519 f. mægenræs forgeaf/hildebille, ' he gave a mighty impetus to his battle-sword.'

1523. þæt se beadoleoma bītan nolde. The she-demon could not be wounded by any weapon (cp. 804) except her own (1557 ff.). See Gering's note (ON. parallels), Panzer 155.

1541. Hēo him eft hraðe etc. We must supply the connecting link, viz., she got up. Only the result of the action is stated. (Intr. lvii.)

1544. fēþecempa necessarily refers to Bēowulf, not to the ogress (cp. 2853). The exceptional intransitive function of *oferweorpan* need not be called in question. (Cf. Schü. xxxix 98; Brett, *MLR.* xiv 7.)

1545. hyre seax (MS. *seaxe*) **getēah/brād [ond] brūnecg.** The lack of concord resulting from the retention of *seaxe* would not be a serious offense, see 2703 f.; note on 48. But *getēon*, unlike *gebregdan*, cannot take the dat. (instr.) case. The scribal error was perhaps caused by the preceding *hyre*.

1550 f. Hæfde ðā forsīðod ... under gynne grund. *gynne grund*, like *eormengrund* 859, ' earth '; i.e.: ' he would have died.'

1555 f. rodera Rǣdend hit on ryht gescēd/ȳðelīce, syþðan hē eft āstōd. For a defense of the punctuation used, see Aant. 25; *ESt.* xxxix 431. Several edd. (Grein, Heyne, Wülker, Schücking, cf. Schü. Sa. 119) have placed a semicolon or comma after *gescēd*, making *ȳðelīce syþðan hē eft āstōd* one independent clause; Ettmüller (E. Sc.), Sievers (ix 140), et al., while punctuating after *ȳðelīce*, likewise consider *syþðan* an adverb, ' afterwards.' This is unsatisfactory because God's help consists in nothing else than showing Bēowulf the marvelous sword (see 1661 ff.), after he had got on his feet again. (The latter fact, though very important, is stated in a subordinate clause, see Intr. lvii, note on 1541. Cp. also 2092.) Sedgefield begins a new sentence with *Syþðan* (conjunct.), which is stylistically objectionable. As to *ȳðelīce*, it goes naturally with the preceding line, see note on 478. — It is of interest to note that in our poem it is God who directs the hero to the victorious sword, whereas in numerous folk-tale versions this rôle falls to the persons (generally women) found in the lower region where the fight takes place, cf. Panzer 154, 288. Moreover, in conformity with the pedigree imposed upon the Grendel race, the good sword of tradition is converted into a *gīganta geweorc* 1562, cp. 1558, 1679, which would seem to go back ultimately to Gen. iv 22; cf. Emerson, *Publ. MLAss.* xxi 915 f., 929; *Angl.* xxxv 260 f. — In the *Gullþórissaga* and the story of *Gullbra* there is sent to the help of the champion a mysterious ray of light which immediately disables the monsters. Such a conception would make the Beowulfian version more intelligible. (Cha. Intr.[2] 466 ff.)

1557. Geseah ðā on searwum sigeēadig bil. Several translations of *on searwum* seem possible; viz. ' among [other] arms ' (see 1613), ' in battle ' (' during the fight,' cp. 419), ' [he] in his armor ' (cp. 2568), or (construing the prepositional phrase with *bil*) ' fully equipped,' ' ready ' (cp. *fūslīc, geatolīc*).

1563. fetelhilt, perhaps 'hilt with chain attached' (Sedgefield). According to J. Schwietering, the hilt was furnished with a cord fastened by a ring (hence: *hring-mǣl*). (*Jahresbericht* . . [*f.*] *germ. Philol.* xli, Part I, p. 50.)

1570. Līxte se lēoma; i.e., the light mentioned in 1516. With *wlāt* 1572 cp. *Ongeat* 1518.

1579. on ǣnne sīð, 'on that one occasion' (122 ff.). — **1583. ōðer swylc,** 'another such [number].' **ūt offerede,** viz., in his *glōf*, 2085 ff.

1584. forgeald, pluperf. — **1585. tō ðæs þe,** see Gloss.: *tō*. The interpretation which would make *tō ðæs þe* ('until') continue the narrative from 1573, after an excessively long parenthesis (Sedgefield, similarly Chambers), is not very tempting.

1588ᵇ–90. On the beheading of Grendel, see Intr. xviii; Panzer 288 f. To an unprejudiced reader it may seem natural enough that the head of Grendel, the chief of the enemies, is cut off and carried home in triumph. But, as an additional reason, the desire of preventing the ghost from haunting Heorot has been cited (see Gering's note). 1590ᵇ. **ond . . þā,** 'and thus (so)'; cp. 2707.

1591 ff. Blackburn proposed an unconvincing conjecture to the effect that, owing to the misplacing of a MS. leaf, the story had become confused, and that originally ll. 1591–1605 followed after l. 1622. See L 5.52, 53.

1596 f. hig þæs æðelinges eft ne wēndon,/þæt hē . . sēcean cōme. . . . So-called proleptic use of a noun, which is preliminary to a clause of an exegetical character; cf. *MPh.* iii 254. *eft* is accounted for by the verbal idea vaguely suggested by the phrase of 1596; it partakes of the proleptic function.

1604. wīston ond ne wēndon; cp. *Par. Lost* ix 422: 'he wish'd, but not with hope.' The formula-like character of the combination is to be gathered from the occurrence of *wȳscað ond wēnaþ, Guðl.* 47, *wilnode and wēnde, Par. Ps.* 24.19, and similar phrases; cf. *MPh.* iii 458, *Arch.* cxxvi 356. *wīston* is apparently a rare form (or spelling) for *wīsctan;* cf. Cosijn viii 571; Pogatscher, *ESt.* xxvii 218; Siev. § 405 n. 8; Bülb. § 507; Schlemilch, *St. EPh.* xxxiv 52 (& K. Sisam, *Arch.* cxxxi 305 ff.); also Braune, *Ahd. Grammatik* § 146 n. 5; Kluge, *P. Grdr.* i², p. 994; W. Horn, *Beiträge zur Geschichte der englischen Gutturallaute* (1901), p. 24; R. Jordan, *Handbuch der mittelenglischen Grammatik I,* § 183 n. The reading *wiston* 'they knew' has been advocated (L 5.61, 62) and opposed (*A.* l 204).

1605 ff. The singular incident of the sword dissolving in the hot blood recalls the melting of the dragon, 897, cp. 3040 f.; see note on 897, Intr. xxiii. While the sword was wasting away, pieces of the blade were hanging down like icicles.

1612 ff. The rich treasures found in the cave belong, of course, to the folk-tale motives; see Panzer 174, Intr. xvi f. (That Bēowulf took Unferð's sword back with him, we learn from 1807 ff.)

NOTES

1616 f. wæs þæt blōd tō þæs hāt,/ættren ellorgǣst. Probably *ættren ellorgǣst* is parallel with *blōd* (logical adjunct and headword forming the terms of variation), though *ættren* could be (and usually is) construed as predicative adj., parallel with *hāt* (cp. 49 f., 2209 f.). Cf. *MPh.* iii 239. The reference is to Grendel, just as in 1614 Grendel's head is meant.

1624 f. The emendation **sǣlāca** (see 1652, 3091 f.) would enable us to connect **þāra þe** directly with that gen. plur. But *þāra* (*þǣra*) may be a late by-form of *þǣre*, cf. Lang. § 22; Bu. 95. [Cf. Hoops 183.]

1649. þǣre idese, dat. sing., i.e. Wealhþēow; not gen. sing. referring to (the head of) Grendel's mother, as sometimes explained (thus by Boer [66], who branded the passage as an interpolation). As to **mid,** cp., e.g., 1642, 923.

1651-1784. Speech-making by Bēowulf and Hrōðgār.

1656. The meaning 'achieve' has been postulated for **genēþan** in this passage (Lorz 60), but this is not necessary, cp. 2350. (See also Varr.)

1657 f. ætrihte wæs/gūð getwǣfed, nymðe mec God scylde. The proper meaning of the rare *ætrihte* appears to be 'immediately' ('right away'), and when used as an adjective, 'close at hand,' cp. *Guðl.* 970, 1125. The vivid indicative of the main clause should not be objected to.

1666. hūses hyrdas. If the plur. here and in 1619: *wīghryre wrāðra* (1669: *fēondum*) is objected to as not entirely consistent with the facts, it could be vindicated as 'generic plural,' see 1074, 565. It has been sometimes regarded as evidence of an earlier, different version of the story; cf. Intr. xviii.

1674-76. him is explained by **eorlum,** cf. Intr. lxv. **on þā healfe;** transl.: 'from that side,' cf. Lang. § 25.5.

1679. ent, entisc. A bold and questionable etymological conjecture by (Schütte and) Olrik (*Danske Studier*, 1914, pp. 9-20) connects these words with the *Anti* (= Circassians) living in the Caucasus district. Lays about their fight with the Goths (Jordanes, ch. 48) are surmised to have given currency to expressions like *entisc helm*, **sweord*. See the discussion, *Beibl.* xl 21 ff.

1681[b]. ond þā (cp. 2707, 1590) **þās worold ofgeaf** (pluperf.). On the possible excision of 1681[b]-84[a], see Intr. cvii.

1688-98. On the wonderful sword, see note on 1555 f.; on Grendel's pedigree, see note on 106 ff. There are a number of doubtful points relating to the curious sword-hilt. 1688 f. **on ðǣm wæs ōr writen/fyrngewinnes.** This signifies either a graphic illustration (which seems, on the whole, probable) or a runic inscription; both kinds are found together on the famous Franks Casket. As regards *ōr . . fyrngewinnes*, the allusion may very well be to the ungodly acts of the giants which preceded the deluge (cp. 113 f.). Cf. *Angl.* xxxv 261 f.; Chambers's note. Kock (*Angl.* xlvi 84 f., cf. *ib.* xliii 307, L 5.44.4.2, *Fornjerm Forskning* 4 f., *AfNF.* xxxvii, 131) understands *ōr* in a wider sense than mere 'beginning,' *ōr fyrngewinnes* being taken as 'all about the ancient strife,' ' an exposition of the ancient strife '; he regards the *syðþan* clause as explanatory of it (' when . . . '). See *Angl.* l 205–07. — 1691. **frēcne gefērdon.** Admitting the perfective function of *gefēran*, we should translate ' they suffered terribly ' (cf. *MPh.* iii 262, also *MLR.* xxiii 208); otherwise, ' they behaved daringly ' would be a possible variant rendering. — 1696 f. **hwām þæt sweord geworht . . . ǣrest wǣre.** Evidently the name of the (first) owner (the one who ordered the sword to be made) was written out in runic characters — a practice confirmed by ancient Scand. and Ags. runic inscriptions, cf. Noreen, *Altnord. Grammatik* i, Appendix, *passim;* Earle, *Ags. Literature*, pp. 48 ff.; Earle, *The Alfred Jewel* (1901) (legend: *Aelfred mec heht gewyrcan*). That the name of the maker of the sword was meant, is less likely. It is true that examples of such inscriptions are to be readily found (cf. Noreen, *l.c.*), but the construction of *hwām* as dat. of agency, ' by whom ' (cf. Green L 6.8.5.99), would be questionable.

1700–84. The much discussed harangue of Hrōðgār, which shows the moralizing, didactic turn of the poem at its very height, falls into four well-marked divisions, viz. a. 1700–9[a]; b. 1709[b]–24[a] (the second Heremōd digression, see 901–15); c. 1724[b]–68 (the ' sermon ' proper); d. 1769–84. It is conspicuous for the blending of heroic and theological motives. There can be no doubt that this address of the king's forms an organic element in the structural plan of the epic, corresponding in its function to Hrōðgār's speech after the first combat together with the first Heremōd episode; cf. Intr. lii. Moreover, it is entirely in harmony with the high moral tone, the serious outlook, and spiritual refinement of the poem. Of course, its excessive length and strong homiletic flavor have laid the third division, and even other parts, open to the charge of having been interpolated by a man versed and interested in theology (Müllenhoff's Interpolator B), and it is, indeed, possible that the ' sermon ' represents a later addition to the text. In that case, the insertion would have necessitated also some changes in the following (and perhaps, the preceding) division. See especially Müllenhoff 130 f.; Earle, pp. lxxxviii, 166 f.; *Angl.* xxxv 474 ff., xxxvi 183 f.; Intr. cxii f.; L 4.146 c. 3; L 5.68.3.

1705 f. Eal . . hit is explained by **mægen mid mōdes snyttrum,** i.e. ' strength and wisdom.' Cp. 2461 f., 287 ff., 1043 ff. See *A.* xxxv 457. As regards the meaning of **geþyldum,** cp. *Cræft.* 79 f.; Otfrid, *Ad Ludowicum* 14: *thaz duit er al mit ebinu.* — [Malone, *A.* lv 271.]

1707[b]–9[a]. Ðū scealt tō frōfre weorþan etc. seems reminiscent of the Bible, see Luke ii 32, 34. Cf. Brandl 1002; *Angl.* xxxv 119.

1709[b]–10. Ne wearð Heremōd swā (namely, *tō frōfre, tō helpe*)/ **eaforum Ecgwelan.** The Danes are named Ecgwela's (descendants, i.e.) men, just as the Frisians are Finn's men (*eaferum* 1068). For the extension of meaning, cp. the use of patronymics like *Scyldingas, Scylfingas, Hrēðlingas.* Nothing is gained by the emendation *eafora* (which has been favored by several scholars). The strange name of Ecgwela

NOTES

occurs nowhere else. (Cf. Notes, p. 164, n. 2.) [Malone, L 5.71.5.]

1714 f. āna hwearf etc. refers to Heremōd's exile and in particular to his death; see note on 902–4ᵃ.

1720. (*bēagas geaf*..) **æfter dōme**, lit. 'in pursuit of glory,' 'in order to obtain glory.' (Cp., e.g., *Runic Poem* 2 f.) Similarly, *drēah æfter dōme* 2179. See Kock in *Studier tillegnade Esaias Tegnér*, 1918, pp. 300 f.; Kock² 113; also *A*. l 213.

1721 f. þæt hē þæs gewinnes weorc þrōwade,/lēodbealo longsum. He suffered everlasting punishment in hell. (Bu. 38; *Angl.* xxxv 267.) Cp. *Gen.* (*B*) 295 f. The veiled form of expression is characteristic.

1724 ff. The author of the 'sermon' has made use of current theological motives, such as God's dispensing of various gifts, the sins of pride and avarice, the shafts of the devil. See *Angl.* xxxv 128 ff., 475 ff. for detailed comments and parallels. On the interesting relation of this homiletic passage to certain parts of *Daniel* and *Christ*, see Intr. cx ff.

1725-27. The meaning is: 'To some men God deals out wisdom, to others wealth and rank.' On **ealra**, see Lang. § 25.9. (Earle: " he holds the disposition of all things.") It is not very likely that *ealra* refers to *manna cynne*.)

1728. Hwīlum hē on lufan lǣteð hworfan. For the scansion, see T.C. §§ 17, 27. The meaning 'wander (i.e., live, cp. 2888) in delight' (*lufu:* concretion of meaning) was proposed, *ESt.* xxxix 464, xli 112. Another explanation: Kock⁵ 88 ff. Connection with *eardlufu* (692, cp. *eard* 1727) was suggested, *A*. l 208, Ed.² 432; so Hoops St. 110 ff.: 'dear home.' (Cp. ll. 2884 ff.)

1730 f. tō healdanne belongs both with **wynne** (cp. 1079 f.) and **hlēoburh.**

1733 f. hē his selfa ne mæg ... ende geþencean, 'he himself cannot imagine that the end of it (i.e., of his kingdom, or his happy state in general) will come.' See *Arch.* cxv 180 f.; *Angl.* xxxv 469.

1737 f. nē gesacu .. /ecghete ēoweð; virtually 'nor does enmity bring about war'; cp. 84 f. Kock (*Angl.* xlvi 90) supports an alternative construction, taking *ēoweð* intransitively and treating *gesacu* and *ecghete* as parallel terms. Cf. *Angl.* l 208.

1740. On the canto division, see Intr. ci.

1741ᵇ–42ᵃ. þonne se weard swefeð,/sāwele hyrde. By the keeper of the soul either man's 'conscience' or (more likely) 'intellect,' 'reason' is meant. Cf. Intr. cxii; *Angl.* xxxv 131 f. [Cook, L 4.146 c 3.394 n. 12: 'custos animae,' Prov. xvi 17, xxii 5.]

1742ᵇ. bið se slǣp tō fæst is treated by Sedgefield and Chambers as a parenthetic clause, which, in this context, does not seem quite satisfactorily stylistically; *gebunden* 1743ᵃ can apply to the sleep as well as to the sleeper.

1743 ff. bona; see *gāstbona*, 177. The devil's mysterious biddings (sinister suggestions, **wōm wundorbedodum** 1747) are equated with his sharp arrows, 1746; cf. *Arch.* cviii 368 f. On the arrows of the devil, see

A. xxxv 128 ff., lvi 423 f.; Crawford, *RESt.* vii 448 ff.; also *Vercelli Hom.* (ed. Förster) iv 340 ff.

1756ᵃ. *unmurnlīce*, and *undyrne* 2000ᵃ are the only sure instances of unstressed prefix *un-* in *Beowulf.* (*ungyfeðe* 2921 is, at least, doubtful.)

1757. egesan ne gȳmeð amplifies the idea of *unmurnlīce*. Cf. Aant. 26; *Angl.* xxviii 455. — Kock² 144: " does not keep anxiously (*egesan*, dat.-instr.) [the hoard]." (?) Cf. *A.* l 208.

1759 f. þæt sēlre gecēos,/ēce rǣdas. See *Angl.* xxxv 457 f. (Luke x 42, etc.); cp. *Hel.* 1201 f.: *feng im wōthera thing,/langsamoron rād; Chr.* 757. — **(oferhȳda) ne gȳm,** ' shun.' (Litotes.)

1763 ff. The enumeration of the different kinds of death (see 1846 ff.) recalls classic and ecclesiastic literature, cf. *Arch.* cxxvi 359 (though some similar Germanic legal formulas might be quoted, see Grimm R. A. 40 ff.). The polysyndetic series suggests the rhetoric of a preacher (such as Wulfstān). The effect is heightened by the repetition of the prefix, *forsiteð ond forsworceð* 1767 (so *forgyteð ond forgȳmeð* 1751), cp. 903 f.; *Dan.* 341, 352, *El.* 208, *Chr.* 270, *Andr.* 614, 1364, *Gen.* (*B*) 452.

1769. Swā introduces an individual exemplification of the preceding general observation; cp. 3066, *Wand.* 19.

1770–72. Although **wigge** could be regarded as parallel with 1771ᵃ, it is a little more natural to take it in an instrumental sense, ' by war ' (and, by readiness for war). But the chief emphasis is laid on the peaceful character of Hrōðgār's long reign, just as in the case of Bēowulf, 2732 ff.; cp. also Otfrid i 1.75 ff. The remarkable parallel, *Ps.* 34.3 (*Benedict. Office*, etc.): (*mē . . .*) *wīge belūc wrāðum fēondum,* Gr.-Wü. iii 331, = ' conclude adversus eos qui persequuntur me,' was first noticed by Heyne. Cf. *ESt.* xxxix 464; *Angl.* xxxv 469; Kock² 114 f. — For the conventional praise of peaceful times, cf. *A.* l 209.

1785-1887. The parting.

1797. þȳ dōgore is perhaps meant in a generic sense, ' in those days,' cp. 197, 790. Hoops 194: ' on that day,' ' on such a day.'

1801. The raven in the peculiar rôle as herald of the morning recalls the proper name *Dæghrefn,* 2501. Cp. *Helgakv. Hund.* ii 42 (Óþin's hawks rejoicing at the coming of morning). Earle thinks the black-cock may have been meant (see his note).

1802ᵇ-3ᵃ. See Varr. **ofer sceadwa** is offered as a slight improvement on Sievers's *æfter sceadwe;* cp. *Phoen.* 209 f.: *sunne hātost/ofer sceadu scīneð.*

1805 f. wolde feor þanon . . . cēoles nēosan; i.e., he wanted to go to the ship ' for a voyage far away ' (Earle).

1807-12. Heht þā se hearda Hrunting beran etc. ' Then the brave son of Ecglāf had Hrunting brought (cp. 1023 f.), bade [him] take his sword, the precious weapon; he [i.e., Bēowulf] thanked him for that gift (see Gloss.: *lēan*), said he considered the war-friend [cp. *hildefrōfor, Wald.* ii 12] good, etc.' It should be noted that the subject of *cwæð* 1810 must be the same as that of *sægde* 1809 (cf. Intr. lvi), and that the abrupt change of subject (from Unferð to Bēowulf) in 1809 is not unparalleled (cf. Intr. lxvii). The fact that Hrunting had been restored to Unferð has been passed over as irrelevant; but the presentation of a parting gift (cp. 1866 ff.) to the hero is appropriately dwelt upon with some emphasis. (*MPh.* iii 460 f.) [For other views, see Varr.; Schröer, *Angl.* xiii 337 ff.; Jellinek & Kraus, *ZfdA.* xxxv 279 ff.; Sedgefield's and Chambers's notes; Kock[5] 90; *A.* l 209.] The question is whether the period begins with Unferð or with Bēowulf as the subject. Of course, if we venture to take *lēanes* = *lǣnes* (Lang. § 9.1; *lǣn*, f., but orig. n., Siev. § 267, 'loan'), the interpretation becomes greatly simplified; *se hearda* = Bēowulf (who restores Hrunting to its owner); *sunu* = *suna*, dat.; for *beran* with dat., see 1192, 2281, 2988; cp. 1023 f.

1814-16. On the punctuation, see *A.* l 209.

1825. Several edd. omit the comma after **gūðgeweorca** and construe the gen. with *gearo*. But **ic bēo gearo sōna** gives the impression of a complete clause. *gūðgeweorca* may have instrumental force like *nīða* 845, 1439, 2206; cf. Aant. 38. Or it could be construed with *tilian*, forming a (kind of vague) parallel of *mōdlufan māran*. Hoops, like Sedgefield, would connect it with (the widely separated) *ōwihte*. (Kock[5] 91 f. notes that *ōwihte* with compar. means ' any,' ' at all ' (greater, etc.).)

1830ᵇ-31ᵃ. Ic on Higelāce wāt,/Gēata dryhten. The lack of concord can be remedied by reading either *Higelāc* (cp. 2650ᵇ) or *dryhtne*, see Varr. But such a congruence is not absolutely necessary in the case of an apposition (Lang. § 25.6; *MPh.* iii 259). Cf. also note on 48; *Hel.* 49 f., etc. Metrically, *Higelāc* would be somewhat more regular, but 1830ᵇ is supported by 501ᵇ.

1831ᵇ. þēah ðe hē geong sȳ. The author is inconsistent in representing Hygelāc here as still young (cp. 1969), whereas several years before he had given his daughter in marriage to Eofor. (See Intr. xxxviii f.) — That a young person is not ordinarily credited with wisdom, is seen from 1927 f., 1842 f.; *Wand.* 64 f.

1833. wordum ond weorcum, largely a formula, see Gloss.: *word;* Sievers's *Heliand*, p. 466. **þæt ic þē wēl herige;** the verb *herian* ' praise ' assumes the sense ' show one's esteem by deeds,' cp. *weorðian* 2096. (*Hel.* 81: *waruhtun lof Goda*, 83: *diuridon ūsan Drohtin*, etc.) [Cf. also Aant. 27; *MPh.* iii 261; Chambers; Kock[5] 92 f., Hoops 199: ' help '; cf. *A.* l 210. (Cp. the different meanings of *ār.*)]

1836 f. Gif him þonne Hrēþrīc tō hofum Gēata/geþingeð, ' . . . determines [to go] to . . .' Exact parallels of this function of (refl.) *geþingan* occur *Bi Domes D.* 5, *Sat.* 598 (see Clubb's note; cf. Aant. 28). For the omission of the verb of motion, see Gloss.: *willan, sculan;* Ælfric's *Saints* xxvi 213: *þider hē gemynt hæfde;* also Laȝamon's *Brut* 28109: *þā þū tō Rōme þohtest;* etc. The meaning ' (arrange to) take service ' has been conjectured for *geþingan* (Ger. ' sich verdingen,' cf. Heyne-Schücking, Lorz 68), but this is not well attested. Kock[5] 93: ' make arrangements for oneself to go.'

1838 f. feorcȳþðe bēoð/sēlran gesōhte þǣm . . . ; 'far countries when visited ' — i.e. ' the visit of far countries is good (cf. Lang. § 25.2) for him . . .' The participial construction accords with Latin syntax (*Arch.* cxxvi 355), yet it makes an idiomatic impression.

1840[b]. him on andsware is, metrically, out of the ordinary (cf. Rie. V. 31; Mö. 141; Holt. Zs. 125), but may be a permissible instance of D2 with the stress on *him* (as in 543[b], cp. 345[b], etc.).

1844–45[a]. Bēowulf is declared perfect in thought, words, and action; see *Angl.* xxxv 457. (Cp. 1705 f.)

1850. þæt þe Sǣ-Gēatas sēlran næbben . . . Several edd. (thus Schücking, Sedgefield, Chambers) write *þē;* but the construction of the dat. (instr.) with a compar. (' better than you ') is found nowhere else in *Beowulf*. The corresponding passage, 858 ff. supports *þæt þe;* cp. 1846. (*Arch.* cxxvi 356 n. 1.) [G. W. Small, *The Germanic Case of Comparison* (1929), 38 ff. argues against it.]

1852 f. gyf þū healdan wylt/māga rīce. Apparently a hint at Bēowulf's future refusal to accept the throne, 2373 ff.

1854[a]. līcað leng swā wēl. Unless *wēl* is a mere scribal blunder for *sēl*, the positive may be due to a contamination of two constructions, viz. *līcað wēl*, and *līcað leng swā sēl* (*bet*); cp. 2423. See B.-T.: *swā, iv 5; Angl.* xxvii 426; Ericson, *The Use of swā in OE.* (1932), 55 f.

1859. wesan; 1861. gegrēttan; scil. *sceal* (1855).

1862. The risky, if tempting interpretation of *heaþu*, or *hēaþu* (from *hēah*) as ' sea ' (also in *heaþolīðende*, see Gloss.) has been generally abandoned in favor of the emendation **heafu**, which is sustained by the occurrence of *ofer heafo* in 2477. Sarrazin's rendering of *ofer heaþu* by ' after the war ' (Sarr. St. 27) is by no means impossible, though otherwise *heaþu* ' war ' is known only as the first element of compounds. (Cp. the very rare use of the noun *heoru* by the side of numerous compounds.)

1865. ealde wīsan. See Glossary: *wīse.* Kock[5] 94: ' the aged leaders '; cf. *A.* l 210; Hoops 201.

1866. inne, ' within '; cp. 390, 1037, 2152, 2190. Bēowulf was still inside the hall.

1873. Him wæs bēga wēn etc. See 1604 f., 2895 f.

1875. þæt h[i]e seoððа(n) [nō]. The addition of the negation improves the sense. Moreover, to judge from the defective state of the MS., a few letters are probably lost at the end of the line (the first line of the page). (Chambers.) Hence, the differentiation of parenthesis and bracket may be illusory in this case.

1884 f. þā wæs on gange gifu Hrōðgāres etc. Cp. 862 f.

1887[b]. (yldo . . .) sē þe. Remembering the use of the masc. designations of Grendel's mother (see note on 1260), we need not be surprised to find the hostile powers of old age and fate (2421) treated in a similar way. [That *sē þe* should refer to Hrōðgār is a very precarious hypothesis.]

1888–1931[a]. Bēowulf's return.

1891[b]. swā hē ǣr dyde. See note on 444[b].

NOTES

1894 f. cwæð þæt wilcuman Wedera lēodum etc.; i.e., ' your people will give you a hearty welcome.' (Cp. 1915 f., 1868 f.)

1900. Hē; i.e., Bēowulf, who has not been mentioned after l. 1880 (1883); see l. 1920. — Is the **bātweard** the same as the *landweard*, 1890?

1918. oncerbendum is illustrated by a quotation from Ælfred's *Soliloquies* (ed. Hargrove) 22.4 ff.: *scipes ancerstreng byð āþenæd on gerihte fram þām scype tō þām ancre . . . , se ancer byð gefastnod on ðǣre eorðan. þēah þæt scyp sī ūte on ðǣre sǣ on þām ȳðum, hyt byð gesund [and] untōslegen gyf se streng āpolað, forðām hys byð se ōðer ende fast on þǣre eorðan and se ōðer on ðām scype.* Cp. also *Whale* 13 ff. (*oncyrrāp*).

1926ᵃ. hēā healle (MS.). The unique plur. of *heal* would be strange, and an emendation like *hēah healreced* (Holthausen[1], cf. Zs. 118) or *hēah *healsele* may well represent the original reading. If 1926ᵃ be considered parallel to 1925ᵇ (rather than to 1925ᵃ), Kock's conjecture *hēah on healle* offers an acceptable improvement. (Cp., e.g., the sequence of half-line units, *Phoen.* 9–10ᵃ.)

1927 f. þēah ðe wintra lȳt/under burhlocan gebiden hæbbe. ' In spite of her youth,' Hygd shows the virtues of a discreet woman and a gracious, open-handed queen, differing therein from Þrȳð in her early, pre-marital stage. *under burhlocan*, ' within the castle (or town) ' (i.e., of Hæreð?).

1931ᵇ–1962. Digression on Þrȳð and Offa.[1]

There remain some obscure points in the cursory allusion to **Þrȳð**,[2] but in all probability this remarkable woman is meant to represent a haughty, violent maiden, who cruelly has any man put to death that is bold enough just to look at her fair (*ǣnlicu* 1941) face, but who, after being wedded to the right husband, becomes an admirable, womanly wife (and kind, generous [1952] queen), — in short, exemplifying the ' Taming of the Shrew ' motive. This specific interpretation — which would put the unapproachable, fierce maiden in a line with Saxo's Hermuthruda (iv 101 f.,[3] 103) and Alvilda (vii 228 ff.), Brünhild of the *Nibelungenlied*, queen Ólof of the *Hrólfssaga* (ch. 6) — derives strong support from ll. 1933–35, 1954. What part the father played in the story, and under what circumstances the daughter left her home, we are left to guess; see notes on 1934, 1950.

Offa, who while still young (1948) married the noble (1949), strong-

---

[1] References: L 4.98-106 d (espec. Suchier, Gough, Rickert, Imelmann, Craigie); also: Grein L 4.69.278 ff.; Müll. 71 ff., 133 f.; ten Brink 115 ff., 221 f., 229 ff.; Chadwick Or. ch. 6; Cha. Wid. 84 ff., 202 ff.; Heusler, *R.-L.* iii 361 f.; Kier L 4.78.65 ff.; *A.* l 233 ff.; Hoops St. 64–71.

[2] This nominative form is not recorded; it has even been doubted that her name is mentioned at all. See note on 1931 f. and Varr. She is ostensibly introduced as a foil to the discreet, decorous, and generous queen Hygd.

[3] ' Sciebat namque eam non modo pudicicia celibem, sed eciam insolencia atrocem, proprios semper exosam procos, amatoribus suis ultimum irrogasse supplicium, adeo ut ne unus quidem e multis exstaret, qui procacionis eius penas capite non luisset.'

minded maiden, is extolled (1955 ff.) as the most excellent hero,[1] famed for his valor, wisdom, and liberality. He is the son of Gārmund and the father of Ēomǣr (Ēomēr), and corresponds to the legendary, prehistoric Angle king Offa (I) of the Mercian genealogies (see Par. § 2).[2] Being removed twelve generations from the historical Offa II, the old Angle Offa may be assigned to the latter half of the fourth century. His great exploit is the single combat by the river Eider which is alluded to in ll. 35 ff. of *Widsið:*

    Offa wēold Ongle,   Alewīh Denum,
    sē wæs þāra manna   mōdgast ealra;
    nō hwæþre hē ofer Offan   eorlscype fremede,
    ac Offa geslōg   ǣrest monna
    cnihtwesende   cynerīca mǣst,
    nǣnig efeneald him   eorlscipe māran[3]
    on ōrette,   āne sweorde[4]
    merce gemǣrde   wið Myrgingum[5]
    bī Fīfeldore;[6]   hēoldon forð siþþan
    Engle ond Swǣfe,   swā hit Offa geslōg.

The details of this fight, by which he saved the kingdom, and the dramatic scene leading up to it, in particular the sudden awakening from his long continued dumbness and torpor,[7] are set forth in one of the most charming stories of Saxo Grammaticus (iv 106, 113-17) and in Sven Aageson's Chronicle (Par. § 8.3). A brief reference is found also in the *Annales Ryenses* (Par. § 8.5).

Stories of Offa as well as of his queen were incorporated in the **Vitae Duorum Offarum,** a Latin work written about the year 1200 by a monk of St. Albans.[8] Here Offa I miraculously gains the power of speech and defeats the Mercian nobles who had rebelled against his old father Warmundus. The story related of his wife, however, is the popular legend of the innocently suffering, patient heroine, who [flees from an

---

[1] Similar, though more moderate, is the praise of Onela, 2382 ff.

[2] The variation Gārmund: Wǣrmund is matched by similar cases in Scand. tradition, see Intr. xxxii n. 4. Sarrazin (*ESt.* xlii 17, Käd. 70) thinks the *Gār-* form due to Celtic influence. The somewhat suspicious Angelþēow is not mentioned in *Beowulf*. (See, besides, Intr. xlii n. 3.) Saxo (Book iv) has the series Vigletus — Wermundus — Uffo. Cf. *Series Runica* (Par. § 8.4) and *Annales Ryenses* (Par. § 8.5).

[3] Perhaps *fremede* or (Holt.:) *geslōg* is to be understood.

[4] In Saxo's version Offa's paternal sword is named *Screp*.

[5] The *Myrgingas* seem to be regarded as a branch of the *Swǣfe* (i.e. North Swabians).

[6] Presumably the river Eider, which for some distance forms the boundary between Schleswig and Holstein.

[7] This widely known motive of the hero's sluggish, unpromising youth (cf. Grimm D. M. 322 (388)) is applied to Bēowulf: 2183 ff. The parallel of the early Irish hero Labhraidh Maen was mentioned by Gerould (L 4.102).

[8] A complete edition by Wats, London, 1640. Some extracts may be found in Gough (L 4.101) and Förster (L 4.34). On pictorial representations, see note on 1948. The *Life of Offa I* and extracts from the *Life of Offa II* ed. by Cha., Intr. 217 ff.

unnatural father,] marries a foreign prince, is banished with her child (or children), but in the end happily rejoins her husband.[1] In the Life of Offa II, i.e. the great historical Mercian king (who reigned from 757 to 796), the prince is similarly cured of his dumbness and, after defeating the rebel Beornred, is elected king. But the account given of the wife of this Offa strangely recalls the Þrýð legend of *Beowulf*, as the following outline will show.

A beautiful but wicked maiden of noble descent, a relative of Charlemagne, is on account of some disgraceful crime condemned to exposure on the sea in a small boat without rudder and sail. She drifts to the shore of Britain. Led before King Offa, she gives her name as Drida and charges her singular banishment to the intrigues of certain men of ignoble blood whose offers of marriage she had proudly rejected. Offa, deceived by the girl's beauty, marries her. From that time she is called Quendrida,[2] 'id est regina Drida.' Now she shows herself a haughty, avaricious, scheming woman, who plots against the king, his councilors, and his kingdom, and treacherously causes the death of Æðelberht, king of East Anglia, a suitor of Offa's third daughter. A few years later she meets a violent death.

In spite of their obvious differences, this narrative and the *Beowulf* version of Þrýð evidently go back to the same source. The shifting of the story from the legendary Offa I to the historical Offa II and the transformation it has undergone are perhaps in part due to the (purely) legendary stories of the cruelty of queen Cyneþrýð, wife of Offa II.[3] Why a legend of the Constance type should have been attached to the Angle Offa, remains a matter of speculation. There are some slight parallelisms between it and the Drida account, but it is difficult to believe, as some scholars do, in their ultimate identity.

There can be no doubt that the stories both of Offa and of Þrýð arose in the ancient continental home of the Angles. The Offa tradition lived on for centuries among the Danes, and it appears in literary, nationalized form (Wermundus figuring as king of Denmark) in the pages of Saxo and Sven Aageson. On the other hand, the Angles migrating to Britain carried the legends of Offa and his queen with them and in course of time localized them in their new home. Offa I became in the *Vita* king of the West Angles (Mercians), the founder of the city of Warwick, and considerable confusion between the two Offas set in, leading to further variations.

[1] I.e., the so-called 'Constance legend,' which is represented by a number of medieval versions (in several languages) and which is best known to students of English literature from Chaucer's *Tale of the Man of Lawe*. Possibly, the OE. poem, *The Banished Wife's Lament*, belongs in this group, see espec. Rickert, *MPh*. ii 365 ff.; Lawrence, *MPh*. v 387 ff. — Cf. Schick L 4.106 c.

[2] OE. *cwēn þrýð*.

[3] And, indirectly, to the odious reputation of the wicked Ēadburg, the daughter of Offa and Cyneþrýð (Rickert, *MPh*. ii 343 ff.).

That the tales of Offa's prowess have a historical basis, is quite believable and antecedently probable. The Þrýð legend has frequently been assigned a mythological origin. Her name and character have called to mind the Valkyria type,[1] and she has been compared directly to the Scandinavian Brynhildr, the person of her father being considered to be no other than Óðinn. Also a Norse myth of Þórr and Þrúðr — a variation of a primitive Indo-European 'day and night' myth — has been put into requisition (L 4.106). But little light on the *Beowulf* version is gained from such hypotheses.

Various scholars have been looking for specific reasons to account for the insertion of this episode in the *Beowulf* narrative. Allusions to CyneÞrýð, wife of Offa II, or to queen ŌsÞrýð (ob. 697)[2] have been detected in it and charged to the account of an interpolator.[3] The passage has been imagined to be a sort of allegory revealing a high moral and educational purpose in its praise of Offa (= Offa II), its rebuke to Þrýð (= CyneÞrýð), its (hidden) admonition to Ēomēr (= prince Ecgferð).[4] But the only conclusion to be drawn from it with reasonable certainty seems to be that the poet was interested in the old Anglian traditions — the only legends in *Beowulf* that are concerned with persons belonging to English (i.e., pre-English) stock. That these enjoyed an especial popularity in the Mercian district, is confirmed by the testimony of the proper names.[5] The author's strong disapproval of Þrýð's behavior (1940 ff.) is quite in keeping with his moralizing, didactic propensities shown in sundry other passages.[6]

1931 f. The introduction of this Episode has received a great deal of varied comment. Schücking's convenient emendational remedy, *mōd Þrýðe ne wæg*, which found its way into four editions, is open to serious objections. Apart from the decided alteration of the text, there is something of the *deus ex machina* character about it, and it has not unjustly been charged (by Kock) with bearing a rather modern stamp. Kock[3] 102 f. made the startling suggestion that the name of the queen may have been *Fremu* of l. 1932 (*fremu folces cwēn*). Craigie ingeniously conjectured that a leaf of the MS. had been lost, and a stray leaf from another poem (containing the Þrýð passage) was erroneously accepted as the continuation of the text. However, only one point was made clear, namely that, according to his view of the case, there is a defect between 1931[a] and 1931[b]. Without doubt, *mōdÞrýðo wæg* (cp. *Gen.* 2238[b] *higeÞrýðe wæg*, etc.; for the spelling *-o*, cf. Lang. §§ 18.3, 24 *ad fin.*) is a thoroughly idiomatic phrase; *mōdÞrýðo* and *firen' ondrysne* would form

---

[1] Þrúþr (i.e. 'strength') is mentioned by the side of Hildr (i.e. 'battle') as one of the Valkyrias in *Grímnismál*, 36. See Grimm D. M. 349 ff. (421 ff.).

[2] ten Brink 229 ff.

[3] L. 1963 would indeed form a faultless continuation of 1924.

[4] Earle, pp. lxxxiv ff.

[5] Binz 169 ff.

[6] Cp., e.g., the characteristic instance of l. 1722.

acceptable parallel objects of *wæg*. If the supposed missing link, i.e., a passage connecting the Episode with the preceding remarks about Hygd and, at the same time, introducing the lady by name, could be discovered, our troubles would be at an end. (*A*. l 233 ff.) A conjectural reconstruction of some missing lines was indulged in years ago, *A*. xxviii 451. Imelmann's shrewd suggestion (L 4.106 a; cf. *Anz.fdA*. xli 33), *mōd þrȳð ō wæg*, fails to give complete satisfaction; for it is doubtful if ' always ' corresponds with the facts of the story (see note on 1945), and it is to be questioned whether the form *ō*, i.e. ' ever ' would be used in this manner, since its proper place seems to be in clauses of negative or conditional import. Besides, the name of *þrȳð* is left without the requisite metrical emphasis (just as in Schücking's emendation). Hoops (St. 64 ff.), in effect returning to Grein's view, proposes *Mōdþrȳð ō wæg* or, for a second choice, *Mōdþrȳðo wæg*. As to the latter, *þrȳð* would, indeed, be the normal form, cf. Hart, *MLN*. xviii 117 f.; but *þrȳðo*, and perhaps even **Mōdþrȳðo**, could be considered possible analogical formations, cf. *A*. xxviii 452; Imelmann, *l.c.*; Holt., *Beibl*. xlii 341. The compound name has been well compared to Saxo's ' Hermuthruda.' The reading *Mōdþrȳðo*, although not certain beyond dispute, seems the best that could be adopted under the trying circumstances.

1932ᵃ. fremu folces cwēn. If she was known to tradition as ' Queen Thryth,' it would not be surprising to find her called *folces cwēn* even in the earlier stage of her life, i.e., before her marriage to Offa. (Or was she married twice??) Again, if (as Patzig suggests, *A*. xlvi 282 ff.) the virago was thought of as having been, before her marriage, an independent ' queen ' after the manner of Brünhild of the *Nibelungenlied*, the chronological impropriety would disappear altogether.

1934. swǣsra gesīða, i.e. the retainers at the court. — **sinfrēa**, either the ' father ' or ' husband.' In the latter case, *nefne sinfrēa* means ' except as husband.' All the unsuccessful suitors were to be executed.

1935. þæt hire an dæges ēagum starede. The construction may be explained from a blending of the absolute (adv.) use of *on*, as in *weras on sāwon* 1650, and the dat. of interest, as in *him āsetton segen . . . hēah ofer hēafod* 47 f.; cp. 2596 f.: *him . . . ymbe gestōdon*. For some parallel instances, see *Arch*. cxxiii 417 n.; *A*. l 237 n. 2. The postpositive *on* takes the strong stress as in 2523, cp. 671. — *dæges* ' by day,' i.e. ' openly.'

1936. . . . him . . . weotode tealde, ' considered . . . (appointed, or) in store for him.' A stereotyped expression. See *Jul*. 357: *ic þæt wēnde ond witod tealde*, 685 f.; *Hel*. 1879 f.; *Wulfst*. 147.26, 241.16.

1938. æfter mundgripe, ' after being seized (arrested).' (?) Or is there an allusion to a fight between maiden (or father) and suitor? (Cf. Stefanović, *ESt*. lxix 23.) With ll. 1936–38ᵃ cp. 963 ff.; *handgewriþene* seems to be meant figuratively.

1944. Hemminges mǣg = Offa; in 1961 = Ēomēr. Was Hemming a brother of Gārmund? Or Gārmund's (or Offa's) father-in-law? (**Cp.**

200   BEOWULF

Nīðhādes mǣg, *Wald.* ii 8.) The name occurs in Ags., ON., and OHG. See Suchier, *Beitr.* iv 511 f.; Sievers, *ib.* x 501 f.; Binz 172; Björkman L 4.31.4.167 f. There is a village named Hemmingstedt in the southwestern part of Schleswig.

1945. ealodrincende ōðer sǣdan. This remark, an individualized variation of the *gefrægn-* formula, used as a phrase of transition, supplies a connecting link between the first part of the story and its continuation: ' beer-drinking men related further,' or ' they set forth another aspect of her character '; it stands in the closest possible relation to the straightforward statement of the preceding line; cp. the stylistic parallel, *Mald.* 116 f. (*MPh.* iii 244, *Angl.* xxviii 449.) [It has often been considered to point to *another*, different version of the Þrýð story, by which interpretation the preceding account (1931–43) was supposed to furnish an especially close parallel to the tale of Drida.]

1946. lǣs, (by litotes:) ' nothing.'

1948. geongum cempan. Offa's youth at the time of his heroic exploit is made much of in the *Widsið* allusion. According to later traditions, curiously both Scandinavian (Sven Aageson, *Annales Ryenses*) and English ones (*Vita Offae I*), he had reached his thirtieth year before he revealed his valor. Still, one of a set of drawings made at St. Albans (in one of the MSS. of the *Vitae*) represents him as a youth, see R. W. Chambers, *Six thirteenth century drawings illustrating the story of Offa and of Thryth (Drida)*, London [privately printed], 1912. [They have been incorporated in Cha.'s Introd.]

1950. ofer fealone flōd. The epithet *fealu* applied to the sea — as is often done (somewhat conventionally) in OE. poetry — denotes " perhaps yellowish green, a common color in the English and Irish Channels " (Mead, *Publ. MLAss.* xiv 199). — **be fæder lāre.** The precise meaning of this allusion is lost. Did the father send Þrýð away, because her excessive violence and cruelty rendered her continued stay at his court impossible? [An interesting suggestion: Stefanović L 4.106.521 f.]

1953. līfgesceafta lifigende brēac. Similarly, *worolde brūceð* 1062; 2097. As to the tautological combination, cp., e.g., *cwice lifdon*, *Andr.* 129, *OS. Gen.* 83.

1960. The reading proposed by Rickert (*MPh.* ii 54 ff.): [*geong*] *ēðel sinne, þonon geōmor wōc*, and interpreted as an allusion to Offa's singular ' awakening,' is very interesting, but clearly impossible.

1963–2151. Bēowulf's arrival and narrative.

1967[b]–70[a]. tō ðæs ðe etc., ' to the place where, as they had heard, the king ... distributed rings.' The familiar *gefrægn-* formula (1969: *gefrūnon*) is of course, strictly speaking, out of place here. **bonan Ongenþēoes** 1968 is not meant in its literal sense, since Hygelāc had performed the deed only by proxy, see Intr. xxxix; Par. § 10: Tacitus, *Germ.* c. xiv. The term is suggestive of the ON. surnames *Hundingsbani*, *Fáfnisbani* (cp. *Ísungs bani*, *Helgakv. Hund.* i 21).

1970 ff. A much abridged form of the ceremonies described in 331 ff.

1978 f. mandryhten is probably acc. (not nom.) sing. It is Bēowulf's part to greet the king in a solemn address, see 407 ff.

1981. By the hook under the *e* in **reced** the scribe seems to have indicated the open character of the *e* (*ę* = *æ*); thus in 2126 *bęl* = *bǣl*, 2652 *fæðmię* = *fæðmiæ*. In *sęcce* 1989 the same sign was added by mistake. (Cf. Intr. xci.) [Did the scribe of the first part use *ę* in 1398[b]? See Varr.]

1983. It has been suggested that the form **hæ(ð)num** (see Varr.) pertains to the tribal name *Hǣðnas* (ON. *Heiðnir*), which occurs *Wids.* 81. But why a term denoting the inhabitants of Hedemarken in Norway (according to Bugge, also the dwellers on the Jutish 'heath') should have been introduced here, has not been explained satisfactorily. Cf. Bu. 9 ff.; Chambers's note. [A guess about a name **Hǣne*, Old Scand. **HainīR*, by J. V. Svensson, *Namn och Bygd* v 125 ff.]

1994 ff. It has not been mentioned before that Hygelāc tried to dissuade Bēowulf from his undertaking (see on the other hand, 202 ff., 415 ff.). The same motive, equally unfounded, appears in the last part, 3079 ff. — Several so-called discrepancies between Bēowulf's own condensed version, 2000 ff., and the original account of his adventures in Denmark are easily detected. Some insignificant variations occur in 2011–13 (?), 2147[b]. A shifting of emphasis (and omission of detail) is observed in 2138 f. Added details, some of which seem to have been purposely reserved for this occasion, are found in 2020 ff. (appearance of Frēawaru and everything told in connection therewith), 2076 (name Hondsciōh), 2085 ff. (Grendel's *glōf*,) 2107 ff. (?), 2131 f., 2157 ff.

1996 f. lēte Sūð-Dene sylfe geweorðan/gūðe wið Grendel may be translated: 'that you should let the Danes themselves settle the war with Grendel.' (Cp. 424 ff.) For the interesting construction see Gloss.: *geweorðan, wið*. [Cf. Aant. 30; Bu. 97.]

2002. uncer Grendles, 'of us two, [me and] Grendel.' An instance of the archaic 'elliptic dual' construction. Cf. Sievers, *Beitr.* ix 271; *Angl.* xxvii 402. (Also Edgerton, *ZfvglSpr.* xliii 110 ff., xliv 23 ff.; Neckel, *GRM.* i 393.)

2004 f. sorge is gen. plur.; probably also **yrmðe**, although the acc. sing. remains a possibility for the latter; cp. 2028 f., 2067 ff.

2018. bǣdde. The emendation *bælde* would be elucidated by 1094. Yet *bǣdde byre geonge*, 'she urged the young men' (viz. 'to accept what was offered,' Kock[5] 96) may be retained. (Cf. also *A*. l 210 f.) [Cl. Hall: 'she kept the young servers (?) going'.]

2021. The most plausible meaning ascribed to **on ende** is 'consecutively,' 'continuously,' 'from end to end' (lit.: [from beginning] to end), i.e. 'to all in succession' (B.-T. Suppl.: *ende, ii 9 d*). The rendering 'at the end of the hall (or tables)' is of doubtful propriety.

2022. Malone's scepticism as to the authenticity of the name **Frēawaru** (*MPh.* xxvii 258, *Kl. Misc.* 150 f.) need not be shared.

2023 f. (næ)gled sinc, presumably 'studded vessel' (Cl. Hall); see 495, 2253 f., 2282, and note on 216. **sinc . . sealde,** a variant expression for *sincfato sealde,* 622.

2024ᵇ–69ᵃ. The Heaðo-Bard Episode. See Intr. xxxiv ff. (L 4.83 ff.; Olrik-Hollander 15 ff.)

The following is a summary of Saxo's narrative (vi 182 ff.).[1] Frotho, who succeeded to the Danish throne when he was in his twelfth year, overcame and subjugated the Saxon kings Swerting and Hanef. He proved an excellent king, strong in war, generous, virtuous, and mindful of honor. Meanwhile Swerting, anxious to free his land from the rule of the Danes, treacherously resolved to put Frotho to death, but the latter forestalled and slew him, though slain by him simultaneously. Frotho was succeeded by his son Ingellus, whose soul was perverted from honor. He forsook the examples of his forefathers, and utterly enthralled himself to the lures of wanton profligacy. He married the daughter of Swerting given him by her brothers, who desired to insure themselves against vengeance on the part of the Danish king. When Starcatherus, the old-time guardian of Frotho's son, heard that Ingellus was perversely minded, and instead of punishing his father's murderers, bestowed upon them kindness and friendship, he was vexed with stinging wrath[2] at so dreadful a crime. He returned from his wanderings in foreign lands, where he had been fighting, and, clad in mean garments, betook himself to the royal hall and awaited the king. In the evening, Ingellus took his meal with the sons of Swerting, and enjoyed a magnificent feast. The tables had been loaded with the profusest dishes. The stern guest, soon recognized by the king, violently spurned the queen's efforts to please him, and when he saw that the slayers of Frotho were in high favor with the king, he could not forbear from attacking Ingellus' character, but poured out the whole bitterness of his reproaches on his head, and thereupon added the following song: 'Thou, Ingellus, buried in sin, why dost thou tarry in the task of avenging thy father? Wilt thou think tranquilly of the slaughter of thy righteous sire? — Why dost thou, sluggard, think only of feasting? Is the avenging of thy slaughtered father a little thing to thee? — I have come from Sweden, traveling over wide lands, thinking that I should be rewarded, if only I had the joy to find the son of my beloved Frotho. — But I sought a brave man, and I have come to a glutton, a king who is the slave of his belly and of vice. — Wherefore, when the honors of kings are sung, and poets relate the victories of captains, I hide my face for shame in my mantle, sick at heart. — I would crave no greater blessing, if I might see those guilty of thy murder, O Frotho, duly punished for such a crime.' Now he prevailed so well by this reproach [clothed by Saxo

---

[1] Literal quotations are from Elton's rendering.

[2] In *Helgakv. Hund.* ii 19 Starkaþr is called *grimmúþgastr;* cp. *Beow.* 2043ᵇ. On Starkaþr, see Heusler, *R.-L.* iv 276–78; Herrmann, L 4.35 a. ii 417 ff.

in seventy Latin stanzas] that Ingellus, roused by the earnest admonition of his guardian, leapt up, drew his sword, and forthwith slew the sons of Swerting.

Compared with the *Beowulf*, Saxo's version marks an advance in dramatic power in that the climax is brought about by a single act (not by exhortations administered on many occasions, *mǣla gehwylce* 2057), and that Ingellus himself executes the vengeance, whereas in the English poem the slaying of one of the queen's attendants by an unnamed warrior ushers in the catastrophe.[1]

2029-31. Oft seldan hwǣr/æfter lēodhryre lȳtle hwīle/bongār būgeð, þēah sēo brȳd duge. The general sense of these lines — which do not stand in need of alteration — is: ' As a rule, the murderous spear will rest only for a short time under such circumstances.' There has been a blending of two conceptions resulting in a somewhat confused expression, viz. 1. ' often (always, as a rule) the spear will rest only a short time '; 2. ' it seldom happens that the spear rests (for any length of time).' Kock's interpretation (*Angl.* xxvii 233 ff.): ' As a rule, it seldom happens that (*seldan hwǣr*, cp. *wundur hwār* 3062) the spear rests when some time has elapsed . . . ' does not take into consideration the natural meaning of *lȳtle hwīle* (cp. 2097, 2240, cp. *Gūðl.* 394, 452, etc.); the combination *seldan hwǣr* simply = ' seldom anywhere.' Hoops's rendering (St. 72 f.) of *lȳtle hwīle* by ' even a short time ' is hardly justified. (Cf. *A. l* 211, *ESt.* lxviii 115.) — For the figurative use of ' spear ' for ' (blood) feud,' cf. Liebermann, *Arch.* cxliii 248. — *sēo brȳd*, the bride (in question), cp. 943, 1758, *Hel.* 310; no *direct* reference to Frēawaru.

2032 f. As *ofþyncan* is regularly construed with the dative, the retention of *ðēoden* appears, after all, quite hazardous, although the joining of different cases (*ðēoden, gehwām*) in itself would not count as an obstacle (*MPh.* iii 259). [It has been suggested that *ðēoden* may stand for *ðēodn(e)* with final *e* elided, cf. Rie.Zs. 404; note on 698[a].]

2034 f. þonne hē mid fǣmnan on flett gǣð:/dryhtbearn Dena, duguða biwenede. Kock[5] 173 f. considers *flett, dryhtbearn, duguða* three parallel terms to be connected with *gān on.* More plausible is the above punctuation, in accordance with Hoops's view (St. 73 f.). That is to say, *dryhtbearn Dena, duguða biwenede* is a loosely joined elliptic clause indicating the cause of the king's displeasure (cf. Ed.[1]), or (simply:) a descriptive phrase explanatory of *þæs* 2032 (cf. Intr. lxv). For a list of earlier interpretations, see Ed.[1] p. 194. [*hē* has sometimes been explained as referring to *dryhtbearn Dena*, i.e. *fǣmnan þegn;* thus recently again by R. Girvan, *MLR.* xxviii 246.] — An entirely different view of the Episode is taken by Malone, see his elaborate study, *MPh.* xxvii 257-76 (cf. L 5.71.4). He, like Olrik, thinks that an event of the past (not of the future) is referred to (but cf. Steadman L 4.85 b), viz. an incident of the wedding feast at the Danish court. (The Scandinavian tradition

---

[1] Cf. Olrik ii 39 f.

relating to Agnarr (son of Ingeld) is thoroughly discussed by him; cf. also Herrmann *l.c.* 168 ff.) However, the scene is naturally held to be at the Heaðo-Bard court. The slayer of the *fǣmnan þegn* 2059 (i.e., of a young Dane who has accompanied the princess to her new home) is a native, *con him land geare* 2062. The noun *fǣmne*, originally perhaps ' maiden,' could (like *mēowle*, *mǣgð*) well be used in the broader sense of ' woman.' [For a renewed, spirited defense of the proposition that the ' Ingeld Episode ' takes place in Denmark, see Malone, *A.* lvii 218–20.]

2036ᵃ. on him gladiað. Type A3; cp. 632ᵃ. As to the accent on the preposition, cf. Rie. V. 31 f. See note on 724ᵇ.

2039 f. If by the subject (*hīe*) we understand the leaders, we need not, with Hoops (St. 70), explain **swǣse gesīðas** specifically as ' swords.'

2041. bēah. There is no doubt that the *mēce* (2047) is meant. It seems entirely possible to credit *bēah*, ' ring,' then ' ornament,' ' precious thing ' (*bēagas* ' things of value,' 80, 523, 2635) with the same development of sense as is seen in the term *māðþum*, ' treasure,' ' anything precious,' which is applied to a sword (see 1528, 2055). Or does *bēag* signify ' hilt-ring '? See Stjer. 25, Gloss.: *fetelhilt, bindan*.

2044 f. geong(um) cempan ... higes cunnian, ' test (tempt) the mind of a young warrior,' cf. Lang. § 25.4. The rather redundant *þurh hreðra gehygd* (cf. *Angl.* xxxv 470) appears to emphasize the intensity of the searching. Gummere: " tests the temper and tries the soul." Cf. Kock[5] 174; *A.*l 212. In Saxo's account it is Ingeld himself that is addressed.

2051ᵇ. syððan Wiðergyld læg; cp. 2201ᵇ, 2388ᵇ, 2978ᵇ. We may imagine that the battle turned after *Wiðergyld*, a great leader, was slain. (It has been conjectured that he was the father of the young warrior, 2044, see G. W. Mead, *MLN.* xxxii 435 f., Schücking, *ESt.* liii 468 ff.) The same name, though apparently not applied to a Bard warrior, occurs *Wids.* 124. A common noun *wiðergyld* (' requital ') is nowhere found.

2053. þāra banena byre nāthwylces. A new generation has grown up in the meantime.

2056. þone þe. The accus., in place of the more regular dat. (instr.) (with *rǣdan*), is the result of attraction to *þone māðþum* 2055. Cp., e.g., 2295, 3003.

2061. se ōðer, the slayer, is no doubt identical with the *geong cempa*, 2044.

2063 f. Þonne bīoð (āb)rocene on bā healfe/āðsweord eorla. This implies that, by way of retaliation, a Dane kills a Heaðo-Bard. Then Ingeld is stirred up.

2065 f. him wīflufan ... cōlran weorðað seems to imply that he sends her away. (Litotes.)

2072ᵃ. hondrǣs hæleða. Note the decidedly conventional use of this gen. plur., cp. 120ᵃ, 1198ᵃ, (2120ᵃ), *Finnsb.* 37ᵇ.

2076ᵃ. **Þǣr wæs Hondsciô** (older *-sceōhe*, cf. Lang. § 17.3 n.). Type C1, cp. (e.g.) 64ᵃ, 2194ᵃ, 2207ᵃ, 2324ᵃ. 2076ᵇ. **hild onsǣge.** Type D1. Cp. 2483ᵇ: (*wearð*) *gūð onsǣge*, ' assailed ' (him); see Gloss.

2085. Does **glōf** appear here in the unique sense of ' bag '? Or is a gigantic ' glove ' meant? Laborde mentions (*MLR*. xviii 202) that the large glove is " a characteristic property of trolls "; he suggests that it was inherited from the story of Skrýmir's glove (*hanzki*) in which Thor slept. Cf. *A*. l 212 f.; Hoops St. 118. For the use of gloves in Ags. times, see Stroebe L 9.45.2.15; Tupper's *Riddles*, p. 96.

2091ᵇ. **hyt ne mihte swā.** The infin. *wesan* is understood (see Gloss.: *eom*), not *gedōn* of 2090, as is proved by the formula-like character of the expression; cp. *Andr*. 1393, *Guðl*. 548, *Rid*. 30.6, etc. (Cf. Sievers, *Angl*. xiii 2.)

2105 ff. The **gyd . . . sōð ond sārlīc** 2108 f., most likely, denotes an elegy (see 2247 ff. and note). What relation there is between this *gyd*, the *syllīc spell*, and the harp playing, we are unable to determine. Was the *gyd* recited by Hrōðgār? The practice of the art of minstrelsy by nobles and kings in the heroic age is attested by Scandinavian (also Middle High German,) and, indeed, Homeric parallels; a celebrated historic example is that of Gelimer, the last king of the Vandals (Procopius, *Histories: Vandal War*). Cf. Köhler, *Germ*. xv 33 ff.; Chadwick H. A. 83 ff., 222; Heusler, *R.-L.* i 455. Still, **hildedēor** 2107 may be taken as an epithet relating to an unnamed retainer (Kock[5] 175 f., Hoops 233). — Kock would rehabilitate *fela fricgende* 2106 (= ' asking many questions '), reminding us that to old Germanic " wisdom and etiquette there belonged a well-balanced interchange of speaking and listening." But see Hoops St. 119 f. — **2111 ff.** The lament over the passing of youth and the misery of old age (cp. 1886 f., 1766 f.) is thoroughly Germanic. Thus, e.g., Saxo viii 269 ff., *Hel*. 150 ff., *Gen*. (*B*) 484 f. Cf. Gummere G. O. 305 f. (But also *Æneid* viii 508 f., 560 ff.)

2131 f. **Þā se ðēoden mec ðīne līfe/healsode,** ' then the king implored me by thy life.' (Cp. 435 f.) A free use of the instrum., cp. the prepositional phrase, *Jul*. 446: *ic þec hālsige þurh þæs Hȳhstan meaht*, *Blickl. Hom*. 189.7 ff., etc. (There may have been some confusion between *hālsian* and *healsian*.) See Kress, *Ueber den Gebrauch des Instrumentalis in der ags. Poesie*, Marburg Diss. (1864), p. 24, n.; Bu. 369 f.; Delbrück, *Synkretismus* (1907), pp. 43, 41.

2137. **Þǣr unc hwīle wæs hand gemǣne.** " There to us for a while was the blending of hands " (W. Morris), or . . . " battle joined " (Sedgefield). Cp. 2473; *Wulfst*. 162.7 f.: *þæt wǣpengewrixl weorðe gemǣne þegene and þrǣle*. The Ger. *handgemein* (*werden*) furnishes a semasiological, though not a syntactical, parallel.

2138. **holm heolfre wēoll, ond ic hēafde becearf . . .** A hysteron proteron. Regarding the decapitation of Grendel's mother, see 1566 ff. and note on 1994 ff.

2147. **on (mīn)ne sylfes dōm.** This is, to say the least, an exaggeration. The poet was yielding to the formula habit; see, e.g., 895, 2776; *Mald.* 38 f.: *syllan sǣmannum on hyra sylfra dōm/feoh*.

2152-2199. Bēowulf and Hygelāc.

2152ᵇ. eafor hēafodsegn. The reading *eafor hēafodsegn* (asyndetic parataxis, see note on 398) is preferable to *eaforhēafodsegn*, which would be a very exceptional double compound (cf. Rie. Zs. 405). The words undoubtedly denote a banner, the first of the four gifts which are enumerated here in the same order as in 1020 ff. The boar banner (a banner with a boar-figure on it) may be compared to the Scand. raven banners (see *OE. Chron.* A.D. 878 (B, C, D, E): *se gūðfana . . . þē hīe Hræfn hēton;* cf. Hartung L 9.50.450). Was it called a ' head sign ' because it was borne aloft in front of the king? (See Baeda, *H.E.* ii, c. 16; *Beow.* 47 f., *El.* 76 [?].) Or does the compound mean ' great banner '? Or, perhaps, an emblem (boar) such as was attached to the helmet which covered the head? (Cf. Siev. xxxvi 417 f.)

2157. þæt ic his ǣrest ðē ēst gesægde. ' That I should first declare to thee his goodwill ' (Schröer, *Angl.* xiii 342 f., Sedgefield, Cl. Hall) would be an altogether supererogatory declaration. Considering the regular way of introducing indirect discourse (see Intr. lv f.), it appears that 2157 must contain a general statement of similar import to that of the following lines introduced by *cwæð*. The noun *ēst* may be ' bequest,' ' bequeathing ' (cp. *syllan* 2160, almost = *unnan*), and *his . . . ēst* may express ' its transmission,' i.e. its history (in which case the use of the adverb *ǣrest* suggests that of *æfter* in 12, 2731), cf. *MPh.* iii 264, 462 f. Or *ēst* may be interpreted as ' gracious gift,' — " that I should describe to thee his gracious gift " (B.-T. Suppl.). The separation of *his* from *ēst* might possibly be cited in favor of the former explanation (see 2579). — When Grettir's mother presented him with a sword, she said: 'This sword was owned by Jǫkull, my father's father, and the earlier Vatnsdal men, in whose hands it was blessed with victory. I give it to you; use it well.' (*Grettissaga*, ch. 17.)

2164 f. lungre, gelīce, according to Kock² 117, ' swift and all alike.' This explanation was called in question (*M L N.* xxxiv 133) on the ground that the two coordinate members of such asyndetic phrases (nouns or adjectives, see note on 398) are commonly synonymous or, at any rate, of distinctly similar scope, and one of them is normally a regular compound. However, as regards the latter objection, Professor Kock (in a private communication) points out that similar combinations are, in fact, not lacking, e.g. *beald, geblētsod, Gr.-Wü.* ii 240.12, *forhte, āfǣrde, Andr.* 1340; and, as to the disparity of meaning between the two adjectives, an exception to the rule may be admitted in view of the fairly analogous cases of the type *īsig ond ūtfūs* 33, cf. *Angl.* xxix 381. It should be mentioned that an adj. **lungor** does not seem to be recorded in OE., except in the compound *cēaslunger* = ' *contentiosus*,' *Rule of Chrodegang* 19.12, but *lungar*, ' quick,' or ' strong ' occurs in the *Heliand;* also OHG. *lungar,* ' quick,' ' strenuous.' (Cf. Kock L 5.44.4.43 f.; Cook's note on *Chr.* 167.) [Grattan, in (Wyatt-) Chambers's edition of 1920, assigns to *lungre* (adverb) its usual sense of ' straightway ': ' straightway four horses all alike followed the other gifts.' This interpretation is rendered doubtful by the position of *lungre.*] — Only in this passage does lāst (*swaðe*) **weardian** carry the meaning of ' follow,' see Gr. Spr.: *weardian.* On the form *weardode*, see Lang. §§ 19.3, 25.6. —**æppelfealuwe**; cf. Lüning L 7.28.208 f. In older German, *apfelgrau* is a favorite epithet of horses. Similarly, ON. *apalgrár* is used of horses (e.g., *Njálssaga,* ch. 157.6). Cf. also Cook, L 4.129 b.2.6 n. 21.

2166 ff. Do these lines allude to Heoroweard (so Cha. Intr.[2] 429)? To judge from the evidence afforded by the *Beowulf*, the author may as well have had Hrōðulf's behavior in mind.

2168[a]. **dyrnum cræfte** may belong as well with the following as with the preceding member of the clause. *hondgesteallan* is clearly variation of *ōðrum*, i.e. *mǣge*.

2172[a]. **Hȳrde ic þæt hē ðone healsbēah.** See 2163 and note on 62 f. For the scansion of **2173**[a], **wrǣtlicne wundurmāððum**, see Intr. lxx & n. 1, T.C. § 19. — How many of the presents did Bēowulf keep for himself?

2179 ff. See note on Heremōd, p. 162.

2181. Does **mǣste cræfte** imply ' with the greatest self-control '? (Cp. *geþyldum healdan* 1705.) Hoops St. 76 ff. ingeniously conjectured that *cræft* was used here as a fem. (as in OHG. and, partly, in OS.), *mǣste cræfte* being parallel with *ginfæstan gife* (cp. 1270 f.), and *ac* carrying the sense of ' and yet ' (or ' although '). (Another instance of the fem. gender, 418 (MS.)? Cf. *ESt.* lxviii 115.)

2183 ff. Hēan wæs lange etc. The introduction of the commonplace story of the sluggish youth is not very convincing (cp. 408 f.). See Intr. xiv n. 3, xxvii n. 6; note on 1931-62 (Offa).

2185 f. nē hyne on medobence micles wyrðne/drihten Wedera gedōn wolde. *wyrðe*, ' having a right to,' assumes, especially in legal language, the pregnant sense of ' possessed of,' see B.-T., p. 1200, viii; Liebermann L 9.10.2. ii 1, Gloss.: *wierðe; MLN.* xviii 246; hence *micles wyrðne gedōn,* ' put in possession of much,' i.e. ' bestow large gifts (on him).' That *wereda* of the MS. is a corruption of *Wedera*, seems all the more natural, as *weoroda Dryhten* is invariably applied to the ' Lord of Hosts ' (Rankin, *JEGPh.* viii 405).

2195. seofan þūsendo. *þūsend* is sometimes used ' of value without expressing the unit ' (B.-T.). In this case, as also, e.g., repeatedly in *Bede*, the *hīd* (' familia ') is evidently understood (see Leo L 4.24.101 n. 2; Ettmüller, Transl.; Kluge ix 191 f.; Plummer's *Saxon Chronicles* ii, p. 23; *Angl.* xxvii 411 f.), so that the size of the land given to Bēowulf would equal that of North Mercia; cp. *OE. Bede* 240.2: *Norðmercum, þāra londes is seofon þūsendo* (= iii, c.24: ' familiarum VII milium '). See note on 2994 f.

2198 f. ōðrum, i.e. Hygelāc; þām = *þām þe* (so 2779); sēlra, ' higher in rank.' Cp. 862 f.

208   BEOWULF

The narrative of the **Second Part** is much broken up by digressions. The main story is contained in ll. 2200–31ᵃ, 2278–2349ᵃ, 2397–2424; 2510–2910ᵃ; 3007ᵇ–50, (3058–68), 3076–3182; the previous history of the dragon hoard, in ll. 2231ᵇ–77, 3051 (or 49ᵇ)–57, 3069–75; episodes of Geatish history, in ll. 2354ᵇ(49ᵇ)–96, 2425–2509, (2611–25ᵃ), 2910ᵇ–3007ᵃ.

2200–2323. The robbing of the hoard and the ravages of the dragon.
2202 ff. On the historical allusions, see Intr. xl, ll. 2378 ff.
2207. syððan is used, in a way, correlatively with *syððan* 2201.
2209. wæs ðā frōd cyning, 'the king was then old.'
2213ᵇ. stīg under læg. Type D4. (See 1416ᵇ.)
2215 ff. The supplied readings are of course conjectural, but there are sufficient grounds for believing that they fairly represent the context. (**sē þe nē)h gefe(al)g/hǣðnum horde,** 'who made his way (forwards) near to the heathen hoard'; cp. 2222, 2225, 2290. To judge from the facsimile, the MS. reading *gefeng* (so Holthausen, Schücking, Chambers) is by no means certain. — 2217. **nē hē þæt syððan (bemāð),** 'nor did he [the dragon] afterwards conceal it,' i.e. he showed it very plainly. For the use of *þ(ēah)* 2218, see 1102.
2220. Malone (see Varr.) argues for *bū folcbeorna;* cp. 2313.
2222. sē ðe him sāre gesceōd. *him* refers to the dragon. Cp. 2295.
2223. þ(ēow). A slave, a fugitive from justice, stole a costly vessel from the dragon's hoard, and upon presenting it to his master — one of Bēowulf's men — obtained his pardon, 2281 ff. The vessel was then sent to Bēowulf himself (2404 f.). In the meantime the dragon had commenced his reign of terror. [According to Lawrence, L 4.62 a. 551, " A warrior [*þegn*] (not a slave), having committed a grievous crime, was forced to flee the court of which he was a member, in order to escape the vengeance of the man whom he had injured, or his kinsmen. He therefore plundered the dragon's hoard, so that he might get objects of value by means of which to compose the feud. The rings were apparently used as atonement for the crime, while the cup was given to the ruler [probably Bēowulf] who arranged the settlement." But why should that person be called a 'captive,' as Lawrence translates *hæft* 2408? (See Gloss.; may he have been a war prisoner?)] Cf. Hubbard L 4.62 b; *A*. l 213 f.
2228–31ᵃ. A hypothetical restoration of the missing words might be attempted as follows.

    hwæðre (earm)sceapen (atolan wyrme
    wræcmon ætwand — him wæs wrōht) sceapen —
    (fūs on fēðe, þā hyne) se fǣr begeat.
    Sincfæt (firde).

With 2229ᵇ cp. 2287, 2913; with 2230ᵃ cp. 970. As to *firde*, see 156: *feorran;* also *hæfde,* or *funde* (proposed by Chambers) would be acceptable. — For 2227 the reading *þæt (him from) ðām gyst(e gryre)brōga stōd* would seem natural (so, except for the omission of *him*, Grein¹).

Cp. 2564 f., 783 f.; as to the meaning of *gyst*, see *gryregiest* 2560.

2231 ff. Supplemented by the account of an earlier stage (3049 ff., 3069 ff.), the history of the hoard is briefly this. Long, long ago (3050[a]) the hoard had been placed in the earth by illustrious chieftains (3070). A curse had been laid on it. After a time, it was discovered and seized by certain warriors (2248 f.), who made good use of it. The last survivor of this race returned the treasures to the earth, placing them in a barrow or cave. There the dragon found them and kept watch over them for three hundred years (2278), until the theft of a cup aroused his anger and brought on the tragic fight, in which both Bēowulf and the dragon lost their lives. The hoard was finally buried in the ground with the ashes of the hero.

It will be observed that the somewhat complicated history of the hoard previous to its seizure by the dragon shows a rather modern motivation. A more primitive conception would have taken a treasure-guarding dragon as an ultimate fact. (*Gnom. Cott.* 26: *draca sceal on hlǣwe,/frōd, frætwum wlanc.*) Regarding the story of the last survivor, it has been suggested that, according to the original notion, the man provided in the cave a burial place for himself as well as for his treasures, and was then transformed into a dragon (cp. the story of Fáfnir); see Ettmüller Transl. 177; Simrock L 3.21.201; Bu. 370; Bugge & Olrik L 4.51; also J. Grimm, *Kleinere Schriften* iv 184. — The cave of the dragon represents one of those ancient, imposing stone graves covered with a mound which by later generations were regarded as *enta geweorc* 2717 (cp. Saxo, *Prefacio*, p. 8; also the mod. Dan. *jættestue*, 'giants' chamber'; Grimm D. M. 442 f. [534 f.]), and which are found in the Scandinavian countries as well as in England. (S. Müller i 55 ff., 77 ff., 95, 122 f.; Wright L 9.3.71 ff.; cf. Schuchhardt, *R.-L.* iii 206 ff.) See Figure 5 inserted in this edition.

The inconsistencies discovered by Stjerna in regard to the place where the hoard was deposited, the nature of the objects composing it, and the depositors (Stjer. 37 ff., 136 ff.) cannot be admitted to exist. [For a study of the whole subject, see also Lawrence L 4.62 a.]

2239[b]–41[a]. wēnde þæs ylcan,/þæt hē lȳtel fæc longgestrēona/brūcan mōste; 'he expected the same [fate as had befallen all his relatives], viz. that he would be permitted to enjoy the ancient treasures only a short time.'

2241[b]. eallgearo. **2243[a].** nīwe. The burial place was specially prepared, not used before — in a way, a distinction; cf. S. Müller i 411. (*A. l* 214.)

2247–66. This characteristic, impressive elegy (see Intr. liii f., note on 2105 ff.) may be compared with the recital of the bereaved father's sorrow, 2444 ff., which is also virtually a sample of elegiac verse but nearer its prototype, viz. the lament for the dead or funeral dirge (see 1117 f., 3152 ff., 3171 ff.). Cf. L 4.126 (Schücking, Sieper).

2252. gesāwon seledrēam. The emendation *secga* could be supported by *Andr.* 1655 f. (*Rid.* 64.1). The series *secga — segan — sēgon — gesāwon* would show the conjectural line of scribal alteration. (*ESt.* xxxix 465.) Kock² 118 pleads for the retention of *gesāwon:* " who had seen [the last of]," cp. 2726 f., si. *Guðl.* 393. (W. Morris: " The hall-joy had they seen.")

2253ᵃ. oððe fe(o)r(mie). Type C2.

2255–56ᵃ. Sceal se hearda helm etc. The inf. *wesan* is understood. See 3021.

2258–60. gē swylce sēo herepād etc. Note the vocalic end rime, enjambment of alliteration, and the use of the same alliteration in two successive lines.

2259. ofer borda gebræc, ' over the crashing shields '; see 2980.

2261. æfter (wīgfruman), lit. ' behind,' ' following,' hence ' along with ' (*JEGPh.* vi 197). Cf. Kock⁵ 179 f.; *A.*l 214 f. The striking personification of the corselet traveling far, by the side of heroes, is matched by *Waldere* ii 18: *standeð mē hēr on eaxelum Ælfheres lāf* (cp. *eaxlgestealla*). Note also *Beow.* 1443 ff.

2262. Næs (adv.) **hearpan wyn.** The verb ' is ' is understood, — ' there is not . . .' See 2297; note on 811.

2263 f. nē gōd hafoc/geond sæl swingeð. It has been established that falcons were tamed in Sweden as early as the seventh century, probably for the chase (Stjer. 36). In England trained hawks (or falcons) seem to have been unknown before the second third of the eighth century, see Cook, *The Date of the Ruthwell and Bewcastle Crosses* (1912), pp. 275 ff. Cf. also Tupper's *Riddles,* p. 110; Roeder, *R.-L.* ii 7 f.; Hoops 246.

2271. opene. According to Lawrence, L 4.62 a.577, " the stones closing the entrance to this ancient tomb had fallen, giving access to the interior."

2278 f. þrēo hund wintra etc. Cp. 1497 f.

2283 f. Đā wæs hord rāsod,/onboren bēaga hord. Merely recapitulation.

2286. fīra fyrngeweorc; i.e., the *fǣted wǣge* 2282, *drincfæt dȳre* 2306.

2287. wrōht wæs genīwad. Probably not ' strife was renewed,' but (lit.) ' strife arose which previously did not exist.' (See, however, also note on 2228 ff.)

2288. stonc ðā æfter stāne. See Gloss.: *stincan.* [The verb form has been thought by various scholars to belong to *stincan* ' emit a smell ' (MnE. *stink*) and has been credited with the unusual sense of ' sniffed,' ' followed the scent.' In case this interpretation is approved, (MHG.) *Ortnit* 570: *als des wurmes houbet vernam des mannes smac* might be cited as a partial parallel.] — **2289. gestōp,** pluperf.

2292 f. sē ðe (' he whom ') **Waldendes/hyldo gehealdeþ.** Cp. 572 f. See Kock² 118 f., Intr. xlix.

2295. þone þe him on sweofote sāre getēode. *sāre* is adverb, not object of the verb, the fem. gender of the noun *sār* being more than

NOTES

doubtful. *getēon*, 'decree,' 'allot,' is used absolutely, perhaps: 'deal with.' (Cp. 2222.) See *A*. l 215.

2297. *hlǣw* is normally masc. (one instance of the neut.: Sievers, *Beitr.* ix 237) and appears as such in all the passages of our poem where the gender can be seen (2803, 2804, 3157 2412?). Hence **ealne** should not be changed to *eal*. Nor should **ūtanweardne** be condemned on metrical grounds.

2298. wīges gefeh, that is to say, by anticipation.

2315. lyftfloga. On the flying dragon, see note on *Finnsb*. 3; *Angl*. xxxvi 188 n. 2.

2324–2537. Preparation for the dragon fight.

2324 ff. Was Bēowulf not at home? Did the author desire to have the tidings announced through a messenger? (Cf. Intr. xxii, cvi.)

2329–31. Bēowulf did not yet know the real cause of the dragon's ravages, see 2403 ff. The phrase **ofer ealde riht**, 'contrary to old law' (cp. Ags. Laws, *Hloðh. & Eadr*. 12: *an eald riht*), is here given a Christian interpretation.

2334. ēalond. Cf. Intr. xxii, xlviii n. 4. Neither Saxo's island (Sievers) nor the islands of Zealand (Boer) or Öland (Stjer. 91 f.), but 'land bordering on water' (Bu. Tid. 68, Bu. 5). An apparently analogous use of *īgland*, *ēalond*: *Andr*. 15, *Phoen*. 9, 287, *Sal*. 1 was pointed out by Krapp, *MPh*. ii 403 f. (See also NED.: *island*.) Also *insula* is found in medieval Latin in this wider sense (cf. *Beitr*. xxxv 541). [Aant. 34.]

2336. wrǣce leornode. From the standpoint of the poem, the defense of the country and desire of revenge is the hero's primary motive. The winning of the hoard (2535 f., 2747 ff., 2794 ff.), which is the sole object in Frotho's dragon fight (Intr. xxi f.), could be easily associated with it. (Cf. *A*. xxxvi 191 and n. 2.) The secondary motive of the hoard in the last part of the *Nibelungenlied* may be recalled.

2338. The form **eallīrenne**, considered acc. masc., was tentatively explained on the supposition that the author had in mind the noun *scyld*. (*ESt*. xxxix 465.) But it is simpler to take it as the weak acc. neut. (Hoops St. 121 f.)

2353ᵇ–54ᵃ. Grendeles mǣgum, i.e. the 'Grendel family,' meaning, of course, Grendel and his mother. (Cp. *Finnes eaferum* 1068.) **lāðan cynnes** 'of (or: 'belonging to') a hateful race'; cp. 1729.

2354ᵇ. Nō þæt lǣsest wæs ...; cp. 1455. There follows here the second of the allusions to Hygelāc's last adventure, see Intr. xxxix f.

2358. hiorodryncum swealt, 'died by sword-drinks,' i.e. by the sword drinking his blood. Cf. Krüger, *Beitr*. ix 574; Rickert, *MPh*. ii 66 ff.; *Arch*. cxxvi 349 & n. 2. The nearest semasiological parallel of the unique compound is *gryrum ecga* 483.

2361 f. hæfde him on earme (āna) **þrītig/hildegeatwa ...** Here Bēowulf is seen to combine his proficiency in swimming with his thirty-men's strength. The extraordinary skill of ancient German tribes in swimming (crossing, e.g., the rivers Rhine and Danube in full armor) is testified to by Roman historians; cf. Müllenhoff L 9.14.1.334 f.; Bjarnason, *R.-L.* iii 150. — Malone, who would read *bēag* ('turned,' 'fled '), not *stāg*, does not think that Bēowulf took those thirty sets of armor with him across the ocean (*Eng. Studies* xv 151).

2367ª. Unless we assume this to be an isolated hypermetrical half-line (cf. Intr. lxx & n. 1), the second part of **sioleða** cannot be connected with *ȳð* (Gr.: 'seals' waves,' see Varr.). Dietrich's explanation of the noun (*ZfdA.* xi 416) on the basis of *sol* 'mud,' 'wet sand ' has been rightly abandoned, especially as the testimony of the form *sole, Beow.* 302 (MS.) cannot be accepted. Bugge (Zs. 214) suggested connection with the stem found in Go. *anasilan* ' become quiet (silent),' Swed. dial. *sil* ' quiet water.' See Falk-Torp, *Etym. Wbch.: sildre;* Hoops St. 123 f.

2379–96. On these Swedish wars, see Intr. xl, xliii f.

2385–86ª. feorhwunde hlēat,/sweordes swengum. This is Kock's punctuation, L 5.44.4.9. The verb *hlēotan* takes the gen., acc., or instr. (so *Chr.* 783). — *orfeorme* (MS.), which Brett tries to vindicate (*MLR.* xiv 2: ' without support ' [?]), is precluded by considerations of meter and sense.

2392 f. Ēadgilse wearð ... frēond; i.e., he supported Ēadgils. Cp. the pregnant meaning of *lufian* 1982, *hatian* 2466, etc.

2395 f. hē refers to Ēadgils. [It has been suggested, as a remote possibility, that Onela (Áli) was killed by Bēowulf himself, who would thus be assigned the rôle of Starkaðr (*Ynglingasaga,* ch. 25 (29), see note on Heremōd, p. 163); cf. Belden, *MLN.* xxviii 153, Intr. xliii n. 2.] **hē gewræc . . /cealdum cearsīðum,** ' he avenged [it, viz. the previous hostile acts] by means of expeditions fraught with harm and distress '? (cp. *sorhfullne sīð* 512, 1278, 1429). As the battle between Aðils and Áli was fought on the ice of Lake Väner (Par. § 5, ch. 55; § 6, ch. 29), Bugge (13) thought of taking *cealdum* in its literal sense of physical cold.

2418. hǣlo ābēad carries no reference to good luck needed on this particular occasion (as in 653), but means, quite in general, ' saluted.'

2419ᵇ–23ª. The expression of gloomy forebodings might recall Mark xiv 33 f. (Mat. xxvi 37 f.). (**wyrd . . .) sē,** see note on 1887 (also 1344). — **sēcean sāwle hord** 2422 comes to the same as *sāwle sēcan* 801.

2423ᵇ. nō þon lange presents, perhaps, a contamination of *nō þon leng* (the normal compar. in connection with *þon*) and *nō . . . lange.* See also note on 968.

2425–2537. Bēowulf speaks.

2428 ff. Ic wæs syfanwintre etc. On the custom (practised with especial frequency in Scandinavia) of placing children in the homes of others for their education, see F. Roeder, *Über die Erziehung der vornehmen ags. Jugend in fremden Häusern,* 1910; cf. L. M. Larson, *JEGPh.* xi 141–43. The training of youths was supposed to begin at the age of seven; cf. Grimm R. A. 411. In the case of Bede we have his own testimony: *mid þȳ ic wæs seofanwintre, þā wæs ic mid gīmene mīnra māga* *seald tō fēdanne ond tō lǣrenne þām ārwyrþan abbude Benedicte ond Cēolferþe æfter þon*, OE. Bede 480.25 ff. (= v, c. 24).

2432 ff. næs ic him . . . lāðra etc. Litotes. — The poet does not state directly that Bēowulf was brought up together with his uncles, but such is the natural interpretation. It involves chronological inconsistency, see Intr. xxxviii, xlv.

2435 ff. On the slaying of **Herebeald** by Hæðcyn, see Intr. xli. Accidental homicide was punishable. Yet Hrēðel cannot fulfill the duty of avenging his son, because he must not lift his hand against his own kin. The king's morbid surrender to his grief is significant. — On the relation of the accidental slaying of Herebeald by Hæðcyn to the Baldr story, see Neckel, L 4.88 b.141 ff.; Nerman, L 4.97 c. 2.71 ff., and *Edda* iii, 1–10. Neckel thinks that an actual occurrence at Hrēðel's court forms the basis of this episode, which, however, was represented in such a manner as to convey a subtle allusion to the fate of Baldr. For another line of comment, see Malone, *Hamlet* 156 ff., L 4.92 e. 783 f., 799.

2436. (wæs . . .) morþorbed strēd; cf. T.C. §§ 1, 6. The phrase recalls the Lat. 'lectum sternere,' cf. *Arch.* cxxvi 353. The corresponding (*hildbedd*) *styred*, *Andr.* 1092 is no doubt an error for *strē(i)d* (Cosijn, *Beitr.* xxi 15).

2438. frēawine is not entirely inappropriate, since Herebeald is the elder brother and heir presumptive.

2444. Swā bið geōmorlīc gomelum ceorle. *Swā* introduces an example or illustration (see note on 1769), in this instance the imaginary case of an old man sorrowing for his son who has been hanged (2444–62[a]). It has been suggested (Holthausen, *Beibl.* iv 35; Gering, note) that the author was thinking of the story of Jǫrmunrekr and his son Randvér (*Vǫlsungasaga*, ch. 40; cp. Saxo viii 280). In both cases the misery of childlessness is emphasized (see 2451 ff.). But there is nothing in the Beowulfian allusion to indicate that the father himself caused the son to be hanged.

2446. þonne hē gyd wrece could be regarded as the continuation of (*þæt*) *his byre rīde*, which would account for the subjunctive (cf. Bu. Tid. 56). But *wreceð* may well be the correct reading.

2448. helpe. The scribe who penned *helpan* expected the infin. of the verb before *ne mæg*. The noun is demanded by *ǣnige* 2449[b]. A wk. fem. *helpe* is unknown in OE. poetry. [Kock 221; *MPh.* iii 463.]

2454. (hafað) dǣda gefondad, '(has) experienced [evil] deeds'; cf. *Arch.* cxv 181.

2455–59. Gesyhð sorhcearig on his suna būre/wīnsele wēstne etc. The wine-hall is apparently thought of as part of the son's *būr*, which must be meant here in the general sense of 'dwelling' or 'mansion.' But why should a number of dead warriors be referred to? (If *rīdend* 2457[b] be taken as 'the one hanging on the gallows,' *swefað* has to be changed to *swefeð*, *Angl.* xxviii 446.) The explanation is that the old man falls into a reverie, seeing with his mind's eye the scene of desolation, or, in other words, the poet passes from the actual, specific situation to a typical motive of elegiac poetry; cf. Schücking, *ESt.* xxxix 10. **2456ᵇ-57ᵃ. windge reste/rēote berofene,** 'the wind-swept resting place deprived of joy.' The hall was also used for sleeping, as the happenings in Heorot show. We are reminded of *Wand.* 76: *winde biwāune weallas stondaþ*, 86: *burgwara breahtma lēase* . . . A fem. *windgerest* (thus, e.g., Schücking, Sedgefield, Chambers) is exceedingly problematical. In place of *reote* (MS., see Varr.), Kock⁵ 178 f. suggested *rōte, on the strength of an ON. noun *rót*, 'the inner part of the roof of the house.' But see Hoops St. 6, 124. For the spelling *reote*, see Lang. § 16 n. — (Longfellow was deeply impressed by this passage, as is shown by his alluding to it in *Hyperion*, Book ii, ch. 10.)

2460. Gewīteð þonne on sealman. The old man goes to his own chamber. **sorhlēoð gæleð.** We cannot be quite sure that this is not merely a high-flown expression implying 'lamentation'; cf. note on 786 ff. — **2461. ān æfter ānum,** strikingly expressive of the father's solitary state. (Leonard: 'chanteth a sorrow-song, the lone one for the lost one.') — **þūhte.** The pret. is fully justified. After a survey of the grounds and buildings the lonely father has retired.

2468. mid þære sorhge, 'with that sorrow in his heart.'

2469 ff. See Intr. cx & n. 3 (parallel passages in *Gen.*).

2472-89. On this first series of Swedish wars, see Intr. xxxviii f.

2475. him, dat. plur. ('ethic dative').

2481. þēah ðe ōðer his/ealdre gebohte. Should the line be metrically divided as *þēah ðe ōðer/his ealdre gebohte* (and similarly, *Finnsb.* 47: *hū ðā wīgend/hyra wunda genǣson*) or should *his* (*hyra*) be placed in the first half-line? The latter division of l. 2481 is defended by Kock, *AfNF.* xxxix 188 f., the former division of *Finnsb.* 47 by Heusler, *Deutsche Versgeschichte* i, § 254; cf. also Bohlen, L 8.24.15 f.; *A. l* 215. The object (*hit*) need not be expressed, cp. 2395ᵇ. *ōðer,* viz. one of the two *mǣgwine* 2479 (Hæðcyn and Hygelāc).

2484 f. þā ic . . . gefrægn mǣg ōðerne . . . on bonan stǣlan, 'then, as I have heard, one kinsman [Hygelāc] avenged the other [Hæðcyn] on the slayer [Ongenþēow]'; cf. Aant. 23; Kock 232 f., Kock⁵ 180 f.; *A. l* 215 f. Hygelāc did not perform the act personally, cf. note on 1968. A detailed narrative of these encounters is given in 2924 ff., 2961 ff.

2490. him must refer to Hygelāc. There is an abrupt change of topics.

2494. The **Gifðas** (Lat. 'Gepidae'), a tribe closely related to the Goths, left their seats near the mouth of the Vistula as early as the third century and settled in the district north of the lower Danube. Their kingdom was destroyed by the Lombards in the latter half of the sixth century. According to this passage, tradition still associated them with their old home.

2497 f. symle ic him on fēðan beforan wolde,/āna on orde. The true heroic note. Cp., e.g., *Iliad* vi 444 f.; *Hildebr.* 27 (*her was eo folches at ente* . . .); *Wald.* i 18 ff.

2501 ff. Another allusion to Hygelāc's Frankish expedition. **Dæghrefn**, very likely the slayer of Hygelāc, was killed by Bēowulf, who took from him his sword (*Nægling* 2680). (Cf. Rie. Zs. 414; *Arch.* cxv 181.) It is decidedly interesting to note that Dæghrefn is a Frankish, non-Ags. name; cf. Schröder, *Anz.fdA.* xii 181, & *Die deutschen Personennamen* (*Festrede*, Göttingen, 1907), p. 9. — It is not quite certain that **for dugeðum** means ' in the presence of the hosts '; *duguð* may have been used in the abstract sense (cf. Gloss.).

2505. in campe (MS. *cempan*). As *cempa* has nowhere the function of a collective noun (cf. Gloss.: *on*), and *in* (*on*) is never found in the sense of ' among ' with a plural denoting ' men,' *cempan* is unacceptable both as dat. sing. and dat. plur. Cf. Siev. xxxvi 409 f. The scribe evidently had in mind *cempan* of 2502.

2514. Though *mǣrðum* ' gloriously ' is not an impossible reading (see Chambers), the emendation **mǣrðu** is antecedently probable; see 2134, 2645, *Seaf.* 84, *Rid.* 73.11. Cf. Bu. 103 f.

2520 f. If **gylpe** is interpreted as ' proudly,' ' gloriously ' (cp. 1749, 868; according to Chambers: ' in such a manner as to fulfill my boast '), no change of the MS. reading is needed.

2523. Cook (*MLN.* xl 137–42) advances the view that the poet knew Aldhelm's *De Virginitate*, both the metrical and the prose version, and derived from the latter the remarkable combination [o]reðes **ond attres**, which answers to Aldhelm's expression applied to a dragon, *virus et flatus* (taken as a *hendiadys* = ' venomous breath '). The evidence can hardly be called adequate, cf. *Angl.* l 241 f.

2525. (Nelle ic beorges weard) oferfleon fōtes trem, ac unc [furður] sceal ... The critics' treatment of this line has been essentially influenced by the parallel passage, *Mald.* 247: (*þæt ic heonon nelle*) *flēon fōtes trym, ac wille furðor gān.* For the scansion of 2525ᵃ, see T.C. § 24. [2526 f. Grein's reading: *wyrd* (acc.) *getēoð/Metod.*]

2538–2711. The dragon fight. On the fight and on the dragon, see Intr. xxi ff., xxv, l; Par. § 7: Saxo ii 38 f. There are three distinct phases of this combat (just as of the fight with Grendel's mother); the second begins at 2591ᵇ (or, a long digression intervening, at 2669), the third at 2688. Cf. *Angl.* xxxvi 193 n. 3.

2538. Ārās ðā bī ronde. The analogy of expressions like *under helme* (see Gloss.: *under*) lends some support to the view that *bī ronde* means ' with the shield (by his side).' Yet the prepositional phrase may be directly connected with the verb (cp. 749), ' leaning on the shield.'

2545 f. strēam, burnan wælm denote the *dracan lēg* 2549. (Hoops St. 127.)

2547. ne meahte; either ' he ' or ' any one ' (*man*) is understood as the subject. See Lang. § 25.4.

2552. Holt. regards this line as parenthetical.

2556ᵇ. From ǣrest cwōm. Type D4.

2558ᵇ. hrūse dynede. In the *Vǫlsungasaga*, ch. 18, at the approach of the dragon, *varþ svá mikill landskjálfti, svá at ǫll jǫrþ skalf í nánd;* cp. *Lied vom Hürnen Seyfrid* 21; *Beues of Hamtoun* (ed. Kölbing, E.E.T.S.) 2737 f.; Gottfried von Strassburg's *Tristan* 9052 ff. (Also *Hel.* 5801: *thiu erða dunida* [=Mat. xxviii 2]. Cf. Cook's notes on *Christ* 826, 881.)

2564. ecgum unslāw. See Varr. The reading *unglāw* or *anglāw* (see note on 357), = ' very sharp ' was advocated, *A.* xxix 380, *ESt.* xxxix 466, Ed.[1] (*glāw* a variant form of *glēaw*, Lang. § 15 n.), although the physical sense of ' sharp ' does not happen to be recorded elsewhere. Somewhat less risky is the emendation *unslāw*, since the meaning ' blunt ' for *slāw* may be inferred from occasional ME. and MnE. instances and from the cognate Germanic languages. (Hoops St. 128.)

2566. gestōd wið stēapne rond. Cp. 749. (*Æn.* xi 283 f.: ' quantus/ in clipeum adsurgat,' *Waltharius* 529: ' [quantus] in clipeum surgat.')

2573-75. ðǣr hē þȳ fyrste forman dōgore/wealdan mōste, swā him wyrd ne gescrāf/hrēð æt hilde. A perplexing passage: *ðǣr* may be adverb or conjunction, *mōste*=' might ' or ' must ' (' had to '), *wealdan* may be construed with *þȳ fyrste* or *forman dōgore* or be used absolutely, also its meaning is debatable. Taking mōste as ' might ' and **ðǣr** as conjunction, ' if ', we obtain for ll. 2573 f. *ðǣr hē þȳ fyrste forman dōgore/wealdan mōste* (a semi-parenthetic clause, i.e., an individualized variety of the formula *gif hē wealdan mōt*, and fairly analogous to *Jul.* 570, *El.* 979) an interpretation which connects them definitely with the preceding lines and which also accounts for the puzzling juxtaposition of *þȳ fyrste* and *forman dōgore*. The expression *forman dōgore* looks like a particular variety of the type *forman sīðe;* as to *þȳ fyrste* (to be construed with *wealdan*), ' the allotted time,' this naturally contains a reference to *lǣssan hwīle* (cp. 2555[b]). The relevance of this seemingly strange clause is fully explained by the emphatic *þonne his myne sōhte*. Accordingly, the general sense would be: ' if he might have controlled events (with particular reference to the length of time his shield would protect him) for the first time (in his life), — but fate decreed otherwise.' The *swā . . . ne* clause may be compared to 2585. Cf. *MPh.* iii 464, *A.* l 216 f. — On the other hand, on the basis of mōste=' must ' and **ðǣr**, adv., we may translate: ' there he had to spend his time (Chambers), (on the first day, i.e.:) for the first time in his life, in such a way that fate did not assign to him glory in battle '; or — taking **wealdan** in an absolute sense — ' there and then (cp. *þā ðǣr* 331, 1280), for the first time, he had to manage (get along) without victory ' (so substantially Müllenhoff xiv 233, Heyne). Or, again: ' there, on that occasion, he lived to see the first day when . . .' (Hoops, in substantial agreement with Kock[5] 181.) As to such function of *wealdan* (i.e., construed with *fyrste* or *dōgore*), perhaps=' make use of,' cp. *Guðl.* 239 *līfe wēoldon*, Laȝamon's *Brut* 1800 *þat heo heora wiildaȝas wælden[d] weoren;* also *Beow.* 1953 *līfgesceafta brēac*.

2577. incge-lāfe (perhaps a compound). *incge* is as obscure as *icge*

1107, with which (as well as with *īsig* 33) it has been conjecturally connected. [Note also *Ex.* 190: *ingemen*, 142: *ingefolc*.] *Inges*, or *Ingwines* (see Proper Names, Intr. xxxvii, and note on Scyld, p. 123 f.), is a desperate remedy for a desperate case. *ē(a)cnan, īcnan*, or *īcnen* (cp. 1663ᵃ, 2140ᵃ, 1104ᵇ [MS.]) could also be proposed. Quite possibly the scribe did not understand the word. [See note on 1107.]

2579. his ... þearfe hæfde, ' had need of it.'

2586–88. It is possible that **grundwong** refers to the dragon's cave (see 2770) or the ground in front of it (cf. Bu. Tid. 298). But it seems on the whole more natural that it should denote the same as *eormengrund*, *ginne grund*, i.e., earth in general (as explained by earlier scholars), or that the phrase ' give up that region,' in this context, implies ' leaving the earth ' (Aant. 36). These lines and the following ones express nearly the same idea, the former negatively, the latter positively. Considering further the contrast between *wolde* 2588 and *sceolde* [*ofer*] *willan* 2589, we may venture to translate literally: ' that was not a pleasant (willing) journey (or, course of action) [i.e.] that the illustrious son of Ecgðēow was willing to leave the earth.' (*ESt.* xxxix 466, *MLN.* xxiv 94 f.)

2595. sē ðe ǣr folce wēold, " he who used to rule a nation ?" (Cl. Hall). Cp. *Æneid* ii 554 ff. [Bu. Zs. 216; Aant. 36.]

2596 ff. The disloyalty of the ten cowardly followers of Bēowulf, who flee for their lives, is not unlike the defection of the disciples of Christ, see Mark xiv 50, Mat. xxvi 56. (Also the injunction to the companions, 2529 may recall Mark xiv 34, Mat. xxvi 38.) Likewise, Wīglāf's heroic assistance is matched by the ἀριστεία of Peter (Mat. xxvi 51, John xviii 10) so nobly glorified in the *Heliand* (4867 ff.). [A note by P. F. Jones, *MLN.* xlv 300 f.]

2599ᵇ. Hiora in ānum. See note on 100ᵇ.

2600 f. sibb' ǣfre ne mæg/wiht onwendan. As the intrans. use of *onwendan* (i.e. ' change ') is not authenticated, *sibb* is now commonly taken as acc., and *wiht* as nom. Still, the possibility of construing *sibb* as the subject of the clause is to be conceded; ' kinship can never change anything,' i.e. ' will always prevent a change (of heart).' For **þām ðe wēl þenceð**, see note on 287 ff.

2602 ff. On **Wīglāf** and **Wēohstān**, see Intr. xliv, xxii; on the form of introducing Wīglāf, *ib.* ci n. 5.

2614. his māgum; *his* probably refers to Ēanmund; the generic term *māgum*, by implication, refers to Onela.

2616. ealdsweord etonisc. This looks like a harking back to the mysterious sword in the Grendel cave (see note on 1555 f.); cf. *Angl.* xxxv 261 n. 1. So 2979.

2618 f. nō ymbe ðā fǣhðe spræc,/þēah ðe hē [i.e. Wēohstān] **his brōðor bearn ābredwade.** *his* refers to Onela, the subject of *spræc*. " Onela's passive attitude was due to the fact that his nephew was a lawless exile, and so no longer entitled to protection from his kin." (Seebohm L 9.17.66 f.) Herein is seen a breaking away from the primitive tribal custom, cf. Chadwick H. A. 347 f. The expression *nō . . . sprǣc* (litotes), by the way, is meant to be more than a mere negative declaration.

2623. gūðgewǣda quite possibly stands for the acc. pl. *-gewǣdu* (Lang. § 18.2). Cp. 3134 f. (also 2028 f., 2067 f.).

2628. mǣges. A general term, instead of 'father.'

2633 ff. On this noble 'comitatus' speech (and certain close parallels), see Intr. lvi, lxii; Par. § 7: Saxo ii 59 ff., § 9: *Hrólfssaga*, chs. 32 f. Cf. Bugge 45 ff.; Phillpotts L 4.146 e (assumes an ultimate Danish source for the *Beowulf*, *Maldon*, and *Bjarkamál* passages).

2638. Ðē hē ūsic on herge gecēas, 'on this account he chose us (from) among the host.' This function of *on* is parallel to that found in combination with *niman*, see Gloss.: *on;* cp. *Vita Guthlaci* 1.7: *him þā āne gecēas on þǣre mǣdena hēape*. *Ðē* is used correlatively with *þē* 2641; see Gloss.: *sē, þē.*

2640ᵃ. onmunde ūsic mǣrða. *onmunan* (with or without the adj. *wyrþe*), 'consider worthy of.' Kock[5] 70 (cf. Gr. Spr.): lit. 'think on someone in connection with something,' 'remember one with something.' There is no basis for the meaning 'remind' very generally ascribed to it.

2640ᵇ. mē implies 'to me as well as to the rest of us.'

2649ᵇ. þenden hyt sȳ. See Varr. That *hyt* should be the 'proleptic' pronoun is not likely (though perhaps not impossible). The assumption of a noun *hit(t)* 'heat' — first definitely proposed by Grein — has been largely approved by modern scholars.

2651. lēofre. See Lang. § 25.2.

2657. þæt nǣron ealdgewyrht, 'he has never deserved it.' *þæt* is probably pronoun.

2658. duguðe, partit. gen. with *hē āna*, 2657.

2659 f. ūrum . . . bām, instead of *unc bām* or **ūre bām* (cp. 2532, 596), is due to attraction. Examples of similar genit. combinations are cited by Cosijn (viii 573) and Chambers; cf. *P. Grdr.*² i 775. The general sense is of course: 'I will join you in the fight.' Gummere's rendering " My sword and helmet . . . for us both shall serve " is perhaps a little too precise. **byrne** and **beaduscrūd** are synonymous, see 1454ᵃ (2321 f., 3163).

2663 ff. There is a singular lack of propriety in making young Wīglāf administer fatherly advice to Bēowulf. It is the author that speaks.

2672 f. Līgȳðum forborn/bord wið rond. It is a question whether *rond* should be rendered here by 'boss' or 'border.' Hoops, like Cook, *MLN*. xli 362 prefers 'border,' 'rim '; also Sedgefield (note) thinks *wið rond[e]* may have meant 'round the edge.' For the meaning 'shield-boss,' see, e.g., Neckel L 10.2.32. As to *rond* or *rond[e]*, cf. T.C. § 22.

2683 ff. A sword in Bēowulf's hands was liable to break on account of his excessive strength. A typical feature frequently met with in old Germanic literature. (E.g., Saxo iv 115 (Offa); Vǫlsungasaga, chs. 15, 35.) Cf. *MPh.* iii 464 f.; also Panzer 35, 41 f., 52 f., 281 n. As to Bēowulf's use of swords, see 435 ff., 679 ff., etc. [Müll. xiv 229; Jellinek & Kraus, *ZfdA.* xxxv 268 f.]

2696[b]. swā him gecynde wæs. A conventional idea. Cp. *Brun.* 7 f.: *swā him geæþele wæs/fram cnēomāgum;* (OHG.) *Ludwigslied* 51: *thaz uuas imo gekunni.*

2697 ff. The statement is not quite clear logically. It involves the anticipation of the result of the action: sīo hand gebarn 2697[b], and a loose use of þæt 2699[a] (see Gloss.). The meaning is this: 'he did not care for (i.e. aim at) the head [of the dragon], but his hand was burned in striking the monster a little lower down, etc.' Dragons are vulnerable in their lower parts; see especially Par. § 7: Saxo ii 38 f. (Frotho's dragon fight). Cf. Bu. 105. [Aant. 37: 'he did not care for his (own) head, i.e. life.']

2705. The context leaves it somewhat undecided whether Bēowulf or Wīglāf is the real victor in the combat with the dragon. But the poet manages to let Bēowulf have the honor of the final blow. Cp. 2835, 2876.

2706. ferh ellen wræc, 'strength drove out life.' Cp. *Gen.* 1385 f.: *ȳða wrǣcon ārlēasra feorh/of flǣschoman.* [Heyne took *ferh* as the subject.] Hoops St. 130 f.: *ferh ellor wræc* (intr.), see Varr.; but cf. *ESt.* lxvii 400.

2710. sīðas (MS.) sigehwīle. As we cannot be sure that the spelling *sīðas* (in place of the grammatically correct *sīðost*) is not due to a scribal misunderstanding of the sense, it seems reasonable to emend it.

2711-2820. Bēowulf's death.

2717-19. seah on enta geweorc,/hū ðā stānbogan stapulum fæste/ēce eorðreced innan healde. One of the difficulties supposed to be in this passage (see Varr.) is removed by construing *eorðreced* (not *stānbogan*) as subject, and *stānbogan* as object (so Kemble, Arnold, Earle, Cl. Hall, Chambers, cf. Sedgefield). The stone chamber is indeed contained in the ever enduring (or, primeval) earth-house. The change from the preterite to the present is not unprecedented (Lang. § 25.6), and the opt. is naturally accounted for by the idea of examining implied by *seah on* (cp. *nēosian* . . . *hū* 115 f.). **stānbogan** seems to refer to a primitive form of vaulting such as is met with in English and Irish stone graves (S. Müller i 95). (B.-T.: 'natural stone arches,' Schü. Bd. 77 ff.: 'rock-curvatures,' i.e. 'cave.') There is certainly no need to take *stānbogan* or *stapulas* as architectural terms pointing to the specific Roman art of vault-building (so Stjer. 37 ff.). *stapulas* may very well denote the upright stones. [Schü. Bd. 78 ff. regards *stānbogan* and *eorðreced* as parallel forms (nom.), supplies the object [it], viz. the *enta geweorc*, by which he understands the dragon hoard; *seah on*, 'looked in the direction of.' (?)] Additional comment: Kock[4] 119; *A.* l 217 f.; Hoops St.

132 f. — Interesting light is shed on **enta geweorc** by Saxo's remark (Prefacio, p. 8): ' Danicam vero regionem giganteo quondam cultu exercitam eximie magnitudinis saxa veterum bustis ac specubus affixa testantur,' which is rendered still more entertaining by his query whether giants could have done this ' post diluvialis inundacionis excursum.'

2723. hilde sædne (commonly treated as a compound) is paralleled by *Brun.* 20: (*wērig*,) *wigges sæd*, *Rid.* 6.2: *beadoweorca sæd*.

2724 ff. On Bēowulf's farewell speeches, see *Angl.* xxxvi 193. (*Arch.* cxxvi 345.) On certain points of resemblance (due to imitation in some form) found in the story of Brynhild's death in *Sigurþarkv. en skamma*, see Bugge, *Beitr.* xxii 129.

2724. hē ofer benne spræc. The original, local sense of *ofer:* ' over the wound ' easily passes into the modal one: ' wounded as he was '; cf. Aant. 37; *Arch.* civ 287 ff. (A partial parallel: *Jul. Cæsar* iii 1. 259.) [Not: ' in spite of,' or ' concerning other things than ' (so Corson, *MLN.* iii 97).]

2730 f. þǣr mē gifeðe swā/ǣnig yrfeweard æfter wurde. A blending of two constructions, viz. a) *þǣr mē swā gifeðe* (neuter) *wurde* and b) *þǣr mē yrfeweard gifeðe* (*gifen*) *wurde*. (Cp. *Gen.* 1726 ff.)

2738 f. nē mē (ethic dative) **swōr fela/āða on unriht.** A conspicuous example of litotes.

2748. gearo, meant to be adv. in the text (see 3074, cf. Aant. 41). An original *gearwe* (see Varr.) could have been taken either as apm. or as adv.

2764ᵇ–66. An apparently uncalled-for ethical reflection on the pernicious influence of gold. The curse resting on the gold (3051 ff., 3069 ff.), and the warning against the sin of avarice (1748 ff.) represent the same general idea. (Cf. *Arch.* cxxvi 342 f.) The unique **oferhīgian** has been hypothetically connected with *hycgan* (E.Sc., Rie. L., Heyne, Kern L 5.9), (*ofer*)*hȳgd* (Kluge), *hēah* (Bu. Tid. 59 f.; *ESt.* xxxix 466), and *hīw*, see Varr. But the best hit was made by Ettmüller (*Lexicon Anglosaxonicum* [1851], p. 464; so Gr. Spr., Holt.), who listed it as a compound of (*higjan*, i.e.) *hīgian* (' strive,' ' hie '). The meaning of this *oferhīgian* is presumably ' overtake ' (corresponding exactly to *overhye* of Northern dialects, see Dial. D.), ' get the better of,' ' overpower ' (Ettm.: ' superare ').

2766ᵇ. hȳde sē ðe wylle. According to Kock[5] 182, this *hȳde* stands for *hēde:* ' let him heed it who will.' Phonological evidence has been added by Malone, Jesp. Misc. 45 ff. (cf. *Beibl.* xlii 134 f., xliii 284 ff., xliv 26 f.). But see also *A.* l 219; Hoops St. 134 f.

2769 ff. of ðām lēoma stōd etc. We are reminded of the light in the Grendel cave, 1516 f., 1570 ff.

2773 f. Ðā ic on hlǣwe gefrægn hord rēafian,/eald enta geweorc ānne mannan. Following after a passage of description and reflection, a new and important event is introduced by means of the *gefrægn*-formula (cp. 2694, 2752). The fact that the ' man ' is well known is

ignored. See note on 100ᵇ (*ān*). By *enta geweorc* either the hoard itself or the stone chamber is meant (cp. 2212 f.).

2778ᵃ. ecg wæs īren. " The formula doubtless had come down from days when, as Tacitus says, metals were rare among the Germans and iron had to be imported." Gummere. (See 1459.) — Note the exceptional parenthetic clause in the first half-line; cf. Intr. lxv, cv.

2784. frætwum gefyrðred; i.e., on account of the precious spoils he is anxious to return to Bēowulf.

2788. mid þām māðmum; i.e., 'with the treasures in his hands.'

2791. wæteres weorpan. A rare, but not unparalleled instance of an instrum. genitive, see note on 1825. Cf. Bu. Zs. 218; Aant. 38.

2792ᵇ. [Biorncyning spræc] is to be regarded as slightly better than Schücking's [*þā se beorn gespræc*]. *gesprecan* is regularly used with an object in *Beowulf.* (*maðelode* never occurs in the second half-line.) Cp. also 3094ᵇ–5ᵃ. — **2793ᵃ.** Some ineffectual speculations concerning a possible basis for the MS. reading *giogoðe* are put forward by Brett, *MLR.* xiv 2 f.

2802 ff. The erection of funeral mounds on elevated places near the sea is well attested for Old Norse and Ags. times. An almost literal parallel of this passage occurs *Odyssey* xxiv 80 ff.; cp. xi 75 ff.; *Iliad* vii 85 ff.; *Æneid* vi 232 ff. Cf. Gummere G. O. 310 f.; Wright L 9.3. 469; Montelius 85.

2806. hit is used loosely without regard to the gender of *hlǣw*. See 779.

2821–3030ᵃ. The spread of the sad tidings.

2829. heaðoscearpe. See Varr.; *heaðosceard* would mean 'notched (hacked) in battle,' cp. MnE. shard, sherd, Ger. Scharte.

2836. Hūru þæt on lande lȳt manna ðāh. We have the choice between (1) taking *lȳt* as dat. with impers. *ðēon*, 'that has prospered with few men' (the accus. would be exceedingly questionable) and (2) construing *lȳt* as the subject, assigning to the verb the sense of 'attain,' 'achieve' (cf. *MPh.* iii 465). In the latter case, it is true, *geðēon* would be expected.

2854. wehte, with 'imperfective' function, perhaps: 'tried to rouse (him)'; cp. 1511.

2857. ðæs Wealdendes wiht, 'anything of the Ruler,' i.e. anything ordained by God. (Generalized, semi-adjectival function of *Wealdend.*) Cp. *Hel.* 1058: *forūtar mankunnies wiht.*

2858 f. wolde dōm Godes dǣdum rǣdan/gumena gehwylcum . . . Cp. 1057 f. *dǣdum* carries instrum. sense.

2860. grim andswaru. Of course, not 'answer' in the strictly literal sense.

2869 f. swylce hē þrȳdlīcost/ōwer feor oððe nēah findan meahte. *þrȳdlīcost* is left uninflected; it may be said to agree, theoretically, with an indefinite object 'it.' Only partial parallels are 3161 f., *Jul.* 571 ff. The change of *ð* (*þrȳð-*) to *d* is paralleled by *þrȳdlīce*, Byrhtferð's

Manual 46.5; cf. Siev. § 201.3 (Hoops St. 7, 136.) [Malone, *Eng. Studies* xv 94 further instances *Hrǣdles, Hrǣdlan: Hrēðel.*]

2880 f. symle wæs þȳ sǣmra, þonne ic sweorde drep/ferhðgeniðlan. *symle* (' ever,' ' regularly ') goes naturally with *þonne*. At the same time, the use of *þȳ sǣmra* suggests a variant construction, viz. *symle wæs þȳ sǣmra, þȳ ic swīðor drep* . . . , cp. *Gen.* 1325 f., *Oros.* 18.29 f. Did Wīglāf really mean to imply that he dealt the dragon several blows? (Cf. Schü. Sa. 89 n.) [Cosijn, Aant. 38 placed 2880ᵃ in parenthesis with Bēowulf as subject.]

2884 ff. On the announcement of punishment to the faithless retainers, see Antiq. § 6; Par. § 10: Tacitus, *Germ.*, cc. 6, 14; cf. Grimm R. A. 40 ff., 731 ff.; Kemble's note; Liebermann L 9.10.2.500, 507. Scherer L 5.5.490 saw in 2890 f. a hint to the cowards to end their own lives. (A certain analogue of Wīglāf's denunciation has been detected in Aldhelm's letter to the clergy of Bishop Wilfriǒ (P. F. Jones, *MLN.* xlvii 378).) [On **lufen** 2886, see also Kock⁵ 88 ff., Hoops St. 111.]

2888. īdel hweorfan. It is doubtful whether the idea of ' going,' ' wandering ' was still present in the phrase. Cp. MnE. *go without*, Ger. *verlustig gehen*. Also *Blickl. Hom.* 97.24: *þæt hē sceole þæs ealles īdel hweorfan; Jul.* 381. Cf. *A.* 1 219.

2899. (sægde) ofer ealle. Earle: " in the hearing of all." See Gloss.: *ofer; Finnsb.* 22.

2909 f. healdeð higemǣðum hēafodwearde/lēofes ond lāðes. *lēofes ond lāðes*, i.e., Bēowulf and the dragon. Kock⁵ 78 — like Rieger Zs. 413 — regards *higemǣðum* as parallel to *lēofes ond lāðes*. This is stylistically admissible. Still, it is hard to believe that the dead dragon (*lāð*) should have been described as *higemǣðe* (*hygemēðe*). The term is far more appropriately applied to Wīglāf's state of mind; cp. 2442, also 2408, 3148.

2911 ff. Prediction of an outbreak of hostilities upon the death of the mighty king; cp. 2474; Ælfric, *Saints* xxvi 11 f.: *Ceadwalla slōh and tō sceame tūcode þā Norðhymbran lēode æfter heora hlāfordes fylle.* The same prediction is made at Roland's death, *Chanson de Roland* 2921 ff.

2912 ff. Last allusion to the Frankish war.

2920. dugoðe, dat. sing.

2920 f. Schücking (*ESt.* lv 95 f.), reviving in an improved form Grundtvig's conjecture, would read *merewīcingas* (instead of **Merewīoingas**), which term could be supported by *sǣwīcingas, Exod.* 333. (Thus also Hecht, *Anz.fdA.* xliii 49.) The sentence 2920 f. would then be an extension of the preceding statement referring to Hygelāc's death, *nalles frætwe geaf/ealdor dugoðe*. But why should the messenger express such a sentimental regret (*ā syððan*) more than fifty years after Hygelāc's death — disregarding, it almost seems, Bēowulf's own beneficent reign? The mention of the Merovingian, on the other hand, provides a fitting transition to the second source of danger, the hostility of the Swedes. We may also compare the summing-up remark of ll. 2999 ff. See Brandl L 4.146 d.

NOTES

2922–98. The (first) Swedish war; **battle at Ravenswood**; cp. 2472–89. Intr. xxxix, xlii f.; Par. § 6: *Ynglingasaga*, ch. 27. The only detailed account of a real battle in *Beowulf*.

An interesting parallel of the fight between Ongenþēow and the two brothers occurs in Saxo's account (iv 111 f.)[1] of the slaying of Athislus by the two Danish brothers Keto and Wigo. (Weyhe, *ESt.* xxxix 21 ff.) There is a striking similarity in the detailed fighting scene. Cf. Cha. Wid. 92–94; Malone Haml. 136 ff., L 4.92 e.780 f. — The fall of Agnerus[2] in a duel with Biarco (Saxo ii 56), which Bugge (17 ff.) adduced as an analogue, is rather far removed from the plot and setting of the *Beowulf* scene. — On some traces of the influence of *Gen.* 1960–2163, see *ESt.* xlii 329 f.

2926 f. The fact that the hostilities had been previously started by the Swedes (see 2475 ff.) is disregarded in this place.

2928. him, probably dat. sing. (i.e., Hæðcen).

2940 f. Probably the text has suffered the loss of at least one line. Attempts at reconstruction by Bugge (107, 372), Holthausen[2-3] (note). — Indulging in a mere conjecture, we might mention the possibility that the original reading was: *sumon* (dat. plur.) *galgtrēowu/gifan tō gamene* (cp. *Gen.* 2069 f., *Mald.* 46), *gēoc eft gelamp*, and that a scribe disturbed the alliteration by substituting *frōfor* for *gēoc*.

2943ᵇ–44ᵃ. horn ond bȳman,/gealdor. See 94ᵇ–95ᵃ.

2946. It has been suggested that the form **Swona** (MS.), for *Swēona*, may be due to the shifting of the accent to the second element of the diphthong (Förster, *Arch.* cxlvi 136).

2950. frōd felageōmor. Cp. *Gen.* 2224: *geōmorfrōd*.

2951. ufor is either 'farther away' (Kock 236) or 'on to higher ground' (cf. *ESt.* xlii 329 f.).

2956. bearn ond brȳde (acc. plur.). Ongenþēow was afraid that women and children would be carried off. Cp. *Gen.* 1969 ff., 2009 ff., 2089 ff., etc. (*ESt.* xlii 329).

2957ᵃ. eorðweall. On earth-walls used as fortifications, see S. Müller ii 225 ff.; Schuchhardt, *R.-L.* iv 434 ff., 476.

2957ᵇ–59. Taking **ǣht** (= *ēht*, Lang. § 9.3) as an analogical formation in place of the normal *ōht*, and construing **segn** as the subject of **oferēodon**, we obtain very satisfactory sense by the slight alteration **Higelāce[s]**. Cf. *A.* l 220. For other interpretations, see Varr.; also Schröer, *Angl.* xiii 346 ff.; Aant. 38; Schücking's and Sedgefield's notes; Green L 6.8.5.101, & L 5.55 (: " then was (the) treasure offered (yielded) by the folk of the Swedes, their banner to H.").

2960. tō hagan seems to refer to the *eorðweall* at the edge of the protected area (*freoðowong*). [Cosijn, Aant. 39 equated *haga* with *wī[g]haga*, *Mald.* 102, 'phalanx.']

---

[1] Cf. also *Annales Ryenses*, Par. § 8.5.
[2] In the brief allusion of the *Hrólfssaga*, ch. 33: *Agnar*, Varr.: *Angar, Angantýr*.

2963 f. ðafian sceolde/Eafores ānne dōm, 'he had to submit to Eofor's decision alone,' i.e., he was completely at the mercy of Eofor. Cf. *A*. l 220.

2973. hē, i.e. Ongenþēow; him, i.e. Wulf.

2977–80. Lēt se hearda Higelāces þegn [i.e. Eofor] .. mēce ... helm/brecan ofer bordweal. Cp. 2258 f.; *Kudrun* 1445: *Der Kūdrūnen vriedel under helme über rant/erreichte Ludewīgen mit ellenthafter hant*. Cf. *A*. l 220.

2982. his mǣg, = *his brōðor* 2978.

2985. rinc (i.e. Eofor) is the subject.

2994–95ᵃ. sealde hiora gehwæðrum hund þūsenda/landes ond locenra bēaga. See note on 2195. In this instance the unit of value represented by the land and rings together is presumably the *sceat*(*t*). Cf. Rie. Zs. 415; Stevenson's ed. of Asser's *Life of King Alfred* (1904), p. 154, n. 6. (Of a valuable ring (*bēag*) given him by Eormanrīc, the Gothic king, Wīdsīð says: *on þām siex hund wæs smǣtes goldes/gescyred sceatta scillingrīme*, *Wids*. 91 f., see Chambers's notes.)

2995ᵇ. ne ðorfte him ðā lēan oðwītan. *him*, dat. sing. (Hygelāc). Cp. 1048, 1884 f. (2995ᵇ–96ᵃ could be taken parenthetically, Kock⁴ 122, Hoops.)

2996. hīe ðā mǣrða geslōgon, probably 'they performed those glorious deeds.' (Cl. Hall: "they had earned the honours by fighting.")

3005. æfter hæleða hryre, hwate Scildingas. See Varr. The line as it stands in the MS. has the air of an intruder. Müllenhoff (xiv 239) denounced it as a thoughtless repetition of 2052. It has been defended as a stray allusion to an ancient story of the Danish king Bēowulf, the hero of a dragon fight (cf. Intr. xxii), or to a possible tradition assigning to Bēowulf the overlordship over the Danes after the fall of Hrōðgār's race (Thorpe's note; cf. Sarrazin, *ESt*. xxiii 245; Chambers, with reference to Saxo iii 75; Brett, *MLR*. xiv 1 f.). But these suppositions are far from being substantiated. Besides, an unprejudiced reader would expect *hwate Scildingas* to be merely a variation of *hord ond rīce*. Again, the emendation *Scilfingas* offers no appreciable improvement in sense, unless, by a violent transposition, we insert the line between 3001 and 3002. (A reference to a temporary authority possibly exercised over the Swedes, as a result of the alliance with Ēadgils, would be strange.) Stylistically, a reading like *Sǣ- Gēatas* (*JEGPh*. viii 259) or scildwigan (Hoops St. 78 ff.) would seem most satisfactory. The latter, being the less drastic emendation, has been allowed a provisional place in the text. [If still another conjecture may be offered, a reading: *hwate* (adv.) *Scildinga/folcrēd fremede* could be considered to contain a passing hint at the Grendel exploit. Similarly, Moore (*JEGPh*. xviii 212) suggests *hwate*[*s*] *Scildingas*, i.e. Hrōðgār's.] For an elaborate attempt to clear up in detail the dark allusions of this entire passage, see Malone Haml. 93 ff.; *A*. liv 1 ff. *Medium Ævum* ii 59 ff.: *hwate Scildingas* to be kept as involving a genuine though obscure historical allusion. It is doubtful whether such a procedure on the part of the poet would have been fair to the readers.

3010. ānes hwæt. See Gloss.: *ān*.

3014. þā sceall brond fretan. In reality the treasures are buried in the mound (3163 ff.). At least, we cannot be quite sure that the arms with which the pyre is hung (3139 f.) have also been taken from the dragon's hoard. There is no necessity to assume (with Stjerna, chs. 6, 8) an imperfect combination of duplicate lays describing different modes of funeral rites. Even granting that the poet was guilty of a slight inaccuracy, the main idea he wished to convey at this point seems to have been that the dearly bought treasures are to be sacrificed with the dead hero. See note on 3137 ff.

3018 f. ac sceal geōmormōd golde berēafod ... elland tredan. Cp. *Iliad* xxiv 730 ff. (lamentation of Andromache); *Gen.* 1969 ff.: *sceolde forht monig/blāchlēor ides bifiende gān/on fremdes fæðm.* — **oft nalles æne.** So *El.* 1252, *Chr.* (iii) 1194; *ib.* 1170: *monge nales fēa* (see Cook's note on Greek parallels); cp. *Jul.* 356.

3022. (gār) morgenceald. Battle begins in the morning. Cf. *ESt.* xlii 335.

3024-27. Of the numerous occasions on which the animals of prey are introduced (in *Gen., Ex., Brun., Mald., El., Jud., Finnsb.*), this is the only one where raven and eagle hold a conversation. The bold and brilliant picture reminds us not only of 'The Twa Corbies' ('The Three Ravens'), but of ON. literature (e.g. *Brot af Sigurþarkv.* 13, *Helgakv. Hund.* i 5 a); cf. Sarrazin, *ESt.* xxiii 255; *MLN.* xvi 18.

3027. þenden hē wið wulf wæl rēafode. The meaning 'contending with' has been postulated for this *wið*. So Sedgefield, note; Cook, L 4.146 c. 1.343 & n. 3 ('he wrenched away the slain from the wolf'); Wyatt, *Threshold* (L 2.23.88). But this would be entirely irregular. In all the other instances the well-known animals of prey act in full harmony.

3028 f. secggende wæs/lāðra spella. The gen. seems to have been caused by the semi-substantival function of the participle; cf. Shipley L 6.8.4.65 f.

3030ª. wyrda nē worda. A variation of a formula (*worda ond weorca*, etc.).

3030ᵇ–3136. Preliminaries of the closing scene.

3034. hlimbed healdan. See 2901 f.; note on 964.

3038. Ǣr hī þǣr gesēgan. The transmitted text should not be tampered with (see Varr.). Even before they came upon Bēowulf, the warriors noticed from a distance the enormously long dragon.

3044. nihtes hwīlum. Hoops: 'at the time of night' (cp. 2320; *Blickl. Hom.* 207.34). It would be the only instance in OE. poetry where *hwīlum* is not used adverbially.

3046. hæfde eorðscrafa ende genyttod; "he had made his last use of earth(ly) caverns" (Earle).

3049 f. swā hīe wið eorðan fæðm/þūsend wintra þǣr eardodon. This does not necessarily mean that the treasures had remained all that time in the same burial cave, but rather that they had lain 'a thousand years' in the bosom of the earth — unless we assume forgetfulness on the part of the author. See note on 2231 ff. [Holt., *Beibl.* xliv 227 conjectures that the Roman numeral symbol for 300 had been misread as 1000.]

3051 ff. The curse laid on the gold is first mentioned in a substantially heathen fashion, though with a saving clause of Christian tenor (3054[b]–57), and, later, is clothed in a Christian formula (3071–73). (Note the term *hǣðen gold* 2276, cp. 2216.) Cf. *Angl.* xxxv 269, xxxvi 171. — The curse resting on the Niblung gold in ON. and MHG. literary tradition is a well-known parallel of the general motive. That the circumstantial history of the Niblung hoard could be traced in *Beowulf* was an erroneous view of Heinzel's (*Anz.fdA.* xv 169 f.).

3051. þonne, 'further,' 'moreover.' **ēacencræftig** is perhaps to be construed predicatively (parallel with *galdre bewunden*), 'of great power,' i.e. powerfully protected. [According to Bugge (374), *þonne* denotes the time when the treasures were placed in the ground; Aant. 40: 'ante tot annos.']

3055 f. The inf. **openian** after **sealde** (Aant. 40) seems to be in part due to the preceding *þām ðe hē wolde.* (Cp. 1730 f.)

3058–62[a]. A recapitulating remark on the end of Bēowulf and of the dragon. The moralizing author denies the dragon the right to the possession of the hoard: **unrihte,** 3059. **Weard ǣr ofslōh/fēara sumne,** i.e., the dragon had slain Bēowulf; *fēara sumne*, 'one and few others' (cp. 1412), by bold litotes, means 'one' only (Aant. 40). (That the dragon was supposed to have killed others on previous occasions, is very unlikely.) Revenge was inflicted on him by Bēowulf (and Wīglāf). [Different interpretations: Bu. 109, 375; Heinzel, *Anz.fdA.* xv 169 f., see note on 3051 ff.]

3062[b]–65. Wundur hwǣr etc., 'it is a mystery where (on what occasion) a man meets death.' Cf. Siev. ix 143; Aant. 40; Kock 233. See *Gnom. Ex.* 29 f.: *Meotud āna wāt,/hwǣr se cwealm cymeþ; Gr.-Wü.* ii 276.59 ff.: *uncūð bið þē þænne,/tō hwan þē þīn Drihten gedōn wille,/þænne þū lenge ne mōst līfes brūcan.*

3066–67[a]. Swā wæs Bīowulfe. See note on 1769. **biorges weard** and **searonīðas** are two parallel objects of **sōhte.**

3067[b]–68. He did not know the ultimate cause of his death (**þurh hwæt . . .**), i.e., he was ignorant of the ancient spell. — It might be questioned why the curse which was visited on Bēowulf and the dragon, did not affect those who had seized the hoard in former times, 2248 f. (Or did it manifest itself in the extinction of that race?) Perhaps the poet failed to take this motive into account until he came to relate the hero's death.

3069[a]. Swā is to be connected with *þæt* 3071. [Holthausen construes *swā* as correlative with *swā* 3066, placing 3067ᵇ–68 in parenthesis.]

3072. hergum and **hellbendum** are used synonymously. As heathen deities were made into devils (*gāstbona* 177), their places of worship were identified with hell. Cp. *hærgtrafum* 175 with *helltrafum*, *Andr.* 1691. [Brett, *MLR.* xiv 5 f.: geheaðerod = 'fenced out from . . .'(?)]

3074–75. Næs hē goldhwæte gearwor hæfde/āgendes ēst ǣr gescēawod. This passage remains, in Bugge's words, a 'locus desperatus.' Cosijn's rendering ' by no means had Bēowulf with gold-greedy eyes before [his death] surveyed the owner's [i.e. the dragon's] inheritance more accurately ² (Aant. 41) makes at least passable sense. (Cp. 2748.) Does the compar. *gearwor* stand for the positive? — Or is the meaning this that 'he had not seen the treasure before more completely than now [at his death],' implying that he had never seen it in its entirety? In its general intent the statement seems to be a declaration of Bēowulf's virtual innocence. — If we accept the change of *Næs hē* to **næfne** (placing a comma after *strude* 3073) and venture to take **āgend** as a kenning for God (cp. *Exod.* 295, *Prayer* (Gr.-Wü. ii 217) 1: *āge mec . . . God*), we obtain the reading *næfne goldhwæte* (or *-hwæt[n]e*) *gearwor hæfde/Āgendes ēst ǣr gescēawod*, i.e. ' unless God's grace (or, kindness) had before (or, first) more readily (or, thoroughly) favored those (or, the one) eager for gold.' (This interpretation was first suggested by Patzig, *Angl.* xlvii 104.) For **scēawian** = ' look with favor upon ² (Lat. ' respicere,' etc.), see, e.g., *Angl.* l 222. In other words, we have here a close stylistic parallel of the clause introduced by *nefne*, 3054 ff. That the ' incantation ' should end with a clause showing a way to avoid the threatened curse, is in line with a practice observed in Formulas of Excommunication. The same feature occurs at the end of Charters. Cf. *Angl.* l 221; also lvi 424. [Cf. further: Bu. Tid. 62 f.; Müll. xiv 241; Rie. Zs. 416; Siev. ix 143; ten Brink 145; Bu. 373 f.; Schü. xxxix 111; Schücking's and Chambers's notes; Brett, *MLR.* xiv 6; Moore, *JEGPh.* xviii 213 ff.; Kock² 123: *goldhwæte* from **goldhwatu*, ' readiness about gold,' ' liberality ' (cf. *A.* lvii 320). Lawrence L 4.62 a. 561: " unless (*næfne*) he, rich in gold (*goldhwæt*), had very zealously given heed in the past to the grace of the Lord "; Siev. L 5.16.11; Furuhjelm L 5.77; Malone L 5.71.5, 6; Holt. L 5.26.23. According to Imelmann, *ESt.* lxvii 331 ff. (lxviii 1 ff.), these lines form part of the curse; *goldhwæt* ' rich in gold ' (so Gr. Spr.); *goldhwæte . . . āgendes ēst* ' the owner's inheritance rich in gold '; the possibility that the lines originally belonged after 3068 is hinted.] *Embarras de richesse.*

3079 ff. Ne meahton wē gelǣran etc. See 1994 ff.

3084. The reading **Hēold on hēah gesceap**, ' he held (on)to his high fate ' (Wyatt-Chambers, similarly Kock, *Angl.* xlvi 183) deserves recommendation, provided the idiomatic character of the phrase can be substantiated. To the hitherto meagre support derived from Middle English examples Kock has added a reference to the Old Norse use of *halda á*.

3094. wīs ond gewittig, 'sound in mind and conscious'; cp. 2703. Though no exact parallel of this use of *wīs* has been adduced, this translation is more appropriate than 'the wise and prudent one' (Scheinert, *Beitr.* xxx 381 n.); cf. *Angl.* xxix 382. (*Hel.* 238 f.: *habda im eft is sprāka giwald,/giwitteas endi wīsun.*)

3104. þæt gē ... scēawiað, 'so that (='and then') you will see.' Contrast with 2747 f.

3108 f. þǣr hē longe sceal/on ðæs Waldendes wǣre geþolian. This expression would be eminently fitting in connection with the Christian mode of interment. Cf. *Angl.* xxxv 263. — *on ðæs Waldendes wǣre* recalls *on Frēan wǣre* 27. In fact, a number of general phrasal analogies connect the obsequies of Bēowulf (and preparations for them) with Scyld's 'sea-burial'; thus 3135 f., 28; 3137 ff., 38 ff.; 3140, 29; 3141 f., 34 ff.; 3166, 3132, 48; also 3112 f., 36 f.

3112. bǣlwudu. See Par. § 10: Tacitus, *Germ.*, c. 27.

3114. gōdum tōgēnes, i.e., to the place where the good one lay (and, for his service).

3115ᵃ. (weaxan wonna lēg). To get rid of the troublesome parenthesis, critics (Grein Spr., Cosijn viii 574; Holthausen, *Arch.* cxxi 293 f.) have conjectured the existence of a verb *weaxan* 'consume,' on the basis of the (somewhat inconclusive) gloss *waxgeorn*='edax,' *Wr.-Wü.* i 102.13, the Go. verbs *wizōn, frawisan,* etc. (The identification of the verb with *wascan* 'wash,' 'bathe,' 'envelop' suggested by Earle and Sedgefield is certainly far-fetched.) However, if an ordinary variation of 3114ᵇ were intended, we might expect either an adj. and noun (e.g. *wonna ǣled*), or a noun and verb (e.g. *wælfȳr þeccan,* cp. 3014 f., 3132 f.). Perhaps the co-ordinate clause may be considered functionally equivalent to a subordinated, appositional phrase, i.e. *weaxende lēg* [Sed. *MLR.* xxviii 230: *weaxen,* pp.] (Note OE. *Bede* 118.4: *þæt fȳr ond þæt lēg swīðe wēox ond miclade.*) A very interesting solution is Holthausen's emendation (*Beibl.* xl 90 f.): **weasan* (= **weosan, *wesan,* 'consume').

3119. fæðergearwum fūs. Leonard: 'swift on feathered wings.' Stern, *ESt.* lxviii 164 refers to *feþrum snel(l), Phoen.* 123, 163, 347.

3121 f. ācīgde of corðre cyniges þegnas/syfone (tō)somne. If the idea of motion is considered negligible in this context, *(æt)somne* may be admitted (cp. 2847).

3126. Næs ðā on hlytme, 'it was not decided by lot,' i.e., they were all very eager. Cf. *ESt.* xxxix 432; *A.* l 223.

3127. orwearde, asn., refers to *hord; ǣnigne dǣl* is co-ordinate with the understood object *hit,* see note on 694ᵇ. The construction could easily be simplified by emending to *orweardne,* and *lǣnne* 3129. (Cf. also note on 48, and 2841.)

3137-3182. Bēowulf's funeral obsequies.[1]

---

[1] On the funeral practices, see Kemble's note on the last line of *Beow.*; Ettmüller Transl. 52 ff.; Grimm L 9.2; Wright L 9.3. chs. 11 & 15; Weinhold L 9.32.474 ff.; du Chaillu L 9.35. i.

NOTES

We know from Tacitus that the Germans of his time burned their dead. (See *Germ.*, c. 27, Par. § 10, and Müllenhoff's commentary, L 9.14.1.)

In the Scandinavian countries[1] the custom of burning was common from the latter half of the bronze age, and though it was temporarily interrupted, more or less, by a period of inhumation, it was for centuries previous to the Viking era the recognized practice in most districts. Splendid examples of this method of disposing of the departed ones — being the more poetical and intrinsically spiritual one — are found in the ON. literature, such as the burning of Brynhildr and Sigurþr (*Sigurþarkv. en skamma* 64 ff.) and that of Harald Hildetan (Saxo viii 264, Par. § 7); see also note on Scyld (p. 122).

The heathen Anglo-Saxons practised both cremation and interment, the latter mode apparently prevailing in the southern districts (Chadwick Or. 73 ff.), but after their conversion to Christianity[2] cremation was of course entirely given up. Yet in their great epos of post-heathen times we find the heathen and heroic practice described in all its impressive splendor.[3]

The obsequies of Bēowulf remind us in several respects of the famous funeral ceremonies of the classical epics (*Iliad* xxiii 138 ff., xxiv 785 ff.; *Odyssey* xxiv 43 ff.; *Æneid* vi 176 ff., xi 59 ff.). More interesting still, certain important features are paralleled by the funeral of Attila (Jordanes, c. 49, Par. § 12), which was carried out after the Gothic fashion — the main points of difference being that Attila's body is not burned but buried, and that the mourning horsemen's songs of praise do not accompany the final ceremony but represent an initial, separate act of the funeral rites.[4]

It is the peculiarity of the *Beowulf* account that two distinct and, as it were, parallel funeral ceremonies are related in detail, the burning and the consigning of the ashes to the monumental mound, and that the greater emphasis is placed on the closing stage, which is made the occasion of rehearsing solemn and inspiring songs sounding an almost Christian note. (Only the former ceremony takes place in the case of

ch. 19; Gummere G. O. ch. 11; Montelius, *passim;* S. Müller, *passim* and i. ch. 10; Stjer. chs. 5 & 8; Schücking L 4.126.1; Helm L 4.42. n. 148 ff.; Seger, *R.-L.* iv 333–38.

[1] See the convenient summarizing statements in Chadwick, *The Cult of Othin* (1899), pp. 40, 59, 64.

[2] Among the continental Saxons the Church labored to suppress the 'heathen' rite as late as the end of the 8th century. (Grimm L 9.2.259.)

[3] On some veiled allusions to the Christian burial (445 f., 1004 ff., 3107 ff.), see *Angl.* xxxv 263, 465 f., xxxvi 174. — The very ancient form of burial in stone graves is suggested by the barrow or mound of the dragon, cf. note on 2231 ff.

[4] Jordanes' story of Attila's funeral was critically examined by E. Schröder, *ZfdA*. lix 240–44. Cf. also Naumann, *GRM*. xv 270 f. Homeric influence on the Beowulfian account was urged by Cook, L 4.146 c. 1. 339 ff. For a comment on the questions involved, see L 4.129 c. There appears to be no necessity to reckon with foreign influences.

the less pompous obsequies of Hnæf and the other fallen warriors of the Finn tale, 1108 ff.)

According to Stjerna (ch. 8) the royal barrow at Gamla Upsala, called Odinshög, which was constructed about 500 A.D., is an exact counterpart of Bēowulf's mound.

3150 ff. On the song of lament, see note on 1117 f. That it should be uttered by a woman is what we expect, see also 3016 ff. If that aged woman was really thought of as Bēowulf's widow (see, e.g., Bu. 111; cp. ll. 2369 ff.?), she was introduced, awkwardly enough, merely in the interest of a conventional motive.

3166 ff. The gold is returned to the earth — *þǣr hit nū gēn lifað/ eldum swā unnyt, swā hit ǣror wæs*. In part this could be explained as a corollary of the motive of the curse resting on the gold. But cp., e.g., *Grettissaga*, ch. 18.16: ' all treasure which is hidden in the earth or buried in a howe is in a wrong place.'

3173–76ª. The lines setting forth the praise of Bēowulf by his faithful thanes sound like an echo of divine service, and closely resemble *Gen.* 1 ff., 15 ff.; cf. *ESt.* xlii 327, *Angl.* xxxv 126 f. See ' The Order of the Holy Communion ' in the Book of Common Prayer (' It is very meet, right, and our bounden duty, etc.').

3180 f. wyruldcyning[a]/manna mildust ond mon(ðw)ǣrust. *manna*, which seems to strengthen the superl. idea (' the mildest of all '), is fundamentally an amplifying (partit.) element. Cp. (OHG.) *Wessobrunner Gebet* 7 f.: *almahtīco Cot,/manno miltisto*, *Beow.* 3098 f., 2645, also 155, 1108 f., 2250 f., 2887, etc. *manna mildost* occurs also *Ex.* 550. Cf. *A.* l 224. As to *wyruldcyning[a]*, cp. 1684 f.

3182. lofgeornost. The reference is either to deeds of valor (cp. 1387 ff., *OE. Bede* 92.4: *se gylpgeornesta* [*cyning*]=' gloriae cupidissimus ' i, c. 34) or to the king's liberality toward his men (see 1719 f., cp. *lofgeorn, Ben. R.* (ed. Schröer) 54.9, 55.3=' prodigus,' also *lofdǣdum, Beow.* 24).

THE FIGHT AT FINNSBURG

INTRODUCTION

I. THE FINN LEGEND[1]

1. THE STORY

By a comparison of the Finn Episode of *Beowulf* and the Fragment of *The Fight at Finnsburg* the perplexing obscurities of both may be cleared up, at least to a considerable extent.

Of the two fights alluded to in the Episode (*B.* 1069 f.; 1151 f. [1068]) it is clearly the former which the fragmentary poem describes, so that the events of the Episode must be considered to follow those of the Fragment.[2] A brief outline of the story is subjoined.

[The antecedents of the conflict are lost to us. But evidently Hildeburh is in some way connected with the hostility between her brother and her husband. Maybe, there existed an old feud between the two tribes, and the Danish princess had been given in marriage to the Frisian chief in the hope of securing permanent peace, but with the same grievous result as in the case of Frēawaru (see *Beow.* Intr. xxxiv f.). Or the ill feeling may have dated from the wedding feast (as in the *Vǫlsungasaga*, ch. 3). It is possible also — though far from probable — that Hildeburh had been abducted like Hildr, Hǫgni's daughter, in Snorri's *Edda* (*Skáldsk.*, ch. 47) and Hilde, Hagene's daughter (and, under different circumstances, Kūdrūn) in the MHG. epic of *Kudrun*. At any rate, at least fifteen or twenty years must have elapsed after the marriage, since Hildeburh's son falls in the battle (*B.* ll. 1074, 1115).]

(The Fragment:) A band of sixty Danes under their chief Hnæf find themselves attacked before daybreak in the hall of the Frisian king Finn, whom they have come to visit. [That the assault was premeditated by

[1] See especially Grein LF. 4.3.1, Möller LF. 4.7, Bugge LF. 4.5.3, Trautmann LF. 4.17, Boer LF. 4.18, Brandl LF. 4.23, Lawrence LF. 4.26; Imelmann LF. 4.30, Williams LF. 4.36, Malone LF. 4.37; Cha. Intr. 245–89; *Angl.* l 224 ff.; Schneider L 4.13 a, 4.22 d; also Finn Bibliography, *passim*.

[2] Möller (who has been followed by some others) tried to prove that the Fragment is concerned with still another battle, one, that is, in which Hengest fell and which — if related in the *Beowulf* Episode — would have found its place between ll. 1145 and 1146. That the *hwapogeong cyning* of the Fragment, l. 2 is Hengest, is also the view of Brandl (cf. Clarke L 4.76.180), who assumes, however, that after Hnæf's fall Hengest, his successor, continued the fight until the treaty was arranged. (Grundtvig in his edition inserted the Fragment between ll. 1106 and 1107 of the *Beowulf*.)

Finn is possibly to be inferred from the opening lines of the Fragment and from *B*. 1125 ff., see Notes, p. 174.[1]] Five days they fight without loss against the Frisians, but (here the Episode sets in:) at the end Hnæf and many of his men as well as of the Frisians are counted among the dead. In this state of exhaustion Finn concludes a treaty with Hengest, who has assumed command over the Danes. The fallen warriors of both tribes are burned together amid appropriate ceremonies. Hengest with his men stays in Friesland during the winter. But deep in his heart burns the thought of revenge. The day of reckoning comes when the Danes Gūðlāf and Ōslāf,[2] unable to keep any longer the silence imposed upon them by the terms of the treaty, openly rebuke their old foes. Finn is set upon (*B*. 1068) and slain, and Hildeburh together with the royal treasure of the Frisians carried home to the land of the Danes. [The part played by Hengest in the last act of the tragedy is not quite clear, see Notes, pp. 175 f.]

2. THE CONTENDING PARTIES

On one side we find the 'Half Danes' (*B*. 1069), or 'Danes' (1090, 1158), also loosely called *Scyldingas* (1069, 1108, 1154),[3] with their king Hnæf, Hōc's son,[4] and his chief thane Hengest. Other Danish warriors mentioned by name are Gūðlāf (1148, *F*. 16), Ōslāf (1148; in the Fragment, l. 16: Ordlāf), Sigeferð of the tribe of the *Secgan* (*F*. 15, 24), Ēaha (*F*. 15), and (probably) Hūnlāfing (*B*. 1143). Their enemies are the Frisians (1093, 1104) or *Ēotan*, 'Jutes' (1072, 1088, 1141, 1145) under King Finn, Folcwalda's son, among whose retainers two only receive individual mention, namely Gārulf, son of Gūðlāf (*F*. 18, 31, 33), and Gūðere (*F*. 18). Between the two parties stands Hildeburh, the wife of Finn (*B*. 1153) and — as we gather from l. 1074 (and 1114, 1117) — sister of Hnæf.

The scene is in Friesland, at the residence of Finn.

It thus appears that the war is waged between a minor branch of the great Danish nation, the one which is referred to in *Widsið* by the term *Hōcingas*,[5] and which seems to have been associated with the tribe of the

---

[1] A new suggestion regarding the occasion for this fight has been advanced by Chambers. Jutish subjects of Finn, he argues, started the trouble. They attack the Danes under King Hnæf by surprise in the hall. Fierce fighting is going on for several days. Finally, Finn is forced to intervene, i.e., to join in the battle. Thus, Finn himself is exonerated from all blame in the tragic happenings. But cf. *A*. l 226 ff. — Still another hypothesis has just been offered by Sedgefield (*MLR*. xxviii 481 f.), who thinks that before *Finnes eaferum*, *B*. 1068 a sentence may have dropped out, something like *Hwæt, þǣm æðelan wæs ende gegongen*.

[2] It has sometimes been inferred from the expression *æfter sǣsīðe* (*B*. 1149) that Gūðlāf and Ōslāf had sailed home and then returned to Friesland with fresh troops. But by *sǣsīð* presumably the original journey of the Danes to Friesland was meant.

[3] Cp. the inaccurate use of *Scyldingas* in the Heremōd episodes (*B*. 913, 1710), see Notes, p. 164.

[4] Cp. *B*. 1076 (1074, 1114, 1117).

[5] *Wids*. 29: *Hnæf [wēold] Hōcingum*

INTRODUCTION

Secgan,[1] and the Frisians, i.e., according to the current view, the ' East ' Frisians between the Zuider Zee and the river Ems (and on the neighboring islands). The interchangeable use of the names ' Frisians ' and ' Jutes '[2] shows that the Jutes, that is the West Germanic tribe which settled in Kent and adjacent parts (Baeda, *H.E.* i, c. 15), were conceived of as quite closely related to the Frisians.[3]

The name of the Danish warrior Ēaha (by emendation: Ēawa[4]) has been connected with the ' Ingvaeonic ' Aviones (Tacitus, *Germ.*, c. 40; see Par. § 10).

However, neither ' Frisians ' nor ' Danes ' are mentioned in the Fragment. It has even been argued that the Danish nationality of Hnæf and Hengest is a Beowulfian innovation,[5] and that the enemies of the Frisians (in history and legend) were really the *Chauci*, their eastern neighbors, or some other Ingvaeonic people. But the names Gūþlāf, Ordlāf (Hūnlāfing) make us think of Danish tradition.[6]

The point of view is distinctly — almost patriotically — Danish. The valor and loyalty of Hnæf's retainers (in the Fragment), Hildeburh's sorrow and Hengest's longing for vengeance (in the Episode) are uppermost in the minds of the poets. It is not without significance, perhaps, that all the direct speech (in the Fragment) has been assigned to the Danes, whereas the utterances of the Frisians are reported as indirect discourse only. On the other hand, no concealment is made of the fact that the ' Jutes ' have shown bad faith (*B.* 1071 f.). The final attack on Finn and his men, culminating in the complete victory

---

[1] Or *Sycgan; Wids.* 31: *Sǣferð [wēold] Sycgum*, cp. *Finnsb.* 24.

[2] Chambers contends that the Jutes were meant to be distinct from the Frisians, though under the command of Finn. Cf. *A.* l 227 (see *B.* 1086 ff.).

[3] This seems to be due to the fact that the Jutes, for some time previous to their migration to Britain, had lived in the vicinity of the Frisians. Cf. Hoops, *Waldbäume und Kulturpflanzen im germ. Altertum*, p. 585; Jordan, *Verhandlungen der 49. Versammlung (1907) deutscher Philologen und Schulmänner*, 1908, pp. 138–40. See also Siebs, *P. Grdr.*[2] i 1158, ii[a] 524; Einenkel, *Angl.* xxxv 419; Björk. Eig. 21 ff., 60 f.; G. Baldwin Brown, *The Arts in Early England* (L 9.28 e) iv 742 f. The Jutes are called by Baeda (*H.E.* i, c. 15; iv, c. 14 (16)): *Iuti, Iutae* — in certain sixth century Latin texts: **Eutii, *Euthiones* — ; in OE.: Angl. *Ēote, Īote* (*Īotan*), LWS. *Ȳte, Ȳtan*. (Björkman L 4.74.2; Cha. Wid. 237 ff.; cf. Intr. xlvi.) Of the forms used in *Beowulf*, the gen. pl. *Ēotena* is entirely regular; the dat. pl. *Ēotenum* (instead of *Ēotum*) 1145 (also 902) is to be explained by the analogical influence of the gen. ending (cf. Siev. § 277 n. 1), unless it is due merely to scribal confusion with the noun *eotenas*. That really in all the instances the *eotenas* ' giants,' hence ' enemies ' (?) were meant (Rieger Zs. 398 ff.), cannot be admitted. [Various interpretations of ' *Eotenas* ' are enumerated by Möller, pp. 96 ff.] — A state of friction between the ' Jutes ' and the Danes is possibly hinted at in the first Heremōd episode, l. 902, see Notes, p. 165. — Wadstein L 4.74.6 thinks the *Ēote, Ȳte* (= *Eutii*) are distinct from the Jutes.

[4] An Ēawa figures in the Mercian genealogy, see Par. § 2.

[5] See below, p. 235 & n. 5.

[6] In Arngrím Jónsson's *Skjǫldungasaga*, ch. 4, the brothers Gunnleifus, Oddleifus, Hunleifus appear in the Danish royal line. (Par. § 8.6.) It is true, Gūðlāf is the name of a Frisian warrior also (*F.* 33).

of the Danes, is regarded as the salient point of the story in *Beowulf* (see ll. 1068, 1146 ff.). Finn himself, the husband of Hildeburh, plays such an insignificant part[1] that the term ' Finn legend ' is rather a misnomer, though ' The Fight at Finnsburg ' is an appropriate enough title for the fragmentary poem such as we know it.

3. POSSIBLE PARALLELS AND GENESIS OF THE LEGEND

The popularity of the legend is attested not only by the preservation of two (in a measure) parallel versions, but also by the mention of certain of its names in *Widsið* (27: *Finn Folcwalding [wēold] Frēsna cynne*, 29: *Hnæf Hōcingum*, 31: *Sǣferð Sycgum*)[2] and by the allusion to Hnæf, Hōc's son, which is implied in the use of the names Huochingus [father] and Nebi (Hnabi) [son] occurring in the Alemannic ducal line of the eighth century.[3] The memory of the Frisian king Finn crops up in a genealogy of Nennius' *Historia Britonum* where Finn the son of Folcwald has been introduced in place of Finn the son of God(w)ulf as known from WS. and Northumbr. (also ON.) genealogies (cf. Par. §§ 1, 3, 5, 8.1).

But no clear traces of any version of the story itself besides the Anglo-Saxon specimens have been recovered. The noteworthy points of agreement between the ' Fight at Finnsburg ' and the second part of the *Nibelungenlied* — as regards the general situation, the relation between the principal persons, the night watch of the two warriors,[4] the mighty hall fight[5] — are no proof that the Finnsburg Fight is an old variant of a continuation of the Sigfrit legend[6] as it was before it became connected with the legend of the Burgundians (Boer, LF. 4.18). Nor can the analogies of the great battle in which Hrólfr Kraki fell (*Hrólfssaga*, chs. 31–34;

[1] Just like Siggeirr, the husband of Signý (*Vǫlsungasaga*), and Etzel, the husband of Kriemhilt (*Nibelungenlied*), in somewhat similar situations. — It deserves to be noted that Hildeburh herself seems to direct the funeral rites (*B.* 1114 ff.).

[2] Of doubtful value is the allusion to Hūn (cf. *B.* 1143?), l. 33: *Hūn Hætwerum*. — The number of names introduced into the Finnsburg tale is surprisingly large. (Chambers conjectured that a meeting of minor chieftains had been called by Finn.)

[3] Thegan's *Life of Louis the Pious*, § 2: ' Godefridus dux genuit Huochingum, Huochingus genuit Nebi, Nebi genuit Immam, Imma vero genuit Hiltigardam, beatissimam reginam.' (Müllenhoff, *ZfdA*. xi 282, xii 285.) On the testimony relating to the names Gūþlāf, Ordlāf, Hūnlāfing, see above, p. 233, n. 6. That the ' Finn legend ' remained popular in Essex, Hampshire, and adjoining districts, has been inferred from the frequent use encountered there of proper names pertaining to it (Binz 179 ff.). For the latest allusion to Hūnlāf, see Intr. xxxiv n. 7.

[4] Hagen(e) and Volkēr, *Nibel.* 1756 ff. This night watch, however, is not followed immediately by the battle.

[5] Extending over two days, *Nibel.* 1888 ff. Also the specific motive of ' the sister's son ' (see note on *F.* 18 ff.) deserves mention.

[6] Uhland (*Germ.* ii 357 ff.) argued for the identity of Sigeferð (*F.* 15, 24) and the celebrated Sigfrit (ON. Sigurðr). — An ancient connection between the elements of the Finn (Hildeburh) and the Hilde-Kūdrūn legend was claimed by Mone L 4.23.134–6; Möller 70 ff.; Much, *Arch.* cviii 406 ff.; cf. Müllenhoff 106 f.

Saxo ii 58 ff.),[1] viz. the Danish nationality of the party suffering the treacherous attack, the family connection between the two kings (brothers-in-law), the attack at night, the rousing of the sleepers, their glorious defense (although outside the hall), the stirring words of exhortation with an appeal to gratitude and loyalty, be construed as evidence of a genetic relation. It is more reasonable to hold that chance similarity in the basic elements of the material (reflecting, in the last analysis, actual conditions of life) naturally resulted in a parallelism of exposition and treatment.

It is commonly supposed that the Finn tale originated among the Ingvaeonic (North Sea) peoples and was carried from Friesland both to Upper Germany (as far as the Lake of Constance[2]) and to the new home of the Anglo-Saxons. If so, the surprisingly thorough Danification of the story in England must have occasioned alterations of considerable importance.

That there was a historical foundation for this recital of warlike encounters among Germanic coast tribes, we may readily believe.[3] But no definite event is known to us that could have served as the immediate model. Taking the Beowulfian version at its full value, an actual parallel of a war between Danes (Geats) and Frisians (and Franks) is supplied by the expedition of Chochilaicus (Hygelāc), see Intr. xxxix f., xlviii. The identification of Hengest with his better known namesake, who together with his brother Horsa led the Jutes to Britain, has been repeatedly proposed;[4] but we should certainly expect a Jutish Hengest to have sided with the Frisians of our Finn tale.[5]

Mythological interpretations[6] may be safely disregarded.

4. GERMANIC CHARACTER

None of the Anglo-Saxon poems equals the ' Finn tale ' in its thorough Germanic and heroic character. The motives and situations are genuinely typical, — mutual loyalty of lord and retainer; bloody feud between relatives by marriage; tragic conflict of duties (the sacred duty of revenge and the obligation of sworn pledges); the rejoicing in the tumult

[1] Cf. Bugge 24.

[2] Cf. the Alemannic genealogy, above, p. 234, n. 3.

[3] " During the Middle Ages, up to the end of the eleventh century, the Danes were the worst enemies of the Frisians." Siebs, *P.Grdr.*² ii^a 524.

[4] Thus, in recent times, by Chadwick Or. 52; cf. Clarke L 4.76.185 ff., Meyer LF. 4.25, Kier L 4.78.25 ff.; Schütte L 4.94 a. 4 ff.; Aurner LF. 4.31; Imelmann; Malone. Cf. the critical study by van Hamel, LF. 4.38.

[5] Is it possible that the Ags. version embodies two distinct strata of early legend reflecting different phases of the history of the Jutes? The settlement of the tribe in Jutland might have tended to link them to the Danes (hence Hengest's position); on the other hand, the sojourn of the Jutes in proximity to the Frisians was apt to suggest an especially close relation between these two tribes (hence *Ēotan=Frȳsan*).

[6] Grimm D. M. 181 (219); Kemble ii, pp. xlvii f.; Möller 70 ff.; ten Brink, *P.Grdr.*¹ ii^a 535; Much, *Arch.* cviii 406 ff.

and pageantry of battle with its birds of prey hovering over the scene, its speeches of exhortation and challenge, the desperate, stubborn defense of the hall until the bitter end, the hardihood of eager youths unwilling to listen to the entreaties of solicitous elders; the burning of the dead amidst lamentations and funeral songs; the faint echoes of merriment and feasting in the hall of the generous chief; and withal a deep undertone of general sadness born of the conviction that joy is bound to turn into sorrow (*B.* 1078 ff.).

By virtue of its heroic spirit of unwavering valor and its central motive of loyalty the late historical poem of *Maldon* alone can be said to approach the Finn poems, and a worthy companion in prose, albeit simple in structure and expression, is easily recognized in the story of Cynewulf and Cyneheard as told in the *OE. Chronicle* (A.D. 755).

II. RELATION BETWEEN THE TWO ANGLO-SAXON VERSIONS

It is possible that the poem of which the fragmentary *Fight at Finnsburg* remains, covered as much narrative ground as the Episode and numbered say about three hundred lines. In what particular form the tale was known to the author of *Beowulf*, cannot be determined. But, at all events, we find no discrepancies in subject-matter between the two versions.[1] At the same time there is no doubt that the author of the Episode has considerably remodeled his material. The Fragment shows the manner of an independent poem, being in fact, apart from the OHG. *Hildebrandslied,* the only specimen in West Germanic literature of the short heroic epic lay.[2] The Episode has been adjusted to its subordinate position in the *Beowulf* epos. It presents in part brief, allusive summaries, passing over the matter of fighting, both at the beginning and at the end, in the most cursory fashion. It has discarded direct discourse. It all but limits its range of actors to the two outstanding figures of Hildeburh and Hengest.[3] But it depicts with evident sympathy their state of mind, brings out the tragic element of the situation, intersperses general reflections, and finds room for picturesque description. In a word, the direct, energetic, dramatic manner (such as we find in the Fragment) has yielded to a somewhat more abstract, sentimental, and ' literary ' treatment of the story.[4]

Entirely in the manner of the *Beowulf* is the litotes in ll. 1071 f., 1076 f., and so are summarizing, retrospective, or semi-explanatory clauses

[1] The variation of names, *Ordlāf* (cp. Arngrím Jónsson's *Oddleifus*): *Ōslāf* is negligible. Cf. *Sigeferð* (*F.* 15, 24): *Sǣferð* (*Wids.* 31, see Möller 86 f.); *Heregār: Heorogār*, cf. Intr. xxxii n. 5. — See also note on *B.* 1077: *syþðan morgen cōm.*

[2] A poem, that is, which was not meant to be read but to be recited.

[3] Möller reckoned with two basic lays, a ' Hildeburh ' and a ' Hengest ' lay — in addition to the lay of the Finnsburg Fight (or an epic poem of which the Fragment is a scanty remnant).

[4] We are not justified in regarding the Episode as the exact version of the scop's recital, though in nearly all editions it is printed within quotation marks.

like *sume on wæle crungon* 1113, *wæs hira blǣd scacen* 1124, *ne meahte wǣfre mōd/forhabban in hreþre* 1150, *þæt wæs geōmuru ides* 1075 (cp. 814 f., 2564 f., 2981, 1727, 11, 1812, 1250, 1372; *Angl.* xxviii 444 f., Intr. lxi). On the literary formula *gǣsta gīfrost* 1123, see Intr. cxii n. 4; on the figurative use of (*foldan*) *bearm*, see *Arch.* cxxvi 353.

Remarkable nonce words of the Episode — some of them still obscure — are: *unflitme* 1097, *unhlitme* 1129, *icge* 1107, *bengeat* 1121, *lāðbite* 1122, *wælfāg* 1128, *torngemōt* 1140, *woroldrǣden* 1142 (n.), *ferhðfrec* 1146, *sweordbealo* 1147, *ingesteald* 1155, *unsynnum* 1072; see also 1106 and note. The relatively numerous words recorded in the Fragment only are listed in the Glossary of *Finnsburg.* An interesting lexical agreement between the two versions is seen in the use of *eorðcyning* 1155, *eorðbūend*, F. 32; *hildelēoma* 1143 (cp. 2583, 1523), *swurdlēoma*, F. 35.

III. THE FIGHT AT FINNSBURG

The Fight at Finnsburg, although a fragment, is in a way the most perfect of the three Old English battle poems. Less polished and rhetorical than the *Battle of Brunanburh*, at the same time truer to the old form of verse and style than the *Battle of Maldon*, it shows complete harmony between subject-matter and form.

It is emphatically a poem of action and moves on directly and swiftly, the consecutive stages being commonly marked by the simple connective *ðā*. Only once does it pause for an exclamation voicing the scop's jubilant admiration of the heroes (37 ff.). Nearly one half of the fragment consists of speech, by which the action is carried on in a wonderfully vivid fashion. The apparent repetition of the question[1] in the answer (1, 4) and the (originally) unassigned speech (24 ff., see note) recall the well-known ballad practice. Quite characteristic are the asyndetic, parallel half-lines (5, 6, 11, 12) following upon each other like short, sharp battle shouts, and the rhetorical repetition and parallelism (37–40) eloquently symbolizing deep emotion. The poet is not sparing in the use of expressive epithets, kennings, and other compounds, nor does he neglect the essential device of variation. Indeed, the general impression is not that of crude workmanship.

The comparative frequency of end-stopped verses is partly accounted for by the use of direct discourse and by the number of distinct divisions of the narrative (introduced by *ðā*). Several groups of 4 lines could be easily arranged as 'stanzas' (sense-units): 14–17, 18–21, 24–27, 37–40; similarly groups of 3 lines could be made out: 10–12, 43–45, 46–48.[2]

Of the rhythmical types the jerky C and the rousing B varieties hold prominent places. We may note especially the striking recurrence of B or C in seven consecutive *a*-lines (16–22), and in six *b*-lines: 40–45. Use of the same type in both half-lines is found seven times: 4, 11, 12, 30,

[1] The opening words have been taken by some scholars as the close of a question. Cf. Hart L 4.125.198 n. 4, 50, 144.
[2] Möller's violent reconstruction is found in his *Altengl. Volksepos* ii, pp. vii–ix.

37, 40, 43. A rather heavy thesis marks the opening of C in 8ᵇ and 37ᵃ (cp. *Beow.* 1027ᵃ, 38ᵃ), and an isolated hypermetrical type is introduced on a highly appropriate occasion: 39ᵃ. (Perhaps also 13ᵃ must be admitted to be hypermetrical.) Irregularities of alliteration: 22ᵃ, 46ᵃ (see T.C. § 18), 28ᵇ, 41ᵇ (T.C. § 27), 39ᵃ (cf. Siev. A.M. § 93) could be set right by transposition or other alterations (see Varr.), but are perhaps naturally explained by the less literary character of this poem which presupposes a far less strictly regulated oral practice. (For the alliteration of 11 and 12, see note on *Beow.* 489 f.)

The language of the text, which unfortunately is transmitted in very bad condition, shows various late forms, such as *Finnsburuh* 36 (for *Finnes-*, cf. Weyhe, *Beitr.* xxx 86 n. 1; quite exceptional), *hlynneð* 6 (for *hlyneð*, cf. Siev. § 410 n. 3), *mænig* 13 (cf. Lang. § 7 n. 1), *sceft* 7 (Lang. § 8.4), *scȳneð* 7 (Lang. § 3.1), also non-WS. forms: *cweþ* 24 (Lang. § 8.1, Siev. § 391 n. 10), *wæg* 43 (Lang. § 7.1), *fæla*¹ 25, 33, *nēfre* 39 (Kent., cf. Siev. § 151; but 37: *nǣfre*), *heordra* 26 (So. Northumbr., cf. Bülb. § 144), *hwearflīcra* 34 (perh. *ea* = *eo*, No. Northumbr., cf. Bülb. § 140), *sword* 15 (Lang. § 8.6; 13: *swurd*). (The analogical *duru* 42, instead of *dura*, is in a line with similar forms in *Beowulf*, 344, 1278; cf. Lang. § 18.2.) But definite localization and dating (both of the Lambeth MS. and of its prototype) are impossible.² General considerations favor, of course, an early date for the original lay, as early at least as that of *Beowulf*.

Some half-lines of a conventional character are common to *Beowulf* and *Finnsburg:* F. 19ᵇ = B. 740ᵇ, 2286ᵇ, F. 38ᵇ = B. 1012ᵇ, F.46ᵇ = B. 610ᵃ, 1832ᵃ, 2981ᵃ. The more striking agreement in the sentences, F. 37 f. and B. 1011 f. (cf. 1027 ff., 38), possibly indicates that the author of the epic knew the Finnsburg poem. Identity or similarity of phrases is further noted in F. 9ᵇ = B. 1832ᵇ, F. 15ᵇ = B. 2610ᵇ, F. 17ᵇ = B. 2945ᵇ, F. 21ᵃ = B. 2170ᵃ, F. 22ᵃ = B. 2899ᵇ, F. 24ᵃ = B. 343ᵇ, F. 24ᵇ = B. 348ᵇ, F. 25ᵃ = B. 2135ᵇ, 2923ᵇ, F. 27ᵇ = B. 200ᵇ, 645ᵇ, F. 33ᵇ = B. 399ᵇ, F. 35ᵇ = B. 2313ᵇ, F. 37ᵇ = B. 2947ᵃ, 3000ᵃ.

The recurrence of F. 11 — in slightly different form — in *Ex.* 218: *habban heora hlencan, hycgan on ellen* (used in a somewhat similar context) need not be construed as direct imitation one way or the other. (Cp. *Mald.* 4, 128.)

---

[1] *fæla* occurs 26 times in the late MS. A of the *WS. Gospels*, cf. G. Trilsbach, *Die Lautlehre der spätwestsächs. Evangelien* (Bonn, 1905), p. 15.

[2] ten Brink (L 4.7.549 f.) advanced the theory that the poem was popular among the East Saxons and was written down in Essex in the latter half of the 10th century. Cf. also Binz 185. — Instructive syntactical features are lacking. The repeated use of the pronoun 'this' (and of the adverb 'here') is fully warranted by the occasion. (See also *Arch.* cxv 182.) Some instances of the personal (and possessive) pronouns are possibly due to the scribe(s) (13, 25, 42); *hyra* in 15ᵇ is metrically necessary. — The metrical laxity and the occurrence of indirect discourse do not afford sufficient evidence of a late date. Nor can the use of *swān* 39 be considered decisive in this connection, since it is merely a guess that its meaning has been influenced by ON. *sveinn* (cf. Mackie LF. 2.12.267).

BIBLIOGRAPHY[1]

I. MANUSCRIPT

The MS. being lost, the text has to be based on George Hickes's transcription in his *Linguarum Vett. Septentrionalium Thesaurus etc.* (L 1.2), Vol. i, pp. 192 f. (Oxford, 1705.) It is preceded by the notice: ' Eodem metro conditum forte reperi fragmenti poetici singulare folium[2] in codice MS. homiliarum Semi-Saxonicarum qui extat in Bibliotheca Lambethana. Fragmentum autem subsequitur.' Cf. H. Wanley's *Catalogus* (L 1.2), pp. 266–69: Catalogus Cod. MSS. Anglo-Saxonicorum Bibliothecæ Lambethanæ. (P. 269: ' Fragmentum Poeticum prœlium quoddam describens in oppido Finnisburgh nuncupato innitum, quod exhibuit D. Hickesius, Gramm. Anglo-Sax. p. 192.')

II. EDITIONS

1. Editions are included in all the complete editions of *Beowulf* except those of Thorkelin, Arnold, and Holder. (In Grundtvig's edition (1861) the text is inserted after l. 1106 of the *Beowulf*.)
2. J. J. Conybeare in (1) *The British Bibliographer* iv, 261 ff. (London, 1814), and in his (2) *Illustrations of Anglo-Saxon Poetry* (L 2.23), pp. 175–79. 1826. [Meant as a republication of Hickes's text.]
3. N. F. S. Grundtvig, *Bjowulfs Drape* (L 3.27), pp. xl–xlv. 1820.
4. L. F. Klipstein, *Analecta Anglo-Saxonica* (L 2.23) ii, 426 f. 1849.
5. L. Ettmüller, *Engla and Seaxna Scopas and Bōceras* (L. 2.20), pp. 130 f. 1850.
6. M. Rieger, *Alt- und angelsächsisches Lesebuch* (L 2.21), pp. 61–3. 1861.
7. R. P. Wülcker, *Kleinere angelsächsische Dichtungen*, pp. 6 f. Halle, 1879. [Unimproved text.]
8. H. Möller, *Das altenglische Volksepos* (L 2.19), Part II, pp. vii–ix. 1883. [In 14 four-line stanzas.]
9. F. Kluge, *Angelsächsisches Lesebuch*, 3d ed., pp. 127 f. Halle, 1902.
10. M. Trautmann, in *Finn und Hildebrand* (Bonn. B. vii). Bonn, 1903. R.: G. Binz (LF. 4.22). Practically identical with this text [slight differences in ll. 10ᵃ, 27ᵃ (28ᵃ), 48 (50)] is the one in Trautmann's *Beowulf* (L 2.14).
11. Bruce Dickins, *Runic and Heroic Poems of the Old Teutonic Peo-*

---

[1] This Bibliography will be referred to as ' LF.' (See Table of Abbreviations, p. clxxxvii.)
[2] Possibly a separate leaf bound up with the MS. and accidentally lost when the MS. was rebound. Cf. Thomas Wright, *Biographia Britannica Literaria* (1842), Vol. i, p. 6, n.

ples, pp. 64–69. Cambridge, 1915. [Contains also an introduction, notes, and a prose translation, besides editions of *Waldere, Deor, Hildebrand*.]

12. W. S. Mackie, "The Fight at Finnsburg." *JEGPh.* xvi (1917), 250–73. [With textual and introductory notes.]

13. L. L. Schücking, *Kleines angelsächsisches Dichterbuch*. Cöthen, 1919, Leipzig, 1933. [Contains sixteen selections, including 'The Fight at Finnsburg,' 'Finn Episode,' and 'Bēowulf's Return.']

14. W. J. Sedgefield, *An Anglo-Saxon Verse-Book*, Manchester, 1922, pp. 25–27, 15–18. ['Fragment' and 'Episode.']

15. W. A. Craigie, *Specimens of Anglo-Saxon Poetry*. III. Edinburgh, 1931, pp. 10 ff. ['Fragment' and 'Episode.']

III. TRANSLATIONS

I. English

1. Translations are included in Thorpe's and Dickins's editions (opposite the text) and in the translations of *Beowulf* by Lumsden [incomplete], Garnett, Clark Hall (L 3.5, the 2d ed. containing a verse and a prose translation), Child (pp. 89 f.), Huyshe, Gummere, Leonard, Moncrieff, Gordon (L 3.9 a), Ayres (L 3.9 c).

2. J. J. Conybeare (LF. 2.2.1 & 2) [rimed paraphrase]; D. H. Haigh (L 4.27), pp. 32 f. [prose]; H. Morley (L 4.2), i 349 f. [prose translation of the Fragment and the Episode]; S. A. Brooke (L 4.6.1), pp. 64 f., (L 4.6.2), pp. 52 f. [four-accent measures; incomplete]; K. M. Warren (L 3.42.1) [prose, incomplete]; W. M. Dixon (*Beow.* Bibliogr., p. cliii, n.), pp. 84 f., 331 f. [verse and prose]; Cosette Faust and Stith Thompson, *Old English Poems Translated into the Original Meter*, Chicago and New York, 1918. — A translation of the 'Finn Episode' by R. W. Chambers is included in G. Sampson's *The Cambridge Book of Prose and Verse* (L 4.10. n.).

II. German

1. In the translations of *Beowulf* by Ettmüller (pp. 36–8), Simrock (pp. 58–60), Hoffmann (pp. 44–6), Vogt (pp. 97–9) [after Möller's text], Gering (pp. 98 f.), and in Trautmann's editions of the text (LF. 2.10).

2. L. Uhland, *Germ.* ii (1857), 354 f. (L 4.26). [Prose.] H. Naumann, *Frühgermanentum, Heldenlieder und Sprüche übersetzt und eingeleitet*, München, 1926 [alliterative verse]; A. Brandl, *För. Misc.*, 1929 [alliterative verse].

III. Danish

In Grundtvig's (L 3.27, LF. 2.3) and Hansen's (L 3.29) translations and Schaldemose's edition (L 2.3) of *Beowulf*. — *Norwegian Landsmaal:* in Rytter's translation (L 3.29 a) of *Beowulf*.

IV. Dutch

In Simons's translation of *Beowulf* (L 3.31).

V. Latin

In Conybeare's edition (LF. 2.2.1 & 2).

VI. French

In Pierquin's edition (L 2.17, 3.34); in W. Thomas's translation (L 3.35).

VII. Italian

In Grion's translation of *Beowulf* (L 3.36), pp. 105 f.; in Olivero's *Traduzioni* (L 3.36 a).

IV. STUDIES EXEGETICAL AND CRITICAL

(Discussions of the FINN EPISODE also are included.)

1. (1) R. Wülker's *Grundriss* (L 4.4), 1885. [Contains a useful summary of critical opinion prior to 1885.] — (2) Nellie Slayton Aurner, *An Analysis of the Interpretations of the Finnsburg Documents*. (Univ. of Iowa Monographs, Humanistic Studies, Vol. i, No. 6.) 1917. 36 pp. [Historical survey and bibliography.]

2. K. Müllenhoff, (1) *Nordalbingische Studien* i (Kiel, 1844), 156 ff. (L 4.19) [on persons and tribes in the Finn legend]; (2) *ZfdA*. xi (1859), 281–82; (3) *ib*. xii (1860), 285–87 (L 4.25) [traces of the legend in Germanic proper names]; (4) *Beovulf* (1889), pp. 97 f., 105–7 (L 4.19).

3. C. W. M. Grein, (1) *Eberts Jahrbuch etc*. iv (1862), 269–71 (L 4.69) [interpretation of the story]; (2) *Germ*. x (1865), 422 [textual criticism].

4. A. Holtzmann, *Germ*. viii (1863), 492–94 (L 5.4). [Textual interpretation and criticism.]

5. S. Bugge, (1) *Tidskrift for Philologi etc*. viii (1869), 304 f. (L 5.6.1) [textual criticism]; (2) *ZfdPh*. iv (1873), 204 (L 5.6.2); (3) *Beitr*. xii (1887), 20–37 (L 5.6.3) [admirable interpretation of the story and textual notes on the Fragment and the Episode].

6. M. Rieger, (1) *ZfdPh*. iii (1871), 394–401 (L 5.7) [textual interpretation of the Episode]; (2) *ZfdA*. xlviii (1905/6), 9–12 [textual notes on the Fragment].

7. H. Möller, *Das altenglische Volksepos* (1883) Part I, pp. 46–100; 151–56. (L 4.134.) [The Finn legend and its basis; composition and interpretation of the texts.] R.: R. Heinzel, *Anz.fdA*. x (1884), 225–30.

8. H. Schilling, *M L N*. i (1886), 89–92, 116 f.; ii (1887), 146–50. [Supports in general Möller's view of the context and opposes that of Bugge.]

9. G. Sarrazin, *Beowulf-Studien* (1888), pp. 174–76. (L 4.16.) [Remarks on the style.]

10. M. H. Jellinek, *Beitr*. xv (1891), 428–31. [Interpretation of the Fragment.]

11. F. Holthausen, (1) *Beitr*. xvi (1892), 549 f. (L 5.26.1); (2) *Beibl*. x (1900), 270 (L 5.26.8); (3) *ZfdPh*. xxxvii (1905), 123 f. (L 5.26.17); (4) *Beibl*. xliii (1932), 256. [Textual criticism.]

12. B. ten Brink, *Altenglische Literatur*, 1893 (see L 4.7), pp. 535 f., 545–50. [The legend of Finn; interpretation of the story.]

13. R. Koegel, *Geschichte der deutschen Litteratur*, I^a (1894), pp. 163–67. (L 4.8.)

14. G. Binz, *Beitr.* xx (1895), 179–86. (L 4.31.1.) [Testimony of proper names.]

15. R. Much (in a review of Panzer's *Hilde-Gudrun*), *Arch.* cviii (1902), 406 ff. [On connection between the Finn and the Kudrun legend.]

16. Th. Siebs in Paul's *Grundriss*, ii^a, 1st ed., pp. 494 f. (1893); 2d ed., pp. 523 f. (1902). [On the legend in general and the tribal names.]

17. M. Trautmann, (1) *Finn und Hildebrand* (1903), pp. 1–64 (LF. 2.10), cf. (2) Bonn. B. xvii (1905), 122. [Interpretation and textual criticism; a serviceable survey of the Fragment and the Episode.]

18. R. C. Boer, " Finnsage und Nibelungensage," *ZfdA.* xlvii (1903), 125–60. [The Finn legend, textual criticism of the Episode and the Fragment.]

19. L. L. Schücking, *Grundzüge der Satzverknüpfung etc.* (1904), pp. 148 f. (L 6.15.)

20. Fr. Klaeber, (1) *Angl.* xxviii (1905), 447, 456; (2) *Arch.* cxv (1905), 181 f. (cf. L 5.35.4); (3) *ESt.* xxxix (1908), 307 f. (4) " Observations on the Finn Episode." *JEGPh.* xiv (1915), 544–49. (5) *Angl.* l (1926), 224–33, lvi (1932), 421–23 (see L 5.35.19, 20).

21. G. L. Swiggett, " Notes on the Finnsburg Fragment." *MLN.* xx (1905), 169–71. [Unconvincing.]

22. G. Binz (in a review of Trautmann's ed.), *ZfdPh.* xxxvii (1905), 529–33.

23. A. Brandl, *Angelsächsische Literatur*, 1908 (see L 4.11), pp. 983–86. [Important.]

24. (1) R. Imelmann, *D.Lit.z.* xxx (1909), 997–1000 (L 2.7.3). [Notes on the Episode.] (2) J. R. R. Hall, *MLN.* xxv (1910), 113 f. (L 5.50.)

25. W. Meyer, *Beiträge zur Geschichte der Eroberung Englands durch die Angelsachsen*. Halle Diss., 1912. [Identifies Hengest with the historical leader of the Jutes.]

26. W. W. Lawrence, " Beowulf and the Tragedy of Finnsburg." *Publ. MLAss.* xxx (1915), 372–431. [Illuminating interpretation.]

27. Alexander Green, " The Opening of the Episode of Finn in *Beowulf*." *Publ. MLAss.* xxxi (1916), 759–97.

28. Harry Morgan Ayres, " The Tragedy of Hengest in *Beowulf*." *JEGPh.* xvi (1917), 282–95. [Interesting analysis.]

29. Carleton Brown, " *Beowulf* 1080–1106." *MLN.* xxxiv (1919), 181–83. [ll. 1084 f.]

30. Rudolf Imelmann, *Forschungen zur altenglischen Poesie*, Berlin, 1920, pp. 342–81. [Hengest=the historic Jutish chief; traces of the influence of the *Æneid;* interpretational notes.]

31. Nellie Slayton Aurner, " Hengest: A Study in Early English

Hero Legend." *Univ. of Iowa Humanistic Studies*, Vol. ii, No. 1. 1921. 76 pp. (and chart). Cf. *id.*, L F. 4.1.2.

32. Ernst A. Kock, *Angl.* xlv (1921), 125-27. [Textual notes.]

33. W. J. Sedgefield, *MLR.* xvi (1921), 59 [Textual notes]; "The Finn 'Episode' in 'Beowulf'," *ib.* xxviii (1933), 480-82.

34. Additional comment by A. Heusler, *R.-L.* ii 505 f., and L 4.124.3; G. Schütte, L 4.94 a; Cha. Intr. 245-89 [elaborate, important discussion]; Malone Haml. 19-23.

35. W. S. Mackie, "The Fight at Finsburg." *MLR.* xvii (1922), 288. [ll. 34 (35), 39 (40).]

36. R. A. Williams, (1) *The Finn Episode in Beowulf. An Essay in Interpretation*. Cambridge, 1924. 171 pp. [Endeavors to trace in the Finn story certain features known from the second part of the Nibelungen legend; suggests a number of novel interpretations. A notably ingenious but unwarranted reconstruction.] R.: W. J. Sedgefield, *MLR.* xx (1925), 338 f.; H. Hecht, *Anz.fdA.* xliv (1925), 121-25; Elsie Blackman, *Review of English Studies* i (1925), 228-31; Fr. Klaeber, *Beibl.* xxxvii (1926), 5-9 (cf. *ib.*, xxxviii, 61-63 and 160); Kemp Malone, *JEGPh.* xxv (1926), 114-17; Hermann M. Flasdieck, *Lit. bl.* xlvii (1926), 156-64; H. Schreuder, *Neophilologus* xi (1926), 294-97. — (2) "'Beowulf,' ll. 1086-1088," *MLR.* xxii (1927), 310-13.

37. Kemp Malone, "The Finn Episode in *Beowulf*." *JEGPh.* xxv (1926), 157-72. [Subtle literary interpretation.] *Id.*, "Hunlafing," *MLN.* xliii (1928), 300-04. [Sword-name.]

38. Anton Gerard van Hamel, "Hengest and his Namesake." *Kl. Misc.* (1929), 159-71. [Critical examination of the accounts of Hengest the invader. The question of his identity with the *Finnsburg* Hengest cannot be decided. But for an Anglo-Saxon of the 7th century (Nennius' informant), " Finn the Frisian, and consequently Hengest the thane, were no contemporaries of Hengest the invader."]

39. H. F. Scott-Thomas, "The Fight at Finnsburg: Guthlaf and the Son of Guthlaf." *JEGPh.* xxx (1931), 498-505. [Unconvincing.] — 39 a. Fr. Klaeber, "Garulf, Guðlafs Sohn im Finnsburg-Fragment." *Arch.* clxii (1932), 116 f. — 39 b. John O. Beaty, *PMLA.* xlix (1934), 372 f. (L 7.25 k.)

40. Cf. Hoops 132 ff., St. 55 ff. [Comments on the Episode.]

41. See also *Beowulf* Bibliography IV, *passim;* thus, Mone L 4.23. 134-36; Uhland L 4.26.351 ff.; Haigh L 4.27. ch. 3; Dederich L 4.70. 215-25; Morley L 4.2. ch. 7; Brooke L 4.6.1.63-6; Ker L 4.120.1.94-7; Heusler L 4.124.1.10 f.; Lawrence L 4.22 c; Schneider L 4.22 d, 4.13 a; also Köhler L 9.5.155-57.

42. Further comments are found in numerous editions and translations of *Beowulf* (and *Finnsburg*), especially those of Grundtvig (transl., pp. xxxix-xlv; ed., pp. l-lii, 138 f.), Kemble (ii, pp. xlvii-xlix), Ettmüller (transl., pp. 35-9), Simrock (pp. 187-90), Arnold (pp. 204-7), Wyatt, Holthausen, Heyne-Schücking, Clark Hall, Child, Vogt, Gering, Gummere, Chambers, Dickins.

THE FIGHT AT FINNSBURG

* * * *

....   (hor)nas byrnað.'
[H]næf hleoþrode ðā   heaþogeong cyning:
'Nē ðis ne dagað ēast*a*n,   nē hēr draca ne flēogeð,
nē hēr ðisse healle   hornas ne byrnað;
5 ac hēr forþ berað,   fugelas singað,
gylleð græghama,   gūðwudu hlynneð,
scyld scefte oncwyð.   Nū scȳneð þes mōna
waðol under wolcnum;   nū ārīsað wēadæda,
ðē ðisne folces nīð   fremman willað.
10 Ac onwacnigeað nū,   wīgend mīne,
habbað ēowre li*n*da,   hicgeaþ on ellen,
win*n*að on orde,   wesað on mōde!'
Ðā ārās mænig goldhladen ðegn,   gyrde hine his
swurde;

NOTE — *Dickins*=LF. 2.11; *Mackie*=LF. 2.12; *Tr.*=LF. 2.10. See also Table of Abbreviations, pp. clxxxiv ff.

1 *Rie.L.* (?), *Gr. Germ. x 422, 4 Edd.* (hor)nas; *Gr. l.c. inserts before it* (beorhtre), *Bu. Tid. 304* (beorhtor). *Tho., Edd.* byrnað næfre. — 2ᵃ *Tr.* Hnæf þā (*for* næfre, *taken as beginning of 2, see Hickes's text*) hleoþrode; *Holt.* Ðā hleoþrode (*metri causa*). *Heusler V.* § 234 Hnæf hleoþrode ðā. — 2ᵇ *Gru.tr., most Edd.* heaþogeong; *Ke.* heorogeong; *Dickins* hearogeong (=heoru-); *Tr.* heaþogeorn. — 3ᵃ *Gru.tr.* ēastan. — 5ᵃ *Gru.tr.* (?) forþ fērað; *E.tr., E.Sc.* fyrd berað; *Gr.¹, Schü.* fēr (=fǣr) *for* hēr. *Before* 5ᵇ *Rie.L. inserts* [fyrdsearu rincas,/ fȳnd ofer foldan], *Gr.²* [feorhgenīðlan/fyrdsearu fūslicu], *Bu.* 23 [fyrdsearu rincas,/flacre flānbogan], *Rie. ZfdA. xlviii 9* [fyrdsearu rincas,/nalles hēr on flyhte]. — 6ᵇ *Klu. LF. 2.9* (?), *Holt.* hlyneð. — 9ᵃ *ten Brink LF. 4.12.545* [þām] ðe. — *Boer ZfdA. xlvii 143 f.* þisses (*so Gru. p. 138) and* 9ᵇ wille. — 11ᵃ *Gr.¹* (?), *He., Tr., Sed.* hebbað. — *Gr.* (*cf. E.Sc.*), *He., Sed.* handa; *Bu. Tid. 305, Schü., Holt.* linda; *Bu.* 23 (?), *Tr., Cha.* hlencan; *Rie. ZfdA. xlviii 10* randas (*cp. Mald. 20*). — 11ᵇ *Gru.tr.* hicgeaþ. — 12ᵃ *Gru.tr., et al., Sed.* windað; *Rieger LF. 4.6.2.10, et al.* þindað (*see note*); *Tho.* (*cf. E.tr.*), *Schü., Holt.* winnað. — 12ᵇ *Gru.tr., et al., Sed.* on mōde; *3 Edd.* onmōde. — 13ᵃ *made into 3 half-lines by Rie.L., Gr.²; Tr.:* Ð. ā. [of reste rondwīgend] m.,/g.ð.; *Holt.:* Ð. ā. [of ræste rūmheort] m./g. [gum]ðegn. — *Tho.* goldhroden.

ðā tō dura ēodon   drihtlīce cempan,
15 Sigeferð and Ēaha,   hyra sword getugon,
and æt ōþrum durum   Ordlāf and Gūþlāf,
and Hengest sylf,   hwearf him on lāste.
Ðā gȳt Gārulf[e]   Gūðere stȳrde,
ðæt hē swā frēolīc feorh   forman sīþe
20 tō ðǣre healle durum   hyrsta ne bǣre,
nū hyt nīþa heard   ānyman wolde;
ac hē frægn ofer eal   undearninga,
dēormōd hæleþ,   hwā ðā duru hēolde.
'Sigeferþ is mīn nama (cweþ hē),   ic eom Secgena lēod,
25 wreccea wīde cūð;   fæla ic wēana gebād,
heordra hilda;   ðē is gȳt hēr witod,
swæþer ðū sylf tō mē   sēcean wylle.'
Ðā wæs on healle   wælslihta gehlyn,
sceolde cellod bord   cēnum on handa,
30 bānhelm berstan,   buruhðelu dynede, —
oð æt ðǣre gūðe   Gārulf gecrang
ealra ǣrest   eorðbūendra,
Gūðlāfes sunu,   ymbe hyne gōdra fæla,
hwearflīcra hrǣw.   Hræfen wandrode
35 sweart and sealobrūn.   Swurdlēoma stōd,
swylce eal Finnsburuh   fȳrenu wǣre.

[15a] *Mö. 86 (cf. Müll. ZfdA. xi 281, Bu. 25), Tr., Holt.* Ēawa. *Dickins supports* Eaha *by ref. to* Echha, Liber Vitae, *etc. (cf. R. Müller, Über die Namen des L.V., Palaestra ix, p. 53)*. — 18a *Tr., Cha.* Gārulf[e]. — 18b *E.Sc. (?), Tr., Holt., Cha.* stȳrde. — 19a *Gr., Schü.* h[ī]e. — 20b *Ke., Holt., Sed., Cha.* bǣre. — 22a *Tr., Holt.* eal[le]. — 25a *Gru.tr.* wreccen, *Tho.* wrecca, *Gr.*[2] wreccea. — 25b *W. D. Conybeare (L 2.23)* wēana. — 26a *Ke., most Edd.* heardra. — 28a *E.tr., most Edd.* wealle. — 29a *Gr.*[1] cēlod; *Rie.L., Tr., Schü., Cha.* cellod; *Jellinek Beitr. xv 431* cēled ('cooled'); *Holt. Zs. 123* ceorlæs; *Holt.*[3] clǣne. — *Ke.* bord. — 29b *Gr.* cēnum. — 30a *Bu. 26* bārhelm ('boar-helmet'). — 33a *Mö.* Gūðulfes, *Tr.* Gūðheres. — 34a *Gru.tr., Gr.*[2]*, Sed., Mackie* hwearflīcra hrǣw; *Bu. 27 f., Schü.,*[10] *Cha.* Hwearf ('moved about,' with acc.) flacra hrǣw (34b *Bu.* hræfen fram ōðrum); *Jellinek l.c.* Hwearf ('crowd') lāðra hrēas; *Tr.* Hrēawblācra hwearf (*and* 34b wundrode); *Holt.*[2-5] Hwearf blācra hrēas. — 36a *Tr.* Finn[e]s buruh, *Dickins* Finn[e]sburuh.

THE FIGHT AT FINNSBURG

Ne gefrægn ic næfre wurþlīcor æt wera hilde
sixtig sigebeorna   sēl gebǣra*n*,
nē nēfre swāna*s* hwītne medo   sēl forgyldan,
40 ðonne Hnæfe guldan   his hægstealdas.

Hig fuhton fīf dagas,   swā hyra nān ne fēol,
drihtgesīða,   ac hig ðā duru hēoldon.
Ðā gewāt him wund hǣleð   on wæg gangan,
sǣde þæt his byrne   ābrocen wǣre,
45 heresceorp u*n*hrōr,   and ēac wæs his helm ðȳr[e]l.
Ðā hine sōna frægn   folces hyrde,
hū ðā wīgend hyra   wunda genǣson,
oððe hwæþer ðǣra hyssa . . . .
　　　*　 *　　　　　　　　 *　 *

HICKES'S TEXT

. . . .   Scyld scefte oncwyð.
. nas byrnað. [geong cyning.   Nu scyneð þes mona.
Næfre hleoþrode ða hearo   Waðol[1] under wolcnum.
Ne ðis ne dagað Eastun.   Nu arisað wea-dæda.
Ne herdraca ne fleogeð.   Ðe ðis ne folces nið.
Ne her ðisse healle hornas   Fremman willað.
ne byrnað.   (10) Ac on wacnigeað nu.
(5) Ac her forþberað.   Wigend mine.
Fugelas singað.   Habbað eowre landa.
Gylleð græghama.   Hie geaþ on ellen.
Guð wudu hlynneð.   Windað on orde.

38[b] *Ke.* gebǣran. — 39[a] *Gr.* swānas; *dropped by Tr.* — *E.tr., most Edd.* swētne (*for* hwītne, *partly metri causa*). — *Gru.* sylfres hwītne mēde. — 41[b] *Holt.* swā ne fēol hira nān (*metri causa*). *Before it lacuna assumed and missing words supplied by Rie.L., Gr.*[3], *Mö., Tr.* — 42[b] *Ke., E.Sc., Tr., Cha.* (?) dura. — 45[a] *Tho., Schü., Cha., Holt.*[6] heresceorp unhrōr; *Tr.* h. āhroren; *Ke., Holt.*[2-5], *Sed.* heresceorpum hrōr. — 45[b] *Tr., Holt., Sed.* þȳr[e]l. (*Or* þyr[e]l, *cf. T.C.* § 3.) — 46[a] *Holt.* Ðā frægn hine sōna (*metri causa*).

[1] For the runic 'wyn' regularly printed in Hickes's text the ordinary *w* has been substituted.

THE FIGHT AT FINNSBURG

Wesað on mode.
Ða aras mænig goldhladen
  ðegn.
Gyrde hine his swurde.
Ða to dura eodon.
Drihtlice cempan.
(15) Sigeferð and Eaha.
Hyra sword getugon.
And æt oþrum durum.
Ordlaf and Guþlaf.
And Hengest sylf.
Hwearf him on laste.
Ða gyt Garulf.
Guðere styrode.
Ðæt he swa freolic feorh.
For-man siþe.
(20) To ðære healle durum.
Hyrsta ne bæran.
Nu hyt niþa heard.
Any man wolde.
Ac he frægn ofer eal.
Undearninga.
Deormod hæleþ.
Hwa ða duru heolde.
Sigeferþ is min Nama cweþ
  he.
Ic eom secgena leod.
(25) Wrecten wide cuð.
Fæla ic weuna gebad.
Heordra hilda.
Ðe is gyt herwitod.
Swæþer ðu sylf to me.
Secean wylle.
Ða wæs on healle.
Wæl-slihta gehlyn.
Sceolde Celæs borð.
Genumon handa.
(30) Banhelm berstan.
Buruhðelu dynede.
Oð æt ðære guðe.
Garulf gecrang.
Ealra ærest.
Eorðbuendra.
Guðlafes sunu.
Ymbe hyne godra fæla.
Hwearflacra hrær.
Hræfen wandrode.
(35) Sweart and sealo brun.
Swurd-leoma stod.
Swylce eal Finnsburuh.
Fyrenu wære.
Ne gefrægn ic.
Næfre wurþlicor.
Æt wera hilde.
Sixtig sigebeorna.
Sel gebærann.
Ne nefre swa noc hwitne
  medo.
Sel forgyldan.
(40) Ðonne hnæfe guldan.
His hægstealdas.
Hig fuhton fif dagas.
Swa hyra nan ne feol.
Drihtgesiða.

THE FIGHT AT FINNSBURG

Ac hig ða duru heoldon. And eac wæs his helm ðyrl.
Ða gewat him wund hæleð. Ða hine sona frægn.
On wæg gangan. Folces hyrde.
Sæde þ his byrne. Hu ða wigend hyra.
Abrocen wære. Wunda genæson.
(45) Here sceorpum hror. Oððe hwæþer ðæra hyssa.

NOTES

1-12. Hnæf announces the approach of enemies and arouses his men.
We may picture to ourselves the situation as follows. One of the Danes, who are distrustful of the Frisians, has been watching outside and reports to the king a suspicious gleam of light. Hnæf replies: 'These are signs of nothing else but armed men marching against us.' Then, by bold anticipation, the realities of battle are sketched by the speaker. It is natural to suppose that Hengest is the watcher addressed by the king.

2. [H]næf hleoþrode ðā. For the scansion, Hel. 4826 *werod sīðoda thō* has been cited as a parallel. (Heusler.) — **heaþogeong.** Evidently Hnæf was thought to be much younger than his sister.

3. ðis ne dagað, 'this is not the dawn.' — **nē hēr draca ne flēogeð;** i.e., a fire-spitting dragon. See *Beow.* 2312, 2522, 2582; *OE. Chron.* A.D. 793 (D, E, F); *Lied vom Hürnen Seyfrid* 18: *Die Burg die ward erleuchtet, Als ob sie wer entprant* (as a result of the flying of a dragon). The exchange of remarks about an alarming light could have suggested itself to the poet by the old belief that an approaching battle was signalized by a reddening of the sky. Cp. *Helgakv. Hund.* ii 22: *verþr vígroþa um víkinga,* and Heusler's note (Thule, No. 1, p. 149).

5 f. forþ berað of the MS. can be justified on the assumption that the war equipments specified afterwards are the object of *berað* (see, e.g., *Beow.* 291, *Ex.* 219, *Mald.* 12) which the poet had in mind but did not take the time to express. [A frankly intrans. use of *forþ beran,* 'press forward' (Schilling, *MLN.* i 116 f., Dickins) can hardly be recognized. The supposedly parallel cases of *beran ūt,* *El.* 45, *Andr.* 1221 were misunderstood by Gr. Spr. Cf. also *Angl.* xxvii 407 f.] — The **fugelas** seem to be the birds of prey (see 34), who gather in expectation of slaughter, as in *Gen.* 1983 ff., *Ex.* 162 ff., *El.* 27 ff., *Jud.* 206 ff. For other interpretations proposed such as 'arrows,' 'morning birds,' see Bu. Tid. 304 f., Bu. 22 f., Möller 47; *Angl.* xxviii 447; Boer, *ZfdA.* xlvii 140 ff.; Rieger, *ZfdA.* xlviii 9. — **grǣghama,** 'the grey-coated one,' i.e. either 'wolf' — the familiar animal of prey, beside raven and eagle, in the regular epic trio, cp., e.g., *Brun.* 64 — or 'coat of mail' (cp. *Beow.* 334). *gyllan* fits both meanings (*Rid.* 25.3; *Andr.* 127).

7-9. Now the moon lights up the scene: the tragic fate is inevitable, **nū ārīsað wēadǣda.** Thus Hildebrand exclaims: *welaga nū . . . wēwurt skihit, Hildebr.* 49. þes (mōna) is thoroughly idiomatic, cp. *Rid.* 58.1: *ðēos lyft, Gen.* 811: *þēos beorhte sunne,* etc. (*Arch.* cxv 182). — **under wolcnum;** the moon is passing 'under,' i.e., 'behind' the clouds, though not really hidden by them. A stereotyped expression is here put to a fine, picturesque use.

9. ðisne folces nīð fremman, 'carry out this enmity of the people.'

12. The 'wyn' form of windað is slightly different from the customary w of Hickes; hence it has sometimes been taken for a þ; so *wrecten* 25 (see Dickins). (*þindað* = 'show your temper' (?).)

13-27. The warriors on both sides make ready for the fight.

13. goldhladen may be meant with reference to helmets, swords, corslets, or (Bu. 24:) bracelets such as Hrólf's warriors are to use in the last fight for their king: 'load your arms with gold; let your right hands receive the bracelets, that they may swing their blows more heavily' (Saxo ii 64, Par. § 7). [Cf. Olrik-Hollander, *The Heroic Legends of Denmark* (1919), pp. 121 f.] Note *Ruin* 33 ff.: *beorn monig/glædmōd and goldbeorht . . . . wīghyrstum scān.* — 13ª is metrically doubtful.

16. æt ōþrum durum, scil. 'stood' or 'drew their swords.' The plural *durum* has singular meaning; cp. 20.

17. and Hengest sylf. Hengest now takes his place inside the hall with the others. (The use of *sylf* is no indication that *he* is the king.)

18 ff. Ðā gȳt marks the progress of the narrative (which now introduces another fighter): 'further,' 'then.' [Or does *gȳt* denote 'as yet' in conjunction with (and partly anticipating) the negative meaning of the sentence (*stȳrde, ne*)?] The Frisian Gūðere tries to restrain the impetuous youth, Gārulf — perhaps his nephew, cp. *Nibel.* 2208 ff., *Waltharius* 846 ff. — from risking his life 'at the first onset' (19ª, cp. *Beow.* 740; or: 'in his first battle'?); but Gārulf, heedless of danger, rushes to one of the doors, encounters the veteran Sigeferþ, and meets a hero's death. There is nothing startling about the fact that Gārulf's father has the same name, Gūðlāf (33), as one of the Danish warriors. (In *Maldon* occur two persons named Godrīc, 187: 321, and two named Wulfmǣr, 113: 155.) Certainly we need not assume that father and son are fighting on opposite sides. See *ESt.* xxxix 308. — Cha. Intr. 283 ff. suggests that Gārulf (possibly miswritten Gefwulf, *Wids.* 26) may have been the chief of the 'Jutes.' Schneider (L 4.13 a, 22 d) conjectures that in the original story Gārulf was the son of Finn. Beaty (L 7.25 k) tries to establish Gārulf as Finn's son by way of taking *gūðlāf* 33 as an adjective designating Finn. [Further, LF. 4.39.]

20. As to hyrsta (parallel with *feorh*) beran, see *Beow.* 291, and note on *F.* 5 f. (*Angl.* xxviii 456.)

21. nīþa heard, scil. Sigeferþ.

22. hē, scil. Gārulf. — ofer eal. The neuter *eal* (in contrast with *ealle*, *Beow.* 2899, cp. *Gen.* 2462, *Dan.* 527, *Sat.* 616, etc. [see *Arch.* civ 291]) includes both the fighters and the scene (and tumult) of fighting. Cp. *Mald.* 256: *ofer eall clypode;* also Ælfric, *Saints* iv 280, xxiii 803.

24. cweþ hē is a parenthetic addition (which during the merely oral existence of such lays was dispensed with). It is to be disregarded metrically. Cf. Rie V. 58 n.; Heusler, *ZfdA.* xlvi 245 ff.

THE FIGHT AT FINNSBURG

26. heordra. Cha. Intr. 245 n. calls attention to the fact that, among numerous unquestionable inaccuracies of Hickes's transcripts of Old English specimens, there is not lacking an erroneous *eo* for *ea* (*Menol.* 121: MS. *bearn*). Thus it will seem to be unnecessary here to find an explanation for such an orthographic irregularity.

27. swæþer, 'which one of two things,' i.e. victory or death. Cp. *Hildebr.* 60 ff.

28-40. The battle rages.

28. on (healle), 'in (the hall)' (cp. 30[b]), or 'at,' 'around'? (cp. *Beow.* 2529, 926[?]). — *wealle* would be metrically more regular.

29. No explanation or really satisfactory emendation of **celæs** has been found. The conjecture *cellod* rests on *Mald.* 283: *cellod bord*, but the meaning of this nonce word is unknown. (Rieger LF. 2.6: 'concave,' 'curved'; Kluge LF. 2.9: from Lat. *celatus;* Trautmann LF. 2.10.46: *cyllod* 'covered with leather'; Grein Spr.: *cēlod* 'keel-shaped,' 'oval'; B.-T. Suppl.: *celod* 'having a boss or beak'; Holt. i[6], ii[5]: *celced* 'white' (from *cealc* 'chalk').) See also Varr.

34. hwearflīc (cf. above, p. 238), perhaps = 'agile,' 'active,' or 'obedient,' 'trusty'; cp. *Gifts of Men* 68: *þegn gehweorf;* Go. *gahwairbs* 'pliant, obedient.' [According to Mackie, 'mortal,' 'dead,' on the basis of *hwerflīc* 'fleeting,' *Boeth.* 25.10 (B). — Cp. ON. *hverfr* 'shifting'; OE. Lind. *Gosp.*: *huoerflīce* = vicissim.] — **hrǣw,** 'body,' not necessarily 'corpse'; cp. *Andr.* 1031: *ǣr þan hrā crunge* (though also *walu fēollon, Beow.* 1042). — Numerous corrections of this passage have been proposed, see Varr. [Also *Hwearfade* (or *Hwearf(t)lade*) *ærn* (= *earn*, cf. Siev. § 158.1) would make sense. Kock[4] 126 f.: *hwearf flacra earn;* Holt. LF. 4.11.4: *hwearf hlacra earn* (*hlacor 'screaming,' cp. *hlacerian* 'to mock, deride'). The eagle is certainly an agreeable newcomer, to whom the raven is not likely to object. — Other guesses: *MLR.* xvi 59 (Sedgefield); *ib.* xix 105 (S. J. Crawford: *ymb hine gōdra fǣla/hwearflīcra hrǣs* (= *hrēas*)).] — **Hræfen wandrode.** Cp. *Mald.* 106: *hremmas wundon.*

36. swylce eal Finnsburuh fȳrenu wǣre. (Cp. 1 ff.) See the parallels: Uhland, *Germ.* ii 356, Lüning L 7.28.73 f., 31; also *Iliad* ii 455 ff.

37 f. On the double comparative (used similarly in the corresponding passage, *Beow.* 1011 f.), see *MPh.* iii 252.

39 f. See *Beow.* 2633 ff. and note. For a defense of the 'white mead' see Mackie (ref. to an 18th cent. quotation in the *NED.*). It is not surprising that critics (Heusler L 4.124.3.28, Holthausen[5], Mackie, *MLR.* xvii 288) should feel strongly tempted to relieve the heavy line (39) by reading (with Trautmann): *nē nēfre swētne medo sēl forgyldan.*

41 ff. The Frisians, weakened and unable to make headway, [seem on the point of preparing for a new move . . .]. — As to **fīf dagas,** see *Beow.* 545 and note on 147.

43 ff. It appears probable that the wounded man who 'goes away' is a Frisian, and **folces hyrde,** Finn. See Rieger, *ZfdA.* xlviii 12; for arguments to the contrary, see Bugge 28, Trautmann 62, Boer, *ZfdA*. xlvii 147. We may imagine a disabled Frisian leaving the front of the battle line and being questioned by his chief as to how the [Danish?] warriors were bearing (or could bear) their wounds.

45ª. Type E. As to the shifting of the stress to the second syllable of **unhrōr,** cp. *Beow.* 1756, 2000. — *heresceorpum hrōr* (see Hickes's text) could refer only to the *wund hæleð* himself, 43.

47. On the metrical division of this line, see note on *B*. 2481.

48. Bugge (28), taking **hwæþer** as 'whether,' would supply [*hild sweðrode*]. If *hwæþer* is = 'which one,' the missing words might be [*hilde gedīgde*]; the names of the two young fighters were then contained in the following line.

The rest is silence. But the outcome is revealed in the *Beowulf* Episode.

It has been surmised by Rieger (*l.c.*) that Finn, anxious to break down the resistance of the besieged at last, orders the hall to be set on fire (as is done, *Vǫlsungasaga*, ch. 8 and *Nibel.* 2048 ff.), whereupon the Danes, forced into the open, have to meet the Frisians on equal ground.

APPENDIX I

PARALLELS

(ANALOGUES AND ILLUSTRATIVE PASSAGES)

I. ANGLO-SAXON GENEALOGIES[1]

§ 1. WEST SAXON GENEALOGY.

§ 1.1. **The Anglo-Saxon Chronicle** (ed. B. Thorpe, 1861; i 126 ff.). A.D. 855. (MS. B, cp. A, C, D.)

Aþelwulf ... gefor ... Se Aþelwulf wæs Ecgbrihting. Ecgbriht ... Ingild ...... (14 more names). Brand — Bældæg — Woden — Frealaf — Finn — God(w)ulf — Geata (A, D: Geat, C: Geatt) — Tætwa — BEAW[2] — SCYLDWA (A: Sceldwea, C: Scealdwa) — HEREMOD — Itermon — Haðra — Hwala — Bedwig[3] SCEAFING, id est filius Noe, se wæs geboren on þære earce Noes. Lamech. Matusalem .... Seth. Adam primus homo et pater noster, id est Christus.

§ 1.2. **Asserius, De Rebus Gestis Ælfredi** (A.D. 893) (ed. W. H. Stevenson, Oxford, 1904). Cap. i.

Genealogia: Ælfred rex, filius Æthelwulfi regis .. Ecgberhti ... Ingild ...... Brond — Beldeag — Uuoden — Frithowald — Frealaf — Frithuwulf — Finn — Godwulf — Geata, quem Getam iamdudum pagani pro deo venerabantur — Tætuua — BEAUU — SCELDWEA — HEREMOD — Itermod — Hathra — Huala — Beduuig — Seth[4] — Noe — Lamech — Mathusalem — Enoch — Malaleel — Cainan — Enos — Seth — Adam.

§ 1.3. **Fabii Ethelwerdi** (ob. cir. 1000 A.D.) Chronicorum libri quatuor (ed. H. Petrie, J. Sharpe, T. D. Hardy; *Monumenta Historica Britannica*, Vol. i, 1848). Lib. iii, cap. iii (p. 512).

Athulf rex .. filius Ecgbyrhti regis ... Ingild ...... Brond — Balder — Uuothen — Frithouuald — Frealaf — Frithouulf — Fin — Goduulfe

---

[1] On the numerous Ags. genealogies, see Grimm D. M. iii 377–401 (1709–36); Kemble ii, pp. v ff., & L 4.43; Earle-Plummer, *Two of the Saxon Chronicles* ii (1899), 1–6 (harmonized genealogical trees); Haack L 4.30. 23 ff.; Chadwick Or. 269 ff.; Cha. Intr. 195 ff., 311 ff.; E. Hackenberg, *Die Stammtafeln der ags. Königreiche*, Berlin Diss., 1918. On ON. genealogies, see *Corpus Poeticum Boreale* (L 10.1) ii 511 ff.; cp. Par. §§ 5, 8.1.

[2] Important names have been marked by the use of capitals or italics.

[3] According to E. Björkman, *ESt.* lii 170, *Beibl.* xxx 23–5, the *d* is a scribal error for *o* (in a form based on a latinized *Beowius*). MS. D has *Beowi*.

[4] Stevenson's note: 'legendum tamen *Sceaf.*'

PARALLELS

— Geat — Tetuua — Beo — Scyld — Scef. Ipse Scef cum uno dromone advectus est in insula oceani quæ dicitur *Scani*,[1] armis circumdatus, eratque valde recens puer, et ab incolis illius terræ ignotus; attamen ab eis suscipitur, et ut familiarem diligenti animo eum custodierunt, et post in regem eligunt; de cuius prosapia ordinem trahit Athulf rex.

(English translation in J. A. Giles's *Six Old English Chronicles* [Bohn's Antiquarian Library].)

§ 1.4. **Willelmi Malmesbiriensis Monachi** (ob. A.D. 1143) **De Gestis Regum Anglorum libri quinque** (ed. W. Stubbs, London, 1887). Lib. ii, § 116.

Ethelwulfus fuit filius Egbirhti ... Ingild[us] ...... Brondius — Beldegius — Wodenius — Fridewaldus — Frelafius — Finnus — Godulfus — Getius — Tetius — Beowius — Sceldius — Sceaf. Iste, ut ferunt, in quandam insulam Germaniæ Scandzam, de qua Jordanes, historiographus Gothorum loquitur, appulsus navi sine remige, puerulus, posito ad caput frumenti manipulo, dormiens, ideoque Sceaf nuncupatus, ab hominibus regionis illius pro miraculo exceptus, et sedulo nutritus; adulta ætate regnavit in oppido quod tunc *Slaswic*, nunc vero Haithebi appellatur. Est autem regio illa *Anglia Vetus* dicta, unde Angli venerunt in Britanniam, inter Saxones et Gothos constituta. Sceaf fuit filius Heremodii . . . .

§ 2. Mercian Genealogy.

The Anglo-Saxon Chronicle (ed. B. Thorpe, i 86). A.D. 755 (MSS. A, B, C).

... Offa feng to rice ond heold xxxix. wintra; ond his sunu Ecgferþ heold xli. daga ond c. daga. Se Offa wæs þincgferþing. Þincgferþ Eanwulfing. Eanwulf — Osmod — Eawa — Pybba — Creoda — Cynewald — Cnebba — Icel — Eomær[2] — Angelþeow — Offa — Wærmund — Wihtlæg Wodening.

See *ib.*, A.D. 626 (MSS. B, C), and Sweet, *The Oldest English Texts*, p. 170.

§ 3. Kentish Genealogy.

Nennii Historia Britonum (redaction dated cir. 800 A.D.) (ed. J. Stevenson, London, 1838), § 31. Cf. Cha. Intr. 199.

Interea venerunt tres ciulæ a Germania expulsæ in exilio, in quibus erant Hors et Hengist, qui et ipsi fratres erant, filii Guictgils, filii Guitta, filii Guectha, filii Vuoden, filii Frealaf, filii Fredulf, filii Finn, filii Folcwald,[3] filii Geta, qui fuit, at aiunt, filius Dei.

---

[1] See Intr. xxxvii; Glossary of Proper Names: *Sceden-íg.*

[2] Sweet, *O.E.T.* 170.93: *Eamer.*

[3] Thus also in Henry of Huntingdon's *Historia Anglorum* (cir. 1135 A.D.), lib. ii, § 1, where the name is corrupted, however, to *Flocwald.*

APPENDIX I

II. SCANDINAVIAN DOCUMENTS

(See L 10.1, 2, 3, 4, 8.)

§ 4. Elder Edda.

Hyndluljóþ (cir. close of the 10th century).[1]

2. Let us pray the Father of the Hosts to be gracious to us, for he grants and gives gold to his servants; he gave Hermóðr a helmet and mail-coat, and Sigmundr a sword.

9. For they have laid a wager of Welsh-ore (i.e., gold), Ōhtere [Óttarr] the young and Ongenþēow [Angantýr]. I am bound to help the former, that the young prince may have his father's heritage after his kinsmen.

11. Now do thou tell over the men of old and say forth in order the races of men. Who of the Shieldings [Skjǫldunga]? Who of the Shelfings [Skilfinga]? who of the Ethelings? who of the Wolfings [Ylfinga]? who of the Free-Born? who of the Gentle-Born are the most chosen of kindred of all upon earth?

14. Onela [Áli] was of old the mightiest of men, and Halfdanr in former days the highest of the Shieldings. Famous are the wars which that king waged, his deeds have gone forth to the skirts of heaven. 15. He [Halfdanr] strengthened himself in marriage with [the daughter of] Eymundr the highest of men, who slew Sigtryggr with the cold blade; he wedded Almweig the highest of ladies; they bred up and had eighteen sons.

§ 5. Prose Edda.*

Prologus, § 3.

..... Vingeþórr, hans sonr Vingener, hans sonr Móda, hans sonr Magi, hans sonr Seskef** — Beðvig — Athra — Ítrmann — Heremóð — Skjaldun, er vér kǫllum Skjǫld — Biáf, er vér kǫllum Bjár — Ját — Guðólfr — Finn — Fríallaf, er vér kǫllum Friðleif — Vóden, þann kǫllum vér Óðin.

Skáldskaparmál. Ch. 40. Skjǫldr hét sonr Óðins, er Skjǫldungar eru frá komnir; hann hafði atsetu[2] ok réð[3] lǫndum, þar sem nú er kǫllu ð Danmǫrk, en þá var kallat Gotland.[4] Skjǫldr átti þann son, er Friðleifr hét, er lǫndum réð eptir hann; sonr Friðleifs hét Fróði [' Frið-Fróði ']. [There follows the story of Fróði's mill (of happiness, peace, and gold), and the *Grottasǫngr*, i.e. Mill Song.[5]] — Ch. 41. Konungr einn í Danmǫrk er nefndr Hrólfr Kraki; hann var ágætastr[6] fornkonunga fyrst af

---

[1] The translation in the *Corpus Poeticum Boreale* is used.

* Finnur Jónsson's edition (1900) is used.

** I.e., OE. *sē Scē(a)f*. See Par. § 8.1.

[2] 'residence.'   [3] 'ruled' (OE. *rēd*).   [4] Rather Jótland, i.e. 'Jutland.'   [5] *Grottasǫngr* 22: ' Let us grind on! Yrsa's child [Rolf Kraki] shall avenge Halfdan's death on Froði. He [Rolfi] shall be called her son and her brother.' (A new rendering by Malone: cf. note on 82 ff.)

[6] ' most renowned.'

mildi ok frœknleik[1] ok lítillæti[2] ...... Konungr réð fyrir Upsǫlum, er
Aðils hét. Hann átti[3] Yrsu, móður Hrólfs kraka. Hann hafði ósætt[4]
við þann konung, er réð fyrir Nóregi, er Áli hét. Þeir stefnðu orrostu[5]
milli sín á ísi vats, þess er *Væni* heitir. [King Aðils had asked Hrólfr
for assistance; the latter, being engaged in another war, sent him his
twelve champions, among whom were Bǫðvar-bjarki, Hjalti hugprúði, Vǫttr, Véseti.] Í þeiri orrostu fell Áli konungr ok mikill hluti[6]
liðs[7] hans. Þá tók Aðils konungr af honum dauðum hjálminn[8] *Hildisvín,* ok hest[9] hans Hrafn ... [There follows the story of Rolf's famous
expedition to Upsala.]

Ch. 55. Þessir [eru hestar] talðir í *Kálfsvísu:*

Vésteinn [reið] Vali,
en Vivill Stúfi,
Meinþjófr Mói,
en Morginn Vakri,
Áli Hrafni,
es til íss riðu,[10]
en annarr austr
und Aðilsi
grár hvarfaði,
geiri undaðr.

Bjǫrn reið Blakki,
en Biárr Kerti,
Atli Glaumi,
en Aðils Slǫngvi,
Hǫgni Hǫlkvi,
en Haraldr Fǫlkvi,
Gunnarr Gota,
en Grana Sigurðr.

§ 6. Ynglingasaga.[11]

Ch. 5. Skjǫld, the son of Óðinn, wedded her [Gefjon], and they dwelt
at *Hleiðra.* — Ch. 23 (27). (*The sea-burial of King Haki.*) Now King
Haki had gotten such sore hurts, that he saw that the days of his life
would not be long; so he let take a swift ship that he had, and lade it with
dead men and weapons, and let bring it out to sea, and ship the rudder,
and hoist up the sail, and then let lay fire in tarwood, and make a bale
aboard. The wind blew offshore, and Haki was come nigh to death, or
was verily dead, when he was laid on the bale, and the ship went blazing
out into the main sea; and of great fame was that deed for long and long
after. — Ch. 27 (31). (*The Fall of King Óttarr vendilkráka.*) [Óttarr
(the son of Egill), king of Sweden, in retaliation for a Danish invasion
made in the preceding year (because Óttarr refused to pay the scat
promised by Egill), went with his warships to the land of the Danes,
while their king Fróði was warring in the East-Countries, and he harried
there, and found nought to withstand him.] Now he heard that men were
gathered thick in Selund [i.e., *Zealand*], and he turned west through
Eyre-Sound, and then sailed south to Jutland, and lays his keels for
Limbfirth, and harries about *Vendil,* and burns there, and lays the land
waste far and wide whereso he came. Vatt [*Vǫttr*] and *Fasti* were Fróði's

---

[1] 'prowess.' [2] 'affability.' [3] 'had (as wife)'; OE. *āhte.* [4] 'quarrel.' [5] 'fight.'
[6] 'portion.' [7] '(of his) following.' [8] 'the helmet.' [9] 'horse.' [10] 'rode to the ice.'
[11] The translation in *The Saga Library* is used.

earls [*jarlar*] whom he had set to the warding of the land whiles he was away thence; so when these earls heard that the Swede king was harrying in Denmark, they gathered force, and leapt a-shipboard, and sailed south to Limbfirth, and came all unawares upon King Óttarr, and fell to fighting; but the Swedes met them well, and folk fell on either side; but as the folk of the Danes fell, came more in their stead from the countrysides around, and all ships withal were laid to that were at hand. So such end the battle had, that there fell King Óttarr, and the more part of his host. The Danes took his dead body and brought it a-land, and laid it on a certain mound, and there let wild things and common fowl tear the carrion. Withal they made a crow of tree and sent it to Sweden, with this word to the Swedes, that that King Óttarr of theirs was worth but just so much as that; so afterwards men called him Óttarr Vendilcrow [*Óttarr vendilkráka*]. So says Thiodolf:[1]

Into the erns' grip	I hear these works
Fell the great Óttarr,	Of Vatt and Fasti
The doughty of deed,	Were set in tale
Before the Danes' weapons:	By Swedish folk:
The glede of war	That Fróði's island's
With bloody foot	Earls between them
At Vendil spurned	Had slain the famous
The one from afar.	Fight-upholder.

— Ch. 29 (33). King HELGI, the son of Halfdan, ruled in *Hleiðra* in those days, and he came to Sweden with so great a host that King Aðils saw nought for it but to flee away. . . . . . King Helgi fell in battle whenas RÓLF KRAKI was eight winters old, who was straightway holden as king at Hleiðra. King AÐILS had mighty strife with a king called ÁLI[2] the Uplander [*Áli inn upplenzki*] from out of Norway. King Aðils and King Áli had a battle on the ice of the *Vener Lake*, and Áli fell there, but Aðils gained the day. Concerning this battle is much told in the Story of the Skjǫldungs [*í Skjǫldunga sǫgu*], and also how Rólf Kraki came to Upsala to Aðils; and that was when Rólf Kraki sowed gold on the Fyrismeads.

§ 7. SAXONIS GRAMMATICI GESTA DANORUM.[3]

II, pp. 38 f.: *Dragon Fight of Frotho (I), father of Haldanus.* A man of the country met him [FROTHO] and roused his hopes [of obtaining money] by the following strain:[4] ' Not far off is an island rising in delicate slopes, hiding treasure in its hills and 'ware of its rich booty. Here a noble pile is kept by the occupant of the mount, who is a snake wreathed in coils, doubled in many a fold, and with a tail drawn out in winding

[1] In the *Ynglingatal* (probably composed cir. 900 A.D.).

[2] Hence Aðils was called *Ála dólgr* (the foe of Áli), *Ynglingatal* 26.

[3] Holder's edition and Elton's English translation are used. — Additional extracts may be found in the Notes, pp. 125 ff., 163, 195 f., 202 f., cf. 223.

[4] In Latin hexameters.

whorls, shaking his manifold spirals and shedding venom. If thou wouldst conquer him, thou must use thy shield and stretch thereon bulls' hides, and cover thy body with the skins of kine, nor let thy limbs lie bare to the sharp poison; his slaver burns up what it bespatters. Though the three-forked tongue flicker and leap out of the gaping mouth, and with awful yawn menace ghastly wounds, remember to keep the dauntless temper of thy mind; nor let the point of the jagged tooth trouble thee, nor the starkness of the beast, nor the venom spat frcm the swift throat. Though the force of his scales spurn thy spears, yet know there is a place under his lowest belly whither thou mayst plunge the blade; aim at this with thy sword, and thou shalt probe the snake to his centre. Thence go fearless up to the hill, drive the mattock, dig and ransack the holes; soon fill thy pouch with treasure, and bring back to the shore thy craft laden.'

Frotho believed, and crossed alone to the island, loth to attack the beast with any stronger escort than that wherewith it was the custom for champions to attack. When it had drunk water and was repairing to its cave, its rough and sharp hide spurned the blow of Frotho's steel. Also the dart that he flung against it rebounded idly, foiling the effort of the thrower. But when the hard back yielded not a whit, he noted the belly heedfully, and its softness gave entrance to the steel. The beast tried to retaliate by biting, but only struck the sharp point of its mouth upon the shield. Then it shot out its flickering tongue again and again, and gasped away life and venom together.[1]

The money which the king found made him rich.

II, p. 51. Cuius [scil. HALDANI] ex eo maxime fortuna ammirabilis fuit, quod, licet omnia temporum momenta ad exercenda atrocitatis officia contulisset, senectute vitam, non ferro finierit. Huius filii ROE et HELGO fuere. A Roe Roskildia condita memoratur. . . . Hic brevi angustoque corpore fuit. Helgonem habitus procerior cepit. Qui diviso cum fratre regno, maris possessionem sortitus, regem Sclavie Scalcum maritimis copiis lacessitum oppressit. . . .

II, pp. 52 f. His filius HOTHBRODUS succedit, qui . . . post immensam populorum cladem Atislum et Hǿtherum filios procreavit . . . . . Daniam petit, eiusque regem ROE tribus preliis provocatum occidit. His cognitis HELGO filium ROLVONEM *Lethrica arce* conclusit, heredis saluti consulturus . . . Deinde presides ab Hothbrodo immissos, ut externo patriam dominio liberaret, missis per oppida satellitibus, cede subegit. Ipsum quoque Hothbrodum cum omnibus copiis navali pugna delevit; nec solum fratris, sed eciam patrie iniuriam plenis ulcionis armis pensavit. Quo evenit, ut, cui nuper ob Hundingi cedem agnomen incesserat, nunc HOTHBRODI strages cognomentum inferret.

II, p. 53. Huic filius ROLVO succedit, vir corporis animique dotibus venustus, qui stature magnitudinem pari virtutis habitu commendaret.

---

[1] A similar, condensed version is the account of Fridlevus' dragon fight, vi, pp. 180 f.

II, p. 56. [BIARCO, one of Rolvo's champions, has protected (H)IALTO against the insults of the wedding guests who were throwing bones at the latter, and has slain Agnerus the bridegroom.] Talibus operum meritis exultanti novam de se silvestris fera victoriam prebuit. Ursum quippe eximie magnitudinis obvium sibi inter dumeta factum iaculo confecit, comitemque suum Ialtonem, quo viribus maior evaderet, applicato ore egestum belue cruorem haurire iussit. Creditum namque erat, hoc pocionis genere corporei roboris incrementa prestari.

II, pp. 59 ff. [When HIARTHWARUS (who has been appointed governor of Sweden) makes his treacherous, fatal attack on ROLVO at Lethra, HIALTO arouses his comrade Biarco to fight for their king: (p. 67) ' Hanc maxime exhortacionum seriem idcirco metrica racione compegerim, quod earundem sentenciarum intellectus Danici cuiusdam carminis (i.e., the *Bjarkamál*) compendio digestus a compluribus antiquitatis peritis memoriter usurpatur.' Some select passages:] P. 59. Ocius evigilet, quisquis se regis amicum/Aut meritis probat, aut sola pietate fatetur. . . . . Dulce est nos domino percepta rependere dona,/Acceptare enses, fameque impendere ferrum. . . . P. 60. Omnia que poti temulento prompsimus ore,/Fortibus edamus animis, et vota sequamur . . . [Words of BIARCO:] P. 64. . . . licet insula memet/Ediderit, stricteque habeam natalia terre,/Bissenas regi debebo rependere gentes,/Quas titulis dedit ille meis. Attendite, fortes! . . . In tergum redeant clypei; pugnemus apertis/Pectoribus, totosque auro densate lacertos./Armillas dextre excipiant, quo forcius ictus/Collibrare queant, et amarum figere vulnus.

VIII, p. 264. [When HARALD HILDETAN, king of Denmark, had been slain in the battle of Bravalla,] RING, king of Sweden, harnessed the horse on which he rode to the chariot of the king [Harald], decked it honorably with a golden saddle, and hallowed it in his honor. Then he proclaimed his vows, and added his prayer that Harald would ride on this and outstrip those who shared his death in their journey to Tartarus; and that he would pray Pluto, the lord of Orcus, to grant a calm abode there for friend and foe. Then he raised a pyre, and bade the Danes fling on the gilded chariot[1] of their king as fuel to the fire. And while the flames were burning the body cast upon them, he went round the mourning nobles and earnestly charged them that they should freely give arms, gold, and every precious thing to feed the pyre in honor of so great a king, who had deserved so nobly of them all. He also ordered that the ashes of his body, when it was quite burnt, should be transferred to an urn, taken to Leire [*Lethram*], and there, together with the horse and armor, receive a royal funeral.

§ 8. CHRONICLES.

§ 8.1. Langfeðgatal. — ' Vetustissima Regum Septentrionis Series

---

[1] Rather, ship; ' inauratam regis sui puppim.'

Langfeðgatal[1] dicta.' (12th century, MS. cir. 1300 A.D.) (*Scriptores Rerum Danicarum Medii Ævi* ed. Jacobus Langebek. Vol. i, Hafniæ, 1772; pp. 1–6.)

Japhet Noa sun, fadir Japhans ... f. Jupiter ... f. Priami Konungs i Troeo ..... hans sun Magi. hans sun Seskef vel SESCEF.[2] Bedvig. Athra. Itermann. HEREMOTR. SCEALDNA. BEAF. Eat. Godulfi. Finn. Frealaf. Voden, þan kǫllum ver Oden. — [The Norwegian line:] Oden. Niordr i Noatunum. Yngvifræyr .... Jorundr. Aun. EGILL Tunnadolgr. OTTARR VENDILKRAKA. Aþils at Uppsaulum.[3] Eysteinn. Yngvarr .... Haralldr Harfagri. — [The Danish line:] Oden — SKIOLDR — Fridleifr — Fridefrode .... Frode F[r]ækni — INGIALDR STARKADAR fostri — HALFDAN brodir hans. HELGI OC HROAR hans synir. ROLFR KRAKI, Helga sun. HRÆREKR Hnauggvanbaugi, Ingiallz sun — Frode — Halfdan — HRÆREKR Slaungvanbaugi — Haralldr Hillditaunn — Sigurdr Hringr. Ragnar Lodbrok — Haurda Knutr.

§ 8.2. **Annales Lundenses.** — 'Annales Rerum Danicarum Esromenses' (ed. J. Langebek, *l.c.*, pp. 212–50; including on pp. 224–27 the 'Chronicle of the Lethra Kings,' composed cir. 1160–1170 A.D.).

P. 226. Non post multum vero temporis animosus ad uxoris exhortacionem HIARWART *Sialandiam* classe peciit. Genero[4] suo ROLFF tributum attulisse simulavit. Die quadam dilucescente ad *Læthram* misit, ut videret tributum, Rolff nunciavit. Qui cum vidisset non tributum sed exercitum armatum, vallatus est Rolff militibus, & a Hyarwardo interfectus est. Hyarwardum autem Syalandenses & Scanienses, qui cum eo erant, in regem assumpserunt. Qui brevi tempore a mane usque ad primam regali nomine potitus est. Tunc venit Haky frater, Hagbradi filius Hamundi, Hyarwardum interfecit & Danorum rex effectus est.

§ 8.3. **Sven Aageson.** — 'Svenonis Aggonis filii Compendiosa Regum Daniæ Historia a Skioldo ad Canutum VI' (cir. 1187 A.D.). (Ed. J. Langebek, *l.c.*, pp. 42–64.)

[Cap. I. 'De primo rege Danorum.'] SKIOLD Danis primum didici præfuisse. Et ut eius alludamus vocabulo, idcirco tali functus est nomine, quia universos regni terminos regiæ defensionis patrocinio affatim egregie tuebatur. A quo primum, modis Islandensibus, SKIOLDUNGER sunt reges nuncupati. Qui regni post se reliquit hæredes, FROTHI videlicet & HALDANUM. Successu temporum fratribus super regni ambitione inter se decertantibus, Haldan, fratre suo interempto, regni monarchiam obtinuit. Hic filium, scilicet HELGHI, regni procreavit hæredem, qui ob eximiam virtutum strenuitatem, pyraticam semper exercuit. Qui cum universorum circumiacentium regnorum fines maritimos classe pyratica depopulatus suo subiugasset imperio, 'Rex maris?' est cognominatus.

---

[1] I.e., 'roll of ancestors.'
[2] From OE. *sē Scē(a)f*. Cf. Sievers, *Beitr.* xvi 361–3.
[3] *au = ǫ*; so repeatedly in this text.
[4] I.e., 'brother-in-law.'

APPENDIX I

Huic in regno successit filius ROLF KRAKI, patria virtute pollens, occisus in *Lethra*, quæ tunc famosissima regis extitit curia, nunc autem Roskildensi vicina civitati, inter abiectissima ferme vix colitur oppida. Post quem regnavit filius eius RÖKIL[1] cognomento dictus Slaghenback. Cui successit in regno hæres, agilitatis strenuitate cognominatus, quem nostro vulgari Frothi hin Frökni nominabant. Huius filius & hæres regni extitit WERMUNDUS. ... Hic filium genuit UFFI nomine, qui usque ad tricesimum ætatis suæ annum fandi possibilitatem cohibuit. ... [In the remainder of this chapter and in ch. II ' De duello Uffonis ? the Offa story is told.]

§ 8.4. **Series Runica Regum Daniæ altera.** (Langebek, *l.c.*, pp. 31–34.)

... Tha var FROTHE Kunung, Hadings sun, han drap en draga, ok skatathe annan time Thydistland, ok Frisland, ok Britanniam. Tha var HALDAN Kunung Frotha sun, han drap sina bröder, fore thy at han vildi hava rikit. Tho var RO Frotha sun, han bygdi föst Roskeldo. Ok HELHE Kunung, hans brother, drap Kunung HOTBROD af Sueriki, ok skatathe thrithia tima Thyhthistland. Tha var ROLF Kunung KRAKE, Helhe sun, i hans tima var HIALTI og BIERGHI, ok hans magh het Jarmar. ...... Tha var VERMUND Kunung Vithlesth sun ... Tha var UFFI Starki, Vermunda sun, han skatathe fiarthe sinni Thydiskulande. Tha var Dan Kunung Uffa sun, ok Huhlek Kunung Uffa sun. ...

§ 8.5. **Annales Ryenses.** — ' Regum & Gentis Danorum Historia a Dano usque ad annum 1288, dicta vulgo *Chronicon Erici Regis*.' (Langebek, *l.c.*, pp. 148–70.)

Pp. 150 f. DAN. HUMBLÆ filius eius. Hic erat vanus & iners, & pauca notabilia fecit. Unde LOTHER, frater eius, facta conspiratione Danorum contra fratrem, eum de regno deposuit, & pro eo regnavit. Tertius Lother nimis durus fuit incolis regni, & in multis se nequiter gessit, & ideo tyrannidem eius Dani non ferentes, eum occiderunt ... SKIOLD. GRAM. ... HALDANUS. RO. HALDAN & HELGI. ... Helgi ... strenuus bellator HOTHBRODUM regem Sveciæ occidit. ... ROLF KRAKI filius Helgi. Ipse post multas præclaras victorias ab HIARTWARO comite Scaniæ, qui sororem eius habuit in uxorem, in lecto suo proditiose est occisus, in *Lethra* curia regali in Sialandia, cum quo & BIARKI & HIALTI, pugiles clarissimi, cum tota familia regia, sunt occisi. Huic successit Hyarwarus. Hyarwarus regnavit brevi tempore, scil. a mane usque ad horam primam. Hunc occidit Haki filius Hamundi, & factus est rex Danorum.

P. 152. Wichlethus ... WERMUNDUS BLINDE ... Huius tempore *Keto & Wiggo*, filii Frowini præfecti Sleswicensis, occiderunt *Athislum* regem Sveciæ, in ultionem patris sui ... UFFO STARKE. Iste a septimo ætatis anno usque ad trigesimum noluit loqui, quousque in loco, qui adhuc Kunengikamp dicitur, super *Eydoram* cum filio regis Teutonicorum & meliore pugile totius Teutoniæ solus certans, ambos occidit. ...

---

[1] 'Nomen ... corruptum est ex *Rörik Slangenboge*.' (Langebek's footnote.)

PARALLELS

§ 8.6. Skjǫldungasaga — 'Arngrím Jónsson's Rerum Danicarum Fragmenta.' (An epitome of a late (13th cent.) version of a Skjǫldungasaga. A.D. 1596. Ed., with Introduction, by A. Olrik, *Aarbøger for Nordisk Oldkyndighed og Historie*, Ser. II, Vol. ix (1894), 83–164. — Cf. Olson, L 4.65.82 ff.)

Cap. I. Rerum Danicarum historiam Norvegorum commentarii . . . a SCIOLDO quodam Odini . . . filio ordiuntur. Tradunt . . . a Scioldo, quos hodie Danos, olim SKIOLLDUNGA fuisse appellatos . . . Scioldus in arce Selandiæ *Hledro* sedes posuit, quæ et sequentium plurimorum regum regia fuit. — Cap. IV enumerates six sons of *Leifus*, the son of Herleifus (the fourth king of Denmark): *Herleifus, Hunleifus, Aleifus, Oddleifus, Geirleifus, Gunnleifus.* — Cap. IX. Perpetrato hoc fratricidio rex FRODO regem Sveciæ *Jorundum* devicit, eique tributa imperavit; similiter etiam baroni cuidam Svecico nomine *Sverting*. Filiam Sveci simul rapuit Frodo, ex qua HALFDANUM filium possedit. Concubina hæc fuit. Postea ducta alia, INGIALLDUM filium legitimum hæredem suscepit. — Cap. X. [Genealogia:] . . . HALFDANUS — HELGO, ROAS vel ROË; [Helgo's son:] ROLPHO KRAG. — Halfdanus . . . ex quadam Sigrida SIGNYAM, ROAM, et HELGONEM habuit. Ingialldus porro Halfdanum regnandi cupiditate cum exercitu ex improviso superveniens occidit. Daniæ igitur monarcha factus relictam fratris viduam uxorem duxit . . . Apud hanc educta est filia Signya, quam Ingialldus vili baroni Selandiæ SEVILLO postea elocavit. — Cap. XI. ROAS filiam Angli uxorem duxit. — Cap. XII. ROLFO cognomento KRAKE vel Krag danice . . . cæso Helgoni patri avoque eidem, octennis successit . . . Rolfo Krake inter ethnicos reges celeberrimus, multa virtute insignis erat: sapientia, potentia seu opibus, fortitudine et modestia atque mira humanitate, statura procera et gracili. — . . . Habuit pugilem celeberrimum Rolfo BODVARUM, Norvegum: hic de omnibus aliis fortitudinis laudem abstulit. . . . Posthæc ortis inter ADILSUM illum Sveciæ regem et ALONEM, Opplandorum regem in Norvegia, inimicitiis, prælium utrinque indicitur: loco pugnæ statuto in stagno *Wæner*, glacie iam obducto . . . Rolpho domi ipse reses, pugiles suos duodecim Adilso in subsidium mittit, quorum etiam opera is alioqui vincendus, victoriam obtinuit. . . . — [Rolfonis] sororius HIØRVARDUS, olim prælio subactus, occultum Rolfonis fovebat odium . . . Hiørvardus in Selandiam aliquot navibus vectus, tributum solvere velle simulat. [He treacherously attacks Rolf.] Ille tamen cum suis heroica virtute arma capescit. . . . Pugnatur usque ad vesperam. . . . Occubuit ROLFO cum suis pæne omnibus. — Cap. XIV. Hiørvardo in ipso regni aditu interfecto, successit Rolfonis consanguineus RÆRECUS, qui Helgoni Rolfonis patri fuit patruelis.

§ 8.7. **Catalogus Regum Sveciæ.** (Ed. by A. Olrik, *l.c.*, pp. 127 ff.) Cap. XXVII. SIGVARDUS RINGO rex Sveciæ 27. . . . Hinc post acerrimam pugnam fortiter occumbentibus Alfo cum Ingvone fratre, Sigvardus etiam male vulneratus est. Qui, Alfsola funere allato, magnam **navim** mortuorum cadaveribus oneratam solus vivorum conscendit,

APPENDIX I

seque et mortuam Alfsolam in puppi collocans navim pice, bitumine et sulphure incendi iubet: atque sublatis velis in altum, validis a continente impellentibus ventis, proram dirigit, simulque manus sibi violentas intulit; sese tot facinorum patratorem, tantorum regnorum possessorem, more maiorum suorum, regali pompa Odinum regem (id est inferos) invisere malle, quam inertis senectutis infirmitatem perpeti, alacri animo ad socios in littore antea relictos præfatus; quidam narrant, eum, antequam littus relinqueret, propria se confodisse manu. Bustum tamen in littore more sui sæculi congeri fecit, quod *Ringshaug* appellari iussit; ipse vero tempestatibus ratem gubernantibus, stygias sine mora tranavit undas.

§ 9. HRÓLFS SAGA KRAKA.

Ch. 1. (3.7 ff.) HÁLFDAN konungr átti þrjú bǫrn, twá syni ok eina dóttur, er SIGNÝ hét; hún var elzt[1] ok gipt[2] SÆVIL jarli, en synir Hálfdanar váru þá ungir, hét annarr HRÓARR, an annarr HELGI.

Ch. 3. (9.4 f.) HRÓARR var þá tólf[3] vetra,[4] en HELGI tíu;[5] hann var þó þeira meiri[6] ok fræknari.[7]

Ch. 5. (17.9 ff.) Konungr hét Norðri; hann réð fyrir nǫkkurum[8] hluta Englands; hans dóttir hét Ǫgn. HRÓARR var lǫngum[9] með Norðra konungi . . . . . ok um síðir[10] gekk[11] Hróarr at eiga[12] Ǫgn ok settiz þar at ríki með Norðra konungi mági[13] sínum.

Ch. 16. (45.25 ff.) HRÓLFR konungr liggr nú í hernaði.[14] . . . ok alla konunga, sem hann finnr, þá gerir hann skattgilda[15] undir sik, ok bar þat mest til, at allir hinir mestu[16] kappar[17] vildu með honum vera ok engum[18] ǫðrum þjóna,[19] því at hann var miklu mildari af fé[20] en[21] nǫkkurir konungar aðrir. Hrólfr konungr setti þar hǫfuðstað sinn, sem *Hleiðargarðr* heitir; þat er í Danmǫrk ok er mikil borg[22] ok sterk,[23] ok meiri rausn[24] ok hoffrakt[25] var þar en nǫkkur staðar, ok í ǫllu því sem til stórlætis[26] kom eða nǫkkurr hafði spurn[27] af.

Chs. 17 ff. BǪÐVAR-BJARKAÞÁTTR. Summary: BǪÐVARR is the son of *Bjǫrn*[28] (the son of Hringr, king of Uppdalir in Norway) and *Bera*,[29] a peasant's daughter. Having passed eighteen winters, he leaves Norway, (ch. 23:) visits his eldest brother Elgfróði and his second brother Þórir, who is king of *Gautland*, and continues on his way to Denmark. He arrives at *Hleiðargarðr*, goes into King Hrólf's hall, seats the simple and cowardly HǪTTR, who is regularly made sport of by the feasters, next to himself, and when one of the men throws a large bone at both of them,

---

[1] 'eldest.' [2] 'given in marriage.' [3] 'twelve.' [4] =OE. *wintra*. [5] 'ten.' [6] =OE. *mára*. [7] 'braver.' [8] dsm. of *nǫkkvorr* (=*ne veit ek hverr*), 'a certain.' [9] 'a long time.' [10] 'at last.' [11] pret. of *ganga*. [12] =OE. *āgan*. [13] 'father-in-law.' [14] 'harrying' (ds.). [15] 'tributary.' [16] =OE. *mǣstan*. [17] 'champions.' [18] 'none' (dsm.). [19] 'serve.' [20] ds. of *fé* (OE. *feoh*). [21] 'than.' [22] =OE. *burg*. [23] 'strong.' [24] 'magnificence.' [25] 'pomp.' [26] 'liberality' (gs.). [27] 'report.' [28] I.e., 'bear'; he was turned into a bear by magic. [29] I.e., 'she-bear.'

returns it with such force as to kill the offender. Whereupon a great outcry is made; but the king settles the matter and even asks Bǫðvarr to become one of his retainers. Bǫðvarr accepts the proposal, insisting at the same time that Hǫttr be allowed to join him.

(68.10 ff.) As the Yule-tide approached, the men seemed greatly depressed. Bǫðvarr, upon asking the reason, was told by Hǫttr that about this time in the two preceding winters a great beast had appeared and caused great damage. It was a terrible monster (*trǫll*), he said, with wings on its back, and no weapon could injure it. Nor would the king's champions come home at this dreadful time. (68.17:) 'The hall is not as well guarded,' said Bǫðvarr, 'as I thought, if a beast can deal destruction to the king's domain and property.' On Yule-eve the king commanded his men to leave the cattle to their fate and on no account to expose themselves to danger. But Bǫðvarr went secretly out at night, taking with him by force the trembling Hǫttr, and attacked the monster as it approached. At first his sword stuck fast in the sheath, but when he pulled very hard, the sword came out, and he struck it with such strength under the shoulder of the beast, that it 'stood' in its heart. The beast fell down dead. Bǫðvarr forced his comrade to drink of the blood and eat of the heart of the beast, whereby Hǫttr became strong and fearless. Both then set up the monster as if it were alive and returned to the hall.

In the morning King Hrólfr found on inquiry that the cattle had been unmolested, and he sent out men to investigate. They quickly returned with the report that at that very moment the monster was charging down upon the hall. When the king called on volunteers to meet the beast, Hǫttr asked him for the loan of his sword *Gullinhjalti*, and with it he struck at the monster, causing it to fall over. Then the king turned to Bǫðvarr and said: 'A great change has come over Hǫttr; but it was you who slew the beast. I knew when you came here, that few were your equals, but this seems to me your bravest deed that you have made a champion of Hǫttr. From this day he shall be called *Hjalti*,—you shall be called after the sword Gullinhjalti.'

Ch. 24. (74.2 ff.) Bǫðvarr var mest metinn[1] ok haldinn,[2] ok sat hann upp á hægri[3] hǫnd konunginum ok honum næst,[4] þá Hjalti hinn hugprúði.[5] — (74.17 f.) ... reyndiz[6] Bǫðvarr mestr allra hans kappa, hvat sem reyna[7] þurfti, ok í svá miklar virðingar[8] komz hann hjá[9] Hrólfi konungi, at hann eignaðiz hans einkadóttur,[10] Drífu.

Chs. 25 ff. Expedition of Hrólfr and his champions (Bǫðvarr among them) to Sweden.

Chs. 32 ff. Fall of King Hrólfr and his champions (Bǫðvarr Bjarki, Hjalti, Vǫttr, and nine others) in defending themselves against Hjǫrvarðr; Hjalti's exhortations. Cp. Saxo ii, pp. 59 ff.

---

[1] =OE. *meten*, pp. [2] =OE. *healden*, pp. [3] 'right (hand).' [4] 'nearest.' [5] 'stouthearted.' [6] 'was proved.' [7] 'try.' [8] 'honor.' [9] 'at,' 'with.' [10] 'only daughter.'

§ 9.1. Bjarkarímur.

IV 58 ff. BJARKI (or BQÐVARR) kills a she-wolf and compels HJALTI to drink her blood.

V 4 ff. HJALTI courageously faces and slays a gray bear which has attacked the folds of *Hleiðargarðr;* he is made one of Hrólf's retainers.

VIII 14 ff. Fight between AÐILS and ÁLI on Lake *Vænir;* Aðils is assisted by Bjarki and the other champions of Hrólfr.

III. (ROMAN, FRANKISH, GOTHIC) HISTORIANS

§ 10. CORNELII TACITI GERMANIA. (A.D. 98.)[1]

Cap. II. Celebrant carminibus antiquis, quod unum apud illos memoriae et annalium genus est, Tuistonem deum terra editum. Ei filium Mannum, originem gentis conditoremque, Manno tris filios assignant, e quorum nominibus proximi Oceano *Ingaevones,*[2] medii Herminones, ceteri Istaevones vocentur.

Cap. VI. Scutum reliquisse praecipuum flagitium, nec aut sacris adesse aut concilium inire ignominioso fas; multique superstites bellorum infamiam laqueo finierunt.

Cap. VII. ... nec regibus infinita aut libera potestas.

Cap. X. Auspicia sortesque ut qui maxime observant.... Et illud quidem etiam hic notum, avium voces volatusque interrogare; proprium gentis equorum quoque praesagia ac monitus experiri.

Cap. XI. ... nec dierum numerum, ut nos, sed noctium computant.

Cap. XIII. Insignis nobilitas aut magna patrum merita principis dignationem etiam adulescentulis assignant; ceteris robustioribus ac iam pridem probatis aggregantur. Nec rubor inter comites aspici. Gradus quin etiam ipse *comitatus* habet iudicio eius quem sectantur; magnaque et comitum aemulatio, quibus primus apud principem suum locus, et principum, cui plurimi et acerrimi comites. Haec dignitas, hae vires, magno semper et electorum iuvenum globo circumdari, in pace decus, in bello praesidium. Nec solum in sua gente cuique, sed apud finitimas quoque civitates id nomen, ea gloria est, si numero ac virtute comitatus emineat; expetuntur enim legationibus et muneribus ornantur et ipsa plerumque fama bella profligant.

Cap. XIV. Cum ventum in aciem, turpe principi virtute vinci, turpe comitatui virtutem principis non adaequare. Iam vero infame in omnem vitam ac probrosum superstitem principi suo ex acie recessisse; illum defendere, tueri, sua quoque fortia facta gloriae eius assignare praecipuum sacramentum est; principes pro victoria pugnant, comites pro principe; ... exigunt enim principis sui liberalitate illum bellatorem equum,

---

[1] A practical edition with a good commentary (in German), by H. Schweizer-Sidler, 7th ed., Halle a.S., 1912. 118 pp. A handy edition with English notes, by H. Furneaux, Oxford. 1894. 131 pp.

[2] Plinius: *Inguaeones.*

illam cruentam victricemque frameam; nam epulae et quamquam incompti, largi tamen apparatus pro stipendio cedunt.

Cap. XX. Sororum filiis idem apud avunculum qui ad patrem honor.

Cap. XXI. Suscipere tam inimicitias seu patris seu propinqui quam amicitias necesse est; nec implacabiles durant; luitur enim etiam homicidium certo armentorum ac pecorum numero, recipitque satisfactionem universa domus, utiliter in publicum, quia periculosiores sunt inimicitiae iuxta libertatem.

Cap. XXVII. *Funerum* nulla ambitio: id solum observatur, ut corpora clarorum virorum certis lignis crementur. Struem rogi nec vestibus nec odoribus cumulant; sua cuique arma, quorundam igni et equus adicitur. Sepulcrum caespes erigit; monumentorum arduum et operosum honorem, ut gravem defunctis, aspernantur. Lamenta ac lacrimas cito, dolorem et tristitiam tarde ponunt. Feminis lugere honestum est, viris meminisse.

Cap. XL.[1] To the Langobardi, on the contrary, their scanty numbers are a distinction. Though surrounded by a host of most powerful tribes, they are safe, not by submitting, but by daring the perils of war. — Next come the Reudigni, the Aviones, the Anglii, the Varini, the Eudoses, the Suardones and Nuithones who are fenced in by rivers or forests. None of these tribes have any noteworthy feature, except their common worship of *Nerthus*, or mother-Earth, and their belief that she interposes in human affairs, and visits the nations in her car. In an island of the ocean there is a sacred grove, and within it a consecrated chariot, covered over with a garment. Only one priest is permitted to touch it. He can perceive the presence of the goddess in this sacred recess, and walks by her side with the utmost reverence as she is drawn along by heifers. It is a season of rejoicing, and festivity reigns wherever she deigns to go and be received. They do not go to battle or wear arms; every weapon is under lock; peace and quiet are known and welcomed only at these times, till the goddess, weary of human intercourse, is at length restored by the same priest to her temple. Afterwards the car, the vestments, and, if you like to believe if, the divinity herself, are purified in a secret lake. Slaves perform the rite, who are instantly swallowed up by its waters. Hence arises a mysterious terror and a pious ignorance concerning the nature of that which is seen only by men doomed to die.

Cap. XLV. (Aestiorum[2] gentes . . .) matrem deum venerantur; insigne superstitionis formas aprorum gestant; id pro armis omniumque tutela securum deae cultorem etiam inter hostis praestat.

§ 11. S. GREGORII EPISCOPI TURONENSIS (cir. 540–594 A.D.) HISTORIA FRANCORUM. (Migne, *Patrologia Latina*, Vol. lxxi.)

Lib. III, cap. I. Defuncto igitur CLODOVECHO rege, quatuor filii eius,

[1] From the translation of A. J. Church and W. J. Brodribb, London & New York, 1877.
[2] A non-Germanic tribe on the coast of the Baltic Sea ('Esthonians'). Cf. T. E. Karsten, *Die Germanen* (*P.Grdr.* 9), 1928, § 31.

id est THEUDERICUS, Chlodomeris, Childebertus, atque Chlothacharius regnum eius accipiunt, et inter se æqua lance dividunt. Habebat iam tunc Theudericus filium, nomine THEUDEBERTUM, elegantem atque utilem. — Cap. III. His ita gestis, Dani cum rege suo, nomine CHLOCHILAICHO,[1] evectu navali per *Gallias* appetunt. Egressique ad terras pagum unum de regno Theuderici[1] devastant atque captivant, oneratisque navibus tam de captivis quam de reliquis spoliis, reverti ad patriam cupiunt. Sed rex eorum in littus[1] residebat, donec naves altum mare comprehenderent, ipse deinceps secuturus. Quod cum Theuderico nuntiatum fuisset, quod scilicet regio eius fuerit ab extraneis devastata, Theudebertum filium suum in illas partes cum valido exercitu ac magno armorum apparatu direxit. Qui interfecto rege, hostes navali prælio superatos opprimit, omnemque rapinam terræ restituit.[2]

§ 11.1. Cf. De Monstris et Belluis Liber. (orig. 7th cent.?) See the texts of Haupt L 4.89 and Müllenhoff L 4.25.5.

Part I. Cap. II. ' De Getarum rege Huiglauco[3] mirae magnitudinis.'

Et sunt mirae magnitudinis, ut rex HUIGLAUCUS,[3] qui imperavit *Getis* et a *Francis* occisus est. Quem equus a duodecimo anno portare non potuit. Cuius ossa in R[h]en*i* fluminis insula, ubi in Oceanum prorumpit, reservata sunt et de longinquo venientibus pro miraculo ostenduntur.

§ 12. JORDANIS DE ORIGINE ACTIBUSQUE GETARUM. (A.D. 551.) (Ed. by A. Holder, Freiburg i.B. & Tübingen, 1882.)

Cap. XLIX. (*Funeral of Attila*.) Cuius manes quibus modis a sua gente honoratae sunt, pauca de multis dicere non omittamus. In mediis siquidem campis et intra tentoria serica cadavere collocato spectaculum admirandum et sollemniter exhibetur. Nam de tota gente Hunorum lectissimi equites in eum locum, quo erat positus, in modum circensium cursibus ambientes, facta eius cantu funereo tali ordine referebant. Praecipuus Hunorum rex Attila, patre genitus Mundzucco, fortissimarum gentium dominus, qui inaudita ante se potentia solus Scythica et Germanica regna possedit. . . . . . Postquam talibus lamentis est defletus, stravam super tumulum eius, quam appellant ipsi, ingenti commessatione concelebrant, et contraria invicem sibi copulantes, luctum fune-

---

[1] *Liber Historiae Francorum* [based on Gregory] (cir. 727 A.D.), cap. xix: *Chochilaico* (and Varr.); — *ib.:* Theuderico pagum *Attoarios* vel alios; — *ib.:* ad litus maris.

[2] The exact date of this event (the all-important starting point of our historical computations in regard to *Beowulf*) cannot be made out. It has commonly been placed at, or about, 516 A.D.; see also *JEGPh*. xxii 424–27 (Cook); Nerman (L 4.97 c 4) 85–87; *A.* l 242–44. (Chlodoweg (who was born in 466) died in 511, Theoderic in 534, Theodebert in 548.) Grion L 3.36 thought it should be placed as late as 527. Fredborg L 4.92 f and P. Severinsen, *Danske Studier*, 1919, p. 96 suggested cir. 526. Cha. (Intr. 381 f., [2]383–87) concludes that " all the evidence points to Hygelac's raid having been after 516 and probably after 520, although perhaps before 522 and certainly before 531." If Gregory's chronology were more definite and more reliable, we could speak with greater confidence about this subject.

[3] Varr.: *Huncglaco, Huncglacus*. (Original reading presumably: *Hugilaicus*.)

reum mixto gaudio celebrant noctuque secreto cadaver terrae recondunt. Cuius fercula primum auro, secundum argento, tertium ferri rigore communiunt, significantes tali argumento potentissimo regi omnia convenisse: ferrum, quod gentes edomuit, aurum et argentum, quod ornatum rei publicae utriusque acceperit; addunt arma hostium caedibus adquisita, faleras variarum gemmarum fulgore pretiosas et diversi generis insignia, quibus colitur aulicum decus. Et, ut tantis divitiis humana curiositas arceretur, operi deputatos detestabili mercede trucidarunt, emersitque momentanea mors sepelientibus cum sepulto.

APPENDIX II

ANTIQUITIES

INDEX OF SUBJECTS PERTAINING TO OLD GERMANIC LIFE[1]

KING AND COMITATUS

§ 1. Kingship.

Terms applied to kings: *cyning, dryhten, þēoden, ealdor, hlāford, frēa, fengel; bealdor, brego, rǣswa;* (*eorla*, etc.) *hlēo, eodor, helm; lēodgebyrgea;* (*folces, rīces*) *hyrde, weard; ēþelweard, landfruma; wine* (*Scyldinga*, etc.); *goldwine gumena, goldgyfa, bēaga brytta, hringa þengel; hildfruma, herewīsa, frumgār, wigena strengel;* besides numerous compounds and combinations. *brego-, ēþel-, gif-, gum-stōl* (= ' cathedra ' or ' solium regni '), cf. Gering's Edda commentary (L 10.1) ii 462.

The ideal king: Hrōðgār (see e.g., 1885 f.); Bēowulf; Hygelāc; Scyld (4 ff.); Offa (1957 ff.). Liberality, 71 f., 1020 ff., 1050 ff., 1089 ff., 1193 ff., 1866 f., 2018 f., 2190 ff., 2633 ff., 2865 ff., 2994 ff. See notes on 20 ff., 660 f. — The antitype: Heremōd.

The loss of the king a national disaster: 14 f., 2999 ff., 3018 ff. (2354 ff.)

Supreme respect for kingship: 862 f., 2198 f.; 2382 f. (praise of an enemy king).

Joint regency: Hrōðgār-Hrōðulf (see Intr. xxxi f.).

Succession to the throne: 53 ff.; 1178 f., 2470 f.; 2369 f., 2207 f., 1851; 910 f. (see note on Heremōd).

Limitation of royal power: 73 (cf. Tacitus, *Germania*, c. 7, Par. § 10). — Councilors of the king: 1098 (*weotena dōme*); 157, 171 f.; 1325, 1407 (Æschere, cp. 1342 ff.); *selerǣdende* 51, 1346; cp. *snotere ceorlas* 202, 416. (Cf. Chadwick H.A. 369, Liebermann L 9.10.2.737 f.; Charles Oman, *England before the Norman Conquest*, pp. 366 ff.) See Comitatus.

§ 2. Comitatus. (Tacitus, *Germania*, cc. 13–14, Par. § 10.)

Terms for retainers: *gesīð(as), þegn(as); ǣðeling(as);* (*ǣðelinga*, etc.) *gedriht; duguð, geoguð; bēod-, heorð-genēat(as), healsittend(e), fletwerod, geselda, hondgesella; fyrd-*(etc.)*gestealla; lēode, þēod; weorod, corðer, handscolu;* — *māgas, winemāgas, wine, gǣdelingas, sibbegedriht;* (*eaforan*). (The body of retainers consisted in part of relatives of the king;

[1] The similarity between Beowulfian and Homeric life and society has been repeatedly pointed out; see especially Chadwick H.A., chs. 15 ff.; also *Arch.* cxxvi 43 ff., 341 ff. (Vergilian parallels).

ANTIQUITIES

besides, the relation of allegiance came to be regarded in the light of kinship.)

Retainers gathered for a special expedition, 205 ff.

Loyalty: Bēowulf (cp. 435 f., 2169 f.); Wīglāf ('comitatus speech,' 2633 ff.); Geats (794 ff., 1602 ff.), Danes (1228 ff., 1246 ff.); see Finn legend. — Disloyalty, 2596 ff., 2864 ff. (ten cowardly comrades). (On Hrōðulf, see Intr. xxxii.)

Gifts received, spoils of war, and credit for brave deeds belong to the king, 1482 ff., 2148 f. (cp. 452 ff.); 2985 ff., 1652 ff.; 1968 (n.), 2484 f., cp. 2875 f.

Court officials and attendants: Æschere, Unferð, Wulfgār, *scop*, chamberlain 1794, cupbearers 494, 1161; servants 993; coast-guard. — Retinue 922 ff. (n.) Etiquette, 331 ff.; 407; 613 ff., etc.

KINSHIP; FAMILY; LAW

§ 3. **Kindred** (the social unit of Germanic life). *cyn(n)*, *mǣgþ (mǣgburg)*, cf. *sib(b)*. See Grønbech L 9.24. i 19 ff.; Liebermann L 9.10.2.651 ff.

Pedigrees, 53 ff., 1960 ff.; 105 ff.; cp. *sunu, maga, mago, eafora, bearn, byre*.

A seven-year-old boy entrusted to another family for his education, 2428 ff. (n.)

The sister's son (cf. L 9.30; Par. § 10: *Germania*, c. 20): Bēowulf (Hygelāc), Fitela (Sigemund), Hildeburh's son (Hnæf), Gārulf (Gūðere, in *Finnsb.*); — a (faithless) brother's son: Hrōðulf (Hrōðgār).

'Adoption' of Bēowulf, 946 ff. (n.), 1175 f.

Fratricide: 587 ff.; 107 f., 1261 f.; 2435 ff.

§ 4. **Women.** *cwēn, ides, mægð, fǣmne, wīf; brȳd; geō-mēowle*. Wealhþēow, Frēawaru; Hildeburh; Þrȳð, Hygd; Bēowulf's widow (?); Grendel's mother; servants, 993. (Cf. Grace F. von Sweringen, "Women in the Germanic Hero-Sagas." *JEGPh.* viii 501–12.)

The only allusions to woman's beauty: *scȳne* 3016, *ǣnlicu* 1941.

Royal ladies at the banquet, taking part in ceremonies and displaying political wisdom, 612 ff. (n.), 1162 ff., 1980 ff., 2016 ff.; cp. 1649.

The king's widow in a position to dispose of the throne, 2369 f.

Marriage for political reasons: Frēawaru, Hildeburh (?); see *friðusib(b), freoðuwebbe*. — Note: 2998.

Carrying off of a queen (in war), 2930 ff.; cp. 3153 ff. (3018 f.); 1153.

§ 5. **Feud.** (Par. § 10: *Germania*, c. 21.)

Tribal wars, blood revenge (cf. Intr. xxix): Danes-Heaðobards, Danes-Frisians; Geats-Swedes; Danes-Grendel kin (note, e.g., 1305 f.).

Composition of feud by payment, 470 ff.; cp. 154 ff., 1053 ff.

No feud or composition within the kindred, 2441 ff.

Duty of revenge nullified, 2618 f.

§ 6. The entire clan responsible for the wrong done by individual members, 2884 ff. Expulsion from right of kinship, *ib.*

APPENDIX II

Granting of the father's estate to the son, 2606 ff. (Cp. *Wids.* 95 f.) —
Hereditary estate, cp. 2885 ff. (*folcscaru*, 73.)
Punishment by hanging, 2445 f. (cp. 2940 f.); putting to the sword,
1937 ff. (cp. 2939). — Punishment averted by a gift, 2224 ff., 2281 ff.
Figurative use of **legal** terms (applied to battle, etc.): *ðing gehēgan*
425 f., *meðelstede* 1082, *geþinge, sacu, wrōht, fāh* (e.g. 811), *fǣhð(o), dōm*
(e.g. 440 f., 2963 f.), *scyldig, stǣlan, sēðan, scȳran, on ryht gescādan* 1555;
heorowearh, grundwyrgen; see 153 ff.; also 2185 f.

WAR

See Intr., *passim*

§ 7. Detailed description of **fight**, 2922–98. — Leaders of army, *folctogan*
839.
Motive of animals of prey, 3024 ff. (Cf. *GRM.* vii 26 ff.)
Spoils of war, 1155 ff., 1205, 1212, 2361 f., 2614 ff., 2955, 2985 ff.
Treaty of peace, 1085 ff., cp. 2028 f., 2063 f. Tribute, 9 ff.
Coast-guard to forestall naval invasion, 229 ff. (1890, 1914).
Fighting on foot, see *fēþa.* King's war-horse with saddle, 1037 ff.; cp.
1399 ff. (Riding, 234, 286, 315, 855 f., 864 f., 2898, 3169; cp. 1035 ff.,
2163 ff.)
§ 8. **Weapons.** Cf. L 9.40–45; Cha. Intr. 357 ff.
Normal equipment of warrior: coat of mail, helmet, shield, spear, 333
ff. (325 ff., 395 ff.), 1242 ff.; cp. 794 ff. (sword). See 1441 ff.
Sword: *sweord, bil(l), mēce, heoru, secg, brond; īren, ecg; wǣpen; brog-
den-, hring-, sceāden-, wunden-mǣl; wǣg-sweord; (lāf); beado-, hilde-
lēoma; (gūðwine); seax.* — Names: Hrunting 1457, 1659, Nægling 2680.
Descriptions, 1455 ff., 1687 ff.; 1900, 1531, 1285; 1563, 1615; 672 f.,
2778, 1533.
Spear: *gār, æsc(-holt), mægen-, þrec-wudu, here-, wæl-sceaft, daroð,
eofersprēot; wælsteng.* See *scēotend.* Cf. Tupper's *Riddles,* p. 212.
Helmet: *helm, beadogrīma* (etc.), *wīgheafola, hlēorbe(o)rg;* see *eofor,
swīn.* Descriptions, 303 ff., 1030 f., 1448 ff.; 1111 f., 1286, 2255 ff., 2615,
2811; cp. 2723. See Figures 2 and 3.
Coat of mail: *byrne; (brēost-,* etc.)*net, hring; syrce, (leoðosyrce),
hrægl, (ge)wǣd(e), beaduscrūd, fyrdhom, hildesceorp, herepād; (searo,
-geatwa;) (lāf).* Descriptions, 321 ff., 406, 1443 ff., 1547 f.; 671, 2986; cp.
2155 ff. Cf. *JEGPh.* xxxiii 194 ff.
Shield: *scyld, rond, bord, lind.* Descriptive, 333, 437 f., 2610; 2337 ff.;
2672 f.
Bow and Arrow: *flān-, horn-boga; flān, gār, strǣl.* See 3116 ff. Cf.
Tupper, *l.c.,* pp. 119 f.; Cook's ed. of *Christ,* pp. 147 f.
Horn and Trumpet: *horn, bȳme.* Cf. Tupper, p. 99. — Banner: *segn,
hēafodsegn, cumbol, hildecumbor; (bēacen).* See 47, 1021 f., 2767 ff.; 1204,
2958 f. Cf. Larson L 9.19.180.

ANTIQUITIES

The Festive Hall

§ 9. Hall. See 307 ff., 327, 402 ff., 491 ff., 704 (cp. 82), 721 ff., 773 ff., 780, 926 f., 997 ff., 1035 f., 1086 ff. (n.), 1188 ff., 1237 ff., 2263 f.; *Finnsb.* 4, 14, 16, 30; *hēahsetl; gif-, brego-, ēþel-, gum-stōl; bēod(-genēat); heorð.* (Cp. *būr, brȳdbūr, in(n)* 1300.)

Court ceremonies, 331–490; cf. § 2. See *cyn(n)* 613, *fǣg(e)re*.

Hall adorned for feast, 991 ff. Entertainment, 491 ff., 611 ff., 1008 ff., 1160 ff., 1647 ff., 1785 ff., 1980 ff., 2011 ff.; cp. 2179 f. (Ladies at banquet, see § 4.) See *medo, bēor, ealo(-benc,* etc.), *wīn (līðwǣge, wered)*; cf. note on 480 f.; *R.-L.* i 279 ff., iii 217 f.; Tupper, pp. 135 f. — Dispensing of gifts, see § 1.

Reciting of lays, 89 ff., 496 f., 1063 ff. (1159 f.), 2105 ff. See *scop, glēoman; lēoð, sang, gid(d); hearpe, gomenwudu, glēobēam.* (Lays recited on another occasion: 867 ff.) On elegies, see notes on 2247 ff., 2444, 2455 ff.

Sports

§ 10. Swimming, 506 ff. (2359 ff.) Horse racing, 864 f., 916 f. Hunting, 1368 ff., 1432 ff. (Boar-hunt, cp. *eoferspreot* 1437; see Tupper, p. 165.) Hawking, 2263 f.

Seafaring

§ 11. Cf. Intr. lix f., xlvi f.; L 9.46–48 a; Cha. Intr. 362 ff. A large number of synonyms for ' sea ' used promiscuously, 506 ff. — Mound on sea-cliff, 2802 ff., 3156 ff.

Voyage, 207 ff., 1896 ff.; 28 ff.; cp. 1130 ff. Warring expeditions over sea, 1202 ff., 2354 ff., 2913 ff. (cf. Intr. xxxix); 1149; cp. 9 f., 1826 ff. (2394, 2472 ff.?) See *flot-, scip-here*.

Ship. Descriptive: *hringedstefna, hringnaca; bunden-, wunden-stefna; wundenhals; sīdfæþme(d), bront; nīwtyrwed.* See *mæst, segl; stefn; bolca; ancor.* Cf. Tupper, pp. 105, 146. See Figure 1 (cf. Notes, p. 122, Boehmer L 9.46.618 ff.).

---

§ 12. Runic Writing, 1694 ff. (Lat. ' scribere ': see *scrīfan*.)
§ 13. Funeral Rites.

See notes on Scyld (p. 122), Bēowulf's obsequies (pp. 228 f.), and ll. 1107 f., 1117 f., 2231 ff. Cf. Intr. xlix.

APPENDIX III

TEXTUAL CRITICISM

NOTE ON CERTAIN GRAMMATICAL AND METRICAL FEATURES BEARING ON TEXTUAL CRITICISM

No attempt has been made to restore the ancient forms of the poem in accordance with the state of the language of the early eighth century and with the specific dialectal character that may be attributed to the original, nor has it been deemed proper to introduce a uniform, normalized orthography.[1]

As regards the system of versification, elaborate rules have been extracted by scholarly investigators from the transmitted poems, in particular from *Beowulf*, which, indeed, shows a remarkable degree of technical regularity and a singularly delicate sense of form. Especially, Sievers's formulations of 1885 and 1893 came to be regarded as practically authoritative. These views, involving a very definite linguistic interpretation and criticism of the text, can no longer be fully maintained, and, accordingly, the value of the following remarks has become somewhat problematic. Still, in the present state of uncertainty in these matters, it seemed best to retain these observations with such changes, however, as are demanded by a more liberal attitude in the treatment of the text.

A. Grammatical Observations

1. Contraction.

(§ 1.) a. Dissyllabic forms called for in place of contractions (Siev. R. 475–80, 268 f., A.M. §76.4; Bülb. §§ 214–16, 529; Morsbach L 4.143.262 ff.; Sarrazin, *ESt.* xxxviii 172 f.; Richter L 6.6.1.13 ff.; Seiffert L 6.6.2) are marked by a circumflex:[2] *gepēon* 25; *tēon* 1036; *flēon* 820, 1264, 2525 (see T.C. § 24), *(tō) beflēonne* 1003ª (cp. 1851ª, 257ª, 174ᵇ), perhaps 755 (Richter 11, 14); *sēon* 1180, 1275; *slēa* 681; *lȳhð* 1048; *hēa(n)* 116, 1926, 3097; *nēan* 528, 839; *ēam* 881; *Hondsciō* 2076 (n.; Lang. § 17.3 n.); *rēon* 512, 539; *ðēon* 2736; *Wealhþēon* 629 (otherwise regularly *Wealhþēo(w)*, *Ongenþīo(w)* [cf. also § 2]); *orcnēas* 112; *gân* 386, 1644, *gæ̂ð* 2034, 2054, *dôn* 1116, 1172, 1534, 2166, *dêð* 1058, 1134, 2859;[3] *strêd* 2436; *frēa(n)*

---

[1] Cf. *MLN.* xvi 17 f.; Kock 220 n. — An interesting sample of a reconstructed passage (ll. 1–25) is found in Holthausen's ed.¹⁻⁵, p. 103.

[2] This device was used in the edition of *The Later Genesis*, 1913; cf. *MLN.* xxiv 95. Also Chambers in his *Beowulf* employs this diacritic.

[3] Note dissyllabic *būan* 3065 by the side of monosyllabic *(ge)būn* 117.

TEXTUAL CRITICISM

16, 271, 359, 168c, 1883, 1934; likewise s͡īe 682 (Siev. § 427 n. 1; Bülb. § 225), sȳ̆ (=s͡īe) 1831, 2649 (plainly monosyllabic sīe 435, sȳ 1941). The diacritics in this, as in the following set of cases, are intended to serve as helps for scansion. They are non-committal as to whether the archetypal forms were something like geþīhan, slāe, rēowun, gāeð, dōeð, strēid, frēga, -þeowan; lǣið (lēið) or lǣhið (lehið); sehon (Holthausen, ed.[1]) or sehan (Kaluza) or seohan (Rieger) or sēoan (Sievers); etc.

(§ 2.) b. Redundant inflexional vowels in contracted forms are marked by a dot underneath. Thus fēaṃm 1081, hrēoṃm 2581, hēa(ṃm) 2212, Ongenþēoẹs 1968 (in 2475ᵃ (oððe him) Ongenðeowes the change to -ðēos is unnecessary). Cf. Siev. §§ 110 ff., R. 234, 489 ff., A.M. §§ 76.5, 77.1 b; Wright §§ 265 f. (Trautm., ESt. xliv 329 ff.) No diacritic is needed in the exceptional but unambiguous spelling -rēouw 58 (uw indicating the vocalization of w, i.e. -rēou [triphthongal], cf. Zupitza, ZfdA. xxi 10 n. 2).

(§ 3.) c. Loss of h after r and before a vowel results in forms of fluctuating vowel quantity (Siev. R. 487 ff., A.M. § 77.1 a; Bülb. § 529; Morsbach l.c. 272 f.; Richter, l.c. 9). Forms of feorh: (-)fēore, fēorum 537, 1152, 1293, 1306, 2664, 3013; all the other instances of oblique cases are doubtful, though the probability is in favor of the short vowel in 73, 933, 1843. Forms of mearh: mēaras, mēarum 855, 865, 917, 1035, 2163; doubtful quantity in mĕ̄arum ond mādmum 1048ᵃ, 1898ᵃ, 2166ᵃ.

2. Syncopation of medial vowels.

(§ 4.) a. Short medial vowels in open syllables following long stem syllables are frequently to be ignored in the scansion (Siev. R. 459, A.M. § 76.1; cf. Bülb. § 433, Wright § 221). This is indicated by a dot below the vowels: Ælmihtịga 92,[1] geōmọre 151,[1] elpēodịge 336, ænịgum 793, 2416, ǣnẹgum 846, mōdẹga 813, mōdịgan 3011 (cp. mōdges 502), gewealdẹne 1732; dōgọres 219, 605, 2896; dōgọre (or dōgor, see Siev. R. 233, 245; Lang. § 20.4) 1797, 2573.

Syncopation appears probable in dōgọra 88, ǣnịge 972, hǣþẹnes 986, tīrēadịgum 2189, nīðhēdịge 3165. There are numerous cases in which merely the possibility of syncopation is to be admitted.

Doubtful are forms of fǣger, since fæger and fǣger (so 773) seem to have been used side by side; thus 522: fægere or fǣgere (or fægẹre); see Siev. § 148, R. 498 f. (Cf. below, 3; § 6–8.)

(§ 5.) b. Syncopation after short stem syllables (Siev. R. 462 f., Bülb. §§ 438 f.) may have occurred in a number of instances, e.g. in forms of fyren, egesa (glēdegesa grim 2650ᵃ, 2780ᵇ; etc.), Sigemund (875, 884), and the like, but positive metrical proof is not obtainable, with the probable exception of nū is ofọst betost 3007ᵇ.[2] The spelling Hȳlāces 1530 presupposes a form Hyglāces. See Lang. § 18.10.

---

[1] Students are reminded of the rule that the final thesis (unstressed part) of types A and C never consists of more than one syllable.

[2] Resolution of the first stress of C2 is avoided, cf. Siev. R. 248. But see also Heusler V. §§ 226, 232 and n. 1; cp. l. 2803ᵇ (1892ᵇ?)

276   APPENDIX III

3. **Forms with vocalic r, l, m, n** to be counted as monosyllabic (Siev. §§ 138 ff., R. *passim*, A.M. § 79.4; Bülb. §§ 440 ff.; Wright § 219; Tr. Kyn. 31 f.; Kal. *passim;* Holt., ed. *passim;* Sarrazin, *ESt.* xxxviii 174 f.; Luick, *Vietor-Festschrift* (*Die Neueren Sprachen*, 1910), pp. 260–62; Richter *l.c.* 9 ff.; Seiffert *l.c.*) are distinguished by a dot below the secondary vowel. (The same diacritic is used in those few cases in which the suppressed vowel is an original one.)

(§ 5.) a. Long stems.

wundǫr- 995, 1681, 2173 (*wundur-*, cf. §§ 7, 19), 3037, *sundǫr-* 667, *hleahtǫr* 611ᵃ (type B, cp. 1063ᵃ, 2105ᵃ, 2472ᵃ, 1008ᵇ), *morþǫr-* 1079. 2436, 2742, *wintęr* 1128, 1132, *wuldǫr-* 1136, *umbǫr-* 1187ᵃ (and probably 46ᵇ: *umbǫrwesende*, cp. *cnihtwesende* 372ᵇ, 535ᵇ, *sāwlberendra* 1004ᵇ, and see Kal. 37, 79), *ātęr-* 1459, *aldǫr-* 1676, *oncęr-* 1918, *baldǫr* 2428, *frōfǫr* (probably) 2941; *-cumbǫr* 1022.

fīfęl- 104, *symbęl*(-) 1782, 2431 (probably so; clearly dissyllabic *symbel* 1010). (Cp. the spelling *ādl* 1763.)

māð(ð)um(-) 1198, 2193, 2405, 2757. (Cp. the spellings *māðm* 1613, 1931, 2833, *bearhtm* 1766.)

īręn- 998, *morgęn-* 2894. (Cp. the spelling *bēcn* 3160.)

(§ 7.) Numerous cases remain doubtful. E.g., *nǣfre hē on aldordagum* 718ᵃ, 757ᵃ, *tō aldorceare* 906ᵇ, *ðæs morþorhetes* 1105ᵃ, *nalles fācenstafas* 1018ᵇ, *þæt hē wið attorsceaðan* 283ᵃ, *ymb aldor Dena* 668ᵃ, *þā wæs wundor micel* 771ᵃ, *þæt wæs tācen sweotol* 833ᵇ, *ðā wæs winter scacen* 1136ᵇ, *þēah þæt wǣpen duge* 1660ᵇ (either type B or C). Again, *wolde on heolster flēon* 755ᵇ, *searowundor sēon* 920ᵃ, *nīðwundor sēon* 1365ᵇ (*flēon? sēon?*). Further, *wǣpen hafenade* 1573ᵇ (*wǣpen* clearly dissyllabic in 685ᵃ), *wundor scēawian* 840ᵇ, 3032ᵇ (cf. § 20) *ceasterbūendum* 768ᵃ (perhaps *ceastęr-*, cp. *foldbūende* 1355ᵃ, *grundbūendʳa* 1006ᵃ; Kal. 36); cf. Fuhr L 8.6.48 f. The monosyllabic function is rather probable in *beorht bēacęn Godes* 570ᵃ (cp. *swutol sang scopes* 90ᵃ); *wīn of wundęrfatum* 1162ᵃ; *wōm wundǫrbebodum* 1747ᵃ; *wundǫrlīc wǣgbora* 1440ᵃ (cp. *lēoflīc lindwiga* 2603ᵃ, *egeslīc eorðdraca* 2825ᵃ); it is by no means impossible in *Ongęnðīoes bearn* (type E) 2387ᵇ (see also § 2). On *wrǣtlicne wundurmāððum* 2173ᵃ, see § 19.

(§ 8.) b. Short stems.

The only decisive cases are *snotǫr* 190ᵇ [1] (Siev., Fuhr *l.c.* 86, Trautm.: *snottor*) and *meðęl-* 1082ᵇ [1] (Trautm., *ESt.* xliv 339: older *mæðlæ-*). The spellings *efn* 2903, *setl* 2013 may be noted. (*wæter* is clearly dissyllabic: 509, 1904, 1989, 2473.)[2]

Note. As a rule, the textual improvements cited in the foregoing sections, being of a generic character, are not included in the variant read-

---

[1] Cp. above, § 5, footnote.

[2] Parasitic vowels developed between *l* and *w* or between *r* and *g* (as in *bealuwa* 281, *-bealewa* 1946, *-byrig* 2471, *herige* 1833; cf. Bülb. §§ 447 ff., Wright § 220) are not found to interfere with the meter.

TEXTUAL CRITICISM

ings. It should be understood that practically all of them are due to Sievers and his example.

4. Variant Forms.

(§ 9.) **a.** *nēosan* and *nēosian*.

The two forms are found side by side; *nēosan* (*nīosan*): 125, 1786, 1791, 1806, 2074, 2366, 2388; *nīosian* (*nēosian*): 2486 (*nīosað*), 1125, 2671, 3045, 115. In no case is a change to *nēosan* (Siev. R. 233, 271) really obligatory. See below, § 20. L. 115[a], *gewāt ðā nēosian* may be scanned like 2569[a], *gewāt ðā byrnende* (type C).

(§ 10.) **b.** (*ge*)*trēowan* and (*ge*)*truwian*.

Cf. Siev. § 416 n. 17, R. 233 f., 298, 486; Cosijn, *Altwests. Gra.* ii § 120; Wright §§ 131, 538 n. However, *truwian* (not *trūwian*) is now considered correct (Sievers L 8.13 d. 105; Luick § 97 n. 3; also Trautmann, *ESt.* xliv 336). The MS. has *trēowde* in 1166[b] only. The forms of (*ge*)*truwian* are deemed metrically unexceptional. (Some instances of the former reading (*ge*)*trūwode* seemed to be objectionable.)

(§ 11.) **c.** Dat. sing. fem. *gehwǣm* and *gehwǣre* (later, analogical formation).

Cf. Siev. § 341 n. 4, R. 485; Tr. Kyn. 84. *gehwǣm*: 1365[a] *þǣr mæg nihta gehwǣm;* — *gehwǣre:* 25[a] *in mǣgþa gehwǣre* (metrically above criticism). See also Gloss.: *gehwā*.

(§ 12.) **d.** The inflected and the uninflected form of the infinitive (after *tō*).

The inflected has been changed to the uninflected form (see 316[a], 2556[a]) by Sievers (R. 255, 312, 482) in 473[a], 1724[b], 1941[a], 2093[a], 2562[a]. But see Hoops St. 9 f.

(§ 13.) **e.** *ymb* (originally preposition and prefix) and *ymbe* (originally adverb). (Cf. Intr. xci.)

See Sweet, *Ags. Dict.;* Wright §§ 594, 645; on the accentuation of *ymb*(*e*)-*sittan*, see Bülb. § 455.

ymb need not be restored in place of *ymbe* (preposition: 2070, 2618, 2883, 3169, prefix: 2734[a] *ymbesittendra*, cp. *ymbsittend* 1827[a], 9[b]), although Sievers (R. 258, 260) called for it in ll. 2296[b]: *hlǣw oft ymbehwearf*, 2691[b]: *heals ealne ymbefēng* (cf., however, e.g. 603[b], 2420[b]). In *ymbe gestōdon* 2597[b] the adverbial form is properly used.

(§ 14.) **f.** *hild-* and *hilde-* in composition.

The normal forms are *hilde* +⏑́ or ⏑́× (e.g., *hilderinc, hildestrengo*), and *hild*+⏑× (e.g., *hildfruma*), see Weyhe, *Beitr.* xxx 79 ff. The emendation of the only exception *hearde hildefrecan* 2205[a] to *hildfrecan* has been proposed by Sievers R. 305, Weyhe, *l.c.*

(§ 15.) **g.** *hraþe* (*hrǣdlīce*, etc.) and *raþe*.

hraþe is established by alliteration in 356, 543, 963, 991, 1576, 1914, 1937; so is *raþe* in 724 (MS. *raþe*) and in 1390, 1975 (MS. *hraþe;* in this edition *hraþe*). See Gloss. Cf. Siev. § 217 n. 1.

(§ 16.) NOTE. It will be seen that the compromise scheme adopted in this edition precludes grammatical consistency. But obvious mistakes have been corrected, of course. It seemed advisable, e.g., to emend forms like *sole* 302 to *sāle, þone* 70 to *þonne, of* 312 to *hof, brimleade* 1051 to *brimlāde, twelfa* 3170 to *twelfe, frecnen* 1104 to *frēcnan, reafeden* 1212 to *rēafedon, gehedde* 505 to *gehēde*, etc., since the exceptional spellings are isolated in the MS. or are easily accounted for by erroneous association (e.g., *gehedde* taken for the preterite of *gehēdan*) or by the influence of neighboring syllables (*frecnen; seomode* on*sole; lead*e *teah; ealr*a *twelf*a). — How to harmonize reasonable respect for the copyists with the presumptive claims of the author is a problem of far from easy solution.

B. Metrical Observations[1]

1. Rare Rhythmical Types.

Certain varieties of types, though not of frequent occurrence, have been considered sufficiently warranted to be left unaltered in the text.

(§ 17.) a. **Type A** admits in the second foot a short stressed syllable:[2] ⊥×|⌣×, a variety not restricted to cases like *wyrd oft nereð, gūðrinc mōnig.* See Siev. R. 453 f., 458, A.M. § 85 1; Fuhr 83 f.; Tupper's *Riddles*, p. lx, n.; also Holt., *Angl.* xxxv 167 f.

Thus in *b*-lines: *Hrunting nama* 1457[b], *æþeling manig* 1112[b], *hwīlum dydon* 1828[b] (cf. Lang. § 23.6); 1807[b], 2430[b], 2457[b], 3135[b]. (Siev. R. 231.)

In *a*-lines: *hlǣw on* [*h*]*līðe* 3157[a] (Siev. R. 275; though more likely, *hlīðe*); *nīða ofercumen* 845[a], *dǣdum gefremed* 954[a] (cf. Siev. R. 312, Kal. 72). — Type A3 (Siev. A.M. § 85 n. 5; Fuhr 25 f.): *hwīlum hē on lufan* 1728[a]; *wæs mīn fæder* 262[a], *þone þīn fæder* 2048[a]; *geslōh þīn fæder* (with anacrusis) 459[a];[3] perhaps *þǣr him nǣnig wæter* 1514[a] (cp. 157[a]), 779[a](?), see § 18.

(§ 18.) b. **Type B** with alliteration on the second stress only is occasionally met with (in *a*-lines). See Siev. A.M. § 85.3.

Possible cases are 459[a], 1514[a] (see § 17); a probable case: *þæt hit ā mid gemete* 779[a] (with transverse alliteration); a clear case: *hē is manna gehyld* 3056[a]. There are two undoubted examples in *Finnsb.*, 22[a], 46[a].

(§ 19.) c. **Type Dx** (D expanded) (in *a*-lines) admits in the first foot two syllables (×× or ⌣×) after the stressed syllable. Cf. Deutschbein L 8.22.33.

---

[1] It is a matter of the greatest difficulty to determine to what extent ' exceptions ' to the ' rules ' should be admitted. In many cases the decision must be left to individual judgment. Some of the emendations formerly supported (see, e.g., §§ 12, 22) may very well represent the original reading. But certainty could not be hoped for. The true archetypal version could never be recovered. Hence, sober resignation teaches us to introduce as few ' metrical ' corrections as possible into the text of our only manuscript. Cf. Hoöps St 9 ff.

[2] There occur several very doubtful instances of a short stressed syllable in the first foot, i.e., ⌣×|⊥×: *kyning mǣnan* 3171[b], *bea(du)weorces* 2299[a], and, according to Grienb. 750, *meoduscencum* 1980[b], *hagustealdra* 1889[a] (?).

[3] Cf. F. Schwarz (*Cynewulfs Anteil am Christ*, Königsberg Diss., 1905, p. 31), who with **Tr. Kyn.** 77 considers the form *fædder* a possibility. Kaluza (34, 76) assigns 262[a] and 459[a] to type C.

TEXTUAL CRITICISM

Thus, *deorc ofer dryhtgumum* 1790[a], *eahtodan eorlscipe* 3173[a], *word wǣron wynsume* 612[a] (cp. 1919[a]); *sellīce sǣdracan* 1426[a]; *fyrdsearu fūslīcu* 232[a] (no call for *fūslīc* (as in 2618[a])); *wrǣtlīcne wundurmāððum* 2173[a] (though possibly hypermetrical [Sievers, Richter]). And see § 12.

Double alliteration in Dx is the rule, but there are exceptions, viz. 768[a], 913[a], 1675[a], 1871[a], 2440[a], 2734[a], 3045[a], which, it is true, could easily be brought into harmony with the majority (*ceaster-, ēþel, þēoden, brōðor, ymb-, nīosan*).

(§ 20.) **d. Type Dx** is found several times also in the second half of the line (cf. Siev. R. 255, A.M. § 84.7; Fuhr 49; Kal. 56): *dohtor Hrōðgāres* 2020[b] (see *Wids.* 98; no need of *dohtor*), *Bēowulf Scyldinga* 53[b] (no need of *Bēow* or *Scylding*), *oftost wīsode* 1663[b] (no need of *oft*), *dēad is Æschere* 1323[b] (n.), *lāðra ōwihte* 2432[b], *ðēodne Heaðo-Beardna* 2032[b]; *wīca nēosian* 1125[b], *fīonda nīos(i)an* 2671[b] (so in 3045[a]); perhaps 840[b], 3032[b], 1573[b] (see above, § 7), 669[b] (but see above, § 10).

(§ 21.) **e. Type E** admits a short syllable with secondary stress: ⏑́⌣×|⏑́. Cf. Siev. A.M. § 84 n. 5, and the references given there. See list of types (p. 281), E2: *Sūð-Dena folc* 463[b]; 623[b], 783[b], 2779[b], (1584[a]).

Thus it would hardly be necessary on metrical grounds alone to change *egsode eorl* 6[a] to *egsode eorlas* (although corresponding forms of weak verbs 2. are elsewhere followed by ⏑́×, ⏑́ ⏑́, or (2085[a]:) ⏑ ×⏑ [i.e., type A]: 560[a], 922[a], 1118[a], 1161[a], 2096[a], 2110[a], 2132[a], 2702[a], 105[b], 1137[b], 1699[b], 1105[b]; on 3173[a], see § 19). Cf. Kock 219 f., *Angl.* xxviii 140 f.; Siev. xxix 560 ff.; Huguenin L 8.20.28 n.; Kal. 70, 97; Graz, *Die Metrik der sog. Cædmonschen Dichtungen* (1894), *passim*. Close parallels from other poems are *lȳtligan eft, Gen.* 1413[a], *ib* 2357[a], *blētsige þec, Az.* 73[a], cp. *Gen.* 180[a], *El.* 394[a], 1259[a], *Jul.* 688[a], *Chr.* 469[a].[1] On *lāðlīcu lāc, Beow.* 1584[a], see Siev. R. 504, A.M. § 84 n. 5, xxix 568; Tr. Kyn. 78, *ESt.* xliv 341; on *īrena cyst* 673[a], 1697[a], see note to l. 673[a].

(§ 22.) **f.** It is a question whether 'catalectic' measures should be allowed. See Siev. A.M. § 180; Vetter, *Zum Muspilli etc.* (1872), p. 33; Cosijn (& Sievers), *Beitr.* xix 441 f.; Trautm., Bonn. B. xxiii 140. Interesting cases are *gegnum fōr* 1404[b], *lissa gelong* 2150[a], *rǣhte ongēan* 747[b] (cf. Kock[5] 187); *bord wið rond* 2673[a]; *þenden hē wið wulf* 3027[a]. Similarly incomplete first feet: *hægstealdra* 1889[a]; *secg betsta* 947[a], 1759[a], cp. *ðegn betstan* 1871[b].

2. Anacrusis (cf. Siev. A.M. § 83 and the references given there).

(§ 23.) **Type A. a.** In the *a*-line: monosyllabic and dissyllabic. Instances of the latter are: 109[a], 1011[a], 1248[a], 1563[a], 1711[a], and 368[a]: *hȳ on wiggetāwum*. See further: 2636[a] *þæt wē him ðā gūðgetāwa;* the emendation *-geatwa* has now been abandoned. The scansion of 2475[a] is doubtful (type A or B).

---

[1] Likewise in the second half of the line: *gyddode þus, Met. Bt.* 1.84[b], *eardian sceal, Rid.* 88.27[b], cp. *Jul.* 626[b], *Phoen.* 506[b], *El.* 330[b], 669[b]. Note also the instances of *andswarode* (D3), *Beow.* 258[b], 340[b]; Siev. A. M. § 85 n. 7; Heusler V. § 197.

b. In the b-line: monosyllabic. There are eight incontestable cases: 93[b], 666[b], 1223[b], 1504[b], 1773[b], 1877[b], 2247[b], 2592[b]; see also 2481[b] (n.). And see further: 395[b] and Varr.

(§ 24.) **Type D. a.** In the a-line: monosyllabic; besides, in Dx, dissyllabic: 1543[a], 2367[a], 2525[a], 2628[a]. L 1027[a] *ne gefrægn ic frēondlīcor* is perhaps to be assigned to type C (like 38[a] *ne hȳrde ic cȳmlīcor*).

b. In the b-line anacrusis occurs only twice: *þā secg wīsode* 402[b], and *þāra ymbsittendra* 9[b]; the latter, being syntactically objectionable, has been emended by dropping *þāra*.

3. Elision.

(§ 25.) Elision is not marked in the text, since it admits of no positive proof. Cf. Schubert L 8.1.47 f.; Siev. R. *passim*, A.M. § 79.5; Fuhr 47 f.; Kaluza *passim*.

Highly probable cases are, e.g., 469[b], 517[b], 609[b], 433[a], 471[a], 525[a], etc. — In several places it appears that an elision-vowel is dropped in the MS.; this is indicated in the text by an apostrophe. Thus *wēn' ic* 338[a], 442[a] (*wēne ic* occurs in 525[a], 1184[a]); *eotonweard' ābēad* 668[b]; *firen' ondrȳsne* 1932[b]; *sibb' æfre* 2600[b]. — *egl unhēoru* 987[a] is more likely a haplographic oversight (originally: *eglu*).

4. Irregularities of Alliteration.

(§ 26.) **a.** A finite verb (in the a-line) followed by a noun or adjective alliterates alone: *gemunde þā se gōda* 758[a]; *gefēng þā be eaxle* 1537[a]. (Cf. Rie. V. 24, 43; Siev. A.M. § 24.3.) [Of this exceptional mode of alliteration some thirty instances have been found by Holthausen (*A.* xlvi 52 ff.) in the entire body of OE. poetry (exclusive of the *Psalms*); in some ten of those cases the verb of the second half of the line also alliterates.] On the alliterating imperative in 489[b], see note on 489 f.

(§ 27.) **b.** A finite verb takes precedence (in alliteration) over an infinitive in 1728[b]: (*hwīlum hē on lufan*) *lǣteð hworfan*. (Cf. Rie. V. 25.) — The second of the stressed syllables in the b-line alliterates in 2615: (*brūnfāgne helm,*) *hringde byrnan*. (Cp. *Finnsb.* 28[b], 41[b].)

Both cases may be justified by the employment of transverse alliteration.

(§ 28.) **c.** Double alliteration in the b-line. Cf. Bu. Tid. 63 f.; Rie V. 8–10; Siev. A.M. § 21 c.

a) Only apparently in 1251[b], 1351[b].

b) Cases to be remedied by fairly certain emendation: *ðā wæs heal hroden* 1151[b] (*roden*); *hilde gehnǣgdon* 2916[b] (*genǣgdon*);[1] *in ēowrum gūðgeatawum* 395[b] (*gūðgetāwum*, cp. *wīggetāwum* 368).[2]

c) *þæt ic mid sweorde ofslōh* 574[b] looks like a real exception. A scribal

---

[1] Cp. 2206[a]: *nīða genǣgdan*, 1274[a]: *gehnǣgde helle gāst*. There seems to have been some confusion between *gehnǣgan* and *genǣgan* (see 1318). Cf. Krapp, *MPh.* ii 405 ff. (possible confusion of *faroð* and *waroð*), Variants: 28[b], 1916[a].

[2] It has been observed (by Schröder, L 8.18) that, excepting *un*-compounds (see note on 1756[a]), the second element of 'noun compounds' never alliterates alone. This rule is applied to 707[a]. Whether it should be extended to 445[a], 1379[a], 2220[a] has been debated. (Cf. Malone, *MLR.* xxv 191, *JEGPh.* xxvii 320 ff.) The proper reading of 1224[a] is not doubtful.

TEXTUAL CRITICISM

substitution of a synonym (*ofslōh* for *ābrēat*, Holt.) is not so easily accounted for in this case as in 965ᵃ (*hand* for *mund*), 1073ᵇ (*hild* for *lind*), cp. 2298ᵇ.

For the convenience of students a list of Sievers's rhythmical types (with some slight modification of the numbering) is appended.

$A \stackrel{\prime}{-}\times|\stackrel{\prime}{-}\times$ hȳran scolde
A 1 bēaga bryttan   ellen fremedon   sceaþena þrēatum
   frumsceaft fīra[1]   frumcyn witan   folcstede frætwan
A 2 **Grendles gūðcræft**   drihtsele drēorfāh
A 3 syðþan hīe þæs lāðan (. lāst scēawedon) [allit. on second arsis]
$B \times\stackrel{\prime}{-}|\times\stackrel{\prime}{-}$ ond Hālga til
B 1 him ðā Scyld gewāt   hē þæs frōfre gebād
B 2 hē is manna gehyld (: hord openian) [allit. on second arsis]
$C \times\stackrel{\prime}{-}|\stackrel{\prime}{-}\times$ oft Scyld Scēfing
C 1 ofer hronrāde   in worold wōcun   tō brimes faroðe
C 2 þæt wæs gōd cyning   in gēardagum
$D \begin{array}{l} a. \stackrel{\prime}{-}|\stackrel{\prime}{-}\stackrel{\backprime}{-}\times \text{ fēond mancynnes} \\ b. \stackrel{\prime}{-}|\stackrel{\prime}{-}\times\stackrel{\backprime}{-} \text{ wēold wīdeferhð} \end{array}$

a:
D 1 weard Scildinga   gumum undyrne
D 2 **hēah Healfdene**   sunu Healfdenes
D 3 **þēodcyninga**   fyll cyninges
b:
D 4 flet innanweard   draca morðre swealt   secg weorce gefeh
D x (expanded D 1, D 2, D 4) **aldres orwēna   mǣre mearcstapa**
    grētte Gēata lēod
$E \stackrel{\prime}{-}\stackrel{\backprime}{-}\times|\stackrel{\prime}{-}$ weorðmyndum þāh
E 1 Scedelandum in   nicorhūsa fela   woroldāre forgeaf
E 2 **Sūð-Dena folc**   mundbora wæs

Scansion of the first 25 lines:

	C 2	C 2		A 1	C 1
	D 3	A 1		A 1	E 1
	C 1	A 1		A 1	D 4
	C 1	A 1		A 1	E 1
5	A 1	E 1	20	C 2	A 1
	A 1	B 1		D 1	C 1
	A 1	B 1		A 3	A 1
	A 1	E 1		A 1	C 2
	A 2 (3?)	D 1		A 1	E 1
10	C 1	A 1	25	A 1	A 1
	A 1	C 2			
	B 1	A 1			
	A 1	C 1			
	A 1	E 1			
15	C 2	A 1			

[1] See Deutschbein L 8.22.32 f.

APPENDIX III

A note on HEUSLER'S system of versification (L 8.13 f).

Heusler's system provides a uniform rhythmical scheme running through all lines, but with varying speech-material, and with pauses (or 'rests,' also 'rest beats') freely admitted. It is of distinct help in the reading of the verses. (Thus, e.g., the troublesome D and E types of Sievers are happily disposed of.) Substantially the same views are set forth in Leonard's less technical discussions of the matter (L 3.44, 8.13 g).[1]

It may be remarked that the practical results of this mode of scansion, so far as textual criticism is concerned, are not seriously at variance with Sievers's well-known findings.

Specimens of scansion.

General pattern. [2]‖×́ × × × | ×́ × × ×

The signs —, ×, U, ∧ represent the equivalents of musical values, viz. half note, quarter note, eighth note, quarter pause respectively.

nȳdwracu nīþgrim	193	nihtbealwa mǣst	
heald þū nū, hrūse,	2247	nū hæleð ne mōstan	
gewāt him ðā se hearda	1963	mid his hondscole	
him ðā Scyld gewāt	26	tō gescæphwīle	
gomban gyldan,	11	þæt wæs gōd cyning	
swā fela fyrena	164	fēond mancynnes	
æþelinga bearn	3170	ealra twelfe	
eahtodan eorlscipe	3173	ond his ellenweorc	

So-called hypermetrical lines:

gān under gyldnum bēage	1163	þǣr þā gōdan twēgen
sǣton suhtergefæderan,	1164	þā gȳt wæs hiera sib ætgædere

---

[1] Leonard (who is a poet and a scholar) feels that the main rhythmical features of the Old Germanic verse can be recognized in the 'Nibelungen couplet.'

[2] All syllables preceding the first stress are to be counted as anacrusis. — The details of the rules formulated by Heusler cannot be stated or applied here. It seemed sufficient to give a general idea of the scheme.

[3] The rest beat may or may not be specially marked.

[4] 'Sixteenth notes.'

APPENDIX IV
THE TEXT OF *WALDERE, DEOR*, SELECT PASSAGES OF *WIDSIÐ*, AND THE OHG. *HILDEBRAND*[1]

WALDERE
I

.... hyrde hyne georne:
' Hūru Wēlande(s)   worc ne geswīceð
monna ǣnigum   ðāra ðe Mimming can
hear[d]ne gehealdan;   oft æt hilde gedrēas
5 swātfāg ond sweordwund   sec[g] æfter ōðrum.
Ætlan ordwyga,   ne lǣt ðīn ellen nū gȳt
gedrēosan tō dæge,   dryhtscipe ......
....   (Nū) is sē dæg cumen,
þæt ðū scealt āninga   ōðer twēga,
10 līf forlēosan,   oððe lang[n]e dōm
āgan mid eldum,   Ælfheres sunu!
Nalles ic ðē, wine mīn,   wordum cīde,
ðȳ ic ðē gesāwe   æt ðām sweord*p*legan
ðurh edwītscype   ǣniges monnes
15 wīg forbūgan,   oððe on weal flēon,
līce beorgan,   ðēah þe lāðra fela
ðīnne byrnhomon   billum hēowun;
ac ðū symle furðor   feohtan sōhtest,
mǣl ofer mearce;   ðȳ ic ðē metod ondrēd,
20 þæt ðū tō fyrenlīce   feohtan sōhtest

---

[1] For critical and explanatory notes on *Waldere* and *Deor*, see Holthausen's and Dickins's editions (L 2.15, LF. 2.11); for an exhaustive study of *Widsið*, Chambers's edition (L 4.77) may be consulted. (Autotype edition of *Waldere* by Holthausen, Göteborg, 1899.) A special edition of *Deor* by Malone, London, 1933; and of *Waldere* by Norman, London, 1933.

æt ðām ætstealle,   ōðres monnes
wīgrædenne.   Weorða ðē selfne
gōdum dǣdum,   ðenden ðīn God recce!
Ne murn ðū for ðī mēce;   ðē wearð māðma cyst
25 gifeðe tō [g]ēoce,   mid[1] ðȳ ðū Gūðhere scealt
bēot forbīgan,   ðæs ðe hē ðās beaduwe ongan
mid unryhte   ǣrest sēcan.
Forsōc hē ðām swurde   ond ðām syncfatum,
bēaga mænigo;   nū sceal bēaga[2] lēas
30 hworfan from ðisse hilde,   hlāfurd sēcan
ealdne ēðel,   oððe hēr ǣr swefan,
gif hē ðā . . . .

II

'. . . . . [mē]ce[2a] bæteran
būton ðām ānum,   ðē ic ēac hafa,
on stānfate   stille gehīded.
Ic wāt þæt [h]it ðōhte   Ðēodrīc Widian
5 selfum onsendon,   ond ēac sinc micel
māðma mid ðī mēce,   monig ōðres mid him
golde gegirwan;[3]   iūlēan genam,
þæs ðe hine of nearwum   Nīðhādes mǣg,
Wēlandes bearn,   Widia ūt forlēt,
10 ðurh fīfela geweald   forð ōnette.'
    Waldere maðelode,   wiga ellenrōf —
hæfde him on handa   hildefrō[f]re,
gūðbilla gripe,   gyddode wordum:
'Hwæt, ðū hūru wēndest,   wine Burgenda,
15 þæt mē Hagenan hand   hilde gefremede
ond getwǣmde fēðewigges.   Feta, gyf ðū dyrre,

[1] Has also been read as unc.   [2] *Dietrich, et al.* bēga.   [2a] Norman: *swilce*.
[3] *Rie.L.* gigirwad, *Cosijn* gegirwed, *see Holt.*

æt ðus heaðuwērigan   hāre byrnan!
Standeð mē hēr on eaxęlum   Ælfheres lāf
gōd ond gēapneb,   golde geweorðod,
20 ealles unscende   æðelinges rēaf
tō habbanne,   þonne ha[n]d wereð
feorhhord fēondum;   ne[1] bið fāh[2] wið mē,
þonne (mē)[3] unmǣgas   eft ongynnað,
mēcum gemētað,   swā gē mē dydon.
25 Ðēah mæg sige syllan   sē ðe symle byð
recon ond rǣdfest   ryhta gehwilces;
sē ðe him tō ðām hālgan   helpe gelīfeð,
tō Gode gīoce,   hē þǣr gearo findeð,
gif ðā earnunga   ǣr geðenceð.
30 Þonne mōten wlance   welan britnian,
ǣhtum wealdan;   þæt is . . . .

DEOR

Wēlund him be wurnan[4]   wrǣces cunnade,
anhȳdig eorl,   earfoþa drēag,
hæfde him tō gesīþþe   sorge ond longaþ,
wintęrcealde wrǣce;   wēan oft onfond,
5 siþþan hine Nīðhād on   nēde legde,
swoncre seonobende   on syllan[5] monn.
    Þæs oferēode: þisses swā mæg!
Beadohilde ne wæs   hyre brōþra dēaþ
on sefan swā sār,   swā hyre sylfre þing,
10 þæt hēo gearolīce   ongieten hæfde,
þæt hēo ēacen wæs;   ǣfre ne meahte
þrīste geþencan,   hū ymb þæt sceolde.
    Þæs oferēode: þisses swā mæg!

[1] *MS*. he.   [2] *Holt.*[2-5] f[l]āh.   [3] *MS. reading doubtful.*
MS. wurman.   [5] *syllan* = *sellan, sēllan*, cf. Bülb. §§ 304, 338.

Wē þæt Mæðhilde[1]   monge gefrugnon,
15 wurdon grundlēase   Gēates frīge,
þæt hī sēo sorglufu   slǣp' ealle binōm.
   Þæs oferēode: þisses swā mæg!
Ðēodrīc āhte   þrītig wintra
Mǣringa burg;   þæt wæs monegum cūþ.
20   Þæs oferēode: þisses swā mæg!
Wē geāscodan   Eormanrīces
wylfenne geþōht;   āhte wīde folc
Gotena rīces;   þæt wæs grim cyning.
Sæt secg monig   sorgum gebunden,
25 wēan on wēnan,   wȳscte geneahhe,
þæt þæs cynerīces   ofercumen wǣre.
   Þæs oferēode: þisses swā mæg!
Siteð sorgcearig,   sǣlum bidǣled,
on sefan sweorceð;   sylfum þinceð,
30 þæt sȳ endelēas   earfoða dǣl.
Mæg þonne geþencan,   þæt geond þās woruld
wītig Dryhten   wendeþ geneahhe,
eorle monegum   āre gescēawað,
wislīcne blǣd,   sumum wēana dǣl.
35 Þæt ic bī mē sylfum   secgan wille,
þæt ic hwīle wæs   Heodeninga scop,
dryhtne dȳre,   mē wæs Dēor noma;
āhte ic fela wintra   folgað tilne,
holdne hlāford,   oþ þæt Heorrenda nū,
40 lēoðcræftig monn   londryht geþāh,
þæt mē eorla hlēo   ǣr gesealde.
   Þæs oferēode: þisses swā mæg!

---

[1] *MS.* mæð hilde; there may be a scribal error in 14[b] (*monge* for *mōd?*) or an omission before it.

WIDSIÐ

Wīdsīð maðolade, wordhord onlēac,
sē þe [monna] mǣst mǣgþa ofer eorþan,
folca geondfērde; oft hē [on] flette geþah
mynelīcne māþþum. Him from Myrgingum
5 æþelo onwōcon. Hē mid Ealhhilde,
fǣlre freoþuwebban forman sīþe
Hrēðcyninges hām gesōhte
ēastan of Ongle, Eormanrīces,
wrāþes wǣrlogan. Ongon þā worn sprecan:
10 ' Fela ic monna gefrægn mǣgþum wealdan;
sceal þēod[n]a gehwylc þēawum lifgan,
eorl æfter ōþrum ēðle rǣdan,
sē þe his þēodenstōl geþēon wile . . . .
18 Ætla wēold Hūnum, Eormanrīc Gotum,
Becca Bāningum, Burgendum Gifica.
20 Cāsere wēold Crēacum ond Cǣlic Finnum,
Hagena Holm-Rygum ond Heoden Glommum.
Witta wēold Swǣfum, Wada Hælsingum,
Meaca Myrgingum, Mearchealf Hundingum.
Þēodrīc wēold Froncum, Þyle Rondingum,
25 Breoca Brondingum, Billing Wernum.
Ōswine wēold Ēowum, ond Ȳtum Gefwulf,
Fin Folcwalding Frēsna cynne.
Sigehere lengest Sǣ-Denum wēold,
Hnæf Hōcingum, Helm Wulfingum,
30 Wald Wōingum, Wōd Þyringum,
Sæferð Sycgum, Swēom Ongendþēow,
Sceafthere Ymbrum, Scēafa Longbeardum,
Hūn Hætwerum ond Holen Wrosnum.
Hringweald wæs hāten Herefarena cyning.
35 Offa wēold Ongle, Alewīh Denum[1] . . . .

[1] See Notes, p. 196.

APPENDIX IV

45 Hrōþwulf ond Hrōðgār　　hēoldon lengest[1] . . . .
57 　Ic wæs mid Hūnum　　ond mid Hrēð-Gotum,
　mid Swēom ond mid Gēatum　　ond mid Sūþ-Denum.
　Mid Wen[d]lum ic wæs ond mid Wærnum　　ond mid
　　　　　　　　　　　　　　　Wīcingum.
60 Mid Gefþum ic wæs ond mid Winedum　　ond mid Gef-
　　　　　　　　　　flegum.
　Mid Englum ic wæs ond mid Swǣfum　　ond mid Ǣnenum.
　Mid Seaxum ic wæs ond [mid] Sycgum　　ond mid Swcord-
　　　　　　　　　　werum.
　Mid Hronum ic wæs ond mid Dēanum　　ond mid Heaþo-
　　　　　　　　　　Rēamum.
　Mid Þyringum ic wæs　　ond mid Þrōwendum
65 ond mid Burgendum;　　þǣr ic bēag geþah;[2]
　mē þǣr Gūðhere forgeaf　　glædlīcne māþþum
　songes tō lēane;　　næs þæt sǣne cyning!
　Mid Froncum ic wæs ond mid Frȳsum　　ond mid Frum-
　　　　　　　　　　　　tingum.
　Mid Rūgum ic wæs ond mid Glommum　　ond mid Rūm-
　　　　　　　　　　walum.
70 Swylce ic wæs on Eatule　　mid Ælfwine;
　sē hæfde moncynnes　　mīne gefrǣge
　lēohteste hond　　lofes tō wyrcenne,
　heortan unhnēaweste　　hringa gedāles,
　beorhtra bēaga,　　bearn Ēadwines . . . .
88 　Ond ic wæs mid Eormanrīce　　ealle þrāge,
　þǣr mē Gotena cyning　　gōde dohte;
90 sē mē bēag forgeaf,　　burgwarena fruma,
　on þām siex hund wæs　　smǣtes goldes
　gescyred sceatta　　scillingrīme, —
　þone ic Ēadgilse　　on ǣht sealde,

---

[1] See Intr. xxxv.　　　　[2] *MS*. geþeah.

WIDSIÐ

   mīnum hlēodryhtne,   þā ic tō hām bicwōm,
95 lēofum tō lēane,   þæs þe hē mē lond forgeaf,
   mīnes fæder ēþel,   frēa Myrginga;
   ond mē þā Ealhhild   ōþerne forgeaf,
   dryhtcwēn duguþe,   dohtor Ēadwines.
   Hyre lof lengde   geond londa fela,
100 þonne ic be songe   secgan sceolde,
   hwǣr ic under swegl[e]   sēlast wisse
   goldhrodene cwēn   giefe bryttian.
   Ðonne wit Scilling   scīran reorde
   for uncrum sigedryhtne   song āhōfan,
105 hlūde bī hearpan,   hlēoþor swinsade,
   þonne monige men   mōdum wlonce
   wordum sprēcan,   þā þe wēl cūþan,
   þæt hī nǣfre song   sēllan ne hȳrdon.
      Ðonan ic ealne geondhwearf   ēþel Gotena;
110 sōhte ic ā [ge]sīþa   þā selestan,
   þæt wæs innweorud   Earmanrīces.
      Heðcan sōhte ic ond Beadecan   ond Herelingas,
   Emercan sōhte ic ond Fridlan   ond Ēastgotan,
   frōdne ond gōdne   fæder Unwēnes . . . .
123 Rǣdhere sōhte ic ond Rondhere,   Rūmstān ond Gīslhere,
   Wiþergield ond Freoþerīc,   Wudgan ond Hāman . . . . . . ʼ
135   Swā scrīþende   gesceapum hweorfað
   glēomen gumena   geond grunda fela,
   þearfe secgað,   þoncword sprecaþ,
   simle sūð oþþe norð   sumne gemētað
   gydda glēawne,   geofum unhnēawne,
140 sē þe fore duguþe wile   dōm ārǣran,
   eorlscipe æfnan,   oþ þæt eal scæceð,
   lēoht ond līf somod;   lof sē gewyrceð,
   hafað under heofonum   hēahfæstne dōm,

APPENDIX IV

OHG. LAY OF HILDEBRAND[1]

Ik gihōrta ðat seggen,
ðat sih urhēttun ǣnon muotīn,
Hiltibra*n*t enti Haðubrant, untar heriun tuēm;
sunufatarungo iro saro rihtun,
5 garutun se iro gūðhamun, gurtun sih iro suert ana,
helidos, ubar [h]ringā, dō sie tō dero hiltiu ritun.
    Hiltibra*n*t gimahalta (Heribrantes sunu) — her uuas hērōro man,
ferahes frōtōro; her frāgēn gistuont
fōhēm uuortum, [h]wer sīn fater wāri
10, 11 fireo in folche, ... ' eddo [h]welīhhes cnuosles dū sīs;
ibu dū mī ęnan sagēs, ik mī dē ōdre uuēt,
chind, in chunincrīche; chūd ist mi*r* al irmindeot.'
    Hadubra*n*t gimahalta, Hiltibrantes sunu:
15 ' Dat sagētun mī ūsere liuti,
alte anti frōte, dea ērhina wārun,
dat Hiltibrant hǣtti mīn fater; ih heittu Hadubrant.
For*n* her ōstar giuueit, flōh her Ōtachres nīd,
hina miti Theotrīhhe, enti sīnero degano filu.
20 Her furlaet in lante luttila sitten
prūt in būre, barn unwahsan,
arbeo laosa; he[r] raet ōstar hina,
sīd Dētrīhhe darbā gistuontu*n*
fate*r*es mīnes, — dat uuas sō friuntlaos man.
25 Her was Ōtachre ummett irri,
degano dechisto *m*iti Deotrīchhe.

[1] Cf. (The Fight at Finnsburg,) p. 236. — For the text and notes, see Braune's *Ahd. Lesebuch*, Holthausen's *Beowulf*[2-5], Dickins's *Runic and Heroic Poems*.

Her was eo folches at ente,   imo was eo feh*t*a ti leop;
chūd was her . . . .   chōnnēm mannum;
ni wāniu ih iū līb habbe ' . . . . .
30 ' Wēttu irmingot (quad Hiltibra*n*t)   obana ab heuane,
dat dū neo dana halt mit sus sippan man
dinc ni gileitōs ' . . . . .
    Want her dō ar arme   wuntane baugā,
cheisuringu gitān,   sō imo se der chuning gap,
35 Hūneo truhtīn: ' dat ih dir it nū bi huldī gibu.'
    Hadubra*n*t gima[ha]lta,   Hiltibrantes sunu:
' Mit gēru scal man   geba infāhan,
ort widar orte . . . . .
Dū bist dir altēr Hūn,   ummet spāhēr,
40 spenis mih mit dīnēm *w*ortun,   wili mih dīnu speru wer-
        pan;
pist alsō gialtēt man,   sō dū ēwīn inwit fuortōs.
Dat sagētun mī   sę̄olīdante
westar ubar wentilsę̄o,   dat *i*nan wīc furnam:
tōt ist Hiltibrant,   Heribrantes suno.'
45   Hiltibra*n*t gimahalta,   Heribra*n*tes suno:
' Wela gisihu ih in dīnēm hrustim,
dat dū habēs hēme   hērron gōten,
dat dū noh bi desemo rīche   reccheo ni wurti ' . . . . . .
    ' Welaga nū, waltant got (quad Hiltibrant),   wēwurt
        skihit.
50 Ih wallōta sumaro enti wintro   sehstic ur lante,
dār man mih eo scerita   in folc sceotantero,
sō man mir at burc ę̄nīgeru   banun ni gifasta;
nū scal mih suāsat chind   suertu hauwan,
bretōn mit sīnu billiu,   eddo ih imo ti banin werdan.
55 Doh maht dū nū aodlīhho,   ibu dir dīn ellen taoc,
in sus hēremo man   hrusti giwinnan,

APPENDIX IV

```
   rauba birahanen,    ibu dū dār ēnīc reht habēs ' . . . . . .
      ' Der sī doh nū argōsto (quad Hiltibrant)    ōstarliuto,
   der dir nū wīges warne,    nū dih es sō wel lustit,
60 gūdea gimeinūn;    niuse dē mōtti,
   [h]werdar sih (hiutu) dero hregilo    hru[o]men muotti
   erdo desero brunnōno    bēdero uualtan.'
      Dō lęttun se ǣrist    asckim scrītan,
   scarpēn scūrim,    dat in dēm sciltim stōnt.
65 Dō stōpun tōsamane,    staimbort chlubun,
   heuwun harmlīcco    huīttę scilti,
   unti im iro lintūn    luttilo wurtun,
   giwigan miti wābnum . . . . . . . .
```

GLOSSARY

The order of words is strictly alphabetical, *æ* coming between *ad* and *af;* but *ð* (as well as *þ*) follows *t*, and the prefix *ge-* of verbs has been disregarded in the arrangement (e.g., *ge-bǣran* follows *bǣr*). Roman numerals indicate the class of ablaut verbs; w 1., etc., that of the weak verbs; rd., the reduplicating, prp., the preterite-present, anv., the so-called anomalous verbs; mi., mja., mc., etc. denote masc. i-, ja-, consonant-stems, etc.; nouns in *-o*, *-u* designated as wk.f. are old fem. abstract nouns in *-īn*, see Wright § 382, Siev. § 279.

When no form of a word is given before a reference, the head-word is to be supplied (the nom. sing. of nouns and the nom. sing. masc. of adjectives being understood unless indicated otherwise); ⌒ signifies the same word(s) as cited before; e.g., s.v. *ā-bregdan: up*⌒ = *up ā-bregdan.* Each designation of mood and tense applies to all citations that follow until another designation is used. The indicative mood of verb forms is understood unless indicated otherwise. In the case of variant forms of a word the one most frequently used in the text is generally chosen as the head-word.

Textual changes by emendation are marked by italicizing (the form or line-number); editorial additions to the text are marked by square brackets wherever conveniently possible. References to words of *The Fight at Finnsburg* (marked ' F.') are added within square brackets.

The dagger, †, designates words (or meanings) found in poetry only; the double dagger, ‡, words not elsewhere found in poetry (or prose); (†) is used when the word is incidentally found in prose (in Glosses or elsewhere) or when closely related words are recorded in prose; (‡) is used when closely related words occur in other poetical texts or in prose, (‡)+ when the word, not elsewhere found in poetry, occurs in prose also, and (‡) (+) when such a use in prose appears to be quite exceptional. In the absence of a complete lexicographical record of OE. prose, it is true, certainty cannot always be attained in these distinctions.

Spaced small capital letters indicate direct modern representatives, slight dialectal differences and similar variations being disregarded. Ordinary small capitals designate related words (or parts of words), also those adopted (directly or indirectly) from a cognate language.

Cpd(*s*). signifies compounds (including ' derivatives '); *ref.*, referring, or reference (to); *s.b.*, somebody; *si.*, similar(ly); *s.t.*, sometimes; *s.th.*, something; — (*n.*) calls attention to a note on the line.

ā, adv., *always;* 881, 1478; ā syþðan, 283, 2920; in general maxims, 455, 930; *at any time* (strengthening a negation), 779. [Go. aiw, OHG. eo, Ger. je.] — Cpd.: (nā), nō.

ā-, prefix, see the following verbs; cp. (stressed) or-. [Go. us-, OHG. ir- (: ur-), Ger. er- (: ur-).] (W. Lehmann, *Das präfix* uz-, *besonders im Altenglischen.* Kiel, 1906.)

ā-belgan, III, *anger;* pret. 3 sg. ābealch, 2280.

ā-bēodan, II, *announce, offer;* pret. 3 sg. ābēad, 390, 668 (*offered*); hǣl(o) ⌒ (cp. 407), *wished good luck, saluted:* 653, 2418.

ā-bīdan, I, w. gen., *await,* A B I D E; 977.

ā-brecan, IV, B R E A K *into, break;* pret. 3 sg. ābræc, *2221;* pp. [ābrocen, *shattered,* F. 44], np. [āb]rocene, 2063.

ā-bredwian(‡), w 2., *kill;* pret. opt. (?) 3 sg. ābredwade, 2619. [Cp. OHG. bretōn, *Hildebr.* 54.]

BEOWULF

ā-bregdan, III, *move rapidly* (trans.); up ∼, *raise;* pret. 3 sg. ābrǣd, 2575.

ā-brēotan(†), II (confus. w. rd.?), *destroy, cut down, kill;* pret. 3 sg. ābrēat, 1298, ābrēot (Lang. § 16.2), 2930; pp. ābroten, *1599*, 2707.

ā-būgan, II, *bend away, start;* pret. 3 sg. ābēag, 775.

ac, conj. (nearly always following a negative clause), *but;* the adversative (mostly contradictory-adversative, cp. Ger. ' sondern ') function appears with varying degrees of logical strictness; occasionally it shades off into the connective-adversative type (almost = *and*, 1448); 109, 135, [159], 339, 438, 446, 565, 595, 599, 601, 683, 694, 696, 708, 740, 773, 804, 813, 863, 975, 1004, 1085, 1300, 1448, 1509, 1524, 1576, 1661, 1711, 1738, 1878, 1893, 1936, 2084, 2142, 2146, 2181, 2223, 2308, 2477, 2505, 2507, 2522, 2525, 2598, 2675, 2697, 2772, 2828, 2834, 2850, 2899, 2923, 2968, 2973, 2976, 3011, 3018, 3024; [F. 5, 22, 42]. Introd. an interrog. clause (Lang. § 26), 1990; [an adhort. clause, F. 10]. Cf. Schü. Sa. § 50; Schuchardt L 6.14.2. 71 ff.; Williams LF. 4.36.1. 148 ff.; Glogauer L 6.15 a. §§ 8 f.

ā-cennan, w I., *beget, bear;* pp. ācenned, 1356.

ā-cīgan, w I., *call forth, summon;* pret. 3 sg. ācīgde, 3121.

ā-cwellan, w I., *kill;* pret. 3 sg. ācwealde, 886, 1055, 2121.

ā-cweðan, v, *say, utter;* pres. 3 sg. (ond þæt word) ācwyð, 2046, pret. 3 sg. (∼) ācwæð, 654 (formula, *ZfdA*. xlvi 267).

ād, m., *funeral pile* or *fire; 1107;* ds. -e, 1110, 1114; as. ād, 3138.

ād-faru‡, f., *way to (onto) the funeral pile;* ds. ādfære, 3010.

ādl, f., *sickness, disease;* ∼ nē yldo, 1736; ∼ oððe ecg, 1763; ∼ oþðe īren, 1848. [Cf. J. Geldner, *Untersuchung einiger ae. Krankheitsnamen*, Würzburg Diss., 1906, pp. 3 ff.]

ā-drēogan, II, *endure;* 3078.

ǣd(e)r, f., *(vein), stream;* dp. ǣdrum 2966, ēdrum 742. [Ger. Ader.]

ǣdre, adv., *early, speedily, forthwith;* 77, 354, 3106.

ǣfen, m.n. (ja.), E V E N*ing;* syþðan ∼ cwōm, 1235, si. 2303. [E V E (N); OHG. āband, Ger. Abend.]

ǣfen-grom‡, adj., *angry (hostile, oppressive) in the* E V E N *ing;* 2074.

ǣfen-lēoht‡, n., E V E N*ing*-L I G H T (' sun '); 413.

ǣfen-ræst‡, f., E V E N*ing*- (or *night*-) R E S T; gs. -e, 1252; *bed*, as. -e, 646.

ǣfen-sprǣc‡, f., E V E N*ing*-S P E E C H; as. -e, 759.

ǣfnan †, w I., *perform, do;* 1464, efnan 1041, 2622; ger. efnanne, 1941; pres. opt. 3 sg. efne, 2535; pret. 1 sg. efnde, 2133; 3 sg. ǣfnde 1254, efnde 3007; *make (ready)*, pp. geǣfned, 1107, 3106. [Holt. Et.]

ge-ǣfnan †, w I., *carry out;* pret. 1 pl. geǣfndon, 538.

ǣfre, adv., E V E R, *at any time (in any case)*; 70, 280, 504, 692, 1101, 1314; in negative clause *(never)*, 2600. [Horn, Pal. cxxxv § 75:* ā-in-fēore.] — Cpd.: nǣfre.

æfter, I. prep., w. dat. (instr.: 724), A F T E R; (1) local: *after, along, through, among, on;* 140, 580, 995,

1067, 1316, 1403, 1425, 1572, 1964, 2288, 2294, 2832; æfter gumcynnum, 944, æfter wīgfruman, 2261 (n.); semi-adv. (verb of motion understood: 'follow') 2816 (ic him æfter sceal.) — (2) (orig. local,) denoting the direction of an inquiry or turn of one's desire or feelings: *after, about;* æfter æþelum frægn, 332, si. 1322; 1879 (langað); (sorrow for the deceased, cp. (4):) 1342 (æfter sincgyfan ... grēoteþ), 2268, 2461, 2463, [3151]; æfter dōme (*in pursuit of, striving after*), 1720 (n.), 2179. — (3) modal: *in accordance with, conformably to;* ∼ rihte, 1049, 2110; 1320, 3096; ∼ wordcwydum, 2753 (cp. temp., (4)). — (4) temporal: *after,* s.t. verging on the sense of *in consequence of, on account of;* 85, 117, 119, 128, 824, 1008, 1149, 1213, 1255, 1258, 1301, 1315, 1589, 1606, 1680, 1775, 1938, 1943, 2030, 2052, 2060, 2066, 2176, 2531, 2581, 2803, 3005; ∼ þǣm wordum, 1492, 2669; ∼ dēaðdæge, 187, 885; cp. (wyrcan) wunder ∼ wundre, 931; ∼ (*after* [*obtaining*]) māðð umwelan, 2750; w. persons: 1257, 2260; — constr. w. instr.: æfter þon, 724.
II. adv., A F T E R (coming after s.b., w. ref. to s.th.); word æfter cwæð, 315 (*thereupon*), si. 341, 2154; 1389; semi-prep.: 12, 2731. (Cf. Schü. Bd. 19 ff.)
æf-þunca(‡) (+), wk.m., *vexation, chagrin;* 502 (n.). [Cp. of-þyncan.]
ǣg-hwā, m., **ǣg-hwæt**, n., pron., *every one, everything;* dsm. ǣghwǣm, 1384; gsn. ǣghwæs (unrīm), 2624, 3135; semi-adv., *in every respect:* ǣghwæs untǣle,

1865, si. 1886 (cf. *Angl.* xxvii 273). [*ā-gi-hwā.]
ǣg-hwǣr, adv., *every*W H E R E, *always;* 1059. [*ā-gi-hwǣr.]
ǣg-hwæðer, pron. subst., *each* (*of two:*) nsm., *2844;* gsn. ǣghwæþres, 287; dsm. ǣghwæðrum, 2564; (*of more than two:*) dsm. ∼, 1636. [*ā-gi-; E I T H E R.]
ǣg-hwylc, pron., *each* (*one*), *every* (*one*); adj.: 1228, 2590; asm. -ne, 621; subst. (absol. or w. gen.): nsm., 9, 984, 987, 1165, 1386, 2887; dsm. -um, 1050. [*ā-gi-.]
ǣg-lǣca, see **āg-lǣca**.
ǣg-weard‡, f., *watch by the sea;* as. -e, 241. [Cp. ēg-, ēagor-; Lang. § 9.2.]
ǣht, fi., *property;* ap. -e, 2248; — *possession, power;* as. ǣht, 1679, (flōdes, wæteres) ∼, 42, 516. [āgan.] — Cpds.: gold-, māðm-.
ǣht(‡), f., *pursuit, chase;* 2957 (n.). [=ōht, OHG. āhta, Ger. Acht; cp. ēhtan, w I.]
ǣhtian, see **eahtian.**
ǣled†, m., *fire;* 3015. [OS. ēld, ON. eldr.]
ǣled-lēoma‡, wk.m., *gleam of fire, torch;* as. -lēoman, 3125.
ǣl-fylce†, nja., *foreign people* or *army;* dp. -fylcum, 2371. [el (cp. el-þēodig); folc.]
ǣl-mihtig, adj., A L M I G H T Y (*God*); wk.: (se) Ælmihtiga, 92. (Cp. Lat. ' omnipotens '; see al-walda.) [Go. ala-; see eall.]
ǣl-wiht‡, fi. (n.), *alien creature, monster;* gp. -a, 1500. [Cp. ellor-gāst; ON. alvitr.] (Malone, *M L N.* xl 35ff.: cp. ' allwyghtys,' Towneley *Secunda Pastorum* 139.)
ǣne, adv., O N C E; 3019. [ān.]
ǣnig, pron., A N Y; adj.: ǣnig ōðer man, 503, 534, si. 1353, 1560; 510, 1099, 2297, 2731; nsf., 802, 2493,

2772; dsm. ǣnegum, 655; asm. ǣnigne, 627, 1772, 1851, 3080, 3127; asf. ǣnige 972, ǣnige 2449, 2548; gpm. ǣnigra, 932; — subst., ǣnig, absol.: 3129; w. gen.: 779, 1356, *2007*, 2734, 3054; dsm. ǣngum 474, 1461, ǣnigum 793, 2416, ǣnęgum 842; isn. (w. partit. gp.:) ǣnige þinga, *in any way, by any means,* 791, 2374, 2905. [ān; Horn, *Arch.* cxlii 128 f.] — Cpd.: nǣnig.

ǣn-līc, adj., *unique, peerless, glorious, beautiful;* nsf. ǣnlīc 251, ǣnlicu 1941. [ān.] (*OE. Glosses* (ed. Napier) 2113: pulcherrima, .i. speciosissima, ' ænlicoste.')

ǣnne, see ān.

ǣppel-fealu‡, adj.wa., 'A P P L E-F A L L O W,' *bay;* npm. -fealuwe, 2165. See fealu.

ǣr, I. adv., (E R E,) *before, formerly, previously;* w. pret. (freq. imparting a pluperf. sense): 15, 655, 694, 757, 778, 825, 831, 941, 1054, 1079, 1187, 1238, 1300, 1356, 1381, 1466, 1525, 1587, 1615, 1618, 1676, 1751, 1858, 1891, 1915, 2248, 2349, 2562, 2595, 2606, 2712, 2777, 2787, 2848, 2861, 2973, 3003, 3060; 3038 (*first*); eft swā ǣr, 642, 1787; ǣr ond sīð, *at all times,* 2500; (nǣfre . . .) ǣr nē siþðan, *at any time,* 718; — w. pluperf.: 3075, 3164; — w. pres.: 1182, 1370 (*sooner,* see II.); — nō þȳ ǣr (w. pret.), *none the sooner, yet . . . not,* 754, 1502, 2081, 2160, 2373, 2466. — Comp. ǣror, *before, formerly,* 809, 2654 (*first*), *3168.* See ǣrra. — Supl. ǣrest, *first,* 616, 1697, 2157, 2556, 2926, [F. 32 (adj.?)]; syððan ǣrest, 6, 1947.

II. conj., *before, ere;* w. pret. opt., 264, 676, 2818; w. pret. ind., 2019, 1496 (opt.?); w. pres. opt.: *rather than* 252, w. correl. adv. ǣr, 1371. (See Siev. xxix 330 f.; B.-T. Suppl., p. 18ᵃ; *Mald.* 60 f.; *Hel.* 3733, 1424 ff.) — ǣr þon, w. pret. opt., 731.

III. prep., w. dat., *ere, before* (temporal); 1388, 2320, 2798.

ǣr-dæg, m., E A R *ly part of the* D A Y, *daybreak;* ds. (mid, samod) ǣrdæge, 126, 1311, 2942.

ǣrende, nja., E R R A N D, *message;* as., 270, 345. [ār? Cf. *Beitr.* xxxv 569; *ZfdPh.* xlii 397 ff.]

ǣrest, see ǣr.

ǣr-fæder‡, mc., *fore* F A T H E R, *old father;* 2622.

ǣr-gestrēon†, n., *ancient treasure* or *wealth;* as. (p.?), 1757; gp. -a, 2232.

ǣr-geweorc†, n., *ancient* W O R K; 1679.

ǣr-gōd‡, adj., G O O D *from old times, very good;* (īren) ǣrgōd, 989, 2586; (applied to: æþeling) ǣrgōd, 130, 1329, 2342. Cf. Hoops St. 20 ff. (*MPh.* xxviii 157 ff.)

ærn, n., *house;* gs. -es, [2225]. See ren-weard. [Go. razn; ON. rann, whence rannsaka, MnE. RANSACK. — Cf. *Angl.* xxiv 386 ff.; *Beitr.* xxx 55 ff.] — Cpds.: heal-, hord-, medo-, þrȳð-, wīn-.

ǣror, see ǣr.

ǣrra, adj. comp., *former,* E A R*lier;* dp. ǣrran (mǣlum), 907, 2237, 3035.

ǣr-wela‡, wk.m., *ancient* WEAL*th;* as. -welan, 2747. [W E A L.]

ǣs, n., *food, carrion, carcass,* ds. ǣse, 1332. [etan; OHG. ās, Ger. Aas.]

æsc, m., (A S H) *spear†;* dp. -um, 1772.

æsc-holt†, n., (A S H *wood,* i.e.) *spear;* np., 330.

GLOSSARY

æsc-wiga†, wk.m., (*spear*) *warrior;* 2042.

æt, prep., w. dat., A T, *near, in* (place, circumstance, time); 32, 45, 81, 175, 224, 500, 517, 1089, 1110, 1114, 1147, 1156, 1166, 1248, 1267, 1588, 1914, 1916, 1923, 2526, 2790, 2803, 2823, 3013, 3026, [F. 16]; hrān æt heortan, 2270; æt hilde (gūðe, sæcce, wīge, etc.), 584, 882, 953, 1073, 1168, 1337, 1460, 1535, 1618, 1659, 1665, 2258, 2353, 2491, 2575, 2585, 2612, 2629, 2659, 2681, 2684, 2878, [F. 31, 37]; æt þearfe, 1477, 1525, 2694, 2709; æt bēore, 2041, si. 617; w. persons: (nū is se rǣd gelang) at þē, 1377, si. 2149; after verbs of taking, receiving, obtaining: *from* (at the hands of) a person, 629, 930, 2374, 2429, 2860. [Go. at.]

ǣt, m. (n.?), *meal;* ds. -e, 3026. [etan.]

æt-beran, IV, B E A R or *carry* (*to*), *bear away;* 1561; pret. 1 sg. ætbær, 3092; 3 sg. ∼, 519, 624, 2127, 2614; 3 pl. ætbǣron, 28.

æt-fēolan, III, w. dat., *stick to, hold firmly;* pret. 1 sg. ætfealh, 968.

æt-ferian(‡) (+), w 1., *carry away* (w. dat., *from*); pret. 1 sg. ætferede, 1669.

æt-gædere, adv., *to* G E T H E R (in connection w. notion of rest); 321, 1190; þā gȳt wæs hiera sib ætgædere, 1164 ('they were still at peace'); samod ætgædere, 329ᵇ, 387ᵇ, 729ᵇ, 1063ᵇ. [Cp. tō-gædre, geador.] (See Dening L 6.10.2.3.)

æt-gifan‡, V, G I V E; 2878. [Go. atgiban.]

æt-grǣpe‡, adj.ja., *grasping* A T, *aggressive;* ∼ weorðan (w. dat.), *lay hold of*, 1269. [grīpan.]

æt-hrīnan(‡)+, 1, w. gen. or dat., *touch;* pret. 3 sg. [æthr]ān, 722.

æt-hweorfan‡, III, *turn* (intr.), *go;* pret. 3 sg. æthwearf, 2299.

æt-rihte†, adv., *immediately,* 'R I G H T *away*'; 1657.

æt-somne, adv., *together;* 307, 402, 544, 2847; geador ∼, 491. [Cp. tō-somne, samod.] (See Dening L 6.10.2.3.)

æt-springan(‡), III, S P R I N G *forth, flow out;* pret. 3 sg. ætspranc, 1121.

æt-standan, VI, S T A N D *fixed, stop;* pret. 3 sg. ætstōd, 891.

æt-steppan‡, VI, S T E P *forth;* pret. 3 sg. ætstōp, 745.

ættren (ǣtren), adj., *poisonous, venomous;* 1617. [ātor, attor.]

æt-wegan‡, V, *carry, carry away;* pret. 3 sg. ætwæg, 1198.

æt-windan(‡)+, III, w. dat., *flee away, escape;* pret. 3 sg. ætwand, 143.

æt-witan, I, w. acc. of thing, *charge, blame* [*s.b.*] *for s. th.;* pret. 3 pl. ætwiton, 1150. [T W I T.] See oð-.

æþele, adj.ja., *noble, excellent, glorious;* 198, 263, 1312; gsn.wk. æðelan, 2234. [Ger. edel.]

æþeling, m., *noble, prince; hero, man;* 1112, 1815, 2188, 2443, 2506, 2715, *3135*, ∼ ǣrgōd 130, [1329], 2342; vs., 1225, 2667; gs. -es, 33, 888, 1596, 2424; ds. -e, 1244, 2374; np. -as, 3, 982, 1804, 2888; gp. -a, 118, 1294, 1920, ∼ bearn, 1408, 2597, 3170; dp. æþellingum, 906. — Cpd.: sib-.

æþelu, nja.p. (sing. *æþele, n., not found; æþelo, f.), (*noble*) *descent, race, nobility, excellence of character;* dp. æþelum, *332*, ∼ gōd 1870, ∼ dīore 1949; ap. æþelu, 392. — Cpd.: fæder-.

ǣðm, m., *breath, breathing;* ds. -e, 2593. [Ger. Atem, Odem.]

ā-fēdan, w I., (F E E D), *bring up;* pp. āfēded, 693.
ā-fyllan, w I., F I L L (instr., *with*); pp. āfylled, 1018.
ā-galan, VI, *sing;* pret. 3 sg. āgōl, 1521.
āgan, prp., *possess, have;* 1088; pres. 3 sg. āh, 1727; pret. 1 sg. āhte, 487, 533; 3 sg. ~, 31, 522, 2608. [o w E.] — Negat. form nāh; pres. 1 sg., 2252.
ā-gangan, rd., *come to pass, befall;* pp. āgangen, 1234.
āgen, adj. (pp. of āgan), O W N; 2676.
āgend, mc. (pres. ptc. of āgan), O W*ner;* gs. -es, 3075 (n.). — Cpds.: blǣd-, bold-, folc-, mǣgen-āgend(e).
āgend-frēa, wk.m., O W*ner, lord;* gs. -freân, *1883.*
ā-gifan, V, G I V E (*in return*); 355; pret. 3 sg. āgeaf, 2929.
āg-lǣca, ǣg-lǣca, †, wk.m., *wretch, monster, demon, fiend* (used chiefly of Grendel and the dragon), cf. *Angl.* xxxv 251); ǣglǣca, 159, 433, atol ~, 592, 816; āglǣca, 739, 1000, 1269, atol ~, 732; gs. āhlǣcan 989, āglǣcean 2557; ds. āglǣcan 425, āhlǣcan 646, āglǣcean 2520, 2534 (as.?), 2905; as. āglǣcan 556, āglǣcean 2534 (?); np. āglǣcan, 1512. — *warrior, hero;* ns. āglǣca, 893; gs. āglǣcan, 1512 (?); np. āglǣcean, 2592 (Bēowulf and the dragon). [*ESt.* xxv 424, xli 24 f.; *IF.* xx 316. — Grein, Trautm., *ESt.* xliv 325: aglǣca.]
āg-lǣc-wīf‡, n., *wretch,* or *monster, of a woman;* 1259.
ā-gyldan, III, *pay; permit, make possible;* pret. 3 sg. āgeald: þā mē sǣl āgeald, ' when I had an opportunity,' 1665, si. 2690.
āh, āhte, see āgan.

ā-hebban, VI, *raise, lift, draw;* pp. āhafen, 128; āhæfen, 1108.
āh-lǣca, see āg-lǣca.
ā-hlēapan, rd., L E A P *up;* pret. 3 sg. āhlēop, 1397.
ā-hli(e)hhan (ā-hlæhhan) †, VI, L A U G H, *exult;* pret. 3 sg. āhlōg, 730.
ā-hreddan, w I., *rescue;* pret. 3 sg. āhredde, *2930.* [*NED.*: R E D D, v.¹ (obs., Sc.); cp. also MnE. rid?; Ger. erretten.]
āhsian (āscian), w 2., A S K, *seek for;* pret. 3 sg. (wēan) āhsode (tō), 1206, 3 pl. (wēan) āhsodon, 423 (' courted trouble,' Cl. Hall, cf. sēcean 1989 f.; see *ESt.* i 488; *MLN.* xvi 15 f., *MPh.* iii 258).
ge-āhsian, w 2., *learn by inquiry* (A S K*ing*), *hear;* pp. geāhsod, 433.
āht, n.(f.)i., *anything,* A U G H T; as., 2314. [ā-wiht.] See ō-wiht.
ā-hyrdan, w I., HARD*en;* pp. āhyrded, 1460.
ā-lǣtan, rd., *leave, give up;* 2591, 2750; — L E T (w. acc. & inf.); pres. opt. 2 sg. ālǣte, 2665.
aldor(-), see ealdor(-).
ā-lecgan, w I., L A Y, *lay down;* pret. 3 sg. ālegde, 834, 2194; 3 pl. ālēdon 34, ālegdon 3141; *lay down, lay aside, give up:* pret. 3 sg. (feorh) ālegde, 851, si. 3020.
ā-lēh, see ā-lēogan.
ā-lēogan, II, *be*L I E, *fail to perform* or *leave unfulfilled* (*a promise*); pret. 3 sg. ālēh, 80.
ā-licgan, v, *fall, fail, cease;* ālicgean, 2886; pret. 3 sg. ālæg, 1528.
ā-limpan†, III, *befall, come* (*to pass*); pret. 3 sg. ālamp, 622; pp. ālumpen, 733.
al-walda†, wk. adj. & m. noun, *omnipotent* (*one*), *the Lord;* Fæder alwalda, 316; Alwalda, 955, *1314;*

ds. Alwealdan, 928. [w(e)aldan.] (Cf. *JEGPh.* viii 414; *Angl.* xxxv 125.)

ā-lȳfan, w 1., *allow, grant, entrust;* pret. 1 sg. ālȳfde, 655; pp. ālȳfed, 3089. [See lēafnes-word. Ger. erlauben.]

ā-lȳsan, w 1., LOOSE*n*, *take off;* pp. ālȳsed, 1630. [lēas; Ger. erlösen.]

an, prep., see on.

an-, prefix, see on-.

an, verb, see unnan.

ān, num. adj. and subst. (1) O N E; (w. partit. gen.: 1037, 1294, 2237, 2599; 1458; w. def. art.: 1053, 2237, 2399, 2453); — nsm. ān, 2237, 2453, ~ æfter eallum, 2268, ~ æfter ānum, 2461; gsm. ānes, 699, 2541, 3077; gsf. ānre, 428; gsn. in: ānes hwæt (*one part*, or *piece, only*, cf. *Angl.* xxvii 140, manages huat, *Hel.* 3173, etc.), 3010; dsm. ānum, 705, 1037, 2461, 2599; asm. ænne 1053, 1579, ānre 1294, 2399, 2964; asf. āne, 135, 1762; plur., *individuals*, gpm. in: ānra gehwylces (*of each one*), 732, ānra gehwylcum, 784; — (*unique*), *peerless;* þæt wæs ān cyning, 1885, si. (nsn.) 1458. — (2) *a certain (one)*; nsm. ān: oð ðæt ān ongan ..., 100, 2210; 2280; asm. ānne, 2410, 2774. — (3) *only, alone;* str. decl.: gsm. ānes, 2533; dsm. ānum, 1377; asm. ænne, 46; dpm. in: fēaum ānum (*few only*, cf. *Angl.* xxvi 493), 1081; wk. decl. (*alone*): nsm. āna, 145, 425, 431, 888, 999, 1714, [2361], 2498, 2643, 2657, 2876. — Cpd.: nān.

ancor, m., A N C H O R; ds. ancre, 303, 1883. [Fr. Lat. ancora.]

ancor-bend‡, fjō. (mi.), A N C H O R-*rope;* dp. oncęrbendum, *1918*.

and-, ond-, stressed prefix, cp. unstressed on-; spelt: and-, 340, 689, 1059, 1287, 1796, 2695, (hand- 1541), ond-, 2938 (hond- 2094, 2929, 2972), otherwise abbreviated: ㄱ. [Gr. ἀντί, Go. anda- (: and-), Ger. ant- (: ent-).]

anda, wk.m., *anger, indignation;* ds. andan, 708; — *vexation, horror;* as. (ds.?) ~, 2314. [OS. ando; cp. Ger. ahnden.]

and-git, n., *understanding, discernment;* 1059. [Cp. on-gitan.]

and-lēan, ond-lēan,†, n., *reward, requital;* as. andlēan (MS. hand-) forgeald, *1541;* ondlēan (MS. hond-) ~, *2094*.

and-long, adj.†, *extending away in the opposite direction* (*NED*.); *standing upright;* asm. -ne, 2695 (Kock² 123: *related, kindred* (?); Girvan, *MLR.* xxviii 246: ' (*the noble*) *at his side*,' cp. gloss ' an[d]langcempa ' = miles ordinarius, B.-T. Suppl.); — *continuous, entire;* asm.: andlangne dæg, 2115; asf.: ondlonge niht, 2938. [Cp. prep. andlang, A L O N G; Ger. entlang; *Beitr.* xviii 233 f.]

and-rysno(†), wk.f. (pl.), *propriety, courtesy;* dp. -um, 1796. [ge-rīsan; cp. gerysne 2653. — Trautm., *ESt.* xliv 325: an-rysno.] (Tho., B.-T., Moore, *JEGPh.* xviii 209 f.: andrysno 'fear,' ie. ' reverence.')

and-saca(†), wk.m., *enemy, adversary;* (Godes) ~, 1682; as. (~) andsacan, 786. [Cp. on-sacan, ge-saca.]

and-swarian (w. chief stress on prefix), w 2., A N S W E R; pret. 3 sg. -swarode, 258, 340. [and-swaru.]

and-swaru, f., A N S W E R; 2860; gs. andsware, 1493; as. ~, 354, 1840. [Cp. swerian.]

and-weard, adj., *opposite, standing*

over against; asn., 1287. [weorþan; cp. Lat. vertere.]
and-wlita, wk.m., *face;* ds. -wlitan, 689. [wlītan; cp. Ger. Antlitz.]
ān-feald, adj., ('O N E F O L D'), *simple, plain;* asm. -ne, 256 (cp. 'plain English').
ānga, wk. adj., *sole,* O N *ly;* dsm. āngan (brēþer), 1262; asm. ~ (eaferan), 1547; asf. ~ (dohtor), 375, 2997. [ān; OS. ēnag.]
an-geat, see on-gitan.
ān-genga(‡)+, wk.m., *one who goes al* O N E*, solitary one* (Grendel); 449, āngengea, 165. (Tr. ed., & *ESt.* xliv 323: angenga 'aggressor.')
an-gyldan, III, w. gen., *pay (a penalty) for;* pret. 3 sg. angeald, 1251. [OS. an(t)-geldan, OHG. in(t)-geltan.] See on-, prefix.
ān-haga(†), wk.m., *solitary one;* 2368.
an-hār‡, adj., *very* H O A R *y;* 357 (n.). (MS. un-.)
an-hȳdig†, adj., *resolute, strong-minded;* 2667. [hycgan.]
ān-pæð†, m., O N E-*by-one* P A T H, *narrow path* (Bu. 94), or *lonely way* (Schü. Bd. 40 ff.); ap. ānpaðas, 1410. (*Epin. Gloss.* 1042: 'termofilas' = fæstin *vel* anstigan; ON. einstigi.)
an-ræd (ān-?), adj., *resolute;* 1529, 1575.
an-sund, adj., S O U N D, *uninjured;* 1000. See ge-sund.
an-sȳn, fi., *appearance, form, sight;* 251, onsȳn 2772; gs. ansȳne, 928; as. ansȳn, 2834. [Go. siuns; cp. OE. sēon, vb.]
ān-tīd‡, fi., *fixed* or *appropriate time, time when something is due;* as., 219. (Siev. xxix 326: cp. āndaga; Gr. Spr.: āntīd = 'hora prima'? (?); Cos. viii 568: an(d)-tīd, *corresponding time,* cf. E., **Tr.**: andtīd; Bonn.B. xvii 169: antīd, *first hour;* Krogmann *ESt.* lxx 40 ff.)
ānunga, adv., *entirely, by all means, certainly;* 634. [ān.]
An-walda, wk.m., *ruler, the Lord;* ds. -waldan, 1272. See al-walda.
ār†, m., *messenger, herald;* 336, 2783.
ār, f., *honor; kindness, benefit, help;* ds. (mid) āre, 2378; as. ~, 1272; gp. ārna, 1187; dp. ārum (healdan), 296, 1182, si. 1099; *property, estate:* as. āre, 2606. [Ger. Ehre.] (See Grønbech L 9.24. i 69 ff., *JEGPh.* ix 277.) — Cpd.: worold-.
ā-rǣran, w 1., *raise up, establish, exalt;* pret. 3 pl. ārǣrdon, 2983; pp. ārǣred, 1703. [rīsan; R E A R.]
ār-fæst, adj., *kind, merciful;* 1168. (Cf. *MPh.* iii 249.) [ār, f.]
ārian, w 2., w. dat., *show mercy, spare;* pres. 3 sg. ārað, 598. [ār, f.]
ā-rīsan, I, *rise,* A R I S E (lit. & fig.); [pres. 3 pl. ārīsað, F. 8]; imp. sg. ārīs, 1390; pret. 3 sg. ārās, 399, 2403, 2538, [F. 13]; we(o)rod eall ārās, 651, 3030, si. 1790.
ār-stafas†, m.p., *kindness, favor, grace;* dp. (mid) ārstafum 317, (for) ~, 382, 458 (*help?*). See fācenstafas.
ā-secgan, w 3., *tell, declare;* 344.
ā-settan, w 1., S E T, *place, appoint;* pret. 3 pl. āsetton, 47; pp. āseted, 667.
ā-singan, III, S I N G (*to an end*); pp. āsungen, 1159.
ā-standan, VI, S T A N D *up, get up;* pret. 1 sg. āstōd, 2092; 3 sg. ~, 759, 1556.
ā-stīgan, I, *ascend, arise* (lit. & fig.); pres. 3 sg. -eð, 1373; pret. 3 sg. āstāg 782, āstāh 1118 (n.), 1160, 3144.
ā-swebban(†), w 1., (*put to sleep,*)

kill; pp. npm. āswefede, 567. [swefan.]

atelīc (=atol-līc) (‡)+, adj., *horrible, dreadful;* 784.

ā-tēon, II, *draw;* sīð ātēon, *take a journey;* pret. 3 sg. (sīð) ātēah, 766 (n.).

āter-tān‡, m., ('*poison twig*'), *poison stripe* (ref. to damascening?); dp. ātẹrtānum, 1459 (n.).

atol, adj., *horrid, dire, terrible* (applied 7 times [marked *] to the fiendish monsters, cf. *Angl.* xxxv 251, 256 f.); *165, 848 (nsn.), *1332, 1766 (nsf.), *2670; atol ǣglǣca, *592, *732, *816; eatol, *2074; asm. eatolne, 2478; asf. atole, 596; dpm.wk.(?) atolan, 1502. [Cp. ON. atall.]

attor (ātor), n., (*animal*) *poison, venom;* 2715; gs. attres, *2523*. [A T T E R (obs., dial.); Ger. Eiter.]

attor-sceaða†, wk.m., *venomous foe* (dragon); gs. -sceaðan, 2839.

āð, m., O A T H; gp. -a, 2739; dp. -um, 1097; ap. -as, 472.

ā-ðencan, W I., T H I N K, *intend;* pret. 3 sg. āðōhte, 2643.

āð-sweord(‡) (+), n., O A T H; np., *2064*. [swerian; ǣþ-swyrd, *Eadw. Cant. Ps.* 104.9, cp. āð-swaru; OHG. eidswurt, -swart. See Lang. § 8.6 n. 1.]

āþum-swēoras‡, m.p., *son-in-law and father-in-law;* dp. āþumswēoran, *84* (n.). [Cp. Ger. Eidam (perh. rel. to āþ, Ger. Eid); swēor, Go. swaíhra, OHG. swehur, Lat. socer.]

āwa(†), adv., *always;* āwa tō aldre, *for ever and ever*, 955. [See ā, *Beibl.* xiii 16.]

ā-wrecan, V, *recite, tell;* pret.: (gid) āwrǣc, I sg. 1724, 3 sg. 2108.

ā-wyrdan, W I., *injure, destroy;* pp. āwyrded, 1113. [weorþan; Go. fra-wardjan, OS. ā-werdian.]

bā, see **bēgen.**

bǣdan W I., *compel, urge on;* pret. 3 sg. bǣdde 2018 (n.); pp. (strengum) gebǣded, 3117; — *press hard, oppress;* pp. (bysigum) gebǣded, 2580; (bealwe) ~, 2826. [Go. baidjan.]

bǣl(†), n., *fire, flame;* ds. -e, 2308, 2322; — *funeral fire, pyre;* ds. -e, 2803; as. bǣl, 1109, 1116, 2126 (bẹ̄l), 2818. [Cf. *NED.*: BALE, sb.² (fr. ON. bál).]

bǣl-fȳr†, n., *funeral* F I R E; gp. -a, 3143.

bǣl-stede‡, mi., *place of the pyre;* ds., 3097.

bǣl-wudu‡, mu., W O O D *for the funeral pile;* as., 3112.

bǣr, f., B I E R; 3105. [beran.]

ge-bǣran, W I., BEAR *oneself, behave, fare;* sēl ~, 1012, [F. *38*]; blēate ~, 2824. [ge-bǣre; beran.]

bærnan, W I., BURN (trans.); 1116, 2313. [See byrnan.] — Cpd.: for-.

(ge-)bǣtan, W I., *bridle,* BIT, (*saddle?*); pp. gebǣted, 1399. [bītan; BAIT, fr. ON. beita.]

bæð, n., B A T H; as. ganotes ~ (= 'sea '), 1861.

baldor, see **bealdor.**

balu, see **bealu.**

bām, see **bēgen.**

bān, n., B O N E; ds. -e, 2578; dp. -um, 2692 (of the dragon's *tusks*).

bana, wk.m., *slayer, murderer;* ns. bana 2613, bona 1743, 2082, 2506, 2824; gs. banan, *158;* ds. banan, 1102, tō banan weorðan, *kill:* 587, 2203 (bonan); as. bonan, 1968, 2485; gp. banena, 2053. [B A N E.] — Cpds.: ecg-, feorh-, gāst-, hand-, mūð-.

bān-cofa†, wk.m., *body;* ds. -cofan, 1445. [cofa 'chamber'; C O V E.]

BEOWULF

bān-fæt†, n., *body;* ap. -fatu, 1116. (Hoops 140: *muscles*.) [fæt 'vessel.']

bān-fāg‡, adj., *adorned with* B O N E (*antlers?*); asn., 780.

bān-hring†, m., (B O N E R I N G), *vertebra;* ap. -as, 1567.

bān-hūs†, n., *body;* as. (p.?), 2508; ap., 3147 (sg. meaning).

bān-loca†, wk.m., (B O N E L O C K-er), *joint; body;* np.-locan, 818; ap. (s.?) ∼, 742. (Cp. Siev. xxxvi 402-4; Hoops 94: *muscles, flesh*.)

ge-bannan, rd., w. dat. of person & acc. of thing, *bid, order;* 74. [See *NED.*: B A N.]

ge-barn, see **ge-byrnan**.

bāt, m., B O A T, *ship;* 211. — Cpd.: sǣ-.

bāt-weard‡, m., B O A T-G U A R D, *boat-keeper;* ds. -e, 1900.

be, bī (1188, 1956, 2538, 2716, 2756, big 3047), prep., w. dat. (instr.: 1722); (1) local: B Y, *beside, near, along, to* (rest, motion); 36, 566, 1188, 1191, 1573, 1905, 2243, 2262, 2538, 2542, 2716, 2756; following its case (prep.-adv.): him big, 3047; be sǣm twēonum, *between the seas* (=*on earth*), 858, 1297, 1685, 1956; (gefēng) be eaxle, 1537; sī. 814, 1574, 1647, 1872. — (2) temporal: be ðē lifigendum, ' during your life,' 2665. — (3) Other uses: *in comparison with*, 1284; *according to:* be fæder lāre, 1950; (ðū þē lǣr) be þon, *from this, thereby*, 1722; (*with reference to*), *for the sake of:* be þē, 1723.

bēacen, n., *sign;* bēacen Godes (=*sun*, cf. *Angl.* xxxv 122), 570; as. bēcn (=*monument*), 3160; gp. bēacna (*banner*), 2777. [B E A-C O N.]

⟨ge-⟩bēacnian, w 2., *point out, show;* pp. gebēacnod, 140. [B E C K O N.]

beado, -u, †, fwō., *battle, fighting;* gs. beadwe, 1539; beaduwe, 2299; gp.(?) beadwa, 709.

beado-grīma‡, wk.m., *war-mask, helmet;* as. -grīman, 2257. See grīm-helm.

beado-hrægl‡, n., *war-garment, coat of mail;* 552.

beado-lēoma‡, wk.m., *battle-light*, i.e. (*flashing*) *sword;* 1523. (Cp. 2492, *Finnsb.* 35 f.; ON. gunnlogi, Intr. xvi; ON. sword-names Ljómi, Sigrljómi, Falk L 9.44.54 & 58.)

beado-mēce‡, mja., *battle-sword;* np. -mēcas, 1454.

beado-rinc†, m., *warrior;* gp. -a, 1109.

beadu-folm‡, f., *battle-hand;* as. -e, 990.

beadu-lāc†, n., (*battle-sport,-exercise*), *battle;* ds. -e, 1561. See (ge-)lāc, lācan.

beadu-rōf†, adj., *bold in battle;* gsm. -es, 3160.

beadu-rūn‡, f., *battle-*R U N E; as.: onband beadurūne, ' commenced fight,' 501.

beadu-scearp‡, adj., *battle-*S H A R P; asn., 2704.

beadu-scrūd‡, n., *war-garment, corslet*, 2660; gp. -a, 453. [S H R O U D.]

beadu-serce‡, wk.f., (*battle-*S A R K), *coat of mail;* as. -sercean, 2755.

bēag, bēah, m., (*precious*) *ring, circlet*, (*bracelet, collar*); used of interlocked rings serving as ' money,' (' treasure '); ns. bēah (*necklace*), 1211, so gs. bēages, 1216; ds. bēage (*diadem, crown?*), 1163; as. bēah, 2041 (n.), 2812, bēg (collect.), 3163; np. bēagas, 3014; gp. bēaga, 2284, locenra bēaga (see Stjer. 34 f.), 2995, bēaga bryttan, 35, 352, 1487; ap. bēagas, 523, 2370, 3105, ∼ dǣlde,

80, ~ geaf, 1719, 2635 (*things of value*), 3009, si. 1750. [būgan; ON. baugr, OHG. boug.] — Cpds.: earm-, heals-.

bēag-gyfa†, wk.m., *ring-*G I V*er, lord, king;* gs.-gyfan, 1102. [Cp. *Hel.*: bōg-gebo.]

bēag-hroden†, adj. (pp.), *ring-adorned* (cp. 1163?); 623. [hrēodan.]

bēah, see bēag, būgan.

bēah-hord‡, n., *ring-*H O A R D, *treasure;* gs. -es, 894; gp. -a, 921; dp. -um, 2826.

bēah-sele†, mi., *ring-hall, hall (in which rings are given)*; 1177. (*Andr.* 1657: bēag-selu, ap.)

bēah-ðegu‡, f., *receiving of a ring;* ds. -ðege, 2176. [þicgan.]

bēah-wriða‡, wk.m., *ring-band, ring, circlet;* as. -wriðan, 2018. [wrīðan.]

bealdian‡, w 2., *show oneself brave* (B O L D); pret. 3 sg. bealdode, 2177.

bealdor†, m., (prec. by gen. pl.), *prince, lord;* 2567; baldor, 2428. [Cp. ON. Baldr; rel. to OE. beald. Cf. *ZfdA.* xxxv 237 ff.]

bealo, bealu,(†), adj.wa., B A L E*ful, evil, pernicious;* dp. balwon, 977. (On the semantic development of Gmc. **balwa-*, see Weisweiler, *IF.* xli 70 ff.)

bealo, bealu,(†), n. (orig. neut. of adj.), (B A L E), *evil, misery, affliction, destruction;* ds. bealwe, 2826; gp. bealwa 909, bealewa 2082, bealuwa 281. — Cpds.: cwealm-, ealdor-, feorh-, hreþer-, lēod-, morð-, morðor-, niht-, sweord-, wīg-.

bealo-cwealm‡, m., B A L E*ful death;* 2265.

bealo-hycgende‡, adj. (pres. ptc.), *intending evil, hostile;* gp. -hycgendra, 2565.

bealo-hȳdig‡, adj., *intending evil, hostile;* 723.

bealo-nīð†, m., *pernicious enmity, wickedness;* ds. -nīð[e] (' with fierce rage '), 2714; as. -nīð, 1758; *dire affliction,* ns. -nīð, 2404.

bearhtm, m.(?), (1) *brightness;* 1766. — (2) *sound, noise;* as., 1431. [Cf. Holt. Et.]

bearm, m., *bosom, lap;* ns. foldan bearm (cp. Lat. ' gremium '), 1137; ds. bearme, 40; as. bearm, 1144, 2194, 2775, (on) bearm scipes (nacan), 35, 214, 896; *possession,* ds. bearme, 21 (n.), 2404. [beran.]

be-arn, 67, see be-irnan.

bearn, n., *child, son;* 888, 910, 1837; bearn Ecgþēowes, 529, 631, 957, 1383, 1473, 1651, 1817, 1999, 2177, 2425, si. 469, 499, *1020*, 2387; ds. bearne, 2370; as. bearn, 1546, 2121, 2619; np. bearn, 59, 1189, 1408, 2184 (Gēata ~), 2597, 3170; gp. bearna, 2433; dp. bearnum, 1074; ap. bearn: Ēotena ~, 1088, 1141; 2956; besides, plural in set (bibl.?) expressions, ' children of men ' (*Angl.* xxxv 467): ylda (yldo) bearn (np.) 70, ~ -um (dp.) 150, ~ bearn (ap.) 605; gumena bearn (np.) 878, ~ -a (gp.) 1367; niþða bearna (gp.) 1005; hæleða bearna (gp.) 2224. [beran; Sc. B A I R N.] — Cpd.: dryht-.

bearn-gebyrdo‡, wk.f. (Siev. § 267 n. 4), *child-bearing;* gs., 946. [BIRTH.]

bearu, mwa., *grove, wood;* np. bearwas, 1363.

bēatan, rd., B E A T, *strike, tramp;* pres. 3 sg. bēateð, 2265; pp. gebēaten, 2359.

be-bēodan, II, *command, order;* pret. 3 sg. bebēad, 401, 1975.
be-beorgan, III, w. refl. dat., *protect or guard oneself,* 1746; w. acc. of thing (*against*), imp. sg. bebeorh, 1758.
be-būgan, II, *encompass, surround;* pres. 3 sg. bebūgeð, 93, 1223.
be-bycgan, w 1., *sell* (on w. acc., *for*); pret. 1 sg. bebohte, 2799.
be-ceorfan(‡)+, III, w. acc. of pers. & dat. (instr.) of thing, *cut off* (*deprive by cutting*); pret. 1 sg. (hēafde) becearf, 2138; 3 sg. (∼) ∼, 1590. [C A R V E.]
bēcn, see **bēacen**.
be-cuman, IV, C O M E; pret. 3 sg. becōm, 115, 192, 2552 (w. inf.), 2992, becwōm 1254, 2116, 2365 (w. inf.); w. acc.: *befall,* pret. 3 sg. becwōm, 2883.
bed(d), nja., B E D; gs. beddes, 1791; as. bed, 140, 676; dp. beddum, 1240. — Cpds.: dēað-, hlim-, leger-, morðor-, wæl-.
be-dǣlan, w 1., w. dat. (instr.) of thing, *deprive;* pp. bedǣled, 721, 1275.
be-fǣstan, w 1., *entrust, commit, give over;* 1115.
be-feallan, rd., F A L L; pp. befeallen, w. dat. (instr.), (‡) *deprived, bereft,* 1126, 2256.
be-flēon, II, F L E E *from, escape;* ger. beflēonne, 1003.
be-fōn, rd., *seize, encompass, encircle, envelop;* pp. befongen, 976, 1451, 2009 (bi-), 2595; befangen, 1295, 2274, 2321.
be-foran, I. adv., B E F O R E, *in front;* 1412, 2497. — II. prep., w. acc., *before, into the presence of;* 1024.
bēg, see **bēag**.
be-gang, see **be-gong**.
bēgen, num., *both;* 536, 769, 2707; gm. bēga, 1124, gn. bēga 1043, 1873, 2895; dm. bām, 2196, 2660; af. bā, 1305, 2063.
be-gitan, V, G E T, *obtain;* pret. 3 pl. begēaton, 2249; *come upon, happen to, befall;* pret. 3 sg. begeat, 1068, 1146, 2230, beget 2872; opt. 3 sg. begēate, 2130.
be-gnornian‡, w 2., *lament, bemoan;* pret. 3 pl. begnornodon, 3178. (Cp. *Gen.* (*B*) 243: begrornian.)
be-gong, m., *circuit, compass, expanse, region;* as. (swegles) begong 860, 1773, (flōda) begong 1497, ∼ begang 1826, (geofenes) begang 362, (sioleða) bigong 2367.
be-gylpan‡, III, w. acc., *boast, exult;* 2006.
be-healdan, rd., *guard,* H O L D, *occupy;* pret. 3 sg. behēold, 1498; *attend to,* ([-]nytte) ∼, 494, 667; *look, observe,* ∼, 736.
be-helan, IV, *hide;* pp. beholen, 414. [Cp. Ger. hehlen.]
be-hōfian, w 2., w. gen., *have need of, require;* pres. 3 sg. behōfað, 2647. [B E H O O V E.]
be-hōn, rd., H A N G (*about with,* instr.): pp. behongen, 3139.
be-hrēosan, II, *fall;* pp. (w. dat. [instr.]), apm. behrorene, ‡*deprived,* 2762.
be-irnan, III, R U N (*into*); pret. 3 sg.: him on mōd bearn, 'came into his mind? (' occurred ' to him), 67. (Cf. *Arch.* cxxvi 355 n. 1.)
bēl, see **bǣl**.
be-lēan, VI, (*blame*); w. dat. of pers. & acc. of thing, *dissuade* or *keep from;* 511.
be-lēosan†, II, L O S E; pp. (w. dat. [instr.]) beloren, *deprived,* 1073. [See losian.]
(ge-)**belgan**, III, *enrage;* pret. opt. 3 sg. gebulge (w. dat.), *offend,*

GLOSSARY

2331; pp. gebolgen, *enraged, angry;* 2401, ðā (þæt) hē gebolgen wæs: *723*, 1539, *2220*, 2550, si. 2304; np. gebolgne, 1431. [Orig. ' swell '; cp. b(i)elg ' bag.'] See bolgen-mōd.

be-limpan(‡)+, III, w. dat., *happen, befall;* pret. 3 sg. belamp, 2468.

be-lūcan, II, LOCK *up, close;* pret. 3 sg. belēac, 1132; *protect against* (dat.), 1 sg. ∼, 1770.

be-mīðan, I, *conceal;* pret. 3 sg. bemāð, [2217]. [Cp. Ger. meiden.]

be-murnan†, III, M O U R N *over, bewail, deplore;* pret. 3 sg. bemearn, 907, 1077.

ben(n)†, fjō., *wound;* as. benne, 2724. [bana.] See wund. — Cpds.: feorh-, sex-.

bēn, fi., *petition, request, favor;* gs. -e, 428, 2284. [BOON, fr. ON. bón.]

bēna, wk.m., *petitioner, petitioning;* ∼ wesan, *ask, request:* bēna, 352, 3140; np. bēnan, 364.

benc, fi., B E N C H; 492; ds. bence, 1188, 1243, bugon þā tō bence: 327, 1013. — Cpds.: ealo-, medu-.

benc-swēg‡, mi., B E N C H-*noise, convivial noise;* 1161.

benc-þel‡, n., B E N C H-*plank*, pl. -þelu, *floor on which benches are placed* (or: *benches?*); np. 486, ap. 1239. (Cf. Heyne L 9.4.1.52.)

bend, fjō. (mi.), BOND, *fetter;* as., 1609; dp. -um, 977. [bindan]. — Cpds.: ancor-, fȳr-, hell-, hyge-, īren-, searo-, wæl-.

be-nemnan, W I., *declare;* pret. 3 sg. (āðum) benemde, 1097; *lay a curse on s.th.*(?) (cp. begalan), pret. 3 pl. benemdon, 3069.

be-nēotan†, II, *deprive of* (dat. [instr.]); (aldre) ∼, 680; pret. 3 sg. (∼) binēat, 2396.

ben-geat‡, n., *wound-opening* (- G A T E), *gash;* np. -geato, 1121.

be-niman, IV, *rob, deprive of* (dat. [instr.]); pret. 3 sg. benam, 1886.

bēodan, II, (1) *offer, tender, give;* 385; pret. 3 pl. budon, 1085; pp. boden, 2957. — (2) *announce;* bīodan, 2892. [See biddan.] — Cpds.: ā-, be-.

ge-bēodan, II, (1) *offer, show;* 603; pret. 3 sg. gebēad, 2369. — (2) *announce*, BID, *command;* gebēodan, 3110.

bēod-genēat‡, m., *table-companion;* np. -as, 343; ap. -as, 1713. [bēodan (but see *IF.* xxiii 395; Feist, *Etym. Wbch. d. got. Spr.:* biuþs); nēotan, cp. Ger. Genosse.]

bēon, bēo(ð), see eom.

beor, n., B E E R; ds. bēore, 480, 531; æt bēore, ' at the beer-drinking,' 2041. [*Beitr.* xxxv 569 ff.; *R.-L.* i 280.]

beorg, beorh, m., (1) *hill, cliff, elevated shore;* ds. beorge, 211, 3143; ap. beorgas, 222. — (2) *mound*, B A R R O W, *cave;* ns. beorh, 2241; gs. beorges, 2304, 2322, 2524, 2580, 2755, biorges, 3066; ds. beorge, 2529, 2546, 2559, 2842; as. beorh, 2299, 3097; (Bīowulfes) biorh, 2807; beorg, 3163; ap. biorgas, 2272. — Cpds.: stān-; Hrēosna-.

beorgan, III, w. dat., *preserve, save, protect;* 1293, [1372], 1445; pret. 3 pl. burgan, 2599. — Cpds.: be-, ymb-.

ge-beorgan, III, w. dat., *protect;* pret. 3 sg. gebearh 1548, gebearg 2570.

beorh, see beorg.

beorht, adj., B R I G H T, *shining, splendid, glorious, magnificent;* 1802, nsn. 570; nsm.wk. beorhta, 1177; nsn.wk. beorhte, 997; gsf. beorhtre, 158; dsf.wk. byrhtan, 1199; asm. beorhtne, 2803; dpf.

beorhtum, 3140; apm. beorhte, 231; apf. beorhte, 214, 896; apn. beorht, 2313; apm.wk. beorhtan, 1243. Supl. beorhtost, 2777. — Cpds.: sadol-, wlite-.
beorhte, adv., B R I G H T *ly;* 1517.
beorhtian, w 2., ‡ *sound clearly or loudly;* pret. 3 sg. beorhtode, 1161. [beorht; cp. meaning of -torht 2553.]
beorn, 1880, see **byrnan**.
beorn†, m., *man, hero, warrior;* 2433, biorn 2559; ds. beorne, 2260; as. beorn, 1024, 1299, 2121; np. -as, 211, 856; gp. beorna 2220, biorna 2404. — Cpd.: gūð-.
beorn-cyning‡, m., (*hero*-) K I N G; vs., 2148; ns. biorn-, [2792].
bēor-scealc‡, m., B E E R-*drinker, feaster* (cf. *A.* xlvi 233 f., l 200); gp. -a, 1240. (See scealc.)
bēor-sele(†), mi., B E E R-*hall, banquet-hall;* ds. (in, on) bēorsele, 482, 492, 1094, (∼) bīorsele, 2635.
bēor-þegu†, f., (B E E R-*taking*), *beer-drinking;* ds. -þege, 117, 617. [þicgan.]
bēot, n., *boast, promise;* as., 80, 523. [*bī-hāt, cp. hātan; Siev. § 43 n. 4.] Cf. Schü. L 7.25 i; Stefán Einarsson, *PMLA.* xlix 975 ff.
ge-bēotian, w 2., *boast, vow;* pret. 1 pl. gebēotedon, 536; 3 pl. ∼, 480.
bēot-word†, n., W O R D *of boasting;* dp. -um, 2510.
beran, IV, B E A R, *carry, wear, bring;* (w. objects denoting armor or weapons s.t. = *go*); 48, 231, 291, 1024, 1807, 1920, 2152, 2518, 2754; pres. 3 sg. byreð, 296, 448, 2055; [3 pl. berað, F. 5]; pres. opt. 1 sg. bere, 437, 1834; 1 pl. beren, 2653; pret. 3 sg. bær, 495, 711, 846, 896, 1405, 1506, 1982, 2021, 2048, 2244, 2281, 2539, 2661, 2686, 2988, 3124; 3 pl. bǣron, 213, 1635, 1889, 2365, bǣran 2850; [opt. 3 sg. bǣre, F. *20*]; pp. boren, 1192, 1647, 3135. — Cpds.: æt-, for-, on-, oþ-; helm-, sāwl-berend.
ge-beran, IV, B E A R (*child*); pp. geboren, 1703.
be-rēafian, w 2., w. dat. (instr.), B E R E A V E, *despoil, deprive;* pp. berēafod, 2746, 2825, 3018.
be-rēofan†, II, w. dat. (instr.), *deprive;* pp. asf. berofene, 2457, 2931. [Cp. be-rēafian.]
berian‡, w 1., BARE, *clear, clear away;* pret. 3 pl. beredon, 1239. [BARE fr. *barian.]
berstan, III, *break,* B U R S T (intr.); [F. 30];pret. 3 pl. burston, 760 (n.), 818; *burst open,* ∼, 1121. — Cpd.: for-.
be-scūfan, II, S H O V E, *thrust;* 184.
be-settan, w 1., S E T *about, adorn;* pret. 3 sg. besette, 1453.
be-sittan, V, *besiege;* pret. 3 sg. besæt, 2936.
be-smiþian(‡) (+), w 2., (*surround with the* S M I T H's *iron work*), *fasten;* pp. besmiþod, 775.
be-snyððan†, w 1., *deprive* (dat. [instr.], *of*); pret. 3 sg. besnyðede, 2924. [Cp. ON. snauðr ' bereft,' ' poor,' sneyða ' deprive.']
be-stȳman†, w 1., *wet;* pp. (blōde) bestȳmed, 486. [stēam (S T E A M); cp. *Rood* 62.]
be-swǣlan, w 1., *scorch, burn;* pp. beswǣled, 3041. [swelan.]
be-syrwan, w 1., *ensnare, entrap, trick;* 713; pp. besyred, *2218;* contrive, accomplish, inf. besyrwan, 942. [searu.]
ge-bētan, w 1., *improve, remedy;* pret. 2 sg. gebēttest, 1991; pret. 3 sg. (or pp. asf.?) gebētte, 830; *put right, settle* (*by punishment*), fǣhðe gebētan, 2465. [bōt.]

GLOSSARY

betera, betost, betst, see **gōd.**
be-timbran‡, w 1., *build, complete the building of;* pret. 3 pl. betimbredon, 3159. (Cp. be-wyrcan.)
bet-līc†, adj., *excellent, splendid;* nsn., 1925; asn., *780.* [Cp. betera.]
be-wægnan‡, w 1., *offer;* pp. bewægned, 1193.
be-wennan‡, w 1., *attend to, entertain;* pp. np. bewenede 1821, biwenede 2035. (See wennan.)
be-weotian, see **be-witian.**
be-werian, w 1., *protect, defend against* (dat.); pret. opt. 3 pl. beweredon, 938.
be-windan, III, W I N D *about, grasp, bind, enclose, encircle, mingle;* pret. 3 sg. bewand, 1461; pp. bewunden, 1031, 2424, 3022, 3052, 3146.
be-witian, w 2., *watch, observe, attend to, watch over;* pres. 3 pl. bewitiað, 1135; pret. 3 sg. beweotede *1796,* beweotode 2212; *perform,* pres. 3 pl. bewitigað, 1428. [Cp. be-witan, prp.; Go. witan, w 3.]
be-wyrcan, w 1., *build around, surround;* pret. 3 pl. beworhton, 3161.
bī, see **be.**
bicgan, see **bycgan.**
bid†, n., ABIDing, *halt;* as.: on bid wrecen, *brought to bay,* 2962. (Bu. 108: cp. ON. bið; Trautm., *ESt.* xliv 322: bīd.)
bīdan, I, B I D E, *wait, stay, remain, dwell;* 2308; pret. 3 sg. bād, 87, 301, 310, 1313, 2568; 3 pl. bidon, 400; — *await, wait for* (gen.); inf., 482, 528, 1268, 1494; pret. 1 sg. bād, 2736; 3 sg. ∼, 82, 709, 1882. — Cpds.: ā-, on-.
ge-bīdan, I, *await;* imp. pl. gebīde, 2529; — *wait for* (gen.); ger. gebīdanne, 2452; — *live to see, experience, live through;* w. acc.: inf., 638, 934, 1060, 1386, 2342; pret. 1 sg. gebād, 929, [F. 25]; 3 sg. ∼, 7, 264, 815, 1618, 2258, 3116; pp. gebiden, 1928; w. þæt-clause: pret. 1 sg. gebād, 1779, 3 sg. ∼, 1720, ger. gebīdanne, 2445.
biddan, V, *ask, request, entreat;* abs.: pres. 1 sg. bidde, 1231; pret. 3 sg. bæd, 29; w. gen. of thing: inf., 427, pret. 3 sg. bæd, 2282; w. acc. and inf. (understood): pret. 3 sg. bæd, 617; w. þæt-clause: pret. 1 sg. bæd, 1994, 3 sg. ∼, 3096, 3 pl. bædon, 176; cp. 427 ff. [B I D fr. blending of biddan and bēodan, see *NED.*]
bi-fōn, see **be-fōn.**
big, see **be.**
[**big**]-**folc(‡),** n., *neighboring people;* 2220. (Cp. bī-fylce, *OE. Bede* 196.1.)
bi-gong, see **be-gong.**
bil(l), n., † *sword, falchion;* bil, 1567, bill, 2777; gs. billes, 2060, 2485, 2508; ds. -e, 2359; as. bil, 1557, bill, 2621; gp. -a, 583, 1144; dp. -um, 40. [*NED.*: B I L L, sb.¹] — Cpds.: gūð-, hilde-, wīg-.
bindan, III, B I N D, *join;* pp. gebunden, 1743, 2111, apn. 871; asm.: wudu bundenne, 216; asn.: bunden golde (swurd), 1900, si. gebunden 1531, nsm.: heoru bunden, 1285 (perh. ' adorned with a gold ring '; Stjer. 25, cf. also Falk L 9.44.22). — Cpd.: on-.
ge-bindan, III, B I N D; pret. 1 sg. geband, 420.
bi-nēotan, see **be-nēotan.**
bīo(ð), see **bēon.**
bīodan, see **bēodan.**
bior-, see **bēor-.**
biorh, see **beorg.**
biorn(-), see **beorn(-).**

bis(i)gu, see bysigu.
bītan, I, *cut*, B I T E; 1454, 1523; pret. 3 sg. bāt, 742, 2578. [Cp. Lat. findere.]
bite, mi., BITE, *cut;* ds., 2060; as., 2259. — Cpd.: lāð-.
biter, adj., *sharp;* asn., 2704; dsm. wk. biteran, 1746; dpn.wk. ~, 2692; *fierce, furious;* np. bitere, 1431. [bītan; B I T T E R.]
bitre, adv., B I T T E R*ly, sorely;* 2331.
bið, see eom.
bi-wennan, see be-wennan.
blāc, adj., *shining, brilliant;* asm. -ne, 1517. [blīcan; B L A K E (North.), BLEAK.] — Cpd.: heoro-.
blæc, adj., B L A C K; nsm.wk. blaca, 1801.
blǣd, m., *power, vigor of life, glory, renown;* 18, 1124, 1703, 1761. [blāwan. Cf. *Neuphilol. Mitteilungen* xxv 109 ff.]
blǣd-āgande‡, pres. ptc. [pl.], *prosperous, glorious;* npm., 1013.
blǣd-fæst(‡), adj., *glorious;* asm. -ne, 1299.
blanca†, wk.m., (*white* or *grey?*, cp. 865) *horse;* dp. blancum, 856. [BLANK, adj., fr. Fr. (fr. OHG.).] Cf. Tupper's *Riddles,* p. 119.
blēate(‡), adv., *wretchedly, pitiably;* 2824. See wæl-blēat. [Cp. OHG. blōz, Ger. bloss.]
blīcan, I, *shine, gleam;* 222.
blīðe, adj. (i.) ja., (1) *joyful,* B L I T H E; asm. blīðne, 617. (2) *kind, gracious;* nsm. blīðe, 436. — Cpd.: un-.
blīð-heort(†), adj., B L I T H E *of* H E A R T, *cheerful;* 1802.
blōd, n., B L O O D; 1121, 1616, 1667; ds. blōde 486, 1422, 1880, ~ fāh 934, 1594, 2974; on blōde, *bloody* 847; as. blōd, 742.
blōd(e)gian(‡)+, w 2., *make*

B L O O D Y; pp. geblōdegod, 2692. [blōdig.]
blōd-fāg†, adj., B L O O D-*stained;* 2060.
blōdig, adj., B L O O D Y, *bloodstained;* dsm.wk. blōdigan, 2440; asf. blōdge, 990; asn. blōdig, 448.
blōdig-tōð‡, adj., *with* B L O O D Y (T O O T H) *teeth;* 2082.
blōd-rēow†, adj., B L O O D-*thirsty;* nsn., 1719.
blonden-feax†, adj., (*having mixed hair,* i.e.) *grey-haired;* 1791; dsm. -um, 1873; npm. -e, 1594; nsm. wk. -fexa, 2962. [blondan.]
bodian, w 2., *announce;* pret. 3 sg. bodode, 1802. [B O D E.]
bolca, wk.m., *gangway of a ship;* i.e., *passageway from the quarter-deck to the forecastle* (or *gangplank,* laid between the ship and the shore); as. bolcan, 231. (See Falk L 9.48.48; Schnepper L 9.47.23, 63; Vogel, *R.-L.* iv 112.)
bold, n., BUILD*ing, house, hall;* 997, 1925; as., 2196; gp. -a, 2326. — Cpd.: fold-.
bold-āgend(e)†, mc. (pres. ptc.) [pl.], *house*-o w*ner (-owning);* gp. -āgendra, 3112.
bolgen-mōd†, adj., *enraged;* 709, 1713. [belgan.]
bolster(‡)+, m.(?), B O L S T E R, *cushion;* dp. bolstrum, 1240. — Cpd.: hlēor-.
bona, see bana.
bon-gār‡, m., *deadly spear;* 2031.
bord, n., (B O A R D), † *shield;* 2673, [F. *29*]; as., 2524; gp. -a, 2259. — Cpds.: hilde-, wīg-.
bord-hæbbend(e)‡, mc. (pres. ptc.) [pl.], (B O A R D-H A V*ing*), *shield-bearer;* npm., 2895.
bord-hrēoða†, wk.m., *shield-covering, shield, phalanx;* ds. -hrēoðan, 2203. [Cp. hroden; Siev. xxxvi

GLOSSARY

408 f.; Keller 226; Cook, note on *Chr.* 675.]

bord-rand‡, m., *shield;* as., 2559.

bord-weal(l)†, m., ' *shield*-W A L L,' (*protecting*) *shield;* as., 2980.

bord-wudu‡, mu., *shield;* ap., 1243.

born, see **byrnan**.

bōt, f., *relief, remedy;* 281; as. -e, 909, 934; *reparation, compensation,* gs. -e, 158. [B O O T; Go. bōta: batiza, OE. bet(e)ra.]

botm, m., B O T T O M; ds. -e, 1506.

brād, adj., B R O A D, *wide, spacious;* 3157; nsn.wk. -e, 2207; asm. -[n]e, 2978; asn. brād, 1546, 3105.

brecan, IV, B R E A K; 2980; pret. 3 sg. bræc, 1511, 1567; opt. 3 sg. bræce, 1100; — *press, torment,* pret. 3 sg.: hine fyrwyt bræc, 232, 1985, 2784; — intr.: *burst forth,* inf. 2546. — Cpds.: ā-, tō-, þurh-.

ge-brecan, IV, B R E A K, *crush, destroy;* pret. 3 sg. gebræc, 2508; pp. gebrocen, 3147.

brecð(‡), f., BREAK*ing,* ‡*grief;* np.: mōdes brecða, 171.

bregdan, III, (1) *move quickly* (trans.), *draw, swing, fling;* 707; pret. 3 sg. brægd, 794, 1539; 2 pl. brugdon (w. dat. [instr.]), 514. — (2) *knit, weave;* inf. bregdon, 2167; pp. brōden (ref. to the interlocked rings of the corslet), 552, 1548, asf. brogdne, 2755. [B R A I D.] — Cpds.: ā-, on-.

ge-bregdan, III, (1) *draw* (sword); w. instr.: pret. 1 sg. gebrǣd, 1664, 3 sg. ∼, 2703; w. acc.: ∼, 2562, gebrægd 1564. — (2) *knit, weave* (see bregdan); pp. gebrōden, 1443.

brego†, m., *chief, lord* (w. gen. pl.); 609; as., 1954; vs., 427.

brego-rōf‡, adj., *very valiant* (or *famous*); 1925.

brego-stōl†, m., *princely seat, throne,* *principality;* as., 2196, 2370, 2389. (See ēþel-stōl.)

brēme, adj.ja., *famous, renowned;* 18. [*Giessener Beiträge* i 139 f.: **be-hrǣme,* cp. **hrōm, hrēmig* (?); Holt. Et.]

brenting‡, m., *ship;* ap. -as, 2807. [bront.]

brēost, n., f. (453), B R E A S T; 2176, 2331; as., 453; pl. (with sg. meaning, cf. Grimm L 6.19.15 ff.): dp. -um, 552, 2550, 2714.

brēost-gehygd†, fni., *thought of the heart;* dp. -um, 2818.

brēost-gewǣde‡, nja. (pl. used w. sg. meaning), B R E A S T-*garment, coat of mail;* np. -gewǣdu, 1211; ap. ∼, 2162.

brēost-hord†, n., (B R E A S T-H O A R D), *breast, mind, heart;* 1719; as., 2792.

brēost-net(t)†, nja., B R E A S T-N E T, *corslet;* -net, 1548.

brēost-weorðung‡, f., B R E A S T-*ornament;* as. -e, 2504.

brēost-wylm(‡)(+), mi., (B R E A S T-W E L L*ing*), *emotion;* as., 1877. [weallan.]

brēotan†, II, (*break*), *cut down, kill;* pret. 3 sg. brēat, 1713. [Cp. brytta; BRITTle.] — Cpd.: ā-.

brim(†), n., *sea, water* (*of sea, lake*); 847, 1594; gs. -es, 28, 2803; np. -u, 570. [Cp. ON. brim; Holt. Et.]

brim-clif‡, n., *sea-*C L I F F; ap. -u, 222.

brim-lād†, f., *sea-passage, voyage;* as. -e, *1051*. [līðan.]

brim-līðend(e)†, mc. (pres. ptc.) [pl.], *seafarer;* ap. -e, 568.

brim-strēam(†), m., *ocean-*S T R E A M, *sea's current, sea;* ap. -as, 1910.

brim-wīsa‡, wk.m., *sea-leader,-king;* as. -wīsan, 2930. [Cp. wīsian.]

brim-wylf‡, fjō., *she-*WOLF *of the sea*

or *lake; 1506*, 1599. (Cf. *Angl.* xxxv 253.) See grund-wyrgen.

brim-wylm‡, mi., *surge of the sea* or *lake;* 1494. [weallan.]

bringan, w 1. (III), B R I N G; 1862, 2148, 2504; pres. 1 sg. bringe, 1829; pret. 1 pl. brōhton, 1653.

ge-bringan, w 1. (III), B R I N G; pres. opt. 1 pl., 3009. (Foll. by on w. dat.; cf. Lorz 74.)

brōden, see **bregdan**.

brōden-mǣl, see **brogden-mǣl**.

brōga, wk.m., *terror, horror;* 1291, 2324, 2565; as. or ap. (cp. 483ᵇ) brōgan, 583 (n.). — Cpds.: gryre-, here-.

brogden-mǣl†, n., (*ornamented with a wavy pattern*, i.e.) *damascened sword;* 1667; brōden-, 1616. (Cp. hring-, wunden-mǣl.) [bregdan; mǣl ' mark.']

brond, m., (1) *burning, fire;* 3014; ds. -e, 2126, 2322; gp. -a, 3160. (2) *sword;* ns., 1454. [*NED*.: B R A N D, sb. I & II.] Cp. ON. brandr (Falk L 9.44.48); brand ' sword ' also: Ælfr., *Hom.* ii 510.19, and perh. *Diplom. Angl.* (ed. Thorpe) 559.24.

bront†, adj., *steep, high;* asm. -ne, 238, 568. [*Dial. D*.: B R A N T, B R E N T. Cp. ON. brattr.] (Cf. Middendorff, *Ae. Flurnamenbuch*, p. 17?)

brosnian, w 2., *decay, fall to pieces;* pres. 3 sg. brosnaδ, 2260.

brōδor, mc., B R O T H E R; 1324, 2440, 2978; gs., 2619; ds. brēþer, 1262; dp. brōδrum, 587, 1074. — Cpd.: ge-.

brūcan, II, w. gen. of object (s.t. understood), *make use of, enjoy;* 894, 1045, 2241, 2812, 3100; pres. 3 sg. brūceδ, 1062; imp. sg. brūc, 1177, 1216, 2162; pret. 1 sg. brēac, 1487; 3 sg. ~, 1953, 2097. [B R O O K.]

brūn, adj., B R O W N, *bright* (sword); 2578. (See Bu.Tid. 67; Mead L 7.29.193 f.; Falk L 9.44.5.) [Cp. BURNish (fr. OFr.).]

brūn-ecg†, adj., *with bright* (B R O W N) E D G E; asn., 1546.

brūn-fāg‡, adj., *of a* B R O W N *color, shining;* asm. -ne, 2615. (Cf. Stjer. 2 & n.)

brȳd, fi., B R I D E; 2031; *wife;* as. brȳd, 2930; †*woman;* ap. -e, 2956. [Cf. Braune, *Beitr.* xxxii 6 ff., 30 ff., 559 ff.]

brȳd-būr(‡)+, m., *woman's apartment;* ds. -e, 921. [B R I D E; B O W E R.]

bryne-lēoma‡, wk.m., *gleam of fire;* 2313. [byrnan.]

bryne-wylm†, mi., *surge of fire;* dp. -um, 2326.

brytnian, w 2., *deal out, dispense;* pret. 3 sg. brytnade, 2383. [Cp. brytta; brēotan.]

brytta(†), wk.m., *distributor, dispenser;* (sinces) brytta, 607, vs. 1170, 2071; as. (bēaga) bryttan, 35, 352, 1487, (sinces) ~, 1922. [brēotan.]

bryttian, w 2., *distribute, dispense;* pres. 3 sg. bryttaδ, 1726.

būan, rd., w 3., (1) *dwell;* būon, 2842. (2) *dwell in, inhabit;* būan, 3065. — Cpds.: ceaster-, feor-, fold-, grund-, land-būend.

ge-būan, rd., (ingressive,) *take possession of, settle in;* pp. gebūn, 117.

būgan, II, B O W (intr.); (1) *sink, fall;* 2918, 2974. (2) *bow down, rest;* pres. 3 sg. būgeδ, 2031. (3) *bend, sit down;* pret. 3 pl. bugon, 327, 1013. (4) *turn, flee;* pret. 3 sg. bēah, 2956; 3 pl. bugon, 2598. — Cpds.: ā-, be-; wōh-bogen.

ge-būgan, II, B O W (intr.); (1) *sink, fall;* pret. 3 sg. gebēah, 1540, 2980. (2) *coil (oneself together);* pret. 3 sg. ~ (tōsomne), 2567; pp. gebogen, 2569. (3) w. acc.: *lie down on;* pret. 3 sg. gebēah 690, gebēag 1241.

bunden-heord‡, adj., *with hair* B O U N D *up* (ref. to an old woman; in contrast with the flowing hair of young women); wk.f. -e, *3151*. (Cf. Kauffmann L 9.26. 451.) [*Beibl.* xii 198, xiii 233 f.]

bunden-stefna‡, wk.m., *ship with* B O U N D *prow;* 1910. ('Bound,' i.e. 'properly joined,' cp. 216; or, possibly, 'ornamented' w. shields [see Figure 1]?) [S T E M.]

bune, wk.f., *cup, drinking vessel;* np. bunan, 3047; ap. ~, 2775.

būr, m., *chamber, apartment, dwelling;* ds. -e, 1310, 2455 (n.); dp. -um, 140. [B O W E R; cp. būan.] — Cpd.: brȳd-.

burh, fc., *fortified place, castle, palace, town;* ds. byrig, 1199; as. burh, 523; dp. (sg. meaning): (on, in) burgum, 53, 2433, si. 1968, 2452. [B O R O U G H, B U R G (H).] — Cpds.: frēo-, freoðo-, hēa-, hlēo-, hord-, lēod-, mǣg-.

burh-loca†, wk.m., *castle enclosure* (LOCK); ds. -locan, 1928.

burh-stede†, mi., *castle court;* as., 2265. [S T E A D.]

burh-wela‡, wk.m., WEAL*th of a castle (town);* gs. -welan, 3100. [W E A L.]

burne, wk.f., *stream;* gs. -an, 2546. [B O U R N, B U R N; Ger. Brunnen.]

būton (būtan), I. prep., w. dat., *except*, B U T; būton, 73, 705. — II. conj.; (1) w. subjunct.: *unless, if — not;* 966 (būtan). (2) w. ind.: *except that, but that;* 1560. (3) without verb (after negat.); *except;* 657, 879; (ne . . . mā . . .) būton, (*not . . . more . . .) than,* 1614.

bycgan, w I., B U Y, *pay for;* bicgan, 1305. — Cpd.: be-.

ge-bycgan, w I., B U Y, *pay for, obtain;* pret. 3 sg. gebohte, 973, 2481; pp. npm. gebohte, *3014*.

byldan, w I., *encourage, cheer;* 1094. [beald.]

bȳme, wk.f., *trumpet;* as. bȳman, 2943. [bēam; *NED.*: B E M E, sb. (obs.)]

byre†, mi., *son;* 2053, 2445, 2621, 2907, 3110; np., 1188; *youth, boy:* ap., 2018. [beran; cp. Go. baúr.]

byrele, mi., *cup*BEAR*er;* np. byrelas, 1161. [beran; *Beitr.* xxx 138.]

byreð, see **beran**.

byrgan, w I., *taste, eat;* byrgean, 448. [Cp. ON. bergja.]

byrht, see **beorht**.

byrig, see **burh**.

byrnan, III, B U R N (intr.); [pres. 3 pl. byrnað, F. 1, 4]; pres. ptc. byrnende, 2272, 2569; pret. 3 sg. beorn, 1880 (Lang. § 13). [B U R N fr. fusion of beornan (byrnan) and bærnan.] — Cpds.: for-; un-byrnende.

ge-byrnan(‡)(+), III, B U R N (intr.), *be consumed;* pret. 3 sg. gebarn, 2697.

byrne, wk.f., *corslet, coat of mail;* 405, 1245, 1629, 2660, 2673, [F. 44]; gs. byrnan, 2260; ds. ~, 2704; as. ~, 1022, 1291, 2153, 2524, 2615, 2621, 2812, 2868; np. ~, 327; dp. byrnum, 40, 238, 2529, 3140. (Note: byrnan hring 2260, hringed byrne 1245, si. 2615; see hring. Cf. Lehmann L 9.40; Keller 93 ff., 255 ff.; Stjer. 34, 258 f.) [*Beitr.* xxx 271; *IF.* xxiii 390 ff. Cp. BYRNIE.] —

Cpds.: gūð-, heaðo-, here-, īren-, īsern-.

byrn-wiga†, wk.m., *mailed warrior;* 2918.

bysigu, wk.f., *affliction, distress, trouble, care, occupation;* gs. bisigu, 281; dp. bisgum, 1743, bysigum, 2580. [B U S I ness.]

byð, see eom.

bȳwan(‡), w 1., *polish, adorn, prepare;* 2257. [Holt. Et.]

camp, m.n., *battle, fight;* ds. -e, *2505.* [Fr. Lat. campus.]

can, see cunnan.

candel, f., C A N D L E, *light;* 1572 (rodores ∼, ' sun,' cf. *Angl.* xxxv 122 f.). [Fr. Lat. candela.] — Cpd.: woruld-.

caru, see cearu.

ceald, adj., C O L D; apm. -e, 1261; supl. nsn. -ost, 546; *painful, pernicious, evil*, dpm. -um, 2396. — Cpd.: morgen-.

cēap, m., *bargain, purchase;* 2415; ds. (heardan) cēape, 2482 (*price*). [C H A P (man), C H E A P; fr. Lat. caupo.]

(ge-)cēapian, w 2., *trade, purchase;* pp. gecēapod, 3012.

cearian, w 2., C A R E, *be anxious;* pres. 3 sg. cearað, 1536.

cear-sīð‡, m., *expedition that brings sorrow* (C A R E); dp. -um, 2396.

cearu, f., C A R E, *sorrow, grief;* 1303; as. care, [3171]. — Cpds.: aldor-, gūð-, mǣl-, mōd-.

cear-wælm, -wylm,†, mi., (C A R E-W E L L*ing*), *seething of sorrow;* np. -wylmas, 282; dp. -wælmum, 2066.

ceaster-būend‡, mc. (pres. ptc.) [pl.], *town-dweller, castle-dweller;* dp. -um, 768. [Lat. castra.]

cempa, wk.m., CHAMPION, *warrior;* 1312, 1551, 1585, 2078; vs. ∼, 1761; ds. cempan, 1948, 2044, 2502, 2626; [np. ∼, F. 14]; ap. ∼, 206. [camp; cp. MnE. champion, fr. OFr. (fr. late Lat. campio).] Cf. Keller L 4.92 g. — Cpd.: fēþe-.

cēne, adj.ja., *bold, brave;* [dsm. (collect.) (or dpm.) cēnum, F. *29*]; gpm. cēnra, 768; supl. apm. cēnoste, 206. [K E E N; Ger. kühn.] — Cpds.: dǣd-, gār-.

cennan, w 1., *declare, show;* imp. sg. cen, 1219. [cunnan; Go. kannjan, ON. kenna; Ger. kennen.]

cennan, w 1., *bring forth, bear* (child); pret. 3 sg. cende, 943; pp. cenned, 12. [Cp. cyn(n).] (On the two verbs cennan, see F. R. Schröder, *Beitr.* xliii 495 ff.) — Cpd.: ā-.

cēnðu‡, f., *boldness;* as., 2696.

cēol, m., *ship;* 1912; gs. -es, 1806; as. cēol, 38, 238. [*NED.*: KEEL, sb.²]

ceorl, m., *man* (orig. *freeman*); (snotor) ∼, 908; ds. (gomelum) -e, 2444, (ealdum) -e, 2972 (ref. to a king); np. (snotere) -as, 202, 416, 1591. [C H U R L.]

cēosan, cīosan, II, C H O O S E, *taste, try;* cīosan, 2376; pret. opt. 3 sg. cure, 2818 (cf. Lorz 47, *Angl.* xxxv 469).

ge-cēosan, II, C H O O S E; *obtain;* imp. sg. gecēos, 1759; ger. gecēosenne, 1851; pret. 3 sg. gecēas, 1201, 2469, 2638; pp. apm. gecorone, 206.

clam(m), clom(m), m., *grasp, grip, clasp;* dp. clammum, 963, 1335, clommum 1502.

clif, n., C L I F F; ap. -u, 1911.— Cpds.: brim-, ecg-, holm-, stān-, weal-.

ge-cnāwan, rd., *recognize;* 2047. [K N O W.]

cniht-wesende(†), adj. (pres. ptc.), *being a boy;* as., 372; np., 535.

(So *OE. Bede* 142.8, 188.1.)
cnyht, m., *boy;* dp. -um, 1219. [K N I G H T.]
cnyssan, w 1., *dash against, strike, smite;* pret. 3(1?) pl. cnysedan, 1328.
cōl, adj., C O O L; comp. np. -ran, 282, 2066.
collen-ferhð†, adj., *bold of spirit, excited;* 1806; collenferð, 2785.
con, const, see **cunnan.**
corðer†, n., *troop, band, host;* ds. corþre 1153, corðre 3121.
costian, w 2., w. gen., *try, make trial of;* pret. 3 sg. costode, 2084. [cēosan; cp. OHG. costōn, Ger. kosten, Lat. gustare.]
cræft, m., (1) *strength, power;* 1283; ds. -e, 982, 1219, 2181 (*ability,* n.), 2360; as. cræft, 418, 699, 2696. — (2) *skill, cunning,* C R A F T, *device;* ds. -e, 2219; dyrnum (-an) ∼, 2168, 2290 (almost = adv. phrase, 'secretly'); dp. -um, 2088. — Cpds.: gūð-, leoðo-, mægen-, nearo-, wīg-.
cræftig, adj., *strong, powerful;* 1466, 1962. — Cpds.: ēacen-, lagu-, wīg-.
ge-cranc, see **ge-cringan.**
cringan†, III, *fall (in battle), die;* pret. 3 pl. (on wæle) crungon, 1113; opt. 1 sg. (on wæl) crunge, 635. [CRINGE (orig. causative deriv.).]
ge-cringan(†), III, *fall (in battle), die;* pret. 3 sg. gecranc (cf. Lang. § 19.1), 1209; gecrang, 1337, [F. 31]; gecrong, 1568, 2505.
cuma, wk.m., C O M*er, visitor;* 1806; np. cuman, 244 (?, see note). — Cpds.: cwealm-, wil-.
cuman, IV, C O M E; (the pret. freq. w. inf. (predicative [as in 2914 f.] or final [as in 268], see Callaway, *The Infinitive in Ags.* (1913), pp. 89 ff., 132 ff.); used w. adv. of motion: hēr 244, 376, feorran 361, 430, 825, 1819, on weg 1382, þonan 2359, from 2556, ūt 3106; w. eft: 281, 1869; of morning, evening, etc.: 569, 731; 1077, 2103, 2124; 1235, 2303; 1133; 2646; 2058;) — inf., 244, 281, 1869; pres. 2 sg. cymest, 1382; 3 sg. cymeð, 2058; opt. 3 sg. cume, 23; 1 pl. cymen, 3106; pret. 1 sg. cwōm, 419, 2009, cōm 430; 3 sg. cwōm, 1162, 1235, 1338, 1774, 1888, 1973, 2073, 2124, 2188, 2303, 2404, 2556, 2669, 2914, cōm 569, 702, 710, 720, 825, 1077, 1133, 1279, 1506, 1600, 1623, 1644, 1802, 2103, 2359, 2944; 1 pl. cwōmon, 268; 2 pl. ∼, 239; 3 pl. ∼, 324, cwōman 650, cōmon 1640; opt. 3 sg. cwōme 731, cōme 1597; pp. cumen 376, 2646, np. (feorran) cumene 361, 1819. — Cpds.: be-, ofer-.
cumbol†, n., *banner, standard;* gs. cumbles, 2505.
cunnan, prp., *know;* (1) w. acc. or clause; pres. 1 sg. can, 1180; 2 sg. const, 1377; 3 sg. can, 392, con 1739, 2062; 3 pl. cunnon, 162, 1355; opt. 2 sg. cunne, 2070; pret. 1 sg. cūðe, 372; 3 sg. ∼, 359, 2012, 3067; 3 pl. cūðon, 119, 180, 418, 1233. — (2) w. inf.: *know how to, be able to;* pres. 3 sg. con, 1746; 3 pl. cunnon, 50; pret. 3 sg. cūþe, 90, 1445, 2372 (opt.?); 3 pl. cūþon, 182. [C A N, C O N; Ger. können.]
cunnian, w 2., w. gen. or acc., *try, make trial of, tempt, explore;* 1426, 1444, 2045; pret. 3 sg. cunnode, 1500; 2 pl. cunnedon, 508.
cure, see **cēosan.**
cūð, adj., *known, well known;* 705, 2178; (undyrne) ∼, 150, 410; (wīde) ∼, 2135, 2923, [F. 25]; asf.

cūþe, 1303, 1634; npm. ~, 867; npf. ~, 1145; apm. ~, 1912. [cunnan; Go. kunþs, Ger. kund.] — Cpds.: un-, wīd-.

cūð-līce, adv., *openly, familiarly;* comp. -līcor, 244.

cwealm, m., *death, killing;* as., 107, *3149.* [cwelan.] — Cpds.: bealo-, dēað-, gār-.

cwealm-bealu‡, nwa., *death-evil* (-B A L E), *death;* as., 1940.

cwealm-cuma‡, wk.m., *murderous visitor;* as. -cuman, 792.

cweccan, w 1., *shake, brandish;* pret. 3 sg. cwehte, 235. [Cp. QUAKE, fr. cwacian.]

cwellan, w 1., *kill;* pret. 2 sg. cwealdest, 1334. [Q U E L L; cp. cwelan, cwalu; Ger. quälen.] — Cpd.: ā-.

cwēn, fi., (1) *wife (of a king);* 62, 613, 923; as., 665. (2) Q U E E N, *lady;* ns., 623, 1153, 1932, 2016.— Cpd.: folc-.

cwēn-līc‡, adj., Q U E E N L Y, *ladylike;* 1940.

cweðan, v, *speak, say;* (1) abs.; pres. 3 sg. cwið, 2041. — (2) w. acc.; pret. 3 sg. (word) cwæð, 315, si. 2246, 2662. — (3) w. subord. clause; (asyndetic:) pret. 3 sg. cwæð, 199, 1810, 2939; [cf. cweþ, F. 24]; (introd. by þæt:) ~, 92, 1894, 2158, 3 pl. cwǣdon, 3180. [Q U O T H; cp. be-Q U E A T H.] Cf. *ZfdA.* xlvi 263 ff. — Cpd.: ā-.

ge-cweðan, v, *say;* pret. 2 sg. gecwǣde, 2664; 3 sg. gecwæð, 857, 874, 987; *agree* (*MPh.* iii 453; cp. Go. ga-qiþan, ga-qiss): 1 pl. gewǣdon, 535.

cwic(o), adj.u., *living, alive;* cwico, 3093; gsn. cwices, 2314; asm. cwicne, 792, 2785; npn. cwice, 98. [Q U I C K.]

cwīðan, w 1., w. acc., *bewail, lament, mourn for;* 2112, 3171.

cyme, mi., COM*ing;* np., 257. — Cpd.: eft-.

cymen, see cuman.

cȳm-līce(†), adv., *beautifully, splendidly, nobly;* comp. -līcor, 38. [Cp. OHG. kūmig 'infirm,' Ger. kaum; ('weak'>'delicate,' 'fine.') MnE. C O M E L Y (cf. *NED.*; Luick § 397 n. 2).]

cyn(n), nja., *race, people, family;* cyn, 461; gs. cynnes, 701, 712, 735, 883, 1058, 1729, 2008, 2234, 2354, 2813; ds. cynne, 107, 810, 914, 1725, 2885; as. cyn, 421, 1093, 1690; gp. cynna, 98. (Note: manna cynne(s), 701, 712, 735, 810, 914, 1725, si. 1058.) [K I N; Go. kuni.] — Cpds.: eormen-, feorh-, fīfel-, frum-, gum-, mon-, wyrm-.

cyn(n), (adj. &) nja., *proper proceeding, etiquette, courtesy;* gp. cynna, 613. See cyn(n) (above), ge-cynde; cp. cunnan.

cyne-dōm, m., *royal power;* as., 2376. [cyn(n).]

cyning, m., K I N G; 11, 619 (kyning), 863, 920, 1010, 1153, 1306, 1870, 1885, 1925, 2110, 2191, 2209, 2390, 2417, 2702, 2980, [F. 2]; (only once w. gen.: Gēata) ~, 2356, (Hiorogār) ~, 2158, (Hrēðel) ~, 2430; gs. cyninges, 867, 1210, 2912, cyniges 3121; ds. cyninge, 3093; as. cyning, 1851, 2396, kyning 3171. [cyn(n).] — Cpds.: beorn-, eorð-, folc-, gūð-, hēah-, lēod-, sǣ-, sōð-, þēod-, worold-, wuldur-; Frēs-.

cyning-bald‡, adj., '*royally brave,*' *very brave;* npm. -e, 1634.

Kyning-wuldor‡, n., *the glory of* K I N G *s* (=cyninga wuldor), i.e., *the most glorious of kings (God);*

GLOSSARY

665. (Cf. *MPh.* iii 454, *Angl.*
xxxv 125.}
ge-cȳpan(†), w 1., *buy;* 2496. [cēap.]
ge-cyssan, w 1., K I S S; pret. 3 sg.
gecyste, 1870.
cyst, f.(m.)i., *choice; the best (of its
class)*, w. gen. pl.: 802, 1232, 1559,
1697; as. ~, 673; *good quality, excellence,* dp. -um, 867, 923. [cēo-
san.] — Cpds.: gum-, hilde-.
cȳðan, w 1., *make known, show;*
1940, 2695; imp. sg. cȳð, 659; pp.
gecȳþed, 700, *(well known:)* 923,
w. dat., 262, 349. [cūð.]
ge-cȳðan, w 1., *make known, announce;* 354; ger. gecȳðanne, 257;
pp. gecȳðed, 1971, 2324. (Cf.
Lorz 48.)

dǣd, fi., D E E D, *action, doing;* as.
dǣd, 585, 940, 2890, dǣde, 889;
gp. dǣda, 181, 479, 2454 (n.),
2646, 2838; dp. dǣdum, 954, 1227,
2059, 2178, 2436, 2467, 2666,
2710, 2858, 2902, 3096; ap. dǣda,
195. — Cpds.: ellen-, fyren-, lof-.
dǣd-cēne‡, adj.ja., *daring in*
D E E D S; 1645.
dǣd-fruma†, wk.m., *doer of (evil)*
D E E D S; 2090.
dǣd-hata‡, wk.m., *one who shows his
H A T red by D E E D S, persecutor;*
275. (Cp. 2466 f.)
dæg, m., D A Y; 485, 731, 2306, 2646;
gs. dæges, 1495, 1600, 2320, adv.:
by day, 1935, 2269; ds.: on þǣm
dæge (*time*) þysses līfes, 197, 790,
806; as. dæg, 2115, 2399, 2894,
3069 (dōmes dæg); dp. dagum,
3159; [ap. dagas, F. 41]. — Cpds.:
ǣr-, dēað-, ealdor-, ende-, fyrn-,
gēar-, hearm-, lǣn-, līf-, swylt-,
win-.
dæg-hwīl‡, f., D A Y -W H I L E, *day;*
ap. -a, 2726.

dæg-rīm†, n., *number of* D A Y S;
823.
dǣl, mi., *part, portion, share, measure, a (great)* D E A L (e.g., oferhygda dǣl 1740 'great arrogance'); 1740, 2843; as., 621,
1150, 1752, 2028, 2068, 2245,
3127; ap. (worolde) dǣlas, *regions,*
1732 (cp. Lat. 'partes,' *Arch.*
cxxvi 354; *Angl.* xxxv 477 n. 4).
dǣlan, w 1., D E A L, *distribute, dispense;* 1970; pres. 3 sg. dǣleþ,
1756; pret. 3 sg. dǣlde, 80, 1686;
share with (wið): pres. opt. 3 sg.
eofoðo dǣle ('fight'), 2534. —
Cpd.: be-.
ge-dǣlan, w 1., *distribute;* 71; *part,
sever* (wið, *from*); 2422; pret. opt.
3 sg. gedǣlde, 731.
daroð†, m., *javelin;* dp. dareðum,
2848. [DART, fr. OFr. (fr. Ger.).
Cf. Falk L 9.44.74.]
dēad, adj., D E A D; 467, 1323, 2372;
asm. -ne, 1309.
ge-dēaf, see **ge-dūfan**.
*****dēagan‡**, rd., *conceal (be con-
cealed?);* pret. 3 sg. dēog, 850
(n.). [See dēogol.]
dēah, see **dugan**.
deal(l)†, adj., *proud, famous;* npm.
dealle, 494.
dear, dearst, see **durran**.
dēað, m., D E A T H; 441, 447, 488,
1491, 1768, 2119, 2236, 2728,
2890; gs. -es, 2269, 2454; ds. -e,
1388, 1589, 2843, 3045; as. dēað,
2168; dēoð (Lang. § 16.2), *1278.*
— Cpds.: gūð-, wæl-, wundor-.
dēað-bed(d)‡, nja., D E A T H-B E D;
ds. -bedde, 2901. (Cf. *Angl.* xxxv
465.)
dēað-cwalu†, f., D E A T H, *destruction;* dp. -cwalum, 1712. [cwelan.]
dēað-cwealm‡, m., D E A T H,
slaughter; as. 1670. [cwelan.]

déað-dæg(†), m., D E A T H-D A Y; ds. -e, 187, 885.

déað-fǣge‡, adj.ja., *doomed to* D E A T H, *dead;* 850.

déað-scua(†), wk.m., D E A T H-*shadow;* 160 (n.).

déað-wērig‡, adj., (D E A T H-W E A R Y), *dead;* asm. -ne, 2125.

déað-wīc‡, n., D E A T H-*place;* as. (p.?), 1275.

dēman, w I., *judge;* — (1) *adjudge, assign;* pres. opt. 3 sg. dēme, 687. (2) *express a (favorable) opinion, appraise, praise;* pret. 3 pl. dēmdon, 3174. [D E E M.]

dēmend, mc. (pres. ptc.), *judge;* as. Dēmend, 181.

den(n)(‡)+, nja., D E N, *lair;* gs. dennes, 3045; as. denn, 2759.

dēofol, m.n., D E V I L, *demon;* gs. dēofles, 2088; gp. dēofla, 756, 1680. [Fr. Lat. (Gr.) diabolus.]

dēog, see dēagan.

dēogol, adj., *secret, hidden, mysterious;* 275; asn. dȳgel, 1357.

dēop, adj., D E E P; asn., 509, 1904.

dēop, n., D E E P; *hollow passage;* 2549.

dēope, adv., D E E P *ly, solemnly;* dīope, 3069.

dēor†, adj., *brave, bold, fierce;* 1933); dīor, 2090. [*NED.:* D E A R (D E R E), a.² (obs.)] — Cpds.: heaðo-, hilde-.

deorc, adj., D A R K; 160, 1790; dpf. -um, 275, 2211.

dēore, adj.ja., D E A R, *precious, excellent, beloved;* nsf. (wk.?) dīore, 1949; gsf. dēorre, 488; dsm. dēorum, 1528, 1879; dsn.wk. dēoran, 561; asn. dēore 2254, dȳre 2050, 2306; npn. dȳre 3048; apm. dēore 2236, dȳre 3131. — Supl. asm. dēorestan, 1309.

dēor-līc‡, adj., *bold;* asf. -e, 585.

dēoð, see dēað.

dēð, see dōn.

ge-dīgan, w I., *pass through safely, survive, endure;* 2291; gedȳgan, 2531, 2549; pres. 2 sg. (aldre) gedīgest, 661; 3 sg. gedīgeð, 300; pret. 1 sg. (fēore) gedīgde, 578, (ealdre) ~, 1655; 3 sg. ~, 2350, 2543.

dīope, see dēope.

dīor, see dēor.

dīore, see dēore.

disc(‡)+, m., D I S H, *plate;* np. -as, 3048; ap. ~, 2775. [Fr. Lat. (Gr.) discus.]

dōgor, n. (Siev. §§ 288 f.), *day;* gs. dōgores, 219, 605; d.(i.)s. dōgor, 1395, dōgore 1797, 2573; gp. dōgora 88, dōgera 823, dōgra 1090; dp. (ufaran) dōgrum, 2200, 2392. [Cp. dæg.] — Cpd.: ende-.

dōgor-gerīm†, n., *number of days;* gs. -es, 2728. Cp. dæg-rīm.

dohte(st), see dugan.

dohtor, fc., D A U G H T E R; 1076, 1929, 1981, 2020, 2174; as. ~, 375, 2997.

dol-gilp‡, n.(m.), *foolish boasting, foolhardiness;* ds. -e, 509. See dol-līc.

dol-līc, adj., *foolhardy, audacious, daring;* gpf. -ra, 2646. [Cp. DULL; Ger. toll.]

dol-sceaða‡, wk.m., *mad ravager, desperate foe;* as. -sceaðan, 479. See dol-līc.

dōm, m., (1) D O O M, *judgment, decree, authority;* 2858; gs. -es, 978, 3069 (~ dæg); ds. -e, 441, 1098; as. dōm, 2964; *discretion, choice;* ds. (selfes) dōme, 895, 2776; as. (sylfes) dōm, 2147. — (2) *glory;* 885, [954], 1528; gs. -es, 1388; ds. -e, 1470, 1645, 1720, 2179; as. dōm, 1491, 2666, 2820. (Cf. Grønbech L 9.24. iii 167.) — Cpds.: cyne-, wīs-.

dōm-lēas†, adj., *inglorious;* asf.wk. -an, 2890.

dōn, anv., (1) *absol.*: D O, *act;* pres. 3 pl. dōð, 1231. — (2) [cp. Gr. τίθημι] *place, put* (w. adv. or prep. phrase); inf. dôn, 1116; pret. 3 sg. dyde, 671, 1144, 2809; 3 pl. dydon, 3070, 3163. — (3) *do (repres. a preceding verb);* inf. (swā sceal man) dôn, 1172, 1534, si. 2166; pres. 3 sg. (swā hē nū gīt) dêð, 1058, si. 1134, si. 2859, dēð 2470; pret. 1 sg. dyde, 1381, 1824, 2521; 2 sg. dydest, 1676; 3 sg. dyde, 444, 956, 1891; 3 pl. dydon, 44, 1238, 1828. — (4) *make* (much, nothing) *of, consider;* pret. 3 sg. dyde, 2348.

ge-dōn, anv., (1) *make, render;* 2186 (n.); pres. 3 sg. gedēð, 1732. — (2) *place, put;* inf., 2090.

dorste, see durran.

draca, wk.m., DRAGON; 892, 2211, [F. 3]; gs. dracan, 2088, 2290, 2549; as. ∼, 2402, 3131. [Fr. Lat. draco; *NED.*: D R A K E[1]; dragon fr. OFr., fr. Lat.] — Cpds.: eorð-, fȳr-, līg-, nīð-, sǣ-. — See wyrm.

drēam, m., *joy, bliss, rejoicing, mirth;* 497; ds. -e, 1275; as. drēam, 88; gp. -a, 850; dp. -um, 99, 721. [See *NED.*: D R E A M, sb.[1,2] Cf. *PMLA.* xlvi 80 ff.] — Cpds.: glēo-, gum-, medu-, mon-, sele-.

drēam-healdende‡, adj. (pres. ptc.), *joyful, blessed;* 1227. (Cf. *MPh.* iii 262.)

drēam-lēas†, adj., *joy*L E S S; 1720.

drēfan, w 1., *stir up, make turbid;* 1904; pp. (of gedrēfan?) gedrēfed, 1417.

drēogan, II, (1) *act, bear oneself;* pret. 3 sg. drēah, 2179. — (2) *perform, be engaged in* (s.t. in periphrasis for plain verb); inf., 1470; pret. 3 sg. (sundnytte) drēah ('swam'), 2360; 3 pl. drugon, 1858, (gewin) ∼ ('fought'), 798, (sīð) ∼ ('journeyed'), 1966. — (3) *experience, pass through;* pp. gedrogen, 2726; *enjoy,* imp. sg. drēoh, 1782; *endure, suffer;* inf., 589; pret. 1 sg. drēah, 422; 3 sg. ∼, 131; 3 pl. drugon, 15, 831. [D R E E (Sc., arch.).] — Cpd.: ā-.

drēor†, m. or n., *dripping blood;* ds. -e, 447. [drēosan.] — Cpds.: heoro-, sāwul-, wæl-.

drēor-fāh‡, adj., *stained with gore;* 485.

drēorig, adj.,† *bloody, gory;* 1417; asm. drīorigne, 2789. [D R E A R Y.] — Cpd.: heoro-.

ge-drēosan(†), II, *fall, decline;* 2666; pres. 3 sg. gedrēoseð, 1754.

drepan, V, (IV), *strike, hit;* pret. 1 sg. drep, 2880; pp. drepen 1745, dropen 2981. [Cp. Ger. treffen.]

drepe†, mi., *blow;* as., 1589.

drīfan, I, D R I V E; 1130; pres. 3 pl. drīfað, 2808. — Cpd.: tō-.

driht-, see dryht-.

drihten, see dryhten.

drincan, III, D R I N K; abs.; pret. 3 pl. druncon, 1648; w. acc.: pret. 3 sg. dranc, 742; 3 pl. druncon, 1233; — pp. druncen, *flushed with drink;* abs.: npm. druncne, 1231; apm. ∼, 2179; w. dat. (instr.): druncen, 531, 1467; npm. druncne, 480. — Cpd.: ealo-drincend(e).

drinc-fæt, see drync-fæt.

drīorig, see drēorig.

drohtoð, m., *way of life, course;* 756. [drēogan.]

dropen, see drepan.

drūsian†, w 2., *stagnate;* pret. 3 sg. drūsade, 1630. (Cf. Sievers, *ZfdPh.* xxi 365; Earle: "sullenly the Mere subsided.") [D R O W S E, cp. OHG. trūrēn; OE. drēosan.]

dryht-bearn‡, n., *noble child;* np., 2035 (n.).
dryhten, m., (1) *lord (retainers' chief), prince* (mostly w. gen. pl.: Gēata [8 times], etc.); 1484 2338, 2402, 2560, 2576, 2901, 2991, drihten 1050, 2186; ds. dryhtne, 2483, 2753; as. dryhten, 1831, 2789; vs. ~, 1824, 2000 (~ Higelāc). — (2) *Lord (God);* ns. Dryhten, 686, 696; Drihten, 108, 1554, 1841; gs. Dryhtnes 441, Drihtnes 940; ds. (ēcean) Dryhtne, 1692, 1779, 2330, 2796; Drihtne, 1398; as. Drihten, 181 (~ God), 187. — Cpds.: frēa-, frēo-, gum-, mon-, sige-, wine-.
dryht-guma, wk.m., †*retainer, warrior, man;* ds. drihtguman, 1388; vs. dryhtguma, 1768; np. drihtguman 99, dryhtguman 1231; dp. dryhtgumum, 1790.
dryht-līc(†), adj., *noble, lordly, splendid;* nsn., 892; asn.wk. drihtlīce, 1158; [npm. ~, F. 14].
dryht-māðum‡, m., *noble treasure, splendid jewel;* gp. dryhtmāðma, 2843.
dryht-scype†, mi., *valor, bravery;* as. driht-, 1470.
dryht-sele‡, mi., *splendid hall* (orig. *retainers' hall*); 767; drihtsele, 485; as. dryhtsele, 2320.
dryht-sib(b)‡, fjō., *peace, alliance;* gs. dryhtsibbe, 2068.
drync-fæt(‡)+, n., DRINK*ing-vessel, cup;* as., 2254, drincfæt 2306. [V A T; see hioro-drync.]
drysmian(‡), w 2., *become gloomy;* pres. 3 sg. drysmaþ, 1375. (Cp. *Ex.* 40?) [Holt. Et.]
ge-dūfan, II, *plunge in, sink in;* pret. 3 sg. gedēaf, 2700. [DIVE fr. deriv. dȳfan.] — Cpd.: þurh-dūfan.
dugan, prp., *avail, be good, be strong;* pres. 3 sg. dēah, 369, 573, 1839; opt. 3 sg. duge, 589, 1660, 2031; pret. opt. 2 sg. dohte, 526; — w. dat., *deal well by, treat well;* pret. 2 sg. dohtest, 1821; 3 sg. dohte, 1344.
duguð, f. (orig. fi.), (1) *body of (noble* or *tried) retainers, host;* 498, 1790, 2254; gs. duguðe, 359, 488, 2238, 2658; duguþe (ond geogoþe): 160, 621, 1674; ds. duguðe, 2020 ('*old retainers*'), dugoðe, 2920, 2945; np. duguða, 2035; dp. dugeðum, 2501(n.). — (2) *power, excellence, manhood, glory;* dp. (semi-adv.) duguðum, 3174 ('praised highly'). [dugan; cp. Ger. Tugend.]
*****durran**, prp., D A R E (in negat., condit., & relat. clauses); pres. 2 sg. dearst, 527; 3 sg. dear, 684; opt. 2 sg. dyrre, 1379; pret. 3 sg. dorste, 1462, 1468, 1933, 2735; 3 pl. dorston, 2848.
duru, fu., D O O R; 721; ds. dura, [389], [F. 14]; as. duru, [F. 23]; [dp. durum (sg. meaning), F. 16, 20; ap. duru, F. 42]. [OE. duru & dor > D O O R.]
dwellan, w 1., *mislead, hinder, stand in one's way;* pres. 3 sg. dweleð, 1735. [D W E L L.]
dyde, dydon, see **dōn**.
ge-dȳgan, see **ge-dīgan**.
dȳgel, see **dēogol**.
dyhtig(†), adj., *strong, good;* 1287. [dugan; DOUGHTY, fr. dohtig.]
dynnan, w 1., *resound;* pret. 3 sg. dynede, 767, 1317, 2558, [F. 30]. [D I N.]
dȳre, see **dēore**.
dyrne, adj.ja., *secret, hidden; mysterious, evil;* 271, 1879; dsm. dyrnum, 2168; dsm.wk.(?) dyrnan, 2290; asm. dyrnne, 2320; gpm dyrnra, 1357. — Cpd.: un-.
dyrre, see **durran.**

GLOSSARY

dyrstig(‡)+, adj., DARing, bold; 2838. [durran.]

ēac, adv., conj. (postposit.), also, moreover; 97, 388, 433, 1683, 2776; ēc, 3131; [and ēac, F. 45]. [E K E (arch.); Ger. auch; cp. EKE (out).]

ēacen, adj. (pp.), †large, mighty; asn., 1663; npm. ēacne, 1621; dpf. ēacnum, 2140; †great, mighty; nsm., 198. [Cp. Go. aukan; see ēac.]

ēacen-cræftig‡, adj., exceedingly powerful, huge; nsn., 3051; asn., 2280.

ēadig, adj., prosperous, happy, blessed; 1225, 2470. [Go. audags.] — Cpds.: sige-, sigor-, tīr-.

ēadig-līce, adv., happily; 100.

eafor, see eofor.

eafora, eafera,†, wk.m., offspring, son; eafera, 12, 19, 897; eafora, 375, 2358, 2992; gs. eaforan, 2451; as. eaferan, 1547, 1847; np. ~, 2475 (?); dp. ~, 1185, eaferum 2470. In a wider sense, pl. = (members of one's household,) retainers, men; dp. Finnes eaferum, 1068, eaforum Ecgwelan, 1710; so perh. np. Ongenðeowes eaferan, 2475.

eafoð†, n., strength, might; eafoð (ond ellen), 902; gs. eafoþes, 1466, 1763; as. eafoð (ond ellen), 602, 2349; eafoð, 960; dp. eafeþum, 1717; ap. eofoðo, 2534. [Cp. ON. afl., Gen. B: abal.]

ēage, wk.n., E Y E; gp. ēagena, 1766; dp. ēagum, 726, 1781, 1935.

ēagor-strēam†, m., sea-S T R E A M, sea; as., 513. [On ēagor, see Siev. § 289 & n. 2; Beitr. xxxi 88 n. Cp. ēg-strēam.]

eahta, num., E I G H T; g., 3123; a., 1035.

eahtian, w 2., consider, deliberate (about s.th.); pret. 3 pl. eahtedon, 172; — watch over, rule; pret. 3 sg.

eahtode, 1407; — esteem, praise; pres. 3 pl. ehtigað, 1222; pret. 3 pl. eahtodan, 3173; pp. geæhted, 1885. [OHG. ahtōn, Ger. achten.]

eal(l), adj. & subst., A L L; nsm. eal, 1424; nsf. eal, 1738, 1790, [F. 36], eall 2087, 2885; nsn. eal, 835, 848, 998, 1567 (or: adv.), 1593, 1608, eall 651, 2149, 2461, 2727, 3030; gsn. ealles, 1955, 2162, 2739, 2794; dsn. eallum, 913; asm. ealne, 1222, 2297, 2691; asf. ealle, 830, 1796 (or pl.?); asn. eal, 523, 744, 1086, 1155, 1185, 1701, 1705, [F. 22], eall 71, 2005, 2017, 2042, 2080, 2427, 2663, 3087, 3094; isn. ealle, 2667; npm. ealle, 111, 699, 705, 941, 1699; npn. eal, 486, 1620; gpm. ealra, [F. 32], ~ twelfe ('twelve in all,' MLN. xvi 17), 3170; gpn. ealra, 1727 (cf. Lang. § 25.9); dpm. eallum, 145, 767, 823, 906, 1057, 1417, 2268; apm. ealle, 649, 1080, 1122, 1717, 2236, 2814, 2899. — eal(l), adv., entirely, quite; eal, 680, 1129, 1708; eall, 3164. (In a few other instances eall, adj., approaches adverbial function.) ealles (gsn.), adv., in every respect, 1000. — [Go. alls.] — Cpd.: n(e)alles.

eald, adj., O L D; (1) of living beings: nsm., 357, 945(?), 1702, 2042, 2210, 2271, 2415, 2449, 2929, 2957; gsm. ealdes, 2760; dsm. ealdum, 1874, 2972; dpm. ealdum, 72. — (2) of material things (time-honored): nsm., 2763; asn., 2774; asf. ealde, 795, 1488, 1688; apm. ealde, 472. — (3) continued from the past, long-standing: asn., 1781; asf. ealde, 1865; asn.wk. ealde, 2330. — See gamol, frōd. — Comp. **yldra,** E L D E R, OLDER; 468, 1324, 2378. — Supl. **yldesta,** E L D E S T, OLDEST; dsm. yldestan, 2435; (se) yldesta, *chief;* 258; asm. yldestan, 363.

ealder-, see ealdor-dagas.

eald-fæder(‡)+, mc., F A T H E R, *ancestor;* 373. Cp. ǣr-fæder.

eald-gesegen‡, f., O L D *tradition* (SAGA); gp. -a, 869.

eald-gesīð†, m., O L D *comrade* or *retainer;* np. -as, 853.

eald-gestrēon, n., *ancient treasure;* gp. -a, 1458; dp. -um, 1381.

eald-gewinna‡, wk.m., O L D *adversary* ('hostis antiquus,' cf. *Angl.* xxxv 251 f.); 1776.

eald-gewyrht†, ni., *desert for former deeds;* np., 2657.

eald-hlāford, m., O L D (perh. ' dear,' or ' rightful ') *lord;* gs. -es, 2778 (i.e., Bēowulf).

Eald-metod‡, m., *God of* O L D; 945. (Cf. *Angl.* xxxv 124.)

ealdor, aldor, m., *chief, lord, prince;* aldor 56, 369, 392, ealdor 1644, 2920; ds. aldre 346, ealdre 592; as. aldor 668, ealdor 1848. [Cp. A L D E R man.]

ealdor, aldor,(†), n., *life;* gs. aldres 822, 1002, 1565, ealdres 1338, 2061, 2443, 2790; ds. aldre 661, 680, 1434 (*vitals*), 1447, 1469, 1478, 1524, ealdre 1442, 1655, 2133, 2396, 2481, 2599, 2624, 2825, 2924; on aldre (*ever*), 1779; tō aldre, *for ever, always, all the time,* 2005, 2498, āwa ⁓, 955; as. aldor, 1371; dp. aldrum, 510, 538.

(e)aldor-bealu†, nwa., *injury to life, death;* as. aldor-, 1676.

(e)aldor-cearu‡, f., *life-*C A R E, *great sorrow;* ds. aldorceare, 906.

(e)aldor-dagas‡, m.p. (sing.: -dæg), D A Y S *of life;* dp. aldordagum 718, ealder-, 757.

(e)aldor-gedāl†, n., *separation from life, death;* aldor-, 805. [Cp. dǣlan; līf-gedāl.]

ealdor-gewinna†, wk.m., *life-enemy, deadly enemy;* 2903.

(e)aldor-lēas(‡)+, adj., ‡*lord-*L E S S, *lacking a king;* npm. aldor[lē]ase, 15. (Cf. B.-T. Suppl.)

ealdor-lēas‡, adj., *life*L E S S, *dead;* asm. aldorlēasne 1587, ealdor-, 3003.

(e)aldor-þegn(†), m., *chief* T H A N E; as. aldor-, 1308.

eald-sweord‡, n., *ancient* S W O R D; as. ealdsweord (eotenisc), 1558, 2616, 2979, (si.) 1663.

eal-fela†, nu. (indecl.), *very much* (w. gen.), *a great many;* acc., 869, 883.

eal(l)-gearo†, adj.wa., *quite ready;* eall-, 2241; eal-, nsf. 1230 (*alert* or *willing*), nsn. 77.

ealgian, w 2., *protect, defend;* (feorh) ⁓, 796, 2655, 2668; pret. 3 sg. ealgode, 1204. [Cp. ealh ' temple '; Lat. arcēre.]

eal(l)-gylden, adj., A L L-GOLDEN; nsn. (swȳn) ealgylden ('entirely covered with gold,' Stjer. 6), 1111; asn. (segn) eallgylden ('gold-wrought,' i.e. ' made of or intermixed with threads of gold wire,' Earle 107), 2767.

eall-īren‡, adj.ja., A L L *of* I R O N; asn.wk. -īrenne, 2338.

ealo-, ealu-benc‡, fi., A L E-B E N C H; ds. ealobence, 1029; ealubence, 2867. [ealu: *R.-L.* i 279.]

ealo-drincend(e)‡, mc. (pres. ptc.) [pl.], A L E-D R I N Ker; np. ealodrincende, 1945.

ēa-lond, n., *water-*L A N D, ‡*seaboard;* as., 2334 (n.). [ISL A N D.]

ealo-, ealu-wǣge,‡, nja., A L E-*cup, -can;* as. ealowǣge 481, 495, ealuwǣge 2021.

ealu-scerwen‡, fjō., (*dispensing of* A L E [*evil drink*], i.e.) *distress,* *terror;* 769 (n.). Cp. meoduscerwen, *Andr.* 1526.

ēam, m., (*maternal*) *uncle;* ēam, 881; ds. ēame, *1117*. [E M E (obs., dial.); Ger. Oheim; *ZfdA.* lxix 46–8; Holt. Et.]

eard, m., *land, estate, region, dwelling, home;* 2198; ds. earde, 56, 2654, 2736; as. eard, 104, 1129, 1377, 1500, 1727, 2493; np. (sg. meaning) eardas, 1621.

eardian, w 2., (1) *dwell, remain;* pret. 3 pl. eardodon, 3050. (2) *inhabit;* inf. eardian, 2589; pret. 3 sg. eardode, 166.

eard-lufu (-lufe)‡, (wk.)f., (*home*-L O V E), *dear home;* as. eardlufan, 692.

earfoþe, nja., *hardship, hard struggle;* ap. earfeþo, 534. [Cf. Go. arbaiþs, Ger. Arbeit.]

earfoð-līce, adv., *with difficulty, painfully, sorrowfully;* 1636, 1657, 2822, 2934; *with torture, impatiently,* 86, 2303.

earfoð-þrāg‡, f., (*time of tribulation*), *distress;* as. -e, 283.

earg, adj., *cowardly, spiritless;* gsm. -es, 2541. [Ger. arg. Cf. *IF.* xli 16 ff.]

earm, m., A R M; ds. -e, 2361; as. earm, 749, 835, 972; dp. -um, 513.

earm, adj., *wretched, distressed, forlorn;* 2368; dsf. -re, 2938. — Comp. asm. -ran, 577. [Ger. arm. Cf. *IF.* xli 304 ff.]

earm-bēag(‡)+, m., A R M-*ring, bracelet;* gp. -a, 2763.

earm-[h]rēad‡, f., A R M-*ornament;* np. -e, 1194. [hrēodan.]

earm-līc, adj., *miserable, pitiable;* 807.

earm-sceapen, adj. (pp.), *wretched, miserable;* 1351, *2228*.

earn, m., *eagle;* ds. -e, 3026. See Earna-næs, 3031. [E R N E; cp. Ger. Aar.]

eart, see eom.

ēastan, adv., *from the* E A S T; 569, [F. *3*].

eatol, see atol.

ēaðe, adj.ja., *easy, pleasant;* nsm. ēðe, 2586; nsn. ȳðe, 1002, 2415; npf. ēaðe, 228. [E A T H (Sc.); cp. OS. ōði. The ēa-form perh. due to the influence of the adv.] (Cp. ȳðe-līce.)

ēaðe, adv., *easily;* ēaþe mæg (*Angl.* xxxv 119 f.), 478, 2291, 2764.

ēað-fynde†, adj.ja., *easy to* FIND; 138 (implying 'a great number,' 'all').

(ge-)ēawan, see (ge-)ȳwan.

eaxl, f., *shoulder;* ds. -e, 816, 1117, 1537, 1547; as. ~, 835, 972; dp. -um, 358, 2853. [Cp. AXLE; Ger. Achsel.]

eaxl-gestealla(†), wk.m., *shoulder-companion, comrade;* 1326; ap. -gesteallan, 1714.

ēc, see ēac.

ēce, adj.ja., *eternal;* ēce (Drihten), 108; nsn. (or m.), 2719; dsm. ēcum (Dryhtne), 2796; dsm.wk. ēcean (~), 1692, 1779, 2330; asm. ēcne (ræd), 1201; apm. ēce (rædas), 1760. [Cp. Go. ajuk-dūþs; Bülb. § 217.]

ecg, fjō, E D G E, *sword;* 1106, 1459, 1524, 1575, 1763, 2506, 2508, 2577, 2772, 2778; ds. ecge, 2876; as. ~, 1549; np. ecga 2828, ecge 1145, 2683; gp. ecga, 483, 805, 1168; dp. ecgum, 1287, 1558, 1772, 2140, 2485, 2564, 2614, 2939, 2961; ap. ecge, 1812. — Cpds.: brūn-, heard-, stȳl-.

ecg-bana‡, wk.m., *slayer with the sword;* ds. -banan, 1262.

ecg-clif‡, n., *sea*-C L I F F (= ēg-clif, cf. *ESt.* xxvii 223 f.), or C L I F F *with an* E D G E *or brink* (B.-T. Suppl.), *steep cliff* (Hoops St. 136 f.); as., 2893.

ecg-hete†, mi., *sword*-HATE, *hostility, war; 84;* as., 1738.

ecg-þracu‡, f., *sword-storm, fight;* as. -þræce, 596.

ēd(e)r, see **ǣd(e)r**.

ed-hwyrft, mi., *return, change, reverse;* 1281. [hweorfan.]

ed-wenden†, fjō., *turning back, reversal, change;* 280, 1774, 2188.

ed-wīt-līf‡, n., L I F E *of disgrace;* 2891.

efn, in **on efn**, prep. phrase, w. preceding dat., (E V E N *with*), *beside;* 2903. [A N E N T; Ger. neben.]

efnan, see **æfnan**.

efne, adv., E V E N, *just;* efne (swā), 943, 1092, 1223, 1283, 1571, 3057; efne (swylc), 1249.

efstan, w 1., *hasten* (intr.); 3101; pret. 3 sg. efste, 1493. [ofost.]

eft, adv., AFTerwards, *back, again; in turn, on the other hand;* 22, 56, 123, 135, 281, 296, 603, 692, 853, 871, 1146, 1160, 1377, 1529, 1541, 1556, 1596, 1753, 1804, 1869, 2111, 2117, 2142, 2200, 2319, 2365, 2368, 2387, 2592, 2654, 2790, 2941, 2956, 3044; eft swā ǣr, 642, 1787; eft sōna (E F T- S O O N (s)), 1762. [Cp. æfter.]

eft-cyme†, mi., *return;* gs. eftcymes, 2896. [cuman.]

eft-sīð‡, m., *journey back, return;* gs. -es, 2783; as. -sīð, 1891; ap. -as tēah, *returned*, 1332.

egesa, wk.m., *terror, fear, horror;* 784; gs. egesan, 1757; ds. ~ (Schü.Bd. 35: *terribly, greatly?*), 1827, 2736; as. ~, 3154; þurh egsan, *in a terrible manner* (*MPh.* iii 451), 276. [ege, cp. AWE.] — Cpds.: glēd-, līg-, wæter-.

eges-full, adj., *terrible;* 2929.

eges-līc₂, adj., *terrible;* nsm., 2309; 2825; nsn., 1649.

egle, adj.ja. (Siev. § 303 n. 2), *hateful, horrible;* nsf. eglu, 987 (n.). [Cp. AIL, vb.]

egsa, see **egesa**.

egsian(‡)+, w 2., *terrify;* pret. 3 sg. egsode, 6.

ēg-strēam†, m., *water-*S T R E A M, (pl.) *sea;* dp. -um, 577. [Cp. ēagor-strēam, ǣg-weard; ēa-lond; Lang. § 10.5.]

ēhtan, w 1., w. gen., *pursue, persecute;* pret. 3 pl. ēhton, 1512; pres. ptc. ēhtende (wæs), 159. [ōht.]

ehti(g)an, see **eahtian**.

elde, eldo, see **ylde, yldo**.

el-land†, n., *foreign country;* as., 3019. [Cp. elra.]

ellen, n., *courage, valor, strength, zeal;* 573, 902, 2706; gs. elnes, 1529, 2876; ds. elne, 893, 1097, 2861; on ~, 2506, 2816; (mid) ~, 1493, 2535; elne (semi-adv.), *valiantly, quickly:* ~ geēode 2676, si. 1967, 2917; as. ellen, 602, 2349, 2695, [F. 11], (*deed*[s] *of valor:*) 3, 637. — Cpd.: mægen-.

ellen-dǣd†, fi., D E E D *of valor;* dp. -um, 876, 900.

ellen-gǣst‡, mi., *powerful* or *bold demon;* 86.

ellen-līce(‡), adv., *valiantly, boldly;* 2122.

ellen-mǣrþu‡, f., *fame for courage; heroic deed;* dp. -mǣrþum, 828, 1471.

ellen-rōf, adj., *brave, strong, famed for courage;* 340, 358, 3063; dpm. -um, 1787.

ellen-sīoc‡, adj., (*strength-*S I C K), *deprived of strength;* asm. -ne, 2787.

ellen-weorc(†), n., W O R K *of valor, courageous deed;* as., 661, 958,

GLOSSARY

1464, 2643; gp. -a, 2399; ap. -weorc, 3173.
elles, adv., E L S E, *otherwise;* 2520; ∼ hwǣr, 138; ∼ hwergen, 2590.
ellor†, adv., E L*sewhither;* 55, 2254.
ellor-gāst, -gǣst,‡, ma., mi., *alien spirit;* -gāst, 807, 1621, -gǣst 1617; ap. -gǣstas, 1349.
ellor-sīð‡, m., *journey* E L*sewhere, death;* 2451.
elne(s), see **ellen**.
elra†, comp. (cf. *MPh.* iii 252), *another;* dsm. elran, 752. [Cp. Go. aljis, Lat. alius. See el-, elles, ellor.]
el-þēodig, adj., *foreign;* apm. elþēodige, 336. [Cp. elra.]
ende, mja., E N D; 822, 1254; ds., 224, 2790, 2823; as., 1386, 1734, 2021 (n.), 2342, 2844, 3046, 3063. — Cpd.: woruld-.
ende-dæg, m., *last* D A Y, *death;* 3035; as., 637.
ende-dōgor†, n., *last day, death;* gs. -dōgores, 2896.
ende-lāf‡, f., *last remnant;* 2813.
ende-lēan(†), n., *final reward* or *retribution;* as., 1692.
ende-sǣta‡, wk.m., *one stationed at the* (E N D) *extremity of a territory* (i.e. *coast-guard*); 241. [sittan.]
ende-stæf(†), m., , E N D; as., 1753. See fācen-stafas.
(ge-)endian, w 2., E N D; pp. geendod, 2311.
enge, adj.ja., *narrow;* apm., 1410 (*cheerless?* cf. Schü.Bd. 37 ff.). [Go. aggwus, Ger. eng.]
ent, mi., *giant;* gp. enta (geweorc), 2717, 2774, si. 1679 (n.). Cf. Grimm D.M. 434 (524), 443 (534).
entisc‡, adj., *made by giants, giant;* asm. -ne, 2979.
(ge-)ēode, see (ge-)gān.
eodor, m., (1) *enclosure, precinct;* ap. (under, 'inside') eoderas, 1037 (Cp. *Gen.* 2445, 2487, *Hel.* 4945.) — (2)† *protector, prince* (w. gen. pl.); ns. eodur, 663, eodor 1044; vs. eodor, 428. (Cp. hlēo; ἕρκος Ἀχαιῶν. See *Beitr.* xli 163-70; Hoops 130.)
eofer, eofor, m., *boar; figure of boar on helmet:* eofer, 1112; ap. eoferas, 1328; *boar banner:* as. eafor, 2152. [Ger. Eber.]
eofer-sprēot(‡)+, m., *boar-spear:* dp. -um, 1437.
eofor-līc‡, n., *figure of a boar;* np., 303. (See līc, swīn-līc.)
eofoð, see **eafoð**.
eolet‡, *sea? voyage?;* gs. -es, 224 (n.).
eom, anv., A M (s.t. used as auxil. w. pp. of trans. or intrans. verbs); 1 sg. eom, 335, 407, 1475, 2527, [F. 24]; 2 sg. eart, 352, 506, 1844, 2813; 3 sg. is 31 times, 248, 256, 272, etc., [F. 24, 26], ys 2093, 2910, 2999, 3084; negat. nis, 249, 1361, 1372, 2458, 2532; 1 pl. synt, 260, 342; 2 pl. syndon, 237, 393; 3 pl. sint 388, synt 364, syndon 257, 361, 1230; opt. 3 sg. sīe 435, 3105, sīe 682, sig 1778, sȳ 1941, sȳ 1831, 2649. — **wesan**, v, *be* (often used as auxil. w. pp. of trans. and s.t. of intrans. verbs); inf. wesan, 272, 1328, 1859, 2708, 2801, 3021; imp. sg. wes, 269, 1170, 1219, 1224, 1480, wæs 407; [pl. wesað, F. 12]; pret. 1 sg. wæs, 240, 1657, 2428, 3087; negat. næs, 2141, 2432; 3 sg. wæs 243 times, 11, 18, 49, 53, 126, 140, etc., [F. 28, 45]; negat. næs 20 times, 134, 1299, etc.; 1 pl. wǣron, 536, 544, 1820; 3 pl. wǣron 15 times, 233, 548, 612, etc., wǣran 2475; negat. nǣron, 2657; opt. 2 sg. wǣre, 1478; 3 sg. wǣre 14 times, 173,

203, 593, etc., [F. 36, 44]; negat. nǣre, 860, 1167; (3 pl. wǣron, 233, 1986?). — Note: pres. ptc. used w. wæs, wǣre ('progressive form,' see note on 159): 159, 1105, 3028. Omission of wesan (cf. *Beitr.* xxxvi 362 ff.): 617, 992, 1783, 1857, 2091, 2256, 2363, 2497, 2659, of is, wæs (in negat. clauses of general import): 2262, 2297; cp. loosely joined elliptic clauses, 936, 1343, 2035, also 3062. — Cpds.: cniht-, umborwesende. — **bēon**, anv., B E; the indic. forms used in 'abstract' clauses; thus in generic and gnomic statements: 3 sg. bið, 183, 186, 1059, 1283, 1384, 1388, 1940, 2541, (cp. w. (n)is, 2532), 2890, 3174, byð 1002, 2277; 3 pl. bēoð, 1838; ref. to 'typical' instances: 3 sg. bið, 1742, 1745, 2444, 2450; w. a future sense: 1 sg. bēo, 1825; 3 sg. bið, 299, 660, 949, 1762, 1767, 1784, 1835, 2043; 3 pl. bīoð, 2063; — imp. sg. bēo, 386, 1173, 1226, bīo 2747. (Auxil. w. pp.: 1745, 2063, 2450.) Cf. K. Jost, *Beon und wesan* (Ang. F. xxvi), §§ 18-34. (L 6.5 a.)

eorclan-stān, m., *precious* S T O N E; ap. -as, 1208. [Cp. eorc(n)anstān. — OHG. erchan 'egregious,' OE. Eorcon- in names of persons; but more likely of oriental origin, cf. *ZfdA.* xi 90, *Beitr.* xii 182 f.]

ēored-geatwe‡, fwō.p., *warlike equipments;* ap., 2866. [ēored (=eoh + rād) 'troop'? (orig., of cavalry). See wīg-getāwa.]

eorl, m., *nobleman, man, warrior, hero;* 761, 795, 1228, 1328, 1512, 1702, 2908, 2951, 3015, 3063, 3077; gs. eorles, 689, 982, 1757; as. eorl, 573, 627, 2695; gp. eorla, 248, 357, 369, 431, 1235, 1238, 1312, 1420, 1891, 2064, 2248, 2891, 3166, ∼ drihten: 1050, 2338, ∼ hlēo: 791, 1035, 1866, 1967, 2142, 2190; dp. eorlum, 769, 1281, 1649, 1676, 2021; ap. eorlas, 6, 2816. [E A R L, cp. ON. jarl.]

eorl-gestrēon†, n., *(noblemen's) treasure, riches;* gp. -a, 2244.

eorl-gewǣde‡, nja., *dress of a warrior, armor;* dp. (sg. meaning) -gewǣdum, 1442.

eorlīc (=eorl-līc) (‡) (+), adj., *manly, heroic, noble;* asn. eorlīc, 637.

eorl-scipe†, mi., *nobility, rank; heroic deed(s);* as., 1727, 3173, ∼ efnan (& si.): 2133, 2535 (-scype), 2622, 3007.

eorl-weorod‡, n., *band of warriors;* 2893.

eormen-cyn(n)†, nja., *man*KIND; gs. -cynnes, 1957. [eormen- 'immense'; K I N.]

eormen-grund(‡), m., *spacious* (G R O U N D) *earth;* as., 859. (*Jul.* 10, *Chr.* 481: yrmenne grund (as.).)

eormen-lāf‡, f., *immense legacy;* as. -lāfe, 2234.

eorre, see **yrre**.

eorð-cyning, m., K I N G *of the land;* gs. -es, 1155.

eorð-draca‡, wk.m., E A R T H-D R A GON; 2712, 2825.

eorðe, wk.f., E A R T H; both *ground* and *the world we live in;* gs. eorþan, 752, 1730, 2727, 3049; ds. ∼, 1532, 1822, 2415, 2822, 2855, 3138; as. ∼, 92, 2834, 3166, ofer ∼, 248, 802, 2007, wīde geond ∼, 266, 3099.

eorð-hūs(‡)+, n., E A R T H-H O U S E; ds. -e, 2232.

eorð-reced‡, m.n., E A R T H-*house;* 2719.

GLOSSARY

eorð-scræf, n., E A R T H-*cavern, cave;* gp. -scrafa, 3046.
eorð-seleᵗ, mi., E A R T H-*hall, cave;* ds., 2515; as., 2410.
eorð-weal(l) (‡)+, m., E A R T H- W A L L, *mound;* as., 2957, 3090.
eorð-weard‡, m., E A R T H-GUARD, *stronghold;* as., 2334. (Cf. Dietrich, *ZfdA.* xi 415 f.)
eoten(‡) (+), m., *giant;* 761 (Grendel); np. -as, 112; gp. -a, 421, 883. [Cp. etan(?). *NED.*: E T E N, E T T I N (obs., dial.).]
eotenisc‡, adj., *made by giants, giant;* asn. (-sweord) ~: 1558, etonisc 2616, eotonisc 2979.
eoton-weard‡, f., *watch against a giant;* as. -weard² (T.C. § 25), 668.
ēow, see þū.
ēowan, see ȳwan.
ēower, poss. pron., Y O U R; 2532; dsn. ēowrum, 2885; asm. ēowerne, 294, 2537, 2889; asn. ēower, 251; npm. ēowre, 257; gpm. ēowra, 634; dpn. ēowrum, 395; [apf. ēowre, F. 11]; apn. (?, see þū) ēower, 392.
ēower, ēowic, (pers. pron.), see þū.
ēst, fi., *favor, good will;* 3075(?); dp. ēstum ('with good will,' 'kindly'), 1194, 2149, 2378, ~ miclum 958; — *gift, legacy, bequest;* as. ēst, 2157 (n.), 2165, 3075 (? n.).[unnan.]
ēste(ᵗ), adj.ja., *kind, gracious* (w. gen.: ' in regard to '), 945.
etan, V, E A T; 444; 3 sg. eteð, 449. — Cpds.: þurh-, fretan.
etonisc, see eotenisc.
ēð-begēte(‡), adj.ja., *easy to obtain* (GET); 2861. [See ēaðe, be-gitan.]
ēðe, see ēaðe.
ēþel, m., *native land, home;* ds. ēþle, 1730, 1774; as. · ⚔ · (Intr. xcvii), 520, 913; ēðel, 1960.
ēðel-rihtᵗ, n., *ancestral* R I G H T, *privileges belonging to a hereditary estate, ancestral domain;* 2198. See folc-, lond-riht (cf. Schü. Bd. 44 ff.).
ēþel-stōlᵗ, m., *native seat, ancestral throne;* ap. -as, 2371. [S T O O L.]
ēþel-turfᵗ, fc., *native soil, country;* ds. -tyrf, 410. [T U R F.]
ēþel-weardᵗ, m., GUARD*ian of the native land, king;* · ⚔ · weard, 1702, ēþelweard, 2210; ds. -e, 616.
ēðel-wyn(n)‡, fi., *enjoyment of hereditary estate, delightful home;* ns. ēðelwyn, 2885; as. ~, 2493.
ēþ-gesȳneᵗ, adj.ja., *easily visible* (with the connotation of 'in abundance'); 1110; ȳþgesēne, 1244. [See ēaðe; S E E N.]

fācen, n., *deceit, malice, crime;* ds. fācne, 2009.
fācen-stafas‡, m.p., *treachery;* ap., 1018. [Cp. ON. feikn-stafir ' baleful runes,' ' crime.'] See ār-stafas, ende-, rūn-stæf.
fæc, n., *space of time;* as., 2240. [Ger. Fach.]
fæder, mc., F A T H E R; 55, 262, 316, 459, 1609, 2048, 2608, 2928; gs. ~, 21, 188, 1479, 1950, 2059; ds. ~, 2429; as. ~, 1355. — Cpds.: ǣr-, eald-.
fæder-æþeluᵗ, nja.p., *paternal rank or excellence;* dp. -æþelum, 911. See æþelu.
fæderen-mǣg(‡)+, m., *paternal relative, kinsman on the* F A T H E R'*s side;* ds. -e, 1263.
fǣge(ᵗ), adj.ja., *doomed to die, fated, near death;* 846, 1241, 1755, 2141, 2975; gsm. fǣges, 1527; dsm. fǣgum, 2077; asm. fǣgne, 1568; *dead:* dpm. fǣgum, 3025. [F E Y (Sc.); Ger. feige.] — Cpds.: dēað-, un-.
fægen, adj., *glad, rejoicing;* npm.

fægne, 1633. [F A I N; cp. ge-fēon.]
fǣger (cf. T.C. § 4), adj., F A I R, *beautiful;* nsm., 1137; nsn. fǣger, 773; asf. -e, 522; npm. -e, 866. — Cpd.: un-.
fǣg(e)re, adv., F A I R *ly, pleasantly, fittingly, courteously;* fægere, 1014, 1788; fægre, 1985, 2989.
(ge-)fægnian, w 2., *rejoice,* i.e. ‡*make glad;* pp. gefægnod (MS. gefrægnod), *1333.* (For the trans. meaning cp. (ge)blissian. — gefrǣgnian is not found elsewhere.) [fægen.]
ge-fǣgon, see ge-fēon.
fǣhð(o), f., FEUD, *enmity, hostile act, battle;* fǣhð, 2403, 3061, fǣhðo 2999; gs. (or ds.) fǣhðe, 109; ds. ∼, 1537; as. ∼, 459, 470, 595, 1207, 1333, 1340, 1380, 2513, 2618, 2948, fǣghðe 2465; fǣhðe ond fyrene, 137, 879 (ap.?), 2480, si. 153; gp. fǣhða, 2689; ap. (s.?) fǣhðo, 2489. [fāh. Cp. Ger. Fehde; *NED.*: FEUD.] — Cpd.: wæl-.
fǣlsian(†), w 2., *cleanse, purge;* 432; pret. 3 sg. fǣlsode, 2352; pp. gefǣlsod, 825, 1176, 1620. [fǣle.]
fǣmne, wk.f., *maiden, woman;* gs. fǣmnan, 2059; d.(a.?)s. ∼, 2034. [Holt. Et.; Pedersen, Jesp. Misc. 55 ff.]
fǣr, n., †*vessel, ship;* 33. [faran.]
fǣr, m., *sudden attack, danger, disaster;* 1068, 2230. [F E A R; Ger. Gefahr.]
fǣr-gripe‡, mi., *sudden* G R I P *or attack;* 1516; dp. -gripum, 738.
fǣr-gryre†, mi., *(terror caused by) sudden attack, awful horror;* dp. -gryrum, 174.
fǣringa, adv., *suddenly;* 1414, 1988. [fǣr.]
fǣr-nīð‡, m., *hostile attack, sudden affliction;* gp. -a, 476.
fæst, adj.. F A S T, *firm, fixed* (often w. dat.); nsm., 137, 636, 1007; 1290, 1364, 1742, 1878, 1906, 2243, 2901, 3045, 3072; nsf., 722, 2086; nsn., 303, 998; asm. -ne, 2069; asf. -e, 1096; asn. fæst, 1918; apm. -e, 2718. — Cpds.: ār-, blǣd-, gin-, sōð-, tīr-, wīs-.
fæste, adv., F A S T, *firmly;* 554, 760, 773, 788, 1295, 1864 (or apm. of adj.?). Comp. fæstor ('more securely'), 143.
fæsten, nja., F A S T *ness, stronghold;* as., 104, 2333, 2950.
fæst-rǣd, adj., *firmly resolved;* asm. -ne, 610.
fæt, n., *vessel, cup;* ap. fatu, 2761. [V A T, (prob.) fr. Kent. dial.] — Cpds.: bān-, drync-, māðþum-, sinc-, wunder-.
fǣt(‡), n., (*gold*) *plate;* dp. fǣtum, 2256, fǣttum (Lang. § 19.4), 716. [See fǣted.]
fǣted(†), adj. (pp. of *fǣtan), *ornamented,* (*gold-*)*plated;* nsn., 2701; gsn.wk. fǣttan (goldes), 1093, 2246; dsn.wk. fǣttan (golde), 2102; asn. fǣted, 2253, 2282; apm. fǣtte, 333, *1750.* [Cp. Go. fētjan 'adorn.'] (See *ZfdA.* xi 420; *Beitr.* xxx 91 n.; Tupper's *Riddles,* pp. 184 f.)
fǣted-hlēor‡, adj., *with ornamented cheeks,* i.e. *with gold-plated headgear* (or *bridle*); apm. -e, 1036.
fǣt-gold‡, n., *plated* G O L D; as., 1921.
fǣttan, fǣtte, see fǣted.
fǣttum, see fǣt.
fæðer-gearwe‡, fwō.p., F E A T H E R-GEAR; dp. -gearwum, *3119.* [GEAR fr. ON. gǫrvi.]
fæþm, m., (*outstretched*) *arms;* dp. -um, 188, 2128; — *embrace:* ns. (līges) fæþm, 781; as. (si.) ∼, 185; — *bosom:* as. (foldan) ∼, 1393, (si.) 3049; — *grasp, power:* as.

GLOSSARY

fæþm, 1210. [F A T H O M.] —Cp. sīd-fæþme(d).

fæðmian(†), w 2., *embrace, enfold;* 3133; opt. 3 sg. fæðmię, 2652.

fāg, fāh, adj., (1) *variegated, decorated, shining;* nsm. fāh, 1038, 2671(?); nsf., 1459; nsn., 2701; asm. fāgne, 725, fāhne 716, 927; asf. fāge, 1615 (cf. Lang. § 21); asn. fāh, 2217; npn. fāh, 305; dpn. fāgum, 586. — (2) *bloodstained;* nsm. fāh, 420 (?), 2974, fāg 1631 (nsn.?); nsn. fāh, 934, 1286, 1594; asm. fāhne, 447. — Cpds.: bān-, blōd-, brūn-, drēor-, gold-, gryre-, searo-, sinc-, stān-, swāt-, wæl-, wyrm-.

fāh, fāg, adj., (1) *hostile,* (F O E); nsm. fāh, 420 (?, Kock[4] 111), 554, 2671(?); asm. fāne, 2655; gpm. fāra, 578, 1463; *in a state of feud with* (wið), nsm. fāg. 811. — (2) *outlawed, guilty;* nsm. fāh, 978, fāg 1001, 1263. — Cpd.: nearo-.

fāmig-heals†, adj., F O A M Y-*necked;* 1909; fāmī-, 218.

(ge-)fandian, w 2., *search out, test, tamper with* (w. gen.); pp. gefandod, 2301; — *experience* (w. acc. or gen.); pp. gefondad, 2454. [findan.] See cunnian.

fāne, fāra, see fāh.

faran, VI, *go, proceed,* F A R E; 124, 865, 2551, 2915, 2945; ger. farenne, *1805;* pret. 3 sg. fōr, 1404, 1908, 2308; 3 pl. fōron, 1895.

ge-faran, VI, *proceed, act;* 738. (Cf. Lorz 22.)

faroð†, m. or n., *current, sea;* ds. -e, 28, 580, 1916. [faran.] Cp. waroð (*Angl.* xxviii 455 f., T.C. § 28 n. 1).

fēa, adj.wa.(a.), pl., F E W, *a few;* gp. fēara, 1412, 3061; dp. fēaum, 1081; a. (w. part. gen.: worda)

fēa, 2246, 2662. [Go. fawai, pl.; cp. Lat. paucus.]

fēa, 156, see feoh.

ge-feah, see ge-fēon.

fealh, ge-fealg, see (ge-)fēolan.

feallan, rd., F A L L; 1070; pret. 3 sg. fēol, 772, [F. 41], fēoll 2919, 2975; 3 pl. fēollon, 1042. — Cpd.: be-.

ge-feallan, rd., F A L L; 3 sg. ge-fealleð, 1755; — w. acc., *fall (on) to:* pret. 3 sg. gefēoll, 2100, 2834.

fealo, 2757, see fela.

fealu, adj.wa., F A L L O W; '*pale yellow shading into red or brown*' (Mead L 7.29.198); asf. fealwe (strǣte, ' covered with pale yellow sand or gravel' (Mead)), 916; apm. ~ (mēaras, ' bay '), 865; ' yellowish green ': asm. fealone (flōd), 1950. — Cpd.: æppel-.

fēa-sceaft(†), adj., *destitute, poor, wretched;* 7, 973; dsm. -um, 2285, 2393; npm. -e, 2373.

feax, n., *hair of the head* (collect.); ds. feaxe, 1647, fexe 2967. — Cpds.: blonden-, gamol-, wunden-.

ge-fēgon, -feh, see ge-fēon.

fēhð, see fōn.

fēl, f., F I L E; gp. -a, 1032 (n.). (=fēol, fīl; Lang. § 10.7.)

fela, nu. (indecl.), *much, many,* nearly always w. part. gen. (pl. or sg.); 36, 992, 995, 1265, 1509, 1783, 2231, 2763, [fǣla, F. 33]; as., 153, 164, 311, 408, 530, 591, 694, 809, 876, 929, 1028, 1060, 1411, 1425, 1525, 1577, 1837, 2003, 2266, 2349, 2426, 2511, 2542, 2620, 2631, 2738, [fǣla, F. 25], fealo, 2757; — adv., *much;* [586], 1385, 2102, 3025, 3029. [Go. filu, Ger. viel.] — Cpd.: eal-. See worn.

fela-fricgende‡, adj. (pres. ptc.), *well informed, wise;* 2106. See ge-

fricgan. (*MPh.* iii 262; Kock: fela fricgende.)
fela-geōmor‡, adj., *very sad, solemn;* 2950.
fela-hrōr‡, adj., *very vigorous, strong;* 27.
fela-mōdig‡, adj., *very brave;* gpm. -ra, 1637, 1888.
fel(l), n., F E L L, *skin;* dp. fellum, 2088.
fen(n), nja., F E N, *marshy region;* ds. fenne, 1295; as. fen, 104.
fen-freoðo‡, wk.f., F E N-*refuge;* as. (ds.?), 851.
feng, mi., *grasp, grip;* 1764; as., 578. [fōn.] — Cpd.: inwit-.
(ge-)fēng, see (ge-)fōn.
fengel‡, m., *prince, king;* 1400, 2156, 2345; vs., 1475. [Cp. fōn? See þengel.]
fen-gelād‡, n., F E N-*path* or -*tract;* as., 1359. [līðan.]
fen-hlið‡, n., F E N-*slope, marshy tract;* ap. -hleoðu, 820.
fen-hop‡, n., F E N-*retreat;* ap. -hopu 764. [*NED.*: H O P E, sb.² Jespersen, *Lang.* 310: cp. hope ' spes '?] (See mōrhop.)
fēo, see **feoh**.
feoh, n., *property, money, riches;* ds. fēo, 470, 1380, fēa 156. [F E E; OHG. fihu, Ger. Vieh.]
feoh-gift‡, fi., *dispensing of treasure; costly* GIFT; gs. -gyfte, 1025; dp. -giftum 21, -gyftum 1089. [MnE. gift prob. fr. ON. gipt.]
feoh-lēas(‡)+, adj., (*money*-L E S S, i.e.)‡ *not to be atoned for with money, inexpiable;* nsn., 2441. Cp. bōt-lēas in *Ags. Laws*.
ge-feohtan, III, F I G H T; 1083 (n.).
feohte, wk.f.†, F I G H T; as. feohtan, 576, 959.
fēolan, III, *penetrate, reach;* pret. 3 sg. (inne) fealh, 1281, 2225. [Go.

filhan. Cf. *Beitr.* xxxvii 314.] — Cpd.: æt-.
ge-fēolan(‡)+, III, *make one's way, pass;* pret. 3 sg. gefealg, 2215.
ge-fēon, v, w. gen. or dat. (instr.), *rejoice;* pret. 3 sg. gefeah, 109, 1624; gefeh, 827, 1569, 2298; 3 pl. gefǣgon, 1014, gefēgon 1627.
fēond, mc., *enemy*, F I E N D; 101, 164, 725, 748, 970, 1276; gs. fēondes, 984, 2128, 2289; ds. fēonde, 143, 439; as. fēond, 279, 698, 962, 1273, 1864, 2706; gp. fēonda, 294, 808, 903, 1152, fīonda 2671; dp. fēondum, 420, 1669. [Go. fijands, Ger. Feind.]
fēond-grāp‡, f., *enemy's* GRIP or *clutch;* dp. -um, 636.
fēond-scaða†, wk.m., *dire foe;* 554. See sceaþa.
fēond-scipe, mi., *enmity, hostility;* 2999.
feor(r), adv., F A R; feor, 42, 109, 542, 808, 1340, 1805, 1916; ~ ond nēah, 1221, si. 2870; feorr, 1988; semi-adj., feor, 1361, 1921; *far back* (time): feor, 1701. — Comp. fyr, 143, 252.
feor-būend‡, mc. [pl.], F A R *dweller;* vp., 254.
feor-cȳðð(u)‡, f. (Wright §§ 371 f.), F A R *country;* np. -cȳþðe, 1838. [cūð; K I T H.]
feorh, (T.C. § 3), m.n., *life;* 2123, 2424; gs. fēores, 1433, 1942; ds. fēore, 578, 1293, 1548, 3013, feore 1843 (*age*); tō wīdan feore, *ever*, 933; as. feorh, 439, 796, 851, 1370, 1849, 2141, 2655, 2668, 2856, [F. 19], ferh 2706; in feorh dropen, 2981 (' mortally wounded,' cp. aldor 1434); wīdan feorh, *ever*, 2014; dp. fēorum, 1306, feorum 73; ap. feorh, 2040; — *living being, body* (cf. *Angl.* xxviii 445); ns. feorh, 1210; dp. fēorum, 1152

GLOSSARY 329

('*life-blood*'). See ealdor. — Cpd.: geogoð-.
feorh-bealu†, nwa., (*life*-B A L E), *deadly evil;* 2077, 2537 (frēcne); -bealo (∼), 2250; as. ∼, 156.
feorh-ben(n)‡, fjō., *life-wound, mortal wound;* dp. -bennum, 2740.
feorh-bona(†), wk.m., (*life-*)*slayer;* ds. -bonan, 2465.
feorh-cyn(n)†, nja., (*life-race*), *race of men;* gp. -cynna, 2266.
feorh-genīðla‡, wk.m., *life-enemy, deadly foe;* ds. -genīðlan, 969; as. ∼, 1540; dp. ∼, 2933.
feorh-lāst‡, m., (*life-track*, i.e.) *track of vanishing life, bloody track;* ap. -as, 846. (Cf. *Angl.* xxviii 445; Hoops St. 104.)
feorh-legu†, wk.f. (Siev. §§ 268, 279), ‡(*allotted*) *life;* as. -lege, 2800. [licgan; cp. LAW. See *Dan.* 139: aldorlegu; Bu. Tid. 69.]
feorh-sēoc‡, adj., (*life*-S I C K), *mortally wounded;* 820.
feorh-sweng‡, mi., *life-blow, deadly blow;* as., 2489.
feorh-wund‡, f., *life-*W O U N D, *mortal wound;* ds. -e, 2385.
feorm, f., *feeding, sustenance, entertaining, taking care of;* ds. feorme, 2385 (*hospitality*; cp. *OE. Bede* 64.16 f.: for feorme ond onfongnesse gæsta ond cumena = 'propter hospitalitatem atque susceptionem'); as. ∼, 451 (n.). [See *NED.:* F A R M, sb.¹ (obs.)]
feormend-lēas‡, adj., *without a cleanser or polisher;* apm. -e, 2761.
feormian, w 2., *cleanse, polish;* pres. opt. 3 sg. feormie, *2253.* **feormynd** (=feormend), mc. (pres. ptc.), *cleanser, polisher;* np., 2256. [*NED.:* F A R M, v.¹ (obs.)]
(ge-)feormian, w 2., †*consume, eat up;* pp. gefeormod, 744.
feormynd, see **feormian**.

feorran(‡**)** (+), w 1., *remove;* 156. [feorr; Lang. § 13.3.]
feorran, adv., *from* aF A R; 430, 825, 1370, 2808, 2889, 3113; ∼ cumen, 361, 1819; ∼ ond nēan, 839; nēan ond ∼, 1174, 2317; *from far back* (time): 91, 2106.
feorran-cund(‡**)**, adj., *of a* F A R *country;* dsm. -um, 1795. [Cf. *Beitr.* xxxvi 414 n.]
feor-weg, m., F A R W A Y, (pl.:) *distant parts;* dp. (of) feorwegum, 37. (Cp. Norw A Y; *Alvíssmál* 10.)
fēower, num., F O U R; 59, 1637, 2163; a., 1027.
fēower-tȳne, num., F O U R T E E N; 1641.
fēran, w 1., *go,* FARE; 27, 301, 316 (tō fēran), 1390, 2261; pres. opt. 2 pl. fēran, 254; pret. 3 pl. fērdon, 839, 1632. [OS. fōrian, Ger. führen.]
ge-fēran, w 1., (*go to*), *reach, attain, bring about;* w. acc.: pres. opt. 3 sg. gefēre, 3063; pret. 3 pl. gefērdon, 1691 (n.); pp. gefēred, 2844; — w. þæt-clause: pp. gefēred, 1221, 1855.
ferh, see **feorh**.
ferhð†, m.n., *mind, spirit, heart;* gs. -es, 1060; ds. -e, 754, 948, 1166, 1718; dp. -um, 1633, 3176. [Cp. feorh.] — Cpds.: collen-, sārig-, swīð-; wīde-.
ferhð-frec‡, adj., *bold in spirit;* asm.wk. -an, 1146. [See freca.]
ferhð-genīðla‡, wk.m., *deadly foe;* as. -genīðlan, 2881.
ferh-weard‡, f., GUARD *over life;* as. -e, 305. See **feorh**.
ferian, w 1., *carry, lead, bring;* pres. 2 pl. ferigeað, 333; pret. 3 pl. feredon, 1154, 1158, fyredon 378; opt. 3 pl. feredon, 3113; pp. npm. gefe-

rede, 361. [F E R R Y; Go. farjan.] — Cpds.: æt-, of-, oð-.

ge-ferian, w 1., *carry;* 1638; imp. (adhort.) 1 pl. ~, 3107; pret. 3 pl. geferedon, 3130.

fetel-hilt‡, n. f., *linked* H I L T, *hilt furnished with a ring or chain* (Stjer. 25; Keller 43, 163 f.); ap. (asf.?) (þā) fetelhilt, 1563. See hilt.

fetian, w 2., F E T C H; pp. fetod, 1310.

ge-fetian, w 2., F E T C H, *bring;* 2190.

fēþa, wk.m., *band on foot, troop;* 1424; ds. fēðan, 2497, 2919; np. ~, 1327, 2544. See fēþe. — Cpd.: gum-.

fēþe, nja., *going, pace;* ds., 970. [OS. fāðí, fōðí. Not rel. to fōt.]

fēþe-cempa‡, wk.m., *foot-warrior;* 1544, 2853.

fēðe-gest†, mi., *foot-*G U E S T *or -warrior* (*Beitr.* xxxii 565 f.); dp. -um, 1976.

fēþe-lāst†, m., *walking-track, step;* dp. -um, 1632.

fēðe-wīg†, n. (or m.), *fight on foot;* gs. -es, 2364.

fex, see feax.

fīf, num., F I V E; uninfl. g., 545; a. fīfe, 420; [fīf, F. 41].

fīfel-cyn(n)‡, nja., *race of monsters;* gs. fīfelcynnes, 104. [Cp. ON. fífl; *MLN.* xxii 235.]

fīftig, num., w. gen., F I F T Y; gs. fīftiges, 3042; a. fīftig (wintra), 2209, 2733.

fīf-tȳne, num., F I F T E E N; g. fīf-tȳna, 207; a. fȳftȳne, 1582.

findan, III, F I N D; 207, 1156, 1378, 1838, 2294, 2870, 3162 (*devise*); pret. 1 sg. fond, 2136, funde 1486; 3 sg. fand, 719, 870, 2789; pp. funden, 7; — w. acc. & inf.; pret. 3 sg. fand, 118, 1267, fond 2270, funde 1415; 3 pl. fundon, 3033; — w. æt, *obtain from, prevail upon;* inf. findan, 2373. — Cpd.: on-.

finger, m., F I N G E R; np. fingras, 760; gp. fingra, 764; dp. fingrum, 1505; ap. fingras, 984.

fīond, see fēond.

fīras†, mja.p., *men, mankind;* gp. fīra, 91, 2001, 2286, 2741, fȳra *2250.* [Cp. feorh.]

firen, see fyren.

firgen-, see fyrgen-.

flǣsc, n., F L E S H; ds. -e, 2424.

flǣsc-homa(†), wk.m., *body;* as. -homan, 1568. See līc-homa.

flān, m. (or f.), *arrow;* ds. -e, 2438, 3119 (*arrowhead,* cf. Moore, Kl. Misc. 212).

flān-boga‡, wk.m., *arrow-*B O W; ds. -bogan, 1433, 1744.

flēah, see flēon.

flēam, m., *flight;* as., 1001, 2889. [Cp. flēon.]

flēogan, II, F L Y; pres. 3 sg. flēogeð, 2273, [F. 3].

flēon, II, F L E E; 755, 764, flēon 820; — w. acc., flēon, 1264; pret. 3 sg. flēah, *1200,* 2224. [OS. fliohan, Ger. fliehen.] — Cpds.: be-, ofer-.

flēotan, II, FLOAT, *swim, sail;* 542; pret. 3 sg. flēat, 1909.

flet(t), nja., (1) *floor (of a 'hall');* as. flet, 1540, 1568. — (2) *hall;* ns., 1976; ds. flette, 1025; as. flet, 1036, 1086 (n.), 1647, 1949, 2017, 2054, flett 2034. See heal(l), sele. (*R.-L.* ii 67; K. Rhamm, *Ethnograph. Beiträge zur german.-slavischen Altertumskunde,* ii 1 (1908), *passim.*) [Cp. FLAT, infl. by adj. flat fr. ON. flatr.]

flet-ræst‡, fjō.(?), (*hall-*R E S T),*couch in the hall;* as. -ræste, 1241.

flet-sittend(e)†, mc. (pres. ptc.) [pl.], S I T T *er in the hall;* dp.

GLOSSARY

-sittendum 1788; ap. -sittende, 2022.
flet-werod‡, n., *hall-troop;* 476.
fliht, mi., FLIGHT, *flying;* 1765. [flēogan.]
flītan, I, *contend, compete;* pres. ptc. npm. flītende, 916; pret. 2 sg. flite, 507. [FLITE, FLYTE (dial.); cp. Ger. Fleiss.] — Cpd.: ofer-.
flōd, m., FLOOD; 545, 580, 1361, 1422, 1689; gs. -es, 42, 1516, 1764; ds. -e, 1366, 1888; as. flōd, 1950, 3133; gp. -a, 1497, 1826, 2808.
flōd-ȳþ‡, fjō., FLOOD-*wave, wave of the sea;* dp. -um, 542.
flōr, m., FLOOR; ds. flōre, 1316; as. flōr, 725.
flota, wk.m., *ship, boat;* 210, 218, 301; as. flotan, 294. ['FLOATer' cp. flēotan.] — Cpd.: wēg-.
flot-here†, mja., *sea-army, naval force;* ds. -herge, 2915. [Cp. flota.] See scip-here.
(ge-)flȳman, w 1., *put to flight;* pp. geflȳmed, 846, 1370. [flēam.]
folc, n., FOLK, *people, nation;* (the pl. s.t. used w. sg. meaning); gs. folces, 1124, 1582, 1932, [F. 9]; ∼ hyrde, 610, 1832, 1849, 2644, 2981, [F. 46], si. 2513; ds. folce, 14, 465, 1701, 2377, 2393, 2595; as. folc, 463, 522, 693, 911, 1179; np. folc, 1422, 2948; gp. folca, 2017, (frēawine) ∼: 2357, 2429, si. 430; dp. folcum, 55, 262, 1855. — Cpds.: big-, sige-.
folc-āgend(e)†, mc. (pres. ptc.), *leader of people, chief;* npm. -āgende, 3113 (or ds.?). See 522.
folc-cwēn‡, fi., FOLK-QUEEN; 641.
folc-cyning†, m., FOLK-KING; 2733, 2873.
folc-rēd†, m., *people's benefit, what is good for the people;* as., 3006.

folc-riht, n., FOLK-RIGHT, *legal share of the 'common' estate;* gp. -a, 2608 (Schü. Bd. 46: *possessions*).
folc-scaru†, f., FOLK-SHARE, *public land;* ds. -scare, 73.
folc-stede†, mi., FOLK-STEAD; *dwelling-place,* as., 76; *battle-place,* as., 1463.
folc-toga†, wk.m., FOLK-*leader, chief;* np. -togan, 839. [tēon, II.]
fold-bold‡, n., BUILD*ing;* 773.
fold-būend(e)† mc. (pres. ptc.) [pl.], *earth-dweller, man;* np. būend, 2274; -būende, 1355; dp. -būendum, 309.
folde(†), wk.f., *earth, ground;* gs. foldan, 96, 1137, 1393; ds. ∼, 1196; as. ∼, 1361, 2975.
fold-weg†, m., WAY, *path;* as., 1633; np. -wegas, 866.
folgian, w 2., w. dat., FOLLOW, *pursue;* pret. 3 sg. folgode, 2933; opt. 3 pl. folgedon, 1102.
folm(†), f., *hand;* ds. -e, 748; as. -e, 970, 1303; dp. -um, 158, 722, 992; ap. -a, 745. — Cpds.: beadu-, gearo-.
fōn, rd., *grasp, grapple, seize;* 439 (wið); pres. 3 sg. fēhð (tō), 1755; pret. 3 sg. fēng (tōgēanes), 1542; — *receive* (cf. *JEGPh.* vi 195 f.); pret. 3 sg. fēng (w. dat.), 2989. —, Cpds.: be-, on-, þurh-, wið-, ymbe-.
ge-fōn, rd., w. acc., *seize, grasp;* pret. 1 sg. gefēng, 3090; 3 sg. ∼. 740, 1501, 1537, 1563, 2609.
fondian, see fandian.
for, prep., I. w. dat. (1) beFORE, *in front of, in the presence of;* 169(?), 358, 1026, 1120, 1649, 2020, 2501(?), 2781(?). — (2) FOR, *out of, because of, on account of;* 110 (w. instr.), 169, 338, 339, 382, 434, 457, 458, 462, 508, 509, 832,

965, 1206, 1515, 1796, 2223, 2501(?), 2549, 2781(?), 2835, 2926, 2966; w. murnan: 1442, 1537; *in return for*, 385, 951, 2385. — II. w. acc., *for, as, in place of;* for (sunu), 947, 1175; (nē ...) for (wiht), 2348. See fore.

foran, adv., *be*FORE, *in front;* 984, 2364; (fig.:) 1458. — Cpd.: be-.

for- (unstressed), **fore-** (stressed), prefix. See the foll. words. (Cf. M. Leopold, *Die Vorsilbe* ver- *und ihre Geschichte*, 1907, pp. 42 f., 274; O. Siemerling, *Das Präfix* for(e) *in der ae. Verbal- u. Nominalkomposition*, Kiel Diss., 1909.)

for-bærnan, w 1., BURN *up* (trans.); 2126.

for-beran, IV, FORBEAR, *restrain;* 1877.

for-berstan, III, BURST *asunder* (intr.), *snap;* pret. 3 sg. forbærst, 2680.

for-byrnan, III, BURN *up* (intr.); pret. 3 sg. forbarn, 1616, 1667, forborn 2672.

ford, m., FORD, ‡*water-way (sea);* as., 568. (Cp. Lat. vadum also used of 'body of water.')

fore, I. adv., *there*FOR, *for it;* 136. II. prep., w. dat., (1) *be* FORE, *in the presence of;* 1064, 1215. — (2) *on account of,* 2059.

fore-mǣre, adj.ja., *very famous, illustrious;* supl. foremǣrost, 309.

fore-mihtig(†), adj., *very powerful;* 969.

fore-snotor‡, adj., *very prudent or clever;* npm. foresnotre, 3162.

fore-þanc, m., FORETHOUGHT; 1060.

for-gifan, V, GIVE, *grant;* pret. 3 sg. forgeaf, 17, 374, 696, 1020, 1519, 2492, 2606, 2616, 2997.

for-grindan, III, GRIND *to pieces, crush* (w. dat. of person); pret. 1 sg. forgrand, 424; — *destroy, consume* (w. acc.); pp. (glēdum) forgrunden, 2335, 2677.

for-grīpan, 1, w. dat. *of person, crush to death;* pret. 3 sg. forgrāp, 2353. [GRIPE.]

for-gyldan, III, *repay, pay for, requite;* 1054, 1577, 2305, [F. 39]; pret. 1 sg. (-lēan) forgeald, 2094; 3 sg. forgeald, 2968, ([-]lēan) ~, 114, 1541, 1584; pp. forgolden, 2843; *recompense, reward* (w. pers. object): pres. opt. 3 sg. forgylde, 956.

for-gȳman, w 1., *neglect, be unmindful of;* pres. 3 sg. forgȳmeð, 1751.

for-gytan, v, FORGET; pres. 3 sg. forgyteð, 1751. [See *NED.* on the form of get.]

for-habban, w 3., *hold oneself back, restrain oneself,* FOR*bear;* (ne meahte ...) forhabban, 1151, 2609.

for-healdan, rd., *disregard, come short in one's duty towards* (Aant. 35), *rebel against;* pp. forhealden, 2381.

for-hicgan, w 3., *despise, scorn;* pres. 1 sg. forhicge (w. þæt-clause), 435.

forht, adj., *afraid;* 754, 2967. [Cp. FRIGHT fr. fyrhtu.] — Cpd.: un-.

for-lācan†, rd., *mislead, betray;* pp. forlācen, 903.

for-lǣdan, w 1., LEAD *to destruction;* pret. 3 pl. forlǣddan, 2039.

for-lǣtan, rd., *leave,* LET; 792 (*let go*); pret. 3 sg. forlēt, 2787; — w. acc. & inf.: ~, 970; 3 pl. forlēton, 3166.

for-lēosan, II, w. dat., LOSE; pret. 3 sg. forlēas, 1470, 2861; pp. forloren, 2145. [See losian.]

forma, adj. supl., *first;* forma (sīð), 716, 1463, 1527, 2625; ds. forman (sīðe), 740, 2286, [F. 19]; ~ (dōgore), 2573. [Cp. FORMer.] —

GLOSSARY

Supl. **fyrmest**, 2077. [Cp. FOREMOST.]
for-niman, IV, *take away, carry off, destroy;* pret. 3 sg. fornam, 488, 557, 695, 1080, 1123, 1205, 1436, 2119, 2236, 2249, 2772; w. dat.: 3 pl. fornāmon, 2828.
for-scrīfan, I, w. dat., *proscribe, condemn;* pp. forscrifen, 106. [See scrīfan. Cp. Lat. proscribere.]
for-sendan(‡)+, w I., S E N D *away, dispatch, put to death;* pp. forsended, 904. See for-sīðian.
for-sittan, V, *fail, diminish* (intr.); pres. 3 sg. forsiteð, 1767.
for-sīðian‡, w 2., *journey amiss (to destruction), perish;* pp. forsīðod, 1550.
forst, m., F R O S T; gs. -es, 1609.
for-standan, VI, (1) *with* S T A N D, *hinder, prevent;* pret. 3 sg. forstōd, 1549; opt. 3 sg. forstōde, 1056. — (2) *defend* (w. dat., *against*); inf., 2955.
for-swāpan†, rd., SWEEP *off;* pret. 3 sg. forswēop, 477, *2814*. [S W O O P.]
for-swelgan, III, S W A L L O W *up;* pret. 3 sg. forswealg, 1122, 2080.
for-sw(e)orcan, III, *become dark* or *dim;* pres. 3 sg. forsworceð, 1767.
for-swerian(‡)+, VI, w. dat., (S W E A R *away*, i.e.) ‡*make useless by a spell;* pp. forsworen, 804. (Cf. B.-T. Suppl.; *A*. l 195.)
forð, adv., F O R T H, *forward, on-(ward), away;* 45, 210, 291, 612, 745, 903, 948 (*henceforth*), 1162, 1179, 1632, 1718, 1795, 1909, 2069 (forð sprecan, 'go on speaking'), 2266, 2289, *2959*, 2967, 3176, [F. 5].
for-ðām, for-ðan, for-ðon, (1) adv., *there*FORE; forþan, 679, 1059; forðon, 2523, 3021(?); forðām, 149. — (2) conj., *because, since,* F O R; forðām, 149(?), 1957, 2645 (MS. forðā), 2741(?) (MS. forðā); forþan, 418, 1336; forðon, 2349, 3021 (?); forþon þe, 503. — (S.t. apparently used as a loose connective, 'so,' 'indeed.' Cf. Lawrence *JGPh*. iv 463 ff. See also Schü. Sa. §§ 11, 54; *Giessener Beitr.* i 77 ff., 133.)
forð-gerīmed(‡), pp. of -rīman, w I., *counted up, all told;* npn., 59.
forð-gesceaft†, fi., *future state, destiny;* as., 1750.
forð-gewiten, pp. of -gewītan, I, *departed, dead;* dsm. -um, 1479.
for-ðon, see **for-ðām.**
for-þringan(‡) (+), III, ‡*rescue, protect* (w. dat., *from*); 1084 (n.).
forð-weg†, m., WAY F O R T H; as., 2625.
for-weorpan, III, *throw away;* pret. opt. 3 sg. forwurpe, 2872.
for-wrecan, V, *drive away, banish;* 1919; pret. 3 sg. forwræc, 109.
for-wrītan‡, I, *cut through;* pret. 3 sg. forwrāt, 2705.
for-wyrnan, w I., *refuse,* (w. dat. of pers. & þæt-clause or gen. of thing); pres. opt. 2 sg. forwyrne, 429; pret. 3 sg. forwyrnde, 1142. [wearn.]
fōt, mc., F O O T; gs. fōtes, 2525; dp. fōtum, 500, 1166; ap. fēt, 745.
fōt-gemearc‡, n., F O O T-M A R K, *length of a foot;* gs. -es, 3042.
fōt-lāst(‡)+, m., F O O T-*print, track;* as., 2289.
fracod, adj., *bad, useless;* nsf., 1575. [cūþ; cp. Go. fra-kunnan 'despise.' See Siev. § 43 n. 4.]
(ge-)frægn, see (ge-)**frignan.**
frætwan, w I., *adorn, make beautiful;* 76.
frætwe, fwō.p., *ornaments, trappings, decorated armor* or *weapons, precious things, treasure;* gp. frætwa, 37, 2794, 3133; dp. frætwum,

BEOWULF

2054, 2163, 2784, 2989, frætewum 962; ap. frætwe, 214, 1207, 1921, 2503, 2620, 2919, frætwa 896.
ge-frætwian, w 2., *adorn, deck;* pret. 3 sg. gefrætwade, 96; pp. gefrætwod, 992.
fram, from, I. prep., w. dat., F R O M; (motion:) (*away*) *from;* fram, 194 (n.), 541, 543, 775, 855, 2366, postposit.: 110; from, 420, 1635, postposit.: 1715; — (origin, source); fram, 2565; *of, concerning:* fram, 581, 875, from 532. — **II. adv.**, *forth, away;* fram, 754, from 2556.
frēa†, wk.m., *lord, king;* 2285; gs. frēan, 2853; gs. or ds.: frēan, 500, 1166, frēan, 359, 1680 (prob. dat., see 1684 f.); ds. frēan, 291, 2662, frēan, 271; as. frēan, 351, 1319, 2537, 3002, 3107; — *consort:* ds. ~, 641 (cp. 1934?); — *the Lord:* gs. ~, 27; ds. ~ (ealles), 2794. [Cp. Go. frauja, ON. Freyr.] — Cpds.: āgend-, Līf-, sin-.
frēa-drihten†, m., *lord;* gs. -drihtnes, 796. See frēo-.
frēa-wine‡, mi., (*friend and*) *lord;* ~ (folca), 2357, 2429; as. ~, 2438. See frēo-.
frēa-wrāsn‡, f., (*lordly,* i.e.) *splendid chain* or *band;* dp. -um, 1451. (See Stjer. 4, 6, 13, 18.)
freca(†), wk.m., *bold one,* †*warrior;* 1563. [Cp. ferhð-frec; *Dial.D.:* F R E C K, F R A C K; Ger. frech.] — Cpds.: gūð-, hild-, scyld-, sweord-, wīg-.
frēcne, adj.ja., (1) *daring, audacious;* dsf.wk. frēcnan, *1104;* asf. frēcne, 889. — (2) *terrible, fearful, dangerous;* nsm. frēcne, 2689; nsn. ~, 2250, 2537; asf. ~, *1378;* asn. ~, 1359, 1691 (n.). [*ESt.* xxxix 330 f.]

frēcne, adv., *daringly, terribly, severely;* 959, 1032.
fremde, adj.ja., *foreign, alien, estranged* (w. dat.); nsf., 1691. [Ger. fremd.]
freme†, adj.i., *good, excellent;* nsf. fremu, 1932. [from, adj.]
fremman, w 1., (1) *further* (w. pers. obj.); 1832. — (2) *do, perform;* abs.: pres. opt. 3 sg. fremme, 1003; — w. obj.: inf., *101,* 2499, 2514, 2627, [F. 9]; pres. 3 sg. fremeð, 1701; imp. pl. fremmað, 2800 (*attend to*); pret. 3 sg. fremede, 3006; 1 pl. fremedon, 959; 3 pl. ~, 3, 1019; opt. 1 sg. fremede, 2134. [from, adj.]
ge-fremman, w 1., (1) *further, advance* (w. pers. obj.); pret. opt. 3 sg. gefremede, 1718. — (2) *do, perform, accomplish;* inf., 636, 1315, 2449, 2674; ger. gefremmanne, 174, 2644; pret. 3 sg. gefremede, 135, 165, 551, 585, 811, 1946, 2004, 2645; 1 pl. gefremedon, 1187; 3 pl. ~, 2478; opt. 3 sg. gefremede, 177, 591, 1552; pp. gefremed, 476, 954 (*brought about,* w. þæt-clause); asf. gefremede, 940.
frēo-burh‡, fc., (F R E E, i.e.) *noble town;* as., 693.
frēod†, f., *friendship;* gs. frēode, 2556; as. ~, 1707, 2476. [Cp. frēogan.]
frēo-drihten, -dryhten,†, m., *noble* (or *dear*) *lord;* ds. -dryhtne, 2627; vs. -drihten, 1169. See frēa-.
frēogan, w 2., †*love;* 948; pres. opt. 3 sg. frēoge, 3176. [Go. frijōn.]
frēo-līc(†), adj., *noble, excellent;* nsn., 615; [asn., F. 19]; nsf. -licu, 641.
frēond, mc., F R I E N D; 2393; as. ~, 1385, 1864; gp. -a, 1306, 1838; dp. -um, 915, 1018, 1126.

GLOSSARY

frēond-lārǂ, f., F R I E N D ly counsel (L O R E); dp. -um, 2377.
frēond-laþuǂ, f., F R I E N D ship, kindness, or invitation; 1192. (Cp. Hávamál 4: þjóðloð 'hearty welcome (cheer).') [Arch. cxv 179.]
frēond-līce, adv., in a F R I E N D L Y manner; comp. -līcor, 1027.
frēond-scipe, mi., F R I E N D S H I P; as., 2069.
freoðo, wk.f. (mu., Siev. §§ 271, 279), protection, safety, peace; gs., 188. [Cf. Lang. § 13.1; Ger. Friede.] — Cpd.: fen-.
freoðo-burh(ǂ)+, fc., town affording protection, stronghold (perh. orig. ref. to 'the sacred peace attaching to the king's dwelling,' cp. Ags. Laws [Chadwick H.A. 330 n.]); as., 522.
freoðo-wongǂ, m., field of refuge, fastness; as., 2959.
freoðu-webbe†, wk.f., peace-WEAVer, i.e. lady (cp. friðu-sibb); 1942.
frēo-wineǂ, mi., noble (or dear) friend; vs. ~ (folca), 430.
fretan, V, E A T up, devour, consume; 3014, 3114; pret. 3 sg. frǣt, 1581. [Go. fra-itan; NED.: F R E T, v.¹]
fricgan(†), V, ask, question; fricgcean, 1985. [Cp. frignan.] — Cpd.: fela-fricgende.
ge-fricgan(†), V, learn (orig. ' by inquiry '), hear of; pres. 1 sg. gefricge, 1826; 3 pl. gefricgeað, 3002; opt. 3 pl. gefricgean, 2889.
friclan(†), w 1., w. gen., desire, ask for; 2556. [Cp. freca; ESt. xxxix 337 f.]
frignan, frīnan, III, ask, inquire; frīnan, 351 (w. acc. of pers. & gen. of thing); imp. sg. frīn, 1322; pret. 3 sg. frægn, 236, 332, 1319, [F. 22, 46]. [Cp. fricgan; Go. fraíhnan.]
ge-frignan, III, learn, (orig. ' by inquiry '), hear of; pret. 1 sg. gefrægn, 575; 3 sg. ~, 194; 1 pl. gefrūnon (Lang. § 19.1), 2; 3 pl. ~, 70, gefrungon 666; pp. gefrægen, 1196, gefrūnen 694, 2403, 2952. — Foll. by inf.: pret. 1 sg. gefrægn, 74; by acc. & inf.: ~, 1011 (gefrægen), 1027, 2484, [2694], 2752, 2773, [F. 37]; 3 pl. gefrūnon, 1969. Cp. fricgan.
frioðo-wǣr†, f., compact of peace; gs. frioðowǣre, 2282; as. frioðuwǣre, 1096.
friðu-sib(b)ǂ, fjō., pledge of peace; friðusibb folca, 2017 (' bond of peace to the nations,' Earle, cp. 2028 f.).
frōd(†), adj., wise, old (' old and wise '); 279, 1306, 1366, 1844, 2209, 2513, 2625, 2950; (wintrum) ~, 1724, 2114, 2277; nsm.wk. -a, 2928; dsm.wk. -an, 2123; asf. -e, 2800 (Kemble, et al.: frōde, adv., ' prudently,' cf. B.-T. Suppl.). [Go. frōþs.] — Cpds.: in-, un-.
frōfor, f., consolation, solace, relief, help; frōfor 2941; gs. frōfre, 185; ds. ~, 14, 1707; as. frōfre, 7, 628, 973, 1273, frōfor 698 (n.; appar. masc.).
from, prep. (adv.), see fram.
from, adj., strenuous, bold, brave; 2527; npm. frome (fyrdhwate): 1641, 2476; dpf. fromum (splendid), 21. — Cpds.: sīð-, un-.
fruma, wk.m., beginning; 2309. (Other meanings: originator, maker, doer, chief.) — Cpds.: dǣd-, hild-, land-, lēod-, ord-, wīg-.
frum-cyn(n)†, nja., lineage, origin; as. -cyn, 252.
frum-gār†, m., chieftain; ds. -e, 2856. (Cp. Lat. ' primipilus '?)
frum-sceaft, fi. (m.?), creation, be-

ginning, origin; ds. -e, 45; as. -sceaft, 91.
ge-frūnen, -frūnon, -frungon, see ge-frignan.
fugol, m., *bird;* ds. fugle, 218; [np. fugelas, F. 5]; dp. fuglum, [2941]. [FOWL.]
full, adj., w. gen., FULL; 2412. — Cpds.: eges-, sorg-, weorð-.
ful, adv., FULL, *very;* ful (oft), 480, 951, 1252.
ful(l), n., (FILLed) *cup, beaker;* ful, 1192; ds. fulle, 1169; as. ful, 615, 628, 1025, ȳða ful ('sea'), 1208. [Cf. *IF.* xxv 152.] — Cpds.: medo-, sele-.
ful-læstan(†), w 1., w. dat., *help, support;* pres. 1 sg. -læstu, 2668. [Cp. fylstan; Siev. § 43 n. 4.]
full-ēode, pret. of ful(l)-gān, anv., w. dat., *follow, serve, aid;* 3119.
fultum, m., *help, support;* as., 698, 1273, 1835, 2662. [ful(l), tēam; Siev. § 43 n. 4.] — Cpd.: mægen-.
fundian, w 2., *strive, be eager to go;* pret. 3 sg. fundode, 1137 (n.); *desire* (w. inf. of motion); pres. 1 pl. fundiaþ, 1819.
furðum, adv., *just* (of time), *first;* 323, 465 (Ries L 6.12.2.378: ðā ... furþum = 'cum primum,' in subord. clause), 2009; (*a short time ago:*) 1707.
furþur, adv., FURTHER, *furthermore, further on;* 254, 761, [2525], 3006.
fūs, adj., *eager to set out, ready, hastening;* 1475, 3025, 3119; nsn., 1966; npm. fūse, 1805; — *longing;* nsm. fūs, 1916; — *ready for death;* nsm. ~, 1241. [Cp. fundian. Stern, *fūslīc and fūs, ESt.* lxviii 162–73.] — Cpds.: hin-, ūt-, wæl-.
fūs-līc(‡), adj., *ready;* asn., 1424; apn. (fyrdsearu) fūslicu, 232 (Gummere: 'war-gear in readiness'), (~) fūslīc 2618 (asn.?).
fȳf-tȳne, see fīf-tȳne.
fyl(l), mi., FALL; 2912; ds. -e, 1544 (see: on). — Cpds.: hrā-, wæl-.
ge-fyllan, w 1., FELL, *kill;* 2655; pret. 3 pl. gefyldan, 2706. [feallan.]
fyllo, wk.f., FILL, *plenty, feast;* gs. fylle, 562; gs. or ds. ~, 1014; ds. ~, 1333. [full.] — Cpds.: wæl-, wist-.
fyl-wērig‡, adj., (FALL-WEARY), *killed;* asm. -ne, 962.
fyr, see feor(r).
fȳr, n., FIRE; 2701, 2881; gs. -es, 185, 1764; ds. -e, 2274, 2309, 2595; as. fȳr, 1366. — Cpds.: bæl-, heaðo-, wæl-.
fȳras, see fīras.
fȳr-bend‡, fjō. (mi.), BAND *forged with* FIRE; dp. -um, 722.
fyrd-gestealla†, wk.m., *war-comrade;* dp. -gesteallum, 2873. [faran; cp. OHG. fart.]
fyrd-hom‡, m., *war-dress, coat of mail;* as., 1504.
fyrd-hrægl‡, n., *war-garment, corslet;* as., 1527.
fyrd-hwæt†, adj., *active in war, warlike;* npm. (frome) fyrdhwate, 1641, 2476.
fyrd-lēoð†, n., *war-song;* as., 1424.
fȳr-draca‡, wk.m., (FIRE-DRAKE), -DRAGON; 2689.
fyrd-searo‡, nwa., *armor;* ap. -searu, 232, -searo 2618 (as.?).
fyrd-wyrðe(‡) (+), adj.ja., *distinguished* (WORTHy) *in war;* 1316.
fyren, firen,(†), f., *crime, sin, wicked deed;* fyren, 915; as. fyrene, 101, 137, 153, 2480, firen' 1932; gp. fyrena, 164, 628, 750, fyrene 811; ap. fyrena, 879; dp. fyrenum, adv., *wickedly:* 1744, *exceedingly, sorely:* 2441 (*MPh.* iii 459). Cf. *IF.* xli 29 ff.; Hoops St. 89.

GLOSSARY

fyren-dǣd(†), fi., *wicked* D E E D, *crime;* dp. -um, 1001; ap. -a, 1669.

fyren-ðearf‡, f., *dire distress;* as. -e, 14.

fyrgen-bēam‡, m., *mountain-tree;* ap. -as, 1414. [Cp. Go. faírguni, see *Beitr.* xxxi 68 f.; Ritter 166 ff.; Holt. Et.; B E A M.]

fyrgen-holt‡, n., *mountain-wood;* as., 1393.

fyrgen-strēam†, m., *mountain*-S T R E A M, *waterfall* (?, Lawrence L 4.62.212; cf. Sarrazin, *ESt.* xlii 4 f.); 1359; as. firgenstrēam, 2128.

fȳr-heard‡, adj., H A R D*ened by* F I R E; npn., 305.

fyrian, see **ferian**.

fȳr-lēoht‡, n., F I R E-L I G H T; as., 1516.

fyrmest, see **forma**.

fyrn-dagas(†), m.p., D A Y S *of old;* dp. -dagum, 1451. [Cp. Go *faírn(ei)s; OE. feor(r).]

fyrn-geweorc†, n., *ancient* W O R K; as., 2286.

fyrn-gewin(n)‡, n., *ancient strife;* gs. -gewinnes, 1689.

fyrn-man(n)‡, mc., M A N *of old;* gp. -manna, 2761.

fyrn-wita†, wk.m., *old counselor;* ds. -witan, 2123.

fyrst, mi., *space of time, time* (granted for doing s.th.); 134, 210, 2555; ds. -e, 76 (n.); as. fyrst, 528, 545; is. -e, 2573. [Ger. Frist.]

(ge-)fyrðran, w I., F U R T H E R, *advance, impel;* pp. gefyrðred, 2784 (cf. Aant. 38). [furðor.]

fyr-wet(t), -wyt(t) [wit(t)], nja., *curiosity;* fyrwet, 1985, 2784; fyrwyt, 232. [Cp. OS. firi-wit(t).]

fȳr-wylm‡, mi., *surge of* F I R E; dp. um, 2671.

(ge-)fȳsan, w I., *make ready, impel, incite;* pp. gefȳsed, 217, 630 (*ready for,* w. gen.), 2309 (*pro-vided with,* w. dat.); nsf. ～, 2561. [fūs.]

gād†, n., *lack, want;* 660, 949.

gǣdeling(†), m., *kinsman, companion;* gs. -es, 2617 (Brett, *MLR.* xiv 5: *nephew*(?), cf. *Corpus Gloss.* 914: ' frat[r]uelis ' = geaduling); dp. -um, 2949. [Go. gadiliggs; OE. geador.]

gǣst, see **gist**.

gǣst, see **gāst**.

galan, VI, *sing, sound;* 786, 1432; pres. 3 sg. gæleð, 2460. [Cp. nightinG A L E.] — Cpd.: ā-.

galdor, see **gealdor**.

galga, wk.m., G A L L O W *s;* ds. galgan, 2446.

galg-mōd(†), adj., *sad in mind, gloomy;* nsf., 1277. [Cf. *IF.* xx 322.]

galg-trēow, nwa., G A L L O W *s*-T R E E; dp. -trēowum, 2940.

gamen, see **gomen**.

gamol†, adj., *old, aged, ancient;* (1) of persons (kings, etc.); 58, 265; gomol, 3095; gomel, 2112, 2793; wk. gamela, 1792; gomela, 1397, 2105, 2487, 2851, 2931, 2968; dsm. gamelum, 1677, gomelum 2444; wk. gomelan, 2817; asm.wk. gomelan, 2421; npm. gomele, 1595; gpm. gomelra (*men of old, ancestors*), 2036. — (2) of material objects (sword); nsn. gomol, 2682; asf. gomele, 2563; asn. gomel, 2610. [Cf. *Zfvgl. Spr.* xxvi 70; *IF.* v 12 f.; Falk-Torp, *Norw.-Dän. Etym. Wbch.*: gammel. — See *Beitr.* xi 562.]

gamol-feax†, adj., *grey-haired;* 608.

gān, anv., G O; 1163, gân 386, 1644; pres. 3 sg. gǣð, 455, 603, gǣð 2034, 2054]; opt. 3 sg. gā, 1394; imp. sg. gā, 1782; pp. (tōgædre) gegān, 2630 (of hostile meeting, cp. *Mald.* 67). — Pret. ēode; 3 sg., 358, [389, 403], 612, 640, 726, 918, 1232, 1312, 1814, 3123; 3 pl. ēodon, 493, 1626, 3031, [F. 14]. [Cp. Go. iddja. See Collitz, *Das schwache Präteritum* (Hesperia i, 1912), § 32.] — Cpds.: full-, ofer-, oð-, ymb-.

ge-gān, anv., (1) G O; pret. 3 sg. geēode, 2676; 3 pl. geēodon, 1967; *enter upon, go to* (w. acc.): inf. gegān, 1277, 1462. — (2) *obtain, gain;* inf. gegān, 1535; *bring to pass* (w. þæt-clause): pret. 3 pl. geēodon, 2917. — (3) *happen;* pret. 3 sg. geīode, 2200.

gang, m., *going;* gs. -es, 968; ds. -e, 1884; — *track;* ns. gang, 1404; as. ~, 1391. [*NED.*: G A N G, sb.[1]] — Cpds.: be-, in-.

gangan, rd., *go;* 314, 324, 395, 1034, [F. 43]; gongan, 711, 1642, 1974, 2083, 2648; imp. sg. geong (Lang. § 13.5), 2743; pret. 3 sg. †gēong, 925, 1785, 2019, 2756, 3125, †gīong, 2214, 2409, 2715; ‡gang (Lang. § 23.4), 1009, 1295, 1316. Pret. gen(g)de, see gengan. [Go. gaggan; G A N G (Sc., dial.).] — Cpd.: ā-.

ge-gangan, rd., (1) (*go to a certain point), reach* (cf. Lorz 24); pp. gegongen, 822, 3036; *obtain, win;* inf. gegangan, 2536; ger. gegangenne, 2416; pp. gegongen, 3085; *bring about* (w. þæt-clause): pp. gegongen, 893. — (2) *happen;* pres. 3 sg. gegangeð, 1846; pp. gegongen, 2821.

ganot, m., G A N N E T, *sea-bird;* gs. -es, 1861.

gār(†), m., (1) *spear*, according to 1765 (gāres fliht), for throwing; 1846, 3021; gs. -es, 1765; ds. -e, 1075; np. -as, 328. (2) *missile;* ds. -e, 2440 (= 'arrow'). [G A R-

(fish, lic), (Ed)-G A R; *NED.*: G A R E, sb.[1] (obs.), GORE, sb.[2], fr. OE. gāra.] — Cpds.: bon-, frum-.

gār-cēnē‡, adj.ja., (*spear-bold*), *brave;* 1958.

gār-cwealm‡, m., *death by the spear;* as., 2043.

gār-holt‡, n., *spear-shaft*, i.e. *spear;* as. (or ap.?), 1834.

gār-secg, mja., *ocean, sea;* as., 49, 515, 537. [*Epin. Gloss.* 966: segg = ' salum ² (' ocean '). Cp. gār, *Gen. (B)* 316? — Etym.: Grimm, *ZfdA.* i 578: secg ' sedge '; Kemble, *Gloss.* s.v. secg: ' spear-man ' (cp. Neptune?); Sweet, *ESt.* ii 315: gāsrīc ' rager.' Redbond, *MLR.* xxvii 204–6: Celtic.]

gār-wiga‡, wk.m., *spear-fighter, warrior;* ds. -wigan, 2674, 2811.

gār-wigend‡, mc., *spear-fighter, warrior;* ap., 2641.

gāst, gǣst, ma., mi., G H O S T, *spirit, sprite, demon;* gǣst, 102, 2073(?), 2312(??); gs. (wergan) gāstes, 133 (Grendel), 1747 (devil); as. gāst, 1274; gp. gāsta 1357, gǣsta 1123 (fire). — (Note. It is s.t. difficult to decide whether (-)gǣst (gist) or (-)gǣst was intended; see Rie. Zs. 383; Emerson L 4.149.880 n. 3; *Angl.* xxxv 251; Chambers, note on 102; Hoops 29 f.) — Cpds.: ellen-, ellor-, geōsceaft-, wǣl-.

gāst-bona‡, wk.m., *soul-slayer, devil;* 177. (Cf. *Angl.* xxxv 249.)

gē, conj., *and;* 1340; gē swylce, 2258; correl. gē ... gē (*both ... and*), 1864; gē ... gē ..., gē 1248.

gē, pron., see þū.

ge-, prefix. See Lorz 11 ff.; W. Lehmann, *Das Präfix uz- im Altenglischen*, p. i, n. 3.

geador(†), adv., *to* G E T H E R; 835;

~ ætsomne, 491. — Cpd.: on-.
ge-æhtle (-a?)‡, wk.f. (m.?), *consideration, esteem;* gs. geæhtlan, 369. [eahtian.]
geald, see gyldan.
gealdor, n., (1) *sound;* as., 2944. — (2) *incantation, spell;* ds. galdre, 3052. [galan.]
gealp, see gilpan.
gēap, adj., *curved, vaulted,* †*spacious;* 1800; asm. -ne, 836. — Cpds.: horn-, sǣ-. (Cf. Hoops 22 f., L 6.27.)
gēar, n., Y E A R; (oþ ðæt ōþer cōm) gēar, 1134 (='spring,' cp. *Guðl.* 716, *Runic Poem* 32). — See winter; missēre.
geāra, adv., gp. of gēar, *long since,* (*of* Y O R E); 2664. — Cpd.: un-.
geara, adj., see gearo.
geard, m., (*enclosure,* hence) *dwelling;* ap. -as, 1134; dp. (sg. meaning) -um, 13, 265, 1138, 2459. [Y A R D.] — Cpd.: middan-, wind-.
gēar-dagas, m.p., D A Y S *of* Y O R E; dp. (in, on) gēardagum, 1, 1354, 2233.
geare, see gear(w)e.
gearo, gearu, adj.wa., *ready, prepared* (*for:* gen., on w. acc.), *alert;* gearo, 121, 1825, 2414; gearu, 1109; geara (Lang. § 18.2), 1914; nsf. gearo, 2118, 3105; asf. gearwe, 1006; np. gearwe, 211, 1247, 1813 (*equipped with,* w. dat.). [Y A R E (dial., arch.); Ger. gar.] See gear(w)e, fæðergearwe. — Cpd.: eal-.
gearo, adv., see gear(w)e.
gearo-folm‡, adj., *with ready hand;* 2085.
gear(w)e, adv., (*readily*), *entirely, well, surely* (w. witan, cunnan, gemunan, scēawian); gearwe, 265, 2339, 2725; gearwe ne . . . , *not at all,* 246, 878; geare (cf. *Beibl.* xv 70), 2062, 2070, 2656; gearo, 2748 (n.). — Comp. gearwor, 3074 (n.). — Supl. gearwost, 715.
geato-līc†, adj., *equipped, adorned, splendid, stately;* 1401; nsn., 1562; asn. ~, 308, 2154; apn. ~, 215. [See geatwa.]
geatwa, fwō.p., *equipment, precious objects;* ap., 3088. [Siev. § 43 n. 4; see wīg-getāwa.] — Cpds.: ēored-, gryre-, hilde-.
ge-bedda, wk.m.f., B E D-*fellow;* ds. gebeddan, 665. — Cpd.: heals-.
ge-bræc, n., *crashing;* as., 2259. [Cp. brecan.]
ge-brōðor, mc.p., B R O T H E R s; dp. gebrōðrum, 1191.
ge-byrd, f.(n.)i., *fate;* as., 1074 (n.). [Cp. BIRTH.]
ge-cynde, adj.ja., *innate, natural, inherited;* nsn., 2197, 2696. [K I N D.]
ge-dāl, n., *separation, parting;* 3068. [Cp. dæl.] — Cpds.: ealdor-, līf-.
ge-dēfe, adj.(i.)ja., *fitting, seemly;* swā hit ~ wæs, 561, 1670, si. 3174; *gentle, kind;* nsm., 1227. [Go. gadōfs.] — Cpd.: (adv.) un-.
ge-dræg†, n., *bearing, concourse,* (*noisy*) *company;* as., 756. [dragan. See Grimm's note on *Andr.* 43; *Angl.* xxxiii 279(?).]
ge-dryht, -driht,†, fi., *troop, band of retainers,* (w. preceding gen. pl.); gedryht, 431; as. gedryht, 662, 1672; gedriht, 118, 357, 633. [drēogan; Go. ga-draúhts.] — Cpd.: sibbe-.
ge-fǣg(?)‡, adj., *satisfactory, pleasing, dear;* comp. gefǣgra, 915 (n.).
ge-fēa, wk.m., *joy;* as. gefēan (habban, w. gen.), 562, 2740. [gefēon.]
ge-feoht, n., F I G H T; 2441; ds. -e, 2048.
ge-flit, n., *contest, rivalry;* as. (on) geflit, 865. [flītan.]

ge-frǣge†, nja., *information through hearsay;* is.: mīne gefrǣge, *as I have heard say,* 776, 837, 1955, 2685, 2837. [ge-fricgan.]

ge-frǣge(†), adj.ja., *well known, renowned;* nsn., 2480; w. dat.: nsm., 55. [ge-fricgan; OS. gi-frāgi.]

gegn-cwide†, mi., *answer;* gp. -cwida, 367. [cweðan.]

gegnum†, adv., *forwards, straight, directly* (gangan, faran); 314, 1404.

gehðo, see giohðo.

ge-hwā, pron., prec. by partit. gen., *each (one);* gsm. gehwæs, 2527, 2838 (ref. to fem.); dsm. gehwǣm, 1365 (ref. to fem.), 1420; gehwām, 882, 2033; dsn. gehwām, 88; dsf. gehwǣre, 25; asm. gehwone, 294, 800 (ref. to fem.), 2765; gehwane, 2397, 2685.

ge-hwǣr, adv., *every*W H E R E, *on every occasion;* 526.

ge-hwæþer, pron., *either, each (of two), both;* 584, 814, 2171; nsn., 1248; gsn. gehwæþres, 1043; dsm. gehwæðrum, 2994. [EITHER fr. ǣg-hwæþer.]

ge-hwelc, see ge-hwylc.

ge-hwylc, pron., *each, every (one),* w. partit. gen. (pl.); 985, 1166, 1673; gsm. gehwylces, 732 (ānra ~, see ān), 1396; gsn. ~, 2094, 2189; dsm. gehwylcum, 412, 768, 784 (ānra ~), *936,* 996, 2859, 2891; dsf. gehwylcre, 805; dsn. gehwylcum, 98; asm. gehwelcne, 148; gehwylcne, 2250, 2516; asf. gehwylce, 1705; asn. gehwylc, 2608; ism. gehwylce, 2450; isn. ~, 1090, 2057.

ge-hygd, fni., *thought;* as., 2045. [hycgan.] — Cpds.: brēost-, mōd-; (ofer-, won-hygd).

ge-hyld, ni.(c.) (Siev. §§ 267a, 288 n. 1), *protection;* (manna) ~, 3056 (cf. *Angl.* xxxv 119 f.). [healdan.]

ge-lāc†, n., *motion, play;* dp. (ecga) gelācum, 1168; ap.(s.?) (sweorda) gelāc, 1040. [lācan.]

ge-lād(†), n., *way, course, tract;* as., 1410. [līþan.] — Cpd.: fen-.

ge-lang, adj., *at hand, dependent on* (æt); 1376; nsn. gelong, 2150. [A L O N G, adj. (arch. & dial.).]

ge-lenge, adj.ja., *be*LONG*ing to* (dat.); 2732.

ge-līc, adj., (A) L Ī K E; npm. -e, 2164 (n.). — Comp. gelīcost, L I K E S T; 218, 985; nsn., 727, 1608. [See *NED.:* alike.]

ge-lōme, adv., *frequently;* 559.

ge-long, see ge-lang.

ge-mǣne, adj.(i.)ja., *common, in common, mutual, shared;* nsf., *1857,* 2137 (n.), 2473, 2660; npm. ~, 1860; gpm. gemǣnra, 1784. [M E A N; Ger. gemein.]

ge-mēde(‡)+, nja., *agreement, consent;* ap. gemēdu, 247. [mōd; OS. gi-mōdi.]

ge-met, n., *measure, faculty, power;* 2533; as. ~, 2879; *means, manner:* mid gemete, *by ordinary means, in any wise,* 779 (*MPh.* iii 455 f.). Cp. mid ungemete, see B.-T. [metan.]

ge-met, adj. (cp. the noun), *fit, proper,* MEET; nsn.: swā him gemet þince, 687, si. 3057. — Cpd.: (adv.) un-gemete(s).

ge-mēting, f., M E E T I N G, *encounter;* 2001.

ge-mong, n., M I N G*ling together, throng, troop;* ds. (on) gemonge, 1643. [A M O N G; cp. mengan.]

ge-mynd, fni., *remembrance, memorial;* dp. -um, 2804, 3016. [M I N D; Go. ga-munds.]

ge-myndig, adj., M I N D*ful (of), intent (on)* (w. gen.); 868, 1173,

GLOSSARY 341

1530, 2082, 2171, 2689; nsf. ~, 613.
gēn, adv., *still, yet, further;* 2070, 2149, 3006; (nū) gēn, 2859, 3167; (ðā) gēn, 2237, 2677, 2702; w. negat., (ðā) gēn, *not yet, by no means,* 83, 734, 2081. See gȳt.
gēna, adv., *still, further;* 2800; (þā) ~, 3093. [Cp. āwa, sōna; -a fr. ā, =Go. aiw; Luick § 313.]
gende, see gengan.
ge-neahhe, adv., *sufficiently, abundantly, frequently;* 783 (*very*), 3152 (perh. *earnestly*); supl. genehost, 794 (n.).
ge-nehost, see ge-neahhe.
gengan(†), w 1., *go, ride* (cp. ærnan); pret. 3 sg. gengde, 1412, gende (Lang. § 19.1), 1401. [gangan.]
ge-nip, n., *darkness, mist;* ap. -u, 1360, 2808. [nīpan.]
ge-nōg, adj., E N O U G H, *abundant, many;* apm. -e, 3104; ap.(s.?)f. -e, 2489.
gēnunga(†), adv., *straightway, directly, completely;* 2871.
geō, adv., *formerly, of old;* 1476; giō, 2521; iū, 2459. [Go. ju.] See geōmēowle, iū-mon(n).
gēoc(†), f., *help;* ds. gēoce, 1834; as. ~, 177, 608, 2674.
gēocor†, adj., *grievous, sad;* 765.
geofon†, m. or n., *sea, ocean;* 515; gifen, 1690; gs. geofenes, 362, gyfenes 1394. [OS. geban.]
geofum, -ena, see gifu.
geogoð, f. (orig. fi.), Y O U T H; (1) abstract; ds. geogoþe, 409, 466, 2512, giogoðe 2426; as. gioguðe, 2112. — (2) concrete: *young persons (warriors);* ns. geogoð, 66, giogoð 1190; gs. (duguþe ond) geogoþe: 160, 621, (~) iogoþe, 1674; as. geogoðe, 1181.
geogoð-feorh†, m.n., (*period of*) Y O U T H; ds. (on) geogoðfēore,

537, (~) geoguðfēore, 2664.
geolo, adj.wa., Y E L L O W; asf. geolwe, 2610.
geolo-rand†, m., Y E L L O W *shield* (ref. to the color of the lindenwood, cp. 2610, or, perh., to a golden band encircling the shield, cf. Keller 73); as., 438.
geō-mēowle‡, wk.f., *old woman or wife;* 3150 (see Varr.); as. iōmēowlan, 2931. [Go. mawilō; cf. Siev. § 73 n. 1.] (Cf. Schü., *ESt.* lv 90 f.)
geōmor(†), adj., *sad, mournful;* 2100, him wæs geōmor sefa: 49, 2419, si. 2632; nsf. geōmuru, 1075. [OHG. jāmar; Ger. Jammer (noun).] — Cpds.: fela-, hyge-, mōd-, wine-.
geōmore†, adv., *sadly;* geōmore, 151.
geōmor-gyd(d)†, nja., *mournful song;* as. giōmorgyd, 3150.
geōmor-līc, adj., *sad;* nsn., 2444.
geōmor-mōd(†), adj., *sad of mind;* 2044, nsf. 3018; nsm. giōmormōd, 2267.
geōmrian, w 2., *mourn, lament;* pret. 3 sg. geōmrode, 1118.
geōmuru, see geōmor.
geond, prep., w. acc., *throughout, through, along, over;* geond þisne middangeard, 75, 1771; wīde geond eorþan, 266, 3099; geond wīdwegas, 840, 1704; geond þæt sæld, 1280, si. 1981, 2264. [Cp. bey O N D; Go. jaind.]
geond-brǣdan(‡) (+), w 1., *overspread;* pp. -brǣded, 1239. [brād.]
geond-hweorfan†, III, *pass through, go about;* pret. 3 sg. -hwearf, 2017.
geond-sēon‡, v, *look over;* pret. 1 sg. -seh, 3087.
geond-wlītan†, I, *look over;* giond-, 2771.
geong, adj., Y O U N G; 13, [20], 854,

1831, giong 2446; nsf. geong, 1926, 2025; wk.m. geonga, 2675; dsm. geongum, 1843, 1948, *2044*, 2674, 2811; dsm.wk. geongan, 2626, *2860*; asm. geongne, 1969; dpm. geongum, 72; apm. geonge, 2018. Supl. wk.n. gingæste (Luick § 169 n. 4), ‡*last*, 2817.

gēong, pret., and **geong**, imp. (2743), see **gangan.**

georn, adj., w. gen., *desirous, eager;* 2783. [Cp. Y E A R N, vb.; see georne.] — Cpd.: lof-.

georne, adv., *eagerly, willingly, earnestly;* 66, 2294; *readily, firmly,* 669, 968; *surely:* comp. geornor, 821. [Ger. gern.]

geō-sceaft‡, fi., *that which has been determined of old, fate;* as., 1234.

geō-sceaft-gāst‡, m., *demon sent by fate, fated spirit;* gp. -a, 1266.

gēotan, II, *pour, flow, rush;* pres. ptc. gēotende, 1690. [Go. giutan, Ger. giessen.]

ge-rād(‡)+, adj., *skilful, apt;* asn. wk. -e, 873. [Go. ga-raiþs; READY.]

ge-rūm-līce(‡), adv., ‡*at a distance, far away;* comp. -līcor, 139. [Cp. R O O M i L Y; on gerūm, *Rid.* 21.14, *El.* 320; OHG. rūmo, rūmor.]

ge-rysne, (-risne), adj.ja., *proper, becoming;* nsn. gerysne, 2653. [ge-rīsan.]

ge-saca, wk.m., *adversary;* as. gesacan, 1773. [sacan; cp. and-saca.]

ge-sacu(‡), f., *contention, enmity;* 1737. (=sacu.)

ge-scād, n., *distinction, discrimination;* gescād witan (w. gen.), *understand, be a judge (of)*, 288. (Cp. Ger. 'Bescheid wissen.') See ge-scādan.

ge-scæp-hwīl‡, f., *fated time (hour);* ds. -e, 26. [See ge-sceap; scyppan.]

ge-sceaft, fi., (*creation*, abstr., & concr. collect.), *world;* as., 1622. [scyppan.] — Cpds.: forð-, līf-, mæl-; cp. won-sceaft.

ge-sceap, n., *creation, creature,* S H A P E, *form;* np. gesceapu, 650. — Cpd.: hēah-.

ge-scipe‡, ni., *fate;* ds., 2570. [Cp. gesceap; *ZföG.* lvi 751.]

ge-selda†, wk.m., (*one of the same dwelling*), *companion, comrade;* as. geseldan, 1984. [See sæld.]

ge-sīð, m., *retainer, companion;* gs. -es, 1297; np. swǣse gesīðas, 29, so ap.: 2040 (n.), 2518; gp. swǣsra gesīða, 1934; dp. gesīðum, 1313, 1924, 2632. [sīð 'journey.'] — Cpds.: eald-, wil-.

ge-slyht(‡), ni., *battle, conflict;* gp. -a, 2398. [slēan; cp. Ger. Schlacht. See ond-slyht, Finnsb. Gloss.: wæl-sliht.]

ge-strēon, n., *wealth, treasure;* ns. (p.?), 2037; as. (p.?), 1920, 3166. [*NED.*: S T R A I N, sb.¹] — Cpds.: ǣr-, eald-, eorl-, hēah-, hord-, long-, māðm-, sinc-, þēod-.

gest-sele†, mi., G U E S T-*hall*, (*royal*) *hall for retainers* (*Beitr.* xxxii 9 ff., 565 ff.); as., 994. [See gist. Cf. Siev. § 75 n. 2.]

ge-sund, adj., S O U N D, *safe, unharmed;* asm. -ne, 1628, 1998; npm. -e, 2075; — w. gen.: apm. (sīða) gesunde, 318. See an-sund.

ge-swing†, n., *vibration, swirl, surf;* 848.

ge-sȳne, adj.(i.)ja., *visible, evident;* 2947, *3158*; nsn., 1255, 2316, 3058; npm., 1403. [S E E N; Go. (ana-)siuns; cp. OE. sēon, vb.] — Cpd.: ēþ-.

ge-synto, f., *health, safety;* dp. ge-syntum, 1869. [ge-sund.]

GLOSSARY 343

gētan(‡), w I., *destroy, kill;* (Kock L 5.44.4.1:) *cut open;* 2940. (Cp. ā-gētan, *Brun.* 18, etc.) [Gmc. *gautian, cp. OE. gēotan. *IF.* xx 327; Holt. Et.]
ge-tǣse, adj.ja., *agreeable;* nsf., 1320.
ge-tenge, adj.ja., *lying on, close to* (w. dat.); asn., 2758.
ge-trum, n., *troop, company;* is. -e, 922.
ge-trȳwe, adj.ja., T R U E, *faithful;* 1228.
ge-þinge, nja., (1) *agreement, compact;* ap. geþingo (*terms*), 1085. — (2) *result, issue;* gs. geþinges, 398, 709; gp. geþingea, 525. [See þing; cp. Ger. Bedingung.]
ge-þōht, m., T H O U G H T; as., 256, 610.
ge-þonc, m.n., THOUGHT; dp. -um, 2332. [See þencan.] — Cpd.: mōd-.
ge-þrǣc(†), n., *press, heap;* as., 3102. [See þrec-wudu; mōd-þracu.]
ge-þring, n., THRONG, *tumult;* as., 2132.
ge-þrūen, see under þ.
ge-þwǣre, adj.ja., *harmonions, united, loyal;* npm., 1230. [geþweran ‘stir,’ ‘mix together.’] See mon-ðwǣre.
ge-þyld, fi., *patience;* as., 1395; dp. geþyldum, *steadily*, 1705. [þolian; Ger. Geduld.]
ge-þȳwe(‡)+, adj.ja., *customary, usual;* nsn., 2332. [þēaw.]
ge-wǣde, nja., *dress, equipment, armor;* ap. gewǣdu, 292. [wǣd > W E E D (s).] — Cpds.: brēost-, eorl-, gūð-.
ge-wealc, n., *rolling;* as., 464. [Cp. WALK, OE. wealc(i)an.]
ge-weald, n., *power, control;* as., 79, 654, 764, 808, 903, 950, 1087, 1610, 1684, 1727; dp. mid ge-wealdum, *of his own accord*, 2221.
ge-wealden, see ge-wealdan.
ge-weorc, n., W O R K; gs. geweorces, 2711; — (*something wrought*), hand-I W O R K; ns. geweorc, 455, 1562, 1681; as. ~, 2717, 2774. — Cpds.: ǣr-, fyrn-, gūð-, hond-, land-, nīþ-.
ge-widre, nja., WEATHER, *storm;* ap. gewidru, 1375. [weder; Ger. Gewitter.]
ge-wif (or **ge-wife**) (‡)+, ni., WEB (*of destiny*), *fortune;* ap. gewiofu, 697. [wefan; cf. *ZfdPh.* xxi 358; Siev. § 263 n. 3.]
ge-win(n), n., *strife, struggle, fight;* gs. gewinnes, 1721; as. gewin, 798 (see drēogan), 877, 1469 (*turmoil*); — *strife, hardship;* ns. gewin, 133, 191; as. ~, 1781. — Cpds.: fyrn-, ȳð-.
ge-wiofu, see ge-wif.
ge-wis-līce, adv., *certainly;* supl. -līcost, 1350. [I W I S, Y W I S (arch.); Ger. gewiss.]
ge-wit(t), nja., *intellect, senses;* ds. gewitte, 2703; — (*seat of intellect*), *head;* ds. ~, 2882. [See wit(t).]
ge-wittig, adj., *wise, conscious;* 3094. (Cf. Ælfric, *Hom.* ii 24.12, 142.19: gewittig ‘in one's senses.’) [wit(t).]
ge-wrixle, nja., *exchange;* 1304. [See wrixl.]
ge-wyrht, fni., *deed done, desert;* dp. um, 457 (n.). [wyrcan.] — Cpd.: eald-.
gid(d), nja., *song, tale,* (*formal*) *speech;* gid 1065, gidd 2105, gyd 1160; as. gid, 1723; gyd, 2108, 2154, 2446; gp. gidda, 868; dp. giddum 1118, gyddum, 151. — Cpds.: geōmor-, word-. (Cf. Merbot L 7.7.25 ff.; *P.Grdr.*[2] ii[a] 36 f.; *R.-L.* i 444. See lēoð, spel(l).)
gif, conj.; (1) I F; w. ind.: gif, 272,

346, 442, 447, 527, 661, 684, 1185, 1822, 1826, 1836, 1846, 2514; gyf, 944, 1182, 1382, 1852; w. opt.: gif, 452, 593, 1379, 1477, 1481, 2519, 2637, 2841; gyf, 280 (ind.?), 1104. — (2) *whether, if*, w. opt.; gif, 1140, 1319.

gifan, v, G I V E; inf. giofan, 2972; pret. 3 sg. geaf, 1719, 2146, 2173, 2431, 2623, 2635, 2640, 2865, 2919, 3009, 3034; 3 pl. gēafon, 49; pp. gyfen, 64, 1678, 1948. [On the prob. Scand. infl. on the form of give, see *NED*.] — Cpds.: ā-, æt-, for-, of-.

gifen, (noun), see geofon.

gifeðe(†), adj.ja. (cf. Kluge, *Nominale Stammbildungslehre* § 233), G I Ven, *granted* (*by fate*); 2730; nsn. 299, 2491, 2682, gyfeþe 555, 819. [Cp. OS. gibiðig.] — Cpd.: un-. — gifeðe †, nja., *fate;* 3085.

gif-heal(l)‡, f., GIFt-H A L L; as. -healle, 838.

gīfre, adj.ja., *greedy, ravenous;* nsf., 1277. — Supl. gīfrost, 1123. — Cpd.: heoro-.

gif-sceat(t)‡, m., GIFt; ap. -sceattas, 378. [See sceat(t).]

gif-stōl†, m., GIFt-*seat, throne;* 2327; as. ~, 168. (See ēþel-stōl.)

gifu, f., GIFt; 1884; as. gife, 1271, 2182; gp. gifa, 1930, geofena 1173; dp. geofum, 1958. — Cpds.: māðm-, swyrd-.

gīgant, m., GIANT; np. -as, 113; gp. -a, 1562, 1690. [Fr. Lat. (Gr.) gigas, acc. gigantem.]

gilp, n. (m.), *boast, boasting;* ds. gylpe, 2521 (n.); as. gilp, 829, gylp 2528; on gylp, *proudly, honorably,* 1749. [OS. gelp.] Cf. Schü. L 7.25 i. — Cpd.: dol-.

gilpan, gylpan, III, w. gen. or dat., *boast, rejoice;* gylpaи, 2874; pres. 1 sg. gylpe, 586; 3 sg. gylpeð,
2055; pret. 3 sg. gealp, 2583. [Y E L P.] — Cpd.: be-.

gilp-cwide†, mi., *boasting speech;* 640. [OS. gelp-quidi.]

gilp-hlæden‡, adj. (pp.), (*vaunt-*L A D E N), *covered with glory, proud;* 868. (*MPh*. iii 456. But see also Gummere's note: ' a man ... who could sing his *bēot*, or vaunt, in good verse....' Bryan, *JEGPh*. xix 85: =gidda gemyndig.)

gim(m), m., GEM, *jewel;* 2072. [Fr. Lat. gemma (>OFr. gemme> MnE. gem).] — Cpd.: searo-.

gin(n)†, adj., *spacious, wide;* asm. gynne, 1551; asn.wk. ginne (MS. gimme), 466.

gin-fæst, gimfæst (Lang. § 19.3),†, adj., *ample, liberal;* asf. gimfæste (gife), 1271; asf.wk. ginfæstan (~), 2182. [gin(n).]

gingæst, see geong.

gið, see geō.

giofan, see gifan.

giogoð, see geogoð.

giohðo †, f., *sorrow, care;* ds. (on) giohðe,°2793, (~) gehðo 3095; as. giohðo, 2267.

giōmor(-), see geōmor(-).

giond-, see geond-.

giong, see geong.

gīong, pret., see gangan.

ge-giredan, see ge-gyrwan.

gist, mi., *stranger, visitor,* G U E S T; gist, 1138, 1522; gæst, 1800, 2073 (??), 2312(?); ds. gyste, *2227;* as. gist, 1441; np. gistas, 1602; ap. gæstas, *1893*. [Cogn. w. Lat. hostis; form guest prob. infl. by ON. gestr.] — Cpds.: fēðe-, gryre-, inwit-, nīð-, sele-.

git, see þū.

gīt, see gȳt.

gladian(‡)+, w 2., ‡*glisten, shine;* pres. 3 pl. gladiað, 2036. [glæd.]

GLOSSARY

glæd, adj., *kind, gracious;* 1173; dsm. gladum, 2025; asm. glædne, 863, 1181; *lordly, glorious:* apm. glæde, 58 (n.). [G L A D (cp. glædmōd); oldest meaning ' shining.']

glæd-man‡, adj., *kind, gracious;* vs., 367. (Wr.-Wü., *Vocab.* i 171.40: ' hilaris ' = glædman; *Beitr.* xii 84; *ESt.* xx 335.)

glæd-mōd, adj., G L A D *at heart;* 1785.

glēd, fi., *fire, flame;* 2652, 3114; dp. glēdum, 2312, 2335, 2677, 3041. [G L E E D (arch., dial.); cp. glōwan.]

glēd-egesa‡, wk.m., *fire-terror, terrible fire;* 2650.

glēo, n. (Siev. §§ 247 n. 3, 250 n. 2), G L E E, *mirth, entertainment;* 2105.

glēo-bēam, m., G L E E-*wood, harp;* gs. -es, 2263. [B E A M.]

glēo-drēam‡, m., *mirth;* as., 3021.

glēo-man(n), mc., G L E E M A N, *singer;* gs. -mannes, 1160.

glīdan, I, G L I D E; pret. 3 sg. glād, 2073; 2 pl. glidon, 515. Cpd.: tō-.

glitinian(‡)+, w 2., GLITT*er, shine;* 2758. [Cp. Go. glitmunjan.]

glōf, f., G L O V E, (*pouch?*); 2085 (n.). [*Arch.* cxxv 159; Th. Kross, *Die Namen der Gefässe bei den Ags.* (1911), pp. 89 f.]

gnēað(‡)+, adj., *niggardly, sparing;* 1930.

gnorn†, m. or n., *sorrow, affliction;* as., 2658.

gnornian, w 2., *mourn, lament;* pret. 3 sg. gnornode, 1117. — Cpd.: be-.

God, m., G O D; 13, 72, 381, 478, 685, 701, 930, 1056, 1271, 1553, 1658, 1716, 1725, 1751, 2182, 2650, 2874, 3054; gs. Godes, 570, 711, 786, 1682, 2469, 2858; ds. Gode, 113, 227, 625, 1397, 1626, 1997; as. God, 181, 811. (Cf. *Angl.* xxxv 123 ff.)

gōd, adj., G O O D (*able, efficient, excellent, strong, brave;* used mostly of persons); 195, 269 (w. gen., ' as regards '), 279 (frōd ond gōd), 1870, 2263, 2543, 2563; þæt wæs gōd cyning: 11, 863, 2390; nsn. gōd, 1562; nsm.wk. gōda, 205, 355, 675, 758, 1190, 1518, 2944, 2949; dsm. gōdum, 3036, 3114; dsm.wk. gōdan, 384, 2327; asm. gōdne, 199, 347, 1486, 1595, 1810, 1969, 2184; npm. gōde, 2249; npm.wk. gōdan, 1163; gpm. gōdra, 2648, [F. 33]; dpf. gōdum, 2178; apm. gōde, 2641. — Cpd.: ǣr-. — Comp. **betera**, B E T T E R, *superior;* 469, 1703 (geboren ∼, cp. (bett) borenra, *Ælfr. Laws* 11.5 [MS. H]). Supl. **bet(o)st**, B E S T; nsm. betst, 1109; nsf. betost, 3007; asn. betst, 453; asm.wk. betstan, 1871; vsm.wk. betsta, 947, 1759. — Comp. **sēlra**, **sēlla**, *better* (only 4 times of persons); sēlra, 860, 2193, 2199 (' higher in rank '); sēlla, 2890; nsn. sēlre, 1384; dsm. sēlran, 1468; asm. sēlran, 1197, 1850; asn. sēlre, 1759; npf. sēlran, 1839. Supl. **sēlest**, *best* (only 6 times of persons); nsf., 256; nsn., 146, 173, 285, 935, 1059, 1389, 2326; nsm. wk. sēlesta, 412; dsm.wk. sēlestan, 1685; asn. sēlest, 454, 658, 1144; asm.wk. sēlestan, 1406, 1956 2382; npm.wk. ∼, 416; apm. ∼, 3122. See sēl. [*sōl¹-; cp. Go. sēls (ablaut).]

gōd, n., G O O D, *goodness, good action, gifts, liberality;* ds. gōde, 20, 956, 1184, 1952; gp. gōda (*advantages,* ' *gentle practices,*' Earle), 681; dp. gōdum, 1861.

gōd-fremmend(e)‡, mc. (pres. ptc.) [pl.], *one doing* G O O D, *acting bravely;* gp. gōdfremmendra, 299.

gold, n., G O L D; 1107, 1193, 2765; 3012, 3052, 3134; gs. goldes, 1093, 1694, 2246, 2301; ds. golde, 304, 553, 777, 927, 1028, 1054, 1382, 1484, 1900, 2102, 2192, 2931, 3018; as. gold, 2276, 2536, 2758, 2793, 3105, 3167. — Cpd.: fæt-.

gold-æht‡, fi., *possessions in* G O L D, *treasure of gold;* as., 2748.

goid-fāg, -fāh,(‡)+, adj., *ornamented with* G O L D; -fāh, 1800; asm. -fāhne, 2811; asn. -fāh, 308; npn. -fāg, 994.

gold-gyfa†, wk.m., G O L D-G I V*er, lord;* as. -gyfan, 2652.

gold-hrōden†, adj. (pp.), G O L D-*adorned;* nsf., 614, 640, 1948, 2025. [hrēodan.]

gold-hwæt‡, adj., *greedy for* G O L D (or *rich in gold?*); apm. -e, 3074 (n.). See hwæt.

gold-māðum‡, m., G O L D-*treasure;* ap. -māðmas, 2414.

gold-sele‡, mi., G O L D-*hall;* ds., 1639, 2083; as., 715, 1253.

gold-weard‡, m., GUARD*ian of* G O L D; as., 3081.

gold-wine†, mi., G O L D-*friend,* (*generous*) *prince;* goldwine gumena: ns., 1602, vs. 1171, 1476; goldwine Gēata: ns., 2419, 2584.

gold-wlanc†, adj., *splendidly adorned with* G O L D; 1881.

gombe (wk.f.?) (-a?, -an?)†, *tribute;* as. gomban (gyldan), 11. (The only other instance: gombon (gieldan), *Gen.* 1978; cp. gambra, *Hel.* 355.)

gomel, gomol, see gamol.

gomen, n., *joy, mirth, sport, pastime;* 2263, 2459, gamen, 1160; ds. gomene, 1775, gamene, 2941; as. gamen, 3021. [G A M E; Falk-Torp, *Etym. Wbch.*: gammen.] — Cpd.: heal-.

gomen-wāþ‡, f., *joyous journey;* ds. -e, 854.

gomen-wudu‡, mu., W O O D *of mirth* (*harp*); 1065; as., *2108.*

(ge-)gongan, see (ge-)gangan.

grǣdig, adj., G R E E D Y, *fierce;* nsf. (grim ond) grǣdig, 121, so 1499 (m.f.); asn. grǣdig, 1522.

grǣg, adj., G R E Y; npn., 330; apf. -e, 334.

grǣg-mǣl‡, adj., G R E Y-*colored* ('-*marked* '); nsn., 2682.

grǣs-molde‡, wk.f., G R A S S-M O L D, *greensward;* as. -moldan, 1881.

gram, adj., *wrathful, hostile;* gsm. -es, 765; npm.wk. -an, 777; dpm. -um, 424, 1034. [Cp. grim(m); Ger. gram.] — Cpd.: ǣfen-.

grāp, f., *grasp, claw;* gs. -e, 836; ds. -e, 438, 555; dp. -um, 765, 1542. [grīpan.] — Cpds.: fēond-, hilde-.

grāpian, W 2., (G R O P E), *grasp;* pret. 3 sg. grāpode, 1566, 2085.

grēot, n., *sand, earth;* ds. -e, 3167. [G R I T.]

grēotan†, II, *weep;* pres. 3 sg. grēoteþ, 1342. [G R E E T (Sc., North.). *Anz.fdA.* xx 244: grēotan fr. blending of grētan (=*grǣtan) and rēotan.]

grētan, W 1., (1) *approach, touch, attack;* 168, 803 (*harm*), 2421, 2735; pret. 3 sg. grētte, 1893, 2108; opt. 2 sg. ~, 1995; 3 sg. ~, 3081; pp. grēted, 1065. — (2) G R E E T, *salute, address;* inf. grētan, 347, 1646, 2010, 3095; pret. 3 sg. grētte, 614, 625, 1816. [OS. grōtian. Cf. *Beitr.* xxxvii 205 ff.]

ge-grētan, W 1., G R E E T, *address;* inf. gegrēttan (Lang. § 19.4), 1861; pret. 3 sg. gegrētte, 652, 1979, 2516.

grim(m), adj., G R I M, *fierce, angry;* grim, 555, 2043, 2650; nsf. ~, 121, 1499 (m.f.), 2860; nsm.wk.

GLOSSARY

grimma, 102; gsf. grimre, 527; asm. grimne, 1148, *2136;* asf. grimme, *1234;* dpm. grimmon, *306;* dpf. wk.(?) grimman, 1542. — Cpds.: heaðo-, heoro-, nīþ-, searo-.

grīm-helm†, m., *mask-*HELM*et*, *(vizored) helmet;* ap. -as, 334. See beado-, here-grīma. ("Visors, in the strict (technical) sense, were unknown in Beowulf's time, but the face was protected by a kind of mask." Cl. Hall. Cf. Keller 92, 246 f.; Stjer. 4 f.; Falk L 9.44. 164.)

grim-līc, adj., *fierce, terrible;* 3041.

grimme, adv., G R I M*ly, terribly;* 3012, 3085.

grīpan, I, G R I P E, *grasp, clutch;* pret. 3 sg. grāp, 1501. — Cpds.: for-, wið-.

gripe, mi., G R I P, *grasp, attack;* 1765; as., 1148. — Cpds.: fǣr-, mund-, nīd-.

grom-heort†, adj., *hostile-*H E A R T*ed;* 1682.

grom-hȳdig†, adj., *angry-minded, hostilely disposed;* 1749. [hycgan.]

grōwan, rd., G R O W; pret. 3 sg. grēow, 1718.

grund, m., G R O U N D, *bottom;* ds. grunde, 553, 2294, 2758, *2765;* as. grund, 1367, 1394; — *plain, earth;* as. (gynne) grund, 1551; ap. grundas, 1404, 2073. — Cpds.: eormen-, mere-, sǣ-.

grund-būend†, mc. [pl.], *inhabitant of the earth, man;* gp. -ra, 1006.

grund-hyrde‡, mja., *guardian of the deep;* as., 2136.

grund-wong‡, m., G R O U N D-*plain; bottom (of the mere),* as., 1496; *surface of floor,* as., 2770; — *earth;* as., 2588 (n.).

grund-wyrgen‡, fjō., *accursed (female) monster of the deep;* as.

-wyrgenne, 1518. (Cf. *Angl.* xxxv 253; Philippson L 4.42. n. 10.53, n. 6.) See werhðo.

gryn(n), see **gyrn**.

gryre(†), mi., *terror, horror;* 1282 (Schü. Bd. 49: *force of attack*); ds. (as.?), 384; as., 478; gp. gryra, 591; dp. gryrum, 483. — Cpds.: fǣr-, wīg-.

gryre-brōga†, wk.m., *horror;* 2227.

gryre-fāh‡, adj., *terrible in its variegated coloring* (rather than *terribly hostile,* cf. *JEGPh.* xii 253); *3041;* asm. -ne, 2576.

gryre-geatwe‡, fwō.p., *terrible armor, warlike equipment;* dp. -geatwum, 324. See wīg-getāwa.

gryre-giest‡, mi., *dreadful stranger;* ds. -e, 2560.

gryre-lēoð†, n., *terrible song;* as. 786.

gryre-līc†, adj., *terrible, horrible,* asm. -ne, 1441, 2136.

gryre-sīð‡, m., *dreadful (perilous) expedition;* ap. -as, 1462.

guma†, wk.m., *man; 20,* 652, 868, 973, 1682, 2178; vs., 1384; ds. guman, *2821;* as. ~, 1843, 2294; np. ~, 215, 306, 666, 1648; gp. gumena, 73, 328, 474, 715, 878, 1058, 1171, 1367, 1476, 1499, 1602, 1824, 2043, 2233, 2301, 2416, 2516, 2859, 3054; dp. gumum, 127, 321; ap. guman. 614. — Cpds.: dryht-, seld-.

gum-cyn(n)†, nja., *man*KIND, *race, men;* gs. -cynnes, 260, 2765; dp. -cynnum, 944. [K I N.]

gum-cyst††, fi., *manly virtue, munificence;* dp. -um (gōd): 1486, 2543; ap. -e, 1723. (Cp. uncyst = 'avaritia,' Ben. R. (ed. Schröer) 55.3, etc.)

gum-drēam‡, m., *joys of men:* as., 2469.

gum-dryhten‡, m., *lord of men;* 1642.
gum-fēþa‡, wk.m., *band on foot;* 1401. See fēþa.
gum-man(n)‡, mc., MAN; gp. -manna, 1028.
gum-stōl‡, m., *throne;* ds. -e, 1952. (See brego-stōl.)
gūð†, f., *war, battle, fight;* 1123, 1658, 2483, 2536; gs. -e, 483, 527, 630, 1997, 2356, 2626; ds. -e, 438, 1472, 1535, 2353, 2491, 2878, [F. 31]; as. -e, 603 (ds.?, cf. *MPh.* iii 453); gp. -a, 2512, 2543; dp. -um, 1958, 2178.
gūð-beorn‡, m., *warrior;* gp. -a, 314.
gūð-bil(l)†, n., *war-sword;* 2584; gp. -billa, 803.
gūð-byrne‡, wk.f., *war-corslet;* 321.
gūð-cearu‡, f., *war-*CARE, *grievous strife;* ds. -ceare, 1258.
gūð-cræft‡, m., *war-strength;* 127.
gūð-cyning†, m., *war-*KING; 2335 (-kyning), 2563, 2677, 3036; as., 199, 1969.
gūð-dēað‡, m., DEATH *in battle;* 2249.
gūð-floga‡, wk.m., *war-*FLI*er;* as. -flogan, 2528. [flēogan.]
gūð-freca†, wk.m., *fighter;* 2414.
gūð-fremmend(e)†, mc. (pres. ptc.) [pl.], *warrior;* gp. -fremmendra, 246.
gūð-getāwa‡, fwō.p., *war-equipments;* ap., 2636; dp. -um, 395. See wīg-getāwa.
gūð-gewǣde‡, nja., *war-dress, armor;* np. -gewǣdo, 227; ap. -gewǣdu, 2617, 2730, 2851, 2871; -gewǣda (gp.?), 2623 (n.).
gūð-geweorc‡, n., *warlike deed;* gp. -a, 678, 981, 1825.
gūð-helm‡, m., *war-*HELM*et;* 2487.
gūð-horn‡, n., *war-*HORN; as., 1432.

gūð-hrēð‡, (orig. n., see hrēð), *glory in battle;* 819.
gūð-lēoð‡, n., *war-song;* as., 1522.
gūþ-mōd‡, adj., *of warlike mind;* 306.
gūð-rǣs†, m., *storm of battle, attack;* as., 2991; gp. -a, 1577, 2426.
gūð-rēow‡, adj., *fierce in battle;* -rēouw, 58. (Cf. T.C. § 2.) [Holt. Et.]
gūð-rinc†, m., *warrior;* 838, 1118 (n.), 1881; as., 1501; gp. -a, 2648.
gūð-rōf†, adj., *brave* (or *famous*) *in battle;* 608.
gūð-scear‡, m., *slaughter* (SHEAR*ing*) *in battle, carnage;* ds. -e, 1213. Cp. inwit-scear.
gūð-sceaða‡, wk.m., *enemy, destroyer;* 2318.
gūð-searo‡, nwa., *armor;* np., 328; ap., 215.
gūð-sele‡, mi., *battle-hall;* ds., 443, 2139.
gūð-sweord‡, n., *war-*SWORD; as., 2154.
gūð-wērig‡, adj., *worn out* (WEARY) *with fighting, dead;* asm. -ne, 1586.
gūð-wiga‡, wk.m., *warrior;* 2112.
gūð-wine‡, mi., *war-friend, warrior, sword;* as., 1810; dp. -winum, 2735.
gyd(d), see gid(d).
gyddian, w 2., *speak, discourse;* pret. 3 sg. gyddode, 630.
gyf, see gif.
gyfen, (noun), see geofon.
gyfen, pp., see gifan.
gyfeþe, see gifeðe.
gyldan, III, *pay, repay;* 11, 1184, 2636; pret. 1 sg. geald, 2491; 3 sg. ~, 1047, 2991; [3 pl. guldan, F. 40]. [YIELD.] — Cpds.: ā-, an-, for-.
gylden, adj., GOLDEN; nsn., 1677; dsm. gyldnum, 1163; asm. gyl-

GLOSSARY

denne, 47, 1021, 2809. [goɪ̌ď; Go. gulþeins.] — Cpd.: eal(l)-.
gylp, gylpan, see gilp, gilpan.
gylp-spræc‡, f., *boasting* S P E E C H; ds. -e, 981.
gylp-word, n., *boasting* W O R D; gp. -a, 675.
gȳman, w 1., w. gen., *care, heed, be intent (on)*; pres. 3 sg. gȳmeð, 1757; imp. sg. gȳm, 1760; w. (tō &) ger.: pres. 3 sg. gȳmeð, 2451. [Go. gaumjan.] — Cpd.: for-.
gyn(n), see gin(n).
gyrdan, w 1., G I R D, *belt;* [pret. 3 sg. gyrde, F. 13]; pp. gyrded, 2078.
gyrede, gegyred, see gyrwan.
gyrn, gryn(n),†, m.f.n.(?), *grief, affliction;* gyrn, 1775; gp. grynna, 930. (Cf. Siev. xxxvi 417.)
gyrn-wracu†, f., *revenge for injury;* gs. -wræce, 2118; ds. ~, 1138.
gyrwan, w 1., *prepare, make ready, dress, equip, adorn;* pret. 3 sg. gyrede, 1441; 3 pl. gyredon, 994; pp. gegyred, 1472; nsf. gegyrwed, 2087, nsn. (golde) ~, 553, asf. (~) gegyrede, 2192, apm. (~) ~, 1028. [gearu; cp. fæðer-gearwe.]
ge-gyrwan, w 1., *make ready, equip;* 38, 199; pret. 3 pl. gegiredan, 3137.
gyst, see gist.
gystran, adv., Y E S T E R *day;* gystran niht (perh. cpd.), 1334.
gȳt, gīt, adv., Y E T, *still, hitherto;* (w. negat., *not yet*); gȳt, 944, 1824, 2512, [F. 26]; gīt, 583, 1377; (nū) gȳt, 956, 1134, (nū) gīt 1058; (þā) gȳt, 1127, 1164, 1256, 1276, 2141, (þā) gīt 536, 2975; þā gȳt, *further, besides:* 47, 1050, [F. 18], so: ðā gīt, 1866. See gēn.
gȳtsian (= gītsian), w 2., *covet, be avaricious, be niggardly;* pres. 3 sg. gȳstað, 1749. [Ger. geizen.]

habban, w 3., (1) H A V E, *hold;* 446, 462 (*keep*), 1176, 1490, 1798, 2740 (gefēan ~), 3017; pres. 1 sg. (wēn) hæbbe, 383, (geweald) ~, 950; hafu 2523, hafo 2150, ([wēn]) ~, 3000; 2 sg. hafast, 1174, 1849; 3 sg. (geweald) hafað, 1610; 1 pl. habbað, 270; opt. 3 sg. hæbbe, 381; 3 pl. negat. næbben, 1850; imp. sg. hafa, 1395, ~ (.. ond geheald), 658; [pl. habbað, F. 11]; pret. 3 sg. hæfde, 79 (geweald .. ~), 518, 554, 814, 1167, 1202, 1625, 2158, 2361, 2430 (hēold .. ond ~), 2579; 1 pl. hæfdon, 539; 3 pl. (gefēan) hæfdon, 562. — (2) *used as auxiliary, have,* w. inflected pp.: pres. 3 sg. hafað, 939; pret. 3 sg. hæfde, 205; — w. uninfl. pp.: pres. 1 sg. hæbbe, 408, 433, 1196; 2 sg. hafast, 953, 1221, 1855; 3 sg. hafað, 474, 595, 975, 1340, 2026, 2265, 2453; opt. 3 sg. hæbbe, 1928; pret. 1 sg. hæfde, 2145; 3 sg. ~, 106, 220, 665, 743, 804, 825, 828 (w. infl. pp. as well (?)), 893, 1294, 1472, 1599 (opt.?), 2301, 2321, 2333, 2397, 2403, 2726, 2844, 2952, 3046, 3074, 3147; 1 pl. hæfdon, 2104; 3 pl. ~, 117 (opt.?), 694, 883, 2381, 2630, 2707, 3165; opt. 3 sg. hæfde, 1550. — Cpds.: for-, wið-habban; bord-, lind-, rond-, searo-hæbbend(e).
hād, m., *manner, state, position, form;* as., 1297 (see: on), 2193; þurh hæstne hād, *in a violent manner,* 1335. [-H O O D; Go. haidus.]
hādor(†), adj., *bright, clear-voiced;* 497. [Ger. heiter.]
hādor, n.(‡), *brightness;* as., 414 (n.).
hādre†, adv., *clearly, brightly;* 1571.
hæft, n., *sea;* ap. heafo, 2477, heafu 1862 (n.). [Falk-Torp, *Etym.*

Wbch.: hav; *Beitr.* xii 561.]
hæfen, see **hebban**.
hæft, m. †*captive;* 2408 (i.e. *slave*), (cp. *Dan.* 266, *Chr.* 154, 360 f.); — ‡wk. (adj.): asm. (helle) hæfton, 788 (= ' captivus inferni,' cf. *Angl.* xxxv 254). [Kluge, *Etym. Wbch.:* Haft.²]
hæft-mēce‡, mja., *hilted sword;* ds., 1457. (See Intr. xviii.) [H A F T; Ger. Heft.]
hæft-nȳd, fi., *captivity;* as., [3155].
hæg-steald, adj., *young;* gpm. -ra, 1889. (Also *Gen.* 1862 used as adj., elsewhere noun [so np. -as, F. 40].) [See haga; Ger. Hagestolz.]
hæl, nc. (Siev. §§ 288 n. 1, 289 n. 2; *Beitr.* xxxi 87), (1) *safety, good luck;* as., 653. — (2) *omen(s);* as., 204. (So *Corpus Gloss.* 1444.) [hāl.] See **hǣlo**.
hæle, hæleð,†, mc. (Siev. §§ 281 n. 4, 263 n. 4; *Beitr.* xxxi 71 ff.), *man, hero, warrior;* hæle (hildedēor): 1646, *1816*, 3111; hæleð, 190, 331, [390], 1069, [F. 23, 43]; np. hæleð, 52, 2247, 2458, 3142; gp. hæleþa, 467, 497, 611, 662, 912, 1047, 1189, 1198, 1296, 1830, 1852, 1954, 2052, 2072, 2224, 3005, 3111; dp. hæleðum, 1709, 1961, *1983*, 2024, 2262. [Ger. Held.]
hǣlo, wk.f., *prosperity, luck,* HAIL; ds. hǣle, 1217; as. ~, 719 (n.); hǣlo, 2418. [hāl; hǣlþ > H E A L T H.] — Cpd.: un-.
hærg-træf‡, n., *heathen temple;* dp. -trafum, *175*. (Cp. *Andr.* 1691: helltrafum.) [See herg; Lat. trabs (?); Holt. Et.]
hǣste†, adj.ja., *violent;* asm. hǣstne, 1335.
hǣþ, mni., H E A T H; ds. -e, *2212*.
hǣþen, adj., H E A T H E N; gsm. hǣþenes, 986; dsn. hǣðnum, 2216; asf. hǣþene, 852; asn. hǣðen, 2276; gpm. hǣþenra, 179. [*NED.*: H E A T H E N; Kluge, *Etym. Wbch.*: Heide; Streitberg, *Got. Elementarbuch*, § 50 n. 3; Braune, *Beitr.* xliii 428 ff.; Hoops, *Braune-Festschrift* 27–35; Wessén, *AfNF.* xliv 86 ff.; Jellinek, *Geschichte der got. Sprache* 190, 196; Velten, *JEGPh.* xxix 491; Krogmann, *ZfdPh.* lix 209 ff.]
hǣð-stapa†, wk.m., H E A T H-*stalker (stag);* 1368. [steppan.]
hafa, see **habban**.
hafela†, wk.m., *head;* gs. heafolan, 2697; ds. hafelan, 672, 1372, 1521, heafolan 2679; as. hafelan, 1327, 1421, 1448, 1614, 1635, 1780, hafalan 446; np. hafelan, 1120. — Cpd.: wīg-.
hafen, see **hebban**.
hafenian†, w 2., *raise, lift up;* pret. 3 sg. hafenade, 1573. [hebban.]
hafo, hafu, see **habban**.
hafoc, m., H A W K; 2263.
haga(‡)+, wk.m., *enclosure, entrenchment;* ds. hagan, 2892, 2960. [*NED.*: H A W, sb.¹·²; Ger. Hag.] See hǣgsteald; ān-haga.
hāl, adj., W H O L E, H A L E, *sound, unhurt;* 300, 1974, wes þū ... hāl (HAIL, cp. WASSAIL), 407; dsn. wk. hālan, 1503.
hālig, adj., H O L Y; hālig (God), 381, 1553, ~ (Dryhten) 686.
hals, see **heals**.
hām, m., H O M E, *dwelling, residence;* *2325;* gs. hāmes, 2366, 2388; ds. hām (after: tō, æt, fram), 124, 194, 374, 1147, 1156, 1248, 1923, 2992; as. hām, 717 1407, 1601 (adv., *home (-wards)*); ap. hāmas, 1127.
hamer, m., H A M M E R; ds. hamere, 1285; gp. homera, 2829.

GLOSSARY 351

hām-weorðung‡, f., *ornament of a* H O M E; as. -e, 2998.
hand, hond, fu., H A N D; hand, 1343, 2099, 2137, 2697; hond, *1520*, 2216, 2488, 2509, 2609, 2684; ds. handa, 495, 540, 746, 1290, 1983, 2720, 3023, 3124, [F. 29], honda 814; as. hand, 558, 983, 1678, 2208; hond, 656 (∼ ond rond), 686, 834, 927, 2405, 2575; dp. hondum, 1443, 2840.
hand-bona‡, wk.m., *slayer with the* H A N D; ds. (tō) handbonan (wearð): 460, 1330 (-banan), 2502.
hand-gestealla‡, wk.m., *comrade, associate;* ds. hondgesteallan, 2169; np. handgesteallan, *2596*.
hand-gewriþen‡, adj. (pp.), *twisted or woven by* H A N D; apf. -e, 1937. [wrīþan.]
hand-scolu, -scalu,‡, f. (H A N D-) *troop, companions;* ds. handscale, 1317 (n.), hondscole 1963. [*NED.*: SHOAL, sb.[2] — For the interchange of vowels in scolu: scalu, cp. rodor: rador, etc.; *Zfvgl.Spr.* xxvi 101 n. 2; *Anz.fdA.* xxv 14.]
hand-sporu‡, wk.f., H A N D-S P U R, *nail* (or *claw*); 986 (n.).
hangian, w 2., H A N G (intr.); 1662; pres. 3 sg. hangað, 2447; 3 pl. hongiað, 1363; pret. 3 sg. hangode, 2085.
hār, adj., H O A R y, *grey, old;* hār (hilderinc), 1307, 3136; gsm. hāres, 2988; dsm. hārum, 1678; asm. hārne (stān), 887, 1415, 2553, 2744; asf. hāre, 2153. [Ger. hehr.] — Cpd.: an-.
hāt, adj., H O T; 897, 2296, 2547, 2558, 2691, 3148; nsn., 1616; gsn. hātes, 2522; dsm.n.wk.(?) hāton, 849, hātan 1423; asm. hātne, 2781; apm. hāte, 2819. — Supl. hātost, 1668.

hāt, n., HEAT; as., 2605.
hātan, rd., (1) *name, call;* pres. opt. 3 pl. hātan, 2806; pp. hāten, 102, 263, 373, 2602. — (2) *order, command* (also shading off into *cause,* cf. J. F. Royster, *JEGPh.* xvii 82 ff.); abs.: pret. 3 sg. heht, 1786; — w. inf.: pret. 3 sg. heht, 1035, 1053, 1807, 1808, 2337, 2892; hēt, 198, 391, 1114, 1920, 2152, 2190, 3095, 3110; passive constr., pp. hāten, 991 (n.); — w. acc. & inf.: inf. hātan, 68; pres. 1 sg. hāte, 293; imp. sg. hāt, 386, pl. hātað, 2802; pret. 3 sg. hēt, 674 (subj. acc. implied), 1868; hēt hine wēl brūcan, 1045, si. 2812; — w. þæt-clause: pret. 3 sg. hēt, 2156. [H I G H T (arch.); Ger. heissen.]
ge-hātan, rd., *promise,* (*vow, threaten*); pres. 1 sg. gehāte, 1392, 1671; pret. 3 sg. gehēt, 2134, 2937, 2989 (w. gen., cp. *Boeth.* 112.4); 1 pl. gehēton, 2634; 3 pl. ∼, 175; pp. nsf. gehāten (*betrothed*), 2024.
hatian, w 2., H A T E, *persecute;* 2466; pret. 3 sg. hatode, 2319. See dǣd-hata, hettend.
hē, hēo, hit, pers. pron., H E, *she* (S H E), I T; hē 282 times, 7, 29, 80, etc.; [F. 3x]; nsf. hēo 18 times (in the A part of the MS. only), hīo 11 times (only 3 times in A), hīe 2019; nsn. hit 18 times, hyt (in B only) 5 times; gsm. his (possessive) 78 times, [F. 4x]; gsf. hire, 722 (or dat.), 1115, 1546, so: hyre, 1188, 1339, 1545, 2121; gsn. his, 2579, poss.; 1733, 2157; dsm. him 167 times, used also as (reflex.) 'ethic dative': him . . gewāt, 26, 234, 662, 1236, 1601, 1903, 1963, 2387, 2949, [F. 43], si. 1880, him . . . losað, 2061, con him, 2062, him

... gelȳfde, 1272, him .. ondrēd, 2347, si. 2348, him selfa dēah, 1839; hym, 1918 (dp.?); dsf. hire, 626, 1521, 1566, 1935, hyre, 945, 2175, 3153 ('ethic dat.'); dsn. him, 78, 313; asm. hine 44 times (only 4 times in B), [F. 13, 46], hyne 30 times (only 6 times in A), [F. 33]; asn. hit 12 times, hyt, 2158, 2248, 3161, [F. 21]; np. hīe 53 times (9 times in B); hī, 28, 43, 1628, 1966, 2707, 2934, 3038, 3130, 3163; hig, 1085, 1596, [F. 41, 42]; hȳ, 307, 364, 368, 2124, 2381, 2598, 2850; gp. (poss. & partit.) hira, 1102, 1124, 1249; heora, 691, 698, 1604, 1636; hiora, 1166, 2599, 2994; hiera, 1164; hyra, 178, 324, 1012, 1055, 1246, 2040, 2311, 2849, [F. 3x]; dp. him 32 times (gewiton him: 301, 1125); [F. 17]; ap. hīe, 477, 694, 706, 1068, 2236; hig, 1770; hȳ, 1048, 2233, 2592.

hēa-burh, fc., (H I G H B U R G H), *great town;* as., 1127.

heafo, -u, see **hæf.**

hēafod, n., H E A D; 1648; as., 48, 1639; ds. hēafde, 1590, 2138, 2290, 2973; dp. hēafdon, 1242.

hēafod-beorg‡, f., H E A D-*protection;* as. -e, 1030.

hēafod-mǣg†, m., (H E A D-, i.e.) *near relative;* gp. -māga, 2151; dp. -mǣgum, 588.

hēafod-segn‡, m.n., H E A D-SIGN, *banner;* as., 2152. [See segn.]

hēafod-weard(‡) (+), f., H E A D-*watch;* as. -e, 2909 (i.e. 'deathwatch,' cp. *Rood* 63; Schücking *L* 4.126.1.4 f.).

heafola, see **hafela.**

hēah, adj., H I G H, *lofty, exalted;* 57, 82, *1926*, 2805, 3157; gsn.wk. hēan, 116; dsm.n. hēaum, *2212;* dsm.wk. (sele þām) hēan: 713, 919, 1016, 1984; asm. hēanne, 983; asn. hēah, 48, 2768; asm.wk. hēan, 3097.

hēah-cyning(†), m., *great* K I N G; gs. -es, 1039.

hēah-gesceap‡, n., (H I G H) *destiny;* as., 3084.

hēah-gestrēon†, n., *splendid treasure;* gp. -a, 2302.

hēah-lufu (-lufe)‡, wk.f., H I G H L O V E; as. -lufan, 1954.

hēah-sele‡, mi., H I G H (*great*) *hall;* ds., 647.

hēah-setl, n., H I G H SEAT, *throne;* as., 1087. [S E T T L E.]

hēah-stede‡, mi., *lofty place;* ds., 285.

heal(l), f., H A L L; heal, 1151, 1214; heall, 487; gs. healle, [F. 4, 20]; ds. ~, 89, 614, 642, 663, 925, 1009, 1288, 1926, [F. 28]; as. ~, 1087. — Cpds.: gif-, medo-.

heal-ærn‡, n., H A L L-*building;* gp. -a, 78.

healdan, rd., H O L D, *keep, guard, occupy, possess, rule;* 230, 296, 319, 704, 1182, 1348, 1852, 2372, 2389, 2477, 3034, 3166; pres. 2 sg. healdest, 1705; 3 sg. healdeð, 2909; opt. 3 sg. healde, 2719; imp. sg. heald, 948, 2247; ger. healdanne, 1731; pret. 1 sg. hēold, 241, 466, 2732, 2737, 2751; 3 sg. ~, 57, 103, 142, 161, 305, 788, 1031, 1079, 1748, 1959, 2183, 2279, 2377, 2414, 2430, 3043, 3084 (n.), 3118; hīold, 1954; 3 pl. hēoldon, 401, 1214, [F. 42]; opt. 3 sg. hēolde, 1099, 2344. [F. 23]. — Cpds.: be-, for-; drēamhealdende.

ge-healdan, rd., H O L D, *keep, guard, rule;* 674, 911, 2856; pres. 3 sg. gehealdeþ, 2293; opt. 3 sg. gehealde, 317; imp. sg. geheald,

658; pret. 3 sg. geheold, 2208, 2620, 3003.

healf, adj., H A L F; gsf. -re, 1087.

healf, f., (H A L F), *side;* ds. -e, 2262; as. -e, 1675; gp. -a, 800; ap. -a, 1095, 1305, -e, 2063.

heal-gamen‡, n., *entertainment in* H A L L; as., 1066.

heal-reced‡, n., H A L L-*building;* as., 68, *1981* (-reced).

heals, m., *neck;* ds. healse, 1872, 2809, 3017, halse, 1566; as. heals, 2691. [Go. Ger. hals.] — Cpds. (adj.): fāmig-, wunden-.

heals-bēag‡, m., *neck-ring, collar;* as. -bēah, 2172; gp. -bēaga, 1195.

heals-gebedda‡, wk.m.f., *dear* B E D-*fellow, consort;* 63. (Cp. *Gen.* 2155: healsmægeð.)

healsian, w 2., *implore;* pret. 3 sg. healsode, 2132 (n.).

heal-sittend(e)‡, mc. (pres. ptc.) [pl.], H A L L-S I T T *er;* gp. -sittendra, 2015; dp. -sittendum, 2868.

heal-ðegn‡, m., H A L L-T H A N E; gs. -ðegnes, 142; ap. -ðegnas, 719.

heal-wudu‡, mu., H A L L-W O O D; 1317.

hēan, adj., *abject, humiliated, wretched, despised;* 1274, 2099, 2183, 2408. [Go. hauns; see hȳnan.]

hēan(ne), see hēah.

hēap, m., *band, troop, company, multitude;* 432, [1889]; (þrȳðlīc þegna) hēap: 400, 1627; ds. hēape, 2596; as. hēap, 335, 730, 1091. [H E A P; Ger. Haufe.] — Cpd.: wīg-.

heard, adj., H A R D, *strong, brave,* HARDy, *severe;* 376; (wīges) heard: 886, si. 1539, [F. 21]; heard (under helme): 342, 404, 2539; nsf. heard, 2914; heard (hondlocen): 322, 551; nsn. heard, 1566 (semiadv. function, *MPh.* iii 251), 2037 (p.?), 2509; nsm.wk. hearda, 401, 432, 1435, 1807, 1963, 2255, 2474, 2977; nsn.wk. hearde, 1343, 1553; dsm. (nīða) heardum, 2170, wk.(?) heardan, 2482; asm. heardne, 1590; asn. heard, 1574, 2687, 2987; npm. hearde, 2205; npf. ~, 2829; gpm. heardra, 988; gpf. ~, 166, [heordra, F. 26(n.)]; dpm. heardum, 1335, wk.(?) heardan, 963; apn. heard, 540, 2638. — Comp. asf. heardran, 576, 719 (n.). [H A R D; HARDy fr. OFr. (fr. Gmc.)] — Cpds.: fȳr-, īren-, nīð-, regn-, scūr-.

hearde, adv., H A R D, *sorely;* 1438, 3153 (~ ondrēde, cp. *Chr.* 1017).

heard-ecg†, adj., H A R D *of* E D G E; nsn., 1288; asn., 1490.

heard-hicgende‡, adj. (pres. ptc.), *brave-minded;* npm., 394, 799. [hycgan.]

hearm, m., H A R M, *injury, insult,* ds. -e, 1892.

hearm-dæg‡, m., *evil* D A Y; ap. -dagas, [3153].

hearm-scaþa‡, wk.m., *pernicious enemy;* 766. See sceaþa.

hearpe, wk.f., H A R P; gs. hearpan (swēg): 89, 2458, 3023, ~ (wyn(ne)): 2107, 2262. [Cf. *IF.* xvi 128 ff.; *Wörter u. Sachen* iii 68 ff.]

heaðerian, w 2., *restrain, confine;* pp. geheaðerod, 3072. [haðor.]

heaðo-byrne†, wk.f., *war-corslet;* 1552. [OHG. Hadu-; ON. Hǫðr.]

heaþo-dēor‡, adj., *battle-brave;* 688; dpm. -um, 772.

heaðo-, heaðu-fȳr,‡, n., *battle-*F I R E, *deadly fire;* gs. heaðufȳres, 2522; dp. heaðofȳrum, 2547.

heaðo-grim(m)†, adj., *battle-*G R I M, *fierce;* -grim, 548, 2691.

heaðo-lāc‡, n., (*battle-sport*), *battle;*

gs. -es, 1974; ds. -e, 584. (Cp. beadu-lāc.)

heaþo-līðend(e)†, mc. (pres. ptc.) [pl.], *war-sailor, sea-warrior;* np. -līðende, 1798; dp. -līðendum, 2955. (See *Beitr.* ix 190; Krapp's note on *Andr.* 426; Tupper's note on *Rid.* 73.19.)

heaðo-mǣre‡, adj.ja., *renowned in battle;* apm., 2802.

heaðo-rǣs‡, m., *storm of battle;* 557; gp. -a, 526; ap. -as, 1047.

heaðo-rēaf‡, n., *war-dress, -equipment, armor;* as., 401. Cp. wælrēaf; rēafian.

heaðo-rinc†, m., *warrior;* [403]; as., 2466; dp. -um, 370.

heaþo-rōf†, adj., *brave* (or *famed*) *in battle;* 381, 2191; npm. -e, 864.

heaðo-scearp‡, adj., *battle-*S H A R P; npf. -e, *2829* (n.).

heaðo-sīoc‡, adj., *battle-*S I C K, *wounded;* dsm. -um, 2754.

heaþo-stēap‡, adj., (S T E E P) *towering in battle;* nsm.wk. -a (helm), 1245; asm. -ne (∼), 2153.

heaþo-swāt‡, m., *battle-*SWEAT, *blood shed in battle;* ds. -e, 1460, 1606; gp. -a, 1668.

heaðo-torht‡, adj., *clear (sounding) in battle;* nsf., 2553.

heaðo-wǣd‡, f., *war-dress, armor;* dp. -um, 39. See ge-wǣde.

heaðo-weorc‡, n., *battle-*W O R K, *fight;* as., 2892.

heaðo-wylm†, mi., (*battle-surge*), *hostile flame;* gp. -a, 82; ap. -as, 2819.

heaðu-sweng‡, mi., *battle-stroke;* ds. -e, 2581.

hēawan, rd., H E W; 800.

ge-hēawan, rd., H E W, *cut* (*to pieces*); opt. 3 sg. gehēawe, 682.

hebban, VI, (H E A V E), *raise, lift;* 656; pp. hafen, 1290; hæfen, 3023. — Cpd.: ā-.

hēdan, w I., w. gen., H E E D, *care for;* pret. 3 sg. hēdde, 2697.

ge-hēde, 505, see ge-hēgan.

hefene, see heofon.

ge-hēgan†, w I., *hold* (*a meeting*), *perform, carry out, achieve;* 425 (∼ ðing); pret. opt. 3 sg. gehēde, 505. [Cp. ON. heyja. Siev. § 408 n. 14.]

heht, see hātan.

hel(l), fjō., H E L L; hel, 852; gs. helle, 788, 1274; ds. ∼, 101, 588; as. ∼, 179.

hell-bend‡, fjō. (mi.), BOND *of* H E L L; dp. -um, 3072.

helm, m., (1) *protection, cover;* as., 1392. — (2) HELM*et;* ns., 1245, 1448, 1629, 2255, 2659, 2762, [F. 45]; gs. helmes, 1030; ds. helme, 342, 404, 1286, 2539; as. helm, 672, 1022, 1290, 1526, 1745, 2153, 2615, *2723*, 2811, 2868, 2973, 2979, 2987; dp. helmum, *3139;* ap. helmas, 2638. — (3)† *protector, lord* (cf. Stjer. 7[?]); ns. helm (Scyldinga, etc.), 371, 456, 1321, 1623, 2462, 2705; as., 182 (heofena Helm), 2381. — See Lehmann L 9.40; Keller 79 ff., 247 ff.; Stjer. 1 ff. [*NED*.: H E L M, sb.¹] — Cpds.: grīm-, gūð-, niht-, scadu-.

helm-berend†, mc. [pl.], (HELM*et-*B E A R *er*), *warrior;* ap. (hwate) helmberend: 2517, 2642.

help, f., H E L P; ds. (hæleðum tō) helpe: 1709, 1961, si. 1830; as. helpe (gefremede): 551, 1552, si. *2448.*

helpan, III, H E L P; w. dat.: *2340*, 2684; w. gen. or dat.: 2649; w. gen.: 2879; pret. 3 sg. healp, 2698.

hel-rūne(‡)+, wk.f., *one skilled in the mysteries of* H E L L, *demon;* np. -rūnan, 163 (n.). Cp. rūn.

hēo (hīo), see hē.

heofon, m., H E A V E N; (pl. used w. sg. meaning); 3155; gs. heofenes, 414; heofones, 576, 1801, 2015, 2072; ds. hefene, 1571; gp. heofena, 182; dp. heofenum, 52, 505.

heolfor†, m. or n., *blood, gore;* ds. heolfre, 849, 1302, 1423, 2138.

heolster(†), m., *hiding-place;* as., 755. [helan.]

heonan, adv., H E N *ce;* 252; heonon, 1361. Cp. hin-fūs.

hēore†, adj.ja., *safe, pleasant, good;* nsf. hēoru, 1372. [Ger. geheuer; Ritter 66.] — Cpd.: un-.

heoro-blāc‡, adj., (*sword-,* i.e.) *battle-pale, mortally wounded;* 2488.

heoro-, heoru-drēor, ‡, m. or n., (*sword-,* i.e.) *battle-blood;* ds. heorodrēore, 849; heorudrēore, 487.

heoro-drēorig†, adj., (*sword-*) *gory, blood-stained;* nsn., 935; asm. -ne, 1780, 2720.

heoro-gīfre†, adj.ja., (*sword-greedy*), *fiercely ravenous;* 1498.

heoro-, heoru-grim(m),†, adj., (*sword-*G R I M), *fierce;* heorogrim, 1564; nsf.wk. heorugrimme, 1847.

heoro-hōcyhte‡, adj.ja., (*sword-*H O O K *ed*), *barbed;* dpm. -hōcyhtum, 1438.

heoro-sweng†, mi., *sword-stroke;* as., 1590.

heorot, m., H A R T, *stag;* 1369. [Ger. Hirsch; cp. Lat. cervus.] (Cp. Heorot.)

heoro-wearh‡, m., *accursed foe, savage outcast;* 1267. (Cf. *Angl.* xxxv 253.) See werhðo.

heor(**r**)(‡)+, m., *hinge;* np. heorras, 999. [H A R (R E) (dial.).]

heorte, wk.f., H E A R T; 2561; gs. heortan, 2463, 2507; ds. ~, 2270. — Cpds.: blīð-, grom-, rūm-, stearc-heort.

heorð, m., H E A R T H, *floor of a fireplace;* ds. -e, *404* (MS. heoðe). (Cf. Kluge, *Etym. Wbch.:* Herd.)

heorð-genēat††, m., H E A R T H-*companion, retainer;* np. -as, 261, 3179; dp. -um, 2418; ap. -as, 1580, 2180. See bēod-genēat.

heoru†, mu., *sword;* 1285. [Go. haírus.] (Only here and *Gnom. Ex.* 202; frequent in cpds.)

hēr, adv., H E R E, *hither;* 244, 361, 376, 397, 1061, 1228, 1654, 1820, 2053, 2796, 2801, [F. 3, 4, 5, 26].

here, mja., *army;* ds. herge, 1248, 2347, 2638. [Go. harjis, Ger. Heer.] — Cpds.: flot-, scip-, sin-.

here-brōga‡, wk.m., *war-terror;* ds. -brōgan, 462.

here-byrne‡, wk.f., *battle-corslet;* 1443.

here-grīma‡, wk.m., *war-mask, helmet;* ds. (under) heregrīman: 396 (dp.?), 2049, 2605. See grīmhelm.

here-net‡, nja., *war-*N E T, *corslet;* 1553.

here-nīð‡, m., *hostility;* 2474.

here-pād‡, f., *coat of mail;* 2258. [Go. paida.]

here-rinc†, m., *warrior;* as., *1176.*

here-sceaft‡, m., *battle-*S H A F T, *spear;* gp. -a, 335.

here-spēd‡, fi., *success in war;* 64. [S P E E D.]

here-strǣl‡, m., *war-arrow;* 1435.

here-syrce‡, wk.f., (*battle-*S A R K), *coat of mail;* as. -syrcan, 1511. Cp. hioro-serce.

here-wǣd‡, f., *war-dress, armor;* dp. -um, 1897. See ge-wǣde.

here-wǣs(t)m‡, m.,(*warlike stature,*) *martial vigor;* dp. -wæsmun (Lang. § 19.6), 677. [weaxan.]

here-wīsa†, wk.m., *army leader;* 3020. [Cp. wīsian.]

herg (hearg), m., *idol-fane;* dp. hergum, 3072 (n.). [ON. hǫrgr, OHG. harug.] (See Cook's note on *Chr.* 485; *Beitr.* xxxv 101 ff.; *R.-L.* ii 313 ff.)

herge, see **here, herian.**

herian, w 1., *praise;* 182, 1071; pres. opt. 3 sg. herge, 3175; *honor;* pres. opt. 1 sg. herige, 1833 (n.). [Go. hazjan.]

hete, mi. (nc., Siev. §§ 263 n. 4, 288 n. 1), HATE, *hostility;* 142, 2554. [Go. hatis, n.] — Cpds.: ecg-, morþor-, wīg-.

hete-līc(‡)+, adj., HATE*ful;* 1267. [Ger. hässlich.]

hetend, see **hettend.**

hete-nīð(†), m., *enmity;* ap. -as, 152.

hete-sweng‡, mi., *hostile blow;* ap. -swengeas, 2224.

hete-þanc†, m., THOUGHT *of* HATE; dp. -um, 475.

hettend†, mc., *enemy;* np. hetende (Lang. § 19.5), 1828; dp. hettendum, 3004. [Cp. hatian; Ger. hetzen.]

hicgean, see **hycgan.**

hider, adv., H I T H E R; 240, 370, 394, 3092.

hige, hyge,†, mi., *mind, heart, soul;* hige, 593; hyge, 755; gs. higes, 2045; as. hige, 267; dp. higum, 3148.

hige-mǣðu (=-mēðu)‡, wk.f., *weariness of mind, distress of soul;* dp. -mǣðum, 2909. Cp. hyge-mēðe.

hige-rōf†, adj., *valiant;* asm. -ne, 204.

hige-þīhtig‡, adj., *strong-hearted, determined;* asm. -ne, 746. See þȳhtig.

hige-þrym(m)‡, mja.(?), *greatness of heart;* dp. -þrymmum, 339.

hild†, fjō., *war, battle;* 1588, 1847, 2076; gif mec hild nime: 452, 1481; gs. hilde, 2723; ds. hilde, 2916; (æt) hilde, 1460, 1659, 2258, 2575, 2684, [F. 37]; as. hilde, 647, 1990; [gp. hilda, F. 26]; — *valor;* ns. hild, 901; as. hilde, 2952.

hilde-bil(l)‡, n., *battle-sword;* -bil, 1666; ds. -bille, 557, 1520, 2679.

hilde-bord‡, n., *battle-shield;* dp. -um, 3139; ap. -bord, 397.

hilde-cumbor‡, n., *battle-banner;* as., *1022* (n.).

hilde-cyst‡, fi., *battle-virtue, valor;* dp. -um, 2598.

hilde-dēor†, adj., *brave in battle;* 312, 834, 2107, 2183; (hæle) hilde-dēor: 1646, 1816, 3111 (-dīor); npm. -dēore, 3169.

hilde-geatwe‡, fwō.p., *war-equipments;* gp. -geatwa, 2362; ap. -geatwe, 674. See wīg-getāwa.

hilde-gicel‡, m., *battle-*ici C L E; dp. -um, 1606.

hilde-grāp‡, f., *hostile grasp;* 1446, 2507.

hilde-hlǣm(m),**-hlem**(m),‡,mja.(?), *crash of battle;* gp. -hlemma, 2351, 2544; dp. -hlæmmum, 2201.

hilde-lēoma‡, wk.m., *battle-light;* as -lēoman (*sword,* cp. beadolēoma 1523), 1143; np. ~ (*flames*), 2583.

hilde-mēce‡, mja., *battle-sword;* np. -mēceas, 2202.

hilde-mecg‡, mja., *warrior;* np. -mecgas, 799.

hilde-rǣs‡, m., *storm of battle;* 300.

hilde-rand‡, m., *battle-shield;* ap. -as., 1242.

hilde-rinc†, m., *warrior;* (hār) hilderinc: 1307, *3136;* gs. -es, 986; ds. -e, 1495, 1576; gp. -a, *3124.*

hilde-sceorp‡, n., *war-dress, armor;* as., 2155.

hilde-setl‡, n., *war-*SEAT, *saddle;* 1039. [S E T T L E.]

hilde-strengo‡, wk.f., *battle-*S T R E N G *th;* as., 2113.

hilde-swāt‡, m., *battle-*SWEAT, *hostile vapor;* 2558.

hilde-tūx (=tūsc)‡, m., *battle-*T U S K; dp. -um, 1511.

hilde-wǣpen‡, n., *war*-W E A P O N; dp. -wǣpnum, 39.

hilde-wīsa‡, wk.m., *leader in battle;* ds. (p.?) -wīsan, 1064. [Cp. wīsian.]

hild-freca†, wk.m., *fighter, warrior;* ds. -frecan, 2366; np. ~, 2205.

hild-fruma†, wk.m., *war-chief;* gs. -fruman, 2649 (ds.?), 2835; ds. ~, 1678.

hild-lata†, wk.m., (adj.), *one sluggish in battle, coward;* np. -latan, 2846. [L A T E.]

hilt, n. f.(m.)i. (Wright §§ 393, 419; Siev. § 267 a, *Beitr.* xxxvi 420), H I L T; (gylden) hilt, 1677 (neut.); as. hilt, 1614 (fem.), 1668 (neut.); hylt, 1687; pl. w. sg. meaning: dp. hiltum, 1574. — Cpds.: fetel-, wreoþen-.

hilted‡, adj., H I L T E D; asn., 2987.

hindema‡, adj. supl. (Wright § 446), *last;* dsm. hindeman (sīðe): 2049, 2517.

hin-fūs†, adj., *eager to get away;* 755. See heonan.

hīofan, II, w 1., *lament;* pres. ptc. npm. hīofende, 3142. [Go. hiufan. Siev. § 384 n. 2, *Beitr.* ix 278.]

hioro-drync‡, mi., *sword*-D R I N K; dp. -um, 2358. [Cp. Ger. Trunk.]

hioro-serce‡, wk.f., (*battle*-S A R K), *coat of mail;* as. -sercean, 2539.

hioro-weallende†, adj. (pres. ptc.), WELL*ing fiercely;* asm. (uninfl.), 2781.

hit (hyt), see hē.

hladan, VI, L A D E, *load, heap up, lay;* 2126; hladon, 2775; pp. hladen, 1897; nsn., 3134. — Cpd.: gilp-hlæden.

ge-hladan, VI, *load;* pret. 3 sg. ge-hlēod, 895 (n.).

hlæst, m. (or n.), *freight, load;* ds. -e, 52. [hladan; *NED.*: L A S T, sb.²]

hlǣw, hlāw, m. (Wright § 419, Siev. §§ 250 n. 1, 288 n. 1), *mound, barrow, cave;* ds. hlāwe, 1120; hlǣwe, 2773; as. hlǣw, 2296, 2411, 2802, 3157, 3169. [*NED.*: L O W, sb.¹; Go. hlaiw.]

hlāford, m., L O R D; 2375, 2642; gs. -es, 3179; ds. -e, 2634; as. hlāford, 267, 2283, 3142. [hlāf-weard (so *Par. Ps.* 104.17).] — Cpd.: eald-.

hlāford-lēas, adj., L O R D-L E S S, *without a chief;* npm. -e, 2935.

hlāw, see **hlǣw**.

hleahtor, m., L A U G H T E R, *merriment;* hleahtor, 611; as. hleahtor, 3020.

hlēapan, rd., L E A P, *gallop;* 864. — Cpd.: ā-.

hlēo(†), m.(n.)wa., *cover, shelter, protection,* hence *protector* (cp. helm, eodor); eorla hlēo: ns., 791, 1035, 1866, 2142, 2190; as., 1967; wīgendra hlēo: ns., 899, 1972, 2337; vs., 429. [L E E.]

hlēo-burh‡, fc., *sheltering town, stronghold;* as., 912, 1731.

ge-hlēod, see ge-hladan.

hleonian (hlinian), w 2., L E A N; hleonian, 1415.

hlēor-berg‡, f., *cheek-guard, helmet;* dp. -an, 304. (Cp. hēafod-beorg; cin-berg, *Ex.* 175; Lang. § 8.5.) See hlēor-bolster.

hlēor-bolster‡, m.(?), *cheek-cushion, pillow;* 688. [*NED.*: L E E R, vb., sb.²; B O L S T E R.] (Cp. wangere, Go. waggareis.)

hlēotan, II, (*cast* LOT*s*), *obtain;* pret. 3 sg. hlēat (w. dat. [instr.]), 2385 (n.).

hlēoðor-cwyde†, mi., *ceremonious speech;* as., 1979. [cweðan.]

hlīfian, w 2., *stand high, tower;* 2805; pret. 3 sg. hlīfade, 81, 1898; hlīuade, 1799.

hlim-bed(d)‡, nja., B E D *of rest;* as.,

3034. (=hlin-, cf. Lang. § 19.3; see hleonian.)
hlið, hlīð, n., *cliff, hill-side, hill;* gs. hlīðes, 1892; ds. -e, *3157.* (Cf. Schü. Bd. 49 ff.) — [Cp. hlid> MnE. lid.] — Cpds.: fen-, mist-, næs-, stān-, wulf-hlīð.
hlīuade, see hlīfian.
hlūd, adj., L O U D; asm. -ne, 89.
hlyn(n), mja., *sound, din;* hlyn, 611.
hlynnan(†), w 1., (hlynian, w 2.), *make a noise, shout, roar;* hlynnan, 2553; [pres. 3 sg. hlynneð, F. 6]; pret. 3 sg. hlynode, 1120.
hlynsian†, w 2., *resound;* pret. 3 sg. hlynsode, 770.
hlytm(‡), mi.(?), LOT (Grein: ' sortitio '); ds. -e, 3126. [hlēotan.] (See un-hlitme.)
ge-hnǣgan, w 1., *lay low, humble, subdue;* pret. 3 sg. gehnǣgde, 1274. [hnīgan; Go. hnaiwjan, Ger. neigen. See hnāh.]
hnāh, adj., *lowly, mean, poor, illiberal;* nsf., 1929. Comp. dsm. hnāhran, 952; asm. hnāgran, 677. [hnīgan; Go. hnaiws.]
hnītan, 1, (*strike*), *clash together;* pret. 3 pl. (þonne) hniton (fēþan): 1327, 2544 (hnitan).
hof, n., *dwelling, house, court;* ds. hofe, 1236, 1507, 1974; as. hof, *312;* dp. hofum, 1836; ap. hofu, 2313. [Ger. Hof.]
(ge-)hogode, see (ge-)hycgan.
hold, adj., *friendly, well-disposed, loyal, trusty; 1229,* 2161, 2170; nsn., 290; asm. -ne, 267, 376, 1979; gpm. -ra, 487. [Ger. hold.]
hōlinga, adv., *in vain, without cause,* 1076.
holm†, m., *sea, water;* 519, 1131, 2138; ds. -e, 543, 1435, 1914, 2362; as. holm, 48, 632, *1592;* gp. -a, 2132; ap. -as, 240. [Cp. ON. hólmr ' islet '; see *NED.:*

HOLM(E)[1]; *JEGPh.* xxi 480 ff.; Wyld L 7.25 f.55.] — Cpd.: wǣg-.
holm-clif‡, n., *sea-*C L I F F, *cliff by the water-side;* ds. -e, 1421, 1635; ap. -u, 230.
holm-wylm‡, mi., *surge of the sea;* ds. -e, 2411.
holt, n., *wood, copse;* as., 2598, 2846. [H O L T; Ger. Holz.] — Cpds.: æsc-, fyrgen-, gār-; Hrefnes-.
holt-wudu†, mu., W O O D; 2340 (*wooden shield*); as., 1369 (*forest*).
homer, see hamer.
hond, hond- (gestealla, scolu), see hand(-).
hond-gemōt‡, n., H A N D-MEET*ing, battle;* gp. -a, 1526, *2355.*
hond-gesella‡, n., *companion (who is close to one's side), comrade;* dp. -gesellum, 1481. [sæl, sele; Ger. Geselle.] Cp. ge-selda; hand-gestealla.
hond-geweorc, n., H A N D I W O R K, *deed of strength;* ds. -e, 2835.
hond-locen‡, adj. (pp.), (LOCK*ed*) *linked by* H A N D; nsf., 322, 551. [lūcan.]
hond-rǣs‡, m., H A N D-*fight;* 2072.
hond-wundor‡, n., W O N D R*ous thing wrought by* H A N D; gp. -wundra, 2768.
hongian, see hangian.
hord, n., H O A R D, *treasure* (orig. *what is hidden*); 2283, 2284, 3011, 3084; gs. hordes, 887; ds. horde, 1108, 2216, 2547, 2768, 2781, 3164; as. hord, 912, 2212, *2276,* 2319, 2422, 2509, 2744, 2773, 2799, 2955, 3056, 3126, hord ond rīce: 2369, 3004. [Go. huzd.] — Cpds.: bēah-, brēost-, word-, wyrm-.
hord-ærn(‡)+, n., *treasure-house;* ds. -e, 2831; gp. -a, 2279.
hord-burh(†), fc., *treasure-city;* as., 467.

hord-gestrēon†, n., *stored-up possessions, treasure;* gp. -a, 3092; dp. -um, 1899.
hord-māðum‡, m., H O A R D-*treasure, jewel;* as. -māðum, *1198*.
hord-weard†, m., GUARD*ian of treasure;* hordweard hæleþa ('king'): ns., 1047, as., 1852; hordweard ('dragon'): ns., 2293, 2302, 2554, 2593.
hord-wela‡, wk.m., H O A R D*ed* WEAL*th;* as. -welan, 2344. [W E A L.]
hord-weorþung‡, f., *honoring with gifts;* as. -e, 952.
hord-wyn(n)‡, fjō., H O A R D-*joy, delightful treasure;* as. -wynne, 2270.
hord-wyrðe‡, adj.ja., WORTH*y of being* H O A R D*ed;* asm. -wyrðne, 2245.
horn, m., H O R N; 1423; as., 2943; [np. -as, 'gables,' F. *1*, 4]; dp. -um, 1369. — Cpd.: gūð-.
horn-boga†, wk.m., H O R N-B O W (i.e. bow 'tipped with horn,' or 'curved like a horn'; see B.-T., Keller 50, Cl. Hall's note, Falk L 9.44.91 f.; Cha. Intr. 361); ds. -bogan, 2437.
horn-gēap†, adj., *wide-gabled;* 82. (Cf. *Angl.* xii 396 f.) See gēap.
horn-reced‡, n., *gabled house;* as., 704.
hors, n., H O R S E; 1399. [OS. hros(s); Ger. Ross.]
hōs‡, f., *troop (of attendants);* ds. -e, 924. [Go. OHG. (Ger.) hansa; *Beitr.* xxix 194 ff., xxx 288.]
hoðma†, wk.m., *concealment, grave;* ds. (p.?) hoðman, 2458.
hrā (hrǣ(w), hrēa(w)), n.(m.) (Siev. § 250 n. 1), *corpse, body;* hrā, 1588; [np. hrǣw, F. *34*]. [Go. hraiwa-.]
hræd-līce, adv., *quickly;* 356, 963. [hraþe.]

hræfen, see **hrefn**.
hrægl, n., *dress, corslet;* 1195; gs. -es, 1217; gp. -a, 454. [R A I L (obs.); night-rail (dial.).] — Cpds.: beado-, fyrd-, mere-.
hrǣðre, see **hreðer**.
hrā-fyl(l)‡, mi., FALL *of corpses, slaughter;* as. -fyl, 277.
hraþe, hræþe, adv., *quickly;* hraðe (hraþe), 224, 740, 748, 1294, 1310, 1541, 1576, 1914, 1937, 2117, 2968; hræþe, 1437; hreþe, 991; raþe (T.C. § 15, cp. Go. raþizō, comp.?), 724; hraþe: 1390, 1975. — Comp. hraþor, 543. [R A T H E R. See Holt. Et.: hræd, ræd.] (Cf. Stern, *Swift, Swiftly, and their Synonyms* (Göteborg, 1921) 17 ff.; *Beitr.* xlviii 79 ff.)
hrēam, m., *cry, outcry;* 1302.
hrēa-wīc‡, n., *place of corpses;* as. (p.?), 1214. [hrā.]
hrefn (hræfn), m., R A V E N; [hræfen, F. 34]; hrefn (blaca), 1801; (wonna) ~, 3024; ds. hrefne, 2448. (Cf. Lang. § 8.1.)
hrēmig†, adj., w. gen. or dat., *exulting;* 124, 1882, 2054; npm. hrēmge, 2363. [OS. hrōm, Ger. Ruhm.]
hrēoh, adj., *rough, fierce, savage, troubled;* 1564, 2180; dsn. hrēoum, 2581, wk. hrēon, 1307; npf. hrēo, 548. (Cp. blōd-, gūð-, wæl-rēow.)
hrēoh-mōd(†), adj., *troubled in mind, fierce;* 2132, 2296.
hrēosan, II, *fall, rush;* pret. 3 sg. hrēas, 2488, 2831; 3 pl. hruron, 1074, 1430, 1872. — Cpd.: be-.
hrēow, f., *sorrow, distress;* 2328; gp. -a, 2129. [*NED.*: R U E, sb.[1]; OHG. (h)riuwa, Ger. Reue.]
hrēð†, orig. n. (Siev. §§ 267 a, 288; *Beitr.* xxxi 82 ff.), *glory, triumph;* as., 2575. See **hrōðor**. — Cpds.: gūð-, sige-. (Hrēð-rīc.)

hreþe, see hraþe.
hreðer†, n.(?), *breast, heart;* 2113, 2593; ds. hreþre, 1151, 1446, 1745, 1878, 2328, 2442, 3148; hræðre, *2819;* gp. hreðra, 2045. [Go. haírþra, n.p.]
hreþer-bealo‡, nwa., (*heart*-B A L E), *distress;* 1343.
hrēð-sigor‡, m.(n.), *glorious victory;* gp. -a, 2583.
hrīnan, I, *touch, reach;* w. dat.: 988, 1515, 3053; pret. opt. 3 sg. hrine, 2976 (*hurt*); w. æt: pret. 3 sg. hrān, 2270. — Cpd.: æt-.
hrinde‡, pp. npm. (of *hrindan, w 1.), *covered with frost;* 1363. [*Dial. D.*: R I N D (North.) 'hoar-frost'; cp. OE. hrīm (*IF.* xiv 339).]
hring, m., (1) R I N G (*ornament*); as., 1202, 2809; np. hringas, 1195; gp. hringa (þengel), 1507, ∼ (hyrde), 2245, ∼ (fengel), 2345; dp. hringum, 1091; ap. hringas, 1970, 3034. — (2) *ring-mail, armor formed of rings;* 1503, 2260 (byrnan hring). (Cf. S. Müller ii 128: corslet consisting of some 20,000 rings.) — Cpd.: bān-.
hringan, W I., R I N G, *resound;* pret. 3 pl. hringdon, 327.
hring-boga‡, wk.m., *coiled creature* (*dragon*); gs. (ds.?) -bogan, 2561. [R I N G; būgan.]
hringed(‡), adj., (pp.), *formed of* R I N G s; hringed (byrne), 1245; asf. hringde (byrnan), 2615.
hringed-stefna‡, wk.m., R I N G-*prowed ship;* 32, 1897; as. -stefnan, 1131. [stefn.] (Perh. a ship furnished w. rings [Weinhold L 9.32.483], or having a curved stem, cp. wundenstefna; hringnaca, ON. Hringhorni [Baldr's ship in Snorri's *Edda*], cf. Falk L 9.48.38. See also Heyne L 9.4.1.42 & n. 3; Neckel L 4.88 b.15 n. 2.)

hring-īren‡, n., R I N G-I R O N, *iron rings (of corslet);* 322. (Falk L 9.44.27: 'sword adorned w. a ring.')
hring-mǣl‡, adj., R I N G-*marked*, i.e. (sword) *adorned with a ring,* see fetelhilt, (or *with wavy patterns?*); nsn. (p.?), 2037; — used as noun (*ring-sword*); ns., 1521; as., 1564. (*Gen.* 1992: hringmǣled.)
hring-naca‡, wk.m., R I N G-*prowed ship;* 1862. See hringed-stefna.
hring-net(t)‡, nja., R I N G-N E T, *coat of mail;* as. -net, 2754; ap. ∼, 1889.
hring-sele‡, mi., R I N G-*hall;* ds., 2010 (cp. bēah-sele); — (of the dragon's cave:) ds., 3053; as., 2840.
hring-weorðung‡, f., R I N G-*adornment;* as. -e, 3017.
hroden†, pp. (of hrēodan, II), *adorned, decorated;* asn., 495, 1022; ge-hroden, npn., 304. — Cpds.: bēag-, gold-.
hrōf, m., R O O F; 999; as., 403, *836,* 926, 983, 1030 (helmes ∼, 'crown'), 2755. — Cpd.: inwit-.
hrōf-sele‡, mi., R O O F ed *hall;* ds., 1515.
hron-fisc (‡) (+), m., *whale* (-F I S H, cp. Ger. Walfisch); ap. -fixas, 540. [Sarrazin Käd. 69: Celt. rhon? But see R. Jordan, *Die ae. Säugetiernamen* (Ang. F. xii), p. 212; Holt. Et.]
hron-rād†, f., *whale*-R O A D, *ocean;* as. -e, 10.
hrōr, adj., *agile, vigorous, strong;* dsm.wk. -an, 1629. [Cp. onhrēran; Ger. rührig.] — Cpd.: fela-.
hrōðor†, n., *joy, benefit;* ds. hrōðre, 2448; gp. hrōþra, 2171. See hrēð. (Hrōð-gār.)

GLOSSARY

hruron, see **hrēosan**.
hrūse†, wk.f., *earth, ground*; 2558; vs., 2247; ds. hrūsan, 2276, *2279*, 2411; as. ~, 772, 2831.
hrycg, mja., *back*, R I D G E; as., 471.
hryre, mi., *fall, death*; ds., 1680, 2052, 3005; as., *3179*. [hrēosan.] — Cpds.: lēod-, wīg-.
hryssan (hrissan), w 1., *shake, rattle* (intr.); pret. 3 pl. hrysedon, 226 (cp. 327). (Elsewhere trans.) [Go. af-, us-hrisjan.]
hū, adv., conj., H O W; in direct question: 1987; — in dependent clauses (indir. interr. or explic.), w. ind., s.t. opt.; 3, 116, 279, 737, 844, 979, 1725, 2093, 2318, 2519, 2718, 2948, 3026, [F. 47].
hund, m., *dog*, H O U N D; dp. -um, 1368.
hund, num., n., H U N D*red*; a., w. partit. gen. (missēra:) 1498, 1769; hund (þūsenda), 2994, (þrēo) hund (wintra), 2278.
hūru, adv., *indeed, at any rate, verily, however*; 182, 369, 669, 862, 1071, 1465, 1944, 2836, 3120.
hūs, n., H O U S E; gs. hūses, 116, 1666; gp. hūsa (sēlest): 146, 285, 658, 935. — Cpds.: bān-, eorð-, nicor-.
hūð, f., *booty, spoil*; ds. (gs.?) -e, 124. [Go. hunþs.]
hwā, m.f., **hwæt**, n., pron., (1) interr., W H O, W H A T; hwā, 52, 2252, 3126, [F. 23]; hwæt, 173, 233 (*who*), w. gp. (*what sort of*): 237; dsm. hwām, 1696; asn. hwæt, 1476, 3068, w. partit. gen.: 474, 1186; isn. (tō) hwan, 2071.
— (2) indef., *some one, any one, something, anything*; asm. hwone, 155; nsn. hwæt, 3010; asn. ~, 880. — hwæt, interj., see hwæt. — Cpds.: ǣg-, ge-.
hwæder, see **hwyder**.

hwǣr, adv., conj., W H E R E, *anywhere*; 2029; hwār, 3062; elles hwǣr, E L S E W H E R E, 138. [OHG. wār, Ger. wo.] — Cpds.: ǣg-, ge-, ō-.
hwæt, adj., *brisk, vigorous, valiant*; nsm.wk. hwata, 3028; dsm. hwatum, 2161; npm. hwate (Scyldingas): 1601, 2052; apm. hwate, 3005; ~ (helmberend): 2517, 2642. [See hwettan.] — Cpds.: fyrd-, gold-.
hwæt, pron., see **hwā**.
hwæt, interj. (=interr. pron.), W H A T, *lo, behold, well*; foll. by pers. or dem. pron.; at the beginning of a speech: 530, 1652; within a speech: [240,] 942, 1774, 2248; at the beginning of the poem (as of many other OE. poems): 1. (Stressed in 1652, 1774.)
hwæðer, pron., (W H E T H E R), *which of two*; 2530; asf. (swā) hwæþere . . . (swā), *whichsoever*, 686. — Cpds.: ǣg-, ge-; nōðer.
hwæþer, conj., W H E T H E R; *1314* (MS. hwæþre), 1356, 2785; [F. 48 (n.)].
hwæþre, hwæþere, adv., *however, yet*; hwæþre, 555, 1270, 2098, 2228, 2298, 2377, 2874, hwæþere, 970, 1718; hwæðre (swā þēah), 2442; *however that may be, anyhow* (*Beitr.* ix 138): hwæþere, 574, *578*, hwæþre, 890. [Horn *ESt.* lxx 46-8.]
hwan, see **hwā**.
hwanan, -on, adv., WHEN*ce*; hwanan, 257, 2403, hwanon, 333.
hwār, see **hwǣr**.
hwata, -e, -um, see **hwæt**.
hwealf, (f.) n., *vault, arch*; as. (heofones) hwealf: 576, 2015. [Cp. Ger. wölben.]
hwēne, adv., *a little, somewhat*;

2699. [Siev. § 237 n. 2; cp. lȳt-hwōn.]

hweorfan, III, *turn, go, move about;* 2888 (n.); hworfan, 1728; pret. 3 sg. hwearf, 55, 356, 1188, 1573, 1714, 1980, 2238, *2268*, 2832, [F. 17]; opt. 3 sg. hwurfe, 264. [Go. hwaírban, Ger. werben.] — Cpds.: æt-, geond-, ond-, ymbe-.

ge-hweorfan, III, *go, pass;* pret. 3 sg. (on æht) gehwearf, 1679, (si.) ~: 1210, 1684, 2208.

hwergen(‡), adv., *some*WHERE; elles hwergen, E L S E WHERE; 2590. [Cp. Ger. irgend.]

hwettan, w I., W H E T, *urge, incite;* pres. opt. 3 sg. hwette, 490; pret. 3 pl. hwetton, 204. [hwæt, adj.]

hwīl, f., W H I L E, *time, space of time;* 146; ds. -e, 2320; as. -e, 16, 1762, 2030, 2097, 2137, 2159, 2548, 2571, 2780; *a long time:* ns. hwīl, *1495*; as. -e, 105, 152, *240;* — dp. hwīlum, adv., *sometimes, at times, now and again,* W H I L O M, *formerly;* 175, 496, 864, 867, 916, 1728, 1828, 2016, 2020, 2107–2108–2109–2111, 2299, 3044 (n.). — Cpds.: dæg-, gescæp-, orleg-, sige-.

hwīt, adj., W H I T E, *shining;* nsm. wk. -a, 1448; [asm. -ne, F. 39].

hworfan, see **hweorfan.**

hwyder, adv., W H I T H E R; 163); hwæder (cf. Lang. § 7 n. 2), *1331.*

hwylc, pron., (1) interr., W H I C H, *what;* 274; nsf., 2002; npm. -e, 1986. — (2) indef., *any (one)* (w. partit. gen.); nsm., 1104; nsn., 2433; — swā hwylc . . swā, *whichever;* nsf., 943; dsm. ~ hwylcum ~, 3057. — Cpds.: ǣg-, ge-, nāt-, wēl-.

hwyrfan, w I., *move about;* pres. 3 pl. hwyrfaþ, 98. (Cf. Lang. § 8 n. 1.) [hweorfan.]

hwyrft, mi., *turning, motion, going;* dp. -um, 163. [hweorfan.] — Cpd.: ed-.

hycgan, w 3., *think, purpose, resolve;* [imp. pl. hi*c*geaþ, F. 11]; pret. 1 sg. hogode, 632. — Cpds.: for-, ofer-; bealo-, heard-, swīð-, þanc-, wīs-hycgende.

ge-hycgan, w 3., *resolve;* pret. 2 sg. gehogodest, 1988.

hȳdan, w I., H I D E; 446; pres. opt. 3 sg. hȳde, 2766.

ge-hȳdan, w I., H I D E; pret. 3 sg. gehȳdde, 2235; *keep secretly,* ~, 3059.

hyge, see **hige.**

hyge-bend‡, fjō. (mi.), *mind's* BOND, *heart-string;* dp. -um, 1878.

hyge-giōmor†, adj., *sad in mind;* 2408.

hyge-mēðe‡, adj.ja., *wearying the mind;* nsn., 2442. [Ger. müde.] (Cp. sǣ-mēþe.) See Hoops 260.

hyge-sorh†, f., *heart-*S O R R O W; gp. -sorga, 2328.

hyht, mi., *hope, solace;* 179.

hyldan, w I., *incline, bend down;* refl.: pret. 3 sg. hylde (hine), 688. [H E E L 'tilt'; OE. heald, 'sloping,' 'inclined.']

hyldo, wk.f., *favor, grace, loyalty, friendship;* 2293; gs., 670, 2998; as., 2067. [hold.]

hylt, see **hilt.**

hȳnan, w I., *humble, ill-treat, injure;* pret. 3 sg. hȳnde, 2319. [hēan; Ger. höhnen; honi soit etc.]

hȳnðu, f., *humiliation, harm, injury;* as. hȳnðu, 277; hȳ[n]ðo, 3155; gp. hȳnða, 166; hȳnðo, 475, 593. [See hȳnan.]

hȳran, w I., (1) H E A R; w. acc., *hear of:* pret. 1 sg. hȳrde, 1197; — w. inf.: pret. 1 sg. hȳrde, 38; (secgan) hȳrde, 582; 3 sg. (~) hȳrde, 875; 1 pl. (~) hȳrdon, 273; — w.

acc. & inf.: pret. 1 sg. hȳrde, 1346, 1842, 2023; — w. þæt-clause: pret. 1 sg., hȳrde ic þæt (formula of transition, 'further'), 62, 2163, 2172. — (2) w. dat., *listen to, obey;* inf., 10, 2754; pret. 3 pl. hȳrdon, 66.

ge-hȳran, w 1., H E A R, *learn;* w. acc.: imp. pl. gehȳrað, 255; pret. 3 sg. gehȳrde, 88, 609; — w. (acc. and) acc. & inf. (*MPh.* iii 238): pret. 3 pl. gehȳrdon, 785; — w. (obj. þæt and) þæt-clause: pres. 1 sg. gehȳre, 290.

hyrde, mja., (H E R D), *guardian, keeper;* 1742, 2245, 2304, 2505; (folces) hyrde (*Arch.* cxxvi 353 n. 3): 610, 1832, 2644, 2981, [F. 46]; (wuldres) Hyrde (=God), 931; (fyrena) hyrde (=Grendel), 750; as. hyrde, 887, 3133, (folces) ∼, 1849, (rīces) ∼: 2027, 3080; ap. hyrdas, 1666. — Cpd.: grund-.

hyrst(†), fi., *ornament, accoutrement, armor;* dp. -um, 2762; ap. -e, 2988; -a, 3164, [F. 20]. [OHG. (h)rust.]

hyrstan(†), w 1., *adorn, decorate;* pp. asn. hyrsted, 672. [Ger. rüsten; see hyrst.]

hyrsted-gold†, n., *fairly-wrought* G O L D; ds. -e, 2255.

hyrtan(‡)+, w 1., *encourage,* refl.: *take* HEART; pret. 3 sg. hyrte (hine), 2593. [heorte.]

hyse†, mi.(ja.) (Siev. § 263 n. 3), *youth, young man;* vs., 1217; [gp. hyssa, F. 48].

hyt(t) (hit(t))‡, fjō., HEAT; 2649 (n.). [Ger. Hitze.]

hȳð, f., *harbor;* ds. -e, 32. [H Y T H E (obs.); cp. Rotherhithe, etc.]

hȳð-weard‡, m., *harbor-*GUARD*ian;* 1914.

ic, pers. pron., *I;* 181 times; [F. 24, 25, 37]; gs. mīn, 2084, 2533; ds. mē 42 times; [F. 27]; as. mec 16 times; mē, 415, 446, 553, 563, 677; — dual nom. wit, 535, 537, 539, 540, 544, 683, 1186, 1476, 1707; g. uncer, 2002 (n.), 2532; d. unc, 1783, 2137, 2525, 2526; a. unc, 540, 545; — plur. wē 24 times; gp. ūser, 2074, ūre, 1386; dp. ūs, 269, 346, 382, 1821, 2635, 2642, 2920, 3001, 3009, 3078, ūrum (w. ending of poss. pron.), 2659 (n.); ap. ūsic, 458, 2638, 2640, 2641.

icge‡, 1107, see note.

īdel, adj., I D L E, *empty, unoccupied;* 413; nsn., 145; *deprived (of,* gen.), 2888.

īdel-hende(‡)+, adj.ja., *empty-*HAND*e*d*;* 2081.

ides(†), f. (orig. fi.), †*woman, lady;* 620, 1075, 1117, 1168, 1259; gs. idese, 1351; ds. ∼, 1649, 1941.

in, I. prep., I N; (1) w. dat. (rest); 1 (the only instance of temporal sense), 13, 25, 87, 89, 107, 180, 323, 324, 395, 443, 482, 588, 695, 713, 728, 851, 976, 1029, 1070, 1151, 1302, [1513], 1612, 1952, 1984, 2139, 2232, 2383, 2433, 2458, 2459, 2495, 2505, 2599, 2635, 2786, 3097; postposit. (stressed), 19; in innan (preced. by dat.), 1968, 2452. — (2) w. acc. (motion), *into, to;* 60, 185, 1134, 1210, 2935, 2981. (W. Krohmer, *Altengl.* in *und* on, Berlin Diss., 1904.) — II. adv., *in, inside;* 386, 1037, 1371, 1502, 1644, 2152, 2190, 2552; inn, 3090.

in(n), n., *dwelling, lodging;* in, 1300. [I N N.]

inc, incer, see þū.

incge-‡, 2577, see note.

in-frōd‡, adj., *very old and wise;* 2449; dsm. -um, 1874.

in-gang, m., *entrance;* as., 1549.

in-genga‡, wk.m., *invader;* 1776.
in-gesteald‡, n., *house-property, possessions in the house;* as., 1155. [See in(n).]
inn, see **in**, adv.
innan, adv., *(from) with*ɪɴ, *inside;* 774, 1017, 2331, 2412, 2719; **in innan**, w. preced. dat. (semiprep.), 1968, 2452; **on innan**, 2715, 1740 (w. preced. dat.); þǣr on innan, 71, denot. motion ('into'): 2089, 2214, 2244.
innan-weard, adj., ɪɴᴡᴀʀᴅ, *interior;* 991; nsn., 1976. Cp. inneweard.
inne, adv., *with*ɪɴ, *inside;* 390, 642, 1281, 1570, 1800, 1866, 2113, 3059; þǣr inne, 118, 1617, 2115, 2225, 3087.
inne-weard, adj., ɪɴᴡᴀʀᴅ, *interior;* nsn., 998.
inwid-sorg, see **inwit-sorh**.
inwit-feng‡, mi., *malicious grasp,* 1447.
inwit-gæst‡, m., *malicious (stranger* or) *foe;* 2670. (Or -gǣst? See gǣst.)
inwit-hrōf‡, m., *evil* (or *enemy's*) ʀᴏᴏғ; as., 3123.
inwit-net(t)‡, nja., ɴᴇᴛ *of malice;* as. -net, 2167. (Cf. *Angl.* xxxv 134.)
inwit-nīð†, m., *enmity, hostile act;* np. -as, 1858; gp. -a, 1947.
inwit-scear‡, m., *malicious slaughter;* as., 2478. See gūð-scear.
inwit-searo‡, nwa., *enmity* (or *malice?*); as., 1101.
inwit-sorh‡, f., *evil care* or ѕᴏʀʀᴏᴡ; 1736; as. inwidsorge, 831.
inwit-þanc†, m., *hostile purpose;* dp. -um, 749.
ge-īode, see **ge-gān**.
iogoð, see **geogoð**.
iō-mēowle, see **geō-**.
īren, nja., ɪʀᴏɴ, †*sword;* 892, 1848, īren ǣrgōd: 989, 2586; ds. īrne, *1141;* as. īren, 1809, 2050; gp. īrenna, 802, (npf. of adj.?:) 2683, 2828; īrena (see note on 673), 673, 1697, 2259. — Cpd.: hring-; cp. īsern-. (Cf. Kluge, *Beitr.* xliii 516 f.: īren fr. *īsren.)
īren, adj.ja., *of* ɪʀᴏɴ; nsf. (ecg wæs) īren: 1459, 2778. — Cpd.: eal-.
īren-bend†, fjō. (mi.), ɪʀᴏɴ ʙᴀɴᴅ; dp. -um, 774, 998 (īrẹn-).
īren-byrne‡, wk.f., ɪʀᴏɴ *corslet;* as. -byrnan, 2986. Cp. īsern-.
īren-heard(‡), adj., ɪʀᴏɴ-ʜᴀʀᴅ; 1112.
īren-þrēat‡, m., *band having* ɪʀᴏɴ *armor, armed troop;* 330.
is, see **eom**.
īs, n., ɪᴄᴇ; ds. -e, 1608.
īsern-byrne‡, wk.f., ɪʀᴏɴ *corslet;* as. -byrnan, 671. Cp. īren-.
īsern-scūr‡, f., ɪʀᴏɴ ѕʜᴏᴡᴇʀ *(of arrows);* as. -e, 3116. [Cp. Go. skūra, f.]
īs-gebind‡, n., ɪᴄʏ ʙᴏɴᴅ; ds. -e, 1133.
īsig(‡)+, adj., ɪᴄʏ, *covered with ice;* 33(n.).
iū, see **geō**.
iū-mon(n), mc. [pl.], ᴍᴀɴ *of old,* gp. -monna, 3052.

kyning(-), see under **C**.

lā, interj., ʟᴏ, *indeed,* þæt lā mæg secgan: 1700, 2864.
lāc, n., *gift, offering;* dp. lācum, 43, 1868; ap. lāc, 1863; *booty:* ap. lāc, 1584. [Go. laiks, OHG. leih.] — Cpds.: ge-, beadu-, heaðo-; sǣ-. See **lācan**. (On the semantic development of lāc (cp. lācan, beadu-lāc, etc.) in connection with ritual practices (processions and the like), see Grimm D. M.

GLOSSARY

32; Heusler L 4.13 a. § 34; B.-T.)
lācan, rd., *move quickly, fly;* pres.
ptc. lācende, 2832; †(*play*, i.e.)
fight; inf. (dareðum) lācan, 2848.
— Cpd.: for-.
lād, f., *way, passage, journey;* gs. -e,
569; ds. -e, 1987. [L O A D, L O D E;
līðan.] — Cpds.: brim-, ge-, sǣ-,
ȳþ-.
lǣdan, w 1., L E A D, *bring;* 239; pret.
3 pl. lǣddon, 1159; pp. [lǣded],
3177, gelǣded, 37. [līðan.] —
Cpd.: for-.
lǣfan, w 1., L E A V E; 2315; imp. sg.
lǣf, 1178; pret. 3 sg. lǣfde, 2470.
[Cp. lāf; (be-)līfan.]
lǣn-dagas‡, m.p., *transitory* D A Y S;
gp. -daga, *2341;* ap. -dagas, 2591.
See lǣne.
lǣne, adj.ja., (LOANed) *transitory,*
perishable, perishing; 1754; gsn.
wk. lǣnan, 2845; asf.wk. ~, 1622;
asn. lǣne, 3129. [lēon; OS. lēhni.]
lǣng, see longe.
lǣran, w 1., *teach;* imp. sg. (þē) lǣr,
1722. [Cp. lār; Go. laisjan, Ger.
lehren.] (Cf. Go. refl. (ga)laisjan
sik, etc., *Zfvgl.Spr.* xlii 317 ff.;
Blickl. Hom. 101.6.)
ge-lǣran, w 1., *teach, advise, persuade* (w. acc. of pers. & of thing,
foll. by þæt- or hū-clause); 278,
3079; pret. 3 pl. gelǣrdon, 415.
lǣs, see lȳt.
lǣsest, lǣssa, see lȳtel.
lǣstan, w 1., (1) w. dat., (*follow*), *do*
service, avail; 812. (2) *perform;*
imp. sg. lǣst, 2663. [lāst; MnE.
L A S T, Ger. leisten.] — Cpd.:
ful-.
ge-lǣstan, w 1., (1) w. acc., *serve,*
stand by; pres. opt. 3 pl. gelǣsten,
24; pret. 3 sg. gelǣste, 2500. (2)
carry out, fulfill; inf., 1706; pret.
3 sg. gelǣste, 524, *2990;* pp. gelǣsted, 829.

læt, adj., *sluggish, slow* (w. gen.);
1529. [L A T E.] — Cpd.: hildlata.
lǣtan, rd., L E T, *allow* (w. acc. &
inf.); pres. 3 sg. lǣteð, 1728; imp.
sg. lǣt, 1488; pl. lǣtað, 397; pret.
3 sg. lēt, 2389, 2550, 2977; 3 pl.
lēton, 48, 864, 3132; opt. 2 sg.
lēte, 1996; 3 sg. ~, 3082. —
Cpds.: ā-, for-, of-, on-.
lāf, f., (1) *what is* LEFt *as an inheritance, heirloom;* ref. to armor, 454;
— ref. to swords: 2611, 2628; ds.
-lāfe, 2577 (n.); as. lāfe, 795, 1488,
1688, 2191, 2563; np. ~, 2036. —
(2) *remnant, remainder; survivors:*
as. (sweorda) lāfe, 2936; *leavings:*
ns. (fēla) lāf (' sword '), 1032; np.
(homera) lāfe (' sword '), 2829; as.
(bronda) lāfe (' ashes '), 3160.
(Cf. *Arch.* cxxvi 348 f.) [See
lǣfan; Go. laiba.] — Cpds.: ende-,
eormen-, wēa-, yrfe-, ȳð-.
ge-lafian(‡)+, w 2., *refresh,* L A V E;
pret. 3 sg. gelafede, 2722. [Lat.
lavare; Ger. laben. See *Prager*
Deutsche Studien viii 81 ff., *ESt.*
xlii 170; Heyne L 9.16. iii 38;
Holt. Et.]
lagu(†), mu., *sea, lake, water;* 1630.
lagu-cræftig‡, adj., *sea-skilled, experienced as a sailor;* 209.
lagu-strǣt‡, f., *sea-road* (-S T R E E T);
as. -e, 239.
lagu-strēam†, m., *sea-*S T R E A M,
sea; ap. -as, 297. Cp. brim-.
lāh, see lēon.
land, n., L A N D; ns. lond, 2197; gs.
landes: 2995; ds. lande, 1623,
1913, 2310, 2836; as. land, 221,
242, 253, 580, 1904, 2062, 2915;
lond, 521, 1357, 2471, 2492; gp.
landa, 311. — Cpds.: ēa-, el-;
Frēs-, Scede-.
land-būend, mc. [pl.], L A N Ddweller, *earth-dweller;* dp. land-

būendum, 95; ap. londbūend, 1345.
land-frumaǂ, wk.m., *prince of the* L A N D, *king;* 31.
land-gemyrce(ǂ)+, nja., L A N D-*boundary;* ap. -gemyrcu (*shore*), 209. [mearc.] (Cp. ende- sǣta.)
land-geweorcǂ, n., L A N D-W O R K, *stronghold;* as., 938.
land-waruǂ, f., *people of the* L A N D; ap. -wara (*country*), 2321 (or apm. =-ware?, cf. Siev. § 263 n. 7).
land-weardǂ, m., L A N D-GUARD, *coast-guard;* 1890. (Cp. 209, 242.)
lang(e), see long(e).
langað, m., L O N G *ing;* 1879.
lang-twīdigǂ, adj., *granted for a* L O N G *time, lasting;* 1708. [*Hel.* 2753 (C): tuīthon ' grant; ' Holt. Et.]
lār, f., *instruction, counsel, precept, bidding;* ds. -e, 1950; gp. -a, 1220; -ena, 269. [L O R E.] — Cpd.: frēond-.
lāst, m., *track, footprint;* as., 132; np. -as, 1402; ap. ∼, 841; — on lāst (faran, w. preced. dat.), *behind, after,* 2945; [si.: on lāste (hwearf), F. 17]; lāst weardian, *remain behind:* 971, *follow:* 2164. [See *NED.*: L A S T, sb.¹; Go. laists.] — Cpds.: feorh-, fēþe-, fōt-, wrǣc-.
lāð, adj., *hateful, grievous, hostile* (used as subst.: *foe*); 440, 511, 815, 2315; nsn., 134, 192; nsm. wk. lāða, 2305; gsm. lāþes, 841, 2910; gsn. ∼, 929, 1061; gsm.wk. lāðan, 83, 132; gsn. wk. lāðan (cynnes): 2008, 2354; dsm. lāþum, 440, 1257; asm. lāðne, 3040; gpm. lāðra, 242, 2672; gpn. ∼, 3029; dpm. lāðum, 550, 938; dpf. ∼, 2467; dpm. wk.(?) lāþan, 1505; apn. lāð, 1375. — Comp. lāðra, 2432. [L O A T H; Ger. leid.]

lāð-biteǂ, mi., *grievous* or *hostile* BITE, *wound;* np., 1122.
lāð-getēonaǂ, wk.m., L O A T H *ly spoiler, evil-doer;* 974; np. -getēonan, 559.
lāð-līc, adj., L O A T H L Y, *hideous;* apn. -licu, 1584.
lēaf, n., L E A F; dp. -um, 97.
lēafnes-wordǂ, n., W O R D *of* L E A V E, *permission;* as. (p. ?), 245.
lēan, n., *reward, requital;* gs. lēanes, 1809 (*gift*, ' present given in appreciation of services rendered,' but see n.); ds. lēane, 1021; as. lēan, 114, 951, 1220, 1584, 2391; gp. lēana, 2990; dp. lēanum, 2145; ap. lēan, 2995. [Go. laun, Ger. Lohn.] — Cpds.: and-, ende-.
lēan(ǂ)+, VI, *blame, find fault with;* pres. 3 sg. lȳhð, 1048; pret. 3 sg. lōg, 1811; 3 pl. lōgon, 862; 203 (w. dat. of pers. & acc. of thing: *blame for, dissuade from*). [OS. lahan.] — Cpd.: be-.
lēanian, w 2., w. dat. of pers. & acc. of thing, *requite, recompense* (*s.b. for s.th.*); pres. 1 sg. lēanige, 1380; pret. 3 sg. lēanode, 2102.
lēas, adj., w. gen., *devoid of, without;* 850; dsm. (winigea) lēasum, 1664 (*friend*L E S S). [Go. laus, Ger. los; LOOSE fr. ON.] — Cpds.: dōm-, drēam-, ealdor-, feoh-, feormend-, hlāford-, sāwol-, sige-, sorh-, tīr-, ðēoden-, wine-, wyn-.
lēas-scēawereǂ, mja., *deceitful observer, spy;* np. -scēaweras, 253. (Cf. *Angl.* xxix 380.)
lēg(-), see līg(-).
leger, n., *lying, place of lying;* ds. -e, 3043. [L A I R; cp. licgan.]
leger-bed(d), nja., B E D, *bed of death, grave;* ds. -bedde, 1007.
lemman (lemian) (ǂ)+, W I., LAME,

hinder, oppress; pret. 3 sg. lemede, 905.
lenge(†), adj. ja., beLONGing, at hand; nsn., 83 (n.).
leng(e), lengest, see **longe.**
lengra, see **long.**
lēod, mi., *man, member of a tribe or nation* (regul. w. gp., Gēata, Scylfinga, etc.: †*prince*[?], cf. *MLN.* xxxiv 129 f.); 341, 348, 669, 829, 1432, 1492, 1538, 1612, 2159, 2551, 2603, [F. 24]; as., 625; vs., 1653. **lēode,** pl., (perh. orig. *freemen,*) *people* (freq. w. gp., Gēata, etc., or poss. pron.); np., 24, 225, 260, 362, 415, 1213, 2125, 2927, 3137, 3156, 3178, lēoda (Lang. § 20.2), 3001; gp. lēoda, 205, 634, 793, 938, 1673, 2033, 2238, 2251, 2333, 2801, 2900, 2945; dp. lēodum, 389, 521, 618, 697, 905, 1159, 1323, 1708, 1712, 1804, 1856, 1894, 1930, 2310, 2368, 2797, 2804, 2910, 2958, 2990, 3182; ap. lēode, 192, 443, 696, 1336, 1345, 1863, 1868, 1982, 2095, 2318, 2732. [Ger. Leute.] —
lēod, f., *people, nation;* gs. lēode, 596, 599. (Cp. 3001.)
lēod-bealo‡, nwa., *harm to a people, great affliction;* as., 1722; gp. -bealewa, 1946.
lēod-burg†, fc., *town;* ap. -byrig, 2471.
lēod-cyning‡, m., K I N G *of a people;* 54.
lēod-fruma†, wk.m., *prince of a people;* as. -fruman, 2130.
lēod-gebyrgea†, wk.m., *protector of a people, prince;* as. -gebyrgean, 269. [beorgan.]
lēod-hryre‡, mi., *fall (of a people or) of a prince, national calamity;* gs. -hryres, 2391; ds. -hryre, 2030.
lēod-sceaða†, wk.m., *people's enemy;* ds. -sceaðan, 2093.

lēod-scipe, mi., *nation, country;* ds., 2197; as., 2751.
lēof, adj., *dear, beloved;* 31, 54, 203, 511, 521, 1876, 2467; gsm. -es, 1994, 2080, 2897, 2910, gsn. 1061; asm. -ne, 34, 297, 618, 1943, 2127, 3079, 3108, 3142; vs.wk. -a, 1216, 1483, 1758, 1854, 1987, 2663, 2745; gpm. -ra, 1915; dp. -um, 1073. — Comp. nsn. lēofre, 2651. Supl. lēofost, 1296; asm.wk. lēofestan, 2823. [L I E F; Go. liufs, Ger. lieb.] — Cpd.: un-.
leofað, see **libban.**
lēof-līc(†), adj., *precious, admirable;* 2603; asn., 1809.
lēogan, II, L I E, *belie;* pres. opt. 3 sg. lēoge, 250; pret. 3 sg. lēag, 3029 (w. gen.). [Go. liugan.] — Cpd.: ā-.
ge-lēogan, II, *deceive, play false* (w. dat.); pret. 3 sg. (him sēo wēn) gelēah, 2323. (Cp. Lat. 'fallere'; *Arch.* cxxvi 355.)
lēoht, n., L I G H T; 569, 727, 1570; ds. lēohte, 95; as. lēoht, 648, 2469. [Cp. Go. liuhaþ.] — Cpds.: ǣfen-, fȳr-, morgen-.
lēoht, adj., L I G H T, *bright, gleaming;* dsn.wk. -an, 2492.
lēoma, wk.m., *light, gleam, luminary;* 311, 1570, 2769; as. lēoman, 1517; ap. ~, 95. [L E A M (Sc., North.); OS. liomo; cp. lēoht.] — Cpds.: ǣled-, beado-, bryne-, hilde-.
leomum, see **lim.**
lēon(‡) (+), I, *lend;* pret. 3 sg. lāh, 1456. [Go. leihwan.] — Cpd.: on-.
leornian, w 2., L E A R N, *devise;* pret. 3 sg. leornode, 2336.
lēoð, n., *song, lay;* 1159. [Go. *liuþ, Ger. Lied.] — Cpds.: fyrd-, gryre-, gūð-, sorh-.
leoðo-cræft†, m., *skill of limbs*

(*hands*); dp. -um, 2769. [OE. liþ>LITH (dial.); Go. liþus, Ger. Glied.]
leoðo-syrce‡, wk.f., (*limb*-SARK), *coat of mail;* as. (locene) leoðosyrcan, 1505; ap. (~) ~, 1890.
lettan(‡)+, w 1., w. acc. of pers. & gen. of thing, (LET), *hinder;* pret. 3 pl. letton, 569. [læt.]
libban, lifgan, w 3., LIVE; pres. 3 sg. lifað, 3167; leofað, 974, 1366, 2008; lyfað, 944, 954; opt. 2 sg. lifige, 1224; pres. ptc. lifigende, 815, 1953, 1973, *2062;* dsm. lifigendum, 2665 (see: be); pret. 3 sg. lifde, 57, 1257; lyfde, 2144; 3 pl. lifdon, 99.— Cpd.: unlifigende.
līc, n., *body* (generally *living*(†)); 966; gs. līces, 451, 1122; ds. līce, 733, 1503, 2423, 2571, 2732, 2743; as. līc, 2080, 2127. [LICH-(gate), etc.; Ger. Leiche.] — Cpds.: eofor-, swīn-. Cp. adj. suffix -līc.
licgan, V, LIE, *lie low, lie dead;* 1586, 3129; licgean, 966, 1427, 3040, 3082; pres. 3 sg. ligeð, 1343, 2745, 2903; pret. 3 sg. læg, 40, 552, 1041 (*failed*), 1532, 1547, 2051, 2077, 2201, 2213 (stīg under læg), 2388, 2824, 2851, 2978; pret. 3 pl. lǣgon, 566, lāgon, 3048. — Cpd.: ā-.
ge-licgan, V, *subside;* pret. 3 sg. gelǣg, 3146 (pluperf.).
līc-homa, wk.m., *body;* 812, 1007, 1754; ds. -haman, *3177;* as. ~, 2651. [Lit. ' body-covering.'] Cp. flǣsc-; fyrd-hom.
līcian, w 2., w. dat., *please;* pres. 3 sg. līcað, 1854; pret. 3 pl. līcodon, 639. [LIKE.]
līc-sār†, n., *bodily pain, wound;* as., 815. [SORE.]
līc-syrce‡, wk.f., (*body*-SARK), *coat of mail;* 550.

lid-man(n)†, mc., *seafarer;* gp. -manna, 1623. [līðan.]
līf, n., LIFE; 2743; gs. līfes, 197, 790, 806, 1387, 2343, 2823, 2845; ds. līfe, 2471, 2571; tō līfe, 2432 (*ever*); as. līf, 97, 733, 1536, [2251], 2423, 2751; is. līfe, 2131. — Cpd.: edwīt-.
līf-bysig‡, adj., *struggling for* LIFE, *in torment of death;* 966. See bysigu.
līf-dæg, m.; pl. **līf-dagas**, LIFE-DAYS; ap., 793, 1622.
Līf-frēa†, wk.m., *Lord of* LIFE (*God*); -frēa, 16.
līf-gedāl(†), n., *parting from* LIFE, *death;* 841. Cp. ealdor-.
līf-gesceaft‡, fi., LIFE (*as ordered by fate*); gp. -a, 1953, 3064.
lifige, lifigende, see libban.
līf-wraðu‡, f., LIFE-*protection;* ds. (tō) līfwraðe (*to save his life*), 971; as. ~, 2877.
līf-wyn(n)†, fi.(jō.), *joy of* LIFE; gp. -wynna, 2097.
līg, mi., *flame, fire;* 1122; lēg, 3115, *3145;* gs. līges, 83, 781; ds. līge, 2305, 2321, 2341, ligge, 727, lēge, 2549. [OHG. loug; cp. Ger. Lohe.]
līg-draca‡, wk.m., *fire*-DRAGON; 2333; lēg-, 3040. Cp. fȳr-.
līg-egesa‡, wk.m., *fire-terror;* as. -egesan, 2780. Cp. glēd-.
lige-torn‡, n., *pretended injury* or *insult;* ds. -e, 1943. [lyge ' lie.']
ligge, see līg.
līg-ȳð‡, fjō., *wave of flame;* dp. -um, 2672.
lim, n., LIMB, *branch* (*of tree*); dp. leomum, 97.
limpan, III, *happen, befall;* pret. 3 sg. lomp, 1987. — Cpds.: ā-, be-.
ge-limpan, III, *happen, come to pass, be forthcoming;* pres. 3 sg. gelimpeð, 1753; opt. 3 sg. gelimpe, 929; pret. 3 sg. gelamp, 626, 1252,

GLOSSARY

2941, gelomp, 76; opt. 3 sg. gelumpe, 2637; pp. gelumpen, 824.
lind, f., (L I N D en),† *shield* (made of linden-wood); 2341; as. -e, 2610; ap. -e, 2365; [-a, F. *11*].
lind-gestealla‡, wk.m., *shield-companion, comrade in battle;* 1973.
lind-hæbbend(e)‡, mc. (pres. ptc.) [pl.], *shield-bearer* (-H A V *ing*), *warrior;* np. -e, 245; gp. -ra, 1402.
lind-plega‡, wk.m., *shield-*P L A Y, *battle;* ds. -plegan, *1073* (MS. hild-), 2039.
lind-wiga‡, wk.m., *shield-warrior;* 2603.
linnan(†), III, w. gen. or dat., *part from, lose;* (aldre) ∼, 1478; (ealdres) ∼, 2443. [Go. af-linnan.]
liss, fjö., *kindness, favor, joy;* gp. -a, 2150. [līðe.]
list, mfi., *skill, cunning;* dp. -um, 781. [Go. lists, Ger. List.]
līðan, I, *go* (*by water*), *traverse* (trans., cp. *Hel.* 2233); pp. liden, 223. līðend, mc. (pres. ptc.), *seafarer, voyager;* np. -e, 221. Cpds.: brim-, heaþo-, mere-, sǣ-, wǣg-līðend(e).
līðe, adj.ja., *gentle, kind* (w. gen., 'as regards'); 1220. Supl. līðost, 3182. [L I T H E; Ger. lind.]
līð-wǣge‡, nja., *can* or *cup of strong drink;* as., 1982. [*R.-L.* iii 358 f.: līð.]
līxan, w 1., *shine, glitter, gleam;* pret. 3 sg. līxte, 311, 485, 1570. [Bülb. § 195.]
locen, see lūcan.
lōcian, w 2., L O O K; pres. 2 sg. lōcast, 1654.
lof, m., *praise, glory;* as., 1536. [Ger. Lob.]
lof-dǣd‡, fi., *praiseworthy* (*glorious*) D E E D; dp. -um, 24.
lof-georn, adj., *eager for praise* (*fame*); supl. -geornost, 3182 (n.).
lōg, lōgon, see lēan.
lond(-), see land(-).
lond-riht, n., L A N D-R I G H T, *privileges belonging to the owner of land, domain;* gs. -es, 2886.
long, adj., L O N G; local; 3043; — temporal: nsn. lang, 2093; næs ðā lang tō ðon: 2845, 2591 (long); asf. lange (hwīle, þrāge, tīd): 16, 114, 1257, 1915, 2159, longe (∼): 54, 2780. — Comp. lengra, 134. — See and-, morgen-, niht-, up-; ge-.
longe, adv., L O N G; 1061, 2751, 3082, 3108; lange, 31, 905, 1336, 1748, 1994, 2130, 2183, 2344, 2423. — Comp. leng, 451 (n.), 974, 1854, 2801, 2826, 3064; læ[n]g, 2307; lenge, 83(?), see note. Supl. lengest, 2008, 2238.
long-gestrēon‡, n., (L O N G-*accumulated,*) *old treasure;* gp. -a, 2240.
long-sum, adj., L O N G, *long-lasting, enduring;* nsn. (lāð ond) longsum: 134, 192; asm. -sumne, 1536; asn. -sum, 1722. [Cp. Ger. langsam.]
losian, w 2., (*be lost*), *escape, get away safely;* pres. 3 sg. losaþ, 1392, 2062; pret. 3 sg. losade, 2096. [LOSE, infl. by -lēosan (cf. Bülb. § 325).]
lūcan, II, LOCK, *intertwine, link;* pp. asf. locene (leoðosyrcan), 1505, so apf., 1890, (see hring); gpm. locenra (bēaga), 2995 (cf. Stjer. 34 f.); asn. (segn) gelocen, 2769 (*woven*). — Cpds.: be-, on-, tō-; hond-locen.
lufen†, f., *joy, comfort* (?); 2886. [Rel. to lufian; *ESt.* xlviii 121; *Beitr.* xxxvi 427 f.; Hoops St. 110 ff.: *dear home, homestead.*] (Cp. *Dan.* 73?) See l. 1728.
lufian, w 2., L O V E, *treat kindly;* pret. 3 sg. lufode, 1982.

luf-tācen‡, n., TOKEN *of* LOVE; ap. 1863.
lufu (lufe), wk.f. (Siev. § 278 n. 1), LOVE; as. lufan, 1728 (n.). See eard-lufu, lufen. — Cpds.: eard-, hēah-, mōd-, wīf-.
lungor(‡), adj., *swift;* npm. lungre, 2164 (n.).
lungre†, adv., *quickly, forthwith;* 929, 1630, 2310, 2743.
lust, m., *joy, pleasure;* as., 599, 618 (on lust, semi-adv.); dp. lustum (*gladly, with joy*), 1653. [LUST.]
ge-lȳfan, w 1., *be* LIEVE *in, trust;* w. dat., 440 (*resign oneself to*); — w. acc., *count on, expect confidently* (*s.th.*); pret. 3 sg. gelȳfde, 608, (on w. acc. or tō, *from s.b.*:) 627, 909, 1272. [Go. ga-laubjan.]
lyfað, lyfde, see libban.
lyft, fmi., *air, sky;* 1375; ds. -e, 2832. [LIFT (Sc., poet.); Go. luftus, ON. lopt>MnE. loft; ON. lypta, vb.>MnE. lift.]
lyft-floga‡, wk.m., *air-*FLI*er;* 2315.
lyft-geswenced‡, adj. (pp.), *driven by the wind;* 1913. [See swencan.]
lyft-wyn(n)‡, fjō.(i.), *air-joy, joyous air;* as. -wynne, 3043.
lȳhð, see lēan.
lystan, w 1., impers., w. acc. of pers., *desire;* pret. 3 sg. lyste, 1793. [LIST (arch.); OE. lust.]
lȳt, (1) n. (indecl.), w. partit. gen. (in 2365 implied), LITT*le, small number;* 2365, 2836 (n.), 2882; as., 1927, 2150. (2) adv., *little, not at all;* 2897, 3129. — Comp. **lǣs**, (1) n., w. partit. gen., LESS; asn. 487, 1946. (2) adv., in: þȳ lǣs, LES *t*, 1918.
lȳtel, adj., LITTLE, *small;* nsn., 1748; asn., 2240; asf. lȳtle, 2877, ∼ (hwīle): 2030, 2097. — Cpd.: un-. — Comp. **lǣssa**, LESS, *lesser;* 1282; dsn. lǣssan, 951; asf. ∼,

2571; dpn. ∼, 43. — Supl. **lǣsest**, LEAST; nsn., 2354.
lȳt-hwōn, adv., *very* LITT*le, not at all;* 203. Cp. hwēne.

mā, (adv. comp.,) subst. n., w. partit. gen., MO*re*, (cp. meanings of Lat. magis and plus); as., 504, 735, 1055, 1613. [Go. mais.] — Supl. **mǣst**, w. partit. gen., MOST; as., 2645. See micel.
mādma(s), -e, -um, see māð(ð)um.
mǣg, m., *kinsman, blood-relative;* 408, 468, 737, 758, 813, 914, 1530, 1944, 1961, 1978, 2166, 2604; gs. mǣges, 2436, *2628*, 2675, *2698*, 2879; ds. mǣge, 1978; as. mǣg, 1339, 2439, 2484, 2982; np. māgas, 1015; gp. māga, 247 (n.), 1079, 1853, 2006, 2742; dp. māgum, 1167, 1178, 2614, *3065;* mǣgum, 2353; ap. māgas, 2815. (See Antiq. §§ 2 ff.) [Go. mēgs.] — Cpds.: fæderen-, hēafod-, wine-.
mǣg-burg, fc., *kinsmen, kindred, clan;* gs. -e, 2887.
mǣgen, n., MAIN, *might, strength;* gs. mǣgenes, 196, 1534, 1716, 1835, 1844, 1887, 2647, mǣgenes cræft, 418 (cf. *Angl.* xxxv 468), si. 1270; mǣgnes, 670, 1761, 2084, 2146; ds. mǣgene, 789, 2667; as. mǣgen, 518, 1706; — *military force, host;* gs. mǣgenes, 155, (perh. 2647); as. mǣgen, 445. — Cpd.: ofer-.
mǣgen-āgende‡, pres. ptc. [pl.], *strong, mighty;* gpm. -āgendra, 2837.
mǣgen-byrþen(n)‡, fjō., *mighty* (BURTHEN,) BURDEN; ds. -byrþenne, 1625; as. ∼, 3091. [beran.]
mǣgen-cræft†, m., *strength;* as., 380.

GLOSSARY

mægen-ellen‡, n., *mighty valor;* as., 659.
mægen-fultum‡, m., *powerful help;* gp. -a, 1455.
mægen-ræs‡, m., *mighty impetus;* as., 1519.
mægen-strengo†, wk.f., *great* S T R E N G *th;* ds., 2678.
mægen-wudu‡, mu., (M A I N-W O O D), *mighty spear;* as., 236.
mægð(†), fc. (Siev. § 284 n. 4; *Beitr.* xxxi 73 ff.), MAID(*en*), *woman;* 3016; gp. mægþa, 924, 943, 1283. [OE. mægden > M A I D (E N).]
mægþ, f., *tribe* (orig. *aggregate of blood-relatives*), *nation, people;* ds. -e, 75; as. -e, 1011; gp. -a, 25, 1771; dp. -um, 5. [mǣg.]
mǣg-wine†, mi., *kinsman* (*and friend*); np., 2479.
mǣl, n., †*time, suitable time, occasion;* 316, 1008 (sǣl ond mǣl); as., 2633; gp. mǣla, 1249, 1611 (sǣla ond mǣla), 2057; dp. (ǣrran) mǣlum: 907, 2237, 3035. [M E A L; cp. dial. ' S E A L S and M E A L S.'] — Cpd.: undern-; cpds. of mǣl= 'mark,' 'sign': brogden-, grǣg-, hring-, sceāden-, wunden-.
mǣl-cearu‡, f., C A R E or *sorrow of the time;* as. -ceare, 189.
mǣl-gesceaft‡, fi., *time-allotment, destiny, fate;* gp. -a, 2737.
mǣnan, w 1., *speak of, utter, relate, complain of;* 1067, 3171; pret. 3 sg. mǣnde, 2267; 3 pl. mǣndon, 1149, 3149; pp. mǣned, 857. [*NED.*: M E A N, v.¹⋅²; MOAN.]
ge-mǣnan, w 1., *mention, complain;* pret. opt. 3 pl. gemǣnden, 1101.
mænigo, see **menigeo**.
mǣre, adj.ja., *famous, glorious, illustrious;* 15 times (marked*) in combination w. þēoden; 129*, 1046*, 1715*; nsf. mǣru, 2016, mǣre (wk.?), 1952; nsn. mǣre. 2405; nsm.wk. mǣra, 2011, 2587; gsm. mǣres, 797*; gsn.wk. mǣran, 1729; dsm. mǣrum, 345*, 1301, 1992*, 2079, 2572*; dsm.wk. mǣran, 270; asm. mǣrne, 36, 201*, 353*, 1598*, 2384*, 2721*, 2788*, 3098, 3141*; asn. mǣre, 1023; vs. mǣre, 1761, (wk.) mǣra, 1474; npm. mǣre, 3070*. Supl. mǣrost, 898; — *well known, notorious;* nsm. mǣre, 103; wk. mǣra, 762. [Go. -mēreis; OHG. māri; cp. Ger. Märchen.] — Cpds.: fore-, heaðo-.
mǣrðo, f., *fame, glory, glorious deed;* 857; as., 659, 687, 2134, mǣrðu, *2514;* gp. mǣrða, 408, 504(?), 1530, 2640, 2645; ap. ~, 504?, *2678*, 2996. [Go. mēriþa.] — Cpd.: ellen-.
mǣst, m., M A S T; 1898; ds. -e, 36, 1905.
mǣst, see **micel**.
mǣte, adj.ja., *moderate, insignificant, small;* supl. mǣtost, 1455. [metan. See *NED.*: MEET, adj.]
maga†, wk.m., (1) *son;* maga (Healfdenes), 189, 2143, si. 2587; vs. (~), 1474. (2) *young man, man;* 978, 2675; as. magan, 943. Cp. mago.
magan, prp., pres. 1 sg. **mæg**, *can,* M A Y, *may well; be able;* 1 sg. mæg, 277, 1822, 2739, 2801; 2 sg. meaht, 2047, miht, 1378; 3 sg. mæg, 930, 942, 1341, 1365, 1484, 1700, 1733, 1837, 2032, 2260, 2448, 2600, 2864, 3064, ēaþe mæg: 478, 2764, si. 2291; opt. 1 sg. mæge, 680, 2749; 3 sg. ~, 2530; 1 pl. mægen, 2654; pret. 1 sg. meahte, 1659, 2877; mihte, 571, 656, 967; 3 sg. meahte, 542, 754, 762(opt.?), *1032*, 1078, 1130, 1150, 1561, 2340, 2464, 2466, 2547, 2673, 2770, 2855, 2870, 2904,

2971; mehte, 1082, 1496, 1515, 1877; mihte, 190, 207, 462, 511, 1446, 1504, 1508, 2091, 2609, 2621, 2954 (opt.?); 1 pl. meahton, 941, 3079; 3 pl. meahton, 648, 797 (opt.?), 1156, 1350, 1454, ˑ911, 2373; mihton, 308, 313 (opt.?), 2683, 3162; opt. 1 sg. meahte, 2520; 3 sg. meahte, 243, 780 (ind.?), 1130(?), 1919; mihte, 1140. — (Without inf.: 754, 762, 797, 2091.)
māgas, -a, -um, see mǣg.
māge (mǣge), wk.f., *kinswoman (mother)*; gs. māgan, 1391. [mǣg.]
magoǂ, mu., *son;* mago (Healfdenes), 1867, 2011, si. 1465. [Go. magus. Cp. hilde-, ōret-, wrǣcmecg (mæcg).]
mago-drihtǂ, fi., *band of young retainers;* 67.
mago-rincǂ, m., *young warrior;* gp. -a, 730.
mago-ðegnǂ, m., *young retainer*, T H A N E; 408, 2757; ds. maguþegne, *2079;* gp. magoþegna, 1405; dp. -um, 1480; ap. maguþegnas, 293.
man(n), man-, see mon(n), mon-.
mān, n., *crime, guilt, wickedness;* ds. -e, 978, 1055; is. -e, 110. [OHG. mein, cp. Ger. Meineid.]
mān-for-dǣdlaǂ, wk.m., *wicked destroyer, evil-doer;* np. -fordǣdlan, 563. [dǣd.]
manian, w 2., *admonish, urge;* pres. 3 sg. manað, 2057. [Ger. mahnen.]
manig, see monig.
man-līceǂ, adv., M A N *ful* L Y, *nobly;* 1046.
mān-scaðaǂ, wk.m., *wicked ravager, evil-doer;* 712, 737, 1339, -sceaða, 2514.
māra, see micel.
maþelian(ǂ), w 2., *speak, discourse, make a speech;* used in introducing direct discourse, see Intr. lv; pret. 3 sg. maþelode, 286[a], 348[a], 360[a], 371[a], 405[a], 456[a], 499[a], 529[a], 631[a], 925[a], 957[a], 1215[a], 1321[a], 1383[a], 1473[a], 1651[a], 1687[a], 1817[a], 1840[a], 1999[a], 2510[a], 2631[a], 2724[a], 2862[a], 3076[a]; maþelade, 2425[a]. [Cp. Go. maþljan. *ZfdA.* xlvi 260 ff.]
māðm-ǣhtǂ, fi., *precious property, treasure;* gp. -a, 1613, 2833.
māþm-gestrēon(ǂ) (+), n., *treasure;* gp. -a, 1931.
māð(ð)um, m., *precious* or *valuable thing, treasure;* ds. māþme, *1902;* mādme, 1528; as. māþðum, 169, 1052, 2055, 3016; np. māþmas, 1860; gp. māþma, 1784, 2143, 2166 (mēara ond ∼), 2779, 2799, 3011; mādma, 36, 41; dp. māðmum, 1898 (mēarum ond ∼), 2103, 2788; mādmum, 1048 (mēarum ond ∼); ap. māþmas, 1867, 2146, 2236, 2490, 2640, 2865, 3131; mādmas, 385, 472, 1027, 1482, 1756. [Go. maiþms. See T.C. § 6.] — Cpds.: dryht-, gold-, hord-, ofer-, sinc-, wundur-.
māðþum-fæt(ǂ)+, n., *precious vessel;* 2405 (māðþum-). [V A T.]
māðþum-gifuǂ, f., *treasure-*G I V*ing;* ds. -gife, 1301.
māððum-sigleǂ, nja., *precious jewel;* gp. māððumsigla, 2757.
māðþum-sweordǂ, n., *precious* S W O R D; as., 1023.
māððum-welaǂ, wk.m., WEAL*th of treasure;* ds. -welan, 2750. [W E A L.]
mē, see ic.
mēagol, adj., *earnest, forceful, hearty;* dp. mēaglum, 1980. [*IF.* xx 317.]
mearc, f., M A R K, *limit;* ([frontier-] *district*); ds. -e, 2384 (*life's end*). — Cpds.: Weder- (see Proper Names); fōt-, mīl-gemearc.

mearcian, w 2., MARK, *make a mark;* pres. 3 sg. mearcað, 450; pp. gemearcod, 1264; nsn., 1695.

mearc-stapa‡, wk.m., ('MARK-' *haunter*), *wanderer in the waste borderland;* 103; ap. -stapan, 1348. [steppan; MARCH.] (See Kemble L 9.1. i 35 ff., 48; Gummere G. O. 54.)

mearh†, m., *horse, steed;* 2264; np. mēaras, 2163; gp. mēara, 2166; dp. mēarum, 855, 917, 1048, 1898; ap. mēaras, 865, 1035. [Cp. MARE.]

mearn, see **murnan**.

mec, see **ic**.

mēce(†), mja., *sword;* 1938; gs. mēces, 1765, 1812, 2614, 2939; as. mēce, 2047, 2978; gp. mēca, 2685; dp. mēcum, 565. [Go. mēkeis.] — Cpds.: beado-, hæft-, hilde-.

mēd, f., MEED, *reward;* ds. -e, 2146; as. -e, 2134; gp. -o (Lang. § 18.3), 1178. [OS. mēda, cp. Go. mizdō.]

medo, medu, mu., MEAD; ds. medo, 604; as. medu, 2633; [medo, F. 39]. (Cf. Schrader L 9.49.2. 85 ff.; *R.-L.* iii 217 f.)

medo-ærn‡, n., MEAD-*hall;* as., 69. [Cf. *Beitr.* xxxv 242.]

medo-benc†, fi., MEAD-BENCH; medu-, 776; ds. medu-bence, 1052, medo-, 1067, 2185, meodu-, 1902. Cp. ealo-.

medo-ful(l)†, n., MEAD-*cup;* as. -ful, 624, 1015.

medo-heal(l)†, f., MEAD-HALL; -heal, 484; ds. meodu-healle, 638.

medo-stīg‡, f., *path to the* MEAD-*hall;* as. -stigge, 924. See stīg.

medu-drēam†, m., MEAD-*joy, festivity;* as., 2016.

medu-seld‡, n., MEAD-*house;* as., 3065. See sæld.

melda, wk.m., *informer;* gs. meldan, 2405. [Cp. Ger. melden.] (*A.* l 241 n. 1.)

meltan, III, MELT; 3011; pret. 3 sg. mealt, 2326; 3 pl. multon, 1120.

ge-meltan, III, MELT; pret. 3 sg. gemealt, 897, 1608, 1615, 2628 (fig., cf. *A.* l 217).

mene(‡)+, mi., *necklace;* as., 1199. [OS. hals-meni; cp. *NED.*: MANE.]

mengan, w 1., *mix*, MINGle, *stir up;* 1449; pp. nsn. gemenged, 848, 1593. [ge-mong.]

menigeo, wk.f., *multitude, a great* MANY; mænigo, 41; as. menigeo, 2143. [monig.]

meodo-setl‡, n., MEAD-(*house-*) SEAT, i.e. *hall-seat;* gp. -a, 5 (n.). See setl.

meodo-wong‡, m., *plain near the* MEAD-*hall;* ap. -as, 1643.

meodu-benc, -heal(l), see **medo-**.

meodu-scenc‡, mi., MEAD-*vessel, -cup*, dp. -um, 1980. See scencan.

meoto, ap. of me(o)tu‡, f., *meditation, thought(s);* 489 (n.)

meotod-, see **metod-**.

mercels, m., MARK, *aim;* gs. -es, 2439. [mearc.]

mere, mi., MERE, *lake, pool,* †*sea;* 1362; ds., 855; as., 845, 1130, 1603. [Go. mari-, Ger. Meer; cp. MER maid.]

mere-dēor‡, n., *sea-beast;* as., 558. [DEER; Ger. Tier.]

mere-fara‡, wk.m., *sea*FARer*;* gs. -faran, 502.

mere-fisc‡, m., *sea-*FISH; gp. -fixa, 549.

mere-grund‡, m., *bottom of a lake;* as., 2100; ap. -as, 1449.

mere-hrægl‡, n., *sea-garment, sail;* gp. -a, 1905.

mere-līðend(e)†, mc. (pres. ptc.) [pl.], *seafarer;* vp. -līðende, 255.

mere-strǣt†, f., *sea-path;* ap. -a, 514. [STREET.]

mere-strengo‡, wk.f., S T R E N G *th in the sea;* as., 533.
mere-wīf‡, n., M E R E-*woman, water-witch;* as., 1519.
mergen, see **morgen**.
metan, v, *measure,* †*traverse* (cp. Lat. ' (e)metiri ', see *MLN*. xxxiii 221 f.); pret. 3 sg. mæt, 924; 2 pl. mǣton, 514; 3 pl. ~, 917, 1633. [M E T E.]
mētan, w 1., M E E T, *find, come upon;* pret. 3 sg. mētte, 751; 3 pl. mētton, 1421. [Go. -mōtjan.]
ge-mētan, w 1., M E E T, *find;* pret. 3 sg. gemētte, 757; 3 pl. (hȳ) gemētton (*met each other*), 2592; opt. 3 sg. gemētte, 2785. Cp. gemēting.
Metod†, m., *God* (perh. orig. *governor*); 110, 706, 967, 979, 1057, 1611, 2527 (*ruler*, cp. 1057 f.); gs. -es, 670; ds. -e, 169, 1778; as. Metod, 180. [metan; cp. OS. Metod; ON. mjǫtuðr ' ordainer of fate,' ' fate '; *Angl.* xxxv 124.] — Cpd.: Eald-.
metod-sceaft†, fi., *decree of fate, death;* ds. -e, 2815; as. meotodsceaft, 1077; metodsceaft (sēon, cf. *Angl.* xxxv 465), 1180 (so *Gen.* 1743).
meþel (mæþel) (†), n., *council, meeting;* ds. meþle, 1876. [Go. maþl.]
meðel-stede†, mi., *place of assembly* (cp. þing-stede), *battle-field;* ds. meðelstede, 1082.
meþel-word‡, n., *formal word;* dp. -um, 236 (' words of parley,' Cl. Hall).
micel, adj., *great, large,* M U C H; 129, 502; nsf., 67, 146, [2001]; nsn., 170, 771; gsn. micles, 2185; gsm. wk. miclan, 978; dsf.wk. ~, 2849; asm. micelne, 3098; asf. micle, 1778, 3091; asn. micel, 69, 270, 1167; isn. micle, 922; dpf. miclum, 958; apm. micle, 1348; — gsn. micles (adv.), *much, far,* 694; isn. micle (adv.), *much,* 1283, 1579, 2651. — [M I C K L E, M U C K L E (arch., dial.); Go. mikils.] — Comp. **māra**, *greater,* M O R E; 1353, 2555; nsn. māre, 1560; gsf. māran, 1823; dsn. ~, 1011; asm. ~, 247, 753, 2016; asf. ~, 533; asn. māre, 136 (*more, additional*), 518. [Go. maiza.] — Supl. **mǣst**, *greatest;* 1195; nsf., 2328; nsn., 78, 193, 1119; asf. mǣste, 459, 1079; asn. mǣst, 2768, 3143; isn. mǣste, 2181. [Go. maists.] — mǣst, subst. n., see mā.
mid, I. **prep.**, *with;* (1) w. acc., *with, together with* (persons); 357, 633, 662, 879, 1672, 2652. — (2) w. dat., a) *among;* 77 (mid yldum), 195 (mid Gēatum), 274, 461, 902, 1145, 2192, 2611, 2623, 2948, [2990]; b) *together with, along with;* (persons:) (125), 923, 1051, 1128, 1313, 1317, 1407, 1592, 1924, 1963, 2034, 2627, 2949, 3011, 3065; postposit., stressed: 41, 889, 1625; (things:) 125, (483), 1868, 2308, 2788, cp. 2468 (n.); 1706 (virtually *and*); c) (manner:) *with* (s.t. semi-adv. phrases); 317, (438), 475, 483, 779, 1217, 1219, 1493, 1892, 2056 (mid rihte, ' by right '), 2221, 2378, 2535; d) (instrument:) *with, by means of;* 243, 438, (475), 574, 746, 748, 1184, 1437, 1461, 1490, 1659, (2535), 2720, 2876, 2917, 2993, 3091; e) (time:) *with, at;* 126 (mid ǣrdæge). — (3) w. instr., *by means of, through;* 2028. — **II. adv.** (cp. prep. foll. its case); 1642 (*among them*), 1649 (*too, with them*). — [Go. miþ, Ger. mit.] Cf. E. Hittle, *Zur Geschichte der ae. Präpos.* mid *und* wið (Ang. F. ii), 1901.

GLOSSARY

middan-geard, m., M I D D *le dwelling* (Y A R D), *world, earth* (considered as the center of the universe, the region between heaven and hell, or the inhabited land surrounded by the sea); gs. -es, 504, 751; ds. -e, 2996; as. (geond þisne) middangeard: 75, 1771. [Go. midjungards, etc.; *NED.*: M I D D E N E R D, M I D D *le*-E R D, (-)earth.] (Cf. Grimm D.M. 662 (794); *P. Grdr.*² iii 377 f.; Chantepie de la Saussaye L 4.42. n. 346; Cleasby-Vigfússon, *Icel.-Eng. Dict.*, & Gering, Glossary of *Edda*, s.v. miðgarðr; *R.-L.* iii 221.)
midde, wk.f.; ds. in **on middan**, *in the* M I D D *le*, 2705.
middel-niht†, fc., M I D D L E *of the* N I G H T; dp. -um, 2782, 2833.
miht, fi., M I G H T, *power, strength;* as., 940; dp. -um, 700. [Go. mahts.]
mihtig, adj., M I G H T Y; 1339; asn., 558, 1519; — applied to God: nsm., 701, 1716, 1725; dsm.wk. -an, 1398. — Cpds.: æl-, fore-.
milde, adj.ja., M I L D, *kind;* 1229; dpn. mildum, 1172. Supl. mildust, 3181. (Cf. *IF.* xli 352 ff.)
mīl-gemearc‡, n., *measure by* M I L E *s;* gs. -es, 1362. [Fr. Lat. milia; M A R K.]
milts, fjō., *kindness;* 2921. [milde.]
mīn, gs. of pers. pron., see **ic**.
mīn, poss. pron., M Y, M I N E; 262, 343, 391, 436, 468, 1325ᵃ, 1325ᵇ, 1776, 2434, [F. 24]; nsf., 550; nsn., 476, 2742; gsn. mīnes, 450; dsm. mīnum, 473, 965, 1226, 2429, 2729, 3093; dsf. mīnre, 410; asm. mīnne, *255, 418*, 445, 638, 1180, 2012, 2147 (on [mīn]ne sylfes dōm), 2651, 2652; asf. mīne, 453, 558, 1706, 2799; asn. mīn, 345,

2737 (absol., *my own*), 2750, 2879; vsm. mīn, 365, 457, 530, 1169, 1704, 2047, 2095; isn. mīne, 776, 837, 1955, 2685, 2837; npm. mīne, 415, 2479; gpm. mīnra, 431, 633, 2251; dpm. mīnum, 1480, 2797, 2804; apm. mīne, 293, 1336, 1345, 2815; [vpm. ~, F. 10].
missan(‡)+, W I., w. gen., ‡M I S S (*a mark*); pret. 3 sg. miste, 2439.
missēre†, n., *half-year;* gp. (fela) missēra: 153, 2620, (hund) ~: 1498, 1769. [ON. misseri. Cp. Go. missō; OE. gēar. *ZfdA.* iii 407, xiii 576.]
mist-hliþ†, n., M I S T *y hill, cover of darkness;* dp. -hleoþum, 710.
mistig(‡) (+), adj., M I S T Y, *dark;* apm. -e, 162.
mōd, n., *mind, spirit, heart;* 50, 549 (*temper*), 730, 1150; gs. mōdes, 171, 436, 810, 1229, 1603, 1706, 2100; ds. mōde, 624, 753, 1307, 1418, 1844, 2281, 2527, 2581; as. mōd, 67; *high spirit, courage:* ns. 1057, as. 1167; [ds. mōde, F. 12]; *pride, arrogance:* as., 1931 (?, see note). [M O O D.] — Cpds.: bolgen-, galg-, geōmor-, glæd-, gūð-, hrēoh-, sārig-, stīð-, swīð-, wērig-, yrre-.
mōd-cearu†, f., *sorrow of soul;* as. -ceare, 1778, 1992, 3149.
mōd-gehygd†, fni., *thought;* dp. -um, 233.
mōd-geþonc(†), m.n., THOUGHT(*s*), *mind;* as., 1729.
mōd-giōmor†, adj., *sad at heart;* nsn., 2894.
mōdig, adj., *high-spirited, courageous, brave;* 604, 1508, 1643, 1812, 2757; wk. mōdęga, 813; gsm. mōdges, 502, mōdiges 2698; gsn.wk. mōdgan, 670; dsm.wk. mōdigan, 3011; npm. mōdge, 855,

mōdige, 1876; gpm. mōdigra, 312. [M O O D Y.] — Cpd.: fela-.

mōdig-līc, adj., *brave, gallant;* comp. apm. -līcran, 337.

mōd-lufu (-lufe) (†), wk.f., *heart's* L O V E, *affection;* gs. -lufan, 1823.

mōdor, fc., M O T H E R; 1258, 1276, 1282, 1683, 2118; as., 1538, 2139, 2932.

mōd-sefa†, wk.m., *mind, spirit, heart, character;* 349, 1853, 2628; ds. -sefan, 180; as. ~, 2012.

mōd-þracu‡, f., *impetuous courage, daring;* ds. -þræce, 385.

mon(n), mc. (s.t., in as., wk.m.), M A N; mon, 209, 510, 1099, 1560, 1645, 2281, 2297, 2355, 2470, 2590, 2996, 3065, 3175; man, 25, 503, 534, 1048, 1172, 1175, 1316, 1353, 1398, 1534, 1876, 1958; gs. monnes, 1729, 2897; mannes, 1057, 1994, 2080, 2533, 2541, 2555, 2698; ds. men, 655, 752, 1879, 2285; menn, 2189; as. man, 1489; mannan, 297, 1943, 2127, 2774, 3108; mannon, 577; np. men, 50, 162, 233, 1634, 3162, 3165; gp. monna, 1413, 2887; manna, 155, 201, 380, 701, 712, 735, 779, 789, 810, 914, 1461, 1725, 1835, 1915, 2527, 2645, 2672, 2836, 3056, 3057, 3098, 3181; ap. men, 69, 337, 1582, 1717. (The ns. used as a kind of indef. pron. [cp. Ger. man], *one, they* (*any one*): 1172, 1175, 2355 (25, 1048, 1534); omission of this pron.: 1365.) — Cpds.: fyrn-, glæd-, glēo-, gum-, iū-, lid-, sǣ-, wǣpned-.

mōna, wk. m., M O O N; [F. 7]; as. mōnan, 94.

mon-cyn(n), nja., M A NKIND; gs. moncynnes, 196, 1955; mancynnes, 164, 1276, 2181; ds. mancynne, 110.

mon-drēam†, m., *joy of life among* MEN; as. mandrēam, 1264; dp. mondrēamum, 1715.

mon-dryhten†, m., (*liege*) *lord;* 2865; mandryhten, 2647; mondrihten, 436; gs. mondryhtnes, 3149, man-, 2849; ds. mandryhtne, 1249, 2281, mandrihtne, 1229; as. mondryhten, 2604, man-, 1978 (ns.?).

monig, adj., (sg.) M A N Y *a,* (pl.) *many;* used as adj. (w. noun): 689, 838, 908, 918, 2762, 3022, 3077; [mænig, F. 13]; nsf., 776; nsn., 1510; nsm. manig, 399, 854 (noun understood), 1112, 1289; dsm. monegum, 1341, 1419; dsf. manigre, 75; asn. manig, 1015; gpf. manigra, 1178; dpm. manegum, 2103; dpf. monegum, 5; apm. manige, 337; apf. monige, 1613 (noun understood); — used as subst., abs.: nsm. monig, 857, 171 (w. adj.); manig, 1860; dsm. manegum, 1887; npm. monige, 2982; manige, 1023; gpm. manigra, 2091; dp.(s.?)m. manegum, 349; apm. monige, 1598; — w. gen.: dp.(s.?)m. monegum, 2001, 3111; manegum, 1235; dpf. manigum, 1771; apm. manige, 728. [Go. manags; Ger. manch.]

mon-ðwǣre, adj.ja., *gentle, kind;* supl. -ðwǣrust, *3181.* Cp. geþwǣre.

mōr, m., M O O R, *marsh, waste land, desert;* ds. -e, 710; as. mōr, 1405; ap. -as, 103, 162, 1348. (Cf. *A.* l 113; L 4.66 b.9.)

morgen, m., (ja.), M O R N *ing,* M O R R O W; 1077, 1784; mergen, 2103, 2124; ds. morgne, 2484; mergenne, 565, 2939; as. morgen, 837; gp. morna, 2450. [Go. maúrgins.]

morgen-ceald‡, adj., C O L D *in the* M O R N *ing;* 3022.
morgen-lēoht(‡), n., M O R N *ing-* L I G H T, *sun;* 604, 917.
morgen-long‡, adj., *lasting the* M O R N *ing;* asm. morgenlongne (dæg, 'the whole forenoon'), 2894. See and-long.
morgen-swēg‡, mi., M O R N *ing-cry;* 129.
morgen-tīd(†), fi., M O R N *ing;* as., 484, 518.
mōr-hop‡, n., M O O R-*retreat;* ap. -u, 450. Cp. fen-hop.
morna, see **morgen**.
morð-bealu‡, nwa., M U R D *er* (-B A L E); as. -beala, 136 (Lang. § 18.2).
morðor, n., M U R D E R, *slaying;* gs. morðres, 1683, 2055; ds. morþre, 1264, morðre (sweart): 892, 2782.
morþor-bealo‡, nwa., M U R D E R, *slaughter;* as. morþor-, 1079, 2742.
morþor-bed(d)‡, nja., B E D *of death (by violence);* morþorbed, 2436.
morþor-hete‡, mi., M U R D E R*ous* HATE or *hostility;* gs. -hetes, 1105.
***mōtan**, prp., (1) *may, have opportunity, be allowed;* pres. 2 sg. mōst, 1671; 3 sg. mōt, 186, 442, 603; 1 pl. mōton, 347 (opt.?); 2 pl. ∼, 395; opt. 1 sg. mōte, 431; 2 sg. ∼, 1177; 3 sg. ∼, 1387; 3 pl. mōton, 365; pret. 1 sg. mōste, 1487, 1998, 2797; 3 sg. ∼, 168, 706, 735, 894, 1939, 2504, 2574(?), 2827, 3053, 3100; 3 pl. mōston, 1628, 2038, 2124, 2984, mōstan, 2247; opt. 2 sg. mōste, 961; 3 sg. ∼, 2241 (ind.?); 3 pl. mōston, 1088, 1875. (With ellipsis of inf.: 603, 1177, 1387, 1487, 2247.) — (2) M U S T; pres. 3 sg. mōt, 2886; pret. 3 sg. mōste, 1939(?), 2574 (?, n.). [M U S T fr. mōste.]

ge-munan, prp., w. acc., *bear in* MIND, *remember, think of;* pres. 1 sg. geman, 1220, 2633, gemon, 2427; 3 sg. geman, 265, *2042;* gemon, 1185, 1701; imp. sg. gemyne, 659; pret. 3 sg. gemunde, 758, 870, 1129, 1259, 1270, 1290, 1465, 2114, 2391, 2431, 2488, 2606, 2678; 3 pl. gemundon, 179; opt. 3 sg. gemunde, 1141. — Cp. onmunan; ge-mynd.
mund, f., †*hand;* dp. -um, 236, 514, 1461, 3022, 3091; (*protection,* in: mund-bora). [Cp. *NED.:* M O U N D, sb.²]
mund-bora, wk.m., *protector, guardian;* 1480, 2779. [beran.]
mund-gripe‡, mi., *hand*-G R I P; ds., 380, *965* (MS. hand-), 1534, 1938; as., 753.
murnan, III, (1) M O U R N, *be sad;* pres. opt. 3 sg. murne, 1385; pres. ptc. nsn. murnende, 50. — (2) *have anxiety* or *fear (about,* for); pret. 3 sg. mearn, 1442; (*shrink from:*) ∼, 136, 1537; (*scruple:*) ∼, 3129 (or *mourn?*). — Cpd.: be-; cp. un-murn-līce.
mūþa, wk.m., M O U T H, *opening,* ([‡]*door*); as. mūþan, 724.
mūð-bona‡, wk.m., *one who destroys with the* M O U T H, *devourer;* ds. -bonan, 2079.
myndgian, w 2., (*recollect*), *re*MIND; pres. 3 sg. myndgað, 2057; pres. ptc. (mc.) myndgiend, 1105. See ge-myndgian. [(ge-)myndig.]
ge-myndgian, w 2., *call to* M I N D; pp. gemyndgad, 2450.
myne†, mi., MIND, *desire,* 2572; *love, kind thought;* as., 169. [Go. muns.]
ge-myne, see **ge-munan**.
myntan, w 1., *intend, think;* pret. 3 sg. mynte, 712, 731, 762. [Cp. munan; M I N T (dial., arch.).]

378 BEOWULF

myrce(†), adj. ja., *dark;* asm. wk. myrcan, 1405. [M U R K.]
myrð(u)‡, f., *disturbance, trouble, affliction;* gp. myrðe, 810 (n.). [m(i)erran > M A R.]
nā, see **nō**.
naca†, wk.m., *boat, ship;* 1896, *1903;* gs. nacan, 214; as. ~, 295. [Ger. Nachen.] — Cpd.: hring-.
nacod, adj., N A K E D, *bare;* 2273 (-draca, *smooth*); nsn. (ref. to sword), 2585; apn. (~), 539.
næbben, see **habban**.
næfne, see **nefne**.
næfre, adv., N E V E R; 247, 583, 591, 655, 718, 1041, 1048; w. ne added before verb, 1460, [F. 37, si. nēfre, F. 39].
nǣgan†, w 1., *accost, address;* pret. 3 sg. (wordum) nǣgde, *1318.* [*IF*. xx 320; Holt. Et.: cp. nēah.]
ge-nǣgan†, w 1., (*approach*), *assail, attack;* pret. 3 pl. genǣgdan, 2206 -don, *2916* (T.C. § 28); pp. genǣged, 1439.
nægl, m., N A I L; gp. -a, 985.
nægl(i)an, w 1. (2.), N A I L; pp. asn. nægled, *2023* (n.).
nǣnig, pron., NO, *no one, none;* adj.: nsn., 1514; asm. nǣnigne, 1197; gpm. nǣnigre, 949; — subst. (w. gen.): nǣnig, 157, 242, 691, 859, 1933; dsm. nǣnegum, 598. [ne, ǣnig.]
nǣre, nǣron, nǣs (=ne wǣs), see **eom**.
nǣs(‡)+, adv., *by* NO *means;* 562, 2262. [=nealles; cf. Horn, Pal. cxxxv § 75.]
nǣs(s), m., *headland, bluff;* ds. nǣsse, 2243, 2417; as. nǣs, 1439, 1600, 2898; gp. nǣssa, 1360; ap. nǣssas, 1358, 1411, 1912. [*NED.*: NESS, cp. ON. nes.] — Cpds.: sǣ-; Earna-, Hrones-.

nǣs-hlið‡, n., (*slope of*) *headland;* dp. -hleoðum, 1427.
nāh, see **āgan**.
nalas, nalæs, nales, nallas, nalles, see **nealles**.
nam, nāman, see **niman**.
nama, wk.m., N A M E; 343, 1457, [F. 24]; as. naman, 78.
nān, pron., adj., N O; nsn., 988; subst., w. partit. gen., N O N E; [F. 41]; nsn., 803. [ne, ān.]
nāt, see **witan**.
nāt-hwylc(†), pron., *some* (*one*), *a certain* (*one*); adj.: dsm. -um, 1513; — subst., w. partit. gen.: nsm., 2215, 2233; gsm. -es, 2053, 2223. [=ne wāt, see 274; cp. ON. nǫkkurr; Lat. ' nescio quis.']
ne, adv., *Not;* immediately prec. the verb, 138 times, 38, 50, 80, 83, 109, 119, 154, 162, 180, etc.; [F. 3ᵃ, 3ᵇ, 4ᵇ, 20, 37, 41]. **nē**, conj., Nor, after (or within) negat. clause, 157, 169, 577, 584, 793, 1084, 1101, 1454, 1736ᵃ'ᵇ, 1737, 1930, 2126, 2185, 2263, 2264, 2348, 2533, 2628ᵇ, 2738ᵇ, 2857, 3016, [F. 39]; w. ne added before verb: 182, 245, 862, 1515, 2922, [F. 3ᵃ, 3ᵇ, 4ᵃ]; disjunct. phrases, nē lēof nē lāð 511, nē . . . nē . . . nē 1393ᵃ'ᵇ, 1394ᵃ, w. first neg. omitted: ǣr nē sipðan 718, sūð nē norð 858, wordum nē worcum 1100, wyrda nē worda 3030, si. 1454ᵃ, 1736ᵃ; — after positive clause: 510, 739, 1071, 2217, 2297. (Cf. L 6.14.)
nēah, *near*, N I G H; I. **adv.**; 1221, 2870. — II. **prep.** (usu. following the noun), w. dat., *near, on, by, close to;* 564, 1924, 2242, 2290, 2547, 2831, 2853; nēh, [2215], 2411. — III. (predic.) **adj.**; 1743, 2420, 2728. — Comp. adv. **nēar**, N E A R *er;* 745. — Supl. **adj.**

GLOSSARY

nīehsta, nȳhsta, *last;* dsm. nīehstan (sīðe), 2511; nȳhstan (∼), 1203. [N E X T.]
nealles, adv., *Not at* A L L; 2145, 2167, 2179, 2221, 2363, 2596, 2873, 3089; nalles, 338, 1018, 1076, 1442, 2503, 2832, 2919, 3015, 3019, 3023; nales, 1811; nallas, 1719, 1749; nalas, 1493, 1529, 1537; nalæs, 43. [ne, ealles.] Cp. næs.
nēan, adv., *from near, near;* nēan, 528, 839; nēan, 1174, 2317; nēon, 3104.
nēar, see **nēah.**
nearo, adj.wa., N A R R O W; ap. (s.?)f. nearwe, 1409.
nearo, nwa., *straits, difficulty, distress;* as., 2350, 2594. [neut. of nearo, adj.]
nearo-cræft‡, m., *art of rendering difficult of access;* dp. -um, 2243.
nearo-fāh‡, adj., *cruelly hostile;* gsm. -fāges, 2317.
nearo-þearf†, f., *severe distress;* as. -e, 422.
nearwe, adv., N A R R O W *ly, closely;* 976.
nearwian, w 2., *press (hard);* pp. genearwod, 1438.
nefa, wk.m., *nephew;* 2170, 1203 (*grandson?*); ds. nefan, 881; as. ∼, 2206; — *grandson:* ns. nefa, 1962. [MnE. nephew fr. OFr., fr. Lat. (acc.) nepotem.]
nefne, nemne, I. conj.; (1) w. subj.: *unless, if — not;* nefne 1056, 3054, næfne *250, 3074,* nemne 1552 (ind.?), 2654. (2) w. ind.: *except that;* næfne, 1353. (3) *without verb (after negat.): except;* nefne, 1934, 2151, 2533. — **II. prep.,** w. dat.: *except;* nemne, 1081. [Cp. Go. niba(i); *Beitr.* xxix 264; *Arch.* cxix 178 ff.] — See nymþe; būton. (Cf. Kock⁴ 115 ff.)

nēh, see **nēah.**
nelle, see **willan.**
nemnan, w 1., NAME, *call;* 2023; pres. 3 pl. nemnað, 364; pret. 3 pl. nemdon, 1354. [nama; Go. namnjan.] — Cpd.: be-.
nemne, see **nefne.**
nēod-laðu‡, f., *desire;* dp. -laðu[m], 1320 (Lang. §20.3). (Cf. *Arch.* cxv 179.) See nīod.
nēon, see **nēan.**
nēosan, nēosian, w 1. 2. (T.C. § 9), w. gen., *seek out, inspect, go to, visit, attack;* nēosan 125, 1786, 1791, 1806, 2074, nīosan 2366, 2388; nēosian 115, 1125, nīosian *2671,* 3045; pres. 3 sg. nīosað, 2486. [Go. niuhsjan.]
nēotan†, II, w. gen., *make use of, enjoy;* imp. sg. nēot, 1217. [Ger. geniessen.] — Cpd.: be-.
neowol, adj., *precipitous, steep;* apm. neowle, 1411. [Cf. Siev. § 73.3; *Beitr.* xxx 135.]
nerian, w 1., *save, protect;* pres. 3 sg. nereð, 572; pp. genered, 827. [(ge-)nesan; Go. nasjan.]
ge-nesan, v, *be saved, survive, get safely through;* abs.: pret. 3 sg. genæs, 999; w. acc.: pret. 1 sg. ∼, 2426; 3 sg. ∼, 1977; [3 pl. genǣson ' bore,' F. 47]; pp. genesen, 2397. [Go. ga-nisan; Ger. genesen.]
nēðan, w 1., *venture (on);* pret. 2 pl. (on .. wæter aldrum) nēþdon, 510; opt. 1 pl. (si.) nēðdon, 538; — w. acc., *brave, dare;* pres. ptc. nēðende, 2350. [Go. ana-nanþjan.]
ge-nēþan, w 1., *venture (on);* (under ȳða gewin aldre) genēþan, 1469; pret. opt. 1 sg. (si.) genēðde, 2133; — w. acc., *engage in, brave, dare;* inf., 1933; pret. 1 sg. genēðde, 1656, 2511; 3 sg. (under

.. stān) ~, 888; 1 pl. genēðdon, 959. Cp. ge-dīgan.
nicor(‡)+, m., *water-monster;* gp. nicera, 845; ap. niceras, 422, 575, nicras 1427. [NICKER (arch.); OHG. nihhus, Ger. Nix(e).] (Cf. *ZfdPh.* iii 388, 399; iv 197; *Angl.* xxxvi 170; *MLR.* x 85 f.; *R.-L.* iii 317 f.)
nicor-hūs‡, n., *abode of water-monsters;* gp. -a, 1411.
nīd-gripe‡ (=nȳd-, cf. Lang. § 1), mi., *forceful* or *coercive* GRIP; ds., 976.
nīehsta, see **nēah**.
nigon, num., NINE; a. nigene, 575.
niht, fc., NIGHT; 115, 547, 649, 1320, 2116; gs. nihtes, adv., *by night;* 422, 2269, 2273, 3044 (n.); ds. niht, 575, 683, 702, 1334 (gystran niht); as. ~, 135, 736, 2938; gp. (fīf) nihta ('days,' cf. Par. § 10, c. xi), 545, nihta 1365; dp. nihtum, 167, 275, 2211; ap. (seofon) niht, SENNIGHT, 517. — Cpds.: middel-, sin-.
niht-bealu‡, nwa., NIGHT-*evil;* gp. -bealwa, 193.
niht-helm†, m., *cover of* NIGHT; 1789.
niht-long, adj., *lasting a* NIGHT; asm. -ne, 528. See and-long.
niht-weorc‡, n., NIGHT-WORK; ds. -e, 827.
niman, IV, *take, seize;* 1808, 3132; pres. 3 sg. nymeð, 598; pret. 3 sg. nōm 1612, nam 746, [2216], 2986; 1 pl. nāman, 2116; pp. numen, 1153; — *carry off* (w. subject: dēað, hild, etc.); pres. 3 sg. nimeð 441, 447, 1491, 2536, nymeð 1846; opt. 3 sg. nime, 452, 1481. [Go. niman, Ger. nehmen; see *NED.*: NIM, NUMB, NIMble.] — Cpds.: be-, for-.
ge-niman, IV, *take, seize, take away;*

pret. 3 sg. genōm, 2776, genam 122, 1302, 1872, 2429; pp. genumen, 3165.
nīod(†), f., *desire, pleasure;* as. -e, 2116.
nīos(i)an, see **nēosan**.
nioðor, see **niþer**.
nīowe, see **nīwe**.
nīpan(†), 1, *grow dark;* pres. ptc. nīpende (niht): 547, 649.
nis, see **eom**.
nīð, m., (*ill-will, envy*), *violence;* ds. nīþe, 2680; *hostility, persecution, trouble, affliction;* ns. 2317; ds. nīðe, 827; as. nīð, 184, 276, 423, [F. 9]; — †*battle, contest;* ds. nīðe, 2585; gp. nīða, 882, 1962, 2170, 2350, 2397, [F. 21], w. verb (instrum. sense): 845, 1439 (*by force?*), 2206. [Go. neiþ, Ger. Neid.] — Cpds.: bealo-, fǣr-, here-, hete-, inwit-, searo-, wæl-.
nīð-draca‡, wk.m., *hostile* or *malicious* DRAGON; 2273.
niþer, adv., *down*(*ward*); 1360; nyðer, 3044. **nioðor**, adv. comp. (based on stem niþ-), *lower down*, 2699. [Cp. NETHER.]
nīð-gæst††, mi., *malicious* (*stranger* or) *foe;* as., 2699. (Or -gǣst?)
nīþ-geweorc(‡), n., *hostile deed, fight;* gp. -a, 683.
nīþ-grim(m)†, adj., GRIM, *cruel,* nsf. -grim, 193.
nīð-heard(†), adj., *brave in battle;* 2417.
nīð-hēdig‡, adj., *hostile;* npm. -hēdige, 3165. [= -hȳdig; hycgan.]
nīð-sele‡, mi., *hostile* or *battle hall;* ds., 1513.
niþðas†, mja.p., *men;* gp. niþða, 1005, 2215. [Go. niþjis 'kinsman.']
nīð-wundor‡, n., *fearful* WONDER, *portent;* as., 1365.
nīwe, adj.ja., NEW; 2243 (n.), 783

GLOSSARY 381

(*unheard of, startling*); asf. ~,
949; gpn. nīwra, 2898; — dsm.
wk. nīwan (stefne) (*afresh, anew*),
2594, nīowan (~), 1789.
(ge-)nīwian, w 2., *re*N E W; pp.
genīwod, 1303, 1322, genīwad,
2287 (n.).
nīw-tyrwed‡, adj. (pp.), N E W-
T A R R *ed;* asm. -tyrwydne, 295.
nō, emphatic neg. adv., N*ot at all,
not, never;* 136, 168, 244, 366, 450,
541: 543 (correl.), 575, 581, 586,
677, 754, 841, 968, 972, 974, 1002,
1025, 1355, 1366, 1392, 1453,
1502, 1508, 1735, [1875], 1892,
1907, 2081, 2160, 2307, 2314,
2347, 2354, 2373, 2423, 2466,
2585, 2618; nā, 445, 567, 1536. —
(nō þȳ ǣr, see ǣr; nō þȳ leng: 974,
si. 2423; syðþan nā (nō): 567,
1453, [1875]. With ne added before verb: 450, 567, 1453, 1508,
2466.) [N O; Go. ni aiw. See ā;
Beibl. xiii 15.]
nolde, see willan.
nōm, see niman.
nōn(‡)+, n.(?), *ninth hour* (= 3
p.m.); 1600. [N O O N; fr. Lat.
nona.]
norð, adv., N O R T H (*wards*); 858.
norþan-wind(‡)+, m., N O R T H
W I N D; 547.
nose, wk.f., ‡*projection, promontory, cape;* ds. nosan, 1892, 2803.
[Cp. nosu; Hoops St. 116; but cf.
Holt. Et.: nōse.]
nōðer, conj., N O R, *and not;* 2124.
[nō-hwæðer.]
nū, I. adv. (conj.), N O W; 251, 254,
375, 395, 424, 489, 602, 658, 939,
946, 1174, 1338, 1343, 1376, 1474,
1761, 1782, 1818, 2053, 2247ᵃ,
2508, 2646, 2666, 2729, 2743,
2747, *2884*, 2900, 2910, *3007*,
3013, 3101, 3114, [F. 7, 8, 10]; nū
gēn, 2859, 3167; nū gȳt, 956, 1058

(gīt), 1134; nū ðā (stressed nū),
426, 657. — II. conj., *now, now
that, since;* 430, 2799, 3020, [F.
21]; correl. w. (preced.) adv. nū:
1475, 2247ᵇ, 2745.
nȳd, fi., *necessity, compulsion, distress;* ds. nȳde, 1005; as. nȳd,
2454. [nēd > N E E D; Go. nauþs,
Ger. Not.] — Cpds.: hæft-, þrēa-.
(ge-)nȳdan, w 1., *compel, force;* pp.
nsn. genȳded, 2680, asf. genȳdde
1005.
nȳd-bād(‡)+, f., *enforced contribution, toll;* as. -e, 598.
nȳd-gesteallaṭ, wk.m., *comrade in
N E E D, i.e. in battle* (cp. *Havelok*
9: at nede); np. -gesteallan, 882.
[OHG. nōt(igi)stallo, MHG. nōt-
gestalle; Uhland L 4.67. n. i 256
n.]
nȳd-wracu†, f., *violent persecution,
dire distress;* 193.
nȳhsta, see nēah.
nyman, see niman.
nyllan, see willan.
nymþe, conj., *unless, if — not;* 781
(w. subj.), 1658 (w. ind.?, *but?*).
Cp. nefne.
nyt(t), fjō., *use, office, duty, service;*
as. nytte, 494, 3118 (~ hēold ' did
its duty '). [Cp. OHG. nuzzī. See
nyt(t), adj.] — Cpds.: sund-, sun-
dor-.
nyt(t), adj.ja., *useful, beneficial;*
apm. nytte, 794. [nēotan; Go.
(un-)nuts, OHG. nuzzi.] — Cpd.:
un-.
ge-nyttian(‡), w 2., w. acc., *use, enjoy;* pp. genyttod, 3046.
nyðer, see niþer.

of, prep., *from* (motion, direction);
37, 56, 229, 265, 419, 672, 710,
726, 785, 854, 921, 1108, 1138,
1162, 1571, 1629, 1892, 2471,
2624, 2743, 2769, 2809, 2819,

2882, 3121, 3177; postposit. (stressed), 671 (O F F); ūt of, 663, 2557; ūt . . . of, 2083, 2546; of . . . ūt, 2515, 2550; of flānbogan ('with an arrow shot) from a bow,' 1433, si. 1744, 2437. [O F, O F F.]
ōfer, m., *bank, shore;* ds. ōfre, 1371. [Ger. Ufer; cp. (Winds)or, etc.]
ofer, prep., (1) w. dat., (rest:) O V E R, *above;* 304, 1244, 1286, 1289, 1363, 1790, 1899, 1907, 2768, 2907, 2908, 3025, 3145.— (2) w. acc., (motion, extension, cf. *M Ph.* iii 256:) *over, across;* 10, 46, 48, 200, 217, 231, 239, 240, 248, 297, 311, 362, 393, 464, 471, 481, 515, 605, 649, 802, 859, 899, 983, 1208, 1404, 1405, 1415, 1705, [1803], 1826, 1861, 1862, 1909, 1910, 1950, 1989, 2007, 2073, 2259, 2380, 2394, 2473, 2477, 2724 (n.), 2808, 2893, 2899 (n.), 2980, 3118, 3132, [F. 22];—*beyond;* 2879, 1717 (*more than*); *contrary to, against:* 2330, 2409, [2589]; *after* (time): 736, 1781; *without,* 685.
ofer-cuman, IV, O V E R C O M E; pret. 3 sg. -cwōm, 1273; 3 pl. -cōmon, 699; pp. -cumen, 845.
ofer-ēode, see **ofer-gān**.
ofer-flēon(‡), II, F L E E *from* (acc.); 2525 (-flēon).
ofer-flītan(‡)+, I, O V E R *come (in a contest);* pret. 3 sg. -flāt, 517.
ofer-gān, anv., *pass* O V E R, *traverse, overrun;* pret. 3 sg. ofereode, 1408; 3 pl. -ēodon, 2959.
ofer-helmian‡, w 2., O V E R *hang, overshadow;* pres. 3 sg. -helmað, 1364.
ofer-hīgian‡, w 2., O V E R *take, overpower;* 2766 (n.). [H I E; *Dial. D.*: O V E R H Y E.]
ofer-hycgan, w 3., *despise, scorn;* pret. 3 sg. -hogode, 2345.

ofer-hygd, -hȳd, fni., *pride, arrogance;* gp. -hygda, 1740; -hȳda, 1760.
ofer-mægen†, n., *superior force;* ds. -e, 2917.
ofer-māð(ð)um‡, m., *exceeding treasure;* dp. -māðmum, 2993.
ofer-sēcan‡, w 1., O V E R *tax, put to too severe a trial;* pret. 3 sg. -sōhte, 2686.
ofer-sēon, V, (O V E R S E E), *look on;* pret. 3 pl. -sāwon, 419.
ofer-sittan(‡)+, v, w. acc., *abstain from, forego (the use of);* 684; pres. 1 sg. -sitte, 2528.
ofer-swimman‡, III, S W I M O V E R; pret. 3 sg. -swam, 2367.
ofer-swȳðan, w 1., O V E R *power, overcome;* pres. 3 sg. -swȳðeþ, 279, 1768. [swīð.]
ofer-weorpan, III, *fall* (O V E R), *stumble* (elsewhere trans.); pret. 3 sg. -wearp, 1543. (Cf. *A.* l 203 f.; *Leuvensche Bijdragen* xvii 3 ff.; *MLR.* xxv 78.)
of-ferian‡, w 1., *carry* O F F; pret. 3 sg. -ferede, 1583.
of-gyfan, V, G I V E *up, leave;* 2588; pret. 3 sg. -geaf, 1681, 1904, 2251, 2469; 3 pl. -gēafon, 1600, -gēfan 2846.
of-lætan, rd., *leave, relinquish;* pres. 2 sg. -lætest, 1183; pret. 3 sg. -lēt, 1622.
ofost, f., *haste, speed;* 256, 3007 (ofost); ds. (on) ofoste, 3090; (bēo on) ofeste, 386, (si:) ofste 1292, ofoste 2747, 2783. [Siev. § 43 n. 4; Bülbr. § 375; *IF.* xx 320; *ESt.* liv 97 ff.]
ofost-līce, adv., *speedily, in haste;* 3130.
of-scēotan, II, S H O O T (*dead*); pret. 3 sg. -scēt, 2439.
of-sittan(‡)+, V, w. acc., S I T *upon;* pret. 3 sg. -sæt, 1545.

GLOSSARY 383

of-slēan, VI, S L A Y, *kill;* pret. 1 sg. -slōh, 574, 1665; 3 sg. ~, 1689, 3060.

oft, adv., O F T *en;* 4, 165, 171, 444, 480, 572, 857, 907, 951, 1065, 1238, 1247, 1252, 1428, 1526, 1885, 1887, 2018, 2029, 2296, 2478, 2500, 2867, 2937, 3019, 3077, 3116. (Implying *as a rule, regularly:* 572, 1247, 2029, etc.) — Comp. oftor, 1579. Supl. oftost, 1663.

of-tēon, I (II), (1) *deny, deprive* (w. dat. of person & gen. of thing): pret. 3 sg. oftēah, 5. (2) *deny, withhold* (w. acc. of thing): pret. 3 sg. oftēah, 1520 (see Varr.), 2489. [Confusion, as to form, meaning, and construction between *oftīhan and *oftēohan. Siev. § 383; *Beitr.* xxix 306 f.]

of-þyncan, W 1., w. dat. of pers. & gen. of thing, *displease;* 2032 (n.).

ō-hwǣr, adv., *anyw* H E R E; 1737; ōwer, 2870. [See ǣg-hwǣr; nō.]

ombeht, m., *servant, officer;* 287; ombiht, 336. [Cp. Go. andbahts; Ger. Amt. Prob. fr. Celt.]

ombiht-þegn†, m., *servant, attendant;* ds. -e, 673.

ōmig(‡)+, adj., *rusty;* 2763; np. ōmige, 3049.

on (an: 677, 1247, 1935), I. prep., O N, *in,* used 373 times; 1. w. dat. (place, time, circumstance, manner, condition), *on, in, at, among;* 21, 22, 40, 53, etc.; [F. 12, 17, 28, 29]; (postpos., stressed, 2357). Note: on him byrne scān, 405, si. on (stressed,) him, 2036; cp. 752; gehȳrde on Bēowulfe . . . geþōht, 609 (transl. *from*), si. 1830; — on searwum, 1557 (n.), 2568, si. 2866 (*in,* postpos., stressed), cp. 2523 (*on,* postpos., stressed); — on ræste genam þrītig þegna, 122, si.: 747, 2986, 3164 (may be rendered by *from*); — *among, in* (w. collect. nouns): on corþre 1153, on herge 1248, 2638 (n.), on gemonge 1643, on folce 1701, 2377, on sigeþēode 2204, cp. 2197, on fēðan 2497, 2919, on ðām ðrēate 2406, on hēape 2596; — on sefan 473, 1342, 1737; on mōde 753, 1418, 1844, 2281, 2527; on ferhðe 754, 948, 1718; on hreþre 1878, 2328; — (time:) on fyrste, 76; on morgne, 2484, si. 565, 2939; on niht, 575, 683, 702; etc.; — on orlege, 1326; on ðearfe, 1456, 2849; — *semi-adj. phrases;* a) predic.: (wæs) on sālum 607, si. 643, 1170; on wynne 2014; on hrēon mōde 1307, 2581, [cp. F. 12]; on ofeste 386, 1292, 2747, 2783 (cp. 3090); on sunde ('swimming'), 1618; on fylle wearð ('fell'), 1544; on blōde, 847; b) attrib., appos.: (fēond) on helle ('hellish fiend'), 101; (secg) on searwum, 249, 2530, 2700, cp. 1557, 2568 (see above), 368; on frætewum, 962; on elne, 2506, 2816; on yrre, 2092; on giohðe, 2793, 3095; — *in respect to, in the matter of;* an herewæsmun, 677; on fēþe, 970; on gylpsprǣce, 981; — on þǣm golde ongitan *(by),* 1484. — 2. w. acc. (motion [actual or fig.], manner, time), cf. *M Ph.* iii 257 f.; *on, to, on to, into, in;* 27, 35, 49, 67, etc., [F. 11]. Note: on (holm) wliton, 1592, 2852; si. (sēon:) 2717, 2863 (cp. 1650), (starian:) 996, 1485, 1603, 1780, (postpos., stressed, on: 2796, cp. an w. dat., semi-adv.: 1935); — (direction), on . . hond 686, on twā healfa 1095, si.: 800, 1305, 1675, 2063; 1728; — on bǣl gearu ('ready to be placed on . . . '),

1109; an wīg gearwe, 1247;—(price, w. bebycgan) *for,* 2799; —*without perception of motion in MnE.;* on wæteres æht... swuncon, 516, si. 242, 507, 2132, on wæl crunge, 635; God wāt on mec, 2650 (see 1830); 627 (gelȳfan, see note); on (gesīðes) hād ('in the position of,' 'as'), 1297, si. 2193; on [mīn]ne sylfes dōm ('at my own discretion'), 2147; (time:) on morgentīd, 484, 518, si. 837, 1428, cp. 1579, 1753; *semi-adverbial phrases:* on gylp, 1749, on lust, 618; on spēd, 873; on ryht, 1555; on unriht, 2739; on geflit, 865; on ende, 2021.—on weg, on lāst, on efn, on innan, see weg, lāst, efn, innan.—[Go. ana, Ger. an.] See in. **II. adv.;** 1650 (see on, prep. (2)), 1903.
on-, prefix, = 1. Go. and- (see and-). 2. Go. ana-. (W. Lüngen, *Das Präfix* on(d)- *in der ae. Verbalkomposition,* Kiel Diss., 1911.)
on-arn, see **on-irnan.**
on-beran, IV, *harm, weaken, diminish;* 990; pp. nsn. onboren, 2284. (Cf. L 4.62 b.14 f.; Kock⁵ 79.)
on-bīdan, I, *wait;* pret. 3 sg. onbād, 2302; (w. gen.:) A B I D E, *await;* inf., 397.
on-bindan, III, U N B I N D, *loose;* pret. 3 sg. onband, 501.
on-bregdan, III, *swing open* (trans.); pret. 3 sg. onbrǣd, 723.
oncer-, see **ancor-.**
on-cirran, w 1., *turn, change* (trans.); 2857;—*turn* (intr.), *go;* pret. 3 sg. oncirde, 2951, 2970.
on-cnāwan, rd., K N O W, *recognize, perceive;* pret. 3 sg. oncnīow, 2554.
on-cȳð(ð)(‡), f., *grief, distress;* oncȳð, 1420; as. oncȳþðe, 830.
ond, conj., A N D; 311 times; spelt: ond, 600, 1148, 2040; otherwise abbreviated: ⁊ ; [and: F. 15, 16ᵃ, 16ᵇ, 17, 35; 45 (and ēac)]. (Cf. Schü. Sa. 80 ff.)
ond-hweorfan‡, III, *turn* (intr.) *against;* pret. 3 sg. ondhwearf, 548 (n.).
ond-lēan, see **and-lēan.**
ond-long, see **and-long.**
on-drǣdan, rd., D R E A D, *fear;* 1674; pres. 3 pl. [ondrǣ]da[ð], 2275; pret. 3 sg. ondrēd, 2347; opt. 3 sg. [ondrē]de, 3153. [ondrǣdan; *Beibl.* xiv 182 ff.; but see also *MLN.* xxxii 290; Holt. Et.]
on-drysne, adj.ja., *terrible, awful;* asf., 1932.
ond-slyht‡, mi., *on*SLAUGHT, *counterblow;* as. (MS. hond-), *2929, 2972.* [slēan.]
ōnettan, w 1., *hasten;* pret. 3 pl. ōnetton, 306, 1803. [*on-hātjan; Siev. § 43 n.4.]
on-findan, III, F I N D, *find out, discover, perceive;* pret. 3 sg. onfand, 1522, 1890, [2219], 2288, 2300, 2629, 2713; onfunde, 750, 809, 1497; opt.(?) 3 sg. ∼, 2841; pp. onfunden, 595, 1293.
on-fōn, rd., w. dat., *receive, take;* 911; imp. sg. onfōh, 1169; pret. 3 sg. onfēng, 52, 688, 748, 852, 1214, 1494.
on-geador‡, adv., *to*G E T H E R; 1595.
on-gēan, I. adv., *opposite (towards s.b.);* 747. **II.** prep., w. dat., A G A I N *st, towards;* 1034; postposit.: 681, 2364. [on-gegn; Ger. entgegen.]
on-ginnan, III, *be*G I N, *undertake;* w. acc.: pp. ongunnen, 409;—w. inf. (s.t. pleonastic); pres. 3 sg. onginneð, 2044; pret. 1 sg. ongan, 2878; 3 sg. ∼, 100, 871, 1605, 1983, 2111, 2210, 2312; ongon, 2701, 2711₁

GLOSSARY

2790; 3 pl. ongunnon, 244 (n.), 3143.

on-gitan, -gytan, v, *perceive, see, hear, understand;* ongitan, 1484, 1911, 2770; ongytan, 1496; ongyton, 308; pres. opt. 1 sg. ongite, 2748; imp. sg. ongit, 1723; pret. 3 sg. ongeat, 14, 1512, 1518; 3 pl. ongēaton, 1431, 2944; — ‡*seize, get hold of;* pret. 3 sg. angeat, 1291.

on-hōhsnian‡, w 2., *check, stop* (?); pret. 3 sg. onhōhsnode, *1944.* [Bu. Tid. 302: fr. hōh-seonu 'hamstring'; for older etymology (cp. OS. hosc), see L 5.3.414 f.; further, Kock[5] 95.]

on-hrēran, w 1., *stir up, arouse;* pp. onhrēred, 549, 2554. [hrōr.]

on-irnan(†), III, †*give way, spring open;* pret. 3 sg. onarn, 721.

on-lǣtan, rd., *loosen, release;* pres. 3 sg. onlǣteð, 1609.

on-lēon, I, w. dat. of pers. & gen. of thing, *lend;* pret. 3 sg. onlāh, 1467.

on-līcnes(s), fjō., L I K E N E S S; onlīcnes, *1351.*

on-lūcan, II, UNLOCK, *disclose;* pret. 3 sg. onlēac, 259.

on-mēdla(†), wk.m., *arrogance, presumption;* ds. onmēdlan, 2926. [mōd.]

on-munan, prp., w. acc. of pers. & gen. of thing, *consider worthy of* (or *fit for*); pret. 3 sg. onmunde, 2640 (n.).

on-sacan, VI, *resist, contest, fight* (dat., *against*); 2954. Cp. 1083.

on-sǣce, see **on-sēcan**.

on-sǣge(‡)+, adj.ja., *attacking, assailing* (cf. Aant. 31), *fatal* (?); nsf., 2076, 2483. [sīgan.]

on-sǣlan, w 1., *untie, loosen, disclose;* imp. sg. onsǣl, 489. [sāl.]

on-sēcan, w 1., w. acc. of pers. & gen. of thing, *exact (s.th. from s.b.), deprive (s.b. of s.th.);* pres. opt. 3 sg. (fēores) onsǣce (cf. Lang. § 9.3), 1942. (*Jul.* 679: fēores onsōhte.)

on-sendan, w 1., S E N D, *send away;* imp. sg. onsend, 452, 1483; pret. 3 sg. onsende, 382; 3 pl. (forð) onsendon, 45; pp. (∼) onsended, 2266.

on-sittan, v, *dread;* 597. [Cp. Go. and-sitan; Ger. sich entsetzen.]

on-sponnan†, rd., *unfasten;* pret. 3 sg. onspēon, 2723. [S P A N.]

on-springan, III, S P R I N G *asunder;* pret. 3 pl. onsprungon, 817.

on-stellan, w 1., *institute, bring about;* pret. 3 sg. onstealde, 2407.

on-swīfan(†), I, *swing, turn* (trans.); pret. 3 sg. onswāf, 2559.

on-sȳn, see **an-sȳn**.

on-tyhtan(‡), w 1., *incite, impel;* pret. 3 sg. ontyhte, 3086. [Cp. tēon, II.]

on-ðēon†, I, *prosper, thrive;* pret. 3 sg. onðāh, 900.

on-wadan(†), VI, *enter, take possession of;* pret. 3 sg. (hine fyren) onwōd, 915. (Cp. *Gen.* 1260, 2579, *Dan.* 17.)

on-wæcnan, pret. onwōc, VI, w 1. (Siev. § 392 n. 2), A W A K E (N) (intr.); pret. 3 sg. onwōc, 2287; — *arise, be born;* pret. 3 sg. ∼, 56; 3 pl. onwōcon, 111. (Cp. swebban.)

on-weald, m., *power, possession;* as., 1044.

on-wendan, w 1., *turn aside* (trans.), *put aside, remove;* 191, 2601.

on-windan(†), III, U N W I N D, *loosen;* pres. 3 sg. onwindeð, 1610.

on-wōc, see **on-wæcnan**.

open, adj., O P E N; asf. opene, 2271.

openian, w 2., O P E N (trans.); 3056.

ōr(†), n.(?), *beginning, origin;* 1688

(n.); ds. ōre *(front)*, 1041; as. ōr, 2407. [Fr. Lat. ora.]

orc, m., *cup, pitcher;* np. orcas, 3047; ap. ~, 2760. [Fr. Lat. orca, cp. urceus. *IF.* xxxii 337; Th. Kross, *Die Namen der Gefässe bei den Ags.* (1911), p. 105.]

orc-nēas‡, m.p., *evil spirits, monsters;* np. -nēǎs, 112. [Fr. Lat. orcus; Grimm D.M. 402 (486) n. 1, iii 402 (1737); *Angl.* xxxvi 169; nēo-; cp. Go. naus.] (Hoops 32, St. 17 ff.; *A.* lvi 40 ff., lvii 110 f., 112, 396.)

ord, m.(?), *point;* 2791; ds. orde, 556; as. ord, 1549; —*front;* ds. orde, 2498, 3125, [F. 12]. [Ger. Ort, ON. oddr; cp. *NED.*: ODD (fr. ON.).]

ord-fruma, wk.m., *leader, chief;* 263. (Rankin, *JEGPh.* viii 407: *father;* Keller, *ESt.* lxviii 335: *front fighter.*)

ōret-mecg(†), mja., *warrior;* np. -as, 363, 481; ap. ~, 332. [*or-hāt, OHG. ur-heiz, ' challenge.' Siev. § 43 n. 4.]

ōretta†, wk.m., *warrior;* 1532, 2538. [See ōret-mecg; (OHG.) *Hildebr.* 2: urhētto.]

oreðe(s), see **oruð**.

or-, stressed prefix, see the following nouns and adjectives; cp. ā-.

or-leahtre(‡)(+), adj.ja., *blameless;* 1886. [Cp. lēan ' blame.']

or-lege(†), ni., *war, battle, strife;* gs. orleges, 2407; ds. orlege, 1326. [OS. urlagi. Cf. Falk-Torp: orlog; Wood, *MLN.* xxxiv 205; Holt. Et.]

orleg-hwīl‡, f., *time of war, fight;* 2002; gs. -e, 2911; gp. -a, 2427.

or-þanc, m., *ingenuity, skill;* dp. -þancum, 406; -ðoncum, 2087.

oruð, n., *breath;* 2557; gs. [o]reðes, 2523; ds. oreðe, 2839. [*or-ōð; cp Go. uz-anan, vb.]

or-weardeǂ, adj., *without* GUARD-*ian;* asn., 3127.

or-wēna, wk.adj., *despairing (of,* gen.); (aidres) orwēna: 1002, 1565. [Go. us-wēna.]

oð, prep., w. acc., *until;* 2399, 3069, 3083. — oð þæt, conj., *until;* 9, 56, 100, 145, 219, 296, 307, 545, 622, 644, 1133, 1254, 1375, 1414, 1640, 1714, 1740, 1801, 1886, 2039, 2058, 2116, 2210, 2269, 2280, 2303, 2378, 2621, 2782, 2791, 2934, 3147; oðð þæt, 66; oþ ðe, 649. [oð, conj., F. 31.] (It specially indicates progress of narrative, ' then,' ' when ': 100, 644, 2210, etc.; s.t. it carries consecutive force, ' so that ': 66, 1375, etc. Cf. Schü. Sa. § 7.) —

oð-, (verbal) prefix, see the foll. verbs; cp. (stressed) ūð-. [Go. unþa-, und. Cf. W. Lüngen, *Das Präfix* on(d)- *etc.*, pp. 73 ff.]

oþ-beran†, IV, B E A R *(off);* pret. 3 sg. oþbær, 579.

oð-ēode, see **oð-gān**.

ōðer, adj. (used as adj. & as subst.), O T H E R, (cp. Lat. alter, alius:) *the other, one of two, another, second, following;* 503, 534, 859, 1338; (correl., ' one . . . the other ':) 1349, 1351; 1353, 1560, 1755, 2481; (se ōþer:) 1815, 2061; nsf., 2117; nsn., 1133, 1300; gsm. ōðres, 2451; gsn. ~, 219, 605, 1874; dsm. ōðrum, 814, 1029, 1165, 1228, 2167, 2171, 2198, 2565, 2908; þǣm ōðrum, 1471; asm. ōþerne, 652, 1860, 2440, 2484, 2985; asn. ōðer, 1086, 1583, 1945; ism. ōðre, 2670, 3101; [dpf. ōþrum, F. 16]; apn. ōþer, 870. [Go. anþar.]

GLOSSARY

oð-ferian, w 1., *bear away;* pret. 1 sg. oðferede, 2141.
oð-gān‡, anv., pret. oð-ēode, *went away, escaped;* 3 pl. oðēodon, 2934.
oððe, conj., OR; 283, 437, 635, 637, 693, 1491, 1763, 1764ª, 1764ᵇ, 1765ª, 1765ᵇ, 1766ª, 1766ᵇ, 1848, 2253, 2376, 2434, 2494, 2495, 2536, 2840, 2870, 2922; [F. 48]; *and*, 2475, 3006. (Cf. Bu. Tid. 57; *Angl.* xxv 268 f.; Schü. Sa. § 48; *ZfdA.* xlviii 193.) [Go. aíþþau.]
oð-wītan, 1, w. dat. of pers. & acc. of thing, *reproach, blame;* 2995. Cp. æt-.
ōwer, see ō-hwǣr.
ō-wiht, (f.)ni., *anything,* A U G H T; ds. -e, 1822, 2432. See āht, ā; note on 1825.

rǣcan, w 1., R E A C H (*out*); pret. 3 sg. rǣhte, 747.
ge-rǣcan, w 1., R E A C H, *hit;* pret. 1 sg. gerǣhte, 556; 3 sg. ∼, 2965.
rǣd, m., *advice, counsel, what is advisable, good counsel, help;* 1376; as., 172, 278, 2027, 3080; *benefit, gain:* as. (ēcne) rǣd, 1201; ap. (ēce) rǣdas, 1760. [R E D E (arch., dial.); Ger. Rat.] Cf. Grønbech L. 9.24. i. 170–74. — Cpds.: folc-; an-, fæst-.
rǣdan, rd., (*counsel*), *provide for, rule, control* (w. dat.), 2858; *possess,* 2056 (n.). [See *NED.*: R E A D, R E D E, v.¹; Go. garēdan, Ger. raten.] — Cpds.: sele-, weorod-rǣdend(e).
rǣd-bora, wk.m., *counselor;* 1325. [beran.]
Rǣdend(†), mc., *Ruler* (God); 1555.
rǣs, m., *rush, onslaught, storm;* as., 2626; dp. -um, 2356. [RACE fr. ON. rás.] — Cpds.: gūð-, heaðo-,
hilde-, hond-, mægen-, wæl-.
rǣsan, w 1., *rush* (upon); pret. 3 sg. rǣsde, 2690.
ge-rǣsan, w 1., *rush* (against); pret. opt.(?) 3 sg. gerǣsde, 2839.
rǣst, fjō.(?), R E S T, *resting-place, bed;* ds. rǣste, 122, 747, 1237, 1298, 1585; as. rǣste, 139, reste 2456. — Cpds.: æfen-, flet-, sele-, wæl-.
rǣswa†, wk.m., (*counselor*), *prince, leader;* ds. rǣswa[n], 60 (Gr. Spr., *et al.*: np.). [Cp. rǣs-bora, rǣdan; ON. rǣsir. Bugge L 4.84.24.]
rand, see rond.
rand-wiga†, wk.m., (*shield-*)*warrior;* 1298; as. -wigan, 1793.
rāsian(‡), w 2., *explore;* pp. nsn. rāsod, 2283. [Holt. Et.]
raþe, see hraþe.
rēafian, w 2., *rob, plunder, rifle;* 2773; pret. 3 sg. rēafode, 2985, 3027; 3 pl. rēafedon, 1212. [R E A V E (arch.); ROB fr. OFr. rob(b)er, fr. Gmc.] — Cpds.: be-; cp. heaðo-, wæl-rēaf.
rēc, mi., *smoke;* ds. -e, 3155. [R E E K.] — Cpds.: wæl-, wudu-.
reccan, w 1., *narrate, tell, unfold;* 91; ger. reccenne, 2093; pret. 3 sg. rehte, 2106, 2110. [racu.]
reccan, w 1., *care* (*for*, gen.); pres. 3 sg. recceð, 434. [R E C K; Siev. § 407 n. 12; cp. OS. rōkian.]
recedt, m.n., *building, hall;* 412 (m.), 770, 1799; gs. recedes, 326, 724, 3088; ds. recede, 720, 728, 1572; as. reced, 1237; gp. receda, 310. [Cp. OS. rakud.] — Cpds.: eorð-, heal-, horn-, wīn-.
regn-heard‡, adj., *wondrously strong;* apm. -e, 326. [Go. ragin. Cf. *JEGPh.* xv 251 ff.]
regnian, rēnian, w 2., *prepare, adorn;* rēn[ian], 2168; pp. geregnad, 777. See regn-heard.
ren-weard‡, m., GUARD*ian of the*

house (see note on 142); np. -as, 770. [See ærn; Lang. § 19.7.]
rēoc‡, adj., *fierce, savage;* 122. [Holt. Et.]
rēodan(†), II, R E D D *en;* pp. roden, *1151.*
rēon, see **rōwan.**
reord, f., *speech, voice;* as. -e, 2555. [Cp. Go. razda.] (*MLR.* xxviii 231 f.)
reordian, w 2., *speak, talk;* 3025.
ge-reordian, w 2., *prepare a feast;* pp. gereorded, 1788.
rēotan†, II, *weep;* pres. 3 pl. rēotað, 1376.
rest, see **ræst.**
restan, w 1., R E S T; 1793, 1857; (w. reflex. acc.:) pret. 3 sg. reste, 1799.
rēotu‡, wk.f., *joy, cheerfulness;* ds. rēote, 2457. (Lang. § 16 n.) [See un-rōt.]
rēþe, adj.ja., *fierce, cruel, furious;* 122, 1585; npm., 770.
rīce, nja., *kingdom, realm, rule;* 2199, 2207; gs. rīces, 861, 1390, 1859, 2027, 3080; as. rīce, 466, 912, 1179, 1733, 1853, 2369, 3004. [Cp. (bishop)R I C; Go. reiki, Ger. Reich.] — (Cpd.: Swīo-.)
rīce, adj.ja., *powerful, mighty, of high rank;* 172, 1209, 1237, 1298; wk. (se) rīca, 310, 399, 1975. [R I C H (cp. OFr. riche); Go. reiks.]
ricone (recene), adv., *quickly, at once;* 2983. [*IF.* xx 329.]
rīcsian, w 2., *rule, hold sway; 2211;* pret. 3 sg. rīxode, 144. [rīce.]
rīdan, I, R I D E; 234, 855; pres. opt. 3 sg. rīde ('swing on gallows'), 2445; pret. 3 sg. rād, 1883 ('ride at anchor'), 1893; 3 pl. riodan, 3169.
ge-rīdan, I, w. acc., R I D E *up to;* pret. 3 sg. gerād, 2898.

rīdend(‡), mc., R I D *er, horseman;* np., 2457 (n.).
riht, n., R I G H T, *what is right;* ds. rihte, 144; mid ~, 2056, æfter ~: 1049, 2110; as. riht, 1700 (sōð ond ~, cf. *Angl.* xxxv 456), 2330 (*law*); on ryht (*rightly*), 1555. — Cpds.: ēðel-, folc-, lond-, un-, word-.
rihte, adv., R I G H T *ly;* 1695. — Cpds.: æt-, un-; cp. upp-riht.
rinc†, *man, warrior;* 399, 720, 2985; ds. rince, 952, 1677; as. rinc, 741, 747; gp. rinca, 412, 728. [ON. rekkr; cp. RANK, adj., fr. OE. ranc.] — Cpds.: beado-, gūð-, heaðo-, here-, hilde-, mago-, sǣ-.
riodan, see **rīdan.**
rīxian, see **rīcsian.**
rodor, m., *sky, heaven;* (pl. used w. sg. meaning); gs. rodores, 1572; np. roderas, 1376; gp. rodera, 1555; dp. roderum, 310. [By-form rador, OS. radur.]
rōf†, adj., *renowned, brave, strong;* 682, 2084, 2538, 2666; asm. rōfne, 1793; asm.wk. rōfan, 2690. — Cpds.: beadu-, brego-, ellen-, gūð-, heaþo-, hige-, sige-.
rond, m., †*boss of shield* (cp. *Gnom. Cott.* 37); as., 2673 (n., *edge?*); †*shield;* ds. ronde, 2538, rande 1209; as. rond, 656, 2566, 2609, rand 682; ap. rondas, 326, 2653, randas 231. [R A N D, see *NED*.] (Cf. Falk L 9.44.131 & 139 f.) — Cpds.: bord-, geolo-, hilde-, sīd-.
rond-hæbbend(e)‡, mc. (pres. ptc.) [pl.], *shield-bearer* (-H A V *ing*), *warrior;* gp. -hæbbendra, 861.
rōwan, rd., R O W (i.e. *swim*); pret. 1 pl. rēon (T.C. § 1), 539; 2 pl. ~, 512.
rūm, m.(?), R O O M, *opportunity;* 2690.

GLOSSARY

rūm, adj., R O O M y, *spacious, large;* nsn., 2461; asm. -ne, 278.
rūm-heort, adj., *large*-H E A R T *ed, noble-spirited;* 1799, 2110.
rūn, f., (RUNE), *(secret) consultation, council;* ds. -e, 172. — Cpd.: beadu-; cp. hel-rūne.
rūn-stæf, m., RUN*ic letter;* ap. -stafas, 1695. [S T A F F, S T A V E.]
rūn-wita†, wk.m., *confidant, trusted counselor;* 1325.
ryht, see **riht**.
(ge-)rȳman, w 1., *clear, vacate, yield;* pret. opt. 3 pl. gerȳmdon, 1086; pp. gerȳmed, 492, 1975; — *allow, grant;* pp. ~, 2983, 3088. [rūm; cp. Ger. (ein)räumen.]

sacan, VI, *contend, fight;* 439. [Go. sakan.] — Cpd.: on-.
sacu, f., *strife, fighting;* 1857, 2472; as. sæce, 154. [S A K E; Ger. Sache; OS. saka 'lawsuit,' 'enmity,' etc.] See sæcc.
sadol(‡)+, m., S A D D L E; 1038.
sadol-beorht‡, adj., S A D D L E-B R I G H T; apn., 2175.
sǣ, mfi., S E A; 579, 1223; ds., 318, 544; as., 507 (masc.), 2380, 2394 (fem., *lake?*); dp. (be) sǣm (twēonum), 858, 1297, 1685, 1956.
sǣ-bāt†, m., S E A-B O A T, *ship;* as., 633, 895.
sæc(c)†, fjō., *fighting, battle, conflict, quarrel;* gs. secce, 600; ds. (æt) sæcce, 953, 1618, 1665, 2612, 2659, 2681, (tō) ~, 2686; as. ~, 1977, 1989, 2347, 2499, 2562; ap. (gp.?) sæcca, 2029. [Go. sakjō. See sacu.]
sæce, see **sacu**.
sǣ-cyning‡, m., S E A-K I N G; gp. -a, 2382. [Cp. ON. sǣ-konungr.]
sǣd, adj., w.gen., *satiated with, having had one's fill of, wearied with;* asm. -ne, 2723. [S A D.]

sǣdan, sǣde, see **secgan**.
sǣ-dēor(‡)+, n., S E A-*beast;* 1510. See **mere**-.
sǣ-draca(‡) (+), wk.m., S E A-*snake;* ap. -dracan, 1426.
sǣgan, w 1., *lay low, slay;* pp. gesǣged, 884. [sīgan.]
sǣ-gēap‡, adj., *curved* (or *spacious*) (for use on the S E A); 1896. See **gēap**.
sǣ-genga(‡)+, wk.m., S E A-*goer,* i.e. ‡*ship;* 1882, 1908. [gangan.]
sǣgon, see **sēon**.
sǣ-grund, m., *bottom of the* S E A; ds. -e, 564.
sǣl†, n. (Siev. §§ 288 f.; Beitr. xxxi 87 n.), *hall;* as. sæl, 307, 2075, 2264; sel (cf. Lang. § 8.1), 167. [Ger. Saal. Cp. sele.]
sǣl, mfi., (1) *time, proper time, opportunity, season;* 622, 1008, 1665, 2058; gp. sǣla, 1611; ap. sēle, 1135. — (2) *happiness, joy;* dp. sǣlum, 1322; on sǣlum 607, on sǣlum 643, 1170 (see: on). [*Dial. D.*: S E A L, sb.² Cp. Go. sēls; — ge-sǣlan, ge-sǣlig.] See **mǣl**.
sǣ-lāc‡, n., S E A-*booty;* ds. -lāce, 1624; ap. -lāc, 1652.
sǣ-lād†, f., S E A-*journey, voyage;* ds. -e, 1139, 1157.
sǣlan(†), w 1., *fasten, moor;* pret. 3 sg. sǣlde, 1917; 3 pl. sǣldon, 226; *twist;* pp. gesǣled, 2764. [sāl.] — Cpd.: on-.
ge-sǣlan, w 1., *befall, chance, turn out favorably;* pret. 3 sg. gesǣlde, 574, 890, 1250. [sǣl.]
sǣld(†), n., *hall;* as., 1280. [Perh. blending of two stems: sæl (cp. Go. saljan, saliþwōs) and seþel — seld 'seat.'] See ge-selda, seldguma, medu-seld.
sǣ-līðend†, mc. [pl.], S E A-*farer;* np., 411, 1818, 2806; -e, 377.
sǣ-man(n), mc., S E A-M A N; gp.

-manna, 329; dp. -mannum, 2954.
sǣ-mēþe‡, adj.ja., S E A-*weary;* npm., 325. See hyge-.
sǣmra, adj. comp., *inferior, worse, weaker;* 2880; dsm. sǣmran, 953. Cp. sǣne.
sǣ-nǣs(s) (‡) (+), m., (S E A-)*headland;* ap. -nǣssas, 223, 571.
sǣne, adj.ja., *slow;* comp. sǣnra, 1436. [Cp. Go. sainjan.]
sǣ-rinc†, m., S E A-*man, -warrior;* 690.
sǣ-sīð‡, m., S E A-*journey, voyage;* ds. -e, 1149.
sǣ-weal(l)†, m., S E A-W A L L, *shore;* ds. -wealle, 1924.
sǣ-wong‡, m., *plain by the* S E A, *shore;* as., 1964.
sǣ-wudu‡, mu., (S E A-W O O D), *ship;* as., 226.
sǣ-wylm‡, mi., S E A-W E L L*ing, billow;* ap. -as, 393. [weallan.]
sāl, m., *rope;* ds. -e, *302,* 1906. [Ger. Seil.]
sālum, see sǣl.
samod, I. adv., *together;* 2196; samod ǣtgǣdere, 329ᵇ, 387ᵇ, 729ᵇ, 1063ᵇ; — *also* (postpos.); somod, 2174; ond . . . somod, 1211, 1614, 2343, 2987. — II. prep., w. dat., *simultaneously with, at,* in: ‡samod ǣrdǣge, 1311, somod ∼, 2942 (cp. mid ∼, 126). [Go. samaþ; cp. SAME, fr. ON.]
sand, n., S A N D, *shore;* ds. -e, 213, 295, 1896, 1917, 1964, 3033.
sang, m., S O N G, *cry;* 90, 1063; as., 787, 2447. [Go. saggws.]
sār, n., (S O R E), *pain, wound;* 975; as., 787. [Go. sair.] — Cpd.: līc-.
sār, adj., S O R E, *grievous, bitter;* nsf., 2468; dpn. -um, 2058.
sāre, adv., S O R E*ly, grievously;* 1251, 2222, 2295, 2311, 2746. [Ger. sehr.]

sārig, adj., *sad, mournful;* asm. -ne, 2447. [S O R R Y.]
sārig-ferð†, adj., *sad at heart;* 2863.
sārig-mōd(‡) (+), adj., *sad-hearted;* dpm. -um, 2942.
sār-līc, adj., *painful, sad;* nsn., 842; asn., 2109.
sāwl-berend‡, mc., (S O U L-B E A R-er), *human being;* gp. -ra, 1004. (Cp. gǣst-, feorh-berend.)
sāwol, f., S O U L, *life;* 2820; gs. sāwele, 1742, sāwle, 2422; as. sāwle, 184, 801, 852. (Cf. *Angl.* xxxv 464 f.) [Go. saiwala.]
sāwol-lēas, adj., *life*L E S S; asm. -ne, 1406, 3033 (sāwul-).
sāwul-drīor†, m. or n., *life-blood;* ds. -e, 2693.
scacan, VI, *hasten, pass, depart;* w. prep. or adv. of local force: 1802; pres. 3 sg. sceaceð, 2742; pret. 3 sg. scōc, 3118, s[c]eōc 2254; — abs., pp. (*gone*): scacen, 1124ᵇ, 1136ᵇ, sceacen, 2306ᵇ, 2727ᵇ. [S H A K E.] (Cf. Wyld L 7.25 f. 85 ff.)
ge-scādan, rd., *decide;* pret. 3 sg. gescēd, 1555. [Go. skaidan; S H E D.]
scadu-helm‡, m., *cover of night* (S H A D O W), *darkness;* gp. -a (gesceapu), 650 ('shapes of darkness,' i.e. 'night,' cf. *Angl.* xxxvi 170). Cp. niht-helm.
scami(g)an, w 2., *be a* S H A M E*d; scamigan* (w. gen.), 1026; pres. ptc. npm. scamiende, 2850.
scaþa, see sceaþa.
sceacen, sceaceð, see scacan.
scead, n., pl. sceadu, S H A D E (*s*); ap., 707. See sceadu.
scēaden-mǣl‡, n., (*ornamented with distinctive* or *branching patterns,* i.e.) *damascened sword;* 1939. Cp. wunden-mǣl. (*Beitr.* xxxvi 429 f.)

GLOSSARY

sceadu, fwō., ap. sceadwa, S H A-
D O W (s), [1803]. See scead.
sceadu-genga‡, wk.m., *walker in
darkness;* 703.
scealc(†), m., *(servant), retainer,
warrior, man;* 918, 939. [Go.
skalks, Ger. Schalk; cp. mar-
SHAL.] — Cpd.: bēor-.
sceapen, see scyppan.
scearp, adj., S H A R P, *acute, smart;*
288. — Cpd.: beadu-, heaðo-.
scēat, m., *corner, lap, district, region;* gp. -a, 752; ap. -as, 96. [Go.
skauts, Ger. Schoss; SHEET (fr.
scīete).] (Cf. *Angl.* xxxv 116.)
sceat(t), m., *property, treasure,
money;* ap. sceattas, 1686. [Go.
skatts, Ger. Schatz.] — Cpd.: gif-.
sceaþa, wk.m., *one who does harm,
enemy;* gp. sceaþena 4, sceaðona
274; — †*warrior;* np. scaþan, 1803,
1895. [sceððan.] — Cpds.: attor-,
dol-, fēond-, gūð-, hearm-, lēod-,
mān-, scyn-, syn-, þēod-, ūht-.
scēawian, w 2., *look at, view, exam-
ine, see, behold;* 840, 1413, 2402,
2744, 3032, scēawigan 1391; pres.
2 pl. scēawiað, 3104; opt. 1 sg.
scēawige, 2748; 1 pl. scēawian,
3008; pret. 3 sg. scēawode, 843,
1687, 2285, 2793; 3 pl. scēawedon,
132, 204, 983, 1440; pp. gescēawod, 3075 (n.), 3084 (perh. 'shown,'
'presented,' fr. ge-scēawian).
[S H O W; Ger. schauen.] — Cp.
lēas-scēawere.
sceft (sceaft), m., S H A F T (*of arrow*); 3118; [ds. -e, F. 7 (*spear*)].
— Cpds.: here-, wæl-sceaft (*spear*).
scel, see sculan.
scencan, w 1., *pour out, give to drink;*
pret. 3 sg. scencte, 496. [SKINK
(dial.); Ger. schenken.]
scenn (scenna, -e?)‡, *sword-guard*
(?), *plate of metal on handle of
sword*(?); dp. scennum, 1694. [L

5.10.1: cp. Du. scheen; *ZföG.* lix
343; Falk L 9.44.30; Holt. Et.]
ge-sceōd, see ge-sceðþan.
scēotan, II, S H O O T; pres. 3 sg.
scēoteð, 1744. — Cpd.: of-.
ge-scēotan(‡)+, II, w. acc.,
(S H O O T), ‡*dart or hasten to;*
pret. 3 sg. gescēat, 2319.
scēotend(†), mc., S H O O T *er, warrior;* np., 703, 1154; dp. -um,
1026.
scepen, see scyppan.
sceran, IV, (S H E A R), *cut;* pres. 3
sg. scireð, 1287.
ge-sceran(‡), IV, *cut through;* pret.
3 sg. gescær, 1526; gescer, 2973.
sceþðan, VI, w 1., *injure, harm;* w.
dat.; 1033, 1524; pret. 3 sg. scōd,
1887; sceþede, 1514; — abs., w.
on & acc.: sceðþan, 243 (*make a
raid,* cf. Lang. § 25.5). [Go.
skaþjan; SCATHE, fr. ON. skaða.]
ge-sceþðan, VI, *injure, harm;* w.
dat.; 1447; pret. 3 sg. gescōd,
1502, 1587, 2777; gesceōd, 2222.
scildig, see scyldig.
scild-weall‡, m., S H I E L D-W A L L,
phalanx(?); as., 3118.
scild-wiga, see scyld-.
scile, see sculan.
scīma, wk.m., *brightness, light;*
[1803]. [Go. skeima.]
scīnan, I, S H I N E; 1517; pres. 3 sg.
scīneð, 606, 1571; [scȳneð, F. 7];
pret. 3 sg. scān, 321, 405, 1965; 3
pl. scinon, 994; scionon, 303.
scinna(†), wk.m., *evil spirit, demon;*
dp. scinnum, 939.
scionon, see scīnan.
scip, n., S H I P; 302; gs. -es, 35, 896;
ds. -e, 1895; as. scip, 1917; dp.
scypon, 1154.
scip-here, mja., S H I P-*army, naval
force;* ds. -herge, 243.
scīr, adj., *bright, resplendent, glorious, clear;* 979; nsn., 322; gsn.wk.

scíran, 1694; asn. scír, 496. [Go. skeirs; SHEER.]

scireð, see sceran.

scír-ham‡, adj., *in bright armor;* npm. -e, 1895.

(ge-)scōd, see (ge-)sceþðan.

scofen, see scúfan.

scop, m., *poet, singer, rhapsodist;* 496, 1066; gs. -es, 90. [Cp. OHG. scof. See *R.-L.* i 445.]

(ge-)sc(e)ōp, see (ge-)scyppan.

scrífan, 1, *decree, adjudge, impose (sentence),* w. dat. of pers.; 979. [Fr. Lat. scribere; S H R I V E.] — Cpd.: for-.

ge-scrífan, 1, *decree, assign,* w. dat. of pers. & acc. of thing; pret. 3 sg. gescráf, 2574.

scríðan, 1, *glide, move, wander, stride;* 650, 703, 2569; pres. 3 pl. scríþað, 163. [Ger. schreiten. Cf. *ESt.* lvi 171 f.; *Beibl.* xxxvii 251.]

scucca, wk.m., *demon, devil;* dp. scuccum, 939. [Holt. Et.; Jente L 6.24. § 106.]

scúfan, II, S H O V E, *push, move forward;* pret. 3 pl. scufon, 215; scufun, 3131; pp. scofen, 918. — Cpds.: be-; wíd-scofen.

sculan, prp., (pres.:) S H A L L, *must, ought, is to,* (pret.:) *had to, was to,* S H O U L D; pres. 1 sg. sceal, 251; 2 sg. scealt, 588, 2666; 3 sg. sceal, 20, 183, 271, 287, 440, 977, 1004, 1060, 1172, 1386, 1534, 2166, 2525, 2590, 2884, 3108, 3114; sceall, 3014, 3077; scel, 455 (inf. to be supplied fr. preced. main clause), 2804, 3010; opt. 3 sg. scyle 2657, scile 3176; pret. 2 sg. sceoldest, 2056; 3 sg. scolde, 10, 85, 805, 819, 1070, 1106, 1443, 1449, 1464; sceolde, 2341, 2400, 2408, 2421, 2442, 2585 (inf. to be supplied fr. preced. main clause), 2589, 2627, 2918, 2963, 2974, [F. 29]; 3 pl. scoldon, 41, 832, 1305, 1637; opt. 3 sg. scolde, 965, 1328, sceolde 2708; — chiefly expressive of futurity: *shall (am determined to);* pres. 1 sg. sceal, 384, 424, 438, 601, 636, 1706, 2069; sceall, 2498, 2535; 2 sg. scealt, 1707; 3 sg. sceal, 1862, 3018, sceall, 2508, 3021; 1 pl. sculon, 683; pret. 3 sg. sceolde (*was to*), 3068; opt. scolde (*should, were to, would*), 1 sg., 1477; 3 sg., 280, 691, 910 (ind.?); — ref. to the performance of an act (or to a state) in accordance w. one's *nature* or *custom* or as a *duty* (semi-periphrastic); pres. 3 sg. sceall ('it is his to . . .'), 2275; pret. 3 sg. scolde, 230, 1034, 1067, 1260; 3 pl. scoldon, 704, 1798 ('were wont to'), sceoldon 2257; suggesting certainty: pres. 3 sg. sceal ('is sure to'), 24. — W. omission of inf. of verb of motion: 1 sg. sceal, 2816, opt. 2 sg. scyle, 1179; of wesan (denot. futur.:) 3 sg. sceal, 1783, 1855, 2255, 2659.

scúr-heard†, adj., S H O W E R-H A R D, *hard in the storm of battle;* nsf., 1033. (See L 5.25; Krapp's note on *Andr.* 1133 (scúrheard); *Jud.* 79: scúrum heard.)

scyld, m., S H I E L D; 2570, [F. 7]; as., 437, 2675; ap. -as, 325, 333, 2850.

scyldan, w 1., *protect;* pret. opt. (ind.?) 3 sg. scylde, 1658. [scyld.]

scyld-freca‡, wk.m., (S H I E L D-) *warrior;* 1033.

scyldig, adj., *guilty;* (synnum) scildig, 3071 (cp. fáh 978, 1001); (w. gen. of crime:) morðres scyldig, 1683; *having forfeited* (w. gen.): ealdres ~, 1338, 2061. [scyld 'guilt'; sculan.]

scyld-wiga‡, wk.m., (S H I E L D-)

GLOSSARY

warrior; 288; scildwigan, ap., *3005* (n.).
scyle, see **sculan.**
scyndan, w 1., *hasten;* intr., 2570; trans., pp. scynded, 918. [ON. skynda.]
scȳne(†), adj.ja., *beautiful, fair;* nsf. (wk.?), 3016. [S H E E N; Go. skauns (adj.i.), Ger. schön.]
scyn-scaþa (scin-)‡, wk.m., *demoniac foe, hostile demon;* 707 (MS. syn-).
scyp, see **scip.**
scyppan, VI, *create,* S H A P E, *make;* pp. sceapen, 2229; scepen, 2913; *assign* (name): pret. 3 sg. scōp, 78. [Go. ga-skapjan.] — Cpd.: earmsceapen.
ge-scyppan, VI, *create;* pret. 3 sg. gesceōp, 97.
Scyppend, mc., *Creator;* 106.
scȳran (scīran), w 1., *clear up, settle;* 1939. [scīr. Cf. also Kock[2] 109.]
sē (se), **sēo, þæt,** dem. pron.; a) dem. adj. & def. article, THE, T H A T: b1) subst., *that one, he, she, that, it;* b2) relat., *that, who, which, what;* b3) sē (etc.) þe, relat. — nsm. sē, se, a) 107 times, 84, 86, 92, 102, 205, 258, etc.; b1) 9 times, 196, 469, 898, etc.; b2) 12 times, 143, 370, 1267, etc.; b3) sē þe 47 times, 79, 87, 90, 103, 230, 289, etc.; 441: sē þe hine (*he whom*); 2292: sē ðe, *he whom.* — nsf. **sēo** 13 times; a) 12 times, 66, 146, etc., 2031, 2258[a], 2323; b3) sēo ðe: 1445; sīo 16 times, 2024, 2087, 2098, 2258[b], 2403, and then regularly; a) 13 times; b1): 2024, 2087, b2): 2258[b]; sīe, a): 2219. — nsn. **þæt** (usually spelt þ) 66 times; a) 18 times, 133, 191, 890, etc.; b1) 46 times; mostly: þæt wæs, 11, 170, 309, etc. (ne wæs þæt, 716, 734, 1455, 1463, 2415, 2586; þæt is (bið), 454, 1002, 1388, 1611, 2000, 2999; nis þæt, 249, 1361, 2532); b2): 453, 2500. — gsm. **þæs** 9 times, ðæs 10 times; a) 18 times, 132, 326 (gsn.?), 989, 1030, etc.; b1): 1145 (gsn.?). — gsf. **þǣre,** a): 109 (d.?), 1025, 2546, 2887; ðǣre, a): 562; [F. 20]. — gsn. **þæs** (incl. ðæs 10 times) 49 times; a) 5 times, 1467, etc.; b1) w. verbs governing the gen.: 350, 586, 778, 1598, 2026, 2032; (semi-adv.) *for that, therefor, because of that,* w. expressions of compensation, reward, thanks, rejoicing, sorrow, etc.; 7, 16, 114, 277, 588, 900, 1220, 1584, 1692, 1774, 1778, 1992, 2335, 2739; (adv.) *to such a degree, so;* 773, 968, 1366, *1508*, 1509, tō þæs 1616; b2) relat.; (semi-adv., *as:*) 272, 383; 1398 (incl. relat. & antecedent); b3) þæs þe (ðe); (semi-conj.) *because, as;* 108, 228, 626, 1628, 1751, 1779 (w. antec. þæs, b1)), 1998, 2797; *according to what, as* (conj.): 1341, 1350, 3000; tō þæs þe (relat. & antec.), see tō. — dsm. **þǣm** 23 times, ðǣm 5 times, þām 19 times ðām 20 times (þǣm, ðǣm in the A part of the MS. only; þām, ðām in the B part, besides þām 425, 713, 824, 919, 1016, 1073, 1421); a) 52 times, 52 (dsn.?), 143, 197, 270, etc.; in (& si.) sele þām hēan: 713, 919, 1016, 1984; b1) 12, 59, 1363, 2612; b2) 310 (dsn.?), 374, (relat. & antec.:) 2199, 2779; b3) þǣm (þām) ðe (relat. & antec.), 183, 186, 1839, 2601, 2861, 3055, 3059. — dsf. **þǣre;** a) 10 times, 109(g.?), 125, 617, etc.; [ðǣre, F. 31]; b3) þāra þe (Lang. § 22), 1625. — dsn.; a) **þǣm** 1215, 1484, 1635, þām 1421, ðām 639, 2232; b1)

ðǽm 1688, þām 137, ðām 2769; see also for-ðām. — asm. þone (incl. ðone 12 times) 65 times; a) 52 times, 107, 168, 202, etc.; ūhthlem þone 2007, si. 2334, 2588, 2959, 2969, 3081; beorh þone héan 3097; b1) 1354, 3009 (þone [allit.] . . . þē); b2): 13, 2048, 2751; b3) þone þe, 1054, 1298, 2056, 2173, 3034; after a noun in the acc., (him) who: 2295, 3003, 3116. — asf. þā 14 times, ðā 4 times; [F. 23]; all a), 189, 354, 470, etc., exc. 2022: b2). — asn. þæt (usually spelt þ) 59 times; a) 17 times, 628, 654, etc.; b1) 36 times, 194, 290, etc.; b2) 6 times, 766, 1456, 1466, etc. — ism. þȳ, a): 2573, isn. þȳ, ðȳ, 19 times; þē (ðē): 821, 1436[a], 2638, 2687; a): 110, 1664, 1797, 2028; b1) *for that reason, therefore:* 1273, 2067, 2638; before comp. (cf. *ESt.* xliv 212 ff.): T H E, *any:* 487, 821, 1436[a], 1902, 2749, 2880; ne . . . ðȳ sēl: 2277, 2687; nō þȳ leng, 974; nō þȳ ǽr, see ǽr; b2) þȳ lǽs, L E S *t*, 1918. þon, b1); þon (mā), *any* (cf. *Beitr.* xxix 286; Small, *The Gmc. Case of Comparison* 89 ff.; Ingerid Dal, *Norske Vidensk.- Akademi i Oslo, Avhandl., Hist.- Filos. Kl.*, 1932, No. 2), 504; 2423 (n.); after prep.: ǽfter þon 724, be þon 1722, tō ðon 2591, 2845; tō þon 1876 (*to that degree, so*); see also for-ðan, for-ðon; ǽr þon (b2), conj.), *before*, 731. — npm. (n.: 639, 1135, 2948) þā 15 times, ðā 9 times, [F. 47]; a) 12 times, 3, 99, 221, etc.; b1) þā (. . . þē) 44 (allit.); b2) 6 times, 41, 113, etc.; b3) þā þe 5 times, 378, 1135, etc. — gpm.f.n. þāra 20 times, ðāra 937, 1578, 1686, 2734, 2779, 2794, þǽra 992, 1266,

ðǽra 1349, [F. 48]; a) 6 times; ymbesittendra ǽnig ðāra 2734; b1) 1015, 1037, 1248, 1266, 1349; þǽra (. . . þē) 992. b3) þāra (etc.) ðe: 206, 878, 1123, 1196, 1578; when containing the subj., (*of those*) *who* (*which*), foll. by the sing.: 843, 996, 1051, 1407, 1461, 1686, 2130, 2251, 2383, or by the plur. of the verb: 98, 785, 937. — dpm.f.n. þǽm, ðǽm 6 times (in A); þām, ðām 7 times (in B, and 1855); all a), 370, 1191, etc. — apm.f.n. þā 9 times, ðā 12 times, [F. 42]; all a), exc. 488, 2148, 3014: b1). — Note. The line of division between the dem. (b1) and relat. (b2) function is occasionally doubtful. As to the use of se, sēo, þæt as def. article, cf. L 6.7. The dem. adj. alliterates: 197[a], 790[a], 806[a]; 736[a]; 1675[b], 1797[b], 2033[b]. — See also relat. part. þē.

sealma (selma) (‡) (+), wk.m., *bedstead, bed, couch;* as. sealman, 2460. [OS. selmo; *Ep.-Erf. Gloss.* 955: selma ' sponda.' (Hoops St. 125.)]

sealt, adj., S A L T; asn., 1989.

searo, nwa., (pl. freq. w. sg. meaning), *contrivance, skill;* dp. searwum, 1038, 2764; — *war-gear, equipment, armor;* np. searo, 329; dp. searwum, 249, 323, 1557 (n.), 1813, 2530, 2568, 2700; — *battle* (cp. searo-grim); dp. ∼, 419, 1557(?). [Go. sarwa, pl.] — Cpds.: fyrd-, gūð-, inwit-.

searo-bend‡, fjō. (mi.), *cunningly wrought* BAND or *clasp;* dp. -um, 2086.

searo-fāh‡, adj., *cunningly decorated;* nsf., 1444.

searo-gim(m), m., *curious* GEM, *precious jewel;* gp. -gimma, 1157.

GLOSSARY

3102; ap. -gimmas, 2749. See gim(m).
searo-grim(m)‡, adj., *fierce in battle;* -grim, 594.
searo-hæbbend(e)†, mc. (pres. ptc.) [pl.], (*armor-*H A V *ing*), *warrior;* gp. -hæbbendra, 237.
searo-net(t)†, nja., *armor-*N E T or *battle-net, corslet;* -net, 406.
searo-nið‡, m., *crafty enmity, treacherous quarrel;* ap. -as, 1200, 2738; — *battle, contest;* gp. -a, 582; ap. -as, 3067.
searo-þonc(†**)**, m., *ingenuity, skill;* dp. -um, 775.
searo-wundor‡, n., *curious* W O N-D E R, *wonderful thing;* as., 920.
seax, n., *knife, short sword;* as., *1545.* [*NED.*: S A X; OS. sahs.] — Cpd.: wæl-.
sēcan, w 1., S E E K; *try to find* or *to get;* abs.: pret. 3 sg. sōhte, 2293 (*search*), 2572 (*desire, demand*); w. obj.: inf. (fǣhðe) sēcan, 2513; ger. (si.) sēceanne, 2562; (cp.) imp. sēc, 1379; pret. 1 sg. sōhte, 2738; 3 sg. ~, [139], 2300, 3067; w. obj. and tō (*from, at*): inf. sēcean, 1989, 2495, [F. 27]; pres. 3 pl. sēceað, 3001; — *try to reach* (*by attack*): inf. (sāwle) sēcan 801, (si.) sēcean 2422 (cf. *Angl.* xxxv 464 f.: 'animam quaerere,' Mat. ii 20, etc.); — *go to, visit;* inf. sēcean, 187, 200, 268, 645, 821, 1597, 1869, 2820, 2950, 3102; sēcan, 664, 756, 1450, 1820; pres. 3 sg. sēceð, 2272; opt. 3 sg. sēce, 1369; pret. 2 sg. sōhtest, 458; 3 sg. sōhte, 208, 376; 2 pl. sōhton, 339; 3 pl. sōhtan, 2380; opt. 1 sg. sōhte, 417. [Go. sōkjan.] — Cpds.: ofer-, on-.
ge-sēcan, w 1., S E E K; gesēcean (wīg), 684; *go to, visit:* ~, 692, 2275; gesēcan, 1004; ger. gesē-canne, 1922; pret. 3 sg. gesōhte, 463, 520, 717, 1951; pp. npf. gesōhte, 1839; — *go to, attack;* pres. 3 sg. gesēceð, 2515; pret. 3 pl. gesōhtan 2204, gesōhton 2926; opt. 3 sg. gesōhte, 2346.
secce, see sæc(c).
secg†, mja., *man;* 208, 249, 402, 871, 980, 1311, 1569, 1812, 2226, 2352, 2406, 2700, 2708, *2863,* 3028, 3071; voc., 947, 1759; ds. secge, 2019; as. secg, 1379; np. secgas, 213, 2530, 3128; gp. secga, 633, 842, 996, 1672, dp. secgum, [149], 490. [ON. seggr; cp. Lat. socius.]
secg†, fjō., *sword;* as. -e, 684. [See *NED.*: S E D G E, sb.[1]; cp. saw, OE. seax; Lat. secare.]
secgan, w 3., S A Y, *tell;* abs.: 273; pret. 3 sg. sægde, 90, 2899; w. acc.: inf. secgan, 582, 875, 880, 1049; pres. 1 sg. secge, 1997, 2795; pret. 2 sg. sægdest, 532; 3 sg. sægde, 1809, 2632; cp. pp. gesægd, 141; w. gen.: pres. ptc. secggende (wæs), 3028; — foll. by indir. question (hū, hwā, hwæt): inf. secgan, 51, 3026; ger. secganne, 473, 1724; pp. gesǣd, 1696; foll. by þæt-clause: inf. secgan, 391, 1818; pres. 1 sg. secge, 590; 3 pl. secgað, 411; pret. 3 sg. sægde, 1175, sǣde, *3152,* [F. 44]; — w. pron. þæt and þæt-clause: inf. secgan, 942, 1346, 1700, 2864; pret. 3 pl. sægdon, 377; w. obj. ōðer and þæt-clause: sǣdan, 1945. [OHG. sagēn.] — Cpd.: ā-.
ge-secgan, w 3., S A Y, *tell;* imp. sg. gesaga, 388; pret. opt. 1 sg. ge-sægde, 2157.
sefa, wk.m., *mind, heart, spirit;* 490, 594, 2600; him wæs geōmor sefa, 49, 2419, si. 2632; si. 2043, 2180; ds. sefan, 473, 1342, *1737;* as. ~,

278, 1726, 1842. [OS. sebo.] —
Cpd.: mōd-.
sēft, see sōfte.
ge-sēgan(-on), see ge-sēon.
segen, see segn.
segl, m.n., S A I L; 1906.
segl-rād‡, f., S A I L-R O A D, *sea,
lake; ds. -e, 1429.
segn, m.n., *banner, standard;* ds.
segne, 1204; as. segn, 2776,
(neut.:) 2767; (masc.:) segen, 47,
1021; np. (neut.) segn, 2958. [Fr.
Lat. signum; SIGN fr. OFr signe.]
— Cpd.: hēafod-.
sel, see sæl.
sēl (noun), see sæl.
sēl, adv. comp., *better;* 1012, 2530,
[F. 38, 39]; ne byð him wihte ðȳ
sēl, 2277, si. 2687. See gōd.
seldan, adv., S E L D O M; 2029 (n.).
seld-guma‡, wk.m., *hall-man, retainer;* 249 (n.). [See sæld.]
sele(†), mi., *hall;* 81, 411; ds., 323,
713; 919, 1016, 1640, 1984, 3128;
as., 826, 2352. [Cp. sæl.] —
Cpds.: bēah-, bēor-, dryht-, eorð-,
gest-, gold-, gūð-, hēah-, hring-,
hrōf-, nīð-, wīn-.
sele-drēam†, m., *joy of the hall;* as.,
2252.
sele-ful(l)‡, n., *hall-cup;* as. -ful,
619.
sele-gyst‡, mi., *hall-visitor*
(- G U E S T); as., 1545.
sele-rædend(e)†, mc. (pres. ptc.)
[pl.], *hall-counselor, -ruler;* np. -e,
51; ap. -e, 1346.
sele-rest‡, fjō.(?), *bed in a hall;* as.
-e, 690. See ræst.
sēlest, see gōd.
sele-þegn‡, m., *hall*-T H A N E, *chamberlain;* 1794.
sele-weard‡, m., *hall*-GUARD*ian;*
as., 667.
self, pron., S E L F; (1) strong infl.;
used abs.: sylf, 1964; gsm. (transl.

'his own') selfes, 700, 895; sylfes,
2222, 2360, 2639, 2710, 2776,
3013; in connect. with a poss.
pron.: on [mīn]ne sylfes dōm,
2147; as. sylfne, 1977; npm. selfe,
419; — w. a noun or pers. pron.;
self, 594, 920, 1010, 1313; sylf
2702, [F. 17, 27]; gsm. selfes,
1147; sylfes, 2013, 2325; gsf.
selfre, 1115; asm. selfne, 961,
1605; sylfne, 2875; gpm. sylfra,
2040; apm. sylfe, 1996; along w.
the dat. of pers. pron.: (þū) þē
self, 953. — (2) weak infl.; nsm.
selfa, 29, 1468, 1733, 1839 (him
~), 1924; sylfa, 505, 3054; seolfa,
3067. (Cf. J. M. Farr, *Intensives
and Reflexives in Ags. and early
ME.,* Johns Hopkins Diss., 1905.)
sēlla, see gōd.
sellan, w 1., *give;* syllan, 2160, 2729;
pres. 3 sg. seleð, 1370 *(give up),*
1730, 1749; pret. 2 sg. sealdest,
1482; 3 sg. sealde, 72, 672, 1271,
1693, 1751, [2019], 2155, 2182,
2490, 2994, 3055, *(proffer, pass:)*
622, 2024; 3 pl. sealdon, 1161
(serve). [S E L L; Go. saljan.]
ge-sellan, w 1., *give, make a present
of;* 1029; pret. 3 sg. gesealde,
1052, 1866, 1901, 2142, 2172,
2195, 2810, 2867, *(proffer, pass:)*
615.
sel-līc, syl-līc, adj., *strange, wonderful;* nsf. syllīc, 2086; asn. ~,
2109; apm. sellice, 1426. Comp.
asf. syllīcran, 3038. [Cp. seldan.]
sēlra, see gōd.
semninga, adv., *straightway, presently;* 1767; oþ þæt ~: 644, 1640.
[Cp. æt-, tō-somne.]
sendan, w 1., S E N D; pret. 1 sg.
sende, 471; 3 sg. ~, 13, 1842. —
Cpds.: for-, on-.
sēo, see sē.
sēoc, adj., S I C K, *weakened;* 2740,

2904; *sad:* npm. -e, 1603. [Go. siuks, Ger. siech.] — Cpds.: ellen-, feorh-, heaðo-.

seofon, num., S E V E N; uninfl.: a., 517, seofan, 2195; syfone, 3122.

seolfa, see **self**.

seomian†, w 2., *rest, lie, remain, hover, hang;* siomian, 2767; pret. 3 sg. seomade, 161 (n.), seomode 302.

sēon, v, *look;* pret. 3 sg. seah (on w. acc.), 2717, 2863; 3 pl. (on) sāwon, 1650; (tō) sǣgon, 1422; — S E E; sēon 387, 920, 1365, 3102, seón 1180, 1275; pret. 1 sg. seah, 336, 2014. [Go. saíhwan.] — Cpds.: geond-, ofer-.

ge-sēon, v, S E E, *behold, perceive;* 396, 571, 648, 961, 1078, 1126 (*go to*), 1485, 1628, 1875 (*see each other*), 1998; pres. 3 sg. gesyhð, 2041, 2455; pret. 1 sg. geseah, 247, 1662; 3 sg. ~, 229, 728, 926, 1516, 1557, 1585, 1613, 2542, 2604, 2756, 2767, 2822; 3 pl. gesāwon, 221, 1023, 1347, 1425, 1591, 2252; gesēgan 3038, gesēgon 3128; opt. 3 pl. gesāwon, 1605.

seonu, fwō., S I N E W; np. seonowe, 817.

sēoðan, II, w. acc., S E E T H E, *boil, cause to well up, brood over;* pret. 1 sg. (-ceare) sēað, 1993; 3 sg. (~) ~, 190(n.).

seoððan, see **siððan**.

sēow(i)an, w 1. 2., S E W, *put together, link;* pp. seowed, 406 (ref. to the 'battle-net,' cp. hrægl, etc.). [Go. siujan. Cf. Siev. § 408 n. 15, Wright § 533.]

ses(s) (‡) (+), m.(n.?), SEAT; ds. sesse, 2717, 2756. [Cp. ON. sess; sittan.]

sētan, see **sittan**.

setl, n., SEAT; gs. -es, 1786; ds. -e, 1232, 1782, 2019; as. setl, 2013; dp. -um, 1289. [S E T T L E. Siev. § 196. 2 & n. 1; *Beitr.* xxx 67 ff.] — Cpds.: hēah-, hilde-, meodo-.

settan, w 1., S E T; pret. 3 pl. setton, 325, 1242; pp. nsn. geseted (*set down*), 1696. [Go. satjan.] — Cpds.: ā-, be-.

ge-settan, w 1., S E T, *establish;* pret. 3 sg. gesette, 94; *settle*, pres. opt. 3 sg. ~, 2029.

sēðan, w 1., *declare, settle; 1106* (n.). [sōð.]

sex-ben(n)‡, fjō., *dagger-wound;* dp. -bennum, *2904.* [See seax; Lang. § 1.]

sib(b), fjō., *kinship, friendship, peace;* sib, 1164, 1857; gs. sibbe, 2922; as. sibbe, 154, 949, 2431; sibb', 2600 (n.) (' ties of kinship '). [Go. sibja. Cp. goss I P.] Cf. Grønbech L 9.24. ¡ 61 f. — Cpds.: dryht-, friðu-.

sib-æðeling‡, m., *related noble;* np. -as, 2708.

sibbe-gedriht†, fi., *band of kinsmen;* as., 387, 729. (Genitival cpd.; earlier form: sibgedriht, *Ex.* 214, etc.)

sīd, adj., *large, spacious, broad, great;* nsf., 1444, 2086; nsn.wk. -e, 2199; dsm.wk. -an, 2347; asm. -ne, 437, 507, 1726; asf. -e, 1291, 2394; asn. [sīd], 2217; asn. wk. sīde, 1733; gpf. -ra, 149; apm. -e, 223, 325.

sīde, adv., *widely;* 1223.

sīd-fæþme‡, adj.ja., *roomy;* asn. 1917. [fæþm.]

sīd-fæþmed‡, adj. (pp.), *roomy;* nsn., 302. [fæþm.]

sīd-rand‡, m., *broad shield;* 1289.

sīe, see **eom**.

sīe, 2219, see **sē**.

sig, see **eom**.

sīgan, I, *sink, fall;* pret. 3 pl. sigon,

BEOWULF

1251; *move (together), march,* ~, 307.
ge-sīgan, I, *sink, fall;* 2659.
sige-drihten†, m., *victorious lord;* 391.
sige-ēadig‡, adj., *victory-blest, victorious;* asn., 1557.
sige-folc†, n., *victorious or gallant people;* gp. -a, 644. See folc.
sige-hrēð‡, (n., see hrēð), *glory of victory;* as., 490 (n.).
sige-hrēþig†, adj., *victorious, triumphant;* 94, 1597, 2756.
sige-hwīl‡, f., *time of victory, victory;* gp. -e, 2710 (cf. Lang. § 18.3).
sigel†, n.(?), *sun;* 1966. (Cp. *Runic Poem* 45 ff.)
sige-lēas, adj., *without victory, of defeat;* asm. -ne, 787.
sige-rōf(†), adj., *victorious, illustrious;* 619.
sige-þēod†, f., *victorious or glorious people;* ds. -e, 2204.
sige-wǣpen‡, n., *victory-*W E A P O N; dp. -wǣpnum, 804.
sigle(‡)+, n., *jewel, brooch, necklace;* as., 1200; gp. sigla, 1157; ap. siglu, 3163. [ON. sigli; — fr. sigel 'brooch,' 'clasp' (orig. 'sun'?, or fr. Lat. sigillum).] — Cpd.: māððum-.
sigor, (nc.) m., *victory;* gs. -es, 1021; gp. -a, 2875, 3055. [Cp. sige(-); Go. sigis, Ger. Sieg; Wright § 419; Siev. § 289 & n. 2; *Beitr.* xxxi 87.] — Cpds.: hrēð-, wīg-.
sigor-ēadig‡, adj., *victorious;* 1311, 2352.
sīn(†), poss. pron. (refl.), *his;* dsm. sīnum, 2160; dsn. ~, 1236, 1507 (*her*); asm. sīnne, 1960, 1984, 2283, 2789. [Go. seins, Ger. sein.]
sinc†, n., *treasure, jewels, something precious, ornament;* 2764; gs. sinces (brytta): 607, 1170, 1922, 2071; ds. since, 1038, 1450, 1615, 1882, 2217, 2746; as. sinc, 81, 1204, 1485, 2023 (n.), 2383, 2431; gp. sinca, 2428. [Cf. Falk, *Altwestnord. Kleiderkunde* (1919) 30.]
sinc-fæt††, n., *precious cup, costly object;* as., 1200 (n.), 2231, 2300; ap. -fato, 622. [V A T.]
sinc-fāg†, adj., *richly decorated;* asn. wk. -e, 167. (Cp. gold-fāg.)
sinc-gestrēon†, n., *treasure;* gp. -a, 1226; dp. -um, 1092.
sinc-gifa†, wk.m., *treasure-*G I V *er;* ds. -gifan, 2311, -gyfan 1342 (Holt., note: ds. of -gyfu[?]); as. ~, 1012.
sinc-māððum‡, m., *treasure, jewel;* -māððum, 2193.
sinc-þego†, f., *receiving of treasure;* 2884. [þicgan.]
sin-frēa‡, wk.m., *great lord;* -frēa, 1934 (n.). [sin- 'continual,' 'great,' see the foll. sin-cpds. and syn-dolh, -snǣd; cp. sym(b)le; Go. sinteins; S E N-(green) (dial.).]
sin-gāl, adj., *continual;* asf. -e, 154.
sin-gāla, sin-gāles,(†), adv., *continually, always;* -gāla, 190; -gāles, 1777; syngāles, 1135.
singan, III, S I N G, *ring (forth);* [pres. 3 pl. singað, F. 5]; pret. 3 sg. sang, 496; song, 323, 1423, [3152]. (Cf. *R.-L.* i 443.) — Cpd.: ā-.
sin-here‡, mja., *huge army;* ds. -herge, 2936.
sinnig, adj., S I N*ful;* asm. -ne, *1379.* [syn(n).]
sin-niht†, fc., *perpetual* N I G H T or *darkness;* ds. -e, 161.
sint, see eom.
sīo, see sē.
siolað‡, m.(?), *water, sea* (?); gp. sioleða, 2367 (n.) (see begong).
siomian, see seomian.

GLOSSARY

sittan, v, S I T; pres. 3 sg. siteð, 2906; pret. 3 sg. sæt, 130, 286, 356, 500, 1166, 1190, 2852, 2894; 3 pl. sǣton, 1164, sētan *1602;* — *sit down;* inf. sittan, 493, 641; imp. sg. site, 489. — Cpds.: be-, for-, of-, ofer-, on-, ymb-; flet-, heal-, ymb(e)-sittend(e).

ge-sittan, v, S I T *down* (ingress.); pret. 3 sg. gesæt, 171, 749 (*sit up,* see note), 1424, 1977, 2417, 2717; pp. geseten, 2104; — w. acc., *sit down in:* pret. 1 sg. gesæt, 633.

sīð, m., (1) *going, journey, voyage; undertaking, venture, expedition;* 501, 765, 1971 (*coming*), 2586, 3089; gs. sīðes, 579, 1475, 1794, 1908; ds. sīðe, 532, 1951, 1993; as. sīð, 353, 512, 872, 908, 1278, 1429, 1966; np. sīðas, 1986; gp. sīða, 318; ap. sīðas, 877; *course (of action), way (of doing);* ns. sīð, 2532, 2541, 3058. — (2) *time, occasion;* ns. (forma) sīð, 716, 1463, 1527, 2625; ds. (forman, nȳhstan, etc.) sīðe, 740, 1203, 2049, 2286, 2511, 2517, 2670, 2688, [3101], [F. 19]; as. sīð, 1579. [Go. sinþs. Cp. sendan.] — Cpds.: cear-, eft-, ellor-, gryre-, sǣ-, wil-, wrǣc-; ge-.

sīð, adv. comp., *later;* 2500 (see ǣr). [Go. (þana-)seiþs; Ger. seit.]

sīðast, sīðest, adj. supl., *latest, last;* sīþas[t], 2710 (n.); dsn.wk. (æt) sīðestan, 3013. [Go. seiþus. Cp. sīð, adv.]

sīð-fæt, m., *expedition, adventure;* ds. -fate, 2639; as. -fæt, 202. [Cp. ON. feta, vb., 'step.']

sīð-from†, adj., *eager to depart;* npm. -e, 1813.

sīðian, w 2., *go, journey;* 720, 808; pret. 3 sg. sīðode, 2119. [sīð.] — Cpd.: for-.

siððan, I. adv., S I N ce, *thereupon, afterwards;* siððan (þð), 470, 685, 718 (see ǣr); syððan (ðþ, þð), 142, 283, 567, 1453, 1901, 1951, *2064,* 2071, 2175, 2207, 2217, 2395, 2702, 2806, 2920; seoððan, 1875, seoþðan, 1937. — II. conj., *since, from the time when, when, after, as soon as* (s.t. shading into *because*); siððan (þð, ðþ, þþ), 106, 413, 604, 648, 656, 850, 901, 982, 1148, 1204, 1253, 1261, 1281, 1784; syððan (þð, ðþ), 6 (∼ ǣrest), 115, 132, 722, 834, 886, 1077, 1198, 1206, 1235, 1308, 1420, 1472, 1556, 1589, 1689(n.), 1947 (∼ ǣrest), 1949, 1978, 2012, 2051, 2072, 2092, 2103, 2124, 2201, 2351, 2356, 2388, 2437, 2474, 2501, 2630, 2888, 2911, 2914, 2943, 2960, 2970, *2996,* 3002, 3127; seoþðan, 1775. See also sōna. [sīð-þon; S I T H, S I N (E), S Y N E (dial.).]

slǣp, m., S L E E P; 1742; ds. -e, 1251.

slǣpan, rd., (w 1.), S L E E P; pres. ptc. slǣpende, 2218; asm. slǣpendne, 741; apm. slǣpende, 1581.

slēac, adj., *slow, slothful;* 2187. [Not rel. to slæc > MnE. slack; *IF.* xx 318, *Angl.* xxxix 366 f.]

slēan, VI, (1) *strike;* abs.: pres. opt. 3 sg. slēa, 681; pret. 3 sg. slōh, 1565, 2678; — w. obj. (acc.): ∼, 2576, 2699, (2179? slōg). — (2) S L A Y; pret. 1 sg. slōg, 421; 3 sg. ∼, 108, 2179; slōh, 1581, 2355; 3 pl. slōgon, 2050; pp. slægen, 1152. — Cpd.: of-.

ge-slēan, VI, *achieve* or *bring about by fighting;* pret. 3 sg. geslōh, 459 (n.); 3 pl. geslōgon, 2996 (n.).

slītan, I, *tear, rend;* pret. 3 sg. slāt, 741. [SLIT.]

slīðe(†), adj.ja., *severe, dangerous,*

terrible; asm. slīðne, 184; gpn. slīðra, 2398. [Go. sleiþs.]
slīðen, adj., *cruel, dire;* nsn., 1147.
smið, m., S M I T H, *worker in metals;* 1452; gs. smiþes, 406. — Cpd.: wundor-.
snēdan(‡)+, w 1., *cut, slice, take food, feast;* pres. 3 sg. snēdeþ, 600 (n.). [Cp. syn-snǣd.]
snel(l), adj., *quick, bold, brave;* nsm.wk. snella, 2971. [S N E L L (Sc., North.); Ger. schnell.]
snel-līc(†), adj., *quick, brave;* 690.
snot(t)or, adj., *prudent, wise;* snotor, 826, 908, 1384 (voc.), snotor 190; wk. snotera, 1313; snotra, 2156, 3120; snottra, 1475 (voc.), 1786; npm. snotere, 202, 416, snottre 1591. [Go. snutrs.] — Cpd.: fore-.
snotor-līce(‡)+, adv., *wisely, prudently,* comp. -līcor, 1842.
snūde, adv., *quickly, straightway;* 904, 1869, 1971, 2325, 2568, 2752. [Cp. Go. sniwan ' hasten.']
snyrian†, w 1., *hasten;* pret. 3 pl. snyredon, 402. [Cp. ON. snarr 'quick.']
snyttru, wk.f., *wisdom, discernment, skill;* as., 1726; dp. snyttrum, 872 (semi-adv.), 942, 1706. [snot(t)or.] — Cpd.: un-.
sōcn, f., (S E E K*ing*), (‡)*persecution, visitation;* gs. sōcne, 1777. [sēcan; Go. sōkns.]
sōfte, adv., S O F T*ly, gently, pleasantly;* comp. sēft, 2749. — Cpd.: un-.
somod, see samod.
sōna, adv., (S O O N), *immediately, at once;* 121, 721, 743, 750, 1280, 1497, 1591, 1618, 1762, 1785, 1794, 1825, 2011, 2226, 2300, 2713, 2928, [F. 46]. (sōna ... siððan: 721, 1280, 2011; cp. sōna ... swā (in prose), ' as soon as.') [OS. sāno.] (Cf. L 6.15 b.)

sorg(-), see sorh(-).
sorgian, w 2., S O R R O W, *grieve, care;* 451; imp. sg. sorga, 1384.
sorh, f., S O R R O W, *grief, trouble;* 473, 1322; ds. sorhge, 2468; as. sorge, 119, 1149, 2463; gp. sorga, 149, sorge 2004; dp. sorgum, 2600. — Cpds.: hyge-, inwit-, þegn-.
sorh-cearig†, adj., S O R R O W*ful, sad;* 2455; nsf. sorg-, 3152.
sorh-ful(l), adj., S O R R O W F U L; nsf. sorhfull, 2119; — *grievous, perilous, sad;* asm. -fullne (sīð) 512, -fulne (~): 1278, 1429.
sorh-lēas, adj., *free from care;* 1672.
sorh-lēoð†, n., *song of* S O R R O W; as., 2460.
sorh-wylm†, mi., *surging* S O R R O W or *care;* np. -as, 904; dp. -um 1993.
sōð, adj., *true;* 1611; asn., 2109. [S O O T H (arch.); ON. sannr; cp. Lat. (prae-)sens.]
sōð, n., *truth;* 700; as., 532, 1049, 1700, 2864; (secgan & si.) tō sōðe, *in* S O O T H, *as a fact:* 51, 590, 2325.
Sōð-cyning†, m., *true* K I N G, *king of truth, God;* 3055.
sōðe(†), adv., *truly, faithfully;* 524, 871.
sōð-fæst, adj., *true, righteous* (cp. Lat. ' iustus '); gp. -ra, 2820.
sōð-līce, adv., *truly, verily, faithfully;* (secgan & si.): 141, 273, 2899.
specan, see sprecan.
spēd, fi., *success;* as. on spēd, *successfully, with skill,* 873. [S P E E D; spōwan.] Cf. Grønbech L 9.24 i 182-85. — Cpds.: here-, wīg-.
spel(l), n., *tale, story, message;* as. spel, 873, spell 2109; gp. spella, 2898, 3029. [*NED.*: S P E L L, sb.¹; Go. spill.] (Cf. *ZfdA.* xxxvii

GLOSSARY

241 ff.; *P. Grdr.*² ii^a 36; *R.-L.* i 442.) — Cpd.: wēa-.

spīwan, I, S P E W, *vomit;* (w. dat.), 2312.

spōwan, rd., impers. w. dat., *succeed, speed;* pret. 3 sg. spēow, *2854,* 3026. [See spēd.]

spræc, f., S P E E C H, *language;* ds. -e, 1104. — Cpds.: æfen-, gylp-.

sprecan, V, S P E A K; abs.: 2069, 3172; imp. sg. spræc, 1171; pret. 3 sg. spræc, 1168, 1215, 1698, 2510, 2618, 2724, [2792]; 1 pl. spræcon, 1707; 3 pl. ⁓, 1595; — w. object (acc.): inf. specan (Lang. § 23.3), 2864; pret. 2 sg. spræce, 531; 3 sg. spræc, 341; 1 pl. spræcon, 1476; pp. sprecen, 643. [OHG. sprehhan, spehhan. Cf. also *Beitr.* xxxii 147 f.]

ge-sprecan, V, S P E A K; w. obj.: pret. 3 sg. gespræc, 675, 1398, 1466, 3094.

springan, III, S P R I N G, *bound, burst forth, spread;* pret. 3 sg. sprang, 18; sprong, 1588, 2966; 3 pl. sprungon, 2582. — Cpds.: æt-, on-.

ge-springan, III, S P R I N G *forth, arise;* pret. 3 sg. gesprang, 1667; gesprong, 884.

stæl, m.(?), *place, position;* ds. -e, 1479. [staþol. Cf. *Beitr.* xxx 73; *NED.*: S T A Lwart.]

stælan, w 1., *(lay to one's charge), avenge;* 2485; pp. gestæled, 1340. (Cf. Kock 229 ff.; *MPh.* iii 261.)

stān, m., S T O N E, *rock;* ds. stāne, 2288, 2557; as. (hārne) stān: 887, 1415, 2553, 2744. — Cpd.: eorclan-.

stān-beorh(‡)+, m., S T O N E-B A R-R O W; as., 2213.

stān-boga‡, wk.m., (S T O N E-B O W), *stone arch;* ap.-bogan, 2545, 2718 (n.).

stān-clif, n., *rocky* C L I F F; ap. -cleofu, 2540.

standan, VI, S T A N D, *continue in a certain state;* 2271; stondan, *2545,* 2760; pres. 3 sg. stande ð, *1362;* 2 pl. standað, 2866; opt. 3 sg. stande, 411; pret. 3 sg. stōd, 32, 145, 926, 935, 1037, 1416, 1434, 1913, 2679; 3 pl. stōdon, 328, stōdan 3047; — w. subjects like lēoht, egesa, (usu. expressing direction, ' ingressive ':) *start, issue, arise, shine forth;* pret. 3 sg. stōd: 726, 783, 1570, 2227, 2313, 2769, [F. 35]. (Si. in ON., OS.; cf. Siev. L 7.34.432.) — Cpds.: ā-, æt-, for-.

ge-standan, VI, S T A N D, *take up one's stand;* pret. 3 sg. gestōd, 358, 404, 2566; 3 pl. gestōdon, 2597.

stān-fāh†, adj., *adorned with* S T O N E *s, paved;* nsf., 320.

stān-hlið†, n., *rocky slope;* ap. -o, 1409.

stapol, m., *post, pillar;* dp. stapulum, 2718 (n.); — *flight of steps;* ds. stapole, 926(n.). Cp. B.-T. Suppl.: fōtstap(p)el. [steppan; *NED.*: S T A P L E, sb.¹; cp. STOOP = ' porch ' etc.]

starian, W 2., *gaze, look;* usu. w. on and acc.; pres. 1 sg. starige, 1781, starie 2796; 3 sg. starað, 996, 1485; pret. 3 sg. starede, 1935 (n.); 3 pl. staredon, 1603. [S T A R E.]

stēap, adj., S T E E P, *high, towering;* asm. stēapne, 926, 2213, 2566; apm. stēape, 222; apn. stēap, 1409. — Cpd.: heaþo-.

stearc-heort‡, adj., *stout-*H E A R T*ed;* 2288, 2552. [S T A R K.]

stefn, m., S T E M, *prow;* as., 212. — Cp. bunden-, hringed-, wundenstefna.

stefn, m., *period, time;* ds. nī(o)wan

stefne (*anew, again*), 1789, 2594.
stefn, f., *voice;* 2552. [Go. stibna, Ger. Stimme.]
stēpan†, w I., *raise, exalt;* pret. opt. 3 sg. stēpte, 1717. [stēap.]
ge-stēpan†, w I., *advance, support;* pret. 3 sg. gestēpte, 2393.
steppan, VI, S T E P, *stride, march;* pret. 3 sg. stōp, 761, 1401.— Cpd.: æt-.
ge-steppan, VI, S T E P, *walk;* pret. 3 sg. gestōp, 2289.
stīg, f., *path;* 320, 2213; ap.(s.?) -e, 1409. [Cp. stīgan.] — Cpd.: medo-.
stīgan, I, *go, step, go up, mount;* pret. 3 sg. stāg, *2362;* 3 pl. stigon, 212, 225; opt. 3 sg. stige, 676. [S T Y (obs.); cp. stile. Ger. steigen.] — Cpd.: ā-.
ge-stīgan, I, *go* (*up*), *set out;* pret. 1 sg. gestāh, 632.
stille, adj.ja., S T I L L, *fixed;* 301, 2830.
stincan†, III, *move rapidly* (intr.); pret. 3 sg. stonc, 2288 (n.). [Go. stigqan.]
stīð, adj., *firm, strong, hard;* nsn., 1533; gpm. -ra, *985* (n.).
stīð-mōd, adj., *stout-hearted, firm;* 2566.
stondan, see **standan.**
stōp, see **steppan.**
storm, m., S T O R M; 3117; ds. -e, 1131.
stōw, f., *place;* 1372; as. -e, 1006, 1378. [Cp. S T O W, vb.; (-)S T O W (E) in place-names.] — Cpd.: wæl-.
stræl, m.(f.), *arrow;* ds. -e, 1746; gp. -a, 3117. [Ger. Strahl.] — Cpd.: here-.
strǣt, f., S T R E E T; 320; as. -e, 916, 1634. [Fr. Lat. strata (sc. via).] — Cpds.: lagu-, mere-.
strang, adj., S T R O N G; (mægenes)

strang, 1844; nsf. strong, 2684; nsn. strang (*severe*), 133. — Supl. strengest: 196 (mægenes ~), 789 (mægene ~), 1543.
strēam, m., S T R E A M, *current* (pl.: †*sea, body of water*); as., 2545; np. strēamas, 212; ap. ~, 1261. — Cpds.: brim-, ēagor-, ēg-, fyrgen-, lagu-.
strēgan(†), w I., STREW, *spread;* pp. strêd, 2436. [Go. straujan. Siev. § 408 n. 14 f.]
strengel‡, m., *chief, ruler;* as. (wigena) ~, 3115. [strang.]
strengest, see **strang.**
strengo, wk.f., S T R E N G *th;* ds., 2540; strenge, 1533; as. ~, 1270; dp. strengum, 3117 (or fr. streng, (*bow-*)*string?*). — Cpds.: hilde-, mægen-, mere-.
strong, see **strang.**
strūdan, II, *plunder;* pret. opt. 3 sg. strude, *3073,* 3126.
ge-strȳnan, w I., *acquire, gain;* 2798. [See ge-strēon.]
stund, f., *time;* dp. stundum, *time and again,* 1423. Cf. Schü. Bd. 84. [S T O U N D (arch., dial.); Ger. Stunde.]
stȳle, nja., S T E E L; ds., *985.* [steel fr. Angl. stēle; cp. OHG. stahal, stāl.]
stȳl-ecg‡, adj., S T E E L-E D G E *d;* nsn., 1533.
styrian, w I., S T I R *up;* pres. 3 sg. styreþ, 1374; — *disturb;* pret. opt. (?) 3 sg. styrede, 2840; — *treat of, recite;* inf., 872.
styrman, w I., STORM, *shout;* pret. 3 sg. styrmde, 2552. [storm.]
suhterge-fæderan†, wk. m.p., *nephew* (*brother's son*) *and* (*paternal*) *uncle;* 1164. (*Wids.* 46: suhtorfædran. See āþum-swēoras.) Cf. Krause, *Zfvgl.Spr.* lii 223 ff. (suhter-gefæderan); Weyhe, *Siev-*

GLOSSARY

ers-Festschrift (1925) 314 (on: suhtria, suhterga).
sum, adj., S O M E (*one*), *one, a certain* (*one*); used as adj.: isn. sume, 2156; — used as subst.; a) abs.: nsm. sum, 1251, 3124; nsn. sum (*anything*), 271; asm. sumne, 1432; npm. sume, 400, 1113; apm. ~, 2940; b) w. partit. gen. (pl., exc. 712 f.; in many cases no partit. relation is perceptible in MnE.): nsm. sum, 248, 314, 1240, 1266, 1312, 1499, 2301; nsn. ~, 1607, 1905; asm. sumne, 713; asn. sum, 675, 2279; w. gen. of numerals: fíftȳna sum (i.e., ' with fourteen others,' cp. MHG. selbe zwelfter, etc.; see *ESt.* xvii 285 ff., xxiv 463), 207; twelfa sum, 2401; eahta sum, 3123; si.: fēara sum, 1412; asm. fēara sumne, 3061 (n.); manigra sumne, 2091. — (S.t., by litotes, *many* (*a one*): 713, 1113, 675(?), 1240(?), 2940(?).) [Go. sums.]
sund, n., (1) *swimming;* gs. sundes, 1436; ds. sunde, 517, 1618 (on ~, *a-swimming*); as. sund, 507. — (2) †*sea, water;* ns. sund, 213, 223; ds. sunde, 1510; as. sund, 512, 539, 1426, 1444. [S O U N D. Cp. swimman.]
sund-gebland‡, n., *commotion of water, surging water;* as., 1450. [blandan.]
sund-nyt(t)‡, fjō., *act of swimming;* as. -nytte, 2360 (see drēogan).
sundor-nyt(t) (‡)+, fjō., *special service;* as. sundornytte, 667.
sundur, adv., *a* S U N D E R; 2422.
sund-wudu†, mu., *sea-*W O O D, i.e. *ship;* 1906; as., 208. Cp. sǣ-.
sunne, wk.f., S U N; 606; gs. sunnan, 648; as. ~, 94.
sunu, mu., S O N; 524, 645, 980, 1009, 1040, 1089, 1485, 1550, 1699, 1808 (ds.?), 2147, 2367, 2386, 2398, 2447, 2602, 2862, 2971, 3076, 3120, [F. 33]; gs. suna, 2455, 2612, sunu (Lang. § 18.2 n.), 1278; ds. suna, 1226, 2025, 2160, 2729, sunu, 344, (1808?); as. sunu, 268, 947, 1115, 1175, 2013 (ap.?), 2119, 2394, 2752; vs. sunu, 590, 1652; np. suna, 2380. (Mostly w. gen. of proper names: sunu Healfdenes, ~ Ecgðēowes, etc.)
sūð, adv., S O U T H (*wards*); 858.
sūþan, adv., *from the* S O U T H; 606, 1966.
swā, I. adv., s o, *thus, in this manner;* at beginning of sentence, usu. at beginn. of *a*-line: 20, 99, 144, 164, 189, 559, 1046, 1142, 1534[b], 1694 (*also*), 1769, 2115, 2144, 2166[b], 2177, 2267, 2278, 2291, 2397, 2444, 2462[b], 3028, 3066, 3069, 3178 (stressed: 559, 1142, 1694, 2115); position within clause: 1103, 2057, 2498; at end of clause and of *b*-line (stressed): 538, 762, 797, 1471, 2091, 2990, si. 1709, 2730; — w. foll. adj., *so;* 585, 1732, 1843, si. 591, [F. 19]; emphat. (*very*), 347; leng swā wēl, 1854; correl. swā . . . swā, see II. — swā þēah (at end of *b*-line), 972, 1929, 2442, 2878, 2967, see þēah. — **II. conj.,** *as;* not foll. by clause; 642, 1787, 2622; — foll. by clause, usu. at beginning of *b*-line (freq. one containing complete clause); 29[b], 93[b](n.), 273[a], 352[b], 401[b]; 444[b] (swā hē oft dyde, si.:) 956[b], 1058[b], 1134[b], 1172[b], 1238[b], 1381[b], 1676[b], 1891[b], 2521[b], 2859[b]; 490[b], 561[b], 666[b], 881[b], 1055[b], 1234[b], 1252[b], 1396[b], [1404[b]], 1451[b], 1571[a] (efne swā), 1587[b], 1670[b], 1707[a], 1786[b], 1828[a], 1975[b], 2233[a], 2310[b], 2332[b], 2470[b], 2480[b],

2491ᵇ, 2526ᵇ, 2585ᵇ, 2590ᵇ, 2608ᵇ, 2664ª, 2696ᵇ, 3049ᵇ, 3078ᵇ, 3098ᵇ, 3140ᵇ, 3161ᵇ, 3174ᵇ; within *b*-line: 455ᵇ, 1231ᵇ; — correl. swā ... swā: 594, 1092 f., 1223, 1283 (efne swā ... swā), 3168; swā hwæþer ... swā, 686 f.; swā hwylc ... swā, 943, 3057; — *as (soon as), when,* 1667ᵇ; — *since,* 2184ª; — *in such a way that, so that* (in negat. clauses), 1048ᵇ, 1508ª, 2006ª, 2574ᵇ, [F. 41]; — w. opt., in asseveration: 435ᵇ (n.). [Go. swa, OHG. sō.] (Cf. Ericson, *The Use of swā in OE.,* 1932.)

swǣs, adj., (†) *(one's) own, dear;* asm. -ne, 520; npm. swǣse (gesīþas), 29, so apm.: 2040, 2518; gpm. -ra (gesīða), 1934; apm. -e, 1868. [Go. swēs.]

swǣs-līce, adv., *in a friendly manner, gently;* 3089.

swancor†, adj., *supple, graceful;* apn., 2175. [*Dial. D.:* S W A N K, adj.²]

swan-rād†, f., S W A N-R O A D, *sea;* as. -e, 200. Cp. hron-.

swāt, m., (SWEAT), (†)*blood;* 2693, 2966; ds. -e, 1286. — Cpds.: heaþo-, hilde-.

swāt-fāh†, adj., *blood-stained;* nsf., 1111.

swātig, adj., (SWEATY), †*bloody;* nsn., 1569.

swāt-swaðu‡, f., *bloody track;* 2946.

swaþrian(†), w 2., *subside, become still;* pret. 3 pl. swaþredon, 570. Cp. sweðrian.

swaðu, f., *track;* as. swaðe (weardade, *remained behind*), 2098. See lāst. [S W A T H (E).] — Cpds.: swāt-, wald-.

swaþul‡, m. or n., *flame, heat;* ds. -e. 782. See swioðol, sweoloð. (Cf. Cha., note; Grein Spr.; B.-T.;

Beitr. xxx 132; Dietrich, *ZfdA.* v 215 f.: *smoke.*)

sweart, adj., S W A R T, *black, dark;* 3145, [F. 35]; dpf. -um, 167.

swebban, w 1., *(put to sleep),* †*kill;* 679; pres. 3 sg. swefeð, 600. [swefan.] — Cpd.: ā-.

swefan(†), v, *sleep, sleep in death;* 119, 729, 1672; pres. 3 sg. swefeþ, 1008, 1741, 2060, 2746; 3 pl. swefað, 2256, 2457; pret. 3 sg. swæf, 1800; 3 pl. swǣfon, 703, swǣfun 1280.

swefeð, 600, see swebban.

swēg, mi., *sound, noise, music;* 644, 782, 1063; hearpan swēg: 89, 2458, 3023; ds. swēge, 1214. [swōgan.] — Cpds.: benc-, morgen-.

swegl†, n., *sky, heaven;* gs. (under) swegles (begong): 860, 1773; ds. (under) swegle: 1078, 1197.

swegl(‡), adj.u.(?), *bright, brilliant;* apm. swegle, 2749. [swegl, n.; cp. OS. swigli. Siev., *ZfdPh.* xxi 357; Tolkien, *Medium Ævum* iii 95 ff.]

swegl-wered‡, adj. (pp.), *clothed with radiance;* nsf. (sunne) ~, 606. [werian ' clothe.'] (Cp. Ps. ciii 2: 'amictus lumine,' etc.; see *Angl.* xxxv 123.)

swelan†, IV, *burn* (intr.); 2713. See be-swǣlan.

swelgan, III, S W A L L O W; w. dat.: pret. 3 sg. swealh, 743; swe[a]lg, 3155; w. ellipsis of pron. obj.: pret. opt. 3 sg. swulge, 782. — Cpd.: for- (w. acc.).

swellan, III, S W E L L; 2713.

sweltan, III, *die;* pret. 3 sg. swealt, 1617, 2474; morðre ~: 892, 2782; -dēaðe ~, 3037; si. 2358. [S W E L T(er); Go. swiltan 'lie dying.']

swencan, w 1., *press hard, harass, afflict;* pret. 3 sg. swe[n]cte, 1510;

pp. geswenced, 975, 1368. [swincan.] — Cpd.: lyft-geswenced.
ge-swencan, w 1., *injure, strike down;* pret. 3 sg. geswencte, 2438.
sweng, mi., *blow, stroke;* ds. -e, 2686, 2966; as. sweng, *1520;* dp. -um, 2386. [swingan.] — Cpds.: feorh-, heaðu-, heoro-, hete-.
sweofot(†), m. or n., *sleep;* ds. -e, 1581, 2295. [swefan.]
sweoloð(‡), m. or n., *heat, flames;* ds. -e, 1115. [swelan.]
sweorcan, III, *become dark, become grievous;* pres. 3 sg. sweorceð, 1737. [OS. swerkan.] — Cpd.: for-.
ge-sweorcan, III, *be dark, lower;* pret. 3 sg. geswearc, 1789.
sweord, swurd, swyrd (cf. Lang. § 8.6), n., S W O R D; sweord, 1286, 1289, 1569, 1605, 1615, 1696, 2499, 2509, 2659, 2681, 2700; swurd, 890; gs. sweordes, 1106, 2193, 2386; ds. sweorde, 561, 574, 679, 2492, 2880, 2904; [swurde, F. 13]; as. sweord, 437, 672, 1808, 2252, 2518, 2562; swurd, 1901; swyrd, 2610, 2987; np. swyrd, 3048; gp. sweorda, 1040, 2936, *2961;* dp. sweordum, *567,* 586, 884; ap. sweord, 2638; swurd, 539; [sword, F. 15]. [OS. swerd, Ger. Schwert.] — Cpds.: eald-, gūð-, māðþum-, wæg-.
sweord-bealo‡, nwa., S W O R D-*evil, death by the sword;* 1147.
sweord-freca‡, wk.m., (S W O R D-) *warrior;* ds. -frecan, 1468.
sweotol, adj., *clear, manifest;* nsm. swutol, 90; nsn. sweotol, 817, 833; dsn.wk. sweotolan, 141.
swerian, VI, S W E A R; pret. 1 sg. swōr, 2738; 3 sg. ~, 472. [Cp. and-swaru.] — Cpd.: for-.
sweðrian, w 2., *subside, diminish, cease;* 2702; pret. 3 sg. sweðrode, 901.
swīcan, I, *depart, escape;* pret. opt. 3 sg. swice, 966; —*fail* (in one's duty to another), *desert;* w. dat.: pret. 3 sg. swāc, 1460.
ge-swīcan, I, *fail, prove inefficient;* w. dat., *fail, desert;* pret. 3 sg. geswāc, 1524, 2584, 2681.
swift, adj., S W I F T; nsm. wk. -a, 2264.
swīge, adj.ja., *silent;* comp. swīgra, 980.
swīgian, w 2., *be silent;* pret. 3 sg. swīgode, 2897 (w. gen.); 3 pl. swīgedon, 1699. [Ger. schweigen.]
swilce, see swylce.
swīn, n., (S W I N E), ‡*image of boar* (*on helmet*); ns. swȳn, 1111; as. swīn, 1286.
swincan, III, *labor, toil;* pret. 2 pl. swuncon, 517. [S W I N K (arch., dial.).]
swingan, III, †*fly;* pres. 3 sg. swingeð, 2264. (Nearly always trans. in OE.) [S W I N G.]
swīn-līc‡, n., *boar-figure;* dp. -um, 1453.
swioðol(‡), m. or n., *fire, flame;* ds. swioðole, 3145. See swaþul, sweoloð. (*Angl.* viii 452: a gloss 'cauma? *vel* 'estus,' swoþel *vel* hæte.)
swīð, adj., *strong, harsh;* nsn. swīð, 3085; swȳð, 191. Comp. nsf. swīðre, *right* (hand), 2098. [Go. swinþs; Ger. geschwind.] — Cpd.: ðrȳð-.
swīðe, adv., (w. adj. or verb), *very, much, very much;* 597, 997, 1092, 1743, 1926, [2275]; swȳðe, 2170, 2187. Comp. swīðor, *more, rather,* 960, 1139; *more especially,* 1874, 2198. — Cpd.: un-.
swīð-ferhð†, adj., *strong-minded, brave;* 826 (swȳð-); gsm. -es, 908;

406 BEOWULF

npm. -e, 493; dpm. -um, 173.
swīð-hicgende‡, adj. (pres. ptc.), *strong-minded, valiant;* 919; npm., 1016.
swīð-mōd(†), adj., *strong-minded, stout-hearted;* 1624.
swōgan, rd., *resound, roar;* pres. ptc. swōgende, 3145. [S O U G H; OS. swōgan, Go. ga-swōgjan.]
swōr, see **swerian**.
swulces, see **swylc**.
swurd, see **sweord**.
swutol, see **sweotol**.
swylc, pron., (1) demonstr., S U C H; 178, 1940, 2541, 2708; gsn. swulces, 880; asn. swylc, 996, 1583, 2798; gpm. swylcra, 582; gpn. ~, 2231; apm. swylce, 1347. — (2) relat., *such as, which (one);* dsm. swylcum, 299 (n.); asf. (pl.?) swylce, 1797; asn. swylc, 72; apm. swylce, 1156 (?, see swylce). —(3) correl., *such . . . as;* nsm. swylc . . . ~, *1328*, 1329; isn. swylce . . . ~, 1249ᵃ·ᵇ; apf. swylce . . . ~, 3164ᵃ·ᵇ. [Go. swa-leiks.]
swylce, I. adv., *likewise, also;* 113, 293, 830, 854, 907, 920, 1146, 1165, 1427, 1482, 2258 (gē ~), 2767, 2824, 3150; swilce, 1152. — II. conj., *(such) as;* 757, 1156(?), 2459, 2869; [*as if*, F. 36, w. opt.]. — (Except in 2824, always at beginning of half-line.)
swylt†, mi., *death;* 1255, 1436. [sweltan; Go. swulta (-waírþja).]
swylt-dæg†, m., D A Y *of death;* ds. -e, 2798.
swymman (swimman), III, S W I M; 1624. — Cpd.: ofer-.
swȳn, see **swīn**.
swynsian (swinsian), w 2., *make a (pleasing* or *cheerful) sound;* pret. 3 sg. swynsode, 611. [swin(n).]
swyrd, see **sweord**.
swyrd-gifu‡, f., G I V*ing of*

S W O R D*s;* 2884. See **sweord**
swȳð(e), see **swīð(e)**.
sȳ, see **eom**.
syfan-wintre(‡)+, adj.ja.(u.), S E V- E N *years old;* 2428. [Go. -wintrus.]
syfone, see **seofon**.
syl(l) (‡)+, fjō., S I L L, *floor;* ds. sylle, 775. [Cp. Go. ga-suljan.]
sylf, see **self**.
syllan, see **sellan**.
syl-līc, see **sel-līc**.
symbel, n., *feast, banquet;* ds. symble, 119, 2104; symle, 81, 489, 1008; as. symbel, 564, 619, 1010, 2431 (symbęl); gp. symbla, 1232. [OS. ds. sumble, ON. sumbl. Fr. Lat. (Gr.) symbola(?); cf. *Beitl.* xiii 226; *Beitr.* xxxvi 99.]
symbel-wyn(n)‡, fjō.(i.), *joy of feasting, delightful feast;* as. symbęlwynne, 1782.
sym(b)le (sim(b)le), adv., *ever, always, regularly;* symble, 2450; symle, 2497, 2880. [Go. simlē.]
symle, ds., see **symbel**.
syn(n), fjō., S I N, *crime;* dp. synnum, 975, 1255, 3071. — *wrong-doing, hostility;* ns. synn, 2472. (Cf. *Angl.* xxxv 128.) [Holt. Et.; *Zfvgl. Spr.* lvi 106 ff.] — Cpd.: un-.
syn-bysig‡, adj., *distressed by* S I N, *guilty;* 2226. [B U S Y.]
syn-dolh (sin-)‡, n., *very great wound;* 817. See the sin-cpds.
syndon, see **eom**.
syn-gāles, see **sin-gāles**.
ge-syngian, W 2., S I N, *do wrong;* pp. gesyngad, 2441.
syn-scaða(†), wk.m., *malefactor, miscreant;* as. -scaðan, 801. Cp. mān-.
syn-snǣd‡, fi., *huge morsel;* dp. -um, 743. [snīðan.] See the sin-cpds.
synt, see **eom**.

GLOSSARY

syrce, wk.f., *shirt of mail;* 1111; np. syrcan, 226; ap. ~, 334. [SARK (Sc., North.); ON. serkr. Fr. Lat.? Cf. *P. Grdr.*² i 344; Stroebe L 9.45. 2.60 f.; Falk, *Altwestnord. Kleiderkunde* 144.] — Cpds.: beadu-, here-, hioro-, leoðo-, līc-.

syrwan, w 1., *plot, ambush;* pret. 3 sg. syrede, 161. [searo.] — Cpd.: be-.

syððan, see **siððan.**

tācen, n., T O K E N, *sign, evidence;* 833; ds. tācne, 141, 1654. [Go. taikns.] — Cpd.: luf-.

ge-tǣcan, w 1., *show, point out, assign;* pret. 3 sg. getǣhte, 313, 2013. [T E A C H; cp. tācen.]

talian, w 2., *suppose, consider* (s.b. or s.th. to be such and such); pres. 1 sg. talige, 532 (*claim, maintain,* cf. *MPh.* iii 261), 677, 1845; 2 sg. talast, 594; 3 sg. talað, 2027. Cp. tellan.

te, 2922, see **tō.**

tēar, m., T E A R; np. -as, 1872. [Go. tagr; OHG. zahar, Ger. Zähre.] — Cpd.: wollen-.

tela, adv., *well, properly;* 948, 1218, 1225, 1820, 2208, 2663, 2737. (Always at end of *b*-line; excepting 2663, always in type C.) [til.]

telge, see **tellan.**

tellan, w 1., *account, reckon, consider* (s.b. or s.th. to be such and such); pres. 1 sg. telge (Lang. § 23.5), 2067; pret. 1 sg. tealde, 1773; 3 sg. ~, 794, 1810, 1936, 2641; 3 pl. tealdon, 2184. Cp. talian. [T E L L.]

teoh(h)†, f., *company, band;* ds. teohhe, 2938. [Cp. Ger. Zeche.]

teohhian, w 2., *appoint, assign;* pret. 1 sg. teohhode, 951; pp. geteohhod, 1300. [teoh(h).]

ge-tēon, 1 (II),†, *confer, bestow, grant;* imp. sg. (wearne) getēoh, 366; pret. 3 sg. (onweald) getēah, 1044, (ēst) ~, 2165. Cp. of-tēon.

tēon, II, *draw;* téôn, 1036 (*lead*); pret. 3 sg. tēah, 553; pp. togen, 1288, 1439; *take (a course)*, i.e. go (*on a journey*): pret. 3 sg. (-lāde) tēah, 1051, (-sīðas) ~, 1332. [Cp. TOW, TUG.] — Cpds.: ā-, þurh-.

ge-tēon, II, *draw;* pret. 3 sg. getēah, 1545, 2610; [3 pl. getugon, F. 15].

tēon, w 2. (or tēogan, Siev. § 414 n. 5; inf. unrecorded), *make, form;* pret. 3 sg. tēode, 1452; —*furnish, provide,* (dat., *with*); pret. 3 pl. tēodan, 43.

ge-tēon, w 2., *assign, allot;* pres. 3 sg. getēoð, 2526; pret. 3 sg. getēode, 2295 (n.).

tīd, fi., *time;* as., 147, 1915. [T I D E; Ger. Zcit.] — Cpds.: ān-, morgen-.

til(†), adj., *good;* 61, till 2721; nsf. tilu, 1250; nsn. til, 1304. [Go. gatils. Cp. tela.]

tilian, w 2., w. gen., *strive after, earn;* 1823. [T I L L; Go. -tilōn, Ger. zielen. Cp. til.]

timbran, w 1., *build;* pp. asn. timbred, 307. [T I M B E R; Go. timrjan, Ger. zimmern.] — Cpd.: be-.

tīr†, m., *glory;* gs. -es, 1654. [Cp. Ger. Zier. Siev. § 58 n. 1.]

tīr-ēadig†, adj., *glorious, famous;* dsm. -ēadigum, 2189.

tīr-fæst†, adj., *glorious, famous;* 922.

tīr-lēas‡, adj., *inglorious, vanquished;* gsm. -es, 843.

tīðian (tigðian), w 2., *grant;* w. dat. of pers. & gen. of thing: pp. nsn. (wæs) getīðad (impers.), 2284.

tō, I. prep. (1) w. dat.; motion, direction: T O, *towards;* 28, 124, 234, 270, 298, 313 (postpos.), 318, 323, 327, 360, 374, 383, [389], 438, 553, 604, 641 (ēode ... sittan, 'by'),

720, 766, 919, 925, 1009, 1013, 1119, 1154, 1158, 1159, 1171, 1199, 1232, 1236, 1237, 1242 ('at'), 1251, 1279, 1295, 1310, 1374, 1506, 1507, 1561, 1578, 1623, 1639, 1640, 1654[b] (postpos.), 1782, 1804, 1815, 1836, 1888, 1895, 1917, 1974, 1983, 2010, 2019, 2039, 2048, 2117, 2362, 2368, 2404, 2519, 2570, 2654, 2686, 2815, 2892, 2960, 2992, 3136, [F. 14, 20]; ((ge)sittan) tō (rūne), 172, ~ (sym(b)le): 489, 2104, (cp. below: aim, object); w. verb of thinking; 1138, 1139; w. verbs of expecting, desiring, seeking, etc. (*from, at, at the hands of*): 158, 188, 525, 601, 647, 1207, 1272, 1990, 2494[a], 2494[b], 2922 (te; cf. Lang. § 18.9), [F. 27], postpos.: 909, 1396, 3001; — aim, object: *to, for, as;* 14, 95, 379, 665, 971, 1021, 1186[a], 1186[b], 1472, 1654[a], 1830, 1834, 1961, 2448, 2639, 2804, 2941, 2998, 3016; — weorðan tō, (*turn to*), *become*, 460, 587, 906, 1262, 1330, 1707, 1709, 2079, 2203, 2384, 2502; si. 1711[a], 1711[b], 1712; — tō sōðe, 'for certain,' 'in truth,' 51, 590, 2325; — time: *at, in* (cf. *A*. l 110); 26; 933 (see feorh); 955, 2005, 2498 (see ealdor); 2432 (see līf). — (2) w. instr.; tō hwan (. . wearð), 2071; tō þon, *to that degree, so*, 1876; (næs ðā long) tō ðon þæt, *until*: 2591, 2845. — (3) w. gen.; tō þæs, *to that degree, so*, 1616; tō þæs þe, *to* (*the point*) *where:* 714, 1967, 2410; *to the point that, until, so that:* 1585. — (4) w. inf. 316, 2556; w. ger.: 174, 257, 473, 1003, 1419, 1724, 1731, 1805, 1851, 1922, 1941, 2093, 2416, 2445, 2452, 2562, 2644. (Cf. T.C. § 12.) — II. adv., (1) where a noun or pron. governed by prep. might be supplied, cp. postpos. tō; *thereto*, etc.; (stressed:) 1422, 1755, 1785, 2648. — (2) T O O; before adj. or adv.: 133, 137, 191, 905, 969, 1336, 1742, 1748, 1930, 2093, 2289, 2461, *2468*, 2684, 3085; si.: 694, 2882.

tō-, prefix, see the following verbs. [OHG. zar-, zir-, Ger. zer-.]

tō-brecan, IV, B R E A K (*to pieces*), *shatter;* 780; pp. tōbrocen, 997. (Cp. Judges ix 53 (A.V.): to(-) brake (pret.).)

tō-drīfan, I, D R I V E *asunder, separate;* pret. 3 sg. tōdrāf, 545.

tō-gædre, adv., T O G E T H E R (in connection w. verb of motion); 2630. See æt-gædere.

tō-gēanes, I. adv., *opposite* (*towards* s.b.); 1501. II. prep., (w. dat. preceding it), *a* G A I N S *t, towards, to meet;* 666, 1542, 1626, 1893; tōgēnes, 3114. Cp. on-gēan.

togen, see tēon, II.

tō-glīdan, I, (G L I D E *asunder*), *split* (intr.); pret. 3 sg. tōglād, 2487.

tō-hlīdan, I, *crack, spring apart;* pp. npm. tōhlidene, 999. [Cp. LID fr. hlid.]

tō-lūcan, II, *pull asunder, destroy;* 781.

tō-middes, adv., *in the* M I D S *t;* 3141.

torht(†), adj., *bright, resplendent;* asn., 313. [OS. torht, OHG. zor(a)ht.] — Cpds.: heaðo-, wuldor-.

torn(†), n., (1) *anger;* ds. -e, 2401. — (2) *grief, affliction, trouble;* as. torn, 147, 833; gp. torna, 2189. [Ger. Zorn.] — Cpd.: lige-.

torn†, adj., *grievous, bitter;* supl. nsf. tornost, 2129.

torn-gemōt‡, n., *hostile* MEET*ing;* as., 1140.

GLOSSARY

tō-somne, adv., T *ogether* (in connection w. idea of motion); 2568, 3122. Cp. æt-somne.

tō-weccan‡, w 1., (WAKE *up*), *stir up;* pret. 3 pl. tōwehton, 2948.

tredan, v, T R E A D, *walk upon, traverse;* 1964, 3019; pret. 3 sg. træd, 1352, 1643, 1881.

treddian(†), w 2., *step, go;* pret. 3 sg. treddode, 725; tryddode, 922. [See tredan, trodu.]

trem(m) (†), m. or n., *step, space;* as. (fōtes) trem, 2525. (*Mald.* 247: fōtes trym. See B.-T.)

trēow, f., T R U *th*, *good faith, fidelity;* gs. trēowe, 2922; as. ~, 1072. [Go. triggwa, OHG. triuwa.]

trēowan, w 1., w. dat., *trust;* pret. 3 sg. trēowde, 1166. [T R O W.] See truwian.

trēow-loga‡, wk.m., *one false to plighted faith* (T R O *th*), *traitor;* np. -logan, 2847. [lēogan.]

trodu(‡)+, f., *track, footprint;* ap. (s.?), trode, 843. [tredan.]

trum, adj., *strong;* 1369.

truwian, w 2. (3.), w. dat. or gen., *trust, have faith in;* pret. 1 sg. truwode, 1993; 3 sg. ~, 669, 2370, 2953. Cp. trēowan. See T.C. § 10.

ge-truwian, w 2. (3.), w. dat. or gen., *trust;* pret. 3 sg. getruwode, 1533, 2322, 2540; — (w. acc.) *confirm, conclude* (a treaty); pret. 3 pl. getruwedon, 1095. See truwian.

tryddian, see treddian.

trȳwe, adj.ja., T R U E, *faithful;* 1165. [Go. triggws, OHG. triuwi.] — Cpd.: ge-.

twā, see twēgen.

ge-twǣfan†, w 1., *separate, part, put an end to;* pp. getwǣfed, 1658; — w. acc. of pers. & gen. of thing: *hinder, restrain, deprive;* inf., 479; pres. 3 sg. getwǣfeð, 1763; pret. 3 sg. getwǣfde, 1433, 1908. [Cp. Go. tweifls.]

ge-twǣman, w 1., *separate, hinder;* 968 (w. acc. of pers. & gen. of thing).

twēgen, m., **twā**, f.(n.), num., T W A I N, T W O; nm. twēgen, 1163; am. ~, 1347; gm. twēga, 2532; dm. twǣm, 1191; nf. twā, 1194; af. ~, 1095.

twelf, num., T W E L V E; uninfl. (gm.): twelf (wintra), 147; nm. twelf*e*, 3170; am. twelfe, 1867; gm. twelfa, 2401. [Go. twa-lif.]

twēone, distrib. num., T W O, in dp.: be (sǣm) twēonum, B E T W E E N (*the seas*, = *on earth*), 858, 1297, 1685, 1956. (Cf. *MLN.* xxxiii 221 n.) [Go. tweihnai.]

tȳdre, adj.ja., *weak, craven;* npm., 2847. [O.Fris. teddre, Du. teeder.]

tȳn, num., T E N; uninfl. (dm.): tȳn (dagum), 3159; nm. tȳne, 2847. [Go. taíhun.] — Cpds.: fēower-, fīf-tȳne.

þā,[1] I. **adv.**, *then, thereupon;* at beginning of sentence 87 times, [& F. 13, 14, 28, 43, 46], exclus. of þā gȳt, gēn combin., (at begin. of 'fit' 10 (11: l. 1050) times); þā (. . .) verb (. . .) subj. 60 times; (þā wæs 46 times, 53, 64, 126, 128, 138, 223, 467, 491, 607, etc.; þā ðǣr . . . , 1280); þā (. . .) subj. (. . .) verb 27 times, 86, 331 (þā ðǣr), 461, 465, 518, etc., ðā ic . . . gefrægn: 74, 2484, 2694, 2752, 2773; — second (s.t. third, in 1011 & 2192 fourth) word in sentence 99 times; (at opening of 'fit' 8 times; always in *a*-line, exc. 1168, 1263, 2192, 2209, 2591,

---

[1] On the distribution of þ and ð in the MS., see Intr. xcvii & n. 2.

2845, 3045); prec. by pers. pron. 10 times, 26, 28, 312, 340, 1263, 2135, 2468, 2720, 2788, 3137; prec. by verb 89 times, 34, 115, 118 (.. þā ðǣr inne), 217, 234, 301, 327, etc. (& F. 2); — ond ðā, 615, 630, 1043, 1681, 1813, 2933, 2997; ond ... þā, 1590, 2707; nū ðā, 426, 657; þā gȳt (gīt), þā gēn, þā gēna, see gȳt, gēn, gēna. — **II. conj.** þā (only 11 times: ðā), *when, since, as;* nearly always in *b*-line; 140, 201, 323, 402, 419, 512, 539, 632, 706, 723, 733, 798, 967, 1068, 1078ᵃ, 1103, 1291, 1293, 1295, 1467, 1506, 1539, 1621, 1665, 1681 (? ond þā), 1813ᵃ (? ond ðā), 1988ᵃ, 2204ᵃ, [2230], 2287ᵃ, 2362, 2372(??), 2428, 2471, 2550, 2567, 2624, 2676, 2690, 2756, 2872, 2876, 2883, 2926ᵃ, 2944, 2978, 2983, 2992, 3066, 3088. (S.t. a slightly correl. use of þā ... þā is found: 138–40, 723, 1506, 1665, 2623–24, 2756, 2982–83. — þā is regul. used w. pret. or pluperf. [nū ðā 426, w. pres.]) Cf. Schü. Sa. §§ 3, 12, 66.

þā, pron., see sē.
ge-þǣgon, see ge-þicgan.
þǣm, þǣre, þǣs, see sē.
þǣr, I. dem. adv., T H E R E, also shading into *then;* 32, 157, 271, 284, 331, 400, 440, 493, 513, 550, 775, 794, 852, 913, 972, 977, 1099, 1123, 1165, 1190, 1243, 1269, 1280, 1365, 1470, 1499, 1613, 1837, 1907, 1951, 1972, 2009, 2095, 2199, 2235, 2238, 2297, 2314, 2369, 2385, 2459, 2522, 2573(?, n.), 2866, 2961, 3008, 3038, 3039, 3050, 3070; þǣr wæs, 36, 89, 497, 611, 835, 847, 856, 1063, 1232, 2076, 2105, 2122, 2231, 2762, si. 2137; ne wæs .. þǣr, 756, 1299, 2555, 2771; þǣr is, 3011; nis þǣr, 2458. (S.t. þǣr appears rather expletive, e.g. 271, 2555; 1123, 2199. þā ðǣr: 331, 1280.) þǣr inne, þǣr on innan, see inne, innan. — **II. rel.,** *where,* occas. shading into *when, as;* 286, 420, 508, 522, 693, 777 (slightly correl. w. dem. þǣr), 866, 1007, 1079, 1279, 1359, 1378, 1394, 1514, 1923, 2003, 2023, 2050, 2276, 2355, 2486, 2633, 2698, 2787, 2893, 2916, 3082, 3167; *to (the place) where,* 356, 1163, 1313, 2851, 3108, perh. in: 1188, 1648, 1815, 2075; conj., *in case that, if;* 762, 797, 1835, 2573 (?), 2730. — (Spelling ðǣr only 30 times.) Cf. Schü. Sa. §§ 30, 72. [Go. þar; OHG. dār, Ger. da.]

þæt, pron., see sē.
þæt (usually spelt þ), conj., T H A T; used 213 times; introd. consecutive clauses, *that, so that;* 22, 65, 567, 571, etc.; after verbs of motion, *until,* 221, 358, 404, 1318, 1911, 2716; s.t. used to indicate vaguely some other kind of relation, 1434, 2528, 2577, 2699, 2806; *provided that:* 1099; — purpose clauses, *that, in order that;* 2070, 2747, 2749; [F. 19]; — substantive clauses; 62, 68, 77, 84, 274, 300, etc., [F. 44]; semi-explanatory, w. refer. to an anticipatory pron. (hit, þæt) or noun of the governing clause; 88, 290, 379, 627, 681, 698, 701, 706, 735, 751, 779 (ref. to þæs), 812, 910, 1167, 1181, 1596, 1671, 1754, 2240, 2325, 2371, 2839, 3036, etc. — Cf. Schü. Sa. §§ 16, 17, 23. — oð þæt, see oð; þæt ðe, see þætte.
þætte (=þæt ðe: 1846, 1850), conj., T H A T; 151, 858, 1256, 1942, 2924.
ðafian, w 2., *consent to, submit to;* 2963.

GLOSSARY

þāh, see þēon, 1.
ge-þah, see ge-þicgan.
þām, see sē.
þanan, see þonan.
þanc, m., T H A N K s; w. gen. (for); 928, 1778; as., 1809, 1997, 2794; — satisfaction, pleasure; ds. (tō) þance, 379; — THOUGHT, in cpds.: fore-, ge-, hete-, inwit-, or-, searo-.
þanc-hycgende‡, adj. (pres. ptc.), THOUGHTful; 2235.
þancian, w 2., T H A N K, w. dat. of pers. & gen. of thing (for); pret. 3 sg. þancode, 625, 1397; 3 pl. þancedon, 227, þancodon 1626.
þanon, see þonan.
þāra, see sē.
þē, pers. pron., see þū.
þē, isn., see sē.
þē, þe (spelling ðe 5 times), rel. particle (repres. any gender, number, and case), *who, which, that*, etc.; *15*, 45, 138, 192, 238, 355, 500, 831, 941, 950, 993, 1271, 1334 (*in* or *by which*), 1482, 1654, 1858, 2135, 2182, 2364, 2400 (*on which, when*), 2468, 2490, 2606, 2635, 2712, 2735, 2796, 2866, 2982, 3001, 3009, 3086, [ðē, F. 9]; conj. *when*, 1000 (cf. Schü. Sa. 7; A. Adams, *The Temporal Clause in OE. Prose* [Yale Studies in English xxxii, 1907], pp. 26 ff.); *because*, 488, 1436ᵇ, 2641; þē ... ne, *that ... not, lest*, 242. Cp. þē, isn. of dem. pron. See also sē (þe), þætte, þēah (þe). — Cf. L 6.13; Schü. Sa. §§ 14, 18a, 24–29, 31. [Cp. Go. þei.]
þēah, I. adv., *nevertheless, however;* swā þēah: 972, 1929, 2878, 2967 (ðēh); hwæðre ∼, 2442. — II. conj., w. opt. or, rarely, ind. (several cases doubtful), THOUGH; 203, 526, 587, 589, 680 (þēah ..

eal, cp. A L THOUGH), 1102, 1660, 2031, 2161, 2467 (ind.), 2855; þēh, 1613 (ind.); þēah þe, 682, 1130 (*if?*, see note), 1167, 1368, 1716, 1831, 1927, 1941, *2218*, 2344, 2481, 2619, 2642, 2838, 2976. [Go. þauh, Ger. doch; ON. *þóh > MnE. though.]
ge-þeah, see ge-þicgan.
þearf, f., *need, want, distress, difficulty, trouble;* 201, 1250, 1835, 2493, 2637, 2876; ds. -e, 1456 (as.?), 1477, 1525, 2694, 2709, 2849; as. -e, 1797 (pl.?), 2579, 2801. [Go. þarba.] — Cpds.: fyren-, nearo-.
þearf, vb., see þurfan.
þearfa, wk.m., adj., *needy, lacking* (w. gen.); 2225.
ge-þearfian(‡), w 2., ‡*necessitate, impose necessity;* pp. geþearfod, 1103.
þearle, adv., *severely, hard;* 560.
þēaw, m., *custom, usage, manner;* 178, 1246, 1940; as., 359; dp þēawum ('in good customs'), 2144. [T H E W (s); OS. thau.] — Cp. ge-þȳwe.
þec, see þū.
þeccean, w 1., *cover, enfold;* 3015 (see B.-T.); pret. 2 pl. þehton, 513. [Cp. THATCH; Ger. decken; Holt. Et.: þeccan 2.]
þegn, m., T H A N E, *follower, attendant, retainer, warrior;* 194, 235, 494, 867, 1574, 2059, 2709, 2721, 2977, [F. 13]; gs. -es, 1797; ds. -e, 1085, 1341, 1419, 2810; as. ðegn, 1871; np. -as, 1230; gp. -a, 123, 400, 1627, 1644, 1673, 1829, 2033; dp. -um, 2869; ap. -as, 1081, 3121. [T H A N E (Sc. spelling); OHG. degan.] — Cpds.: ealdor-, heal-, mago-, ombiht-, sele-.
þegn-sorg‡, f., S O R R O W *for* T H A N E s; as. -e, 131.

þegon, -un, see **þicgan**
þēh, see **þēah.**
þehton, see **þeccean.**
þencan, w 1., T H I N K; abs.: pres. 3 sg. þenceð, 289, 2601; w. þæt-clause: pret. 3 sg. þōhte, 691; w. tō (*be intent on*): ~, 1139; — w. inf., *mean, intend;* pres. 3 sg. þenceð, 355, 448, 1535; pret. 1 sg. þōhte, 964; 3 sg. ~, 739; 1 pl. þōhton, 541; 3 pl. ~, 800. — Cpd.: ā-.
ge-þencan, w 1., T H I N K, *remember;* imp. sg. geþenc, 1474; w. acc., *conceive;* inf. geþencean, 1734.
þenden, I. conj., *while, as long as;* ~ lifde 57, si. 1224; ~ . . wēold 30, si. 1859, 2038; ~ . . mōte 1177, si. (2038), 3100; 284, 2499, 2649, 3027. **II. adv.**, *meanwhile, then;* 1019, 2418, 2985. [Go. þandē.]
þengel†, m., *prince;* as., 1507. [þēon, 1; ON. þengill.]
þēnian, w 2., *serve;* pret. 1 sg. þēnode, 560. [þegn.]
þēod, f., *people, nation, troop of warriors;* 643, 1230, 1250, 1691; ðīod, 2219; gp. þēoda, 1705. [Go. þiuda.] — Cpds.. sige-, wer-; Swēo-; el-þēodig.
þēod-cyning(†), m., K I N G *of a people;* 2963, 2970; ðīod-, 2579; ðēod-kyning, 2144; gs. -cyninges, 2694; as. -cyning, 3008, [3086]; gp. -cyninga, 2.
þēoden(†), m., *chief, lord, prince, king;* 15 times w. mǣre, see mǣre; 7 times w. gp. (Scyldinga, etc.); 129, 1046, 1209, 1715, 1871, 2131, 2869, 3037; þīoden, 2336, 2810; ǥs. þēodnes, 797, 910, 1085, 1627, 1837, *2174*, 2656; ds. þēodne, 345, 1525, 1992, *2032*, 2572, 2709; as. þēoden, 34, 201, 353, 1598, 2384, 2721, 2786, 2883, 3079, 3141; þīoden, 2788; vs. þēoden (mīn):

365, 2095; ~ (Hrōðgār), 417; ~ (Scyldinga), 1675; np. þēodnas, 3070. [þēod; Go. þiudans.]
ðēoden-lēas‡, adj., *lord-*L E S S, *deprived of one's chief;* npm. -e, 1103.
þēod-gestrēon‡, n., *people's treasure, great treasure;* gp. -a, *1218;* dp. -um, 44.
ðēod-kyning, see **þēod-cyning.**
þēod-sceaða, wk.m., *people's foe* or *spoiler;* 2278, 2688. (Cf. *Angl.* xxxv 251.)
þēod-þrēa‡, fwō., wk.m. (Siev. §§ 259 n., 277 n. 2 & 3), *distress of the people, great calamity;* dp. -þrēaum, 178.
þēof, m., T H I E F; gs. -es, 2219.
þēon, 1, *thrive, prosper;* pret. 3 sg. þāh, 8, 2836 (n.), 3058 (*turn to profit*); pp. nsf. geþungen, *excellent,* 624. [Go. þeihan.] — Cpds.: on-; wēl-þungen.
ge-þēon, 1, *prosper, flourish;* 910; geþéon, 25; imp. sg. geþēoh, 1218.
þēon, w 1., see **þȳwan.**
þēos, see **þēs.**
þēostre, adj.ja. (Lang. § 10.1), *dark, gloomy;* dp. (m.n.) þēostrum, 2332. [Ger. düster.]
þēow, m., *servant, slave;* þ[ēow], 2223. — (Cpds.: Ecg-, Ongen-, Wealh-.)
þēs, þēos, þis, dem. pron. (adj., exc. 290), T H I S; þes, 432, 1702, [F. 7], þæs (Lang. § 7.1), 411; nsf. þēos, 484; nsn. þis, 290, 2499, [F. 3]; gsm. ðisses, 1216; gsf. ðisse, 928, [F. 4]; gsn. þisses, 1217, þysses 197, 790, 806; dsm. ðys-sum, 2639; dsf. þisse, 638; dsn. þissum, 1169; asm. þisne, 75, [F. 9], þysne 1771; asf. þās, 1622, 1681; asn. þis, 1723, 2155, 2251, 2643; isn. ðȳs, 1395; dpm. ðys-sum, 1062, 1219; apm. ðās, 2635,

GLOSSARY

2640, 2732; apn. ~, 1652. (Alliter.: 197, 790, 806; 1395.)

þicgan, v, *receive, take, partake of (food, drink)*; 1010; ðicgean, 736; pret. 1 pl. þēgun, 2633; 3 pl. þēgon, 563. [OS. thiggian.]

ge-þicgan, v, *receive, partake of, drink;* pret. 3 sg. geþeah, 618, 628; geþah (Lang. § 23.3), 1024; 3 pl. geþǣgon, 1014.

þīn, poss. pron., T H Y (T H I N E); 459, 490, 593, 954, 1705, 1853, 2048; nsn., 589; gsf. -re, 1823; gsn. -es, 1761; dsm. -um, 346, 592; dsf. -re, 1477; asm. -ne, 267, 353, 1848; asn. þīn, 1849; isn. -e, 2131; gpm. -ra, 367, 1672, 1673; dpm. -um, 587, 1178, 1708; apm. -e, 2095.

þincean, see þyncan.

þing, n., T H I N G, *affair*, 409 (n.); — *meeting (judicial assembly)*; as., 426 (n.); — gp. in: ænige þinga, *in any way, by any means:* 791, 2374, 2905. — See ge-þinge.

ge-þingan(†), w 1., *determine, appoint, purpose;* pp. geþinged, 647 (n.), 1938; w. refl. dat., *determine (to go to,* tō); pres. 3 sg. geþingeð, 1837 (n.).

þingian, w 2., *compound, settle;* (fēa) ~, 156; pret. 1 sg. (fēo) þingode, 470; — †*speak, make an address;* inf., 1843.

ðīod(-), þīoden, see þēod(-), þēoden.

þis, see þěs.

þolian, w 2., *suffer, endure;* 832; pres. 3 sg. þolað, 284; pret. 3 sg. þolode, 131, 1525; — intr., *hold out;* pres. 3 sg. þolað, 2499. [T H O L E (arch., North.); Go. þulan.]

ge-þolian, w 2., *suffer, endure;* ger. geþolianne, 1419; pret. 3 sg. geþolode, 87, 147; — intr., *abide, remain;* inf., 3109.

þon, see sē.

þon, 44, see þonne, II, 2.

þonan, adv., in many cases (marked*) at the end of the line, THENce (motion [accord. to modern notions s.t. redundant], origin: *from him* 111, 1265, 1960); þonan, 819*, 2061*, 2099*, 2140*, 2359, 2545*, 2956*; ðonon, 520, 1373, 1601*, 1632 (at the end of the *a*-line), 1960, 2408*; þanon, 111, 123, 224, 463, 691, 763*, 844*, 853, 1265, 1292*, 1805*, 1921*; þanan, 1668*, 1880*.

þone, see sē.

þonne (ðonne only 15 times), adv., conj. (used mostly ' where the time of an action is indefinite, and is found w. the future, the indefinite present and the indefinite past,' B.-T.), **I. adv.**, T H E N; (time); 1484, 1741, 1745, 2032, 2041, 2063, 2446, 2460, 3062, 3107; 1106 (*in that case*); — (succession in narrative:) *then, further;* 377, 1455, 3051; — (conclusion:) *then, therefore;* 435, 525, 1671, 1822 (2063); — (contrast:) *however, on the other hand;* (gyf) þonne: 1104, 1836; ðonne, 484 (*but then*). — **II. conj.** (1) *when, at such times as, whenever;* 23, 485, 573, 880, 934, 1033, 1040, 1042, 1066, 1121, 1143, 1179, 1285, 1326, 1327, 1374, 1485, 1487 (*while*), 1535, 1580, 1609, 2034, 2114, 2447, 2453, 2544, 2634, 2686, 2742, 2867 (þonne ... oft, cp. *Wand.* 39 f.), 2880, 3064, 3106, 3117, 3176. (Correl. þonne (adv.) ... þonne (conj.): 484 f., 1484 f., 2032–34, 2446 f., 3062–64; gyf þonne ... þonne, 1104–06.) — (2) T H A N (after comp.); without foll. clause: 469, 505, 534, 678, 1139, 1182, 1353, 1579, 2433,

2891; with foll. clause: *70*, 248, (cp. 678), 1385, 1560, 1824, 2572, 2579, [F. 40]; þon, 44 (n.).
þonon, see **þonan**.
þorfte, see **þurfan**.
þrāg, f., *time;* as. (longe) þrāge: 54, 114, 1257; — *evil time, hardship, distress;* ns., 2883; as. þrāge, 87. (Cf. *MPh.* iii 254.) [Cp. Go. þragjan?] — Cpd.: earfoð-.
þrēa-nēdla†, wk.m., *sore stress, distress;* ds. -nēdlan, 2223. See nȳd.
þrēa-nȳd†, fi., *distress, sad necessity;* as., 284; dp. -um, 832.
ðrēat, m., *crowd, troop, company;* ds. -e, 2406; dp. -um, 4. [*NED.*: T H R E A T, sb.] — Cpd.: īren-.
þrēatian, w 2., *press, harass;* pret. 3 pl. þrēatedon, 560. [*NED.*: T H R E A T, vb., T H R E A T en. Cp. þrēat.]
þrec-wudu‡, mu., (*might-*W O O D), *spear;* 1246. Cp. mægen-. See geþræc.
þrēo, num., n., T H R E E; a. þrēo, 2278; þrīo, 2174.
þreottēoða, num., T H I R T E E *n* T H; 2406.
þridda, num., T H I R D; dsm. þriddan, 2688.
þringan, III, intr., THRONG, *press forward;* pret. 3 sg. þrong, 2883; 3 pl. þrungon, 2960. [Ger. dringen.] — Cpd.: for-.
ge-þringan, III, intr., *press (forward*); pret. 3 sg. geþrang, 1912.
þrīo, see **þrēo**.
þrīst-hȳdig†, adj., *bold-minded, brave;* 2810. [Ger. dreist.]
þrītig, num., n., w. partit. gen., T H I R T Y; as., 123, 2361; gs. -es, 379.
þrōwian, w 2., *suffer;* 2605, 2658; pret. 3 sg. þrōwade, 1589, 1721; ðrōwode, 2594.
ge-þrūen†, pp., †*forged, hammered;*

1285 (MS. geþuren). Cp. geþrūen (MS. geþ^uruen), *Met. Bt.* 20.134; geþuren (MS.), *Rid.* 91.1; Siev. §§ 385 n. 1, 390 n. 1. [Cp. (ge-)-þweran, see ge-þwǣre; *ZföG.* lix 345?]
þrȳd-līc, see **þrȳð-līc**.
ðrym(m), mja.(?), *might, force;* 1918; dp. þrymmum (semi-adv.), 235; — *greatness, glory;* as. þrym, 2. [Cp. ON. þrymr.] — Cpd.: hige-.
þrym-līc, adj., *mighty, magnificent;* 1246.
þrȳð†, fi., (pl.), *might, strength;* dp. -um, 494. [ON. -þrúðr, þrúð-.] See Proper Names: Mōd-Þrȳðo.
ðrȳþ-ærn‡, n., *mighty house, splendid hall;* as., 657.
þrȳð-līc(‡) (+), adj., *mighty, splendid;* 400, 1627. Supl. acc. þrȳdlīcost, 2869 (n.).
ðrȳð-swȳð (-swīð)‡, adj., *strong, mighty;* 131, 736. (Conjectured by Grein Spr. [?], Hold., Earle to be a noun, 'great pain,' w. ref. to ON. sviði 'smart from burning'; unconvincing.)
þrȳð-word‡, n., *strong (brave, noble)* W O R D (*s*); 643.
þū, pers. pron., T H O U; þū 43 times, ðū 19 times [& F. 27]; ds. þē 24 times, ðē 9 times [& F. 26]; as. þec (ðec), 946, 955, 1219, 1763, 1768, 1827, 1828, 2151; þē (ðē), 417, 426, 517, 1221, 1722, 1833, 1994, 1998; dual git, 508, 512, 513, 516; g. incer, 584; d. inc, 510; plur. **gē**, 237, 245, 252, 254, 333, 338, 393, 395, 2529, 2866, 3096, 3104; gp. ēower, 248, 392(?), 596; dp. ēow, 292, 391, 1344, 1987, 2865, 3103; ap. ēowic, 317, 3095.
þūhte, see **þyncan**.
ge-þungen, see **þēon**, 1.

GLOSSARY 415

þunian, w 2., (T H U N der), *creak, groan;* pret. 3 sg. þunede, 1906.
*þurfan, prp., (in negat. clauses,) *need, have good cause or reason;* pres. 2 sg. þearft, 445, 450, 1674; 3 sg. þearf, 595, 2006, 2741; opt. 3 sg. þurfe, 2495; pret. 3 sg. þorfte, 157, 1026, 1071, 2874, 2995; 3 pl. þorf[t]on, 2363. [Go. þaúrban.]
þurh, prep., w. acc., T H R O U G H; local: 2661; means, instrument: 276(?), 558, 699, 940, 1693, 1695, 1979, 2045, 2405; cause, motive, *through, from, because of:* 267, 278, 1726(?), 1101(?), 3068; state, manner, accompanying circumstances, *in, with, by way of:* 184 (n.), 276, 1335, 2454; 267(?), 278(?), 1101, 1726.
þurh-brecan(‡), IV, B R E A K T H R O U G H; pret. 3 sg. -bræc, 2792.
þurh-dūfan(‡), II, (DIVE) *swim* T H R O U G H; pret. 3 sg. -dēaf, 1619.
þurh-etan(†), V, E A T T H R O U G H; pp. np. þurhetone (cf. Lang. § 18.6), 3049.
ðurh-fōn(‡), rd., *penetrate;* 1504.
þurh-tēon, II, *bring about, effect;* 1140.
þurh-wadan(†), VI, *go* T H R O U G H, *penetrate;* pret. 3 sg. -wōd, 890, 1567.
þus, adv., T H U S, *so;* 238, 337, 430.
þūsend, n., T H O U S A N D; as., 3050; ap. (seofan) þūsendo, 2195 (n.); þūsenda (Lang. §18.2), 1829; (hund) þūsenda, 2994 (n.).
þȳ, see sē.
þyder (þider), adv., T H I T H E R; þyder, 379, 2970, 3086.
þȳhtig(‡), adj., *strong, firm;* asn., 1558. [þēon, I.] — Cpd.: hige-.
þyle(‡) (+), mi., *orator, spokesman, official entertainer* (see Notes, p. 149); 1165, 1456. [ON. þulr.]

þyncan, w I., *seem, appear;* impers. (marked*), w. dat., M E T H I N K S, etc.; þincean, 1341*; pres. 3 sg. þynceð, 2653*, þinceð 1748; 3 pl. þinceað, 368; opt. 3 sg. þince, 687*; pret. 3 sg. þūhte, 842, 2461, 3057*; 3 pl. þūhton, 866. [Go. þugkjan. Cp. þencan.] — Cpd.: of-.
þyrs, mi., *giant, demon;* ds. -e, 426. [ON. þurs.]
þys-līc, adj., *such;* nsf. þyslicu, 2635. [þus.]
þȳs, þysne, þysses, þyssum, see þĕs.
þȳstru, wk.f., *darkness;* dp. þȳstrum, 87. [þēostre.]
þȳwan, þēon, w I., *oppress, threaten;* ðēon, 2736; pres. 3 pl. þȳwað, 1827. (Siev. §§ 117.2 & n., 408 n. 12 & 18.)

ufan, adv., *from* abo V E; 330 (n.), 1500.
ufera, ufara,(‡)+, comp., *(higher), later;* dpn. uferan (dōgrum), 2392, ufaran (~), 2200.
ufor, adv. comp., *higher up, farther away;* 2951.
ūhta or ūhte, wk.m. or n. (Siev. § 280 n. 2), *time just before daybreak, dawn;* ds. (on) ūhtan, 126. [Go. ūhtwō, wk.f.] (Cf. Tupper, *Publ. MLAss.* x 146 ff.)
ūht-floga‡, wk.m., *(dawn-* or*) night-*FLIer; gs. -flogan, 2760.
ūht-hlem(m)‡, mja.(?), *din* or *crash at (dawn) night;* as. -hlem, 2007.
ūht-sceaða‡, wk.m., *depredator at (dawn) night;* 2271.
umbor-wesende‡, adj. (pres. ptc.), *being a child;* dsm. umborwesendum, 1187; asm. umborwesende, 46. Cp. cniht-; T.C. § 6. (umbor also *Gnom. Ex.* 31.) [*umb, cp. ymb(e), see Bright, *MLN.* xxxi 82 f.; other etymologies: *ib.*:

Grimm D.M. 322 (389); Simrock L 3.21.170 f.; also H. Schröder, *Ablautstudien* (1910), p. 46; Grienb., *ZföG*. lix 345: cp. wamb.]
un-blīðe, adj.(i.)ja., *joyless, sorrowful;* 130, 2268; npm., 3031.
un-byrnende(‡), adj. (pres. ptc.), *without* B U R N *ing;* 2548.
unc, see **ic.**
uncer, pers. pron., see **ic.**
uncer, poss. pron., *of us two;* dpm. uncran, 1185.
un-cūð, adj., *unknown;* nsf., 2214; — *strange, forbidding, awful;* gsn. -es, 876 (*unknown?*); asm. -ne, 276; asn. uncūð, 1410; *uncanny* (*foe*), gsm. -es 960. (Cf. Schü. Bd. 42–4.) [U N C O U T H.]
under, I. prep., (1) w. dat., (position:) U N D E R; under (wolcnum, heofenum, roderum, swegle): 8, 52, 310, 505, 651, 714, 1078, 1197, 1631, 1770, [F. 8]; 1656, 2411, 2415, 2967, 3060, 3103; under (helme, 'covered by'): 342, 404, 2539, si.: 396, 1163, 1204, 1209, 2049, 2203, 2605; si. 1302; *at the lower part (foot) of,* 211, 710, 2559; *within,* 1928, cp. 3060, 3103; (attending circumstances:) *with,* 738 (n.). — (2) w. acc., (motion, cf. *MPh.* iii 256 f.:) *under* (also *to the lower part of*); 403, 820, 836, 887, 1360, 1361, 1469, 1551, 1745, *2128,* 2540, 2553, 2675, 2744, 2755, 3031, 3123; (*to the*) *inside* (*of*), 707 (n.), 1037, 2957, 3090; (extension:) *under;* under (heofones hwealf): 576, 2015, si. 414, 860, 1773. — II. adv., *beneath;* 1416, 2213.
undern-mǣl(‡) (+), n., *morningtime;* as., 1428. (undern, orig.: '3rd hour,' 'mid-forenoon.' Cf. Tupper, *Publ. MLAss.* x 160 ff.) [U N D E R N (obs., dial.), ▪ N-

D E R M E A L (obs.), Chaucer, *C.T.*, D 875; Go. undaúrni-.]
un-dyrne, -derne, adj.ja., *not hidden, manifest;* undyrne, 127; under[ne], 2911; nsn. undyrne, 2000; in: undyrne cūð, 150, 410 (hardly adv.; see note on 398; *Angl.* xxviii 440, Kock² 104).
un-fǣcne(‡)+, adj.ja., *without deceit, sincere;* as. (f. or m.), 2068.
un-fǣge(‡), adj.ja., *undoomed, not fated to die;* 2291; asm. unfǣgne, 573.
un-fǣger(‡)+, adj., U N F A I R, *horrible;* nsn., 727.
un-flitme(?)‡, *undisputed* (?), 1097 (n.).
un-forht, adj., *fearless, brave;* 287.
un-forhte(‡), adv., *fearlessly, without hesitation;* 444.
un-frōd(‡), adj., *not old, young;* dsm. -um, 2821.
un-from†, adj., *inactive, feeble;* 2188.
un-geāra, adv., (1) *not long ago, recently;* 932. — (2) *erelong, soon;* 602 (~ nū). See geāra.
un-gedēfe-līce(‡), adv., U N *fittingly;* 2435.
un-gemete, adv.(†), *without measure, exceedingly;* 2420, 2721, 2728. [metan. Cp. OS.; *Hildebr.* 25: ummet.]
un-igmetes (= un-gemetes, Lang. §18.8), adv.(‡), *without measure, exceedingly;* 1792.
un-gyfeðe (-gifeðe)‡, adj.ja., *not granted, denied;* nsf., 2921.
un-hǣlo(‡)+, wk.f., ‡*evil, destruction;* gs., 120. [hāl.]
un-hēore, -hīore, -hȳre, adj.ja., *awful, frightful, monstrous;* -hīore, 2413; nsf. -hēoru, 987; nsn. -hȳre, 2120.
un-hlitme(?)‡, 1129, see note.
un-lēof†, adj., *not loved;* apm. -e,

2863. (Schü. Bd. 8 n.: 'faithless'?)
un-lifigende, -lyfigende, adj. (pres. ptc.), *not* L I V *ing, dead;* -lifigende, 468; gsm. -lyfigendes, 744; dsm. -lifgendum, 1389, -lifigendum 2908; asm. -lyfigendne, 1308.
un-lȳtel, adj., *not* L I T T L E, *great;* 885; nsf., 498; asn., 833.
un-murn-līce†, adv., *ruthless*L Y, 449 (cp. 136); *recklessly,* 1756. [murnan.]
unnan, prp., *not begrudge, wish* (s.b. to have s.th.), *grant;* w. dat. of pers. & gen. of thing: pres. 1 sg. an, 1225; w. dat. of pers. & þæt-clause: pret. 3 sg. ūðe, 2874; — *like, wish;* abs.: pret. opt. 3 sg. ūðe, 2855; w. þæt-clause: pret. 1 sg. ūþe, 960 (opt.?); 3 sg. ~, 503. [OS. OHG. unnan.]
ge-unnan, prp., *grant;* w. dat. of pers. & þæt-clause; 346; pret. 3 sg. geūðe, 1661. [OHG. gi-unnan, Ger. gönnen.]
un-nyt(t), adj.ja., *useless;* 413; nsn., 3168.
un-riht, n., *wrong;* as., 1254; (on) ~ (*wrongfully*), 2739.
un-rihte, adv. (or ds. of unriht, n.), *wrongfully;* 3059.
un-rīm, n., *countless number;* 1238, 3135; as., 2624.
un-rīme, adj.ja., *countless;* nsn., 3012.
un-rōt, adj., *sad, depressed;* npm. -e, 3148.
un-slāw, adj. wa., *not* S L O W, (‡)*not blunt, sharp;* asn., 2564 (n.).
un-snyttru, wk.f., U N*wisdom, folly;* dp. unsnyttrum, 1734.
un-sōfte, adv., (U N S O F T *ly*), *hardly, with difficulty;* 1655, 2140.
un-swīðe(‡), adv., *not strongly;* comp. unswīðor, *less strongly,* 2578, 2881.

un-synnig(‡)+, adj., *guiltless;* asm. -ne, 2089. [syn(n).]
un-synnum‡, adv. (dp.), *guiltlessly;* 1072. See syn(n).
un-tǣle(‡)+, adj.ja., *blameless;* apm., 1865.
un-tȳdre‡, mja., *evil progeny, evil brood;* np. -tȳdras, 111. [tūdor.]
un-wāc-līc(‡), adj., *not* (WEAK) *mean, splendid;* asm. -ne, 3138.
un-wearnum†, adv. (dp.), *without hindrance, irresistibly;* or: *eagerly, greedily* (Schuchardt L 6.14.2.14); 741. See wearn.
un-wrecen(‡)+, adj. (pp.), U N-*avenged;* 2443.
up, adv., U P (*wards*); 128, 224, 519, 782, 1373, 1619, 1912, 1920, 2575, 2893.
up-lang, adj., U P *right;* 759. See and-long. (Cp. upp-riht.)
uppe, adv., U P, *above;* 566.
upp-riht(‡)+, adj., U P R I G H T; 2092.
ūre, pers. pron., see ic.
ūre, poss. pron., O U R; 2647; gsn. ūsses, 2813; dsm. ūssum, 2634; asm. ūserne, 3002, 3107.
ūrum, ūs, ūser, see ic.
ūserne, see ūre.
ūsic, see ic.
ūsses, ūssum, see ūre.
ūt, adv., O U T (motion); 215, 537, 663, 1292, 1583, 2081, 2515, 2545, 2551, 2557, 3092, 3106, 3130. [Go. ūt.]
ūtan, adv., *from with*O U T, *outside;* 774, 1031, 1503, 2334. [Go. ūtana.]
ūtan-weard(‡)+₂ adj., O U T*side;* asm. -ne, 2297.
ūt-fūs‡, adj., *ready* (*eager*) *to set* O U T; 33.
uton, see wutun.
ūt-weard(‡)+, adj., *turning* O U T-

W A R D s, *striving to escape;* 761. [Cp. weorðan.]
ūþe, see unnan.
ūð-genge, adj.ja., *departing;* wæs .. ūðgenge, w. dat., *departed from,* 2123. [Go. unþa-. Cp. oð-.]
wā, adv., W O E, *ill;* 183. [Go. wai.]
wacian, w 2., *keep* WATCH; imp. sg. waca, 660. See wæccan.
wada, -o, -u, see wæd.
wadan, VI, *go, advance;* pret. 3 sg. wōd, 714, 2661. [W A D E.] — Cpds.: on-, þurh-.
ge-wadan, VI, *go, advance* (to a certain point); pp. gewaden, 220.
wæccan, w 3. 2. (Siev. § 416 n. 10), W A T C H, *be awake;* pres. ptc. wæccende, 708; asm., uninfl. 2841, wæccendne, 1268. See wacian.
wæcnan(†), VI, w 1. (Siev. § 392 n. 2), W A K E N, *arise, spring, be born;* 85; pret. 3 sg. wōc, 1265, 1960; 3 pl. wōcun, 60. [Go. wakan, -waknan.] — Cpd.: on-.
wæd†, n., *water, sea;* (pl. w. sg. meaning); np. wadu, 581, wado 546; gp. wada, 508. [Cp. wadan.]
wæfre†, adj.ja., *restless;* 2420; nsn., 1150; *wandering,* nsm., 1331 (cf. *Angl.* xxxv 256).
wǣg-bora‡, wk.m., *wave-roamer;* 1440. [See wēg; beran. (borian?)] (Etymological meanings proposed: 'wave-bearer, -bringer, -traveler, -piercer, -disturber,' 'offspring of the waves.' Cf. Grein Spr.; Schröer, *Angl.* xiii 335; Siev., *Angl.* xiv 135; Aant. 24; Holt., *Beibl.* xiv 49, xxi 300; Grienb., *Beitr.* xxxvi 99; Siev., *ib.* 431; Hoops 171. See Varr.)
wǣge(†), nja., *cup, flagon;* as., [2216], (fǣted) wǣge: 2253, 2282. [OS. wēgi. Cf. Th. Kross, *Die Namen der Gefässe bei den Ags.*

(1911), pp. 26, 129 f.] — Cpds.: ealo-, līð-.
wǣg-holm‡, m., *(billowy) sea;* as., 217.
wǣg-līðend(e)†, mc. (pres. ptc.) [pl.], *seafarer;* dp. -līðendum, *3158.*
wǣg-sweord‡, n., S W O R D *with wavy ornamentation;* as., 1489. (Cf. Hoops 174.)
wæl, n., *those slain in battle* (collect.), *corpse(?);* as., 448 (n.), 1212, 3027; np. walu, 1042; — *slaughter, field of battle;* ds. wæle, 1113; as. wæl, 635. [Cp. wōl. Valhalla.] — Cpd.: Frēs-.
wæl-bed(d)†, nja., B E D *of death;* ds. bedde, 964.
wæl-bend‡, fjō., *deadly* BOND; ap. -e, 1936.
wæl-blēat‡, adj., *deadly, mortal;* asf. -e, 2725. See blēate.
wæl-dēað‡, m., *murderous* D E A T H; 695.
wæl-drēor†, m. or n., *blood of slaughter;* ds. -e, 1631.
wæl-fǣhð‡, f., *deadly* FEUD; gp. -a, 2028.
wæl-fāg‡, adj., *slaughter-stained* (?); asm. -ne, 1128 (n.).
wæl-feal(l) (‡), m., *slaughter;* ds. -fealle, 1711. See wæl-fyl(l).
wæl-fūs‡, adj., *ready for death;* 2420.
wæl-fyl(l), mi., *slaughter;* gp. -fylla, 3154. See wæl-feal(l).
wæl-fyllo‡, wk.f., *abundance of slain,* F I L L *of slaughter;* ds. -fylle, 125. [full.]
wæl-fȳr‡, n., *murderous* F I R E; ds. -e, 2582; *funeral fire;* gp. -a, 1119.
wæl-gǣst‡, mi., *murderous sprite;* 1331; as., 1995. See gāst.
wæl-hlem(m)‡, mja.(?), *slaughter-blow, onslaught;* as. -hlem, 2969.
wæll-seax‡, n., *battle-knife;* ds. -e, 2703.

GLOSSARY

wælm, see wylm.
wæl-nīð†, m., *deadly hate, hostility;* 3000; ds. -e, 85; np. -as, 2065.
wæl-rǣs‡, m., *murderous onslaught, bloody conflict;* 2947; ds. -e, 824, 2531; as. -rǣs, 2101.
wǣl-rāp‡, m., *water-fetter (ice);* ap. -as, 1610. [wǣl 'deep pool,' 'stream,' see *Dial. D.*: W E E L, sb.[1]; R O P E.] (Kock, Kl. Misc. 19: wæl-rāpas, 'quelling chains.')
wæl-rēaf, n., *spoil of battle;* as., 1205.
wæl-rēc‡, mi., *deadly* (R E E K) *fumes;* as., 2661.
wæl-rēow, adj., *fierce in battle;* 629.
wæl-rest†, fjō.(?), *bed of slaughter;* as. -e, 2902.
wæl-sceaft‡, m., *battle-*(S H A F T, i.e.) *spear;* ap. -as, 398.
wæl-steng‡, mi., *battle-pole, shaft of spear;* ds. -e, 1638.
wæl-stōw, f., *battle-field;* ds. (or gs.) -e, 2051, 2984. [Cp. Ger. Wa(h)lstatt.]
wǣn (wægn), m., WAGON; as., 3134. [W A I N.]
wǣpen, n., W E A P O N; 1660; gs. wǣpnes, 1467; ds. wǣpne, 2965, 1664 (is.); as. wǣpen, 685, 1573, 2519, 2687; gp. wǣpna, 434, 1045, 1452, 1509, 1559; dp. wǣpnum, 250, 331, 2038, 2395; ap. wǣpen, 292. [Go. wēpn.] — Cpds.: hilde-, sige-.
wǣpned-mon(n), mc., M A N; ds. -men, 1284. [W E A P O N E D, i.e. male.]
wǣr, f., *agreement, treaty;* as. -e, 1100; — *protection, keeping;* ds. -e, 3109; as. -e, 27. [OHG. wāra, cp. OS. OHG. wār.] — Cpd.: frioðo-.
wǣre, wǣran, -on, wæs, see eom.
wæstm, m., *growth, stature, form;* dp. -um, 1352. [weaxan.] — Cpd.: here-.

wæter, n., W A T E R, *sea;* 93, 1416, 1514, 1631; gs. wæteres, 471, 516, 1693, 2791; ds. wætere, 1425, 1656, 2722, wætre 2854; as. wæter, 509, 1364, 1619, 1904, 1989, 2473.
wæter-egesa†, wk.m., W A T E R-*terror, dreadful water;* as. -egesan, 1260.
wæter-ȳð‡, fjō., *wave of the sea;* dp. -um, 2242.
wāg, m., *wall;* ds. -e, 1662; dp. -um, 995. [Go. -waddjus, OS. wēg.]
wala(‡), wk.m. (or mu.?), ‡*rounded projection on helmet, rim, roll;* 1031 (n.) (see Varr.). [Cp. walu 'mark of blow,' 'ridge' > W A L E; Go. walus 'staff'; Hoops 129.]
Waldend, see Wealdend.
wald-swaþu‡, f. (or -swæþ, n.), *forest-track, -path;* dp. -swaþum, 1403. [W O L D; see swaðu.]
walu, pl., see wæl.
wan, adj., see won(n).
wang, see wong.
wanian, w 2., (1) intr., W A N E, *diminish, waste away;* 1607. — (2) trans., *diminish, lessen;* pret. 3 sg. wanode, 1337; pp. gewanod, 477. [Cp. won-.]
wānigean, w 2., *bewail;* 787. [OHG. weinōn, Ger. weinen.]
warian, w 2., †*guard, occupy, inhabit;* pres. 3 sg. warað, 2277; 3 pl. warigeað, 1358; pret. 3 sg. warode, 1253, 1265. [OS. warōn, Ger. wahren.]
waroð, m., *shore;* ds. -e, 234; ap. -as, 1965. [OHG. werid; Ger. Werder. Cf. *MLN.* xxxii 223; Pal. cxlvii 67 ff.]
wāst, wāt, see witan.
wē, see ic.
wēa, wk.m., WOE, *misery, trouble;* 936; as. wēan, 191, 423, 1206, 1991, 2292, 2937; gp. wēana, 148, 933, 1150, 1396, [F. 25]. Cp. wā.

weal(1), m., W A L L (artificial or natural; of building, cave, rock, elevated shore [229, 572, 1224]); gs. wealles, 2323; ds. wealle, 229, 785, 891, 1573, 2307, 2526, 2542, 2716, 2759, 3060, 3103, 3161; as. weal, 326; ap. weallas, 572, 1224. [Fr. Lat. vallum.] — Cpds.: bord-, eorð-, sǣ-, scild-.
wēa-lāf(†), f., *survivors of calamity;* as. -e, 1084, 1098. (So *Met. Bt.* 1.22; *Wulfst.* 133.13.)
wealdan, rd., *control, have power over, rule,* WIELD, *possess;* w. dat. (instr.); 2038, 2390, 2574 (instr., (n.)), 2827, 2984 (gen.?); pret. 1 sg. wēold, 465; 3 sg. ~, 30, 1057, 2379, 2595; 3 pl. wēoldon, 2051 (gen.?); — w. gen.; pres. 1 sg. wealde, 1859; pret. 1 sg. wēold, 1770; 3 sg. ~, 702; — abs.; inf., 2574(?); 442ᵇ: gif hē wealdan (*manage*) mōt (a set expression, see *Gen.* 2786ᵇ, *Hel.* 220ᵇ; B.-T.: wealdan, V, d.).
ge-wealdan, rd., *control,* WIELD; w. dat.; pret. 3 sg. gewēold, 2703; — w. gen.; inf., 1509; — w. acc.; pret. 3 sg. gewēold, 1554 (*bring about,* cf. Lang. § 20.4); pp. apm. gewealdęne (*subject*), 1732 (cp. Lat. ' subditum facere ').
Wealdend, mc., *ruler, the Lord;* abs., Waldend, 1693; gs. Wealdendes, 2857, Waldendes 2292, 3109; ds. Wealdende, 2329; — w. gen. (wuldres, ylda, etc.); ns. Wealdend, 17, Waldend 1661, 1752, 2741, 2875; as. ~, 183.
weallan, rd., WELL, *surge, boil;* pres. ptc. nsn. weallende, 847, npn. ~, 546, weallendu 581; pret. 3 sg. wēol, 515, 849, 1131, 1422, wēoll 2138, 2593, 2693, 2714, 2882; — fig., of emotions; (subject: hreðer, brēost,) pret. 3 sg. wēoll, 2113,

2331, 2599 (~ sefa wið sorgum); (subject: wælnīðas,) pres. 3 pl. weallað, 2065; pres. ptc. asf. (sorge) weallinde, 2464.
weall-clif‡, n., C L I F F (see weal(1)); as., 3132.
weard, m., GUARD*ian, watchman, keeper, lord, possessor;* 229, 286, 921, 1741, 2239, 2413, 2513, 2580, 3060; as. ~, 2524, 2841, 3066; vs. ~, 1390. [Go. (daúra-)wards.] — Cpds.: bāt-, eorð-, ēþel-, gold-, hord-, hȳð-, land-, ren-, sele-, yrfe-; hlāford; or-wearde.
weard, f., W A R D, *watch;* as. -e, 319. — Cpds.: ǣg-, eoton-, ferh-, hēafod-.
weardian, w 2., (W A R D), GUARD, (†)*occupy;* pret. 3 sg. weardode, 105, 1237; 1 pl. weardodon, 2075; — lāst weardian: (1) *follow;* pret. 3 sg. weardode, 2164 (w. dat.). (2) *remain behind;* inf., 971; so: swaðe weardian; pret. 3 sg. weardade, 2098 (w. dat.).
wearn, f., (*hindrance*), ‡*refusal;* as. wearne (getēoh, *refuse,* cp. forwyrnan), 366. — Cpd.: un-wearnum.
wēa-spel(1)‡, n., *tidings of* WOE; ds. -spelle, 1315.
weaxan, rd., W A X, *grow, increase, flourish;* 3115 (n.); pres. 3 sg. weaxeð, 1741; pret. 3 sg. wēox, 8.
ge-weaxan, rd., W A X, *increase;* pret. 3 sg. gewēox, 66; *develop (so as to bring s.th. about,* tō): ~, 1711.
web(b) (‡)+, nja., W E B, *tapestry;* np. web, 995. — Cp. freoðuwebbe, ge-wif.
weccan, W 1., WAKE, *rouse, stir up;* weccean, 2046, 3024; weccan, 3144 (*kindle*); pret. 3 sg. wehte, 2854 (n.). [Go. (us-)wakjan. See wæccan, wæcnan.] — Cpd.: tō-.

GLOSSARY 421

wed(d), nja., *pledge;* ds. wedde, 2998. [Go. wadi; weddian > W E D.]
weder, n., W E A T H E R; np., 1136; gp. -a, 546.
weg, m., W A Y; as. in on weg, A W A Y, 264, 763, 844, 1382, 1430, 2096; [on wæg, F. 43]. [Go. wigs.] — Cpds.: feor-, fold-, forð-, wīd-.
wēg (wǣg) (†), m., *wave;* as., 3132. [Go. wēgs, Ger. Woge.]
wegan, V, *carry, wear, have* (feelings); 3015; pres. 3 sg. wigeð, 599; opt. 3 sg. wege, 2252; pret. 1 sg. wæg, 1777; 3 sg. ~, 152 (*carry on*), 1207, 1931, 2464, 2704, 2780. [W E I G H; Go. (ga-)wigan.] — Cpd.: æt-.
ge-wegan‡, V, *fight;* 2400. [ON. vega; cp. wīgan. Cf. *Beitr.* xii 178 f.; Falk-Torp: veie II; *JEGPh.* xx 22 ff.; Hoops 256.]
wēg-flota (wǣg-)†, wk.m., *waveFLOATer, ship;* as. -flotan, 1907.
wehte, see **weccan**.
wēl, well, adv. (always stressed), W E L L, *very much, rightly;* wēl, 186, 289, 639, 1045, 1792, 1821, 1833, 1854, 2570, 2601, 2855; well, 1951, 2162, 2812. [W E L L, dial. W E E L; Go. waíla. Cf. *Beibl.* xiii 16 ff., *IF.* xvi 503 f., but also Bülb. § 284, Wright § 145; *ESt.* xliv 326; *Beitr.* li 304 f.]
wēl-hwylc(†), pron., *every* (*one*); adj.: gpm. -ra, 1344; — subst., nsm. wēlhwylc, 266; asn. (*everything*) ~, 874.
welig, adj., WEAL*thy, rich;* asm. -ne, 2607.
wēl-þungen(†), adj. (pp.), *accomplished, excellent;* nsf., 1927 (or: wēl þungen?). [See þēon, 1.]
wēn, fi., *expectation;* 734, 1873, 2323, 2910; as., 383, 1845 (*s.th. to be expected, likely*), [3000]; dp. wēnum, 2895. [Ger. Wahn.] — Cp. orwēna.
wēnan, w 1., W E E N, *expect, think;* w. inf.: pret. 1 sg. wēnde, 933; w. þæt-clause: pres. 1 sg. wēn' ic (T.C. § 25), 338, 442, wēne (ic) 1184; pret. 3 sg. wēnde, 2329; 3 pl. wēndon, 937, 1604, *2187;* — (*expect;*) w. gen.: pres. 1 sg. wēne, 272 (*think*), 2522; w. gen. & inf.: inf., 185; w. gen. & tō (*from*): inf., 157; pres. 1 sg. wēne (ic), 525, wēne 2923; 3 sg. wēneþ, 600; w. gen. & þæt-clause: pret. 3 sg. wēnde, 2239; 3 pl. wēndon, 778, 1596; w. tō: pres. 1 sg. wēne, 1396.
wendan, w 1., *turn;* pres. 3 sg. wendeð, 1739 (intr.). [W E N D; windan; Go. wandjan.] — Cpd.: on-.
ge-wendan, w 1., *turn* (trans.); pret. 3 sg. gewende, 315; *change* (trans.), inf. 186.
wennan, w 1., (*accustom, attach to oneself*), †*entertain, present;* pret. opt. 3 sg. wenede, 1091. [ON. venja.] Cf. Rooth, *Språkvetensk. Sällskap. i Uppsala Förhandl.,* 1922–24, pp. 93 ff. — Cpd.: be-.
weora, gp., see **wer**.
weorc, n., W O R K, *deed;* (see word); gs. weorces, 2299; ds. weorce, 1569; as. weorc, 74, 1656; gp. worca, 289; dp. weorcum, *1833,* 2096; worcum, 1100; — *labor, difficulty, distress;* as. weorc, 1721; dp. weorcum, 1638. — *weorce* (is.), adv., in: weorce wesan, *be painful, grievous;* 1418. — Cpds.: ellen-, heaðo-, niht-; ge-weorc.
weorod, see **werod**.
weorod-rǣdend‡, mc., *ruler of the host, king;* ds. -e, *1142* (n.).
weorpan, III, *throw;* w. acc., pret. 3

sg. wearp, 1531; w. instr. (*throw out*), ~ 2582; — ‡w. acc. of pers. & (instr.) gen. of thing (wæteres), *sprinkle;* inf., 2791 (cf. Bu. Zs. 218; Aant. 38). [Go. waírpan; WARP.] — Cpds.: for-, ofer-.
weorð, adj., *valued, dear, honored;* 1814; comp. weorþra, 1902. [Go. waírþs; W O R T H.] See wyrðe, weorðian.
weorð, n., W O R T H, *price, treasure;* ds. -e, 2496. [Go. waírþ(s).]
weorðan, III, *happen, come to pass, arise;* 2526, 3068; pret. 3 sg. wearð, 767, 1280, 1302, 2003; pp. geworden, 1304, 3078. — w. tō & dat., (*turn to*), *become, prove a source of;* inf., 1707; pret. 1 sg. wearð, 2501; 3 sg. ~, 460, 905, 1261, 1330, 1709 (si.), 2071, 2078, 2384; 3 pl. wurdon, 2203; opt.(?) 2 sg. wurde, 587; — w. pred. adj. or noun, *become;* inf., wurðan, 807; pres. 3 sg. weorðeð, 2913; 3 pl. weorðað, 2066, wurðaþ 282; pret. 3 sg. wearð, 77, 149, 409, 555, 753, 816, 818, 913, 1255, 1269, 1775, 2378, 2392, 2482, 2612; 3 pl. wurdon, 228; opt. 3 sg. wurde, 2731; si. pret. 3 sg.: on fylle wearð ('fell'), 1544; — *auxiliary*, w. pp. of trans. verbs; inf. weorðan, 3177; pres. 3 sg. weorþeð, 414; pret. 3 sg. wearð, 6, 902, 1072, 1239, 1437, 1947, 2310, 2692, 2842, 2961, 2983; opt. 3 sg. [wur]de, 2218; w. pp. of intr. verbs: pret. 3 sg. wearð, 823, 1234. [Go. waírþan, Ger. werden; cp. Lat. vertere; woe W O R T H the day, Ezek. xxx 2.]
ge-weorðan, III, *auxiliary*, w. pp. of trans. verb: pret. 3 sg. gewearð, 3061. — impers., w. acc. of pers. & gen. of thing, *suit, seem good,* (pers.:) *agree upon, decide;* (w.

foll. þæt-clause:) pret. 3 sg. gewearð, 1598 (transl.: *agree in thinking*); pp. ([h]afað) geworden, 2026; (*agree upon*), *settle,* inf. 1996. (Cf. *J EGPh.* xvii 119 ff., xviii 264 ff.)
weorð-ful(l) (‡)+, adj., W O R T H y, *illustrious;* supl. -fullost, 3099.
weorðian, w 2., *honor, exalt, adorn;* pret. 1 sg. weorðode, 2096; opt. 3 sg. weorþode, 1090; pp. geweorðad, 250, 1450; geweorðod, 1959, 2176; gewurþad, 331, 1038, 1645. [weorð.] — Cpd.: wīg-geweorþad.
weorð-līce, adv., W O R T H *i* L Y, *splendidly;* supl. -līcost, 3161; [comp. wurþlīcor, F. 37].
weorð-mynd, f.n.(m.) i., *honor, glory;* 65; as., 1559 (wigena ~, i.e. 'sword'; cf. *Arch.* cxxvi 354: Lat. 'decus,' 'gloria'); gp. -a, 1752; dp. -um, 8, worðmyndum 1186.
weotena, see wita.
weotian (witian), w 2., in weotod, pp., *appointed, ordained, assured, destined;* apf. -e, 1936; [witod, F. 26]. [OS. witod, pp.; Go. witōþ 'law.'] — Cp. be-witian.
wer, m., *man;* 105; gs. weres, 1352 (*male person*); as. wer, 1268, *3172;* np. weras, 216, 1222, 1233, 1440, 1650; gp. wera, 120, 993 (~ ond wīfa), 1731, 3000, [F. 37], weora 2947; dp. werum, 1256. [Cf. *Angl.* xxxi 261.]
wered(‡), n., *sweet drink;* as., 496. (Elsewhere adj., 'sweet.')
werga (wērga?), wk.adj., *accursed, evil;* gsm. wergan (gāstes): 133 (n.), 1747. See werhðo.
wērge, -um, see wērig.
wergend, mc. (pres. ptc.), *defender;* gp. -ra, *2882.* See werian.
(ge-)wērgian, w 2., W E A R Y, *fa-*

GLOSSARY

tigue; pp. gewērgad, 2852. [wē-rig.]
werhðo(†), f., *damnation, punishment in hell;* as., 589. [Go. wargiþa.] See heoro-wearh, grund-wyrgen.
werian, w 1., *defend, protect;* 541; pres. 3 sg. wereð, 453; pret. 3 sg. werede, 1205, 1448; 1 pl. weredon, 1327; pp. npm. (byrnum) werede: 238, 2529. See wergend. [Go. warjan.] — Cpd.: be-.
wērig, adj., W E A R Y; w. gen. (*from*); (sīþes) wērig, 579; dsm. (∼) wērgum, 1794; w. dat., *exhausted* (*by*); asf. wērge, 2937. [OS. (sīð-)wōrig.] — Cpds.: dēað-, fyl-, gūð-.
wērig-mōd†, adj., W E A R Y, *disheartened;* 844, 1543.
werod, n., *band, host, company;* 651; weorod, 290, 2014, 3030; gs. werodes, 259; ds. werede, 1215, weorode 1011, 2346; as. (or ap.) werod, 319; gp. weoroda, 60. [wer 'man'? See Holt. Et.] — Cpds.: eorl-, flet-.
wer-þēod(†), f., *people, nation;* ap. (ofer) werþēode, 899 (cp. 1705).
wesan, see eom.
wēste, adj.ja., *waste, deserted;* asm. wēstne, 2456. [OS. wōsti.]
wēsten(n), nja., *waste, desert, wilderness;* as. wēsten, 1265; fjō. (Siev. § 248 n. 3), ds. wēstenne, 2298.
wīc, n., *dwelling-place, abode;* (pl. freq. w. sg. meaning); gp. wīca, 125, 1125; dp. wīcum, 1612, 3083, wīcun 1304; ap. (as.?) wīc, 821, 2589. [Fr. Lat. vicus; W I C K.] — Cpds.: dēað-, hrēa-.
ge-wīcan(†), 1, *give way, fail;* pret. 3 sg. gewāc, 2577, 2629. [Cp. un-wāc-līc; Ger. weichen.]
wicg(†), nja., *horse;* 1400; ds. wicge, 234, 286; as. wicg, 315; gp. wicga, 1045; ap. wicg, 2174.
wīc-stede†, mi., *dwelling-place, home;* 2462; as., 2607.
wīd, adj., W I D E, *extended, spacious*, gsn.wk.wīdan, 1859; asn. wīd, *2473;* apm. wīde, 877, 1965; (of time,) ds.wk. wīdan, 933, asm.wk. ∼, 2014 (see feorh). — Comp. asn. wīdre, 763, see gewindan.
wīd-cūþ(‡)+, adj., W I D E *ly known, famous;* [390]; nsn., 1256; gsm. -es, 1042; asm. -ne, 1489, *1991.*
wīde, adv., W I D E *ly, far and wide, far;* 74, 79, 898, *1959,* 2261, 2913; wīde geond eorþan: 266, 3099; wīde sprang: 18, 1588, (si.) 2582; wīde gesȳne: 1403, 2316, 2947, 3158; wīde cūð: 2135, 2923, [F. 25].
wīde-ferhð(†), m. n., in: as., adv., *for a long time, for ever, ever;* 702, 937, 1222.
wīd-floga‡, wk.m., *far-*FLI*er;* 2830; as. -flogan, 2346.
wīd-scofen‡, adj. (pp.), *pushed far, far-reaching, great;* 936. [scūfan.] (Cf. *ESt.* xlii 326.)
wīd-wegas†, m.p., W I D E-*stretched* W A Y S (Gummere), *distant* or *far-extending regions;* ap. (geond) ∼, 840, 1704.
wīf, n., *woman, lady;* 615, 2120; gs. wīfes, 1284; ds. wīfe, 639, 2028 (is.); as. wīf, 1158; gp. wīfa, 993. [W I F E.] — Cpds.: āglǣc-, mere-.
wīf-lufu (-lufe)†, wk.f., *love for a woman* (or W I F E); np. -lufan, 2065.
wīg, n. (or m.), *war, fight, warfare;* 23, 1080, 2316, 2872; gs. wīges, 65, 886, 1268, *2298;* ds. wīge, 1084, 1337, 2629; wigge 1656, 1770; as. wīg, 685, 1083, 1247; — *fighting force, valor;* ns. wīg, 350,

1042; gs. wīges, 2323; as. wīg, 2348. — Cpd.: fēðe-.
wiga, wk.m., *warrior;* 629; gp. wigena, 1543, 1559, 3115; dp. wigum, 2395. [Sc. W I E, W Y (E), see Jamieson, *Etym. Dict.*] — Cpds.: æsc-, byrn-, gār-, gūð-, lind-, rand-, scyld-.
wīgan(‡), 1, *fight;* 2509. [Go. weihan.] See wīgend; ge-wegan.
wīg-bealu‡, nwa., *war-*B A L E, *war;* as., 2046.
wīg-bil(l)‡, n., *battle-sword;* -bil, 1607.
wīg-bord†, n., *battle-shield;* as., 2339.
wīg-cræft(‡)+, m., *prowess;* as., 2953.
wīg-cræftig‡, adj., *strong in battle;* asm. -ne, 1811.
wīgend(†), mc., *warrior;* 3099; gs. [wīgen]des, 3154; np. wīgend, 1125, 1814, 3144, [F. 47]; gp. wīgendra, 429, 899, 1972, 2337; ap. wīgend, 3024; [vp. ~, F. 10]. — Cpd.: gār-.
wigeð, see wegan.
wīg-freca‡, wk.m., *warrior;* as. -frecan, 2496; np. ~, 1212.
wīg-fruma‡, wk.m., *war-chief;* 664; ds. -fruman, 2261.
wigge, see wīg.
wīg-getāwa‡, fwō.p., *war-equipments;* dp. -getāwum, 368. [Cp. Go. tēwa. Siev. § 43 n. 4; Keller 116 f.] See gūð-getāwa, ēored-, gryre-, hilde-geatwe.
wīg-geweorþad(‡), adj. (pp.), *distinguished in battle;* 1783. See weorðian.
wīg-gryre‡, mi., *war-horror, martial power;* 1284.
wīg-heafola‡, wk.m., *war-head,* i.e. *helmet;* as. -heafolan, 2661.
wīg-hēap‡, m., *band of warriors;* 477.

wīg-hete‡, mi., (*war-*HATE), *war;* 2120.
wīg-hryre‡, mi., *fall in fight;* as., 1619.
wīg-sigor†, (nc.)m., (*war-*) *victory;* as. (or ds., cf. Lang. § 20.4), 1554.
wīg-spēd†, fi., *success in war, victory;* gp. -a, 697. [S P E E D.]
wigtig, see wītig.
wīg-weorþung†, f., *honor to idols, sacrifice;* ap. -a, 176. [wīh, wēoh, 'idol'; cp. Go. weihs 'holy.']
wiht, fni. (Siev. § 267 b & n. 3), (1) W I G H T), *creature, being;* 120; as., 3038 (fem.). (2) *anything* (in negat. clauses); ns. wiht, 2601; as. ~, 581, 1660, 2348, 2857; — ds. wihte used adverbially, *in any way, at all,* in negat. clauses: 186, 1514, 1995, 2277, 2464, 2687, 2923, in interr. clause: 1991; as. wiht used adverbially (in negat. clauses), *at all,* 541, 862, 1083, 1735, 2854. [W I G H T, W H I T (?); Go. waíhts.] — Cpds.: āht, æl-, ō-wiht.
wil-cuma, wk.m., *welc* O M E *person,* also used like adj.; np. -cuman, 388, 394, 1894. [willa.]
wildēor [wild-dēor], n., W I L D *beast;* ap., 1430. [D E E R. Cf. Siev. § 289.]
wil-geofa†, wk.m., *joy-*G I Ver, *lord;* 2900. [willa.]
wil-gesīþ†, m., *dear companion;* np. -gesīþas, 23. [willa.]
willa, wk.m., W I L L, *wish, desire;* ds. (ānes) willan ('for the sake of one'), 3077; as. willan, 635 (*good will*); on ~, 1739; ofer ('against') ~, 2409, 2589; gp. wilna, 1344(?); dp. (sylfes) willum ('of his own will'), 2222, 2639; — *gratification, pleasure, delight, joy;* ns., 626, 824; ds. willan, 1186, 1711;

as. ~, 2307; dp. willum (' delightfully '), 1821; — *desirable* or *good thing;* gp. wilna, 660, 950, 1344.
willan, anv., W I L L, *wish, desire, be about to;* (1) w. inf.; pres. 1 sg. wille, 344, 351, 427; wylle, 947, 2148, 2512; neg.: nelle, 679, 2524; 2 sg. wylt, 1852; 3 sg. wille, 442, 1184; wile, 346, 446, 1049, 1181, 1832; wyle, 2864; 1 pl. wyllaðˇ, 1818; [3 pl. willaðˇ, F. 9]; opt. [2 sg. wylle, F. 27]; 3 sg. wille, 979, 1314; pret. 1 sg. wolde, 2497; 3 sg. ~, 68, 154, 200, 645, 664, 738, 755, 796, 880, 1010, 1041, 1094 (opt.?), 1277, 1292, 1339, 1494, 1546, 1576, 1791, 1805, 2083, 2090, 2160, 2186, 2294, 2305, 2308, 2315, 2588, 2858, 2940, [F. 21, opt.?]; neg.: nolde, 791, 803, 812, 1523; 3 pl. woldon, 3171; opt. 1 sg. wolde, 2729; neg.: nolde, 2518; 2 sg. wolde, 1175; 3 sg. ~, 988, 990, 2376; 1 pl. woldon, 2636; 3 pl. ~, 482. — (2) without inf.; w. omission of verb of motion: pres. 1 sg. wille, 318; opt. 3 sg. ~, 1371; pret. 1 sg. wolde, 543, cp. 2497 (wesan understood); w. inf. understood fr. prec. verb: pres. 3 sg. (fremme sē þe) wille, 1003, si.: 1394, 2766 (wylle); pret. 3 sg. wolde, 1055, 3055; neg., abs.: (þā Metod) nolde (' willed it not '), 706, 967.
wilnian, w 2., *desire, ask for* (gen.); w. tō (*from, at*); 188.
wil-sīðˇ(†), m., *wished-for journey;* as., 216. [willa.]
wīn, n., W I N E; ds. wīne, 1467; as. wīn, 1162, 1233. [Fr. Lat. vinum.]
wīn-ærn(‡)+, n., W I N E-*hall;* gs. -es, 654.
wind, m., W I N D; 1374, 1907; ds. -e, 217, 1132. — Cpd.: norþan-.
win-dæg(‡), m., D A Y *of labor or strife;* dp. windagum, 1062 (cf. *Angl.* xxxv 460 f.). See winnan, ge-win(n).

windan, III, (1) intr., W I N D, *fly, curl, eddy;* pret. 3 sg. wand, 1119; 3 pl. wundon, 212. — (2) trans., *twist;* pp. wunden (gold, ' made into rings '), 1193, 3134; dsn. wund*num* (golde), 1382. — Cpds.: æt-, be-, on-.
ge-windan III, *go, turn;* pret. 3 sg. (on flēam) gewand, 1001; — inf. (wīdre) gewindan, *reach by flight* (*a more remote place*), 763 (cf. *M Ph.* iii 263).
wind-blond‡, n., *tumult of* W I N D *s;* 3146.
wind-geard‡, m., *home of the* W I N D *s;* 1224 (n.).
windig, adj., W I N D Y; asf. windge, 2456; apm. windige, 572, 1358.
wine(†), mi., *friend*, (*friendly*) *lord;* 30, 148, 2101; gs. wines, 3096; ds. wine, 170; as. ~, 350, 376, 2026; vs. ~, 1183, wine (mīn): 457, 530, 1704, (mīn) wine 2047; gp. winigea, 1664; — applied to retainers (cp. māgas): gp. winia 2567, dp. winum 1418. [OS. wini, ON. vinr, Dan. ven.] — Cpds.: frēa-, frēo-, gold-, gūðˇ-, mǣg-; Ing-.
wine-drihten†, m., (*friendly*) *lord;* ds. -drihtne, 360; as. -drihten, 862, 1604; -dryhten, 2722, 3175.
wine-gēomor‡, adj., *mourning one's friends;* 2239.
wine-lēas†, adj., *friend*L E S S (ref. to exile); dsm. -um, 2613.
wine-mǣg†, m., *friend and kinsman, retainer;* np. -māgas, 65. See Antiq. § 2.
winia, winigea, see wine.
winnan, III, *contend, fight;* [imp. pl. winnað, F. 12]; pret. 2 sg. wunne, 506; 3 sg. wan, 144, 151, won

1132; 3 pl. wunnon, 113, 777. [(ge-)winnan > W I N.]
wīn-recedǂ, n., W Ī N E-*hall;* as., 714, 993.
wīn-seleǂ, mi., W I N E-*hall;* 771; ds., 695; as., 2456.
winter, m., (1) W I N T E R; 1132 (wintęr), 1136; gs. wintrys, 516; as. wintęr, 1128. (2) pl. (in reckoning), *years;* gp. wintra, 147, 264, 1927, 2209, 2278, 2733, 3050; dp. wintrum (frōd), 1724, 2114, 2277. — Cp. syfan-wintre.
wīrǂ, m., W I R E, *metal band, ornament;* gp. -a, 2413; dp. -um, 1031. (Cf. Stjer. 2 f., 143.)
wīs, adj., W I S E; 1845, 3094 (*sound in mind,* see note); nsf., 1927; nsm. wk. wīsa, 1400, 1698, 2329; asm.wk. wīsan, 1318; gpm. wīsra, 1413.
wīsaǂ, wk.m., *leader;* 259. [Cp. wīsian.] — Cpds.: brim-, here-, hilde-.
wīscan (wȳscan), W I., W I S H; pret. 3 pl. wīston, 1604 (n.).
wīs-dōm, m., W I S D O M; 350; ds. -e, 1959.
wīse, wk.f., W I S E, *way, manner;* as. ealde wīsan (semi-adv.), 'after the old fashion,' 1865. (Cp. *Blickl. Hom.* 177.33: ōðre wīsan.)
wīs-fæst(ǂ), adj., W I S E; nsf., 626.
wīs-hycgendeǂ, adj. (pres. ptc.), W I S E *in thought;* 2716.
wīsian, w 2., *show the way, guide, direct, lead;* abs.: pret. 3 sg. wīsode, 402; w. dat. of pers.: pres. 1 sg. wīsige, 292, 3103; pret. 3 sg. wīsode, 320, 1663; wīsade (w. adv. of motion): 370, 1795; — w. acc., *show* or *lead the way to* (a place); inf., 2409; pret. 3 sg. wīsade, 208.
wisse, -on, see witan.
wist, fi., (*sustenance*), *feast*(*ing*), *abundance, prosperity;* ds. -e, 128, 1735. [wesan.]
wiste, -on, see witan.
wist-fylloǂ, wk.f., F I L L *of feasting, plentiful meal;* gs. -fylle, 734.
wīston, see wīscan.
wit(t), nja., W I T, *intelligence;* wit, 589. — Cpds.: fyr-, ge-.
wit, pers. pron., see ic.
wita, wk.m., *wise man, councilor;* np. witan, 778; gp. witena, 157, 266, 936; weotena, 1098. [witan.] — Cpds.: fyrn-, rūn-.
witan, prp., *know;* witan, 252, 288; pres. 1 sg. wāt, 1331, 1830, 1863, 2656; neg. (ic) nāt (hwylc, cp. nāthwylc), 274; 2 sg. wāst, 272; 3 sg. wāt, 2650; neg. nāt, 681; opt. 3 sg. wite, 1367; pret. 3 sg. wisse, 169 (n.), 715, 1309, 2339, 2410, 2725; wiste, 646, 764 (n.), 821; 2 pl. wisson, 246; 3 pl. wiston, 181, 798, 878; opt. 1 sg. wiste, 2519. [(to) W I T, W O T, W I S T.]
ge-witan, prp., *know, ascertain;* 1350.
wītan, 1, w. dat. of pers. & acc. of thing, *lay to (s.b.'s) charge;* 2741. — Cpds.: æt-, oð-.
ge-wītan, 1, *depart, go;* in many instances (marked*) followed by verb of motion; freq. w. reflex. pron.; 42; pres. 3 sg. gewīteð, 1360, 2460; imp. pl. gewītaþ, 291*; pret. 3 sg. gewāt, 26*, 115*, 123*, 210, 217, 234*, 662, 1236, 1263*, 1274*, 1601, 1903*, 1963*, 2387*, 2401*, 2471, 2569*, 2624 (of caldre ~), 2819*, 2949*, 3044*, [F. 43*]; 3 pl. gewiton, 301*, 853*, 1125*. See forðgewiten, wutun.
wītig(ǂ), adj., *wise;* wītig (God): 685, 1056; ~ (Drihten), 1554; wigtig (~), 1841.

GLOSSARY

wītnian, w 2., *punish, torment;* pp. gewītnad, 3073. [wīte.]
witod, see weotian.
wið, prep., w. dat. & w. acc. (marked*); basic meaning *against;* (motion:) *against, opposite, near, towards;* 213, 326*, 749* (n.), 1977*, 1978, 2013*, 2560, 2566*, 2673* (*as far as*), 2925*, 3049 (*in*); (w. fōn, grāpian, wiðgrīpan:) 439, 1566, 2520, 2521; — (opposition, fighting, defense, protection:) *against*, W I T H; 113, 144, 145, 152*, 174, 178, 294*, 319*, 384 (*?), 440, 506(*?), 540*, 550, 660, 827, 1132, 1549ᵃ*, 1549ᵃ*, (1997*), 2341, 2371, 2400, 2839, 2914*, 3004; — (mutual relation, behavior:) *towards, with;* 155*, 811*, 1173*, 1864ᵃ*, 1864ᵃ*, 1954*; (conversation, transaction:) *with*, 365, 424*, 425, 426, cp. 1997* (agreement); (si.:) 523, 2528*; — (association, sharing:) *with;* 1088*, 2534(*?), 3027*; — (mingling, close contact:) 1880 (*within*, cf. *ZfdPh.* xxi 363, Aant. 33), 2600 (*with*); — (separation:) *from*, 733, 2423. — (Note interchange of acc. & dat.: 424–25 f.; 1977–78.) [Cp. Dan. ved, Swed. vid.]
wiðer-ræhtes‡, adv., *opposite;* 3039. [wið; Go. wiþra; riht (Lang. § 7.5); cf. *Beitr.* xxxvi 432.]
wið-fōn‡, rd., w. dat., *lay hold on;* pret. 3 sg. -fēng, 760.
wið-grīpan‡, 1, *grapple* W I T H; 2521.
wið-habban, w 3., w. dat., *hold out against*, W I T H *stand;* pret. 3 sg. -hæfde, 772.
wiðre†, nja., *resistance;* gs. wiðres, 2953.
wlanc, see wlonc.
wlātian†, w 2., *gaze, look out for* (w. gen., cf. *Beitr.* xii 97); pret. 3 sg.

wlātode, 1916. [wlītan; Go. wlaitōn.]
wlenco, wk.f., *pride, high spirit, daring;* ds. (for) wlenco: 338, 1206, (∼) wlence, 508. [wlonc.]
wlītan†, 1, *look, gaze;* pret. 3 sg. wlāt, 1572; 3 pl. wliton, 1592, wlītan 2852. — Cpd.: giond-.
wlite, mi., *countenance, appearance, beauty;* 250. [Go. wlits; wlītan.]
wlite-beorht†, adj., *beautiful;* asm. -ne, 93.
wlite-sēon‡, fi., *sight, spectacle;* 1650. Cp. wundor-sīon.
wlitig, adj., *beautiful;* asn., 1662.
wlonc, adj., *proud, high-spirited, bold;* 331; wlanc, 341; gs. wlonces, 2953; *proud of, glorying in*, w. gen.: wlonc 2833, w. dat.: wlanc 1332. — Cpd.: gold-.
wōc, see wæcnan.
wōh, adj., *crooked, perverse;* dpn. wōm, 1747. [Go. (un-)wāhs; *IF.* xli 333 ff.]
wōh-bogen‡, adj. (pp.), *bent, coiled;* 2827. [būgan.]
wolcen, n., *cloud;* pl. *clouds, sky*, WELKIN; dp. (tō) wolcnum: 1119, 1374; (under) wolcnum: 8, 651, 714, 1631, 1770 (in 8 & 1770 = ' on earth '); [F. 8].
wolde, see willan.
wollen-tēar‡, adj., *with gushing* T E A R s; npm. -e, 3032. [pp. of *wellan, ON. vella; cp. weallan.]
wōm, see wōh.
wom(m), m., *stain, blot, evil;* dp. womum, 3073 (perh. semi-adv., *grievously*). [Go. wamm, or wamms; *IF.* xli 46 ff.]
won, pret., see winnan.
won(n), adj., *dark, black;* nsn. won, 1374; wk.m. wonna, 3024, 3115; dsf. wanre, 702; npn. wan, 651. [W A N.]
wong(†), m., *plain, field, land, coun-*

try, place; ds. wonge, 2242, 3039; wange 2003; as. wong, 1413, 2409, 3073, wang 93, 225; np. wongas, 2462. [Go. waggs.] — Cpds.: freoðo-, grund-, meodo-, sǣ-.

wong-stede†, mi., *place;* ds., 2786.

won-hȳd (-hygd)†, fni., *recklessness;* dp. -um, 434. [Cp. wana; Go. wans; WANT.]

won-sǣlī (-sǣlig)†, adj., *unhappy;* 105.

won-sceaft(†), fi., *misery;* as., 120.

wōp, m., WEEP*ing, lamentation;* 128; ds. wōpe, 3146; as. wōp, 785.

worc, see **weorc**.

word, n., W O R D; 2817; gs. -es, 79, 2791; ds. (is.) -e, 2156; as. word, 315, 341, 390, 654, 2046, 2551; np. ∼, 612, 639; gp. worda, 289 (∼ ond worca), 398, 2246, 2662, 3030 (wyrda nē ∼); dp. wordum, 30, 176, 366, 388, 626, 874, 1172, 1193, 1318, 1492, 1811, 1980, 2058, 2669, 2795, 3175; ∼ (nē worcum), 1100, ∼ (ond ∼), *1833;* ap. word, 870. — Cpds.: bēot-, gylp-, lēafnes-, meþel-, þrȳð-.

word-cwide(†), mi., W O R D S, *speech;* gp. -cwida, 1845; dp. -cwydum, 2753; ap. -cwydas, 1841. [cweðan.]

word-gyd(d)‡, nja., *lay, elegy;* as. -gyd, 3172.

word-hord†, n., W O R D-H O A R D, *store of words;* as., 259.

word-riht††, n., (W O R D-R I G H T), *right word, censure;* gp. -a, 2631.

worhte, see **wyrcan**.

worn, m., *large number, great quantity;* freq. w. partit. gen.; as., 264, 870, 2114 (*many things*), *3154;* — combined w. eall: as. worn eall, 3094 (*a great many things*), w. fela: ns. worn fela, 1783; as., 530, cᴅ. 870; — gp. (partit. gen. depend. on fela): worna fela, 2003, 2542 (cp. Go. manageins filu).

worold, f., W O R L D; (eal) worold, 1738 ('everything'); gs. worolde, 950, 1062 (∼ brūceð, cp. Lat. mundo uti, 'live'), 1080, 1387, 1732; worulde, 2343, 3068, worlde 2711; as. worold, 60, 1183, 1681. [OHG. weralt, Ger. Welt.]

worold-ār(‡)+, f., W O R L D *ly honor* (*Angl.* xxxv 116); as. -e, 17.

worold-cyning†, m., (*earthly*) K I N G; gp. -a, 1684, wyruldcyning[a], 3180.

worðig, m., *enclosed homestead, precinct*(*s*); as., 1972. (Cf. Middendorff, *Ae. Flurnamenbuch*, pp. 148 f.; Holt., *Beibl.* xxxiv 349; Hoops, Pal. cxlvii 72 f.)

worð-mynd, see **weorð-mynd**.

woruld-candel‡, f., W O R L D-C A N-D L E (*sun*); 1965.

woruld-ende‡, mja., E N D *of the* W O R L D; ds., 3083.

wracu, f., *revenge, punishment;* as. wrǣce, 2336. [wrecan; Go. wraka.] — Cpds.: gyrn-, nȳd-.

wrǣc, n. (f.?, see B.-T.), *misery, distress;* 170; as., 3078. [Cp. WRACK, WRECK; wrecan; Go. wrēkei.]

wrǣcca, see **wrecca**.

wrǣce, see **wracu**.

wrǣc-lāst (wrǣc-?)†, m., *track or path of exile;* ap. -as, 1352.

wrǣc-mǣcg (wrǣc-?)†, mja., *banished man, outcast;* np. -as, 2379. See **mago**.

wrǣc-sīð (wrǣc-?), m., *exile, misery;* as., 2292; dp. -um, 338. [OS. wrak-sīð.]

wrǣt(t)†, f., *ornament, work of art;* gp. wrǣtta, 2413; dp. wrǣttum, 1531; ap. wrǣ́te, 2771, 3060. [Holt., *Beibl.* xxxv 253: *wraitiþu, cp. wrītan.]

wrǣt-līc(†), adj., *ornamental, splen-*

GLOSSARY

did, wondrous; nsf., 1650; asm.
-ne, 891, 2173; asn. -līc, 1489,
2339.
wrāð, adj., hostile (subst.: foe);
fierce; dsm. wrāþum, 660, 708;
asn. (or p.) wrāð, 319; gp. wrāðra,
1619. [W R O T H; OS. wrēð; cp.
wrīþan.]
wrāðe, adv., grievously; 2872.
wrāð-līce(‡), adv., cruelly, severely;
3062.
wrecan, v, drive, force; pp. wrecen,
2962; drive out; pret. 3 sg. wræc,
2706; — recite, utter; inf., 873,
3172; pres. opt. 3 sg. wrece, 2446;
pret. 3 sg. wræc, 2154; pp. wrecen,
1065; — avenge; inf., 1278, 1339,
1546; pres. opt. 3 sg. wrece, 1385;
pret. 1 sg. wræc, 423, 1669; 3 sg.
∼, 1333. [W R E A K.] — Cpds.:
ā-, for-; un-wrecen. See wrecend.
ge-wrecan, v, avenge, punish; pret.
1 sg. gewræc, 2005; 3 sg. ∼, 107,
2121, 2395, 2875; 3 pl. gewrǣcan,
2479; pp. gewrecen, 3062.
wrecca, wk.m., exile, adventurer, hero
(cf. Beitr. xxxv 483); 1137; [wrec-
cea, F. 25]; ds. wrǣcca[n], 2613;
gp. wreccena, 898. [W R E T C H;
OS. wrekkio, Ger. Recke. Cp.
wrecan.]
wrecend, mc., avenger; 1256.
wreoþen-hilt‡, adj., with twisted
H I L T; nsn., 1698. [wrīþan.]
(Cf. Stjer. 23 f.)
wrīdian, w 2., grow, flourish; pres.
3 sg. wrīdað, 1741.
wrītan, I, cut, engrave (W R I T E);
pp. writen, 1688. — Cpd.: for-.
wrīþan, I, (twist), bind; 964; — bind
up; pret. 3 pl. wriðon, 2982.
[W R I T H E.] — Cp. hand-gewri-
þen; bēah-wriða.
wrixl, f., exchange; ds. -e, 2969. [Cp.
Ger. Wechsel.]
wrixlan, w 1., w. dat., change, vary,

exchange; (wordum) wrixlan: 366,
874.
wrōht, f., (accusation), quarrel,
strife; 2287, 2473, 2913. [Cp.
wrēgan; Go. wrōhs.]
wudu, mu., W O O D; tree(s); ns.,
1364; as., 1416; — spear; as. (or
p.), 398; — ship; ns., 298; as.,
216, 1919. — Cpds.: bæl-, bord-,
gomen-, heal-, holt-, mægen-, sǣ-,
sund-, þrec-; Hrefna-.
wudu-rēc‡, mi., W O O D-smoke; 3144.
[R E E K.]
wuldor, n., glory, heaven (cp. Lat.
' gloria '); gs. wuldres, 17, 183,
931, 1752. [Go. wulþrs, cp. wul-
þus.] — Cpd.: Kyning-.
wuldor-torht†, adj., gloriously bright;
npn. wk. wuldortorhtan, 1136.
Wuldur-cyning(†), m., K I N G of
glory; ds. -e, 2795. (Cf. Angl.
xxxv 124 f.)
wulf, m., W O L F; as., 3027. [Go.
wulfs.]
wulf-hliþ‡, n., W O L F-slope, retreat
of wolves; ap. -hleoþu, 1358. (Cf.
J E G Ph. xxxiv 2c-23.)
wund, f., W O U N D; 2711, 2976; as.
-e, 2531, 2725, 2906; dp. -um,
1113, 2830, 2937; [ap. -a, F. 47].
— Cpd.: feorh-.
wund, adj., W O U N Ded; 2746, [F.
43]; dsm. -um, 2753; npm. -e, 565,
1075. [Go. wunds.]
wunden-feax‡, adj., with (W O U N D)
braided hair, or with curly mane;
nsn., 1400. (Cp. wundenloc(c);
Siev. xxxvi 432 f., Tupper's Riddles, pp. 125 f.)
wunden-hals‡, adj., with (W O U N D)
curved (neck, i.e.) prow; 298.
wunden-mǣl‡, n., sword with
(W O U N D) curved markings (ornaments); as., 1531. See brogden-
mǣl.
wunden-stefna‡, wk.m., ship with

(w o u n d) *curved* (s t e m) *prow;* 220.
wunder-fæt‡, n., w o n d e R*ful vessel;* dp. wunderfatum, 1162. [v a t.]
wundor, n., w o n d e r, *wonderful thing;* 771, 1724, wundur 3062 (n.); ds. wundre, 931; as. wundor, 840; wunder, 931; wundur, 2759 (?), 3032, 3103 (?); gp. wundra, 1509 (*strange beings, monsters*), 1607; dp. (adv.) wundrum, *wonderfully,* 1452, *2687;* ap. wundur, 2759, 3103. — Cpds.: hond-, nīð-, searo-.
wundor-bebod‡, n., *strange* or *mysterious command* (*advice*); dp. wundorbebodum, 1747 (n.).
wundor-dēað‡, m., w o n d r *ous* d e a t h; ds. wundordēaðe, 3037.
wundor-līc, adj., w o n d e r *ful, strange;* 1440 (wundor-).
wundor-sīon‡, fi., w o n d r *ous sight;* gp. wundorsīona, 995.
wundor-smiþ‡, m., w o n d e r- s m i t h, i.e. *smith who makes wonderful things,* or *who works by wondrous art* (B.-T.); gp. wundorsmiþa, 1681. (Cf. Earle's note; *Angl.* xxxv 260 n. 4.)
wundur-māððum‡, m., w o n d r *ous jewel;* as. wundurmāððum, 2173.
wunian, w 2., *dwell, live, remain, continue, be situated;* 3083 (w. dat. [instr.]: wīcum), 3128; pres. 3 sg. wunað, 284, 1735, 1923; pret. 3 sg. wunode, 1128, 2242; — w. acc., (†)*inhabit, occupy;* inf., 1260; pres. 3 sg. wunað, 2902. [w o n (Sc., obs.), w o N t; Ger. wohnen.]
ȝe-wunian, w 2., w. acc., †*remain with, stand by* (*s.b.*); pres. opt. 3 pl. gewunigen, 22.
wurð-, see **weorð-**.
wutun, uton, w. inf., introd. ad- hortative clause, *let us;* wutun, 2648; uton, 1390, 3101. [OS. wita; cp. ge-wītan.]
wyl(l)e, wyllað, wylt, see **willan.**
wylm, mi., w e l l *ing, surging, flood;* 1764, 2269, wælm 2546; gs. wælmes, 2135 (*surging water*); as. wylm, 1693; dp. wylm[um], 516; ap. wylmas, 2507. [weallan.] — Cpds.: brēost-, brim-, bryne-, cear-, fȳr-, heaðo-, holm-, sǣ-, sorh-.
wyn(n), fjō.(i.), *joy, delight, pleasure;* wyn, 2262; ds. wynne, 2014; as. ∼, 1080, 1730, 1801 (heofones ∼, ' sun '), 2107, 2727; dp. wynnum, 1716, 1887. [See wyn-sum; Ger. Wonne.] — Cpds.: ēðel-, hord-, līf-, lyft-, symbel-.
wyn-lēas†, adj., *joy*L E S S; asm. -ne, 1416; ap.(s.?)n. -lēas, 821.
wyn-sum, adj., *joyous, pleasant, fair;* asm.wk. -an, 1919; npn. -e, 612. [w i n s o m e.]
wyrcan, w 1., w o r k, *do, make;* 930; pret. 3 sg. worhte, *92*, 1452; w. gen., *acquire, endeavor to win:* pres. opt. 3 sg. wyrce, 1387 (cp. 1491). [Go. waúrkjan.] — Cpd.: be-.
ge-wyrcan, w 1., *make, perform, carry out, accomplish, achieve;* 1660; gewyrcean, 69, 2337, 2802, 2906; pres. 1 sg. gewyrce, 1491; pret. 3 sg. geworhte, 1578, 2712; 3 pl. geworhton, 3156; opt. 1 sg. geworhte, 635 ('gain'); 2 pl. geworhton, 3096; pp. geworht, 1696; apm. (fæste) geworhte ('disposed'), 1864 (cf. *Aant.* 28, *MPh.* iii 461); w. þæt-clause, *bring* (it) *about* (that): inf. gewyrcean, 20.
wyrd, fi., *fate, destiny;* 455, 477, 572, 734 (*destined*), 1205, 2420, 2526, 2574, 2814; as., 1056, 1233; *event,*

GLOSSARY

fact, gp. -a, 3030. [W E I R D; weorðan.] (Cf. Intr. xlviii f.)

wyrdan, w I., *injure, destroy;* pret. 3 sg. wyrde, 1337. [Go. (fra-)wardjan; weorðan.] Cpd.: ā-.

wyrm, mi., *serpent;* ap. -as, 1430; (*dragon:*) ns., 897, 2287, 2343, 2567, 2629, 2669, 2745, 2827; gs. wyrmes, 2316, 2348, 2759, 2771, 2902; ds. wyrme, 2307, 2400, 2519; as. wyrm, 886, 891, 2705, 3039, 3132. [W O R M.] — See draca.

wyrm-cyn(n), nja., *race of serpents;* gs. -cynnes, 1425.

wyrm-fāh‡, adj., *with serpentine ornamentation;* nsn., 1698. (Cf. Stjer. 22, 29.)

wyrm-hord‡, n., *dragon's* H O A R D; as., 2221.

wyrp, fjō., *change (for the better);* as. -e, 1315. [weorpan.]

ge-wyrpan, w I., refl., *recover;* pret. 3 sg. (hyne) gewyrpte, 2976. [See wyrp.]

wyrsa, compar. (cp. posit. yfel), W O R S E; gsn. (or p.) wyrsan, 525 (n.); dsf. ~, 2969; asn. wyrse, 1739; *inferior* (applied to foreigners, enemies): asm. wyrsan (wīgfrecan), 2496; npm. ~ (~), 1212.

wyrt, fi., *root;* dp. -um, 1364. [W O R T.]

wyrðe, adj.ja., w. gen., W O R T H y *of, fit for;* npm., 368; comp. nsm. wyrðra, 861; — *entitled to, possessed of;* asm. wyrðne (gedōn), 2185 (n.). [weorð.] — Cpds.: fyrd-, hord-.

wyruld-, see worold-.

yfel, n., E V I L; gp. yfla, 2094. [Go. ubils.]

ylca, pron., (*the*) *same;* gsn.(wk.) ylcan, 2239. [I L K.]

yldan, w I., *delay* (trans.); 739. [eald.]

ylde†, mi.p., *men;* gp. ylda, 1661, ylda (bearn): 150, 605, yldo (~), 70 (n.); dp. yldum, 77, 705, 2117; eldum, 2214, 2314, 2611, 3168. [eald; OS. eldi.]

yldesta, see eald.

yldo, wk.f., *age, old age;* 1736, 1766, 1886; ds. ylde, 22; eldo, 2111. [E L D; eald.]

yldra, see eald.

ylfe, mi.p., E L V E s; 112. (Cf. Grimm D.M. 365 ff. [442 ff.]; *R.-L.* i 551 ff.) See Ælf-here.

ymb, ymbe, prep., w. acc.; (place:) *about, around, near;* ymb, 399, 568, 668, 689 (postpos., stressed), 838, 1012, 1030, 2477; ymbe, 2883, 3169, [F. 33]; postpos., stressed, w. dat. (semi-adv.): 2597; — (time:) *after* (cf. Siev. xxix 323 ff.); ymb, 135, 219; — (fig.:) *about, concerning;* ymb, 353, 439, 450, 507, 531, 1536, 1595, 2509, 3172; ymbe, 2070, 2618. [OS. OHG. umbi. See T.C. § 13.]

ymb-beorgan‡, III, *protect (round about);* pret. 3 sg. -bearh, 1503.

ymbe-fōn, rd., *clasp, enclose;* pret. 3 sg. -fēng, 2691.

ymbe-hweorfan, III, *move* (intr.) *about* (w. acc.); pret. 3 sg. -hwearf, 2296.

ymb-ēode, anv., pret. (see gān), *went round* (w. acc.); 3 sg., 620.

ymb-sittan, V, S I T *round* (w. acc.); pret. 3 pl. -sǣton, 564.

ymb(e)-sittend†, mc.p., *neighboring peoples* (*those living* [S I T T *ing*] *about,* or *on the borders*); np. ymbsittend, 1827; gp. ymbsittendra, 9; ymbesittendra, 2734.

yppe(‡)+, wk.f., *raised floor, high seat;* ds. yppan, 1815. [up, uppe.]

yrfe, nja., *heritage;* 3051. [Go. arbi.]
yrfe-lāf†, f., *heirloom;* ds. -e, 1903; as. -e, 1053.
yrfe-weard, m., (GUARDian *of an inheritance*), *heir;* 2731; gs. -as, 2453.
yrmþ(u), f., *misery;* as. yrmþe, 1259; gp. ~, 2005 (n.). [earm.]
yrre, nja., *anger;* ds., 2092; as., 711.
yrre, adj.ja., *angry;* 1532, 1575, 2073, 2669; gsm. eorres, 1447; npm. yrre, 769. [Go. aírzeis.]
yrre-mōd‡, adj., *angry (of* MOOD); 726.
yrringa, adv., *angrily;* 1565, 2964.
ys, see eom.
ȳð, fjō., *wave;* np. ȳþa, 548; gp.~, 464, 848, 1208, 1469, 1918; dp. ȳðum, 210, 421, 515, 534, 1437, 1907, 2693; ap. ȳðe, 46, 1132, 1909. [OS. ūðia.] — Cpds.: flōd-, līg-, wæter-.
ȳðan, w 1., *destroy;* pret. 1 sg. ȳðde, 421. [Go. auþs, Ger. öde.]

ȳðe, adj., see ēaðe.
ȳðe-līce, adv., *easily;* 1556.
ȳð-geblond‡, n., *tossing waves, surge, surging water;* 1373, 1593; np. -gebland, 1620. [blandan.]
ȳþ-gesēne, see ēþ-gesȳne.
ȳð-gewin(n)‡, n., *wave-strife; swimming,* gs. -es, 1434; *tossing water,* ds. -e, 2412.
ȳþ-lād†, f., *way across the waves, voyage;* np. -e, 228. [līðan.]
ȳð-lāf†, f., LEAVing *of waves, (sand on) shore;* ds. -e, 566. (Cf. Aant. 11 f.; Hoops 81, St. 98 f.)
ȳð-lida‡, wk.m., *wave-traverser, ship;* as. -lidan, 198. [līðan.]
ȳwan, w 1., *show, manifest;* pres. 3 sg. ēaweð, 276; ēoweð, 1738; pret. 3 sg. ȳwde, 2834.
ge-ȳwan, w 1., *show, present, bestow;* (ēstum) geȳwan, 2149; pp. (~) geēawed 1194.

PROPER NAMES

[Note the abbreviation, Schönf. =L 4.79.4.]

Ābel, m., *biblical person;* as., 108.
Ælf-here, mja., *kinsman of Wīglāf;* gs. -es, 2604. [ælf- ' elf,' cf. Lang. § 7 n. 3; here ' army.'] (Cf. Bu. 51.)
Æsc-here, mja., *a counselor and warrior of Hrōðgār's;* 1323, 1329; gs. -es, 1420; ds. -e, 2122. [æsc (ON. askr), (' ash '-)' spear ' (Scand. ' boat '; see *Mald.* 69).]
Ār-Scyldingas, see **Scyldingas.**
Bēan-stān, m., *father of Breca;* gs. -es, 524. [Icel. bauni ' shark,' ' dogfish ' (or OE. bēan ' bean '?). Cf. *ZfdA.* vii 421; *MLN.* xviii 118, xx 64; Varr.: 524; Notes, p. 148, n. 4.]
Beorht-Dene, see **Dene.**
Bēowulf, m., *Danish king, son of Scyld;* 18, 53. [Prob. for Bēow, cf. bēow ' barley '; see Intr. xxvi, xxviii; Björkman L 4.82 a, & *ESt.* lii 145 ff.]
Bēowulf, Bīowulf, m., (Bēowulf Gēata 676, 1191), *the hero of the poem.* (The *īo* form is confined to the second part of the MS., in which it is regularly used with the exception of ll. 1971, 2207, 2510; cf. Lang. § 17.1 b, Intr. xc.) — ns., 343 (Bēowulf is mīn nama), 405, 506, 529, 631, 676, 957, 1024, 1191, 1299, 1310, 1383, 1441, 1473, 1651, 1817, 1880, 1999, 2359, 2425, 2510, 2724; gs. -es, 501, 795, 856, 872 & 1971 (sīð Bēowulfes), 2194, 2681, 2807 (Bīowulfes biorh); ds. -e, 609, 623, 818, 1020, 1043, 1051, 2207, 2324, 2842, 2907, 3066, [3151]; as. -, 364, 653, 2389; vs. -, 946; wine mīn B.: 457, 1704; B. lēofa: 1216, 1758; lēofa B.: 1854, 1987, 2663. — Note: Bēowulf maðelode: 405, 2510, 2724; Bēowulf maþelode, bearn Ecgþēowes: 529, 631, 957, 1383, 1473, 1651, 1817, 1999, 2425. — [' bee-wolf '; see Intr. xxv ff.]
Breca, wk.m., *chief of the Brondingas;* 583; d.(a.?)s. Brecan, 506; as. ~, 531. [Cf. brecan ofer bæðweg, *El.* 244, *Andr.* 223, 513; Björkman, *Beibl.* xxx 170 ff.: perh. brecan = ' rush ', ' storm '; ON. breki, ' breaker.']
Brondingas, m.p., *tribal name;* gp. -a, 521. [brond ' sword '?; ON. brandr, ' ship's beak (prow).' Cf. Cha. Wid. 111; Björkman, *Beibl.* xxx 174 ff.]
Brōsinga (gp.) mene, 1199, see Notes, p. 178. [Etym. of ON. Brísinga (men), brísingr: Bu. 75; *R.-L.* i 314.] (Müllenhoff, *ZfdA.* xii 304: Breosingas, = Brisingas.)

Cāin, m., *biblical person; 1261* (MS. camp); gs. Cāines (altered fr. cames), 107.

Dæg-hrefn, m., *a warrior of the Hūgas;* ds. Dæghrefne, 2501 (n.). [dæg ' day '; hrefn ' raven '; see 1801 f.]
Dene, mi.p., *Danes* (national and geographical designation); np., 2050; gp. Dena, Denig(e)a, Denia, 155, 498, 657, 1670, 2035; land

~, 242, 253, si. 1904; folce(s) ~, 465, 1582; ~ lēode (-um), 389, 599, 696, 1323, 1712, 2125; wine ~, 350; aldor ~, 668; ~ frēan, 271, 359, 1680; dp. Denum, 767, 823, 1158, 1417, 1720, 1814, 2068; ap. Dene, 1090. [ON. Danir. Cf. OE. denu 'valley'? See Much, *R.-L.* i 388; Noreen, *Spridda Studier* ii 138 ff.; Zachrisson, *Acta philol. Scandinavica* i 284 ff., and *Studier tillägnade Axel Kock* (1929) 494 ff.: 'woodlanders'; O. Scand. dan, cp. OE. dæn(n).] — Cpds.: a) **Beorht-Dene**; gp. -a, 427, 609. [beorht 'bright.'] **Gār-Dene**; gp. -a, 1; dp. -um, 601, 1856, 2494. [gār 'spear'; for names of persons compounded w. gār, see Sweet, *Oldest Engl. Texts*, p. 586; Keller 140; cp. Gārmund (l. 1962), Hrōðgār.] **Hring-Dene**; np., 116, 1279; gp. -a, 1769. [hring 'corslet.'] — b) **Ēast-Dene**; gp. -a, 392, 616; dp. -um, 828. **Norð-Dene**; dp. -um, 783. **Sūð-Dene**; gp. -a, 463; ap. -e, 1996. **West-Dene**; dp. -um, 383, 1578. — Cp. Healf-Dene. — See Scyldingas, Ingwine.

Ēad-gils, m., *Swedish prince, son of Ōhthere;* ds. -e, 2392. [ēad 'wealth'; gīs(e)l 'hostage.']

Eafor, see Eofor.

Ēan-mund, m., *Swedish prince, son of Ōhthere;* gs. -es, 2611.

Earna-næs, m., *a promontory in the land of the Geats*, near the scene of the dragon fight; as., 3031. [earn 'eagle.']

Ēast-Dene, see Dene.

Ecg-lāf, m., *a Dane, father of Unferð;* gs. Ecglāfes: ~ bearn, 499; sunu ~, 590, 980, 1808; mago ~, 1465. [ecg 'sword'; lāf 'remnant.']

Ecg-þēow, mwa., *father of Bēowulf;* 263, 373 (Ecgþēo); gs. Ecgþēowes: bearn ~, 529, 631, 957, 1383, 1473 1651, 1817, 1999 (-ðīoes), 2177, 2425; sunu ~, 1550, 2367, 2398 (-ðīowes); maga ~, 2587. [ecg 'sword'; þēow 'servant.' Cf. ON. Eggþér.]

Ecg-wela, wk.m., *(unknown) Danish king;* gs. -an, 1710 (n.). [ecg 'sword'; wela 'wealth'; L5.71.5?]

Eofor, m., *a Geat, the slayer of Ongenþēow;* gs. Eofores 2486, Eafores 2964; ds. Iofore, 2993, 2997. [eofor 'boar.']

Ēo-mēr, m., *son of the Angle king Offa; 1960.* [eoh 'horse'; mǣre 'famous.'] (Baeda, *H.E.* ii, c. 9: Eumer, *OE. Bede* 122.9: Ēomǣr.)

Eormen-rīc, m., *king of the East Goths;* gs. -es, 1201. [eormen- 'immense'; rīce 'powerful,' cf. Go. reiks 'ruler.'] (Baeda, *H.E.* ii, c. 5: Irminricus; Sweet, *Oldest English Texts*, p. 171: Iurmenrīc.)

Ēotan, wk.m.p., *'Jutes'; the people of Finn, the Frisian king:* gp. Ēotena, 1072, 1088, 1141; dp. Ēotenum, 1145; — *Jutes:* dp. ~, 902. (Cf. Introd. to *The Fight at Finnsburg*, p. 233; *Zfvgl. Spr.* l 142; *Beitr.* li 10 f.)

Fin(n), m., *king of the East Frisians;* Fin, 1096, 1152; gs. Finnes, 1068, 1081, 1156; ds. Finne, 1128; as. Fin, 1146.

Finnas, m.p., *Finns (Lapps)*; gp. -a, 580. See Notes, p. 148. [Cf. Schönf, 275 f.]

Fitela, wk.m., *nephew (and son) of Sigemund;* 879, 889. [Etym. of Fitela, ON. Sinfjǫtli, OHG. Sintarfizzilo: Grimm, *ZfdA.* i 2–6;

PROPER NAMES

Raszmann, *Die deutsche Heldensage* i 66; Müllenhoff, *ZfdA.* xxiii 161–163; *P. Grdr.*[1] ii[a] 185,[2] ii[a] 87; *ESt.* xvi 433 f.; *Beitr.* xvi 363–66, 509 f., xxx 97 f.; Koegel L 4.8. i[a] 173, i[b] 200; — Gering L 10.1.2. 183 n.; *Beitr.* xviii 182 n. 2; *ZfdPh.* xl 392 ff.; — *Beitr.* xxxv 265. Björk. Eig. 27 ff.; Much, *ZfdA.* lxvi 15 ff. (kenning for 'wolf'; Fitela shortened from the compound form as found in OHG. and ON.).]

Folc-walda, wk.m., *father of Finn;* gs. -an, 1089. [Cf. 2595.]

Francan, wk.m.p., *Franks;* gp. Francna, 1210; dp. Froncum, 2912. ['spear-men'? (cf. OE. franca 'spear')?? Or 'freemen'? Or 'bold ones'? Cf. Schönf. 91; Cha. Wid. 195 f.; Much, *R.-L.* ii 83; Björkman, *Beibl.* xxx 177.]

Frēa-waru, f., *daughter of Hrōðgār;* as. -e, 2022. [waru 'watchful care,' wær '(a)ware.'] (Cp. *Liber Vitae:* Berct-, Ecg-, Hroth-, Sigwaru.)

Frēsan, Frȳsan, wk.m.p., *Frisians; West Frisians* (Intr. xxxix): gp. Frēsna, 2915; dp. Frȳsum, 1207, 2912; — *East Frisians* (Introd. to *The Fight at Finnsburg*, p. 233): gp. Frēsena, 1093, Frȳsna 1104. [Schönf. 95 f.; Much, *R.-L.* ii 101.]

Frēs-cyning, m., *king of the (West) Frisians;* ds. -[e], 2503.

Frēs-lond, n., *Friesland; land of the West Frisians:* dp. Frēslondum, 2357; — *land of the East Frisians:* as. Frȳsland, 1126.

Frēs-wæl, n., *Frisian battle-field;* ds. -e, 1070.

Frōda, wk.m., *Heaðo-Bard chief, father of Ingeld;* gs. -an, 2025. [frōd 'wise'? ('old').]

Froncan, see **Francan**.

Frȳsan, Frȳs-land, see **Frēsan, Frēs-lond**.

Gār-Dene, see **Dene**.

Gār-mund, m., *father of the Angle king Offa;* gs. -es, 1962. [gār 'spear'; mund 'hand,' 'protection.']

Gēatas, m.p., *Scandinavian tribe in South 'Sweden,'* = ON. *Gautar* (see Intr. xlvi ff.); gp. Gēata, 374, 378, 601, 676, 1191, 1202, 1551, 1642, 1836, 1911, 2184, 2327, 2472, 2658, 2946; ~ lēode (-a, -um), 205, 260, 362, 443 (Gēotena, cf. Lang. § 16.2), 1213, 1856, 1930, 2318, 2927, 3137, 3178; ~ lēod, 625, 669, 1432; ~ dryhten (cyning, goldwine), 1484, 1831, 2356, 2402, 2419, 2483, 2560, 2576, 2584, 2901, 2991; dp. Gēatum, 195, 1171, 2192, 2390, 2623; ap. Gēatas, 1173. **Gēat** (i.e. Bēowulf), ns., 1785; gs. Gēates, 640; ds. Gēate, 1301; as. Gēat, 1792. — [Ablaut form: Gotan 'Goths.' Schönf. 104 f. ON. Gautar derived from Gautland, the land near the river Gautelfr; cp. ON. gjóta, OE. gēotan. Cf. Tamm, *Etym. Ordbok*, s.v. Göte; von Grienberger, *ZfdA.* xlvi 158; Noreen, *Spridda Studier* ii 91, 139.] — Cpds.: **Gūð-Gēatas**; gp. -a, 1538. [gūð 'war.'] **Sæ-Gēatas**; np., 1850; gp. -a, 1986. [sæ 'sea.'] **Weder-Gēatas**; gp. -a, 1492, 1612, 2551; dp. -um, 2379. [weder 'weather.'] — See Wederas; Hrēðlingas.

Gēat-mæcgas, mja.p., *men of the Geats;* gp. -mecga, 829; dp. -mæcgum, 491.

Gēotena, see **Gēatas**.

Gifðas, m.p., *East Germanic tribe;* dp. -um, 2494 (n.). (*Wids.* 60:

Gefþas, Lat. form Gepidae.) [Schönf. 109 f.; Much, *R.-L.* ii 157; Malone, *MLR.* xxviii 315 ff.]

Grendel, m., *monster slain by Bēowulf;* 102, 151, 474, *591*, 678, 711, 819, 1054, 1253, 1266, 1775, 2078; gs. Grendles, 127, 195, 384, 409, 478, 483, 527, 836, 927, 1258, 1282, 1391, 1538, 1639, 1648, 2002; Grendeles, 2006, 2118, 2139, 2353; ds. Grendle, 666, 930, 1577, 2521; as. Grendel, 424, 1334, 1354, 1586, 1997, 2070. [*grandil, fr. *grand, ' sand,' ' bottom (ground) of a body of water '; see Intr. xxviii f.]

Gūð-Gēatas, see Gēatas.

Gūð-lāf, m., *a Danish warrior;* 1148. [gūð ' war '; lāf ' remnant.']

Gūð-Scilfingas, see Scylfingas.

Hæreð, m., *father of Hygd;* gs. Hæreþes 1929, Hæreðes 1981. [Binz 162 f.; J. Köpke, *Altnord. Personennamen bei den Ags.* (Berlin Diss., 1909), pp. 26 f.; Björk. Eig. 49 ff.]

Hæðcyn, -cen, m., *Geatish prince, second son of Hrēðel;* Hæðcyn, 2434, 2437; ds. Hæðcynne, 2482; as. Hæðcen, 2925. [h(e)aðu- ' war '; Björkman, *ESt.* liv 24 ff.: ON. *Haþu-kuniR. Cf. Lang. § 18.7 n.; Binz 165; *ESt.* xxxii 348; but also: Bu.Tid. 289; *ZföG.* lvi 758; Gering L 3.26.117.]

Hālga, wk.m., *Danish prince, younger brother of Hrōðgār;* Hālga til, 61. [ON. Helgi, from ON. heilagr, OE. hālig, i.e. ' consecrated,' ' inviolable.']

Hāma, wk.m., *a person of the Gothic cycle of legends;* 1198; see Notes, pp. 177 f.

Healf-Dene, mi., *king of the Danes;* hēah ~, 57; gs. -es, 1064; maga ~, 189, 1474, 2143; mago ~, 1867, 2011; sunu ~, 268, 344, 645, 1040, 1652, 1699, 2147; ~ sunu, 1009; bearn ~, 469, 1020. [O. (West) N. Hálfdan(r), O.Dan. Haldan (Lat. Haldanus). See Intr. xxxiii f.]

Healf-Dene, mi.p., ' *Half-Danes,*' *tribe (of the Finnsburg story) to which Hōc, Hnæf, Hildeburh belong;* gp. -Dena, 1069. See note on 82–85. [Named after the king, 57.]

Heard-rēd, m., *Geatish king, son of Hygelāc;* 2388; ds. -e, 2202, 2375.

Heaðo-Beardan, wk.m.p., *a Germanic tribe* (see Intr. xxxv f., *R.-L.* iii 123-25); gp. -Beardna 2032; (MS. bearna:) *2037* (Heaða-), *2067*. [heaðo- ' war.']

Heaþo-lāf, m., *a man of the Wylfing tribe;* ds. -e, 460. [heaþo- ' war '; lāf ' remnant.']

Heaþo-Rǣmas, m.p., *a people living in southern Norway (Romerike);* ap. -Rǣmes, 519. (*Wids.* 63: Heaþo-Rēamum, dp.; ON. Raumar.) See Notes, p. 148.

Heaðo-Scilfingas, see Scylfingas.

Helmingas, m.p., *the family to which Wealhþēow belongs;* gp. -a, 620. (*Wids.* 29: Helm. Cf. Cha. Wid. 198.)

Hemming, m., *a kinsman of Offa and of Ēomēr;* gs. -es, *1944* (n.), *1961*.

Hengest, m., *leader of the (Half-) Danes;* 1127; gs. -es, 1091; ds. -e, 1083, 1096. [hengest ' horse.']

Heoro-gār, m., *Danish king, elder brother of Hrōðgār;* 61; Hioro-, 2158; Here-, 467. [heoro ' sword,' here ' army '; gār ' spear.'] (Cp. hioro-serce 2539: here-syrce 1511.)

Heorot, m., *the famous hall of the Danish king Hrōðgār (corresponding to the royal seat of Hleiðr*

PROPER NAMES

(*Zealand*) *in Norse tradition,* cf. Intr. xxxvii); 1017, 1176, Heort 991; gs. Heorotes, 403; ds. Heorote, 475, 497, 593, 1267, 1279, 1302, 1330, 1588, 1671, Heorute 766, Hiorote 1990, Hiorte 2099; as. Heorot 166, 432, Heort 78. [heorot ' hart '; see note on 78.]
Heoro-weard, m., *son of Heorogār;* ds. -e, 2161.
Here-beald, m., *Geatish prince, eldest son of Hrēðel;* 2434; ds. -e, 2463. [here ' army '; beald ' bold.']
Here-gār, see **Heoro-gār.**
Here-mōd, m., *a king of the Danes;* 1709; gs. -es, 901. [here ' army '; mōd ' mind,' ' courage.'] See Notes, pp. 162 ff.
Here-rīc, m., (prob.) *uncle of Heardrēd* (i.e. *brother of Hygd,* cf. Seebohm L 9.17.69); gs. -es, 2206. [here ' army '; rīce ' powerful.']
Here-Scyldingas, see **Scyldingas.**
Het-ware, mi.p., *a Frankish people on the lower Rhine* (see Intr. xxxix f.); 2363, 2916. (*Wids.* 33: Hætwerum, dp.) [hæt(t) ' hat ' (perh. ' helmet ')?; -ware ' inhabitants.' Cf. Lat. forms Chatti: Chattuarii; Much, *R.-L.* i 371 f.; Schönf. 130 f.]
Hige-lāc, see **Hyge-lāc.**
Hilde-burh, f., *wife of the Frisian king Finn;* 1071, 1114. [hild ' battle '; burg ' fortified place.']
Hiorot, see **Heorot.**
Hnæf, m., *chief of the* (*Half-*)*Danes,* 1069; gs. -es, 1114. [Cf. *ZfdA.* xii 285.]
Hōc, m., *father of Hildeburh* (*and of Hnæf*); gs. -es, 1076. [Cf. Bu. Zs. 204; Much, *ZfdA.* lxii 133 f.: cp. OE. hēcen, ' kid.']
Hond-sciōh, m., *a Geat warrior, one of the comrades of Bēowulf;* ds.

-sciō, 2076. [Cf. Ger. Handschuh, ' glove.'] (First recognized as a proper name by Gru. See Holtzm. 496; Bu. Zs. 209 f. For the ON. name Vǫttr, i.e. ' glove,' see Par. § 5: *Skáldsk.,* ch. 41, Par. § 6: *Ynglingas.,* ch. 27.)
Hrædlan, Hrædles, see **Hrēðel.**
Hrefna-wudu, mu., *a forest in Sweden* (' *Ravenswood* '); as. (or ds.?), 2925.
Hrefnes-holt, n., *a forest in Sweden* (' *Ravenswood* '); as., 2935.
Hrēosna-beorh, m., *a hill in Geatland;* as., 2477.
Hrēðel (-ǣ-, **Hrǣdla**), m., *king of the Geats, father of Hygelāc, grandfather of Bēowulf;* 374 (Hrēþel Gēata), 2430 (Hrēðel cyning), 2474; gs. Hrēþles, 1847, 2191, 2358, 2992; Hrǣdles, 1485; Hrǣdlan, 454. [For the interchange of Hrēð- and Hrǣd-, see Binz 164; Cha. Wid. 252 f.; Intr. xxxii n. 5; Lang. § 9.3; note on 2869 f.]
Hrēð-men, mc., *a name for the Geats;* gp. -manna, 445 (n.).
Hrēþling, m., *son of Hrēþel;* as., 1923 (Higelāc), 2925 (Hæðcen).
Hrēðlingas, m.p., *Geat people,* 2960.
Hrēð-rīc, m., *a son of Hrōðgār;* 1189, *1836.* [hrōð-: hrēð ' glory,' see Sievers, *Beitr.* xxvii 207. Cp. Roderick.]
Hring-Dene, see **Dene.**
Hrones-næs(s), m, *a headland on the coast of Geatland;* ds. -næsse, 2805, 3136. [hron ' whale.']
Hrōð-gār, m., *king of the Danes;* 61, 356, 371, 456, 653, 662, 925, 1017, 1236, 1321, 1687, 1840, 2155; gs. -es, 235, 335, 613, 717, 826, 1066, 1456, 1580, 1884, 1899, 2020, 2351; ds. -e, 64, 1296, 1399, 1407, 1592, 1990, 2129; as. -, 152, 277,

339, 396, 863, 1646, 1816, 2010; vs., 367, 407, 417 (þēoden H.), 1483. — Note: Hrōðgār maþelode: 925, 1687, 1840; Hrōðgār maþelode, helm Scyldinga: 371, 456, 1321. — [hrōðor, hrēð (see Olrik i 25; Intr. xxxii); gār. Cf. ON. Hrōðgeirr, MHG. Rüedegēr, Anglo-Norman Roger (see OE. Chronicle, A.D. 1075).]

Hrōð-mund, m., *a son of Hrōðgār;* 1189. [mund 'hand,' 'protection.']

Hrōþ-ulf, m., *son of Hālga;* 1017; as., 1181. [wulf. ON. Hrólfr, ME. Rolf. Cf. Ralph.]

Hrunting, m., *Unferð's sword;* 1457; ds. -e, 1490, 1659; as., 1807. [Cf. ON. Hrotti, sword-name; ON. (OE.) hrinda(n) 'thrust.' See Noreen, *Urgerm. Lautlehre,* p. 188; also Falk L 9.44.52.]

Hūgas, m.p., *a name applied to the Franks;* gp. -a, 2502; ap. -as, 2914. [Cf. Intr. xxxix f.; Schönf. 132.]

Hūn-lāfing, m., (*son of Hūnlāf*), *a warrior in Hengest's band;* 1143 (n.). [*hūn- 'high,' see Hoops in *Germ. Abhandlungen für H. Paul* (1902), pp. 167 ff.; Schönf. 143; Holt. Et.]

Hygd, fi., *wife of Hygelāc;* 1926, 2369; ds. -e, 2172. [ge-hygd 'thought,' 'deliberation.'] (Cf. Schönf. 142?)

Hyge-lāc, Hige-lāc, (Hȳlāc(es) 1530 pointing to the form Hyglāc, see Siev. R. 463, Lang. §§ 18.10, 19.1; the form Hyge- occurs only betw. 2001 and 2434, besides 813, 2943), m., *king of the Geats;* 435, 1202, 1983, 2201, 2372, 2434, 2914; gs. -es, 261, 342, 2386, 2943, 2952, 2958; ~ þegn, 194, 1574, 2977; mǣg ~, 737, 758, 813, 914, 1530, (si.) 407; ds. -e, 452, 1483, 1830, 1970, 2169, 2988; as. -, 1820, 1923, 2355; vs., 2000 (dryhten H.), 2151. [Cf. ON. Hugleikr.]

In-geld, m., *prince of the Heaðo-Bards, son of Frōda;* ds. -e, 2064. [Schönf. 146 f.; Björk. Eig. 77 ff.: *Ing-geld.]

Ing-wine, mi.p., (*Ing's friends*), *Danes;* gp.: (eodor) Ingwina, 1044, (frēan) ~, 1319. [Schönf. 147; Intr. xxxvii & n. 6; Holt. Et. (and Suppl.).]

Iofor, see Eofor.

Mere-wīoing, m., *Merovingian* (i.e. *king of the Franks*); gs. -as, 2921. [Schönf. 139, 167 f., 12; Holt., *ESt.* liv 89; cp. Ōswīo. As to the patronymic ending -ing, cp. Scylding.]

Mōd-þrȳðo, f., *wife of the Angle king Offa;* 1931 (n.). [þrȳð ' strength.'] See notes, pp. 195 ff.

Nægling, m., *Bēowulf's sword;* 2680. [nægl, see 2023; cp. sword-names Nagelrinc, -ring, Nagelung in *þidrekssaga* & MHG. epics; Falk L 9.44.31 & 57.]

Norð-Dene, see Dene.

Offa, wk.m., *king of the (continental) Angles;* 1957; gs. Offan, 1949. [Ekwall, *ESt.* liv 310: cp. Wulf-? (Saxo: Uffo).]

Ōht-(h)ere, mja., *son of the Swedish king Ongenþēow;* gs. Ōhteres, 2380, 2394, 2612; Ōhtheres, 2928, 2932. [ōht 'pursuit'? (or 'terror'?); here 'army'; ON. Óttarr. Cf. Björkman L 4.31.4.104; Sarrazin, *ESt.* xlii 17.]

Onela, wk.m., *king of the Swedes, son of Ongenþēow;* 2616; gs. Onelan,

62, 2932. [ON. Áli. Cf. Björk. Eig. 85 f.]
Ongen-þēow, mwa., *king of the Swedes;* 2486, -ðīo, 2924, 2951, -ðīow 2961; gs. -þēoes, 1968, Ongęnðīoes, 2387; -ðeowes, 2475; ds. -ðīo, 2986. [þēow ' servant.' Cf. ON. Angantýr.]
Ōs-lāf, m., *a Danish warrior;* 1148. [ōs, ON. áss ' god.' Cf. Krappe, *Beitr.* lvi 1 ff.]
Sǣ-Gēatas, see **Gēatas.**
Scede-land (=Sceden-), n., see **Sceden-īg;** dp. -landum, 19.
Sceden-īg, fjō., *name of the southernmost part of the Scandinavian peninsula (Skåne), applied to the Danish realm;* ds. -igge, 1686. [ON. Skán-ey, Lat. Sca(n)dinavia, mod. Swed. Skåne, see Intr. xxxvii; Gloss.: ēg-strēam. Cf. Müllenhoff, *Deutsche Altertumskunde* ii 359 ff.; Much, *ZfdA*. xxxvi 126 ff.; Bugge, *Beitr.* xxi 424; Schrader in *Philol. Studien, Festgabe für E. Sievers* (1896), pp. 2–5; Holt., *Beibl.* xxix 256; but also Lindroth, *Namn och Bygd* iii 10 ff. (connection of ' Scadinavia ' and ' Skåne'denied); Björkman *L* 4.31.8; Much, *R.-L.* iv 87 f.; Kretschmer, *Glotta* xvii 148–51; Malone, *Eng. Studies* xv 149.]
Scēfing, m., *appellation of Scyld;* 4. [scēaf, MnE. sheaf; see Notes, p. 123; Lang. § 10.4.]
Scyld, m., *mythical Danish king;* 4, 26; gs. -es, 19. [scyld ' shield '; see Notes, pp. 121 ff.]
Scyldingas (Scild-, 229, 351, 1183, 2101, 2105), m.p., *(descendants of Scyld, members of Danish dynasty), Danes* (poet. name); np. hwate ~, 1601, 2052 (Scyldungas); gp. Scyldinga, 53, 229, 913, 1069, 1154, 1168, 1563; wine ~, 30, 148, 170, 1183, 2026, 2101 (Scildunga); frēan ~, 291, 351, 500, 1166; helm ~, 371, 456, 1321; eodor ~, 428, 663; þēoden ~, 1675, 1871; lēod ~, 1653, 2159 (Scyldunga); witan ~, 778; winum ~, 1418; dp. Scyldingum, 274; ap. Scyldingas, 58. **Scylding,** ns.: gamela ~ (i.e. Hrōðgār), 1792, 2105. [scyld, Scyld; ON. Skjǫldungar; see Notes, p. 121.]
— Cpds.: **Ār-Scyldingas;** gp. -a, 464; dp. -um, 1710. [ār ' honor.'] **Here-Scyldingas;** gp. -a, 1108. [here ' army.'] **Sige-Scyldingas;** gp. -a, 597; dp. -um, 2004. [sige ' victory.'] **Þēod-Scyldingas;** np., 1019. [þēod ' people.'] — See **Dene.**
Scylfingas (Scilf-), m.p., *(Swedish dynasty), Swedes;* gp. Scylfinga: helm ~, 2381, lēod ~, 2603. **Scylfing,** ns.: gomela ~ (i.e. Ongenþēow), 2487, 2968 (Scilfing). [ON. Skilfing(a)r, see Par. § 4: *Hyndl.* 11; ON. -skjálf, OE. scielf, scylf, ' peak, crag, pinnacle '; cf. MHG. (*Nibel.*) Schilbunc (-ung). See Bu. 12; Björk. Eig. 100 ff.; Hoops 255.] — Cpds.: **Gūð-Scilfingas;** ap. 2927. **Heaðo-Scilfingas;** np. 2205; **Heaðo-Scilfing;** gs. -as, 63 (i.e. Onela). — See **Swēon.**
Sige-mund, m., *son of Wæls, uncle (and father) of Fitela;* gs. -es, *875;* ds. -e, 884. [sige ' victory '; mund ' hand,' ' protection.']
Sige-Scyldingas, see **Scyldingas.**
Sūð-Dene, see **Dene.**
Swēon, wk.m.p., *Swedes;* i.e. *inhabitants of the east central part of the present Sweden (northeast of Lakes Väner and Vätter)*; gp. Swēona, 2472, 2946 (n.); ~ lēodum (-e),

BEOWULF

2958, 3001. [O. Icel. Svíar, O. Swed. Swēar, Swīar. Cf. Go. swēs, OE. swǣs 'one's own '; Noreen, *Altschwed. Gram.* § 169 n.; Wadstein, *Fornvännen*, 1930, pp. 193 ff.] — See Scylfingas.

Swēo-ðēod, f., *the Swedish people;* ds. -e, 2922. [ON. Sví-þjóð; cf. *Leges Edwardi Confessoris* 32E: Suetheida, ' Sweden.'] See Swīorīce.

Swerting, m., *(maternal) uncle* (Seebohm L 9.17.69) or *grandfather*(?) *of Hygelāc;* gs. -es, 1203. [sweart 'black'; ON. Svertingr.]

Swīo-rīce, nja., *Sweden;* ds., 2383, 2495. [Mn.Swed. Sverige.] (Cf. Langenfelt, *Neuphilol. Mitteilungen* xxxiii 92 ff.)

þēod-Scyldingas, see Scyldingas.

Un-ferð, m., *courtier (þyle) of Hrōðgār;* 499, 1165; as., 1488; vs., 530. (MS.:Hun-.) [Cf. Notes,pp. 148 f.]

Wǣg-mundingas, m.p. *the family to which Wīhstān, Wīglāf, and Bēowulf belong;* gp. -a, 2607, 2814.

Wǣls, m., *father of Sigemund;* gs. -es, 897. [Cf. Goth, walis, γνήσιος, 'genuine,' 'legitimate.' See also Björk. Eig. 114 f.]

Wǣlsing, m., *son of Wǣls* (i.e. Sigemund); gs. -es, 877. [Cf. ON. Vǫlsungr.]

Wealh-þēo(w) (the form with final *w* in 612 only), str. & wk.f., *Hrōðgār's queen;* 612, 1162, 1215, 2173; ds. -þēōn, 629; as. -þēo, 664. [wealh ' Celtic,' ' foreign '; þēow = ' captive ' (carried off in war). See Intr. xxxiii & n. 2; Björkman, *Beibl.* xxx 177 ff.; Wessén L 4.31.9. 110 ff.]

Wederas, m.p., = Weder-Gēatas (cf.

Hrēðas, *El.* 58 = Hrēð-Gotan, *ib.* 20); gp. Wedera, and (in the second part of the MS., except 2186 & 2336, regularly:) Wedra (cf. Lang. § 18.10 n.); 423, *461*, 498, 2120, *2186;* ~ lēode (-a, -um), 225, 697, 1894, 2900, 3156; ~ lēod, 341; ~ þīoden (helm), 2336, 2462, 2656, 2705, 2786, 3037. Weder-Gēatas, see Gēatas.

Weder-mearc, f., *land of the (Weder-) Geats;* ds. -e, 298. (Cf. (Den-) mark.)

Wēland, m., *famous smith of Germanic legend;* gs. -es, 455. [Cf. ON. vél ' artifice ' (Grimm)?; High Ger. Wielant(d), ON. Vǫlundr (Jiriczek L 4.116.7; Heusler, *ZfdA.* lii 97 f.); MnE. Wayland (dial. pronunc., cf. Förster, *Arch.* cxix 106).] See Notes, p. 145.

Wendlas (or **Wendle**), m.p., *Vandals(?)* (cp. *Greg. Dial.* 179.14: Wandale, Var.: Wendle, 182.11: Wǣndla, etc.), or *inhabitants of Vendel in Uppland, Sweden,* or *inhabitants of Vendill in North Jutland (mod. Vendsyssel);* gp. Wendla, 348. (See Intr. xxx, xliv, xlviii; Müll. 89 f., Cha. Wid. 208.)

Wēoh-stān (**Wēox-**), see Wīh-stān.

West-Dene, see Dene.

Wīg-lāf, m., *a Wǣgmunding, kinsman of Bēowulf;* 2602, 2631, 2862, 2906, 3076; vs., 2745; as. Wīlāf, 2852.

Wīh-stān, **Wēoh-stān**, m., *father of Wīglāf;* Wēohstān, 2613; gs. Wīhstānes (sunu): 2752, 3076, 3120, 2862 (Wēoh-), 2602 (Wēox-); (byre) Wīhstānes: 2907, 3110. [wīg, wēoh (see wīg-weorþung), cp. Alewīh, *Wids.* 35; ON. Vésteinn, see Par. § 5: *Kálfsvísa*.]

Wilfingas, see Wylfingas.

PROPER NAMES

Wiðer-gyld, m., *a Heaðo-Bard warrior;* 2051 (n.).

Won-rēd, m., *a Geat, father of Wulf and Eofor;* gs. -es, 2971. [won ' wanting,' ' void of.']

Won-rēding, m., *son of Wonrēd* (i.e. *Wulf*); 2965.

Wulf, m., *a Geat (warrior);* 2965; ds. -e, 2993.

Wulf-gār, m., *an official at the court of Hrōðgār;* 348, 360.

Wylfingas, m.p., *a Germanic tribe (prob. south of the Baltic sea);* dp. Wylfingum, 471, Wilfingum 461. [wulf; ON. Ylfingar.] (Cf. Müllenhoff, *ZfdA.* xi 282, xxiii 128, 169 f.; Jiriczek L 4.116.273, 291 f.; Bugge L 4.84.175; Cha. Wid. 198; Heusler, *R.-L.* iv 572.)

Yrmen-lāf, m., *a Dane;* gs. -es. 1324. [Cf. Eormen-(rīc).]

GLOSSARY OF *THE FIGHT AT FINNSBURG*

Only the words not occurring in *Beowulf* are listed here. References to the others have been incorporated in the Glossary of *Beowulf*.

ā-nyman (-niman) (‡)+, IV, *take away;* 21.

bān-helm‡, m., B O N E-HELM*et* (or *-protection*), i.e. *shield(?)*; 30. (Dickins: 'helmet decorated w. horns,' cf. Stjer. 8.)

buruh-ðelu‡, f., *castle-floor;* 30.

cellod, *29*, see note.

dagian(‡)+, w 2., D A W *n;* pres. 3 sg. dagað, 3. [dæg; *NED.*: D A W, v.¹ (obs., Sc.)]

dēor-mōd†, adj., *bold, brave;* 23.

driht-gesīð‡, m., *retainer, comrade;* gp. -a, 42.

eorð-būend(e) (†), mc. (pres. ptc.) [pl.], (E A R T H-*dweller*), *man, native;* gp. -ra, 32. (Cp. *Jud.* 226, 315: landbūend(e) = ' land-dwellers,' i.e., ' natives.')

feohtan, III, F I G H T; pret. 3 pl. fuhton, 41.

fȳren, adj., F I E R *y, on fire;* nsf. fȳrenu, 36.

ge-hlyn(n) (‡), nja., *loud sound, din;* 28.

gold-hladen‡, adj. (pp.), (L A D E N) *adorned with* G O L D; 13.

grǣg-hama‡, wk.m. (adj.), *the* G R E Y-*coated one:* 6 (n.).

gūð-wudu‡, mu., *battle-*W O O D, *spear;* 6.

gyllan(†), III, Y E L L, *cry out, resound;* pres. 3 sg. gylleð, 6.

heaþo-geong‡, adj., Y O U N G (*in war*); 2.

here-sceorp‡, n., *war-dress, armor;* 45.

hlēoþrian, w 2., *speak, exclaim;* pret. 3 sg. hlēoþrode, 2.

hwearf-līc(‡), adj., *active(?), trusty(?)*; gpm. -ra, *34* (n.).

on-cweðan, v, *answer;* pres. 3 sg. oncwyð, 7.

on-wacnian, w 2., A W A K E (intr.); imp. pl. onwacnigeað, 10.

sealo-brūn‡, adj., [S A L L O W- or] *dark-*B R O W N; 35.

sige-beorn‡, m., *victorious warrior;* gp. -a, 38.

sixtig, num., S I X T Y; as., 38.

stȳran, w 1., w. dat., (S T E E R), *restrain;* pret. 3 sg. stȳrde, *18.*

swæþer(‡)+ (=swā hwæþer), pron., *whichever of two;* asn., 27. (Cp. *Beow.* 686.)

swān(‡)+, m., *young man* (in prose: ' herdsman '); ap. -as, *39.* [Cp. SWAIN, from ON. sveinn.]

swurd-lēoma‡, wk.m., S W O R D-*light;* 35.

ðȳrel, adj., *pierced through;* ðȳr[el]; 45. [þurh.]

un-dearninga, adv., *without con-*

cealment, openly; 22. [Cp. undyrne, Beow.]
un-hrōr(‡) (+), adj., weak, (made)
useless; nsn., 45. (Nonce meaning.) (Another conjectural meaning, 'firm' [orig. 'not stirring']
is mentioned by Chambers.)
wæl-sliht, mi., SLAUGHTer; gp. -a,
28. [slēan; ON. *slahtr>slaugh-
ter.]

wandrian, w 2., WANDER, rove,
circle; pret. 3 sg. wandrode, 34.
waðol‡, adj., wandering; 8. [Cp.
MHG. wadel, OHG. wadalōn,
wallōn, OE. weallian, see IF. iv
337, Beitr. xxx 132, xxxvi 99 f.,
431.] (B.-T., Cl. Hall [Dict.],
Mackie: wāðol, from wāð, f.,
'wandering.')
wēa-dǣd†, fi., DEED of WOE; np.
-a. 8.

PROPER NAMES

Ēaha, wk.m., *a Danish warrior;* 15.
Finns-buruh, fc., *Finn's castle;* 36.
Gār-ulf, m., *a Frisian warrior;* 31; ds. -e, *18*. [gār; wulf.]
Gūð-ere, mja., *a Frisian warrior;* 18. [gūð; here.]
Gūþ-lāf, m., 1) *a Danish warrior;* 16. 2) *a Frisian warrior;* gs. -es, 33.
Hengest, m., *a leading Danish warrior;* 17. [hengest 'horse.']
Hnæf, m., *Danish chief; 2;* ds. -e, 40.
Ord-lāf, m., *a Danish warrior;* 16.
Secgan, wk.m.p., *a Germanic (coast) tribe;* gp. Secgena, 24. [secg 'sword'; Cf. seax; Seaxe.]
Sige-ferð, m., *one of Hnæf's warriors (of the tribe of the Secgan);* 15, 24. [ferð=frið(u).]

SUPPLEMENT

This supplement makes available to students the additions to the Bibliography, Introduction, Notes, and Glossary which the author deems desirable to bring the book up to date. For latest additions see pp. 460-461.

BIBLIOGRAPHY[1]

MANUSCRIPT. EDITIONS. TRANSLATIONS

(L 1.5a.) A new facsimile publication of the *Beowulf* MS. to be edited by R. Flower, F. Norman, and A. H. Smith, is contemplated.

(L 1.14.) A. H. Smith, "The Photography of Manuscripts." *London Mediæval Studies* i (Part 2, 1938), 179-207. [Description of some of the highly refined modern methods. Several photographs of the last page of *Beowulf* are given together with an independent transcript in two forms.]

(L 2.15.) F. Holthausen's *Beowulf*, 7th ed., Part I, 1938. R.: Fr. Klaeber, *Beibl.* l (1939), 161 f.

(L 2.16.) W. J. Sedgefield's 3d ed. of *Beowulf*, 1935. [Favors textual emendations. Suggestive notes.] R.: K. Malone, *Eng. Studies* xviii (1936), 257 f.; H. Marcus, *Beibl.* xlvii (1936), 129-31; E. van K. Dobbie, *MLN.* liii (1938), 456 f.; F. Holthausen, *Lit. bl.* lix (1938), 163-67; D. E. M. Clarke, *Year's Work* xvi, 74-6.

(L 2.17a.) Reviews of Fr. Klaeber's 3d ed. (1936): F. Holthausen, *Beibl.* xlviii (1937), 65 f.; A. Brandl, *Arch.* clxxi (1937), 221 f.

(L 2.17c.) An (unprinted) ed. [on the basis of *Schallanalyse*] by the late Eduard Sievers is kept at the University of Leipzig library. Cf. Holthausen, *Lit. bl.* lix, 163 ff.

(L 2.23.) Martin Lehnert, *Beowulf: Auswahl* [some 1000 lines, with introduction, translation of some 600 lines, notes, and glossary]. (Sammlung Göschen, No. 1135.) Berlin, 1939.

(L 3.9d.) A translation by A. Wigfall Green, Boston, 1935. [Extremely literal, half-line for half-line rendering, intended as a practical aid to struggling students; arranged as verse.]

(L 3.35a.) A French translation of Federico Olivero's translation and edition (L 3.36a, 2.17b) by Camille Monnet, Torino, 1937. R.: Fr. Klaeber, *Arch.* clxxiii (1938), 80-82.

(L 3.42. n. (8).) Strafford Riggs, *The Story of Beowulf*. (Quite freely adapted for the entertainment of boys and girls.) With fantastic woodcuts by Henry C. Pitz. New York and London, 1933.

---
[1] This supplementary Bibliography will be referred to as ' Su.'; thus, L 1.14. Su. (See p. clxxxv for explanation of abbreviations.)

LITERARY CRITICISM. FABULOUS AND HISTORICAL ELEMENTS

(L 4.13.4.) J. R. Hulbert, *A Sketch of Anglo-Saxon Literature*, in Bright's *Anglo-Saxon Reader*, revised ed., New York, 1935, pp. lxxxvii–cxxxii.
(L 4.13a.) Review of H. Schneider's *Germanische Heldensage*, Vol. ii. 2: A. Heusler, *Anz. fdA*. liv (1935), 102–08.
(L 4.13c.) E. E. Wardale, *Chapters on Old English Literature*. London, 1935. 310 pp.
(L 4.13d.) Walter F. Schirmer, *Geschichte der englischen Literatur*. Halle, 1937. 679 pp. Book I: Old English Literature (pp. 1–44).
(L 4.22.2.) H. M. Chadwick and N. K. Chadwick, *The Growth of Literature*. Vol. ii, 1936. 783 pp. [Russian oral literature, Yugoslav oral poetry, Early Indian literature, Early Hebrew literature.]
(L 4.22e.) Ritchie Girvan, *Beowulf and the Seventh Century*. London, 1935. 86 pp. [1. The language. 2. The background (7th cent. Northumbria). 3. Folk-tale and history (e.g., arguments for historicity of Bēowulf). — [Very stimulating studies.] R.: W. W. Lawrence, *Speculum* xi (1936), 297 f.; J. R. Hulbert, *MPh*. xxxiv (1936), 76 f.; F. Mossé, *Revue germanique* xxvii (1936), 398 f.; K. Malone, *Eng. Studies* xviii (1936), 223; J. Raith, *Beibl*. xlviii (1937), 68–70; R. C. L. Wrenn, *RESt*. xiii (1937), 465–67; E. van K. Dobbie, *MLN*. liii (1938), 455 f.; D. E. M. Clarke, *Year's Work* xvi, 73 f.
(L 4.42. n. (7).) Karl Helm, *Altgermanische Religionsgeschichte. II. Die nachrömische Zeit*. 1. 'Die Ostgermanen.' Heidelberg, 1937. 76 pp. — (11.) Ernst A. Philippson, "Neuere Forschung auf dem Gebiet der germanischen Mythologie." *Germanic Review* xi (New York, 1936), 4–19. [Sketch of modern methods and results.] — (12.) Jan de Vries, *Altgermanische Religionsgeschichte*, Vol. i. (*P. Grdr*. 12.1.): ' Einleitung. Die vorgeschichtliche Zeit. Religion der Südgermanen.' Berlin, 1935. 335 pp. Vol. ii. (*P. Grdr*. 12.2): ' Religion der Nordgermanen.' Berlin, 1937. 460 pp. — Cf. (13.) Hermann Schäfer, *Götter und Helden. Ueber religiöse Elemente in der germanischen Heldendichtung*. Tübingen, 1937. 126 pp.
(L 4.62d.) *The Times Literary Supplement*, Nov. 9, 1935, p. 722, Constance Davies (on a Welsh legend resembling Bēowulf's Fight with Grendel), cf. Katherine M. Buck, Dec. 14, p. 859; Nov. 23, p. 770, Donald A. Mackenzie (on Scottish analogues).
(L 4.66b 4.) Gustav Hübener, "Beowulf's ' Seax,' the Saxons and an Indian Exorcism." *RESt*. xii (1936), 429–39. A German version (with illustrations) in *Englische Kultur in sprachwissenschaftlicher Deutung, Festschrift für Max Deutschbein*. Leipzig, 1936, pp. 60–71. [On exorcistic rites performed with a knife as observable in India. However, the story of *Beowulf* is immeasurably removed from such conditions.] — Cf. D. E. M. Clarke, " The Office of Thyle in *Beowulf*." *RESt*. xii (1936), 61–66. [Connects Unferð with the exorcist theory. (?)] — F. P. Magoun, Jr., " Zum heroischen Exorzismus des Beowulfepos." *AfNF*. liv (1939), 215–28. [A detailed, scholarly refutation of the exorcist theory.]

(L 4.66b 10.) J. R. R. Tolkien, "Beowulf: the Monsters and the Critics." *Proceedings of the British Academy* (1936), xxii, 245–95. London, 1938. [Justifies the dominant rôle of the fights with the fabulous monsters as involving a highly significant symbolism. The true meaning of the poem (*līf is lǣne*). Beowulf an heroic-elegiac poem. Remarks on the Christian elements. P. 259: "Something more significant than a standard hero, a man faced with a foe more evil than any human enemy of house or realm, is before us, and yet incarnate in time, walking in heroic history, and treading the named lands of the North."] R.: Fr. Klaeber, *Beibl.* xlviii (1937), 321–23; R. W. Chambers, *MLR.* xxxiii (1938), 272 f. ("the finest appreciation which has yet been written of our finest Old English poem"); H. R. Patch, *MLN.* liv (1939), 217 f.

(L 4.77a.) Kemp Malone, *Widsith edited.* London, 1936. 202 pp. [A very learned, stimulating publication.]

(L 4.78b 1.) Stephen J. Herben, Jr., "Heorot." *PMLA.* l (1935), 933–45. [Localization of Heorot on a hill-top farm in Vixø Parish which appears on a map of 1780 with the names *Store Hiort* and *Lille Hiorte*.]

(L 4.78b 2.) Stephen J. Herben, "Beowulf, Hrothgar and Grendel." *Arch.* clxxiii (1938), 24–30. [Grendel and his dam represent the powerful and cruel priesthood of the Nerthus cult which called for the immolation of human victims and involved a temporary taboo on the use of weapons. Fanciful.]

(L 4.78d 1.) E. V. Gordon, "Wealhþeow and Related Names." *Medium Ævum* iv (1935), 169–75. [ON. Valþjófr.]

(L 4.79.6.) Gudmund Schütte, *Our Forefathers the Gothonic Nations.* 2 vols. Cambridge (Engl.), 1929, 1933. 290, 482 pp. — Supplementary: *id.*, *Gotthiod und Utgard, Altgermanische Sagengeographie in neuer Auffassung.* 2 vols. Kjøbenhavn & Jena, 1935, 1936. 336, 372 pp. — (L 4.79.7.) Kemp Malone, L 4.77a. Su.

(L 4.82c.) This paper as well as L 4.118, 129e, 146d, LF. 3.2.2 may be found reprinted in *Forschungen und Charakteristiken* by A. Brandl, Berlin, 1936.

(L 4.85a 1.) Kemp Malone, "Time and Place in the Ingeld Episode of Beowulf." *JEGPh.* xxxix (1940), 76–92. [A somewhat modified version of Malone's former interpretation.]

(L 4.85c.) Bernard F. Huppé, "A Reconsideration of the Ingeld Passage in Beowulf." *JEGPh.* xxxviii (1939), 217–25. [Disapproves of Malone's interpretation.]

(L 4.85d.) Cf. L 5.35.22. Su: *A.* lxiii, 422 f.; *Beibl.* l, 223 f.

(L 4.88b 1.) Cf. S. Gutenbrunner, *Die germanischen Götternamen der antiken Inschriften*, Halle, 1936, pp. 63 ff.

(L 4.92i.) Henry B. Woolf, "The Name of Beowulf." *ESt.* lxxii (1937), 7–9. [The true name may have been Ælfhere (l. 2604). Cf. Malone *Haml.* 236 f.]

(L 4.92k.) Kemp Malone, "Hygelac." *Eng. Studies* xxi (1939), 108–19. [Hygelāc ultimately identical with Hugleikr of *Ynglingasaga* and Huglecus

(Holder's text: Hugletus) of Saxo, book VI, perhaps also with Huglecus of Saxo, book IV.]

(L 4.97e.) W. F. Bryan, "The Wægmundings — Swedes or Geats?" *MPh.* xxxiv (1936), 113–18. [Geats.]

(L 4.102a.) A. H. Krappe, "Der blinde König." *ZfdA.* lxxii (1935), 161–71.

(L 4.106c 1.) A. H. Krappe, "The Offa-Constance Legend." *A.* lxi (1937), 361–69.

(L 4.129e 1.) Alois Brandl, "Beowulf-Epos und Aeneis in systematischer Vergleichung." *Arch.* clxxi (1937), 161–73. [Shows parallelism in the general plan of the two epics; suggests a political purpose in the writing of *Beowulf.*]

(L 4.129i.) Ingeborg Schröbler, "Beowulf und Homer." *Beitr.* lxiii (1939), 305–46. [A comprehensive study. Acquaintance with Homer considered unlikely.]

(L 4.129k.) Hertha Marquardt, "Zur Entstehung des *Beowulf.*" *A.* lxiv (1940), 152–58. [The general idea of the poem was inspired by religious epic poetry of the *Exodus* type.]

(L 4.141.3.) Walter A. Berendsohn, *Zur Vorgeschichte des "Beowulf."* Kopenhagen, 1935. 302 pp. [The analysis of the original strata has been carried out on a large scale. Heroic lays and popular stories, it is held, were merged in a considerable poem of some 750–850 lines. This straightforward heroic narrative fell into the hands of an incompetent Christian (Anglian) author marked by a love of moral reflection and sentiment, who recast, enlarged, and altered it for the worse. The distinction set up between the old poem and the work of the adapter is largely based on stylistic criteria (in a wide sense). Even 506 lines of the transmitted text (some 100 fragments) are singled out as definitely belonging to the former. — The careful, minute observations on the style are of decided value. But, considering the insufficient material at our disposal, the investigation as a whole — in a way, a refined and modified renewal of the old patchwork theories — could not lead to convincing results.] R.: L. L. Schücking, *Anz. fdA.* lv (1936), 117–21; F. Norman, *MLR.* xxxi (1936), 414 f.; E. A. Philippson, *Germanic Review* xi (New York, 1936), 294–96; F. Mossé, *Revue germanique* xxvii (1936), 399; J. de Vries, *Neophilologus* xxi (1936), 212–19; K. Malone, *Eng. Studies* xix (1937), 24–26; W. F. Bryan, *MLN.* lii (1937), 374–78; A. Brandl, *Arch.* clxxv (1939), 228. Cf. W. A. Berendsohn, "Stilkritik am Beowulf-Epos," *AfNF.* liv (1939), 235–37 (brief reiteration of the stylistic argument).

(L 4.146d 1.) Alois Brandl, "Das Beowulfepos und die mercische Königskrisis um 700." *Forschungen und Fortschritte* xii (1936), 165–68. An English Version: "The Beowulf Epic and the Crisis in the Mercian Dynasty about the year 700 A.D." *Research and Progress* ii (1936), 195–203. [A revolutionary thesis. Mercian history is seen reflected in the references to Heremōd (Penda), Scyld (Wulfhere), etc. The author's purpose was to arouse the kings to the duty of a firm, vigorous, soldierly rule.]

(L 4.159.) Cf. Tolkien, L 4.66b 10. Su.; Brandl, L 4.129e 1. Su., L 4.146d 1 Su.

BIBLIOGRAPHY

TEXTUAL CRITICISM AND INTERPRETATION

(L 5.25.6.) B. Colgrave, "scūrheard." *MLR.* xxxii (1937), 281. (Cf. *A.* lxiii, 414.)

(L 5.35.22.) Fr. Klaeber, "Beowulfiana minora." *A.* lxiii (1939), 400-25. [Notes on numerous passages.] " A Notelet on the Ingeld Episode in *Beowulf,*" *Beibl.* l (1939), 223 f. — (L 5.35.23.) *id.*, " Beowulf 769 und Andreas 1526 ff." *ESt.* lxxiii (1939), 185-89. — (L 5.35.24.) *id.*, " A Few *Beowulf* Jottings." *Beibl.* l (1939), 330-32.

(L 5.51.) W. J. Sedgefield, "The Scenery in Beowulf." *JEGPh.* xxxv (1936), 161-69.[1] [" In his description of . . . scenery . . . the poet was drawing on his own knowledge; . . . it is . . . probable that he combined things he had himself seen or heard from friends into one composite picture." Incidentally the suggestion is ventured that the author's father may have been a Dane married to an Anglo-Saxon woman. Cf. also Sedgefield's ed.[3], p. xxxi, n. 1.]

(L 5.60.5.) Review of Hoops's *Beowulfstudien* by E. von Schaubert, *Lit. bl.* lvii (1936), 26-31. — (L 5.60.6.) Review of *Beowulfstudien* and *Kommentar* by G. Hübener, *Lit. bl.* lvi (1935), 241-43.

(L 5.67a.) W. S. Mackie, "The Demons' Home in Beowulf." *JEGPh.* xxxvii (1938), 455-61. [" A supernatural cave at the bottom of a deep inlet of the sea."]

(L 5.71.7.) Kemp Malone, "Young Beowulf." *JEGPh.* xxxvi (1937), 21-23. [l. 2177 ff., etc.] — (L 5.71.8.) *id.*, " The Burning of Heorot." *RESt.* xiii (1937), 462 f. [Confirms, in opposition to Girvan, L 4.22e. Su. 66 f., the poet's accuracy.] — (L 5.71.9.) *id.*, "Notes on *Beowulf.*" *A.* lxiii (1939), 103-12. [1. *herericˉ* 1176, ' army commander ' (cp. Goth. *reiks*); *heaðori(n)c* 2466, ' war ruler,' cp. *Heaþoricˉ, Wids.* 116. — 2. *Hemning* 1944, *Heming* 1961, and *Hemming* are legitimate variants. — 3. Ingeld Episode again.] — And see L 4.85a 1. Su.

(L 5.81.) W. Krogmann, *A.* lxiii (1939), 398. [Reiterates Holthausen's earlier suggestion: *weaxan* 3115, i.e. *waxan*,=**waskan*, **was-skan*, ' consume.']

(L 5.84.) Else von Schaubert, "Zur Gestaltung und Erklärung des Beowulf-textes." *A.* lxii (1938), 173-89. [1931 f.; 932 ff., 2032 ff., 28 ff., 2105 f.; 1169 ff.] And see L 5.60.5.

(L 5.85.) Carleton Brown, "*Beowulf* and the *Blickling Homilies*, and Some Textual Notes." *PMLA.* liii (1938), 905-16. [1357 ff. (very important); 305 f., 403[b], 457, 987, 1106, 1146-53, 1174, 1247[b], 1372[a], 1399, 1465-69, 2251[b]-54, 2556[b]-60, 2589.]

LANGUAGE. STYLE. VERSIFICATION

(L 6.12.4.) Hans Kuhn, "Zur Wortstellung und -betonung im Altger-

---

[1] For the reference (under L 5.51, also on p. 170, note on 1066-70), to ' L F. 4.41 ' read: 'L F. 4.33.'

manischen." *Beitr.* lvii (1933), 1–109. R.: G. Neckel, *Anz. fdA.* lii (1933), 161–163; K. Jost, *Beibl.* xlvii (1936), 225–31.
(L 6.12.5.) S. O. Andrew, "Some Principles of Old English Word-Order.". *Medium Ævum* iii (1934), 167–88; *id.*, "Relative and Demonstrative Pronouns in Old English." *Language* xii (1936), 283–93. [Unacceptable.]
(L 6.24a.) Bruce Dickins, "English Names and English Heathenism." *Essays and Studies by Members of the English Association* xix (1934), 148–60. Cf. Philippson, L 4.42. n. (10).
(L 7.25d 1.) Hertha Marquardt, *Die altenglischen Kenningar. Ein Beitrag zur Stilkunde altgermanischer Dichtung.* Halle, 1938. 4to, 238 pp. [A thorough study.] R.: Fr. Klaeber, *Beibl.* xlix (1938), 321–26; J. W. Rankin, *JEGPh.* xxxviii (1939), 282–85; K. Malone, *MLN.* lv (1940), 73 f. — *id.*, "Fürsten- und Kriegerkenning im Beowulf," *A.* lx (1936), 390–95. [Discussion of a few terms.]
(L 7.25g 1.) Gudmund Schütte, "Ethnische Prunknamen." *ZfdA.* lxvii (1930), 129–39. [Such compound names (e.g., *Gār-Dene*) are used to mark ethnic rank, importance of a person, or significance of a situation.]
(L 7.25l.) Adeline C. Bartlett, *The Larger Rhetorical Patterns in Anglo-Saxon Poetry.* New York, 1935. 130 pp. [Suggestive observations on the rhetorical building up of long passages.]
(L 7.25m.) C. C. Batchelor, "The Style of the *Beowulf*: a Study of the Composition of the Poem.". *Speculum* xii (1937), 330–42. [Arrives at the familiar conclusion that *Beowulf* is essentially Christian.]
(L 7.25n.) Frederick Bracher, "Understatement in Old English Poetry." *PMLA.* lii (1937), 915–34. (Cf. *MPh.* iii, 248 f.) See also Lee M. Hollander, 'Litotes in Old Norse," *PMLA.* liii (1938), 1–33.
(L 7.25o.) Joan Blomfield, "The Style and Structure of *Beowulf*." *RESt.* xiv (1938), 396–403. [A stimulating essay.] Cf. Tolkien, L 4.66b 10. Su. 271 ff.; also Bartlett, L 7.25l.Su.
(L 8.5.) A revised edition of Bright's *Anglo-Saxon Reader* (with its account of "Anglo-Saxon versification") by J. R. Hulbert. New York, 1935.

LIFE OF THE TIMES. OLD NORSE PARALLELS

(L 9.14.3.) Rudolf Much, *Die Germania des Tacitus erläutert.* Heidelberg, 1937. 464 pp. R.: H. Rosenfeld, *Arch.* clxxiii (1938), 74–78.
(L 9.24.) A German translation of Grønbech's work, entitled *Kultur und Religion der Germanen,* Hamburg, 1937, 1939.
(L 9.28e 1.) Suse Pfeilstücker, *Spätantikes und germanisches Kunstgut in der frühangelsächsischen Kunst.* Berlin, 1936. 244 pp.
(L 9.28g.) R. H. Hodgkin, *A History of the Anglo-Saxons.* Oxford, 1935. (2 vols.) 748 pp. With numerous plates and text figures. Pp. 201–44: 'Heathen Society.' Cf. also Charles Oman, *England before the Norman Conquest,* London, 5th ed., 1921.
(L 9.34a.) Haakon Shetelig and Hjalmar Falk, *Scandinavian Archaeology.* Translated by E. V. Gordon. Oxford, 1937. 458 pp. [A helpful handbook.]

(Ch. 21 'Seafaring,' cf. L 9.48; ch. 22 'Weapons,' cf. L 9.44.) R.: Joan Blomfield, *RESt.* xiv (1938), 333-37.
(L 9.34b.) Haakon Shetelig, *Préhistoire de la Norvège*. Oslo, 1926. 280 pp.
(L 9.40a.) Stephen J. Herben, Jr., "A Note on the Helm in Beowulf." *MLN.* lii (1937), 34-36. [On recent illustrative finds in Sweden.]
(L 10.1.) *The Elder Edda:* G. Neckel's 3d ed., 1936; Vol. ii, 2d ed., 1936. — *Codex Regius of the Elder Edda MS. No. 2365, 4to, in the Old Royal Collection in the Royal Library of Copenhagen.* [Facsimile.] Introd. by A. Heusler. Copenhagen, 1937.
(L 10.6.) A French translation of the *Grettissaga*, with introduction and notes, by F. Mossé, Paris, 1933. lxxvi, 272 pp.

FINNSBURG BIBLIOGRAPHY

(L F.3.) A translation (alliterating) of the Fragment and the Episode into Frisian, with brief comment, by D. Kalma in his *Kening Finn (Frisia-Rige,* No. 3, 1937, Snits (Sneek)).
Note. The Finnsburg Story, supplemented by miscellaneous Beowulfian material and combined with the Hengest-Horsa tradition, has been cleverly treated as fiction in John O. Beaty's *Swords in the Dawn: a Story of the First Englishmen.* New York, 1937; London, 1938.
(L F. 4.37a.) George Sanderlin, "A Note on *Beowulf* 1142." *MLN.* liii (1938), 501-03. [Supports Malone.]
(L F. 4.39c.) Fr. Klaeber, *ESt.* lxx (1936), 334 f. (A note on Gārulf.)
(L F. 4.43.) A. C. Bouman, "The Heroes of the Fight at Finnsburh." *Acta Philol. Scand.* x (1935), 130-44. [*Ēotan*, Jutes, i.e., 'Danes' (by annexation or assimilation).] See *A.* lxiii, 415.

NOTES ON THE INTRODUCTION

Page xix, n. 1. The importance of the *Hrólfssaga* has been elaborated again by Berendsohn, L. 4.40a, L. 4.141.3. Su.
Page xxvii. Girvan, L 4.22e. Su. (ch. 3) endeavors to vindicate the historicity of Béowulf.
Page xxix, n. 3. The importance of basic historical elements in the formation of Germanic heroic legends is strongly urged and exemplified by Schütte, see esp. L 4.79.6. Su. (*Gotthiod und Utgard*).
Page xxxv, n. 2. The complete text of Alcuin's letter to bishop Higbald (Speratus): *Monumenta Alcuiniana* ed. Wattenbach et Duemmler (Berlin, 1873), Epistolae, No. 81.
Page xxxvi, n. 1. and n. 3. *Heaðo-Bards* (Langobards): see Malone, *Widsith*, pp. 155 ff., 174; *Myrgingas: ib.*, pp. 176 ff.
Page xxxvii. As to the original seat of Danish power, see also Schütte, L 4.79.6. Su. (*Our Forefathers*, ii, 353 ff.); Malone, *Widsith*, p. 132.
Page xli. On the tradition of Hygelāc in Scandinavian sources (*Ynglingasaga*, Saxo), see Malone, L 4.92k. Su.

SUPPLEMENT

Page xliv. The *Wǣgmundingas* are best considered simply Geats (L 4.97e. Su., see note on *lēod Scylfinga* 2603, below). Wulfgār most likely came from the Vendel district in Jutland. (Cf. n. 1.)

Page xlvi, n. 1. On the question of Geatish immigration to Jutland, see also Schütte, L 4.79.6. Su. (*Our Forefathers*, ii, 382 ff., *Gotthiod*, i, 172 f.) Cf. also note on l. 445ª, below.

Page l, n. 1. On the nicely differentiated use of the Christian elements, see Tolkien, L 4.66b. 10. Su. 284 f. Cf. also *A*. xxxv, 471 ff.

Page li. Chambers's felicitous term '[almost] a Christian knight' (L 4.22b) might well be accepted as an apt description of the hero. — The prevalent view of the strange weakness of the main plot is vigorously opposed in Tolkien's brilliant study. Cf. also p. cxx, n. 2.

Page lxiii. Girvan (ch. 2) stresses the Anglo-Saxon background of the poem. See also note on *stānbogan* 2718, below.

Page lxiv, n. 5. The entire passage, 2444–62, may be viewed as an extended comparison.

Page lxxiii, Language, § 3. The interchange of *Frēsan* and *Frȳsan* (i.e., *ī*) has been explained from an original Ablaut (*Beitr*. xvii, 150, lx, 374; see Glossary). Malone regards it as an instance of an OE. raising of close *ē* to *ī* (*Jesp. Misc*. 49).

Page lxxviii, Language, § 11. Anglian smoothing of *īu* to *ī* (*Bülb*., § 195): *līxan* 311, 485, 1570.

Page ciii, below. " the more primitive ballads "; i.e., not ballads in a strict technical sense.

Page cix, n. 5. Further criticism of Morsbach's tests: Girvan, pp. 19 ff.

Page cxiii, n. 1. Carleton Brown (L 5.85. Su.) argues for Beowulfian influence on *Maldon*. (He also recognizes such influence in the 17th *Blickling Homily*, see note on ll. 1357 ff., below.) — n. 4. Girvan would place *Beowulf* about A.D. 680–700 (and in Northumbria).

Page cxiv, below. As to the old spear-warrior's speech, 2047 ff., we may venture to guess that it represents an approximation to the basic verse material (of a short lay), especially as the end-stopt line arrangement (*Zeilenstil*) is strikingly carried out here. By the same token, the opening lines of the *comitatus* speech, 2633 ff. may be taken as a survival of ancient traditional verses; cf. also p. lvi. See further *A*. lxiii, 422.

Page cxv. The fact of a direct intercourse in the 5th and 6th centuries between England and Scandinavian countries has been established by archaeological evidence. (Shetelig, L 9.34b. Su. 177; Shetelig and Falk, L 9.34a. Su. 261, 267.) — n. 3. A similar suggestion by Girvan, p. 80. A clever guess by Sedgefield, L 5.51. Su.

Page cxix, n. 1. The description of the chambered tomb (see note on 2718, below) possibly points to the southern part of Scotland which from the 7th to the 10th century was under Northumbrian rule.

Page cxx, n. 2. A hazardous theory: L 4.78b 2. Su. A political purpose in the writing of *Beowulf* was suggested by Brandl, L 4.129e 1. Su., L 4.146d 1. Su. Also Tolkien's thoughtful lecture is to be remembered.

Page cxxii, n. 1. Note the thorough study by Ingeborg Schröbler, *Beowulf und Homer*, L 4.129i. Su.

Page cxxiii. n. 4. 'Pointed parallels' from English history are cited by Girvan, pp. 48 f. (Brandl, L 4.146d 1. Su.)

NOTES ON THE TEXT

4-52 (p. 122, n. 5). A burial ship apparently dating from the 7th century has been dug up in East Suffolk, see *Antiquity* xiii (September, 1939), 260.

62 f. The name of Healfdene's daughter (conjecturally *Yrse*) in our poem does not alliterate with that of her father and brothers. (It may be remembered that the true name of Hrōðgār's daughter has been conjectured [by Malone] to be not Fréawaru, but Hrūt.) Henry B. Woolf, "The Naming of Women in Old English Times," *MPh.* xxxvi, 113-20, has found abundant illustration of father-daughter alliteration and variation in historical monuments; "49 out of 60 father-daughter pairs in the OE. royal families are marked by alliteration, and 18 such pairs are joined by variation." Which, however, seems to show that alliteration was indeed the rule, but not an absolute law. (Note also *Nīðhād, Beadohild*. Absence of father-son alliteration, e.g., *Frōda, Ingeld; Gārmund [Wǣrmund], Offa*.) (*Beibl.* l, 330.)[1]

83 ff. *ne wæs hit lenge þā gēn*, etc., 'the time was not yet come.' Similarly the reader is advised that a tragic event which may be feared for the future has not yet come to pass, 1018 f. *nalles fācenstafas / þēod-Scyldingas þenden fremedon;* 1164 f. — As to the burning of Heorot, see L 5.71.8. Su.

159 f. *ēhtende wæs*. Cf. Fernand Mossé, *Histoire de la forme périphrastique être+participe présent en Germanique*, 2 vols., Paris, 1938 (note *Beibl.* L 261-66).

168 f. *nō hē þone gifstōl grētan mōste*. Grendel was imagined in the (impossible) rôle of a retainer. Note also *healðegn* 142, *renweard* 770.

172-74. *rǣd eahtedon, / hwæt swīðferhðum sēlest wǣre / wið fǣrgryrum tō gefremmanne*. Cp., e.g., OE. *Bede* 50. 9 ff. *þā gesomnedon hī gemōt ond þeahtedon ond rǣddon, hwæt him tō dōnne wǣre* (=I, c. 14 *initum . . . est consilium, quid agendum esset*), and similar instances; see *A*. lxiii, 404. In these Beowulfian lines we recognize a scholar's hand.

194. *Higelāces þegn*. His name *Bēowulf* is not mentioned before l. 343. The same device, ll. 86: 102, 331: 348, 1294: 1323; also 12: 18. Thus, e.g., also *Helgakv. Hund.* i, 17 *Họgna dóttir:* 30 *Sigrún; Nibel.* (ed. Bartsch) 326.1 *ein küneginne:* 329.2 (*ze*) *Prünhilde*. A similar practice is found in Vergil and

---

[1] Also in a number of the following notes use has been made of the papers, L 5.35.22 and 24. Su.

SUPPLEMENT

Homer (see Schücking, *Heldenstolz und Würde im Angelsächsischen*, pp. 29 f.). The origin of such epic usage invites speculation. Cf. Introd., p. lxv; (notes on ll. 100, 314).

305 f. Carleton Brown (*PMLA*. liii, 910 f.), in combining certain emendations suggested by Cosijn (Lübke, Trautmann) and Holthausen, proposes to read: *fǣrwearde hēold / gūþmōd gummon*, ' a warlike man held boat-watch.' If we follow Brown in understanding by *gūþmōd gummon* not the chief coastguard himself, but one of his young men (see l. 293), the text thus improved makes perfectly smooth reading. Stylistically, the entire passage, 301–319, illustrates the typical forward-backward movement (Heinzel's ABA, etc.). It is, of course, to be borne in mind that we have to pay for the agreeable result by two textual changes and a rather odd sequence of words, *gummon, guman*.

389b–390a. A more likely reading would be: [*þā tō* (or *wið*) *dura efste* (cp. 386a) / *wīdcūð hæleð*.] (Carleton Brown, *l.c.*, 911 f. called attention to the fact that *ēode* in *Beowulf* never stands at the end of a half-line, and *ēodon* only once, 493).

403. An improved reading: [*herewīsa* (cp. 259, 370) *gēong*.]. Previous emendations, *hygerōf ēode, heaþorinc ēode*, are rendered doubtful (as observed by Sedgefield,[3] p. 110) by the fact that this particular variety of the metrical type A is generally avoided in the second half-line, only one case, 3065, being found out of 21 instances; see also note on 389b–390a, above.

443. The unique form *Gēotena* — though it might be explained as a permissible variant of *Gēata*, Language, § 16.2 — looks like a blending of *Gēata* and *Ēotena*. Could this temporary confusion have led to the unique use of *Hrēðmen* 445?

445a (p. 144). A critical note on the ' Alfredian ' *Gēata, Gēatum: A.* lxiii, 403 f.

455a (p. 145, n. 5). See also G. Baesecke, *Beitr.* lxi (1937), 368–78.

457. Hoops (*ESt.* lxx, 77–80) has justly pointed out that *for werefyhtum* (' for defensive fight ') as proposed by Grundtvig most naturally accounts for the scribal corruption to *fere fyhtum*. Thus *for* is used to mark purpose (as in *for ārstafum* 458, 382, ' for help ').

499 ff. (p. 148, n. 6). Cf. Malone, *Widsith*, p. 158. — (p. 148, n. 7.) Cf. Schütte, L 4.79.6. Su. (*Gotthiod* ii, 285, 307 ff.); Girvan, p. 67.

600. *sendeþ* (MS.). It seems after all safer not to give the emendation *snēdeþ* a place in the text. A form like *snēdeþ* (Language, § 10.1a) would be unique in *Beowulf;* cf. von Schaubert, *Lit. bl.* lvii, 28. The note on this use of *sendan, Beibl.* xl (1929), 24 may be recalled. Cp. also *onsendan*, ' offer to ' (in *Vercelli Homilies*), Willard, *A.* liv, 18.

670. *mōdgan mægnes, Metodes hyldo*. Is this a case of apposition (Tolkien, L 4.66b 10. Su. 287: parallel expressions) or addition ? Tolkien: " the favour of God *was* the possession of *mægen*." [Again, " where Béowulf's (own) thoughts are revealed by the poet we can observe that his real trust was in his own might." Yet, as Tolkien himself notes, ll. 1658–61 form a decided

NOTES ON THE TEXT

exception.] That no *and* is needed to mark addition appears from ll. 397 f. 2809 ff., 2850 f., 3139 f.

694–96. *þæt hīe ǣr tō fela micles / in þǣm wīnsele wældēað fornam, / Denigea lēode.* Perhaps *fela* should be taken as adverb; *fela*='multi' is hardly ever used without partitive genitive. Cp. *Jul.* 444: *tō late micles.*

708 f. The meaning of *wrāþum on andan,* 'for vexation to the foe,' is illustrated by its opposite, *wyrme on willan* 2306 f. See the discussion, *A.* lxiii 409 f.

769. For an attempt to clear up the puzzling relation between *ealuscerwen* and *meoduscerwen, Andr.* 1526, see *ESt.* lxxiii, 185 ff. There it was suggested that *ealuscerwen,* which had been coined solely as an allusion to ll. 4ᵇ–6ᵃ ('taking away of the ale[-hall],' i.e., consternation), was understood by the author of *Andreas* in the sense of 'dispensing of ale' and quaintly applied to a singular situation. The form of the nonce-word, it is held, might lend itself to either interpretation. [Prof. Holthausen, in a personal letter, suggests that *ealu-* may have been meant originally as *alu,* 'good luck,' 'safety,' occurring in Norse runic inscriptions and, possibly, in Germanic proper names.]

836. *under gēapne hrōf.* Another attempt at an explanation: Sedgefield³, p. 115. Cf. the old note, *MPh.* iii, 256.

870 f. A defense of *word ōþer fand / sōðe gebunden* taken as a parenthetical clause: von Schaubert, *l.c.,* 31.

901–15 (p. 162, n. 1). Malone, "Humblus and Lotherus," *Acta Philol. Scand.* xiii (1939), 201–14 considers it "obviously impossible" to identify Lotherus and Heremōd.

1020. *brand* (MS.) *Healfdenes.* H. Marquardt, *A.* lx, 391 ff., argues for the retention, or rather rehabilitation, of *brand*='sword,' i.e., 'he who uses the sword'; 'Healfdene's sword,' i.e., 'H.'s distinguished warrior.' In the same way, in l. 1064 *fore Healfdenes hildewīsan,* a title inherited from the reign of Hrōðgār's father is used. Similarly, the memory of Atli's father is kept up: *Atlam.* 63 *tóko þeir brás Buðla,* 38 *bæ sá þeir standa. er Buðli átti.* Cf. *A.* lxiii, 413 f., and see note on *lēod Scylfinga* 2603, below.

1066–68. von Schaubert, *l.c.,* 30 suggests for *mǣnan* the sense of 'direct (to),' 'devote (to)'; *healgamen,* 'entertainment in the hall'; thus the insertion of *be* would be rendered unnecessary.

1082. The use of the article in *on þǣm meðelstede* supports the assumption that some of the fighting had taken place in the open (outside the hall); see p. 253.

1106. *þonne hit sweordes ecg syððan* (MS.) *scolde.* Meter no less than sense demands an important, predicational word before *scolde.* (Cp. *þæt hit sceādenmǣl scȳran mōste* 1939). A non-essential adverb, 'afterwards' (*syððan*), won't do, whether we supply mentally, with Schücking, *myndgiend wesan,* or, with W. Krause (cf. H. Marquardt, *Die altenglischen Kenningar,* p. 208), *wesan* ('it should be sword's edge, i.e., fight'). The recently proposed verb *sidian,* 'arrange,' 'determine' (Sievers, cf. Holthausen, *Lit. bl.*

lix, 164) — a nonce-word, it is true, in OE. poetry — is somewhat nearer to the transmitted *syððan* than previous emendations.

1151 f. von Schaubert, *l.c.*, 27 f., could keep *hroden: Đā wæs heal hroden / fēonda fēorum*. (Cf. Textual Criticism, p. 280, § 28.) Cp. *Gen.* 2931 f. *brynegield onhrēad, / rēc(c)endne wēg rommes blōde;* but *Andr.* 1003 *dēaðwong rudon, Exod.* 412 *rēodan*. A scribe's replacing *roden* by the very common *hroden* would not be surprising.

1176. Malone, *A*. lxiii, 103 would retain the MS. reading, *hererīc* (a nonce-word), ' army commander ' (cp. Gothic *reiks*).

1197 ff. (p. 177, n. 1). Cf. Malone, *Widsith*, pp. 141 ff., 151 ff. (162 ff.), on Eormenrīc, Hāma. He argues that OE. *Brōsingas* may have passed into **Brēsingas*, then **Brīsingas* (*Jesp. Misc.* 47 ff.), hence ON. *Brísinga men*. — On ll. 1199 ff., see also *A*. lxiii, 417 f.

1210. *Gehwearf þā in Francna fæþm feorh cyninges*. In this connection the Frankish tradition of the Liber Monstrorum (Par. § 11.1) is to be remembered. It appears that the notion of Bēowulf's fabulous strength had been transferred to Hygelāc. Cf. W. Keller, L 4.92g.

1247. *þæt hīe oft wǣron an wīg gearwe*. For this reading, see *MPh*. iii, 458; *A*. lxiii, 418. (Brown, *l.c.*, 914: *andwīggearwe*.)

1351. *idese onlicnes, ōðer earmsceapen*. von Schaubert, *l.c.*, 27, who contends for the admission of double alliteration in the second half-line (see note on 1151 f., above), assigns strong stress and alliteration to *ōðer*. Cf. *A*. lxiii, 418 f.

1357 ff. Recent comment on the monsters' haunts: Sedgefield, L 5.51. Su., Mackie, L 5.67a. Su. — Carleton Brown, in a highly significant discussion (*l.c.*, 905 ff.), stresses the fact that the incident of the trees — and they are fiery trees, . . . ' arbores igneas, in quarum ramis peccatores cruciati pendebant ' — to which the well-known descriptive passage in (the closing portion of) the 17th *Blickling Homily* is attached, does not occur in the earlier versions of the *Visio S. Pauli;* besides, the close verbal agreement between the description in *Beowulf* and in the *Blickling Homily* argues for a *direct* connection between the homiletic and the Beowulfian passage. Hence he draws the important conclusion — confirming in fact the impression of the editor of the Homilies, R. Morris — that the homilist was influenced by the striking landscape description in *Beowulf*. That the author of the 17th Homily appreciated poetry in the vernacular is to be inferred also from the rhythmical and alliterative quality of his prose (cf. Förster, *Arch*. xci, 194 f.).

1375. Sedgefield[3] reads *ðrysmaþ*, to which he attributes the meaning ' is stifling.' (?)

1379. *fela sinnigne* (MS.) *secg*. Malone and Hoops strongly urge the retention of *fela*. Against this is to be noted not only Sievers's statement, *A.M.*, § 23.2, but also, and in particular, the important fact that *fela*-compounds invariably bear *f* alliteration; there are 11 instances in OE. poetry and 2 in OS. If anywhere, here a definite rule is to be recognized.

1563. *fetelhilt* is supposed to refer to a type of swordhilt described by G.

Baldwin Brown, L 9.28e. 221 (and which is regarded by him as an Ags. invention); cf. Girvan, p. 39; Pfeilstücker, L 9.28e 1. Su. 202.

1605 ff. The incident of the sword up to the hilt dissolving in the hot blood recalls a certain Vergilian parallel, *Aen.* xii, 740 f., 734; cf. *Arch.* cxxvi, 348; Berendsohn, L 4.141. 3. Su. 69 f.

1636. *ǣghwǣþrum*, according to Sedgefield, perhaps refers to each of two pairs carrying the head. A plausible explanation.

1850. *þæt þe Sǣ-Gēatas sēlran nǣbben*, etc. It is impossible to prove or disprove that *þe* is=*þē*. The dative of comparison cannot be called un-Germanic (as is shown most clearly by the Old Norse), but it was no doubt reinforced by Latin models (cf. *Beibl.* xlviii, 162). No example of that construction (leaving the debated case out of discussion) occurs in *Beowulf* or *Widsið*. The lack of stress might be taken as an argument for *þe*, cp. 469, 505, 534, 1182, 1353.

1865. *ǣghwæs untǣle ealde wīsan.* It cannot be denied that the semi-adverbial use of *ealde wīsan* (instead of *on ealde wīsan*) in our poem is questionable. Kock's rendering 'the aged leaders' appears satisfactory if, with Hoops, we understand by *ealde wīsan* not the kings (note l. 1831), but the leading retainers, *selerǣdende, ealdgesīðas, snotere ceorlas*. A third possibility, slightly less plausible (note l. 1858), is advocated by Sedgefield, who translates ' the old custom.'

1931 ff. (p. 196, n. 3). *onōrette, Wids.* 41, may be taken as the verb of the clause, ' accomplished by fight '; so B.-T., Grein, Schücking, Malone, *et al.;* cf. *Gr. Spr.*, p. 890. — (p. 197.) As to queen Cyneþrȳð, wife of Offa II, Bruce Dickins (*Proceedings of the Leeds Philosophical Society*, Vol. IV, Part I) calls attention to the fact that she is the only Old English queen who is known to have issued coins with her own image and superscription — ' Cyneðryð Regina.' "Had Cynethryth enjoyed the substance of power during her son's short reign, or did she attempt to seize the throne after his death?"

1932. von Schaubert, *A.* lxii, 175 f. proposes *firen-ondrysne* (cp. l. 1796). 'terrible usage (practice).' (?)

2032 ff. Renewed discussion of the Ingeld episode by Malone, *A.* lxiii, 105 ff. (L 5.71.9. Su.), *JEGPh.* xxxix, 76 ff. (L 4.85a 1. Su.) See, on the other hand, *A.* lxiii, 422 f., *Beibl.* l, 223 f. (L 5.35.22. Su.); *JEGPh.* xxxviii, 217 ff. (L 4.85c. Su.) If we insist on the rigid interpretation of *fǣmne*=virgo (see also Malone, *Eng. Studies* xvii, 226 f.), its use here (2034, 2059) might well be held to indicate that Bēowulf, who is foretelling an event of the future, applies to *Frēawaru* an epithet suitable to her at the time of his report to Hygelāc — he knows her only as a *fǣmne*. — As to *bēah* 2041, it seems to signify a hilt-ring by which the *eald æscwiga* recognizes the sword (2047) of the Heaðobard warrior of former days. (Cp. *Aen.* xii, 940 ff., *Nibel.* 1783.)

2106. A new attempt to explain *fela fricgende (sic)*: von Schaubert, *A.* lxii, 186. See *A.* lxiii, 423 f.

2178. (*Swā bealdode bearn Ecgðēowes, / guma gūðum cūð,*) *gōdum dǣdum.* Is this an instance of what Tolkien (p. 286) in his penetrating discussion of the Christian elements calls 're-paganization'? Cp. bona opera; *Gen.* 1507 *gōdum dǣdum.* (*Waldere* i 22 f.) In the same category would seem to belong terms and expressions like *synn* (*ond sacu*), *unsynnum, firen, geþyld, woroldār,* cp. *mǣgenes crǣft, morðre swealt* (modeled after *dēaðe swealt, Gen.* 1205, morte morieris, Gen. ii 17), and others.

2183 ff. *Hēan wæs lange,* etc. Malone, *JEGPh.* xxxvi, 21–23 would explain this phase of Bēowulf's life in the light of his spiritual development.

2207 ff. By having folio 179 examined under the ultra-violet lamp Sedgefield[3] (Preface, and p. 135 f.) established the fact that no freshening up by a later hand had taken place; he made out such readings as 2212 *heaum hofe,* 2215 *neh gefeng* (but *þ* visible under a later *f*, possibly pointing to an intended *geþrang*), 2220 *bu* or *by;* he conjectured 2226 *þonan* (*s*)*wāt ī*(*o*)*de;* he emended *nīwe* 2243 to *nīwel,* 'lying down,' 'deep down.'

2212 f. Motives for depositing gold hoards in the earth: Shetelig and Falk, L 9.34a. Su. 235 f. Cp. ll. 3166 ff. and note.

2435 ff. (p. 213). The accidental slaying of Herebeald by Hæðcyn. Add: Malone, *Wids.,* p. 160.

2466. MS.: *heaðo ri,* $^n c$; "the correction with a lighter ink," Zupitza; Malone (*A.* lxiii, 103 f.), who besides notes a difference in the shape of *n*, reads *heaðorīc* (see l. 1176), 'war ruler,' cp. *Heaporīc, Wids.* 116 (cf. Malone, *Wids.,* pp. 158 ff.).

2558 f. A pleasing variant punctuation offered by Brown, *l.c.,* 916: *hāt hildeswāt-hrūse dynede — / biorn* ('burned') *under beorge. Bordrand onswāf.*

2577. Sedgefield[3] guesses *mid egelāfe.*

2603. *lēod Scylfinga.* W. F. Bryan (*MPh.* xxxiv, 113 ff.) ably supports the view that Wēohstān — as often happened in those days — temporarily took service with a foreign prince, viz. the Swedish king, and thus had to fight even against his own countrymen; he was unquestionably a Geat. The term *lēod Scylfinga,* it is explained, which might have been applied to him on account of his famous exploit in the Swedish service (ll. 2611 ff.), clung to his son, who strictly speaking had no right to it. Cf. *freca Scyldinga* 1563; also ll. 1020, 1064.

2687. *wǣpen wundum* (MS.) *heard* has recently been upheld again; thus Holthausen, note; von Schaubert, *Lit. bl.* lvii, 29. Cp. *āhyrded heaþoswāte* 1460, *scūrheard* 1033.

2718. *stānbogan,* 'stone arches.' The vaulting or corbeling in megalithic chambered tombs is not infrequently met with in Ireland and Scotland (Alexander Keiller and Stuart Piggott, *Antiquity,* xiii (1939) 360 f.) [Cf. John Thurnam, *Archaeologia* xlii (1869), 202–4.]

2922–98 (p. 223). The fall of Ongenþēow in a fight against two brothers. Add: Malone, *Wids.,* pp. 133–35.

3071 f. *þæt se secg wǣre . . . hergum gehearðerod, hellbendum fæst.* See *A.* xxxv, 268–70, lxiii, 425.

3074. Sedgefield[3] conjectures *goldwǣge.* See his note.

3115. *weaxan.* See L 5.81. Su.

3146. The expression *windblond gelæg* has given trouble to various critics.

NOTES ON THE TEXT

See, e.g., an earlier comment, *JEGPh.* vi, 196; a recent note by Girvan, p. 37. Perhaps *wōpe bewunden* helps to explain it; the wind 'subsided' when the lamentation set in, 3146ª, 3148ᵇ ff., — so the wailing could be clearly heard. Thus *windblond gelæg* would practically serve the same purpose as the very appropriate *swīgedon ealle* 1699. (Note *Elene* 1272 ff.)

3150 ff. A. H. Smith, L 1.14. Su. has been able to establish some new MS. readings; thus, e.g., 3153 : : : : : : . *g* : : : . *gas*, which may reasonably be reconstructed as *hefige dagas;* 3154 *werudes* (for *wigendes*); besides 3157 *hleo on hoe*, 'a shelter on the promontory,' which, however, seems problematical; in fact, the variant 'text by visual examination' shows *lide* instead of *hoe;* the noun *hōh* in the sense of 'promontory' occurs nowhere else in the OE. poetry.

3156 ff. On memorial cairns, see Sedgefield, *JEGPh.* xxxv, 168. On two conspicuous grave mounds in the Thames valley, see Hodgkin, L 9.28g. Su. 227.

THE FIGHT AT FINNSBURG

Introduction

P. 235, n. 4. Cf. also the mention, Introd. xxxiv, n. 7.

Notes on the Text

6. *grǣghama*. Of the two possible meanings, 'wolf' and 'coat of mail,' the former is by all means to be preferred.

16. *æt ōþrum durum*. It has been repeatedly pointed out that there were two doors opposite each other in the hall of the Northumbrian king Ēadwine (Bede, *H.E.* ii, c. 13).

34. The conjecture *Hwearf flacra* (or **hlacra*) *ærn* (with period after *fǣla* 33) is too tempting to be resisted.

APPENDIX II

Page 270, n. Cf. Girvan, ch. 2 (conditions of life predominantly Anglo-Saxon).

APPENDIX III

Page 280. § 28. Double alliteration in the *b*-line advocated: von Schaubert, *Lit.bl.* lvii, 27 (1251ᵇ, type Db; 1351ᵇ, type Da, see note, above; 1151ᵇ MS., see note, above; 2916ᵇ MS.).

APPENDIX IV

Page 283, n. Add: Malone's edition of *Widsið*, London, 1936.

Page 286, n. On *Deor* 14 ff., see further *Jour. of Eng. Liter. Hist.* iii, 253 ff., *Eng. Studies* xix, 193 ff.; *MLR.* xxxii, 374 ff., *London Mediæval Studies* i (Part 2), 165 ff.

Page 287. *Wids.* 34: Hringwald (MS.: *hringwęald*).

ADDITIONS TO THE SUPPLEMENT

Bibliography

(L 2.7.4.) The Heyne-Schücking *Beowulf* re-edited by Else von Schaubert: 15th ed., 1940; issued in three parts: text (105 pp.), commentary and glossary of proper names (144 pp.), glossary (232 pp.). [Completely and carefully revised; notes very largely rewritten. Distinctly conservative treatment of the text.] R.: Fr. Klaeber, *ESt.* lxxiv (1941), 219-23; K. Schneider, *Beibl.* lii (1941), 1-6.

(L 3.16e.) Charles W. Kennedy, *Beowulf Translated into Alliterative Verse, with a Critical Introduction.* New York and London, 1940. lxvi, 121 pp.*

(L 4.13e.) W. L. Renwick and Harold Orton, *The Beginnings of English Literature to Skelton 1509.* London, 1939. 431 pp. [Largely bibliographical, intended as a students' guide.]

(L 4.66b 3.) James R. Caldwell, "The Origin of the Story of Bothvar-Bjarki." *AfNF.* lv (1939), 223-75. ['Bjarki' originally derived from some version of the folk-tale, The Two Brothers (Grimm, No. 60).]

(L 4.66b 11.) L. Whitbread, "Grendel's Abode: an Illustrative Note." *Eng. Studies,* xxii (1940), 64-66. [Description of the land of purgatorial torment in the Old Irish prose text, Fís Adamnáin.]**

(L 4.85a 2.) Kemp Malone, "Freawaru." *Jour. of Eng. Lit. Hist.* vii (1940), 39-44. [Name coined by the *Beowulf* poet, in place of the original Hrūt.]

(L 4.92.l.) Kemp Malone, "Ecgtheow." *Mod. Lang. Quarterly* i (1940), 37-44. [Ecgþēow a Wylfing. See note on l. 461, below. Cf. L 4.97d; L 4.97e. Su.]

(L 5.86.) H. Lamar Crosby, Jr., *MLN.* lv (1940), 605-06. [*stefn* 212, '*prow*,' or 'forecastle'; (*wudu*) *bunden* 216 applies to the 'tied up' or 'laced' structure of North German and Scandinavian vessels.]

(L 5.87.) Calvin S. Brown, Jr., "Beowulf's Arm-Lock." *PMLA.* lv (1940), 621-27. [Explains Beowulf's mode of fighting Grendel in the light of modern wrestling technique. See note on l. 748 f., below.]

(L 6.12.6.) Karl Schneider, *Die Stellungstypen des finiten Verbs im urgermanischen Haupt- und Nebensatz.* Heidelberg, 1938. 73 pp.

(L 6.12.7.) J. Fourquet, *L'ordre des éléments de la phrase en germanique ancien.* Paris, 1938. 300 pp. R.: K. Schneider, *Beibl.* l. (1939) 225-33.

(L 7.25p.) Anton Pirkhofer, "Figurengestaltung im Beowulf-Epos." (*Ang.* F. lxxxvii.) Heidelberg, 1940, 160 pp.

(L 8.13l.) W. H. Vogt, "Altgermanische Druck-'Metrik.'" *Beitr.* lxiv (1940), 124-64. [Skeptical attitude toward Heusler; attempts new ways. Examples chosen from ON. and OHG.]

(L 9.28h.) Hermann Schneider (and seven collaborators), *Germanische Altertumskunde.* München, 1938. 504 pp. [Including, e.g., Helmut de

---

* Has not yet been seen by me.
** W. W. Lawrence's article, "Grendel's Lair," *JEGPh.* xxxviii (1939), 477-80 has been out of reach.

ADDITIONS TO THE SUPPLEMENT

Boor's 'Old Germanic Poetry,' pp. 306-430, Hermann Schneider's 'Religion,' pp. 222-305.] R.: L. Wolff, *Anz. fdA*. lviii (1939), 101-10.

Note. (See Intr., p. cii.) Franklin Cooley, in a paper, "Early Danish Criticism of Beowulf" [chiefly: Thorkelin and Grundtvig], *Jour. of Eng. Lit. Hist.* vii (1940), 45-67, points out (p. 61 f.) that the title 'Bjowulfs Drape' (see p. cii, n.1.) first appeared in Dannevirke ii, in 1817.

Notes on the Text

62 f. It should be added that the absence of alliteration in the names, Frōda, Ingeld recalls Langobard practice; see H. B. Woolf, *The Old Germanic Principles of Name-Giving*, Baltimore, 1939, pp. 231 f.

445 a. (p. 144). Malone, *Beibl*. li, 262-64, objects to *Angl*. lxiii, 403 f. (p. 454).

461. *gara* (MS., commonly emended to *Wedera*) *cyn*. Malone, *Mod. Lang. Quarterly* i (1940), 37 f. proposes to read *Wulgara cyn*. (*Wulgaras*, **Wulgwaras*, = *Wylfingas*.) It is certainly difficult to account for a scribal blunder *gara* in place of *Wedera*. In this connection it is suggested by Malone that Ecgþeow was a Wylfing by birth.

748 f. C. S. Brown (L 5.87) translates: " he grasped quickly, with hostile thoughts, and sat up against (Grendel's) arm," explaining it to mean that " Bēowulf put an arm-lock onto Grendel at the latter's first attack, and never released it." He also takes *wrīþan* 964 as 'twist.' Cf. Grattan's note in Chambers' edition; also Dehmer, L 4.66 b5.2.59 ff.

2041. On *bēah*, ' hilt-ring,' see *Beibl*. li (1940), 206 f.

Finnsburg **34.** Holthausen's suggestion *hlacra* may be supported by Vǫluspá 50, *ari hlakkar*.

Finnsburg **36.** Francis P. Magoun, *ZfdA*. lxxvii (1940), 65 f. argues for *Finns buruh*, cf. *Etzeln burc* (Nibel.) and, perhaps, *Brun(n)an* (or *Brūnan*) *burg* (OE. Chron., A.D. 937).

Note. On *Wids.* 111, *innweorud Earmanrīces* and its close relation to the following lines, see Caroline Brady, *Speculum* xv (1940), 454-59.

GLOSSARY

æfen-ræst, fjō. (?)
anda. See note on 708 f., above.
(ge-)bætan. Brown, *PMLA*. liii, 914 f.: *saddle*.
be-nemnan. Cp. *Par. Ps.* 88.43 *dēope āðe benemdest* (=jurasti), 88.3, 94.11, 131.11, *Husb. Mess.* 49.
bēod-genēat. [*ZfdA.* lx, 70; *Beitr.* lx, 398 f.]
brūn. See Ingerid Dal, *Norsk Tidsskrift for Sprogvidenskap* ix (1937), 219–30.
*****dēagan.** Flasdieck, *A.* lx, 267: **dugan* or **dēogan*.
eaxl. 1117: (as.?)
eom, wesan, bēon. Cf. Flasdieck, *ESt.* lxxi, 336–40.
fǣhð(o). On the origin of 'feud,' see Malone, *Eng. Studies* xxi, 269–71. [Su.
frēa-wrāsn. See Herben, L 9.40a.
fyrgen(-strēam). Malone: *mountainous, huge*. [*ture.*
gāst, gǣst. Tolkien, p. 279: *creagēn*, w. negat. (ðā) gēn, *not yet, no more*. [1. Su. 106.
gombe. Cf. Gutenbrunner, L 4.88b
grom-heort, grom-hȳdig. Prose examples (in *Vercelli Homilies*): Willard, *A.* liv, 14.
hæft-mēce, and *hepti-sax*. Cf. Shetelig and Falk, L 9.34a. Su. 385.
hē. him 1056 is dat. plur., not sing.
herg (hearg). [Cp. Harrow(-) in place-names.]
hild-fruma. Perh. *warrior, hero*, (Marquardt *A.* lx, 390).
hōs. [Cf. *Arch.* clxix, 1 ff.]
hring. hringa þengel, fengel, perh. *corslet owner, warrior* (?) (Marquardt, *A.* lx, 394 f.; cf. *Beibl.* xlix, 325).
lāf. On fēla, homera lāf, etc., see Marquardt, *Kenningar*, L 7.25d 1. Su. 131 f.

lēod w. gen. plur. (Gēata, etc.), perh. *representative of a people* (Marquardt, *l.c.*, 251).
ge-licgan. gelǣg 3146, *strike out:* (pluperf.)
mǣgen-fultum, perh. *support of one's strength,* cp. l. 1835 (Marquardt, *l.c.,* 223).
on-sǣlan, *disclose.*
on-sēcan. Cp. *wyllað mē lāðe līfes āsēcean, Par. Ps.* 118.95 (=ut perderent me).
scūr-heard. See *A.* lxiii, 414.
seomian. [OHG. gi-semōn; *Beitr.* lv, 311 f.]
sin-nihte, nja.; 161, acc. sing. (*A.* lxiii, 404.)
(snēdan, see note on l. 600, above).
synn. See Heusler, *Germanentum,* L 9.28c. 56.
tō. On the origin of the meaning *too* (from negat. clauses), see L. G. Downs, *JEGPh.* xxxviii, 64–68.
þenden. Cf. *A.* xxvii, 273.
þonne. For þonne used with the definite past tense (1121, 1143, cp. 2880), see Möllmer, *Konjunktionen und Modus im Temporalsatz des Altenglischen* (Breslau, 1937), pp. 24 f.
ge-þrūen. Flasdieck, *A.* lx, 345.
wǣg-bora. Cf. *A.* lxiii, 420, *Beibl.* l, 331.
wala. See Herben, L 9.40a. Su.
wīg-fruma. Perh. *warrior, hero* (Marquardt, *A.* lx, 390).
wrēoþen-hilt, wyrm-fāh. See Girvan, p. 39.
Breca, Brondingas. Malone, *Wids.,* p. 192. **Brōsinga(s),** *ib.,* p. 152 (see note on 1197 ff., above).
Ecg-wela. [L 5.71.5. (?)]
Ongen-þēow. Malone, *Wids.,* pp. 172, 180. [Su.
Wealh-þēow. Gordon, L 4.78d 1.
Wylfingas. Malone, *Wids.,* pp. 199 f.

SECOND SUPPLEMENT*

BIBLIOGRAPHY

(L 1.3a.) Kemp Malone, "Thorkelin's Transcripts of *Beowulf*." *Studia Neophilologica* xiv (1942), 25–30. [The pointing of the text.] R.: Fr. Klaeber, *ib.* xv (1943), 339 f.

(L 1.3b.) Kemp Malone, "Readings from the Thorkelin Transcripts of *Beowulf*." *PMLA*. lxiv (1949), 1190–1218. [E.g., 47^b *ge(l)denne*, 1287^a, 1734^a *for his unsnyttrum* (A), 1737^a, 2042^b *genam* (B), 2186^a *(drih)ten* (Thk. emend.), 3179^a.]

(L 2.15.) F. Holthausen's *Beowulf*, 8th ed., Part I, 1948. R.: Fr. Klaeber, *D. Lit. z.* lxx (1949), 210–213.

(L 2.17d.) An edition of *Beowulf* and *Judith*, forming Vol. iv of *The Anglo-Saxon Poetic Records*, by Elliott Van Kirk Dobbie is in preparation. Cf. Intr., p. cxxix.

(L 2.17e.) A *Variorum Edition* of *Beowulf* by Kemp Malone is in preparation.

(L 3.16e.) Philip W. Souers, *Speculum* xvi (1941), 351 f.: review of Kennedy's translation of *Beowulf*.

(L 4.10a.) George Sampson, *The Concise Cambridge History of English Literature*. Cambridge and New York, 1941. 1094 pp.

(L 4.13a.) Andreas Heusler, *Die altgermanische Dichtung*. 2. ed. (augmented). Babelsberg, 1943. 250 pp. Cf. also Georg Baesecke, *Vor- und Frühgeschichte des deutschen Schrifttums*. Vol. i: *Vorgeschichte*. Halle, 1940. 557 pp. *Passim*.

(L 4.13f.) *A Literary History of England*, ed. by Albert C. Baugh. New York and London, 1948. Book I, Part I: Kemp Malone, *The Old English Period*. 105 pp. [A brilliant scholarly account.] (Pp. 92–94: *Beowulf*; pp. 49–52: *Finnsburg*.)

(L 4.22.2.) H. M. Chadwick and N. K. Chadwick, *The Growth of Literature*. Vol. iii, 1940. xxvi, 928 pp. [Oral literature of the Tartars and of certain Polynesian and African peoples; a "note on English ballad poetry"; a "general survey" (of 207 pages). R.: Kemp Malone, *MLN*. lvi (1941), 401 f.

(L 4.66b 11.) Kemp Malone, "Grendel and Grep." *PMLA*. lvii (1942), 1–14. [The Grep story in Saxo (book v) a somewhat remote parallel to the Grendel story.]

(L 4.85a 3.) Kemp Malone, "Hagbard and Ingeld." *Essays and Studies in Honor of Carleton Brown* (1940), 1–22. [Seems to point out parallels of Saxo's story of Hagbard and Signe to the Ingeld story.] — *id.*, "Swerting." *Germanic Review* xiv (1939), 235–57. (Both papers have been out of reach.)

---

* This supplement was prepared in 1949–50. Owing to the unusual conditions, various books have been inaccessible to the editor, and completeness cannot be vouched for. The titles of some papers which could not be consulted: M. Hamilton, "The Religious Principle in *Beowulf*," *PMLA*., June, 1946; James R. Hulbert, "*Beowulf* and the Classical Epic," *MPh*., November, 1946.

(L 4.92m.) Kemp Malone, "Hygd." *MLN.* lvi (1941), 356–58. [The character of Hygd as developed by the poet. New translation of some lines. " Hygd and Þrȳð are presumably historical characters. We have no means of knowing what they were actually like; but it is a safe presumption that their names contributed largely to the development of their characters and careers in story." If it is argued that Hygd's name properly alliterates with her father's name, it is only fair to point out that the initial agreement of the names Hygelāc: Hygd is suspicious.]

(L 4.100.3.) Inger M. Boberg, " Die Sage von Vermund und Uffe." *Acta Philol. Scand.* xvi (1942), 129–57. [The Danish version (Saxo, Sven, Annales Ryenses) derived from continental Anglian, not Old English, tradition.]

(L 4.145b.) Fr. Klaeber, " Noch einmal *Exodus* 56–58 und *Beowulf* 1408–10." *Arch.* clxxxvii (1950), 71 f.

(L 4.156a.) (Cf. L 6.23.) B. J. Timmer, " *Wyrd* in Anglo-Saxon Prose and Poetry." *Neophilologus* xxvi (1940–41), 24–33, 213–28. — Hans Galinsky, " Sprachlicher Ausdruck und künstlerischer Gehalt germanischer Schicksalsauffassung in der angelsächsischen Dichtung." *ESt.* lxxiv (1941), 273–323.

(L 5.26.25.) F. Holthausen, *ESt.* lxxiv (1941), 324–25. [*icge* 1107 = *ītge*, weak adj., *ītig ' resplendent,' cf. ON. *ítr* (a return to his 2. ed.); *Widsið* 126: *æt nīhstan.*] — (L 5.26.26.) *id.*, *Studia Neophil.* xiv (1942), 160. [461 *wigana*; 3168 *swā heom æror wæs* (cf. L 1.14. Su.).] — (L 5.26.27.) *id.*, *Beibl.* liv/lv (1943), 27–30. [404 *hēoð* ' interior,' 461, 769, 1174, 3075, 3168.]

(L 5.35.25.) Fr. Klaeber, *Beibl.* li (1940), 206 f. [*bēah* 2041, ' hilt-ring.'] — (L 5.35.26.) *id.*, *Beibl.* lii (1941), 216–19. [Function of *oð þæt.*] — (L 5.35.27.) *id.*, " Unferð's Verhalten im *Beowulf.*" *Beibl.* liii (1942), 270–72. — (L 5.35.28) *id.*, *Beibl.* liv/lv (1944), 173–76. [404 *heorð* ' floor of a fireplace? answers in meaning to ON. *gólf*, cf. *Volundarkviða* 16.5.] — (L 5.35.29.) *id.*, " Randglossen zur Texterklärung des *Beowulf.*" *Beitr.* lxxii (1950), 120–26.

(L 5.71.10) (Cf. L 4.85a 1. Su.) Kemp Malone, *Angl.* lxv (1941), 227–29. [2041–43, 445, 991.] — (L 5.71.11.) *id.*, " Old English *beagas.*" *Beibl.* lii (1941), 179 f. [The plur. of *bēah* occurs in a primary sense ' rings ' and a secondary sense ' valuables,' but the sing. *bēah* nowhere means ' thing of value ' (see l. 2041).]

(L 7.25q.) B. J. Timmer, " Irony in Old English Poetry." *Eng. Studies* xxiv (1942), 171–75. [" There is very little, if any, humor in OE. poetry. Some examples of irony, but of a grim nature and mostly contained in one word; sometimes it arises from the context."]

(L 7.25r.) Henry B. Woolf, " On the characterization of Beowulf." *ELH.* xv (1948), 85–92.

(L 7.25s.) Kemp Malone, " *Beowulf.*" *Eng. Studies* xxix (1948), 162–172. [A critical analysis of the poem.]

(L 8.13m.) John Collins Pope, *The Rhythm of Beowulf. An Interpretation of the Normal and Hypermetric Verse-Forms in Old English Poetry.* New Haven, 1942. 386 pp. [A very thorough, important treatise.]

(L 8.13n.) Kemp Malone, L 4.13f., pp. 23–31: a brief sketch of versification and style.

SECOND SUPPLEMENT

(L 8.130.) Paull F. Baum, "The Meter of the *Beowulf*." *MPh.* xlvi (1948), 73–91.

(L 9.28i.) Elizabeth Martin Clarke, *Culture in Early Anglo-Saxon England*. Baltimore, 1947.

(L 9.39a.) Sune Lindqvist, "Sutton Hoo and *Beowulf*." *Antiquity*, No. 87 (Sept., 1948), pp. 131–140, = *Fornvännen*, 1948, pp. 94–110. [The Sutton Hoo burial-ship finds used for dating the poem. The helmet and shield dating from *c*. 600 A.D. and closely resembling Swedish workmanship point to early relations between England and Sweden (Uppland, Gotland).] Cf. Supplement, pp. 452 and 453.

(L 10.9.) Jan de Vries, *Altnordische Literaturgeschichte*. (P. Grdr. 15.) i, Berlin, 1941; ii, 1942.

FINNSBURG BIBLIOGRAPHY

(L F.2.16.) *Finnsburg*, ed. by Elliott Van Kirk Dobbie, in *The Anglo-Saxon Minor Poems* (Vol. vi of *The Anglo-Saxon Poetic Records*). New York, 1942.

(L F.4.44.) Helge Kökeritz, *Studia Neophil.* xiv (1942), 277–79. [Ll. 4–5.] Cf. Fr. Klaeber, *ib*. xv (1943), 341.

(L F.4.45.) Willy Meyer, *Beibl*. liv/lv (1943), 125 f. [Ll. 5–6.]

(L F.4.46.) Kemp Malone, "Hildeburg and Hengest." *ELH*. x (1943), 257–84. — *id*., "Finn's Stronghold." *MPh.* xliii (1945), 83–85.

Note. (See Intr., p. clxxxiii.) Fredrik Gadde, "Viktor Rydberg and Some *Beowulf* Questions." *Studia Neophil*. xv (1943), 71–90. [Cites some of the theories propounded in Rydberg's *Undersökningar i germansk mytologi* (1886, 1889); mentions, *inter alia*, a comment on them to the effect that "the poet in him had a fatal influence on the scholar."] — Franklin Cooley, "William Taylor of Norwich and *Beowulf*." *MLN*. lv (1940), 210 f. [W. Taylor the author of an anonymous review of Thorkelin's edition in the *Monthly Review* of 1816.]

NOTES ON THE TEXT

168 f. (A final statement.) The general meaning is: (Grendel "inhabited" Heorot at night, but) in the daytime he let the hall alone. This thought is expressed in a strikingly concrete and ironical way: he did not approach the king's throne (like a retainer) nor did he receive gifts from him, — the latter idea being implied by *nē his myne wisse*, 'nor did he feel (affection) gratitude for it'; *his* refers to *gifstōl* = 'gifts' (cf. *Gnom. Ex*. 68; *Beow*. 1177 f.; and *Wand*. 44). There is no reason why *myne wisse* might not be used as well of the retainer as of the chief who bestows gifts on him (*Wand*. 27). It was God who prevented the accursed fiend from entering in broad daylight. (Cf., by the way, 646 ff.)

404. *þæt hē on heo[r]ðe gestōd*. The Geats had entered the hall. Beowulf then proceeded, until he took his stand (stopped) on the floor of the fireplace, in front of Hrōðgār (see 358 f.). Cf. *Vǫlundarkviða* 16 *hon inn um gekk enlangan sal, / stóð á gólfi*. The MS. form *heoðe* possibly represents phonetic spelling; cf. 567 *sweodum;* also *MLN*. xviii, 244 f., *Beibl*. xxxii, 37 f.

414. *heofenes hādor* ' the clear sky ' is more expressive than *heofenes haðor*. Of course, if we can be sure that " the very faint ð " (Pope 323) written above the line denotes an authorized correction, we must write *haðor*.

457ᵃ. If the eminently plausible reading *F[or w]erefyhtum* is adopted, it may be questioned whether *þū* is to be dropped (or, possibly, to be assigned to the second half-line).

461. None of the three emendations, *Wedera*, *Wulgara* (Malone), *wigana* (Holthausen), is entirely satisfactory.

473. *tō secganne*. It seems entirely proper (though contrary to the orthodox practice) to retain the inflected infinitive as purposely used by the author. No need to emend to *tō secgan*. The difference between the two varieties appears to be due to a difference of context. The short forms, 316 *mǣl is mē tō fēran*, 2555 f. *næs ðǣr māra fyrst / frēode tō friclan:* a cleancut close. The fuller forms, 473ᵃ *sorh is mē tō secganne on sefan mīnum . . .* , 1724ᵇ, 1805ᵃ, 1941ᵃ, 2093ᵃ: a minor rest within the main clause. (2562 as transmitted looks like an exception.) To reduce these two groups to a rigid metrical uniformity (in favor of the short forms) would not be fair to the author. A third set of forms, occupying an entire half-line, weighty, solemn, 173 f. *hwæt swīðferhðum sēlest wǣre / wið fǣrgryrum tō gefremmanne*, generally representing the type, 1417 ff. *Đenum eallum wæs, / winum Scyldinga weorce on mōde / tō geþolianne*, 257ᵃ, 1003ᵃ, 1731ᵃ, 1851ᵃ, 1922ᵃ, 2416ⁿ, 2445ᵃ, 2452ᵃ, 2644ᵃ, occurs with remarkable frequency. (A striking example, *Christ* 1621 f.) Thus there are three nicely discriminated sets of metrical grades answering to three sets of textual context. The systematic distinction may be considered a Beowulfian peculiarity. (Similarly, a delicate artistic feeling seems to have prompted the duality of 9 *oð þæt him ǣghwylc ymbsittendra* and 2733 f. *næs sē folccyning, / ymbesittendra ǣnig ðāra*. Cf. also T. C. § 13.

600ᵃ. A daringly brilliant guess by Holt.⁸: *swendeþ*. Cf. *Lit. bl.* xvi (1895), 82.

747. On the basis of some uncertain traces of letters in the MS. Pope (372) would insert *him swā* before *rǣhte ongēan*, which, however, hardly makes acceptable sense.

769. Holthausen (L 5.26.27) refers to names like OHG. *Alu-berht*, OE. *Alu-*, *Ealu-berht*, *-burg*, *-wine*, ON. *Ql-bjǫrn*, *-valdr*, and runic *alu*, frequently met with in runic inscriptions and apparently meaning ' good luck,' ' safety.' Thus *ealuscerwen* ' taking away of good luck.' (Cf. note on p. 455.) Thus the annoying riddle of *ealuscerwen* (*meoduscerwen*) seems to be happily solved by a twofold misunderstanding: 1) (taking away of) good luck: ale; 2) taking away: dispensing (of ale, mead). The actual meaning of the noun in l. 769 is, most likely, ' disaster,' with a subaudition of ' terror.'

779. *þæt hit ā mid gemete manna ǣnig* and 2615 *brūnfāgne helm, hringde byrnan*. The exceptional form of alliteration can hardly be objected to. (Transverse alliteration.) Cf. also T. C. § 18, § 27.

870 f. The text as printed needs revision; *word ōþer* as contrast to *ealdge-segena* seems rather weak, and the uncalled-for *eft* decidedly awkward. A return to the punctuation of the first two editions (*word ōþer fand / sōðe* *gebunden* taken parenthetically, no semicolon after *gebunden*), as fully explained in *MPh.* iii, 456, is recommended.

963. In this line as well as in 2377 and 2828 Malone (*Eng. Studies* xviii, 257) takes *him* (= *hine*) as modern forms foreshadowing the general later English status. However, the dative in 2828 *ac him īrenna ecga fornāmon* possibly represents an archaic construction comparable to the dative with *forgrīpan, forgrindan, forswerian, forlēosan, foreldan, forscrīfan* (?).

982 ff. Malone (*Angl.* lvii, 315) regards *eorles cræfte* as "dative of accompaniment" going with *hand* and *fingras*, "the hand and fingers of the foe and the strength of the hero." Such a dative (or rather instrumental), for which he pleads in numerous instances, is no doubt to be recognized in connection with verbs (mostly of motion) and applied particularly to nouns of collective sense, as, e.g., 922 *tryddode tīrfæst getrume micle*, 924 *medostigge mæt mægþa hōse*, 2914 f. *cwōm / faran flotherge, Elene* 150 f. *cōm þā wigena hlēo / þegna prēate*, 691 *heht þā swā cwicne corðre lǣdan*, also *Beow.* 1011 f. *ne gefrægen ic þā mǣgþe māran weorode / ymb hyra sincgyfan sēl gebǣran*. (Cf. Heusler, *Altisl. Elementarbuch* § 382.4. Correspondingly, the ablative in Latin, as *Aeneid* i, 497 *incessit magna iuvenum stipante caterva*.) By extension also, e.g., *Gen.* 1652 *oð þæt hīe becōmun corðrum miclum / folc fērende* (cf. 1986 *on mægencorðrum*), *Guðl.* 894 *weorude cwōmun . . . hlōþum þringan.* A case like *Beow.* 1980 *meoduscencum hwearf* or 2672 *līgȳðum fōr* (or *Andr.* 1205, *Elene* 24) probably represents the utmost limit of such a usage. A plain sense of 'addition' (= 'and') is very doubtful. In that case *mid* is to be expected, as *Beow.* 1706 *mægen mid mōdes snyttrum* (or *ēac*, as *Guðl.* 206).

1118. *gūðrinc āstāh.* Which one? Unquestionably, Hildeburh's son.

1174. Holthausen (L 5.26.27) proposes *þū nū [frēode] hafast*. (So Brown, *PMLA.* liii (1938), 913.) Holthausen also (*metri causa*) changes *nēan ond feorran* to *feorran ond nēan*. A lacuna after *hafast* 1174 seems a far from improbable assumption (cf. Bugge 92).

1382. It may, after all, be advisable to give *wundini* (instead of *wundnum*) as an archaic instrumental form a place in the text.

1610. *wælrāpas* or *wǣlrāpas* (cf. the numerous *wǣl* compounds)? Both are admissible.

1688 f. *ōr . . . fyrngewinnes.* If *ōr* is understood to refer to the ungodly acts of the giants which preceded the deluge (cf. 113 f.), or even to the fratricide (as the "prima causa"), the clause introduced by *syðþan* might be held to refer to *fyrngewinnes*, not to *ōr fyrngewinnes.* Of course, if we venture to take *ōr* in a broader sense and translate 'all about the ancient strife,' the situation is certainly simplified.

1734. *for his unsnyttrum.* Malone (L 1.3b.Su.²) has established the fact that *for* is not an emendation of Thorkelin's, but was found in Thorkelin transcript A.

1783. *wīggeweorþad.* The entire body of OE. poetry yields, by the side of very many examples of *geweorðod*, only two instances of *weorðod*, sc. *Elene* 1195 *wigge weorðod* and *Beow.* 1783 *wigge weorþad*. In both cases presumably a compound was intended; cf. *lyftgeswenced* 1913, *handgewriþene* 1937; Intr., p. cv and n. 3.

1809. Against *lǣnes* it is to be noted that, in contrast to the very common adjective *lǣne*, the noun *lǣn* is never found in OE. poetry, except in *Gen. B* 601, 692, where it is a loan-word from Old Saxon.

1931 f. Malone's view (L 4.92m) of the old *crux* is strikingly original: " the good folk-queen had weighed (implying ' criticized,' ' disapproved of ') the arrogance and terrible wickedness of Thryth." By this interpretation the harshness of transition from Hygd to Þrȳð is moderated. But the meaning assigned to *wegan* is problematic; in the earliest example given in *NED.*, *Poema Morale* 63, the idea of weighing the good against the bad qualities is still clearly recognizable. Besides, the whole idea, interesting enough psychologically, strikes one as altogether too modern. — For the reading *Mōd þrȳðo wæg*, see note on 2706 below.

1981. Who is meant by *Hǣreðes dohtor*, could not be understood without reference to 1926 ff. This shows the structural connection of the Þrȳð episode with the main narrative.

2032. *ðeoden* (MS.) is taken by Malone (L 5.71.9) = *þēodan*, dative of an assumed noun *þēoda*, ' military leader,' ' lord,' which he supports by *Widsið* 11, *þēoda gehwylc* (see note in his edition). However, apart from a very few negligible instances, *gehwilc*, when used in OE. poetry with a noun or *ān*, appears invariably with a preceding partitive genit. plur. — there are more than a hundred such passages. Hence, *þēoda* must be understood as genit. plur. of *þēod* or should be emended to *þēodna*.

2041 f. Malone (L 5.71.10) remarks that the scribe seems to have intended *genam* (not *geman*); he translates ' he who took all '; *bēah*, pret. of *būgan*, ' fled,' *gesyhð* = *ge* ' and,' *syhþ* = *segþ*. (?) " Starkad was he who endured everything, even the supreme humiliation of having to fall back before the enemy." He thinks the reference is to Starkað's flight before the Danes after the fall of Regnald in a hard-fought battle (Saxo vii, v). He adds: " In a forthcoming study I try to show that Regnald is the Scandinavian counterpart of Wiðergyld." But it is not very likely that the poet would have singled out for allusion a far from creditable episode in the life of the grim old warrior.

2150. [*mīnra*] *lissa gelong*. The insertion of *mīnra* (*JEGPh*. viii, 257) improves the sense appreciably, but even a metrical rigorist (Pope 320 f.) is willing to tolerate the unemended text, pointing out the parallel half-line, *Guðl*. 313 *lēofes gelong*.

2237. *sē ān*. The remarkable *si* of the MS. is explained by Malone (*Eng. Studies* xv, 151) as an early instance of the common change of *ē* to *ī*. Cf., e.g., *Chr. and Sat.* 274 *sic* (*i* altered to *e* and *o* added above the line).

2252. The smooth emendation *secga seledrēam* (cf. *ESt*. xxxix, 465) makes perfect sense, but such a drastic change is, at any rate, debatable, especially as the transmitted text admits of a suitable interpretation.

2255. Both (*hyr*)*stedgolde* and (*hyr*)*sted golde* (' adorned with gold ') are presentable.

2297. The genuineness of the text, *ealne ūtanweardne*, is vouched for by

SECOND SUPPLEMENT 469

the context. Neither can *ealne* be spared nor should *ūtanweardne* be tampered with.

2299. *bea(dwe) weorces.* The Thorkelin transcripts show no letter between *bea* and *weorces*. (*A* leaves some space after *bea* blank.)

2356. *gūðe rǣsum*, 2626 *gūðe rǣs*. Hoops recommends composition, *gūðerǣs*, referring to *hilderǣs* 300. Still, *hild* (fjō.) is on a somewhat different basis; no *hildrǣs* is possible (Weyhe, *Beitr.* xxx, 79 ff.). The duality of *gūðe rǣs* and *gūðrǣs* (1577, 2426, 2991) is matched by *līfes wynn: līfwyn, heriges wīsa: herewīsa, wuldres cyning: wuldorcyning, beaduwe weorc: beaduweorc,* etc.

2372. *ðā wæs Hygelāc dēad.* The same unusual word order occurs 2301 *ðæt hæfde gumena sum goldes gefandod.* (Rhythmical reason?)

2435. *ungedēfelīce* a nonce word, and 1379 *felasinnigne* (MS. *fela sinnigne*). Evidently a copyist wished to " improve " his text by adding a suffix and prefix respectively. These flourishes may be legitimately removed.

2488. [*heoro-*] *blāc*, [*hilde-*] *blāc*. Von Schaubert, in her commentary, argues for [*hilde-*] *blāc* = ' war bright,' ' shining in armor,' as in *Exod.* 204 *wīgblāc*. This is not incompatible with the context. Yet the second meaning of *blāc* (Grein: pallidus [de moribundis et mortuis]) is here by no means precluded, but seems on the whole even preferable; *heoro-, hilde-blāc* are paralleled by *flōdblāc, Exod.* 498 (Grein: ' durch die Flut erbleichend, ertrinkend '). There could be no objection to assigning entirely different meanings to *hildeblāc* and *wīgblāc* according to the context in which they are used. (Also ON. *bleikr* shows the two meanings.) It may be added that a scribal omission of *heoro* after *hrēas* appears more likely than that of *hilde*. Still more natural would be the loss of *hrēa* (Bugge), but a *hrēablāc* would be hardly suitable in this context.

2573 ff. (A final decision.) " There he had to spend the (allotted) time (his time) for the first time (*forman dōgore*) in such a way that fate did not assign to him glory in battle." A semicolon is to be placed after *sōhte* 2572.

2600 f. *sibb ǣfre ne mæg/ wiht onwendan.* The interpretation provisionally suggested (p. 217): " kinship can never change anything," i.e., " will always prevent a change (of heart)," seems to me the preferable one. It involves a sort of energetic abbreviation. Similarly, e.g., *Rood* 44 *āhōf ic rīcne cyning; Muspilli* 45 (*der antichristo . . . stet pi demo Satanase,*) *der inan varsenkan scal*, ' shall bring it about that he is hurled down,' cf. *ZfdA.* lxxv, 189; *OS. Gen.* 185 f. *sculun sia hira firinsundeon/ suara bisenkian;* Renan, *Die Apostel* (German translation) 324: *Götter haben Sokrates getötet;* and the like.

2672 f. Pope (320) ably proposes *līgȳðum fōr./ Born bord wið rond.*

2706. *ferh ellen wræc.* (The martial exertions are strongly emphasized in this passage.) For metrically and syntactically identical half-lines, see *Exod.* 463 *flōd blōd gewōd, Beow.* 2119 *sunu dēað fornam.* One is also reminded of the much discussed *mōd þrȳðo wæg* 1931; the tempting argument that the name should receive the principal stress is perhaps not weighty enough to enforce the reading *Mōdþrȳðo*.

2794 f. *Ic ðāra frætwa Frēan ealles þanc . . . secge.* Connect *ðāra frætwa . . . ealles* with *þanc*. Cf. *Jul.* 593, *Gen. B* 238 f. (Glossary, s. v. *frēa* to be corrected accordingly.)

2817 f. *þæt wæs þām gomelan gingæste word / brēostgehygdum.* Cf., e.g., **232 f.** *hine fyrwyt bræc / mōdgehygdum,* 2044 ff., 2280 f., *Andr.* 996 *se hālga gebæd bilwytne Fæder brēostgehygdum, Christ* 261 f.; also *Ps.* xiv: 1, liii: 1 *dixit insipiens in corde suo,* Eccl. i: 16 *locutus sum in corde meo,* etc. (*Angl.* xxxv, 470 f.)

3027. *þenden hē wið wulf wæl rēafode.* 3056 — *hē is manna gehyld — hord openian.* These two metrically parallel lines support each other.

3150 ff. Pope (232 f.), by close scrutiny of the MS. with the aid of modern photographic devices (cf. L 1.14. Su.), has succeeded in recovering some probable readings: 3150ᵇ (*gē*)*at*(*isc*) *mēowle,* 3152ᵇ *s*(*w*)*ĭðe* (?) *geneahhe,* 3153ᵃ (*hēofun*)*g*(*da*)*gas* (?).

Finnsburg 47. It seems after all more in conformity with the *Finnsburg* style to read: *hū ðā wīgend / hyra wunda genǣson.*

A LIST OF TEXTUAL CHANGES

389ᵇ [þā tō dura efste
403ᵇ [herewīsa gēong,]
457ᵃ F[or w]erefyhtum þū,
870 f. worn gemunde (word ōþer fand / sōðe gebunden), secg eft ongan
1382ᵃ wundini
1734ᵃ for his unsnyttrum
2042ᵇ ge*man*
2435ᵇ ungedēfe
2672 f. lāðra manna; līgȳðum fōr. / Born bord wið rond,
3150ᵇ (gē)at(isc) mēowle
3154ᵇ werudes egesan
3168ᵇ swā he(om) ǣ(r)or wæs.
Finnsburg 34 Hwearf [h]lacra ær[n], hræfen wandrode (period after *fæla* 33)

GLOSSARY

āg-lǣca. Lotspeich, *JEGPh.* xl (1941), 1.
and-long 2695, von Schaubert (commentary): 'excellent.'
(ge-)bǣtan. Cf. *Beibl.* liv/lv, 175.
bearhtm 1) and 2). M. Foerster, ed. of *Vercelli Homilies* i, 78.
brūn (used of weapons). Krogmann, *ZfdPh.* lxvii (1942), 1–10; Holthausen, *Beibl.* liv/lv, 133 f.
camp 2505 (*in campe*), 'battle-field,' cf. von Schaubert (commentary).
drēam (and its relation to 'dream'). Cf. B. von Lindheim, *RESt.* xxv (1949), 193–209.

eolet(e). Lotspeich, *JEGPh.* xl (1941), 1 f. [*el-wite, *ewlite, 'a going elsewhere,' 'a foreign journey.']
fetel-hilt. Swaen, *Neophilologus* xxviii (1942), 43: 'belted hilt.'
gār-secg. Malone, *Eng. Studies* xxviii (1947), 42–45: *gār* 'storm,' cf. *gās-rīc.*
gūð-getǣwa, wīg-getǣwa (short *a*).
sin-nihte, nja.; as., 161.
weardian. On *lāst weardian* 2164, see *Beibl.* liv/lv, 173. (*Aen.* ii, 711.)
wom(m) 3073, 'torment.'

PROPER NAMES

Hrunting. Cf. Malone, *AfNF*. lxi (1946), 284 f.
Ōht-(h)ere. Cf. M. Foerster, *Der Flussname Themse und seine Sippe*. Muenchen, 1941, pp. 257 ff.
On the names of tribes, cf. M. Deutschbein, " Geographie der Wortbildung der germanischen Völkernamen nach ags. Ueberlieferung.", *Zs. f. Mundartforschung* xvi (1940), 113–22.